&

THE PRODIGAL
DAUGHTER

Jeffrey Archer is a master storyteller, the author of eleven novels which have all been worldwide bestsellers. *Not a Penny More, Not a Penny Less* was his first book, and it achieved instant success. Next came the tense and terrifying thriller *Shall We Tell the President?*, followed by his triumphant bestseller *Kane and Abel*. His first collection of short stories, *A Quiver Full of Arrows*, came next, and then *The Prodigal Daughter*, the superb sequel to *Kane & Abel*. This was followed by *First Among Equals*, considered by the *Scotsman* to be the finest novel about parliament since Trollope, the thrilling chase story *A Matter of Honour*, his second collection of stories, *A Twist in the Tale*, and the novels *As the Crow Flies* and *Honour Among Thieves*. *Twelve Red Herrings*, his third collection of stories, was followed by the novels *The Fourth Estate* and *The Eleventh Commandment*. A collected edition of his short stories was published in 1997, followed by another collection, *To Cut a Long Story Short*. His latest novel, *Sons of Fortune*, was published by Macmillan in 2002.

Jeffrey Archer was born in 1940 and educated at Wellington School, Somerset, and Brasenose College, Oxford. He represented Great Britain in the 100 metres in the early sixties, and entered the House of Commons when he won the by-election at Louth in 1969. He wrote his first novel, *Not a Penny More, Not a Penny Less*, in 1974. From September 1985 to October 1986 he was Deputy Chairman of the Conservative Party, and he was created a Life Peer in the Queen's Birthday Honours of 1992. He is married with two children.

JEFFREY ARCHER

AS THE CROW FLIES

&

THE PRODIGAL DAUGHTER

PAN BOOKS

As the Crow Flies first published 1991 by Hodder and Stoughton.
First published by Pan Books 2003
The Prodigal Daughter first published 1982 by Hodder and Stoughton.
First published by Pan Books 2004

This omnibus edition published 2005 by Pan Books
an imprint of Pan Macmillan Ltd
Pan Macmillan, 20 New Wharf Road, London N1 9RR
Basingstoke and Oxford
Associated companies throughout the world
www.panmacmillan.com

ISBN 0 330 44088 8

1 3 5 7 9 8 6 4 2

A CIP catalogue record for this book is available from
the British Library.

Printed and bound in Great Britain by
Mackays of Chatham plc, Chatham, Kent

AS THE
CROW FLIES

To James

CHARLIE

1900-1919

CHAPTER 1

"I don't offer you these for twopence," my Granpa would shout, holding up a cabbage in both hands, "I don't offer 'em for a penny, not even a ha'penny. No, I'll give 'em away for a farthin'."

Those were the first words I can remember. Even before I had learned to walk my eldest sister used to dump me in an orange box on the pavement next to Granpa's pitch just to be sure I could start my apprenticeship early.

"Only stakin' 'is claim," Granpa used to tell the customers as he pointed at me in the wooden box. In truth, the first word I ever spoke was "Granpa", the second "farthing", and I could repeat his whole sales patter word for word by my third birthday. Not that any of my family could be that certain of the exact day on which *I* was born, on account of the fact that my old man had spent the night in gaol and my mother had died even before I drew breath. Granpa thought it could well have been a Saturday, felt it most likely the month had been January, was confident the year was 1900, and knew it was in the reign of Queen Victoria. So we settled on Saturday, 20 January 1900.

I never knew my mother because, as I explained, she died on the day I was born. "Childbirth" our local priest called it, but I didn't really understand what he was on about until several years later when I came up against the problem again. Father O'Malley never

11

stopped telling me that she was a saint if ever he'd seen one. My father – who couldn't have been described as a saint by anyone – worked on the docks by day, lived in the pub at night and came home in the early morning because it was the only place he could fall asleep without being disturbed.

The rest of my family was made up of three sisters – Sal, the eldest who was five and knew when she was born because it was in the middle of the night and had kept the old man awake, Grace who was three and didn't cause anyone to lose sleep, and red-headed Kitty who was eighteen months and never stopped bawling.

The head of the family was Granpa Charlie, whom I was named after. He slept in his own room on the ground floor of our home in Whitechapel Road, not only because he was the oldest but because he always paid the rent. The rest of us were herded all together in the room opposite. We had two other rooms on the ground floor, a sort of kitchen and what most people would have called a large cupboard, but which Grace liked to describe as the parlour.

There was a lavatory in the garden – no grass – which we shared with an Irish family who lived on the floor above us. They always seemed to go at three o'clock in the morning.

Granpa – who was a costermonger by trade – worked the pitch on the corner of Whitechapel Road. Once I was able to escape from my orange box and ferret around among the other barrows, I quickly discovered that he was reckoned by the locals to be the finest trader in the East End.

My dad, who, as I have already told you, was a docker by trade, never seemed to take that much interest in any of us and though he could sometimes earn as much as a pound a week, the money always seemed to end up in the Black Bull, where it was spent on pint after pint of ale, and gambled away on games of cribbage or dominoes in the company of our next-door neighbour, Bert Shorrocks, a man who never seemed to speak, just grunt.

In fact, if it hadn't been for Granpa I wouldn't even have been made to attend the local elementary school in Jubilee Street, and "attend" was the right word, because I didn't do a lot once I'd got there, other than bang the lid of my little desk and occasionally pull the pigtails of "Posh Porky", the girl who sat in front of me. Her real name was Rebecca Salmon and she was the daughter of Dan Salmon who owned the baker's shop on the corner of Brick Lane. Posh Porky knew exactly when and where she was born and never stopped reminding us all that she was nearly a year younger than anyone else in the class.

I couldn't wait for the bell to ring at four in the afternoon when class would end and I could bang my lid for the last time before running all the way down the Whitechapel Road to help out on the barrow.

On Saturdays as a special treat Granpa would allow me to go along with him to the early morning market in Covent Garden, where he would select the fruit and vegetables that we would later sell from his pitch, just opposite Mr Salmon's and Dunkley's, the fish and chippy that stood next to the baker's.

Although I couldn't wait to leave school once and for all so I could join Granpa permanently, if I ever played truant for as much as an hour he wouldn't take me to watch West Ham on Saturday afternoon or, worse, he'd stop me selling on the barrow in the morning.

"I 'oped you'd grow up to be more like Rebecca Salmon," he used to say. "That girl will go a long way —"

"The further the better," I would tell him, but he never laughed, just reminded me that she was always top in every subject.

"'cept 'rithmetic," I replied with bravado, "where I beat her silly." You see, I could do any sum in my head that Rebecca Salmon had to write out in long-hand; it used to drive her potty.

My father never visited Jubilee Street Elementary once in all the years I was there, but Granpa used to pop along at least once a term and have a word with Mr Cartwright my teacher. Mr Cartwright told Granpa that with my head for figures I could end up an accountant or a clerk. He once said that he might even be able to "find me a position in the City". Which was a waste of time really, because all I wanted to do was join Granpa on the barrow.

I was seven before I worked out that the name down the side of Granpa's barrow – Charlie Trumper, the honest trader, founded in 1823 – was the same as mine. Dad's first name was George, and he had already made it clear on several occasions that when Granpa retired he had no intention of taking over from him as he didn't want to leave his mates on the docks.

I couldn't have been more pleased by his decision, and told Granpa that when I finally took over the barrow we wouldn't even have to change the name.

Granpa just groaned and said, "I don't want you to end up workin' in the East End, young 'un. You're far too good to be a barrow boy for the rest of your life." It made me sad to hear him speak like that; he didn't seem to understand that was all I wanted to do.

School dragged on for month after month, year after year, with Rebecca Salmon going up to collect prize after prize on Speech Day. What made the annual gathering even worse was we always had to listen to her recite the twenty-third psalm, standing up there on the stage in her white dress, white socks, black shoes. She even had a white bow in her long black hair.

"And I expect she wears a new pair of knickers every day," little Kitty whispered in my ear.

"And I'll bet you a guinea to a farthin' she's still a virgin," said Sal.

I burst out laughing because all the costermongers

in the Whitechapel Road always did whenever they heard that word, although I admit that at the time I didn't have a clue what a virgin was. Granpa told me to "shhh" and didn't smile again until I went up to get the arithmetic prize, a box of coloured crayons that were damned-all use to anyone. Still, it was them or a book.

Granpa clapped so loud as I returned to my place that some of the mums looked round and smiled, which made the old fellow even more determined to see that I stayed on at school until I was fourteen.

By the time I was ten, Granpa allowed me to lay out the morning wares on the barrow before going off to school for the day. Potatoes on the front, greens in the middle and soft fruits at the back was his golden rule.

"Never let 'em touch the fruit until they've 'anded over their money," he used to say. "'ard to bruise a 'tato, but even 'arder to sell a bunch of grapes that's been picked up and dropped a few times."

By the age of eleven I was collecting the money from the customers and handing them the change they were due. That's when I first learned about palming. Sometimes, after I'd given them back their money, the customer would open the palm of their hand and I would discover that one of the coins I had passed over had suddenly disappeared so I ended up having to give them even more bees and honey. I lost Granpa quite a bit of our weekly profit that way, until he taught me to say, "Twopence change, Mrs Smith," then hold up the coins for all to see before handing them over.

By twelve, I had learned how to bargain with the suppliers at Covent Garden while displaying a poker face, later selling the same produce to the customers back in Whitechapel with a grin that stretched from ear to ear. I also discovered that Granpa used to switch suppliers regularly, "just to be sure no one takes me for granted".

By thirteen, I had become his eyes and ears as I already knew the name of every worthwhile trader of fruit and vegetables in Covent Garden. I quickly sussed out which sellers just piled good fruit on top of bad, which dealers would attempt to hide a bruised apple and which suppliers would always try to short-measure you. Most important of all, back on the pitch I learnt which customers didn't pay their debts and so could never be allowed to have their names chalked up on the slate.

I remember that my chest swelled with pride the day Mrs Smelley, who owned a boarding house in the Commercial Road, told me that I was a chip off the old block and that in her opinion one day I might even be as good as my Granpa. I celebrated that night by ordering my first pint of beer and lighting up my first Woodbine. I didn't finish either of them.

I'll never forget that Saturday morning when Granpa first let me run the barrow on my own. For five hours he didn't once open his mouth to offer advice or even give an opinion and, when he checked the takings at the end of the day, although we were two shillings and fivepence light from a usual Saturday, he still handed over the sixpenny piece he always gave me at the end of the week.

I knew Granpa wanted me to stay on at school and improve my readin' and writin', but on the last Friday of term in December 1913 I walked out of the gates of Jubilee Street Elementary, with my father's blessing. He had always told me that education was a waste of time and he couldn't see the point of it. I agreed with him, even if Posh Porky had won a scholarship to some place called St Paul's, which in any case was miles away in Hammersmith. And who wants to go to school in Hammersmith when you can live in the East End?

Mrs Salmon obviously wanted her to because she told everyone who was held up in the bread queue of her daughter's "interlectual prowess", whatever that meant.

"Stuck-up snob," Grandpa used to whisper in my ear. "She's the sort of person who 'as a bowl of fruit in the 'ouse when no one's ill."

I felt much the same way about Posh Porky as Grandpa did about Mrs Salmon. Mr Salmon was all right, though. You see, he'd once been a costermonger himself, but that was before he married Miss Roach, the baker's daughter.

Every Saturday morning, while I was setting up the barrow, Mr Salmon used to disappear off to the Whitechapel synagogue leaving his wife to run the shop. While he was away she never stopped reminding us at the top of her voice that she wasn't a five by two.

Posh Porky seemed to be torn between going along with her old man to the synagogue and staying put at the shop, where she'd sit by the window and start scoffing cream buns the moment he was out of sight.

"Always a problem, a mixed marriage," Granpa would tell me. It was years before I worked out that he wasn't talking about the cream buns.

The day I left school I told Granpa he could lie in while I went off to Covent Garden to fill up the barrow, but he wouldn't hear of it. When we got to the market, for the first time he allowed me to bargain with the dealers. I quickly found one who agreed to supply me with a dozen apples for threepence as long as I could guarantee the same order every day for the next month. As Granpa Charlie and I always had an apple for breakfast, the arrangement sorted out our own needs and also gave me the chance to sample what we were selling to the customers.

From that moment on, every day was a Saturday and between us we could sometimes manage to put the profits up by as much as fourteen shillings a week.

After that, I was put on a weekly wage of five shillings – a veritable fortune – four of which I kept locked in a tin box under Granpa's bed until I had saved up my first guinea: a man what's got a guinea got security, Mr Salmon once told me as he stood outside his shop, thumbs in his waistcoat pockets, displaying a shiny gold watch and chain.

In the evenings, after Granpa had come home for supper and the old man had gone off to the pub, I soon became bored just sitting around listening to what my sisters had been up to all day; so I joined the Whitechapel Boys' Club. Table tennis Mondays, Wednesdays and Fridays; boxing Tuesdays, Thursdays and Saturdays. I never did get the hang of table tennis but I became quite a useful bantam-weight and once even represented the club against Bethnal Green.

Unlike my old man I didn't go much on pubs, the horses or cribbage but I still went on supporting West Ham most Saturday afternoons. I even made the occasional trip into the West End of an evening to see the latest music-hall star.

When Granpa asked me what I wanted for my fifteenth birthday I replied without a moment's hesitation, "My own barrow," and added that I'd nearly saved enough to get one. He just laughed and told me that his old one was well good enough for whenever the time came for me to take over. In any case, he warned me, it's what a rich man calls an asset and, he added for good measure, never invest in something new, especially when there's a war on.

Although Mr Salmon had already told me that we had declared war against the Germans almost a year ago – none of us having heard of Archduke Franz Ferdinand – we only found out how serious it was when a lot of young lads who had worked in the market began to disappear off to "the front" to be replaced by their younger brothers – and sometimes even sisters. On a Saturday morning there were often more lads down the East End dressed in khaki than in civvies.

My only other memory of that period was Schultz's,

the sausage-maker – a Saturday night treat for us, especially when he gave us a toothless grin and slipped an extra sausage in free. Lately he had always seemed to start the day with a broken window-pane, and then suddenly one morning the front of his shop was boarded up and we never saw Mr Schultz again. "Internment," my granpa whispered mysteriously.

My old man occasionally joined us on a Saturday morning, but only to get some cash off Granpa so that he could go to the Black Bull and spend it all with his mate Bert Shorrocks.

Week after week Granpa would fork out a bob, sometimes even a florin, which we both knew he couldn't afford. And what really annoyed me was that he never drank and certainly didn't go a bundle on gambling. That didn't stop my old man pocketing the money, touching his cap and then heading off towards the Black Bull.

This routine went on week after week, and might never have changed, until one Saturday morning a toffee-nosed lady who I had noticed standing on the corner for the past week, wearing a long black dress and carrying a parasol, strode over to our barrow, stopped and placed a white feather in Dad's lapel.

I've never seen him go so mad, far worse than the usual Saturday night when he had lost all his money gambling and came home so drunk that we all had to hide under the bed. He raised his clenched fist to the lady but she didn't flinch and even called him "coward" to his face. He screamed back at her some choice words that he usually saved for the rent collector. He then grabbed all her feathers and threw them in the gutter before storming off in the direction of the Black Bull. What's more, he didn't come home at midday, when Sal served us up a dinner of fish and chips. I never complained as I went off to watch West Ham that afternoon, having scoffed his portion of chips. He still wasn't back when I returned that night, and when I woke the next morning, his side of the bed hadn't been slept in. When Granpa brought us all home from midday mass there was still no sign of Dad, so I had a second night with the double bed all to myself.

"'e's probably spent another night in gaol," said Granpa on Monday morning as I pushed our barrow down the middle of the road, trying to avoid the horse shit from the buses that were dragged backwards and forwards, to and from the City along the Metropolitan Line.

As we passed Number 110, I spotted Mrs Shorrocks staring at me out of the window, sporting her usual black eye and a mass of different coloured bruises which she collected from Bert most Saturday nights.

"You can go and bail 'im out round noon," said Granpa. "'e should have sobered up by then."

I scowled at the thought of having to fork out the half-crown to cover his fine, which simply meant another day's profits down the drain.

A few minutes after twelve o'clock I reported to the police station. The duty sergeant told me that Bert Shorrocks was still in the cells and due up in front of the beak that afternoon, but they hadn't set eyes on my old man the whole weekend.

"Like a bad penny, you can be sure 'e'll turn up again," said Granpa with a chuckle.

But it was to be over a month before Dad "turned up" again. When I first saw him I couldn't believe my eyes – he was dressed from head to toe in khaki. You see, he had signed up with the second battalion of the Royal Fusiliers. He told us that he expected to be posted to the front at some time in the next few weeks but he would still be home by Christmas; an officer had told him that the bloody Huns would have been sent packing long before then.

Granpa shook his head and frowned, but I was so proud of my dad that for the rest of the day I just strutted around the market by his side. Even the lady who stood on the corner handing out white feathers gave him an approving nod. I scowled at her and promised Dad that if the Germans hadn't been sent packing by Christmas – I would leave the market and join up myself to help him finish off the job. I even went with him to the Black Bull that night, determined to spend my weekly wages on whatever he wanted. But no one would let him buy a drink so I ended up not spending a ha'penny. The next morning he had left us to rejoin his regiment, even before Granpa and I started out for the market.

The old man never wrote because he couldn't write, but everyone in the East End knew that if you didn't get one of those brown envelopes pushed under your door the member of your family who was away at the war must still be alive.

From time to time Mr Salmon used to read to me from his morning paper, but as he could never find a mention of the Royal Fusiliers I didn't discover what the old man was up to. I only prayed that he wasn't at some place called Ypres where, the paper warned us, casualties were heavy.

Christmas Day was fairly quiet for the family that year on account of the fact that the old man hadn't returned from the front as the officer had promised.

Sal, who was working shifts in a café on the Commercial Road, went back to work on Boxing Day, and Grace remained on duty at the London hospital throughout the so-called holiday, while Kitty mooched around checking on everyone else's presents before going back to bed. Kitty never seemed to be able to hold down a job for more than a week at a time, but somehow she was still better dressed than any of us. I suppose it must have been because a string of boyfriends seemed quite willing to spend their last penny on her before going off to the front. I couldn't imagine what she expected to tell them if they all came back on the same day.

Now and then, Kitty would volunteer to do a couple of hours' work on the barrow, but once she had eaten her way through the day's profits she would soon disappear. "Couldn't describe that one as an asset," Granpa used to say. Still, I didn't complain. I was sixteen without a care in the world and my only thoughts at that time were on how soon I could get hold of my own barrow.

Mr Salmon told me that he'd heard the best barrows were being sold off in the Old Kent Road, on account of the fact that so many young lads were heeding Kitchener's cry and joining up to fight for King and country. He felt sure there wouldn't be a better time to make what he called a good *metsieh*. I thanked the baker and begged him not to let Granpa know what I was about, as I wanted to close the *metsieh* before he found out.

The following Saturday morning I asked Granpa for a couple of hours off.

"Found yourself a girl, 'ave you? Because I only 'ope it's not the boozer."

"Neither," I told him with a grin. "But you'll be the first to find out, Granpa, I promise you." I touched my cap and strolled off in the direction of the Old Kent Road.

I crossed the Thames at Tower Bridge and walked further south than I had ever been before, and when I arrived at the rival market I couldn't believe my eyes. I'd never seen so many barrows. Lined up in rows, they were. Long ones, short ones, stubby ones, in all the colours of the rainbow and some of them displaying names that went back generations in the East End. I spent over an hour checking out all those that were for sale but the only one I kept coming back to had displayed in blue on gold down its sides, "The biggest barrow in the world".

The woman who was selling the magnificent object told me that it was only a month old and her old man, who had been killed by the Huns, had paid three quid for it: she wasn't going to let it go for anything less.

I explained to her that I only had a couple of quid to my name, but I'd be willing to pay off the rest before six months were up.

"We could all be dead in six months," she replied, shaking her head with an air of someone who'd heard those sort of stories before.

"Then I'll let you 'ave two quid and sixpence, with my granpa's barrow thrown in," I said without thinking.

"Who's your granpa?"

"Charlie Trumper," I told her with pride, though if the truth be known I hadn't expected her to have heard of him.

"Charlie Trumper's your granpa?"

"What of it?" I said defiantly.

"Then two quid and sixpence will do just fine for now, young un'," she said. "And see you pay the rest back before Christmas."

That was the first time I discovered what the word "reputation" meant. I handed over my life's savings and promised that I would give her the other nineteen and six before the year was up.

We shook hands on the deal and I grabbed the handles and began to push my first cock sparrow back over the bridge towards the Whitechapel Road. When Sal and Kitty first set eyes on my prize, they couldn't stop jumping up and down with excitement and even helped me to paint down one side, "Charlie Trumper, the honest trader, founded in 1823".

Once we had finished our efforts and long before the paint was dry, I wheeled the barrow triumphantly off towards the market. By the time I was in sight of Granpa's pitch my grin already stretched from ear to ear.

The crowd around the old fellow's barrow seemed larger than usual for a Saturday morning and I couldn't work out why there was such a hush the moment I showed up. "There's young Charlie," shouted a voice and several faces turned to stare at me. Sensing trouble, I let go of the handles of my new barrow and ran into the crowd. They quickly stood aside, making a path for me. When I had reached the front, the first thing I saw was Granpa lying on the pavement, his head propped up on a box of apples and his face as white as a sheet.

I ran to his side and fell on my knees. "It's Charlie, Granpa, it's me, I'm 'ere," I cried. "What do you want me to do? Just tell me what and I'll do it."

His tired eyelids blinked slowly. "Listen to me careful, lad," he said, between gasps of breath. "The barrow now belongs to you, so never let it or the pitch out of your sight for more than a few hours at a time."

"But it's your barrow and your pitch, Granpa. 'ow will you work without a barrow and a pitch?" I asked. But he was no longer listening.

Until that moment I never realised anyone I knew could die.

CHAPTER 2

ranpa Charlie's funeral was held on a cloudless morning in early February at the church of St Mary's and St Michael's on Jubilee Street. Once the choir had filed into their places there was standing room only, and even Mr Salmon, wearing a long black coat and deep-brimmed black hat, was among those who were to be found huddled at the back.

When Charlie wheeled the brand-new barrow on to his granpa's pitch the following morning, Mr Dunkley came out of the fish and chip shop to admire the new acquisition.

"It can carry almost twice as much as my granpa's old barrow," Charlie told him. "What's more, I only owe nineteen and six on it." But by the end of the week Charlie had discovered that his barrow was still half-full of stale food that nobody wanted. Even Sal and Kitty turned up their noses when he offered them such delicacies as black bananas and bruised apples. It took several weeks before the new trader was able to work out roughly the quantities he needed each morning to satisfy his customers' needs, and still longer to realise that those needs would vary from day to day.

It was a Saturday morning, after Charlie had collected his produce from the market and was on his way back to Whitechapel, that he heard the raucous cry.

"British troops slain on the Somme," shouted out the boy who stood on the corner of Covent Garden waving a paper high above his head.

Charlie parted with a halfpenny in exchange for the *Daily Chronicle*, then sat on the pavement and started to read, picking out the words he recognised. He learned of the death of thousands of British troops who had been involved in a combined operation with the French against Kaiser Bill's army. The ill-fated exchange had ended in disaster. General Haig had predicted an advance of four thousand yards a day, but it had ended in retreat. The cry of "We'll all be home for Christmas" now seemed an idle boast.

Charlie threw the paper in the gutter. No German would kill his dad, of that he felt certain, though lately he had begun to feel guilty about his own war efforts since Grace had signed up for a spell in the hospital tents, a mere half-mile behind the front line.

Although Grace wrote to Charlie every month, she was unable to supply any news on the whereabouts of their father. "There are half a million soldiers out here," she explained, "and cold, wet and hungry they all look alike." Sal continued her job as a waitress in the Commercial Road and spent all her spare time looking for a husband, while Kitty had no trouble in finding any amount of men who were happy to satisfy her every need. In fact, Kitty was the only one of the three who had enough time off during the day to help out on the barrow, but as she never got up until the sun rose and slipped away long before it had set, she still wasn't what Granpa would have called an asset.

It was to be weeks before young Charlie would stop turning his head to ask, "'ow many, Granpa?", "'ow much, Granpa?", "Is Mrs Ruggles good for credit, Granpa?" And only after he had paid back every penny of his debt on the new barrow and been left with hardly any spare cash to talk of did he begin to realise just how good a costermonger the old fellow must have been.

For the first few months they earned only a few pennies a week between them and Sal became convinced they would all end up in the workhouse if they kept failing to cough up the rent. She begged Charlie to sell Granpa's old barrow to raise another pound, but Charlie's reply was always the same – "Never" – before adding that he would rather starve and leave the relic to rot in the back yard than let another hand wheel it away.

Soon business began to look up, and the biggest barrow in the world even returned enough of a profit to allow Sal to buy a second-hand dress, Kitty a pair of shoes and Charlie a third-hand suit.

Although Charlie was still thin – now a flyweight – and not all that tall, once his seventeenth birthday had come and gone he noticed that the ladies on the corner of the Whitechapel Road, who were still placing white feathers on anyone wearing civilian clothes who looked as if they might be between the ages of eighteen and forty, were beginning to eye him like impatient vultures.

Charlie wasn't frightened of any Germans, but he still hoped that the war might come to an end quickly and that his father would return to Whitechapel and his routine of working at the docks during the day and drinking in the Black Bull at night. But with no letters and only restricted news in the papers even Mr Salmon couldn't tell him what was really happening at the front.

As the months passed, Charlie became more and more aware of his customers' needs and in turn they were discovering that his barrow was now offering better value for money than many of its rivals. Even Charlie felt things were on the up when Mrs Smelley's smiling face appeared, to buy more potatoes for her boarding house in one morning than he would normally have hoped to sell a regular customer in a month.

"I could deliver your order, Mrs Smelley, you know," he said, raising his cap. "Direct to your boarding 'ouse every Monday mornin'."

"No, thank you, Charlie," she replied. "I always like to see what I'm buyin'."

"Give me a chance to prove myself, Mrs Smelley, and then you wouldn't 'ave to come out in all weathers, when you suddenly discover you've taken more bookin's than you expected."

She stared directly at him. "Well, I'll give it a go for a couple of weeks," she said. "But if you ever let me down, Charlie Trumper –"

"You've got yourself a deal," said Charlie with a grin, and from that day Mrs Smelley was never seen shopping for fruit or vegetables in the market again.

Charlie decided that, following this initial success, he should extend his delivery service to other customers in the East End. Perhaps that way, he thought, he might even be able to double his income. The following morning, he wheeled out his Granpa's old barrow from the back yard, removed the cobwebs, gave it a lick of paint and put Kitty on to house-to-house calls taking orders, while he remained on his pitch in Whitechapel.

Within days Charlie had lost all the profit he had made in the past year and suddenly found himself back to square one. Kitty, it turned out, had no head for figures and, worse, fell for every sob story she was told, often ending up giving the food away. By the end of that month Charlie was almost wiped out and once again unable to pay the rent.

"So what you learn from such a bold step?" asked Dan Salmon as he stood on the doorstep of his shop, skull cap on the back of his head, thumbs lodged in the black waistcoat pockets that proudly displayed his half-hunter watch.

"Think twice before you employ members of your own family and never assume that anyone will pay their debts."

"Good," said Mr Salmon. "You learn fast. So how much you need to clear rent and see yourself past next month?"

"What are you getting at?" asked Charlie.

"How much?" repeated Mr Salmon.

"Five quid," said Charlie, lowering his head.

On Friday night after he had pulled down the blind Dan Salmon handed over five sovereigns to Charlie along with several wafers of matzos. "Pay back when possible, boychik, and don't ever tell the missus or we both end up in big trouble."

Charlie paid back his loan at a rate of five shillings a week and twenty weeks later he had returned the full amount. He would always remember handing over the final payment, because it was on the same day as the first big aeroplane raid over London and he spent most of that night hiding under his father's bed, with both Sal and Kitty clinging on to him for dear life.

The following morning Charlie read an account of the bombing in the *Daily Chronicle* and learned that over a hundred Londoners had been killed and some four hundred injured in the raid.

He dug his teeth into a morning apple before he dropped off Mrs Smelley's weekly order and returned to his pitch in the Whitechapel Road. Monday was always busy with everybody stocking up after the weekend and by the time he arrived back at Number 112 for his afternoon tea he was exhausted. Charlie was sticking a fork into his third of a pork pie when he heard a knock on the door.

"Who can that be?" said Kitty, as Sal served Charlie a second potato.

"There's only one way we're going to find out, my girl," said Charlie, not budging an inch.

Kitty reluctantly left the table only to return a moment later with her nose held high in the air. "It's that Becky Salmon. Says she 'desires to have a word with you'."

"Does she now? Then you had better show Miss Salmon into the parlour," said Charlie with a grin.

Kitty slouched off again while Charlie got up from the kitchen table carrying the remainder of the pie in his fingers. He strolled into the only other room that wasn't a bedroom. He lowered himself into an old leather chair and continued chewing while he waited. A moment later Posh Porky marched into the middle of the room and stood right in front of him. She didn't speak. He was slightly taken aback by the sheer size of the girl. Although she was two or three inches shorter than Charlie, she must have weighed at least a stone more than he did; a genuine heavyweight. She so obviously hadn't given up stuffing herself with Salmon's cream buns. Charlie stared at her gleaming white blouse and dark blue pleated skirt. Her smart blue blazer sported a golden eagle surrounded by words he had never seen before. A red ribbon sat uneasily in her short dark hair and Charlie noticed that her little black shoes and white socks were as spotless as ever.

He would have asked her to sit down but as he was occupying the only chair in the room he couldn't. He ordered Kitty to leave them alone. For a moment she stared defiantly at Charlie, but then left without another word.

"So what do you want?" asked Charlie once he heard the door close.

Rebecca Salmon began to tremble as she tried to get the words out. "I've come to see you because of what has happened to my parents." She enunciated each word slowly and carefully and, to Charlie's disgust, without any trace of an East End accent.

"So what 'as 'appened to your parents?" asked Charlie gruffly, hoping she wouldn't realise that his voice had only recently broken. Becky burst into tears. Charlie's only reaction was to stare out of the window because he wasn't quite sure what else to do.

Becky continued shaking as she began to speak again. "Tata was killed in the raid last night and Mummy has been taken to the London hospital." She stopped abruptly, adding no further explanation.

Charlie jumped out of his chair. "No one told me," he said as he began pacing round the room.

"There's no way that you could possibly have known," said Becky. "I haven't even told the assistants at the shop yet. They think he's off sick for the day."

"Do you want me to tell them?" asked Charlie. "Is that why you came round?"

"No," she said, raising her head slowly and pausing for a moment. "I want you to take over the shop."

Charlie was so stunned by this suggestion that although he stopped pacing he made no attempt to reply.

"My father always used to say that it wouldn't be that long before you had your own shop, so I thought . . ."

"But I don't know the first thing about baking," stammered Charlie as he fell back into his chair.

"Tata's two assistants know everything there is to know about the trade, and I suspect you'll know even more than they do within a few months. What that shop needs at this particular moment is a salesman. My father always considered that you were as good as old Granpa Charlie and everyone knows he was the best."

"But what about my barrow?"

"It's only a few yards away from the shop, so you could easily keep an eye on both." She hesitated before adding, "Unlike your delivery service."

"You knew about that?"

"Even know you tried to pay back the last five shillings a few minutes before my father went to the synagogue one Saturday. We had no secrets."

"So 'ow would it work?" asked Charlie, beginning to feel he was always a yard behind the girl.

"You run the barrow and the shop and we'll be fifty-fifty partners."

"And what will you do to earn your share?"

"I'll check the books every month and make sure that we pay our tax on time and don't break any council regulations."

"I've never paid any taxes before," said Charlie, "and who in 'ell's name cares about the council and their soppy regulations?"

Becky's dark eyes fixed on him for the first time. "People who one day hope to be running a serious business enterprise, Charlie Trumper, that's who."

"Fifty-fifty doesn't seem all that fair to me," said Charlie, still trying to get the upper hand.

"My shop is considerably more valuable than your barrow and it also derives a far larger income."

"Did, until your father died," said Charlie, regretting the words immediately he had spoken them.

Becky bowed her head again. "Are we to be partners or not?" she muttered.

"Sixty-forty," said Charlie.

She hesitated for a long moment, then suddenly thrust out her arm. Charlie rose from the chair and shook her hand vigorously to confirm that his first deal was closed.

After Dan Salmon's funeral, Charlie tried to read the *Daily Chronicle* every morning in the hope of discovering what the second battalion, Royal Fusiliers, were up to and where his father might be. He knew the regiment was fighting somewhere in France, but its exact location was never recorded in the paper, so Charlie was none the wiser.

The daily broadsheet began to have a double fascination for Charlie, as he started to take an interest in the advertisements displayed on almost every page. He couldn't believe that those nobs in the West End were willing to pay good money for things that seemed to him to be nothing more than unnecessary luxuries. However, it didn't stop Charlie wanting to taste Coca-Cola, the latest drink from America, at a cost of a penny a bottle; or to try the new safety razor from Gillette – despite the fact that he hadn't even started shaving – at sixpence for the holder and twopence for six blades: he felt sure his father, who had only ever used a cut-throat, would consider the whole idea sissy. And a woman's girdle at two guineas struck Charlie as quite ridiculous. Neither Sal nor Kitty would ever need one of those – although Posh Porky might soon enough, the way she was going.

So intrigued did Charlie become by these seemingly endless selling opportunities that he started to take a tram up to the West End on a Sunday morning just to see for himself. Having ridden on a horse-drawn vehicle to Chelsea, he would then walk slowly back east towards Mayfair, studying all the goods in the shop windows on the way. He also noted how people dressed and admired the motor vehicles that belched out fumes but didn't drop shit as they travelled down the middle of the road. He even began to wonder just how much it cost to rent a shop in Chelsea.

On the first Sunday in October 1917 Charlie took Sal up West with him – to show her the sights, he explained.

Charlie and his sister walked slowly from shop window to shop window, and he was unable to hide his excitement at every new discovery he came across. Men's clothes, hats, shoes, women's dresses, perfume, undergarments, even cakes and pastries could hold his attention for minutes on end.

"For Gawd's sake, let's get ourselves back to Whitechapel where we belong," said Sal. "Because one thing's for sure – I'm never going to feel at 'ome 'ere."

"But don't you understand?" said Charlie. "One day I'm going to own a shop in Chelsea."

"Don't talk daft," said Sal. "Even Dan Salmon couldn't 'ave afforded one of these."

Charlie didn't bother to reply.

When it came to how long Charlie would take to master the baking trade, Becky's judgment proved accurate. Within a month he knew almost as much about oven temperatures, controls, rising yeast and the correct mixture of flour to water as either of the two assistants, and as they were dealing with the same customers as Charlie was on his barrow, sales on both dropped only slightly during the first quarter.

Becky turned out to be as good as her word, keeping the accounts in what she described as "apple-pie order" and even opening a set of books for Trumper's barrow. By the end of their first three months as partners they declared a profit of four pounds eleven shillings, despite having a gas oven refitted at Salmon's and allowing Charlie to buy his first second-hand suit.

Sal continued working as a waitress in a café on the Commercial Road, but Charlie knew she couldn't wait to find someone willing to marry her – whatever physical shape he was in – just as long as I can sleep in a room of my own, she explained.

Grace never failed to send a letter on the first of every month, and somehow managed to sound cheerful despite being surrounded by death. She's just like her mother, Father O'Malley would tell his parishioners. Kitty still came and went as she pleased, borrowing money from both her sisters as well as Charlie, and never paying them back. Just like her father, the priest told the same parishioners.

"Like your new suit," said Mrs Smelley, when Charlie dropped off her weekly order that Monday afternoon. He blushed, raised his cap and pretended not to hear the compliment, as he dashed off to the baker's shop.

The second quarter promised to show a further profit on both Charlie's enterprises, and he warned Becky that he had his eye on the butcher's shop, since the owner's only boy had lost his life at Passchendaele. Becky cautioned him against rushing into another venture before they had discovered what their profit margins were like, and then only if the rather elderly assistants knew what they were up to. "Because one thing's for certain, Charlie Trumper," she told him as they sat down in the little room at the back of Salmon's to check the monthly accounts, "you don't know the first thing about butchery. 'Trumper, the Honest Trader, founded in 1823' still appeals to me," she added. "'Trumper, the Foolish Bankrupt, folded in 1917' doesn't."

Becky also commented on the new suit, but not until she had finished checking a lengthy column of figures. He was about to return the compliment by suggesting that she might have lost a little weight when she leaned across and helped herself to another jam tart.

She ran a sticky finger down the monthly balance-sheet, then checked the figures against the handwritten bank statement. A profit of eight pounds and fourteen shillings, she wrote in thick black ink neatly on the bottom line.

"At this rate we'll be millionaires by the time I'm forty," said Charlie with a grin.

"Forty, Charlie Trumper?" Becky repeated disdainfully. "Not exactly in a hurry, are you?"

"What do you mean?" asked Charlie.

"Just that I was rather hoping we might have achieved that long before then."

Charlie laughed loudly to cover the fact that he wasn't quite certain whether or not she was joking. Once Becky felt sure the ink was dry she closed the books and put them back in her satchel while Charlie prepared to lock up the baker's shop. As they stepped out on to the pavement Charlie bade his partner goodnight with an exaggerated bow. He then turned the key in the lock before starting his journey home. He whistled "It's a Long Way to Tipperary" out of tune as he pushed the few remains left over from the day towards the setting sun. Could he really make a million before he was forty, or had Becky just been teasing him?

As he reached Bert Shorrocks's place Charlie came to a sudden halt. Outside the front door of 112, dressed in a long black cassock, black hat, and with black bible in hand, stood Father O'Malley.

CHAPTER 3

harlie sat in the carriage of a train bound for Edinburgh and thought about the actions he had taken during the past four days. Becky had described his decision as foolhardy. Sal hadn't bothered with the hardy. Mrs Smelley didn't think he should have gone until he had been called up, while Grace was still tending the wounded on the Western Front, so she didn't even know what he had done. As for Kitty, she just sulked and asked how she was expected to survive without him.

Private George Trumper had been killed on 2 November 1917 at Passchendaele, the letter had informed him: bravely, while charging the enemy lines at Polygon Wood. Over a thousand men had died that day attacking a ten-mile front from Messines to Passchendaele, so it wasn't surprising that the lieutenant's letter was short and to the point.

After a sleepless night, Charlie was the first to be found the following morning standing outside the recruiting office in Great Scotland Yard. The poster on the wall called for volunteers between the ages of eighteen and forty to join up and serve in "General Haig's" army.

Although not yet eighteen, Charlie prayed that they wouldn't reject him.

When the recruiting sergeant barked, "Name?" Charlie threw out his chest and almost shouted, "Trumper." He waited anxiously.

"Date of birth?" said the man with three white stripes on his arm.

"Twentieth of January, 1899," replied Charlie without hesitation, but his cheeks flushed as he delivered the words.

The recruiting sergeant looked up at him and winked. The letters and numbers were written on a buff form without comment. "Remove your cap, lad, and report to the medical officer."

A nurse led Charlie through to a cubicle where an elderly man in a long white coat made him strip to the waist, cough, stick out his tongue and breathe heavily before prodding him all over with a cold rubber object. He then proceeded to stare into Charlie's ears and eyes before going on to hit his kneecaps with a rubber stick. After taking his trousers and underpants off – for the first time ever in front of someone who wasn't a member of his family – he was told he had no transmittable diseases – whatever they were, thought Charlie.

He stared at himself in the mirror as they measured him. "Five foot nine and a quarter," said the orderly.

And still growing, Charlie wanted to add, as he pushed a mop of dark hair out of his eyes.

"Teeth in good condition, eyes brown," stated the elderly doctor. "Not much wrong with you," he added. The old man made a series of ticks down the right-hand side of the buff form before telling Charlie to report back to the chap with the three white stripes.

Charlie found himself waiting in another queue before coming face to face with the sergeant again.

"Right, lad, sign up here and we'll issue you with a travel warrant."

Charlie scrawled his signature on the spot above where the sergeant's finger rested. He couldn't help noticing that the man didn't have a thumb.

"The Honourable Artillery Company or Royal Fusiliers?" the sergeant asked.

"Royal Fusiliers," said Charlie. "That was my old man's regiment."

"Royal Fusiliers it is then," said the sergeant without a second thought, and put a tick in yet another box.

"When do I get my uniform?"

"Not until you get to Edinburgh, lad. Report to King's Cross at zero eight hundred hours tomorrow morning. Next."

Charlie returned to 112 Whitechapel Road to spend another sleepless night. His thoughts dotted from Sal to Grace and then on to Kitty and how two of his sisters would survive in his absence. He also began thinking about Rebecca Salmon and their bargain, but in the end his thoughts always returned to his father's grave on a foreign battlefield and the revenge he intended to inflict on any German who dared to cross his path. These sentiments remained with him until the morning light came shining through the windows.

Charlie put on his new suit, the one Mrs Smelley had commented on, his best shirt, his father's tie, a flat cap and his only pair of leather shoes. I'm meant to be fighting the Germans, not going to a wedding, he said out loud, as he looked at himself in the cracked mirror above the wash-basin. He had already written a note to Becky – with a little help from Father O'Malley – instructing her to sell the shop along with the two barrows if she possibly could and to hold on to his share of the money until he came back to Whitechapel. No one talked about Christmas any longer.

"And if you don't return?" Father O'Malley had asked, head slightly bowed. "What's to happen to your possessions then?"

"Divide anything that's left over equally between my three sisters," Charlie said.

Father O'Malley wrote out his former pupil's instructions and for the second time in as many days Charlie signed his name to an official document.

After Charlie had finished dressing, he found Sal and Kitty waiting for him by the front door, but he refused to allow them to accompany him to the station, despite their tearful protest. Both his sisters kissed him – another first – and Kitty had to have her hand prised out of his before

Charlie was able to pick up the brown paper parcel that contained all his worldly goods.

Alone, he walked to the market and entered the baker's shop for the last time. The two assistants swore that nothing would have changed by the time he returned. He left the shop only to find another barrow boy, who looked about a year younger than himself, was already selling chestnuts from his pitch. He walked slowly through the market in the direction of King's Cross, never once looking back.

He arrived at the Great Northern station half an hour earlier than he had been instructed and immediately reported to the sergeant who had signed him up on the previous day. "Right, Trumper, get yourself a cup of char, then 'ang about on platform three." Charlie couldn't remember when he had last been given an order, let alone obeyed one. Certainly not since his grandfather's death.

Platform three was already crowded with men in uniforms and civilian clothes, some chatting noisily, others standing silent and alone, each displaying his own particular sense of insecurity.

At eleven, three hours after they had been ordered to report, they were finally given instructions to board a train. Charlie grabbed a seat in the corner of an unlit carriage and stared out of the grimy window at a passing English countryside he had never seen before. A mouth-organ was being played in the corridor, all the popular melodies of the day slightly out of tune. As they travelled through city stations, some he hadn't even heard of – Peterborough, Grantham, Newark, York – crowds waved and cheered their heroes. In Durham the engine came to a halt to take on more coal and water. The recruiting sergeant told them all to disembark, stretch their legs and grab another cup of char, and added that if they were lucky they might even get something to eat.

Charlie walked along the platform munching a sticky bun to the sound of a military band playing "Land of Hope and Glory". The war was everywhere. Once they were back on the train there was yet more waving of handkerchiefs from pin-hatted ladies who would remain spinsters for the rest of their lives.

The train chugged on northwards, further and further away from the enemy, until it finally came to a halt at Waverley station in Edinburgh. As they stepped from the carriage a captain, three NCOs and a thousand women were waiting on the platform to welcome them.

Charlie heard the words, "Carry on, Sergeant-Major," and a moment later a man who must have been six feet six inches in height, and whose beer-barrel chest was covered in medal ribbons, took a pace forward.

"Let's 'ave you in line then," the giant shouted in an unintelligible accent. He quickly – but, Charlie was to learn later, by his own standards, slowly – organised the men into ranks of four before reporting back to someone who Charlie assumed must have been an officer. He saluted the man. "All present and correct, sir," he said and the smartest-dressed man Charlie had ever seen in his life returned the salute. He appeared slight standing next to the sergeant-major, although he must have been a shade over six feet himself. His uniform was immaculate, but paraded no medals, and the creases on his trousers were so sharp that Charlie wondered if they had ever been worn before. The young officer held a short leather stick in a gloved hand and occasionally thumped the side of his leg with it, as if he thought he were on horseback. Charlie's eyes settled on the officer's Sam Browne belt and brown leather shoes. They shone so brightly they reminded him of Rebecca Salmon.

"My name is Captain Trentham," the man informed the expectant band of untrained warriors, in an accent that Charlie suspected would have sounded more in place in Mayfair than at a railway station in Scotland. "I'm the battalion adjutant," he went on to explain, as he swayed from foot to foot, "and will be responsible for this intake for the period that you are billeted in Edinburgh. First we will march to the barracks, where you will be issued with supplies so that you can get yourselves bedded down. Supper will be served at nineteen hundred hours and lights out will be at twenty-one hundred hours. Tomorrow morning reveille will be sounded at zero five hundred, when you will rise and have breakfast before you begin your basic training at zero six hundred. This routine will last for the next twelve weeks. And I can promise you that it will be twelve weeks of absolute hell," he added, sounding as if the idea didn't altogether displease him. "During this period Sergeant-Major Philpott will be the senior warrant officer in charge of the unit. The sergeant-major fought on the Somme, where he was awarded the Military Medal, so he knows exactly what you can expect when we eventually end up in France and have to face the enemy. Listen to his every word carefully, because it might be the one thing that saves your life. Carry on, Sergeant-Major."

"Thank you, sir," said Sergeant-Major Philpott in a clipped bark.

The motley band stared in awe at the figure who would be in charge of their lives for the next three months. He was, after all, a man who had seen the enemy and come home to tell the tale.

"Right, let's be having you then," he said, and proceeded to lead his recruits – carrying everything from battered suitcases to brown paper parcels – through the streets of Edinburgh at the double, only to be sure that the locals didn't realise just how undisciplined this rabble really was. Despite their amateur appearance, passers-by still stopped to cheer and clap. Out of the corner of one eye Charlie couldn't help noticing that one of them was resting his only hand against his only leg. Some twenty minutes later, after a climb up the biggest hill Charlie had ever seen, one that literally took his breath away, they entered the barracks of Edinburgh Castle.

That evening Charlie hardly opened his mouth as he listened to the different accents of the men babbling around him. After a supper of pea soup – "One pea each," the duty corporal quipped – and bully beef, he was quartered – and learning new words by the minute – in a large gymnasium that temporarily housed four hundred beds, each a mere two feet in width and set only a foot apart. On a thin horsehair mattress rested one sheet, one pillow and one blanket. King's Regulations.

It was the first time Charlie had thought that 112 Whitechapel Road might be considered luxurious. Exhausted, he collapsed on to the unmade bed, fell asleep, but still woke the next morning at four thirty. This time, however, there was no market to go to, and certainly no choice as to whether he should select a Cox's or a Granny Smith for breakfast.

At five a lone bugle woke his companions from their drowsy slumber. Charlie was already up, washed and dressed when a man with two stripes on his sleeve marched in. He slammed the door behind him and shouted, "Up, up, up," as he kicked the end of any bed that still had a body supine on it. The raw recruits leapt up and formed a queue to wash in basins half full of freezing water, changed only after every third man. Some then went off to the latrines behind the back of the hall, which Charlie thought smelled worse than the middle of Whitechapel Road on a steaming summer's day.

Breakfast consisted of one ladle of porridge, half a cup of milk and a dry biscuit, but no one complained. The cheerful noise that emanated from that hall wouldn't have left any German in doubt that these recruits were all united against a common enemy.

At six, after their beds had been made and inspected, they all trudged out into the dark cold air and on to the parade ground, its surface covered in a thin film of snow.

"If this is bonny Scotland," Charlie heard a Cockney accent declare, "then I'm a bloody Dutchman." Charlie laughed for the first time since he had left Whitechapel and strolled over to a youth far smaller than himself who was rubbing his hands between his legs as he tried to keep warm.

"Where you from?" Charlie asked.

"Poplar, mate. And you?"

"Whitechapel."

"Bloody foreigner."

Charlie stared at his new companion. The youth couldn't have been an inch over five feet three, skinny with dark curly hair and flashing eyes that never seemed to be still, as if he were always on the lookout for trouble. His shiny, elbow-patched suit hung on him, making his shoulders look like a coathanger.

"Charlie Trumper's the name."

"Tommy Prescott," came back the reply. He stopped his exercises and thrust out a warm hand. Charlie shook it vigorously.

"Quiet in the ranks," hollered the sergeant-major. "Now let's get you formed up in columns of three. Tallest on the right, shortest on the left. Move." They parted.

For the next two hours they carried out what the sergeant-major described as "drill". The snow continued to drop unceasingly from the sky, but the sergeant-major showed no inclination to allow one flake to settle on his parade ground. They marched in column of fours, which Charlie later learned were called platoons, arms swinging to waist height, heads held high, one hundred and twenty paces to the minute. "Look lively, lads," and "Keep in step," were the words Charlie had shouted at him again and again. "The Bosche are also marching out there somewhere, and they can't wait to have a crack at you lot," the sergeant-major assured them as the snow continued to fall.

Had he been in Whitechapel, Charlie would have been happy to run up and down the market from five in the morning to seven at night and still box a few rounds at the club, drink a couple of pints of beer and carry out the same routine the next day without a second thought, but when at nine o'clock the sergeant-major gave them a ten-minute break for cocoa he collapsed on to the verge exhausted. Looking up, he found Tommy Prescott peering at him. "Fag?"

"No, thanks," said Charlie. "I don't smoke."

"What's your trade then?" asked Tommy, lighting up.

"I own a baker's shop on the corner of Whitechapel Road," replied Charlie, "and a —"

"Ring the other one, it's got bells on," interrupted

Tommy. "Next you'll be telling me your dad's Lord Mayor of London."

Charlie laughed. "Not exactly. So what do you do?"

"Work for a brewery, don't I? Whitbread and Co, Chiswell Street, EC1. I'm the one who puts the barrels on the carts, and then the shire 'orses pulls me round the East End so that I can deliver my wares. Pay's not good, but you can always drink yourself silly before you get back each night."

"So what made you join up?"

"Now that's a long story, that is," replied Tommy. "You see, to start with – "

"Right. Back on parade, you lot," shouted Sergeant-Major Philpott, and neither man had the breath to speak another word for the next two hours as they were marched up and down, up and down, until Charlie felt that when they eventually stopped his feet must surely fall off.

Lunch consisted of bread and cheese, neither of which Charlie would have dared to offer for sale to Mrs Smelley. As they munched hungrily he learned how Tommy at the age of eighteen had been given the choice of two years at His Majesty's pleasure or volunteering to fight for King and country. He tossed a coin and the King's head landed face up.

"Two years?" said Charlie. "But what for?"

"Nicking the odd barrel 'ere and there and making a side deal with one or two of the more crafty landlords. I'd been getting away with it for ages. An 'undred years ago they would 'ave 'anged me on the spot or sent me off to Australia, so I can't complain. After all, that's what I'm trained for, ain't it?"

"What do you mean?" asked Charlie.

"Well, my father was a professional pick-pocket, wasn't 'e? And 'is father before 'im. You should have seen Captain Trentham's face when 'e found out that I had chosen a spell in the Fusiliers rather than going back to gaol."

Twenty minutes was the time allocated for lunch and then the afternoon was taken up with being fitted with a uniform. Charlie, who turned out to be a regular size, was dealt with fairly quickly, but it took almost an hour to find anything that didn't make Tommy look as if he was entering a sack race.

Once they were back in the billet Charlie folded up his best suit and placed it under the bed next to the one Tommy had settled on, then swaggered around the room in his new uniform.

"Dead men's clothes," warned Tommy, as he looked up and studied Charlie's khaki jacket.

"What do you mean?"

"Been sent back from the front, 'asn't it? Cleaned and sewn up," said Tommy, pointing to a two-inch mend just above Charlie's heart. "About wide enough to thrust a bayonet through, I reckon," he added.

After another two-hour session on the now freezing parade ground they were released for supper.

"More bloody stale bread and cheese," said Tommy morosely, but Charlie was far too hungry to complain as he scooped up every last crumb with a wet finger. For the second night running he collapsed on his bed.

"Enjoyed our first day serving King and country, 'ave we?" asked the duty corporal of his charges, when at twenty-one hundred hours he turned down the gas lights in the barrack room.

"Yes, thank you, Corp," came back the sarcastic cry.

"Good," said the corporal, "because we're always gentle with you on the first day."

A groan went up that Charlie reckoned must have been heard in the middle of Edinburgh. Above the nervous chatter that continued once the corporal had left, Charlie could hear the last post being played on a bugle from the castle battlements. He fell asleep.

When Charlie woke the next morning he jumped out of bed immediately and was washed and dressed before anyone else had stirred. He had folded up his sheets and blankets and was polishing his boots by the time reveille sounded.

"Aren't we the early bird?" said Tommy, as he turned over. "But why bother, I ask myself, when all you're goin' to get for breakfast is a worm."

"If you're first in the queue at least it's an 'ot worm," said Charlie. "And in any case – "

"Feet on the floor. *On* the *floor*," the corporal bellowed, as he entered the billet and banged the frame on the end of every bed he passed with his cane.

"Of course," suggested Tommy, as he tried to stifle a yawn, "a man of property like yourself would need to be up early of a mornin', to make sure 'is workers were already on parade and not shirkin'."

"Stop talking you two and look sharpish," said the corporal. "And get yourselves dressed or you'll find yourself on fatigues."

"I am dressed, Corp," insisted Charlie.

"Don't answer me back, laddie, and don't call me 'Corp' unless you want a spell cleaning out the latrines." That threat was even enough to get Tommy's feet on the floor.

The second morning consisted of more drill accompanied by the ever-falling snow, which this time had a two-inch start on them, followed by another lunch of bread and cheese. The afternoon, however, was designated on company orders as 'Games and Recreation'. So it was a change of kit before jogging in step over to the gymnasium for physical jerks followed by boxing instruction.

Charlie, now a light middleweight, couldn't wait to get in the ring while Tommy somehow managed to keep himself out of the firing line, although both of them became aware of Captain Trentham's menacing presence as his swagger stick continually struck the side of his leg. He always seemed to be hanging about, keeping a watchful eye on them. The only smile that crossed his lips all afternoon was when he saw someone knocked out. And every time he came across Tommy he just scowled.

"I'm one of nature's seconds," Tommy told Charlie later that evening. "You've no doubt 'eard the expression 'seconds out'. Well, that's me," he explained as his friend lay on his bed, staring up at the ceiling.

"Do we ever escape from this place, Corp?" Tommy asked when the duty corporal entered the barracks a few minutes before lights out. "You know, for like good behaviour?"

"You'll be allowed out on Saturday night," said the corporal. "Three hours' restricted leave from six to nine, when you can do what you please. However, you will go no further than two miles from the barracks, you will behave in a manner that befits a Royal Fusilier and you will report back to the guardroom sober as a judge at one minute before nine. Sleep well, my lovelies." These were the corporal's final words before he went round the barracks turning down every one of the gas lights.

When Saturday night eventually came, two swollen-footed, limb-aching, shattered soldiers covered as much of the city as they possibly could in three hours with only five shillings each to spend, a problem that limited their discussions on which pub to select.

Despite this, Tommy seemed to know how to get more beer per penny out of any landlord than Charlie had ever dreamed possible, even when he couldn't understand what they were saying or make himself understood. While they were in their last port of call, the Volunteer, Tommy even disappeared out of the pub followed by the barmaid, a pert, slightly plump girl called Rose. Ten minutes later he was back.

"What were you doin' out there?" asked Charlie.

"What do you think, idiot?"

"But you were only away for ten minutes."

"Quite enough time," said Tommy. "Only officers need more than ten minutes for what I was up to."

During the following week they had their first rifle lesson, bayonet practice and even a session of map-reading. While Charlie quickly mastered the art of map-reading it was Tommy who took only a day to find his way round a rifle. By their third lesson he could strip the barrel and put the pieces back together again faster than the instructor.

On Wednesday morning of the second week Captain Trentham gave them their first lecture on the history of the Royal Fusiliers. Charlie might have quite enjoyed the lesson if Trentham hadn't left the impression that none of them was worthy of being in the same regiment as himself.

"Those of us who selected the Royal Fusiliers because of historic links or family ties may feel that allowing criminals to join our ranks simply because we're at war is hardly likely to advance the regiment's reputation," he said, looking pointedly in the direction of Tommy.

"Stuck-up snob," declared Tommy, just loud enough to reach every ear in the lecture theatre except the captain's. The ripple of laughter that followed brought a scowl to Trentham's face.

On Thursday afternoon Captain Trentham returned to the gym, but this time he was not striking the side of his leg with a swagger stick. He was kitted up in a white gym singlet, dark blue shorts and a thick white sweater, the new outfit just as neat and tidy as his uniform. He walked around watching the instructors putting the men through their paces and, as on his last visit, seemed to take a particular interest in what was going on in the boxing ring. For an hour the men were placed in pairs while they received basic instructions, first in defence and then attack. "Hold your guard up, laddie," were the words barked out again and again whenever fists reached chins.

By the time Charlie and Tommy climbed through the ropes, Tommy had made it clear to his friend that he hoped to get away with three minutes' shadow-boxing.

"Get stuck into each other, you two," shouted Trentham, but although Charlie started to jab away at Tommy's chest he made no attempt to inflict any real pain.

"If you don't get on with it, I'll take on both of you, one after the other," shouted Trentham.

"I'll bet 'e couldn't knock the cream off a custard puddin'," said Tommy, but this time his voice did carry, and to the instructor's dismay, Trentham immediately leapt up into the ring and said, "We'll see about that." He asked the coach to fit him up with a pair of boxing gloves.

"I'll have three rounds with each of these two men," Trentham said as a reluctant instructor laced up the captain's gloves. Everyone else in the gymnasium stopped to watch what was going on.

"You first. What's your name?" asked the captain, pointing to Tommy.

"Prescott, sir," said Tommy, with a grin.

"Ah yes, the convict," said Trentham, and removed the grin in the first minute, as Tommy danced around him trying to stay out of trouble. In the second round Trentham began to land the odd punch, but never hard enough to allow Tommy to go down. He saved that humiliation for the third round, when he knocked Tommy out with an uppercut that the lad from Poplar never saw. Tommy was carried out of the ring as Charlie was having his gloves laced up.

"Now it's your turn," said Trentham. "What's your name?"

"Trumper, sir."

"Well. Let's get on with it, Trumper," was all the captain said before advancing towards him.

For the first two minutes Charlie defended himself well, using the ropes and the corner as he ducked and dived, remembering every skill he had learned at the Whitechapel Boys' Club. He felt he might even have given the captain a good run for his money if it hadn't been for the damn man's obvious advantage of height and weight.

By the third minute Charlie had begun to gain confidence and even landed a punch or two, to the delight of the onlookers. As the round ticked to an end, he felt he had acquitted himself rather well. When the bell sounded he dropped his gloves and turned to go back to his corner. A second later the captain's clenched fist landed on the side of Charlie's nose. Everyone in that gymnasium heard the break as Charlie staggered against the ropes. No one murmured as the captain unlaced his gloves and climbed out of the ring. Never let your guard down was the only solace he offered.

When Tommy studied the state of his friend's face that night as Charlie lay on his bed, all he said was, "Sorry, mate, all my fault. Bloody man's a sadist. But don't worry, if the Germans don't get the bastard, I will."

Charlie could only manage a thin smile.

By Saturday they had both recovered sufficiently to fall in with the rest of the company for pay parade, waiting in a long queue to collect five shillings each from the paymaster. During their three hours off duty that night the pennies disappeared more quickly than the queue, but Tommy somehow continued to get better value for money than any other recruit.

By the beginning of the third week, Charlie could only just fit his swollen toes into the heavy leather boots the army had supplied him with, but looking down the rows of feet that adorned the barrack room floor each morning he could see that none of his comrades was any better off.

"Fatigues for you, my lad, that's for sure," shouted the corporal. Charlie shot him a glance, but the words were being directed at the occupant of the next bed.

"What for, Corp?" asked Tommy.

"For the state of your sheets. Just look at them. You might have had three women in there with you during the night."

"Only two, to be 'onest with you, Corp."

"Less of your lip, Prescott, and see that you report for latrines duty straight after breakfast."

"I've already been this morning, thank you, Corp."

"Shut up, Tommy," said Charlie. "You're only makin' things more difficult for yourself."

"I see you're gettin' to understand my problem," whispered Tommy. "It's just that the corp's worse than the bloody Germans."

"I can only 'ope so, lad, for your sake," came back the corporal's reply. "Because that's the one chance you've got of coming through this whole thing alive. Now get yourself off to the latrines – at the double."

Tommy disappeared, only to return an hour later smelling like a manure heap.

"You could kill off the entire German army without any of us having to fire a shot," said Charlie. "All you'd 'ave to do is stand in front of 'em and 'ope the wind was blowin' in the right direction."

It was during the fifth week – Christmas and the New Year having passed with little to celebrate – that Charlie was put in charge of the duty roster for his own section.

"They'll be makin' you a bleedin' colonel before you've finished," said Tommy.

"Don't be stupid," replied Charlie. "Everyone gets a chance at runnin' the section at some time durin' the twelve weeks."

"Can't see them takin' that risk with me," said Tommy. "I'd turn the rifles on the officers and my first shot would be aimed at that bastard Trentham."

Charlie found that he enjoyed the responsibility of having to organise the section for seven days and was only sorry when his week was up and the task was handed on to someone else.

By the sixth week, Charlie could strip and clean a rifle almost as quickly as Tommy, but it was his friend who turned out to be a crack shot and seemed to be able to hit anything that moved at two hundred yards. Even the sergeant-major was impressed.

"All those hours spent on rifle ranges at fairs might 'ave somethin' to do with it," admitted Tommy. "But what I want to know is, when do I get a crack at the Huns?"

"Sooner than you think, lad," promised the corporal.

"Must complete twelve weeks' trainin'," said Charlie. "That's King's Regulations. So we won't get the chance for at least another month."

"King's Regulations be damned," said Tommy. "I'm

told this war could be all over before I even get a shot at them."

"Not much 'ope of that," said the corporal, as Charlie reloaded and took aim.

"Trumper," barked a voice.

"Yes, sir," said Charlie, surprised to find the duty sergeant standing by his side.

"The adjutant wants to see you. Follow me."

"But, Sergeant, I haven't done anythin' –"

"Don't argue, lad, just follow me."

"It 'as to be the firin' squad," said Tommy. "And just because you wet your bed. Tell 'im I'll volunteer to be the one who pulls the trigger. That way at least you can be certain it'd be over quick."

Charlie unloaded his magazine, grounded his rifle and chased after the sergeant.

"Don't forget, you can insist on a blindfold. Just a pity you don't smoke," were Tommy's last words as Charlie disappeared across the parade ground at the double.

The sergeant came to a halt outside the adjutant's hut, and an out-of-breath Charlie caught up with him just as the door was opened by a colour-sergeant who turned to Charlie and said, "Stand to attention, lad, remain one pace behind me and don't speak unless you're spoken to. Understood?"

"Yes, Colour-Sergeant."

Charlie followed the colour-sergeant through the outer office until they reached another door marked "Capt Trentham, Adj". Charlie could feel his heart pumping away as the colour-sergeant knocked quietly on the door.

"Enter," said a bored voice and the two men marched in, took four paces forward and came to a halt in front of Captain Trentham.

The colour-sergeant saluted.

"Trumper, Private 7312087, reporting as ordered, sir," he bellowed, despite neither of them being more than a yard away from Captain Trentham.

The adjutant looked up from behind his desk.

"Ah, yes, Trumper. I remember, you're the baker's lad from Whitechapel." Charlie was about to correct him when Trentham turned away to stare out of the window, obviously not anticipating a reply. "The sergeant-major has had his eye on you for several weeks," Trentham continued, "and feels you'd be a good candidate for promotion to lance-corporal. I have my doubts, I must confess. However, I do accept that occasionally it's necessary to promote a volunteer in order to keep up morale in the ranks. I presume you will take on this responsibility, Trumper?" he added, still not bothering to look in Charlie's direction.

Charlie didn't know what to say.

"Yes, sir, thank you, sir," offered the colour-sergeant before bellowing, "About turn, quick march, left, right, left, right."

Ten seconds later Lance-Corporal Charlie Trumper of the Royal Fusiliers found himself back out on the parade ground.

"Lance-Corporal Trumper," said Tommy in disbelief after he had been told the news. "Does that mean I 'ave to call you 'sir'?"

"Don't be daft, Tommy. 'Corp' will do," Charlie said with a grin, as he sat on the end of the bed sewing a single stripe on to a sleeve of his uniform.

The following day Charlie's section of ten began to wish that he hadn't spent the previous fourteen years of his life visiting the early morning market. Their drill, their boots, their turn-out and their weapons training became the benchmark for the whole company, as Charlie drove them harder and harder. The highlight for Charlie, however, came in the eleventh week, when they left the barracks to travel to Glasgow where Tommy won the top prize for rifle shooting, beating all the officers and men from seven other regiments.

"You're a genius," said Charlie, after the colonel had presented his friend with the silver cup.

"Wonder if there's an 'alf good fence to be found in Glasgow," was all Tommy had to say on the subject.

* * *

The passing out parade was held on Saturday, 23 February 1918, which ended with Charlie marching his section up and down the parade ground keeping step with the regimental band, and for the first time feeling like a soldier – even if Tommy still resembled a sack of potatoes.

When the parade finally came to an end, Sergeant-Major Philpott congratulated them all and before dismissing the parade told the troops they could take the rest of the day off, but they must return to barracks and be tucked up in bed before midnight.

The assembled company was let loose on Edinburgh for the last time. Tommy took charge again as the lads of Number Eleven Platoon lurched from pub to pub becoming drunker and drunker, before finally ending up in their established local, the Volunteer, on Leith Walk.

Ten happy soldiers stood around the piano sinking pint after pint as they sang, "Pack up your troubles in your old kit bag" and repeating every other item in their limited repertoire. Tommy, who was accompanying them on the mouth-organ, noticed that Charlie couldn't take his eyes off Rose the barmaid who, although on the wrong side of thirty, never stopped flirting with the young recruits. Tommy broke away from the group to join his friend at the bar. "Fancy 'er, mate, do you?"

"Yep, but she's your girl," said Charlie as he continued to stare at the long-haired blonde who pretended to ignore their attentions. He noticed that she had one button of her blouse more than usual undone.

"I wouldn't say that," said Tommy. "In any case, I owe you one for that broken nose."

Charlie laughed when Tommy added, "So we'll 'ave to see what I can do about it." Tommy winked at Rose, then left Charlie to join her at the far end of the bar.

Charlie found that he couldn't get himself to look at them, although he was still able to see from their reflection in the mirror behind the bar that they were deep in conversation. Rose on a couple of occasions turned to look in his direction. A moment later Tommy was standing by his side.

"It's all fixed, Charlie," he said.

"What do you mean, fixed?"

"Exactly what I said. All you 'ave to do is go out to the shed at the back of the pub where they pile up them empty crates, and Rose should be with you in a jiffy."

Charlie sat glued to the bar stool.

"Well, get on with it," said Tommy, "before the bleedin' woman changes her mind."

Charlie slipped off his stool and out of a side door without looking back. He only hoped that no one was watching him, as he almost ran down the unlit passage and out of the back door. He stood alone in the corner of the yard feeling more than a little stupid as he stamped up and down to keep warm. A shiver went through him and he began to wish he were back in the bar. A few moments later he shivered again, sneezed and decided the time had come to return to his mates and forget it. He was walking towards the door just as Rose came bustling out.

"'ello, I'm Rose. Sorry I took so long, but a customer came in just as you darted off." He stared at her in the poor light that filtered through a tiny window above the door. Yet another button was undone, revealing the top of a black girdle.

"Charlie Trumper," said Charlie, offering her his hand.

"I know," she giggled. "Tommy told me all about you, said you were probably the best lay in the platoon."

"I think 'e might 'ave been exaggeratin'," said Charlie, turning bright red, as Rose reached out with both her hands, taking him in her arms. She kissed him first on his neck, then his face and finally his mouth. She then parted Charlie's lips expertly before her tongue began to play with his.

To begin with Charlie was not quite sure what was happening, but he liked the sensation so much that he just continued to hold on to her, and after a time even began to press his tongue against hers. It was Rose who was the first to break away.

"Not so hard, Charlie. Relax. Prizes are awarded for endurance, not for strength."

Charlie began to kiss her again, this time more gently as he felt the corner of a beer crate jab into his buttocks. He tentatively placed a hand on her left breast, and let it remain there, not quite sure what to do next as he tried to make himself slightly more comfortable. It didn't seem to matter that much, because Rose knew exactly what was expected of her and quickly undid the remaining buttons of her blouse, revealing ample breasts well worthy of her name. She lifted a leg up on to a pile of old beer crates, leaving Charlie faced with an expanse of bare pink thigh. He placed his free hand tentatively on the soft flesh. He wanted to run his fingers up as far as they would go, but he remained motionless, like a frozen frame in a black and white film.

Once again Rose took the lead, and removing her arms from around his neck started to undo the buttons on the front of his trousers. A moment later she slid her hand inside his underpants and started to rub. Charlie couldn't believe what was happening although he felt it was well worth getting a broken nose for.

Rose began to rub faster and faster and started to pull down her knickers with her free hand. Charlie felt more and more out of control until suddenly Rose stopped, pulled herself away and stared down the front of her dress. "If you're the best lay the platoon has to offer, I can only hope the Germans win this bloody war."

The following morning battalion orders were posted on the board. The new battalion of Fusiliers was now considered to be of fighting strength and was expected to join the Allies on the Western Front. Charlie wondered if the comradeship that had bound such a disparate bunch of lads together during the past three months was quite enough to make them capable of joining combat with the elite of the German army.

On the train journey back south they were cheered once

again as they passed through every station, and this time Charlie felt they were more worthy of the hatted ladies' respect. Finally that evening the engine pulled into Maidstone where they disembarked, and were put up for the night at the local barracks of the Royal West Kents.

At zero six hundred hours the following morning Captain Trentham gave them a full briefing: they were to be transported by ship to Boulogne, they learned, and after ten days' further training they would be expected to march on to Etaples, where they would join their regiment under the command of Lieutenant-Colonel Sir Danvers Hamilton DSO, who, they were assured, was preparing for a massive assault on the German defences. They spent the rest of the morning checking over their equipment before being herded up a gangplank and on to the waiting troop carrier.

After the ship's foghorn had blasted out six times, they set sail from Dover, one thousand men huddled together on the deck of HMS *Resolution* singing, "It's a Long Way to Tipperary".

"Ever been abroad before, Corp?" Tommy asked.

"No, not unless you count Scotland," replied Charlie.

"Neither 'ave I," said Tommy nervously. After a few more minutes he mumbled, "You frightened?"

"No, of course not," said Charlie. "Bleedin' terrified."

"Me too," said Tommy.

"Goodbye Piccadilly, farewell Leicester Square. It's a long, long way to . . ."

CHAPTER 4

harlie felt seasick only a few minutes after the English coast was out of sight. "I've never been on a boat before," he admitted to Tommy, "unless you count the paddle steamer at Brighton." Over half the men around him spent the crossing bringing up what little food they had eaten for breakfast.

"No officers coughin' up as far as I can see," said Tommy.

"Perhaps that lot are used to sailin'."

"Or doing it in their cabins."

When at last the French coast came in sight, a cheer went up from the soldiers on deck. By then all they wanted to do was set foot on dry land. And dry it would have been if the heavens hadn't opened the moment the ship docked and the troops set foot on French soil. Once everyone had disembarked, the sergeant-major warned them to prepare for a fifteen-mile route-march.

Charlie kept his section squelching forward through the mud with songs from the music-halls, accompanied by Tommy on the mouth-organ. When they reached Etaples and had pitched their tents for the night, Charlie decided that perhaps the gymnasium in Edinburgh had been luxury after all.

Once the last post had been played two thousand eyes closed, as soldiers under canvas for the first time tried to sleep. Each platoon had placed two men on guard duty, with orders to change them every two hours, to ensure that no one went without rest. Charlie drew the four o'clock watch with Tommy.

After a restless night of tossing and turning on lumpy, wet French soil, Charlie was woken at four, and in turn kicked Tommy, who simply turned over and went straight back to sleep. Minutes later Charlie was outside the tent, buttoning up his jacket before continually slapping himself on the back in an effort to keep warm. As his eyes slowly became accustomed to the half-light, he began to make out row upon row of brown tents stretching as far as the eye could see.

"Mornin', Corp," said Tommy, when he appeared a little after four twenty. "Got a lucifer, by any chance?"

"No, I 'aven't. And what I need is an 'ot cocoa, or an 'ot somethin'."

"Whatever your command, Corp."

Tommy wandered off to the cookhouse tent and returned half an hour later with two hot cocoas and two dry biscuits.

"No sugar, I'm afraid," he told Charlie. "That's only for sergeants and above. I told them you were a general in disguise but they said that all the generals were back in London sound asleep in their beds."

Charlie smiled as he placed his frozen fingers round the hot mug and sipped slowly to be sure that the simple pleasure lasted.

Tommy surveyed the skyline. "So where are all these bleedin' Germans we've been told so much about?"

"'eaven knows," said Charlie. "But you can be sure they're out there somewhere, probably askin' each other where we are."

At six o'clock Charlie woke the rest of his section. They were up and ready for inspection, with the tent down and folded back into a small square by six thirty.

Another bugle signalled breakfast, and the men took their place in a queue that Charlie reckoned would have gladdened the heart of any barrow boy in the Whitechapel Road.

When Charlie eventually reached the front of the queue, he held out his billycan to receive a ladle of lumpy porridge and a stale piece of bread. Tommy winked at the boy in his long white jacket and blue check trousers. "And to think I've waited all these years to sample French cookin'."

"It gets worse the nearer you get to the front," the cook promised him.

For the next ten days they set up camp at Etaples, spending their mornings being marched over dunes, their afternoons being instructed in gas warfare and their evenings being told by Captain Trentham the different ways they could die.

On the eleventh day they gathered up their belongings, packed up their tents and were formed into companies so they could be addressed by the Commanding Officer of the Regiment.

Over a thousand men stood in a formed square on a muddy field somewhere in France, wondering if twelve weeks of training and ten days of "acclimatisation" could possibly have made them ready to face the might of the German forces.

"P'raps they've only had twelve weeks' trainin' as well," said Tommy, hopefully.

At exactly zero nine hundred hours Lieutenant-Colonel Sir Danvers Hamilton DSO trotted in on a jet black mare and brought his charger to a halt in the middle of the man-made square. He began to address the troops. Charlie's abiding memory of the speech was that for fifteen minutes the horse never moved.

"Welcome to France," Colonel Hamilton began, placing a monocle over his left eye. "I only wish it were a day trip you were on." A little laughter trickled out of the ranks. "However, I'm afraid we're not going to be given much time off until we've sent the Huns back to Germany where they belong, with their tails between their legs." This time cheering broke out in the ranks. "And never forget, it's an away match, and we're on a sticky wicket. Worse, the Germans don't understand the laws of cricket." More laughter, although Charlie suspected the colonel meant every word he said.

"Today," the colonel continued, "we march towards Ypres where we will set up camp before beginning a new and I believe final assault on the German front. This time I'm convinced we will break through the German lines, and the glorious Fusiliers will surely carry the honours of the day. Fortune be with you all, and God save the King."

More cheers were followed by a rendering of the National Anthem from the regimental band. The troops joined in lustily with heart and voice.

It took another five days of route-marching before they heard the first sound of artillery fire, could smell the trenches and therefore knew they must be approaching the front. Another day and they passed the large green tents of the Red Cross. Just before eleven that morning Charlie saw his first dead soldier, a lieutenant from the East Yorkshire Regiment.

"Well, I'll be damned," said Tommy. "Bullets can't tell the difference between officers and enlisted men."

Within another mile they had both witnessed so many stretchers, so many bodies and so many limbs no longer attached to bodies that no one had the stomach for jokes. The battalion, it became clear, had arrived at what the newspapers called the "Western Front". No war correspondent, however, could have described the gloom that pervaded the air, or the look of hopelessness ingrained on the faces of anyone who had been there for more than a few days.

Charlie stared out at the open fields that must once have been productive farmland. All that remained was the odd burnt-out farmhouse to mark the spot where civilisation had once existed. There was still no sign of the enemy. He tried to take in the surrounding countryside that was to be his home during the months that lay ahead – if he lived that long. Every soldier knew that average life expectancy at the front was seventeen days.

Charlie left his men resting in their tents while he set out to do his own private recce. First he came across the reserve trenches a few hundred yards in front of the hospital tents, known as the "hotel area" as they were a quarter of a mile behind the front line, where each soldier spent four days without a break before being allowed four days of rest in the reserve trenches. Charlie strolled on up to the front like some visiting tourist who was not involved in a war. He listened to the few men who had survived for more than a few weeks and talked of "Blighty" and prayed only for a "cushy wound" so they could be moved to the nearest hospital tent and, if they were among the lucky ones, eventually be sent home to England.

As the stray bullets whistled across no-man's-land, Charlie fell on his knees and crawled back to the reserve trenches, to brief his section on what they might expect once they were pushed forward another hundred yards.

The trenches, he told his men, stretched from horizon to horizon and at any one time could be occupied by ten thousand troops. In front of them, about twenty yards away, he had seen a barbed-wire fence some three feet high which an old corporal told him had already cost a thousand lives of those who had done nothing more than erect it. Beyond that lay no-man's-land, consisting of five hundred acres once owned by an innocent family, caught in the centre of someone else's war. Beyond that lay the Germans' barbed-wire, and beyond that still the Germans, waiting for them in their trenches.

Each army, it seemed, lay in its own sodden, rat-infested dug-outs for days, sometimes months, waiting for the other side to make a move. Less than a mile separated them. If a head popped up to study the terrain, a bullet followed from the other side. If the order was to advance, a man's chances of completing twenty yards would not have been considered worth chalking up on a bookie's blackboard. If you reached the wire there were two ways of dying; if you reached the German trenches, a dozen.

If you stayed still, you could die of cholera, chlorine gas, gangrene, typhoid or trench foot that soldiers stuck bayonets through to take away the pain. Almost as many men died behind the lines as did from going over the top, an old sergeant told Charlie, and it didn't help to know that the Germans were suffering the same problems a few hundred yards away.

Charlie tried to settle his ten men into a routine. They carried out their daily duties, bailed water out of their trenches and cleaned equipment. Charlie picked up rumours and counter-rumours of what the future might hold for them. He suspected that only the colonel seated in HQ, a mile behind the lines, really had much idea of what was going on.

Whenever it was Charlie's turn to spend four days in the advance trenches his section seemed to occupy most of their time filling their billycans with pints of water, as they struggled to bail out the gallons that dropped daily from the heavens. Sometimes the water in the trenches would reach Charlie's kneecaps.

"The only reason I didn't sign up for the navy was because I couldn't swim," Tommy grumbled. "And no one warned me I could drown just as easily in the army."

Even soaked, frozen and hungry, they somehow remained cheerful. For four weeks Charlie and his section endured such conditions, waiting for fresh orders that would allow them to advance. The only advance they learned of during that time was von Ludendorff's. The German general had caused the Allies to retreat some forty miles, losing 400,000 men while another 80,000 were captured. Captain Trentham was generally the bearer of such news, and what annoyed Charlie even more was that he always looked so smart, clean, and worse – warm and well fed.

Two men from his own section had already died without even seeing the enemy. Most soldiers would have been only too happy to go over the top, as they no longer believed they would survive a war some were saying would last for ever. The boredom was broken only by bayoneting rats, bailing more water out of the trench or having to listen to Tommy repeat the same old melodies on a now rusty mouth-organ.

It wasn't until the ninth week that orders finally came through and they were called back to the man-made square. The colonel, monocle in place, once again briefed them from his motionless horse. The Royal Fusiliers were to advance on the German lines the following morning, having been given the responsibility for breaking through their northern flank. The Irish Guards would give them support from the right flank, while the Welsh would advance from the left.

"Tomorrow will be a day of glory for the Fusiliers," Colonel Hamilton assured them. "Now you must rest, as the battle will commence at first light."

On returning to the trenches, Charlie was surprised to find that the thought of at last being involved in a real fight had put the men in better humour. Every rifle was stripped, cleaned, oiled, checked and then checked again, every bullet placed carefully into its magazine, every Lewis gun tested, oiled and re-tested and then the men finally shaved before they faced the enemy. Charlie's first experience of a razor was in near-freezing water.

No man finds it easy to sleep the night before a battle, Charlie had been told, and many used the time to write long letters to their loved ones at home; some even had the courage to make a will. Charlie wrote to Posh Porky – he wasn't sure why – asking her to take care of Sal, Grace and Kitty if he didn't return. Tommy wrote to no one, and not simply because he couldn't write. At midnight Charlie collected all the section's efforts and handed them in a bundle to the orderly officer.

Bayonets were carefully sharpened, then fixed; hearts began to beat faster as the minutes passed, and they waited in silence for the command to advance. Charlie's own feelings raced between terror and exhilaration, as he watched Captain Trentham strolling from platoon to platoon to deliver his final briefing. Charlie downed in one gulp the tot of rum that was handed out to all the men up and down the trenches just before a battle.

A Second Lieutenant Makepeace took his place behind Charlie's trench, another officer he had never met. He looked like a fresh-faced schoolboy and introduced himself to Charlie as one might do to a casual acquaintance at a cocktail party. He asked Charlie to gather the section together a few yards behind the line so he could address them. Ten cold, frightened men climbed out of their trench and listened to the young officer in cynical silence. The day had been specially chosen because the meteorologists had assured them that the sun would rise at five fifty-three and there would be no rain. The meteorologists would prove to be right about the sun, but as if to prove their fallibility at four eleven a steady drizzle began. "A German drizzle," Charlie suggested to his comrades. "And whose side is God on, anyway?"

Lieutenant Makepeace smiled thinly. They waited for a Verey pistol to be fired, like some referee blowing a whistle before hostilities could officially commence.

"And don't forget, 'bangers and mash' is the password," said Lieutenant Makepeace. "Send it down the line."

At five fifty-three, as a blood-red sun peeped over the horizon, a Verey pistol was fired and Charlie looked back to see the sky lit up behind him.

Lieutenant Makepeace leapt out of the trench and cried, "Follow me, men."

Charlie climbed out after him and, screaming at the top of his voice – more out of fear than bravado – charged towards the barbed-wire.

The lieutenant hadn't gone fifteen yards before the first bullet hit him, but somehow he still managed to carry on until he reached the wire. Charlie watched in horror as Makepeace fell across the barbed barrier and another burst of enemy bullets peppered his motionless body. Two brave men changed direction to rush to his aid, but neither of them even reached the wire. Charlie was only a yard behind them, and was about to charge through a gap in the barrier when Tommy overtook him. Charlie turned, smiled, and that was the last thing he remembered of the Battle of the Lys.

Two days later Charlie woke up in a hospital tent, some three hundred yards behind the line, to find a young girl in a dark blue uniform with a royal crest above her heart hovering over him. She was talking to him. He knew only because her lips were moving: he couldn't hear a word she said. Thank God, Charlie thought, I'm still alive, and surely now I'll be sent back to England. Once a soldier had been certified medically deaf he was always shipped home. King's Regulations.

Charlie's hearing was fully restored a week later and a smile appeared on his lips for the first time when he saw Grace standing by his side pouring him a cup of tea. They had granted her permission to move tents once she'd heard that an unconscious soldier named Trumper was lying down the line. She told her brother that he had been one of the lucky ones, blown up by a land-mine, and only lost a toe – not even a big one, she teased. He was disappointed by her news as the loss of the big one also meant you could go home.

"Otherwise only a few grazes and cuts. Nothing serious and very much alive. Ought to have you back at the front in a matter of days," she added sadly.

He slept. He woke. He wondered if Tommy had survived.

"Any news of Private Prescott?" Charlie asked the orderly officer after he had completed his rounds.

The lieutenant checked his clipboard and a frown came over his face. "He's been arrested. Looks as if he might have to face a court-martial."

"What? Why?"

"No idea," replied the young lieutenant, and moved on to the next bed.

The following day Charlie managed a little food, took

a few painful steps the day after and could run a week later. He was sent back to the front only twenty-one days after Lieutenant Makepeace had leapt up and shouted, "Follow me."

Once Charlie had returned to the relief trenches he quickly discovered that only three men in his section of ten had survived the charge, and there was no sign of Tommy. A new batch of soldiers had arrived from England that morning to take their places and begin the routine of four days on, four days off. They treated Charlie as if he were a veteran.

He had only been back for a few hours when company orders were posted showing that Colonel Hamilton wished to see Lance-Corporal Trumper at eleven hundred hours the following morning.

"Why would the commanding officer want to see me?" Charlie enquired of the duty sergeant.

"It usually means a court-martial or a decoration – the governor hasn't time for anything else. And never forget that he also means trouble, so watch your tongue when you're in his presence. I can tell you, he's got a very short fuse."

At ten fifty-five hours sharp Lance-Corporal Trumper stood trembling outside the colonel's tent, almost as fearful of his commanding officer as of going over the top. A few minutes later the company sergeant-major marched out of the tent to collect him.

"Stand to attention, salute and give your name, rank and serial number," barked CSM Philpott. "And remember, don't speak unless you're spoken to," he added sharply.

Charlie marched into the tent and came to a halt in front of the colonel's desk. He saluted and said, "Trumper, Lance-Corporal 7312087 reporting, sir." It was the first time he had seen the colonel sitting on a chair, not on a horse.

"Ah, Trumper," said Colonel Hamilton, looking up. "Good to have you back. Delighted by your speedy recovery."

"Thank you, sir," said Charlie, aware for the first time that only one of the colonel's eyes actually moved.

"However, there's been a problem involving a private from your section that I'm hoping you might be able to throw some light on."

"I'll 'elp if I can, sir."

"Good, because it seems," said the colonel, placing his monocle up to his left eye, "that Prescott" – he studied a buff form on the desk in front of him before continuing – "yes, Private Prescott, may have shot himself in the hand in order to avoid facing the enemy. According to Captain Trentham's report, he was picked up with a single bullet wound in his right hand while lying in the mud only a few yards in front of his own trench. On the face of it such an action appears to be a simple case of cowardice in the face of the enemy. However, I was not willing to order the setting up of a court-martial before I had heard your version of what took place that morning. After all, he was in your section. So I felt you might have something of substance to add to Captain Trentham's report."

"Yes, sir, I certainly do," Charlie said. He tried to compose himself and go over in his mind the details of what had taken place almost a month before. "Once the Verey pistol 'ad been fired Lieutenant Makepeace led the charge and I went over the top after 'im followed by the rest of my section. The lieutenant was the first to reach the wire but was immediately 'it by several bullets, and there were only two men ahead of me at the time. They bravely went to 'is aid, but fell even before they could reach 'im. As soon as I got to the wire I spotted a gap and ran through it, only to see Private Prescott overtake me as he charged on towards the enemy lines. It must have been then that I was blown up by the land-mine, which may well have knocked out Private Prescott as well."

"Can you be certain it was Private Prescott that overtook you?" asked the colonel, looking puzzled.

"In the 'eat of a battle, it's 'ard to remember every detail, sir, but I will never forget Prescott overtakin' me."

"Why's that?" asked the colonel.

"Because 'e's my mate, and it annoyed me at the time to see 'im get ahead of me."

Charlie thought he saw a faint smile come over the colonel's face.

"Is Prescott a close friend of yours?" the colonel asked, fixing his monocle on him.

"Yes, sir, 'e is, but that would not affect my judgment, and no one 'as the right to suggest it would."

"Do you realise who you are talkin' to?" bellowed the sergeant-major.

"Yes, Sergeant-Major," said Charlie. "A man interested in finding out the truth, and therefore seeing that justice is done. I'm not an educated man, sir, but I am an 'onest one."

"Corporal, you will report –" began the sergeant-major.

"Thank you, Sergeant-Major, that will be all," said the colonel. "And thank you, Corporal Trumper, for your clear and concise evidence. I shall not need to trouble you any further. You may now return to your platoon."

"Thank you, sir," said Charlie. He took a pace backwards, saluted, did an about-turn and marched out of the tent.

"Would you like me to 'andle this matter in my own way?" asked the sergeant-major.

"Yes, I would," replied Colonel Hamilton. "Promote Trumper to full corporal and release Private Prescott immediately."

Tommy returned to his platoon that afternoon, his left hand bandaged.

"You saved my life, Charlie."

"I only told the truth."

"I know, so did I. But the difference is, they believed you."

Charlie lay in his tent that night wondering why Captain Trentham was so determined to be rid of Tommy.

Could any man believe he had the right to send another to his death simply because he had once been to gaol?

Another month passed while they continued the old routines before company orders revealed that they were to march south to the Marne and prepare for a counter-attack against General von Ludendorff. Charlie's heart sank when he read the orders; he knew the odds against surviving two attacks were virtually unknown. He managed to spend the odd hour alone with Grace, who told him she had fallen for a Welsh corporal who had stood on a land-mine and ended up blind in one eye.

Love at first sight, quipped Charlie.

Midnight on Wednesday, 17 July 1918, and an eerie silence fell over no-man's-land. Charlie let those who could, sleep, and didn't attempt to wake anyone until three o'clock the next morning. Now an acting sergeant, he had a platoon of forty men to prepare for battle, all of whom still came under the overall command of Captain Trentham, who hadn't been seen since the day Tommy had been released.

At three thirty, a Lieutenant Harvey joined them behind the trenches, by which time they were all on full battle alert. Harvey, it turned out, had arrived at the front the previous Friday.

"This is a mad war," said Charlie after they had been introduced.

"Oh, I don't know," said Harvey lightly. "I can't wait to have a go at the Hun myself."

"The Germans 'aven't an 'ope in 'ell, as long as we go on producin' nutcases like 'im," whispered Tommy.

"By the way, sir, what's the password this time?" asked Charlie.

"Oh, sorry, quite forgot. Little Red Riding Hood," said the lieutenant.

They all waited. At zero four hundred hours they fixed bayonets and at zero four twenty-one the Verey pistol shot a red flame into the sky somewhere behind the lines and the air was filled with whistles blowing.

"Tally-ho," cried Lieutenant Harvey. He fired his pistol in the air and charged over the top as if he were chasing some errant fox. Once again, Charlie scrambled up and out of the trench only yards behind. The rest of the platoon followed as he stumbled through mud over barren land that no longer bore a single tree to protect them. To the left Charlie could see another platoon ahead of him. The unmistakable figure of the immaculate Captain Trentham brought up the rear. But it was Lieutenant Harvey who was still leading the charge as he hurdled elegantly over the wire and into no-man's-land. It made Charlie feel curiously confident that anyone could survive such stupidity. On and on Harvey went, as if somehow indestructible, or charmed. Charlie assumed that he must fall with every pace he took, as he watched the lieutenant treat the German wire as just another hurdle, before running on towards the enemy trenches as if they were the finishing line in some race being held at his public school. The man got within twenty yards of the tape before a hail of bullets finally brought him down. Charlie now found himself in front and began firing at the Germans as their heads popped up from behind the dug-outs.

He had never heard of anyone actually reaching the German trenches, so he wasn't sure what he was supposed to do next, and despite all the training he still found it hard to shoot on the run. When four Germans and their rifles came up at once he knew that he was never going to find out. He shot straight at the first one, who fell back into the trench, but by then he could only watch the other three take aim. He suddenly became aware of a volley of shots from behind him, and all three bodies fell back like tin ducks on a rifle range. He realised then that the winner of the shooting prize must still be on his feet.

Suddenly he was in the enemy's trench and staring down into a young German's eyes, a terrified boy even younger than himself. He hesitated only for a moment before thrusting his bayonet down the middle of the German's mouth. He pulled the blade out and drove it home once again, this time into the boy's heart, then ran on. Three of his men were now ahead of him, chasing a retreating enemy. At that moment Charlie spotted Tommy on his right flank pursuing two Germans up a hill. He disappeared into some trees and Charlie distinctly heard a single shot somewhere above the noise of battle. He turned and charged quickly off into the forest to rescue his friend, only to find a German splayed out on the ground and Tommy still running on up the hill. A breathless Charlie managed to catch him up when he came finally to a halt behind a tree.

"You were bloody magnificent, Tommy," said Charlie, throwing himself down by his side.

"Not 'alf as good as that officer, what was 'is name?"

"'arvey, Lieutenant 'arvey."

"In the end we were both saved by 'is pistol," said Tommy, brandishing the weapon. "More than can be said for that bastard Trentham."

"What do you mean?" said Charlie.

"He funked the German trenches, didn't 'e? Bolted off into the forest. Two Germans saw the coward and chased after 'im, so I followed. Finished off one of them, didn't I?"

"So where's Trentham now?"

"Somewhere up there," said Tommy, pointing over the brow of the hill. "'e'll be 'iding from that lone German, no doubt."

Charlie stared into the distance.

"So what now, Corp?"

"We 'ave to go after that German and kill 'im before he catches up with the captain."

"Why don't we just go 'ome, and 'ope he finds the captain before I do?" said Tommy.

But Charlie was already on his feet advancing up the hill.

Slowly they moved on up the slope, using the trees for protection, watching and listening until they had reached the top, and open ground.

"No sign of either of them," whispered Charlie.

"Agreed. So we'd better get back behind our lines, because if the Germans catch us I can't believe they'll invite us to join 'em for tea and crumpet."

Charlie took his bearings. Ahead of them was a little church not unlike the many they had passed on the long route-march from Etaples to the front.

"Maybe we'd better check that church first," he said. "But don't let's take any unnecessary risks."

"What the 'ell do you think we've been doin' for the last hour?" asked Tommy.

Inch by inch, foot by foot, they crawled across the open ground until they reached the vestry door. Charlie pushed it open slowly, expecting a volley of bullets to follow but the loudest sound they heard was the screech of the hinges. Once inside, Charlie crossed himself the way his grandfather always had when entering St Mary's and St Michael's in Jubilee Street. Tommy lit a cigarette.

Charlie remained cautious as he began to study the layout of the little church. It had already lost half its roof, courtesy of a German or English shell, while the rest of the nave and porch remained intact.

Charlie found himself mesmerised by the mosaic patterns that covered the inner walls, their tiny squares making up life-size portraits. He moved slowly round the perimeter staring at the seven disciples who had so far survived the ungodly war.

When he reached the altar he fell on his knees and bowed his head, a vision of Father O'Malley coming into his mind. It was then that the bullet flew past him, hitting the brass cross and sending the crucifix crashing to the ground. As Charlie dived for cover behind the altar, a second shot went off. He glanced round the corner of the altar and watched a German officer who had been hit in the side of the head slump through the curtains and out of a wooden box on to the stone floor. He must have died instantly.

"I only 'ope he 'ad time to make a full confession," said Tommy.

Charlie crawled out from behind the altar.

"For Gawd's sake, stay put, you fool, because someone else is in this church and I've got a funny feelin' it isn't just the Almighty."

They both heard a movement in the pulpit above them and Charlie quickly scurried back behind the altar.

"It's only me," said a voice they immediately recognised.

"'o's me?" said Tommy, trying not to laugh.

"Captain Trentham. So whatever you do, don't fire."

"Then show yourself, and come down with your 'ands above your 'ead so that we can be certain you're 'o you say you are," Tommy said, enjoying every moment of his tormentor's embarrassment.

Trentham rose slowly from the top of the pulpit and began to descend the stone steps with his hands held high above his head. He proceeded down the aisle towards the fallen cross, that now lay in front of the altar, before stepping over the dead German officer and continuing until he came face to face with Tommy, who was still holding a pistol pointing straight at his heart.

"Sorry, sir," said Tommy, lowering the pistol. "I 'ad to be sure you weren't a German."

"Who spoke the King's English," said Trentham sarcastically.

"You did warn us against being taken in by that in one of your lectures, sir," said Tommy.

"Less of your lip, Prescott. And how did you get hold of an officer's pistol?"

"It belonged to Lieutenant 'arvey," interjected Charlie, "who dropped it when –"

"You bolted off into the forest," said Tommy, his eyes never leaving Trentham.

"I was pursuing two Germans who were attempting to escape."

"It looked the other way round to me," said Tommy. "And when we get back, I intend to let anyone know who cares to listen."

"It would be your word against mine," said Trentham. "In any case, both Germans are dead."

"Only thanks to me and try not to forget that the corp 'ere also witnessed everything what 'appened."

"Then you know my version of the events is the accurate one," said Trentham, turning directly to face Charlie.

"All I know is that we ought to be up in that tower, plannin' how we get back to our own lines, and not wastin' any more time quarrellin' down 'ere."

The captain nodded his agreement, turned, ran to the back of the church and up the stone stairs to the safety of the tower. Charlie quickly followed him. They both took look-out positions on opposite sides of the roof, and although Charlie could still hear the sound of the battle, he was quite unable to make out who was getting the better of it on the other side of the forest.

"Where's Prescott?" asked Trentham after a few minutes had passed.

"Don't know, sir," said Charlie. "I thought he was just behind me." It was several minutes before Tommy, wearing the dead German's *pickelhaube*, appeared at the top of the stone steps.

"Where have you been?" asked Trentham suspiciously.

"Searchin' the place from top to bottom in the 'ope that there might 'ave been some grub to be found, but I couldn't even find any communion wine."

"Take your position over there," said the captain, pointing to an arch that was not yet covered, "and keep a look-out. We'll stay put until it's pitch dark. By then I'll have worked out a plan to get us back behind our own lines."

The three men stared out across the French countryside as the light turned first murky, then grey and finally black.

"Shouldn't we be thinkin' of moving soon, Captain?" asked Charlie, after they had sat in pitch darkness for over an hour.

"We'll go when I'm good and ready," said Trentham, "and not before."

"Yes, sir," said Charlie, and sat shivering as he continued to stare out into the darkness for another forty minutes.

"Right, follow me," said Trentham without warning. He rose and led them both down the stone steps, coming to a halt at the entrance to the vestry door. He pulled the door open slowly. The noise of the hinges sounded to Charlie like a magazine emptying on a machine-gun. The three of them stared into the night and Charlie wondered if there was yet another German out there, rifle cocked, waiting. The captain checked his compass.

"First we must try to reach the safety of those trees at the top of the ridge," Trentham whispered. "Then I'll work out a route for getting us back behind our own lines."

By the time Charlie's eyes had become accustomed to the darkness he began to study the moon and, more importantly, the movement of the clouds.

"It's open ground to those trees," the captain continued, "so we can't risk a crossing until the moon disappears behind some cover. Then we'll each make a dash for the ridge separately. So, Prescott, when I give the order, you'll go first."

"Me?" said Tommy.

"Yes, you, Prescott. Then Corporal Trumper will follow the moment you've reached the trees."

"And I suppose you'll bring up the rear, if we're lucky enough to survive?" said Tommy.

"Don't be insubordinate with me," said Trentham. "Or you'll find this time that you will be court-martialled and end up in the gaol you were originally intended for."

"Not without a witness, I won't," said Tommy. "That much of King's Regulations I do understand."

"Shut up, Tommy," said Charlie.

They all waited in silence behind the vestry door until a large shadow moved slowly across the path and finally enveloped the church all the way to the trees.

"Go!" said the captain, tapping Prescott on the shoulder. Tommy bolted off like a greyhound released from the slips, and the two other men watched as he scampered across the open ground, until some twenty seconds later he reached the safety of the trees.

The same hand tapped Charlie on the shoulder a moment later, and off he ran, faster than he had ever run before, despite having to carry a rifle in one hand and a pack on his back. The grin didn't reappear on his face until he had reached Tommy's side.

They both turned to stare in the direction of the captain.

"What the 'ell's he waitin' for?" said Charlie.

"To see if we get ourselves killed would be my guess," said Tommy as the moon came back out.

They both waited but said nothing until the circular glow had disappeared behind another cloud, when finally the captain came scurrying towards them.

He stopped by their side, and leaning against a tree rested until he had got his breath back.

"Right," he eventually whispered, "we'll advance slowly down through the forest, stopping every few yards to listen for the enemy, while at the same time using the trees for cover. Remember, never move as much as a muscle if the moon is out, and never speak unless it's to answer a question put by me."

The three of them began to creep slowly down the hill, moving from tree to tree, but no more than a few yards at a time. Charlie had no idea he could be so alert to the slightest unfamiliar sound. It took the three of them over an hour to reach the bottom of the slope, where they came to a halt. All they could see in front of them was a vast mass of barren open ground.

"No-man's-land," whispered Trentham. "That means we'll have to spend the rest of our time flat on our bellies." He immediately sank down into the mud. "I'll lead," he said. "Trumper, you'll follow, and Prescott will bring up the rear."

"Well at least that proves 'e knows where 'e's goin'," whispered Tommy. "Because 'e must 'ave worked out exactly where the bullets will be comin' from, and 'o they're likely to 'it first."

Slowly, inch by inch, the three men advanced the half mile across no-man's-land, towards the Allied front line, pressing their faces back down into the mud whenever the moon reappeared from behind its unreliable screen.

Although Charlie could always see Trentham in front of him, Tommy was so silent in his wake that from time to time he had to look back just to be certain his friend was still there. A grin of flashing white teeth was all he got for his trouble.

During the first hour the three of them covered a mere hundred yards. Charlie could have wished for a more cloudy night. Stray bullets flying across their heads from both trenches ensured that they kept themselves low to the ground. Charlie found he was continually spitting out mud and once even came face to face with a German who couldn't blink.

Another inch, another foot, another yard – on they crawled through the wet, cold mud across a terrain that still belonged to no man. Suddenly Charlie heard a loud squeal from behind him. He turned angrily to remonstrate with Tommy, only to see a rat the size of a rabbit lying between his legs. Tommy had thrust a bayonet right through its belly.

"I think it fancied you, Corp. Couldn't have been for the sex if Rose is to be believed, so must have wanted you for dinner."

Charlie covered his mouth with his hands for fear the Germans might hear him laughing.

The moon slid out from behind a cloud and again lit up the open land. Once more the three men buried themselves in the mud and waited until another passing cloud allowed them to advance a few more yards. It was two more hours before they reached the barbed-wire perimeter that had been erected to stop the Germans breaking through.

Once they had reached the spiky barrier Trentham

changed direction and began to crawl along the German side of the fence searching for a breach in the wire between them and safety. Another eighty yards had to be traversed – to Charlie it felt more like a mile – before the captain eventually found a tiny gap which he was able to crawl through. They were now only fifty yards from the safety of their own lines.

Charlie was surprised to find the captain hanging back, even allowing him to crawl past.

"Damn," said Charlie under his breath, as the moon made another entrance on to the centre of the stage and left them lying motionless only a street's length away from safety. Once the light had been turned out again, slowly, inch by inch, Charlie continued his crab-like advance, now more fearful of a stray bullet from his own side than from the enemy's. At last he could hear voices, English voices. He never thought the day would come when he would welcome the sight of those trenches.

"We've made it," shouted Tommy, in a voice that might even have been heard by the Germans. Once again Charlie buried his face in the mud.

"Who goes there?" came back the riposte. Charlie could hear rifles being cocked up and down the trenches as sleepy men quickly came to life.

"Captain Trentham, Corporal Trumper and Private Prescott of the Royal Fusiliers," called out Charlie firmly.

"Password?" demanded the voice.

"Oh, God, what's the pass – ?"

"Little Red Riding Hood," shouted Trentham from behind them.

"Advance and be recognised."

"Prescott first," said Trentham, and Tommy pushed himself up on to his knees and began to crawl slowly towards his own trenches. Charlie heard the sound of a bullet that came from behind him and a moment later watched in horror as Tommy collapsed on his stomach and lay motionless in the mud.

Charlie looked quickly back through the half-light

towards Trentham who said, "Bloody Huns. Keep down or the same thing might happen to you."

Charlie ignored the order and crawled quickly forward until he came to the prostrate body of his friend. Once he had reached his side he placed an arm around Tommy's shoulder. "There's only about twenty yards to go," he told him. "Man wounded," said Charlie in a loud whisper as he looked up towards the trenches.

"Prescott, don't move while the moon's out," ordered Trentham from behind them.

"How you feelin', mate?" asked Charlie as he tried to fathom the expression on his friend's face.

"Felt better to be 'onest," said Tommy.

"Quiet, you two," said Trentham.

"By the way, that was no German bullet," choked Tommy as a trickle of blood began to run out of his mouth. "So just make sure you get the bastard if I'm not given the chance to do the job myself."

"You'll be all right," said Charlie. "Nothin' and nobody could kill Tommy Prescott."

As a large black cloud covered the moon, a group of men jumped including two Red Cross orderlies who were carrying a stretcher over the top and ran towards them. They dropped the stretcher by Tommy's side and dragged him on to the canvas before jogging back towards the trench. Another volley of bullets came flying across from the German lines.

Once they had reached the safety of the dug-out, the orderlies dumped the stretcher unceremoniously on the ground. Charlie shouted at them, "Get 'im to the 'ospital tent – quickly for God's sake, quickly."

"Not much point, Corp," said the medical orderly. "'e's dead."

CHAPTER 5

"HQ is still waiting for your report, Trumper."

"I know, Sarge, I know."

"Any problems, lad?" asked the colour-sergeant, which Charlie recognised as a coded message for, "Can you write?"

"No problems, Sarge."

For the next hour he wrote out his thoughts slowly, then rewrote the simple account of what had taken place on 18 July 1918 during the second battle of the Marne.

Charlie read and re-read his banal offering, aware that although he extolled Tommy's courage during the battle he made no mention of Trentham fleeing from the enemy. The plain truth was that he hadn't witnessed what was going on behind him. He might well have formed his own opinion but he knew that would not bear cross-examination at some later date. And as for Tommy's death, what proof had he that one stray bullet among so many had come from the pistol of Captain Trentham? Even if Tommy had been right on both counts and Charlie voiced those opinions, it would only be his word against that of an officer and a gentleman.

The only thing he could do was make sure that Trentham received no praise from his pen for what had taken place on the battlefield that day. Feeling like a traitor, Charlie scribbled his signature on the bottom of the second page before handing in his report to the orderly officer.

Later that afternoon the duty sergeant allowed him an hour off to dig the grave in which they would bury Private

Prescott. As he knelt by its head he cursed the men on either side who could have been responsible for such a war.

Charlie listened to the chaplain intone the words, "Ashes to ashes, dust to dust", before the last post was played yet again. Then the burial party took a pace to the right and began digging the grave of another known soldier. A hundred thousand men sacrificed their lives on the Marne. Charlie could no longer accept that any victory was worth such a price.

He sat cross-legged at the foot of the grave, unaware of the passing of time as he hewed out a cross with his bayonet. Finally he stood and placed it at the head of the mound. On the centre of the cross he had carved the words, "Private Tommy Prescott".

A neutral moon returned that night to shine on a thousand freshly dug graves, and Charlie swore to whatever God cared to listen that he would not forget his father or Tommy, or, for that matter, Captain Trentham.

He fell asleep among his comrades. Reveille stirred him at first light, and after one last look at Tommy's grave he returned to his platoon, to be informed that the Commanding Officer would be addressing the troops at zero nine hundred hours.

An hour later he was standing to attention in a depleted square of those who had survived the battle. Colonel Hamilton told his men that the Prime Minister had described the second battle of the Marne as the greatest victory in the history of the war. Charlie found himself unable to raise a voice to join his cheering comrades.

"It was a proud and honourable day to be a Royal Fusilier," continued the colonel, his monocle still firmly in place. The regiment had won a VC, six MCs and nine MMs in the battle. Charlie felt indifferent as each of the decorated men was announced and his citation read out until he heard the name of Lieutenant Arthur Harvey who, the colonel told them, had led a charge of Number Eleven Platoon all the way up to the German trenches, thus allowing those behind him to carry on and break through the enemy's defences. For this he was posthumously awarded the Military Cross.

A moment later Charlie heard the colonel utter the name of Captain Guy Trentham. This gallant officer, the colonel assured the regiment, careless of his own safety, continued the attack after Lieutenant Harvey had fallen, killing several German soldiers before reaching their dug-outs, where he wiped out a complete enemy unit single-handed. Having crossed the enemy's lines, he proceeded to chase two Germans into a nearby forest. He succeeded in killing both enemy soldiers before rescuing two Fusiliers from German hands. He then led them back to the safety of the Allied trenches. For this supreme act of courage Captain Trentham was also awarded the Military Cross.

Trentham stepped forward and the troops cheered as the colonel removed a silver cross from a leather case before pinning the medal on his chest.

One sergeant-major, three sergeants, two corporals and four privates then had their citations read out, each one named and his acts of heroism recalled in turn. But only one of them stepped forward to receive his medal.

"Among those unable to be with us today," continued the colonel, "is a young man who followed Lieutenant Harvey into the enemy trenches and then killed four, perhaps five German soldiers before later stalking and shooting another, finally killing a German officer before being tragically killed himself by a stray bullet when only yards from the safety of his own trenches." Once again the assembled gathering cheered.

Moments later the parade was dismissed and while others returned to their tents Charlie walked slowly back behind the lines until he reached the mass burial ground.

He knelt down by a familiar mound and after a moment's hesitation yanked out the cross that he had placed at the head of the grave.

Charlie unclipped a knife that hung from his belt and beside the name Tommy Prescott he carved the letters MM.

* * *

A fortnight later one thousand men, with a thousand legs, a thousand arms and a thousand eyes between them, were ordered home. Sergeant Charles Trumper of the Royal Fusiliers was detailed to accompany them, perhaps because no man had been known to survive three charges on the enemy's lines.

Their cheerfulness and delight at still being alive only made Charlie feel more guilty. After all, he had only lost one toe. On the journey back by land, sea and land, he helped the men dress, wash, eat and be led without complaint or remonstration.

At Dover they were greeted on the quayside by cheering crowds welcoming their heroes home. Trains had been laid on to despatch them to all parts of the country, so that for the rest of their lives they would be able to recall a few moments of honour, even glory. But not for Charlie. His papers only instructed him to travel on to Edinburgh where he was to help train the next group of recruits who would take their places on the Western Front.

On 11 November 1918, at eleven hundred hours, hostilities ceased and a grateful nation stood in silence for three minutes when, on a railway carriage in the forest of Compiègne, the Armistice was signed. When Charlie heard the news of victory he was training some raw recruits on a rifle range in Edinburgh. Some of them were unable to hide their disappointment at being cheated out of the chance of facing the enemy.

The war was over and the Empire had won – or that is how the politicians presented the result of the match between Britain and Germany.

"More than ten million men have died for their country, and some even before they had finished growing," Charlie wrote in a letter to his sister Sal. "And what has either side to show for such carnage?"

Sal wrote back to let him know how thankful she was he was still alive and went on to say that she had become engaged to a pilot from Canada. "We plan to marry in the next few weeks and go to live with his parents in Toronto. Next time you get a letter from me it will be from the other side of the world.

"Grace is still in France but expects to return to the London hospital some time in the New Year. She's been made a ward sister. I expect you know her Welsh corporal caught pneumonia. He died a few days after peace had been declared.

"Kitty disappeared off the face of the earth and then without warning turned up in Whitechapel with a man in a motor car; neither of them seemed to be hers but she looked very pleased with life."

Charlie couldn't understand his sister's PS: "Where will you live when you get back to the East End?"

Sergeant Charles Trumper was discharged from active service on 20 February 1919, one of the early ones: the missing toe had at last counted for something. He folded up his uniform, placed his helmet on top, boots by the side, marched across the parade ground and handed them in to the quartermaster.

"I hardly recognised you, Sarge, in that old suit and cap. Don't fit any longer, do they? You must have grown during your time with the Fussies."

Charlie looked down and checked the length of his trousers: they now hung a good inch above the laces of his boots.

"Must have grown durin' my time with the Fussies," he repeated, pondering the words.

"Bet your family will be glad to see you when you get back to civvy street."

"Whatever's left of them," said Charlie as he turned to go. His final task was to report to the paymaster's office and receive his last pay packet and travel voucher before relinquishing the King's shilling.

"Trumper, the orderly officer would like a word with you," said the sergeant-major, after Charlie had completed what he had assumed was his last duty.

Lieutenants Makepeace and Harvey would always be his duty officers, thought Charlie as he made his way back across the parade ground in the direction of the company offices. Some fresh-faced youth, who had not been properly introduced to the enemy, now had the nerve to try and take their place.

Charlie was about to salute the lieutenant when he remembered he was no longer in uniform, so he simply removed his cap.

"You wanted to see me, sir?"

"Yes, Trumper, a personal matter." The young officer touched a large box that lay on his desk. Charlie couldn't quite see what was inside.

"It appears, Trumper, that your friend Private Prescott made a will in which he left everything to you."

Charlie was unable to hide his surprise as the lieutenant pushed the box across the table.

"Would you be kind enough to check through its contents, and then sign for them?"

Another buff form was placed in front of him. Above the typed name of Private Thomas Prescott was a paragraph written in a bold large hand. An "X" was scrawled below it, witnessed by Sergeant-Major Philpott.

Charlie began to remove the objects from the box one by one. Tommy's mouth-organ, rusty and falling apart, seven pounds eleven shillings and sixpence in back pay, followed by a German officer's helmet. Next Charlie took out a small leather box and opened the lid to discover Tommy's Military Medal and the simple words "For bravery in the field" printed across the back. He removed the medal and held it in the palm of his hand.

"Must have been a jolly brave chap, Prescott," said the lieutenant. "Salt of the earth and all that."

"And all that," agreed Charlie.

"A religious man as well?"

"No, can't pretend 'e was," said Charlie, allowing himself a smile. "Why do you ask?"

"The picture," said the lieutenant, pointing back into

the box. Charlie leaned forward and stared down in disbelief at a painting of the Virgin Mary and Child. It was about eight inches square and framed in black teak. He took the portrait out and held it in his hands.

He gazed at the deep reds, purples and blues that dominated the central figure in the painting, feeling certain he'd seen the image somewhere before. It was several moments before he replaced the little oil in the box along with Tommy's other possessions.

Charlie put his cap back on and turned to go, the box under one arm, a brown paper parcel under the other and a ticket to London in his top pocket.

He marched out of the barracks to make his way to the station – he wondered how long it would be before he could walk at a normal pace. When he reached the guardroom he stopped and turned round for one last look at the parade ground. A set of raw recruits was marching up and down with a new drill instructor, who sounded every bit as determined as the late Sergeant-Major Philpott had been to see that the snow was never allowed to settle.

Charlie turned his back on the parade ground and began his journey to London. He was nineteen years of age and had only just qualified to receive the King's shilling; but now he was a couple of inches taller, shaved and had even come near to losing his virginity.

He'd done his bit, and at least felt able to agree with the Prime Minister on one matter. He had surely taken part in the war to end all wars.

The night sleeper from Edinburgh was full of men in uniform who eyed the civilian-clad Charlie with suspicion, as a man who hadn't yet served his country or, worse, was a "conshi".

"They'll be calling him up soon enough," said a corporal to his mate in a loud whisper from the far side of the carriage. Charlie smiled but didn't comment.

He slept intermittently, amused by the thought that he might have found it easier to rest in a damp, muddy trench with rats and cockroaches for companions. By the time the train pulled into King's Cross station at seven the following morning, he had a stiff neck and an aching back. He stretched himself before he picked up his large paper parcel along with Tommy's life possessions.

On the station he bought a sandwich and a cup of tea. He was surprised when the girl asked him for threepence. "Twopence for those what are in uniform," he was told with undisguised disdain. Charlie downed the tea and left the station without another word.

The roads were busier and more hectic than he remembered, but he still jumped confidently on a tram that had "City" printed across the front. He sat alone on a trestled wooden bench, wondering what changes he would find on his return to the East End. Did his shop flourish, was it simply ticking over, had it been sold, or even gone bankrupt? And what of the biggest barrow in the world?

He jumped off the tram at Poultry, deciding to walk the final mile. His pace quickened as the accents changed; City gents in long black coats and bowlers gave way to professional men in dark suits and trilbies, to be taken over by rough lads in ill-fitting clothes and caps, until Charlie finally arrived in the East End, where even the boaters had been abandoned by those under thirty.

As Charlie approached the Whitechapel Road, he stopped and stared at the frantic bustle taking place all around him. Hooks of meat, barrows of vegetables, trays of pies, urns of tea passed him in every direction.

But what of the baker's shop, and his grandfather's pitch? Would they be "all present and correct"? He pulled his cap down over his forehead and slipped quietly into the market.

When he reached the corner of the Whitechapel Road he wasn't sure he had come to the right place. The baker's shop was no longer there but had been replaced by a bespoke tailor who traded under the name of Jacob Cohen. Charlie pressed his nose against the window but couldn't recognise anyone who was working inside. He swung round to stare at the spot where the barrow of "Trumper, the honest trader" had stood for nearly a century, only to find a gaggle of youths warming themselves round a charcoal fire where a man was selling chestnuts at a penny a bag. Charlie parted with a penny and was handed a bagful, but no one even gave him a second glance. Perhaps Becky had sold everything as he instructed, he thought, as he left the market to carry on down Whitechapel Road where at least he would have a chance to catch up with one of his sisters, rest and gather his thoughts.

When he arrived outside Number 112 he was pleased to find that the front door had been repainted. God bless Sal. He pushed the door open and walked straight into the parlour, where he came face to face with an overweight, half-shaven man dressed in a vest and trousers who was brandishing an open razor.

"What's your game then?" asked the man, holding up the razor firmly.

"I live 'ere," said Charlie.

"Like 'ell you do. I took over this dump six months ago."

"But —"

"No buts," said the man and without warning gave Charlie a shove in the chest which propelled him back into the street. The door slammed behind him, and Charlie heard a key turn in the lock. Not certain what to do next, he was beginning to wish he had never come home.

" 'ello, Charlie. It is Charlie, isn't it?" said a voice from behind him. "So you're not dead after all."

He swung round to see Mrs Shorrocks standing by her front door.

"Dead?" said Charlie.

"Yes," replied Mrs Shorrocks. "Kitty told us you'd been killed on the Western Front and that was why she 'ad to sell 112. That was months ago — 'aven't seen 'er since. Didn't anyone tell you?"

"No, no one told me," said Charlie, at least glad to

find someone who recognised him. He stared at his old neighbour trying to puzzle out why she looked so different.

"'ow about some lunch, luv? You look starved."

"Thanks, Mrs Shorrocks."

"I've just got myself a packet of fish and chips from Dunkley's. You won't 'ave forgotten how good they are. A threepenny lot, a nice piece of cod soaked in vinegar and a bag full of chips."

Charlie followed Mrs Shorrocks into Number 110, joined her in the tiny kitchen and collapsed on to a wooden chair.

"Don't suppose you know what 'appened to my barrow or even Dan Salmon's shop?"

"Young Miss Rebecca sold 'em both. Must 'ave been a good nine months back, not that long after you left for the front, come to think of it." Mrs Shorrocks placed the bag of chips and the fish on a piece of paper in the middle of the table. "To be fair, Kitty told us you were listed as killed on the Marne and by the time anyone found out the truth it was too late."

"May as well 'ave been," said Charlie, "for all there is to come 'ome to."

"Oh, I don't know," said Mrs Shorrocks as she flicked the top off a bottle of ale, took a swig and then pushed it over to Charlie. "I 'ear there's a lot of barrows up for sale nowadays and some still goin' for bargain prices."

"Glad to 'ear it," said Charlie. "But first I must catch up with Posh Porky as I don't 'ave much capital left of my own." He paused to take his first mouthful of fish. "Any idea where she's got to?"

"Never see her round these parts nowadays, Charlie. She always was a bit 'igh and mighty for the likes of us, but I did 'ear mention that Kitty had been to see her at London University."

"London University, eh? Well, she's about to discover Charlie Trumper's very much alive, however 'igh and mighty she's become. And she'd better have a pretty convincing story as to what 'appened to my share of our money." He rose from the table and gathered up his belongings, leaving the last two chips for Mrs Shorrocks.

"Shall I open another bottle, Charlie?"

"Can't stop now, Mrs Shorrocks. But thanks for the beer and grub – and give my best to Mr Shorrocks."

"Bert?" she said. "'aven't you 'eard? 'e died of an 'eart attack over six months ago, poor man. I do miss 'im." It was then that Charlie realised what was different about his old neighbour: no black eye and no bruises.

He left the house and set out to find London University, and see if he could track down Rebecca Salmon. Had she, as he'd instructed if he were listed as dead, divided the proceeds of the sale between his three sisters – Sal, now in Canada, Grace, still somewhere in France, and Kitty, God knows where? In which case there would be no capital for him to start up again other than Tommy's back pay and a few pounds he'd managed to save himself. He asked the first policeman he saw the way to London University and was pointed in the direction of the Strand. He walked another half-mile until he reached an archway that had chiselled in the stone above it: KING'S COLLEGE. He strolled through the opening and knocked on a door marked Enquiries, walked in and asked the man behind the counter if they had a Rebecca Salmon registered at the college. The man checked a list and shook his head. "Not 'ere," he said. "But you could try the university registry in Malet Street."

After another penny tram ride Charlie was beginning to wonder where he would end up spending the night.

"Rebecca Salmon?" said a man who stood behind the desk of the university registry dressed in a corporal's uniform. "Doesn't ring no bells with me." He checked her name in a large directory he pulled out from under the desk. "Oh, yes, 'ere she is. Bedford College, 'istory of Art." He was unable to hide the scorn in his voice.

"Don't have an address for 'er, do you, Corp?" asked Charlie.

"Get some service in, lad, before you call me corp," said the older man. "In fact the sooner you join up the better."

Charlie felt he had suffered enough insults for one day and suddenly let rip, "Sergeant Trumper, 7312087. I'll call you corp and you'll call me sergeant. Do I make myself clear?"

"Yes, Sergeant," said the corporal, springing to attention.

"Now, what's that address?"

"She's in digs at 97 Chelsea Terrace, Sergeant."

"Thank you," said Charlie, and left the startled ex-serviceman staring after him as he began yet another journey across London.

A weary Charlie finally stepped off a tram on the corner of Chelsea Terrace a little after four o'clock. Had Becky got there before him, he wondered, even if she were only living in digs?

He walked slowly up the familiar road admiring the shops he had once dreamed of owning. Number 131 – antiques, full of mahogany furniture, tables and chairs all beautifully polished. Number 133, women's clothes and hosiery from Paris, with garments displayed in the window that Charlie didn't consider it was right for a man to be looking at. On to Number 135 – meat and poultry hanging from the rods at the back of the shop that looked so delicious Charlie almost forgot there was a food shortage. His eyes settled on a restaurant called Mr Scallini which had opened at 139. Charlie wondered if Italian food would ever catch on in London.

Number 141 – an old bookshop, musty, cobwebbed and with not a single customer to be seen. Then 143 – a bespoke tailor. Suits, waistcoats, shirts and collars could, the message painted on the window assured him, be purchased by the discerning gentleman. Number 145 – freshly baked bread, the smell of which was almost enough to draw one inside. He stared up and down the street in incredulity as he watched the finely dressed women going about their daily tasks, as if a world war had never taken place. No one seemed to have told them about ration books.

Charlie came to a halt outside 147 Chelsea Terrace. He gasped with delight at the sight that met his tired eyes — rows and rows of fresh fruit and vegetables that he would have been proud to sell. Two well-turned-out girls in green aprons and an even smarter-looking youth waited to serve a customer.

Charlie took a pace backwards and stared up at the name above the shop. He was greeted by a sign printed in blue on gold which read: "Charlie Trumper, the honest trader. Founded 1823."

BECKY

1918-1920

CHAPTER 6

"From 1480 to 1532," he said.

I checked through my notes to make sure I had the correct dates, aware I had been finding it hard to concentrate. It was the last lecture of the day, and all I could think about was getting back to Chelsea Terrace.

The artist under discussion that afternoon was Bernardino Luini. I had already decided that my degree thesis would be on the life of this underrated painter from Milan. Milan . . . just another reason to be thankful that the war was finally over. Now I could plan excursions to Rome, Florence, Venice and yes, Milan, and study Luini's work at first hand. Michelangelo, da Vinci, Bellini, Caravaggio, Bernini – half the world's art treasures in one country, and I hadn't been able to travel beyond the walls of the Victoria and Albert.

At four thirty a bell rang to mark the end of lectures for the day. I closed my books and watched Professor Tilsey as he pottered towards the door. I felt a little sorry for the old fellow. He had only been dragged out of retirement because so many young dons had left to fight on the Western Front. The death of Matthew Makepeace, the man who *should* have been lecturing that afternoon, "one of the most promising scholars of his generation", the old Professor used to tell us, was "an inestimable loss to the department and the university as a whole". I had to agree with him: Makepeace was one of the few men in England acknowledged as an authority on Luini. I had only attended three of his lectures before he had signed up to go to France ... The irony of such a man being riddled with German bullets while stretched over a barbed-wire fence somewhere in the middle of France was not lost on me.

I was in my first year at Bedford. It seemed there was never enough time to catch up, and I badly needed Charlie to return and take the shop off my hands. I had written to him in Edinburgh when he was in Belgium, to Belgium when he was in France and to France the very moment he arrived back in Edinburgh. The King's mail never seemed to catch up with him, and now I didn't want Charlie to find out what I had been up to until I had the chance to witness his reaction for myself.

Jacob Cohen had promised to send Charlie over to Chelsea the moment he reappeared in the Whitechapel Road. It couldn't be too soon for me.

I picked up my books and stuffed them away in my old school satchel, the one my father – Tata – had given me when I won my open scholarship to St Paul's. The R.S. he had had so proudly stamped on the front was fading now, and the leather strap had almost worn through, so lately I had been carrying the satchel under my arm: Tata would never have considered buying me a new one while the old one still had a day's life left in it.

How strict Tata had always been with me as a child; even taken the strap to me on a couple of occasions, once for pinching "fress", or buns as Mother called them, behind his back – he didn't mind how much I took from the shop as long as I asked – and once for saying "Damn" when I cut my finger peeling an apple. Although I wasn't brought up in the Jewish faith – my mother wouldn't hear of it – he still passed on to me all those standards that were part of his own upbringing and would never tolerate what he from time to time described as my "unacceptable behaviour".

It was to be many years later that I learned of the strictures Tata had accepted once he had proposed marriage to my mother, a Roman Catholic. He adored her and never once complained in my presence of the fact that he always had to attend *shul* on his own. "Mixed marriage" seems such an outdated expression nowadays but at the turn of the century it must have been quite a sacrifice for both of them to make.

I loved St Paul's from the first day I walked through the gates, I suppose partly because no one told me off for working too hard. The only thing I didn't like was being called "Porky". It was a girl from the class above me, Daphne Harcourt-Browne, who later explained its double connotation. Daphne was a curly-headed blonde known as "Snooty", and although we were not natural friends, our predilection for cream buns brought us together – especially when she discovered that I had a never-ending source of supply. Daphne would happily have paid for them but I wouldn't allow her to as I wanted my classmates to think we were pals. On one occasion she even invited me to her home in Chelsea, but I didn't accept as I knew if I did I would only have to ask her back to my place in Whitechapel.

It was Daphne who gave me my first art book, *The Treasures of Italy*, in exchange for several cream wafers, and from that day on I knew I had stumbled across a subject I wanted to study for the rest of my life. I never asked Daphne but it always puzzled me why one of the pages at the front of the book had been torn out.

Daphne came from one of the best families in London, certainly from what I understood to be the upper classes, so once I left St Paul's I assumed we would never come across each other again. After all, Lowndes Square was hardly a natural habitat for me. Although to be fair neither was the East End while it remained full of such people as the Trumpers and Shorrocks.

And when it came to those Trumpers I could only agree with my father's judgment. Mary Trumper, by all accounts, must have been a saint. George Trumper was a man whose behaviour was unacceptable, not in the same class as his father, whom Tata used to describe as a "mensch". Young Charlie – who was always up to no good as far as I could see – nevertheless had what Tata called "a future". The magic must have skipped a generation, he suggested.

"The boy's not bad for a goy," he would tell me. "He'll run his own shop one day, maybe even more than one, believe me." I didn't give this observation a lot of thought until my father's death left me with no one else to whom I could turn.

Tata had complained often enough that he couldn't leave his two assistants at the shop for more than an hour before something was certain to go wrong. "No *saychel*," he would complain of those unwilling to take responsibility. "Can't think what would happen to the shop if I take one day off."

As Rabbi Glikstein read out the last rites at his *levoyah*, those words rang in my ears. My mother was still unconscious in hospital and they couldn't tell me when or if she might recover. Meanwhile I was to be foisted on my reluctant Aunt Harriet, whom I had only previously met at family gatherings. It turned out that she lived in some place called Romford and as she was due to take me back there the day after the funeral I had only been left with a few hours to make a decision. I tried to work out what my father would have done in the same circumstances and came to the conclusion that he would have taken what he so often called "a bold step".

By the time I got up the next morning, I had determined to sell the baker's shop to the highest bidder – unless Charlie Trumper were willing to take on the responsibility himself. Looking back, I certainly had my doubts about whether Charlie was capable of doing the job but in the end they were outweighed by Tata's high opinion of him.

During my lessons that morning I prepared a plan of action. As soon as school was over I took the train from Hammersmith to Whitechapel, then continued the rest of the journey on foot to Charlie's home.

Once at Number 112 I banged on the door with the palm of my hand and waited – I remember being surprised that the Trumpers didn't have a knocker. My call was eventually answered by one of those awful sisters, but I wasn't quite sure which one it was. I told her I needed to speak to Charlie, and wasn't surprised to be left standing on the doorstep while she disappeared back into the house. She returned a few minutes later and somewhat grudgingly led me into a little room at the back.

When I left twenty minutes later I felt I had come off with rather the worst of the bargain but another of my father's aphorisms came to mind: shnorrers no choosers.

The following day I signed up for an accountancy course as an "extra option". The lessons took place during the evening and then only after I had finished my regular school work for the day. To begin with I found the subject somewhat tedious, but as the weeks passed I became fascinated by how meticulously recording each transaction could prove to be so beneficial even to our little business. I had no idea so much money could be saved by simply understanding a balance-sheet, debt repayments and how to make claims against tax. My only worry was that I suspected Charlie had never bothered to pay any tax in the first place.

I even began to enjoy my weekly visits to Whitechapel, where I would be given the chance to show off my new-found skills. Although I remained resolute that my partnership with Charlie would come to an end the moment I was offered a place at university, I still believed that with his energy and drive, combined with my level-headed approach in all matters financial, we would surely have impressed my father and perhaps even Granpa Charlie.

As the time approached for me to concentrate on my matriculation, I decided to offer Charlie the opportunity to buy out my share of the partnership and even arranged for a qualified accountant to replace me in order that they could take over the book-keeping. Then, yet again, those Germans upset my best laid plans.

This time they killed Charlie's father, which was a silly mistake because it only made the young fool sign up to fight the lot of them on his own. Typically he didn't even bother to consult anyone. Off he went to Great Scotland Yard, in that frightful double-breasted suit, silly flat cap and flashy green tie, carrying all the worries of the Empire on his shoulders, leaving me to pick up the pieces. It was little wonder I lost so much weight over the next year, which my mother considered a small compensation for having to associate with the likes of Charlie Trumper.

To make matters worse, a few weeks after Charlie had boarded the train for Edinburgh, I was offered a place at London University.

Charlie had left me with only two choices: I could try to run the baker's shop myself and give up any thought of taking a degree, or I could sell out to the highest bidder. He had dropped me a note the day he left advising me to sell, so sell I did, but despite many hours spent traipsing round the East End I could only find one interested party: Mr Cohen, who had for some years conducted his tailor's business from above my father's shop and wanted to expand. He made me a fair offer in the circumstances and I even picked up another two pounds from one of the street traders for Charlie's huge barrow; but hard though I tried I couldn't find a buyer for Granpa Charlie's dreadful old nineteenth-century relic.

I immediately placed all the money I had collected on deposit in the Bow Building Society at 102 Cheapside for a period of one year at a rate of four per cent. I had had no intention of touching it while Charlie Trumper was still away at war, until some five months later Kitty Trumper visited me in Romford. She burst into tears and told me that Charlie had been killed on the Western Front. She added that she didn't know what would become of the family now that her brother was no longer around to take care of them. I immediately explained to her what my arrangement with Charlie had been, and that at least brought a smile to her face. She agreed to accompany me to the building society the next day so that we could withdraw Charlie's share of the money.

It was my intention to carry out Charlie's wishes and see that his share of the money was distributed equally between his three sisters. However, the under-manager of the society pointed out to us both in the politest possible terms that I was unable to withdraw one penny of the deposit until the first full year had been completed. He even produced the document I had signed to that effect, bringing to my attention the relevant clause. On learning this Kitty immediately leapt up, let out a stream of obscenities that caused the under-manager to turn scarlet, and then flounced out.

Later, I had cause to be grateful for that clause. I could so easily have divided Charlie's sixty per cent between Sal, Grace, and that awful Kitty, who had so obviously lied about her brother's death. I only became aware of the truth when in July Grace wrote from the front to let me know that Charlie was being sent home following the second battle of the Marne. I vowed there and then to give him his share of the money the day he set foot in England; I wanted to be rid of all those

Trumpers and their distracting problems once and for all.

I only wish Tata had lived to see me take up my place at Bedford College. His daughter at London University; Whitechapel would never have heard the end of it. But a German aeroplane put paid to that and crippled my mother into the bargain. As it turned out, Mother was still delighted to remind all her friends that I had been among the first women from the East End to sign the register.

After I had written my letter of acceptance to Bedford I began to look for digs nearer the university: I was determined to show some independence. My mother, whose heart had never fully recovered from the shock of losing Tata, retired to the suburbs to live with Aunt Harriet in Romford. She couldn't understand why I needed to lodge in London at all, but insisted that any accommodation I settled on had to be approved by the university authorities. She emphasised that I could only share rooms with someone Tata would have considered "acceptable". Mother never stopped telling me she didn't care for the lax morals that had become so fashionable since the outbreak of the war.

Although I had kept in contact with several school friends from St Paul's, I knew only one who was likely to have surplus accommodation in London, and I considered she might well turn out to be my one hope of not having to spend the rest of my life on a train somewhere between Romford and Regent's Park. I wrote to Daphne Harcourt-Browne the following day.

She replied inviting me round to tea at her little flat in Chelsea. When I first saw her again I was surprised to find that I was now a little taller than Daphne but that she had lost almost as much weight as I had. Daphne not only welcomed me with open arms but to my surprise expressed delight at the thought of my occupying one of her spare rooms. I insisted that I should pay her a rent of five shillings a week and also asked her, somewhat tentatively, if she felt able to come and have tea with my mother in Romford. Daphne seemed amused by the thought and travelled down to Essex with me on the following Tuesday.

My mother and aunt hardly uttered a word the entire afternoon. A monologue that centred on hunt balls, riding to hounds, polo and the disgraceful decline of the manners of Guards officers were hardly subjects about which they were often invited to give an opinion. By the time Aunt Harriet had served a second round of muffins I wasn't at all surprised to see my mother happily nodding her approval.

In fact, the only embarrassing moment the entire afternoon came when Daphne carried the tray out into the kitchen – something I suspected she had seldom done before – and spotted my final school report pinned to the pantry door. Mother smiled and added to my humiliation by reading its contents out loud: "Miss Salmon displays an uncommon capacity for hard work which, combined with an inquiring and intuitive mind, should augur well for her future at Bedford College. Signed Miss Potter, Headmistress."

"Ma certainly didn't bother to display my final report anywhere," was all Daphne had to say on the subject.

After I had moved into Chelsea Terrace, life for both of us quickly settled into a routine. Daphne flitted from party to party while I walked at a slightly faster pace from lecture hall to lecture hall, our two paths rarely crossing.

Despite my apprehension, Daphne turned out to be a wonderful companion to share digs with. Although she showed little interest in my academic life – her energies were spent in the pursuit of foxes and Guards officers – she was always brimful of common sense on every subject under the sun, not to mention having constant contact with a string of eligible young men who seemed to arrive in a never-ending convoy at the front door of 97 Chelsea Terrace.

Daphne treated them all with the same disdain, confiding in me that her one true love was still serving on the Western Front − not that she once mentioned his name in my presence.

Whenever I found time to break away from my books, she could always manage to supply a spare young officer to escort me to a concert, a play, even the occasional regimental dance. Although she never showed any interest in what I was up to at university, she often asked questions about the East End and seemed fascinated by my stories of Charlie Trumper and his barrow.

It might have continued like this indefinitely if I hadn't picked up a copy of the *Kensington News*, a paper Daphne took so she could find out what was showing at the local picture-house.

As I flicked through the pages one Friday evening an advertisement caught my eye. I studied the wording closely to be sure the shop was exactly where I thought it was, folded up the paper and left the flat to check for myself. I strolled down Chelsea Terrace to find the sign in the window of the local greengrocer's. I must have walked past it for days without noticing: "For sale. Apply John D. Wood, 6 Mount Street, London W1."

I remembered that Charlie had always wanted to know how prices in Chelsea compared with those in Whitechapel, so I decided to find out for him.

The following day, having asked some leading questions of our local newsagent − Mr Bales always seemed to know exactly what was going on in the terrace and was only too happy to share his knowledge with anyone who wanted to pass the time of day − I presented myself at the offices of John D. Wood in Mount Street. For some time I was left standing at the counter but eventually one of four assistants came over, introduced himself to me as Mr Palmer and asked how he could help.

After a closer inspection of the young man, I doubted that he could help anyone. He must have been about seventeen and was so pale and thin he looked as if a gust of wind might blow him away.

"I'd like to know some more details concerning Number 147 Chelsea Terrace," I said.

He managed to look both surprised and baffled at the same time.

"Number 147 Chelsea Terrace?"

"Number 147 Chelsea Terrace."

"Would madam please excuse me," he said and walked over to a filing cabinet, shrugging exaggeratedly as he passed one of his colleagues. I could see him thumb through several papers before returning to the counter with a single sheet; he made no attempt to invite me in or even to offer me a chair.

He placed the single sheet on the counter top and studied it closely.

"A greengrocer's shop," he said.

"Yes."

"The shop frontage," the young man went on to explain in a tired voice, "is twenty-two feet. The shop itself is a little under one thousand square feet, which includes a small flat on the first floor overlooking the park."

"What park?" I asked, not certain we were discussing the same property.

"Princess Gardens, madam," he said.

"That's a patch of grass a few feet by a few feet," I informed him, suddenly aware that Mr Palmer had never visited Chelsea Terrace in his life.

"The premises are freehold," he continued, not responding to my comment, but at least no longer leaning on the counter. "And the owner would allow vacant possession within thirty days of contracts being signed."

"What price is the owner asking for the property?" I asked. I was becoming more and more annoyed by being so obviously patronised.

"Our client, a Mrs Chapman –" continued the assistant.

"Wife of Able Seaman Chapman, late of HMS *Boxer*," I informed him. "Killed in action on 8 February 1918, leaving a daughter aged seven and a son aged five."

Mr Palmer had the grace to turn white.

"I also know that Mrs Chapman has arthritis which makes it almost impossible for her to climb those stairs to the little flat," I added for good measure.

He now looked considerably perplexed. "Yes," he said. "Well, yes."

"So how much is Mrs Chapman hoping the property will fetch?" I insisted. By now Mr Palmer's three colleagues had stopped what they were doing in order to follow our conversation.

"One hundred and fifty guineas is being asked for the freehold," stated the assistant, his eyes fixed on the bottom line of the schedule.

"One hundred and fifty guineas," I repeated in mock disbelief, without a clue as to what the property was really worth. "She must be living in cloud cuckoo land. Has she forgotten there's a war on? Offer her one hundred, Mr Palmer, and don't bother me again if she expects a penny more."

"Guineas?" he said hopefully.

"Pounds," I replied as I wrote out my name and address on the back of the particulars and left it on the counter. Mr Palmer seemed incapable of speech, and his mouth remained wide open as I turned and walked out of the office.

I made my way back to Chelsea only too aware that I had no intention of buying a shop in the terrace. In any case, I hadn't got one hundred pounds, or anything like it. I had just over forty pounds in the bank and not much prospect of raising another bean, but the silly man's attitude had made me so angry. Still, I decided, there wasn't much fear of Mrs Chapman accepting so insulting an offer.

Mrs Chapman accepted my offer the following morning. Blissfully unaware that I had no obligation to sign any agreement, I put down a ten-pound deposit the same afternoon. Mr Palmer explained that the money was not returnable, should I fail to complete the contract within thirty days.

"That won't be a problem," I told him with bravado, though I hadn't a clue how I would get hold of the balance of the cash.

For the following twenty-seven days I approached everyone I knew, from the Bow Building Society to distant aunts, even fellow-students, but none of them showed the slightest interest in backing a young woman undergraduate to the tune of sixty pounds in order that she could buy a fruit and vegetable shop.

"But it's a wonderful investment," I tried to explain to anyone who would listen. "What's more, Charlie Trumper comes with the deal, the finest fruit and vegetable man the East End has ever seen." I rarely got beyond this point in my sales patter before expressions of incredulity replaced polite interest.

After the first week I came to the reluctant conclusion that Charlie Trumper wasn't going to be pleased that I had sacrificed ten pounds of our money – six of his and four of mine – just to appease my female vanity. I decided I would carry the six-pound loss myself rather than admit to him I'd made such a fool of myself.

"But why didn't you talk it over with your mother or your aunt before you went ahead with something quite so drastic?" enquired Daphne on the twenty-sixth day. "After all, they both seemed so sensible to me."

"And be killed for my trouble? No, thank you," I told her sharply. "In any case, I'm not that sure they have sixty pounds between them. Even if they did, I don't think they'd be willing to invest a penny in Charlie Trumper."

At the end of the month I crept back round to John D. Wood to explain that the ninety pounds would not be forthcoming and they should feel free to place the property back on the market. I dreaded the "I knew as much" smirk that would appear on Mr Palmer's face once he learned my news.

"But your representative completed the transaction yesterday," Mr Palmer assured me, looking as if he would never understand what made me tick.

"My representative?" I said.

The assistant checked the file. "Yes, a Miss Daphne Harcourt-Browne of –"

"But why?" I asked.

"I hardly feel that I'm the person to answer that particular question," offered Mr Palmer, "as I've never set eyes on the lady before yesterday."

"Quite simple really," Daphne replied when I put the same question to her that evening. "If Charlie Trumper is half as good as you claim then I'll have made a very sound investment."

"Investment?"

"Yes. You see, I require that my capital plus four per cent interest should be returned within three years."

"Four per cent?"

"Correct. After all, that's the amount I am receiving on my War Loan Stock. On the other hand, should you fail to return my capital plus interest in full, I will require ten per cent of the profits from the fourth year onwards."

"But there may not be any profits."

"In which case I will automatically take over sixty per cent of the assets. Charlie will then own twenty-four per cent and you sixteen. Everything you need to know is in this document." She handed over several pages of tightly worded copy, the last page of which had a seven on the top. "All it now requires is your signature on the bottom line."

I read through the papers slowly while Daphne poured herself a sherry. She or her advisors seemed to have considered every eventuality.

"There's only one difference between you and Charlie Trumper," I told her, penning my signature between two pencilled crosses.

"And what's that?"

"You were born in a four-poster bed."

As I was quite unable to organise the shop myself and continue with my studies at the university, I quickly came to the conclusion that I would have to appoint a temporary manager. The fact that the three girls who were already employed at Number 147 just giggled whenever I gave any instructions, only made the appointment more pressing.

The following Saturday I began a tour of Chelsea, Fulham and Kensington, staring into shop windows up and down the three boroughs and watching young men going about their business in the hope of eventually finding the right person to run Trumper's.

After keeping an eye on several possible candidates who were working in local shops, I finally selected a young man who was an assistant at a fruiterer's in Kensington. One evening in November I waited for him to finish his day's work. I then followed him as he began his journey home.

The ginger-haired lad was heading towards the nearest bus stop when I managed to catch him up.

"Good evening, Mr Makins," I said.

"Hello?" He looked round startled and was obviously surprised to discover that an unintroduced young woman knew his name. He carried on walking.

"I own a greengrocer's shop in Chelsea

Terrace . . ." I said, keeping up with him stride for stride as he continued on towards the bus stop. He showed even more surprise but didn't say anything, only quickened his pace. ". . . and I'm looking for a new manager."

This piece of information caused Makins to slow down for the first time and look at me more carefully.

"Chapman's," he said. "Was it you who bought Chapman's?"

"Yes, but it's Trumper's now," I told him. "And I'm offering you the job as manager at a pound a week more than your present salary." Not that I had any idea what his present salary was.

It took several miles on the bus and a lot of questions still to be answered outside his front door before he invited me in to meet his mother. Bob Makins joined us two weeks later, as manager of Trumper's.

Despite this coup I was disappointed to find at the end of our first month that the shop had made a loss of over three pounds which meant I wasn't able to return a penny piece to Daphne.

"Don't be despondent," she told me. "Just keep going and there must still be an outside chance the penalty clause will never come into force, especially if on Mr Trumper's return he proves half as good as you claim he is."

During the previous six months I had been able to keep a more watchful eye on the whereabouts of the elusive Charlie, thanks to the help of a young officer Daphne had introduced me to who worked in the War Office. He always seemed to know exactly where Sergeant Charles Trumper of the Royal Fusiliers could be located at any time of the day or night. However, I still remained determined to have Trumper's running smoothly and declaring a profit long before Charlie set foot in the premises.

However I learned from Daphne's friend that my errant partner was to be discharged on 20 February

1919, leaving me with little or no time to balance the books. And worse, we had recently found it necessary to replace two of the three giggling girls who had sadly fallen victim to the Spanish flu epidemic, and sack the third for incompetence.

I tried to recall all the lessons Tata had taught me when I was a child. If a queue was long then you must serve the customers quickly, but if short you had to take your time: that way the shop would never be empty. People don't like to go into empty shops, he explained; it makes them feel insecure.

"On your awning," he would insist, "should be printed in bold lettering the words 'Dan Salmon, freshly baked bread, Founded 1879'. Repeat name and date at every opportunity; the sort of people who live in the East End like to know you've been around for some time. Queues and history: the British have always appreciated the value of both."

I tried to implement this philosophy, as I suspected Chelsea was no different from the East End. But in our case the blue awning read, "Charlie Trumper, the honest trader, founded 1823". For a few days I had even considered calling the shop Trumper and Salmon, but dropped that idea when I realised that would only tie me in with Charlie for life.

One of the big differences I discovered between the East and the West End was that in Whitechapel the names of debtors were chalked up on a slate, whereas in Chelsea they opened an account. To my surprise, bad debts turned out to be more common in Chelsea than in Whitechapel. By the following month I was still unable to pay anything back to Daphne. It was becoming daily more apparent that my only hope now rested with Charlie.

On the day he was due back I had lunch in the college dining hall with two friends from my year. I munched away at my apple and toyed with a piece of cheese as I tried to concentrate on their views on Karl

Marx. Once I had sucked my third of a pint of milk dry I picked up my books and returned to the lecture theatre. Despite being normally mesmerised by the subject of the early Renaissance artists, on this occasion I was grateful to see the professor stacking up his papers a few minutes before the lecture was scheduled to end.

The tram back to Chelsea seemed to take for ever, but at last it came to a halt on the corner of Chelsea Terrace.

I always enjoyed walking the full length of the street to check how the other shops were faring. First I had to pass the antique shop where Mr Rutherford resided. He always raised his hat when he saw me. Then there was the women's clothes shop at Number 133 with its dresses in the window that I felt I would never be able to afford. Next came Kendrick's, the butchers, where Daphne kept an account; and a few doors on from them was the Italian restaurant with its empty cloth-covered tables. I knew the proprietor must be struggling to make a living, because we could no longer afford to extend him any credit. Finally came the bookshop where dear Mr Sneddles tried to eke out a living. Although he hadn't sold a book in weeks he would happily sit at the counter engrossed in his beloved William Blake until it was time to turn the sign on the front door from "Open" to "Closed". I smiled as I passed by but he didn't see me.

I calculated that if Charlie's train had arrived at King's Cross on time that morning, he should have already reached Chelsea by now, even if he had had to cover the entire journey on foot.

I hesitated only for a moment as I approached the shop, then walked straight in. To my chagrin, Charlie was nowhere to be seen. I immediately asked Bob Makins if anyone had called in asking for me.

"No one, Miss Becky," Bob confirmed. "Don't worry, we all remember exactly what was expected of us if Mr Trumper shows up." His two new assistants, Patsy and Gladys, nodded their agreement.

I checked my watch – a few minutes past five – and decided that if Charlie hadn't turned up by now he was unlikely to appear before the next day. I frowned and told Bob he could start closing up. When six chimed on the clock above the door, I reluctantly asked him to push the blind back in, and to lock up while I checked over the day's takings.

"Strange that," said Bob as he arrived by my side at the front door clutching on to the shop door keys.

"Strange?"

"Yes. That man over there. He's been sitting on the bench for the last hour and has never once taken his eyes off the shop. I only hope there's nothing wrong with the poor fellow."

I glanced across the road. Charlie was sitting, arms folded, staring directly at me. When our eyes met he unfolded his arms, stood up and walked slowly over to join me.

Neither of us spoke for some time until he said "So what's the deal?"

CHAPTER 7

"How do you do, Mr Trumper? Pleased to make your acquaintance, I'm sure," said Bob Makins, rubbing his palm down a green apron before shaking his new master's outstretched hand.

Gladys and Patsy both stepped forward and gave Charlie a half-curtsey, which brought a smile to Becky's lips.

"There'll be no need for anything like that," said Charlie. "I'm up from Whitechapel and the only bowing and scraping you'll be doing in future will be for the customers."

"Yes, sir," said the girls in unison, which left Charlie speechless.

"Bob, will you take Mr Trumper's things up to his room?" Becky asked. "While I show him round the shop."

"Certainly, miss," said Bob, looking down at the brown paper parcel and the little box that Charlie had left on the floor by his side. "Is that all there is, Mr Trumper?" he asked in disbelief.

Charlie nodded.

He stared at the two assistants in their smart white blouses and green aprons. They were both standing behind the counter looking as if they weren't quite sure what to do next. "Off you go, both of you," said Becky. "But be sure you're in first thing tomorrow morning. Mr Trumper's a stickler when it comes to time-keeping."

The two girls collected their little felt bags and scurried

away as Charlie sat himself down on a stool next to a box of plums.

"Now we're alone," he said, "you can tell me 'ow all this came about."

"Well," replied Becky, "foolish pride was how it all began but . . ."

Long before she had come to the end of her story Charlie was saying, "You're a wonder, Becky Salmon, a positive wonder."

She continued to tell Charlie everything that had taken place during the past year and the only frown to appear on his forehead came when Charlie learned the details of Daphne's investment.

"So I've got just about two years and nine months to pay back the full sixty pounds plus interest?"

"Plus the first six months' losses," said Becky sheepishly.

"I repeat, Rebecca Salmon, you're a wonder. If I can't do something that simple then I'm not worthy to be called your partner."

A smile of relief crossed Becky's face.

"And do you live 'ere as well?" Charlie asked as he looked up the stairs.

"Certainly not. I share digs with an old school friend of mine, Daphne Harcourt-Browne. We're just up the road at 97."

"The girl who supplied you with the money?" asked Charlie.

Becky nodded.

"She must be a good friend," said Charlie.

Bob reappeared at the bottom of the stairs.

"I've put Mr Trumper's things in the bedroom and checked over the flat. Everything seems to be in order."

"Thank you, Bob," said Becky. "As there's nothing else you can do today, I'll see you in the morning."

"Will Mr Trumper be coming to the market, miss?"

"I doubt it," said Becky. "So why don't you do the

ordering for tomorrow as usual? I'm sure Mr Trumper will join you some time later in the week."

"Covent Garden?" asked Charlie.

"Yes, sir," said Bob.

"Well, if they 'aven't moved it I'll see you there at four thirty tomorrow morning."

Becky watched Bob turn white. "I don't suppose Mr Trumper will expect you to be there every morning at four thirty," she laughed. "Just until he's got back in the swing of things. Goodnight, Bob."

"Goodnight miss, goodnight sir," said Bob, who left the shop with a perplexed look on his face.

"What's all this 'sir' and 'miss' nonsense?" asked Charlie. "I'm only about a year older than Bob."

"So were many of the officers on the Western Front who you called 'sir'."

"But that's the point. I'm not an officer."

"No, but you are the boss. What's more, you're no longer in Whitechapel, Charlie. Come on, it's time you saw your rooms."

"Rooms?" said Charlie. "I've never had 'rooms' in my life. It's been just trenches, tents and gymnasiums lately."

"Well, you have now." Becky led her partner up the wooden staircase to the first floor and began a guided tour. "Kitchen," she said. "Small, but ought to serve your purposes. By the way, I've seen to it that there are enough knives, forks and crockery for three and I've told Gladys that it's also her responsibility to keep the flat clean and tidy. The front room," she announced, opening a door, "if one has the nerve to describe something quite this small as a front room."

Charlie stared at a sofa and three chairs, all obviously new. "What happened to all my old things?"

"Most of them were burnt on Armistice Day," admitted Becky. "But I managed to get a shilling for the horsehair chair, with the bed thrown in."

"And what about my granpa's barrow? You didn't burn that as well?"

"Certainly not. I tried to sell it, but no one was willing to offer me more than five shillings, so Bob uses it for picking up the produce from the market every morning."

"Good," said Charlie, with a look of relief.

Becky turned and moved on to the bathroom. "Sorry about the stain below the cold water tap," she said. "None of us could find anything that would shift it however much elbow grease we used. And I must warn you, the lavatory doesn't always flush."

"I've never 'ad a toilet inside the 'ouse before," said Charlie. "Very posh."

Becky continued on into the bedroom.

Charlie tried to take in everything at once, but his eyes settled on a coloured picture that had hung above his bed in Whitechapel Road and had once belonged to his mother. He felt there was something familiar about it. His eyes moved on to a chest of drawers, two chairs and a bed he had never seen before. He desperately wanted to show Becky how much he appreciated all she had done, and settled for bouncing up and down on the corner of the bed.

"Another first," said Charlie.

"Another first?"

"Yes, curtains. Granpa wouldn't allow them, you know. He used to say –"

"Yes, I remember," said Becky. "Kept you asleep in the morning, and prevented you from doing a proper day's work."

"Well, somethin' like that, except I'm not sure my granpa would 'ave known what the word 'prevented' meant," said Charlie as he began to unpack Tommy's little box. Becky's eyes fell on the picture of the Virgin Mary and Child the moment Charlie placed the little painting on the bed. She picked up the oil and began to study it more closely.

"Where did you get this, Charlie? It's exquisite."

"A friend of mine who died at the front left it to me," he replied matter-of-factly.

"Your friend had taste." Becky kept holding on to the picture. "Any idea who painted it?"

"No, I 'aven't." Charlie stared up at his mother's framed photo that Becky had hung on the wall. "Blimey," he said, "it's exactly the same picture."

"Not quite," said Becky, studying the magazine picture above his bed. "You see, your mother's is a photograph of a masterpiece by Bronzino, while your friend's painting, although it looks similar, is actually a damned good copy of the original." She checked her watch. "I must be off," she said without warning. "I've promised I'd be at the Queen's Hall by eight o'clock. Mozart."

"Mozart. Do I know 'im?"

"I'll arrange an introduction in the near future."

"So you won't be 'anging around to cook my first dinner then?" asked Charlie. "You see, I've still got so many questions I need to 'ave answered. So many things I want to find out about. To start with –"

"Sorry, Charlie. I mustn't be late. See you in the morning though – when I promise I'll answer all your questions."

"First thing?"

"Yes, but not by your standards," laughed Becky. "Some time round eight would be my guess."

"Do you like this fellow Mozart?" Charlie asked, as Becky felt his eyes studying her more closely.

"Well, to be honest I don't know a lot about him myself, but Guy likes him."

"Guy?" said Charlie.

"Yes, Guy. He's the young man who's taking me to the concert and I haven't known him long enough to be late. I'll tell you more about both of them tomorrow. Bye, Charlie."

On the walk back to Daphne's flat Becky couldn't help feeling a little guilty about deserting Charlie on his first night home and began to think perhaps it had been selfish of her to accept an invitation to go to a concert with Guy that night. But the battalion didn't give him that many evenings off during the week, and if she didn't see him when he was free it often turned out to be several days before they could spend another evening together.

As she opened the front door of 97, Becky could hear Daphne splashing around in the bath.

"Has he changed?" her friend shouted on hearing the door close.

"Who?" asked Becky, walking through to the bedroom.

"Charlie, of course," said Daphne, pushing open the bathroom door. She stood leaning against the tiled wall with a towel wrapped around her body. She was almost enveloped in a cloud of steam.

Becky considered the question for a moment. "He's changed, yes; a lot, in fact, except for his clothes and voice."

"What do you mean?"

"Well, the voice is the same – I'd recognise it anywhere. The clothes are the same – I'd recognise them anywhere. But he's not the same."

"Am I meant to understand all that?" asked Daphne, as she began to rub her hair vigorously.

"Well, as he pointed out to me, Bob Makins is only a year younger than he is, but Charlie seems about ten years older than either of us. It must be something that happens to men once they've served on the Western Front."

"You shouldn't be surprised by that, but what I want to know is: did the shop come as a surprise to him?"

"Yes, I think I can honestly say it did." Becky slipped out of her dress. "Don't suppose you've got a pair of stockings I could borrow, have you?"

"Third drawer down," said Daphne. "But in exchange I'd like to borrow your legs."

Becky laughed.

"What's he like to look at?" Daphne continued as she threw her wet towel on the bathroom floor.

Becky considered the question. "An inch, perhaps two, under six foot, every bit as large as his father, only in his case it's muscle, not fat. He's not exactly Douglas Fairbanks, but some might consider him handsome."

"He's beginning to sound my type," said Daphne as she rummaged around among her clothes to find something suitable.

"Hardly, my dear," said Becky. "I can't see Brigadier Harcourt-Browne welcoming Charlie Trumper to morning sherry before the Cottenham Hunt."

"You're such a snob, Rebecca Salmon," said Daphne, laughing. "We may share rooms, but don't forget you and Charlie originate from the same stable. Come to think of it, you only met Guy because of me."

"Too true," Becky said, "but surely I get a little credit for St Paul's and London University?"

"Not where I come from, you don't," said Daphne, as she checked her nails. "Can't stop and chatter with the working class now, darling," she continued. "Must be off. Henry Bromsgrove is taking me to a flapper dance in Chelsea. And wet as our Henry is, I do enjoy an invitation to stalk at his country home in Scotland every August. Tootle pip!"

As Becky drew her bath, she thought about Daphne's words, delivered with humour and affection but still highlighting the problems she faced when trying to cross the established social barriers for more than a few moments.

Daphne had indeed introduced her to Guy, only a few weeks before, when Daphne had persuaded her to make up a party to see *La Bohème* at Covent Garden. Becky could still recall that first meeting clearly. She had tried so hard not to like him as they shared a drink at the Crush Bar, especially after Daphne's warning about his reputation. She had tried not to stare too obviously at the slim young man who stood before her. His thick blond hair, deep blue eyes and effortless charm had probably captivated the hearts of a host of women that evening, but as Becky assumed that every girl received exactly the same treatment, she avoided allowing herself to be flattered by him.

The following evening Daphne asked her what she had thought of the young officer she had met at the Opera.

"Remind me of his name," said Becky.

"Oh, I see," said Daphne. "Affected you that badly, did he?"

"Yes," she admitted. "But so what? Can you see a

young man with a background like his taking any interest in a girl from Whitechapel?"

"Yes, I can actually, although I suspect he's only after one thing."

"Then you'd better warn him I'm not that sort of girl," said Becky.

"I don't think that's ever put him off in the past," replied Daphne. "However, to start with he's asking if you would care to accompany him to the theatre along with some friends from his regiment. How does that strike you?"

"I'd love to."

"I thought you might," said Daphne. "So I told him 'yes' without bothering to consult you."

Becky laughed but had to wait another five days before she actually saw the young officer again. After he had come to collect her at the flat they joined a party of junior officers and debutantes at the Haymarket Theatre to see *Pygmalion* by the fashionable playwright George Bernard Shaw. Becky enjoyed the new play despite a girl called Amanda giggling all the way through the first act and then refusing to hold a conversation with her during the interval.

Over dinner at the Café Royal, she sat next to Guy and told him everything about herself from her birth in Whitechapel through to winning a place at Bedford College the previous year.

After Becky had bade her farewells to the rest of the party, Guy drove her back to Chelsea and having said, "Goodnight, Miss Salmon," shook her by the hand.

Becky assumed that she would not be seeing the young officer again.

But Guy dropped her a note the next day, inviting her to a reception at the mess. This was followed a week later by a dinner, then a ball, and after that regular outings took place, culminating in an invitation to spend the weekend with his parents in Berkshire.

Daphne did her best to brief Becky fully on the family. The major, Guy's father, was a sweetie, she assured her, farmed seven hundred acres of dairy land in Berkshire, and was also Master of the Buckhurst Hunt.

It took Daphne several attempts to explain what "riding to hounds" actually meant, though she had to admit that even Eliza Doolittle would have been hard pushed to understand fully why they bothered with the exercise in the first place.

"Guy's mother, however, is not graced with the same generous instincts as the major," Daphne warned. "She is a snob of the first order." Becky's heart sank. "Second daughter of a baronet, who was created by Lloyd George for making things they stick on the end of tanks. Probably gave large donations to the Liberal Party at the same time, I'll be bound. Second generation, of course. They're always the worst." Daphne checked the seams on her stockings. "My family have been around for seventeen generations, don't you know, so we feel we haven't an awful lot to prove. We're quite aware that we don't possess a modicum of brain between us, but by God we're rich, and by Harry we're ancient. However, I fear the same cannot be said for Captain Guy Trentham."

CHAPTER 8

ecky woke the next morning before her alarm went off, and was up, dressed and had left the flat long before Daphne had even stirred. She couldn't wait to find out how Charlie was coping on his first day. As she walked towards 147 she noticed that the shop was already open, and a lone customer was receiving Charlie's undivided attention.

"Good mornin', partner," shouted Charlie from behind the counter as Becky stepped into the shop.

"Good morning," Becky replied. "I see you're determined to spend your first day just sitting back and watching how it all works."

Charlie, she was to discover, had begun serving customers before Gladys and Patsy had arrived, while poor Bob Makins looked as if he had already completed a full day's work.

"'aven't the time to chatter to the idle classes at the moment," said Charlie, his Cockney accent seeming broader than ever. "Any 'ope of catching up with you later this evening?"

"Of course," said Becky.

She checked her watch, waved goodbye and departed for her first lecture of the morning. She found it hard to concentrate on the history of the Renaissance era, and even slides of Raphael's work, reflected from a magic lantern on to a white sheet, couldn't fully arouse her interest. Her mind kept switching from the anxiety of having to spend a weekend with Guy's parents to the problems of Charlie making enough of a profit to clear their debt with Daphne. Becky admitted to herself that she felt more confident of the latter. She was relieved to see the black hand of the clock pass four thirty. Once again she ran to catch the tram on the corner of Portland Place – and continued to run after the trudging vehicle had deposited her in Chelsea Terrace.

A little queue had formed at Trumper's and Becky could hear Charlie's familiar old catch-phrases even before she reached the front door.

"'alf a pound of your King Edward's, a juicy grapefruit from South Africa, and why don't I throw in a nice Cox's orange pippin, all for a bob, my luv?" Grand dames, ladies-in-waiting and nannies, all who would have turned their noses up had anyone else called them "luv", seemed to melt when Charlie uttered the word. It was only after the last customer had left that Becky was able to properly take in the changes Charlie had already made to the shop.

"Up all night, wasn't I?" he told her. "Removin' 'alf-empty boxes and unsaleable items. Ended up with all the colourful vegetables, your greens, all soft, placed at the back; while all your 'ardy unattractive variety you put up front. Potatoes, swedes, and turnips. It's a golden rule."

"Granpa Charlie –" she began with a smile, but stopped herself just in time.

Becky began to study the rearranged counters and had to agree that it was far more practical the way Charlie had insisted they should be laid out. And she certainly couldn't argue with the smiles on the faces of the customers.

Within a month, a queue stretching out on to the pavement became part of Charlie's daily routine and within two he was already talking to Becky of expanding.

"Where to?" she asked. "Your bedroom?"

"No room for vegetables up there," he replied with a grin. "Not since we've 'ad longer queues at Trumper's than what they 'ave outside *Pygmalion*. What's more, *we're* goin' to run for ever."

After she had checked and rechecked the takings for

the first quarter, Becky couldn't believe how much they had turned over; she decided perhaps the time had come for a little celebration.

"Why don't we all have dinner at that Italian restaurant?" suggested Daphne, after she had received a far larger cheque for the past three months than she had anticipated.

Becky thought it a wonderful idea, but was surprised to find how reluctant Guy was to fall in with her plans, and also how much trouble Daphne took getting herself ready for the occasion.

"We're not expecting to spend all the profits in one evening," Becky assured her.

"More's the pity," said Daphne. "Because it's beginning to look as if it might be the one chance I'm given to enforce the penalty clause. Not that I'm complaining. After all, Charlie will be quite a change from the usual chinless vicars' sons and stable boys with no legs that I have to endure most weekends."

"Be careful he doesn't end up eating you for dessert."

Becky had warned Charlie that the table had been booked for eight o'clock and made him promise he would wear his best suit. "My only suit," he reminded her.

Guy collected the two girls from Number 97 on the dot of eight, but seemed unusually morose as he accompanied them to the restaurant, arriving a few minutes after the appointed hour. They found Charlie sitting alone in the corner, fidgeting and looking as if it might be the first time he had ever been to a restaurant.

Becky introduced first Daphne to Charlie and then Charlie to Guy. The two men just stood and stared at each other like prizefighters.

"Of course, you were both in the same regiment," said Daphne. "But I don't suppose you ever came across each other," she added, staring at Charlie. Neither man commented on her observation.

If the evening started badly, it was only to become worse, as the four of them were quite unable to settle on any subject with which they had something in common. Charlie, far from being witty and sharp as he was with the customers in the shop, became surly and uncommunicative. If Becky could have reached his ankle she would have kicked him, and not simply because he kept putting a knife covered with peas in his mouth.

Guy's particular brand of sullen silence didn't help matters either, despite Daphne laughing away, bubbly as ever, whatever anyone said. By the time the bill was finally presented, Becky was only too relieved that the evening was coming to an end. She even had discreetly to leave a tip, because Charlie didn't seem to realise it was expected of him.

She left the restaurant at Guy's side and the two of them lost contact with Daphne and Charlie as they strolled back towards 97. She assumed that her companions were only a few paces behind, but stopped thinking about where they might be when Guy took her in his arms, kissed her gently and said, "Goodnight, my darling. And don't forget, we're going down to Ashurst for the weekend." How could she forget? Becky watched Guy look back furtively in the direction that Daphne and Charlie had been walking, but then without another word he hailed a hansom and instructed the cabbie to take him to the Fusiliers' barracks in Hounslow.

Becky unlocked the front door and sat down on the sofa to consider whether or not she should return to 147 and tell Charlie exactly what she thought of him. A few minutes later Daphne breezed into the room.

"Sorry about this evening," said Becky before her friend had had the chance to offer an opinion. "Charlie's usually a little more communicative than that. I can't think what came over him."

"Not easy for him to have dinner with an officer from his old regiment, I suspect," said Daphne.

"I'm sure you're right," said Becky. "But they'll end up friends, I feel sure of that."

Daphne stared down at Becky thoughtfully.

*   *   *

The following Saturday morning, Guy arrived at 97 Chelsea Terrace to collect Becky and drive her down to Ashurst. The moment he saw her in one of Daphne's stylish red dresses he remarked on how beautiful she looked, and he was so cheerful and chatty on the journey down to Berkshire that Becky even began to relax. They arrived in the village of Ashurst just before three and Guy turned to wink at her as he swung the car into the mile-long drive that led up to the Hall.

Becky hadn't expected the house to be quite that large.

A butler, under-butler, and two footmen were waiting on the top step to greet them. Guy brought the car to a halt on the gravelled drive and the butler stepped forward to remove Becky's two small cases from the boot, before handing them over to a footman who whisked them away. The butler then led Captain Guy and Becky at a sedate pace up the stone steps, into the front hall, and on up the wide wooden staircase to a bedroom on the first-floor landing.

"The Wellington Room, madam," he intoned as he opened the door for her.

"He's meant to have spent the night here once," explained Guy, as he strolled up the stairs beside her. "By the way, no need for you to feel lonely. I'm only next door, and much more alive than the late general."

Becky walked into a large comfortable room where she found a young girl in a long black dress with a white collar and cuffs unpacking her bags. The girl turned, curtsied and announced, "I'm Nellie, your maid. Please let me know if you need anything, ma'am."

Becky thanked her, walked over to the bay window and stared out on to the green acres that stretched as far as her eye could see. There was a knock on the door and Becky turned to find Guy entering the room before she had been given the chance to say, "Come in."

"Room all right, darling?"

"Just perfect," said Becky as the maid curtsied once again. Becky thought she detected a slight look of apprehension in the young girl's eyes as Guy walked across the room.

"Ready to meet Pa?" he asked.

"As ready as I'm ever likely to be," Becky admitted, as she accompanied Guy back downstairs to the morning room where a man in his early fifties stood in front of a blazing log fire waiting to greet them.

"Welcome to Ashurst Hall," said Major Trentham.

Becky smiled at her host and said, "Thank you."

The major was slightly shorter than his son, but had the same slim build and fair hair, though there were some strands of grey appearing at the side. But that was where the likeness ended. Whereas Guy's complexion was fresh and pale, Major Trentham's skin had the ruddiness of a man who had spent most of his life outdoors, and when Becky shook his hand she felt the roughness of someone who obviously worked on the land.

"Those fine London shoes won't be much good for what I have in mind," declared the major. "You'll have to borrow a pair of my wife's riding boots, or perhaps Nigel's wellingtons."

"Nigel?" Becky enquired.

"Trentham minor. Hasn't Guy told you about him? He's in his last year at Harrow, hoping to go on to Sandhurst – and outshine his brother, I'm told."

"I didn't know you had a –"

"The little brat isn't worthy of a mention," Guy interrupted with a half-smile, as his father guided them back through the hall to a cupboard below the stairs. Becky stared at the row of leather riding boots that were even more highly polished than her shoes.

"Take your pick, m'dear," said Major Trentham.

After a couple of attempts Becky found a pair that fitted perfectly, then followed Guy and his father out into the garden. It took the best part of the afternoon for Major Trentham to show his young guest round the seven-hundred-acre estate and by the time Becky returned she was more than ready for the hot punch that awaited them in a large silver tureen in the morning room.

The butler informed them that Mrs Trentham had

phoned to say that she had been held up at the vicarage and would be unable to join them for tea.

By the time Becky returned to her room in the early evening to take a bath and change for dinner, Mrs Trentham still hadn't made an appearance.

Daphne had loaned Becky two dresses for the occasion, and even an exquisite semi-circular diamond brooch about which Becky had felt a little apprehensive. But when she looked at herself in the mirror, all her fears were quickly forgotten.

When Becky heard eight o'clock chiming in chorus from the numerous clocks around the house she returned to the drawing room. The dress and the brooch had a perceptible and immediate effect on both men. There was still no sign of Guy's mother.

"What a charming dress, Miss Salmon," said the major.

"Thank you, Major Trentham," said Becky, as she warmed her hands by the fire before glancing around the room.

"My wife will be joining us in a moment," the major assured Becky, as the butler proffered her a glass of sherry on a silver tray.

"I did enjoy being shown round the estate."

"Hardly warrants that description, my dear," the major replied with a warm smile. "But I'm glad you enjoyed the walk," he added as his attention was diverted over her shoulder.

Becky swung round to see a tall, elegant lady, dressed in black from the nape of her neck to her ankles, enter the room. She walked slowly and sedately towards them.

"Mother," said Guy, stepping forward to give her a kiss on the cheek, "I should like you to meet Becky Salmon."

"How do you do?" said Becky.

"May I be permitted to enquire who removed my best riding boots from the hall cupboard?" asked Mrs Trentham, ignoring Becky's outstretched hand. "And then saw fit to return them covered in mud?"

"I did," said the major. "Otherwise Miss Salmon would have had to walk around the farm in a pair of high heels. Which might have proved unwise in the circumstances."

"It might have proved wiser for Miss Salmon to have come properly equipped with the right footwear in the first place."

"I'm so sorry . . ." began Becky.

"Where have you been all day, Mother?" asked Guy, jumping in. "We had rather hoped to see you earlier."

"Trying to sort out some of the problems that our new vicar seems quite unable to cope with," replied Mrs Trentham. "He has absolutely no idea of how to go about organising a harvest festival. I can't imagine what they are teaching them at Oxford nowadays."

"Theology, perhaps," suggested Major Trentham.

The butler cleared his throat. "Dinner is served, madam."

Mrs Trentham turned without another word and led them through into the dining room at a brisk pace. She placed Becky on the right of the major and opposite herself. Three knives, four forks and two spoons shone up at Becky from the large square table. She had no trouble in selecting which one she should start with, as the first course was soup but from then on she knew she would simply have to follow Mrs Trentham's lead.

Her hostess didn't address a word to Becky until the main course had been served. Instead she spoke to her husband of Nigel's efforts at Harrow – not very impressive; the new vicar – almost as bad; and Lady Lavinia Malim – a judge's widow who had recently taken residence in the village and had been causing even more trouble than usual.

Becky's mouth was full of pheasant when Mrs Trentham suddenly asked, "And which of the professions is your father associated with, Miss Salmon?"

"He's dead," Becky spluttered.

"Oh, I am sorry to hear that," she said indifferently.

"Am I to presume he died serving with his regiment at the front?"

"No, he didn't."

"Oh, so what *did* he do during the war?"

"He ran a baker's shop. In Whitechapel," added Becky, mindful of her father's warning: "If you ever try to disguise your background, it will only end in tears."

"Whitechapel?" Mrs Trentham queried. "If I'm not mistaken, isn't that a sweet little village, just outside Worcester?"

"No, Mrs Trentham, it's in the heart of the East End of London," said Becky, hoping that Guy would come to her rescue, but he seemed more preoccupied with sipping his glass of claret.

"Oh," said Mrs Trentham, her lips remaining in a straight line. "I remember once visiting the Bishop of Worcester's wife in a place called Whitechapel, but I confess I have never found it necessary to travel as far as the East End. I don't suppose they have a bishop there." She put down her knife and fork. "However," she continued, "my father, Sir Raymond Hardcastle – you may have heard of him, Miss Salmon –"

"No, I haven't actually," said Becky honestly.

Another disdainful look appeared on the face of Mrs Trentham, although it failed to stop her flow. "– Who was created a baronet for his services to King George V . . ."

"And what were those services?" asked Becky innocently, which caused Mrs Trentham to pause for a moment before explaining, "He played a small part in His Majesty's efforts to see that we were not overrun by the Germans."

"He's an arms dealer," said Major Trentham under his breath.

If Mrs Trentham heard the comment she chose to ignore it.

"Did you come out this year, Miss Salmon?" she asked icily.

"No, I didn't," said Becky. "I went up to university instead."

"I don't approve of such goings-on myself. Ladies shouldn't be educated beyond the three 'Rs' plus an adequate understanding of how to manage servants and survive having to watch a cricket match."

"But if you don't have servants —" began Becky, and would have continued if Mrs Trentham hadn't rung a silver bell that was by her right hand.

When the butler reappeared she said curtly, "We'll take coffee in the drawing room, Gibson." The butler's face registered a hint of surprise as Mrs Trentham rose and led everyone out of the dining room, down a long corridor and back into the drawing room where the fire no longer burned so vigorously.

"Care for some port or brandy, Miss Salmon?" asked Major Trentham, as Gibson poured out the coffee.

"No, thank you," said Becky quietly.

"Please excuse me," said Mrs Trentham, rising from the chair in which she had just sat down. "I seem to have developed a slight headache and will therefore retire to my room, if you'll forgive me."

"Yes, of course, my dear," said the major flatly.

As soon as his mother had left the room Guy walked quickly over to Becky, sat down, and took her hand. "She'll be better in the morning, when her migraine has cleared up, you'll see."

"I doubt it," replied Becky in a whisper, and turning to Major Trentham said, "Perhaps you'll excuse me as well. It's been a long day, and in any case I'm sure the two of you have a lot to catch up on."

Both men rose as Becky left the room and climbed the long staircase to her bedroom. She undressed quickly and, after washing in a basin of near freezing water, crept across the unheated room to slide between the sheets of her cold bed.

Becky was already half asleep when she heard the door handle turning. She blinked a few times and tried to focus on the far side of the room. The door opened slowly, but all she could make out was the figure of a man entering, then the door closing silently behind him.

"Who's that?" she whispered sharply.

"Only me," murmured Guy. "Thought I'd pop in and see how you were."

Becky pulled her top sheet up to her chin. "Goodnight, Guy," she said briskly.

"That's not very friendly," said Guy, who had already crossed the room and was now sitting on the end of her bed. "Just wanted to check that everything was all right. Felt you had rather a rough time of it tonight."

"I'm just fine, thank you," said Becky flatly. As he leaned over to kiss her she slid away from him so he ended up brushing her left ear.

"Perhaps this isn't the right time?"

"Or place," added Becky sliding even further away so that she was nearly falling out of the far side of the bed.

"I only wanted to kiss you goodnight."

Becky reluctantly allowed him to take her in his arms and kiss her on the lips, but he held on to her far longer than she had anticipated and eventually she had to push him away.

"Goodnight, Guy," she said firmly.

At first Guy didn't move, but then he rose slowly and said, "Perhaps another time." A moment later she heard the door close behind him.

Becky waited for a few moments before getting out of bed. She walked over to the door, turned the key in the lock and removed it before going back to bed. It was some time before she was able to sleep.

When Becky came down for breakfast the following morning she quickly discovered from Major Trentham that a restless night had not improved his wife's migraine: she had therefore decided to remain in bed until the pain had completely cleared.

Later, when the major and Guy went off to church,

leaving Becky to read the Sunday newspapers in the drawing room, she couldn't help noticing that the servants were whispering among themselves whenever she caught their eye.

Mrs Trentham appeared for lunch, but made no attempt to join in the conversation that was taking place at the other end of the table. Unexpectedly, just as the custard was being poured on to the summer pudding she asked, "And what was the vicar's text this morning?"

"Do unto others as you expect them to do unto you," the major replied with a slight edge to his voice.

"And how did you find the service at our local church, Miss Salmon?" asked Mrs Trentham, addressing Becky for the first time.

"I didn't . . ." began Becky.

"Ah, yes, of course, you are one of the chosen brethren."

"No, actually if anything I'm a Roman Catholic," said Becky.

"Oh," said Mrs Trentham, feigning surprise "I assumed, with the name of Salmon . . . in any case you wouldn't have enjoyed St Michael's. You see, it's very down to earth."

Becky wondered if every word Mrs Trentham uttered and every action she took was rehearsed in advance.

Once lunch had been cleared away Mrs Trentham disappeared again and Guy suggested that he and Becky should take a brisk walk. Becky went up to her room and changed into her oldest shoes, far too terrified to suggest she might borrow a pair of Mrs Trentham's wellingtons.

"Anything to get away from the house," Becky told him when she returned downstairs and didn't open her mouth again until she felt certain that Mrs Trentham was well out of earshot.

"What does she expect of me?" Becky finally asked.

"Oh, it's not that bad," Guy insisted, taking her hand. "You're overreacting. Pa's convinced she'll come round given time and in any case, if I have to choose between you and her I know exactly which one of you is more important to me."

Becky squeezed his hand. "Thank you, darling, but I'm still not certain I can go through another evening like the last one."

"We could always leave early and spend the rest of the day at your place," Guy said. Becky turned to look at him, unsure what he meant. He added quickly, "Better get back to the house or she'll only grumble that we left her alone all afternoon." They both quickened their pace.

A few minutes later they were climbing the stone steps at the front of the hall. As soon as Becky had changed back into her house shoes and checked her hair in the mirror on the hallstand, she rejoined Guy in the drawing room. She was surprised to find a large tea already laid out. She checked her watch: it was only three fifteen.

"I'm sorry you felt it necessary to keep everyone waiting, Guy," were the first words that Becky heard as she entered the room.

"Never known us to have tea this early before," offered the major, from the other side of the fireplace.

"Do you take tea, Miss Salmon?" Mrs Trentham asked, even managing to make her name sound like a petty offence.

"Yes, thank you," replied Becky.

"Perhaps you could call Becky by her first name," Guy suggested.

Mrs Trentham's eyes came to rest on her son. "I cannot abide this modern-day custom of addressing everyone by their Christian name, especially when one has only just been introduced. Darjeeling, Lapsang or Earl Grey, Miss Salmon?" she asked before anyone had been given a chance to react. She looked up expectantly for Becky's reply, but no answer was immediately forthcoming because Becky still hadn't quite recovered from the previous jibe. "Obviously you're not given that much choice in Whitechapel," Mrs Trentham added.

Becky considered picking up the pot and pouring the contents all over the woman, but somehow she managed to hold her temper, if only because she knew that making her lose it was exactly what Mrs Trentham was hoping to achieve.

After a further silence Mrs Trentham asked, "Do you have any brothers or sisters, Miss Salmon?"

"No, I'm an only child."

"Surprising, really."

"Why's that?" asked Becky innocently.

"I always thought the lower classes bred like rabbits," said Mrs Trentham, dropping another lump of sugar into her tea.

"Mother, really –" began Guy.

"Just my little joke," she said quickly. "Guy will take me so seriously at times, Miss Salmon. However, I well remember my father, Sir Raymond, once saying . . ."

"Not again," said the major.

". . . that the classes were not unlike water and wine. Under no circumstances should one attempt to mix them."

"But I thought it was Christ who managed to turn water into wine," said Becky.

Mrs Trentham chose to ignore this observation. "That's exactly why we have officers and other ranks in the first place; because God planned it that way."

"And do you think that God planned that there should be a war, in order that those same officers and other ranks could then slaughter each other indiscriminately?" asked Becky.

"I'm sure I don't know, Miss Salmon," Mrs Trentham replied. "You see, I don't have the advantage of being an intellectual like yourself. I am just a plain, simple woman who speaks her mind. But what I do know is that we *all* made sacrifices during the war."

"And what sacrifices did you make, Mrs Trentham?" Becky enquired.

"A considerable number, young lady," Mrs Trentham replied, stretching to her full height. "For a start, I had to go without a lot of things that were quite fundamental to one's very existence."

"Like an arm or a leg?" said Becky, quickly regretting her words the moment she realised that she had fallen into Mrs Trentham's trap.

Guy's mother rose from her chair, walked slowly over to the fireplace, where she tugged violently on the servants' bell-pull. "I do not have to sit around and be insulted in my own home," she said. As soon as Gibson reappeared she turned to him and added, "See that Alfred collects Miss Salmon's belongings from her room. She will be returning to London earlier than planned."

Becky remained silently by the fire not sure what she should do next. Mrs Trentham stood coolly staring at her until finally Becky walked over to the major, shook him by the hand and said, "I'll say goodbye, Major Trentham. I have a feeling we won't be seeing each other again."

"My loss, Miss Salmon," he said graciously before kissing her hand. Then Becky turned and walked slowly out of the drawing room without giving Mrs Trentham a second look. Guy followed Becky into the hall.

On their journey back to London Guy made every excuse he could think of for his mother's behaviour, but Becky knew he didn't really believe his own words. When the car came to a halt outside Number 97 Guy jumped out and opened the passenger door.

"May I come up?" he said. "There's something I still have to tell you."

"Not tonight," said Becky. "I need to think and I'd rather like to be on my own."

Guy sighed. "It's just that I wanted to tell you how much I love you and perhaps talk about our plans for the future."

"Plans that include your mother?"

"To hell with my mother," he replied. "Don't you realise how much I love you?"

Becky hesitated.

"Let's announce our engagement in *The Times* as soon as possible, and to hell with what she thinks. What do you say?"

She turned and threw her arms around him. "Oh, Guy, I do love you too, but you'd better not come up tonight. Not while Daphne is expected back at any moment. Another time perhaps?"

A look of disappointment crossed Guy's face. He kissed her before saying, "Goodnight." She opened the front door and ran up the stairs.

Becky unlocked the flat door to find that Daphne had not returned from the country. She sat alone on the sofa, not bothering to turn the gas up when the light faded. It was to be a further two hours before Daphne sailed in.

"How did it all go?" were the first words Daphne uttered as she entered the drawing room, a little surprised to find her friend sitting in the dark.

"A disaster."

"So it's all over?"

"No, not exactly," said Becky. "In fact I have a feeling Guy proposed to me."

"But did you accept?" asked Daphne.

"I rather think I did."

"And what do you intend to do about India?"

The following morning when Becky unpacked her overnight case, she was horrified to discover that the delicate brooch Daphne had lent her for the weekend was missing. She assumed she must have left it at Ashurst Hall.

As she had no desire to make contact with Mrs Trentham again, she dropped a note to Guy at his regimental mess to alert him of her anxiety. He replied the next day to assure her that he would check on Sunday when he planned to have lunch with his parents at Ashurst.

Becky spent the next five days worrying about whether Guy would be able to find the missing piece: thankfully Daphne didn't seem to have noticed its absence. Becky only hoped she could get the brooch back before her friend felt the desire to wear it again.

Guy wrote on Monday to say that despite an extensive search of the guest bedroom he had been unable to locate the missing brooch, and in any case Nellie had informed him that she distinctly remembered packing all of Becky's jewellery.

This piece of news puzzled Becky because she remembered packing her own case following her summary dismissal from Ashurst Hall. With considerable trepidation she sat up late into the night, waiting for Daphne to return from her long weekend in the country so that she could explain to her friend what had happened. She feared that it might be months, even years before she could save enough to replace what was probably a family heirloom.

By the time her flatmate breezed into Chelsea Terrace a few minutes after midnight, Becky had already drunk several cups of black coffee and almost lit up one of Daphne's cigarettes.

"You're up late, my darling," were Daphne's opening words. "Are exams that close?"

"No," said Becky, then blurted out the whole story of the missing diamond brooch. She finished by asking how long she thought it might take to repay her.

"About a week would be my guess," said Daphne.

"A week?" said Becky, looking puzzled.

"Yes. It was only stage jewellery — all the rage at the moment. If I remember correctly, it cost me every penny of three shillings."

A relieved Becky told Guy over dinner on Tuesday why finding the missing piece of jewellery was no longer of such importance.

The following Monday Guy brought the piece round to Chelsea Terrace, explaining that Nellie had found it under the bed in the Wellington Room.

CHAPTER 9

ecky began to notice small changes in Charlie's manner, at first subtle and then more obvious.

Daphne made no attempt to hide her involvement in what she described as: "The social discovery of the decade, my very own Charlie Doolittle. Why, only this weekend," she declared, "I took him down to Harcourt Hall, don't you know, and he was a wow. Even Mother thought he was fantastic."

"Your mother approves of Charlie Trumper?" said Becky in disbelief.

"Oh, yes, darling, but then you see Mummy realises that I have no intention of marrying Charlie."

"Be careful, I had no intention of marrying Guy."

"My darling, never forget you spring from the romantic classes, whereas I come from a more practical background, which is exactly why the aristocracy have survived for so long. No, I shall end up marrying a certain Percy Wiltshire and it's got nothing to do with destiny or the stars, it's just good old-fashioned common sense."

"But is Mr Wiltshire aware of your plans for his future?"

"Of course the Marquess of Wiltshire isn't. Even his mother hasn't told him yet."

"But what if Charlie were to fall in love with you?"

"That's not possible. You see, there's another woman in his life."

"Good heavens," said Becky. "And to think I've never met her."

The shop's six-monthly figures showed a considerable improvement on the first quarter's, as Daphne discovered to her cost when she received her next dividend. She told Becky that at this rate she couldn't hope to make any long-term profit from her loan. As for Becky herself, she spent less and less of her time thinking about Daphne, Charlie or the shop as the hour drew nearer for Guy's departure to India.

India . . . Becky hadn't slept the night she had learned of Guy's three-year posting and she certainly might have wished to discover something that would so disrupt their future from his lips and not Daphne's. In the past Becky had accepted, without question, that because of Guy's duties with the regiment it would not be possible for them to see each other on a regular basis; but as the time of his departure drew nearer she began to resent guard duty, night exercises and, most of all, any weekend operations in which the Fusiliers were expected to take part.

Becky had feared that Guy's attentions would cool after her distressing visit to Ashurst Hall, but if anything he became even more ardent and kept repeating how different it would all be once they were married.

But then, as if without warning, the months became weeks, the weeks days, until the dreaded circle Becky had pencilled around 3 February 1920 on the calendar by the side of her bed was suddenly upon them.

"Let's have dinner at the Café Royal, where we spent our first evening together," Guy suggested, the Monday before he was due to leave.

"No," said Becky. "I don't want to share you with a hundred strangers on our last evening." She hesitated before adding, "If you can face the thought of my cooking, I'd rather give you dinner at the flat. At least that way we can be on our own."

Guy smiled.

*   *   *

Once the shop seemed to be running smoothly Becky didn't drop in every day, but she couldn't resist a glance through the window whenever she passed Number 147. She was surprised to find that that particular Monday morning Charlie wasn't to be seen behind the counter.

"Over here," she heard a voice cry and turned to find Charlie sitting on the same bench opposite the shop where she had first spotted him the day she returned to London. She crossed the road to join him.

"What's this, taking early retirement before we've repaid the loan?"

"Certainly not. I'm working."

"Working? Please explain, Mr Trumper, how lounging about on a park bench on a Monday morning can be described as work?"

"It was Henry Ford who taught us that 'For every minute of action, there should be an hour of thought,'" said Charlie, with only a slight trace of his old Cockney accent; Becky also couldn't help noticing how he had pronounced Henry.

"And where are those Fordian-like thoughts taking you at this particular moment?" she asked.

"To that row of shops opposite."

"All of them?" Becky looked over at the block. "And what conclusion would Mr Ford have come to had he been sitting on this bench, pray?"

"That they represent thirty-six different ways of making money."

"I've never counted them, but I'll take your word for it."

"But what else do you see when you look across the road?"

Becky's eyes returned to Chelsea Terrace. "Lots of people walking up and down the pavement, mainly ladies with parasols, nannies pushing prams, and the odd child with a skipping rope or hoop." She paused. "Why, what do you see?"

"Two 'For Sale' signs."

"I confess I hadn't noticed them." Once again she looked across the road.

"That's because you're looking with a different pair of eyes," Charlie explained. "First there's Kendrick's the butcher. Well, we all know about him, don't we? Heart attack, been advised by his doctor to retire early or he can't hope to live much longer."

"And then there's Mr Rutherford," said Becky, spotting the second 'For Sale' sign.

"The antique dealer. Oh, yes, dear Julian wants to sell up and join his friend in New York, where society is a little more sympathetic when it comes to his particular proclivities – like that word?"

"How did you find –?"

"Information," said Charlie, touching his nose. "The life-blood of any business."

"Another Fordian Principle?"

"No, much nearer home than that," admitted Charlie. "Daphne Harcourt-Browne."

Becky smiled. "So what are you going to do about it?"

"I'm going to get hold of them both, aren't I?"

"And how do you intend to do that?"

"With my cunning and your diligence."

"Are you being serious, Charlie Trumper?"

"Never more." Charlie turned to face her once again. "After all, why should Chelsea Terrace be any different from Whitechapel?"

"Just the odd decimal point, perhaps," suggested Becky.

"Then let's move that decimal point, Miss Salmon. Because the time has come for you to stop being a sleeping partner and start fulfilling your end of the bargain."

"But what about my exams?"

"Use the extra time you'll have now that your boyfriend has departed for India."

"He goes tomorrow, actually."

"Then I'll grant you a further day's leave. Isn't that

how officers describe a day off? Because tomorrow I want
you to return to John D. Wood and make an appointment to see that pimply young assistant – what was his
name?"

"Palmer," said Becky.

"Yes, Palmer," said Charlie. "Instruct him to negotiate
a price on our behalf for both those shops, and warn him
that we're also interested in anything else that might come
up in Chelsea Terrace."

"Anything else in Chelsea Terrace?" said Becky, who
had begun making notes on the back of her textbook.

"Yes, and we'll also need to raise nearly all the money
it's going to cost to purchase the freeholds, so visit several
banks and see that you get good terms. Don't consider anything above four per cent."

"Nothing above four per cent," repeated Becky. Looking up, she added, "But thirty-six shops, Charlie?"

"I know, it could take an awful long time."

In the Bedford College library, Becky tried to push
Charlie's dreams of being the next Mr Selfridge to one
side as she attempted to complete an essay on the influence
of Bernini on seventeenth-century sculpture. But her mind
kept switching from Bernini to Charlie and then back to
Guy. Unable to grapple with the modern, Becky felt she
was having even less success with the ancient so she came
to the conclusion that her essay would have to be postponed until she could find more time to concentrate on
the past.

During her lunch break she sat on the red brick wall
outside the library, munching a Cox's orange pippin while
continuing to think. She took one last bite before tossing
the core into a nearby wastepaper-basket and everything
else back into her satchel before beginning her journey west-
ward to Chelsea.

Once she had reached the terrace her first stop was
the butcher's shop, where she picked up a leg of lamb and
told Mrs Kendrick how sorry she was to hear about her

husband. When she paid the bill she noted that the assistants, though well trained, didn't show a great deal of initiative. Customers escaped with only what they had come in for, which Charlie would never have allowed them to do. She then joined the queue at Trumper's and drew Charlie to serve her.

"Something special, madam?"

"Two pounds of potatoes, one pound of button mushrooms, a cabbage and a melon."

"It's your lucky day, madam. The melon should be eaten this very evening," he said, just pressing the top lightly. "Can I interest madam in anything else? A few oranges, a grapefruit perhaps?"

"No, thank you, my good man."

"Then that'll be three shillings and fourpence, madam."

"But don't I get a Cox's orange pippin thrown in, like all the other girls?"

"No, sorry, madam, such privileges are reserved only for our regular customers. Mind you, I could be persuaded, if I was asked to share that melon with you tonight. Which would give me the chance to explain in detail my master plan for Chelsea Terrace, London, the world – "

"Can't tonight, Charlie. Guy's leaving for India in the morning."

"Of course, 'ow silly of me, sorry. I forgot." He sounded uncharacteristically flustered. "Tomorrow, perhaps?"

"Yes, why not?"

"Then as a special treat I'll take you *out* to dinner. Pick you up at eight?"

"It's a deal, partner," said Becky, hoping she sounded like Mae West.

Charlie was suddenly distracted by a large lady who had taken her place at the front of the queue.

"Ah, Lady Nourse," said Charlie, returning to his Cockney accent, "your usual swedes and turnips, or are we going to be a little more adventurous today, m'lady?"

Becky looked back to watch Lady Nourse, who wasn't a day under sixty, blush as her ample breast swelled with satisfaction.

Once she had returned to her flat, Becky quickly checked the drawing room over to be sure that it was clean and tidy. The maid had done a thorough job and as Daphne hadn't yet returned from one of her long weekends at Harcourt Hall there was little for her to do other than plumping up the odd cushion and drawing the curtains.

Becky decided to prepare as much of the evening meal as possible before having a bath. She was already regretting turning down Daphne's offer of the use of a cook and a couple of maids from Lowndes Square to help her out, but she was determined to have Guy to herself for a change, although she knew her mother wouldn't approve of having dinner with a male friend without Daphne or a chaperone to keep an eye on them.

Melon, followed by leg of lamb with potatoes, cabbage and some button mushrooms: surely that would have met with her mother's approval. But she suspected that approval would not have been extended to wasting hard-earned money on the bottle of Nuits-St-Georges 1912 that she had purchased from Mr Cuthbert at Number 101. Becky peeled the potatoes, basted the lamb and checked she had some mint before removing the stalk on the cabbage.

As she ran her bath she decided that in future she would have to purchase all her goods locally, to be sure that her information on what was taking place in the terrace was as up to date as Charlie's. Before going to undress she also checked there was still some brandy left over in the bottle she had been given the previous Christmas.

She lay soaking in a hot bath for some time as she thought through which banks she would approach and, more importantly, how she would present her case. The detailed figures of Trumper's income and a time schedule required for the repayment of any loan . . . Her mind drifted back from Charlie to Guy, and why it was that neither of them would ever talk about the other.

When Becky heard the bedroom clock chime the half-hour she leapt out of the bath in a panic, suddenly realising how much time her thoughts must have occupied and only too aware that Guy was certain to appear on the doorstep as the clock struck eight. The one thing you could guarantee with a soldier, Daphne had warned her, was that they always turned up on time.

Clothes were strewn all over both their bedroom floors as Becky emptied half Daphne's wardrobe and most of her own in a desperate attempt to find something to wear. In the end she chose the dress Daphne had worn at the Fusiliers' Ball, and never worn since. Once she had managed to do up the top button she checked herself in the mirror. Becky felt confident she would pass muster. The clock on the mantelpiece struck eight and the doorbell rang.

Guy, wearing a double-breasted regimental blazer and cavalry twills, entered the room carrying another bottle of wine as well as a dozen red roses. Once he had placed both offerings on the table, he took Becky in his arms.

"What a beautiful dress," he said. "I don't think I've seen it before."

"No, it's the first time I've worn it," said Becky, feeling guilty about not asking Daphne's permission to borrow it.

"No one to help you?" asked Guy, looking around.

"To be honest, Daphne volunteered to act as chaperone, but I didn't accept as I hadn't wanted to share you with anyone on our last evening together."

Guy smiled. "Can I do anything?"

"Yes, you could uncork the wine while I put the potatoes on."

"Trumper's potatoes?"

"Of course," replied Becky, as she walked back through into the kitchen and dropped the cabbage into a pot of boiling water. She hesitated for a moment before calling back, "You don't like Charlie, do you?"

Guy poured out a glass of wine for each of them but either hadn't heard what she had said, or made no attempt to respond.

"What's your day been like?" Becky asked when she returned to the drawing room and took the glass of wine he handed her.

"Packing endless trunks in preparation for tomorrow's journey," he replied. "They expect you to have four of everything in that bloody country."

"Everything?" Becky sipped the wine. "Um, good."

"Everything. And you, what have you been up to?"

"Talked to Charlie about his plans for taking over London without actually declaring war; dismissed Caravaggio as second-rate; and selected some button mushrooms, not to mention Trumper's deal of the day." As she finished speaking, Becky placed half a melon on Guy's mat and the other half in her place as he refilled their glasses.

Over a lingering dinner, Becky became more and more conscious that this would probably be their last evening together for the next three years. They talked of the theatre, the regiment, the problems in Ireland, Daphne, even the price of melons, but never India.

"You could always come and visit me," he said finally, bringing up the taboo subject himself as he poured her another glass of wine, nearly emptying the bottle.

"A day trip, perhaps?" she suggested, removing the empty dinner plates from the table and taking them back to the kitchen.

"I suspect even that will be possible at some time in the future."

Guy filled his own glass once again, then opened the bottle he had brought with him.

"What do you mean?"

"By aeroplane. After all, Alcock and Brown have crossed the Atlantic non-stop, so India must be any pioneer's next ambition."

"Perhaps I could sit on a wing," said Becky when she returned from the kitchen.

Guy laughed. "Don't worry. I'm sure three years will pass by in a flash, and then we can be married just as soon as I return." He raised his glass and watched her take another drink. For some time they didn't speak.

Becky rose from the table feeling a little giddy. "Must put the kettle on," she explained.

When she returned Becky didn't notice that her glass had been refilled. "Thank you for a wonderful evening," Guy said, and for a moment Becky was anxious that he might be thinking of leaving.

"Now I fear the time has come to do the washing-up, as you don't seem to have any staff around tonight and I left my batman back at barracks."

"No, don't let's bother with that." Becky hiccuped. "After all, I can spend a year on the washing-up, followed by a year on the drying and still put aside a year for stacking."

Guy's own laugh was interrupted by the rising whistle of the kettle.

"Won't be a minute. Why don't you pour yourself some brandy?" Becky added, as she disappeared back into the kitchen and selected two cups that didn't have chips in them. She returned with them full of strong hot coffee, and thought for a moment that the gaslight might have been turned down a little. She placed the two cups on the table next to the sofa. "The coffee's so hot that it will be a couple of minutes before we can drink it," she warned.

He passed her a brandy balloon that was half full. He raised his glass and waited. She hesitated, then took a sip before sitting down beside him. For some time again neither of them spoke and then suddenly he put down his glass, took her in his arms and this time began kissing her passionately, first on her lips, then on her neck and then on her bare shoulders. Becky only began to resist when she felt a hand move from her back on to one of her breasts.

Guy broke away and said, "I have a special surprise for you, darling, which I've been saving for tonight."

"What's that?"

"Our engagement is to be announced in *The Times* tomorrow."

For a moment Becky was so stunned she could only stare at Guy. "Oh, darling, how wonderful." She took him back in her arms and made no effort to resist when his hand returned to her breast. She broke away again. "But how will your mother react?"

"I don't give a damn how she reacts," said Guy, and once again began to kiss her neck. His hand moved to her other breast as her lips parted and their tongues touched.

She began to feel the buttons on the back of her dress being undone, slowly at first, then with more confidence before Guy released her again. She blushed as he removed his regimental blazer and tie and threw them over the back of the sofa, and began to wonder if she shouldn't make it clear they had already gone too far.

When Guy started to undo the front of his shirt she panicked for a moment: things were getting a little out of control.

Guy leaned forward and slipped the top of Becky's dress off her shoulders. Once he had returned to kissing her again, she felt his hand trying to undo the back of her bodice.

Becky felt she might be saved by the fact that neither of them knew where the fasteners were. However, it became abundantly clear that Guy had overcome such problems before, as he deftly undid the offending clips and hesitated only for a moment before transferring his attention to her legs. He stopped quite suddenly when he reached the top of her stockings, and looking into her eyes murmured, "I had only imagined until now what this would be like, but I had no idea you would be quite so beautiful."

"Thank you," said Becky, and sat bolt upright. Guy handed over her brandy and she took another sip, wondering if it might not be wise for her to make some excuse about the coffee going cold and slip back into the kitchen to make another pot.

"However there's still been a disappointment for me this evening," he added, one hand still on her thigh.

"A disappointment?" Becky put down her brandy glass. She was beginning to feel distinctly woozy.

"Yes," said Guy. "Your engagement ring."

"My engagement ring?"

"I ordered it from Garrard's over a month ago, and they promised it would be ready for me to collect by this evening. But only this afternoon they informed me that I wouldn't be able to pick it up until first thing tomorrow."

"It doesn't matter," said Becky.

"It does," said Guy. "I'd wanted to slip it on your finger tonight, so I do hope you can be at the station a little earlier than we had planned. I intend to fall on one knee and present it to you then."

Becky stood up and smiled as Guy quickly rose and took her in his arms. "I'll always love you, you know that, don't you?" Daphne's dress slipped off and fell to the floor. Guy took her by the hand and she led him into the bedroom.

He quickly pushed back the top sheet, jumped in and held up his arms. Once she had climbed in to join him Guy quickly removed the rest of her clothes and began kissing her all over her body before making love with an expertise that Becky suspected could only have come from considerable practice.

Although the act itself was painful, Becky was surprised how quickly the promised sensation was over and she clung on to Guy for what seemed an eternity. He kept repeating how much he cared for her which made Becky feel less guilty – after all, they were engaged.

Becky was half asleep when she thought she heard a door slam, and turned over, assuming it must have come from the flat above them. Guy hardly stirred. Quite suddenly the bedroom door was flung open, and Daphne appeared in front of them.

"So sorry, I didn't realise," she said in a whisper and closed the door quietly behind her. Becky looked across at her lover apprehensively.

He smiled and took her in his arms. "No need to worry about Daphne. She won't tell anyone." He stretched out an arm and pulled her towards him and they made love once again.

Waterloo station was already crowded with men in uniforms when Becky walked on to platform one. She was a couple of minutes late, so a little surprised not to find Guy waiting for her. Then she remembered that he'd have had to go to Albemarle Street to pick up the ring.

She checked the board: chalked up in white capital letters were the words "*Southampton Boat Train*, P & O to India, departure time 11.30". Becky continued to look anxiously up and down the platform before her eyes settled on a band of helpless girls. They were huddled together under the station clock, their shrill, strained voices all talking at once of hunt balls, polo and who was coming out that season – each of them only too aware that farewells must be said at the station because it wasn't the done thing for a girl to accompany an officer on the train to Southampton unless they were married or officially engaged. But *The Times* that morning would prove that she and Guy were engaged, thought Becky, so perhaps she would be invited to travel on as far as the coast . . .

She checked her watch yet again: eleven twenty-one. For the first time she began to feel slightly uneasy. Then suddenly she saw him striding across the platform towards her followed by a man dragging two cases, and a porter wheeling even more luggage.

Guy apologised, but gave no explanation as to why he was so late, only ordering his batman to place his trunks on the train and wait for him. For the next few minutes they talked of nothing in particular and Becky even felt he was a little distant, but she was well aware that there were several brother officers on the platform, also bidding their farewells, some even to their wives.

A whistle blew and Becky noticed a guard check his watch. Guy leaned forward, brushed her cheek with his lips, then suddenly turned away. She watched him as he stepped quickly on to the train, never once looking back, while all she could think of was their naked bodies lodged together in that tiny bed and Guy saying, "I'll always love you. You know that, don't you?"

A final whistle blew and a green flag was waved. Becky stood quite alone. She shivered from the gust of wind that came as the engine wound its snake-like path out of the station and began its journey to Southampton. The giggling girls also departed, but in another direction, towards their hansom cabs and chauffeur-driven cars.

Becky walked over to a booth on the corner of platform seven, purchased a copy of *The Times* for threepence, and checked, first quickly, then slowly, down the list of forthcoming weddings.

From Arbuthnot to Yelland there was no mention of a Trentham, or a Salmon.

CHAPTER 10

Even before the first course had been served Becky regretted accepting Charlie's invitation to dinner at Mr Scallini's, the only restaurant he knew. Charlie was trying so hard to be considerate, which only made her feel more guilty.

"I like your dress," he said, admiring the pastel-coloured frock she had borrowed from Daphne's wardrobe.

"Thank you."

A long pause followed.

"I'm sorry," he said. "I should have thought twice before inviting you out the same day as Captain Trentham was leaving for India."

"Our engagement will be announced in *The Times* tomorrow," she said, not looking up from her untouched bowl of soup.

"Congratulations," said Charlie without feeling.

"You don't like Guy, do you?"

"I never was much good with officers."

"But your paths had crossed during the war. In fact, you knew him before I did, didn't you?" said Becky without warning. Charlie didn't reply, so she added, "I sensed it the first time we all had dinner together."

"'Knew him' would be an exaggeration," said Charlie. "We served in the same regiment, but until that night we'd never eaten at the same table."

"But you fought in the same war."

"Along with four thousand other men from our regiment," said Charlie, refusing to be drawn.

"And he was a brave and respected officer?"

A waiter appeared uninvited by their side. "What would you like to drink with your fish, sir?"

"Champagne," said Charlie. "After all, we do have something to celebrate."

"Do we?" said Becky, unaware that he had used the ploy simply to change the subject.

"Our first year's results. Or have you forgotten that Daphne's already been paid back more than half her loan?"

Becky managed a smile, realising that while she had been worrying about Guy's departure for India, Charlie had been concentrating on solving her other problem. But despite this news the evening continued in silence, occasionally punctuated with comments from Charlie that didn't always receive a reply. She occasionally sipped the champagne, toyed with her fish, ordered no dessert, and could barely hide her relief when the bill was eventually presented.

Charlie paid the waiter and left a handsome tip. Daphne would have been proud of him, Becky thought.

As she rose from her chair, she felt the room starting to go round in circles.

"Are you all right?" asked Charlie, placing an arm around her shoulder.

"I'm fine, just fine," said Becky. "I'm not used to drinking so much wine two nights in a row."

"And you didn't eat much dinner either," said Charlie, guiding her out of the restaurant and into the cold night air.

They proceeded arm in arm along Chelsea Terrace and Becky couldn't help thinking any casual passer-by might have taken them for lovers. When they arrived at the entrance to Daphne's flat Charlie had to dig deep into Becky's bag to find her keys. Somehow he managed to get the door open, while at the same time keeping her propped up against the wall. But then Becky's legs gave way and he had to cling on to stop her from falling. He gathered her up and carried her in his arms to the first floor. When he reached her flat, he had to perform a contortion to open the door without actually dropping her. At last he staggered into the drawing room and lowered her on to the sofa. He stood up and took his bearings, not sure whether to leave her on the sofa or to investigate where her bedroom might be.

Charlie was about to leave when she slipped off on to the floor, muttering something incoherent, the only word of which he caught was "engaged".

He returned to Becky's side, but this time lifted her firmly up over his shoulder. He carried her towards a door which, when he opened it, he discovered led to a bedroom. He placed her gently on top of the bed. As he began to tiptoe back to the door, she turned and Charlie had to rush back and pull her on to the middle of the bed to prevent her falling off. He hesitated, then bent over to lift up her shoulders before undoing the buttons down the back of her dress with his free hand. Once he had reached the bottom button he lowered her back on the bed, then lifted up her legs high in the air with one hand before he pulled with the other, inch by inch, until her dress was off. He left her only for a moment while he placed the dress neatly over a chair.

"Charlie Trumper," he said in a whisper, looking down at her, "you're a blind man, and you've been blind for an awfully long time."

He pulled back the blanket and placed Becky between the sheets, the way he had seen nurses on the Western Front carry out the same operation with wounded men.

He tucked her in securely, making sure that the whole process could not repeat itself. His final action was to lean over and kiss her on the cheek.

You're not only blind, Charlie Trumper, you're a fool, he told himself as he closed the front door behind him.

"Be with you in a moment," said Charlie as he threw some potatoes on to the weighing machine, while Becky waited patiently in the corner of the shop.

"Anythin' else, madam?" he asked the customer at the

front of the queue. "A few tangerines, per'aps? Some apples? And I've got some lovely grapefruit straight from South Africa, only arrived in the market this mornin'."

"No, thank you, Mr Trumper, that will be all for today."

"Then that'll be two shillings and fivepence, Mrs Symonds. Bob, could you carry on serving the next customer while I 'ave a word with Miss Salmon?"

"Sergeant Trumper."

"Sir," was Charlie's instant reaction when he heard the resonant voice. He turned to face the tall man who stood in front of him, straight as a ramrod, dressed in a Harris tweed jacket, cavalry twill trousers and carrying a brown felt hat.

"I never forget a face," the man said, although Charlie would have remained perplexed if it hadn't been for the monocle.

"Good God," said Charlie, standing to attention.

"No, Colonel will do," the other man said, laughing. "And no need for any of that bull. Those days have long gone. Although it's been some time since we last met, Trumper."

"Nearly two years, sir."

"Seems longer than that to me," the colonel said wistfully. "You certainly turned out to be right about Prescott, didn't you? And you were a good friend to him."

"'e was a good friend to me."

"And a first class soldier. Deserved his MM."

"Couldn't agree with you more, sir."

"Would have got one yourself, Trumper, but the rations were up after Prescott. Afraid it was only 'mentioned in dispatches' for you."

"The right man got the medal."

"Terrible way to die, though. The thought of it still haunts me, you know," said the colonel. "Only yards from the tape."

"Not your fault, sir. If anyone's, it was mine."

"If it was anyone's fault, it was certainly not yours,"

said the colonel. "And best forgotten, I suspect," he added without explanation.

"So 'ow's the regiment comin' along?" asked Charlie. "Survivin' without me?"

"And without me, I'm afraid," said the colonel, placing some apples into the shopping bag he was carrying. "They've departed for India, but not before they put this old horse out to grass."

"I'm sorry to 'ear that, sir. Your 'ole life was the regiment."

"True, though even Fusiliers have to succumb to the Geddes's axe. To be honest with you, I'm an infantry man myself, always have been, and I never did get the hang of those newfangled tanks."

"If we'd only 'ad 'em a couple of years earlier, sir, they might 'ave saved a few lives."

"Played their part, I'm bound to admit," the colonel nodded. "Like to think I played my part as well." He touched the knot of his striped tie. "Will we be seeing you at the regimental dinner, Trumper?"

"I didn't even know there was one, sir."

"Twice annually. First one in January, men only, second one in May with the memsahibs, which is also a ball. Gives the comrades a chance to get together and have a chinwag about old times. Would be nice if you could be on parade, Trumper. You see, I'm the president of the ball committee this year and rather hoping for a respectable turn-out."

"Then count me in, sir."

"Good man. I'll see that the office gets in touch with you pronto, ten shillings a ticket, and all you can drink thrown in, which I'm sure will be no hardship for you," added the colonel, looking round the busy shop.

"And can I get you anythin' while you're 'ere, sir?" Charlie asked, suddenly aware a long queue was forming behind the colonel.

"No, no, your able assistant has already taken excellent care of me, and as you can see I have completed the memsahib's written instructions." He held up a thin slip of paper bearing a list with a row of ticks down one side.

"Then I'll look forward to seeing you on the night of the ball, sir," said Charlie.

The colonel nodded and then stepped out on to the pavement without another word.

Becky strolled over to join her partner, only too aware that he had quite forgotten that she had been waiting to have a word with him. "You're still standing to attention, Charlie," she teased.

"That was my commanding officer, Lieutenant-Colonel Sir Danvers Hamilton," said Charlie a little pompously. "Led us at the front, 'e did, a gentleman, and 'e remembered my name."

"Charlie, if you could only hear yourself. A gentleman he may be, but he's the one who's out of work, while you're running a thriving business. I know which I'd rather be."

"But 'e's the Commanding Officer. Don't you understand?"

"Was," said Becky. "And he was also quick to point out the regiment have gone to India without him."

"That doesn't change anythin'."

"Mark my words, Charlie Trumper, that man will end up calling you 'sir'."

Guy had been away almost a week, and sometimes Becky could now go a whole hour without thinking about him.

She had sat up most of the previous night composing a letter to him, although when she left for her morning lecture the following day she walked straight past the pillar-box. She had managed to convince herself that the blame for failing to complete the letter should be placed firmly on the shoulders of Mr Palmer.

Becky had been disappointed to find their engagement had not been announced in *The Times* the next day, and became quite desperate when it failed to appear on any other day during that week. When in desperation she phoned Garrard's on the following Monday they claimed they knew nothing of a ring ordered in the name of a Captain Trentham of the Royal Fusiliers. Becky decided she would wait a further week before she wrote to Guy. She felt there must be some simple explanation.

Guy was still very much on her mind when she entered the offices of John D. Wood in Mount Street. She palmed the flat bell on the counter and asked an enquiring assistant if she could speak to Mr Palmer.

"Mr Palmer? We don't have a Mr Palmer any longer," she was told. "He was called up nearly a year ago, miss. Can I be of any assistance?"

Becky gripped the counter. "All right then, I'd like to speak to one of the partners," she said firmly.

"May I know the nature of your enquiry?" asked the assistant.

"Yes," said Becky. "I've come to discuss the instructions for the sale of 131 and 135 Chelsea Terrace."

"Ah yes, and may I ask who it is enquiring?"

"Miss Rebecca Salmon."

"I won't be a moment," the young man promised her, but didn't return for several minutes. When he did he was accompanied by a much older man, who wore a long black coat and horn-rimmed spectacles. A silver chain dangled from his waistcoat pocket.

"Good morning, Miss Salmon," the older man said. "My name is Crowther. Perhaps you'd be good enough to join me." He raised the counter lid and ushered her through. Becky duly followed in his wake.

"Good weather for this time of the year, wouldn't you say, madam?"

Becky stared out of the window and watched the umbrellas bobbing up and down along the pavement, but decided not to comment on Mr Crowther's meteorological judgment.

Once they had reached a poky little room at the back of the building he announced with obvious pride, "This is my office. Won't you please be seated, Miss Salmon?" He gestured towards an uncomfortably low chair placed opposite his desk. He then sat down in his own high-backed chair. "I'm a partner of the firm," he explained, "but I must confess a very junior partner." He laughed at his own joke. "Now, how can I help you?"

"My colleague and I want to acquire Numbers 131 and 135 Chelsea Terrace," replied Becky.

"Quite so," said Mr Crowther, looking down at his file. "And on this occasion will Miss Daphne Harcourt-Browne –"

"Miss Harcourt-Browne will not be involved in this transaction and if, because of that, you feel unable to deal with Mr Trumper or myself, we shall be happy to approach the vendors direct." Becky held her breath.

"Oh, please don't misunderstand me, madam. I'm sure we will have no trouble in continuing to do business with you."

"Thank you."

"Now, let us start with Number 135," said Mr Crowther, pushing his spectacles back up his nose before he leafed through the file in front of him. "Ah, yes, dear Mr Kendrick, a first-class butcher, you know. Sadly he is now considering an early retirement."

Becky sighed, and Mr Crowther looked up at her over his spectacles.

"His doctor has told him that he has no choice if he hopes to live more than a few more months," she said.

"Quite so," said Mr Crowther, returning to his file. "Well, it seems that his asking price is one hundred and fifty pounds for the freehold, plus one hundred pounds for the goodwill of the business."

"And how much will he take?"

"I'm not quite sure I catch your drift, madam." The junior partner raised his eyebrows.

"Mr Crowther, before we waste another minute of each other's time I feel I should let you know in confidence that it is our intention to purchase, if the price is right, every shop that becomes available in Chelsea Terrace, with the long-term aim of owning the entire block, even if it takes us a lifetime to achieve. It is not my intention to visit your office regularly for the next twenty years for the sole purpose of shadow-boxing with you. By then I suspect you will be a senior partner, and both of us will have better things to do. Do I make myself clear?"

"Abundantly," said Mr Crowther, glancing at the note Palmer had attached to the sale of 147: the lad hadn't exaggerated in the forthright opinion of his client. He pushed his spectacles back up his nose.

"I think Mr Kendrick might be willing to accept one hundred and twenty-five pounds if you would also agree to a pension of twenty-five pounds a year until his death."

"But he might live for ever."

"I feel I should point out, madam, that it was you, not I, who referred to Mr Kendrick's present state of health." For the first time the junior partner leaned back in his chair.

"I have no desire to rob Mr Kendrick of his pension," Becky replied. "Please offer him one hundred pounds for the freehold of the shop and twenty pounds a year for a period of eight years as a pension. I'm flexible on the latter part of the transaction but not on the former. Is that understood, Mr Crowther?"

"It certainly is, madam."

"And if I'm to pay Mr Kendrick a pension I shall also expect him to be available to offer advice from time to time as and when we require it."

"Quite so," said Crowther, making a note of her request in the margin.

"So what can you tell me about 131?"

"Now that is a knotty problem," said Crowther, opening a second file. "I don't know if you are fully aware of the circumstances, madam, but . . ."

Becky decided not to help him on this occasion. She smiled sweetly.

"Um, well," continued the junior partner, "Mr Rutherford is off to New York with a friend to open an antique gallery, in somewhere called 'the Village'." He hesitated.

"And their partnership is of a somewhat unusual nature?" assisted Becky after a prolonged silence. "And he might prefer to spend the rest of his days in an apartment in New York, rather than a cell in Brixton."

"Quite so," said Mr Crowther, as a bead of perspiration appeared on his forehead. "And in this particular gentleman's case, he wishes to remove everything from the premises, as he feels his merchandise might well fetch a better price in Manhattan. Therefore all that he would leave for your consideration would be the freehold."

"Then can I presume in his case, there will be no pension?"

"I think we may safely presume that," said Crowther.

"And may we therefore expect his price to be a little more reasonable, remembering some of the pressures he is under?"

"I would have thought not," replied Mr Crowther, "as the shop in question is rather larger than most of the others in Chelsea –"

"One thousand, four hundred and twenty-two square feet, to be precise," said Becky, "compared with one thousand square feet at Number 147, which we acquired for –"

"A very reasonable price at the time, if I may be so bold as to suggest, Miss Salmon."

"However . . ."

"Quite so," said Mr Crowther. Another bead of sweat appeared on his forehead.

"So how much is he hoping to raise for the freehold, now that we have established that he won't be requiring a pension?"

"His asking price," said Mr Crowther, whose eyes had once again returned to the file, "is two hundred pounds. However, I suspect," he added before Becky had the chance to challenge him, "that if you were able to close the negotiations quickly, he might allow the property to go for as little as one hundred and seventy-five." His eyebrows arched. "I am given to understand that he is anxious to join his friend as quickly as possible."

"If he's that anxious to join his friend I suspect he will be only too happy to lower his price to one hundred and fifty for a quick sale, and he might even accept one hundred and sixty, despite it taking a few days longer."

"Quite so." Mr Crowther removed his handkerchief from his top pocket and mopped his brow. Becky couldn't help noticing that it was still raining outside. "Will there be anything else, madam?" he asked, the handkerchief having been returned to the safety of his pocket.

"Yes, Mr Crowther," said Becky. "I should like you to keep a watching brief on all the properties in Chelsea Terrace and approach either Mr Trumper or myself the moment you hear of anything likely to come on the market."

"Perhaps it might be helpful if I were to prepare a full assessment of the properties on the block, then let you and Mr Trumper have a comprehensive written report for your consideration?"

"That would be most useful," said Becky, hiding her surprise at this sudden piece of initiative.

She rose from her chair to make it clear she considered the meeting to be over.

As they walked back to the front desk, Mr Crowther ventured, "I am given to understand that Number 147 is proving most popular with the inhabitants of Chelsea."

"And how would you know that?" asked Becky, surprised for a second time.

"My wife," Mr Crowther explained, "refuses to shop for her fruit and vegetables anywhere else, despite the fact that we live in Fulham."

"A discerning lady, your wife," said Becky.

"Quite so," said Mr Crowther.

Becky assumed that the banks would react to her approach with much the same enthusiasm as the estate agent had. However, having selected eight she thought might be possibilities, she quickly discovered that there is a considerable difference between offering yourself as a buyer to prostrating oneself as a borrower. Every time she presented her plans – to someone so junior as to be most unlikely to be able to make a decision – she received only a dismissive shake of the head. This included the bank that already held the Trumper account. "In fact," as she recounted to Daphne later that evening, "one of the junior assistants at the Penny Bank even had the nerve to suggest that should I ever become a married woman then they'd be only too delighted to do business with my husband."

"Come up against the world of men for the first time, have we?" asked Daphne, dropping her magazine on the floor. "Their cliques, their clubs? A woman's place is in the kitchen, and, if you're half attractive, perhaps occasionally in the bedroom."

Becky nodded glumly as she placed the magazine back on a side table.

"It's an attitude of mind that's never worried me, I must confess," Daphne admitted as she pushed her feet into a pair of shoes with stylish pointed toes. "But then I wasn't born overly ambitious like you, my darling. However, perhaps it's time to throw you another lifeline."

"Lifeline?"

"Yes. You see, what you need to solve your problem is an old school tie."

"Wouldn't it look a bit silly on me?"

"Probably look rather fetching actually, but that's not the point. The dilemma you seem to be facing is your gender – not to mention Charlie's accent, although I've nearly cured the dear boy of that problem. However, one thing's for sure, they haven't yet found a way to change people's sex."

"Where is all this leading?" asked Becky innocently.

"You're so impatient, darling. Just like Charlie. You must allow us lesser mortals a little more time to explain what we're about."

Becky took a seat on the corner of the sofa and placed her hands in her lap.

"First you must realise that all bankers are frightful snobs," continued Daphne. "Otherwise they'd be out there like you, running their own businesses. So what you require, to have them eating out of your hand, is a respectable front man."

"Front man?"

"Yes. Someone who'll accompany you on your trips to the bank whenever it should prove necessary." Daphne rose and checked herself in the mirror before continuing. "Such a person may not be blessed with your brains, but then on the other hand he won't be encumbered by your gender or by Charlie's accent. What he *will* have, however, is an old school tie, and preferably a title of some kind to go with it. Bankers do like a 'Bart', but most important of all you must secure someone who has a definite need of cash. For services rendered, you understand."

"Do such people exist?" asked Becky in disbelief.

"They most certainly do. In fact, there are far more of that type around than there are those who are willing to do a day's work." Daphne smiled reassuringly. "Give me a week or two and I feel confident I'll be able to come up with a short list of three. You'll see."

"You're a wonder," said Becky.

"In return I shall expect a small favour from you."

"Anything."

"Never use that word when dealing with a praying mantis like myself, darling. However, my request on this occasion is quite simple, and well within your power to grant. If Charlie should ask you to accompany him to his regimental dinner and dance, you are to accept."

"Why?"

"Because Reggie Arbuthnot has been stupid enough to invite me to the blithering occasion and I can't refuse him if I'm to hope for a little stalking on his estate in Scotland come November." Becky laughed as Daphne added, "I don't mind being taken to the ball by Reggie, but I do object to having to leave with him. So, if we have reached an agreement, I'll supply you with your necessary chinless

Bart and all you have to do when Charlie asks you, is say 'yes'."

"Yes."

Charlie wasn't surprised when Becky agreed without hesitation to be escorted to the regimental ball. After all, Daphne had already explained the details of their agreement to him. But it did come as a shock that, when Becky took her seat at the table, his fellow-sergeants couldn't take their eyes off her.

The dinner had been laid out in a massive gymnasium, which prompted Charlie's mates to tell story after story of their early days of training in Edinburgh. However, there the comparison ended, because the food was of a far higher standard than Charlie remembered being offered in Scotland.

"Where's Daphne?" asked Becky, as a portion of apple pie liberally covered in custard was placed in front of her.

"Up there on the top table with all the nobs," said Charlie, pointing over his shoulder with his thumb. "Can't afford to be seen with the likes of us, can she?" he added with a grin.

Once the dinner was over there followed a series of toasts – to everyone, it seemed to Becky, except the King. Charlie explained that the regiment had been granted dispensation from the loyal toast by King William IV in 1836 as their allegiance to the crown was without question. However, they did raise their glasses to the armed forces, each battalion in turn, and finally to the regiment, coupled with the name of their former colonel, each toast ending in rousing cheers. Becky watched the reactions of the men seated around her at the table and came to realise for the first time how many of that generation considered themselves lucky simply to be alive.

The former Commanding Officer, Sir Danvers Hamilton Bt, CBE, DSO, monocle in place, made a moving speech about all their fellow-comrades who were for different reasons unable to be present that night. Becky saw Charlie visibly stiffen at the mention of his friend Tommy Prescott. Finally they all rose and toasted absent friends. Becky found herself unexpectedly moved.

Once the colonel had sat down the tables were cleared to one side so that dancing could begin. No sooner had the first note struck up from the regimental band than Daphne appeared from the other end of the room.

"Come on, Charlie. I haven't the time to wait for you to find your way up to the top table."

"Delighted, I'm sure, madam," said Charlie, when he rose from his seat, "but what has happened to Reggie what's-his-name?"

"Arbuthnot," she said. "I have left the silly man clinging on to a deb from Chelmsford. And quite dreadful she was, I can tell you."

"What was so 'dreadful' about her?" mimicked Charlie.

"I never thought the day would come," said Daphne, "when His Majesty would allow anyone from Essex to be presented at court. But worse than that was her age."

"Why? How old is she?" asked Charlie, as he waltzed Daphne confidently round the floor.

"I can't altogether be certain, but she had the nerve to introduce me to her widowed father."

Charlie burst out laughing.

"You're not supposed to find it funny, Charles Trumper, you're meant to show some sympathy. There's still so much you have to learn."

Becky watched Charlie as he danced smoothly round the floor. "That Daphne's a bit of all right," said the man sitting next to her, who had introduced himself as Sergeant Mike Parker and turned out to be a butcher from Camberwell who had served alongside Charlie on the Marne. Becky accepted his judgment without comment, and when he later bowed and asked Becky for the pleasure of the next dance she reluctantly accepted. He proceeded to march her around the ballroom floor as if she were a leg of mutton on the way to the refrigeration room. The only thing he managed to do in time with the music was to tread on her toes.

At last he returned Becky to the comparative safety of their beer-stained table. Becky sat in silence while she watched everyone enjoying themselves, hoping that no one else would ask her for the pleasure. Her thoughts returned to Guy, and the meeting that she could no longer avoid if in another two weeks . . .

"May I have the honour, miss?"

Every man round the table shot to attention as the Commanding Officer escorted Becky on to the dance floor.

She found Colonel Hamilton an accomplished dancer, and an amusing companion, without showing any of those tendencies to patronise her that the string of bank managers had recently displayed. After the dance was over he invited Becky to the top table and introduced her to his wife.

"I must warn you," Daphne told Charlie, glancing over her shoulder in the direction of the Colonel and Lady Hamilton. "It's going to be quite a challenge for you to keep pace with the ambitious Miss Salmon. But as long as you stick with me and pay attention we'll give her a damn good run for her money."

After a couple more dances Daphne informed Becky that she had more than done her duty and the time had come for them all to leave. Becky, for her part, was only too pleased to escape the attention of so many young officers who had seen her dance with the colonel.

"I've some good news for you," Daphne told the two of them as the hansom trundled down the King's Road in the direction of Chelsea Terrace, with Charlie still clinging on to his half-empty bottle of champagne.

"What's that, my girl?" he asked, after a burp.

"I'm not your girl," Daphne remonstrated. "I may be willing to invest in the lower classes, Charlie Trumper, but never forget I'm not without breeding."

"So what's your news?" asked Becky laughing.

"You've kept your part of the bargain, so I must keep to mine."

"What do you mean?" asked Charlie, half asleep.

"I can now produce my short list of three to be considered as your front man, and thus, I hope, solve your banking problem."

Charlie immediately sobered up.

"My first offer is the second son of an earl," began Daphne. "Penniless but presentable. My second is a Bart, who will take the exercise on for a professional fee, but my *pièce de résistance* is a viscount whose luck has run out at the tables in Deauville and now finds it necessary to involve himself in the odd piece of vulgar commercial work."

"When do we get to meet them?" asked Charlie, trying not to slur his words.

"As soon as you wish," promised Daphne. "Tomorrow – "

"That won't be necessary," said Becky quietly.

"Why not?" asked Daphne, surprised.

"Because I have already chosen the man who will front for us."

"Who've you got in mind, darling? The Prince of Wales?"

"No. Lieutenant-Colonel Sir Danvers Hamilton, Bart, DSO, CBE."

"But 'e's the bleedin' Colonel of the Regiment," said Charlie, dropping the bottle of champagne on the floor of the hansom cab. "It's impossible, 'e'd never agree."

"I can assure you he will."

"What makes you so confident?" asked Daphne.

"Because we have an appointment to see him tomorrow morning at eleven o'clock."

CHAPTER 11

aphne waved her parasol as a hansom approached them. The driver brought the cab to a halt and raised his hat. "Where to, miss?"

"Number 172 Harley Street," she instructed, before the two women climbed aboard.

He raised his hat again, and with a gentle flick of his whip headed the horse off in the direction of Hyde Park Corner.

"Have you told Charlie yet?" Becky asked.

"No, I funked it," admitted Daphne.

They sat in silence as the cabbie guided the horse towards Marble Arch.

"Perhaps it won't be necessary to tell him anything."

"Let's hope not," said Becky.

There followed another prolonged silence until the horse trotted into Oxford Street.

"Is your doctor an understanding man?"

"He always has been in the past."

"My God, I'm frightened."

"Don't worry. It will be over soon, then at least you'll know one way or the other."

The cabbie came to a halt outside Number 172 Harley Street, and the two women got out. While Becky stroked the horse's mane Daphne paid the man sixpence. Becky turned when she heard the rap on the brass knocker and climbed the three steps to join her friend.

A nurse in a starched blue uniform, white cap and collar

answered their call, and asked the two ladies to follow her. They were led down a dark corridor, lit by a single gaslight, then ushered into an empty waiting room. Copies of *Punch* and *Tatler* were displayed in neat rows on a table in the middle of the room. A variety of comfortable but unrelated chairs circled the low table. They each took a seat, but neither spoke again until the nurse had left the room.

"I –" began Daphne.

"If –" said Becky simultaneously.

They both laughed, a forced sound that echoed in the high-ceilinged room.

"No, you first," said Becky.

"I just wanted to know how the colonel's shaping up."

"Took his briefing like a man," said Becky. "We're off to our first official meeting tomorrow. Child and Co in Fleet Street. I've told him to treat the whole exercise like a dress rehearsal, as I'm saving the one I think we have a real chance with for later in the week."

"And Charlie?"

"All a bit much for him. He can't stop thinking of the colonel as his commanding officer."

"It would have been the same for you, if Charlie had suggested that the man teaching you accountancy should drop in and check the weekly takings at 147."

"I'm avoiding that particular gentleman at the moment," said Becky. "I'm only just putting in enough academic work to avoid being reprimanded; lately my commendeds have become passes, while my passes are just not good enough. If I don't manage to get a degree at the end of all this there will be only one person to blame."

"You'll be one of the few women who's a Bachelor of Arts. Perhaps you should demand they change the degree to SA."

"SA?"

"Spinster of Arts."

They laughed at what they both knew to be a hoary chestnut, as they continued to avoid the real reason they were in that waiting room. Suddenly the door swung open and they looked up to see that the nurse had returned.

"The doctor will see you now."

"May I come as well?"

"Yes, I'm sure that will be all right."

Both women rose and followed the nurse further down the same corridor until they reached a white door with a small brass plate almost worn away with rubbing which read "Fergus Gould, MD". A gentle knock from the nurse elicited a "yes" and Daphne and Becky entered the room together.

"Good morning, good morning," said the doctor cheerfully in a soft Scottish burr, shaking hands with the two of them in turn. "Won't you please be seated? The tests have been completed and I have excellent news for you." He returned to the seat behind his desk and opened a file in front of him. They both smiled, the taller of the two relaxing for the first time in days.

"I'm happy to say that you are physically in perfect health, but as this is your first child" – he watched both women turn white – "you will have to behave rather more cautiously over the coming months. But as long as you do, I can see no reason why this birth should have any complications. May I be the first to congratulate you?"

"Oh, God, no," she said, nearly fainting. "I thought you said the news was excellent."

"Why, yes," replied Doctor Gould. "I assumed you would be delighted."

Her friend interjected. "You see, Doctor, there's a problem. She's not married."

"Oh, yes, I do see," said the doctor, his voice immediately changing tone. "I'm so sorry, I had no idea. Perhaps if you had told me at our first meeting –"

"No, I'm entirely to blame, Doctor Gould. I had simply hoped –"

"No, it is I who am to blame. How extremely tactless of me." Doctor Gould paused thoughtfully. "Although it remains illegal in this country, I am assured that there are excellent doctors in Sweden who –"

"That is not possible," said the pregnant woman. "You see, it's against everything my parents would have considered 'acceptable behaviour'."

"Good morning, Hadlow," said the colonel as he marched into the bank, handing the manager his topcoat, hat and cane.

"Good morning, Sir Danvers," replied the manager, passing the hat, coat and cane on to an assistant. "May I say how honoured we are that you thought our humble establishment worthy of your consideration."

Becky couldn't help reflecting that it was not quite the same greeting she had received when visiting another bank of similar standing only a few weeks before.

"Would you be kind enough to come through to my office?" the manager continued, putting his arm out as if he were guiding wayward traffic.

"Certainly, but first may I introduce Mr Trumper and Miss Salmon, both of whom are my associates in this venture."

"Delighted, I'm sure," the manager said as he pushed his glasses back up his nose before shaking hands with Charlie and Becky in turn.

Becky noticed that Charlie was unusually silent and kept pulling at his collar, which looked as though it might be half an inch too tight for comfort. However, after spending a morning in Savile Row the previous week being measured from head to foot for a new suit, he had refused to wait a moment longer when Daphne suggested he should be measured for a shirt, so in the end Daphne was left to guess his neck size.

"Coffee?" enquired the manager, once they had all settled in his office.

"No, thank you," said the colonel.

Becky would have liked a cup of coffee but realised that the manager had assumed Sir Danvers had spoken for all three of them. She bit her lip.

"Now, how can I be of assistance, Sir Danvers?" The manager nervously touched the knot of his tie.

"My associates and I currently own a property in Chelsea Terrace – Number 147 – which although a small venture at present is nevertheless progressing satisfactorily." The manager's smile remained in place. "We purchased the premises some eighteen months ago at a cost of one hundred pounds and that investment has shown a profit this year of a little over forty-three pounds."

"Very satisfactory," said the manager. "Of course, I have read your letter and the accounts you so kindly had sent over by messenger."

Charlie was tempted to tell him who the messenger had been.

"However, we feel the time has come to expand," continued the colonel. "And in order to do so we will require a bank that can show a little more initiative than the establishment with which we're presently dealing – as well as one that has its eye on the future. Our current bankers, I sometimes feel, are still living in the nineteenth century. Frankly, they are little more than holders of deposits, while what we are looking for is the service of a real bank."

"I understand."

"It's been worrying me –" said the colonel, suddenly breaking off and fixing his monocle to his left eye.

"Worrying you?" Mr Hadlow sat forward anxiously in his chair.

"Your tie."

"My tie?" The manager once again fingered the knot nervously.

"Yes, your tie. Don't tell me – the Buffs?"

"You are correct, Sir Danvers."

"Saw some action, did you, Hadlow?"

"Well, not exactly, Sir Danvers. My sight, you understand." Mr Hadlow began fiddling with his glasses.

"Bad luck, old chap," said the colonel, his monocle dropping back down. "Well, to continue. My colleagues and I are of a mind to expand, but I feel it would only be the honourable thing to let you know that we have an appointment with a rival establishment on Thursday afternoon."

"Thursday afternoon," repeated the manager, after dipping his quill pen once more into the ink-well on the front of his desk and adding this to the other pieces of information he had already recorded.

"But I had rather hoped it would not have gone unnoticed," continued the colonel, "that we chose to come and see you first."

"I'm most flattered," said Mr Hadlow. "And what terms were you hoping this bank might offer, Sir Danvers, that your own could not?"

The colonel paused for a moment and Becky glanced towards him alarmed, as she couldn't remember if she had briefed him on terms. Neither of them had expected to have reached quite this far at the first meeting.

The colonel cleared his throat. "We would naturally expect competitive terms, if we are to move our business to your bank, being aware of the long-term implications."

This answer seemed to impress Hadlow. He looked down at the figures in front of him and pronounced, "Well, I see you are requesting a loan of two hundred and fifty pounds for the purchase of 131 and 135 Chelsea Terrace, which, bearing in mind the state of your account, would require an overdraft facility" – he paused, appearing to be making a calculation – "of at least one hundred and seventy pounds."

"Correct, Hadlow. I see you have mastered our present predicament admirably."

The manager allowed himself a smile. "Given the circumstances, Sir Danvers, I feel we could indeed advance such a loan, if a charge of four per cent interest per annum would be acceptable to you and your colleagues."

Again the colonel hesitated, until he caught Becky's half-smile.

"Our present bankers provide us with a facility of three and a half per cent," said the colonel. "As I'm sure you know."

"But they are taking no risk," pointed out Mr Hadlow. "As well as refusing to allow you to be overdrawn more than fifty pounds. However," he added before the colonel could reply, "I feel in this particular case we might also offer three and a half per cent. How does that sound to you?"

The colonel did not comment until he had observed the expression on Becky's face. Her smile had widened to a grin.

"I think I speak for my colleagues, Hadlow, when I say we find your proposition acceptable, most acceptable."

Becky and Charlie nodded their agreement.

"Then I shall begin to process all the paperwork. It may take a few days, of course."

"Of course," said the colonel. "And I can tell you, Hadlow, that we look forward to a long and profitable association with your bank."

The manager somehow rose and bowed all in one movement, an action Becky felt even Sir Henry Irving would have found difficult to accomplish.

Mr Hadlow then proceeded to escort the colonel and his young associates to the front hall.

"Old Chubby Duckworth still with this outfit?" enquired the colonel.

"Lord Duckworth is indeed our chairman," murmured Mr Hadlow reverentially.

"Good man – served with him in South Africa. Royal Rifles. I shall, with your permission, mention our meeting to him, when I next see Chubby at the club."

"That would be most kind of you, Sir Danvers."

When they reached the door the manager dispensed with his assistant and helped the colonel on with his topcoat himself, then handed him his hat and cane before bidding farewell to his new customers. "Do feel free to call me at any time," were his final words as he bowed once again. He stood there until the three of them were out of sight.

Once they were back on the street the colonel marched quickly round the corner, coming to a halt behind the nearest tree. Becky and Charlie ran after him, not quite sure what he was up to.

"Are you feeling all right, sir?" Charlie asked, as soon as he had caught up.

"I'm fine, Trumper," replied the colonel. "Just fine. But I can tell you, I would rather face a bunch of marauding Afghan natives than go through that again. Still, how did I do?"

"You were magnificent," said Becky. "I swear, if you had taken off your shoes and told Hadlow to polish them, he would have removed his handkerchief and started rubbing little circles immediately."

The colonel smiled. "Oh, good. Thought it went all right, did you?"

"Perfect," said Becky. "You couldn't have done better. I shall go round to John D. Wood this afternoon and put down the deposit on both shops."

"Thank God for your briefing, Miss Salmon," said the colonel, standing his full height. "You know what? You would have made a damned fine staff officer."

Becky smiled. "I take that as a great compliment, Colonel."

"Don't you agree, Trumper? Some partner you've found yourself," he added.

"Yes, sir," said Charlie as the colonel began to stride off down the road. "But may I ask you something that's been worrying me?"

"Of course, Trumper, fire away."

"If you're a friend of the chairman of the bank," said Charlie, matching him stride for stride, "why didn't we go direct to him in the first place?"

The colonel came to a sudden halt. "My dear Trumper," he explained, "you don't visit the chairman of the bank when you require a loan of only two hundred and fifty pounds. Nevertheless, let it be said that I have every confidence that it will not be long before we shall need to seek him out. However, at this very moment other needs are more pressing."

"Other needs?" said Charlie.

"Yes, Trumper. I require a whisky, don't you know?" said the colonel, eyeing a sign flapping above a pub on the opposite side of the road. "And while we're at it, let's make it a double."

"How far gone are you?" asked Charlie, when the following day Becky came round to tell him the news.

"About three months." She avoided looking him directly in the eye.

"Why didn't you tell me earlier?" He sounded a little hurt as he turned the Open sign to Closed, and marched up the stairs.

"I hoped I wouldn't need to," said Becky as she followed him into the flat.

"You've written to tell Trentham, of course?"

"No. I keep meaning to, but I haven't got round to it yet." She began to tidy up the room rather than face him.

"Keep meaning to?" said Charlie. "You should have told the bastard weeks ago. He's the first person who ought to know. After all, he's the one who's responsible for the bleedin' mess, if you'll excuse the expression."

"It's not that easy, Charlie."

"Why not, for heaven's sake?"

"It would mean the end of his career, and Guy lives for the regiment. He's like your colonel: it would be unfair to ask him to give up being a soldier at the age of twenty-three."

"He's nothing like the colonel," said Charlie. "In any case, he's still young enough to settle down and do a day's work like the rest of us."

"He's married to the army, Charlie, not to me. Why ruin both our lives?"

"But he should still be told what has happened and at least be given the choice."

"He wouldn't be left with any choice, Charlie, surely you see that? He'd sail home on the next boat and marry me. He's an honourable man."

"An honourable man, is he?" said Charlie. "Well, if he's so honourable you can afford to promise me one thing."

"What's that?"

"You'll write to him tonight and tell him the truth."

Becky hesitated for some time before saying, "All right, I will."

"Tonight?"

"Yes, tonight."

"And you should also let his parents know while you're at it."

"No, I can't be expected to do that, Charlie," she said, facing him for the first time.

"So what's the reason this time? Some fear that their careers might be ruined?"

"No, but if I did his father would insist that Guy return home and marry me."

"And what's so wrong with that?"

"His mother would then claim that I had tricked her son into the whole thing, or worse –"

"Worse?"

"– that it wasn't even his child."

"And who'd believe her?"

"All those who wanted to."

"But that isn't fair," said Charlie.

"Life isn't, to quote my father. I had to grow up some time, Charlie. For you it was the Western Front."

"So what are we going to do now?"

"We?" said Becky.

"Yes, we. We're still partners, you know. Or had you forgotten?"

"To start with I'll have to find somewhere else to live; it wouldn't be fair on Daphne –"

"What a friend she's turned out to be," said Charlie.

"To both of us," said Becky as Charlie stood up, thrust his hands in his pockets, and began to march around the little room. It reminded Becky of when they had been at school together.

"I don't suppose . . ." said Charlie. It was his turn to be unable to look her in the face.

"Suppose? Suppose what?"

"I don't suppose . . ." he began again.

"Yes?"

"You'd consider marrying me?"

There was a long silence before a shocked Becky felt able to reply. "But what about Daphne?" she eventually said.

"Daphne? You surely never believed we had that sort of relationship? It's true she's been giving me night classes but not the type you think. In any case, there's only ever been one man in Daphne's life, and it's certainly not Charlie Trumper, for the simple reason she's known all along that there's only been one woman in mine."

"But –"

"And I've loved you for such a long time, Becky."

"Oh, my God," said Becky, placing her head in her hands.

"I'm sorry," said Charlie. "I thought you knew. Daphne told me women always know these things."

"I had no idea, Charlie. I've been so blind as well as stupid."

"I haven't looked at another woman since the day I came back from Edinburgh. I suppose I just 'oped you might love me a little," he said.

"I'll always love you a little, Charlie, but I'm afraid it's Guy I'm in love with."

"Lucky blighter. And to think I saw you first. Your father once chased me out of 'is shop, you know, when he 'eard me calling you 'Posh Porky' behind your back." Becky smiled. "You see, I've always been able to grab everything I really wanted in life, so 'ow did I let you get away?"

Becky was unable to look up at him.

"He's an officer, of course, and I'm not. That would explain it." Charlie had stopped pacing round the room and came to a halt in front of her.

"You're a general, Charlie."

"It's not the same, though, is it?"

CHAPTER 12

97 Chelsea Terrace,
London SW3

May 20th, 1920

My Darling Guy

This is the hardest letter I have ever had to write in
my life. In fact, I'm not sure where to begin. Just over three
months have passed since you left for India, and
something has happened that I felt you would want to know
about at once. I have just been to see Daphne's doctor in
Harley Street and

Becky stopped, checked carefully over the few sentences
she had written, groaned, scrumpled up the notepaper and
dropped it in the wastepaper-basket that rested at her feet.
She stood up, stretched and started to pace around the room
in the hope that she might be able to dream up some new
excuse for not continuing with her task. It was already
twelve thirty so she could now go to bed, claiming that she
had been too weary to carry on – only Becky knew that she
wouldn't be able to sleep until the letter had been completed. She returned to her desk and tried to settle herself
again before reconsidering the opening line. She picked up
her pen.

97 Chelsea Terrace,
London SW3

May 20th, 1920

My Dear Guy,

I fear that this letter may come as something of a surprise, especially after all the irrelevant gossip that I was able to share with you only a month ago. I have been postponing writing anything of consequence to you in the hope that my fears would prove unfounded. Unhappily that has not proved to be the case, and circumstances have now overtaken me.

After spending the most wonderful time with you the night before you left for India, I then missed my period the following month, but did not trouble you with the problem immediately in the hope that

Oh no, thought Becky, and tore up her latest effort before once again dropping the scraps of paper into the wastepaper-basket. She traipsed off to the kitchen to make herself a pot of tea. After her second cup, she reluctantly returned to her writing desk and settled herself again.

97 Chelsea Terrace,
London SW3

May 20th, 1920

Dear Guy,

I do hope everything is going well for you in India, and that they are not working you too hard. I miss you more than I can express, but what with exams looming and Charlie seeing himself as the next Mr. Selfridge, these first three months since you left have just shot by. In fact I feel sure you'll be fascinated to learn that your old Commanding Officer, Lieutenant-Colonel Sir Danvers Hamilton, has become

"And by the way I'm pregnant," said Becky out loud, and tore up her third attempt. She replaced the top back on her pen, deciding the time had come to take a walk round the square. She picked up her coat from its hook in the hall, ran down the stairs and let herself out.

She strolled aimlessly up and down the deserted road, seemingly unaware of the hour. She was pleased to find that "Sold" signs now appeared in the windows of Numbers 131 and 135. She stopped outside the old antique shop for a moment, cupped her hands round her eyes and peered in through the window. To her horror she discovered that Mr Rutherford had removed absolutely everything, even the gas fittings and the mantelpiece that she had assumed were fixed to the wall. That'll teach me to study an offer document more carefully next time, she thought. She continued to stare at the empty space as a mouse scurried across the floorboards. "Perhaps we should open a pet shop," she said aloud.

"Beg pardon, miss."

Becky swung round to find a policeman rattling the door knob of 133, to be certain the premises were locked.

"Oh, good evening, Constable," said Becky sheepishly, feeling guilty without any reason.

"It's nearly two in the morning, miss. You just said, 'Good evening'."

"Oh, is it?" said Becky, looking at her watch. "Oh, yes, so it is. How silly of me. You see, I live at 97." Feeling some explanation was necessary, she added, "I couldn't sleep, so I decided to take a walk."

"Better join the force then. They'll be happy to keep you walking all night."

Becky laughed. "No, thank you, Constable. I think I'll just go back to my flat and try and get some sleep. Goodnight."

"Goodnight, miss," said the policeman, touching his helmet in a half-salute before checking the empty antique shop was also safely locked up.

Becky turned and walked determinedly back down

Chelsea Terrace, opened the front door of 97, climbed the staircase to the flat, took off her coat and returned immediately to the little writing desk. She paused only for a moment before picking up her pen and starting to write.

For once the words flowed easily because she now knew exactly what needed to be said.

97 Chelsea Terrace,
London SW3

May 20th, 1920

Dear Guy,

I have tried to think of a hundred different ways of letting you know what has happened to me since you left for India, and finally came to the conclusion that only the simple truth makes any sense.

I am now some fourteen weeks pregnant with your child, the idea of which fills me with great happiness but I confess more than a little apprehension. Happiness because you are the only man I have ever loved, and apprehension because of the implications such a piece of news might have on your future with the regiment.

I must tell you from the outset that I have no desire to harm that career in any way by forcing you into marriage. A commitment honoured only out of some feeling of guilt, which then caused you to spend the rest of your life participating in a sham after what happened between us on one occasion, must surely be unacceptable to either of us.

For my part, I make no secret of my total devotion to you, but if it is not reciprocated, I can never be a party to sacrificing such a promising career on the altar of hypocrisy.

But, my darling, be left in no doubt of my complete love for you and my abiding interest in your future and well-being, even to the point of denying your involvement in this affair, should that be the course you wish me to follow.

Guy, I will always adore you, and be assured of my utmost loyalty whatever decision you should come to.

With all my love

Becky

She was unable to control her tears as she read her words through a second time. As she folded the notepaper the bedroom door swung open and a sleepy Daphne appeared in front of her.

"You all right, darling?"

"Yes. Just felt a little queasy," explained Becky. "I decided that I needed a breath of fresh air." She deftly slipped the letter into an unmarked envelope.

"Now I'm up," said Daphne, "would you care for a cup of tea?"

"No, thank you. I've already had two cups."

"Well, I think I will." Daphne disappeared into the kitchen. Becky immediately picked up her pen again and wrote on the envelope:

Captain Guy Trentham, M.C.,
2nd Battalion Royal Fusiliers,
Wellington Barracks,
Poona,
INDIA

She had left the flat, posted the letter in the pillar-box on the corner of Chelsea Terrace and returned to Number 97 even before the kettle had boiled.

Although Charlie received the occasional letter from Sal in Canada to tell him of the arrival of his latest nephew or niece, and the odd infrequent call from Grace whenever she could get away from her hospital duties, a visit from Kitty was rare indeed. But when she came to the flat it was always with the same purpose.

"I only need a couple of quid, Charlie, just to see me through," explained Kitty as she lowered herself into the one comfortable chair only moments after she had entered the room.

Charlie stared at his sister. Although she was only eighteen months older than himself she already looked like a woman well into her thirties. Under the baggy shapeless cardigan there was no longer any sign of the figure that had attracted every wandering eye in the East End, and without make-up her face was already beginning to look splotchy and lined.

"It was only a pound last time," Charlie reminded her. "And that wasn't so long ago."

"But my man's left me since then, Charlie. I'm on my own again, without even a roof over my head. Come on, do us a favour."

He continued to stare at her, thankful that Becky was not yet back from her afternoon lecture, although he suspected Kitty only came when she could be sure the till was full and Becky was safely out of the way.

"I won't be a moment," he said after a long period of silence. He slipped out of the room and headed off downstairs to the shop. Once he was sure the assistants weren't looking, he removed two pounds ten shillings from the till. He walked resignedly back upstairs to the flat.

Kitty was already waiting by the door. Charlie handed over the three notes. She almost snatched the money before tucking the notes in her glove and leaving without another word.

Charlie followed her down the stairs and watched her remove a peach from the top of a neat pyramid in the corner of the shop before taking a bite, stepping out on to the pavement and hurrying off down the road.

Charlie would have to take responsibility for checking the till that night; no one must find out the exact amount he had given her.

"You'll end up having to buy this bench, Charlie Trumper," said Becky as she lowered herself down beside him.

"Not until I own every shop in the block, my lovely," he said, turning to look at her. "And how about you? When's the baby due?"

"About another five weeks, the doctor thinks."

"Got the flat all ready for the new arrival, have you?"

"Yes, thanks to Daphne letting me stay on."

"I miss her," said Charlie.

"So do I, although I've never seen her happier since Percy was discharged from the Scots Guards."

"Bet it won't be long before they're engaged."

"Let's hope not," said Becky, looking across the road.

Three Trumper signs, all in gold on blue, shone back at her. The fruit and vegetable shop continued to make an excellent return and Bob Makins seemed to have grown in stature over the past year. The butcher's had lost a little custom after Mr Kendrick retired, but had picked up again since Charlie had employed Mike Parker to take his place.

"Let's hope he's a better butcher than a dancer," Becky had remarked when Charlie told her the news of Sergeant Parker's appointment.

As for the grocer's, Charlie's new pride and joy, it had flourished from the first day, although as far as his staff could tell, their master seemed to be in all three shops at once.

"Stroke of genius," said Charlie, "turning that old antique shop into a grocer's."

"So now you consider yourself to be a grocer, do you?"

"Certainly not, I'm a plain fruit and vegetable man, and always will be."

"I wonder if that's what you'll tell the girls when you own the whole block."

"That could take some time yet. So how is the balance-sheet shaping up for the new shops?"

"They're both in the books to show a loss during their first year."

"But they could still make a profit, certainly break even." Charlie's voice rose in protest. "And the grocer's shop is set to –"

"Not so loud. I want Mr Hadlow and his colleagues at the bank to discover that we've done far better than we originally predicted."

"You're an evil woman, Rebecca Salmon, that's no mistake."

"You won't be saying that, Charlie Trumper, when you need me to go begging for your next loan."

"If you're so clever, then explain to me why I can't get hold of the bookshop," said Charlie, pointing across the road at Number 141, where a single light was the only proof the building was still inhabited. "The place hasn't seen a customer in weeks from what I can tell, and even when they do it's only because someone had gone in to find directions back to Brompton Road."

"I've no idea," said Becky, laughing. "I've already had a long chat to Mr Sneddles about buying the premises, but he just wasn't interested. You see, since his wife died, running the shop has become the only reason for him to carry on."

"But carry on doing what?" asked Charlie. "Dusting old books and stacking up ancient manuscripts?"

"He's happy just to sit around and read William Blake and his beloved war poets. As long as he sells a couple of books every month he's quite content to keep the shop open. Not everyone wants to be a millionaire, you know – as Daphne never stops reminding me."

"Possibly. So why not offer Mr Sneddles one hundred

and fifty guineas for the freehold, then charge him a rent of say ten guineas a year? That way it'll automatically fall into our hands the moment he dies."

"You're a hard man to please, Charlie Trumper, but if that's what you want, I'll give it a try."

"That is what I want, Rebecca Salmon, so get on with it."

"I'll do my best, although it may have slipped your notice that I'm about to have a baby while also trying to sit a bachelor's degree."

"That combination doesn't sound quite right to me. However, I still may need you to pull off another coup."

"Another coup?"

"Fothergill's."

"The corner shop."

"No less," said Charlie. "And you know how I feel about corner shops, Miss Salmon."

"I certainly do, Mr Trumper. I am also aware that you know nothing about the fine art business, let alone being an auctioneer."

"Not a lot, I admit," said Charlie. "But after a couple of visits to New Bond Street, where I watched how they earn a living at Sotheby's, followed by a short walk down the road to St James's to study their only real rivals, Christie's, I came to the conclusion that we might eventually be able to put that art degree of yours to some use."

Becky raised her eyebrows. "I can't wait to learn what you have planned for the rest of my life."

"Once you've finished that degree of yours," continued Charlie, ignoring the comment, "I want you to apply for a job at Sotheby's or Christie's, I don't mind which, where you can spend three to five years learning everything they're up to. The moment you consider that you're good and ready to leave, you could then poach anyone you felt was worth employing and return to run Number 1 Chelsea Terrace and open up a genuine rival to those two establishments."

"I'm still listening, Charlie Trumper."

"You see, Rebecca Salmon, you've got your father's

business acumen. I hope you liked that word. Combine that with the one thing you've always loved and also have a natural talent for, how can you fail?"

"Thank you for the compliment, but may I, while we're on the subject, ask where Mr Fothergill fits into your master plan?"

"He doesn't."

"What do you mean?"

"He's been losing money hand over fist for the past three years," said Charlie. "At the moment the value of the property and sale of his best stock would just about cover his losses, but that state of affairs can't last too much longer. So now you know what's expected of you."

"I certainly do. Mr Trumper."

When September had come and gone, even Becky began to accept that Guy had no intention of responding to her letter.

As late as August Daphne reported to them that she had bumped into Mrs Trentham at Goodwood. Guy's mother had claimed that her son was not only revelling in his duties in India but had every reason to expect an imminent announcement concerning his promotion to major. Daphne found herself only just able to keep her promise and remain silent about Becky's condition.

As the day of the birth drew nearer, Charlie made sure that Becky didn't waste any time shopping for food and even detailed one of the girls at Number 147 to help her keep the flat clean, so much so that Becky began to accuse them both of pampering her.

By the eighth month Becky didn't even bother to check the morning post, as Daphne's long-held view of Captain Trentham began to gain more credibility. She was surprised to find how quickly he faded from her memory, despite the fact that it was his child she was about to give birth to.

Becky also felt embarrassed that most people assumed Charlie was the father, and it wasn't helped by the fact that, whenever he was asked, he refused to deny it.

Meanwhile, Charlie still had his eye on a couple of

shops whose owners he felt might soon be willing to sell but Daphne wouldn't hear of any further business transactions until after the child had been born.

"I don't want Becky involved in any of your dubious business enterprises before she's had the child and completed her degree. Do I make myself clear?"

"Yes, ma'am," said Charlie, clicking his heels. He didn't mention that only the week before Becky had herself closed the deal with Mr Sneddles so that the bookshop would be theirs once the old man died. There was only one clause in the agreement that Charlie remained concerned about, because he wasn't quite sure how he would get rid of that number of books.

"Miss Becky has just phoned," whispered Bob into the boss's ear one afternoon when Charlie was serving in the shop. "Says could you go round immediately. Thinks the baby's about to arrive."

"But it's not due for another two weeks," said Charlie as he pulled off his apron.

"I'm sure I don't know about that Mr Trumper but all she said was to hurry."

"Has she sent for the midwife?" Charlie asked, deserting a half-laden customer before grabbing his coat.

"I've no idea, sir."

"Right, take charge of the shop, because I may not be back again today." Charlie left the smiling queue of customers and ran down the road to 97, flew up the stairs, pushed open the door and marched straight on into Becky's bedroom.

He sat down beside her on the bed and held her hand for some time before either of them spoke.

"Have you sent for the midwife?" he eventually asked.

"She certainly has," said a voice from behind them, as a vast woman entered the room. She wore an old brown raincoat that was too small for her and carried a black leather bag. From the heaving of her breasts she had obviously had a struggle climbing the stairs. "I'm Mrs

Westlake, attached to St Stephen's hospital," she declared. "I do hope I've got here in time." Becky nodded as the midwife turned her attention to Charlie. "Now you go away and boil me some water, and quickly." Her voice sounded as if she wasn't in the habit of being questioned. Without another word Charlie jumped off the end of the bed and left the room.

Mrs Westlake placed her large Gladstone bag on the floor and started by taking Becky's pulse.

"How long between the spasms?" she asked matter-of-factly.

"Down to twenty minutes," Becky replied.

"Excellent. Then we don't have much longer to wait."

Charlie appeared at the door carrying a bowl of hot water. "Anything else I can do?"

"Yes, there certainly is. I need every clean towel you can lay your hands on, and I wouldn't mind a cup of tea."

Charlie ran back out of the room.

"Husbands are always a nuisance on these occasions," Mrs Westlake declared. "One must simply keep them on the move."

Becky was about to explain to her about Charlie when another contraction gripped her.

"Breathe deeply and slowly, my dear," encouraged Mrs Westlake in a gentler voice, as Charlie came back with three towels and a kettle of hot water.

Without turning to see who it was, Mrs Westlake continued. "Leave the towels on the sideboard, pour the water in the largest bowl you've got, then put the kettle back on so that I've always got more hot water whenever I call for it."

Charlie disappeared again without a word.

"I wish I could get him to do that," gasped Becky admiringly.

"Oh, don't worry, my dear. I can't do a thing with my own husband and we've got seven children."

A couple of minutes later Charlie pushed open the door

with a foot and carried another bowl of steaming water over to the bedside.

"On the side table," said Mrs Westlake, pointing. "And try not to forget my tea. After that I shall still need more towels," she added.

Becky let out a loud groan.

"Hold my hand and keep breathing deeply," said the midwife.

Charlie soon reappeared with another kettle of water, and was immediately instructed to empty the bowl before refilling it with the new supply. After he had completed the task, Mrs Westlake said, "You can wait outside until I call for you."

Charlie left the room, gently pulling the door closed behind him.

He seemed to be making countless cups of tea, and carrying endless kettles of water, backward and forward, always arriving with the wrong one at the wrong time until finally he was shut out of the bedroom and left to pace up and down the kitchen fearing the worst. Then he heard the plaintive little cry.

Becky watched from her bed as the midwife held up her child by one leg and gave it a gentle smack on the bottom. "I always enjoy that," said Mrs Westlake. "Feels good to know you've brought something new into the world." She wrapped up the child in a tea-towel and handed the bundle back to its mother.

"It's – ?"

"A boy, I'm afraid," said the midwife. "So the world is unlikely to be advanced by one jot or tittle. You'll have to produce a daughter next time," she said, smiling broadly. "If he's still up to it, of course." She pointed a thumb towards the closed door.

"But he's –" Becky tried again.

"Useless, I know. Like all men." Mrs Westlake opened the bedroom door in search of Charlie. "It's all over, Mr Salmon. You can stop skulking around and come and have a look at your son."

Charlie came in so quickly that he nearly knocked the midwife over. He stood at the end of the bed and stared down at the tiny figure in Becky's arms.

"He's an ugly little fellow, isn't he?" said Charlie.

"Well, we know who to blame for that," said the midwife. "Let's just hope this one doesn't end up with a broken nose. In any case, as I've already explained to your wife, what you need next is a daughter. By the way, what are you going to call this one?"

"Daniel George," said Becky without hesitation. "After my father," she explained, looking up at Charlie.

"And mine," said Charlie, as he walked to the head of the bed and placed an arm round Becky.

"Well, I'll have to go now Mrs Salmon. But I shall be back first thing in the morning."

"No, it's Mrs Trumper actually," said Becky quietly. "Salmon was my maiden name."

"Oh," said the midwife, looking flustered for the first time. "They seem to have got the names muddled up on my call sheet. Oh, well, see you tomorrow, Mrs Trumper," she said as she closed the door.

"Mrs Trumper?" said Charlie.

"It's taken me an awful long time to come to my senses, wouldn't you say, Mr Trumper?"

DAPHNE

1918-1921

CHAPTER 13

hen I opened the letter, I confess I didn't immediately recall who Becky Salmon was. But then I remembered that there had been an extremely bright, rather plump pupil by that name at St Paul's, who always seemed to have an endless supply of cream cakes. If I remember, the only thing I gave her in return was an art book that had been a Christmas present from an aunt in Cumberland.

In fact, by the time I had reached the upper sixth, the precocious little blighter was already in the lower sixth, despite there being a good two years difference in our age.

Having read her letter a second time, I couldn't imagine why the girl should want to see me, and concluded that the only way I was likely to find out was to invite her round to tea at my little place in Chelsea.

When I first saw Becky again I hardly recognised her. Not only had she lost a couple of stone, but she would have made an ideal model for one of those Pepsodent advertisements that one saw displayed on the front of every tram – you know, a fresh-faced girl showing off a gleaming set of perfect teeth. I had to admit I was quite envious.

Becky explained to me that all she needed was a room in London while she was up at the university. I was only too happy to oblige. After all, the mater had made it clear on several occasions how much she disapproved of my being in the flat on my own, and that she couldn't for the life of her fathom what was wrong with 26 Lowndes Square, our family's London residence. I couldn't wait to tell Ma, and Pa for that matter, the news that I had, as they so often requested, found myself an appropriate companion.

"But who is this girl?" enquired my mother, when I went down to Harcourt Hall for the weekend. "Anyone we know?"

"Don't think so, Ma," I replied. "An old school chum from St Paul's. Rather the academic type."

"Bluestockin', you mean?" my father chipped in.

"Yes, you've got the idea, Pa. She's attending some place called Bedford College to read the history of the Renaissance, or something like that."

"Didn't know girls could get degrees," my father said. "Must all be part of that damned little Welshman's ideas for a new Britain."

"You must stop describing Lloyd George in that way," my mother reprimanded him. "He is, after all, our Prime Minister."

"He may be yours, my dear, but he's certainly not mine. I blame it all on those suffragettes," my father added, producing one of his habitual non sequiturs.

"My dear, you blame most things on the suffragettes," my mother reminded him, "even last year's harvest. However," she continued, "coming back to this girl, she sounds to me as if she could have a very beneficial influence on you, Daphne. Where did you say her parents come from?"

"I didn't," I replied. "But I think her father was a businessman out East somewhere, and I'm going to take tea with her mother some time next week."

"Singapore possibly?" said Pa. "There's a lot of business goin' on out there, rubber and all that sort of thing."

"No, I don't think he was in rubber, Pa."

"Well, whatever, do bring the girl round for tea one afternoon," Ma insisted. "Or even down here for the weekend. Does she hunt?"

"No, I don't think so, Ma, but I'll certainly invite her to tea in the near future, so that you can both inspect her."

I must confess that I was equally amused by the idea of being asked along to tea with Becky's mother, so that she could be sure that I was the right sort of girl for *her* daughter. After all, I was fairly confident that I wasn't. I had never been east of the Aldwych before, as far as I could recollect, so I found the idea of going to Essex even more exciting than travelling abroad.

Luckily the journey to Romford was without incident, mainly because Hoskins, my father's chauffeur, knew the road well. It turned out he had originated from somewhere called Dagenham, which he informed me was even deeper inside the Essex jungle.

I had no notion until that day that such people existed. They were neither servants nor from the professional classes nor members of the gentry, and I can't pretend that I exactly fell in love with Romford. However, Mrs Salmon and her sister Miss Roach couldn't have been more hospitable. Becky's mother turned out to be a practical, sensible, God-fearing woman who could also produce an excellent spread for tea, so it was not an altogether wasted journey.

Becky moved into my flat the following week, and I was horrified when I discovered how hard the girl worked. She seemed to spend all day at that Bedford place, returning home only to nibble a sandwich, sip a glass of milk and then continue her studies until she fell asleep, long after I had gone to bed. I could never quite work out what it was all in aid of.

It was after her foolish visit to John D. Wood that I first learned about Charlie Trumper and his ambitions. All that fuss, simply because she had sold off his barrow without consulting him. I felt it nothing less than my duty to point out that two of my ancestors had been beheaded for trying to steal counties, and one sent to the Tower for high treason; well, at least, I reflected, I had a kinsman who had spent his final days in the vicinity of the East End.

As always, Becky knew she was right. "But it's only a hundred pounds," she kept repeating.

"Which you don't possess."

"I've got forty and I feel confident it's such a good investment that I ought to be able to raise the other sixty without much trouble. After all, Charlie could sell blocks of ice to the Eskimos."

"And how are you planning to run the shop in his absence?" I asked. "Between lectures perhaps?"

"Oh, don't be so frivolous, Daphne. Charlie will manage the shop just as soon as he gets back from the war. After all, it can't be long now."

"The war has been over for some weeks," I reminded her. "And there doesn't seem to be much sign of your Charlie."

"He's not my Charlie" was all she said.

Anyway, I kept a close eye on Becky during the next thirty days and it quickly became plain for anyone to see that she wasn't going to raise the money. However, she was far too proud to admit as much to me. I therefore decided the time had come to pay another visit to Romford.

"This is an unexpected pleasure, Miss Harcourt-Browne," Becky's mother assured me, when I arrived unannounced at their little house in Belle Vue Road. I should point out, in my own defence, that I would have informed Mrs Salmon of my imminent arrival if she had possessed a telephone. As I sought certain information that only she could supply before the thirty days were up – information that would save not only her daughter's face but also her finances – I was unwilling to put my trust in the postal service.

"Becky isn't in any trouble, I hope?" was Mrs Salmon's first reaction when she saw me standing on the doorstep.

"Certainly not," I assured her. "Never seen the girl in perkier form."

"It's just that since her father's death I do worry about her," Mrs Salmon explained. She limped just slightly as she guided me into a drawing room that was as spotless as the day I had first accepted their kind invitation to tea. A bowl of fruit rested on the table in the centre of the room. I only prayed that Mrs Salmon would never drop into Number 97 without giving me at least a year's notice.

"How can I be of assistance?" Mrs Salmon asked, moments after Miss Roach had been despatched to the kitchen to prepare tea.

"I am considering making a small investment on a greengrocer's shop in Chelsea," I told her. "I am assured by John D. Wood that it is a sound proposition, despite the current food shortage and the growing problems with trade unions – that is, as long as I can install a first-class manager."

Mrs Salmon's smile was replaced by a puzzled expression.

"Becky has sung the praises of someone called Charlie Trumper, and the purpose of my visit is to seek your opinion of the gentleman in question."

"Gentleman he certainly is not," said Mrs Salmon without hesitation. "An uneducated ruffian might be nearer the mark."

"Oh, what a disappointment," I said. "Especially as Becky led me to believe that your late husband thought rather highly of him."

"As a fruit and vegetable man he certainly did. In fact I'd go as far as to say that Mr Salmon used to consider that young Charlie might end up being as good as his grandfather."

"And how good was that?"

"Although I didn't mix with those sort of people, you understand," explained Mrs Salmon, "I was told, second-hand of course, that he was the finest Whitechapel had ever seen."

"Good," I said. "But is he also honest?"

"I have never heard otherwise," Mrs Salmon admitted. "And heaven knows, he's willing to work all the hours God gave, but he's hardly your type, I would have thought, Miss Harcourt-Browne."

"I was considering employing the man as a shop-keeper, Mrs Salmon, not inviting him to join me in the Royal Enclosure at Ascot." At that moment Miss Roach reappeared with a tray of tea – jam tarts and eclairs smothered in cream. They turned out to be so delicious that I stayed far longer than I had planned.

The following morning I paid a visit to John D. Wood and handed over a cheque for the remaining ninety pounds. I then visited my solicitor and had a contract drawn up, which when it was completed I didn't begin to understand.

Once Becky had found out what I had been up to I drove a hard bargain, because I knew the girl would resent my interference if I wasn't able to prove that I was getting something worthwhile out of the deal.

As soon as she had been convinced of that, Becky immediately handed over a further thirty pounds to help reduce the debt. She certainly took her new enterprise most seriously, because within days she had stolen a young man from a shop in Kensington to take over Trumper's until Charlie returned. She also continued to work hours I didn't even know existed. I could never get her to explain to me the point of rising before the sun did.

After Becky had settled into her new routine I even invited her to make up a foursome for the opera one night to see *La Bohème*. In the past she had shown no inclination to attend any of my outings, especially since her new responsibilities with the shop. But on this occasion I pleaded with her to join the group because a chum of mine had cancelled at the last minute and I desperately needed a spare girl.

"But I've nothing to wear," she said helplessly.

"Take your pick of anything of mine you fancy," I told her, and ushered her through to my bedroom.

I could see that she found such an offer almost irresistible. An hour later she re-emerged in a long turquoise dress that brought back memories of what it had originally looked like on the model.

"Who are your other guests?" Becky enquired.

"Algernon Fitzpatrick. He's Percy Wiltshire's best friend. You remember, the man who hasn't yet been told I'm going to marry him."

"And who makes up the party?"

"Guy Trentham. He's a captain in the Royal Fusiliers, an acceptable regiment, just," I added. "He's recently returned from the Western Front where it's said he had a rather good war. MC and all that. We come from the same village in Berkshire, and grew up together, although I confess we don't really have a lot in common. Extremely good-looking, but has the reputation of being a bit of a ladies' man, so beware."

La Bohème, I felt, had been a great success, even if Algernon wasn't able to give me much news about what Percy was up to. Guy couldn't take his eyes off Becky throughout the second act – not that she seemed to show the slightest interest in him.

However, to my surprise, as soon as we got back home, Becky couldn't stop talking about Guy – his looks, his sophistication, his charm and how solicitous he had been throughout the entire evening. Eventually I managed to get to bed, but not before I had assured Becky to her satisfaction that her feelings were undoubtedly reciprocated.

In fact, I became, unwittingly, Cupid for the budding romance. The following day I was asked by Guy to invite Miss Salmon to accompany him to a West End play. Becky accepted, of course, but then I had already assured Guy she would.

After their outing to the Haymarket, I seemed to bump into the two of them all the time, and began to fear that if the relationship became any more serious it could only, as my nanny used to say, end in tears. I began to regret having ever introduced them in the first place, although there was no doubt, to quote the modern expression: she was head over heels in love.

Despite this, for a few weeks equilibrium returned to the residents of 97 – and then Charlie was demobbed.

I wasn't formally introduced to the man for some time after his return, and when I was I had to admit they didn't make them like that in Berkshire. The occasion was a dinner we all shared at that awful little Italian restaurant just up the road from my flat.

To be fair, the evening was not what one might describe as a wow, partly because Guy made no effort to be sociable, but mainly because Becky didn't bother to bring Charlie into the conversation at all. I found myself asking and then answering most of the questions, and, as for Charlie, he appeared on first sighting to be somewhat gauche.

When we were all walking back to the flat after dinner, I suggested to him that we should leave Becky and Guy to themselves. When Charlie escorted me into his shop he couldn't resist stopping to explain how he had changed everything around since he had taken over. His enthusiasm would have convinced the most cynical investor, but what impressed me most was his knowledge of a business which until that moment I hadn't given a second thought to. It was then that I made the decision to assist Charlie with both his causes.

I wasn't in the least surprised to discover how he felt about Becky, but that for her part she was so infatuated with Guy she wasn't even aware of Charlie's

existence. It was during one of his interminable mono-
logues on the virtues of the girl that I began to form a
plan for Charlie's future. I was determined that he
must have a different type of education, perhaps not
as formal as Becky's, but no less valuable for the future
he had decided on.

I assured Charlie that Guy would soon become
bored with Becky – as that had proved to be the
invariable pattern with girls who had crossed his path
in the past. I added that he must be patient and the
apple would eventually fall into his lap. I also
explained who Newton was.

I assumed that those tears to which Nanny had so
often referred might indeed begin to flow soon after
Becky was invited to spend the weekend with Guy's
parents at Ashurst. I made sure that I was asked to join
the Trenthams for afternoon tea on the Sunday, to give
whatever moral support Becky might feel in need of.

I arrived a little after three forty, which I have
always considered a proper hour for taking tea, only
to find Mrs Trentham surrounded by silverware and
crockery but sitting quite alone.

"Where are the starstruck lovers?" I enquired, as
I entered the drawing room.

"If you're referring, in that coarse way of yours,
Daphne, to my son and Miss Salmon, they have already
departed for London."

"Together, I presume?" I asked.

"Yes, although for the life of me I can't imagine
what the dear boy sees in her." Mrs Trentham poured
me a cup of tea. "As for myself, I found her exceedingly common."

"Perhaps it could be her brains and looks," I
volunteered as the major entered the room. I smiled
at a man I had known since I was a child and had come
to treat as an uncle. The one mystery about him as far
as I was concerned was how he could possibly have
fallen for someone like Ethel Hardcastle.

"Guy left too?" he asked.

"Yes, he's returned to London with Miss Salmon," said Mrs Trentham for a second time.

"Oh, pity really. She seemed such a grand girl."

"In a parochial type of way," said Mrs Trentham.

"I get the impression Guy rather dotes on her," I said, hoping for a reaction.

"Heaven forbid," said Mrs Trentham.

"I doubt if heaven will have a lot to do with it," I told her, as I warmed to the challenge.

"Then *I* shall," said Mrs Trentham. "I have no intention of letting my son marry the daughter of an East End street trader."

"I can't see why not," interjected the major. "After all, isn't that what your grandfather was?"

"Gerald, really. My grandfather founded and built up a highly successful business in Yorkshire, not the East End."

"Then I think that it's only the location we are discussing," said the major. "I well recall your father tellin' me, with some pride I might add, that his old dad had started Hardcastle's in the back of a shed somewhere near Huddersfield."

"Gerald – I feel sure he was exaggerating."

"Never struck me as the type of man who was prone to exaggerate," retorted the major. "On the contrary, rather blunt sort of fellow. Shrewd with it, I always considered."

"Then that must have been a considerable time ago," said Mrs Trentham.

"What's more, I suspect that we shall live to see the children of Rebecca Salmon doing a bloody sight better than the likes of us," added the major.

"Gerald, I do wish you wouldn't use the word 'bloody' so frequently. We're all being influenced by that socialist playwright Mr Shaw and his frightful *Pygmalion*, which seems to be nothing more than a play about Miss Salmon."

"Hardly," I told her. "After all, Becky will leave London University with a Bachelor of Arts degree, which is more than my whole family has managed between them in eleven centuries."

"That may well be the case," Mrs Trentham concurred, "but they are hardly the qualifications that I feel appropriate for advancing Guy's military career, especially now his regiment will be completing a tour of duty in India."

This piece of information came as a bolt out of the blue. I also felt pretty certain Becky knew nothing of it.

"And when he returns to these shores," continued Mrs Trentham, "I shall be looking for someone of good breeding, sufficient money and perhaps even a little intelligence to be his matrimonial partner. Gerald may have failed, by petty prejudice, to become Commanding Officer of the Regiment, but I will not allow the same thing to happen to Guy, of that I can assure you."

"I simply wasn't good enough," said the major gruffly. "Sir Danvers was far better qualified for the job, and in any case it was only you who ever wanted me to be commanding officer in the first place."

"Nevertheless, I feel after Guy's results at Sandhurst – "

"He managed to pass out in the top half," the major reminded her. "That can hardly be described as carrying off the Sword of Honour, my dear."

"But he was awarded the Military Cross on the field of battle and his citation – "

The major grunted in a manner that suggested that he had been trotted round this particular course several times before.

"And so you see," Mrs Trentham continued, "I have every confidence that Guy will in time become Commanding Officer of the Regiment and I don't mind telling you that I already have someone in mind who will assist him in that quest. After all, wives can make or break a career, don't you know, Daphne."

"At least on that I am able to concur fully, my dear," murmured her husband.

I travelled back to London somewhat relieved that, after such an encounter, Becky's relationship with Guy must surely come to an end. Certainly the more I had seen of the damn man the more I distrusted him.

When I returned to the flat later that evening, I found Becky sitting on the sofa, red-eyed and trembling. She told me her version of what had taken place at the weekend, which she considered had been a disaster, but added that she thought Guy had proposed to her.

I was about to mention India when she said, "She hates me."

"She doesn't yet appreciate you," was how I remembered phrasing my reply. "But I can tell you that the major thinks you're a grand girl."

"How kind of him," said Becky. "He showed me round the estate, you know."

"My dear, one does not describe seven hundred acres as an estate. A freeholding, perhaps, but certainly not an estate."

"Do you think Guy will stop seeing me after what took place at Ashurst?"

I wanted to say, I hope so, but managed to curb my tongue. "Not if the man has any character," I replied diplomatically.

And indeed Guy did see her the following week, and as far as I could determine never raised the subject of his mother or that unfortunate weekend again.

However, I still considered my long-term plan for Charlie and Becky was proceeding rather well, until I returned home after a long weekend to find one of my favourite dresses strewn across the drawing room floor. I followed a trail of clothes until I reached Becky's door, which I opened tentatively to find, to my horror, that even more of my garments lay by the side of her bed, along with Guy's. I had rather hoped Becky would have seen him for the bounder he was long before she had allowed it to reach the terminal stage.

Guy started out on his journey to India the following day, and as soon as he had taken his leave Becky began telling everyone who cared to listen that she was engaged to the creature, although there was no ring on her finger and no announcement in any paper to confirm her version of the story. "Guy's word is good enough for me," she asserted, which left one simply speechless.

I arrived home that night to find her asleep in my bed. Becky told me over breakfast that Charlie had put her there – without further explanation.

The following Sunday afternoon I invited myself back to tea with the Trenthams, only to learn from Guy's mother that she had been assured by her son that he had not been in contact with Miss Salmon since her premature departure from Ashurst some nine months before.

"But that isn't –" I began, but stopped in midsentence when I recalled my promise to Becky not to inform Guy's mother that they were still seeing each other.

A few weeks later Becky told me that she had missed her period. I swore that I would keep her secret but did not hesitate to inform Charlie the same day. When he heard the news he nearly went berserk. What made matters worse was that he had to go on pretending whenever he saw the girl that he wasn't aware of anything untoward.

"I swear if that bastard Trentham were back in England I'd kill him," Charlie kept repeating, as he went on one of his route-marches round the drawing room.

"If he were in England I can think of at least three girls whose fathers would happily carry out the job for you," I retorted.

"So what am I meant to do about it?" Charlie asked me at last.

"Not a lot," I advised. "I suspect time – and eight thousand miles – may well turn out to be your greatest allies."

The colonel also fell into the category of those who would have happily shot Guy Trentham, given half a chance, in his case because of the honour of the regiment and all that. He even murmured something sinister about going to see Major Trentham and giving it to him straight. I could have told him that the major wasn't the problem. However, I wasn't sure if the colonel, even with his vast experience of different types of enemy, had ever come up against anyone as formidable as Mrs Trentham.

It must have been around this time that Percy Wiltshire was finally discharged from the Scots Guards. Lately I had stopped worrying about his mother telephoning me. During those dreadful years between 1916 and 1919 I always assumed it would be a message to say that Percy had been killed on the Western Front, as his father and elder brother had been before him. It was to be years before I admitted to the dowager marchioness whenever she called how much I dreaded hearing her voice on the other end of the line.

Then quite suddenly Percy asked me to marry him. I fear from that moment on I became so preoccupied with our future together and being expected to visit so many of his family that I quite neglected my duty to Becky, even though I had allowed her to take over the flat. Then, almost before I could look round, she had given birth to little Daniel. I only prayed that she could face the inevitable stigma.

It was some months after the christening that I decided to pay a surprise visit to the flat on my way back from a weekend in the country with Percy's mother.

When the front door opened I was greeted by Charlie, a newspaper tucked under his arm while Becky, who was sitting on the sofa, appeared to be darning a sock. I looked down to watch Daniel crawling towards me at a rate of knots. I took the child in my arms before he had the chance to head off down the stairs and out into the world.

"How lovely to see you," Becky said, jumping up. "It's been ages. Let me make you some tea."

"Thank you," I said, "I only came round to make sure you are free on . . ." My eyes settled on a little oil that hung above the mantelpiece. "What a truly beautiful picture," I remarked.

"But you must have seen the painting many times before," Becky said. "After all, it was in Charlie's –"

"No, I've never seen it before," I replied, not sure what she was getting at.

CHAPTER 14

T he day the gold-edged card arrived at Lowndes Square Daphne placed the invitation between the one requesting her presence in the Royal Enclosure at Ascot and the command to attend a Garden Party at Buckingham Palace. However, she considered that this particular invitation could well remain on the mantelpiece for all to gaze upon long after Ascot and the palace had been relegated to the wastepaper-basket.

Although Daphne had spent a week in Paris selecting three outfits for the three different occasions, the most striking of them was to be saved for Becky's degree ceremony which she now described to Percy as "the great event".

Her fiancé – though she hadn't yet become quite used to thinking of Percy in that way – also admitted that he had never been asked to such a ceremony before.

Brigadier Harcourt-Browne suggested that his daughter should have Hoskins drive them to the Senate House in the Rolls, and admitted to being a little envious at not having been invited himself.

When the morning finally dawned, Percy accompanied Daphne to lunch at the Ritz, and once they had been over the guest list and the hymns that would be sung at the service for the umpteenth time, they turned their attention to the details of the afternoon outing.

"I do hope we won't be asked any awkward questions," said Daphne. "Because one thing's for certain, I will not know the answers."

"Oh, I'm sure we won't be put to any trouble like that, old gel," said Percy. "Not that I've ever attended one of these shindigs before. We Wiltshires aren't exactly known for troubling the authorities on these matters," he added, laughing which so often came out sounding like a cough.

"You must get out of that habit, Percy. If you are going to laugh, laugh. If you're going to cough, cough."

"Anything you say, old gel."

"And do stop calling me 'old gel'. I'm only twenty-three, and my parents endowed me with a perfectly acceptable christian name."

"Anything you say, old gel," repeated Percy.

"You haven't been listening to a word I've said." Daphne checked her watch. "And now I do believe it's time we were on our way. Better not be late for this one."

"Quite right," he replied, and called a waiter to bring them their bill.

"Do you have any idea where we are going, Hoskins?" asked Daphne, as he opened the back door of the Rolls for her.

"Yes, m'lady, I took the liberty of going over the route when you and His Lordship were up in Scotland last month."

"Good thinking, Hoskins," said Percy. "Otherwise we might have been going round in circles for the rest of the afternoon, don't you know."

As Hoskins turned on the engine Daphne looked at the man she loved, and couldn't help thinking how lucky she had been in her choice. In truth she had chosen him at the age of sixteen, and never faltered in her belief that he was the right partner – even if he wasn't aware of the fact. She had always thought Percy quite wonderful, kind, considerate and gentle and, if not exactly handsome, certainly distinguished. She thanked God each night that he had escaped that fearful war with every limb intact. Once Percy had told her he was going off to France to serve with the Scots Guards, Daphne had spent three of the unhappiest years of her life. From that moment on she assumed every letter, every message, every call could only be to inform her of his death. Other men tried to court her in his absence, but they all failed as Daphne waited, not unlike Penelope, for her chosen partner to return. She would only accept that he was still alive when she saw him striding down the gangplank at Dover. Daphne would always treasure his first words the moment he saw her.

"Fancy seeing you here, old gel. Dashed coincidence don't you know."

Percy never talked of the example his father had set, though *The Times* had devoted half a page to the late marquess's obituary. In it they described his action on the Marne in the course of which he had single-handedly over-run a German battery as "one of the great VCs of the war". When a month later Percy's elder brother was killed at Ypres it came home to her just how many families were sharing the same dreadful experience. Now Percy had inherited the title: the twelfth Marquess of Wiltshire. From tenth to twelfth in a matter of weeks.

"Are you sure we're going in the right direction?" asked Daphne as the Rolls entered Shaftesbury Avenue.

"Yes, m'lady," replied Hoskins, who had obviously decided to address Daphne by the title even though she and Percy were not yet married.

Percy coughed again. "He's only helping you to get accustomed to the idea, old gel."

Daphne had been delighted when Percy told her that he had decided to resign his commission with the Scots Guards in order to take over the running of the family estates. Much as she admired him in that dark blue uniform with its four brass buttons evenly spaced, stirruped boots, and funny red, white and blue checked cap, it was a farmer she wanted to marry, not a soldier. A life spent in India, Africa and the colonies had never really appealed to her.

As they turned into Malet Street, they saw a throng of people making their way up some stone steps to enter a monumental building. "That must be the Senate House," she exclaimed, as if she had come across an undiscovered pyramid.

"Yes, m'lady," replied Hoskins.

"And do remember, Percy – " began Daphne.

"Yes, old gel?"

"– not to speak unless you're spoken to. On this occasion we are not exactly on home ground, and I object to either of us being made to look foolish. Now, did you remember the invitation and the special tickets that show our seat allocation?"

"I know I put them somewhere." He began to search around in his pockets.

"They're in the left-hand inside top pocket of your jacket, Your Lordship," said Hoskins as he brought the car to a halt.

"Yes, of course they are," said Percy. "Thank you, Hoskins."

"A pleasure, m'lord," Hoskins intoned.

"Just follow the crowd," instructed Daphne. "And look as if you do this sort of thing every week."

They passed several uniformed doorkeepers and ushers before a clerk checked their tickets, then guided them to row M.

"I've never been seated this far back in a theatre before," said Daphne.

"I've only tried to be this far away in a theatre once myself," admitted Percy. "And that was when the Germans were on centre stage." He coughed again.

The two remained sitting in silence as they stared in front of them, waiting for something to happen. The stage was bare but for fourteen chairs, two of which, placed at its centre, might almost have been described as thrones.

At two fifty-five, ten men and two women, all of whom were dressed in what looked to Daphne like long black dressing-gowns with purple scarves hanging from their necks, proceeded across the stage in a gentle crocodile before taking their allocated places. Only the two thrones remained unoccupied. On the stroke of three Daphne's attention was drawn to the Minstrels' Gallery, where a fanfare of trumpets struck up to announce the arrival of the Visitors, and all those present rose as the King and Queen entered to take their places in the centre of the Senate. Everyone remained standing until after the National Anthem had been played.

"The King looks very well, considering," said Percy, resuming his seat.

"Do be quiet," said Daphne. "No one else knows him."

An elderly man in a long black gown, the only person who remained standing, waited for everyone to settle before he took a pace forward, bowed to the royal couple and then proceeded to address the audience.

After the vice-chancellor, Sir Russell Russell-Wells, had been speaking for some considerable time Percy enquired of his fiancée, "How is a fellow expected to follow all this piffle when he gave up Latin as an option in his fourth half?"

"I only survived a year of the subject myself."

"Then you won't be much help either, old gel," admitted Percy in a whisper.

Someone seated in the row in front turned round to glare at them ferociously.

Throughout the remainder of the ceremony Daphne and Percy tried to remain silent, although Daphne did find it necessary from time to time to place a firm hand on Percy's knee as he continued to shift uncomfortably from side to side on the flat wooden chair.

"It's all right for the King," whispered Percy. "He's got a dam' great cushion to sit on."

At last the moment came for which they had both been bidden.

The vice-chancellor, who continued to call out a list of names from the Roll of Honour, had at last come to the Ts. He then declared, "Bachelor of Arts, Mrs Charles Trumper of Bedford College." The applause almost doubled, as it had done every time a woman had walked up the steps to receive her degree from the Visitor. Becky curtsied before the King as he placed what the programme described as a "hood of purple" over her gown and handed her a parchment scroll. She curtsied again and took two paces backwards before returning to her seat.

"Couldn't have done it better myself," said Percy as he joined in the applause. "And no prizes for guessing who tutored her through that little performance," he added. Daphne blushed as they remained in their places for some time to allow all the Us, Vs, Ws and Ys to receive their degrees, before being allowed to escape into the garden for tea.

"Can't see them anywhere," said Percy, as he turned a slow circle in the middle of the lawn.

"Nor I," said Daphne. "But keep looking. They're bound to be here somewhere."

"Good afternoon, Miss Harcourt-Browne."

Daphne spun round. "Oh, hello, Mrs Salmon, how super to see you. And what a simply charming hat, and dear Miss Roach. Percy, this is Becky's mother, Mrs Salmon, and her aunt, Miss Roach. My fiancé –"

"Delighted to meet you, Your Lordship," said Mrs Salmon, wondering if anyone from the Ladies Circle at Romford would believe her when she told them.

"You must be so proud of your daughter," said Percy.

"Yes, I am, Your Lordship," said Mrs Salmon.

Miss Roach stood like a statue and didn't offer an opinion.

"And where is our little scholar?" demanded Daphne.

"I'm here," said Becky. "But where have you been?" she asked, emerging from a group of new graduates.

"Looking for you."

The two girls threw their arms around each other.

"Have you seen my mother?"

"She was with us a moment ago," said Daphne, looking around.

"She's gone to find some sandwiches, I think," said Miss Roach.

"Typical of Mum," said Becky, laughing.

"Hello, Percy," said Charlie. "How are things?"

"Things are spiffing," said Percy, coughing. "And well done, Becky, I say," he added as Mrs Salmon returned carrying a large plate of sandwiches.

"If Becky has inherited her mother's common sense, Mrs Salmon," said Daphne as she selected a cucumber sandwich for Percy, "she ought to do well in the real world, because I suspect there won't be many of these left in fifteen minutes' time." She picked out one of the smoked salmon variety for herself. "Were you very nervous when you marched up on to that stage?" Daphne asked, turning her attention back to Becky.

"I certainly was," replied Becky. "And when the King placed the hood over my head, my legs almost gave way. Then, to make matters worse, the moment I returned to my place I discovered Charlie was crying."

"I was not," protested her husband.

Becky said nothing more as she linked her arm through his.

"I've rather taken to that purple hood thing," said Percy. "I think I'd look quite a swell were I to sport one of those at next year's Hunt Ball. What do you think, old gel?"

"You're expected to do rather a lot of hard work before you're allowed to adorn yourself with one of those, Percy."

They all turned to see who it was who had offered this opinion.

Percy lowered his head. "Your Majesty is, as always, quite correct. I might add, sir, that I fear, given my present record, I am unlikely ever to be considered for such a distinction."

The King smiled, then added, "In fact I'm bound to say, Percy, that you seem to have strayed somewhat from your usual habitat."

"A friend of Daphne's," explained Percy.

"Daphne, my dear, how lovely to see you," said the King. "And I haven't yet had the opportunity to congratulate you on your engagement."

"I received a kind note from the Queen only yesterday,

Your Majesty. We are honoured that you are both able to attend the wedding."

"Yes, simply delighted," said Percy. "And may I present Mrs Trumper, who was the recipient of the degree?" Becky shook hands with the King for a second time. "Her husband, Mr Charles Trumper, and Mrs Trumper's mother, Mrs Salmon; her aunt Miss Roach."

The King shook hands with all four before saying, "Well done, Mrs Trumper. I do hope you're going to put your degree to some useful purpose."

"I shall be joining the staff of Sotheby's, Your Majesty. As an apprentice in their fine art department."

"Capital. Then I can only wish you continued success, Mrs Trumper. I look forward to seeing you at the wedding, if not before, Percy." With a nod the King moved on to another group.

"Decent fellow," said Percy. "Good of him to come over like that."

"I had no idea you knew –" began Becky.

"Well," explained Percy, "to be honest, *my* great-great-great-great-grandfather tried to murder *his* great-great-great-great-grandfather, and had he succeeded our roles might well have been reversed. Despite that he's always been jolly understanding about the whole affair."

"So what happened to your great-great-great-great-grandfather?" asked Charlie.

"Exiled," said Percy. "And I'm bound to add, quite rightly. Otherwise the blighter would only have tried again."

"Good heavens," said Becky, laughing.

"What is it?" said Charlie.

"I've just worked out who Percy's great-great-great-great-grandfather was."

Daphne didn't get a chance to see Becky again before the marriage ceremony, as the last few weeks of preparation for her wedding seemed to be totally occupied. However, she did manage to keep abreast of the goings-on in Chelsea

Terrace, after bumping into the colonel and his wife at Lady Denham's reception in Onslow Square. The colonel was able to inform her, *sotto voce*, that Charlie was beginning to run up a rather large overdraft with the bank – "even if he had cleared every other outstanding creditor". Daphne smiled when she recalled that her last payment had been returned in typical Charlie fashion several months before it was due. "And I've just learned that the man has his eye on yet another shop," added the colonel.

"Which one this time?"

"The bakery – Number 145."

"Becky's father's old trade," said Daphne. "Are they confident of getting their hands on it?"

"Yes, I think so – although I fear Charlie's going to have to pay a little over the odds this time."

"Why's that?"

"The baker is right next door to the fruit and vegetable shop, and Mr Reynolds is only too aware just how much Charlie wants to buy him out. However, Charlie has tempted Mr Reynolds with an offer to remain as manager, plus a share of the profits."

"Hmmm. How long do you think that little arrangement will last?"

"Just as long as it takes for Charlie to master the bakery trade once again."

"And how about Becky?"

"She's started her job at Sotheby's. As a counter clerk."

"A counter clerk?" said Daphne on a rising note. "What was the point of taking all that trouble to get a degree if she ends up as a counter clerk?"

"Apparently everybody starts off that way at Sotheby's, whatever qualifications they bring to the job. Becky explained it all to me," replied the colonel. "It seems that you can be the son of the chairman, have worked in a major West End art gallery for several years, possess a degree or even have no qualifications at all, but you still start on the front desk. Once they discover you're any good you get promoted into a specialist department. Not unlike the army, actually."

"So which department does Becky have her eye on?"

"Seems she wants to join some old fellow called Pemberton who's the acknowledged expert on Renaissance paintings."

"My bet," said Daphne, "is that she'll last on the front desk for about a couple of weeks."

"Charlie doesn't share your low opinion of her," said the colonel.

"Oh, so how long does he give her?"

The colonel smiled. "Ten days at the most."

CHAPTER 15

hen the morning mail arrived at Lowndes Square, Wentworth, the butler, would place the letters on a silver tray and take them to the brigadier in his study, where his master would remove those addressed to himself before handing the tray back to the butler. He, in turn, would deliver the remaining letters to the ladies of the house.

However, since the announcement of his daughter's engagement in *The Times*, and the subsequent sending out of over five hundred invitations for the forthcoming wedding, the brigadier had become bored with the sorting-out process and instructed Wentworth to reverse his route, so that he would be handed only those letters addressed to him.

Thus it was on a Monday morning in June 1921 that Wentworth knocked on Miss Daphne's bedroom door, entered when bidden and handed her a large bundle of mail. Once Daphne had extracted the letters addressed to her mother and herself she returned the few that remained to Wentworth, who bowed slightly and proceeded on his anti-clockwise route.

As soon as Wentworth had closed the door behind him Daphne climbed out of bed, placed the stack of letters on her dressing-table and wandered into the bathroom. A little after ten thirty, feeling ready for the rigours of the day, she returned to her dressing-table and began slitting open the letters. Acceptances and regrets had to be placed in separate piles before they could be ticked or crossed off on a master list; her mother would then be able to calculate the exact numbers to cater for and proceed to work on a seating plan. The breakdown of the thirty-one letters that particular morning produced twenty-two yeses, including a princess, a viscount, two other lords, an ambassador and dear Colonel and Lady Hamilton. There were also four noes, comprising two couples who would be abroad, an elderly uncle who was suffering from advanced diabetes and another whose daughter had been foolish enough to select the same day as Daphne on which to be married. Having ticked and crossed their names off the master list, Daphne turned her attention to the five remaining letters.

One turned out to be from her eighty-seven-year-old Aunt Agatha, who resided in Cumberland and had some time previously stated that she would not be attending the wedding as she felt the journey to London might prove too much of a strain. However, Aunt Agatha went on to suggest that perhaps Daphne should bring Percy up north to visit her just as soon as they returned from their honeymoon, as she wished to make his acquaintance.

"Certainly not," said Daphne out loud. "Once I am back in England I shall have far more important things to worry myself with than ageing aunts." She then read the PS:

And while you are in Cumberland, my darling, it will be a good opportunity for you to advise me on my will, because I'm not sure which of the pictures to give to whom, especially the Canaletto, which I do feel deserves a good home.

Wicked old lady, thought Daphne, well aware that Aunt Agatha wrote an identical PS to every one of her relations, however distant, thus guaranteeing that she rarely spent a weekend alone.

The second letter was from Michael Fishlock and Co, the catering specialists, who enclosed an estimate for supplying tea to eight hundred guests in Vincent Square immediately preceding the wedding. Three hundred guineas seemed an outrageous sum to Daphne, but without a second thought she placed the estimate on one side, to be dealt with by her father at some later date. Two other letters addressed to her mother that were from friends and no concern of Daphne's were also placed on one side.

The fifth letter she saved until last, because the envelope was enriched by the most colourful stamps, the King's crown set in an oval on the right-hand corner above the words "Ten Annas".

She slit the envelope open slowly and extracted several sheets of heavy notepaper, the first of which was embossed with the crest and legend of the Royal Fusiliers.

"Dear Daphne", the letter began. She hurriedly turned to the last page in order to check the salutation which read, "Your friend, as always, Guy".

Returning to the first page, she glanced at the address before beginning to read Guy's words with apprehension.

Officers' Mess
2nd Battalion
Royal Fusiliers
Wellington Barracks
Poona
India

May 15th, 1921

Dear Daphne,

    I hope you will forgive me for presuming on our long family friendship, but a problem has arisen of which I am sure you are only too aware, and unfortunately I now

---

find that I must turn to you for help and guidance.

Some time ago I received a letter from your friend Rebecca Salmon

Daphne placed the unread pages back on her dressing-table, wishing that the letter had arrived a few days after she had set out on her honeymoon rather than before. She fiddled around with the guest list for some time, but realised she would eventually have to find out what Guy expected of her. She returned to his letter.

informing me that she was pregnant and that I was the father of her child.

Let me assure you from the outset that nothing could be further from the truth, as on the only occasion I remained overnight in your flat, Rebecca and I had no physical contact.

As a matter of record, it was she who insisted we had dinner together at 97, Chelsea Terrace that evening, despite the fact that I had already booked a table for us at the Ritz.

As the evening progressed, it became obvious that she was trying to get me drunk, and indeed when I thought to leave. I confess I did feel a little queasy, and wasn't certain that I would be able to make the journey safely back to my barracks.

Rebecca immediately suggested that I remain overnight in order to "sleep it off". I use her exact words. Naturally I refused, until she pointed out that I could stay in your room as you were not expected to return from the country until the following afternoon – a fact which you later confirmed.

Indeed, I took up Rebecca's kind offer, and on retiring to bed, quickly fell into a deep sleep only to be awoken later by the banging of a door. To my horror I awoke to find you standing there in front of me. I was even more shocked to discover that Rebecca, quite unbeknown to me had crept into bed beside me.

You were naturally embarrassed and left immediately.

Without uttering another word I rose, dressed and returned to my barracks, arriving back in my own room by one-fifteen, at the latest.

On arriving at Waterloo station later in the morning to begin my journey to India I was, as you can imagine, somewhat surprised to find Rebecca waiting for me on the platform. I spent only a few moments with her but left her in no doubt as to how I felt about the trick she had played on me the previous evening. I then shook her by the hand and boarded the boat train for Southampton, never for one moment expecting to hear from her again. The next contact I had with Miss Salmon came a few months later when I received this unwarranted scurrilous letter, which brings me to the reason why I now need your assistance.

Daphne turned the page and stopped to look at herself in the mirror. She had no desire to find out what Guy expected of her. He had even forgotten in whose room he had been discovered. Yet it was only seconds before her eyes returned to the top of the next page and she began reading again.

No further action would have proved necessary had it not been for the fact that Lieutenant-Colonel Sir Danvers Hamilton took it upon himself to drop a note to my new Commanding Officer, Colonel Forbes, informing him of Miss Salmon's version of the story, which resulted in my being called upon to defend myself in front of a special enquiry made up of my brother officers.

Naturally, I told them exactly what had taken place that night, but because of Colonel Hamilton's continuing influence with the regiment some of them remained unwilling to accept my version of events. Fortunately my mother was able to write to Colonel Forbes a few weeks later to let him know that Miss Salmon had married her long-time lover, Charlie Trumper, and that he was not denying that the child that had been born out of wedlock was his. If the Colonel had not accepted my mother's word, I might have been forced to resign my commission immediately, but fortunately that injustice has been avoided.

However, since then my mother has informed me of your intention to visit India while you are on your honeymoon (on which my sincere congratulations). You are therefore almost certain to come across Colonel Forbes who, I fear, may well refer to this matter, as your name has already been mentioned in connection with the affair.

I therefore beg you to say nothing that might harm my career. In fact, if you felt able to confirm my story, the whole sorry business might finally be laid to rest.

Your friend, as always,

Guy.

Daphne placed the letter back on the dressing-table and began to brush her hair as she considered what should be done next. She did not want to discuss the problem with her mother or father and certainly had no desire to drag Percy into it. She also felt certain that Becky should not be made aware of Trentham's missive until she had thought out exactly what course of action needed to be taken. She was amazed at how short a memory Guy assumed she must have as he distanced himself from reality.

She put down the hairbrush and looked at herself in the mirror before returning to the letter for a second and then a third reading. Eventually she placed the letter back in the envelope and tried to dismiss its contents from her thoughts; but whatever distraction she turned her attention to, Guy's words continued to prey on her mind. It particularly aggravated her that he should imagine she was so gullible.

Suddenly Daphne realised from whom she should seek advice. She picked up the telephone, and after asking the operator for a Chelsea number, was delighted to find the colonel was still at home.

"I was just off to my club, Daphne," he told her. "But do let me know how I can be of help."

"I need to talk to you urgently but it's not something I feel I can discuss over the telephone," she explained.

"I understand," said the colonel, who paused for a moment before adding, "If you're free why don't you join me for lunch at the In and Out? I'll just change my booking to the Ladies Room."

Daphne accepted the offer gratefully, and once she had checked her make-up Hoskins drove her to Piccadilly, arriving at the Naval and Military a few minutes after one.

The colonel was standing in the entrance hall waiting to greet her. "This is a pleasant surprise," said Sir Danvers. "It's not every day I'm seen lunching with a beautiful young woman. It will do my reputation at the club no end of good. I shall wave at every brigadier and general I come across."

The fact that Daphne didn't laugh at the colonel's little aside brought about an immediate change in his demeanour. He took his guest gently by the arm and guided her through to the ladies' luncheon room. Once he had written out their order and handed it to a waitress, Daphne removed Guy's letter from her bag and without another word passed it over to her host.

The colonel fixed the monocle to his good eye and began to read, occasionally looking up at Daphne, only to observe that she hadn't touched the Brown Windsor soup that had been placed in front of her.

"Rum business this," he said, as he placed the letter in its envelope and handed it back to Daphne.

"I agree, but what do you suggest I do?"

"Well, one thing's for certain, my dear, you can't discuss the contents with Charlie or Becky. I also don't see how you can avoid letting Trentham know that should the question of who fathered the child be put to you directly you would feel beholden to tell the truth." He paused and took a sip of his soup. "I swear I'll never speak to Mrs

Trentham again as long as I live," he added without explanation.

Daphne was taken aback by this remark; until that moment she had not been aware that he had ever come across the woman.

"Perhaps we should use our combined efforts to come up with a suitable reply, my dear?" the colonel suggested after some further thought. He broke off to allow a waitress to serve up two helpings of the club's dish of the day.

"If you felt able to help, I would be eternally grateful," said Daphne nervously. "But first I think I ought to tell you everything I know."

The colonel nodded.

"As I'm sure you're only too aware it is I who am to blame for the two of them meeting in the first place . . ."

By the time Daphne had come to the end of her story the colonel's plate was empty.

"I knew most of that already," he admitted as he touched his lips with a napkin. "But you still managed to fill in one or two important gaps for me. I confess I had no idea Trentham was that much of a bounder. Looking back on it, I should have insisted on further corroboration before I agreed to allow his name being put forward for an MC." He rose. "Now, if you'll be good enough to amuse yourself for a few minutes by reading a magazine in the coffee room, I'll see what I can come up with as a first draft."

"I'm sorry to be such a nuisance," said Daphne.

"Don't be silly. I'm flattered that you consider me worthy of your confidence." The colonel stood up and strode off into the writing room.

He didn't reappear for nearly an hour, by which time Daphne was re-reading advertisements for nannies in the *Lady*.

She hastily dropped the magazine back on the table and sat bolt upright in her chair. The colonel handed over the results of his labours, which Daphne studied for several minutes before speaking.

"God knows what Guy would do if I were to write such a letter," she said at last.

"He'll resign his commission, my dear, it's as simple as that. And none too soon, in my opinion." The colonel frowned. "It's high time Trentham was made aware of the consequences of his misdeeds, not least because of the responsibilities he still has to Becky and the child."

"But now that she's happily married that's hardly fair on Charlie," Daphne pleaded.

"Have you seen Daniel lately?" asked the colonel, lowering his voice.

"A few months ago, why?"

"Then you'd better take another look, because there aren't many Trumpers, or Salmons for that matter, who have blond hair, a Roman nose and deep blue eyes. I fear the more obvious replicas are to be found in Ashurst, Berkshire. In any case, Becky and Charlie will eventually have to tell the child the truth or they'll only store up more trouble for themselves at some later date. Send the letter," he said, tapping his fingers on the side table, "that's my advice."

Once Daphne had returned home to Lowndes Square she went straight up to her room. She sat down at her writing desk and, pausing only for a moment, began to copy out the colonel's words.

When she had completed her task Daphne re-read the one paragraph of the colonel's deliberations that she had left out and prayed that his gloomy prognosis would not prove to be accurate.

Once she had completed her own version she tore up the colonel's transcript and rang for Wentworth.

"Just one letter to be posted," was all she said.

The preparations for the wedding became so frantic that once Daphne had passed over the letter to Wentworth she quite forgot about the problems of Guy Trentham. What with selecting the bridesmaids without offending half her family, enduring endless dress fittings that never ran to time, studying seating arrangements so as to be certain that those members of the family who hadn't spoken to each other in years were not placed at the same table – or for that matter in the same pew as each other – and finally having to cope with a future mother-in-law, the dowager marchioness, who, having married off three of her own daughters, always had three opinions to offer on every subject, she felt quite exhausted.

With only a week to go Daphne suggested to Percy that they should pop along to the nearest register office and get the whole thing over with as quickly as possible – and preferably without bothering to tell anyone else.

"Anything you say, old gel," said Percy, who had long ago stopped listening to anyone on the subject of marriage.

On 16 July 1921 Daphne woke at five forty-three feeling drained but by the time she stepped out into the sunshine in Lowndes Square at one forty-five she was exhilarated and actually looking forward to the occasion.

Her father helped her up the steps into an open carriage that her grandmother and mother had travelled in on the day they were married. A little crowd of servants and well-wishers cheered the bride as she began her journey to Westminster, while others waved from the pavement. Officers saluted, toffs blew her a kiss and would-be brides sighed as she passed by.

Daphne, on her father's arm, entered the church by the north door a few minutes after Big Ben had struck two, then proceeded slowly down the aisle to the accompaniment of Mendelssohn's Wedding March. She paused only for a moment before joining Percy, curtseying to the King and Queen, who sat alone in their private pews beside the altar. After all those months of waiting the service seemed over in moments. As the organ struck up "Rejoice, rejoice" and the married couple were bidden to an anteroom to sign the register, Daphne's only reaction was to want to go through the entire ceremony again.

Husband and wife left the church to a thunderous peal

of bells and strolled on through the streets of Westminster in the bright afternoon sun. Once they had arrived at the large marquee that had been set up on the lawn in Vincent Square, they began to welcome their guests.

Trying to have a word with every one of them resulted in Daphne almost failing to sample a piece of her own wedding cake, and no sooner had she taken a bite than the dowager marchioness swept up to announce that if they didn't get on with the speeches they might as well dispense with any hope of sailing on the last tide.

Algernon Fitzpatrick praised the bridesmaids and toasted the bride and groom. Percy made a surprisingly witty and well-received reply. Daphne was then ushered off to 45 Vincent Square, the home of a distant uncle, so that she could change into her going-away outfit.

Once again the crowds flocked out on to the pavement to throw rice and rose petals, while Hoskins waited to despatch the newly-weds off to Southampton.

Thirty minutes later Hoskins was motoring peacefully down the A307 past Kew Gardens, leaving the wedding guests behind them to continue their celebrations without the bride and groom.

"Well, now you're stuck with me for life, Percy Wiltshire," Daphne told her husband.

"That, I suspect, was ordained by our mothers before we even met," said Percy. "Silly, really."

"Silly?"

"Yes. I could have stopped all their plotting years ago, by simply telling them that I never wanted to marry anyone else in the first place."

Daphne was giving the honeymoon serious thought for the first time when Hoskins brought the Rolls to a halt on the dockside a good two hours before the *Mauretania* was due even to turn her pistons. With the help of several porters Hoskins unloaded two trunks from the boot of the car – fourteen having been sent down the previous day – while Daphne and Percy headed towards the gangplank where the ship's purser was awaiting them.

Just as the purser stepped forward to greet the marquess and his bride someone from the crowd shouted, "Good luck, Your Lordship! And I'd like to say on behalf of the missus and myself that the marchioness looks a bit of all right."

They both turned and burst out laughing when they saw Charlie and Becky, still in their wedding outfits, standing among the crowd.

The purser guided the four of them up the gangplank and into the Nelson stateroom, where they found yet another bottle of champagne waiting to be opened.

"How did you manage to get here ahead of us?" asked Daphne.

"Well," said Charlie in a broad Cockney accent, "we may not 'ave a Rolls-Royce, my lady, but we still managed to overtake 'oskins in our little two-seater just the other side of Winchester, didn't we?"

They all laughed except Becky who couldn't take her eyes off the little diamond brooch that looked exquisite on the lapel of Daphne's suit.

Three toots on the foghorn, and the purser suggested that the Trumpers might care to leave the ship, assuming it was not their intention to accompany the Wiltshires to New York.

"See you in a year or so's time," shouted Charlie, as he turned to wave at them from the gangplank.

"By then we will have travelled right round the world, old gel," Percy confided to his wife.

Daphne waved. "Yes, and by the time we get back heaven knows what those two will have been up to."

COLONEL HAMILTON

1920-1922

CHAPTER 16

'm usually good on faces, and the moment I saw the man weighing those potatoes I knew at once that I recognised him. Then I recalled the sign above the shop door. Of course, Trumper, Corporal C. No, he ended up a sergeant, if I remember correctly. And what was his friend called, the one who got the MM? Ah, yes, Prescott, Private T. Explanation of death not altogether satisfactory. Funny the details one's mind considers worthy of retention.

When I arrived back home for lunch I told the memsahib I'd seen Sergeant Trumper again, but she didn't show a great deal of interest until I handed over the fruit and vegetables. It was then that she asked me where I'd bought them. "Trumper's," I told her. She nodded, making a note of the name without further explanation.

The following day I duly instructed the regimental secretary to send Trumper two tickets for the annual dinner and dance, then didn't give the man another thought until I spotted the two of them sitting at the sergeants' table on the night of the ball. I say "the two of them", because Trumper was accompanied by an extremely attractive girl. Yet for most of the evening he seemed to ignore the lady in favour of someone whose name I didn't catch, a young woman I might add who had previously been seated a few places away from me on the top table. When the adjutant asked Elizabeth for a dance I took my chance, I can tell you.

I marched right across the dance floor, aware that half the battalion had their eyes on me, bowed to the lady in question and asked her for the honour. Her name, I discovered, was Miss Salmon, and she danced like an officer's wife. Bright as a button she was too, and gay with it. I just can't imagine what Trumper thought he was up to, and if it had been any of my business I would have told him so.

After the dance was over I took Miss Salmon up to meet Elizabeth, who seemed equally enchanted. Later the memsahib told me that she had learned the girl was engaged to a Captain Trentham of the regiment, who was now serving in India. Trentham, Trentham . . . I remembered that there was a young officer in the battalion by that name – won an MC on the Marne – but there was something else about him that I couldn't immediately recall. Poor girl, I thought, because I had put Elizabeth through the same sort of ordeal when they posted me to Afghanistan in 1882. Lost an eye to those bloody Afghans and nearly lost the only woman I've ever loved at the same time. Still, it's bad form to marry before you're a captain – or after you're a major, for that matter.

On the way home, Elizabeth warned me that she had invited Miss Salmon and Trumper round to Tregunter Road the following morning.

"Why?" I asked.

"It seems they have a proposition to put to you."

They arrived at our little house in Tregunter Road even before the grandfather clock had finished chiming eleven and I settled them down in the drawing room before saying to Trumper, "So what's all this about, Sergeant?" He made no attempt to reply – it was Miss Salmon who turned out to be the spokesman for the two of them. Without a wasted word she set about presenting a most convincing case for my joining their little enterprise, in a non-executive capacity you understand, on a salary of one hundred pounds per annum. Although I didn't consider the proposition was quite up my street, I was touched by their confidence in me and promised I would give their proposal a great deal of thought. Indeed I said I would write to them and let them know my decision in the near future.

Elizabeth fully concurred with my judgment but felt the least I could do was conduct a little field reconnaissance of my own before I decided finally to turn down the offer.

For the next week I made sure I was somewhere in the vicinity of 147 Chelsea Terrace every working day. I quite often sat on a bench opposite the shop, from where without being seen I could watch how they went about their business. I chose different times of the day to carry out my observation, for obvious reasons. Sometimes I would appear first thing in the morning, at others during the busiest hour, then again perhaps later in the afternoon. On one occasion I even watched them close up for the day, when I quickly discovered that Sergeant Trumper was no clock-watcher: Number 147 turned out to be the last shop in the row to close its doors to the public. I don't mind telling you that both Trumper and Miss Salmon made a most favourable impression on me. A rare couple, I told Elizabeth after my final recce.

I had been sounded out some weeks before by the curator of the Imperial War Museum regarding an invitation to become a member of their council, but frankly Trumper's offer was the only other approach I'd received since hanging up my spurs the previous year. As the curator had made no reference to remuneration I assumed there wasn't any, and from the recent council papers they had sent me to browse through it looked as if their demands wouldn't exercise my time for more than about an hour a week.

After considerable soul-searching, a chat with Miss Daphne Harcourt-Browne and encouraging noises from Elizabeth – who didn't take to having me hanging about the house all hours of the day – I dropped Miss Salmon a note to let them know I was their man.

The following morning I discovered exactly what I had let myself in for when the aforementioned lady reappeared in Tregunter Road to brief me on my first assignment. Jolly good she was too, as thorough as any staff officer I ever had under my command, I can tell you.

Becky – she had told me that I should stop calling her "Miss Salmon" now that we were "partners" – said that I should treat our first visit to Child's of Fleet Street as a "dry run", because the fish she really wanted to land wasn't being lined up until the following week. That was when we would "move in for the kill". She kept using expressions I simply couldn't make head or tail of.

I can tell you that I came out in a muck sweat on the morning of our meeting with that first bank, and if the truth be known I nearly pulled out of the front line even before the order had been given to charge. Had it not been for the sight of those two expectant young faces waiting for me outside the bank I swear I might have withdrawn from the whole campaign.

Well, despite my misgivings, we walked out of the bank less than an hour later having successfully carried out our first sortie, and I think I can safely say, in all honesty, that I didn't let the side down. Not that I thought a lot of Hadlow, who struck me as an odd sort of cove, but then the Buffs were never what one might describe as a first-class outfit. More to the point, the damn man had never seen the whites of their eyes, which in my opinion always sorts a fellow out.

From that moment I kept a close eye on Trumper's activities, insisting on a weekly meeting at the shop so I could keep myself up to date on what was happening. I even felt able to offer the odd word of advice or encouragement from time to time. A fellow doesn't like to accept remuneration unless he feels he's pulling his weight.

To begin with everything seemed to be going swimmingly; in fact the quarterly accounts were downright impressive. Then late in May of 1920 Trumper requested a private meeting. I knew he had got his eyes fixed on another establishment in Chelsea Terrace and the account was a bit stretched so I assumed that was what he wanted to discuss with me.

I agreed to visit Trumper at his flat, as he never appeared completely at ease whenever I invited him round to my club or to Tregunter Road. When I arrived that evening I found him in quite a state, and assumed something must have been troubling him at one of our three establishments, but he assured me that was not the case.

"Well, out with it then, Trumper," I said.

"It's not that easy, to be honest, sir," he replied, so I remained silent in the hope that it might help him relax and get whatever it was off his chest.

"It's Becky, sir," he blurted out eventually.

"First-class girl," I assured him.

"Yes, sir, I agree. But I'm afraid she's pregnant."

I confess that I had already learned this news some days before from Becky herself but as I had given the lady my word not to tell anyone, including Charlie, I feigned surprise. Although I realise times have changed, I knew Becky had been strictly brought up and in any case she had never struck me as that sort of girl, if you know what I mean.

"Of course, you'll want to know who the father is," Charlie added.

"I had assumed –" I began, but Charlie immediately shook his head.

"Not me," he said. "I only wish it was. Then at least I could marry her and wouldn't have to bother you with the problem."

"Then who is the culprit?" I asked.

He hesitated before saying, "Guy Trentham, sir."

"Captain Trentham? But he's in India, if I remember correctly."

"That's right, sir. And I've had the devil's own job persuading Becky to write and let him know what's happened; says it would only ruin his career."

"But if she doesn't tell him, it could well ruin her whole life," I suggested testily. "Just imagine the stigma of being an unmarried mother, not to mention having to bring up an illegitimate child. In any case, Trentham's bound to find out eventually, don't you know."

"He may never learn the truth from Becky, and I certainly don't have the sort of influence that would make him do the decent thing."

"Are you holding anything else back about Trentham that I ought to know about, Trumper?"

"No, sir."

Trumper replied a little too quickly for me to be totally convinced.

"Then you'll have to leave the problem of Trentham to me," I told him. "Meanwhile you get on with running the shops. But be sure to let me know the moment it's all out in the open so I don't go around looking as if I haven't a clue what's going on." I rose to leave.

"The whole world will know before much longer," Charlie said.

I had said "leave the problem to me" without the slightest idea of what I was going to do about it, but when I had returned home that night I discussed the whole affair with Elizabeth. She advised me to have a chat with Daphne, who she felt confident would know considerably more about what was going on than Charlie did. I suspected she was right.

Elizabeth and I duly invited Daphne to tea at Tregunter Road a couple of days later. She confirmed everything Charlie had said and was also able to fill in one or two missing pieces of the jigsaw.

In Daphne's opinion Trentham had been Becky's first serious romance, and certainly to her knowledge Becky had never slept with any other man before they had met, and only once with Trentham. Captain Trentham, she assured us, was unable to boast the same blameless reputation.

The rest of her news did not augur well for a simple solution, as it turned out that Guy's mother could not be relied on to insist that her son do the decent thing by Becky.

"But what about Trentham's father?" I asked. "Do you think I should have a word with him? Although we were in the same regiment we were never in the same battalion, don't you know."

"He's the only member of that family I really care for," Daphne admitted. "He's the MP for Berkshire West, a Liberal."

"Then that has to be my approach route," I replied. "I can't abide the man's politics, but that won't stop him from knowing the difference between right and wrong."

Yet another letter sent on club notepaper elicited an immediate reply from the major, inviting me to drinks at Chester Square the following Monday.

I arrived punctually at six, and was taken into the drawing room where I was greeted by a quite charming lady who introduced herself as Mrs Trentham. She was not at all what I expected after Daphne's description; in fact she was a rather handsome woman. She was profuse in her apologies: it seemed that her husband had been held up at the House of Commons by a running three-line whip, which even I knew meant he was unable to leave the Palace of Westminster on pain of death. I made an instant decision – wrongly I realise in retrospect – that this matter couldn't wait a moment longer and I must relay my message to the major through his wife.

"I find this is all rather embarrassing actually," I began.

"Do feel free to speak quite openly, Colonel. I can assure you that I am fully in my husband's confidence. We have no secrets from each other."

"Well, to be frank with you, Mrs Trentham, the matter I wish to touch on concerns your son Guy."

"I see," was all she said.

"And his fiancée, Miss Salmon."

"She is not, and never has been, his fiancée," said Mrs Trentham, her voice revealing a sudden edge.

"But I was given to understand –"

"That promises were made to Miss Salmon by my son? I can assure you, Colonel, that nothing could be further from the truth."

Slightly taken aback, I was unable to think of a diplomatic way of letting the lady know the real purpose behind my wanting to see her husband. So I simply said, "Whatever promises were or were not made, madam, I do feel that you and your husband should be aware that Miss Salmon is expecting a child."

"And what has that to do with me?" Mrs Trentham stared directly at me with no fear showing in her eyes.

"Simply that your son is undoubtedly the father."

"We only have her word for that, Colonel."

"That, madam, was unworthy of you," I told her. "I know Miss Salmon to be a thoroughly decent and honest girl. And in any case, if it were not your son, who else could it have possibly been?"

"Heaven knows," said Mrs Trentham. "Any number of men, I would have thought, judging by her reputation. After all, her father was an immigrant."

"So was the King's grandfather, madam," I reminded her. "But he still would have known how to conduct himself had he been faced with the same predicament."

"I'm sure I don't know what you mean, Colonel."

"I mean, madam, that your son must either marry Miss Salmon or at least resign from the regiment and make suitable arrangements to see the child is properly provided for."

"It seems I must make it clear to you once again, Colonel, that this sad state of affairs has nothing whatsoever to do with my son. I can assure you that Guy stopped seeing the girl some months before he sailed for India."

"I know that is not the case, madam, because —"

"Do you, Colonel? Then I must ask what exactly this whole business has to do with you in the first place?"

"Simply that Miss Salmon and Mr Trumper are both colleagues of mine," I explained.

"I see," she said. "Then I suspect you will not have to look much further to discover who is the real father."

"Madam, that was also uncalled for. Charlie Trumper is not —"

"I cannot see any purpose in continuing this conversation, Colonel," Mrs Trentham said, rising from her chair. She began to walk towards the door, not even bothering to glance in my direction. "I must warn you, Colonel, that should I hear this slander repeated in any quarter I shall not hesitate to instruct solicitors to take the necessary action to defend my son's good reputation."

Although shaken, I followed her into the hall, determined to see that the matter was not allowed to rest there. I now felt Major Trentham was my only hope. As Mrs Trentham opened the front door to show me out I said firmly, "May I presume, madam, that you will recount this conversation faithfully to your husband?"

"You may presume nothing, Colonel," were her final words as the front door was slammed in my face. The last occasion I received such treatment from a lady had been in Rangoon, and I'm bound to say that the girl in question had considerably more reason to be aggrieved.

When I repeated the conversation to Elizabeth – as accurately as I could recall – my wife pointed out to me in that clear, concise way of hers that I had been left with only three choices. The first was to write to Captain Trentham direct and demand he do the decent thing, the second would be to inform his commanding officer of everything I knew.

"And the third?" I asked.

"Never to refer to the subject again."

I considered her words carefully, and chose the middle course, dropping a note to Ralph Forbes – acquainting him with the facts, as I knew them – a first-class fellow who had succeeded me as commanding officer. I chose my words most judiciously, aware that if Mrs Trentham were to carry out her threat any legal action she took could only bring the regiment's good name into disrepute perhaps even ridicule. However, I did at the same time decide to keep a fatherly eye on Becky, as she now seemed to be burning the candle at both ends, not to mention in the middle. After all, the girl was trying to prepare for her exams, as well as act as an unpaid secretary and accountant to a thriving little business, while everyone who passed her in the street must have known that it could only be a matter of weeks before she was due to give birth.

As those weeks passed, it worried me that nothing seemed to be happening on the Trentham front despite the fact that I had received a reply from Forbes assuring me that he had set up a panel of enquiry. Certainly when I enquired further of Daphne or Charlie neither of them seemed to be any better informed than I was.

It was in mid October that year that Daniel George was born and I was touched that Becky invited me to be a godparent, along with Bob Makins and Daphne. I was even more delighted when I learned from Becky that she and Charlie were to be married the following week. It wouldn't stop wagging tongues, of course, but at least the child would be considered legitimate in the eyes of the law.

Elizabeth and I, along with Daphne, Percy, Mrs Salmon, Miss Roach and Bob Makins, attended the simple civic service at Chelsea Register Office, followed by a boisterous reception in Charlie's flat above the shop.

I began to think that perhaps everything had worked out for the best until some months later Daphne telephoned, asking to see me urgently. I took her to lunch at the club, where she produced a letter that she had received from Captain Trentham that morning. As I read his words I became painfully aware that Mrs Trentham must have learned of my own letter to Forbes warning him of the consequences of a breach of promise suit and immediately taken matters into her own hands. I felt the time had come to let her son know that he had not got away with it.

I left my guest to have coffee while I retired to the writing room and with the help of a stiff brandy began to compose an even stiffer letter, I can tell you. I felt my final effort covered all the necessary points in as diplomatic and realistic a way as was possible given the circumstances. Daphne thanked me, and promised she would send the letter on to Trentham verbatim.

I didn't have another conversation with her again until we met at her wedding a month later, and that was hardly an appropriate time to broach the subject of Captain Trentham.

After the service was over I strolled round to Vincent Square where the reception was being held. I kept a wary eye out for Mrs Trentham who I assumed had also been invited. I had no desire to hold a second conversation with that particular lady.

I was, however, delighted to catch up with Charlie and Becky in the large marquee that had been erected especially for the occasion. I have never seen the girl looking more radiant, and Charlie could almost have been described as suave standing there in his morning coat, grey cravat and topper. The fine half-hunter that hung from his waistcoat turned out to be a wedding gift from Becky, left to her by her father, she explained, although the rest of the outfit, Charlie reported, had to be returned to Moss Bros first thing the following morning.

"Has the time not come, Charlie," I suggested, "for you to purchase a morning coat of your own? After all, there are likely to be considerably more of these occasions in the future."

"Certainly not," he replied. "That would only be a waste of good money."

"May I enquire why?" I asked. "Surely the cost of a —"

"Because it is my intention to purchase a tailor's shop of my own," he interjected. "I've had my eye on Number 143 for some considerable time, and I hear from Mr Crowther that it might come on the market at any moment."

I couldn't argue with this piece of logic, although his next question baffled me completely.

"Have you ever heard of Marshall Field, Colonel?"

"Was he in the regiment?" I asked, racking my brain.

"No, he was not," replied Charlie with a grin. "Marshall Field is a department store in Chicago, where you can purchase anything you could ever want for the rest of your life. What's more they have two million square feet of selling space all under one roof."

I couldn't think of a more ghastly concept, but I

didn't attempt to stop the boy's enthusiastic flow. "The building takes up an entire block," he informed me. "Can you imagine a store that has twenty-eight entrances? According to the advertisements there's nothing you can't buy, from an automobile to an apple, and they have twenty-four varieties of both. They've revolutionised retailing in the States by being the first store to give full credit facilities. They also claim that if they don't have it they'll get it for you within a week. Field's motto is: 'Give the lady what she wants'."

"Are you suggesting that we should purchase Marshall Field in exchange for 147 Chelsea Terrace?" I asked ingenuously.

"Not immediately, Colonel. But if in time I was able to get my hands on every shop in Chelsea Terrace we could then carry out the same operation in London, and perhaps even remove the first line from their current cheeky advertisement."

I knew I was being set up so I duly asked what the line proclaimed.

"The biggest store in the world," Charlie replied.

"And how do *you* feel about all this?" I asked, turning my attention to Becky.

"In Charlie's case," she replied, "it would have to be the biggest barrow in the world."

CHAPTER 17

T he first annual general meeting of Trumper's
was held above the fruit and vegetable shop
in the front room of 147 Chelsea Terrace. The
colonel, Charlie and Becky sat round a small
trestle table, not quite sure how to get things
started until the colonel opened the proceedings.

"I know there are only three of us, but I still
consider all our future meetings should be conducted in a
professional manner." Charlie raised his eyebrows but made
no attempt to stop the colonel's flow. "I have therefore taken
the liberty," he began, "of setting out an agenda. Otherwise
I find one can so easily forget to raise quite important issues."
The colonel proceeded to pass both his colleagues a sheet of
paper with five items neatly written in his own hand. "To
that end the first item to come under discussion is headed
'financial report' and I'll begin by asking Becky to let us know
how she sees the current fiscal position."

Becky had carefully written out her report word for
word, having the previous month purchased two large
leather-bound books, one red, one blue, from the stationer's
at 137 and for the past fortnight having risen only minutes
after Charlie had left for Covent Garden in order to be sure
she could answer any questions that might arise at their first
meeting. She opened up the cover of the red book and began
to read slowly, occasionally referring to the blue book, which
was just as large and authoritative-looking. This had the
single word "Accounts" stamped in gold on the outside.

"In the year ending 31 December 1921 we showed a

turnover on the seven shops of one thousand three hundred and twelve pounds and four shillings, on which we declared a profit of two hundred and nineteen pounds eleven shillings, showing seventeen per cent profit on turnover. Our debt at the bank currently stands at seven hundred and seventy-one pounds, which includes our tax liability for the year, but the value of the seven shops remains in the books at one thousand two hundred and ninety pounds, which is the exact price we paid for them. This therefore does not reflect their current market value.

"I have made a breakdown of the figures on each of the shops for your consideration," said Becky, handing copies of her efforts to Charlie and the colonel, both of whom studied them carefully for several minutes before either spoke.

"Grocery is still our number one earner, I see," said the colonel, as he ran his monocle down the profit and loss column. "Hardware is only just breaking even, and the tailor's is actually eating into our profits."

"Yes," said Charlie. "I met up with a right holy friar when I bought that one."

"Holy friar?" said the colonel, perplexed.

"Liar," said Becky, not looking up from her book.

"Afraid so," said Charlie. "You see, I paid through the nose for the freehold, too much for the stock, then got myself landed with poor staff who weren't properly trained. But things have taken a turn for the better since Major Arnold took over."

The colonel smiled at the knowledge that the appointment of one of his former staff officers had been such an immediate success. Tom Arnold had returned to Savile Row soon after the war only to find that his old job as under-manager at Hawkes had been taken up by someone who had been demobbed a few months earlier than himself, and he was therefore expected to be satisfied with the status of senior assistant. He wasn't. When the colonel told him there just might be an opening for him at Trumper's, Arnold had jumped at the opportunity.

"I'm bound to say," said Becky, studying the figures, "that people seem to have a totally different moral attitude to paying their tailor than they would ever consider applying to any other tradesman. Just look at the debtors' column."

"Agreed," said Charlie. "And I fear we won't be able to show a great deal of improvement on that until Major Arnold has managed to find replacements for at least three members of his present staff. I don't expect him to declare a profit during the next six months, although I would hope they might be able to break even by the end of the third quarter."

"Good," said the colonel. "Now what about hardware? I see Number 129 declared a decent enough profit last year, so why should the figures have fallen back so badly this? They're down over sixty pounds on 1920, declaring a loss for the first time."

"I'm afraid there's a simple enough explanation," said Becky. "The money was stolen."

"Stolen?"

"I fear so," replied Charlie. "Becky began to notice as long ago as October of last year that the weekly receipts were falling, at first only by a little but then the amount grew as a pattern began to evolve."

"Have we discovered who the culprit is?"

"Yes, that was simple enough. We switched Bob Makins from grocery when one of the staff at hardware was on holiday, and he spotted the tea leaf in no time."

"Stop it, Charlie," said Becky. "Sorry, Colonel, thief."

"It turned out the manager, Reg Larkins, has a gambling problem," Charlie continued, "and was using our money to cover his debts. The bigger those debts became the more he needed to steal."

"You sacked Larkins, of course," said the colonel.

"The same day," said Charlie. "He turned rather nasty at the time and tried to deny that he'd ever taken a penny. But we haven't heard a word from him since and in the last three weeks we've even begun to show a small profit again.

However, I'm still looking for a new manager to take over as soon as possible. I've got my eye on a young man who works at Cudsons just off the Charing Cross Road."

"Good," said the colonel. "That covers last year's problems, Charlie, so now you can frighten us with your plans for the future."

Charlie opened the smart new leather case that Becky had given him on 20 January and took out the latest report from John D. Wood. He cleared his throat theatrically and Becky had to put a hand to her mouth to stifle a laugh.

"Mr Crowther," began Charlie, "has prepared a comprehensive survey of all the properties in Chelsea Terrace."

"For which, incidentally, he has charged us ten guineas," said Becky, checking the accounts book.

"I have no quarrel with that, if it turns out to be a good investment," said the colonel.

"It already has," said Charlie. He handed over copies of Crowther's report. "As you both already know, there are thirty-six shops in Chelsea Terrace, of which we currently own seven. In Crowther's opinion a further five could well become available during the next twelve months. However, as he points out, all the shopkeepers in Chelsea Terrace are now only too aware of my role as a buyer, which doesn't exactly help keep the price down."

"I suppose that was bound to happen sooner or later."

"I agree, Colonel," said Charlie, "but it's still far sooner than I'd hoped for. In fact, Syd Wrexall, the chairman of the Shops Committee, is becoming quite wary of us."

"Why Mr Wrexall in particular?" asked the colonel.

"He's the publican who owns the Musketeer on the other corner of Chelsea Terrace. He's started telling his customers that it's my long-term aim to buy up all the property in the block and drive out the small shopkeepers."

"He has a point," said Becky.

"Maybe, but I never expected him to form a co-operative with the sole purpose of stopping me purchasing certain properties. I was rather hoping to get my hands on the Musketeer itself in time but whenever the subject comes up he just says, 'Over my dead body'."

"That comes as rather a blow," said the colonel.

"Not at all," said Charlie. "No one can expect to go through life without facing a moment of crisis. The secret will be spotting Wrexall's when it comes and then moving in quickly. But it does mean for the time being that I'm occasionally going to have to pay over the odds if a shop owner decides the time has come to sell."

"Not a lot we can do about that I suspect," said the colonel.

"Except call their bluff from time to time," said Charlie.

"Call their bluff? I'm not sure I catch your drift."

"Well, we've had an approach from two shops recently with an interest in disposing of their freehold and I turned them both down out of hand."

"Why?"

"Simply because they were demanding such outrageous prices, not to mention Becky nagging me about our present overdraft."

"And have they reconsidered their position?"

"Yes and no," said Charlie. "One has already come back with a far more realistic demand, while the other is still holding out for his original price."

"Who is holding out?"

"Cuthbert's, Number 101, the wine and spirits merchant. But there's no need to make any sort of move in that direction for the time being, because Crowther says that Mr Cuthbert, the owner, has recently been looking at several properties in Pimlico, and he'll be able to keep us informed of any progress on that front. We can then make a sensible offer the moment Cuthbert commits himself."

"Well done, Crowther I say. By the way, where do you pick up all your information?" the colonel asked.

"Mr Bales the newsagent, and Syd Wrexall himself."

"But I thought you said Wrexall wasn't proving that helpful."

"He isn't," said Charlie, "but he'll still offer his opinion on any subject for the price of a pint, so Bob Makins has become a regular and learned never to complain about being short-measured. I even get a copy of the Shops Committee minutes before they do."

The colonel laughed. "And what about the auctioneers at Number 1? Have we still got our eye on them?"

"We most certainly have, Colonel. Mr Fothergill, the proprietor, continues to go deeper and deeper into debt, having had another bad year. But somehow he manages to keep his head above water, if only just, but I anticipate he will finally go under some time next year, at the latest the year after, when I will be standing on the quayside waiting to throw him a lifeline. Especially if Becky feels she is ready to leave Sotheby's by then."

"I'm still learning so much," confessed Becky. "I'd rather like to stay put for as long as I can. I've completed a year in Old Masters," she added, "and now I'm trying to get myself moved to Modern, or Impressionist as they've started calling that department. You see, I still feel I need to gain as much experience as possible before they work out what I'm up to. I attend every auction I can, from silverware to old books, but I'd be far happier if we could leave Number 1 until the last possible moment."

"But if Fothergill does go under for a third time, Becky, you're our lifeboat. So what if the shop were suddenly to come on the market?"

"I could just about handle it, I suppose. I've already got my eye on the man who ought to be our general manager. Simon Matthews. He's been with Sotheby's for the past twelve years and is disenchanted at being passed over once too often. There's also a bright young trainee who's been around for about three years who I think will be the pick of the next generation of auctioneers. He's only two years younger than the chairman's son so he might be only too happy to join us if we were able to make him an attractive offer."

"On the other hand, it may well suit us for Becky to

remain at Sotheby's for as long as possible," said Charlie. "Because Mr Crowther has identified a further problem we're going to have to face in the near future."

"Namely?" queried the colonel.

"On page nine of his report, Crowther points out that Numbers 25 to 99, a block of thirty-seven flats bang in the middle of Chelsea Terrace – one of which Daphne and Becky shared until a couple of years ago – may well come on the market in the not too distant future. They're currently owned by a charitable trust who are no longer satisfied with the return they receive on their investment, and Crowther says they're considering disposing of them. Now, remembering our long-term plan, it might be wise to purchase the block as soon as possible rather than risk waiting for years when we would have to pay a far higher price or, worse, never be able to get hold of them at all."

"Thirty-eight flats," said the colonel. "Hm, how much is Crowther expecting them to fetch?"

"His guess would be around the two-thousand-pound mark; they're currently only showing an income of two hundred and ten pounds a year and what with repairs and maintenance they're probably not even declaring a profit. If the property does come on the market, and we're able to afford them, Crowther also recommends that we only issue ten-year leases in future, and try to place any empty flats with staff from embassies or foreign visitors, who never make any fuss about having to move at a moment's notice."

"So the profit on the shops would end up having to pay for the flats," said Becky.

"I'm afraid so," said Charlie. "But with any luck it would only take me a couple of years, three at the outside, before I could have them showing a profit. Mind you, if the charity commissioners are involved, the paperwork could take that long."

"Nevertheless, remembering our current overdraft limit a demand on our resources like that may well require another lunch with Hadlow," said the colonel. "Still, I can see if we need to get hold of those flats I'm left with little choice. Might even take the opportunity to bump into Chubby Duckworth at the club and drop a word in his ear." The colonel paused. "To be fair to Hadlow, he's also come up with a couple of good ideas himself, both of which I feel are worthy of our consideration, and accordingly I have placed them next on the agenda."

Becky stopped writing and looked up.

"Let me begin by saying that Hadlow is most satisfied with the way our first two years' figures have worked out, but nevertheless he feels strongly that because of the state of our overdraft and for taxation reasons we should stop being a partnership and form ourselves into a company."

"Why?" asked Charlie. "What advantage could there possibly be in that?"

"It's the new Finance Bill that has just gone through the Commons," explained Becky. "The change in the tax laws could well be used to our advantage, because at the moment we're trading as seven different businesses and taxed accordingly, whereas if we were to put all our shops into one company we could run the losses of, say, the tailor's shop and hardware against any gains made by the grocery store and the butcher's, and thus reduce our tax burden. It could be especially beneficial in a bad year."

"That all makes good sense to me," said Charlie. "So let's go ahead and do it."

"Well, it's not quite that easy," said the colonel, placing his monocle to his good eye. "To start with, if we were to become a company Mr Hadlow is advising us to appoint some new directors to cover those areas in which we currently have little or no professional experience."

"Why would Hadlow expect us to do that?" asked Charlie sharply. "We've never needed anyone else to interfere with our business before."

"Because we're growing so rapidly, Charlie. We may need other people to advise us in the future, who can offer expertise we simply don't at present possess. The purchasing of the flats is a good example."

"But we have Mr Crowther for that."

"And perhaps he would feel a greater commitment to our cause if he were on the board." Charlie frowned. "I can well understand how you feel," continued the colonel. "It's your show, and you believe you don't need any outsiders to tell you how to run Trumper's. Well, even if we did form a company it would still be your show, because all the shares would be lodged in the names of you and Becky, and any assets would therefore remain totally under your control. But you would have the added advantage of non-executive directors to call on for advice."

"And to spend our money and overrule our decisions," said Charlie. "I just don't like the idea of outsiders telling me what to do."

"It wouldn't necessarily work like that," said Becky.

"I'm not convinced it will work at all."

"Charlie, you should listen to yourself sometimes. You're beginning to sound like a Luddite."

"Perhaps we should take a vote," said the colonel, trying to calm things down. "Just to see where we all stand."

"Vote? What on? Why? The shops belong to me."

Becky looked up. "To both of us, Charlie, and the colonel has more than earned his right to give an opinion."

"I'm sorry, Colonel, I didn't mean –"

"I know you didn't, Charlie, but Becky's right. If you want to realise your long-term aims you'll undoubtedly need some outside help. It just won't be possible to achieve such a dream all on your own."

"And it will with outside interferers?"

"Think of them as inside helpers," said the colonel.

"So what are we voting on?" asked Charlie touchily.

"Well," began Becky, "someone should propose a resolution that we turn ourselves into a company. If that is passed we could then invite the colonel to be chairman, who can in turn appoint you as managing director and myself as secretary. I think Mr Crowther should also be invited to join the board, along with a representative from the bank."

"I can see you've given this a lot of thought," said Charlie.

"That was my side of the bargain, if you remember our original deal correctly, Mr Trumper," Becky replied.

"We're not Marks and Spencer, you know."

"Not yet," said the colonel, with a smile. "Remember it's you, Charlie, who has taught us to think like this."

"I knew somehow it would all end up being my fault."

"So I propose the resolution that we form a company," said Becky. "Those in favour?"

Becky and the colonel each placed a hand in the air, and a few seconds later Charlie reluctantly raised his and added, "Now what?"

"My second proposal," said Becky, "is that Lieutenant-Colonel Sir Danvers Hamilton should be our first chairman."

This time Charlie's hand shot straight up.

"Thank you," said the colonel. "And my first action as chairman is to appoint Mr Trumper as managing director and Mrs Trumper as company secretary. And with your permission I shall approach Mr Crowther, and I think also Mr Hadlow, with a view to asking them to join the board."

"Agreed," said Becky, who was scribbling furiously in the minutes book as she tried to keep up.

"Any other business?" asked the colonel.

"May I suggest, Mr Chairman," said Becky – the colonel couldn't resist a smile – "that we fix a date for our first monthly meeting of the full board?"

"Any time suits me," said Charlie. "Because one thing's for certain, we won't be able to get them all round this table at any one time, unless of course you propose to hold the meetings at four thirty in the morning. At least that way we might find out who the real workers are."

The colonel laughed. "Well, that's another way you could guarantee that all your own resolutions are passed without us ever finding out, Charlie. But I must warn you, one will no longer constitute a quorum."

"A quorum?"

"The minimum number of people needed to pass a resolution," explained Becky.

"That used to be just me," said Charlie wistfully.

"That was probably true of Mr Marks before he met Mr Spencer," said the colonel, "so let's settle on our next meeting being a month today."

Becky and Charlie nodded.

"Now if there is no other business I will declare the meeting closed."

"There is," said Becky, "but I don't think such information should be minuted."

"The floor's all yours," said the chairman, looking puzzled.

Becky stretched across the table and took Charlie's hand. "It comes under miscellaneous expenses," she said. "You see, I'm going to have another baby."

For once Charlie was speechless. It was the colonel who eventually asked if there were a bottle of champagne anywhere near at hand.

"I'm afraid not," said Becky. "Charlie won't let me buy anything from wine and spirits until we own the shop."

"Quite understandably," said the colonel. "Then we shall just have to walk round to my place," he added, rising from his seat and picking up his umbrella. "That way Elizabeth can join the celebration. I declare the meeting closed."

A few moments later the three of them stepped out on to Chelsea Terrace just as the postman was entering the shop. Seeing Becky he handed her a letter.

"It can only have come from Daphne with all those stamps," she told them as she ripped the envelope open and began reading its contents.

"Come on, then, what's she been up to?" asked Charlie, as they walked towards Tregunter Road.

"She's covered America and China, and as far as I can tell India's next," Becky announced. "She's also put on half a stone and met a Mr Calvin Coolidge, whoever he is."

"The Vice-President of the United States," said Charlie.

"Is that so? And they still hope to be home sometime in August, so it won't be that long before we are able to learn everything firsthand." Becky looked up to discover that only the colonel was still by her side. "Where's Charlie?" They both turned round to see him staring up at a small town house that had a "For Sale" sign attached to the wall.

They walked back towards him. "What do you think?" he asked, continuing to stare at the property.

"What do you mean, 'what do I think'?"

"I suspect, my dear, what Charlie is enquiring of you is your opinion of the house."

Becky stared up at the little house that was on three floors and the front was covered in Virginia creeper.

"It's wonderful, quite wonderful."

"It's better than that," said Charlie, placing his thumbs in his waistcoat pockets. "It's ours, and also ideal for someone with a wife and three children who is the managing director of an expanding business in Chelsea."

"But I don't have a second child yet, let alone a third."

"Just planning ahead," said Charlie. "Something you taught me."

"But can we afford it?"

"No, of course we can't," he said. "But I'm confident that the value of property will soon be going up in this area, once people realise they will have their own department store within walking distance. In any case, it's too late now, because I put down the deposit this morning." He placed a hand in his jacket pocket and removed a key.

"But why didn't you consult me first?" asked Becky.

"Because I knew you'd only say we couldn't afford it, as you did with the second, third, fourth, fifth and every subsequent shop."

He walked towards the front door with Becky still a yard behind him.

"But —"

"I'll leave you two to sort things out," said the colonel. "Come over to my place and have that glass of champagne just as soon as you've finished looking over your new home."

The colonel continued on down Tregunter Road, swinging his umbrella in the morning sun, pleased with himself and the world, arriving back just in time for his first whisky of the day.

He imparted all his news to Elizabeth, who had many more questions about the baby and the house than about the present state of the company accounts or her husband's appointment as chairman. Having acquitted himself as best he could, the colonel asked his manservant to place a bottle of champagne in a bucket of ice. He then retired to his study to check through the morning mail while he awaited the Trumpers' arrival.

There were three letters unopened on his desk: a bill from his tailor — which reminded him of Becky's strictures on such matters — an invitation to the Ashburton Shield to be held at Bisley, an annual event he always enjoyed, and a letter from Daphne, which he rather expected might simply repeat the news that Becky had already relayed to him.

The envelope was postmarked Delhi. The colonel slit it open in anticipation. Daphne dutifully repeated how much she was enjoying the trip, but failed to mention her weight problem. She did, however, go on to say that she had some distressing news to impart concerning Guy Trentham. She wrote that while they were staying in Poona, Percy had come across him one evening at the officers' club dressed in civilian clothes. He had lost so much weight that her husband hardly recognised him. He informed Percy that he had been forced to resign his commission and there was only one person to blame for his downfall: a corporal who had lied about him in the past, and was happy to associate with known criminals. Guy was claiming that he had even caught the man stealing himself. Once he was back in England Trentham intended to . . .

The front door bell rang.

"Can you answer it, Danvers?" Elizabeth said, leaning over the banisters. "I'm upstairs arranging the flowers."

The colonel was still seething with anger when he opened the front door to find Charlie and Becky waiting on the top step in anticipation. He must have looked surprised to see them because Becky had to say, "Champagne, Chairman. Or have you already forgotten my physical state?"

"Ah, yes, sorry. My thoughts were some distance away." The colonel stuffed Daphne's letter into his jacket pocket. "The champagne should be at the perfect temperature by now," he added, as he ushered his guests through to the drawing room.

"Two and a quarter Trumpers have arrived," he barked back up the stairs to his wife.

CHAPTER 18

It always amused the colonel to watch Charlie spending so much of his time running from shop to shop, trying to keep a close eye on all his staff, while also attempting to concentrate his energy on any establishment that wasn't showing a worthwhile return. But whatever the various problems he faced, the colonel was only too aware that Charlie couldn't resist a spell of serving at the fruit and vegetable shop, which remained his pride and joy. Coat off, sleeves rolled up and Cockney accent at its broadest, Charlie was allowed an hour a day by Bob Makins to pretend he was back on the corner of Whitechapel Road peddling his wares from Granpa's barrow.

"'alf a pound of tomatoes, some runner beans, and your usual pound of carrots, Mrs Symonds, if I remember correctly."

"Thank you so much, Mr Trumper. And how's Mrs Trumper?"

"Never better."

"And when's the baby expected?"

"In about three months, the doctor thinks."

"Don't see you serving in the shop so much nowadays."

"Only when I know the important customers are around, my luv," said Charlie. "After all, you were one of my first."

"I was indeed. So have you signed the deal on the flats yet, Mr Trumper?"

Charlie stared at Mrs Symonds as he handed back her change, unable to hide his surprise. "The flats?"

"Yes, you know, Mr Trumper. Numbers 25 to 99."

"Why do you ask, Mrs Symonds?"

"Because you're not the only person who's showing an interest in them."

"How do you know that?"

"I know because I saw a young man holding a bunch of keys waiting outside the building for a client last Sunday morning."

Charlie recalled that the Symondses lived in a house on the far side of the terrace immediately opposite the main entrance to the flats.

"And did you recognise them?"

"No. I watched a car draw up but then my husband seemed to think his breakfast was more important than me being nosey, so I didn't see who it was who got out."

Charlie continued to stare at Mrs Symonds as she picked up her bag, waved a cheery goodbye and walked out of the shop.

Despite Mrs Symonds's bombshell and Syd Wrexall's efforts to contain him, Charlie went about plotting his next acquisition. Through the combination of Major Arnold's diligence, Mr Crowther's inside knowledge and Mr Hadlow's loans, by late July Charlie had secured the freehold on another shop in the terrace – Number 39, women's clothes. At the August board meeting Becky recommended that Major Arnold be promoted to deputy managing director of the company, with the task of keeping a watching brief on everything that was taking place in Chelsea Terrace.

Charlie had desperately needed an extra pair of eyes and ears for some time, and with Becky still working at Sotheby's during the day, Arnold had begun to fill that role to perfection. The colonel was delighted to ask Becky to minute the confirmation of the major's appointment. The monthly meeting continued very smoothly until the colonel asked, "Any other business?"

"Yes," said Charlie. "What's happening about the flats?"

"I put in a bid of two thousand pounds as instructed," said Crowther. "The agent said they would recommend their clients should accept the offer, but to date I've been unable to close the deal."

"Why?" asked Charlie.

"Because Savill's rang back this morning to let me know that they have received another offer far in excess of what they had anticipated for this particular piece of property. They thought I might want to alert the board to the present situation."

"They were right about that," said Charlie. "But how much is this other offer? That's what I want to know."

"Two thousand five hundred pounds," said Crowther.

It was several moments before anyone round the board-room table offered an opinion.

"How on earth can they hope to show a return on that kind of investment?" Hadlow eventually asked.

"They can't," said Crowther.

"Offer them three thousand pounds."

"What did you say?" said the chairman, as they all turned to face Charlie.

"Offer them three thousand," Charlie repeated.

"But Charlie, we agreed that two thousand was a high enough price only a few weeks ago," Becky pointed out. "How can the flats suddenly be worth so much more?"

"They're worth whatever someone is willing to pay for them," Charlie replied. "So we've been left with no choice."

"But Mr Trumper –" began Hadlow.

"If we end up with the rest of the block but then fail to get our hands on those flats, everything I have worked for will go up the spout. I'm not willing to risk that for three thousand pounds – or, as I see it, five hundred."

"Yes, but can we afford such a large outlay just at this moment?" asked the colonel.

"Five of the shops are now showing a profit," said Becky, checking her inventory. "Two are breaking even and only one is actually losing money consistently."

"We must have the courage to go ahead," said Charlie.

"Buy the flats, knock 'em down and then we can build half a dozen shops in their place. We'll be making a return on them before anyone can say 'Bob's your uncle'."

Crowther gave them all a moment to allow Charlie's strategy to sink in, then asked, "So what are the board's instructions?"

"I propose that we offer three thousand pounds," said the colonel. "As the managing director has pointed out, we must take the long view, but only if the bank feels able to back us on this one. Mr Hadlow?"

"You can just about afford three thousand pounds at the moment," said the bank manager, checking over the figures. "But that would stretch your overdraft facility to the limit. It would also mean that you couldn't consider buying any more shops for the foreseeable future."

"We don't have a choice," said Charlie, looking straight at Crowther. "Someone else is after those flats and we can't at this stage allow a rival to get their hands on them."

"Well, if those are the board's instructions I shall attempt to close the deal later today, at three thousand pounds."

"I think that's precisely what the board would wish you to do," confirmed the chairman, as he checked around the table. "Well, if there's no other business, I declare the meeting closed."

Once the meeting had broken up, the colonel took Crowther and Hadlow on one side. "I don't like the sound of this flats business at all. An offer coming out of the blue like that requires a little more explanation."

"I agree," said Crowther. "My instinct tells me that it's Syd Wrexall and his Shops Committee trying to stop Charlie taking over the whole block before it's too late."

"No," said Charlie as he joined them. "It can't be Syd because he doesn't have a car," he added mysteriously. "In any case, Wrexall and his cronies would have reached their limit long before two thousand five hundred pounds."

"So do you think it's an outside contractor," asked

Hadlow, "who has his own plans for developing Chelsea Terrace?"

"More likely to be an investor who's worked out your long-term plan and is willing to hang on until we have no choice but to pay the earth for them," said Crowther.

"I don't know who or what it is," said Charlie. "All I'm certain of is that we've made the right decision to outbid them."

"Agreed," said the colonel. "And Crowther, let me know the moment you've closed the deal. Afraid I can't hang about now. I'm taking a rather special lady to lunch at my club."

"Anyone we know?" asked Charlie.

"Daphne Wiltshire."

"Do give her my love," said Becky. "Tell her we're both looking forward to having dinner with them next Wednesday."

The colonel raised his hat to Becky, and left his four colleagues to continue discussing their different theories as to who else could possibly be interested in the flats.

Because the board meeting had run on later than he anticipated the colonel only managed one whisky before Daphne was ushered through to join him in the Ladies Room. She had, indeed, put on a few pounds, but he didn't consider she looked any the worse for that.

He ordered a gin and tonic for his guest from the club steward, while she chatted about the gaiety of America and the heat of Africa, but he suspected that it was another continent entirely that Daphne really wanted to talk about.

"And how was India?" he eventually asked.

"Not so good, I'm afraid," said Daphne before pausing to sip her gin and tonic. "In fact, awful."

"Funny, I always found the natives rather friendly," said the colonel.

"It wasn't the natives who turned out to be the problem," replied Daphne.

"Trentham?"

"I fear so."

"Hadn't he received your letter?"

"Oh, yes, but events had long superseded that, Colonel. Now I only wish I had taken your advice and copied out your letter word for word warning him that if the question were ever put to me directly I would have to tell anyone who asked that Trentham was Daniel's father."

"Why? What has caused this change of heart?"

Daphne drained her glass in one gulp. "Sorry, Colonel, but I needed that. Well, when Percy and I arrived in Poona the first thing we were told by Ralph Forbes, the Commanding Officer of the Regiment, was that Trentham had resigned his commission."

"Yes, you mentioned as much in your letter." The colonel put his knife and fork down. "What I want to know is why."

"Some problem with the adjutant's wife, Percy later discovered, but no one was willing to go into any detail. Evidently the subject's taboo – not the sort of thing they care to discuss in the officers' mess."

"The unmitigated bastard. If only I –"

"I couldn't agree with you more, Colonel, but I must warn you that there's worse to come."

The colonel ordered another gin and tonic for his guest and a whisky for himself before Daphne continued.

"When I visited Ashurst last weekend, Major Trentham showed me the letter that Guy had sent to his mother explaining why he had been forced to resign his commission with the Fusiliers. He claimed this had come about because you had written to Colonel Forbes informing him that he, Guy, had been responsible for putting 'a tart from Whitechapel' in the family way. I saw the exact wording of the sentence."

The colonel's cheeks suffused scarlet with rage.

"'Whereas time has proved conclusively that Trumper was the father of the child all along.' Anyway, that's the story Trentham is putting about."

"Has the man no morals?"

"None, it would seem," said Daphne. "You see, the

letter went on to suggest that Charlie Trumper is now employing you in order to make sure that you keep your mouth shut. 'Thirty pieces of silver' was the precise expression he used."

"He deserves to be horsewhipped."

"Even Major Trentham might add 'Hear, hear' to that. But my greatest fear isn't for you or even Becky for that matter, but for Charlie himself."

"What are you getting at?"

"Before we left India, Trentham warned Percy when they were on their own at the Overseas Club that Trumper would regret this for the rest of his life."

"But why blame Charlie?"

"Percy asked the same question, and Guy informed him that it was obvious that Trumper had put you up to it in the first place simply to settle an old score."

"But that's not true."

"Percy explained as much, but he just wouldn't listen."

"And in any case what did he mean by 'to settle an old score'?"

"No idea, except that later that evening Guy kept asking me about a painting of the Virgin Mary and Child."

"Not the one that hangs in Charlie's front room?"

"The same, and when I finally admitted I had seen it he dropped the subject altogether."

"The man must have gone completely out of his senses."

"He seemed sane enough to me," said Daphne.

"Well, let's at least be thankful that he's stuck in India, so there's still a little time to consider what course of action we should take."

"Not that much time, I fear," said Daphne.

"How come?"

"Mrs Trentham tells me that Guy is expected to return to these shores some time next month."

After lunch with Daphne the colonel returned to Tregunter Road. He was fuming with anger when his butler opened the front door to let him in but he remained uncertain as to what he could actually do about it. The butler informed his master that a Mr Crowther awaited him in the study.

"Crowther? What can he possibly want?" mumbled the colonel to himself before straightening a print of the Isle of Skye that hung in the hall and joining him in the study.

"Good afternoon, Chairman," Crowther said as he rose from the colonel's chair. "You asked me to report back as soon as I had any news on the flats."

"Ah, yes, so I did," said the colonel. "You've closed the deal?"

"No, sir. I placed a bid of three thousand pounds with Savill's, as instructed, but then received a call from them about an hour later to inform me that the other side had raised their offer to four thousand."

"Four thousand," said the colonel in disbelief. "But who – ?"

"I said we were quite unable to match the sum, and even enquired discreetly who their client might be. They informed me that it was no secret whom they were representing. I felt I ought to let you know immediately, Chairman, as the name of Mrs Gerald Trentham meant nothing to me."

CHARLIE

1919-1926

CHAPTER 19

A s I sat alone on that bench in Chelsea Terrace staring across at a shop with the name "Trumper's" painted over the awning, a thousand questions went through my mind. Then I saw Posh Porky – or, to be accurate, I thought it must be her, because if it was, during my absence she'd changed into a woman. What had happened to that flat chest, those spindly legs, not to mention the spotty face? If it hadn't been for those flashing brown eyes I might have remained in doubt.

She went straight into the shop and spoke to the man who had been acting as if he was the manager. I saw him shake his head; she then turned to the two girls behind the counter who reacted in the same way. She shrugged, before going over to the till, pulling out the tray and beginning to check the day's takings.

I had been watching the manager carry out his duties for over an hour before Becky arrived, and to be fair he was pretty good, although I had already spotted several little things that could have been done to help improve sales, not least among them moving the counter to the far end of the shop and setting up some of the produce in boxes out on the pavement so that the customers could be tempted to buy. "You must advertise your wares, not just hope people will come across them," my granpa used to say. However, I remained patiently on that bench until the staff began to empty the shelves prior to closing up the premises.

A few minutes later Becky came back out on to the pavement and looked up and down the street as if she was waiting for someone. Then the young man, who was now holding a padlock and key, joined her and nodded in my direction. Becky looked over towards the bench for the first time.

Once she had seen me I jumped up and crossed the road to join her. For some time neither of us spoke. I wanted to hug her, but we ended up just shaking hands rather formally, before I asked, "So what's the deal?"

"Couldn't find anyone else who would supply me with free cream buns," she told me, before going on to explain why she had sold the baker's shop and how we had come to own 147 Chelsea Terrace. When the staff had left for the night, she showed me round the flat. I couldn't believe my eyes – a bathroom with a toilet, a kitchen with crockery and cutlery, a front room with chairs and a table, and a bedroom – not to mention a bed that didn't look as if it would collapse when you sat down on it.

Once again I wanted to hug her, but I simply asked if she could stay and share dinner, as I had a hundred other questions that still needed answering.

"Sorry, not tonight," she said as I opened my parcel and began to unpack. "I'm off to a concert with a gentleman friend." No sooner had she added some remark about Tommy's picture than she smiled and left. Suddenly I was on my own again.

I took off my coat, rolled up my sleeves, went downstairs to the shop and for several hours moved things around until everything was exactly where I wanted it. By the time I had packed away the last box I was so exhausted that I only just stopped myself collapsing on the bed and grabbing some kip fully dressed. I didn't draw the curtains so as to be sure I would wake by four.

I dressed quickly the following morning, excited by the thought of returning to a market I hadn't seen for nearly two years. I arrived at the Garden a few minutes before Bob Makins, whom I quickly discovered knew his way around – without actually knowing his way about. I accepted that it would take me a few days before I could work out which dealers were being supplied by the most reliable farmers, who had the real contacts at the docks and ports, who struck the most sensible price day in, day out, and, most important of all, who would take care of you whenever there was any sort of real shortage. None of these problems seemed to worry Bob, as he strolled around the market in an uninterrupted, undemanding circle, collecting his wares.

I loved the shop from the moment we opened that first morning, my first morning. It took me a little time to get used to Bob and the girls calling me "sir" but it also took them almost as long to become used to where I'd put the counter and to having to place the boxes out on the pavement before the customers were awake. However, even Becky agreed that it was an inspiration to place our wares right under the noses of potential buyers, although she wasn't sure how the local authority would react when they found out.

"Hasn't Chelsea ever heard of passing trade?" I asked her.

Within a month I knew the name of every regular customer who patronised the shop, and within two I was aware of their likes, dislikes, passions and even the occasional fad that each imagined must be unique to them. After the staff had packed up at the end of each day I would often walk across the road and sit on the bench opposite and just watch the comings and goings in Chelsea Terrace SW3. It didn't take long to realise that an apple was an apple whoever wanted to take a bite out of it, and Chelsea Terrace was no different from Whitechapel when it came to understanding a customer's needs: I suppose that must have been the moment I thought about owning a second shop. Why not? Trumper's was the only establishment in Chelsea Terrace that regularly had a queue out on to the street.

Becky, meanwhile, continued her studies at the university and kept attempting to arrange for me to meet her gentleman friend. If the truth be known, I was trying to avoid Trentham altogether, as I had no desire to come in contact with the man I was convinced had killed Tommy.

Eventually I ran out of excuses and agreed to have dinner with them. When Becky entered the restaurant with Daphne and Trentham, I wished that I had never agreed to spend the evening with them in the first place. The feeling must have been mutual, for Trentham's face registered the same loathing I felt for him, although Becky's friend, Daphne, tried to be friendly. She was a pretty girl and it wouldn't have surprised me to find that a lot of men enjoyed that hearty laugh. But blue-eyed, curly-headed blondes never were my type. I pretended for form's sake that Trentham and I hadn't met before.

I spent one of the most miserable evenings of my life wanting to tell Becky everything I knew about the bastard, but aware as I watched them together that nothing I had to reveal could possibly have any influence on her. It didn't help when Becky scowled at me for no reason. I just lowered my head and scooped up some more peas.

Becky's roommate, Daphne Harcourt-Browne, continued to do her best, but even Charlie Chaplin would have failed to raise a smile with the three of us as an audience.

Shortly after eleven I called for the bill, and a few minutes later we all left the restaurant. I let Becky and Trentham walk ahead in the hope that it would give me a chance to slip away, but to my surprise double-barrelled Daphne hung back, claiming she wanted to find out what changes I'd made to the shop.

From her opening question as I unlocked the front door I realised she didn't miss much.

"You're in love with Becky, aren't you?" she asked quite matter-of-factly.

"Yes," I replied without guile, and went on to reveal my feelings in a way I would never have done to someone I knew well.

Her second question took me even more by surprise.

"And just how long have you known Guy Trentham?"

As we climbed the steps to my little flat I told her that we had served together on the Western Front, but because of the difference in our rank our paths had rarely crossed.

"Then why do you dislike him so much?" Daphne asked, after she had taken the seat opposite me.

I hesitated again but then in a sudden rush of uncontrollable anger I described what had happened to Tommy and myself when we were trying to reach the safety of our own lines, and how I was convinced that Guy Trentham had shot my closest friend.

When I'd finished we both sat in silence for some time before I added, "You must never let Becky know what I've just told you as I've no real proof."

She nodded her agreement and went on to tell me about the only man in her life, as if swopping one secret for another to bond our friendship. Her love for the man was so transparent that I couldn't fail to be touched. And when Daphne left around midnight she promised that she'd do everything in her power to speed up the demise of Guy Trentham. I remembered her using the word "demise", because I had to ask her what it meant. She told me, and thus I received my first tutorial – with the warning that Becky had a good start on me as she had not wasted the last ten years.

My second lesson was to discover why Becky had scowled at me so often during dinner. I would have protested at her cheek, but realised she was right.

I saw a lot of Daphne during the next few months, without Becky ever becoming aware of our true relationship. She taught me so much about the world of my new customers and even took me on trips to clothes shops, picture houses and to West End theatres to see plays that didn't have any dancing girls on the stage but I still enjoyed them. I only drew the line when she tried to get me to stop spending my Saturday afternoons watching West Ham in favour of some rugby team called the Quins. However, it was her introduction to the National Gallery and its five thousand canvases that was to start a love affair that was to prove as costly as any woman. It was to be only a few months before I was dragging her off to the latest exhibitions: Renoir, Manet and even a young Spaniard called Picasso who was beginning to attract attention among London's fashionable society. I began to hope that Becky would appreciate the change in me, but her eyes never once wavered from Captain Trentham.

On Daphne's further insistence I started reading two daily newspapers. She selected the *Daily Express* and the *News Chronicle*, and occasionally when she invited me round to Lowndes Square I even delved into one of her magazines, *Punch* or *Strand*. I began to discover who was who and who did what, and to whom. I even went to Sotheby's for the first time and watched an early Constable come under the hammer for a record price of nine hundred guineas. It was more money than Trumper's and all its fixtures and fittings were worth put together. I confess that neither that magnificent country scene nor any other painting I came across in a gallery or auction house compared with my pride in Tommy's picture of the Virgin Mary and Child, which still hung above my bed.

When in January 1920 Becky presented the first year's accounts, I began to realise my ambition to own a second shop no longer had to be a daydream. Then without warning two sites became available in the same month. I immediately instructed Becky that somehow she had to come up with the money to purchase them.

Daphne later warned me on the QT that Becky was having considerable trouble raising the necessary cash, and although I said nothing I was quite expecting her to tell me that it simply wasn't possible, especially as her mind seemed to be almost totally preoccupied with Trentham and the fact that he was about to be posted to India. When Becky announced the day he left that they had become officially engaged, I could have willingly cut his throat – and then mine – but Daphne assured me that there were several young ladies in London who had at one time or another entertained the illusion that they were about to marry Guy Trentham. However, Becky herself remained so confident of Trentham's intentions that I didn't know which of the two women to believe.

The following week my old commanding officer appeared on the premises with a shopping list to complete for his wife. I'll never forget the moment he took a purse from his jacket pocket and fumbled around for some loose change. Until then it had never occurred to me that a colonel might actually live in the real world. However, he left with a promise to put me down for two ten-bob tickets at the regimental ball; he turned out to be as good as his word.

My euphoria – another Harcourt-Browne word – at meeting up with the colonel again lasted for about twenty-four hours. Then Daphne told me Becky was expecting. My first reaction was to wish I'd killed Trentham on the Western Front instead of helping to save the bloody man's life. I assumed that he would return immediately from India in order to marry her before the child was born. I hated the idea of his coming back into our lives, but it was the only course of action a gentleman could possibly consider, otherwise the rest of Becky's life would be spent as a social outcast.

It was around this time that Daphne explained that if we hoped to raise some real money from the banks then we were definitely in need of a front man. Becky's sex was now militating – another of Daphne's words – against her, although she was kind enough *not* to mention my accent "militating" against me.

On the way home from the regimental ball Becky breezily informed Daphne that she had decided that the colonel was the obvious man to represent us whenever we had to go cap in hand seeking loans from one of the banks. I wasn't optimistic, but Becky insisted after her conversation with the colonel's wife that we at least go round to see him and present our case.

I fell in line and to my surprise we received a letter ten days later saying that he was our man.

A few days after that Becky admitted she was going to have a baby. From that moment on my consuming interest became in finding out what news Becky had of Trentham's intentions. I was horrified to discover that she hadn't even written to tell him her news, although she was almost four months pregnant. I made her swear that she would send a letter that night, even if she did refuse to consider threatening him with a breach of promise suit. The following day Daphne assured me that she had watched from the kitchen window as Becky posted the letter.

I made an appointment to see the colonel and briefed him on Becky's state before the whole world knew. He said somewhat mysteriously, "Leave Trentham to me."

Six weeks later Becky told me that she had still heard nothing from the man, and I sensed for the first time that her feelings for him were beginning to wane.

I even asked her to marry me, but she didn't take my proposal at all seriously although I had never been more sincere about anything in my life. I lay awake at night wondering what else I could possibly do to make her feel I was worthy of her.

As the weeks passed Daphne and I began to take more and more care of Becky, as daily she increasingly resembled a beached whale. There was still no word from India but long before the child was due she had stopped referring to Trentham by name.

When I first saw Daniel I wanted to be his father and was overjoyed when Becky said she hoped I still loved her.

Hoped I still loved her!

We were married a week later with the colonel, Bob Makins and Daphne agreeing to be godparents.

The following summer Daphne and Percy were themselves married, not at Chelsea Register Office but at St Margaret's, Westminster. I watched out for Mrs Trentham just to see what she looked like, but then I remembered that Percy had said she hadn't been invited.

Daniel grew like a weed, and I was touched that one of the first words he repeated again and again was "dad". Despite this I could only wonder how long it would be before we had to sit down and tell the boy the truth. "Bastard" is such a vicious slur for an innocent child to have to live with.

"We don't have to worry about that for some time yet," Becky kept insisting, but it didn't stop me being fearful of the eventual outcome if we remained silent on the subject for much longer, after all some people in the terrace already knew the truth.

Sal wrote from Toronto to congratulate me, as well as to inform me that she herself had stopped having babies. Two girls – Maureen and Babs – and two boys – David and Rex – seemed to her quite enough, even for a good Catholic. Her husband, she wrote, had been promoted to areas sales rep for E. P. Taylor so altogether they seemed to be doing rather well. She never made mention of England in her letters or of any desire to return to the country of her birth. As her only real memories of home must have been sleeping three to a bed, a drunken father and never having enough food for a second helping I couldn't really blame her.

She went on to chastise me for allowing Grace to be a far better letter-writer than I was. I couldn't claim the excuse of work, she added, as being a ward sister in a London teaching hospital left my sister with even less time than I had. After Becky had read the letter and nodded her agreement I made more of an effort over the next few months.

Kitty made periodic visits to Chelsea Terrace, but only with the purpose of talking me out of more money, her demands rising on each occasion. However, she always made certain that Becky was not around whenever she turned up. The sums she extracted, although exorbitant, were always just possible.

I begged Kitty to find a job, even offered her one myself, but she simply explained that she and work didn't seem to get along together. Our conversations rarely lasted for more than a few minutes because as soon as I'd handed over the cash she immediately sloped off. I realised that with every shop I opened it would become harder and harder to convince Kitty that she should settle down, and once Becky and I moved into our new home on Gilston Road her visits only became more frequent.

Despite Syd Wrexall's efforts to thwart my ambition of trying to buy up every shop that became available in the terrace – I was able to get hold of seven before I came across any real opposition – I now had my eyes on Numbers 25 to 99, a block of flats which I intended to purchase without Wrexall ever finding out what I was up to; not to mention my desire to get my hands on Number 1 Chelsea Terrace, which, given its position on the street, remained crucial as part of my long-term plan to own the entire block.

During 1922 everything seemed to be falling neatly into place and I began to look forward to Daphne's return from her honeymoon so I could tell her exactly what I had been up to in her absence.

The week after Daphne arrived back in England she invited us both to dinner at her new home in Eaton Square. I couldn't wait to hear all her news, knowing that she would be impressed to learn that we now owned eight shops, a new home in Gilston Road and at any moment would be adding a block of flats to the Trumper portfolio. However, I knew the question she would ask me as soon as I walked in their front door, so I had my reply ready: "It will take me about another ten years before I own the entire block – as long as you can guarantee no floods, pestilence or the outbreak of war."

Just before Becky and I set out for our reunion dinner an envelope was dropped through the letter-box of 11 Gilston Road.

Even as it lay on the mat I could recognise the bold hand. I ripped it open and began to read the colonel's words. When I had finished the letter I suddenly felt sick and could only wonder why he should want to resign.

CHAPTER 20

harlie stood alone in the hall and decided not to mention the colonel's letter to Becky until after they had returned from their dinner with Daphne. Becky had been looking forward to the occasion for such a long time that he feared the colonel's unexplained resignation could only put a blight on the rest of the evening.

"You all right, darling?" asked Becky when she reached the bottom of the stairs. "You look a bit pale."

"I'm just fine," said Charlie, nervously tucking the letter into an inside pocket. "Come on or we'll be late, and that would never do." Charlie looked at his wife and noticed that she was wearing the pink dress with a massive bow on the front. He remembered helping her choose it. "You look ravishing," he told her. "That gown will make Daphne green with envy."

"You don't look so bad yourself."

"When I put on one of these penguin suits I always feel like the head waiter of the Ritz," admitted Charlie as Becky straightened his white tie.

"How could you possibly know when you've never been to the Ritz?" she said, laughing.

"At least the outfit came from my own shop this time," Charlie replied as he opened the front door for his wife.

"Ah, but have you paid the bill yet?"

As they drove over to Eaton Square Charlie found it difficult to concentrate on his wife's chatty conversation while he tried to fathom why the colonel could possibly want to resign just at the point when everything was going so well.

"So how do you feel I should go about it?" asked Becky.

"Whichever way you think best," began Charlie.

"You haven't been listening to a word I've said since we left the house, Charlie Trumper. And to think we've been married for two years."

"Sorry," said Charlie, as he parked his little Austin Seven behind the Silver Ghost that stood directly in front of 14 Eaton Square. "Wouldn't mind living here," Charlie added, as he opened the car door for his wife.

"Not quite yet," suggested Becky.

"Why not?"

"I've a feeling that Mr Hadlow might not feel able to sanction the necessary loan."

A butler opened the door for them even before they had reached the top step. "Wouldn't mind one of those either," said Charlie.

"Behave yourself," said Becky.

"Of course," he said. "I must remember my place."

The butler ushered them through to the drawing room where they found Daphne sipping a dry martini.

"Darlings," she said. Becky ran forward and threw her arms around her and they bumped into each other.

"Why didn't you tell me?" said Becky.

"My little secret." Daphne patted her stomach. "Still, you seem to be well ahead of me, as usual."

"Not by that much," said Becky. "So when's yours due?"

"Doctor Gould is predicting some time in January. Clarence if it's a boy, Clarissa if it's a girl."

Her guests both laughed.

"Don't you two dare snigger. Those are the names of Percy's most distinguished ancestors," she told them, just as her husband entered the room.

"True, by Jove," said Percy, "though I'm damned if I can remember what they actually did."

"Welcome home," said Charlie, shaking him by the hand.

"Thank you, Charlie," said Percy, who then kissed Becky on both cheeks. "I don't mind telling you I'm damned pleased to see you again." A servant handed him a whisky and soda. "Now, Becky, tell me everything you've been up to and don't spare me any details."

They sat down together on the sofa as Daphne joined Charlie, who was slowly circling the room studying the large portraits that hung on every wall.

"Percy's ancestors," said Daphne. "All painted by second-rate artists. I'd swap the lot of them for that picture of the Virgin Mary you have in your drawing room."

"Not this one, you wouldn't," said Charlie, as he stopped in front of the second Marquess of Wiltshire.

"Ah, yes, the Holbein," said Daphne. "You're right. But since then I'm afraid it's been downhill all the way."

"I wouldn't begin to know, M'Lady," said Charlie with a grin. "You see, my ancestors didn't go a bundle on portraits. Come to think of it, I don't suppose Holbein was commissioned by that many costermongers from the East End."

Daphne laughed. "That reminds me, Charlie, what's happened to your Cockney accent?"

"What was you 'oping for, Marchioness, a pound ov tomatoes and 'alf a grapefruit, or just a night on the razzle?"

"That's more like it. Mustn't let a few night classes go to our head."

"Shhh," said Charlie, looking over to his wife who was seated on the sofa. "Becky still doesn't know and I'm not saying anything until –"

"I understand," said Daphne. "And I promise you that she won't hear a thing from me. I haven't even told Percy." She glanced towards Becky who was still deep in conversation with her husband. "By the way, how long before – ?"

"Ten years would be my guess," said Charlie, delivering his prepared answer.

"Oh, I thought that these things usually took about

nine months," said Daphne. "Unless of course you're an elephant."

Charlie smiled, realising his mistake. "Another two months would be my guess. Tommy if it's a boy and Debbie if it's a girl. So with a bit of luck whatever Becky delivers let's hope it turns out to be the ideal partner for Clarence or Clarissa."

"A nice idea but the way the world is going at the moment," said Daphne, "I wouldn't be surprised if mine ended up as your sales assistants."

Despite Daphne bombarding him with questions Charlie still couldn't take his eyes off the Holbein. Eventually Daphne bribed him away by saying, "Come on, Charlie, let's go and have something to eat. I always seem to be famished nowadays."

Percy and Becky stood up and followed Daphne and Charlie towards the dining room.

Daphne led her guests down a long corridor and through into another room that was exactly the same size and proportion as the one they had just left. The six full-length canvases that hung from the walls were all by Reynolds. "And this time only the ugly one is a relation," Percy assured them as he took his place at one end of the table and gestured to a long grey figure of a lady that hung on the wall behind him. "And she would have found it exceedingly difficult to land a Wiltshire had she not been accompanied by an extremely handsome dowry."

They took their places at a table that had been laid for four but would have comfortably seated eight, and proceeded to eat a four-course dinner that could have happily fed sixteen. Liveried footmen stood behind each chair to ensure the slightest need was administered to. "Every good home should have one," whispered Charlie across the table to his wife.

The conversation over dinner gave the four of them a chance to catch up with everything that had taken place during the past year. By the time a second coffee had been poured Daphne and Becky left the two men to enjoy a cigar and Charlie couldn't help thinking that it was as if the Wiltshires had never been away in the first place.

"Glad the girls have left us alone," said Percy, "as I feel there is something less pleasant we ought perhaps to touch on."

Charlie puffed away at his first cigar, wondering what it must be like to suffer in this way every day.

"When Daphne and I were in India," Percy continued, "we came across that bounder Trentham." Charlie coughed as some smoke went down the wrong way and began to pay closer attention as his host revealed the conversation that had taken place between Trentham and himself. "His threat that he would 'get you, come what may' could have been no more than an idle boast, of course," said Percy, "but Daphne felt it best that you were put fully in the picture."

"But what can I possibly do about it?" Charlie knocked an extended column of ash into a silver saucer that had been placed in front of him just in time.

"Not a lot, I suspect," said Percy. "Except to remember that forewarned is forearmed. He's expected back in England at any moment, and his mother is now telling anyone who still cares to enquire that Guy was offered such an irresistible appointment in the City that he was willing to sacrifice his commission. I can't imagine that anyone really believes her and anyway most decent-minded people think the City's about the right place for the likes of Trentham."

"Do you think I ought to tell Becky?"

"No, I don't," said Percy. "In fact I never told Daphne about my second encounter with Trentham at the Overseas Club. So why bother Becky with the details? From what I've learned from her this evening she's got quite enough on her plate to be going on with."

"Not to mention the fact that she's about to give birth," added Charlie.

"Exactly," said Percy. "So let's leave it at that for the time being. Now, shall we go and join the ladies?"

Over a large brandy in yet another room filled with

ancestors including a small oil of Bonnie Prince Charlie, Becky listened to Daphne describe the Americans, whom she adored, but felt we should never have given the darlings away; the Africans, whom she considered delightful, but who ought to be given away as soon as was convenient; and the Indians, who she understood couldn't wait to be given away, according to the little man who kept arriving at Government House in a dishcloth.

"Are you by any chance referring to Gandhi?" asked Charlie, as he puffed away more confidently at his cigar. "I find him rather impressive."

On the way back to Gilston Road Becky chatted happily as she revealed all the gossip she had picked up from Daphne. It became obvious to Charlie that the two women had not touched on the subject of Trentham, or the threat he currently posed.

Charlie had a restless night, partly caused by having indulged in too much rich food and alcohol, but mainly because his mind kept switching from why the colonel should want to resign to the problem that had to be faced with Trentham's imminent return to England.

At four o'clock in the morning he rose and donned his oldest clothes before setting off to the market, something he still tried to do at least once a week, convinced there was no one at Trumper's who could work the Garden the way he did, until, quite recently, when a trader at the market called Ned Denning had managed to palm him off with a couple of boxes of overripe avocados and followed it up the next day by pressing Charlie into buying a box of oranges he'd never wanted in the first place. Charlie decided to get up very early on the third day and see if he could have the man removed from his job once and for all.

The following Monday Ned Denning joined Trumper's as the grocery shop's first general manager.

Charlie had a successful morning stocking up with provisions for both 131 and 147 and Bob Makins arrived an hour later to drive him and Ned back to Chelsea Terrace in their newly acquired van.

Once they arrived at the fruit and vegetable shop, Charlie helped unload and lay out the goods before returning home for breakfast a few minutes after seven. He still considered it was a little early to place a phone call through to the colonel.

Cook served him up eggs and bacon for breakfast which he shared with Daniel and his nanny. Becky didn't join them, as she had not yet recovered from the after-effects of Daphne's dinner party.

Charlie happily spent most of breakfast trying to answer Daniel's string of unrelated, never-ending questions until Nanny picked up the protesting child and carried him back upstairs to the playroom. Charlie flicked open the cover of his half-hunter to check the time. Although it was still only a few minutes before eight, he felt he couldn't wait any longer so he walked through to the hall, picked up the stem phone, unhooked the earpiece and asked the operator to connect him with Kensington 1729. A few moments later he was put through.

"Can I have a word with the colonel?"

"I'll tell him you're on the line, Mr Trumper," came back the reply. Charlie was amused by the thought that he was never going to be able to disguise his accent over the telephone.

"Good morning, Charlie," came back another accent that was also immediately recognisable.

"I wonder if I might come round and see you, sir?" Charlie asked.

"Of course," said the colonel. "But could you leave it until ten, old fellow? By then Elizabeth will have gone off to visit her sister in Camden Hill."

"I'll be there at ten on the dot," promised Charlie. After he had put the phone back on the hook, he decided to occupy the two hours by completing a full round of the shops. For a second time that morning and still before Becky had stirred, he left for Chelsea Terrace.

Charlie dug Major Arnold out of hardware before beginning a spot check on all eight establishments. As he passed the block of flats he began to explain in detail to his deputy the plans he had to replace the building with six new shops.

After they had left Number 129, Charlie confided in Arnold that he was worried about wines and spirits, which he considered was still not pulling its weight. This was despite their now being able to take advantage of the new delivery service that had originally been introduced only for fruit and vegetables. Charlie was proud that his was one of the first shops in London to take orders by telephone, then drop off the goods on the same day for account customers. It was another idea he had stolen from the Americans, and the more he read about what his opposite numbers were up to in the States the more he wanted to visit that country and see how they went about it first-hand.

He could still recall his first delivery service when he used his granpa's barrow for transport and Kitty as the delivery girl. Now he ran a smart blue three-horsepower van with the words, "Trumper, the honest trader, founded 1823", emblazoned in blue letters down both sides.

He stopped on the corner of Chelsea Terrace and stared at the one shop that would always dominate Chelsea with its massive bow window and great double door. He knew the time must almost be ripe for him to walk in and offer Mr Fothergill a large cheque to cover the auctioneer's debts: a former employee of Number 1 had recently assured Charlie that his bank balance was overdrawn by more than two thousand pounds.

Charlie marched into Number 1 to pay a far smaller bill and asked the girl behind the counter if they had finished reframing the Virgin Mary and Child, which was already three weeks overdue.

He didn't complain about the delay as it gave him another excuse to nose around. The paper was still peeling off the wall behind the reception area, and there was only one girl assistant left at the desk, which suggested to Charlie that the weekly wages were not always being met.

Mr Fothergill eventually appeared with the picture in

its new gilt frame and handed the little oil over to Charlie.

"Thank you," said Charlie as he once again studied the bold brushwork of reds and blues that made up the portrait and realised just how much he had missed it.

"Wonder what it's worth?" he asked Fothergill casually as he passed over a ten-shilling note.

"A few pounds at the most," the expert declared as he touched his bow tie. "After all, you can find countless examples of the subject by unknown artists right across the continent of Europe."

"I wonder," said Charlie as he checked his watch and stuffed the receipt into his pocket. He had allowed himself sufficient time for a relaxed walk across Princess Gardens and on to the colonel's residence, expecting to arrive a couple of minutes before ten. He bade Mr Fothergill "Good morning," and left.

Although it was still quite early, the pavements in Chelsea were already bustling with people and Charlie raised his hat to several customers he recognised.

"Good morning, Mr Trumper."

"Good morning, Mrs Symonds," said Charlie as he crossed the road to take a short cut through the garden.

He began to try and compose in his mind what he would say to the colonel once he'd discovered why the chairman felt it had been necessary to offer his resignation. Whatever the reason, Charlie was determined not to lose the old soldier. He closed the park gate behind him and started to walk along the man-made path.

He stood aside to allow a lady pushing a pram to pass him and gave a mock salute to an old soldier sitting on a park bench rolling a Woodbine. Once he had crossed the tiny patch of grass, he stepped into the Gilston Road, closing the gate behind him.

Charlie continued his walk towards Tregunter Road and began to quicken his pace. He smiled as he passed his little home, quite forgetting he still had the picture under his arm, his mind still preoccupied with the reason for the colonel's resignation.

Charlie turned immediately he heard the scream and a door slam somewhere behind him, more as a reflex than from any genuine desire to see what was going on. He stopped in his tracks as he watched a dishevelled figure dash out on to the road and then start running towards him.

Charlie stood mesmerised as the tramp-like figure drew closer and closer until the man came to a sudden halt only a few feet in front of him. For a matter of seconds the two men stood and stared at each other without uttering a word. Neither ruffian nor gentleman showed on a face half-obscured by rough stubble. And then recognition was quickly followed by disbelief.

Charlie couldn't accept that the unshaven, slovenly figure who stood before him wearing an old army greatcoat and a battered felt hat was the same man he had first seen on a station in Edinburgh some five years before.

Charlie's abiding memory of that moment was to be the three clean circles on both epaulettes of Trentham's greatcoat from which the three pips of a captain must recently have been removed.

Trentham's eyes dropped as he stared at the painting for a second and then suddenly, without warning, he lunged at Charlie, taking him by surprise, and wrested the picture from his grasp. He turned and started running back down the road in the direction he had come. Charlie immediately set off in pursuit and quickly began to make up ground on his assailant who was impeded by his heavy greatcoat, while having also to cling on to the picture.

Charlie was within a yard of his quarry and about to make a dive for Trentham's waist when he heard the second scream. He hesitated for a moment as he realised the desperate cry must be coming from his own home. He knew he had been left with no choice but to allow Trentham to escape with the picture as he changed direction and dashed up the steps of Number 11. He charged on into the drawing room to find the cook and nanny standing over Becky. She was lying flat out on the sofa screaming with pain.

Becky's eyes lit up when she saw Charlie. "The baby's coming," was all she said.

"Pick her up gently, Cook," said Charlie, "and help me get her to the car."

Together they carried Becky out of the house and down the path as Nanny ran ahead of them to open the car door so they could place her on the back seat. Charlie stared down at his wife. Her face was drained of colour and her eyes were glazed. She appeared to lose consciousness as he closed the car door.

Charlie jumped into the front of the car and shouted at Cook, who was already turning the handle to get the engine started.

"Ring my sister at Guy's hospital and explain we're on our way. And tell her to be prepared for an emergency."

The motor spluttered into action and Cook jumped to one side as Charlie drove the car out into the middle of the road, trying to keep a steady pace as he avoided pedestrians, bicycles, trams, horses and other cars as he crashed through the gears on his journey south towards the Thames.

He turned his head every few seconds to stare at his wife, not even sure if she were still alive. "Let them both live," he shouted at the top of his voice. He continued on down the Embankment as fast as he could manage, honking his horn and several times screaming at people who were casually crossing the road unaware of his plight. As he drove across Southwark Bridge he heard Becky groan for the first time.

"We'll soon be there, my darling," he promised. "Just hold on a little longer."

Once over the bridge he took the first left and maintained his speed until the great iron gates of Guy's came into view. As he swung into the courtyard and round the circular flower-bed he spotted Grace and two men in long white coats standing waiting, a stretcher by their side. Charlie brought the car to a halt almost on their toes.

The two men lifted Becky gently out and placed her on the stretcher before rushing her up the ramp and into the hospital. Charlie jumped out of the car and marched by the stretcher, holding Becky's hand as they climbed a flight of stairs, Grace running by his side explaining that Mr Armitage, the hospital's senior obstetrician, was waiting for them in an operating theatre on the first floor.

By the time Charlie reached the door of the theatre, Becky was already inside. They left him outside in the corridor on his own. He began to pace up and down, unaware of others bustling past him as they went about their work.

Grace came out a few minutes later to reassure him that Mr Armitage had everything under control and that Becky could not be in better hands. The baby was expected at any moment. She squeezed her brother's hand, then disappeared back into the theatre. Charlie continued his pacing, thinking only of his wife and their first child, the sight of Trentham already becoming a blur. He prayed for a boy, Tommy, who would be a brother for Daniel and perhaps one day even take over Trumper's. Pray God that Becky was not going through too much pain as she delivered their son. He paced on up and down that long green-walled corridor mumbling to himself, aware once again how much he loved her.

It was to be another hour before a tall, thickset man emerged from behind the closed doors, followed by Grace. Charlie turned to face them but as the surgeon had a mask over his face he had no way of knowing how the operation had gone. Mr Armitage removed the mask: the expression on his face answered Charlie's silent prayer.

"I managed to save your wife's life," he said, "but I am so very sorry, Mr Trumper, I could do nothing about your stillborn daughter."

CHAPTER 21

or several days after the operation Becky never left her room in the hospital.

Charlie later learned from Grace that although Mr Armitage had saved his wife's life it might still be weeks before she was fully recovered, especially since it had been explained to Becky that she could never have another child without risking her own life.

Charlie visited her every morning and evening, but it was over a fortnight before she was able to tell her husband how Guy Trentham had forced his way into the house and then threatened to kill her unless she told him where the picture was.

"Why? I simply can't understand why," said Charlie. "Has the picture turned up anywhere?"

"No sign of it so far," he said, just as Daphne came in bearing a huge basket of provisions. She kissed Becky on the cheek before confirming that the fruit had been purchased at Trumper's that morning. Becky managed a smile as she munched her way through a peach. Daphne sat on the end of the bed and immediately launched into all her latest news.

She was able to let them know, following one of her periodic visits to the Trenthams, that Guy had disappeared off to Australia and that his mother was claiming he had never set foot in England in the first place, but travelled to Sydney direct from India.

"Via the Gilston Road," said Charlie.

"That's not what the police think," said Daphne.

"They remain convinced that he left England in 1920 and they can find no proof he ever returned."

"Well, we're certainly not going to enlighten them," said Charlie, taking his wife's hand.

"Why not?" asked Daphne.

"Because even I consider Australia far enough away for Trentham to be left to his own devices: in any case nothing can be gained from pursuing him now. If the Australians give him enough rope I'm sure he'll hang himself."

"But why Australia?" asked Becky.

"Mrs Trentham's telling everyone who cares to listen that Guy has been offered a partnership in a cattle brokers – far too good a position to turn down, even if it did mean having to resign his commission. The vicar is the only person I can find who believes the story." But even Daphne had no simple answer as to why Trentham should have been so keen to get his hands on the little oil painting.

The colonel and Elizabeth also visited Becky on several occasions and as he continually talked of the company's future and never once referred to his resignation letter, Charlie didn't press him on the subject.

It was to be Crowther who eventually enlightened Charlie as to who had purchased the flats.

Six weeks later Charlie drove his wife home to Gilston Road – at a more stately pace – Mr Armitage having suggested a quiet month resting before she considered returning to work. Charlie promised the surgeon that he would not allow Becky to do anything until he felt sure she had fully recovered.

The morning Becky returned home Charlie left her propped up in bed with a book and headed back to Chelsea Terrace where he went straight to the jewellery shop he had acquired in his wife's absence.

Charlie took a considerable time selecting a string of cultured pearls, a gold bracelet and a lady's Victorian watch, which he then instructed to be sent to Grace, to the staff nurse and to the nurse who had taken care of Becky during her unscheduled stay at Guy's. His next stop was the greengrocer's shop where he asked Bob to make up a basket of the finest fruit, while he personally selected a bottle of vintage wine from Number 101 to accompany it. "Send them both round to Mr Armitage at 7 Cadogan Square, London SW1, with my compliments," he added.

"Right away," said Bob. "Anything else while I'm at it?"

"Yes, I want you to repeat that order every Monday for the rest of his life."

It was about a month later in November 1922 that Charlie learned of the problems Arnold was facing with the simple task of replacing a shop assistant. In fact, selecting staff had become one of Arnold's biggest headaches of late, because for every job that became vacant fifty to a hundred people were applying to fill it. Arnold would then put together a shortlist as Charlie still insisted that it was he who interviewed the final candidates before any position was confirmed.

On that particular Monday, Arnold had already considered a number of girls for the position as sales assistant at the flower shop, following the retirement of one of the company's longest-serving employees.

"Although I've already shortlisted three for the job," said Arnold, "I thought you would be interested in one of the applicants I rejected. She didn't seem to have the appropriate qualifications for this particular position. However –"

Charlie glanced at the sheet of paper Arnold passed to him. "Joan Moore. Why would I – ?" began Charlie, as his eyes ran swiftly down her application. "Ah, I see," he said. "How very observant of you, Tom." He read a few more lines. "But I don't need a – well, on the other hand perhaps I do." He looked up. "Arrange for me to see Miss Moore within the next week."

The following Thursday Charlie interviewed Joan Moore for over an hour at his home in Gilston Road and his first impression was of a cheery, well-mannered if somewhat immature girl. However, before he offered her the position as lady's maid to Mrs Trumper he still had a couple of questions he felt needed answering.

"Did you apply for this job because you knew of the relationship between my wife and your former employer?" Charlie asked.

The girl looked him straight in the eyes. "Yes, sir, I did."

"And were you sacked by your previous employer?"

"Not exactly, sir, but when I left she refused to supply me with a reference."

"What reason did she give for that?"

"I was walkin' out with the second footman, 'aving failed to inform the butler who is in charge of the 'ousehold."

"And are you still walking out with the second footman?"

The girl hesitated. "Yes, sir," she said. "You see, we're 'oping to be married as soon as we've saved up enough."

"Good," said Charlie. "Then you can report for duty next Monday morning. Mr Arnold will deal with all the necessary arrangements."

When Charlie told Becky he had employed a lady's maid for her she laughed at first, then asked, "And what would I want with one of those?" Charlie told her exactly why she wanted "one of those". When he had finished all Becky said was, "You're an evil man, Charlie Trumper, that's for sure."

It was at the February board meeting in 1924 that Crowther warned his colleagues that Number 1 Chelsea Terrace might well come on the market earlier than anticipated.

"Why's that?" asked Charlie, a little anxiously.

"Your estimate of another two years before Fothergill would have to cave in is beginning to look prophetic."

"So how much does he want?"

"It's not quite as simple as that."

"Why not?"

"Because he's decided to auction the property himself."

"Auction it?" enquired Becky.

"Yes," said Crowther. "That way he avoids paying any fees to an outside agent."

"I see. So what are you expecting the property to fetch?" asked the colonel.

"Not an easy one to answer, that," replied Crowther. "It's four times the size of any other shop in the terrace, it's on five floors and it's even bigger than Syd Wrexall's pub on the other corner. It also has the largest shop frontage in Chelsea and a double entrance on the corner facing the Fulham Road. For all those reasons it's not that simple to estimate its value."

"Even so, could you try and put a figure on it?" asked the chairman.

"If you were to press me I'd say somewhere in the region of two thousand, but it could be as much as three, if anyone else were to show an interest."

"What about the stock?" asked Becky. "Do we know what's happening to that?"

"Yes, it's being sold along with the building."

"And what's it worth?" asked Charlie. "Roughly?"

"More Mrs Trumper's department than mine, I feel," said Crowther.

"It's no longer that impressive," said Becky. "A lot of Fothergill's best works have already gone through Sotheby's, and I suspect Christie's have seen just as many during the past year. However, I would still expect what's left over to fetch around a thousand pounds under the hammer."

"So the face value of the property and the stock together appears to be around the three thousand pound mark," suggested Hadlow.

"But Number 1 will go for a lot more than that," said Charlie.

"Why?" queried Hadlow.

"Because Mrs Trentham will be among the bidders."

"How can you be so sure?" asked the chairman.

"Because our lady's maid is still walking out with her second footman."

The rest of the board laughed, but all the chairman volunteered was, "Not again. First the flats, now this. When will it end?"

"Not until she's dead and buried, I suspect," said Charlie.

"Perhaps not even then," added Becky.

"If you're referring to the son," said the colonel, "I doubt if he can cause too much trouble from twelve thousand miles away. But as for the mother, hell hath no fury –" he said testily.

"Commonly misquoted," said Charlie.

"What's that?" asked the chairman.

"Congreve, Colonel. The lines run, 'Heav'n has no rage, like love to hatred turn'd, Nor Hell a fury, like a woman scorn'd.'" The Colonel's mouth remained open but he was speechless. "However," Charlie continued, "more to the point, I need to know what is the limit the board will allow me to bid for Number 1."

"I consider five thousand may well prove necessary given the circumstances," said Becky.

"But no more," said Hadlow, studying the balance sheet in front of him.

"Perhaps one bid over?" suggested Becky.

"I'm sorry, I don't understand," said Hadlow. "What does 'one bid over' mean?"

"Bids never go to the exact figure you anticipate, Mr Hadlow. Most people who attend an auction usually have a set figure in their minds which inevitably ends in round numbers, so if you go one above that figure you often end up securing the lot."

Even Charlie nodded, as Hadlow said in admiration, "Then I agree to one bid over."

"May I also suggest," said the colonel, "that Mrs Trumper should carry out the bidding, because with her experience –"

"That's kind of you, Colonel, but I shall nevertheless need the help of my husband," said Becky with a smile. "And, in fact, the whole board's, come to that. You see, I have already formulated a plan." She proceeded to brief her colleagues on what she had in mind.

"What fun," said the colonel when she had finished. "But will I also be allowed to attend the proceedings?"

"Oh, yes," said Becky. "All of you must be present, and, with the exception of Charlie and myself, you ought to be seated silently in the row directly behind Mrs Trentham a few minutes before the auction is due to commence."

"Bloody woman," said the colonel, before adding hastily, "I do apologise."

"True. But, more important, we must never forget that she is also an amateur," Becky added.

"What's the significance of that statement?" asked Hadlow.

"Sometimes amateurs get carried away by the occasion, and when that happens the professionals have no chance because the amateur often ends up going one bid too far. We must remember that it may well be the first auction Mrs Trentham has ever placed a bid at, even attended, and as she wants the premises every bit as much as we do, and has the advantage of superior resources, we will have to secure the lot by sheer cunning." No one seemed to disagree with this assessment.

Once the board meeting was over Becky took Charlie through her plan for the forthcoming auction in greater detail, and even made him attend Sotheby's one morning with orders to bid for three pieces of Dutch silver. He carried out his wife's instructions but ended up with a Georgian mustard pot he had never intended to buy in the first place.

"No better way of learning," Becky assured him. "Just be thankful that it wasn't a Rembrandt you were bidding for."

She continued to explain to Charlie the subtleties of auctions over dinner that night in far greater detail than she had with the board. Charlie learned that there were different signs you could give the auctioneer, so that rivals remained unaware that you were still bidding, while at the same time you could discover who was bidding against you.

"But isn't Mrs Trentham bound to spot you?" said Charlie after he had cut his wife a slice of bread. "After all, you'll be the only two left bidding by that stage."

"Not if you've already put her off balance before I enter the fray," said Becky.

"But the board agreed that you . . ."

"That I should be allowed to go one bid over five thousand."

"But –"

"No buts, Charlie," said Becky as she served her husband up another portion of Irish stew. "On the morning of the auction I want you on parade, dressed in your best suit and sitting in the seventh row on the gangway looking very pleased with yourself. You will then proceed to bid ostentatiously up to one over three thousand pounds. When Mrs Trentham goes to the next bid, as undoubtedly she will, you must stand up and flounce out of the room, looking defeated, while I continue the bidding in your absence."

"Not bad," said Charlie as he put his fork into a couple of peas. "But surely Mrs Trentham will work out exactly what you're up to?"

"Not a chance," said Becky. "Because I will have an agreed code with the auctioneer that she could never hope to spot, let alone to decipher."

"But will *I* understand what you are up to?"

"Oh, yes," said Becky, "because you'll know exactly what I'm doing when I use the glasses ploy."

"The glasses ploy? But you don't even wear glasses."

"I will be on the day of the auction, and when I'm wearing them you'll know I'm still bidding. If I take them off, I've finished bidding. So when you leave the room all the auctioneer will see when he looks in my direction is that I still have my glasses on. Mrs Trentham will think you've gone, and will, I suspect, be quite happy to let someone else continue with the bidding so long as she's confident they don't represent you."

"You're a gem, Mrs Trumper," said Charlie as he rose to clear away the plates. "But what if she sees you chatting to the auctioneer or, worse, finds out your code even before Mr Fothergill calls for the first bid?"

"She can't," said Becky. "I'll agree the code with Fothergill only minutes before the auction begins. In any case, it will be at that moment that you will make a grand entrance, and then only seconds after the other members of the board have taken their seats directly behind Mrs Trentham, so with a bit of luck she'll be so distracted by everything that's going on around her that she won't even notice me."

"I married a very clever girl," said Charlie.

"You never admitted as much when we were at Jubilee Street Elementary."

On the morning of the auction, Charlie confessed over breakfast that he was very nervous, despite Becky's appearing to be remarkably calm, especially after Joan had informed her mistress that the second footman had heard from the cook that Mrs Trentham had placed a limit of four thousand pounds on her bidding.

"I just wonder . . ." said Charlie.

"Whether she planted the sum in the cook's mind?" said Becky. "It's possible. After all, she's every bit as cunning as you are. But as long as we stick to our agreed plan – and remember everyone, even Mrs Trentham, has a limit – we can still beat her."

The auction was advertised to begin at ten a.m. A full twenty minutes before the bidding was due to commence Mrs Trentham entered the room and swept regally down the aisle. She took her place in the centre of the third row, and placed her handbag on one seat and a catalogue on the other to be certain that no one sat next to her. The colonel and his two colleagues entered the half-filled room at nine-fifty a.m. and, as instructed, filed into the seats immediately behind their adversary. Mrs Trentham appeared to show

no interest in their presence. Five minutes later Charlie
made his entrance. He strolled down the centre aisle, raised
his hat to a lady he recognised, shook hands with one of his
regular customers and finally took his place on the gangway
at the end of the seventh row. He continued to chat noisily
with his next-door neighbour about England's tour of Australia, explaining once again that he was not related to the
great Australian batsman whose name he bore. The minute
hand on the grandfather clock behind the auctioneer's box
moved slowly towards the appointed hour.

Although the room was not much larger than Daphne's
hall in Eaton Square, they had still somehow managed to
pack in over a hundred chairs of different shapes and sizes.
The walls were covered in a faded green baize that displayed several hook marks where pictures must have hung
in the past and the carpet had become so threadbare that
Charlie could see the floorboards in places. He began to feel
that the cost of bringing Number 1 up to the standard he
expected for all Trumper's shops was going to be greater
than he had originally anticipated.

Glancing around, he estimated that over seventy people
were now seated in the auction house, and wondered just
how many had no interest in bidding themselves but had
simply come to see the showdown between the Trumpers
and Mrs Trentham.

Syd Wrexall, as the representative of the Shops Committee, was already in the front row, arms folded, trying to look
composed, his vast bulk almost taking up two seats. Charlie
suspected that he wouldn't go much beyond the second or
third bid. He soon spotted Mrs Trentham seated in the third
row, her gaze fixed directly on the grandfather clock.

Then, with two minutes to spare, Becky slipped into
the auction house. Charlie was sitting on the edge of his
seat waiting to carry out his instructions to the letter. He
rose from his place and walked purposefully towards the
exit. This time Mrs Trentham did glance round to see what
Charlie was up to. Innocently he collected another bill of
sale from the back of the room, then returned to his seat at

a leisurely pace, stopping to talk to another shop owner who had obviously taken an hour off to watch the proceedings.

When Charlie returned to his place he didn't look in the direction of his wife, who he knew must now be hidden somewhere towards the back of the room. Nor did he once look at Mrs Trentham, although he could feel her eyes fixed on him.

As the clock chimed ten, Mr Fothergill – a tall thin man with a flower in his buttonhole and not a hair of his silver locks out of place – climbed the four steps of the circular wooden box. Charlie thought he looked an impressive figure as he towered over them. As soon as he had composed himself he rested a hand on the rim of the box and beamed at the packed audience, picked up his gavel and said, "Good morning, ladies and gentlemen." A silence fell over the room.

"This is a sale of the property known as Number 1, Chelsea Terrace, its fixtures, fittings and contents, which have been on view to the general public for the past two weeks. The highest bidder will be required to make a deposit of ten per cent immediately following the auction, then complete the final transaction within ninety days. Those are the terms as stated on your bill of sale, and I repeat them only so that there can be no misunderstanding."

Mr Fothergill cleared his throat and Charlie could feel his heart beat faster and faster. He watched the colonel clench a fist as Becky removed a pair of glasses out of her bag and placed them in her lap.

"I have an opening bid of one thousand pounds," Fothergill told the silent audience, many of whom were standing at the side of the room or leaning against the wall as there were now few seats vacant. Charlie kept his eyes fixed on the auctioneer. Mr Fothergill smiled in the direction of Mr Wrexall, whose arms remained folded in an attitude of determined resolution. "Do I see any advance on one thousand?"

"One thousand, five hundred," said Charlie, just a little too loudly. Those not involved in the intrigue looked around to see who it was who had made the bid. Several turned to their neighbours and began talking in noisy whispers.

"One thousand, five hundred," said the auctioneer. "Do I see two thousand?" Mr Wrexall unfolded his arms and raised a hand like a child in school determined to prove he knows the answer to one of teacher's questions.

"Two thousand, five hundred," said Charlie, even before Wrexall had lowered his hand.

"Two thousand, five hundred in the centre of the room. Do I see three thousand?"

Mr Wrexall's hand rose an inch from his knee, then fell back. A deep frown formed on his face. "Do I see three thousand?" Mr Fothergill asked for a second time. Charlie couldn't believe his luck. He was going to get Number 1 for two thousand, five hundred. Each second felt like a minute as he waited for the hammer to come down.

"Do I hear three thousand bid anywhere in the room?" said Mr Fothergill, sounding a little disappointed. "Then I am offering Number 1 Chelsea Terrace at two thousand, five hundred pounds for the first time . . ." Charlie held his breath. "For the second time." The auctioneer started to raise his gavel ". . . Three thousand pounds," Mr Fothergill announced with an audible sigh of relief, as Mrs Trentham's gloved hand settled back in her lap.

"Three thousand, five hundred," said Charlie as Mr Fothergill smiled in his direction, but as soon as he looked back towards Mrs Trentham she nodded to the auctioneer's enquiry of four thousand pounds.

Charlie allowed a second or two to pass before he stood up, straightened his tie and, looking grim, walked slowly down the centre of the aisle and out on to the street. He didn't see Becky put her glasses on, or the look of triumph that came over Mrs Trentham's face. "Do I see four thousand, five hundred pounds?" asked the auctioneer, and with only a glance towards where Becky was seated he said, "I do."

Fothergill returned to Mrs Trentham and asked, "Five thousand pounds, madam?" Her eyes quickly searched round the room, but it became obvious for all to see that she couldn't work out where the last bid had come from. Murmurs started to turn into chatter as everyone in the auction house began the game of searching for the bidder. Only Becky, safely in her back row seat, didn't move a muscle.

"Quiet, please," said the auctioneer. "I have a bid of four thousand, five hundred pounds. Do I see five thousand anywhere in the room?" His gaze returned to Mrs Trentham. She raised her hand slowly, but as she did so swung quickly round to see if she could spot who was bidding against her. But no one had moved when the auctioneer said, "Five thousand, five hundred. I now have a bid of five thousand, five hundred." Mr Fothergill surveyed his audience. "Are there any more bids?" He looked in Mrs Trentham's direction, but she in turn looked baffled, her hands motionless in her lap.

"Then it's five thousand, five hundred for the first time," said Mr Fothergill. "Five thousand, five hundred for a second time" – Becky pursed her lips to stop herself from breaking into a large grin – "and for a third and final time," he said, raising his gavel.

"Six thousand," said Mrs Trentham clearly, while at the same time waving her hand. A gasp went up around the room: Becky removed her glasses with a sigh, realising that her carefully worked-out ploy had failed even though Mrs Trentham had been made to pay triple the price any shop in the terrace had fetched in the past.

The auctioneer's eyes returned to the back of the room but the glasses were now clasped firmly in Becky's hand, so he transferred his gaze back to Mrs Trentham, who sat bolt upright, a smile of satisfaction on her face.

"At six thousand for the first time," said the auctioneer, his eyes searching the room. "Six thousand for the second time then, if there are no more bids, it's six thousand for the last time . . ." Once again the gavel was raised.

"Seven thousand pounds," said a voice from the back of the room. Everyone turned to see that Charlie had returned and was now standing in the aisle, his right hand high in the air.

The colonel looked round, and when he saw who the new bidder was began to perspire, something he didn't like to do in public. He removed a handkerchief from his top pocket and mopped his brow.

"I have a bid of seven thousand pounds," said a surprised Mr Fothergill.

"Eight thousand," said Mrs Trentham, staring straight at Charlie belligerently.

"Nine thousand," barked back Charlie.

The chatter in the room quickly turned into a babble. Becky wanted to jump up and push her husband back out into the street.

"Quiet, please," said Mr Fothergill. "Quiet!" he pleaded, almost shouting. The colonel was still mopping his brow, Mr Crowther's mouth was open wide enough to have caught any passing fly and Mr Hadlow's head was firmly buried in his hands.

"Ten thousand," said Mrs Trentham, who Becky could see, like her husband, was now totally out of control.

The auctioneer asked, "Do I see eleven thousand?"

Charlie had a worried look on his face but he simply wrinkled his brow, shook his head and placed his hands back in his pocket.

Becky sighed with relief and, unclasping her hands, nervously put her glasses back on.

"Eleven thousand," said Mr Fothergill, looking towards Becky, while pandemonium broke out once again as she rose to protest, having quickly removed her glasses. Charlie looked totally bemused.

Mrs Trentham's eyes had now come to rest on Becky, whom she had finally located. With a smile of satisfaction Mrs Trentham declared, "Twelve thousand pounds."

The auctioneer looked back towards Becky, who had placed her glasses in her bag and closed the catch with a snap. He glanced towards Charlie whose hands remained firmly in his pockets.

"The bid is at the front of the room at twelve thousand pounds. Is anyone else bidding?" asked the auctioneer.

Once again his eyes darted from Becky to Charlie before returning to Mrs Trentham. "Then at twelve thousand for the first time" – he looked around once more – "for the second time, for the third and final time . . ." His gavel came down with a thud. "I declare the property sold for twelve thousand pounds to Mrs Gerald Trentham."

Becky ran towards the door, but Charlie was already out on the pavement.

"What were you playing at, Charlie?" she demanded even before she caught up with him.

"I knew she would bid up to ten thousand pounds," said Charlie, "because that's the amount she still has on deposit at her bank."

"But how could you possibly know that?"

"Mrs Trentham's second footman passed on the information to me this morning. He will, by the way, be joining us as our butler."

At that moment the chairman walked out on to the pavement. "I must say, Rebecca, your plan was brilliant. Had me completely fooled."

"Me too," said Charlie.

"You took an awful risk, Charlie Trumper," said Becky, not letting her husband off the hook.

"Perhaps, but at least I knew what her limit was. I had no idea what you were playing at."

"I made a genuine mistake," said Becky. "When I put my glasses back on . . . what are you laughing at, Charlie Trumper?"

"Thank God for genuine amateurs."

"What do you mean?"

"Mrs Trentham thought you really were bidding, and she had been tricked, so she went one bid too far. In fact, she wasn't the only one who was carried away by the occasion. I even begin to feel sorry for –"

"For Mrs Trentham?"

"Certainly not," said Charlie. "For Mr Fothergill. He's about to spend ninety days in heaven before he comes down to earth with an almighty thump."

MRS TRENTHAM

1919-1927

CHAPTER 22

I don't believe anyone could describe me as a snob. However, I do believe that the maxim, "There's a place for everything, and everything in its place" applies equally well to human beings.

I was born in Yorkshire at the height of the Victorian Empire, and I think I can safely say that during that period in our island's history my family played a considerable role.

My father, Sir Raymond Hardcastle, was not only an inventor and industrialist of great imagination and skill, but he also built up one of the nation's most successful companies. At the same time he always treated his workers as if they were all part of the family, and indeed it was this example that he set, whenever he dealt with those less fortunate than himself, that has been the benchmark by which I have attempted to conduct my own life.

I have no brothers and just one elder sister, Amy. Although there were only a couple of years between us I cannot pretend that we were ever particularly close, perhaps because I was an outgoing, even vivacious child, while she was shy and reserved, to the point of being retiring, particularly whenever it came to contact with members of the opposite sex. Father and I tried to help her find an appropriate spouse, but it was to prove an impossible task, and even he gave up once Amy had passed her fortieth birthday. Instead she has usefully occupied her time since my mother's untimely death taking care of my beloved father in his old age – an arrangement, I might add, that has suited them both admirably.

I, on the other hand, had no problem in finding myself a husband. If I remember correctly, Gerald was the fourth or perhaps even the fifth suitor who went down on bended knee to ask for my hand in marriage. Gerald and I first met when I had been a house guest at Lord and Lady Fanshaw's country home in Norfolk. The Fanshaws were old friends of my father, and I had been seeing their younger son Anthony for some considerable time. As it turned out, I was warned that he was not going to inherit his father's land or title, so it seemed to me there was little purpose in letting the young man entertain any hopes of a lasting relationship. If I remember correctly, Father was not overwhelmed with my conduct and may even have chastised me at the time, but as I tried to explain to him, at length, although Gerald may not have been the most dashing of my paramours, he did have the distinct advantage of coming from a family that farmed land in three counties, not to mention an estate in Aberdeen.

We were married at St Mary's, Great Ashton, in July 1894 and our first son, Guy, was conceived a year later; one does like a proper period of time to elapse before one's firstborn takes his place in the world, thus giving no one cause for idle chatter.

My father always treated both my sister and myself as equals, although I was often given to believe that I was his favourite. Had it not been for his sense of fair play he would surely have left everything to me, because he simply doted on Guy, whereas in fact Amy will, on my father's demise, inherit half his vast fortune. Heaven knows what possible use she could make of such wealth, her only interests in life being gardening, crochet work and the occasional visit to the Scarborough festival.

But to return to Guy, everyone who came into contact with the boy during those formative years
invariably commented on what a handsome child he
was, and although I never allowed him to become
spoilt, I did consider it nothing less than my duty to
ensure that he was given the sort of start in life that
would prepare him for the role I felt confident he was
bound eventually to play. With that in mind, even
before he'd been christened, he was registered with
Aysgarth Preparatory School, and then Harrow, from
where I assumed he would enter the Royal Military
Academy. His grandfather spared no expense when it
came to his education, and indeed, in the case of his
elder grandson, was generous to a fault.

Six years later I gave birth to a second son, Nigel,
who arrived somewhat prematurely, which may
account for why he took rather longer to progress than
his elder brother. Guy, meanwhile, was going through
several private tutors, one or two of whom found him
perhaps a little too boisterous. After all, what child
doesn't at some time put toads in your bathwater or cut
shoe-laces in half?

At the age of nine Guy duly proceeded to Aysgarth,
and from there on to Harrow. The Reverend Preben-
dary Anthony Wood was his headmaster at the time
and I reminded him that Guy was the seventh generation of Trenthams to have attended that school.

While at Harrow Guy excelled both in the combined cadet force – becoming a company sergeant-
major in his final year – and in the boxing ring, where
he beat every one of his opponents with the notable
exception of the match against Radley, where he came
up against a Nigerian, who I later learned was in his
mid-twenties.

It saddened me that during his last term at school
Guy was not made a monitor. I understood that he had
become involved in so many other activities that it was
not considered to be in his own best interests. Although

I might have hoped that his exam results would have been a little more satisfactory, I have always considered that he was one of those children who can be described as innately intelligent rather than academically clever. Despite a rather biased housemaster's report that suggested some of the marks Guy had been awarded in his final exams came as a surprise to him, my son still managed to secure his place at Sandhurst.

At the Academy Guy proved to be a first-class cadet and also found time to continue with his boxing, becoming the cadet middleweight champion. Two years later, in July 1916, he passed out in the top half of the Roll of Honour before going on to join his father's old regiment.

Gerald, I should point out, had left the Fusiliers on the death of his father in order that he might return to Berkshire and take over the running of the family estates. He had been a brevet colonel at the time of his forced retirement, and many considered that he was the natural successor to be the Commanding Officer of the Regiment. As it turned out, he was passed over for someone who wasn't even in the first battalion, a certain Danvers Hamilton. Although I had never met the gentleman in question, several brother officers expressed the view that his appointment had been a travesty of justice. However, I had every confidence that Guy would redeem the family honour and in time go on to command the regiment himself.

Although Gerald was not directly involved in the Great War he did nevertheless serve his country during those arduous years by allowing his name to be put forward as a parliamentary candidate for Berkshire West, a constituency that in the middle of the last century his grandfather had represented for the Liberals under Palmerston. He was returned unopposed in three elections and worked for his party diligently from the back benches, having made it clear to all concerned that he had no desire to hold office.

After Guy had received the King's Commission, he was despatched to Aldershot as a second lieutenant where he continued with his training in preparation for joining the regiment on the Western Front. On being awarded his second pip in less than a year he was transferred to Edinburgh and seconded to the second battalion a few weeks before they were ordered to sail for France.

Nigel, meanwhile, had just entered Harrow and was attempting to follow in his brother's footsteps – I fear, however, not with quite the same obvious flair. In fact during one of those interminable holidays they will give children nowadays he complained to me of being bullied. I told the boy to buckle down and remember that we were at war. I also pointed out that I could never recall Guy making a fuss on that particular score.

I watched my two sons closely during that long summer of 1917 and cannot pretend that Guy found Nigel an amiable companion while he was at home on leave; in fact he barely tolerated his company. I kept telling Nigel that he had to strive to gain his elder brother's respect, but this only resulted in Nigel running off to hide in the garden for hours on end.

During his leave that summer I advised Guy to visit his grandfather in Yorkshire and even found a first edition of *Songs of Innocence* to present him with, which I knew my father had long wanted to add to his collection. Guy returned a week later and confirmed that securing a William Blake the old man did not have had indeed put Granpa "in good salts".

Naturally, like any mother, during that particular inspiring period in our history I became anxious that Guy should be seen to acquit himself well in the face of the enemy, and eventually, God willing, return home in one piece. As it turned out, I think I can safely say that no mother, however proud, could have asked for more of a son.

Guy was promoted to the rank of captain at a very young age and, following the second battle of the Marne, was awarded the Military Cross. Others who read the citation felt he had been a touch unlucky not to have been put forward for the VC. I have resisted pointing out to them that any such recommendation would have had to be countersigned by his commanding officer in the field, and as he was a certain Danvers Hamilton, the injustice was readily explicable.

Soon after the Armistice was signed Guy returned home to serve a tour of duty at the Regimental Barracks in Hounslow. While he was on leave I asked Spink's to engrave both of his MCs, dress and miniature, with the initials G.F.T. Meanwhile, his brother Nigel was, after some influence being exercised by Gerald, finally accepted as a cadet at the Royal Military Academy.

During the time Guy was back in London, I feel certain he sowed a few wild oats – what young man of that age doesn't? – but he well understood that marriage before the age of thirty could only harm his chances of promotion.

Although he brought several young ladies down to Ashurst at the weekends, I knew none of them was serious and anyway, I already had my eye on a particular girl from the next village who had been known to the family for some considerable time. Despite being without a title she could trace her family back to the Norman Conquest. More important, they could walk on their own land from Ashurst to Hastings.

It thus came as a particularly unpleasant shock for me when Guy turned up one weekend accompanied by a girl called Rebecca Salmon, who, I found it hard to believe, was at that time sharing rooms with the Harcourt-Brownes' daughter.

As I have already made abundantly clear, I am not a snob. But Miss Salmon is, I fear, the type of girl who always manages to bring out the worst in me. Don't misunderstand me. I have nothing against anyone simply because they wish to be educated. In fact I'm basically in favour of such goings-on – in sensible proportions – but at the same time that doesn't allow one to assume one automatically has a right to a place in society. You see, I just can't abide anyone who pretends to be something that they obviously are not, and I sensed even before meeting Miss Salmon that she was coming down to Ashurst with one purpose in mind.

We all understood that Guy was having a fling while he was based in London – after all, Miss Salmon was that type of girl. Indeed, when the following weekend I had Guy to myself for a few moments I was able to warn him never to allow the likes of Miss Salmon to get their hooks into him, and that he must realise he would be a marvellous catch for someone from her background.

Guy laughed at such a suggestion and assured me that he had no long-term plans for the baker's daughter. In any case, he reminded me, he would be departing to serve with the Colours in Poona before too long, so marriage was out of the question. He must have sensed, however, that my fears were still not fully assuaged, because after further thought he added, "It may interest you to know, Mother, that Miss Salmon is presently walking out with a sergeant from the regiment with whom she has an understanding."

In fact two weeks later Guy appeared at Ashurst with a Miss Victoria Berkeley, a far more suitable choice whose mother I had known for years; indeed, if the girl hadn't had four other sisters and an impoverished archdeacon for a father, she might in time have suited admirably.

To be fair, after that single unfortunate occasion Guy never mentioned the name of Rebecca Salmon in my presence again, and as he sailed for India a few months later I assumed I had heard the last of the wretched girl.

When Nigel eventually left Sandhurst he didn't follow Guy into the regiment, as it had become abundantly clear during his two-year period at the Academy that he was not cut out to be a soldier. However, Gerald was able to secure him a position with a firm of stockbrokers in the City where one of his cousins was the senior partner. I have to admit that the reports that filtered back to me from time to time were not encouraging, but once I had mentioned to Gerald's cousin that I would eventually be needing someone to manage his grandfather's portfolio, Nigel started to progress slowly up the firm's ladder.

It must have been about six months later that Lieutenant-Colonel Sir Danvers Hamilton dropped Gerald that note through the letter-box at 19 Chester Square. The moment Gerald told me that Hamilton wanted a private word with him, I sensed trouble. Over the years I had come in contact with many of Gerald's brother-officers so I knew exactly how to handle them. Gerald, on the other hand, is quite naïve when it comes to matters of a personal nature, invariably giving the other fellow the benefit of the doubt. I immediately checked my husband's whip commitments in the Commons for the following week and arranged for Sir Danvers to visit us on the Monday evening at six, knowing only too well that, because of his commitments in the House, Gerald would almost certainly have to cancel the meeting at the last moment.

Gerald phoned soon after five on the day in question to say that he couldn't possibly get away and suggested the colonel might come on over to the House of Commons. I said I would see what I could do. An hour later Sir Danvers arrived at Chester Square. After I had apologised and explained my husband's absence I was able to convince him that he should convey his message to me. When the colonel informed me that Miss Salmon was going to have a child I naturally asked of what interest that could possibly be to Gerald or myself. He hesitated only for a moment before suggesting that Guy was the father. I realised immediately that if such a slander was allowed to spread abroad it might even reach the ears of his brother-officers in Poona and that could only do immense harm to my son's chances of further promotion. Any such suggestion I therefore dismissed as ridiculous, along with the colonel in the same breath.

It was during a rubber of bridge at Celia Littlechild's house a few weeks later that she let slip that she had employed a private detective called Harris to spy on her first husband, once she was convinced he was being unfaithful. After learning this piece of information I found myself quite unable to concentrate on the game, much to my partner's annoyance.

On returning home I looked up the name in the London directory. There he was: Max Harris, Private Detective – ex-Scotland Yard, all problems considered. After some minutes staring at the phone, I finally picked up the headpiece and asked the operator to get me Paddington 3720. I waited for several moments before anyone spoke.

"Harris," said a gruff voice without further explanation.

"Is that the detective agency?" I asked, nearly replacing the phone back on the hook before I had given the man a chance to reply.

"Yes, madam, it is," said the voice, sounding a little more enthusiastic.

"I may be in need of your help – for a friend, you understand," I said, feeling rather embarrassed.

"A friend," said the voice. "Yes, of course. Then perhaps we should meet."

"But not at your office," I insisted.

"I quite understand, madam. Would the St Agnes Hotel, Bury Street, South Kensington, four o'clock tomorrow afternoon suit?"

"Yes," I said and put the phone down, suddenly aware that he didn't know my name and I didn't know what he looked like.

When the following day I arrived at the St Agnes, a dreadful little place just off the Brompton Road, I walked round the block several times before I finally felt able to enter the lobby. A man of about thirty perhaps thirty-five was leaning on the reception desk. He straightened up the moment he saw me.

"Are you looking for a Mr Harris, by any chance?" he enquired.

I nodded and he quickly led us through to the tea room and ushered me into a seat in the furthest corner. Once he had sat down in the chair opposite me I began to study him more carefully. He must have been about five foot ten, stocky with dark brown hair and an even browner moustache. He wore a brown check Harris Tweed jacket, cream shirt and thin yellow tie. As I began to explain why I might be in need of his services I became distracted as he started to click the knuckles of his fingers, one by one, first the left hand and then the right. I wanted to get up and leave, and would have done so had I believed for a moment that finding anyone less obnoxious to carry out the task would have proved easy.

It also took me some considerable time to convince Harris that I was not looking for a divorce. At that first meeting I explained to him as much of my dilemma as I felt able. I was shocked when he demanded the extortionate fee of five shillings an hour just to begin his investigation. However, I did not feel I had been left with a great deal of choice in the matter. I agreed that he should start the following day and that we would meet again a week later.

Mr Harris's first report informed me that, in the view of those who spent most of their working hours at a pub in Chelsea called the Musketeer, Charlie Trumper was the father of Rebecca Salmon's child, and indeed when the suggestion was put to him directly he made no attempt to deny it. As if to prove the point, within days of the child's birth he and Miss Salmon were married – quietly in a register office.

Mr Harris had no trouble in obtaining a copy of the child's birth certificate. It confirmed that the child, Daniel George Trumper, was the son of Rebecca Salmon and Charlie George Trumper of 147 Chelsea Terrace. I also noted that the child had been named after both his grandparents. In my next letter to Guy I enclosed a copy of the birth certificate along with one or two other little snippets that Harris had supplied, such as details of the wedding and Colonel Hamilton's appointment as chairman of the Trumper board. I must confess that I assumed that was an end of the matter.

However, two weeks later I received a letter from Guy: I presume it must have crossed with mine in the post. He explained that Sir Danvers had been in communication with his commanding officer, Colonel Forbes, and because of Forbes's insistence that there might be a breach of promise suit pending Guy had been made to appear in front of a group of his fellow-officers to explain the relationship between himself and Miss Salmon.

I immediately sat down and wrote a long letter to Colonel Forbes – Guy was obviously not in a position to present the full evidence I had managed to secure. I included a further copy of the birth certificate so that he would be left in no doubt that my son could not have possibly been involved with the Salmon girl in any way. I added – without prejudice – that Colonel Hamilton was now employed as chairman of the board of Trumper's, a position from which he certainly derived some remuneration. The long information sheets now sent to me on a weekly basis by Mr Harris were, I had to admit, proving of considerable value.

For some little time matters returned to normal. Gerald busied himself with his parliamentary duties while I concentrated on nothing more demanding than the appointment of the new vicar's warden and my bridge circle.

The problem, however, went deeper than I had imagined, for quite by chance I discovered that we were no longer to be included on the guest list for Daphne Harcourt-Browne's marriage to the Marquess of Wiltshire. Of course, Percy would never have become the twelfth marquess had it not been for his father and brother sacrificing their lives on the Western Front. However, I learned from others who were present at the ceremony that Colonel Hamilton as well as the Trumpers were to be seen at St Margaret's, and at the reception afterwards.

During this period, Mr Harris continued to supply me with memoranda about the comings and goings of the Trumpers and their growing business empire. I must confess that I had no interest whatsoever in any of their commercial transactions: it was a world that remained totally alien to me but I didn't stop him going beyond his brief as it gave me a useful insight into Guy's adversaries.

A few weeks later I received a note from Colonel Forbes acknowledging my letter but otherwise I heard nothing further concerning Guy's unfortunate misrepresentation. I therefore assumed everything must be back on an even keel and that Colonel Hamilton's fabrication had been treated with the disdain it merited.

Then one morning in June the following year, Gerald was called away to the War Office on what he thought at the time must be another routine parliamentary briefing.

When my husband returned to Chester Square unexpectedly that afternoon he made me sit down and drink a large whisky before he explained that he had some unpleasant news to impart. I had rarely seen him looking so grim as I sat there silently wondering what could possibly be important enough to cause him to return home during the day.

"Guy has resigned his commission," announced Gerald tersely. "He will be returning to England just as soon as the necessary paperwork has been completed."

"Why?" I asked, quite stunned.

"No reason was given," Gerald replied. "I was called to the War Office this morning, and tipped off by Billy Cuthbert, a brother-Fusilier. He informed me privately that if Guy hadn't resigned he would undoubtedly have been cashiered."

During the time I waited for Guy's return to England I went over every snippet of information on the rapidly growing Trumper empire that Mr Harris was able to supply me with, however minute or seemingly insignificant it seemed at the time. Among the many pages of material that the detective sent, no doubt in order to justify his outrageous fees, I came across one item which I suspected might have been almost as important to the Trumpers as my son's reputation was to me.

I carried out all the necessary enquiries myself, and having checked over the property one Sunday morning I phoned Savill's on the Monday and made a bid of two thousand, five hundred pounds for the property in question. The agent rang back later in the week to say someone else – who I realised had to be Trumpers – had offered three thousand. "Then bid four thousand," I told him, before replacing the phone.

The estate agents were able to confirm later that afternoon that I was in possession of the freehold on 25 to 99 Chelsea Terrace, a block of thirty-seven flats. Trumper's representative, I was assured, would be informed immediately who their next-door neighbour was to be.

CHAPTER 23

uy Trentham arrived back on the doorstep of 19 Chester Square on a chilly afternoon in September 1922, just after Gibson had cleared away afternoon tea. His mother would never forget the occasion, because when Guy was shown into the drawing room she hardly recognised him. Mrs Trentham had been writing a letter at her desk when Gibson announced, "Captain Guy."

She turned to see her son enter the room and walk straight over to the fireplace where he stood, legs astride, with his back to the coals. His glazed eyes stared in front of him but he didn't speak.

Mrs Trentham was only thankful that her husband was taking part in a debate at the Commons that afternoon and was not expected back until after the ten o'clock vote that night.

Guy obviously hadn't shaved for several days. He could also have made excellent use of a scrubbing brush, while the suit he wore was barely recognisable as the one that only three years before had been tailored by Gieves. The dishevelled figure stood with his back to the blazing coal fire, his body visibly shivering, as he turned to face his mother. For the first time Mrs Trentham noticed that her son was holding a brown paper parcel under one arm.

Although she was not cold, Mrs Trentham also shuddered. She remained at her desk, feeling no desire to embrace her first-born, or be the one who broke the silence between them.

"What have you been told, Mother?" Guy uttered at last, his voice shaky and uncertain.

"Nothing of any real substance." She looked up at him quizzically. "Other than that you have resigned your commission, and that had you not done so you would have been cashiered."

"That much is true," he admitted, at last releasing the parcel he had been clutching and placing it on the table beside him. "But only because they conspired against me."

"They?"

"Yes, Colonel Hamilton, Trumper and the girl."

"Colonel Forbes preferred the word of Miss Salmon even after I had written to him?" asked Mrs Trentham icily.

"Yes – yes, he did. After all, Colonel Hamilton still has a lot of friends in the regiment and some of them were only too happy to carry out his bidding if it meant a rival might be eliminated."

She watched him for a moment as he swayed nervously from foot to foot. "But I thought the matter had been finally settled. After all, the birth certificate – "

"That might have been the case had it been signed by Charlie Trumper as well as the girl, but the certificate only bore the single signature – hers. What made matters worse, Colonel Hamilton advised Miss Salmon to threaten a breach of promise suit naming me as the father. Had she done so, of course, despite my being innocent of any charge they could lay at my door, the good name of the regiment would have suffered irredeemably. I therefore felt I'd been left with no choice but to take the honourable course and resign my commission." His voice became even more bitter. "And all because Trumper feared that the truth might come out."

"What are you talking about, Guy?"

He avoided his mother's direct gaze as he moved from the fireplace to the drinks cabinet where he poured himself a large whisky. He left the soda siphon untouched and took a long swallow. His mother waited in silence for him to continue.

"After the second battle of the Marne I was ordered by Colonel Hamilton to set up an enquiry into Trumper's cowardice in the field," said Guy as he moved back to the fireplace. "Many thought he should have been court-martialled, but the only other witness, a Private Prescott, was himself killed by a stray bullet when only yards from the safety of our own trenches. I had foolishly allowed myself to lead Prescott and Trumper back towards our lines, and when Prescott fell I looked round to see a smile on Trumper's face. All he said was, 'Bad luck, Captain, now you haven't got your witness, have you?'"

"Did you tell anyone about this at the time?"

Guy returned to the drinks cabinet to refill his glass. "Who could I tell without Prescott to back me up? The least I could do was to make sure that he was awarded a posthumous Military Medal. Even if it meant letting Trumper off the hook. Later, I discovered Trumper wouldn't even confirm my version of what had happened on the battlefield which nearly prevented my being awarded the MC."

"And now that he's succeeded in forcing you to resign your commission, it can only be your word against his."

"That would have been the case if Trumper had not made one foolish mistake which could still cause his downfall."

"What are you talking about?"

"Well," continued Guy, his manner slightly more composed, "while the battle was at its height I came to the rescue of the two men in question. I found them hiding in a bombed-out church. I made the decision to remain there until nightfall, when it was my intention to lead them back to the safety of our own trenches. While we were waiting on the roof for the sun to go down and Trumper was under the impression that I was asleep, I saw him slope off back to the chancel and remove a magnificent picture of the Virgin Mary from behind the altar. I continued to watch him as he placed the little oil in his haversack. I said nothing at the time because I realised that this was the proof I needed of his duplicity; after all, the picture could always be returned to the church at some later date. Once we were back behind our own lines I immediately had Trumper's equipment searched so I could have him arrested for the theft. But to my surprise it was nowhere to be found."

"So how can that be of any use to you now?"

"Because the picture has subsequently reappeared."

"Reappeared?"

"Yes," said Guy, his voice rising. "Daphne Harcourt-Browne told me that she had spotted the painting on the drawing room wall in Trumper's house, and was even able to give me a detailed description of it. There was no doubt in my mind that it was the same portrait of the Virgin Mary and Child that he had earlier stolen from the church."

"But there's little anyone can do about that while the painting is still hanging in his home."

"It isn't any longer. Which is the reason I'm disguised like this."

"You must stop talking in riddles," said his mother. "Explain yourself properly, Guy."

"This morning I visited Trumper's home, and told the housekeeper that I had served alongside her master on the Western Front."

"Was that wise, Guy?"

"I told her my name was Fowler, Corporal Denis Fowler, and I had been trying to get in touch with Charlie for some time. I knew he wasn't around because I'd seen him go into one of his shops on Chelsea Terrace only a few minutes before. The maid – who stared at me suspiciously – asked if I would wait in the hall while she went upstairs to tell Mrs Trumper I was there. That gave me easily enough time to slip into the front room and remove the picture from where Daphne had told me it was hanging. I was out of the house even before they could possibly have worked out what I was up to."

"But surely they will report the theft to the police and you will be arrested."

"Not a chance," said Guy as he picked up the brown

paper parcel from the table and started to unwrap it. "The last thing Trumper will want the police to get their hands on is this." He passed the picture over to his mother.

Mrs Trentham stared at the little oil. "From now on you can leave Mr Trumper to me," she said without explanation. Guy smiled for the first time since he had set foot in the house. "However," she continued, "we must concentrate on the more immediate problem of what we are going to do about your future. I'm still confident I can get you a position in the City. I have already spoken to –"

"That won't work, Mother, and you know it. There's no future for me in England for the time being. Or, at least, not until my name has been cleared. In any case, I don't want to hang around London explaining to your bridge circle why I'm no longer with the regiment in India. No, I'll have to go abroad until things have quietened down a little."

"Then I'll need some more time to think," Guy's mother replied. "Meanwhile, go up and have a bath and shave, and while you're at it find yourself some clean clothes and I'll work out what has to be done."

As soon as Guy had left the room Mrs Trentham returned to her writing desk and locked the little picture in the bottom left-hand drawer. She placed the key in her bag, then began to concentrate on the more immediate problem of what should be done to protect the Trentham name.

As she stared out of the window a plan began to form in her mind which, although it would require using even more of her dwindling resources, might at least give her the breathing space she required to expose Trumper for the thief and liar he was, and at the same time to exonerate her son.

Mrs Trentham reckoned she only had about fifty pounds in cash in the safe-deposit box in her bedroom, but she still possessed sixteen thousand of the twenty thousand that her father had settled on her the day she was married. "Always there in case of some unforeseen emergency," he had told her prophetically.

Mrs Trentham took out a piece of writing paper from her drawer and began to make some notes. She was only too aware that once her son left Chester Square that night she might not see him again for some considerable time. Forty minutes later she studied her efforts:

> £50 (cash)
> Sydney
> Max Harris
> Greatcoat
> £5,000 (cheque)
> Bentley's
> Picture
> Local police

Her thoughts were interrupted by the return of Guy looking a little more like the son she remembered. A blazer and cavalry twills had replaced the crumpled suit and the skin, although pale, was at least cleanshaven. Mrs Trentham folded up the piece of paper, having finally decided on exactly what course of action needed to be taken.

"Now, sit down and listen carefully," she said.

Guy Trentham left Chester Square a few minutes after nine o'clock, an hour before his father was due to return from the Commons. He had fifty-three pounds in cash along with a cheque for five thousand pounds lodged in an inside pocket. He had agreed that he would write to his father the moment he landed in Sydney, explaining why he had travelled direct to Australia. His mother had vowed that while he was away she would do everything in her power to clear her son's name, so that he might eventually return to England vindicated and take up his rightful place as head of the family.

The only two servants who had seen Captain Trentham that evening were instructed by their mistress not to mention his visit to anyone, especially her husband, on pain of losing their positions in the household.

Mrs Trentham's final task before her husband returned home that night was to phone the local police. A Constable Wrigley dealt with the reported theft.

During those weeks of waiting for her son's letter to arrive, Mrs Trentham did not sit around idly. The day after Guy sailed to Australia she made one of her periodic visits to the St Agnes Hotel – a rewrapped parcel under one arm – and handed over her prize to Mr Harris before giving him a series of detailed instructions.

Two days later the detective was able to confirm that the portrait of the Virgin Mary and Child had been left with Bentley's the pawnbroker, and could not be sold for at least five years when the date on the pawn ticket would have expired. He handed over a photo of the picture and the receipt to prove it. Mrs Trentham placed the photo in her handbag but didn't bother to ask Harris what had become of the five pounds he had been paid for the picture.

"Good," she said, placing her handbag by the side of her chair. "In fact highly satisfactory."

"So would you like me to point the right man at Scotland Yard in the direction of Bentley's?" asked Harris.

"Certainly not," said Mrs Trentham. "I need you to carry out a little research on the picture before anyone else will set eyes on it, and then if my information proves correct the next occasion that painting will be seen by the public will be when it comes under the hammer at Sotheby's."

CHAPTER 24

"ood morning, madam. I do apologise for having to bother you in this way."

"It's no bother," said Mrs Trentham to the police officer whom Gibson had announced as Inspector Richards.

"It's not you I was hoping to see actually, Mrs Trentham," explained the inspector. "It's your son, Captain Guy Trentham."

"Then you'll have a very long journey ahead of you, Inspector."

"I'm not sure I understand you, madam."

"My son," said Mrs Trentham, "is taking care of our family interests in Australia, where he is a partner in a large firm of cattle brokers."

Richards was unable to hide his surprise. "And how long has he been out there, madam?"

"For some considerable time, Inspector."

"Could you be more precise?"

"Captain Trentham left England for India in February 1920, to complete his tour of duty with the regiment. He won the MC at the second battle of the Marne, you know." She nodded towards the mantelpiece. The inspector looked suitably impressed. "Of course," Mrs Trentham continued, "it was never his intention to remain in the army, as we had always planned that he would have a spell in the colonies before returning to run our estates in Berkshire."

"But did he come back to England before taking up this position in Australia?"

"Sadly not, Inspector," said Mrs Trentham. "Once he had resigned his commission he travelled directly to Australia to take up his new responsibilities. My husband, who as I am sure you know is the Member of Parliament for Berkshire West, would be able to confirm the exact dates for you."

"I don't feel it will be necessary to bother him on this occasion, madam."

"And why, may I ask, did you wish to see my son in the first place?"

"We are following up enquiries concerning the theft of a painting in Chelsea."

Mrs Trentham offered no comment so the detective continued. "Someone who fits your son's description was seen in the vicinity wearing an old army greatcoat. We hoped he might therefore be able to help us with our enquiries."

"And when was this crime committed?"

"Last September, madam, and as the painting has not yet been recovered we are still pursuing the matter – " Mrs Trentham kept her head slightly bowed as she learned this piece of information and continued to listen carefully. "– but we are now given to understand that the owner will not be preferring charges, so I expect the file should be closed on this one fairly shortly. This your son?" The inspector pointed to a photograph of Guy in full dress uniform that rested on a side table.

"It is indeed, Inspector."

"Doesn't exactly fit the description we were given," said the policeman, looking slightly puzzled. "In any case, as you say, he must have been in Australia at the time. A cast-iron alibi." The inspector smiled ingratiatingly but Mrs Trentham's expression didn't alter.

"You're not suggesting that my son was in any way involved in this theft, are you?" she asked coldly.

"Certainly not, madam. It's just that we've come across

a greatcoat which Gieves, the Savile Row tailors, have confirmed they made for a Captain Trentham. We found an old soldier wearing it who . . ."

"Then you must have also found your thief," said Mrs Trentham with disdain.

"Hardly, madam. You see, the gentleman in question has only one leg."

Mrs Trentham still showed no concern. "Then I suggest you ring Chelsea police station," she said, "as I feel sure they will be able to enlighten you further on the matter."

"But I'm from Chelsea police station myself," replied the inspector, looking even more puzzled.

Mrs Trentham rose from the sofa and walked slowly over to her desk, pulled open a drawer and removed a single sheet of paper. She handed it to the inspector. His face reddened as he began to take in the contents. When he had finished reading the document he passed the piece of paper back.

"I do apologise, madam. I had no idea that you had reported the loss of the greatcoat the same day. I shall have a word with young Constable Wrigley just as soon as I get back to the station." Mrs Trentham showed no reaction to the policeman's embarrassment. "Well, I won't take up any more of your time," he said. "I'll just show myself out."

Mrs Trentham waited until she heard the door close behind him before picking up the phone and asking for a Paddington number.

She made only one request of the detective before replacing the receiver.

Mrs Trentham knew that Guy must have arrived safely in Australia when her cheque was cleared by Coutts and Co through a bank in Sydney. The promised letter to his father arrived on the doormat a further six weeks after that. When Gerald imparted to her the contents of the letter explaining that Guy had joined a firm of cattle brokers she feigned surprise at her son's uncharacteristic action, but her husband didn't seem to show a great deal of interest either way.

During the following months Harris's reports continued to show that Trumper's newly formed company was going from strength to strength, but it still brought a smile to Mrs Trentham's lips when she recalled how for a mere four thousand pounds she had stopped Charles Trumper right in his tracks.

The same smile was not to return to Mrs Trentham's face again until she received a letter from Savill's sometime later presenting her with an opportunity to repeat for Rebecca Trumper the same acute frustration as she had managed in the past for Charlie Trumper, even if this time the cost to herself might be a little higher. She checked her bank balance, satisfied that it would prove more than adequate for the purpose she had in mind.

Over the years Savill's had kept Mrs Trentham well informed of any shops that came up for sale in Chelsea Terrace but she made no attempt to stop Trumper from purchasing them, reasoning that her possession of the flats would be quite adequate to ruin any long-term plans he might have for the whole terrace. However, when the details of Number 1 Chelsea Terrace were sent to her she realised that here the circumstances were entirely different. Not only was Number 1 the corner shop, facing as it did towards the Fulham Road, and the largest property on the block, it was also an established if somewhat run-down fine art dealer and auctioneer. It was the obvious outlet for all those years of preparation Mrs Trumper had put in at Bedford College and more recently at Sotheby's.

A letter accompanying the bill of sale asked if Mrs Trentham wished to be represented at the auction that Mr Fothergill, the present owner, was proposing to conduct himself.

She wrote back the same day, thanking Savill's but explaining that she would prefer to carry out her own bidding and would be further obliged if they could furnish her with an estimate of how much the property might be expected to fetch.

Savill's reply contained several ifs and buts, as in their view the property was unique. They also pointed out that they were not qualified to offer an opinion as to the value of the stock. However, they settled on an upper estimate in the region of four thousand pounds.

During the following weeks Mrs Trentham was to be found regularly seated in the back row of Christie's, silently watching the various auctions as they were conducted. She never nodded or raised a hand herself. She wanted to be certain that when the time came for her to bid she would be thoroughly familiar with the protocol of such occasions.

On the morning of the sale of Number 1 Chelsea Terrace Mrs Trentham entered the auctioneer's wearing a long dark red dress that swept along the ground. She selected a place in the third row and was seated some twenty minutes before the bidding was due to commence. Her eyes never remained still as she watched the different players enter the room and take their places. Mr Wrexall arrived a few minutes after she had, taking a seat in the middle of the front row. He looked grim but determined. He was exactly as Mr Harris had described him, mid-forties, heavily built and balding. Being so badly overweight he looked considerably older than his years, she considered. His flesh was swarthy and whenever he lowered his head several more chins appeared. It was then that Mrs Trentham decided that should she fail to secure Number 1 Chelsea Terrace a meeting with Mr Wrexall might prove advantageous.

At nine fifty precisely Colonel Hamilton led his two colleagues down the aisle and filed into the vacant seats immediately behind Mrs Trentham. Although she glanced at the colonel he made no effort to acknowledge her presence. At nine fifty there was still no sign of either Mr or Mrs Trumper.

Savill's had warned Mrs Trentham that Trumper might be represented by an outside agent, but from all she had gathered about the man over the years she couldn't believe he would allow anyone else to carry out the bidding for him. She was not to be disappointed, for when the clock behind the auctioneer's box showed five minutes before the hour, in he strode. Although he was a few years older than he had been at the time of the photograph she held in her hand, she was in no doubt that it was Charlie Trumper. He wore a smart, well-tailored suit that helped disguise the fact that he was beginning to have a weight problem. A smile rarely left his lips though she had plans to remove it. He seemed to want everyone to know he had arrived, as he shook hands and chatted with several people before taking a reserved seat on the aisle about four rows behind her. Mrs Trentham half turned her chair so she could observe both Trumper and the auctioneer without having continually to look round.

Suddenly Mr Trumper rose and made his way towards the back of the room, only to pick up a bill of sale from the table at the entrance before returning to his reserved place on the aisle. Mrs Trentham suspected that this performance had been carried out for some specific reason. Her eyes raked each row and although she could see nothing untoward she nevertheless felt uneasy.

By the time Mr Fothergill had climbed the steps of the auctioneer's box the room was already full. Yet despite almost every place having been taken Mrs Trentham was still unable to see if Mrs Trumper was seated among the large gathering.

From the moment Mr Fothergill called for the first bid the auction did not proceed as Mrs Trentham had imagined, or indeed planned. Nothing she had experienced at Christie's during the previous month could have prepared her for the final outcome – Mr Fothergill announcing a mere six minutes later, "Sold for twelve thousand pounds to Mrs Gerald Trentham."

She was angry at having made such a public spectacle of herself, even if she had secured the fine art shop and dealt a satisfying blow to Rebecca Trumper. It had certainly been done at a considerable cost, and now she wasn't even certain she had enough money to cover the full amount she had committed herself to.

After eighty days of soul-searching, in which she considered approaching her husband and even her father to make up the shortfall, Mrs Trentham finally decided to sacrifice the one thousand and two hundred pounds deposit, retreat, and lick her wounds. The alternative was to admit to her husband exactly what had taken place at Number 1 Chelsea Terrace that day.

There was one compensation, however. She would no longer need to use Sotheby's when the time came to dispose of the stolen painting.

As the months passed, Mrs Trentham received regular letters from her son, first from Sydney, then later from Melbourne, informing her of his progress. They often requested her to send more money. The larger the partnership grew, Guy explained, the more he needed extra capital to secure his share of the equity. Overall some six thousand pounds found its way across the Pacific Ocean to a bank in Sydney during a period of four years, none of which Mrs Trentham resented giving since Guy appeared to be making such a success of his new profession. She also felt confident that once she could expose Charles Trumper for the thief and liar he was, her son could return to England with his reputation vindicated, even in the eyes of his father.

Then suddenly, just at the point when Mrs Trentham had begun to believe that the time might be right to put the next stage of her plan into action, a cable arrived from Melbourne. The address from which the missive had been sent left Mrs Trentham with no choice but to leave for that distant city without delay.

When, over dinner that night, she informed Gerald that she intended to depart for the Antipodes on the first possible tide her news was greeted with polite indifference. This came as no surprise, as Guy's name had rarely passed her husband's lips since that day he had visited the War Office over four years before. In fact, the only sign that still remained of their firstborn's existence at either Ashurst Hall or Chester Square was the one picture of him in full dress uniform that stood on her bedroom table and the MC that Gerald had allowed to remain on the mantelpiece.

As far as Gerald was concerned, Nigel was their only child.

Gerald Trentham was well aware that his wife told all his and her friends that Guy was a successful partner in a large firm of cattle brokers that had offices right across Australia. However, he had long ago stopped believing such stories, and had lately even stopped listening to them. Whenever the occasional envelope, in that all too familiar hand, dropped through the letter-box at Chester Square, Gerald Trentham made no enquiry as to his elder son's progress.

The next ship scheduled to sail for Australia was the SS *Orontes*, which was due out of Southampton on the following Monday. Mrs Trentham cabled back to an address in Melbourne to let them know her estimated time of arrival.

The five-week trip across two oceans seemed interminable to Mrs Trentham, especially as for most of the time she chose to remain in her cabin, having no desire to strike up a casual acquaintanceship with anyone on board – or, worse, bump into someone who actually knew her. She turned down several invitations to join the captain's table for dinner.

Once the ship had docked at Sydney, Mrs Trentham only rested overnight in that city before travelling on to Melbourne. On arrival at Spencer Street station she took a taxi directly to the Royal Victoria hospital where the sister in charge told her matter-of-factly that her son had only another week to live.

They allowed her to see him immediately, and a police officer escorted her to the special isolation wing. She stood by his bedside, staring down in disbelief at a face she could barely recognise. Guy's hair was so thin and grey and the lines on his face so deep that Mrs Trentham felt she might have been at her husband's death-bed.

A doctor told her that such a condition was not uncommon once the verdict had been delivered and the person concerned realised there was no hope of a reprieve. After standing at the end of the bed for nearly an hour she left without having been able to elicit a word from her son. At no time did she allow any of the hospital staff to become aware of her true feelings.

That evening Mrs Trentham booked herself into a quiet country club on the outskirts of Melbourne. She made only one enquiry of the young expatriate owner, a Mr Sinclair-Smith, before retiring to her room.

The next morning she presented herself at the offices of the oldest firm of solicitors in Melbourne, Asgarth, Jenkins and Co. A young man she considered far too familiar asked "what was her problem".

"I wish to have a word with your senior partner," Mrs Trentham replied.

"Then you'll have to take a seat in the waiting room," he told her.

Mrs Trentham sat alone for some time before Mr Asgarth was free to see her.

The senior partner, an elderly man who from his dress might have been conducting his practice in Lincoln's Inn Fields rather than Victoria Street, Melbourne, listened in silence to her sad story and agreed to deal with any problems that might arise from handling Guy Trentham's estate. To that end he promised to lodge an immediate application for permission to have the body transported back to England.

Mrs Trentham visited her son in hospital every day of that week before he died. Although little conversation passed between them, she did learn of one problem that would have to be dealt with before she could hope to travel back to England.

On the Wednesday afternoon Mrs Trentham returned to the offices of Asgarth, Jenkins and Co to seek the advice of the senior partner on what could be done following her latest discovery. The elderly lawyer ushered his client to a chair before he listened carefully to her revelation. He made the occasional note on a pad in front of him. When Mrs Trentham had finished he did not offer an opinion for some considerable time.

"There will have to be a change of name," he suggested, "if no one else is to find out what you have in mind."

"And we must also be sure that there is no way of tracing who her father was at some time in the future," said Mrs Trentham.

The old solicitor frowned. "That will require you to place considerable trust in" – he checked the scribbled name in front of him – "Miss Benson."

"Pay Miss Benson whatever it takes to assure her silence," said Mrs Trentham. "Coutts in London will handle all the financial details."

The senior partner nodded and by dint of remaining at his desk until nearly midnight for the next four days he managed to complete all the paperwork necessary to fulfil his client's requirements only hours before Mrs Trentham was due to return to London.

Guy Trentham was certified as dead by the doctor in attendance at three minutes past six on the morning of 23 April 1927, and the following day Mrs Trentham began her sombre journey back to England, accompanied by his coffin. She was relieved that only two people on that continent knew as much as she did, one an elderly gentleman only months away from retirement, the other a woman who could now spend the rest of her life in a style she would never have believed possible only a few days before.

Mrs Trentham cabled her husband with the minimum information she considered necessary before sailing back to Southampton as silently and as anonymously as she had come. Once she had set foot on English soil Mrs Trentham was driven directly to her home in Chester Square. She briefed her husband on the details of the tragedy, and he reluctantly accepted that an announcement should be placed in *The Times* the following day. It read:

The death is announced of Captain Guy Trentham MC, tragically from tuberculosis after suffering a long illness. The funeral will take place at St Mary's, Ashurst, Berkshire, on Tuesday, 8 June 1927.

The local vicar conducted the ceremony for the dear departed. His death, he assured the congregation, was a tragedy for all who knew him.

Guy Trentham was laid to rest in the plot originally reserved for his father. Major and Mrs Trentham, relations, friends of the family, parishioners and servants left the burial ground with their heads bowed low.

During the days that followed Mrs Trentham received over a hundred letters of condolence, one or two of which pointed out that she could at least be consoled with the knowledge that there was a second son to take Guy's place.

The next day Nigel's photograph replaced his elder brother's on the bedside table.

CHARLIE

1926-1945

CHAPTER 25

I was walking down Chelsea Terrace with Tom Arnold on our Monday morning round when he first offered an opinion.

"It will never happen," I said.

"You could be right, sir, but at the moment a lot of the shopkeepers are beginning to panic."

"Bunch of cowards," I told him. "With nearly a million already unemployed there'll be only a handful who would be foolish enough to consider an all-out strike."

"Perhaps, but the Shops Committee is still advising its members to board up their windows."

"Syd Wrexall would advise his members to board up their windows if a pekinese put a leg up against the front door of the Musketeer. What's more, the bloody animal wouldn't even have to piss."

A smile flickered across Tom's lips. "So you're prepared for a fight, Mr Trumper?"

"You bet I am. I'll back Mr Churchill all the way on this one." I stopped to check the window of hats and scarves. "How many people do we currently employ?"

"Seventy-one."

"And how many of those do you reckon are considering strike action?"

"Half a dozen, ten at the most would be my bet – and then only those who are members of the Shop-workers' Union. But there could still be the problem for some of our employees who wouldn't find it easy to get to work because of a public transport stoppage."

"Then give me all the names of those you're not sure of by this evening and I'll have a word with every one of them during the week. At least that way I might be able to convince one or two of them about their long-term future with the company."

"What about the company's long-term future if the strikes were to go ahead?"

"When will you get it into your head, Tom, that nothing is going to happen that will affect Trumper's?"

"Syd Wrexall thinks –"

"I can assure you that's the one thing he doesn't do."

"– thinks that at least three shops will come on the market during the next month, and if there were to be a general strike there might be a whole lot more suddenly available. The miners are persuading –"

"They're not persuading Charlie Trumper," I told him. "So let me know the moment you hear of anyone who wants to sell, because I'm still a buyer."

"While everyone else is a seller?"

"That's exactly when you *should* buy," I replied. "The time to get on a tram is when everyone else is getting off. So let me have those names, Tom. Meanwhile, I'm going to the bank." I strode off in the direction of Knightsbridge.

In the privacy of his new Brompton Road office Hadlow informed me that Trumper's were now holding a little over twelve thousand pounds on deposit: an adequate buttress, he considered, were there to be a general strike.

"Not you as well," I said in exasperation. "The strike will never take place. Even if it does, I predict it'll be over in a matter of days."

"Like the last war?" said Hadlow as he peered back at me over his half-moon spectacles. "I am by nature a cautious man, Mr Trumper –"

"Well, I'm not," I said, interrupting him. "So be

prepared to see that cash being put to good use."

"I have already earmarked around half the sum, should Mrs Trentham fail to take up her option on Number 1," he reminded me. "She still has" – he turned to check the calendar on the wall – "thirty-two days left to do so."

"Then I would suggest this is going to be a month for keeping our nerve."

"If the market were to collapse, it might be wise not to risk everything. Don't you think, Mr Trumper?"

"No, I don't, but that's why I'm –" I began, only just managing to stop myself venting my true feelings.

"It is indeed," replied Hadlow, making me feel even more embarrassed. "And that is also the reason I have backed you so wholeheartedly in the past," he added magnanimously.

As the days passed I had to admit that a general strike did look more and more likely. The air of uncertainty and lack of confidence in the future meant that first one shop and then another found its way on to the market.

I purchased the first two at knock-down prices, on the condition that the settlement was immediate, and thanks to the speed with which Crowther completed the paperwork and Hadlow released the cash, I was even able to add boots and shoes, followed by the chemist's, to my side of the ledger.

When the general strike finally began – on Tuesday, 4 May 1926 – the colonel and I were out on the streets at first light. We checked over every one of our properties from the north end to the south. All Syd Wrexall's committee members had already boarded up their shops, which I considered tantamount to giving in to the strikers. I did agree, however, to the colonel's plan for "operation lock-up", which on a given signal from me allowed Tom Arnold to have all thirteen shops locked and bolted within three minutes. On the previous Saturday I had watched Tom carry out several "practice runs", as he called them, to the amusement of the passers-by.

Although on the first morning of the strike the weather was fine and the streets were crowded the only concession I made to the milling throng was to keep all foodstuff from Numbers 147 and 131 off the pavements.

At eight Tom Arnold reported to me that only five employees had failed to turn up for work, despite spectacular traffic jams causing public transport to be held up for hours on end, and even one of those was genuinely ill.

As the colonel and I strolled up and down Chelsea Terrace we were met by the occasional insult but I didn't sense any real mood of violence and, everything considered, most people were surprisingly good-humoured. Some of the lads even started playing football in the street.

The first sign of any real unrest came on the second morning, when a brick was hurled through the front window of Number 5, jewellery and watches. I saw two or three young thugs grab whatever they could from the main window display before running off down the terrace. The crowd became restless and began shouting slogans so I gave the signal to Tom Arnold, who was about fifty yards up the road, and he immediately blew six blasts on his whistle. Within the three minutes the colonel had stipulated every one of our shops was locked and bolted. I stood my ground while the police moved in and several people were arrested. Although there was a lot of hot air blowing about, within an hour I was able to instruct Tom that the shops could be reopened and that we should continue serving customers as if nothing had happened. Within three hours hardware had replaced the window of Number 5 – not that it was a morning for buying jewellery.

By the Thursday, only three people failed to turn up for work, but I counted four more shops in the terrace that had been boarded up. The streets seemed a lot calmer. Over a snatched breakfast I learned from Becky that there would be no copy of *The Times* that morning because the printers were on strike, but in defiance the government had brought out their own paper, the *British Gazette*, a brainchild of Mr Churchill, which informed its readers that the railway and transport workers were now returning to work in their droves. Despite this, Norman Cosgrave, the fishmonger at Number 11, told me that he'd had enough, and asked how much I was prepared to offer him for his business. Having agreed on a price in the morning we walked over to the bank that same afternoon to close the deal. One phone call made sure that Crowther had the necessary documents typed up, and Hadlow had filled in a cheque by the time we arrived, so all that was required of me was a signature. When I returned to Chelsea Terrace I immediately put Tom Arnold in charge of the fishmonger's until he could find the right manager to take Cosgrave's place. I never said anything to him at the time, but it was to be several weeks after Tom had handed over to a lad from Billingsgate before he finally rid himself of the lingering smell.

The general strike officially ended on the ninth morning, and by the last day of the month I had acquired another seven shops in all. I seemed to be running constantly backwards and forwards to the bank, but at least every one of my acquisitions was at a price that allowed Hadlow an accompanying smile, even if he warned me that funds were running low.

At our next board meeting, I was able to report that Trumper's now owned twenty shops in Chelsea Terrace, which was more than the Shops Committee membership combined. However Hadlow did express a view to the board that we should now embark on a long period of consolidation if we wanted our recently acquired properties to attain the same quality and standard as the original thirteen. I made only one other proposal of any significance at that meeting, which received the unanimous backing of my colleagues – that Tom Arnold be invited to join the board.

I still couldn't resist spending the odd hour sitting on the bench opposite Number 147 and watching the transformation of Chelsea Terrace as it took place before my eyes. For the first time I could differentiate between those shops I owned and those that I still needed to acquire, which included the fourteen owned by Wrexall's committee members – not forgetting either the prestigious Number 1 or the Musketeer.

Seventy-two days had passed since the auction, and although Mr Fothergill still purchased his fruit and vegetables regularly from Number 147 he never uttered a word to me as to whether or not Mrs Trentham had fulfilled her contract. Joan Moore informed my wife that her former mistress had recently received a visit from Mr Fothergill, and although the cook had not been able to hear all the conversation there had definitely been raised voices.

When Daphne came to visit me at the shop the following week I enquired if she had any inside information on what Mrs Trentham was up to.

"Stop worrying about the damned woman," was all Daphne had to say on the subject. "In any case," she added, "the ninety days will be up soon enough, and frankly, you should be more worried about your Part II than Mrs Trentham's financial problems."

"I agree. But if I go on at this rate, I won't have completed the necessary work before next year," I said, having selected twelve perfect plums for her before placing them on the weighing machine.

"You're always in such a hurry, Charlie. Why do things always have to be finished by a certain date?"

"Because that's what keeps me going."

"But Becky will be just as impressed by your achievement if you manage to finish a year later."

"It wouldn't be the same," I told her. "I'll just have to work harder."

"There are only a given number of hours in each day," Daphne reminded him. "Even for you."

"Well, that's one thing I can't be blamed for."

Daphne laughed. "How's Becky's thesis on Luini coming along?"

"She's completed the bloody thing. Just about to check over the final draft of thirty thousand words, so she's still well ahead of me. But what with the general strike and acquiring all the new properties, not to mention Mrs Trentham, I haven't even had time to take Daniel to see West Ham this season." Charlie started placing her order in a large brown paper bag.

"Has Becky discovered what you're up to yet?" Daphne asked, passing over a ten-shilling note.

"No, and I make sure I only disappear completely whenever she's working late at Sotheby's or off cataloguing some grand collection. She still hasn't noticed that I get up every morning at four thirty, which is when I put in the real work." I passed over the bag and seven and tenpence change.

"Proper little Trollope, aren't we?" remarked Daphne. "By the way, I still haven't let Percy in on our secret, but I can't wait to see the expression on their faces when –"

"Shh, not a word . . ."

When you have been chasing something for a long time it's strange how the final prize so often lands in your lap just when you least expect it.

I was serving at Number 147 that morning. It always annoyed Bob Makins to see me roll up my sleeves, but I do enjoy a little chat with my old customers, and lately it was about the only chance I had to catch up on the gossip, as well as an occasional insight into what the customers really thought of my other shops. However, I confess that by the time I served Mr Fothergill the queue stretched nearly all the way to the grocery shop which I knew Bob still regarded as a rival.

"Good morning," I said, when Mr Fothergill reached the front of the queue. "And what can I offer you today, sir? I've got some lovely –"

"I wondered if we could have a word in private, Mr Trumper?"

I was so taken by surprise that I didn't reply immediately. I knew Mrs Trentham still had another nine days to go before she had to complete her contract and I had assumed I would hear nothing before then. After all, she must have had her own Hadlows and Crowthers to do all the paperwork.

"I'm afraid the storeroom is the only place available at the moment," I warned. I removed my green overall, rolled down my sleeves and replaced my jacket. "You see, my manager now occupies the flat above," I explained as I led the auctioneer through to the back of the shop.

I offered him a seat on an upturned orange box while pulling up another box opposite him. We faced each other, just a few feet apart, like rival chess players. Strange surroundings, I considered, to discuss the biggest deal of my life. I tried to remain calm.

"I'll come to the point straight away," said Fothergill. "Mrs Trentham has not been in touch for several weeks and lately she has been refusing to answer my calls. What's more, Savill's have made it abundantly clear that they have had no instruction to complete the transaction on her behalf. They have gone as far as to say that they are now given to understand that she is no longer interested in the property."

"Still, you got your one thousand, two hundred pounds deposit," I reminded him, trying to stifle a grin.

"I don't deny it," replied Fothergill. "But I have

since made other commitments, and what with the general strike – "

"Hard times, I agree," I told him. I felt the palms of my hands begin to sweat.

"But you've never hidden your desire to be the owner of Number 1."

"True enough, but since the auction I've been buying up several other properties with the cash I had originally put on one side for your shop."

"I know, Mr Trumper. But I would now be willing to settle for a far more reasonable price – "

"And three thousand, five hundred pounds is what I was willing to bid, as no doubt you recall."

"Nine thousand was your final bid, if I remember correctly."

"Tactics, Mr Fothergill, nothing more than tactics. I never had any intention of paying nine thousand, as I feel sure you are only too aware."

"But your wife bid five thousand, five hundred pounds, even forgetting her later bid of eleven thousand."

"I can't disagree with that," I told him, dropping back into my Cockney accent. "But if you 'ad ever married, Mr Fothergill, you would know only too well why we in the East End always refer to them as the trouble and strife."

"I'd let the property go for seven thousand pounds," he said. "But only to you."

"You'd let the property go for five thousand," I replied, "to anyone who'd cough up."

"Never," said Fothergill.

"In nine days' time would be my bet, but I'll tell you what I'll do," I added, leaning forward and nearly falling off my box. "I'll honour my wife's commitment of five thousand, five 'undred pounds, which I confess was the limit the board 'ad allowed us to go to, but only if you 'ave all the paperwork ready for me to sign before midnight." Mr Fothergill opened his mouth indignantly. "Of course," I added before he could protest, "it shouldn't be too much work for you. After all, the contract's been sitting on your desk for the last eighty-one days. All you have to do is change the name and knock off the odd nought. Well, if you'll excuse me, Mr Fothergill, I must be getting back to my customers."

"I have never been treated in such a cavalier way before, sir," declared Mr Fothergill, jumping up angrily. He turned and marched out, leaving me sitting in the storeroom on my own.

"I have never thought of myself as a cavalier," I told the upturned orange box. "More of a roundhead, I would have said."

Once I had read another chapter of *Through the Looking-Glass* to Daniel and waited for him to fall asleep, I went downstairs to join Becky for dinner. While she served me a bowl of soup I told her the details of my conversation with Fothergill.

"Pity," was her immediate reaction. "I only wish he'd approached me in the first place. Now we may never get our hands on Number 1" – a sentiment she repeated just before climbing into bed. I turned down the gaslight beside me, thinking that perhaps Becky could be right. I was just beginning to feel drowsy when I heard the front door bell sound.

"It's past eleven thirty," Becky said sleepily. "Who could that possibly be?"

"A man who understands deadlines?" I suggested as I turned the gaslight back up. I climbed out of bed, donned my dressing-gown and went downstairs to answer the door.

"Do come through to my study, Peregrine," I said, after I had welcomed Mr Fothergill.

"Thank you, Charles," he replied. I only just stopped myself laughing as I moved a copy of *Mathematics, Part Two* from my desk, so that I could get to the drawer that housed the company cheques.

"Five thousand, five hundred, if I remember correctly," I said, as I unscrewed the top of my pen and checked the clock on the mantelpiece. At eleven thirty-seven I handed over the full and final settlement to Mr Fothergill in exchange for the freehold of Number 1 Chelsea Terrace.

We shook hands on the deal and I showed the former auctioneer out. Once I had climbed back up the stairs and returned to the bedroom I found to my surprise that Becky was sitting at her writing desk.

"What are you up to?" I demanded.

"Writing my letter of resignation to Sotheby's."

Tom Arnold began going through Number 1 with far more than a fine-tooth comb in preparation for Becky joining us a month later as managing director of Trumper's Auctioneers and Fine Art Specialists. He realised that I considered our new acquisition should quickly become the flagship of the entire Trumper empire, even if – to the dismay of Hadlow – the costs were beginning to resemble those of a battleship.

Becky completed her notice at Sotheby's on Friday, 16 July 1926. She walked into Trumper's, *née* Fothergill's, the following morning at seven o'clock to take over the responsibility of refurbishing the building, at the same time releasing Tom so that he could get back to his normal duties. She immediately set about turning the basement of Number 1 into a storeroom, with the main reception remaining on the ground floor and the auction room on the first floor.

Becky and her team of specialists were to be housed on the second and third floors while the top floor, which had previously been Mr Fothergill's flat, became the company's administrative offices, with a room left over that turned out to be ideal for board meetings.

The full board met for the first time at Number 1 Chelsea Terrace on 17 October 1926.

Within three months of leaving Sotheby's Becky had "stolen" seven of the eleven staff she had wanted to join her and picked up another four from Bonham's and Phillips. At her first board meeting she warned us all that it could take anything up to three years to clear the debts incurred by the purchase and refurbishment of Number 1, and it might even be another three before she could be sure they would be making a serious contribution to the group's profits.

"Not like my first shop," I informed the board. "Made a profit within three weeks, you know, Chairman."

"Stop looking so pleased with yourself, Charlie Trumper, and try to remember I'm not selling potatoes," my wife told me.

"Oh, I don't know," I replied and on 21 October 1926, to celebrate our sixth wedding anniversary, I presented my wife with an oil painting by Van Gogh called *The Potato Eaters*.

Mr Reed of the Lefevre Gallery, who had been a personal friend of the artist, claimed it was almost as good an example as the one that hung in the Rijksmuseum. I had to agree even if I felt the asking price a little extravagant, but after some bargaining we settled on a price of six hundred guineas.

For some considerable time everything seemed to go quiet on the Mrs Trentham front. This state of affairs always worried me, because I assumed she must be up to no good. Whenever a shop came up for sale I expected her to be bidding against me, and if there was ever any trouble in the terrace I wondered if somehow she might be behind it. Becky agreed with Daphne that I was becoming paranoid, until Arnold told me he had been having a drink at the pub when Wrexall had received a call from Mrs Trentham. Arnold was unable to report anything of significance because Syd went into a back room to take it. After that my wife was willing to admit that the passing of time had obviously not lessened Mrs Trentham's desire for revenge.

It was some time in March that Joan informed us that her former mistress had spent two days packing before being driven to Southampton where she boarded a liner for Australia. Daphne was able to confirm this piece of information when she came round to dinner at Gilston Road the following week.

"So one can only assume, darlings, that she's paying a visit to that dreadful son of hers."

"In the past she's been only too willing to give lengthy reports on the bloody man's progress to anyone and everyone who cared to listen, so why's she not letting us know what she's up to this time?"

"Can't imagine," said Daphne.

"Do you think it's possible Guy might be planning to return to England now that things have settled down a little?"

"I doubt it." Daphne's brow furrowed. "Otherwise the ship would have been sailing in the opposite direction, wouldn't it? In any case, if his father's feelings are anything to go by, should Guy ever dare to show his face at Ashurst Hall he won't exactly be treated like the prodigal son."

"Something's still not quite right," I told her. "This veil of secrecy Mrs Trentham's been going in for lately requires some explanation."

It was three months later, in June 1927, that the colonel drew my attention to the announcement in *The Times* of Guy Trentham's death. "What a terrible way to die," was his only comment.

Daphne attended the funeral at Ashurst parish church – because, as she explained later, she wanted to see the coffin lowered into the grave before she was finally convinced that Guy Trentham was no longer among us.

Percy informed me later that he had only just been

able to restrain her from joining the gravediggers as they filled up the hole with good English sods. However, Daphne told us that she remained sceptical about the cause of death, despite the absence of any proof to the contrary.

"At least you'll have no more trouble from that quarter," were Percy's final words on the subject.

I scowled. "They'll have to bury Mrs Trentham alongside him before I'll believe that."

CHAPTER 26

In 1929 the Trumpers moved to a larger house in the Little Boltons. Daphne assured them that although it was "the Little", at least it was a step in the right direction. With a glance at Becky she added, "However, it's still a considerable way from being Eaton Square, darlings."

The house-warming party the Trumpers gave held a double significance for Becky, because the following day she was to be presented with her Master of Arts degree. When Percy teased her about the length of time she had taken to complete the thesis on her unrequited lover, Bernardino Luini, she cited her husband as the co-respondent.

Charlie made no attempt to defend himself, just poured Percy another brandy before clipping off the end of a cigar.

"Hoskins will be driving us to the ceremony," Daphne announced, "so we'll see you there. That is, assuming on this occasion they've been considerate enough to allow us to be seated in the first thirty rows."

Charlie was pleased to find that Daphne and Percy had been placed only a row behind them so this time were close enough to the stage to follow the entire proceedings.

"Who are they?" demanded Daniel, when fourteen dignified old gentlemen walked on to the platform wearing long black gowns and purple hoods, and took their places in the empty chairs.

"The Senate," explained Becky to her eight-year-old son. "They recommend who shall be awarded degrees. But you mustn't ask too many questions, Daniel, or you'll only annoy all the people sitting around us."

At that point, the vice-chancellor rose to present the scrolls.

"I'm afraid we'll have to sit through all the BAs before they reach me," said Becky.

"Do stop being so pompous, darling," said Daphne. "Some of us can remember when you considered being awarded a degree was the most important day in your life."

"Why hasn't Daddy got a degree?" asked Daniel as he picked up Becky's programme off the floor. "He's just as clever as you are, Mummy."

"True," said Becky. "But his daddy didn't make him stay at school as long as mine did."

Charlie leaned across. "But his granpa taught him instead how to sell fruit and vegetables, so he could do something useful for the rest of his life."

Daniel was silenced for a moment, as he weighed the value of these two contrary opinions.

"The ceremony's going to take an awfully long time if it keeps going at this rate," whispered Becky when after half an hour they had only reached the Ps.

"We can wait," whispered Daphne cheerfully. "Percy and I haven't a lot planned before Goodwood."

"Oh, look, Mummy," said Daniel. "I've found another Arnold, another Moore and another Trumper on my list."

"They're all fairly common names," said Becky, not bothering to check the programme as she placed Daniel on the edge of her seat.

"Wonder what he looks like?" asked Daniel. "Do all Trumpers look the same, Mummy?"

"No, silly, they come in all shapes and sizes."

"But he's got the same first initial as Dad," Daniel said, loudly enough for everyone in the three rows in front of them to feel they were now part of the conversation.

"Shh," said Becky, as one or two people turned round and stared in their direction.

"Bachelor of Arts," declared the vice-chancellor.

"Mathematics Second Class, Charles George Trumper."

"And he even looks like your dad," said Charlie as he rose from his place and walked up to receive his degree from the vice-chancellor. The applause increased once the assembled gathering became aware of the age of this particular graduate. Becky's mouth opened wide in disbelief, Percy rubbed his glasses, while Daphne showed no surprise at all.

"How long have you known?" demanded Becky through clenched teeth.

"He registered at Birkbeck College the day after you were awarded your degree."

"But when has he found the time?"

"It's taken him nearly eight years and an awful lot of early mornings while you were sound asleep."

By the end of her second year Becky's financial forecasts for Number 1 were beginning to look a little too optimistic. As each month passed by the overdraft seemed to remain constant, and it was not until the twenty-seventh month that she first began to make small inroads on the capital debt.

She complained to the board that although the managing director was continually helping with the turnover he was not actually contributing to the profits, because he always assumed he could purchase their most sought-after items at the buy-in cost.

"But we are at the same time building a major art collection, Mrs Trumper," he reminded her.

"And saving a great deal on tax while also making a sound investment," Hadlow pointed out. "Might even prove useful as collateral at some later date."

"Perhaps, but in the meantime it doesn't help my balance sheet, Chairman, if the managing director is always making off with my most saleable stock – and it certainly doesn't help that he's worked out the auctioneer's code so that he always knows what our reserve price is."

"You must look upon yourself as part of the company

and not as an individual, Mrs Trumper," said Charlie with a grin, adding, "though I confess it might have been a lot cheaper if we had left you at Sotheby's in the first place."

"Not to be minuted," said the chairman sternly. "By the way, what is this auctioneer's code?"

"A series of letters from a chosen word or words that indicate numbers; for example, Charlie would be C-1, H-2, A-3, but if any letter is repeated then it has to be ignored. So once you've worked out the two words we are substituting for one to zero and can get your hands on our master catalogue you will always know the reserve price we have set for each painting."

"So why don't you change the words from time to time?"

"Because once you've mastered the code, you can always work out the new words. In any case, it takes hours of practice to glance down at QNHH, and know immediately it's . . ."

"One thousand three hundred pounds," said Charlie with a smile of satisfaction.

While Becky had been trying to build up Number 1, Charlie had captured four more shops, including the barber and the newsagent, without any further interference from Mrs Trentham. As he told his fellow-directors, "I no longer believe she possesses the finances to challenge us."

"Until her father dies," Becky pointed out. "Once she inherits that fortune she could challenge Mr Selfridge and then there will be nothing Charlie can do about it."

Charlie agreed, but went on to assure the board that he had plans to get his hands on the rest of the block long before that eventuality. "No reason to believe the man hasn't got a good few years left in him yet."

"Which reminds me," said the colonel, "I'll be sixty-five next May, and feel that would be an appropriate time for me to step down as chairman."

Charlie and Becky were stunned by this sudden announcement, as neither of them had ever given a moment's thought as to when the colonel might retire.

"Couldn't you at least stay on until you're seventy?" asked Charlie quietly.

"No, Charlie, though it's kind of you to suggest it. You see, I've promised Elizabeth that we will spend our last few years on her beloved Isle of Skye. In any case, I think it's time you became chairman."

The colonel officially retired the following May. Charlie threw a party for him at the Savoy to which he invited every member of staff along with their husbands or wives. He laid on a five-course dinner with three wines for an evening that he hoped the colonel would never forget.

When the meal came to an end, Charlie rose from his place to toast the first chairman of Trumper's, before presenting him with a silver barrow which held a bottle of Glenlivet, the colonel's favourite brand of whisky. The staff all banged on their tables and demanded the outgoing chairman should reply.

The colonel rose, still straight as a ramrod, and began by thanking everyone present for their good wishes for his retirement. He went on to remind those present that when he had first joined Mr Trumper and Miss Salmon in 1920 they only possessed one shop in Chelsea Terrace, Number 147. It sold fruit and vegetables, and they had acquired it for the princely sum of one hundred pounds. Charlie could see as he glanced around the tables that many of the younger staff – and Daniel who was wearing long trousers for the first time – just didn't believe the old soldier.

"Now," the colonel continued, "we have twenty-four shops and a staff of one hundred and seventy-two. I told my wife all those years ago that I hoped I would live to see Charlie" – there was a ripple of laughter – "Mr Trumper, own the whole block, and build the biggest barrow in the world. Now I'm convinced I will." Turning to Charlie he raised his glass and said, "And I wish you luck, sir."

They cheered when he resumed his seat as chairman for the last time.

Charlie rose to reply. "Chairman," he began, "let no one in this room be in any doubt that Becky and I could not have built up Trumper's to the position it enjoys today without your support. In fact, if the truth be known, we wouldn't even have been able to purchase shops numbers two and three. I am proud to follow you and be the company's second chairman, and whenever I make a decision of any real importance I shall always imagine you are looking over my shoulder. The last proposal you made as chairman of the company will take effect from tomorrow. Tom Arnold will become managing director and Ned Denning and Bob Makins will join the board. Because it will always be Trumper's policy to promote from within.

"You are the new generation," said Charlie as he looked out into the ballroom at his staff, "and this is the first occasion at which we have all been together under the same roof. So let us set a date tonight for when we will all *work* under one roof, Trumper's of Chelsea Terrace. I give you – 1940."

The entire staff rose as one and all cried "1940" and cheered their new chairman. As Charlie sat down the conductor raised his baton to indicate that the dancing would begin.

The colonel rose from his place and invited Becky to join him for the opening waltz. He accompanied her on to an empty dance floor.

"Do you remember when you first asked me to dance?" said Becky.

"I certainly do," said the colonel. "And to quote Mr Hardy, 'That's another fine mess you've got us into.'"

"Blame him," said Becky as Charlie glided by, leading Elizabeth Hamilton around the dance floor.

The colonel smiled. "What a speech they'll make when Charlie retires," he said wistfully to Becky. "And I can't imagine who will dare follow him."

"A woman, perhaps?"

CHAPTER 27

The Silver Jubilee of King George V and Queen Mary in 1935 was celebrated by everyone at Trumper's. There were coloured posters and pictures of the royal couple in every shop window, and Tom Arnold ran a competition to see which shop could come up with the most imaginative display to commemorate the occasion.

Charlie took charge of Number 147, which he still looked upon as his personal fiefdom, and with the help of Bob Makins's daughter, who was in her first year at the Chelsea School of Art, they produced a model of the King and Queen made up of every fruit and vegetable that hailed from the British Empire.

Charlie was livid when the judges, the colonel along with the Marquess and Marchioness of Wiltshire, awarded Number 147 second place behind the flower shop, which was doing a roaring trade selling bunches of red, white and blue chrysanthemums; what had put them in first place was a vast map of the world made up entirely of flowers, with the British Empire set in red roses.

Charlie gave all the staff the day off and he escorted Becky and Daniel up the Mall at four thirty in the morning so that they could find a good vantage point to watch the King and Queen proceed from Buckingham Palace to St Paul's Cathedral, where a service of thanksgiving was to be conducted.

They arrived at the Mall only to discover that thousands of people were already covering every inch of the pavements with sleeping-bags, blankets and even tents, some having already begun their breakfast or simply fixed themselves to the spot.

The hours of waiting passed quickly as Charlie made friends with visitors who had travelled from all over the Empire. When the procession finally began, Daniel was speechless with delight as he watched the different soldiers from India, Africa, Australia, Canada and thirty-six other nations march past him. When the King and Queen drove by in the royal carriage Charlie stood to attention and removed his hat, an action he repeated when the Royal Fusiliers marched past playing their regimental anthem. Once they had all disappeared out of sight, he thought enviously of Daphne and Percy, who had been invited to attend the service at St Paul's.

After the King and Queen had returned to Buckingham Palace – well in time for their lunch, as Daniel explained to those around him – the Trumpers began their journey home. On the way back they passed Chelsea Terrace where Daniel spotted the big "2nd place" in the window of Number 147.

"Why's that there, Dad?" he immediately demanded. His mother took great delight in explaining to her son how the competition had worked.

"Where did you come, Mum?"

"Sixteenth out of twenty-six," said Charlie. "And then only because all three judges were long-standing friends."

Eight months later the King was dead.

Charlie hoped that with the accession of Edward VIII, a new era would begin, and decided that the time was well overdue for him to make a pilgrimage to America.

He warned the board of his proposed trip at their next meeting.

"Any real problems for me to worry about while I'm away?" the chairman asked his managing director.

"I'm still looking for a new manager at jewellery and

a couple of assistants for women's clothes," replied Arnold. "Otherwise it's fairly peaceful at the moment."

Confident that Tom Arnold and the board could hold the fort for the month they planned to be away, Charlie was finally convinced he should go when he read of the preparation for the launching of the *Queen Mary*. He booked a cabin for two on its maiden voyage.

Becky spent five glorious days on the *Queen* during the journey over, and was delighted to find that even her husband began to relax once he realised he had no way of getting in touch with Tom Arnold, or even Daniel, who was settling into his first boarding school. In fact, once Charlie accepted that he couldn't bother anyone he seemed thoroughly to enjoy himself as he discovered the various facilities that the liner had to offer a slightly overweight, unfit middle-aged man.

The great *Queen* sailed into the port of New York on the Monday morning to be greeted by a crowd of thousands; Charlie could only wonder how different it must have been for the Pilgrim Fathers bobbing along in the *Mayflower*, with no welcoming party and unsure of what to expect from the natives. In truth, Charlie wasn't quite sure what to expect from the natives either.

Charlie had booked in to the Waldorf Astoria Hotel, on the recommendation of Daphne, but once he and Becky had unpacked their suitcases, there was no longer any necessity to sit around and relax. He rose the following morning at four thirty and, browsing through the *New York Times*, learned of the name of Mrs Wallis Simpson for the first time. Once he had devoured the newspapers, Charlie left the Waldorf Astoria and strolled up and down Fifth Avenue studying the different displays in the shop windows. He quickly became absorbed by how inventive and original the Manhattaners were compared with their opposite numbers in Oxford Street.

As soon as the shops opened at nine, he was able to explore everything in greater detail. This time he walked up and down the aisles of the fashionable stores that made up most street corners. He checked their stock, watched the assistants and even followed certain customers around the store to see what they purchased. After each of those first three days in New York he arrived back at the hotel in the evening exhausted.

It was not until the third morning that Charlie, having completed Fifth Avenue and Madison, moved on down to Lexington, where he discovered Bloomingdale's, and from that moment Becky realised that she had lost her husband for the rest of their stay in New York.

Throughout the first two hours Charlie did nothing more than travel up and down the escalators until he had completely mastered the layout of the building. He then began to study each floor, department by department, making copious notes. On the ground floor they sold perfume, leather goods, jewellery; on the first floor, scarves, hats, gloves, stationery; on the second floor were men's clothes and on the third floor women's clothes; on the fourth floor, household goods and on up and up until he discovered that the company offices were on the twelfth floor, discreetly hidden behind a "No Entry" sign. Charlie longed to discover how that floor was laid out, but had no means of finding out.

On the fourth day he made a close study of how each of the counters was positioned, and began to draw their individual layouts. As he proceeded up the escalator to the third floor that morning, he found two athletic young men blocking his way. Charlie had no choice but to stop or try to go back down the escalator the wrong way.

"Something wrong?"

"We're not sure, sir," said one of the thickset men. "We are store detectives and wondered if you would be kind enough to come along with us."

"Delighted," said Charlie, unable to work out what their problem might be.

He was whisked up in a lift to the one floor he'd never had a chance to look round and led down a long corridor through an unmarked door and on into a bare room. There were no pictures on the wall, no carpet on the floor, and the only furniture consisted of three wooden chairs and a table. They left him alone. Moments later two older men came in to join him.

"I wonder if you would mind answering a few questions for us, sir?" began the taller of the two.

"Certainly," said Charlie, puzzled by the strange treatment he was receiving.

"Where do you come from?" asked the first.

"England."

"And how did you get here?" asked the second.

"On the maiden voyage of the *Queen Mary*." He could see that they both showed signs of nervousness when they learned this piece of information.

"Then why, sir, have you been walking all over the store for two days, making notes, but not attempted to purchase a single item?"

Charlie burst out laughing. "Because I own twenty-six shops of my own in London," he explained. "I was simply comparing the way you do things in America to the way I conduct my business in England."

The two men began to whisper to each other nervously.

"May I ask your name, sir?"

"Trumper, Charlie Trumper."

One of the men rose to his feet and left. Charlie had the distinct feeling that they found his story hard to believe. It brought back memories of when he had told Tommy about his first shop. The man who remained seated opposite him still did not offer an opinion, so the two of them sat silently opposite each other for several minutes before the door burst open and in walked a tall, elegantly dressed gentleman in a dark brown suit, brown shoes and a golden cravat. He almost ran forward, arms outstretched to engulf Charlie.

"I must apologise, Mr Trumper," were his opening words. "We had no idea you were in New York, let alone on the premises. My name is John Bloomingdale, and this is my little store which I hear you've been checking out."

"I certainly have," said Charlie.

Before he could say another word, Mr Bloomingdale added, "That's only fair, because I also checked over your famous barrows in Chelsea Terrace, and took one or two great ideas away with me."

"From Trumper's?" said Charlie in disbelief.

"Oh, certainly. Didn't you see the flag of America in our front window with all forty-eight states represented by different coloured flowers?"

"Well, yes," began Charlie, "but . . ."

"Stolen from you when my wife and I made a trip to see the Silver Jubilee. So consider me at your service, sir."

The two detectives were now smiling.

That night Becky and Charlie joined the Bloomingdales at their brownstone house on Sixty-First and Madison for dinner and John Bloomingdale answered Charlie's many questions until the early hours.

The following day Charlie was given an official tour of "my little store" by its owner while Patty Bloomingdale introduced Becky to the Metropolitan Museum of Art and the Frick, pumping her with endless questions about Mrs Simpson, to which Becky was unable to offer any answers as she had never heard of the lady before they'd set foot in America.

The Trumpers were sorry to say goodbye to the Bloomingdales before they continued their journey on to Chicago by train, where they had been booked into the Stevens. On their arrival in the windy city they found their room had been upgraded to a suite and Mr Joseph Field, of Marshall Field, had left a handwritten note hoping that they would be able to join them for a meal the following evening.

Over dinner in the Fields' home on Lake Shore Drive, Charlie reminded Mr Field of his advertisement describing his store as one of the biggest in the world, and warned him that Chelsea Terrace was seven feet longer.

"Ah, but will they let you build on twenty-one floors, Mr Trumper?"

"Twenty-two," countered Charlie, without the slightest

idea of what the London County Council were likely to permit.

The next day Charlie added to his growing knowledge of a major store by seeing Marshall Field's from the inside. He particularly admired the way the staff appeared to work as a team, all the girls dressed in smart green outfits with a gold "MF" on their lapels and all the floor walkers in grey suits, while the managers wore dark blue double-breasted blazers.

"Makes it easy for a customer to spot a member of my staff when they're in need of someone to help them, especially when the store becomes overcrowded," explained Mr Field.

While Charlie became engrossed in the workings of Marshall Field, Becky spent countless hours at the Chicago Art Institute, and came away particularly admiring the works of Wyeth and Remington, whom she felt should be given exhibitions in London. She was to return to England with one example of each artist tucked into newly acquired suitcases, but the British public never saw either the oil or the sculpture until years later, because once they had been unpacked Charlie wouldn't let them out of the house.

By the end of the month they were both exhausted, and sure of only one thing: they wanted to return to America again and again, though they feared they could never match the hospitality they had received, should either the Fields or the Bloomingdales ever decide to turn up in Chelsea Terrace. However, Joseph Field requested a small favour of Charlie which he promised he would deal with personally the moment he got back to London.

The rumours of the King's affair with Mrs Simpson that Charlie had seen chronicled in such detail by the American press were now beginning to reach the ears of the English, and Charlie was saddened when the King finally felt it necessary to announce his abdication. The unexpected responsibility was suddenly placed on the unprepared shoulders of the Duke of York, who became King George VI.

The other piece of news that Charlie followed on the front pages was the rise to power of Adolf Hitler in Nazi Germany. He could never understand why the Prime Minister, Mr Chamberlain, didn't use a little street sense and give the man a good thump on the nose.

"Neville Chamberlain's not a barrow boy from the East End," Becky explained to her husband over breakfast. "He's the Prime Minister."

"More's the pity," said Charlie. "Because that's exactly what would happen to Herr Hitler if he ever dared show his face in Whitechapel."

Tom Arnold didn't have a great deal to report to Charlie on his return, but he quickly became aware of the effect that the visit to America had had on his chairman by the ceaseless rat-tat-tat of orders and ideas that came flying at him from all directions during the days that followed.

"The Shops Committee," Arnold warned the chairman at their Monday morning meeting, after Charlie had finished extolling the virtues of America once again, "is now talking seriously of the effect a war with Germany might have on business."

"That lot would," said Charlie, taking a seat behind his desk. "Appeasers to a man. In any case, Germany won't declare war on any of Britain's allies – they wouldn't dare. After all, they can't have forgotten the hiding we gave them last time. So what other problems are we facing?"

"At a more mundane level," replied Tom from the other side of the desk, "I still haven't found the right person to manage the jewellery shop since Jack Slade's retirement."

"Then start advertising in the trade magazines and let me see anyone who appears suitable. Anything else?"

"Yes, a Mr Ben Schubert has been asking to see you."

"And what does he want?"

"He's a Jewish refugee from Germany, but he refused to say why he needed to see you."

"Then make an appointment for him when he gets back in touch with you."

"But he's sitting in the waiting room outside your office right now."

"In the waiting room?" said Charlie in disbelief.

"Yes. He turns up every morning and just sits there in silence."

"But didn't you explain to him I was in America?"

"Yes, I did," said Tom. "But it didn't seem to make a blind bit of difference."

"Sufferance is the badge of all our tribe," murmured Charlie. "Show the man in."

A small, bent, tired-looking figure whom Charlie suspected was not much older than himself entered the office and waited to be offered a seat. Charlie rose from behind his desk and ushered his visitor into an armchair near the fireplace before asking him how he could help.

Mr Schubert spent some time explaining to Charlie how he had escaped from Hamburg with his wife and two daughters, after so many of his friends had been sent off to concentration camps, never to be heard of again.

Charlie listened to Mr Schubert's account of his experiences at the hands of the Nazis without uttering a word. The man's escape and his description of what was taking place in Germany could have come straight off the pages of a John Buchan novel and was far more vivid than any newspaper report of recent months.

"How can I help?" asked Charlie when Mr Schubert appeared to have finished his sad tale.

The refugee smiled for the first time, revealing two gold teeth. He picked up the little briefcase by his side, placed it on Charlie's desk and then slowly opened it. Charlie stared down at the finest array of stones he had ever seen, diamonds and amethysts, some of them in the most magnificent settings. His visitor then removed what turned out to be nothing more than a thin tray to reveal loose stones, more rubies, topaz, diamonds, pearls and jade filling every inch of the deep box.

"They are but a tiny sample of what I had to leave behind, in a business that was built up by my father and his father before him. Now I must sell everything that is left to be sure that my family doesn't starve."

"You were in the jewellery business?"

"Twenty-six years," replied Mr Schubert. "Man and boy."

"And how much are you hoping to get for this lot?" Charlie pointed to the open case.

"Three thousand pounds," Mr Schubert said without hesitation. "That is far less than they are worth, but I am no longer left with the time or the will to bargain."

Charlie pulled open the drawer by his right hand, removed a cheque book and wrote out the words "Pay Mr Schubert three thousand pounds". He pushed it across the desk.

"But you have not checked their value," said Mr Schubert.

"Not necessary," said Charlie, as he rose from his chair. "Because you're going to sell them as the new manager of my jewellery shop. Which also means that you'll have to explain to me personally if they don't fetch the price you claim they are worth. Once you've repaid the advance, then we'll discuss your commission."

A smile came over Mr Schubert's face. "They teach you well in the East End, Mr Trumper."

"There are a lot of you down there to keep us on our toes," replied Charlie with a grin. "And don't forget, my father-in-law was one."

Ben Schubert stood up and hugged his new boss.

What Charlie hadn't anticipated was just how many Jewish refugees would find their way to Trumper's the Jeweller, closing deals with Mr Schubert that ensured Charlie never had to worry about the jewellery side of the business again.

It must have been about a week later that Tom Arnold entered the chairman's office without knocking. Charlie could see what an agitated state his managing director was in so he simply asked, "What's the problem, Tom?"

"Shoplifting."

"Where?"

"Number 133 – women's clothes."

"What's been stolen?"

"Two pairs of shoes and a skirt."

"Then follow the standard procedure as laid down in company regulations. First thing you do is call in the police."

"It's not that easy."

"Of course it's that easy. A thief is a thief."

"But she's claiming –"

"That her mother is ninety and dying of cancer, not to mention the fact that her children are all crippled?"

"No, that she's your sister."

Charlie rocked back in his chair, paused for a moment and then sighed heavily. "What have you done?"

"Nothing yet. I told the manager to hold on to her while I had a word with you."

"Then let's get on with it," said Charlie. He rose from behind his desk and began to march towards the door.

Neither man spoke again until they had reached Number 133 where an agitated manager was waiting for them by the front door.

"Sorry, Chairman," were Jim Grey's opening words.

"There's nothing for you to be sorry about, Jim," said Charlie as he was led through to the back room where they found Kitty sitting at a table, compact in hand, checking her lipstick in a hand mirror.

The moment she saw Charlie she clicked the compact lid closed and dropped it into her bag. On the table in front of her lay two pairs of fashionable leather shoes and a purple pleated skirt. Kitty clearly still liked the best as her selection was all from the top price range. She smiled up at her brother. The lipstick didn't help.

"Now that the big boss himself has arrived you'll find out exactly 'o I am," said Kitty, glaring at Jim Grey.

"You're a thief," said Charlie. "That's what you are."

"Come on, Charlie, you can afford it." Her voice showed no sign of remorse.

"That's not the point, Kitty. If I –"

"If you put me up in front of the beak claimin' I'm a tea leaf the press'll 'ave a field day. You wouldn't dare 'ave me arrested, Charlie, and you know it."

"Not this time, perhaps," said Charlie, "but it's the last occasion, that I promise you." He turned to the manager and added, "If this lady ever tries to leave again without paying for something, call in the police and see that she is charged without any reference to me. Do I make myself clear, Mr Grey?"

"Yes, sir."

"Yes, sir, no, sir, three bags full, sir. Don't worry yourself, Charlie, I won't be botherin' you again."

Charlie looked unconvinced.

"You see, I'm off to Canada next week where it seems there's at least one member of our family who actually cares about what happens to me."

Charlie was about to protest when Kitty picked up the skirt and both pairs of shoes and dropped them in the bag. She walked straight past the three men.

"Just a moment," said Tom Arnold.

"Bugger off," said Kitty over her shoulder as she marched through the shop.

Tom turned towards the chairman who stood and watched his sister as she stepped out on to the pavement without even looking back.

"Don't bother yourself, Tom. It's cheap at the price."

On 30 September 1938 the Prime Minister returned from Munich where he had been in talks with the German Chancellor. Charlie remained unconvinced by the Peace in our Time, Peace with Honour document that Chamberlain kept waving in front of the cameras, because after listening to Ben Schubert's first-hand description of what was taking place in the Third Reich he had become convinced that war with Germany was inevitable. Introducing conscription for those over twenty had already been debated in Parliament, and with Daniel in his last year at St Paul's waiting to sit his university entrance papers, Charlie couldn't bear the thought of losing a son to another war with the Germans. When a few weeks later Daniel was awarded a scholarship to Trinity College, Cambridge it only added to his fears.

Hitler marched into Poland on 1 September 1939 and Charlie realised that Ben Schubert's stories had not been exaggerated. Two days later Britain was at war.

For the first few weeks after the declaration of hostilities there was a lull, almost an anticlimax, and if it hadn't been for the increased number of men in uniforms marching up and down Chelsea Terrace and a drop in sales Charlie might have been forgiven for not realising Britain was engaged in a war at all.

During this time only the restaurant came up for sale. Charlie offered Mr Scallini a fair price, which he accepted without question before fleeing back to his native Florence. He was luckier than some, who were interned for no more reason than that they possessed a German or an Italian name. Charlie immediately locked up the restaurant because he wasn't sure what he could do with the premises – eating out was hardly a top priority for Londoners in 1940. Once the Scallini lease had been transferred only the antiquarian bookshop and the syndicate chaired by Mr Wrexall still remained in other traders' hands; but the significance of Mrs Trentham's large block of unoccupied flats became more obvious for all to see as each day went by.

On 7 September 1940 the false lull ended when the Luftwaffe carried out its first mass raid on the capital. After that Londoners started to emigrate to the country in droves. Charlie still refused to budge, and even ordered that "Business as usual" signs be placed in every one of his shop windows. In fact, the only concessions he made to Herr Hitler were to move his bedroom to the basement and have all the curtains changed to black drape.

Two months later, in the middle of the night, Charlie was woken by a duty constable to be told that the first bomb had fallen on Chelsea Terrace. He ran all the way from the Little Boltons down Tregunter Road in his dressing-gown and slippers to inspect the damage.

"Anyone killed?" he asked while on the move.

"Not that we know of," replied the constable, trying to keep up with him.

"Which shop did the bomb land on?"

"Can't tell you the answer to that, Mr Trumper. All I know is that it looks as if the whole of Chelsea Terrace is on fire."

As Charlie turned the corner of Fulham Road he was confronted by bright flames and dark smoke soaring up into the sky. The bomb had landed right in the middle of Mrs Trentham's flats, completely demolishing them, while at the same time shattering three of Charlie's shop windows and badly damaging the roof of Hats and Scarves.

By the time the fire brigade finally departed from the terrace all that was left of the flats was a grey, smouldering, bombed-out shell, right in the middle of the block. As the weeks passed, Charlie became only too aware of the obvious – Mrs Trentham had no intention of doing anything about the heap of rubble that now dominated the centre of Chelsea Terrace.

In May 1940 Mr Churchill took over from Mr Chamberlain as Prime Minister which gave Charlie a little more confidence about the future. He even talked to Becky of joining up again.

"Have you looked at yourself in the mirror lately?" asked his wife, laughing.

"I could get fit again, I know I could," said Charlie, pulling in his stomach. "In any case they don't only need troops for the front line."

"You can do a far more worthwhile job by keeping those shops open and stocked up for the general public."

"Arnold could do that just as well as me," said Charlie. "What's more, he's fifteen years older than I am."

However, Charlie reluctantly came to the conclusion

that Becky was right when Daphne came round to tell them that Percy had rejoined his old regiment. "Thank God they've told him he's too old to serve abroad this time," she confided in them. "So he's landed a desk job at the War Office."

The following afternoon, while Charlie was carrying out an inspection of repairs after another night of bombing, Tom Arnold warned him that Syd Wrexall's committee had begun to make noises about selling the remaining eleven of their shops, as well as the Musketeer itself.

"There's no hurry to do anything about them," said Charlie. "He'll be giving those shops away within a year."

"But by then Mrs Trentham could have bought them all at a knock-down price."

"Not while there's a war on, she won't. In any case, the damn woman knows only too well that I can't do a lot while that bloody great crater remains in the middle of Chelsea Terrace."

"Oh, hell," said Tom as the klaxon whine of the siren started up. "They must be on their way again."

"They certainly are," said Charlie, as he looked towards the sky. "You'd better get all the staff into the basement – sharpish." Charlie ran out on to the street, to find an ARP man cycling down the middle of the road, shouting instructions that everyone should head for the nearest Underground as quickly as possible. Tom Arnold had trained his managers to lock up the shops and have all the staff and customers safely in the basement with their torches and a small supply of food within five minutes. It always put Charlie in mind of the general strike. As they sat in the large storeroom under Number 1 waiting for the all-clear Charlie looked around the gathering of his fellow-Londoners and became aware of just how many of his best young men had already left Trumper's to join up; he was now down to fewer than two-thirds of his permanent staff, the majority of whom were women.

Some cradled young children in their arms, while others tried to sleep. Two regulars in a corner continued a game of chess as if the war were no more than an inconvenience. A couple of young girls practised the latest dance step on a small space left unoccupied in the centre of the basement, while others just slept.

They could all hear the bombs falling above them, and Becky told Charlie she felt sure one had landed nearby. "On Syd Wrexall's pub, perhaps?" said Charlie, trying to hide a grin. "That'll teach him to serve short measures." The all-clear klaxon eventually sounded, and they emerged back into an evening air filled with dust and ashes.

"You were right about Syd Wrexall's pub," said Becky, looking at the far corner of the block, but Charlie's eyes were not fixed on the Musketeer.

Becky's gaze eventually turned to where Charlie was staring. A bomb had landed right in the middle of his fruit and vegetable shop.

"The bastards," he said. "They've gone too far this time. Now I will join up."

"But what good will that do?"

"I don't know," said Charlie, "but at least I'll feel I'm involved in this war and not just sitting around watching."

"And what about the shops? Who's going to take charge of them?"

"Arnold can take care of them while I'm away."

"But what about Daniel and myself? Can Tom take care of us while you're away?" she asked, her voice rising.

Charlie was silent for a moment while he considered Becky's plea. "Daniel's old enough to take care of himself, and you'll have your time fully occupied seeing that Trumper's keeps its head above water. So don't say another word, Becky, because I've made up my mind."

After that nothing his wife could say or do would dissuade Charlie from signing up. To her surprise the Fusiliers were only too happy to accept their old sergeant back in the ranks, and immediately sent him off to a training camp near Cardiff.

With Tom Arnold looking anxiously on, Charlie kissed

his wife, hugged his son and shook hands with his managing director before waving goodbye to all three of them.

As he travelled down to Cardiff in a train full of fresh-faced eager youths not much older than Daniel – most of whom insisted on calling him "sir" – Charlie felt like an old man. A battered truck met the new recruits at the station and delivered them safely into barracks.

"Nice to have you back, Trumper," said a voice, as he stepped on to the parade ground for the first time in more than twenty years.

"Stan Russell. Good heavens, are you the company sergeant-major now? You were only a lance-corporal when –"

"I am, sir," Stan said. His voice dropped to a whisper. "And I'll see to it that you don't get the same treatment as the others, me old mate."

"No, you'd better not do that, Stan. I need worse than the same treatment," said Charlie, placing both hands on his stomach.

Although the senior NCOs were gentler on Charlie than they were on the raw recruits, he still found the first week of basic training a painful reminder of how little exercise he had done over the previous twenty years. When he became hungry he quickly discovered that what the NAAFI had to offer could hardly be described as appetising, while trying to get to sleep each night on a bed of unrelenting springs held together by a two-inch horsehair mattress made him less than delighted with Herr Hitler.

By the end of the second week Charlie was made up to corporal and told that if he wanted to stay on in Cardiff as an instructor they would immediately commission him as a training officer, with the rank of captain.

"The Germans are expected in Cardiff, are they, boyo?" asked Charlie. "I had no idea they played rugby football."

His exact words on the subject were relayed back to the commanding officer, so Charlie continued as a corporal, completing his basic training. By the eighth week he had been promoted to sergeant and given his own platoon to knock into shape, ready for wherever it was they were going to be sent. From that moment on there wasn't a competition, from the rifle range to the boxing ring, that his men were allowed to lose, and "Trumper's Terriers" set the standard for the rest of the battalion for the remaining four weeks.

With only ten days left before they completed their training, Stan Russell informed Charlie that the battalion was destined for Africa, where they would join Wavell in the desert. Charlie was delighted by the news, as he had long admired the reputation of the Poet General.

Sergeant Trumper spent most of that final week helping his lads write letters to their families and girlfriends. He didn't intend to put pen to paper himself until the last moment. With a week to go he admitted to Stan that he wasn't ready to take on the Germans in anything much more than a verbal battle.

He was in the middle of a Bren demonstration with his platoon, explaining cocking and reloading, when a red-faced lieutenant came running up.

"Trumper."

"Sir," said Charlie, leaping to attention.

"The commanding officer wants to see you immediately."

"Yes, sir," said Charlie. He instructed his corporal to carry on with the lesson and then chased after the lieutenant.

"Why are we running so fast?" asked Charlie.

"Because the commanding officer was running when he came looking for me."

"Then it has to be at least high treason," said Charlie.

"Heaven knows what it is, Sergeant, but you'll find out soon enough," said the lieutenant, as they arrived outside the CO's door. The lieutenant, closely followed by Charlie, entered the colonel's office without knocking.

"7312087 Sergeant Trumper reporting –"

"You can cut all that bullshit out, Trumper," said the

colonel, as Charlie watched the commanding officer pacing up and down, slapping his side with a swagger stick. "My car is waiting for you at the gate. You are to go straight to London."

"London, sir?"

"Yes, Trumper, London. Mr Churchill's just been on the blower. Wants to see you soonest."

CHAPTER 28

The colonel's driver did everything in his power to get Sergeant Trumper to London as quickly as possible. He pressed his foot to the floor again and again as he tried to keep the speedometer above eighty. However, as they were continually held up en route by convoys of troops, transportation lorries, and even at one point Warrior tanks, the task was daunting. When Charlie finally reached Chiswick on the outskirts of London they were then faced with the blackout, followed by an air-raid, followed by the all-clear, followed by countless more road blocks all the way to Downing Street.

Despite having six hours to ponder as to why Mr Churchill could possibly want to see him, when the car came to a halt outside Number 10 Charlie was no nearer a conclusion than he had been when he left the barracks at Cardiff earlier that afternoon.

When he explained to the policeman on the door who he was, the constable checked his clipboard, then gave a sharp rap on the brass knocker before inviting Sergeant Trumper to step into the hall. Charlie's first reaction on being inside Number 10 was surprise at discovering how small the house was compared with Daphne's home in Eaton Square.

A young Wren officer came forward to greet the middle-aged sergeant before ushering him through to an anteroom.

"The Prime Minister has the American ambassador

with him at the moment," she explained. "But he doesn't expect his meeting with Mr Kennedy to last much longer."

"Thank you," said Charlie.

"Would you like a cup of tea?"

"No, thank you." Charlie was too nervous to think about drinking tea. As she closed the door, he picked up a copy of *Lilliput* from a side table and leafed through the pages, but didn't attempt to take in the words.

After he had thumbed through every magazine on the table – and they were even more out of date at Number 10 than at his dentist – he began to take an interest in the pictures on the wall. Wellington, Palmerston and Disraeli: all inferior portraits that Becky would not have bothered to offer for sale at Number 1. Becky. Good heavens, he thought, she doesn't even know I'm in London. He stared at the telephone that rested on the sideboard, aware that he couldn't possibly call her from Number 10. In frustration he began to pace round the room feeling like a patient waiting for the doctor to tell him if the diagnosis was terminal. Suddenly the door swung open and the Wren reappeared.

"The Prime Minister will see you now, Mr Trumper," she said, then proceeded to lead him up a narrow staircase, past the framed photographs of former Prime Ministers. By the time he reached Chamberlain he found himself on the landing facing a man of five feet nine inches in height who stood, arms on hips, legs apart, staring defiantly at him.

"Trumper," said Churchill, thrusting out his hand. "Good of you to come at such short notice. Hope I didn't tear you away from anything important."

Just a Bren lesson, thought Charlie, but decided not to mention the fact as he followed the shambling figure through to his study. Churchill waved his guest into a comfortable winged chair near a roaring fire; Charlie looked at the burning logs and remembered the Prime Minister's strictures to the nation on wasting coal.

"You must be wondering what this is all about," the

Prime Minister said, as he lit up a cigar and opened a file that was resting on his knee. He started to read.

"Yes, sir," said Charlie, but his reply failed to elicit any explanation. Churchill continued to read from the copious notes in front of him.

"I see we have something in common."

"We do, Prime Minister?"

"We both served in the Great War."

"The war to end all wars."

"Yes, wrong again, wasn't he?" said Churchill. "But then he was a politician." The Prime Minister chuckled before continuing to read from the files. Suddenly he looked up. "However, we both have a far more important role to play in *this* war, Trumper, and I can't waste your time on teaching recruits Bren lessons in Cardiff."

The damn man knew all along, thought Charlie.

"When a nation is at war, Trumper," said the Prime Minister, closing the file, "people imagine victory will be guaranteed so long as we have more troops and better equipment than the enemy. But battles can be lost or won by something that the generals in the field have no control over. A little cog that stops the wheels going round smoothly. Only today I've had to set up a new department in the War Office to deal with code-breaking. I've stolen the two best professors they have at Cambridge, along with their assistants, to help solve the problem. Invaluable cogs, Trumper."

"Yes, sir," said Charlie, without a clue as to what the old man was talking about.

"And I have a problem with another of those cogs, Trumper, and my advisors tell me you're the best man to come up with a solution."

"Thank you, sir."

"Food, Trumper, and more important its distribution. I understand from Lord Woolton, the minister in charge, that supplies are fast running out. We can't even get enough potatoes shipped over from Ireland. So one of the biggest problems I'm facing at this moment is how to keep the nation's stomach full while waging a war on the enemy's shores and at the same time keeping our supply routes open. The minister tells me that when the food arrives in the ports it can often be weeks before the damn stuff is moved, and sometimes even then it ends up in the wrong place.

"Added to this," continued the Prime Minister, "our farmers are complaining that they can't do the job properly because we're recruiting their best men for the armed forces, and they're not receiving any back-up from the government in exchange." He paused for a moment to relight his cigar. "So what I'm looking for is a man who has spent his life buying, selling and distributing food, someone who has lived in the market place and whom the farmers and the suppliers will both respect. In short, Trumper, I need you. I want you to join Woolton as his right-hand man, and see that we get the supplies, and then that those supplies are distributed to the right quarters. Can't think of a more important job. I hope you'll be willing to take on the challenge."

The desire to get started must have shown in Charlie's eyes, because the Prime Minister didn't even bother to wait for his reply. "Good, I can see you've got the basic idea. I'd like you to report to the Ministry of Food at eight tomorrow morning. A car will come to pick you up from your home at seven forty-five."

"Thank you, sir," said Charlie, not bothering to explain to the Prime Minister that if a car did turn up at seven forty-five the driver would have missed him by over three hours.

"And, Trumper, I'm going to make you up to a brigadier so you've got some clout."

"I'd prefer to remain plain Charlie Trumper."

"Why?"

"I might at some time find it necessary to be rude to a general."

The Prime Minister removed his cigar and roared with laughter before he accompanied his guest to the door. "And,

Trumper," he said, placing a hand on Charlie's shoulder, "should the need ever arise, don't hesitate to contact me direct, if you think it could make the difference. Night or day. I don't bother with sleep, you know."

"Thank you, sir," said Charlie, as he proceeded down the staircase.

"Good luck, Trumper, and see you feed the people."

The Wren escorted Charlie back to his car and saluted him as he took his place in the front seat, which surprised Charlie because he was still dressed as a sergeant.

He asked the driver to take him to the Little Boltons via Chelsea Terrace. As they travelled slowly through the streets of the West End, it saddened him to find old familiar landmarks so badly damaged by the Luftwaffe, although he realised no one in London had escaped the Germans' relentless air bombardment.

When he arrived home, Becky opened the front door and threw her arms around her husband. "What did Mr Churchill want?" was her first question.

"How did you know I was seeing the Prime Minister?"

"Number 10 rang here first to ask where they could get hold of you. So what did he want?"

"Someone who can deliver his fruit and veg on a regular basis."

Charlie liked his new boss from the moment they met. Although James Woolton had come to the Ministry of Food with the reputation of being a brilliant businessman, he admitted that he was not an expert in Charlie's particular field but said his department was there to see that Charlie was given every assistance he required.

Charlie was allocated a large office on the same corridor as the minister and supplied with a staff of fourteen headed by a young personal assistant called Arthur Selwyn who hadn't been long down from Oxford.

Charlie soon learnt that Selwyn had a brain as sharp as a razor, and although he had no experience of Charlie's world he only ever needed to be told something once.

The navy supplied Charlie with a personal secretary called Jessica Allen, who appeared to be willing to work the same hours as him. Charlie wondered why such an attractive, intelligent girl appeared to have no social life until he studied her file more carefully and discovered that her young fiancé had been killed on the beach at Dunkirk.

Charlie quickly returned to his old routine of coming into the office at four thirty, even before the cleaners had arrived, which allowed him to read through his papers until eight without fear of being disturbed.

Because of the special nature of his assignment and the obvious support of his minister, doors opened whenever he appeared. Within a month most of his staff were coming in by five, although Selwyn turned out to be the only one of them who also had the stamina to stick with him through the night.

For that first month Charlie did nothing but read reports and listen to Selwyn's detailed assessment of the problems they had been facing for the best part of a year, while occasionally popping in to see the minister to clarify a point that he didn't fully understand.

During the second month Charlie decided to visit every major port in the kingdom to find out what was holding up the distribution of food, food that was sometimes simply being left to rot for days on end in the storehouses on the docksides throughout the country. When he reached Liverpool he quickly discovered that supplies were rightly not getting priority over tanks or men when it came to movement, so he requested that his ministry should operate a fleet of its own vehicles, with no purpose other than to distribute food supplies across the nation.

Woolton somehow managed to come up with sixty-two trucks, most of them, he admitted, rejects from war surplus. "Not unlike me," Charlie admitted. However, the minister still couldn't spare the men to drive them.

"If men aren't available, Minister, I need two hundred women," Charlie suggested, and despite the cartoonists' gentle jibes about women drivers it only took another month before the food started to move out of the docks within hours of its arrival.

The dockers themselves responded well to the women drivers, while trade union leaders never found out that Charlie spoke to them with one accent while using quite another when he was back at the ministry.

Once Charlie had begun to solve the distribution problem, he came up against two more dilemmas. On the one hand, the farmers were complaining that they couldn't produce enough food at home because the armed forces were taking away all their best men; on the other, Charlie found he just wasn't getting enough supplies coming in from abroad because of the success of the German U-boat campaign.

He came up with two solutions for Woolton's consideration. "You supplied me with lorry girls, now you must give me land girls," Charlie told him. "I need five thousand this time, because that's what the farmers are saying they're short of."

The next day Woolton was interviewed on the BBC and made a special appeal to the nation for land girls. Five hundred applied in the first twenty-four hours, and the minister had the five thousand Charlie requested within ten weeks. Charlie allowed the applications to continue pouring in until he had seven thousand, and could clearly identify a smile on the face of the president of the National Farmers' Union.

Over the second problem of lack of supplies, Charlie advised Woolton to buy rice as a substitute staple diet because of the hardship the nation was facing with a potato shortage. "But where do we find such a commodity?" asked Woolton. "China and the Far East is much too hazardous a journey for us even to consider right now."

"I'm aware of that," said Charlie, "but I know a supplier in Egypt who could let us have a million tons a month."

"Can he be trusted?"

"Certainly not," said Charlie. "But his brother still works in the East End, and if we were to intern him for a few months I reckon I could pull off some sort of deal with the family."

"If the press ever found out what we were up to, Charlie, they'd have my guts for garters."

"*I'm* not going to tell them, Minister."

The following day Eli Calil found himself interned in Brixton Prison while Charlie flew off to Cairo to close a deal with his brother for a million tons of rice per month, rice that had been originally earmarked for the Italians.

Charlie agreed with Nasim Calil that the payments could be made half in pounds sterling and half in piastres, and, as long as the shipments always arrived on time, no paperwork concerning the money needed be evident at the Cairo end. Failing this, Calil's government would be informed of the full details of their transaction.

"Very fair, Charlie, but then you always were. But what about my brother Eli?" asked Nasim Calil.

"We'll release him at the end of the war but then only if every shipment is delivered on time."

"Also most considerate," Nasim replied. "A couple of years in gaol will do Eli no harm. He is, after all, one of the few members of my family who hasn't yet been detained at His Majesty's pleasure."

Charlie tried to spend at least a couple of hours a week with Tom Arnold so that he could be kept up to date on what was happening in Chelsea Terrace. Tom had to report that Trumper's was now losing money steadily and he had found it necessary to close five of the premises and board up another four; this saddened Charlie because Syd Wrexall had recently written to him offering his entire group of shops and the bombed-out corner pub for only six thousand pounds, a sum Wrexall was claiming Charlie had once made him a firm offer on. All Charlie had to do now, Wrexall reminded Arnold in an accompanying letter, was to sign the cheque.

Charlie studied the contract that Wrexall had enclosed and said, "I made that offer long before the outbreak of war. Send all the documents back. I'm confident he'll let those shops go for around four thousand by this time next year. But try and keep him happy, Tom."

"That might prove a little difficult," replied Tom. "Since that bomb landed on the Musketeer Syd's gone off to live in Cheshire. He's now the landlord of a country pub in some place called Hatherton."

Charlie had to leave Tom and travel on down to Southampton where Calil's first shipment of rice had arrived. His lorry girls had gone to pick up the bags, but the manager of the port was refusing to release them without proper signed documentation. It was a trip Charlie could have well done without, and one he certainly didn't intend to make every month.

When he arrived on the dockside he quickly discovered that there was no problem with the trade unions, who were quite willing to unload the entire cargo, or with his girls, who were just sitting on the mudguards of their lorries waiting to take delivery.

Over a pint at the local pub, Alf Redwood, the dockers' leader, warned Charlie that Mr Simkins, the general manager of the Docks and Harbour Board, was a stickler when it came to paperwork and liked everything done by the book.

"Does he?" said Charlie. "Then I'll have to stick by the book, won't I?" After paying for his round, he walked over to the administration block where he asked to see Mr Simkins.

"He's rather busy at the moment," said a receptionist, not bothering to look up from painting her nails. Charlie walked straight past her and into Simkins's office, to find a thin, balding man sitting alone behind a very large desk dipping a biscuit into a cup of tea.

"And who are you?" asked the port's official, taken so completely by surprise that he dropped his biscuit into the tea.

"Charlie Trumper. And I'm here to find out why you won't release my rice."

"I don't have the proper authority," said Simkins, as he tried to rescue his biscuit which was now floating on the top of his morning beverage. "No official papers have come from Cairo, and your forms from London are inadequate, quite inadequate." He gave Charlie a smile of satisfaction.

"But it could take days for me to get the necessary paperwork sorted out."

"That's not my problem."

"But we're at war, man."

"Which is why we must all try to keep to the regulations. I'm sure the Germans do."

"I don't give a damn what the Germans do," said Charlie. "I've got a million tons of rice coming through this port every month, and I want to distribute every last grain of it as quickly as possible. Do I make myself clear?"

"You certainly do, Mr Trumper, but I shall still require the official papers correctly completed before you get your rice."

"I order you to release that rice immediately," said Charlie, barking at him for the first time.

"No need to raise your voice, Mr Trumper, because as I've already explained you don't have the authority to order me to do anything. This is the Docks and Harbour Board and it doesn't, as I'm sure you know, come under the Ministry of Food. I should go back to London, and this time do try a little harder to see that we get the correct forms properly filled in."

Charlie felt he was too old to hit the man, so he simply picked up the telephone on Simkins's desk and asked for a number.

"What are you doing?" demanded Simkins. "That's my telephone – you don't have the proper authority to use my telephone."

Charlie clung on to the phone and turned his back on

Simkins. When he heard the voice on the other end of the line, he said, "It's Charlie Trumper. Can you put me through to the Prime Minister?"

Simkins's cheeks turned first red, then white, as the blood drained quickly from his face. "There's really no need –" he began.

"Good morning, sir," said Charlie. "I'm down in Southampton. The rice problem I mentioned to you last night. There turns out to be a bit of a hold-up at this end. I don't seem to be able –"

Simkins was now frantically waving his hands like a semaphore sailor in an attempt to gain Charlie's attention, while at the same time nodding his head energetically up and down.

"I've got a million tons coming in every month, Prime Minister, and the girls are just sitting on their –"

"It will be all right," whispered Simkins as he began to circle Charlie. "It will be all right, I can assure you."

"Do you want to speak to the man in charge yourself, sir?"

"No, no," said Simkins. "That won't be necessary. I have all the forms, all the forms you need, all the forms."

"I'll let him know, sir," said Charlie, pausing for a moment. "I'm due back in London this evening. Yes, sir, yes, I'll brief you the moment I return. Goodbye, Prime Minister."

"Goodbye," said Becky as she put down the telephone. "And no doubt you'll tell me what all that was about when you do get home tonight."

The minister roared with laughter when Charlie repeated the whole story to him and Jessica Allen later that evening.

"You know, the Prime Minister would have been quite happy to speak to the man if you had wanted him to," said Woolton.

"If he'd done that Simkins would have had a heart

attack," said Charlie. "And then my rice, not to mention my drivers, would have been stuck in that port for ever. In any case, with the food shortage the way it is I wouldn't have wanted the wretched man to waste another of his biscuits."

Charlie was in Carlisle attending a farmers' conference when an urgent call came through for him from London.

"Who is it?" he asked as he tried to concentrate on a delegate who was explaining the problems of increasing turnip yields.

"The Marchioness of Wiltshire," whispered Arthur Selwyn.

"Then I'll take it," said Charlie, and left the conference room to return to his bedroom where the hotel operator put the call through.

"Daphne, what can I do for you, my luv?"

"No, darling, it's what I can do for you, as usual. Have you read your *Times* this morning?"

"Glanced at the headlines. Why?" asked Charlie.

"Then you'd better check the obituaries page more carefully. In particular, the last line of one of them. I won't waste any more of your time, darling, as the Prime Minister keeps reminding us just what a vital role you're playing in winning the war."

Charlie laughed as the line went dead.

"Anything I can do to help?" asked Selwyn.

"Yes, Arthur, I need a copy of today's *Times*."

When Selwyn returned with a copy of the morning paper, Charlie flicked quickly through the pages until he came to the obituaries: Admiral Sir Alexander Dexter, a First World War commander of outstanding tactical ability; J. T. Macpherson, the balloonist and author; and Sir Raymond Hardcastle, the industrialist . . .

Charlie skimmed through the bare details of Sir Raymond's career: born and educated in Yorkshire; built up his father's engineering firm at the turn of the century.

During the twenties Hardcastle's had expanded from a fledgling company into one of the great industrial forces in the north of England. In 1938 Hardcastle sold his shareholding to John Brown and Co for seven hundred and eighty thousand pounds. But Daphne was right – the last line was the only one that really concerned Charlie.

"Sir Raymond, whose wife died in 1914, is survived by two daughters, Miss Amy Hardcastle and Mrs Gerald Trentham."

Charlie picked up the telephone on the desk beside him and asked to be put through to a Chelsea number. A few moments later Tom Arnold came on the line.

"Where the hell did you say Wrexall was to be found?" was the only question Charlie asked.

"As I explained when you last enquired, Chairman, he now runs a pub in Cheshire, the Happy Poacher, in a village called Hatherton."

Charlie thanked his managing director and replaced the receiver without another word.

"Can I be of any assistance?" asked Selwyn drily.

"What's my programme for the rest of the day looking like, Arthur?"

"Well, they haven't quite finished with the turnips yet, then you're meant to be attending more sessions all afternoon. This evening you're proposing the health of the government at the conference dinner before finally presenting the farmers' annual dairy awards tomorrow morning."

"Then pray I'm back in time for the dinner," said Charlie. He stood up and grabbed his overcoat.

"Do you want me to come with you?" asked Selwyn, trying to keep up with his master.

"No, thank you, Arthur. It's a personal matter. Just cover for me if I'm not back in time."

Charlie ran down the stairs and out into the yard. His driver was dozing peacefully behind the wheel.

Charlie jumped into his car and the slammed door woke him up. "Take me to Hatherton."

"Hatherton, sir?"

"Yes, Hatherton. Head south out of Carlisle, and by then I should be able to point you in the right direction." Charlie flicked open the road map, turned to the back and began running his finger down the Hs. There were five Hathertons listed but luckily just the one in Cheshire. The only other word Charlie uttered on the entire journey was "Faster," which he repeated several times. They passed through Lancaster, Preston and Warrington before coming to a halt outside the Happy Poacher half an hour before the pub was due to close for the afternoon.

Syd Wrexall's eyes nearly popped out of his head when Charlie strolled in the front door.

"A Scotch egg and a pint of your best bitter, landlord, and no short measures," Charlie said with a grin, placing a briefcase by his side.

"Fancy seeing you in these parts, Mr Trumper," declared Syd after he had shouted over his shoulder, "Hilda, one Scotch egg, and come and see who's 'ere."

"I was just on my way to a farmers' conference in Carlisle," explained Charlie. "Thought I'd drop by and have a pint and a snack with an old friend."

"That's right neighbourly of you," said Syd as he placed the pint of bitter on the counter in front of him. "Of course, we read about you in the papers a lot nowadays, and all the work you're doing with Lord Woolton for the war effort. You're becoming quite a celebrity."

"It's a fascinating job the Prime Minister has given me," said Charlie. "I can only hope that I'm doing some good," he added, hoping he sounded pompous enough.

"But what about your shops, Charlie? Who's taking care of them with you away so much of the time?"

"Arnold's back at base doing the best he can in the circumstances, but I'm afraid I've got four or five closed, not to mention those that were already boarded up. I can tell you, Syd, in confidence" – Charlie lowered his voice – "if things don't start brightening up before too long I shall soon be looking for a buyer myself." Wrexall's wife came bustling in carrying a plate of food.

"Hello, Mrs Wrexall," said Charlie, as she put down a Scotch egg and a plate of salad in front of him. "Good to see you again, and why don't you and your husband have a drink on me?"

"Don't mind if I do, Charlie. Can you see to it, Hilda?" he said, as he leaned over the bar conspiratorially. "Don't suppose you know anyone who'd be interested in purchasing the syndicate's shops, and the pub, for that matter?"

"Can't say I do," said Charlie. "If I remember rightly, Syd, you were asking an awful lot of money for the Musketeer which is now nothing more than a bomb site. Not to mention the state of the few shops the syndicate still have boarded up."

"I came down to your figure of six thousand, which I thought we had already shaken hands on, but Arnold told me you were no longer interested," said Syd as his wife placed two pints on the counter before going off to serve another customer.

"He told you that?" said Charlie, trying to sound surprised.

"Oh, yes," said Wrexall. "I accepted your offer of six thousand, even sent the signed contract for your approval, but he just returned the documents without so much as a by your leave."

"I don't believe it," said Charlie. "After I'd given my word, Syd. Why didn't you get in touch with me direct?"

"Not that easy nowadays," said Wrexall, "what with your new exalted position I didn't think you'd be available for the likes of me."

"Arnold had no right to do that," said Charlie. "He obviously didn't appreciate how long our relationship goes back. I do apologise, Syd, and remember, for you I'm always available. You don't still have the contract, by any chance?"

"Certainly do," said Wrexall. "And it'll prove I'm as good as my word." He disappeared, leaving Charlie to take a bite of Scotch egg and a slow swig of the local brew.

The publican returned a few minutes later and slammed down some documents on the bar top. "There you are, Charlie, true as I stand here."

Charlie studied the contract that he had been shown by Arnold some eighteen months before. It already bore the signature "Sydney Wrexall", with the figures "six thousand" written in after the words "for the consideration of –"

"All that it needed was the date and your signature," said Syd. "I never thought you'd do that to me, Charlie, after all these years."

"As you well know, Syd, I'm a man of my word. I'm only sorry my managing director wasn't properly acquainted with our personal arrangement." Charlie removed a wallet from his pocket, took out a cheque book, and wrote out the words Syd Wrexall on the top line and six thousand pounds on the line below before signing it with a flourish.

"You're a gentleman, Charlie, I always said you were. Didn't I always say he was, Hilda?"

Mrs Wrexall nodded enthusiastically as Charlie smiled, picked up the contract, placed all the papers inside his briefcase and then shook hands with the publican and his wife.

"How much is the damage?" he asked after he had drained the last drop of his beer.

"It's on the house," said Wrexall.

"But, Syd –"

"No, I insist, wouldn't dream of treating an old friend like a customer, Charlie. On the house," he repeated as the telephone rang and Hilda Wrexall went off to answer it.

"Well, I must be on my way," said Charlie. "Otherwise I'll be late for this conference, and I'm meant to be delivering another speech tonight. Nice to have done business with you, Syd." He had just reached the door of the pub as Mrs Wrexall came rushing back to the counter.

"There's a lady on the line for you, Syd. Calling long distance. Says her name is Mrs Trentham."

As the months passed Charlie became the master of his brief. No port director could be sure when he might burst into his office, no supplier was surprised when he demanded to check his invoices and the president of the National Farmers' Union positively purred whenever Charlie's name came up in conversation.

He never found it necessary to phone the Prime Minister, although Mr Churchill did phone him on one occasion. It was four forty-five in the morning when Charlie picked up the receiver on his desk.

"Good morning," he said.

"Trumper?"

"Yes, who's that?"

"Churchill."

"Good morning, Prime Minister. What can I do for you, sir?"

"Nothing. I was just checking that it was true what they say about you. By the way, thank you." The phone went dead.

Charlie even managed from time to time to have lunch with Daniel. The boy was now attached to the War Office, but would never talk about the work he was involved in. After he was promoted to captain, Charlie's only worry became what Becky's reaction would be if she ever saw him in uniform.

When Charlie visited Tom Arnold at the end of the month he learned that Mr Hadlow had retired as manager of the bank and his replacement, a Mr Paul Merrick, was not proving to be quite as amenable. "Says our overdraft is reaching unacceptable levels and perhaps it's time we did something about it," explained Tom.

"Does he?" said Charlie. "Then I shall obviously have to see this Mr Merrick and tell him a few home truths."

Although Trumper's now owned all the shops in Chelsea Terrace, with the exception of the bookshop, Charlie was still faced with the problem of Mrs Trentham and her bombed-out flats, not to mention the additional worry of Herr Hitler and his unfinished war: these he tended to place in roughly the same category, and nearly always in that order.

The war with Herr Hitler began to take a step in the right direction towards the end of 1942 with the victory of the eighth army at El Alamein. Charlie felt confident that Churchill was right when he declared that the tide had turned, as first Africa, then Italy, France and finally Germany were invaded.

But by then it was Mr Merrick who was insisting on seeing Charlie.

When Charlie entered Mr Merrick's office for the first time he was surprised to find how young Mr Hadlow's replacement was. It also took him a few moments to get used to a bank manager who didn't wear a waistcoat or a black tie. Paul Merrick was a shade taller than Charlie and every bit as broad in everything except his smile. Charlie quickly discovered that Mr Merrick had no small-talk.

"Are you aware, Mr Trumper, that your company account is overdrawn by some forty-seven thousand pounds and your present income doesn't even cover . . ."

"But the property must be worth four or five times that amount."

"Only if you're able to find someone who's willing to buy it."

"But I'm not a seller."

"You may be left with no choice, Mr Trumper, if the bank decides to foreclose on you."

"Then I'll just have to change banks, won't I?" said Charlie.

"You have obviously not had the time recently to read the minutes of your own board meetings because when they last met, your managing director Mr Arnold reported that he had visited six banks in the past month and none of them had showed the slightest interest in taking over Trumper's account."

Merrick waited for his customer's response but as Charlie remained silent he continued. "Mr Crowther also explained to the board on that occasion that the problem you are now facing has been caused by property prices being lower now than they have been at any time since the 1930s."

"But that will change overnight once the war is over."

"Possibly, but that might not be for several years and you could be insolvent long before then . . ."

"More like twelve months would be my guess."

". . . especially if you continue to sign cheques to the value of six thousand pounds for property worth about half that amount."

"But if I hadn't . . ."

"You might not be in such a precarious position."

Charlie remained silent for some time. "So what do you expect me to do about it?" he asked finally.

"I require you to sign over all the properties and stock held by your company as collateral against the overdraft. I have already drawn up the necessary papers."

Merrick swivelled round a document that lay on the middle of his desk. "If you feel able to sign," he added, pointing to a dotted line near the bottom of the page marked by two pencil crosses, "I would be willing to extend your credit for a further twelve months."

"And if I refuse?"

"I'll be left with no choice but to issue an insolvency notice within twenty-eight days."

Charlie stared down at the document and saw that Becky had already signed on the line above his. Both men remained silent for some time as Charlie weighed up the alternatives. Then, without offering any further comment, Charlie took out his pen, scrawled a signature between the two pencilled crosses, swivelled the document back round, turned, and marched out of the room without another word.

The surrender of Germany was signed by General Jodl and accepted on behalf of the Allies by General Bedell Smith at Reims on 7 May 1945.

Charlie would have joined the VE Day celebrations in Trafalgar Square had Becky not reminded him that their overdraft had reached nearly sixty thousand pounds and Merrick was once again threatening them with bankruptcy.

"He's got his hands on the property and all our stock. What else does he expect me to do?" demanded Charlie.

"He's now suggesting that we sell the one thing that could clear the debt, and would even leave some capital over to see us through the next couple of years."

"And what's that?"

"Van Gogh's *The Potato Eaters*."

"Never!"

"But Charlie, the painting belongs to . . ."

Charlie made an appointment to see Lord Woolton the following morning and explained to the Minister he was now faced with his own problems that required his immediate attention. He therefore asked, now the war in Europe was over, if he could be released from his present duties.

Lord Woolton fully understood Charlie's dilemma, and made it clear how sad he and all at the department would be to see him go.

When Charlie left his office a month later the only thing he took with him was Jessica Allen.

Charlie's problems didn't ease up during 1945 as property prices continued to fall and inflation continued to rise. He was nevertheless touched when, after peace had been declared with Japan, and after Winston Churchill's General Election defeat, the former Prime Minister held a dinner in his honour, before he left Number 10. Daphne admitted that she had never entered the building, and told Becky that she wasn't even sure she wanted to. Percy admitted he wanted to, and was envious.

There were several leading cabinet ministers present for the occasion. Becky was placed between Churchill and the rising young star Rab Butler, while Charlie was seated next to Mrs Churchill and Lady Woolton. Becky watched her husband as he chatted in a relaxed way with the Prime

Minister and Lord Woolton, and had to smile when Charlie had the nerve to offer the old man a cigar he had specially selected that afternoon from Number 139. No one in that room could possibly have guessed that they were on the verge of bankruptcy.

When the evening finally came to an end, Becky thanked the Prime Minister, who in turn thanked her.

"What for?" asked Becky.

"Taking telephone calls in my name, and making excellent decisions on my behalf," he said, as he accompanied them both down the long corridor to the front hall.

"I had no idea you knew," said Charlie, turning scarlet.

"Knew? Woolton told the entire cabinet the next day. Never seen them laugh so much."

When the Prime Minister reached the front door of Number 10, he gave Becky a slight bow and said, "Goodnight, Lady Trumper."

"You know what that means, don't you?" said Charlie as he drove out of Downing Street and turned right into Whitehall.

"That you're about to get a knighthood?"

"Yes, but more important, we're going to have to sell the Van Gogh."

DANIEL

1931-1947

CHAPTER 29

"Y ou're a little bastard," remains my first memory. I was five and three-quarters at the time and the words were being shouted by a small girl on the far side of the playground as she pointed at me and danced up and down. The rest of the class stopped and stared, until I ran across and pinned her against the wall.

"What does it mean?" I demanded, squeezing her arms.

She burst into tears and said, "I don't know. I just heard my mum tell my dad that you were a little bastard."

"I know what the word means," said a voice from behind me. I turned round to find myself surrounded by the rest of the pupils from my class, but I was quite unable to work out who had spoken.

"What does it mean?" I said again, even louder.

"Give me sixpence and I'll tell you."

I stared up at Neil Watson, the form bully who always sat in the row behind me.

"I've only got threepence."

He considered the offer for some time before saying, "All right then, I'll tell you for threepence."

He walked up to me, thrust out the palm of his hand, and waited until I'd slowly unwrapped my handkerchief and passed over my entire pocket money for the week. He then cupped his hands and whispered into my ear, "You don't have a father."

"It's not true!" I shouted, and started punching him on the chest. But he was far bigger than me and only laughed at my feeble efforts. The bell sounded for the end of break and everyone ran back to class, several of them laughing and shouting in unison, "Daniel's a little bastard."

Nanny came to pick me up from school that afternoon and when I was sure none of my classmates could overhear me I asked her what the word meant. She only said, "What a disgraceful question, Daniel, and I can only hope that it's not the sort of thing they're teaching you at St David's. Please don't let me ever hear you mention the word again."

Over tea in the kitchen, when Nanny had left to go and run my bath, I asked Cook to tell me what bastard meant. All she said was, "I'm sure I don't know, Master Daniel, and I would advise you not to ask anyone else."

I didn't dare ask my mother or father in case what Neil Watson had said turned out to be true, and I lay awake all night wondering how I could find out.

Then I remembered that a long time ago my mother had gone into hospital and was meant to come back with a brother or sister for me, and didn't. I wondered if that's what made you a bastard.

About a week later Nanny had taken me to visit Mummy at Guy's hospital but I can't recall that much about the outing, except that she looked very white and sad. I remember feeling very happy when she eventually came home.

The next episode in my life that I recall vividly was going to St Paul's School at the age of eleven. There I was made to work really hard for the first time in my life. At my prep school I came top in almost every subject without having to do much more than any other child, and although I was called "swot" or "swotty", it never worried me. At St Paul's there turned out to be lots of boys who were clever, but none of them could touch me when it came to maths. I not only enjoyed a subject so many of my classmates seemed to dread but the marks I was awarded in the end of term exams appeared always to delight my mum and dad. I couldn't wait for the next algebraic equation, a further geometric puzzle or the challenge of solving an arithmetic test in my head while others in the form sucked their pencils as they considered pages of longhand figures.

I did quite well in other subjects and although I was not much good at games I took up the cello and was invited to join the school orchestra, but my form master said none of this was important because I was obviously going to be a mathematician for the rest of my life. I didn't understand what he meant at the time, as I knew Dad had left school at fourteen to run my great-grandfather's fruit and vegetable barrow in Whitechapel, and even though Mum had gone to London University she still had to work at Number 1 Chelsea Terrace to keep Dad "in the style to which he'd become accustomed". Or that's what I used to hear Mum telling him at breakfast from time to time.

It must have been around that time that I discovered what the word "bastard" really meant. We were reading *King John* out loud in class, so I was able to ask Mr Quilter, my English master, without drawing too much attention to the question. One or two of the boys looked round and sniggered, but this time there were no pointed fingers or whispers, and when I was told the meaning I remember thinking Neil Watson hadn't been that far off the mark in the first place. But of course such an accusation could not be levelled at me, because my very first memories had involved my mum and dad being together. They had always been Mr and Mrs Trumper.

I suppose I would have dismissed the whole memory of that early incident if I hadn't come down to the kitchen one night for a glass of milk and overheard Joan Moore talking to Harold the butler.

"Young Daniel's doing well at school," said Harold. "Must have his mother's brains."

"True, but let's pray that he never finds out the truth about his father." The words made me freeze to the stair rail. I continued to listen intently.

"Well, one thing's for certain," continued Harold, "Mrs Trentham's never going to admit the boy's her grandson, so heaven knows who'll end up with all that money."

"Not Captain Guy any longer, that's for sure," said Joan. "So perhaps that brat Nigel will be left the lot."

After that the conversation turned to who should lay up for breakfast so I crept back upstairs to my bedroom; but I didn't sleep. Although I sat on those steps for many hours during the next few months, patiently waiting for another vital piece of information that might fall from the servants' lips, the subject never arose between them again.

The only other occasion I could recall having heard the name "Trentham" had been some time before, when the Marchioness of Wiltshire, a close friend of my mother's, came to tea. I remained in the hall when my mother asked, "Did you go to Guy's funeral?"

"Yes, but it wasn't well attended by the good parishioners of Ashurst," the Marchioness assured her. "Those who remembered him well seemed to be treating the occasion more as if it were a blessed release."

"Was Sir Raymond present?"

"No, he was conspicuous by his absence," came back the reply. "Mrs Trentham claimed he was too old to travel, which only acted as a sad reminder that she still stands to inherit a fortune in the not too distant future."

New facts learned, but they still made little sense. The name of Trentham arose in my presence once more when I heard Daddy talking to Colonel Hamilton as he was leaving the house after a private meeting that had been held in his study. All Daddy said was, "However much we offer Mrs Trentham, she's never going to sell those flats to us."

The colonel vigorously nodded his agreement, but all he had to say on the subject was, "Bloody woman."

When both my parents were out of the house, I looked up "Trentham" in the telephone directory. There was only one listing: Major G. H. Trentham, MP, 19 Chester Square. I wasn't any the wiser.

When in 1939 Trinity College offered me the Newton Mathematics Prize Scholarship I thought Dad was going to burst, he was so proud. We all drove up to the university city for the weekend to check my future digs, before strolling round the colleges' cloisters and through Great Court.

The only cloud on this otherwise unblemished horizon was the thunderous one of Nazi Germany. Conscription for all those over twenty was being debated in Parliament, and I couldn't wait to play my part if Hitler dared to plant as much as a toe on Polish soil.

My first year at Cambridge went well, mainly because I was being tutored by Horace Bradford who, along with his wife Victoria, were considered to be the pick of the bunch among a highly talented group of mathematicians who were teaching at the university at that time. Although Mrs Bradford was rumoured to have won the Wrangler's Prize for coming out top of her year, her husband explained that she was not given the prestigious award, simply because she was a woman. The man who came second was deemed to have come first, a piece of information that made my mother puce with anger.

Mrs Bradford rejoiced in the fact that my mother had been awarded her degree from London University in 1921, while Cambridge still refused to acknowledge hers even existed in 1939.

At the end of my first year I, like many Trinity undergraduates, applied to join the army, but my tutor asked me if I would like to work with him and his wife at the War Office in a new department that would be specialising in code-breaking.

I accepted the offer without a second thought, relishing the prospect of spending my time sitting in a dingy little back room somewhere in Bletchley Park attempting to break German codes. I felt a little guilty that I was going to be one of the few people in uniform who was actually enjoying the war. Dad gave me enough money to buy an old MG which meant I could get up to London from time to time to see him and Mum.

Occasionally I managed to grab an hour for lunch with him over at the Ministry of Food, but Dad would only eat bread and cheese accompanied by a glass of milk as an example to the rest of his team. This may have been considered edifying but it certainly wasn't nourishing, Mr Selwyn warned me, adding that my father even had the minister at it.

"But not Mr Churchill?" I suggested.

"He's next on his list, I'm told."

In 1943 I was made up to captain, which was simply the War Office acknowledging the work we were all doing in our fledgling department. Of course, my father was delighted but I was sorry that I couldn't share with my parents our excitement when we broke the code used by the German U-boat commanders. It still baffles me to this day why they continued to go on using the four-wheel Enigma key long after we'd made our discovery. The code was a mathematician's dream that we finally broke on the back of a menu at Lyons Corner House just off Piccadilly. The waitress serving at our table described me as a vandal. I laughed, and remember thinking that I would take the rest of the day off and go and surprise my mother by letting her see what I looked like in my captain's uniform. I thought I looked rather swish, but when she opened the front door to greet me I was shocked by her response. She stared at me as if she'd seen a ghost. Although she recovered quickly enough, that first reaction on seeing me in uniform became just another clue in an ever more complex puzzle, a puzzle that was never far from the back of my thoughts.

The next clue came in the bottom line of an obituary, to which I wasn't paying much attention until I discovered that a Mrs Trentham would be coming into a fortune; not an important clue in itself, until I reread the entry and learned that she was the daughter of someone called Sir Raymond Hardcastle, a name that allowed me to fill in several little boxes that went in both directions. But what puzzled me was there being no mention of a Guy Trentham among the surviving relatives.

Sometimes I wish I hadn't been born with the kind of mind that enjoyed breaking codes and meddling with mathematical formulae. But somehow "bastard", "Trentham", "hospital", "Captain Guy", "flats", "Sir Raymond", "that brat Nigel", "funeral", and Mother turning white when she saw me dressed in a captain's uniform seemed to have some linear connection. Although I realised I would need even more clues before logic would lead me to the correct solution.

Then suddenly I worked out to whom they must have been referring when the Marchioness had come to tea all those years before, and told Mother that she had just attended Guy's funeral. It must have been Captain Guy's burial that had taken place. But why was that so significant?

The following Saturday morning I rose at an ungodly hour and travelled down to Ashurst, the village in which the Marchioness of Wiltshire had once lived – not a coincidence, I concluded. I arrived at the parish church a little after six, and as I had anticipated at that hour there was no one to be seen in the churchyard. I strolled around the graveyard checking the names: Yardley, Baxter, Flood, and Harcourt-Brownes aplenty. Some of the graves were overgrown with weeds, others were well cared for and even had fresh flowers at the head. I paused for a moment at the grave of my godmother's grandfather. There must have been over a hundred parishioners buried around the clock tower, but it didn't take that long to find the neatly kept Trentham family plot, only a few yards from the church vestry.

When I came across the most recent family gravestone I broke out in a cold sweat:

CAPTAIN GUY TRENTHAM, M.C.
1896–1927
After a long illness.
Sadly missed by all his family.

And so the mystery had come literally to a dead end, at the grave of the one man who surely could have answered all my questions had he still been alive.

When the war ended I returned to Trinity and was granted an extra year to complete my degree. Although my father and mother considered the highlight of the year to be my passing out as senior Wrangler with the offer of a prize fellowship at Trinity, I thought Dad's investiture at Buckingham Palace wasn't to be sneezed at.

The ceremony turned out to be a double delight because I was also able to witness my old tutor, Professor Bradford, being knighted for the role he had played in the field of code-breaking – although there was nothing for his wife, my mother noted. I remember feeling equally outraged on Doctor Bradford's behalf. Dad may have played his part in filling the stomachs of the British people, but as Churchill had stated in the House of Commons our little team had probably cut down the length of the war by as much as a year.

We all met up afterwards for tea at the Ritz, and not unnaturally at some point during the afternoon the conversation switched to what career I proposed to follow now the war was over. To my father's abiding credit he had never once suggested that I should join him at Trumper's, especially as I knew how much he had longed for another son who might eventually take his place. In fact during the summer vacation I became even more conscious of my good fortune, as Father seemed to be preoccupied with the business and Mother was unable to hide her own anxieties about the future of Trumper's. But whenever I asked if I could help all she would say was: "Not to worry, it will all work out in the end."

Once I had returned to Cambridge, I persuaded myself that should I ever come across the name Trentham again I would no longer allow it to worry me. However, because the name was never mentioned freely in my presence it continued to nag away in the back of my mind. My father had always been such an open man that there was no simple explanation as to why on this one particular subject he remained so secretive – to such an extent, in fact, that I felt I just couldn't raise the subject with him myself.

I might have gone years without bothering to do anything more about the conundrum if I hadn't one morning picked up an extension to the phone in the Little Boltons and heard Tom Arnold, my father's right-hand man, say, "Well, at least we can be thankful that you got to Syd Wrexall before Mrs Trentham." I replaced the head set immediately, feeling that I now had to get to the bottom of the mystery once and for all – and what's more, without my parents finding out. Why does one always think the worst in these situations? Surely the final solution would turn out to be something quite innocuous.

Although I had never met Syd Wrexall I could still remember him as the landlord of the Musketeer, a pub that had stood proudly on the other end of Chelsea Terrace until a bomb had landed in the snug bar. During the war my father bought the freehold and later converted the building into an up-market furnishing department.

It didn't take a Dick Barton to discover that Mr Wrexall had left London during the war to become the landlord of a pub in a sleepy village called Hatherton, hidden away in the county of Cheshire.

I spent three days working out my strategy for Mr Wrexall, and only when I was convinced that I knew all the questions that needed to be asked did I feel confident enough to make the journey to Hatherton. I had to word every query I needed answering in such a way that they didn't appear to be questions; but I still waited for a further month before I drove up north, by which time I had grown a beard that was long enough for me to feel confident that Wrexall would not recognise me. Although I was unaware of having seen him in the past, I realised that it was possible Wrexall might have come across me as recently as three or four years ago, and would therefore have known who I was the moment I walked into his pub. I even purchased a modern pair of glasses to replace my old specs.

I chose a Monday to make the trip as I suspected it would be the quietest day of the week on which to have a pub lunch. Before I set out on the journey I telephoned the Happy Poacher to be sure Mr Wrexall would be on duty that day. His wife assured me that he would be around and I put the phone down before she could ask why I wanted to know.

During my journey up to Cheshire I rehearsed a

series of non-questions again and again. Having arrived in the village of Hatherton I parked my car down a side road some way from the pub before strolling into the Happy Poacher. I discovered three or four people standing at the bar chatting and another half-dozen enjoying a drink around a mean-looking fire. I took a seat at the end of the bar and ordered some shepherd's pie and a half-pint of best bitter from a buxom, middle-aged lady who I later discovered was the landlord's wife. It took only moments to work out who the landlord was, because the other customers all called him Syd, but I realised that I would still have to be patient as I listened to him chat about anybody and everybody, from Lady Docker to Richard Murdoch, as if they were all close friends.

"Same again, sir?" he asked eventually, as he returned to my end of the bar and picked up my empty glass.

"Yes, please," I said, relieved to find that he didn't appear to recognise me.

By the time he had come back with my beer there were only two or three of us left at the bar.

"From around these parts, are you, sir?" he asked, leaning on the counter.

"No," I said. "Only up for a couple of days on an inspection. I'm with the Ministry of Agriculture, Fisheries and Food."

"So what brings you to Hatherton?"

"I'm checking out all the farms in the area for foot and mouth disease."

"Oh, yes, I've read all about that in the papers," he said, toying with an empty glass.

"Care to join me, landlord?" I asked.

"Oh, thank you, sir. I'll have a whisky, if I may." He put his empty half-pint glass in the washing-up water below the counter and poured himself a double. He charged me half a crown, then asked how my findings were coming along.

"All clear so far," I told him. "But I've still got a few more farms in the north of the county to check out."

"I used to know someone in your department," he said.

"Oh, yes?"

"Sir Charles Trumper."

"Before my time," I said, taking a swig from my beer, "but they still talk about him back at the ministry. Must have been a tough customer if half the stories about him are true."

"Bloody right," said Wrexall. "And but for him I'd be a rich man."

"Really?"

"Oh, yes. You see, I used to own a little property in London before I moved up here. A pub, along with an interest in several shops in Chelsea Terrace, to be exact. He picked the lot up from me during the war for a mere six thousand. If I'd waited another twenty-four hours I could have sold them for twenty thousand, perhaps even thirty."

"But the war didn't end in twenty-four hours."

"Oh, no, I'm not suggesting for one moment that he did anything dishonest, but it always struck me as a little more than a coincidence that having not set eyes on him for years he should suddenly show up in this pub on that very morning."

Wrexall's glass was now empty.

"Same again for both of us?" I suggested, hoping that the investment of another half-crown might further loosen his tongue.

"That's very generous of you, sir," he responded, and when he returned he asked, "Where was I?"

"On that very morning . . ."

"Oh, yes, Sir Charles – Charlie, as I always called him. Well, he closed the deal right here at this bar, in under ten minutes, when blow me if another interested party didn't ring up and ask if the properties were still for sale. I had to tell the lady in question that I had just signed them away."

I avoided asking who "the lady" was, although I suspected I knew. "But that doesn't prove that she would have offered you twenty thousand pounds for them," I said.

"Oh, yes, she would," responded Wrexall. "That Mrs Trentham would have offered me anything to stop Sir Charles getting his hands on those shops."

"Great Scott," I said, once again avoiding the word "why?"

"Oh, yes, the Trumpers and the Trenthams have been at each other's throats for years, you know. She still owns a block of flats right in the middle of Chelsea Terrace. It's the only thing that's stopped him building his grand mausoleum, isn't it? What's more, when she tried to buy Number 1 Chelsea Terrace, Charlie completely outfoxed her, didn't he? Never seen anything like it in my life."

"But that must have been years ago," I said. "Amazing how people go on bearing grudges for so long."

"You're right, because to my knowledge this one's been going on since the early twenties, ever since her posh son was seen walking out with Miss Salmon."

I held my breath.

"She didn't approve of that, no, not Mrs Trentham. We all had that worked out at the Musketeer, and then when the son disappears off to India the Salmon girl suddenly ups sticks and marries Charlie. And that wasn't the end of the mystery"

"No?"

"Certainly not," said Wrexall. "Because none of us are sure to this day who the father was."

"The father?"

Wrexall hesitated. "I've gone too far. I'll say no more."

"Such a long time ago, I'm surprised anyone still

cares," I offered as my final effort before draining my glass.

"True enough," said Wrexall. "That's always been a bit of a mystery to me as well. But there's no telling with folks. Well, I must close up now, sir, or I'll have the law after me."

"Of course. And I must get back to those cattle."

Before I returned to Cambridge I sat in the car and wrote down every word I could remember the landlord saying. On the long journey back I tried to piece together the new clues and get them into some sort of order. Although Wrexall had supplied a lot of information I hadn't known before he had also begged a few more unanswered questions. The only thing I came away from that pub certain of was that I couldn't possibly stop now.

The next morning I decided to return to the War Office and ask Sir Horace's old secretary if she knew of any way that one could trace the background of a former serving officer.

"Name?" said the prim middle-aged woman who still kept her hair tied in a bun, a style left over from the war.

"Guy Trentham," I told her.

"Rank and regiment?"

"Captain and the Royal Fusiliers would be my guess."

She disappeared behind a closed door, but was back within fifteen minutes clutching a small brown file. She extracted a single sheet of paper and read aloud from it. "Captain Guy Trentham, MC. Served in the first war, further service in India, resigned his commission in 1922. No explanation given. No forwarding address."

"You're a genius," I said, and to her consternation kissed her on the forehead before leaving to return to Cambridge.

The more I discovered, the more I found I needed

to know, even though for the time being I seemed to have come to another dead-end.

For the next few weeks I concentrated on my job as a supervisor until my pupils had all safely departed for their Christmas vacation.

I returned to London for the three-week break and spent a happy family Christmas with my parents at the Little Boltons. Father seemed a lot more relaxed than he had been during the summer and even Mother appeared to have shed her unexplained anxieties.

However, another mystery arose during that holiday and as I was convinced it was in no way connected with the Trenthams, I didn't hesitate to ask my mother to solve it.

"What's happened to Dad's favourite picture?"

Her reply saddened me greatly and she begged me never to raise the subject of *The Potato Eaters* with my father.

The week before I was due to return to Cambridge I was strolling back down Beaufort Street towards the Little Boltons, when I spotted a Chelsea Pensioner in his blue serge uniform trying to cross the road.

"Allow me to help you," I offered.

"Thank you, sir," he said, looking up at me with a rheumy smile.

"And who did you serve with?" I asked casually.

"The Prince of Wales Own," he replied. "And you?"

"The Royal Fusiliers." We crossed the road together. "Got any of those, have you?"

"The Fussies," he said. "Oh, yes, Banger Smith who saw service in the Great War, and Sammy Tomkins who joined up later, twenty-two, twenty-three, if I remember, and was then invalided out after Tobruk."

"Banger Smith?" I said.

"Yes," replied the pensioner as we reached the other side of the road. "A right skiver, that one." He chuckled chestily. "But he still puts in a day a week at your regimental museum, if his stories are to be believed."

I was first to enter the small regimental museum the following day, only to be told by the curator that Banger Smith only came in on Thursdays, and even then, couldn't always be relied on. I glanced around a room filled with regimental mementoes, threadbare flags parading battle honours, a display case with uniforms, out-of-date implements of war from a bygone age and large maps covered in different coloured pins depicting how, where and when those honours had been won.

As the curator was only a few years older than me I didn't bother him with any questions about the First World War.

I returned the following Thursday when I found an old soldier seated in a corner of the museum pretending to be fully occupied.

"Banger Smith?"

The old contemptible couldn't have been an inch over five feet and made no attempt to get up off his chair. He looked at me warily.

"What of it?"

I produced a ten-bob note from my inside pocket.

He looked first at the note and then at me with an enquiring eye. "What are you after?"

"Can you remember a Captain Guy Trentham, by any chance?" I asked.

"You from the police?"

"No, I'm a solicitor dealing with his estate."

"I'll wager Captain Trentham didn't leave anything to anybody."

"I'm not at liberty to reveal that," I said. "But I don't suppose you know what happened to him after he left the Fusiliers? You see, there's no trace of him in regimental records since 1922."

"There wouldn't be, would there? He didn't

exactly leave the Fussies with the regimental band playing him off the parade ground. Bloody man should have been horse-whipped, in my opinion."

"Why?"

"You won't get a word out of me," he said. "Regimental secret," he added, touching the side of his nose.

"But have you any idea where he went after he left India?"

"Cost you more than ten bob, that will," said the old soldier, chuckling.

"What do you mean?"

"Buggered off to Australia, didn't he? Died out there, then got shipped back by his mother. Good riddance, is all I can say. I'd take his bloody picture off the wall if I had my way."

"His picture?"

"Yes. MCs next to the DSOs, top left-hand corner," he said, managing to raise an arm to point in that direction.

I walked slowly over to the corner Banger Smith had indicated, past the seven Fusilier VCs, several DSOs and on to the MCs. They were in chronological order: 1914 – three, 1915 – thirteen, 1916 – ten, 1917 – eleven, 1918 – seventeen. Captain Guy Trentham, the inscription read, had been awarded the MC after the second battle of the Marne on 18 July 1918.

I stared up at the picture of a young officer in captain's uniform and knew I would have to make a journey to Australia.

CHAPTER 30

"When were you thinking of going?"

"During the long vacation."

"Have you enough money to cover such a journey?"

"I've still got most of that five hundred pounds you gave me when I graduated. In any case, a bachelor with his own rooms in college is hardly in need of a vast private income." Daniel looked up as his mother entered the drawing room.

"Daniel's thinking of going to America this summer."

"How exciting," said Becky, placing some flowers on a side table next to the Remington. "Then you must try and see the Fields in Chicago and the Bloomingdales in New York, and if you have enough time you could also –"

"Actually," said Daniel, leaning against the mantelpiece, "I think I'll be trying to see Waterstone in Princeton and Stinstead at Berkeley."

"Do I know them?" Becky frowned as she looked up from her flower-arranging.

"I wouldn't have thought so, Mother. They're both college professors who teach maths, or math, as they call it."

Charlie laughed.

"Well, be sure you write to us regularly," said his mother. "I always like to know where you are and what you're up to."

"Of course I will, Mother," said Daniel, trying not to sound exasperated. "If you promise to remember that I'm now twenty-six years old."

Becky looked across at him with a smile. "Are you really, my dear?"

Daniel returned to Cambridge that night trying to work out how he could possibly keep in touch from America while he was in fact travelling to Australia. He disliked the thought of deceiving his mother, but knew it would have pained her even more to tell him the truth about Captain Trentham.

Matters weren't helped when Charlie sent him a first-class ticket for New York on the *Queen Mary* for the exact date he had mentioned. It cost one hundred and three pounds and included an open-ended return.

Daniel eventually came up with a solution. He worked out that if he took the *Queen Mary* bound for New York the week after term had ended, then continued his journey on the Twentieth Century Limited and the Super Chief across the States to San Francisco, he could pick up the SS *Aorangi* to Sydney with a day to spare. That would still give him four weeks in Australia before he would have to repeat the journey south to north, allowing him just enough time to arrive back in Southampton a few days before the Michaelmas term began.

As with everything on which Daniel embarked, he spent hours of research and preparation long before he even set off for Southampton. He allocated three days to the Australian High Commission Information Department in the Strand, and made sure he regularly sat next to a certain Dr Marcus Winters, a visiting professor from Adelaide, whenever he came to dine at Trinity High Table. Although the first secretary and deputy librarian at Australia House remained puzzled by some of Daniel's questions and Doctor Winters curious as to the motives of the young mathematician, by the end of the Trinity term Daniel felt confident that he had learned enough to ensure that his time wouldn't be wasted once he had set foot on the sub-continent. However, he realised the whole enterprise was still a huge gamble: if the first question he needed to be answered yielded the reply, "There's no way of finding that out."

Four days after the students had gone down and he had completed his supervision reports, Daniel was packed and ready. The following morning his mother arrived at the college to drive him to Southampton. On the journey down to the south coast he learned that Charlie had recently applied to the London County Council for outline planning permission to develop Chelsea Terrace as one gigantic department store.

"But what about those bombed-out flats?"

"The council have given the owners three months to proceed with an application to rebuild or they have threatened to issue a compulsory purchase order and put the site up for sale."

"Pity we just can't buy the flats ourselves," said Daniel, trying out one of his non-questions in the hope that it might elicit some response from his mother but she just continued to drive on down the A30 without offering an opinion.

It was ironic, Daniel reflected, that if only his mother had felt able to confide in him the reason Mrs Trentham wouldn't co-operate with his father she could have turned the car around and taken him back to Cambridge.

He returned to safer territory. "So how's Dad hoping to raise the cash for such a massive enterprise?"

"He can't make up his mind between a bank loan and going public."

"What sort of sum are you talking about?"

"Mr Merrick estimates around a hundred and fifty thousand pounds."

Daniel gave a low whistle.

"The bank are happy enough to loan us the full amount now that property prices have shot up," Becky continued, "but they're demanding everything we own as collateral including the property in Chelsea Terrace, the house, our art collection, and on top of that they want us to sign a personal guarantee and charge the company four per cent on the overdraft."

"Then perhaps the answer is to go public."

"It's not quite that easy. If we were to take that route the family might end up with only fifty-one per cent of the shares."

"Fifty-one per cent means you still control the company."

"Agreed," said Becky, "but should we ever need to raise some more capital at a future date, then further dilution would only mean we could well lose our majority shareholding. In any case, you know only too well how your father feels about outsiders being given too much of a say, let alone too large a stake. And his having to report regularly to even more non-executive directors, not to mention shareholders, could be a recipe for disaster. He's always run the business on instinct, while the Bank of England may well prefer a more orthodox approach."

"How quickly does the decision have to be made?"

"It should have been settled one way or the other by the time you get back from America."

"What about the future of Number 1?"

"There's a good chance I can knock it into shape. I've the right staff and enough contacts, so if we're granted the full planning permission we have applied for I believe we could, in time, give Sotheby's and Christie's a run for their money."

"Not if Dad keeps on stealing the best pictures –"

"True." Becky smiled. "But if he goes on the way he is now, our private collection will be worth more than the business, as selling my Van Gogh back to the Lefevre Gallery proved only too cruelly. He has the best amateur's eye I've ever come across – but don't ever tell him I said so."

Becky began to concentrate on the signs directing her to the docks and finally brought the car to a halt alongside the liner, but not quite so close as Daphne had once managed, if she remembered correctly.

Daniel sailed out of Southampton on the *Queen Mary* that evening, with his mother waving from the dockside.

While on board the great liner he wrote a long letter to his parents, which he posted five days later from Fifth Avenue. He then purchased a ticket on the Twentieth Century Limited for a Pullman to Chicago. The train pulled out of Penn station at eight the same night, Daniel having spent a total of six hours in Manhattan where his only other purchase was a guide book of America.

Once they had reached Chicago, the Pullman carriage was attached to the Super Chief which took him all the way to San Francisco.

During the four-day journey across America he began to regret he was going to Australia at all. As he passed through Kansas City, Newton City, La Junta, Albuquerque and Barstow, each city appeared more interesting than the last. Whenever the train pulled into a new station Daniel would leap off, buy a colourful postcard that indicated exactly where he was, fill in the white space with yet more information gained from the guide book before the train reached the next station. He would then post the filled-in card at the following stop and repeat the process. By the time the express had arrived at Oakland station, San Francisco, he had posted twenty-seven different cards back to his parents in the Little Boltons.

Once the bus had dropped him off in St Francis Square, Daniel booked himself into a small hotel near the harbour after checking the tariff was well within his budget. As he still had a thirty-six-hour wait before the SS *Aorangi* was due to depart, he travelled out to Berkeley and spent the whole of the second day with Professor Stinstead. He became so engrossed with Stinstead's research on tertiary calculus that he began to regret once again that he would not be staying longer, as he suspected he might learn far more by remaining at Berkeley than he would ever discover in Australia.

On the evening before he was due to sail, Daniel bought

twenty more postcards and sat up until one the following morning filling them in. By the twentieth his imagination had been stretched to its limit. The following morning, after he had settled his bill, he asked the head porter to post one of the postcards every three days until he returned. He handed over ten dollars and promised the porter that there would be a further ten when he came back to San Francisco, but only if the correct number of cards remained, as precisely when he would be back remained uncertain.

The senior porter was puzzled but pocketed the ten dollars, commenting in an aside to his young colleague on the desk that he had been asked to do far stranger things in the past, for far less.

By the time Daniel boarded the SS *Aorangi* his beard was no longer a rough stubble and his plan was as well prepared as it could be, given that his information had been gathered from the wrong side of the globe. During the voyage Daniel found himself seated at a large circular table with an Australian family who were on their way home from a holiday in the States. Over the next three weeks they added greatly to his store of knowledge, unaware that he was listening to every word they had to say with uncommon interest.

Daniel sailed into Sydney on the first Monday of August 1947. He stood out on the deck and watched the sun set behind Sydney Harbour Bridge as a pilot boat guided the liner slowly into the harbour. He suddenly felt very homesick and, not for the first time, wished he had never embarked on the trip. An hour later he had left the ship and booked himself into a guest-house which had been recommended to him by his travelling companions.

The owner of the guest-house, who introduced herself as Mrs Snell, turned out to be a big woman, with a big smile and a big laugh, who booked him into what she described as her de luxe room. Daniel was somewhat relieved that he hadn't ended up in one of her ordinary rooms, because when he lay down the double bed sagged in the centre, and when he turned over the springs followed him, clinging to the small of his back. Both taps in the wash-basin produced cold water in different shades of brown, and the one naked light that hung from the middle of the room was impossible to read by, unless he stood on a chair directly beneath it. Mrs Snell hadn't supplied a chair.

When Daniel was asked the next morning, after a breakfast of eggs, bacon, potatoes and fried bread whether he would be eating in or out, he said firmly, "Out," to the landlady's evident disappointment.

The first – and critical – call was to be made at the Immigration Office. If they had no information to assist him, he knew he might as well climb back on board the SS *Aorangi* that same evening. Daniel was beginning to feel that if that happened he wouldn't be too disappointed.

The massive brown building on Market Street that housed the official records of every person who had arrived in the colony since 1823 opened at ten o'clock. Although he arrived half an hour early Daniel still had to join one of the eight queues of people attempting to establish some fact about registered immigrants, which ensured that he didn't reach the counter for a further forty minutes.

When he eventually did get to the front of the queue he found himself looking at a ruddy-faced man in an open-necked blue shirt who was slumped behind the counter.

"I'm trying to trace an Englishman who came to Australia at some time between 1922 and 1925."

"Can't we do better than that, mate?"

"I fear not," said Daniel.

"You fear not, do you?" said the assistant. "Got a name, have you?"

"Oh, yes," said Daniel. "Guy Trentham."

"Trentham. How do you spell that?"

Daniel spelt the name out slowly for him.

"Right, mate. That'll be two pounds." Daniel extracted his wallet from inside his sports jacket and handed over the cash. "Sign here," the assistant said, swivelling a form round and placing his forefinger on the bottom line. "And come back Thursday."

"Thursday? But that's not for another three days."

"Glad they still teach you to count in England," said the assistant. "Next."

Daniel left the building with no information, merely a receipt for his two pounds. Once back out on the pavement, he picked up a copy of the *Sydney Morning Herald* and began to look for a café near the harbour at which to have lunch. He selected a small restaurant that was packed with young people. A waiter led him across a noisy, crowded room and seated him at a little table in the corner. He had nearly finished reading the paper by the time a waitress arrived with the salad he had ordered. He pushed the paper on one side, surprised to have found that there hadn't been one piece of news about what was taking place back in England.

As he munched away at a lettuce leaf and wondered how he could best use the unscheduled hold-up constructively, a girl on the next table leaned across and asked if she could borrow the sugar.

"Of course, allow me," said Daniel, handing over the shaker. He wouldn't have given the girl a second glance had he not noticed that she was reading *Principia Mathematica*, by A. N. Whitehead and Bertrand Russell.

"Are you a mathematics student, by any chance?" he asked once he had passed the sugar across.

"Yes," she said, not looking back in his direction.

"I only asked," said Daniel, feeling the question might have been construed as impolite, "because I teach the subject."

"Of course you do," she said, not bothering to turn round. "Oxford, I'm sure."

"Cambridge, actually."

This piece of information did make the girl glance across and study Daniel more carefully. "Then can you explain Simpson's Rule to me?" she asked abruptly.

Daniel unfolded his paper napkin, took out a fountain pen and drew some diagrams to illustrate the rule, stage by stage, something he hadn't done since he'd left St Paul's.

She checked what he had produced against the diagram

in her book, smiled and said, "Fair dinkum, you really do teach maths," which took Daniel a little by surprise as he wasn't sure what fair dinkum meant, but as it was accompanied by a smile he assumed it was some form of approval. He was taken even more by surprise when the girl picked up her plate of egg and beans, moved across and sat down next to him.

"I'm Jackie," she said. "A bushwhacker from Perth."

"I'm Daniel," he replied. "And I'm . . ."

"A Pom from Cambridge. You've already told me, remember?"

It was Daniel's turn to look more carefully at the young woman who sat opposite him. Jackie appeared to be about twenty. She had short blonde hair and a turned-up nose. Her clothes consisted of shorts and a yellow T-shirt that bore the legend "PERTH" right across her chest. She was quite unlike any undergraduate he had ever come across at Trinity.

"Are you up at university?" he enquired.

"Yeah. Second year, Perth. So what brings you to Sydney, Dan?"

Daniel couldn't think of an immediate response, but it hardly mattered that much because Jackie was already explaining why she was in the capital of New South Wales long before he had been given a chance to reply. In fact Jackie did most of the talking until their bills arrived. Daniel insisted on paying.

"Good on you," said Jackie. "So what are you doing tonight?"

"Haven't got anything particular planned."

"Great, because I was thinking of going to the Theatre Royal," she told him. "Why don't you join me?"

"Oh, what's playing?" asked Daniel, unable to hide his surprise at being picked up for the first time in his life.

"Noël Coward's *Tonight at Eight-Thirty* with Cyril Ritchard and Madge Elliott."

"Sounds promising," said Daniel non-committally.

"Great. Then I'll see you in the foyer at ten to eight,

Dan. And don't be late." She picked up her rucksack, threw it on her back, strapped up the buckle and in seconds was gone.

Daniel watched her leaving the café before he could think of an excuse for not agreeing to her suggestion. He decided it would be churlish not to turn up at the theatre, and in any case he had to admit he had rather enjoyed Jackie's company. He checked his watch and decided to spend the rest of the afternoon looking round the city.

When Daniel arrived at the Theatre Royal that evening, a few minutes before seven forty, he purchased two six-shilling tickets for the stalls then hung around in the foyer waiting for his guest – or was she his host? When the five-minute bell sounded Jackie still hadn't arrived and Daniel began to realise that he had been looking forward to seeing her again rather more than he cared to admit. There was still no sign of his lunch-time companion when the two-minute bell rang, so Daniel assumed that he would be seeing the play on his own. With only a minute to spare before the curtain went up, he felt a hand link through his arm and heard a voice say, "Hello, Dan. I didn't think you'd turn up." Another first, he had never taken a girl to the theatre who was wearing shorts.

Daniel smiled. Although he enjoyed the play, he found he enjoyed Jackie's company during the interval, after the show and then later over a meal at Romano's – a little Italian restaurant she seemed acquainted with – even more. He had never come across anyone who, after only knowing him for a few hours, could be so open and friendly. They discussed everything from mathematics to Clark Gable, and Jackie was never without a definite opinion, whatever the subject.

"May I walk you back to your hotel?" Daniel asked when they eventually left the restaurant.

"I don't have one," Jackie replied with a grin, and throwing the rucksack over her shoulder added, "so I may as well walk you back to yours."

"Why not?" said Daniel. "I expect Mrs Snell will be able to supply another room for the night."

"Let's hope not," said Jackie.

When Mrs Snell opened the door, after Jackie had pressed the night bell several times, she told them, "I hadn't realised there would be two of you. That will mean extra, of course."

"But we're not –" began Daniel.

"Thank you," said Jackie, seizing the key from Mrs Snell as the landlady gave Daniel a wink.

Once they were in Daniel's little room, Jackie removed her rucksack and said, "Don't worry about me, Dan, I'll sleep on the floor."

He didn't know what to say in reply, and without uttering another word went off into the bathroom, changed into his pyjamas and cleaned his teeth. He reopened the bedroom door and walked quietly over to his bed without even glancing in Jackie's direction. A few moments later he heard the bedroom door close, so he crept out of bed again, tiptoed over to the door and turned out the light before slipping back under the sheets. A few more minutes passed before he heard the bedroom door reopen. He closed his eyes pretending to be asleep. A moment later he felt a body slide in next to his and two arms encircle him.

"Oh, Daniel" – in the darkness Jackie's voice took on an exaggerated English accent – "do let's get rid of these frightful pyjamas." As she pulled at the cotton cord on his pyjama bottoms, he turned over to protest, only to find himself pressed up against her naked body. Daniel didn't utter a word as he lay there, eyes closed, doing almost nothing as Jackie began to move her hands slowly up and down his legs. He became utterly exhilarated, and soon after exhausted, unsure quite what had taken place. But he had certainly enjoyed every moment.

"You know, I do believe you're a virgin," Jackie said, when he eventually opened his eyes.

"No," he corrected. "*Was* a virgin."

"I'm afraid you still are," said Jackie. "Strictly speaking. But don't get worked up about it; I promise we'll have that sorted out by the morning. By the way, next time, Dan, you are allowed to join in."

Daniel spent most of the next three days in bed being tutored by a second-year undergraduate from the University of Perth. By the second morning he had discovered just how beautiful a woman's body could be. By the third evening Jackie let out a little moan that led him to believe that although he might not have graduated he was no longer a freshman.

He was sad when Jackie told him the time had come for her to return to Perth. She threw her rucksack over her shoulder for the last time, and after he had accompanied her to the station Daniel watched the train pull away from the platform as she began her journey back to Western Australia.

"If I ever get to Cambridge, Dan, I'll look you up," were the last words he remembered her saying.

"I do hope so," he said, feeling there were several members of Trinity High Table who would have benefited from a few days of Jackie's expert tuition.

On the Thursday morning Daniel reported back to the Immigration Department as instructed, and after another hour's wait in the inevitable queue, handed his receipt over to the assistant who was still slumped across the counter wearing the same shirt.

"Oh, yes, Guy Trentham, I remember. I discovered his particulars a few minutes after you'd left," the clerk told him. "Pity you didn't come back earlier."

"Then I can only thank you."

"Thank me, what for?" asked the assistant, suspiciously.

Daniel took the little green card the assistant handed to him. "For three of the happiest days of my life."

"What are you getting at, mate?" said the other man; but Daniel was already out of earshot.

He sat alone on the steps outside the tall colonial building and studied the official card. As he feared, it revealed very little:

Name: Guy Trentham (registered as immigrant)
             18 November 1922
Occupation: Land agent
Address: 117 Manley Drive
             Sydney

Daniel soon located Manley Drive on the city map which Jackie had left with him, and took a bus to the north side of Sydney where he was dropped off in a leafy suburb overlooking the harbour. The houses, although fairly large, looked a little run-down, leaving Daniel with the impression that the suburb might at some time in the past have been a fashionable area.

When he rang the bell of what could have been a former colonial guest-house, the door was answered by a young man wearing shorts and a singlet. Daniel was coming to accept that this was the national dress.

"It's a long shot, I know," Daniel began, "but I'm trying to trace someone who may have lived in this house in 1922."

"Bit before my time," said the youth cheerily. "Better come in and talk to my Aunt Sylvia – she'll be your best bet."

Daniel followed the young man through the hall into a drawing room that looked as if it hadn't been tidied for several days and out on to the verandah, which showed indications of having once been painted white. There, seated in a rocking chair, was a woman who might have been a shade under fifty but whose dyed hair and over-made-up face made it impossible for Daniel to be at all sure of her age. She continued to rock backwards and forwards, eyes closed, enjoying the morning sun.

"I'm sorry to bother you –"

"I'm not asleep," said the woman, her eyes opening to

take in the intruder. She stared suspiciously up at him. "Who are you? You look familiar."

"My name is Daniel Trumper," he told her. "I'm trying to trace someone who may have stayed here in 1922."

She began to laugh. "Twenty-five years ago. You're a bit of an optimist, I must say."

"His name was Guy Trentham."

She sat up with a start and stared straight at him. "You're his son, aren't you?" Daniel went ice cold. "I'll never forget that smooth-tongued phoney's face if I live to be a hundred."

The truth was no longer possible to deny, even to himself.

"So have you come back after all these years to clear up his debts?"

"I don't understand – " said Daniel.

"Scarpered with nearly a year's rent owing, didn't he? Always writing to his mother back in England for more money, but when it came I never saw any of it. I suppose he thought that bedding me was payment enough, so I'm not likely to forget the bastard, am I? Especially after what happened to him."

"Does that mean you know where he went after he left this house?"

She hesitated for some time looking as if she was trying to make up her mind. She turned to look out of the window while Daniel waited. "The last I heard," she said after a long pause, "was that he got a job working as a bookie's runner up in Melbourne, but that was before – "

"Before – ?" queried Daniel.

She stared up at him again with quizzical eyes.

"No," she said, "you'd better find that out for yourself because I wouldn't want to be the one who tells you. But if you want my advice, you'll take the first boat back to England and not bother yourself with Melbourne."

"But you may turn out to be the only person who can help me."

"I was taken for a ride by your father once so I'm not

going to wait around to be conned by his son, that's for sure. Show him the door, Kevin."

Daniel's heart sank. He thanked the woman for seeing him and left without another word. Once back on the street he took the bus into Sydney and walked the rest of the journey to the guest-house. He spent a lonely night missing Jackie while wondering why his father had behaved so badly when he came to Sydney, and whether he should heed "Aunt Sylvia's" advice.

The following morning Daniel left Mrs Snell and her big smile, but not before she had presented him with a big bill. He settled it without complaint and made his way to the railway station.

When the train from Sydney pulled into Spencer Street station in Melbourne that evening, Daniel's first action was to check the local telephone directory, just in case there was a Trentham listed, but there was none. Next he telephoned every bookmaker who was registered in the city, but it was not until he spoke to the ninth that Daniel came across anyone to whom the name meant anything.

"Sounds familiar," said a voice on the other end of the line. "But can't remember why. You could try Brad Morris, though. He ran this office around that time, so he may be able to help you. You'll find his number in the book."

Daniel looked up his number. When he was put through to Mr Morris his conversation with the old man was so short that it didn't require a second coin.

"Does the name Guy Trentham mean anything to you?" he asked once again.

"The Englishman?"

"Yes," Daniel replied, feeling his pulse quicken.

"Spoke with a posh accent and told everyone he was a major?"

"Might well have done."

"Then try the gaolhouse, because that's where he finished up." Daniel would have asked why but the line had already gone dead.

He was still shaking from head to toe when he dragged

his trunk out of the station and checked into the Railway Hotel on the other side of the road. Once again, he lay on a single bed, in a small dark room, trying to make up his mind whether he should continue with his enquiries or simply avoid the truth and do as Sylvia had advised, "take the first boat back to England".

He fell asleep in the early evening, but woke again in the middle of the night, to find he was still fully dressed. By the time the early morning sun shone through the window he had made up his mind. He didn't want to know, he didn't need to know, and he would return to England immediately.

But first he decided to have a bath, and a change of clothes, and by the time he had done that he had also changed his mind.

Daniel came down to the lobby half an hour later and asked the receptionist where the main police station was located. The man behind the desk directed him down the road to Bourke Street.

"Was your room that bad?" he enquired.

Daniel gave a false laugh. He set off slowly and full of apprehension in the direction he had been shown. It took him only a few minutes to reach Bourke Street but he circled the block several times before he finally climbed the stone steps of the police station and entered the building.

The young duty sergeant showed no recognition when he heard the name of Trentham and simply enquired who it was who wanted to know.

"A relation of his from England," replied Daniel. The sergeant left him at the counter and walked over to the far side of the room to speak to a senior officer seated behind a desk who was patiently turning over photographs. The officer stopped what he was doing and listened carefully, then appeared to ask the sergeant something. In response the sergeant turned and pointed at Daniel. Bastard, thought Daniel. You're a little bastard. A moment later the sergeant returned to the front desk.

"We've closed the file on Trentham," he said. "Any

further enquiries would have to be made at the Prison Department."

Daniel almost lost his voice, but somehow managed, "Where's that?"

"Seventh floor," he said, pointing up.

When he stepped out of the lift on the seventh floor Daniel was confronted by a larger-than-life poster showing a warm-faced man bearing the name Hector Watts, Inspector-General of Prisons.

Daniel walked over to the enquiry desk and asked if he could see Mr Watts.

"Do you have an appointment?"

"No," said Daniel.

"Then I doubt –"

"Would you be kind enough to explain to the inspector-general that I have travelled from England especially to see him?"

Daniel was kept waiting for only a few moments before he was shown up to the eighth floor. The same warm smile that appeared in the picture now beamed down at him in reality, even if the lines in the face were a little deeper. Daniel judged Hector Watts to be near his sixtieth birthday and, although overweight, he still looked as if he could take care of himself.

"Which part of England do you come from?" Watts asked.

"Cambridge," Daniel told him. "I teach mathematics at the university."

"I'm from Glasgow myself," Watts said. "Which won't come as a surprise to you, with my name and accent. So, please have a seat and tell me what I can do for you."

"I'm trying to trace a Guy Trentham, and the Police Department have referred me to you."

"Oh, yes, I remember that name. But why do I remember it?" The Scotsman rose from his desk and went over to a row of filing cabinets that lined the wall behind him. He pulled open the one marked "STV", and extracted a large box file.

"Trentham," he repeated, as he thumbed through the papers inside the box, before finally removing two sheets. He returned to his desk and, having placed the sheets in front of him, began reading. After he had absorbed the details, he looked up and studied Daniel more carefully.

"Been here long, have you, laddie?"

"Arrived in Sydney less than a week ago," said Daniel, puzzled by the question.

"And never been to Melbourne before?"

"No, never."

"So what's the reason for your enquiry?"

"I wanted to find out anything I could about Captain Guy Trentham."

"Why?" asked the inspector-general. "Are you a journo?"

"No," said Daniel, "I'm a teacher but –"

"Then you must have had a very good reason for travelling this far."

"Curiosity, I suppose," said Daniel. "You see, although I never knew him, Guy Trentham was my father."

The head of the prison service looked down at the names listed on the sheet as next of kin: wife, Anna Helen (deceased), one daughter, Margaret Ethel. There was no mention of a son. He looked back up at Daniel and, after a few moments of contemplation, came to a decision.

"I'm sorry to tell you, Mr Trentham, that your father died while he was in police custody."

Daniel was stunned, and began shaking.

Watts looked across his desk and added, "I'm sorry to have to give you such unhappy news, especially when you've travelled all this way."

"What was the cause of his death?" Daniel whispered.

The inspector-general turned the page, checked the bottom line of the charge sheet in front of him and re-read the words: Hanged by the neck until dead. He looked back up at Daniel.

"A heart attack," he said.

CHAPTER 31

aniel took the sleeper back to Sydney but he didn't sleep. All he wanted to do was get as far away from Melbourne as he possibly could. As every mile slipped by he relaxed a little more, and after a time was even able to eat half a sandwich from the buffet car. When the train pulled into the station of Australia's largest city he jumped off, loaded his trunk into a taxi and headed straight for the port. He booked himself on the first boat sailing to the west coast of America.

The tiny tramp steamer, only licensed to carry four passengers, sailed at midnight for San Francisco, and Daniel wasn't allowed on board until he had handed over to the captain the full fare in cash, leaving himself just enough to get back to England – as long as he wasn't stranded anywhere on the way.

During that bobbing, swaying, endless crossing back to America, Daniel spent most of his time lying on a bunk, which gave him easily enough time to consider what he should do with the information he now possessed. He also tried to come to terms with the anxieties his mother must have suffered over the years and what a fine man his step-father was. How he hated the word step-father. He would never think of Charlie that way. If only they had taken him into their confidence from the beginning he could surely have used his talents to help rather than waste so much of his energy trying to find out the truth. But he was now even more painfully aware that he couldn't let them become aware what he had discovered, as he probably knew more than they did.

Daniel doubted that his mother realised that Trentham had died in gaol leaving a string of disgruntled debtors across Victoria and New South Wales. Certainly there had been no indication of that on the gravestone in Ashurst.

As he stood on the deck and watched the little boat bob along on its chosen course under the Golden Gate and into the bay, Daniel finally felt a plan beginning to take shape.

Once he had cleared immigration he took a bus into the centre of San Francisco and booked himself back into the hotel at which he had stayed before travelling on to Australia. The porter produced two remaining cards and Daniel handed over the promised ten-dollar note. He scribbled something new and posted them both before boarding the Transcontinental Express destined for New York.

With each hour and each day of solitude his ideas continued to develop although it still worried him how much more information his mother must have that he still daren't ask her about. But now at least he was certain that his father was Guy Trentham and had left India or England in disgrace. The fearsome Mrs Trentham must therefore be his grandmother, who had for some unfathomable reason blamed Charlie for what had happened to her son.

On arriving in New York Daniel was exasperated to find that the *Queen Mary* had sailed for England the previous day. He transferred his ticket to the *Queen Elizabeth*, leaving himself with only a few dollars in cash. His final action on American soil was to telegraph his mother with an estimated time of arrival at Southampton.

Daniel began to relax for the first time once he could no longer see the Statue of Liberty from the stern of the ocean liner. Mrs Trentham, however, remained constantly in his thoughts during the five-day journey. He couldn't think of her as his grandmother and when the time came to disembark at Southampton he felt he needed several more questions answered by his mother before he would be ready to carry out his plan.

As he walked down the gangplank and back on to English soil he noticed that the leaves on the trees had turned from green to gold in his absence. He intended to have solved the problem of Mrs Trentham before they had fallen.

His mother was there on the dockside waiting to greet him. Daniel had never been more happy to see her, giving her such a warm hug that she was unable to hide her surprise. On the drive back to London he learned the sad news that his other grandmother had died while he had been in America and although his mother had received several postcards she couldn't remember the name of either of the professors he had said he was visiting so she had been unable to contact him to pass on the news. However, she had enjoyed receiving so many postcards.

"There are some more still on their way, I suspect," said Daniel, feeling guilty for the first time.

"Will you have time to spend a few days with us before you return to Cambridge?"

"Yes. I'm back a little earlier than I expected, so you could be stuck with me for a few weeks."

"Oh, your father will be pleased to hear that."

Daniel wondered how long it would be before he could hear anyone say "your father" without a vision of Guy Trentham forming in his mind.

"What decision did you come to about raising the money for the new building?"

"We've decided to go public," said his mother. "In the end it was a case of simple arithmetic. The architect has completed the outline plan, and of course your father wants the best of everything, so I'm afraid the final cost is likely to be nearer a half a million pounds."

"And are you still able to keep fifty-one per cent of the new company?"

"Only just, because based on those figures it's going to be tight. We could even end up having to pawn your great-grandfather's barrow."

"And the flats – any news of them?" Daniel was gazing

out of the car window for his mother's reaction in the reflection of the glass. She seemed to hesitate for a moment.

"The owners are carrying out the council's instructions and have already begun knocking down what remains of them."

"Does that mean Dad is going to be granted his planning permission?"

"I hope so, but it now looks as if it might take a little longer than we'd originally thought as a local resident – a Mr Simpson on behalf of the Save the Small Shops Federation – has lodged an objection to our scheme with the council. So please don't ask about it when you see your father. The very mention of the flats brings him close to apoplexy."

And I presume it's Mrs Trentham who is behind this Mr Simpson? was all Daniel wanted to say but simply asked, "And how's the wicked Daphne?"

"Still trying to get Clarissa married off to the right man, and Clarence into the right regiment."

"Nothing less than a royal duke for one and a commission in the Scots Guards for the other would be my guess."

"That's about right," agreed his mother. "She also expects Clarissa to produce a girl fairly quickly so she can marry her off to the future Prince of Wales."

"But Princess Elizabeth has only just announced her engagement."

"I am aware of that, but we all know how Daphne does like to plan ahead."

Daniel adhered to his mother's wishes and made no mention of the flats when he discussed with Charlie the launching of the new company over dinner that night. He also noticed that a picture entitled *Apples and Pears* by an artist called Courbet had replaced the Van Gogh that had hung in the hall. Something else he didn't comment on.

Daniel spent the following day at the planning department of the LCC (Enquiries) at County Hall. Although a clerk supplied him with all the relevant papers he was quick to point out, to Daniel's frustration, that he could not remove any original documents from the building.

In consequence he spent the morning repeatedly going over the papers, making verbatim notes of the relevant clauses and then committing them to memory so it wouldn't prove necessary to carry anything around on paper. The last thing he wanted was for his parents to stumble across any notes he had made by accident. By five o'clock, when they locked the front door behind him, Daniel felt confident he could recall every relevant detail.

He left County Hall, sat on a low parapet overlooking the Thames and repeated the salient facts to himself.

Trumper's, he had discovered, had applied to build a major department store that would encompass the entire block known as Chelsea Terrace. There would be two towers of twelve storeys in height. Each tower would consist of eight hundred thousand square feet of floor space. On top of that would be a further five floors of offices and walkways that would span the two towers and join the twin structures together. Outline planning permission for the entire scheme had been granted by the LCC. However, an appeal had been lodged by a Mr Martin Simpson of the Save the Small Shops Federation against the five floors that would bring together the two main structures over an empty site in the centre of the terrace. It didn't take a great deal of hypothesising to decide who was making sure Mr Simpson was getting the necessary financial backing.

At the same time Mrs Trentham herself had been given outline planning permission to build a block of flats to be used specifically for low-rent accommodation. Daniel went over in his mind her detailed planning application which had showed that the flats would be built of rough-hewn concrete, with the minimum of internal or external facilities – the expression "Jerry-built" immediately sprang to mind. It wasn't hard for Daniel to work out that Mrs Trentham's purpose was to build the ugliest edifice the council would allow her to get away with, right in the middle of Charlie's proposed palace.

Daniel looked down to check his memory against the notes. He hadn't forgotten anything, so he tore the crib sheet into tiny pieces and dropped them into a litter bin on the corner of Westminster Bridge, then returned home to the Little Boltons.

Daniel's next move was to telephone David Oldcrest, the resident law tutor at Trinity who specialised in town and country planning. His colleague spent over an hour explaining to Daniel that, what with appeals and counter-appeals that could go all the way up to the House of Lords, permission for such a building as Trumper Towers might not be granted for several years. By the time a decision had been made Dr Oldcrest reckoned that only the lawyers would have ended up making any money.

Daniel thanked his friend and having considered the problem he now faced came to the conclusion that the success or failure of Charlie's ambitions rested entirely in the hands of Mrs Trentham. That was unless he could . . .

For the next couple of weeks he spent a considerable amount of his time in a telephone box on the corner of Chester Square, without ever once making a call. For the remainder of each day, he followed an immaculately dressed lady of obvious self-confidence and presence around the capital, trying not to be seen but often attempting to steal a glimpse of what she looked like, how she behaved, and the kind of world she lived in.

He quickly discovered that only three things appeared to be sacrosanct to the occupant of Number 19 Chester Square. First, there were the meetings with her lawyers in Lincoln's Inn Fields – which seemed to take place every two or three days, though not on a regular basis. Second came her bridge gatherings, which were always at two o'clock, three days a week: on Monday at 9 Cadogan Place, on Wednesday at 117 Sloane Avenue and on Friday at her own home in Chester Square. The same group of elderly women appeared to arrive at all three establishments. Third was the occasional visit to a seedy hotel in South Kensington where she sat in the darkest corner of the tea room and held a conversation with a man who looked to Daniel a most unlikely companion for the daughter of Sir Raymond Hardcastle. Certainly she did not treat him as a friend, even an associate, and Daniel was unable to work out what they could possibly have in common.

After a further week he decided that his plan could only be executed on the last Friday before he returned to Cambridge. Accordingly he spent a morning with a tailor who specialised in army uniforms. During the afternoon he set about writing a script which he later that evening rehearsed. He then made several telephone calls, including one to Spink's, the medal specialists, who felt confident they could have his order made up in time. On the last two mornings – but only after he was sure his parents were safely out of the house – he carried out a full dress rehearsal in the privacy of his bedroom.

Daniel needed to be certain that not only would Mrs Trentham be taken by surprise but also she would remain off balance for at least the twenty minutes he felt would prove necessary to see the whole exercise through.

That Friday over breakfast, Daniel confirmed that neither of his parents was expected to return home until after six that evening. He readily agreed that they should all have dinner together as he was returning to Cambridge the following day. He hung around patiently waiting for his father to leave for Chelsea Terrace, but then had to wait another half-hour before he could depart himself because his mother was held up by a phone call just as she was on her way out. Daniel left the bedroom door open and marched around in endless circles.

At last his mother's conversation came to an end and she left for work. Twenty minutes later Daniel strolled out of the house carrying a small suitcase containing the uniform he had obtained from Johns and Pegg the previous day. Cautiously he walked three blocks in the wrong direction before hailing a taxi.

On arrival at the Royal Fusiliers Museum Daniel spent

a few minutes checking the picture of his father that hung on the wall. The hair was wavier than his own, and looked from the sepia photo to be a touch fairer. He suddenly feared he might not be able to remember the exact details. Daniel waited until the curator's back was turned, then, despite feeling a tinge of guilt, quickly removed the little photograph and placed it in his briefcase.

He took another taxi to a barber in Kensington, who was only too delighted to bleach the gentleman's hair, switch his parting and even to add a wave or two, creating as near as possible a duplicate of the sepia photograph from which he had been asked to work. Every few minutes Daniel checked the changing process in the mirror, and once he believed the effect was as close as could be achieved he paid the bill and left. The next cabbie he directed to Spink's, the medal specialists in King Street, St James. On arrival he purchased for cash the four ribbons that he had ordered over the phone; to his relief the young assistant did not enquire if he was entitled to wear them. Another taxi took him from St James to the Dorchester Hotel. There he booked himself into a single room and informed the girl on the desk that he intended to check out of the hotel by six that night. She handed him a key marked 309. Daniel politely refused the porter's offer to carry his case and merely asked for directions to the lift.

Once safely in his room he locked the door and laid the contents of his suitcase carefully on the bed. The moment he had finished changing from his suit into the uniform he fixed the row of ribbons above the left-hand breast pocket exactly as they were in the photograph and finally checked the effect in the long mirror attached to the bathroom door. He was every inch a First World War captain of the Royal Fusiliers, and the purple and silver ribbon of the MC and the two campaign medals simply added the finishing touch.

Having checked over every last detail against the stolen photograph Daniel began to feel unsure of himself for the first time. But if he didn't go through with it . . . He sat on the end of the bed, checking his watch every few minutes. An hour passed before he stood up, took a deep breath and pulled on his long trenchcoat – almost the only article of clothing he had the right to wear – locked the door behind him and went down to the lobby. Once he had pushed his way through the swing doors, he hailed another taxi which took him to Chester Square. He paid off the cabbie and checked his watch. Three forty-seven. He estimated that he still had at least another twenty minutes before the bridge party would begin to break up.

From his now familiar telephone box on the corner of the square Daniel watched as the ladies began to depart from Number 19. Once he had counted eleven of them leave the house he felt confident that Mrs Trentham must, servants apart, now be on her own; he already knew from the parliamentary timetable detailed in the *Daily Telegraph* that morning that Mrs Trentham's husband would not be expected back in Chester Square until after six that night. He waited for another five minutes before he came out of the telephone box and marched quickly across the road. He knew that if he hesitated, even for a moment, he would surely lose his nerve. He rapped firmly on the knocker and waited for what felt like hours before the butler finally answered.

"Can I help you, sir?"

"Good afternoon, Gibson. I have an appointment with Mrs Trentham at four fifteen."

"Yes, of course, sir," said Gibson. As Daniel had anticipated, the butler would assume that someone who knew his name must indeed have an appointment. "Please come this way, sir," he said before taking Daniel's trenchcoat. When they reached the door of the drawing room Gibson enquired, "May I say who is calling?"

"Captain Daniel Trentham."

The butler seemed momentarily taken aback but opened the door of the drawing room and announced, "Captain Daniel Trentham, madam."

Mrs Trentham was standing by the window when

Daniel entered the room. She swung round, stared at the young man, took a couple of paces forward, hesitated and then fell heavily on to the sofa.

For God's sake don't faint, was Daniel's first reaction as he stood in the centre of the carpet facing his grandmother.

"Who are you?" she whispered at last.

"Don't let's play games, Grandmother. You know very well who I am," said Daniel, hoping he sounded confident.

"She sent you, didn't she?"

"If you are referring to my mother, no, she did not. In fact she doesn't even know I'm here."

Mrs Trentham's mouth opened in protest, but she did not speak. Daniel swayed from foot to foot during what seemed to him to be an unbearably long silence. His eye began to focus on an MC that stood on the mantelpiece.

"So what do you want?" she asked.

"I've come to make a deal with you, Grandmother."

"What do you mean, a deal? You're in no position to make any deals."

"Oh, I think I am, Grandmother. You see, I've just come back from a trip to Australia." He paused. "Which turned out to be very revealing."

Mrs Trentham flinched, but her eyes did not leave him for a moment.

"And what I learned about my father while I was there doesn't bear repeating. I won't go into any details, as I suspect you know every bit as much as I do."

Her eyes remained fixed on him and she slowly began to show signs of recovery.

"Unless, of course, you want to know where they had planned to bury my father originally, because it certainly wasn't in the family plot at Ashurst parish church."

"What do you want?" she repeated.

"As I said, Grandmother, I've come to make a deal."

"I'm listening."

"I want you to abandon your plans for building those dreadful flats in Chelsea Terrace, and at the same time withdraw any objections you may have to the detailed planning permission Trumper's have applied for."

"Never."

"Then I fear the time may have come for the world to be informed of the real reason for your vendetta against my mother."

"But that would harm your mother every bit as much as me."

"Oh, I don't think so, Grandmother," said Daniel. "Especially when the press find out that your son resigned his commission with far from glowing testimonials, and later died in Melbourne in even less auspicious circumstances – despite the fact he was finally laid to rest in a sleepy village in Berkshire after you had shipped the body home, telling your friends that he had been a successful cattle broker and died tragically of tuberculosis."

"But that's blackmail."

"Oh, no, Grandmother, just a troubled son, desperate to discover what had really happened to his long-lost father and shocked when he found out the truth behind the Trentham family secret. I think the press would describe such an incident quite simply as 'an internal feud'. One thing's for certain – my mother would come out smelling of roses, though I'm not sure how many people would still want to play bridge with you once they learned all the finer details."

Mrs Trentham rose quickly to her feet, clenched both her fists and advanced towards him menacingly. Daniel stood his ground.

"No hysterics, Grandmother. Don't forget I know everything about you." He felt acutely aware that he actually knew very little.

Mrs Trentham stopped, and even retreated a pace. "And if I agree to your demands?"

"I shall walk out of this room and you will never hear from me again as long as you live. You have my word on it."

She let out a long sigh, but it was some time before she replied.

"You win," she eventually said, sounding remarkably composed. "But I have a condition of my own if I am expected to comply with your demands."

Daniel was taken by surprise. He hadn't planned for any conditions coming from her side. "What is it?" he asked suspiciously.

He listened carefully to her request and, although puzzled by it, could see no cause for any alarm.

"I accept your terms," he said finally.

"In writing," she added quietly. "And now."

"Then I shall also require our little arrangement in writing," said Daniel, trying to score a point of his own.

"Agreed."

Mrs Trentham walked shakily towards the writing desk. She sat down, opened the centre drawer, and took out two sheets of purple headed paper. Painstakingly she wrote out separate agreements before passing them over for Daniel to consider. He read through the drafts slowly. She had covered all the points he had demanded and had left nothing out, including the one rather long-winded clause she had herself insisted upon. Daniel nodded his agreement and passed the two pieces of paper back to her.

She signed both copies, then handed Daniel her pen. He in turn added his signature below hers on both sheets of paper. She returned one of the agreements to Daniel before rising to pull the bell rope by the mantelpiece. The butler reappeared a moment later.

"Gibson, we need you to witness our signatures on two documents. Once you have done that the gentleman will be leaving," she announced. The butler penned his signature on both sheets of paper without question or comment.

A few moments later Daniel found himself out on the street with an uneasy feeling everything hadn't gone exactly as he had anticipated. Once he was seated in a taxi and on his way back to the Dorchester Hotel he re-read the sheet of paper they had both signed. He could not reasonably have asked for more but remained puzzled by the clause Mrs Trentham had insisted on inserting as it made no sense to him. He pushed any such disquiet to the back of his mind.

On arrival at the Dorchester Hotel, in the privacy of room 309, he quickly changed out of the uniform and back into his civilian clothes. He felt clean for the first time that day. He then placed the uniform and cap in his suitcase before going back down to reception, where he handed in the key, paid the bill in cash and checked out.

Another taxi returned him to Kensington where the hairdresser was disappointed to be told that his new customer now wished all signs of the bleach to be removed, the waves to be straightened out and the parting to be switched back.

Daniel's final stop before returning home was to a deserted building site in Pimlico. He stood behind a large crane and when he was certain no one could see him he dropped the uniform and cap into a rubbish tip and set light to the photograph.

He stood shivering as he watched his father disappear in a purple flame.

MRS TRENTHAM

1938 - 1948

CHAPTER 32

y purpose in inviting you up to Yorkshire this weekend is to let you know exactly what I have planned for you in my will." My father was seated behind his desk while I sat in a leather chair facing him, the one my mother had always favoured. He had named me after her, Margaret Ethel, but there the resemblance ended, as he never stopped reminding me. I watched him as he carefully pressed some tobacco down into the well of his briar pipe, wondering what he could possibly be going to say. He took his time before looking up at me again and announcing, "I have made the decision to leave my entire estate to Daniel Trumper."

I was so stunned by this revelation that it was several seconds before I could think of an acceptable response.

"But, Father, now that Guy has died surely Nigel must be the legitimate heir?"

"Daniel would have been the legitimate heir if your son had done the honourable thing. Guy should have returned from India and married Miss Salmon the moment he realised she was having his child."

"But Trumper is Daniel's father," I protested. "Indeed, he has always admitted as much. The birth certificate –"

"He has never denied it, I grant you that. But don't take me for a fool, Ethel. The birth certificate only proves that, unlike my late grandson, Charlie Trumper has some sense of responsibility. In any case, those of us who have watched Guy in his formative years and have also followed Daniel's progress can be in little doubt about the relationship between the two men."

I wasn't certain I had heard my father correctly. "You've actually seen Daniel Trumper?"

"Oh, yes," he replied matter-of-factly, picking up a box of matches from his desk. "I made a point of visiting St Paul's on two separate occasions. Once when the boy was performing in a concert I was able to sit and watch him at close quarters for over two hours – he was rather good, actually. And then a year later on Founders' Day when he was awarded the Newton Mathematics Prize, I shadowed him while he accompanied his parents to afternoon tea in the headmaster's garden. So I can assure you that not only does he look like Guy, but he's also inherited some of his late father's mannerisms."

"But surely Nigel deserves to be treated as his equal?" I protested, racking my brains to think of some rational response that would make my father reconsider his position.

"Nigel is not his equal and never will be," replied my father, as he struck a match before beginning that endless sucking that always preceded his attempt to light a pipe. "Don't let's fool ourselves, Ethel. We've both known for some time that the lad isn't even worthy of a place on the board of Hardcastle's, let alone to be considered as my successor."

While my father puffed energetically at his pipe, I stared blindly at the painting of two horses in a paddock that hung on the wall behind him and tried to collect my thoughts.

"I'm sure you haven't forgotten, my dear, that Nigel even failed to pass out of Sandhurst, which I'm told takes some doing nowadays. I have also recently been informed that he's only holding down his present job with Kitcat and Aitken because you led the senior partner to believe that in time they will be administering the Hardcastle portfolio." He punctuated each statement with a puff from his pipe. "And I can assure you that will not be the case."

I found myself unable to look straight at him. Instead my eyes wandered from the Stubbs on the wall behind his desk to the row upon row of books he had spent a lifetime collecting. Dickens, every first edition; Henry James, a modern author he admired, and countless Blakes of every description from treasured handwritten letters to memorial editions. Then came the second blow.

"As there isn't a member of the family who can readily replace me as head of the firm, I have reluctantly come to the conclusion that with war daily becoming more likely I will have to reconsider the future of Hardcastle's." The pungent smell of tobacco hung in the air.

"You would never allow the business to fall into anyone else's hands?" I said in disbelief. "Your father would – "

"My father would have done what was best for all concerned, and no doubt expectant relations would have been fairly low down on his list of priorities." His pipe refused to stay alight so a second match was brought into play. He gave a few more sucks before a look of satisfaction appeared on his face and he began to speak again. "I've sat on the boards of Harrogate Haulage and the Yorkshire Bank for several years, and more recently John Brown Engineering where I think I've finally found my successor. Sir John's son may not be an inspired chairman of the company but he's capable and more important he's a Yorkshireman. Any road, I have come to the conclusion that a merger with that company will be best for all concerned."

I was still unable to look directly at my father as I tried to take in all that he was saying.

"They've made me a handsome offer for my

shares," he added, "which will in time yield an income for you and Amy that will more than take care of your needs once I've gone."

"But, Father, we both hope you will live for many more years."

"Don't bother yourself, Ethel, with trying to flatter an old man who knows death can't be far away. I may be ancient but I'm not yet senile."

"Father," I protested again but he simply returned to the sucking of his pipe, showing total lack of concern at my agitation. So I tried another ploy.

"Does that mean Nigel will receive nothing?"

"Nigel will receive what I consider right and proper in the circumstances."

"I'm not sure I fully understand you, Father."

"Then I shall explain. I've left him five thousand pounds which after my death he may dispose of in any manner he wishes." He paused as if considering whether he should add to this piece of information. "I have at least saved you one embarrassment," he offered at last. "Although, following your death, Daniel Trumper will inherit my entire estate, he won't learn of his good fortune until his thirtieth birthday, by which time you will be well over seventy and perhaps find it easier to live with my decision."

Twelve more years, I thought, as a tear fell from my eye and began to run down my cheek.

"You needn't bother with crying, Ethel, or hysterics, or even reasoned argument for that matter." He exhaled a long plume of smoke. "I have made up my mind, and nothing you can say or do is going to budge me."

His pipe was now puffing away like an express train. I removed a handkerchief from my handbag in the hope it would give me a little more time to think.

"And should it cross your mind to try and have the will revoked at some later date, on the grounds of my insanity" – I looked up aghast – "of which you are quite capable, I have had the document drawn up by Mr Baverstock and witnessed by a retired judge, a cabinet minister and, perhaps more relevant, a specialist from Sheffield whose chosen subject is mental disorders."

I was about to protest further when there was a muffled knock on the door and Amy entered the room.

"I do apologise for interrupting you, Papa, but should I have tea served in the drawing room or would you prefer to take it in here?"

My father smiled at his elder daughter. "The drawing room is just fine, my dear," he said in a far gentler tone than he ever adopted when addressing me. He rose unsteadily from behind his desk, emptied his pipe in the nearest ashtray and, without another word, followed my sister slowly out of the room.

I remained fairly uncommunicative during tea while I tried to think through the implications of all my father had just told me. Amy, on the other hand, prattled happily on about the effect the recent lack of rain was having on the petunias in the flower-bed directly under my father's room. "They don't catch the sun at any hour of the day," she confided to us in worried tones as her cat jumped up on to the sofa and settled in her lap. The old tortoise-shell whose name I could never remember had always got on my nerves but I never said as much because I knew Amy loved the creature second only to my father. She began to stroke the animal, obviously unaware of the unease caused by the conversation that had just taken place in the study.

I went to bed early that evening and spent a sleepless night trying to work out what course of action had been left open to me. I confess I hadn't expected anything substantial from the will for Amy or myself, as we were both women in our sixties and without a great need of any extra income. However, I had always assumed that I would inherit the house and the estate while the company would be left to Guy and, following his death, Nigel.

By the morning I had come to the reluctant conclusion that there was little I could do about my father's decision. If the will had been drawn up by Mr Baverstock, his long-serving solicitor and friend, F. E. Smith himself would not have been able to find a loophole. I began to realise that my only hope of securing Nigel's rightful inheritance would have to involve Daniel Trumper himself.

After all, my father would not live for ever.

We sat alone almost unsighted in the darkest corner of the room. He began clicking the knuckles of his right hand one by one.

"Where is it at this moment?" I asked, looking across at a man to whom I had paid thousands of pounds since we had first met almost twenty years ago. He still turned up for our weekly meetings at the St Agnes wearing the same brown tweed jacket and shiny yellow tie, even if he did seem to have acquired one or two more shirts lately. He put down his whisky, pulled out a brown paper package from under his chair and handed it over to me.

"How much did you have to pay to get it back?"

"Fifty pounds."

"I told you not to offer him more than twenty pounds without consulting me."

"I know, but there was a West End dealer nosing around the shop at the time. I just couldn't risk it, could I?"

I didn't believe for one moment that it had cost Harris fifty pounds. However, I did accept that he realised how important the picture was to my future plans.

"Would you like me to hand the painting over to the police?" he asked. "I could then drop a hint that perhaps –"

"Certainly not," I said without hesitation. "The police are far too discreet in these matters. Besides, what I have in mind for Mr Trumper will be a great deal more humiliating than a private interview in the privacy of Scotland Yard."

Mr Harris leaned back in the old leather chair and began clicking the knuckles of his left hand.

"What else do you have to report?"

"Daniel Trumper has taken up his place at Trinity College. He's to be found on New Court, staircase B, room seven."

"That was all in your last report."

Both of us stopped speaking while an elderly guest selected a magazine from a nearby table.

"Also, he's started seeing quite a lot of a girl called Marjorie Carpenter. She's a third-year mathematician from Girton College."

"Is that so? Well, if it begins to look at all serious let me know at once and you can start a file on her." I glanced around to be sure no one could overhear our conversation. The clicking began again and I looked back to find Harris staring fixedly at me.

"Is something worrying you?" I asked as I poured myself another cup of tea.

"Well, to be honest with you there is one thing, Mrs Trentham. I feel the time might have come for me to ask for another small rise in my hourly rate. After all, I'm expected to keep so many secrets" – he hesitated for a moment – "secrets that might . . ."

"That might what?"

"Prove to be invaluable to other equally interested parties."

"Are you threatening me, Mr Harris?"

"Certainly not, Mrs Trentham, it's just that – "

"I'll say this once and once only, Mr Harris. If you ever reveal anything to anyone that has passed between us it won't be an hourly rate that you'll be worrying about but the length of time you'll be spending in prison. Because I also have kept a file on you which I suspect some of your former colleagues might well be interested to learn about. Not least the pawning of a stolen picture and the disposal of an army greatcoat after a crime had been committed. Do I make myself clear?"

Harris didn't reply, just clicked his fingers back into place, one by one.

Some weeks after war was declared I learned that Daniel Trumper had avoided being called up. It transpired that he was now to be found serving behind a desk in Bletchley Park and was therefore unlikely to experience the wrath of the enemy unless a bomb were to land directly on top of him.

As it happened, the Germans did manage to drop a bomb, right in the middle of *my* flats, destroying them completely. My initial anger at this disaster evaporated when I saw the chaos it left behind in Chelsea Terrace. For several days I gained considerable satisfaction from just standing on the opposite side of the road admiring the Germans' handiwork.

A few weeks later it was the turn of the Musketeer and Trumper's greengrocery shop to feel the brunt of the Luftwaffe. The only perceptible outcome of this second bombing was that Charlie Trumper signed up for the Fusiliers the following week. However much I might have desired to see Daniel disposed of by a stray bullet, I required Charlie Trumper to remain very much alive: it was a more public execution I had in mind for him.

It didn't require Harris to brief me on Charlie Trumper's new appointment at the Ministry of Food because it was fully reported in every national paper. However, I made no attempt to take advantage of his prolonged absence as I reasoned there could be little purpose in acquiring further property in the terrace while war was still being waged, and in any case

Harris's monthly reports revealed that Trumper's was steadily losing money.

Then, when I was least prepared for it, my father died of a heart attack. I immediately dropped everything and hurried off to Yorkshire in order to help oversee the arrangements for the burial.

Two days later Amy and I led the mourners at the funeral, which was held in Wetherby parish church. As titular head of the family, Amy was placed on the left-hand end of the front pew with Gerald and Nigel on her right. The service was well attended by family, friends and business associates alike, including the solemn Mr Baverstock, clutching on to his inevitable Gladstone bag that I noticed he never let out of his sight. Amy, who sat in the row directly in front of me, became so distressed during the archdeacon's address that I don't believe she would have got through the rest of the day had I not been there to comfort her.

After the mourners had left I decided to stay on in Yorkshire for a few more days while Gerald and Nigel returned to London. Amy spent most of the time in her bedroom which gave me the chance to look around the house and check if there was anything of real value that could be rescued before I returned to Ashurst. After all, the property would – once the will had been administered – at worst end up being divided between us.

I came across my mother's jewellery, which had obviously never been touched since her death, and the Stubbs that still hung in my father's study. I removed the jewellery from my father's bedroom, and as for the Stubbs Amy agreed – over a light supper in her room – that for the time being I could hang the painting at Ashurst. The only other item left of any real value, I concluded, was my father's magnificent library. However, I already had long-term plans for the collection that did not involve the sale of a single book.

On the first of the month I travelled down to

London to attend the offices of Baverstock, Dickens and Cobb to be informed officially of the contents of my father's will.

Mr Baverstock seemed disappointed that Amy had felt unable to make the journey but accepted the fact that my sister had not yet recovered sufficiently from the shock of my father's death to contemplate such a trip. Several other relations, most of whom I saw only at christenings, weddings and funerals, sat around looking hopeful. I knew exactly what they could expect.

Mr Baverstock took over an hour performing what seemed to me a simple enough responsibility, though to be fair he managed with some considerable dexterity not to reveal the name of Daniel Trumper when it came to explaining what would eventually happen to the estate. My mind began to wander as minor relations were informed of the thousand pound windfalls they would inherit and was only brought sharply back to the droning voice of Mr Baverstock when he uttered my own name.

"Mrs Gerald Trentham and Miss Amy Hardcastle will both receive during their lifetime in equal part any income derived from the Trust." The solicitor stopped to turn a page before placing the palms of his hands on the desk. "And finally, the house, the estate in Yorkshire and all its contents plus the sum of twenty thousand pounds," he continued, "I bequeath to my elder daughter, Miss Amy Hardcastle."

CHAPTER 33

"Good morning, Mr Sneddles."

The old bibliophile was so surprised the lady knew his name that for a moment he just stood and stared at her.

Eventually he shuffled across to greet the lady, giving her a low bow. She was, after all, the first customer he had seen for over a week – that is if he did not count Doctor Halcombe, the retired headmaster who would happily browse around the shop for hours on end but who had not actually purchased a book since 1937.

"Good morning, madam," he said in turn. "Was there a particular volume that you were hoping to find?" He looked at the lady, who wore a long lace dress and a large wide-brimmed hat with a veil that made it impossible to see her face.

"No, Mr Sneddles," said Mrs Trentham. "I have not come to purchase a book, but to seek your services." She stared at the stooping old man in his mittens, cardigan and overcoat, which she assumed he was wearing because he could no longer afford to keep the shop heated. Although his back seemed to be permanently semicircular and his head stuck out like a tortoise from its overcoat shell, his eyes were clear and his mind appeared sharp and alert.

"My services, madam?" the old man repeated.

"Yes. I have inherited an extensive library that I require to be catalogued and valued. You come highly recommended."

"It's kind of you to say so, madam."

Mrs Trentham was relieved that Mr Sneddles did not enquire as to who had made the particular recommendation.

"And where is this library, might I be permitted to ask?"

"A few miles east of Harrogate. You will find that it is quite an extraordinary collection. My late father, Sir Raymond Hardcastle – you may have heard of him? – devoted a considerable part of his life to putting it together."

"Harrogate?" said Sneddles as if it was a few miles east of Bangkok.

"Of course I would cover all your expenses, however long the enterprise might take."

"But it would mean having to close the shop," he murmured as if talking to himself.

"I would naturally also compensate you for any loss of earnings."

Mr Sneddles removed a book from the counter and checked its spine. "I fear it's out of the question, madam, quite impossible, you see –"

"My father specialised in William Blake, you know. You will find that he managed to get hold of every first edition, some still in mint condition. He even secured a handwritten manuscript of . . ."

Amy Hardcastle had gone to bed even before her sister arrived back in Yorkshire that evening.

"She gets so tired nowadays," the housekeeper explained.

Mrs Trentham was left with little choice but to have a light supper on her own before retiring to her old room a few minutes after ten. As far as she could tell nothing had changed: the view over the Yorkshire dales, the black clouds, even the picture of York Minster that hung above the walnut-framed bed. She slept soundly enough and returned downstairs at eight the following morning. The cook explained to her that Miss Amy had not yet risen so she ate breakfast alone.

Once all the covered dishes had been cleared away Mrs Trentham sat in the drawing room reading the *Yorkshire Post* while she waited for her sister to make an appearance. When over an hour later the old cat wandered in, Mrs Trentham shooed the animal away with a vicious wave of the folded newspaper. The grandfather clock in the hall had already struck eleven when Amy finally entered the room. She walked slowly towards her sister with the aid of a stick.

"I'm so sorry, Ethel, that I wasn't here to greet you when you arrived last night," she began. "I fear my arthritis has been playing me up again."

Mrs Trentham didn't bother to reply, but watched her sister as she came hobbling towards her, unable to believe the deterioration in her condition in less than three months.

Although Amy had in the past appeared slight she was now frail. And even if she had always been quiet she was now almost inaudible. If she had been perhaps a little pale, she was now grey and the lines on her face were so deeply etched she looked far older than her sixty-nine years.

Amy lowered herself on to the chair next to her sister and for some seconds continued to breathe deeply, leaving her visitor in no doubt that the walk from the bedroom to the drawing room had been something of an ordeal.

"It's so kind of you to leave your family and come up to be with me in Yorkshire," Amy said as the tortoise-shell cat climbed up on to her lap. "I must confess that since dear Papa died I don't know where to turn."

"That's quite understandable, my dear." Mrs Trentham smiled thinly. "But I felt it was nothing more than my duty to be with you – as well as being a pleasure, of course. In any case, Father warned me this might happen once he had passed away. He gave me specific instructions, you know, as to exactly what should be done in the circumstances."

"Oh, I'm so glad to hear that." Amy's face lit up for the first time. "Please do tell me what Papa had in mind."

"Father was adamant that you should sell the house as

quickly as possible and either come and live with Gerald and myself at Ashurst –"

"Oh, I could never dream of putting you to so much trouble, Ethel."

"– or alternatively you could move into one of those nice little hotels on the coast that cater specially for retired couples and single people. He felt that way you could at least make new friends and indeed even have an extended lease of life. I would naturally prefer you to join us in Ashurst, but what with the bombs –"

"He never mentioned selling the house to me," murmured Amy anxiously. "In fact, he begged me –"

"I know, my dear, but he realised only too well what a strain his death would be on you and asked me to break the news gently. You will no doubt recall the long meeting we held in his study when I last came up to see him."

Amy nodded her acknowledgment but the look of bewilderment remained on her face.

"I remember every word he said," Mrs Trentham went on. "Naturally, I shall do my utmost to see his wishes are carried out."

"But I wouldn't know how or where to begin."

"There's no need for you to give it a second thought, my dear." She patted her sister's arm. "That's exactly why I'm here."

"But what will happen to the servants and my dear Garibaldi?" Amy asked anxiously as she continued stroking the cat. "Father would never forgive me if they weren't all properly taken care of."

"I couldn't agree more," Mrs Trentham said. "However, as always he thought of everything and gave me explicit instructions as to what should be done with all the staff."

"How thoughtful of dear Papa. However, I am not altogether certain . . ."

It took Mrs Trentham two more days of patient encouragement before she was finally able to convince her sister that her plans for the future would all work out for the best and, more important, it was what "dear Papa" wanted.

From that moment on Amy only came down in the afternoons to take a short walk around the garden and occasionally attend to the petunias. Whenever Mrs Trentham came across her sister she begged her not to overdo things.

Three days later Amy dispensed with her afternoon walk.

The following Monday Mrs Trentham gave the staff a week's notice, with the exception of the cook whom she told to stay on until Miss Amy had been settled. That same afternoon she sought out a local agent and placed the house and the sixty-acre estate on the market.

On the following Thursday Mrs Trentham made an appointment to see a Mr Althwaite, a solicitor in Harrogate. On one of her sister's infrequent visits downstairs she explained to Amy that it had not been necessary to bother Mr Baverstock: she felt certain any problem that arose concerning the estate could be more easily dealt with by a local man.

Three weeks later Mrs Trentham was able to move her sister and a few of her belongings into a small residential hotel overlooking the east coast a few miles north of Scarborough. She agreed with the proprietor that it was unfortunate that they could not allow pets but felt sure that her sister would fully understand. Mrs Trentham's final instruction was to send the monthly bills direct to Coutts in the Strand, where they would be settled immediately.

Before Mrs Trentham bade farewell to Amy she got her sister to sign three documents. "So that you will have nothing more to worry about, my dear," Mrs Trentham explained in a gentle tone.

Amy signed all three of the forms placed in front of her without bothering to read them. Mrs Trentham quickly folded up the legal papers prepared by the local solicitor and deposited them in her handbag.

"I'll see you soon," she promised Amy before kissing

her sister on the forehead. A few minutes later she began her journey back to Ashurst.

The bell above the door clanged noisily in the musty silence as Mrs Trentham stepped smartly into the shop. At first there was no sign of movement until at last Mr Sneddles appeared from his little room at the rear carrying three books under his arm.

"Good morning, Mrs Trentham," he said. "How kind of you to respond to my note so quickly. I felt I had to contact you as a problem has arisen."

"A problem?" Mrs Trentham drew back the veil that covered her face.

"Yes. As you are aware, I have almost completed my work in Yorkshire. I am sorry it has taken so long, madam, but I fear I have been over-indulgent with my time, such was my appreciation of—"

Mrs Trentham waved a hand in a manner that indicated she was not displeased.

"And I fear," he continued, "that despite enlisting the good services of Doctor Halcombe as my assistant and also remembering the time it takes to travel up and down to Yorkshire it may still take us several more weeks both to catalogue and value such a fine collection – always aware that your late father spent a lifetime putting the library together."

"It's of no consequence," Mrs Trentham assured him. "You see, I'm not in a hurry. Do take your time, Mr Sneddles, and just let me know when you have completed the task."

The antiquarian smiled at the thought of being allowed to continue his cataloguing uninterrupted.

He escorted Mrs Trentham back to the front of the shop and opened the door to let her out. No one who saw them together would have believed they had been born in the same year. She stared up and down Chelsea Terrace before quickly dropping the veil across her face.

Mr Sneddles closed the door behind her and rubbed

his mittens together, then shuffled back to his room to join Doctor Halcombe.

Lately he had been annoyed whenever a customer entered the shop.

"After thirty years, I have no intention of changing stockbrokers," Gerald Trentham said curtly as he poured himself a second cup of coffee.

"But can't you understand, my dear, just what a boost it would give Nigel to secure your account for his company?"

"And what a blow it would be for David Cartwright and Vickers da Costa to lose a client whom they have served so honourably for over a hundred years? No, Ethel, it's high time Nigel carried out his own dirty work. Damn it all, he's over forty."

"All the more reason to help," his wife suggested as she buttered a second piece of toast.

"No, Ethel. I repeat, no."

"But can't you see that one of Nigel's responsibilities is to bring new clients into the firm? It's particularly important at this moment, as I feel sure that now the war is over, they will soon be offering him a partnership."

Major Trentham didn't try to hide his incredulity at this piece of news. "If that is the case, he should be making more use of his own contacts – preferably the ones he made at school and at Sandhurst, not to mention the City. He shouldn't always expect to fall back on his father's friends."

"That's hardly fair, Gerald. If he can't rely on his own flesh and blood, why should he expect anyone else to come to his aid?"

"Come to his aid? That just about sums it up." Gerald's voice rose with every word. "Because that's exactly what you've been doing since the day he was born, which is perhaps the reason he is still unable to stand on his own two feet."

"Gerald," Mrs Trentham said, removing a handkerchief from her sleeve. "I never thought –"

"In any case," the major replied, trying to restore some calm, "it's not as if my portfolio is all that impressive. As you and Mr Attlee know only too well, all our capital is bound up in land and has been for generations."

"It's not the amount that matters," Mrs Trentham chided him. "It's the principle."

"Couldn't agree with you more," said Gerald as he folded his napkin, rose from the breakfast table and left the room before his wife could utter another word.

Mrs Trentham picked up her husband's morning paper and ran her finger down the names of those who had been awarded knighthoods in the Birthday Honours. Her shaking finger stopped at the Ts.

During his summer vacation, according to Max Harris, Daniel Trumper had taken the *Queen Mary* to America. However, the private detective was quite unable to answer Mrs Trentham's next question – why? All that Harris could be sure of was that Daniel's college still expected the young don back for the start of the new academic year.

During the weeks that Daniel was away in America Mrs Trentham spent a considerable amount of time closeted with her solicitors in Lincoln's Inn Fields while they prepared a building application for her.

She had already sought out three architects, all of whom had recently qualified. She instructed them to prepare outline drawings for a block of flats to be built in Chelsea. The winner, she assured them, would be offered the commission while the other two would receive one hundred pounds each in compensation. All three happily agreed to her terms.

Some twelve weeks later, each presented his portfolio but only one of them had come up with what Mrs Trentham was hoping for.

In the opinion of the senior partner of the law practice, the submission by the youngest of the three, Justin Talbot, would have made Battersea Power Station look like the Palace of Versailles. Mrs Trentham did not divulge to her solicitor that she had been influenced in her selection by the fact that Mr Talbot's uncle was a member of the Planning Committee of the London County Council.

Even if Talbot's uncle were to come to his nephew's aid, Mrs Trentham remained unconvinced that a majority of the committee would accept such an outrageous offering. It resembled a bunker that even Hitler might have rejected. However, her lawyers suggested that she should state in her application that the primary purpose of the new building was to create some low-cost housing in the centre of London to help students and single unemployed men who were in dire need of temporary accommodation. Second, any income derived from the flats would be placed in a charitable trust to help other families suffering from the same problem. Third, she should bring to the committee's attention the painstaking efforts that had been made to give a young, recently qualified architect his first break.

Mrs Trentham didn't know whether to be delighted or appalled when the LCC granted its approval. After long deliberation over several weeks, they insisted on only a few minor modifications to young Talbot's original plans. She gave her architect immediate instructions to clear the bombed-out site so that the building could begin without delay.

The application to the LCC by Sir Charles Trumper for a new store to be erected in Chelsea Terrace came in for considerable national publicity, most of it favourable. However, Mrs Trentham noted that in several articles written about the proposed new building, there was mention of a certain Mr Martin Simpson who described himself as the president of the Save the Small Shops Federation, a body that objected to the whole concept of Trumper's. Mr Simpson claimed it could only harm the little shopkeeper in the long run; their livelihoods were, after all, being put at risk. He went on to complain that what made it even more unfair was that none of the local shopkeepers had the means of taking on a man as powerful and wealthy as Sir Charles Trumper.

"Oh, yes, they have," Mrs Trentham said over breakfast that morning.

"Have what?"

"Nothing important," she reassured her husband, but later that day she supplied Harris with the financial wherewithal to allow Mr Simpson to lodge an official objection to the Trumper scheme. Mrs Trentham also agreed to cover any out-of-pocket costs Mr Simpson might incur while carrying out his endeavours.

She began to follow the results of Mr Simpson's efforts daily in the national press, even confiding to Harris that she would have been happy to pay the man a fee for the service he was rendering; but like so many activists the cause was all he seemed to care about.

Once the bulldozers had moved in on Mrs Trentham's site and work had come to a standstill on Trumper's, she turned her attention back to Daniel and the problem of his inheritance.

Her lawyers had confirmed that there was no way of reversing the provisions in the will unless Daniel Trumper were voluntarily to resign all his rights. They even presented her with a form of words that would be necessary for him to sign in such circumstances, leaving Mrs Trentham the daunting task of actually getting his signature affixed to the paper.

As Mrs Trentham was unable to imagine any situation in which she and Daniel would ever meet, she considered the whole exercise futile. However, she carefully locked the lawyer's draft in the bottom drawer of her desk in the drawing room along with all the other Trumper documents.

"How nice to see you again, madam," said Mr Sneddles. "I cannot apologise too profusely over the length of time I have taken to complete your commission. I shall naturally charge you no more than the sum on which we originally agreed."

The bookseller was unable to see the expression on Mrs Trentham's face as she had not yet removed her veil. She followed the old man past shelf after shelf of dust-covered books until they reached his little room at the back of the shop. There she was introduced to Doctor Halcombe who, like Sneddles, was wearing a heavy overcoat. She declined to take the offered chair when she noticed that it too was covered in a thin layer of dust.

The old man proudly pointed to eight boxes that lay on his desk. It took him nearly an hour to explain, with the occasional interjection from Doctor Halcombe, how they had catalogued her late father's entire library, first alphabetically under authors, then by categories and finally with a separate cross-section under titles. A rough valuation of each book had also been pencilled neatly in the bottom right-hand corner of every card.

Mrs Trentham was surprisingly patient with Mr Sneddles, occasionally asking questions in whose answer she had no interest, while allowing him to indulge in a long and complicated explanation as to how he had occupied his time during the past five years.

"You have done a quite remarkable job, Mr Sneddles," she said after he flicked over the last card, "Zola, Emile (1840–1902)". "I could not have asked for more."

"You are most kind, madam," said the old man, bowing low, "but then you have always shown such a genuine concern in these matters. Your father could have found no more suitable person to be responsible for his life's work."

"Fifty guineas was the agreed fee, if I remember correctly," said Mrs Trentham, removing a cheque from her handbag and passing it over to the owner of the bookshop.

"Thank you, madam," Mr Sneddles replied, taking the cheque and placing it absent-mindedly in an ash-tray. He refrained from adding, "I would happily have paid *you* double the sum for the privilege of carrying out such an exercise."

"And I see," she said, studying the accompanying papers closely, "that you have placed an overall value on the entire collection of a little under five thousand pounds."

"That is correct, madam. I should warn you, however,

that if anything I have erred on the conservative side. You see, some of these volumes are so rare it would be difficult to say what they might fetch on the open market."

"Does that mean you would be willing to offer such a sum for the library should I wish to dispose of it?" asked Mrs Trentham, looking directly at him.

"Nothing would give me greater pleasure, madam," replied the old man. "But alas, I fear that I quite simply do not have sufficient funds to do so."

"What would your attitude be were I to entrust you with the responsibility for their sale?" asked Mrs Trentham, her eye never leaving the old man.

"I can think of no greater privilege, madam, but it might take me many months – possibly even years to carry out such an enterprise."

"Then perhaps we should come to some arrangement, Mr Sneddles."

"Some arrangement? I'm not sure I fully understand you, madam."

"A partnership perhaps, Mr Sneddles?"

CHAPTER 34

rs Trentham approved of Nigel's choice of bride; but then it was she who had selected the young lady in the first place.

Veronica Berry possessed all the attributes her future mother-in-law considered necessary to become a Trentham. She came from a good family: her father was a vice-admiral who had not yet been placed on the reserve list and her mother was the daughter of a suffragan bishop. They were comfortably off without being wealthy and, more important, of their three children, all daughters, Veronica was the eldest.

The wedding was celebrated at Kimmeridge parish church in Dorset where Veronica had been christened by the vicar, confirmed by the suffragan bishop and was now to be married by the Bishop of Bath and Wells. The reception was grand enough without being lavish and "the children", as Mrs Trentham referred to them, would, she told everyone, be spending their honeymoon on the family estate in Aberdeen before returning to a mews house in Cadogan Place that she had selected for them. It was so convenient for Chester Square, she explained when asked, and also when not asked.

Every one of the thirty-two partners of Kitcat and Aitken, the stockbrokers for whom Nigel worked, was invited to the nuptial feast, but only five felt able to make the journey to Dorset.

During the reception, held on the lawn of the vice-admiral's home, Mrs Trentham made a point of speaking to all those partners present. To her consternation none was particularly forthcoming about Nigel's future.

Mrs Trentham had rather hoped that her son might have been made a partner soon after his fortieth birthday as she was well aware that several younger men had seen their names printed on the top left-hand side of the letterpaper despite having joined the firm some time after Nigel.

Just before the speeches were about to begin a shower sent the guests scurrying back into the marquee. Mrs Trentham felt the bridegroom's speech could have been received a little more warmly. However, she allowed that it was quite hard to applaud when you were holding a glass of champagne in one hand and an asparagus roll in the other. Indeed, Nigel's best man, Hugh Folland, hadn't done a great deal better.

After the speeches were over Mrs Trentham sought out Miles Renshaw, the senior partner of Kitcat and Aitken, and after taking him on one side revealed that in the near future she intended to invest a considerable sum of money in a company that was planning to go public. She would therefore be in need of his advice as to what she described as her long-term strategy.

This piece of information did not elicit any particular response from Renshaw who still remembered Mrs Trentham's assurance over the future management of the Hardcastle portfolio once her father had died. However, he suggested that perhaps she should drop in to their City office and go over the details of the transaction once the official tender document had been released.

Mrs Trentham thanked Mr Renshaw and continued to work her way round the assembled gathering as if it were she who was the hostess.

She didn't notice Veronica's scowl of disapproval on more than one occasion.

It was the last Friday in September 1947 that Gibson tapped quietly on the door of the living room, entered and announced, "Captain Daniel Trentham."

When Mrs Trentham first saw the young man dressed in the uniform of a captain in the Royal Fusiliers, her legs almost gave way. He marched in and came to a halt in the middle of the carpet. The meeting that had taken place in that room some twenty-five years before immediately sprang to her mind. Somehow she managed to get herself across the room before collapsing on to the sofa.

Gripping its arm to make sure she didn't pass out completely Mrs Trentham stared up at her grandson. She was horrified at his resemblance to Guy, and felt quite sick at the memories he evoked. Memories which for so many years she had managed to keep at the back of her mind.

Once she had composed herself Mrs Trentham's first reaction was to order Gibson to throw him out, but she decided to wait for a moment as she was anxious to discover what the young man could possibly want. As Daniel delivered his carefully rehearsed sentences she began to wonder if possibly the meeting might be turned to her advantage.

Her grandson started by telling her how he had been to Australia that summer, not America as Harris had led her to believe. He went on to show he knew of her ownership of the flats, her attempt to block the planning permission for the store and the wording on the grave in Ashurst and even details of her meetings at the St Agnes Hotel. He continued his rendering with an assurance that his parents were unaware he had come to visit her that afternoon.

Mrs Trentham concluded that he must have discovered the full circumstances of her son's death in Melbourne. Otherwise why would he have stressed that, if the information he possessed were to fall into the hands of the popular press, it could only result in – to put it mildly – embarrassment for all concerned?

Mrs Trentham allowed Daniel to continue his speech while at the same time thinking furiously. It was during his prognosis on the future development of Chelsea Terrace that she wondered just how much the young man standing before her actually did know. She decided there was only one way of finding out, and that would require her to take one big risk.

When Daniel had finally come out with his specific demand, Mrs Trentham simply replied, "I have a condition of my own."

"What condition?"

"That you relinquish any claim you might have to the Hardcastle estate."

Daniel looked uncertain for the first time. It was obviously not what he had expected. Mrs Trentham suddenly felt confident that he had no knowledge of the will: after all, her father had briefed Baverstock not to allow the young man to be privy to its contents until his thirtieth birthday; and Mr Baverstock was not a man to break his word.

"I can't believe you ever intended to leave me anything in the first place," was Daniel's first response.

She didn't reply and waited until Daniel at last nodded his agreement.

"And it must be in writing," she added.

"So must my part of the deal," he demanded brusquely.

Mrs Trentham felt certain that he was no longer relying on the safety of a prepared script and was now simply reacting to events as they took place.

She rose, walked slowly over to her desk and unlocked a drawer. Daniel remained in the middle of the room, swaying slightly from foot to foot.

Having located two sheets of paper and retrieved the lawyer's draft wording that she had left locked in the bottom drawer, Mrs Trentham wrote out two identical agreements which included Daniel's demand for her withdrawal both of her application to build the flats and her objections to his father's application for planning permission to build Trumper Towers. She also included in the agreements her lawyer's exact words for Daniel's waiver of his rights to his great-grandfather's estate.

She handed over the first draft for her grandson to study. At any moment she expected him to work out what he must be sacrificing by signing such a document.

Daniel finished reading the first copy of the agreement then checked to see that both drafts were identical in every detail. Though he said nothing, Mrs Trentham still felt he must surely fathom out why she needed the agreement so badly. In fact, had he demanded that she also sell the land in Chelsea Terrace to his father at a commercial rate she would happily have agreed, just to have Daniel's signature on the bottom of the agreement.

The moment Daniel had signed both documents Mrs Trentham rang the bell and called for the butler to witness the two signatures. Once this task had been completed she said curtly, "Show the gentleman out, Gibson." As the uniformed figure left the room she found herself wondering just how long it would be before the boy realised what a poor bargain he had struck.

When on the following day Mrs Trentham's solicitors studied the one-page document they were stunned by the simplicity of the transaction. However, she offered no explanation as to how she had managed to achieve such a coup. A slight bow of the head from the senior partner acknowledged that the agreement was watertight.

Every man has his price, and once Martin Simpson realised his source of income had dried up, a further fifty pounds in cash convinced him that he should withdraw his objection to Trumper Towers from proceeding as planned.

The following day Mrs Trentham turned her attention to other matters: the understanding of offer documents.

In Mrs Trentham's opinion Veronica became pregnant far too quickly.

Her daughter-in-law produced a son, Giles Raymond, only nine months and three weeks after she and Nigel had been married. At least the child had not been born prematurely. As it was, Mrs Trentham had already observed the servants counting the months on their fingers on more than one occasion.

It was after Veronica had returned from hospital with

the child that Mrs Trentham had the first difference of opinion with her daughter-in-law.

Veronica and Nigel had wheeled Giles round to Chester Square for the proud grandmother to admire. After Mrs Trentham had given the infant a cursory glance Gibson pushed the pram out and the tea trolley in.

"Of course you'll want the boy to be put down for Aysgarth and Harrow without delay," said Mrs Trentham, even before Nigel or Veronica had been given a chance to select a sandwich. "After all, one wants to be certain that his place is guaranteed."

"Actually, Nigel and I have already decided how our son will be educated," said Veronica, "and neither of those schools have entered our deliberations."

Mrs Trentham placed her cup back on its saucer and stared at Veronica as if she had announced the death of the King. "I'm sorry, I don't think I heard you correctly, Veronica."

"We are going to send Giles to a local primary school in Chelsea and then on to Bryanston."

"Bryanston? And where is that, may one ask?"

"In Dorset. It's my father's old school," Veronica added before removing a salmon sandwich from the plate in front of her.

Nigel looked anxiously across at his mother as he touched his blue and silver striped tie.

"That may well be the case," said Mrs Trentham. "However, I feel sure we still need to give a little more consideration as to how young Raymond – she stressed the name – should start off in life."

"No, that will be unnecessary," said Veronica. "Nigel and I have already given quite sufficient thought as to how Giles should be educated. In fact, we registered him for Bryanston last week. After all, one wants to be certain that his place is guaranteed."

Veronica leant forward and helped herself to another salmon sandwich.

* * *

Three chimes echoed from the little carriage clock that stood on the mantelpiece on the far side of the room.

Max Harris pushed himself up out of the armchair in the corner of the lounge the moment he saw Mrs Trentham enter the hotel lobby. He gave a half-bow as he waited for his client to be seated in the chair opposite him.

He ordered tea for her and another double whisky for himself. Mrs Trentham frowned her disapproval as the waiter scurried off to carry out the order. Her attention fixed on Max Harris the moment she heard the inevitable clicks.

"I assume you would not have requested this meeting, Mr Harris, unless you had something important to tell me."

"I think I can safely say that I am the bearer of glad tidings. You see, a lady by the name of Mrs Bennett has recently been arrested and charged with shoplifting. A fur coat and a leather belt from Harvey Nichols, to be exact."

"And of what possible interest could this lady be to me?" asked Mrs Trentham as she looked over his shoulder, annoyed to see that it had started raining and remembering that she had left the house without an umbrella.

"She turns out to have a rather interesting relationship with Sir Charles Trumper."

"Relationship?" said Mrs Trentham, looking even more puzzled.

"Yes," said Harris. "Mrs Bennett is none other than Sir Charles's youngest sister."

Mrs Trentham turned her gaze back on Max Harris. "But Trumper only has three sisters if I remember correctly," she said. "Sal, who is in Toronto and married to an insurance salesman; Grace, who has recently been appointed matron of Guy's hospital, and Kitty who left England some time ago to join her sister in Canada."

"And has now returned."

"Returned?"

"Yes, as Mrs Kitty Bennett."

"I don't begin to understand," said Mrs Trentham, becoming exasperated by the cat and mouse game Harris was so obviously enjoying.

"While she was in Canada," Harris continued, oblivious to his client's irritation, "she married a certain Mr Bennett, a longshoreman. Not unlike her old man, in fact. It lasted for almost a year before ending in a messy divorce in which several men were petitioned. She returned to England a few weeks ago, but only after her sister Sal had refused to take her back."

"How did you come by this information?"

"A friend of mine at Wandsworth nick pointed me in the right direction. Once he had read the charge sheet in the name of Bennett, *née* Trumper, he decided to double-check. It was 'Kitty' that gave the game away. I popped round immediately to be sure we had the right woman." Harris stopped to sip his whisky.

"Go on," said Mrs Trentham impatiently.

"For five pounds she sang like a canary," said Harris. "If I were in a position to offer her fifty I've a feeling she'd sound awfully like a nightingale."

When Trumper's announced they were preparing to go public Mrs Trentham was holidaying on her husband's estate in Aberdeenshire. Having read the short piece in the *Telegraph* she concluded that, although she now had control over the combined monthly incomes left to her sister as well as herself and a further windfall of twenty thousand pounds, she would still need all the capital she had acquired from the sale of the Yorkshire estate if she were going to be able to purchase a worthwhile holding in the new company. She made three trunk calls that morning.

Earlier in the year she had given instructions for her own portfolio to be transferred to Kitcat and Aitken, and after several months of continually badgering her husband she had finally bludgeoned him into following suit. Despite this further commitment on her son's behalf Nigel was still not offered a partnership. Mrs Trentham would have advised him to resign had she been confident his prospects elsewhere would have been any better.

Despite this setback she continued to invite the partners of Kitcat to dinner at Chester Square in regular rotation. Gerald left his wife in no doubt that he did not approve of such tactics, and remained unconvinced that they helped their son's cause. He had been, however, aware that his opinion in such matters had made little impression on her for some time. In any case, the major had now reached an age when he had become too weary to put up more than token resistance.

After Mrs Trentham had studied the finer details of the Trumper's proposals in her husband's copy of *The Times*, she instructed Nigel to apply for five per cent of the company's shares the moment the prospectus was launched.

However, it was a paragraph towards the end of an article in the *Daily Mail* written by Vincent Mulchrone headed "The Triumphant Trumpers" that reminded her that she was still in possession of a picture that needed to fetch its proper price.

Whenever Mr Baverstock requested a meeting with Mrs Trentham it always seemed to her to be more of a summons than an invitation. Perhaps it was because he had acted for her father for over thirty years.

She was only too aware that, as her father's executor, Mr Baverstock still wielded considerable influence, even if she had managed to clip his wings recently over the sale of the estate.

Having offered her the seat on the other side of the partner's desk Mr Baverstock returned to his own chair, replaced his half-moon spectacles on the end of his nose and opened the cover of one of his inevitable grey files.

He seemed to conduct all his correspondence, not to mention his meetings, in a manner that could only be described as distant. Mrs Trentham often wondered if he had treated her father in the same way.

"Mrs Trentham," he began, placing the palms of his

hands on the desk in front of him and pausing to stare down at the notes he had written the previous evening. "May I first thank you for taking the trouble to come and see me in my offices and add how sad I am that your sister felt she had to once again decline my invitation. However, she has made it clear to me in a short letter I received last week that she is happy for you to represent her on this and indeed on any future occasion."

"Dear Amy," said Mrs Trentham. "The poor creature took the death of my father rather badly, even though I have done everything in my power to soften the blow."

The solicitor's eyes returned to the file which contained a note from a Mr Althwaite of Bird, Collingwood and Althwaite in Harrogate, instructing them to see that in future Miss Amy's monthly cheque should be sent direct to Coutts in the Strand for an account number that differed by only one digit from that to which Mr Baverstock already sent the other half of the monthly revenue.

"Although your father left you and your sister the income derived from his Trust," the solicitor continued, "the bulk of his capital will, as you know, in time be passed on to Doctor Daniel Trumper."

Mrs Trentham nodded, her face impassive.

"As you are also aware," Mr Baverstock continued, "the Trust is currently holding stocks, shares and gilts that are being administered for us by the merchant bankers Hambros and Co. Whenever they consider it prudent to make a sizeable investment on behalf of the Trust, we feel it equally important to keep you informed of their intentions, despite the fact that Sir Raymond gave us a free hand in these matters."

"That's most considerate of you, Mr Baverstock."

The solicitor's eyes returned to the file where he studied another note. This time it was from an estate agent in Bradford. The estate, house and contents of the late Sir Raymond Hardcastle had without his knowledge been sold for forty-one thousand pounds. After deducting commissions and legal fees, the agent had sent the balance of the monies direct to the same account at Coutts in the Strand as received Miss Amy's monthly payment.

"Bearing this in mind," continued the family lawyer, "I felt it nothing less than my duty to inform you that our advisors are recommending a considerable investment in a new company that is about to come on to the market."

"And which company might that be?" enquired Mrs Trentham.

"Trumper's," said Baverstock, watching carefully for his client's reaction.

"And why Trumper's in particular?" she asked, the expression on her face revealing no particular surprise.

"Principally because Hambros consider it a sound and prudent investment. But, perhaps more important, in time the bulk of the company's stock will be owned by Daniel Trumper, whose father, as I feel sure you know, is currently chairman of the board."

"I was aware of that," said Mrs Trentham, without further comment. She could see that it worried Mr Baverstock that she took the news so calmly.

"Of course, if you and your sister were both to object strongly to such a large commitment being made by the Trust it is possible our advisors might reconsider their position."

"And how much are they thinking of investing?"

"Around two hundred thousand pounds," the solicitor informed her. "This would make it possible for the Trust to purchase approximately ten per cent of the company's shares."

"Is that not a considerable stake for us to be holding in one company?"

"It certainly is," said Mr Baverstock. "But still well within the Trust's budget."

"Then I am happy to accept Hambros' judgment," said Mrs Trentham. "And I feel sure I speak for my sister in this matter."

Once again Mr Baverstock looked down at the file

where he studied an affidavit signed by Miss Amy Hardcastle, virtually giving her sister *carte blanche* when it came to decisions relating to the estate of the late Sir Raymond Hardcastle, including the transfer of twenty thousand pounds from her personal account. Mr Baverstock only hoped that Miss Amy was happy at the Cliff Top Residential Hotel. He looked up at Sir Raymond's other daughter.

"Then all that is left for me to do," he concluded, "is to advise Hambros of your views in this matter and brief you more fully when Trumper's eventually allocate their shares."

The solicitor closed the file, rose from behind his desk and began to walk towards the door. Mrs Trentham followed in his wake, happy in the knowledge that both the Hardcastle Trust and her own advisors were now working in tandem to help her fulfil her long-term purpose without either side being aware of what she was up to. It pleased her even more to think that the day Trumper's went public she would have control of fifteen per cent of the company.

When they reached the door Mr Baverstock turned to shake Mrs Trentham by the hand.

"Good day, Mrs Trentham."

"Good day, Mr Baverstock. You have been most punctilious, as always."

She made her way back to the car where a chauffeur held open the back door for her. As she was driven away she turned to look out of the rear window. The lawyer was standing by the door of his offices, the worried expression remaining on his face.

"Where to, madam?" asked the chauffeur as they joined the afternoon traffic.

She checked her watch: the meeting with Baverstock had not taken as long as she had anticipated and she now found herself with some spare time before her next appointment. Nevertheless she still gave the instruction, "The St Agnes Hotel," as she placed a hand on the brown paper parcel that lay on the seat beside her.

She had told Harris to book a private room in the hotel

and slip Kitty Bennett up in the lift at a time when he felt confident that no one was watching them.

When she arrived at the St Agnes clutching the parcel under one arm, she was annoyed to find that Harris was not waiting for her in his usual place by the bar. She intensely disliked standing alone in the corridor and reluctantly went over to the hall porter to ask the number of the room Harris had booked.

"Fourteen," said a man in a shiny blue uniform with buttons that did not shine. "But you can't –"

Mrs Trentham was not in the habit of being told "You can't" by anyone. She turned and slowly climbed the stairs that led up to the bedrooms on the first floor. The hall porter quickly picked up the phone on the counter beside him.

It took Mrs Trentham a few minutes to locate Number 14 and Harris almost as long to respond to her sharp knock. When Mrs Trentham was eventually allowed to enter the room she was surprised to discover how small it was: only just large enough to accommodate one bed, one chair and a wash-basin. Her eyes settled on the woman who was sprawled across the bed. She was wearing a red silk blouse and a black leather skirt – far too short in Mrs Trentham's opinion, not to mention the fact that two of the top buttons of the blouse were undone.

As Kitty made no attempt to remove an old raincoat that had been thrown across the chair, Mrs Trentham was left with little choice but to remain standing.

She turned to Harris, who was checking his tie in the only mirror. He had obviously decided that any introduction was superfluous.

Mrs Trentham's only reaction was to get on with the business she had come to transact so that she could return to civilisation as quickly as possible. She didn't wait for Harris to start the proceedings.

"Have you explained to Mrs Bennett what is expected of her?"

"I most certainly have," said the detective, as he put

on his jacket. "And Kitty is more than ready to carry out her part of the bargain."

"Can she be trusted?" Mrs Trentham glanced doubtfully down at the woman on the bed.

"'course I can, long as the money's right," were Kitty's first words. "All I want to know is, 'ow much do I get?"

"Whatever it sells for, plus fifty pounds," said Mrs Trentham.

"Then I expect twenty quid up front."

Mrs Trentham hesitated for a moment, then nodded her agreement.

"So what's the catch?"

"Only that your brother will try to talk you out of the whole idea," said Mrs Trentham. "He may even attempt to bribe you in exchange for . . ."

"Not an 'ope," said Kitty. "'e can talk 'is 'ead off as far as I'm concerned but it won't make a blind bit of difference. You see, I 'ate Charlie almost as much as you do."

Mrs Trentham smiled for the first time. She then placed the brown paper parcel on the end of the bed.

Harris smirked. "I knew you two would find you had something in common."

BECKY

1947-1950

CHAPTER 35

ight after night I would lie awake worrying that Daniel must eventually work out that Charlie wasn't his father.

Whenever they stood next to each other, Daniel tall and slim, with fair wavy hair and deep blue eyes, Charlie at least three inches shorter, stocky, with dark wiry hair and brown eyes, I assumed Daniel must in time comment on the disparity. It didn't help that my complexion is also dark. The dissimilarities might have been comic had the implications not been so serious. Yet Daniel has never once mentioned the differences in physical make-up or character between himself and Charlie.

Charlie wanted to tell Daniel the truth about Guy right from the start, but I convinced him that we should wait until the boy was old enough to understand all the implications. But when Guy died of tuberculosis there no longer seemed any point in burdening Daniel with the past.

Later, after years of anguish and Charlie's continued remonstrations, I finally agreed to tell Daniel everything. I phoned him at Trinity the week before he was due to sail for America and asked if I could drive him down to Southampton; that way at least I knew we would be uninterrupted for several hours. I mentioned that there was something important I needed to discuss with him.

I set out for Cambridge a little earlier than was

necessary and arrived well in time to help Daniel with his packing. By eleven we were heading down the A10. For the first hour he chatted away happily enough about his work at Cambridge – too many students, not enough time for research – but the moment the conversation switched to the problems we were facing with the flats, I knew he had presented me with the ideal opportunity to tell him the truth about his parentage. Then quite suddenly he changed the subject and I lost my nerve. I swear I would have broached the topic right there and then, but the moment had passed.

Because of all the unhappiness we subsequently experienced with the death of my mother and with the life of Mrs Trentham while Daniel was away in America, I decided my best chance of ever being frank with my son had been squandered. I begged Charlie to allow the matter to drop once and for all. I have a fine husband. He told me I was wrong; that Daniel was mature enough to handle the truth but he accepted that it had to be my decision. He never once referred to the matter again.

When Daniel returned from America I travelled back down to Southampton to pick him up. I don't know what it was about him but he seemed to have changed. For a start he looked different – more at ease – and the moment he saw me he gave me a big hug, which quite took me by surprise. On the way back to London we discussed his visit to the States, which he had obviously enjoyed, and without going into great detail I brought him up to date on what was happening to our planning application for Chelsea Terrace. He didn't seem all that interested in my news, but to be fair Charlie never involved Daniel in the day-to-day working of Trumper's once we both realised he was destined for an academic career.

Daniel spent the next few weeks with us before returning to Cambridge, and even Charlie, not always the most observant of people, commented on how much he had changed. He was just as serious and quiet, even as secretive, but he was so much warmer towards us both that I began to wonder if he had met a girl while he had been away. I hoped so, but despite the odd hint clumsily dropped, Daniel made no mention of anyone in particular. I rather liked the idea of him marrying an American. He had rarely brought girls home in the past and always seemed so shy when we introduced him to the daughters of any of our friends. In fact he was never to be found if Clarissa Wiltshire put in an appearance – which was quite often nowadays, as during their vacations from Bristol University both the twins were to be found working behind the counter at Number 1.

It must have been about a month after Daniel returned from America that Charlie told me Mrs Trentham had withdrawn all her objections to our proposed scheme for joining the two tower blocks together. I leapt with joy. When he added that she was not going ahead with her own plans to rebuild the flats I refused to believe him and immediately assumed that there had to be some catch. Even Charlie admitted, "I've no idea what she's up to this time." Certainly neither of us accepted Daphne's theory that she might be mellowing in her old age.

Two weeks later the LCC confirmed that all objections to our scheme had been withdrawn and we could begin on our building programme. That was the signal Charlie had been waiting for to inform the outside world that we intended to go public.

Charlie called a board meeting so that all the necessary resolutions could be passed.

Mr Merrick, whom Charlie had never forgiven for causing him to sell the Van Gogh, advised us to appoint Robert Fleming to be our merchant bankers in the run-up to the flotation. The banker also added that he hoped the newly formed company would continue to use Child and Co as their clearing bank. Charlie would have liked to have told him to "get lost" but knew only too well that if he changed banks a few weeks before going public, eyebrows would be raised in the City. The board accepted both pieces of advice, and Tim Newman of Robert Fleming's was duly invited to join the board. Tim brought a breath of fresh air to the company, representing a new breed of bankers. However, although I, like Charlie, immediately took to Mr Newman, I never really got on the same wavelength as Paul Merrick.

As the day for issuing the tender documents drew nearer, Charlie spent more and more of his time with the merchant banker. Meanwhile Tom Arnold took overall control of the running of the shops, as well as overseeing the building programme – with the exception of Number 1, which still remained my domain.

I had decided several months before the final announcement that I wanted to mount a major sale at the auction house just before Charlie's declaration of going public, and I was confident that the Italian collection to which I had been devoting a great deal of my time would prove to be the ideal opportunity to place Number 1 Chelsea Terrace on the map.

It had taken my chief researcher Francis Lawson nearly two years to gather some fifty-nine canvases together, all painted between 1519 and 1768. Our biggest coup was a Canaletto – *The Basilica of St Mark's* – a painting that had been left to Daphne by an old aunt of hers from Cumberland. "It isn't," she characteristically told us, "as good as the two Percy already has in Lanarkshire. However, I still expect the painting to fetch a fair price, my darling. Failure will only result in offering any future custom to Sotheby's," she added with a smile.

We placed a reserve on the painting of thirty thousand pounds. I had suggested to Daphne that this was a sensible figure, remembering that the record for a

Canaletto was thirty-eight thousand guineas, bid at Christie's the previous year.

While I was in the final throes of preparation for the sale Charlie and Tim Newman spent most of their time visiting institutions, banks, finance companies and major investors, to brief them on why they should take a stake in the "biggest barrow in the world".

Tim was optimistic about the outcome and felt that when the stock applications came to be counted we would be heavily oversubscribed. Even so, he thought that he and Charlie should travel to New York and drum up some interest among American investors. Charlie timed his trip to the States so that he would be back in London a couple of days before my auction was to take place and a clear three weeks before our tender document was to be offered to the public.

It was a cold Monday morning in January, and I may not have been at my brightest but I could have sworn I recognised the customer who was in deep conversation with one of our new counter assistants. It worried me that I couldn't quite place the middle-aged lady who was wearing a coat that would have been fashionable in the thirties and looked as if she had fallen on hard times and might be having to sell off one of the family heirlooms.

Once she had left the building I walked over to the desk and asked Cathy, our most recent recruit, who she was.

"A Mrs Bennett," said the young girl behind the counter.

The name meant nothing to me so I asked what she had wanted.

Cathy handed me a small oil painting of the Virgin Mary and Child. "The lady asked if this could still be considered for the Italian sale. She knew nothing of its provenance and looking at her I have to say I wondered if it might have been stolen. I was about to have a word with Mr Lawson."

I stared at the little oil and immediately realised it had been Charlie's youngest sister who had brought the painting in.

"Leave this one to me."

"Certainly, Lady Trumper."

I took the lift to the top floor and walked straight past Jessica Allen and on into Charlie's office. I handed over the picture for him to study and quickly explained how it had come into our possession.

He pushed the paperwork on his desk to one side and stared at the painting for some time without saying a word.

"Well, one thing's for certain," Charlie eventually offered, "Kitty is never going to tell us how or where she got hold of it, otherwise she would have come to me direct."

"So what shall we do?"

"Put it in the sale as she instructed, because you can be sure that no one is going to bid more for the picture than I will."

"But if all she's after is some cash, why not make her a fair offer for the picture?"

"If all Kitty is after was some cash, she would be standing in this office now. No, she would like nothing better than to see me crawling to her for a change."

"But if she stole the painting?"

"From whom? And even if she did there's nothing to stop us stating the original provenance in our catalogue. After all, the police must still have all the details of the theft on their files."

"But what if Guy gave it to her?"

"Guy," Charlie reminded me, "is dead."

I was delighted by the amount of interest the press and public were beginning to take in the sale. Another good omen was that several of the leading art critics and collectors were spotted during the preview week study-ing the pictures on display in the main gallery.

Articles about Charlie and myself began to appear, first in the financial sections, then spreading over to the feature pages. I didn't care much for the sound of "The Triumphant Trumpers", as one paper dubbed us, but Tim Newman explained to us the importance of public relations when trying to raise large sums of money. As feature after feature appeared in news-papers and magazines, our new young director became daily more confident that the flotation was going to be a success.

Francis Lawson and his new assistant Cathy Ross worked on the auction catalogue for several weeks, painstakingly going over the history of each painting, its previous owners and the galleries and exhibitions in which each had been exhibited before they were offered to Trumper's for auction. To our surprise, what went down particularly well with the public was not the paintings themselves but our catalogue, the first with every plate in colour. It cost a fortune to produce, but as we had to order two reprints before the day of the sale and we sold every catalogue at five shillings a time, it wasn't long before we recovered our costs. I was able to inform the board at our monthly meeting that following two more reprints we had actually ended up making a small profit. "Perhaps you should close the art gallery and open a publishing house," was Charlie's helpful comment.

The new auction room at Number 1 held two hun-dred and twenty comfortably. We had never managed to fill every seat in the past, but now, as applications for tickets kept arriving by every post, we quickly had to sort out the genuine bidders from the hangers-on.

Despite cutting, pruning, being offhand and even downright rude to one or two persistent individuals, we still ended up with nearly three hundred people who expected to be found seats. Several journalists were among them, but our biggest coup came when the arts editor of the Third Programme phoned to enquire if they could cover the auction on radio.

Charlie arrived back from America two days before the sale and told me in the brief moments we had together that the trip had proved most satisfactory – whatever that meant. He added that Daphne would be accompanying him to the auction – "Got to keep the major clients happy." I didn't mention the fact that I had quite forgotten to allocate him a seat, but Simon Matthews, who had recently been appointed as my deputy, squeezed a couple of extra chairs on the end of the seventh row and prayed that no one from the fire department would be among the bidders.

We decided to hold the sale at three o'clock on a Tuesday afternoon, after Tim Newman advised us that timing was all-important if we were to ensure the maximum coverage in the national papers the following day.

Simon and I were up all night before the auction with the saleroom staff, removing the pictures from the walls and placing them in the correct order ready for sale. Next we checked the lighting of the easel which would display each painting and finally placed the chairs in the auction room as close together as possible. By pulling the stand from which Simon would conduct the auction back by a few feet we were even able to add another row. It may have left less room for the spotters – who always stand by the side of the auctioneer during a sale searching for the bidders – but it certainly solved fourteen other problems.

On the morning of the auction we carried out a dress rehearsal, the porters placing each picture on the easel as Simon called the lot number, then removing it once he had brought the hammer down and called for the next lot. When eventually the Canaletto was lifted up on to the easel, the painting displayed all the polished technique and minute observation which had been the hallmark of the master. I could only smile when a moment later the masterpiece was replaced by Charlie's little picture of the Virgin Mary and Child. Despite considerable research by Cathy Ross she had been quite unable to trace its antecedents, so we had merely re-framed the painting and attributed it in the catalogue as sixteenth-century school. I marked it up in my book at an estimated two hundred guineas, although I was fully aware that Charlie intended to buy back the little picture whatever the price. It still worried me how Kitty had got hold of the oil, but Charlie told me continually to "stop fussing". He had bigger problems on his mind than how his sister had come into possession of Tommy's gift.

On the afternoon of the auction some people were already in their seats by two fifteen. I spotted more than one major buyer or gallery-owner who had not previously encountered a packed house at Trumper's and consequently had to stand at the back.

By two forty-five there were only a few seats left, and latecomers were already crammed shoulder to shoulder down the side walls, with one or two even perched on their haunches in the centre aisle. At two fifty-five Daphne made a splendid entrance, wearing a finely tailored cashmere suit of midnight blue which I had seen featured in *Vogue* the previous month. Charlie, who I felt looked a little tired, followed only a pace behind. They took their seats on the end of the seventh row, for sentimental reasons he had explained. Daphne appeared very satisfied with herself while Charlie fidgeted impatiently.

At exactly three o'clock I took my place next to the auctioneer's stand while Simon climbed the steps to his little box, paused for a moment as he scrutinised the crowd to work out where the major buyers were seated, then banged his gavel several times.

"Good afternoon, ladies and gentlemen," he

announced. "Welcome to Trumper's, the fine art auctioneers." He managed somehow to emphasise "the" in a most agreeable fashion. As he called for lot number one a hush came over the room. I checked the painting in my catalogue – although I think I knew the details of all fifty-nine lots by heart. It was a depiction of St Francis of Assisi by Giovanni Battista Crespi, dated 1617. I had the little oil marked in our code as QIHH pounds, so when Simon brought down the hammer at two thousand two hundred, seven hundred pounds more than I had estimated, I felt we were off to a good start.

Of the fifty-nine works on sale the Canaletto had been left until lot number thirty-seven as I wanted an atmosphere of excitement to build before the painting reached the stand, while not leaving it so late that people started to drift away. The first hour had raised forty-seven thousand pounds and we still had not come to the Canaletto. When eventually the four-foot-wide canvas was placed in the glare of the spotlight, a gasp came from those in the audience who were seeing the masterpiece for the first time.

"A painting of St Mark's Basilica by Canaletto," said Simon, "dated 1741" – as if we had another half-dozen stored away in the basement. "Considerable interest has been shown in this item and I have an opening bid of ten thousand pounds." His eyes scanned the hushed room, as I and my spotters searched to see where the second bid might come from.

"Fifteen thousand," said Simon as he looked towards a representative from the Italian government who was seated in the fifth row.

"Twenty thousand pounds at the back of the room" – I knew it had to be the representative from the Mellon Collection. He always sat in the second to back row, a cigarette dangling from his lips to show us he was still bidding.

"Twenty-five thousand," said Simon, turning again towards the Italian government representative.

"Thirty thousand." The cigarette was still emitting smoke: Mellon remained in the chase.

"Thirty-five thousand." I spotted a new bidder, sitting in the fourth row to my right: Mr Randall, the manager of the Wildenstein Gallery in Bond Street.

"Forty thousand," said Simon as a fresh puff of smoke emanated from the back. We were past the estimate I had given Daphne, although no emotion showed on her face.

"Fifty thousand." This was far too big a hike at this stage in my opinion. Looking towards the box, I noticed that Simon's left hand was shaking.

"Fifty thousand," he repeated a little nervously, when a new bidder in the front row, whom I didn't recognise, started nodding furiously.

The cigarette puffed once again. "Fifty-five thousand."

"Sixty thousand." Simon had turned his attention back in the direction of the unknown bidder, who confirmed with a sharp nod that he remained in the hunt.

"Sixty-five thousand." The Mellon representative still kept puffing away, but when Simon turned his attention back to the bidder in the front row he received a sharp shake of the head.

"Sixty-five thousand then, the bid is at the back of the room. Sixty-five thousand, are there any more bidders?" Once again Simon looked towards the under-bidder in the front row. "Then I'm offering the Canaletto at sixty-five thousand pounds, sixty-five thousand pounds for the second time, then it's sold for sixty-five thousand pounds." Simon brought the gavel down with a thud less than two minutes after the first bid had been offered, and I marked ZIHHH in my catalogue as a round of applause spontaneously burst from the audience – something I had never experienced before at Number 1.

Noisy chatter broke out all over the room as Simon turned round to me and said in a low voice, "Sorry about the mistake, Becky," and I realised that the jump from forty to fifty thousand had been nothing more than a bout of auctioneer's nerves.

I began to compose a possible headline in tomorrow's papers: "Record amount paid for Canaletto in auction at Trumper's". Charlie would be pleased.

"Can't see Charlie's little picture fetching quite that sum," Simon added with a smile, as the Virgin Mary and Child replaced the Canaletto on the stand and he turned to face his audience once again.

"Quiet please," he said. "The next item, lot number thirty-eight in your catalogue, is from the school of Bronzino." He scanned the room. "I have a bid of one hundred and fifty" – he paused for a second – "pounds for this lot. Can I ask for one hundred and seventy-five?" Daphne, who I assumed was Charlie's plant, raised her hand and I stifled a smile. "One hundred and seventy-five pounds. Do I see two hundred?" Simon looked around hopefully but received no response. "Then I'll offer it for the first time at one hundred and seventy-five pounds, for the second time, for the third time then . . ."

But before Simon could bring the gavel down a stocky man with a brownish moustache, greying hair, dressed in a tweed jacket, checked shirt and a yellow tie leaped up from the back of the room and shouted, "That painting is not 'from the school of', it's an original Bronzino, and it was stolen from the Church of St Augustine, near Reims, during the First World War."

Pandemonium broke out as people stared first at the man in the yellow tie, then at the little picture. Simon banged his gavel repeatedly but could not regain control as the journalists began to scribble furiously across their pads. I glanced across to see Charlie and Daphne, their heads bowed in frantic conversation.

Once the outcry had died down, attention began to focus on the man who had made the claim. He remained standing in his place.

"I believe you are mistaken, sir," said Simon firmly. "As I can assure you, this painting has been known to the gallery for some years."

"And I assure you, sir," replied the man, "the painting is an original, and although I do not accuse the previous owner of being a thief, I can nevertheless prove it was stolen." Several in the audience immediately glanced down at their catalogues to see the name of the most recent owner. "From the private collection of Sir Charles Trumper" was printed in bold letters along the top line.

The hubbub, if anything, was now even louder, but still the man remained standing. I leaned forwards and tugged Simon's trouser leg. He bent over and I whispered my decision in his ear. He banged his gavel several times and at last the audience began to quieten. I looked across at Charlie who was as white as a sheet, then at Daphne, who remained quite calm and was holding his hand. As I believed there had to be a simple explanation to the mystery, I felt curiously detached. When Simon had finally restored order he announced, "I am advised that this lot will be withdrawn until further notice."

"Lot number thirty-nine," he added quickly as the man in the brown tweed jacket rose and hurriedly departed from the room, pursued by a gaggle of journalists.

None of the remaining twenty-one items reached their reserve prices, and when Simon brought the gavel down for the final time that afternoon, although we had broken every house record for an Italian sale, I was only too aware what the story in the next day's papers was bound to be. I looked across at Charlie who was obviously trying his best to appear unruffled. Instinctively I turned towards the chair which had been occupied by the man in the brown tweed jacket. The room was beginning to empty as people drifted towards the doors and I noticed for the first time that directly behind the chair sat an elderly lady sitting bolt upright, leaning forward, her two hands resting on the head of a parasol. She was staring directly at me.

Once Mrs Trentham was sure she had caught my eye, she rose serenely from her place and glided slowly out of the gallery.

The following morning the press had a field day. Despite the fact that neither Charlie nor I had made any statement our picture was on every front page except *The Times* alongside the little oil of the Virgin Mary and Child. There was hardly a mention of the Canaletto in the first ten paragraphs of any report and certainly no accompanying photograph.

The man who made the accusation had apparently disappeared without trace and the whole episode might have died down if Monsignor Pierre Guichot, the Bishop of Reims, hadn't agreed to be interviewed by Freddie Barker, the saleroom correspondent of the *Daily Telegraph*, who had uncovered the fact that Guichot had been the priest at the church where the original picture had hung. The bishop confirmed to Barker that the painting had indeed mysteriously disappeared during the Great War and, more important, he had at the time reported the theft to the appropriate section of the League of Nations responsible for seeing that, under the Geneva Convention, stolen works of art were returned to their rightful owners once hostilities had ceased. The bishop went on to say that of course he would recognise the picture if he ever saw it again – the colours, the brushwork, the serenity of the Virgin's face; indeed the genius of Bronzino's composition would remain clearly in his memory until the day he died. Barker quoted him word for damning word.

The *Telegraph* correspondent rang my office the day the interview appeared and informed me that his paper intended to fly the distinguished cleric over at their expense so that he could study the painting at first hand and thus establish its provenance beyond doubt. Our legal advisors warned us that we would be unwise not to allow the bishop to view the painting; to deny him access would be tantamount to acknowledging we were trying to hide something. Charlie agreed without hesitation and simply added, "Let the man see the picture. I'm confident that Tommy left that church with nothing other than a German officer's helmet."

The next day, in the privacy of his office, Tim Newman warned us that if the Bishop of Reims identified the picture as the original Bronzino, then the launch of Trumper's as a public company would have to be held up for at least a year, while the auction house might never recover from such a scandal.

The following Thursday the Bishop of Reims flew into London, to be greeted by a bank of photographers whose flash-bulbs popped again and again before the monsignor was driven off to Westminster, where he was staying as a guest of the archbishop.

The bishop had agreed to visit the gallery at four the same afternoon, and anyone walking through Chelsea Terrace that Thursday might have been forgiven for thinking Frank Sinatra was about to make a personal appearance. A large gathering had formed on the kerbside as they waited keenly for the cleric's arrival.

I met the bishop at the entrance to the gallery and introduced him to Charlie, who bowed before kissing the episcopal ring. I think the bishop was somewhat surprised to discover that Charlie was a Roman Catholic. I smiled nervously at our visitor who appeared to have a perpetual beam on his face – a face that was red from wine, not sun, I suspected. He glided off down the passage in his long purple cassock as Cathy led him in the direction of my room, where the picture awaited him. Barker, the reporter from the *Telegraph*, introduced himself to Simon as if he were dealing with someone from the underworld. He made no attempt to be civil when Simon tried to strike up a conversation with him.

The bishop came through to my little office and accepted a proffered cup of coffee. I had already placed the picture on an easel, having at Charlie's insistence refitted the original old black frame on the painting. We all sat round the table in silence as the priest stared at the Virgin Mary.

"*Vous permettez?*" he asked, holding out his arms.

"Certainly," I replied, and handed over the little oil.

I watched his eyes carefully as he held the painting in front of him. He seemed to take just as much interest in Charlie, whom I had never seen so nervous, as he did in the picture itself. He also glanced at Barker, who in contrast had a look of hope in his eyes. After that the bishop returned his attention to the painting, smiled and seemed to become transfixed by the Virgin Mary.

"Well?" enquired the reporter.

"Beautiful. An inspiration for any non-believer."

Barker also smiled and wrote his words down.

"You know," the priest added, "this painting brings back many memories" – he hesitated for a moment and I thought my heart was going to stop before he pronounced – "but, *hélas*, I must inform you, Mr Barker, that it is not the original. A mere copy of the madonna I knew so well."

The reporter stopped writing. "Only a copy?"

"Yes, *je le regrette*. An excellent copy, *peut-être* painted by a young pupil of the great man, would be my guess, but none the less a copy."

Barker was unable to hide his disappointment as he placed his pad down on the table, looking as if he wished to make some protest.

The bishop rose and bowed in my direction. "It

is my regret that you have been troubled, Lady Trumper."

I too rose and accompanied him to the door, where he was faced once again with the assembled press. The journalists fell silent as they waited for the priest to utter some revelation and I felt for a moment that he might actually be enjoying the experience.

"Is it the real thing, Bishop?" shouted a reporter in the crowd.

He smiled benignly. "It is indeed a portrait of the Blessed Virgin, but this particular example is only a copy, and of no great significance." He did not add a word to this statement before climbing back into his car to be whisked away.

"What a relief," I said once the car was out of sight. I turned round to look for Charlie, but he was nowhere to be seen. I rushed back to my office and found him holding the picture in his hands. I closed the door behind me so that we could be alone.

"What a relief," I repeated. "Now life can return to normal."

"You realise, of course, that this *is* the Bronzino," Charlie said, looking straight at me.

"Don't be silly," I said. "The bishop – "

"But did you see the way he held her?" said Charlie. "You don't cling on to a counterfeit like that. And then I watched his eyes while he came to a decision."

"A decision?"

"Yes, as to whether or not to ruin our lives, in exchange for his beloved Virgin."

"So we've been in possession of a masterpiece without even knowing it?"

"It would seem so, but I'm still not sure who removed the painting from the chapel in the first place."

"Surely not Guy . . ."

"Why not, he's more likely to have appreciated its value than Tommy."

"But how did Guy discover where it ended up, let alone what it was really worth?"

"Company records, perhaps, or a chance conversation with Daphne might have put him in the right direction."

"But that still doesn't explain how he found out it was an original."

"I agree," said Charlie. "I suspect he didn't, and simply saw the picture as another way of discrediting me."

"Then how the blazes . . . ?"

"Whereas Mrs Trentham has had several years to stumble across . . ."

"Good God, but where does Kitty fit in?"

"She was a distraction, nothing more, used by Mrs Trentham simply to set us up."

"Will that woman go to any lengths to destroy us?"

"I suspect so. And one thing's for certain, she isn't going to be pleased when she discovers her 'best laid plans' have once again been scuppered."

I collapsed on the chair beside my husband. "What shall we do now?"

Charlie continued to cling to the little masterpiece as if he were afraid someone might try to seize it from him.

"There's only one thing we can do."

I drove us to the archbishop's house that night and parked the car outside the tradesmen's entrance. "How appropriate," Charlie remarked, before knocking quietly on an old oak door. A priest answered our call and without a word ushered us in before leading us through to see the archbishop, whom we found sharing a glass of wine with the Bishop of Reims.

"Sir Charles and Lady Trumper," the priest intoned.

"Welcome, my children," said the archbishop as he came forward to greet us. "This is an unexpected pleasure," he added, after Charlie kissed his ring. "But what brings you to my home?"

"We have a small gift for the bishop," I said as I handed over a little paper parcel to His Grace.

The bishop smiled the same smile as when he had declared the picture to be a copy. He opened the parcel slowly, like a child who knows he's being given a present when it isn't his birthday. He held the little masterpiece in his hands for some time before passing it to the archbishop for his consideration.

"Truly magnificent," said the archbishop who studied it carefully before handing it back to the bishop. "But where will you display it?"

"Above the cross in the chapel of St Augustine I consider would be appropriate," the bishop replied. "And possibly in time someone far more scholarly on such matters than myself will declare the picture to be an original." He looked up and smiled, a wicked smile for a bishop.

The archbishop turned towards me. "Would you and your husband care to join us for dinner?"

I thanked him for the kind offer and muttered some excuse about a previous engagement before we both bade them goodnight and quietly slipped out the way we had come.

As the door closed behind us I heard the archbishop say, "You win your bet, Pierre."

CHAPTER 36

"Twenty thousand pounds?" said Becky as she came to a halt outside Number 141. "You must be joking."

"That's the price the agent is demanding," said Tim Newman.

"But the shop can't be worth more than three thousand at most," said Charlie, staring at the only building on the block he still didn't own. "And in any case I signed an agreement with Mr Sneddles that when –"

"Not for the books, you didn't," said the banker.

"But we don't want the books," said Becky, noticing for the first time that a heavy chain and bolt barred them from entering the premises.

"Then you can't take possession of the shop, because until the last book is sold your agreement with Mr Sneddles cannot come into operation."

"What are the books really worth?" Becky asked.

"In his typical fashion, Mr Sneddles has pencilled a price in every one of them," said Tim Newman. "His colleague, Doctor Halcombe, tells me the total comes to around five thousand pounds with the exception –"

"So buy the lot," said Charlie, "because knowing Sneddles he probably undervalued them in the first place. Then Becky can auction the entire collection some time later in the year. That way the shortfall shouldn't be more than about a thousand."

"With the exception of a first edition of Blake's *Songs of Innocence*," added Newman. "Vellum bound, that are marked up in Sneddle's inventory at fifteen thousand pounds."

"Fifteen thousand pounds at a time when I'm expected to watch every penny. Who imagines that . . . ?"

"Someone who realises you can't go ahead with the building of a department store until you are in possession of this particular shop?" suggested Newman.

"But how could she – ?"

"Because the Blake in question was originally purchased from the Heywood Hill bookshop in Curzon Street for the princely sum of four pounds ten shillings and I suspect the inscription solves half the mystery."

"Mrs Ethel Trentham, I'll be bound," said Charlie.

"No, but not a bad guess. The exact words on the flyleaf, if I remember correctly, read: From your loving grandson, Guy. 9 July 1917."

Charlie and Becky stared at Tim Newman for some time until Charlie finally asked, "What do you mean – half the mystery?"

"I also suspect she needs the money," replied the banker.

"What for?" asked Becky incredulously.

"So she can purchase even more shares in Trumper's of Chelsea."

On 19 March 1948, two weeks after the bishop had returned to Reims, the official tender document for Trumper's was released to the press to coincide with full-page advertisements taken in *The Times* and the *Financial Times*. All Charlie and Becky could do now was sit and wait for the public's response. Within three days of the announcement the share issue was oversubscribed and within a week the merchant bankers had received double the applications necessary. When all the requests had been counted, Charlie and Tim Newman were left with only one problem: how to allocate the shares. They agreed that institutions who had applied for a large holding should be taken up first, as that would give the board easy access to the majority of shares should any problem arise in the future.

The only application that puzzled Tim Newman came from Hambros who offered no explanation as to why they should wish to purchase one hundred thousand shares which would give them control of ten per cent of the company. However, Tim recommended that the chairman should accept their application in full while at the same time offering them a place on the board. This Charlie agreed to do, but only after Hambros had confirmed that the bid had not come from Mrs Trentham or one of her proxies. Two other institutions applied for five per cent: Prudential Assurance which had serviced the company from its outset, and a United States source which Becky discovered was simply a front for one of the Field family trusts. Charlie readily accepted both these applications and the rest of the shares were then divided between another one thousand seven hundred ordinary investors, including one hundred shares, the minimum allowed, which were taken up by an old-age pensioner living in Chelsea. Mrs Symonds had dropped Charlie a line to remind him that she had been one of his original customers when he opened his first shop.

Having distributed the shares, Tim Newman felt the next matter Charlie should consider was further appointments to the board. Hambros put up a Mr Baverstock, a senior partner of the solicitors Baverstock, Dickens and Cobb, whom Charlie accepted without question. Becky suggested that Simon Matthews, who virtually ran the auction house whenever she was absent, should also be appointed. Again Charlie acquiesced, bringing the full complement on the board to nine.

It was Daphne who told Becky that 17 Eaton Square was coming on the market, and Charlie only needed to see the eight-bedroomed house once before he decided that was where he wanted to spend the rest of his life. It didn't seem to cross Charlie's mind that someone would have to supervise the move at the same time as Trumper's was being built. Becky might have complained if she too hadn't fallen in love with the house.

A couple of months later Becky held a house-warming party at Eaton Square. Over a hundred guests were invited to join the Trumpers for a dinner that had to be served in five different rooms.

Daphne arrived late and complained about being held up in a traffic jam on her way back from Sloane Square, while the colonel travelled down from Skye without a murmur. Daniel came over from Cambridge accompanied by Marjorie Carpenter and to Becky's surprise Simon Matthews arrived with Cathy Ross on his arm.

After dinner, Daphne made a short speech and presented Charlie with a scale model of Trumper's crafted in the form of a silver cigar case.

Becky judged the gift to be a success because after the last guest had left, her husband carried the case upstairs and placed it on his bedside table.

Charlie climbed into bed and took one last look at his new toy as Becky came out of the bathroom.

"Have you considered inviting Percy to be a director?" she said as she climbed into bed.

Charlie looked across at her sceptically.

"The shareholders might appreciate having a marquess on the company letterhead. It would give them a feeling of confidence."

"You're such a snob, Rebecca Salmon. Always were and always will be."

"You didn't say that when I suggested the colonel should be our first chairman twenty-five years ago."

"True enough," said Charlie, "but I didn't think he'd say yes. In any case, if I wanted another outsider I'd rather have Daphne on the board. That way we get the name as well as her particular brand of common sense."

"I should have thought of that."

When Becky approached Daphne with an invitation to join the board of Trumper's as a non-executive director the

Marchioness was overwhelmed and accepted without a second thought. To everyone's surprise, Daphne approached her new responsibilities with immense energy and enthusiasm. She never missed a board meeting, always read the papers thoroughly and whenever she considered Charlie hadn't fully covered an item under discussion or, worse, was trying to get away with something, she nagged at him until she got a full explanation as to what he was up to.

"Are you still hoping to build Trumper's at the price you recommended in your original offer document, Mr Chairman?" she asked time and time again during the next two years.

"I'm not so sure it was a good idea of yours to invite Daphne to become a director," Charlie grumbled to Becky following one particularly raucous meeting in which the marchioness had got the better of him.

"Don't blame me," Becky replied. "I would have happily settled for Percy, but then I'm a snob."

It took nearly two years for the architects to complete the twin towers of Trumper's, their adjoining walkway and the five floors of offices above Mrs Trentham's empty space. The task was not made any easier by Charlie's expecting business in the remaining shops to proceed as if nothing was going on around them. It was a source of wonder to all concerned that during the changeover period Trumper's lost only nineteen per cent of its annual revenue.

Charlie set about supervising everything, from the exact siting of the one hundred and eighteen departments to the colour of the twenty-seven acres of carpet, from the speed of the twelve lifts to the wattage of the one hundred thousand light bulbs, from the displays in the ninety-six windows to the uniforms of over seven hundred employees, each of whom displayed a little silver barrow on their lapel.

Once Charlie realised how much storage space he would need, not to mention facilities for an underground car park now so many customers had their own vehicles, the costs went considerably over budget. However, the contractors somehow managed to complete the building by 1 September 1949, mainly because Charlie appeared on the site at four thirty every morning and often didn't leave to go back home much before midnight.

On 18 October 1949 the Marchioness of Wiltshire, escorted by her husband, performed the official opening ceremony.

A thousand people raised their glasses once Daphne had declared the building open. The assembled guests then did their best to eat and drink their way through the company's first year's profits. But Charlie didn't seem to notice; he moved happily from floor to floor checking that everything was exactly as he expected it to be and made sure that the major suppliers were being properly looked after.

Friends, relations, shareholders, buyers, sellers, journalists, hangers-on, gatecrashers and even customers were celebrating on every floor. By one o'clock Becky was so tired that she decided to start looking for her husband in the hope that he might agree to go home. She found her son in the kitchen department examining a refrigerator that would have been too large for his room in Trinity. Daniel assured his mother that he had seen Charlie leaving the building about half an hour before.

"Leaving the building?" Becky said, in disbelief. "Surely your father wouldn't have gone home without me?" She took the lift to the ground floor and walked quickly towards the main entrance. The doorman saluted her as he held open one of the massive double doors that led out on to Chelsea Terrace.

"Have you seen Sir Charles, by any chance?" Becky asked him.

"Yes, m'lady." He nodded in the direction of the far side of the road.

Becky looked across to see Charlie seated on his bench, an old man perched by his side. They were chatting animatedly as they stared across at Trumper's. The old man pointed at something that had attracted his attention and

Charlie smiled. Becky quickly crossed the road but the colonel had sprung to attention long before she had reached his side.

"How lovely to see you, my dear," he said as he leaned forward to kiss Becky on the cheek. "I only wish Elizabeth had lived to see it."

"As I understand it, we're being held to ransom," said Charlie. "So perhaps it's time we took a vote on the issue."

Becky looked around the boardroom table, wondering which way the vote would fall. The full board had been working together for three months since Trumper's had opened its doors to the public, but this was the first major issue on which there had been any real disagreement.

Charlie sat at the head of the table, looking unusually irritable at the thought of not getting his own way. On his right was the company secretary, Jessica Allen. Jessica did not have a vote but was there to see that whenever there was one it would be faithfully recorded. Arthur Selwyn, who had worked with Charlie at the Ministry of Food during the war, had recently left the civil service to replace Tom Arnold on his retirement as managing director. Selwyn was proving to be an inspired choice, shrewd and thorough, while being the ideal foil to the chairman as he tended to avoid confrontation whenever possible.

Tim Newman, the company's young merchant banker, was sociable and friendly and almost always backed Charlie, though he was not averse to giving a contrary view if he felt the company finances might suffer. Paul Merrick, the finance director, was neither sociable nor friendly and continued to make it abundantly clear that his first loyalty would always be to Child's Bank and its investment. As for Daphne, she rarely voted the way anyone might expect her to, and certainly was no placeman for Charlie – or anyone else, for that matter. Mr Baverstock, a quiet, elderly solicitor who represented ten per cent of the company stock on behalf of Hambros, spoke rarely, but when he did everyone listened, including Daphne.

Ned Denning and Bob Makins, both of whom had now served Charlie for nearly thirty years, would rarely go against their chairman's wishes, while Simon Matthews often showed flashes of independence that only confirmed Becky's initial high opinion of him.

"The last thing we need at the moment is a strike," said Merrick. "Just at a time when it looks as if we've turned the corner."

"But the union's demands are simply outrageous," said Tim Newman. "A ten-shilling rise, a forty-four-hour week, before overtime becomes automatic – I repeat, they're outrageous."

"Most of the other major stores have already agreed to those terms," interjected Merrick, consulting an article from the *Financial Times* that lay in front of him.

"Chucked the towel in would be nearer the mark," came back Newman. "I must warn the board that this would add to our wages bill by some twenty thousand pounds for the current year – and that's even before we start to consider overtime. So there's only one group of people who will suffer in the long run, and that's our share-holders."

"Just how much does a counter assistant earn nowadays?" asked Mr Baverstock quietly.

"Two hundred and sixty pounds a year," said Arthur Selwyn without having to check. "With incremental rises so that if they have completed fifteen years' service with the company, the sum could be as high as four hundred and ten pounds a year."

"We've been over these figures on countless occasions," said Charlie sharply. "The time has come to decide – do we stand firm or just give in to the union's demands?"

"Perhaps we're all overreacting, Mr Chairman," said Daphne, who hadn't spoken until then. "It may not prove to be quite as black or white as you imagine."

"You have an alternative solution?" Charlie made no attempt to hide his incredulity.

"I might have, Mr Chairman. First, let's consider

what's at stake if we do give our staff the rise. An obvious drain on resources, not to mention what the Japanese would call 'face'. On the other hand, if we don't agree to their demands, it's possible that we might lose some of the better as well as the weaker brethren to one of our main rivals."

"So what are you suggesting, Lady Wiltshire?" asked Charlie, who always addressed Daphne by her title whenever he wished to show he didn't agree with her.

"Compromise, perhaps," replied Daphne, refusing to rise. "If Mr Selwyn considers that to be at all possible at this late stage. Would the trade unions, for example, be willing to contemplate an alternative proposal on wages and hours, drawn up in negotiation with our managing director?"

"I could always have a word with Don Short, the leader of USDAW, if the board so wishes," said Arthur Selwyn. "In the past I've always found him a decent, fair-minded man and he's certainly shown a consistent loyalty to Trumper's over the years."

"The managing director dealing direct with the trade union's representative?" barked Charlie. "Next you'll want to put him on the board."

"Then perhaps Mr Selwyn should make an informal approach," said Daphne. "I'm confident *he* can handle Mr Short with consummate skill."

"I agree with Lady Wiltshire," said Mr Baverstock.

"Then I propose that we allow Mr Selwyn to negotiate on our behalf," continued Daphne. "And let's hope he can find a way of avoiding an all-out strike without actually giving in to everything the unions are demanding."

"I'd certainly be willing to have a try," said Selwyn. "I could report back to the board at our next meeting."

Once again Becky admired the way Daphne and Arthur Selwyn between them had defused a time-bomb the chairman would have been only too happy to let explode on the boardroom table.

"Thank you, Arthur," Charlie said a little begrudgingly. "So be it. Any other business?"

"Yes," said Becky. "I would like to bring to the board's attention a sale of Georgian silver that will be taking place next month. Catalogues will be sent out during the coming week and I do hope any directors who are free on that particular day will try to attend."

"How did the last antiques sale work out?" asked Mr Baverstock.

Becky checked her file. "The auction raised twenty-four thousand seven hundred pounds, of which Trumper's kept seven and a half per cent of everything that came under the hammer. Only three items failed to reach their reserve prices, and they were called back in."

"I'm only curious about the success of the sale," said Mr Baverstock, "because my dear wife purchased a Charles II court cupboard."

"One of the finest items in the sale," said Becky.

"My wife certainly thought so because she bid far more for the piece than she had intended. I'd be obliged if you didn't send her a catalogue for the silver sale."

The other members of the board laughed.

"I've read somewhere," said Tim Newman, "that Sotheby's are considering raising their commission to ten per cent."

"I know," said Becky. "That's exactly why I can't contemplate the same move for at least another year. If I'm to go on stealing their best customers I must stay competitive in the short term."

Newman nodded his understanding.

"However," Becky continued, "by remaining at seven and a half per cent, my profits for 1950 won't be as high as I might have hoped. But until the leading sellers are willing to come to us, that's a problem I'll continue to face."

"What about the buyers?" queried Paul Merrick.

"They aren't the problem. If you have the product to sell, the buyers will always beat a path to your door. You see, it's the sellers that are the life-blood of an auction house, and they're every bit as important as the buyers."

"Funny old outfit you're running," said Charlie with a grin. "Any other business?"

As no one spoke, Charlie thanked all the members of the board for their attendance and rose from his place, a signal he always gave to indicate that the meeting was finally over.

Becky collected up her papers and started walking back to the gallery with Simon.

"Have you completed your estimates on the silver sale yet?" she asked as they jumped into the lift just before the doors closed. She touched the "G" and the lift began its slow journey to the ground floor.

"Yes. Finished them last night. One hundred and thirty-two items in all. I reckon they might raise somewhere in the region of seven thousand pounds."

"I saw the catalogue for the first time this morning," said Becky. "It looks to me as if Cathy has done another first-class job. I was only able to pick up one or two minor errors but I'd still like to check over the final proofs before they go back to the printer."

"Of course," said Simon. "I'll ask her to bring all the loose sheets up to your office this afternoon." They stepped out of the lift.

"That girl has turned out to be a real find," said Becky. "Heaven knows what she was doing working in a hotel before she came to us. I shall certainly miss her when she goes back to Australia."

"Rumour has it that she's thinking of staying."

"That's good news," said Becky. "I thought she was only hoping to spend a couple of years in London before she returned to Melbourne?"

"That's what she had originally planned. However, I may have been able to convince her that she should stay on a little longer."

Becky would have asked Simon to explain in greater detail but once they had set foot in the gallery she was quickly surrounded by staff anxious to gain her attention.

After Becky had dealt with several queries, she asked

one of the girls who worked on the counter if she could locate Cathy.

"She's not actually around at the moment, Lady Trumper," the assistant told her. "I saw her go out about an hour ago."

"Do you know where she went?"

"No idea, I'm sorry."

"Well, ask her to come to my office the moment she returns. Meanwhile, could you send up those catalogue proofs for the silver sale?"

Becky stopped several times on the way back to her room to discuss other gallery problems that had arisen in her absence, so that by the time she sat down at her desk, the proofs for the silver sale were already awaiting her. She began to turn the pages slowly, checking each entry against its photograph and then the detailed description. She was studying the photograph of the Georgian mustard pot that Charlie had overbid for at Christie's some years before when there was a knock on the door and a young woman popped her head in.

"You asked to see me?"

"Yes. Do come in, Cathy." Becky looked up at a tall, slim girl with a mass of curly fair hair and a face that hadn't quite lost all its freckles. She liked to think that her own figure had once been as good as Cathy's but the bathroom mirror unflatteringly reminded her that she was fast approaching her fiftieth birthday. "I only wanted to check over the final catalogue proofs for the silver sale before they went back to the printer."

"I'm sorry I wasn't around when you returned from the board meeting," Cathy said. "It's just that something's come up that worried me. I may be overreacting, but I felt you ought to know about it in any case."

Becky took off her glasses, placed them on the desk and looked up intently. "I'm listening."

"Do you remember that man who stood up during the Italian auction and caused all that trouble over the Bronzino?"

"Will I ever forget him?"

"Well, he was in the gallery again this morning."

"Can you be sure?"

"I'm fairly confident. Well-built, greying hair, a brownish moustache and sallow complexion. He even had the nerve to wear that awful tweed jacket and yellow tie again."

"What did he want this time?"

"I can't be certain of that, although I kept a close eye on him. He didn't speak to any member of the staff, but took a great deal of interest in some of the items that were coming up in the silver sale – in particular lot nineteen."

Becky replaced her glasses and turned the catalogue pages over quickly until she came to the item in question: "A Georgian silver tea-set made up of four pieces, teapot, sugar bowl, tea strainer and sugar tongs, hallmarked with an anchor." Becky looked down at the letters "AH" printed in the margin. "Estimated value seventy pounds. One of our better items."

"And he obviously agrees with you," Cathy replied, "because he spent a considerable time studying each individual piece, then made copious notes before he left. He even checked the teapot against a photograph he had brought with him."

"Our photograph?"

"No, he seemed to have one of his own."

"Did he now?" said Becky· as she rechecked the catalogue photo.

"And the reason I wasn't around when you came back from the board meeting was because when he left the gallery I decided to follow him.

"Quick thinking," said Becky, smiling. "And where did our mystery man disappear to?"

"Ended up in Chester Square," said Cathy. "A large house halfway down on the right-hand side. He dropped a package through the letter-box but didn't go in."

"Number 19?"

"That's right," said Cathy, looking surprised. "Do you know the house?"

"Only from the outside," said Becky without explanation.

"Is there anything else I can do to help?"

"Yes, there is. To start with, can you remember anything about the customer who brought that particular lot in for sale?"

"Certainly can," replied Cathy, "because I was called to the front desk to deal with the lady." She paused for a moment before adding, "Can't remember her name but she was elderly and rather – genteel is the way I think you would describe her." Cathy hesitated then continued, "As I remember, she had taken a day trip down from Nottingham. She told me that she'd been left the tea-set by her mother. She didn't want to sell a family heirloom but 'needs must'. I remember that expression, because I'd never heard it before."

"And what was Mr Fellowes's opinion when you showed him the set?"

"As fine an example of the period as he'd seen come under the hammer – each piece is still in almost mint condition. Peter's convinced the lot will fetch a good price, as you can see from his estimate."

"Then we'd better call in the police straight away," said Becky. "We don't need our mystery man standing up again announcing that this particular item has been stolen too."

She picked up the telephone on her desk and asked to be put through to Scotland Yard. A few moments later an Inspector Deakins of the CID came on the line and, having listened to the details of what had taken place that morning, agreed to come round to the gallery during the afternoon.

The inspector arrived a little after three, accompanied by a sergeant. Becky took them both straight through to meet the head of the department. Peter Fellowes pointed to a minute scratch he had come across on a silver salver. Becky frowned. He stopped what he was doing and walked over to the centre table where the four-piece tea-set was already out on display.

"Beautiful," said the inspector as he bent over and checked the hallmark. "Birmingham around 1820 would be my guess."

Becky raised an eyebrow.

"It's my hobby," the inspector explained. "That's probably why I always end up getting these jobs." He removed a file from the briefcase he was carrying and checked through several photographs along with detailed written descriptions of recently missing pieces of silverware from the London area. An hour later he had to agree with Fellowes: none of them fitted the description of the Georgian tea-set.

"Well, we've had nothing else reported as stolen that matches up with this particular lot," he admitted. "And you've polished them so superbly," he said, turning to Cathy, "that there's no hope of our identifying any prints."

"Sorry," said Cathy, blushing slightly.

"No, miss, it's not your fault, you've done a fine job. I only wish my little pieces looked so good. Still, I'd better check with the Nottingham police in case they have something on their files. If they haven't, I'll issue a description to all forces throughout the United Kingdom, just in case. And I'll also ask them to check on Mrs . . . ?"

"Dawson," said Cathy.

"Yes, Mrs Dawson. That may take a little time, of course, but I'll come back to you the moment I hear anything."

"Meanwhile our sale takes place three weeks next Tuesday," Becky reminded the inspector.

"Right, I'll try and give you the all-clear by then," he promised.

"Should we leave that page in the catalogue, or would you prefer the pieces to be withdrawn?" asked Cathy.

"Oh, no, don't withdraw anything. Please leave the catalogue exactly as it is. You see, someone might recognise the set and then get in touch with us."

Someone has already recognised the set, thought Becky.

"While you're at it," continued the inspector, "I'd be obliged if you could give me a copy of the catalogue picture, as well as use of one of the negatives for a day or two."

When Charlie was told about the Georgian tea-set over dinner that night, his advice was simple: withdraw the pieces from the sale – and promote Cathy.

"Your first suggestion isn't quite that easy," said Becky. "The catalogue is due to be sent out to the general public later this week. What explanation could we possibly give to Mrs Dawson for removing her dear old mother's family heirloom?"

"That it wasn't her dear old mother's in the first place and you withdrew it because you've every reason to believe that it's stolen property."

"If we did that, we could find ourselves being sued for breach of contract," said Becky, "when we later discover that Mrs Dawson's totally innocent of any such charge. If she then took us to court we wouldn't have a leg to stand on."

"If this Dawson lady is as totally innocent as you think, then why is Mrs Trentham showing such an interest in her tea-set? Because I can't help feeling she already has one of her own."

Becky laughed. "She certainly has. I know, because I've even seen it, though I never did get the promised cup of tea."

Three days later Inspector Deakins telephoned Becky to let her know that the Nottingham police had no record of anything that had been stolen in their patch fitting the tea-set's description and they were also able to confirm that Mrs Dawson was not previously known to them. He had therefore sent the details out to every other constabulary in the land. "But," he added, "outside forces aren't always that co-operative with the Met when it comes to trading information."

As Becky put the phone down, she decided to give the green light and send the catalogues out, despite Charlie's apprehension. They were posted the same day along with invitations to the press and selected customers.

A couple of journalists applied for tickets to the sale. An unusually sensitive Becky checked them out, only to find that both worked for national newspapers, and had covered Trumper's sales several times in the past.

Simon Matthews considered that Becky was over-reacting, while Cathy tended to agree with Sir Charles that the wise course would be to withdraw the tea-set from the auction until they had been given the all-clear by Deakins.

"If we're to withdraw a lot every time that man takes an interest in one of our sales we may as well close our front doors and take up star-gazing," Simon told them.

The Monday before the sale was to take place Inspector Deakins telephoned to ask if he could see Becky urgently. He arrived at the gallery thirty minutes later, again accompanied by his sergeant. This time the only item he removed from his briefcase was a copy of the Aberdeen *Evening Express* dated 15 October 1949.

Deakins asked to be allowed to inspect the Georgian tea-set once more. Becky nodded her agreement and the policeman studied each piece carefully against a photograph that was on an inside page of the newspaper.

"That's them all right," he said, after double-checking. He showed Becky the photograph.

Cathy and Peter Fellowes also studied each item while looking carefully at the picture from the newspaper and had to agree with Deakins that the match was perfect.

"This little lot was stolen from the Aberdeen Museum of Silver some three months ago," the inspector informed them. "The bloody local police didn't even bother to let us know. No doubt they considered it was none of our business."

"So what happens now?" asked Becky.

"The Nottingham constabulary have already visited Mrs Dawson, where they found several other pieces of silver and jewellery hidden around the house. She's been taken to her local station in order to, as the press would have it, help the police with their enquiries." He placed the newspaper back in his briefcase. "After I've phoned them back to confirm my piece of news, I expect that she'll be charged later today. However, I'm afraid I shall have to take the tea-set away with me for processing at Scotland Yard."

"Of course," said Becky.

"My sergeant will write out a receipt for you, Lady Trumper, and I'd like to thank you for your co-operation." The inspector hesitated as he looked lovingly at the tea-set. "A month's salary," he said with a sigh, "and stolen for all the wrong reasons." He raised his hat and the two policemen left the gallery.

"So what do we do now?" said Cathy.

"Not much we can do," Becky sighed. "Carry on with the auction as if nothing had taken place and when the lot comes up, simply announce that the piece has been withdrawn."

"But then our man will leap up and say, 'Isn't this yet another example of advertising stolen goods and then having to withdraw them at the last moment?' We won't look so much like an auction house," said Simon, his voice rising with anger. "More like a pawnbroker. So why don't we just put three balls outside the front door, and a fence to give a clue as to the class of person we're hoping to attract?"

Becky didn't react.

"If you feel so strongly about it, Simon, why not try and turn the whole episode to our advantage?" suggested Cathy.

"What do you mean?" asked Becky as both she and Simon swung round to face the young Australian.

"We must get the press on our side for a change."

"I'm not sure I understand what you're getting at."

"Phone that journalist from the *Telegraph* – what was his name? Barker – and give him the inside story."

"What good would that do?" asked Becky.

"He'll have our version of what happened this time, and he'll be only too pleased to be the one journalist on the inside, especially after that fiasco with the Bronzino."

"Do you think he'd be at all interested in a silver set worth seventy pounds?"

"With a Scottish museum involved and a professional fence arrested in Nottingham? He'll be interested all right. Especially if we don't tell anyone else."

"Would you like to handle Mr Barker yourself, Cathy?" Becky asked.

"Just give me the chance."

The following morning, the *Daily Telegraph* had a small but prominent piece on page three reporting that Trumper's, the fine art auctioneers, had called in the police after they had become suspicious about the ownership of a Georgian tea-set that was later discovered to have been stolen from the Aberdeen Museum of Silver. The Nottingham police had since arrested a woman whom they later charged with handling stolen goods. The article went on to say that Inspector Deakins of Scotland Yard had told the *Telegraph*: "We only wish every auction house and gallery in London were as conscientious as Trumper's."

The sale that afternoon was well attended, and despite losing one of the centre-pieces of the auction Trumper's still managed to exceed several of the estimates. The man in the tweed coat and yellow tie didn't make an appearance.

When Charlie read the *Telegraph* in bed that night he remarked, "So you didn't take my advice?"

"Yes and no," said Becky. "I admit I didn't withdraw the tea-set immediately, but I did promote Cathy."

CHAPTER 37

O n 9 November 1950 Trumper's held their second AGM. The directors met at ten o'clock in the boardroom so that Arthur Selwyn could take them slowly through the procedure he intended to follow once they faced the shareholders.

At eleven o'clock sharp he guided the chairman and his eight directors out of the boardroom and into the main hall as if they were school children being led in a crocodile on their way to morning assembly.

Charlie introduced each member of the board to the assembled gathering, who numbered around one hundred and twenty – a respectable turn-out for such an occasion, Tim Newman whispered in Becky's ear. Charlie went through the agenda without a prompt from his managing director and was only asked one awkward question. "Why have your costs gone so much over budget in the first full year of trading?"

Arthur Selwyn rose to explain that the expense of the building had exceeded their original estimate and launching had incurred certain one-off costs which would not arise again. He also pointed out that strictly on a trading basis Trumper's had managed to break even in the first quarter of their second year. He added that he remained confident about the year ahead, especially with the anticipated rise in the number of tourists attracted to London by the Festival of Britain. However, he warned shareholders it might be necessary for the company to raise more capital, if they hoped to increase their facilities.

When Charlie declared the AGM closed he remained seated because the board received a small ovation, which quite took the chairman by surprise.

Becky was about to return to Number 1 and continue with her work on an Impressionist sale she had planned for the spring when Mr Baverstock came over and touched her gently on the elbow.

"May I have a word with you in private, Lady Trumper?"

"Of course, Mr Baverstock." Becky looked around for a quiet spot where they could talk.

"I feel that perhaps my office in High Holborn would be more appropriate," he suggested. "You see, it's a rather delicate matter. Would tomorrow, three o'clock suit you?"

Daniel had phoned from Cambridge that morning and Becky couldn't remember when she had heard him sounding so chatty and full of news. She, on the other hand, was not chatty or full of news: she still hadn't been able to fathom why the senior partner of Baverstock, Dickens and Cobb should want to see her on "a rather delicate matter".

She couldn't believe that Mr Baverstock's wife wanted to return the Charles II court cupboard or required more details on the forthcoming Impressionist sale, but as in her case anxiety always ruled over optimism, Becky spent the next twenty-six hours fearing the worst.

She didn't burden Charlie with her troubles, because the little she did know of Mr Baverstock made her certain that if her husband were involved the lawyer would have asked to see them both. In any case, Charlie had quite enough problems of his own to deal with without being weighed down with hers.

Becky couldn't manage any lunch and arrived at the solicitor's office a few minutes before the appointed hour. She was ushered straight through to Mr Baverstock's rooms.

She was greeted with a warm smile by her fellow-director, as if she were some minor relation of his large family. He offered her the seat opposite his on the other side of a large mahogany desk.

Mr Baverstock, Becky decided, must have been about fifty-five, perhaps sixty, with a round, friendly face and the few strands of grey hair that were left were parted neatly down the centre. His dark jacket, waistcoat, grey striped trousers and black tie could have been worn by any solicitor who practised within five square miles of the building in which they now sat. Having returned to his own chair he began to study the pile of documents that lay in front of him before removing his half-moon spectacles.

"Lady Trumper," he began. "It's most kind of you to come and see me." In the two years they had known each other he had never once addressed her by her christian name.

"I shall," he continued, "come straight to the point. One of my clients was the late Sir Raymond Hardcastle." Becky wondered why he had never mentioned this fact before and was about to protest when Mr Baverstock quickly added, "but I hasten to say that Mrs Gerald Trentham is not and never has been a client of this firm."

Becky made no effort to disguise her relief.

"I must also let you know that I had the privilege of serving Sir Raymond for over thirty years and indeed considered myself not only to be his legal advisor but towards the end of his life a close friend. I tell you this as background information, Lady Trumper, for you may feel such facts are relevant when you've heard all that I have to say."

Becky nodded, still waiting for Mr Baverstock to get to the point.

"Some years before he died," continued the solicitor, "Sir Raymond drew up a will. In it he divided the income from his estate between his two daughters – an income, I might add, that has grown considerably since his death, thanks to some prudent investment on his behalf. The elder of his daughters was Miss Amy Hardcastle, and the younger, as I feel sure you know, Mrs Gerald Trentham. The income from the estate has been sufficient to give both these ladies a standard of living equal to, if not considerably higher, than the one to which they had grown accustomed to before his death. However – "

Will dear Mr Baverstock ever get to the point? Becky was beginning to wonder.

"– Sir Raymond decided, in his wisdom, that the share capital should remain intact, after he allowed the firm that his father had founded and he had built up so successfully to merge with one of his greatest rivals. You see, Lady Trumper, Sir Raymond felt there was no member of the family who could obviously fill his shoes as the next chairman of Hardcastle's. Neither of his two daughters, or his grandsons for that matter – of whom I shall have more to say in a moment – did he consider competent to run a public company."

The solicitor removed his glasses, cleaned them with a handkerchief which he took out of his top pocket and peered through the lenses critically before returning to the task at hand.

"Sir Raymond, you see, had no illusions about his immediate kith and kin. His elder daughter, Amy, was a gentle, shy lady who nursed her father valiantly through his final years. When Sir Raymond died she moved out of the family house into a small seaside hotel where she resided until her death last year.

"His younger daughter, Ethel Trentham," he continued, "let me put this as delicately as I can – Sir Raymond considered had perhaps lost touch with reality and certainly she no longer acknowledged any attachment to her past. Anyway, I know it particularly saddened the old man not to have produced a son of his own, so when Guy was born his hopes for the future became focused on the young grandson. From that day he lavished everything on him. Later he was to blame himself for the boy's eventual downfall. He did not make the same mistake when Nigel was born, a child for whom he had neither affection nor respect.

"However, this firm was instructed to keep Sir Raymond briefed at all times with any information that came into our hands concerning members of his immediate family. Thus when Captain Trentham resigned his commission in 1922, somewhat abruptly, we were asked to try to find out the real cause behind his leaving the colours. Sir Raymond certainly did not accept his daughter's story about an appointment as a partner with an Australian cattle broker, and indeed at one stage was sufficiently concerned that he even contemplated sending me to that continent to find out the real story. Then Guy died."

Becky sat in her chair wanting to wind Mr Baverstock up like a gramophone and set him going well above 78 rpm, but she had already come to the conclusion that nothing she said was going to accelerate him along the track he had set himself.

"The result of our investigations," continued Baverstock, "led us to believe – and at this point, Lady Trumper, I must apologise for any indelicacy, for I do not intend to offend – that Guy Trentham and not Charles Trumper was the father of your child."

Becky bowed her head and Mr Baverstock apologised once again before he continued.

"Sir Raymond, however, needed to be convinced that Daniel was his great-grandson, and to that end he made two separate visits to St Paul's after the boy had won a scholarship to that school."

Becky stared at the old lawyer.

"On the first occasion he watched the boy perform in a school concert – Brahms, if I remember correctly – and on a second saw Daniel receive the Newton Prize for Mathematics from the High Master on Founders' Day. I believe you were also present on that occasion. On both visits Sir Raymond went out of his way to be sure that the boy was unaware of his presence. After the second visit, Sir Raymond was totally convinced that Daniel was his great-grandchild. I'm afraid all the men in that family are stuck with that Hardcastle jaw, not to mention a tendency to sway from foot to foot when agitated. Sir Raymond accordingly altered his will the following day."

The solicitor picked up a document bound in a pink ribbon which lay on his desk. He untied the ribbon slowly. "I was instructed, madam, to read the relevant clauses of his will to you at a time I considered appropriate but not until the boy had celebrated his thirtieth birthday. Daniel was thirty a few weeks ago, if I am not mistaken."

Becky nodded.

Baverstock acknowledged the nod and slowly unfolded the stiff sheets of parchment.

"I have already explained to you the arrangements concerning the disposal of Sir Raymond's estate. However, since Miss Amy's death Mrs Trentham has had the full benefit of any interest earned from the Trust, now amounting to some forty thousand pounds a year. At no time to my knowledge did Sir Raymond make any provision for his elder grandson, Mr Guy Trentham, but since he is now deceased that has become irrelevant. Subsequently he made a small settlement on his other grandson, Mr Nigel Trentham." He paused. "And now I must quote Sir Raymond's exact words," he said, looking down at the will. He cleared his throat before continuing.

"After all other commitments have been honoured and bills paid, I leave the residue of my messuage and estate to Mr Daniel Trumper of Trinity College, Cambridge, the full benefit of which will come into his possession on the death of his grandmother, Mrs Gerald Trentham."

Now that the lawyer had at last come to the point Becky was stunned into silence. Mr Baverstock paused for a moment in case Becky wished to say something, but as she suspected that there was still more to be revealed she remained silent. The lawyer's eyes returned to the papers in front of him.

"I feel I should add at this point that I am aware – as

indeed Sir Raymond was – of the treatment you have suffered at the hands both of his grandson and his daughter, so I must also let you know that although this bequest to your son will be considerable, it does not include the farm at Ashurst in Berkshire or the house in Chester Square. Both properties, since the death of her husband, are now owned by Mrs Gerald Trentham. Nor does it include – and I suspect this is of more importance to you – the vacant land in the centre of Chelsea Terrace, which forms no part of Sir Raymond's estate. However, everything else he controlled will eventually be inherited by Daniel, although, as I explained, not until Mrs Trentham has herself passed away."

"Is she aware of all this?"

"Indeed, Mrs Trentham was made fully conversant with the provisions in her father's will some time before his death. She even took advice as to whether the new clauses inserted after Sir Raymond's visits to St Paul's could be contested."

"Did that result in any legal action?"

"No. On the contrary, she quite suddenly, and I must confess inexplicably, instructed her lawyers to withdraw any objections. But whatever the outcome, Sir Raymond stipulated most clearly that the capital could never be used or controlled by either of his daughters. That was to be the privilege of his next of kin."

Mr Baverstock paused and placed both palms down on the blotting paper in front of him.

"Now I will finally have to tell him," murmured Becky under her breath.

"I feel that may well be the case, Lady Trumper. Indeed, the purpose of this meeting was to brief you fully. Sir Raymond was never quite sure if you had informed Daniel who his father was."

"No, we never have."

Baverstock removed his glasses and placed them on the desk. "Please take your time, dear lady, and just let me know when I have your permission to contact your son and acquaint him with his good fortune."

"Thank you," said Becky quietly, sensing the inadequacy of her words.

"Finally," said Mr Baverstock, "I must also let you know that Sir Raymond became a great admirer of your husband and his work, indeed of your partnership together. So much so that he left a recommendation with this office that, were Trumper's ever to go public, which he anticipated they would, we were to invest a sizeable stake in the new company. He was convinced that such an enterprise could only flourish and therefore prove to be a first-class investment."

"So that's why Hambros invested ten per cent when we went public," said Becky. "We always wondered."

"Precisely," Mr Baverstock added with a smile, almost of satisfaction. "It was on my specific instructions that Hambros applied for the shares on behalf of the Trust, so that there could never be any reason for your husband to be apprehensive about such a large outside shareholder.

"The amount was in fact considerably less than the estate received from dividends during that year. However, more important, we were aware from the offer documents that it was Sir Charles's intention to retain fifty-one per cent of the company, and we therefore felt it might be some relief for him to know that he would have a further ten per cent under his indirect control should any unforeseen problem arise at some time in the future. I can only hope that you feel we have acted in your best interests, as it was always Sir Raymond's wish that you should be told the full facts at a time that I considered appropriate, the only stipulation as I have already explained was that such information was not to be revealed to your son before his thirtieth birthday."

"You couldn't have been more considerate, Mr Baverstock," said Becky. "I know Charlie will want to thank you personally."

"That is most kind of you, Lady Trumper. May I also add that this meeting has been a genuine delight for me. Like Sir Raymond, I have had considerable pleasure over the years in following the careers of all three of you, and I am delighted to be playing a small part in the company's future."

Having completed his task, Mr Baverstock rose from his side of the desk and accompanied Becky silently to the front door of the building. Becky began to wonder if the solicitor spoke only when he had a brief.

"I shall wait to hear from you, dear lady, as to when I may be permitted to contact your son."

CHAPTER 38

The weekend after Becky's visit to Mr Baverstock she and Charlie drove to Cambridge to see Daniel. Charlie had insisted that they could procrastinate no longer and had telephoned Daniel that evening to warn him that they were coming up to Trinity as there was something of importance they needed to tell him. On hearing this piece of news Daniel had replied, "Good, because I've also got something rather important to tell you."

On the journey to Cambridge, Becky and Charlie rehearsed what they would say and how they were going to say it; but still came to the conclusion that however carefully they tried to explain what had happened in the past, they could not anticipate how Daniel would react.

"I wonder if he'll ever forgive us?" said Becky. "You know, we should have told him years ago."

"But we didn't."

"And now we're only letting him know at a time when it could be to our financial benefit."

"And ultimately to his. After all, he'll eventually inherit ten per cent of the company, not to mention the entire Hardcastle estate. We'll just have to see how he takes the news and react accordingly." Charlie accelerated when he came to a stretch of dual carriageway. For some time neither of them spoke until Charlie suggested, "Let's go through the order once again. You'll start by telling him how you first met Guy –"

"Perhaps he already knows," said Becky.

"Then he surely would have asked –"

"Not necessarily. He's always been so secretive in the past, especially when dealing with us."

The rehearsal continued until they had reached the outskirts of the city.

Charlie drove slowly down the Backs past Queens' College, avoiding a bunch of undergraduates who had strayed on to the road, and finally right into Trinity Lane. He brought his car to a halt in New Court and he and Becky walked across to entrance C and on up the worn stone staircase until they reached the door with "Doctor Daniel Trumper" painted above it. It always amused Becky that she hadn't even discovered that her son had been awarded his PhD until someone addressed him as Doctor Trumper in her presence.

Charlie gripped his wife's hand. "Don't worry, Becky," he said. "Everything will be all right, you'll see." He gave her fingers a squeeze before knocking firmly on Daniel's door.

"Come on in," shouted a voice that could only have been Daniel's. The next moment he pulled open the heavy oak door to greet them. He gave his mother a huge hug before ushering them both through to his untidy little study where tea was already laid out on a table in the centre of the room.

Charlie and Becky sat down in two of the large and battered leather chairs the college had provided. They had probably been owned by the past six inhabitants of the room, and brought back memories for Becky of the chair that she had once removed from Charlie's home in Whitechapel Road and sold for a shilling.

Daniel poured them both a cup of tea and began to toast a crumpet over the open fire. Nobody spoke for some time and Becky wondered where her son had come across such a modern cashmere sweater.

"Good journey down?" Daniel asked eventually.

"Not bad," said Charlie.

"And how's the new car running in?"

"Fine."

"And Trumper's?"

"Could be worse."

"Quite a little conversationalist, aren't you, Dad? You ought to apply for the recently vacated chair of Professor of English."

"Sorry, Daniel," said his mother. "It's just that he's got rather a lot on his mind at the moment, not least the subject we have to discuss with you."

"Couldn't be better timing," said Daniel, turning the crumpet over.

"Why's that?" asked Charlie.

"Because, as I warned you, there's something rather important I have to discuss with you. So – who goes first?"

"Let's hear your news," said Becky quickly.

"No, I think it might be wise if we went first," Charlie intervened.

"Suits me." Daniel dropped a toasted crumpet on to his mother's plate. "Butter, jam and honey," he added, pointing to three small dishes that rested on the table in front of her.

"Thank you, darling," said Becky.

"Get on with it then, Dad. The tension's becoming too much for me to bear." He turned a second crumpet over.

"Well, my news concerns a matter we should have told you about many years ago and indeed would have done so only –"

"Crumpet, Dad?"

"Thank you," said Charlie, ignoring the steaming offering that Daniel dropped on to his plate "– circumstances and a chain of events somehow stopped us from getting round to it."

Daniel placed a third crumpet on the end of his long toasting fork. "Eat up, Mum," he said. "Otherwise yours will only get cold. In any case, there'll be another one on its way soon."

"I'm not all that hungry," admitted Becky.

"Well, as I was saying," said Charlie. "A problem has arisen concerning a large inheritance that you will eventually –"

There was a knock on the door. Becky looked desperately towards Charlie, hoping that the interruption was nothing more than a message that could be dealt with quickly. What they didn't need at that moment was an undergraduate with an interminable problem. Daniel rose from the fender and went over to the door.

"Come in, darling," they heard him say and Charlie stood up as Daniel's guest entered the room.

"How nice to see you, Cathy," Charlie said. "I had no idea you were going to be in Cambridge today."

"Isn't that typical of Daniel," said Cathy. "I wanted to warn you both, but he wouldn't hear of it." She smiled nervously at Becky.

Becky glanced across at the two of them seated next to each other – something worried her.

"Pour yourself some tea, darling," said Daniel. "You're just in time for the next crumpet and you couldn't have arrived at a more exciting moment. Dad was just about to let me into the secret of how much I might expect to be left in his will. Am I to inherit the Trumper empire or shall I have to be satisfied with his season ticket to the West Ham Football Club?"

"Oh, I'm so sorry," said Cathy, half rising from her seat.

"No, no," said Charlie, waving her back down. "Don't be silly, it wasn't that important. Our news can wait until later."

"They're very hot, so watch it," said Daniel, dropping a crumpet on to Cathy's plate. "Well, if my inheritance is of such monumental insignificance then I shall have to impart my own little piece of news first. Roll of drums, curtain up, opening line" – Daniel raised the toasting fork as if it were a baton – "Cathy and I are engaged to be married."

"I don't believe it," said Becky, immediately springing

up from her chair to hug Cathy in delight. "What wonderful news."

"How long has this been going on?" asked Charlie. "I must have been blind."

"Nearly two years," admitted Daniel. "And to be fair, Dad, even you couldn't expect to have a telescope capable of focusing on Cambridge every weekend. I'll let you into another little secret: Cathy wouldn't allow me to tell you until Mum had invited her to join the management committee."

"As someone who's always been a dealer, my boy," said Charlie beaming, "I can tell you you've got the better of this bargain." Daniel grinned. "In fact, I think Cathy's probably been short-changed. But when did all this happen?"

"We met at your house-warming party nearly eighteen months ago. You won't remember, Sir Charles, but we bumped into each other on the stairs," Cathy said, nervously fingering the little cross that hung around her neck.

"Of course I remember, and please call me Charlie. Everyone else does."

"So have you decided on a date?" asked Becky.

"We were planning to be married during the Easter vacation," said Daniel. "If that suits you?"

"Next week suits me," said Charlie. "I couldn't be happier. And where do you plan to hold the wedding?"

"The College chapel," said Daniel without hesitation. "You see, both Cathy's parents are dead so we thought down here in Cambridge might be best, in the circumstances."

"And where will you live?" asked Becky.

"Ah, that all depends," said Daniel mysteriously.

"On what?" asked Charlie.

"I've applied for a chair in mathematics at King's, London – and I'm reliably informed that their choice will be announced to the world in two weeks' time."

"Are you at all hopeful?" asked Becky.

"Well, let me put it this way," said Daniel. "The Principal has asked me to have dinner with him next Thursday at his lodgings, and as I've never set eyes on the gentleman in question before –" He broke off as the telephone interrupted his flow.

"Now, whoever can that be?" he asked rhetorically. "The monsters don't usually bother me on a Sunday." He picked up the receiver and listened for a moment.

"Yes, she is," he said after a few more seconds. "May I say who's calling? I'll let her know." He turned to face his mother. "Mr Baverstock for you, Mum."

Becky pushed herself out of her chair and took the telephone from Daniel as Charlie looked on apprehensively.

"Is that you, Lady Trumper?"

"Yes, it is."

"Baverstock here. I'll be brief. But first, have you informed Daniel about the details of Sir Raymond's will?"

"No. My husband was just about to do so."

"Then please don't mention the subject to him until I have had the chance to see you again."

"But – why not?" Becky realised it was now going to be necessary to conduct a one-sided conversation.

"It isn't something I feel comfortable about discussing over the telephone, Lady Trumper. When are you expecting to be back in town?"

"Later this evening."

"I think we should meet as soon as possible."

"Do you consider it's that important," said Becky, still mystified.

"I do. Would seven o'clock this evening suit you?"

"Yes, I feel sure we'll be back by then."

"In that case I'll come round to Eaton Square at seven. And please, whatever you do, don't mention anything about Sir Raymond's will to Daniel. I apologise about the mystery but I fear I have been left with little choice. Goodbye, dear lady."

"Goodbye," said Becky and put the receiver down.

"Problem?" asked Charlie, raising an eyebrow.

"I don't know." Becky looked her husband straight in the eye. "It's just that Mr Baverstock wants to see us about those papers he briefed me on last week." Charlie grimaced. "And he doesn't wish us to discuss the details with anyone else for the time being."

"Now that does sound mysterious," said Daniel, turning to Cathy. "Mr Baverstock, my darling, is on the board of the barrow, a man who would consider phoning his wife during office hours a breach of contract."

"That sounds like the right qualifications for a place on the board of a public company."

"You've met him once before, as a matter of fact," said Daniel. "He and his wife were also at Mum's housewarming party, but I fear he isn't exactly memorable."

"Who painted that picture?" said Charlie suddenly, staring at a watercolour of the Cam that hung above Daniel's desk.

Becky only hoped the change of subject hadn't been too obvious.

On the journey back to London Becky was torn between delight at the thought of having Cathy as a daughter-in-law and anxiety over what Mr Baverstock could possibly want to see them about.

When Charlie asked yet again for details, Becky tried to repeat the conversation she'd conducted with Baverstock word for word, but it left neither of them any the wiser.

"We'll know soon enough," said Charlie as they left the A10 to go through Whitechapel and on into the City. It always gave Charlie a thrill whenever he passed all the different barrows displaying their colourful wares and heard the cries of the merchants shouting their outrageous claims.

I don't offer you these for . . .

Suddenly Charlie brought the car to a halt, turned off the engine and stared out of the window.

"Why are you stopping?" asked Becky. "We haven't any time to spare."

Charlie pointed at the Whitechapel Boys' Club: it

looked even more run-down and dilapidated than usual.

"You've seen the club a thousand times before, Charlie. And you know we mustn't be late for Mr Baverstock."

He took out his diary and began unscrewing the top of his fountain pen.

"What *are* you up to?"

"When will you learn, Becky, to look more carefully?" Charlie was busy scribbling down the number of the estate agent on the "For Sale" sign.

"You surely don't want to open a second Trumper's in Whitechapel?"

"No, but I do want to find out why they're closing my old boys' club," said Charlie. He returned the pen to his inside pocket and pressed the button to start up the engine.

The Trumpers arrived back at 17 Eaton Square with just over half an hour to spare before Mr Baverstock was due to visit them; and Mr Baverstock, they both were painfully aware, was never late.

Becky immediately set about dusting the tables and plumping up the cushions in the drawing room.

"Everything looks fine to me," said Charlie. "Do stop fussing. In any case, that's what we employ a housekeeper for."

"But it's a Sunday night," Becky reminded him. She continued to check under objects she hadn't touched for months and finally put a match to the well-laid fire.

At exactly seven the front door bell rang and Charlie left to greet his guest.

"Good evening, Sir Charles," said Mr Baverstock, removing his hat.

Ah, yes, thought Charlie, there *is* someone I know who never calls me Charlie. He took Mr Baverstock's coat, scarf and hat and hung them on the hallstand.

"I am sorry to bother you on a Sunday evening," Mr Baverstock said as he followed his host into the drawing room carrying his Gladstone bag. "But I hope when you learn my news, you will feel I came to the right decision."

"I'm sure we will. We were naturally both intrigued by

your call. But first let me offer you a drink. Whisky?"

"No, thank you," said Mr Baverstock. "But a dry sherry would be most acceptable."

Becky poured Mr Baverstock a Tio Pepe and her husband a whisky before she joined the two men round the fire and waited for the lawyer to explain his uncharacteristic interruption.

"This isn't easy for me, Sir Charles."

Charlie nodded. "I understand. Just take your time."

"Can I first confirm with you that you did not reveal to your son any details of Sir Raymond's will?"

"We did not. We were saved that embarrassment first by the announcement of Daniel's engagement to be married and then by your fortuitous telephone call."

"Oh, that is good news," said Mr Baverstock. "To the charming Miss Ross, no doubt. Please do pass on my congratulations."

"You knew all along?" said Becky.

"Oh, yes," said Mr Baverstock. "It was obvious for everyone to see, wasn't it?"

"Everyone except us," said Charlie.

Mr Baverstock permitted himself a wry smile before he removed a file from his Gladstone bag.

"I'll waste no more words," continued Mr Baverstock. "Having talked to the other side's solicitors during the past few days, it has come to light that at some time in the past Daniel paid a visit to Mrs Trentham at her home in Chester Square."

Charlie and Becky were unable to hide their astonishment.

"Just as I thought," said Baverstock. "Like myself, you were both obviously quite unaware that such a meeting had taken place."

"But how could they have met when – ?" asked Charlie.

"That we may never get to the bottom of, Sir Charles. However, what I do know is that at that meeting Daniel came to an agreement with Mrs Trentham."

"And what was the nature of this agreement?" asked Charlie.

The old solicitor extracted yet another piece of paper from the file in front of him and re-read Mrs Trentham's handwritten words: "'In exchange for Mrs Trentham's withdrawing her opposition to any planning permission for the building to be known as Trumper Towers, and in addition for agreeing not to proceed with her own scheme for the rebuilding of a block of flats in Chelsea Terrace, Daniel Trumper will waive any rights he might be entitled to now or at any time in the future from the Hardcastle estate.' At that time, of course, Daniel had no idea that he was the main beneficiary of Sir Raymond's will."

"So that's why she gave in without putting up a fight?" said Charlie eventually.

"It would seem so."

"He did all that without even letting us know," said Becky as her husband began to read through the document.

"That would appear to be the case, Lady Trumper."

"And is it legally binding?" were Charlie's first words after he had finished reading the page of Mrs Trentham's handwriting.

"Yes, I'm afraid it is, Sir Charles."

"But if he didn't know the full extent of the inheritance – ?"

"This is a contract between two people. The courts would have to assume Daniel had relinquished his interest to any claim in the Hardcastle estate, once Mrs Trentham had kept her part of the bargain."

"But what about coercion?"

"Of a twenty-six-year-old man by a woman over seventy when he went to visit her? Hardly, Sir Charles."

"But how did they ever meet?"

"I have no idea," replied the lawyer. "It seems that she didn't confide the full circumstances of the meeting even to her own solicitors. However, I'm sure you now understand why I considered this wasn't the most appropriate time to raise the subject of Sir Raymond's will with Daniel."

"You made the right decision," said Charlie.

"And now the subject must be closed for ever," said Becky, barely louder than a whisper.

"But why?" asked Charlie, placing an arm around his wife's shoulder.

"Because I don't want Daniel to spend the rest of his life feeling he betrayed his great-grandfather when his only purpose in signing that agreement must have been to help us." The tears flowed down Becky's cheeks as she turned to face her husband.

"Perhaps I should have a word with Daniel, man to man."

"Charlie, you will never even consider raising the subject of Guy Trentham with my son again. I forbid it."

Charlie removed his arm from around his wife and looked at her like a child who has been unfairly scolded.

"I'm only glad it was you who has brought us this unhappy news," said Becky, turning back to the solicitor. "You've always been so considerate when it comes to our affairs."

"Thank you, Lady Trumper, but I fear I have yet more unpalatable news to impart."

Becky gripped Charlie's hand.

"I have to report that on this occasion Mrs Trentham has not satisfied herself with one blow at a time."

"What else can she do to us?" asked Charlie.

"It seems that she is now willing to part with her land in Chelsea Terrace."

"I don't believe it," said Becky.

"I do," said Charlie. "But at what price?"

"That is indeed the problem," said Mr Baverstock, who bent down to remove another file from his old leather bag.

Charlie and Becky exchanged a quick glance.

"Mrs Trentham will offer you the freehold on her site in Chelsea Terrace in exchange for ten per cent of Trumper's shares" – he paused – "and a place on the board for her son Nigel."

"Never," said Charlie flatly.

"If you should reject her offer," the solicitor continued, "she intends to sell the property on the open market and accept the highest bidder – whoever that might be."

"So be it," said Charlie. "We would undoubtedly end up buying the land ourselves."

"At a far higher price than the value of ten per cent of our shares, I suspect," said Becky.

"That's a price worth paying after what she's put us through."

"Mrs Trentham has also requested," continued Mr Baverstock, "that her offer should be presented to the board in detail at your next meeting and then voted on."

"But she doesn't have the authority to make such a demand," said Charlie.

"If you do not comply with this request," said Mr Baverstock, "it is her intention to circulate all the shareholders with the offer and then call an extraordinary general meeting at which she will personally present her case and bring the issue to a vote."

"Can she do that?" For the first time Charlie sounded worried.

"From everything I know about that lady, I suspect she wouldn't have thrown down such a gauntlet before taking legal advice."

"It's almost as if she can always anticipate our next move," said Becky with feeling.

Charlie's voice revealed the same anxiety. "She wouldn't need to bother about our next move if her son was on the board. He could just report back to her direct after every meeting."

"So what it comes to is that we may well *have* to give in to her demands," said Becky.

"I agree with your judgment, Lady Trumper," said Mr Baverstock. "However, I felt it was only proper that I should give you as much notice as possible of Mrs Trentham's demands as it will be my painful duty to acquaint the board with the details when we next meet."

There was only one "apologies for absence" when the board met the following Tuesday. Simon Matthews had to be in Geneva to conduct a rare gems sale and Charlie had assured him that his presence would not be vital. Once Mr Baverstock had finished explaining the consequences of Mrs Trentham's offer to the board, everyone around the table wanted to speak at once.

When Charlie had restored some semblance of order, he said, "I must make my position clear from the outset. I am one hundred per cent against this offer. I don't trust the lady in question and never have. What's more, I believe that in the long term her only purpose is to harm the company."

"But, surely, Mr Chairman," said Paul Merrick, "if she is considering selling her land in Chelsea Terrace to the highest bidder, she could always use the cash from that sale to purchase another ten per cent of the company's shares at any time that suited her. So what real choice are we left with?"

"Not having to live with her son," said Charlie. "Don't forget, part of this package means offering him a place on the board."

"But if he were in possession of ten per cent of the company," said Merrick, "and perhaps an even higher stake for all we know, it would be nothing less than our duty to accept him as a director."

"Not necessarily," said Charlie. "Especially if we believed his sole reason for joining the board was eventually to take over the company. The last thing we need is a hostile director."

"The last thing we need, is to pay more than is necessary for a hole in the ground."

For a moment no one spoke while the rest of the board considered these contrary statements.

"Let's assume for one moment," said Tim Newman, "the consequences of not accepting Mrs Trentham's terms but instead bidding for the empty plot ourselves on the open market. That might not prove to be the cheapest route, Sir

Charles, because I can assure you, that Sears, Boots, the House of Fraser and John Lewis – to name but four – would derive considerable pleasure from opening a new store right in the middle of Trumper's."

"Rejecting her offer may therefore turn out to be even more expensive in the long run, whatever your personal views are of the lady, Mr Chairman," said Merrick. "In any case, I have another piece of information that the board may feel is relevant to this discussion."

"What's that?" asked Charlie, warily.

"My fellow-directors may be interested to know," began Merrick rather pompously, "that Nigel Trentham has just been made redundant by Kitcat and Aitken, which is simply a euphemism for being sacked. It seems he's not proved up to the task in these leaner times. So I can't imagine his presence around this table is likely to provide us with a great deal of anxiety now or at any time in the future."

"But he could still keep his mother briefed on every move we make," said Charlie.

"Perhaps she needs to know how well the knickers are selling on the seventh floor?" suggested Merrick. "Not to mention the trouble we had with that burst water main in the gents' lavatory last month. No, Mr Chairman, it would be foolish, even irresponsible, not to accept such an offer."

"As a matter of interest, Mr Chairman, what would you do with the extra space, should Trumper's suddenly get hold of Mrs Trentham's land?" asked Daphne, throwing everyone off balance for a moment.

"Expand," said Charlie. "We're already bulging at the seams. That piece of land would mean at least fifty thousand square feet. If I could only get my hands on it it would be possible for me to open another twenty departments."

"And what would such a building programme cost?" Daphne continued.

"A lot of money," Paul Merrick interjected, "which we may not have at our disposal if we are made to pay well over the odds for that vacant site in the first place."

"May I remind you that we're having an exceptionally good year," said Charlie, banging the table.

"Agreed, Mr Chairman. But may I also remind you that when you last made a similar statement within five years you were facing bankruptcy."

"But that was caused by an expected war," insisted Charlie.

"And this isn't," said Merrick.

The two men stared at each other, unable to disguise their mutual loathing.

"No, our first duty must always be to the share-holders," continued Merrick, as he looked around the boardroom table. "If they were to find out that we had paid an excessive amount for that piece of land simply because of – and I put this as delicately as I can – a personal vendetta between the principals, we could be heavily censured at the next AGM and you, Mr Chairman, might even be called on to resign."

"I'm willing to take that risk," said Charlie, by now almost shouting.

"Well, I'm not," said Merrick calmly. "What's more, if we don't accept her offer we already know that Mrs Trentham will call an extraordinary general meeting in order to put her case to the shareholders, and I've little doubt where their interests will lie. I consider the time has come to take a vote on this matter, rather than carry on with any further pointless discussion."

"But wait a moment –" Charlie began.

"No. I will not wait, Mr Chairman, and I propose that we accept Mrs Trentham's generous offer of releasing her land, in exchange for ten per cent of the company's shares."

"And what do you propose we do about her son?" asked Charlie.

"He should be invited to join the board without delay," replied Merrick.

"But –" began Charlie.

"No buts, thank you, Mr Chairman," said Merrick. "The time has come to vote. Personal prejudices shouldn't be allowed to cloud our better judgment."

There was a moment's silence before Arthur Selwyn said, "As a formal proposal has been made will you be kind enough to record the votes, Miss Allen?" Jessica nodded and glanced round at the nine members of the board.

"Mr Merrick?"

"For."

"Mr Newman?"

"For."

"Mr Denning?"

"Against."

"Mr Makins?"

"Against."

"Mr Baverstock?"

The lawyer placed the palms of his hands on the table and seemed to hesitate, as if in some considerable dilemma over the decision.

"For," he said finally.

"Lady Trumper?"

"Against," Becky said without hesitation.

"Lady Wiltshire?"

"For," said Daphne quietly.

"Why?" said Becky, unable to believe her response.

Daphne turned to face her old friend. "Because I'd rather have the enemy inside the boardroom causing trouble, than outside in the corridor causing even more."

Becky couldn't believe her ears.

"I assume you're against, Sir Charles?"

Charlie nodded vigorously.

Mr Selwyn raised his eyes.

"Does that mean it's four votes each?" he enquired of Jessica.

"Yes, that's correct, Mr Selwyn," said Jessica after she had run her thumb down the list of names a second time.

Everyone stared across at the managing director. He

placed the pen he had been writing with on the blotting pad in front of him. "Then I can only do what I consider to be in the best long-term interests of the company. I cast my vote in favour of accepting Mrs Trentham's offer."

Everyone round the table except Charlie started to talk.

Mr Selwyn waited for some time before adding, "The motion has been carried, Mr Chairman, by five votes to four. I will therefore instruct our merchant bankers and solicitors to carry out the necessary financial and legal arrangements to ensure that this transaction takes place smoothly and in accordance with company regulations."

Charlie made no comment, just continued to stare in front of him.

"And if there is no other business, Mr Chairman, perhaps you should declare the meeting closed."

Charlie nodded but didn't move when the other directors rose to leave the boardroom. Only Becky remained in her place, halfway down the long table. Within moments they were alone.

"I should have got my hands on those flats thirty years ago, you know."

Becky made no comment.

"And we should never have gone public while that bloody woman was still alive."

Charlie rose and walked slowly over to the window, but his wife still didn't offer an opinion as he stared down at the empty bench on the far side of the road.

"And to think I told Simon that his presence wouldn't be vital."

Still Becky said nothing.

"Well, at least I now know what the bloody woman has in mind for her precious Nigel."

Becky raised an eyebrow as Charlie turned to face her.

"She plans that he will succeed me as the next chairman of Trumper's."

CATHY

1947-1950

CHAPTER 39

The one question I was never able to answer as a child was, "When did you last see your father?" Unlike the young cavalier, I simply didn't know the answer. In fact I had no idea who my father was, or my mother for that matter. Most people have no idea how many times a day, a month, a year one is asked such a question. And if your reply is always, "I simply don't know, because they both died before I can remember," you are greeted with looks of either surprise or suspicion – or, worse still, disbelief. In the end you learn how to throw up a smoke-screen or simply avoid the issue by changing the subject. There is no variation on the question of parentage for which I haven't developed an escape route.

The only vague memory I have of my parents is of a man who shouted a lot of the time and of a woman who was so timid she rarely spoke. I also have a feeling she was called Anna. Other than that, both of them remain a blur.

How I envied those children who could immediately tell me about their parents, brothers, sisters, even second cousins or distant aunts. All I knew about myself was that I had been brought up in St Hilda's Orphanage, Park Hill, Melbourne. Principal: Miss Rachel Benson.

Many of the children from the orphanage did have relations and some received letters, even the occasional visit. The only such person I can ever recall was an elderly, rather severe-looking woman, who wore a long black dress, black lace gloves up to her elbows and spoke with a strange accent. I have no idea what her relationship to me was, if any.

Miss Benson treated this particular lady with considerable respect and I remember even curtsied when she left; but I never learned her name and when I was old enough to ask who she was Miss Benson claimed she had no idea what I was talking about. Whenever I tried to question Miss Benson about my own upbringing, she would reply mysteriously, "It's best you don't know, child." I can think of no sentence in the English language more likely to ensure that I tried even harder to find out the truth about my background.

As the years went by I began to ask what I thought were subtler questions on the subject of my parents – of the vice-principal, my house matron, kitchen staff, even the janitor – but I always came up against the same blank wall. On my fourteenth birthday I requested an interview with Miss Benson in order to ask her the question direct. Although she had long ago dispensed with "It's best you don't know, child," she now replaced this sentiment with, "In truth, Cathy, I don't know myself." Although I didn't question her further, I didn't believe her, because some of the older members of the staff would from time to time give me strange looks, and on at least two occasions began to whisper behind my back once they thought I was out of earshot.

I had no photographs or mementoes of my parents, or even any proof of their past existence, except for a small piece of jewellery which I convinced myself was silver. I remember that it was the man who shouted a lot who had given me the little cross and since then it had always hung from a piece of string around my neck. One night when I was undressing in the dormitory Miss Benson spotted my prize and demanded to know where the pendant had come from; I told her Betsy Compton had swopped it with me for a dozen marbles, a fib that seemed to satisfy her at the time. But from that day onwards I kept my treasure well hidden from anyone's prying eyes.

I must have been one of those rare children who loved going to school from the first day its doors were opened to me. The classroom was a blessed escape from my prison and its warders. Every extra minute I spent at the local school was a minute I didn't have to be at St Hilda's, and I quickly discovered that the harder I worked the longer the hours I was allowed to remain behind. These became even more expandable when, at the age of eleven, I won a place at Melbourne Church of England Girls' Grammar School, where they had so many extra-curricular activities going on, from first thing in the morning until late every evening, that St Hilda's became little more than the place where I slept and had breakfast.

While at MGS I took up painting, which made it possible for me to spend several hours in the art room without too much supervision or interference; tennis, where by dint of sheer hard work and application I managed to gain a place in the school second six, which produced the bonus of being allowed to practise in the evening until it was dusk; and cricket, for which I had no talent, but as team scorer not only was I required never to leave my place until the last ball had been bowled but every other Saturday I was able to escape on a bus for a fixture against another school. I was one of the few children who enjoyed away matches in preference to home fixtures.

At sixteen I entered the sixth form and began to work even harder: it was explained to Miss Benson that I might possibly win a scholarship to the University of Melbourne – not an everyday occurrence for an inmate from St Hilda's.

Whenever I received any academic distinction or

reprimand – the latter became rarer once I had discovered school – I was made to report to Miss Benson in her study, where she would deliver a few words of encouragement or disapproval, before placing the slip of paper that marked these occurrences in a file which she would then return to a cabinet that stood behind her desk. I always watched her most carefully as she carried out this ritual. First she would remove a key from the top left-hand drawer of her desk, then she would go over to the cabinet, check my file under QRS, place the credit or misdemeanour inside my entry, lock the cabinet and then replace the key in her desk. It was a routine that never varied.

Another fixed point in Miss Benson's life was her annual holiday, when she would visit "her people" in Adelaide. This took place every September and I looked forward to it as others might a holiday.

Once war had been declared I feared she might not keep to her schedule, especially as we were told we would all have to make sacrifices.

Miss Benson appeared to make no sacrifices and despite travel restrictions and cutbacks departed for Adelaide on exactly the same day that summer as she always had. I waited until five days after the taxi had driven her off to the station before I felt it was safe to carry out my little escapade.

On the sixth night I lay awake until just after one in the morning, not moving a muscle until I was certain all sixteen girls in the dormitory were fast asleep. Then I rose, borrowed a pen torch from the drawer of the girl who slept next to me and headed off across the landing towards the staircase. Had I been spotted en route, I already had an excuse prepared about feeling sick, and as I had rarely entered the sanatorium at any time during my twelve years at St Hilda's, I felt confident I would be believed.

I crept cautiously down the staircase without having to use the torch: since Miss Benson had departed for Adelaide, I had practised the routine each morning with my eyes closed. Once I had reached the principal's study, I opened the door and slipped in, only then switching on the pen torch. I tiptoed over to Miss Benson's desk and cautiously pulled open the top left-hand drawer. What I hadn't been prepared for was to be faced with about twenty different keys, some in groups on rings while others were detached but unmarked. I tried to remember the size and shape of the one Miss Benson had used to unlock the filing cabinet, but I couldn't, and with only a pen torch to guide me several trips to the cabinet and back were necessary before I discovered the one that would turn one hundred and eighty degrees.

I pulled open the top drawer of the filing cabinet as slowly as I could but the runners still seemed to rumble like thunder. I stopped, and held my breath as I waited to hear if there were any movement coming from the house. I even looked under the door to be sure no light was suddenly switched on. Once I felt confident I hadn't disturbed anyone I leafed through the names in the QRS box file: Roberts, Rose, Ross . . . I pulled out my personal folder and carried the heavy bundle back to the principal's desk. I sat down in Miss Benson's chair and, with the help of the torch began to check each page carefully. As I was sixteen and had now been at St Hilda's for around twelve years, my file was necessarily thick. I was reminded of misdemeanours as long ago as wetting my bed as well as several credits for painting, including the rare double credit for one of my watercolours that still hung in the dining room. Yet however much I searched through that folder there was no trace of anything about me before the age of three. I began to wonder if this was a general rule that applied to everyone who had come to live at St Hilda's. I took a quick glance at the details of Jennie Rose's record. To my dismay, I found the names of both her father (Ted, deceased) and her mother

(Susan). An attached note explained that Mrs Rose had three other children to bring up and since the death of her husband from a heart attack had been quite unable to cope with a fourth child.

I locked the cabinet, returned the key to the top left-hand drawer of Miss Benson's desk, switched off the pen torch, left the study and walked quickly up the stairs to my dormitory. I put the pen torch back in its rightful place and slipped into bed. I began to wonder what I could possibly do next to try and find out who I was and where I'd come from.

It was as if my parents had never existed, and I had somehow started life aged three. As the only alternative was virgin birth and I didn't accept that even for the Blessed Mary, my desire to know the truth became irrepressible. I must eventually have fallen asleep, because all I remember after that is being woken by the school bell the following morning.

When I was awarded my place at the University of Melbourne I felt like a long-term prisoner who has finally been released. For the first time, I was given a room of my own and was no longer expected to wear a uniform – not that the range of clothes I could afford was going to set the Melbourne fashion houses alight. I remember working even longer hours at university than I had done at school, as I was apprehensive that if I didn't pass my first year general papers they would send me back to spend the rest of my days at St Hilda's.

In my second year I specialised in the history of art, and English while continuing with painting as a hobby, but I had no idea what career I wanted to pursue after leaving university. My tutor suggested I should consider teaching, but that sounded to me rather like an extension of St Hilda's, with me ending up as Miss Benson.

I didn't have many boyfriends before going to university, because the boys at St Hilda's were kept in a

separate wing of the house and you were not allowed
to talk to them before nine in the morning and after
five o'clock at night. Until the age of fifteen I thought
kissing made you pregnant so I was determined not to
make that mistake, especially after my experience of
growing up with no family of my own.

My first real boyfriend was Mel Nicholls, who was
captain of the university football team. Having finally
succeeded in getting me into bed he told me that I was
the only girl in his life and, more important, the first.
After I had admitted it was true for me too and lay
back on the pillow Mel leant over and began to take an
interest in the only thing I was still wearing.

"I've never seen anything quite like that before,"
he said, taking my little piece of jewellery between his
fingers.

"Another first."

"Not quite." He laughed. "Because I've seen one
very similar."

"What do you mean?"

"It's a medal," he explained. "My father won three
or four of them himself but none of them's made of
silver."

Looking back on it now, I consider that this particular piece of information was well worth losing my
virginity for.

In the library of the University of Melbourne there
is a large selection of books covering the First World
War, biased not unnaturally towards Gallipoli. However, tucked away among the pages of heroic deeds
performed by Australian infantrymen was a chapter
on British gallantry awards, complete with several
coloured plates.

I discovered that there were VCs, DSOs, DSCs,
CBEs, OBEs – the variations seemed endless until
finally on page four hundred and nine I found what I
was searching for: the Military Cross, a ribbon of white
watered silk and purple vertical stripes and a medal

forged in silver with the Imperial crown on each of its four arms. It was awarded to officers below the rank of major "for conspicuous gallantry when under fire". I began to hypothesise that my father was a war hero who had died at an early age from terrible wounds. At least that would have explained his perpetual shouting as something that had been brought on by so much suffering.

My next piece of detective work came when I visited an antique shop in Melbourne. The man behind the counter simply studied the medal, then offered me five pounds for it. I didn't bother to explain why I wouldn't have parted with my prize had he offered me five hundred pounds, but at least he was able to inform me that the only real medal dealer in Australia was a Mr Frank Jennings, of Number 47 Mafeking Street, Sydney.

At that time I considered Sydney to be the other side of the globe, and I certainly couldn't afford to make such a long journey on my tiny grant. So I had to wait patiently until the summer term when I applied to be scorer for the university cricket team. They turned me down on account of my sex. Women couldn't really be expected to understand the game fully, it was explained to me by a youth who used to sit behind me in lectures so that he could copy my notes. This left me with no choice but to spend hours of practice on my ground strokes and almost as many on my overhead smash until I was selected for the ladies' second tennis team. Not a major achievement but there was only one match on the calendar that interested me: Sydney (A).

On the morning we arrived in Sydney, I went straight to Mafeking Street and was struck by how many young men who passed me on the street were in uniform. Mr Jennings himself studied the medal with considerably more interest than the dealer from Melbourne had shown.

"It's a miniature MC all right," he told me, peering at my little prize through a magnifying glass. "It would have been worn on a dress uniform for guest nights in the regimental mess. These three initials printed down the edge of one of the arms, barely discernible to the naked eye, ought to give us a clue as to who was awarded the decoration."

I stared through Mr Jennings' magnifying glass at something I had never been aware of until then, but I could now clearly see the initials "G.F.T.".

"Is there any way of finding out who G.F.T. is?" I asked hopefully.

"Oh, yes," said Mr Jennings, turning to a shelf behind him, from which he removed a leather-bound book and flicked through its pages until he came to Godfrey S. Thomas and George Victor Taylor, but could find no trace of anyone with the initials G.F.T.

"Sorry, but I can't help you on this one," he said. "Your particular medal can't have been awarded to an Australian, otherwise it would be catalogued right here." He tapped the leather cover. "You'll have to write to the War Office in London if you want any further information. They still keep on file the names of every member of the armed forces awarded any decoration for gallantry."

I thanked him for his help but not before he had offered me ten pounds for the medal. I smiled and returned to join the tennis team for my match against Sydney University. I lost 6-0, 6-1, being quite unable to concentrate on anything except G.F.T. I wasn't selected for the university tennis team again that season.

The next day I followed Mr Jennings's advice and wrote to the War Office in London. I didn't get a letter back from them for several months, which was hardly surprising as everyone knew they had other things on their mind in 1944. However, a buff envelope eventually came and when opened informed me that the holder of my medal could have been either Graham

Frank Turnbull of the Duke of Wellington's regiment or Guy Francis Trentham of the Royal Fusiliers.

So was my real name Turnbull or Trentham?

That same evening I wrote to the British High Commissioner's office in Canberra asking whom I should contact for information regarding the two regiments referred to in the letter. I received a reply a couple of weeks later. With the new leads I had acquired I despatched two more letters to England: one to Halifax, the other to London. I then sat back again and resigned myself to another long wait. When you have already spent eighteen years of your life trying to discover your true identity, another few months doesn't seem all that important. In any case, now that I had begun my final year at university I was up to my eyes in work.

The Duke of Wellington's were the first to reply, and they informed me that Lieutenant Graham Frank Turnbull had been killed at Passchendaele on 6 November 1917. As I was born in 1924 that let Lieutenant Turnbull off the hook. I prayed for Guy Francis Trentham.

It was several weeks later that I received a reply from the Royal Fusiliers to inform me that Captain Guy Francis Trentham had been awarded the MC on 18 July 1918, following the second battle of the Marne. Fuller details could be obtained from the Regimental Museum library at their headquarters in London, but this had to be done in person as they had no authority to release information about members of the regiment by post.

As I had no way of getting to England I immediately began a new line of investigation, only this time I drew a complete blank. I took a whole morning off in order to search for the name of Trentham in the birth records of the Melbourne city registry on Queen Street. I found there was not one Trentham listed. There were several Rosses but none came anywhere near my date of birth. I began to realise that someone had gone to considerable lengths to make sure I was unable to trace my roots. But why?

Suddenly my sole purpose in life switched to how I could get myself to England, despite the fact that I had no money and the war had only recently ended. I checked every graduate and undergraduate course that was on offer and all that my tutor considered it might be worth applying for was a scholarship to the Slade School of Art in London, which offered three places each year to students from Commonwealth countries. I began to put in hours that even I hadn't realised existed, and was rewarded by a place on the short list of six for a final interview to be held in Canberra.

Although I became extremely nervous on the train journey to the Australian capital, I felt the interview went well and indeed the examiners told me that my papers on the history of art were of particular merit, even if my practical work was not of the same high standard.

An envelope marked The Slade was dropped in my cubbyhole a month later. I ripped it open in anticipation and extracted a letter that began:

Dear Miss Ross,

We are sorry to inform you

The only worthwhile thing that came out of all the extra work I had put in was that I sailed through my finals and was awarded a First Class honours degree when the graduation results were announced. But I was still no nearer to getting myself to England.

In desperation I telephoned the British High Commission and was put through to the labour attaché. A lady came on the line and informed me that with my qualifications there would be several teaching posts on offer. She added that I would have to sign a three-year contract and be responsible for my own travel arrangements – nicely worded, I considered, as I still wasn't able to afford the trip to Sydney, let alone the United Kingdom. In any case, I felt I would only need to spend about a month in England to track down Guy Francis Trentham.

The only other jobs that were available, the lady explained the second time I called, were known as "slave traders". These consisted of positions in hotels, hospitals or old people's homes, where you were virtually unpaid for one year in return for your passage to England and back. As I still had no plans for any particular career and realised this was virtually the only chance I might ever have of getting myself to England and finding someone I was related to, I called into the labour attaché's department and signed on the dotted line. Most of my friends at university thought I had taken leave of my senses, but then they had no idea of my real purpose in wanting to visit Britain.

The boat we sailed to Southampton on couldn't have been much of an improvement on the one the first Australian immigrants took coming the other way some one hundred and fifty years before. They put three of us "slave traders" to a cabin no larger than my room on the university campus, and if the ship listed more than ten degrees Pam and Maureen ended up in my bunk. We had all signed on to work at the Melrose Hotel in Earl's Court, which we were assured was in central London. After a journey of some six weeks we were met at the dockside by a clapped-out army lorry which took us up to the capital and deposited us on the steps of the Melrose Hotel.

The housekeeper allocated our accommodation and I ganged up with Pam and Maureen, again. I was surprised to discover that we were expected to share a room of roughly the same size as the cabin in which we had suffered together on board ship. At least this time we didn't fall out of bed unexpectedly.

It was over two weeks before they gave me enough time off to visit Kensington Post Office and check through the London telephone directory. There wasn't a Trentham to be found.

"Could be ex-directory," the girl behind the counter explained. "Which means they won't take your call in any case."

"Or there just isn't a Trentham living in London," I said, and accepted that the Regimental Museum was now my only hope.

I thought I had worked hard at the University of Melbourne, but the hours they expected us to do at the Melrose would have brought a combat soldier to his knees. All the same, I was damned if I was going to admit as much, especially after Pam and Maureen gave up the struggle within a month, cabled their parents in Sydney for some money and returned to Australia on the first available boat. At least it meant I ended up with a room to myself until the next boatload arrived. To be honest I wish I could have packed up and gone home with them, but I hadn't anyone in Australia to whom I could cable back for more than about ten pounds.

The first full day I had off and wasn't totally exhausted, I took a train to Hounslow where the museum was situated now. When I left the station the ticket collector directed me to the Royal Fusiliers' Depot and Museum. After walking about a mile I eventually reached the building I was looking for. It seemed to be uninhabited except for a single receptionist. He was dressed in khaki uniform, with three stripes on both arms. He sat dozing behind a counter.

I walked noisily over and pretended not to wake him.

"Can I 'elp you, young lady?" he asked, rubbing his eyes.

"I hope so."

"Australian?"

"Is it that obvious?"

"I fought alongside your chaps in North Africa," he explained. "Damn great bunch of soldiers, I can tell you. So 'ow can I help you, miss?"

"I wrote to you from Melbourne," I said, producing a handwritten copy of the letter. "About the holder of this medal." I slipped the piece of string over my head and handed my prize to him. "His name was Guy Francis Trentham."

"Miniature MC," said the sergeant without hesitation as he held the medal in his hand. "Guy Francis Trentham, you say?"

"That's right."

"Good. So let's look 'im up in the great book: 1914–1918, yes?"

I nodded.

He went over to a massive bookshelf weighed down by heavy volumes and removed a large leather-bound book. He placed it on the counter with a thud, sending dust in every direction. On the cover were the words, printed in gold, "Royal Fusiliers, Decorations 1914–1918".

"Let's have a butcher's, then," he said as he started to flick through the pages. I waited impatiently. "There's our man," he announced triumphantly. "Guy Francis Trentham, Captain." He swung the book round so that I could study the entry more carefully. I was so excited it was several moments before I could take the words in.

Captain Trentham's citation went on for twenty-two lines and I asked if I might be allowed to copy out the details in full.

"Of course, miss," he said. "Be my guest." He

handed over a large sheet of ruled paper and a blunt army-issue pencil. I began to write:

On the morning of 18th July, 1918, Captain Guy Trentham of the Second Battalion of the Royal Fusiliers led a company of men from the Allied trenches towards the enemy lines, killing several German soldiers before reaching their dug-outs, where he wiped out a complete army unit single-handed. Captain Trentham continued in pursuit of two other German soldiers and chased them into a nearby forest where he succeeded in killing them both.

The same evening, despite being surrounded by the enemy, he rescued two men of his own company, Private T. Prescott and Corporal C. Trumper, who had strayed from the battlefield, and were hiding in a nearby church. After nightfall, he led them back across open terrain while the enemy continued to fire intermittently in their direction.

Private Prescott was killed by a stray German tracer bullet before he managed to reach the safety of his own trenches. Corporal Trumper survived despite a continual barrage of firepower from the enemy.

For this singular act of leadership and heroism in the face of the enemy, Captain Trentham was awarded the MC.

Having written out every word of the citation in my neatest hand, I closed the heavy cover and turned the book round to face the sergeant.

"Trentham," he said. "If I remember correctly, miss, 'e still 'as 'is picture up on the wall." The sergeant picked up some crutches, manoeuvred himself from behind the counter and limped slowly to the far corner of the museum. I hadn't realised until that moment that the poor man only had one leg. "Over 'ere, miss," he said. "Follow me."

My palms began to sweat and I felt a little sick at the thought of discovering what my father looked like. I wondered if I might resemble him in any way.

The sergeant hobbled straight past the VCs before we came to a row of MCs. They were all lined up, old sepia pictures, badly framed. His finger ran along them – Stevens, Thomas, Tubbs. "That's strange. I could have sworn 'is photo was there. Well, I'll be damned. Must 'ave got lost when we moved from the Tower."

"Could his picture be anywhere else?"

"Not to my knowledge, miss," he said. "I must 'ave imagined it all along, but I'd swear I'd seen 'is photo when the museum was at the Tower. Well, I'll be damned," he repeated.

I asked him if he could supply me with any more details of Captain Trentham and what might have happened to him since 1918. He hobbled back to the counter and looked up his name in the regimental handbook. "Commissioned 1916, promoted to second lieutenant 1916, captain 1917, India 1920–1922, resigned 'is commission August 1922. Since then nothing known of 'im, miss."

"So he could still be alive?"

"Certainly could, miss. 'e'd only be fifty, fifty-five, most."

I checked my watch, thanked him and ran quickly out of the building, suddenly aware of how much time I had spent at the museum and fearful that I might miss the train back to London and wouldn't be in time to clock on for my five o'clock shift.

After I had settled in a corner of a dingy third-class compartment I read over the citation again. It pleased me to think that my father had been a First World War hero; but I still couldn't fathom out why Miss Benson had been so unwilling to tell me anything about him. Why had he gone to Australia? Had he changed his

name to Ross? I felt I would have to return to
Melbourne if I was ever going to find out exactly what
had happened to Guy Francis Trentham. Had I possessed the money to pay for my return fare, I would
have gone back that night, but as I had to work out my
contract at the hotel for another nine months before
they would advance me enough cash to cover the one-
way ticket home I settled down to complete my
sentence.

London in 1947 was an exciting city for a twenty-
three-year-old so despite the dreary work there were
many compensations. Whenever I had any time off I
would visit an art gallery, a museum or go to a cinema
with one of the girls from the hotel. On a couple of
occasions I even accompanied a group of friends to a
dance at the Mecca ballroom just off the Strand. One
particular night I remember a rather good-looking
bloke from the RAF asked me for a dance and, just
moments after we had started going round the hall, he
tried to kiss me. When I pushed him away he became
even more determined and only a firm kick on his ankle
followed by a short dash across the dance floor made it
possible for me to escape. A few minutes later I found
myself out on the pavement and heading back to the
hotel on my own.

As I strolled through Chelsea in the general direction of Earl's Court I stopped from time to time to
admire the unattainable goods on display in every shop
window. I particularly craved a long blue silk shawl
draped over the shoulders of an elegant slim man-
nequin. I stopped window-shopping for a moment and
glanced up at the name over the door: "Trumper's".
There was something familiar about the name but I
couldn't think what. I walked slowly back to the hotel
but the only Trumper I could recall was the legendary
Australian cricketer who had died before I was born.
Then in the middle of the night it came back to me.
Trumper, C. was the corporal mentioned in the citation

written about my father. I jumped out of bed, opened the bottom drawer of my little desk and checked the words I had copied out during my visit to the Royal Fusiliers Museum.

The name was not one I'd come across since arriving in England, so I wondered if the shopkeeper might be related in some way to the corporal and therefore might help me find him. I decided to return to the museum in Hounslow on my next day off and see if my one-legged friend could be of any further assistance.

"Nice to see you again, miss," he said as I walked up to the counter. I was touched that he remembered me.

"More information you're after?"

"You're right," I told him. "Corporal Trumper, he's not the . . . ?"

"Charlie Trumper the 'onest trader. Certainly is, miss; but now 'e's Sir Charles and owns that large group of shops in Chelsea Terrace."

"I thought so."

"I was about to tell you all about 'im when you ran off last time, miss." He grinned. "Could 'ave saved you a train journey and about six months of your time."

The following evening, instead of going to see Greta Garbo at the Gate Cinema in Notting Hill, I sat on an old bench on the far side of Chelsea Terrace and just stared at a row of windows. Sir Charles seemed to own almost every shop on the street. I could only wonder why he had allowed such a large empty space to remain right in the middle of the block.

My next problem was how I could possibly get to see him. The only idea that occurred to me was that I might take my medal into Number 1 for a valuation – and then pray.

During the next week I was on the day shift at the hotel so I was unable to return to Number 1 Chelsea Terrace before the following Monday afternoon, when I presented the girl on the front counter with my MC and asked if the medal could be valued. She considered my tiny offering, then called for someone else to examine it more carefully. A tall, studious-looking man spent some time checking the piece before he offered an opinion. "A miniature MC," he declared, "sometimes known as a dress MC because it would be worn on a mess or dinner jacket for regimental nights, value approximately ten pounds." He hesitated for a moment. "But of course Spink's at 5 King Street SW1 would be able to give you a more accurate assessment should you require it."

"Thank you," I said, having learned nothing new and finding myself quite unable to think of any way I might phrase a question about Sir Charles Trumper's war record.

"Anything else I can help you with?" he asked as I remained rooted to the spot.

"How do you get a job here?" I bleated out, feeling rather stupid.

"Just write in, giving us all the details of your qualifications and past experience and we'll be back in touch with you within a few days."

"Thank you," I said and left without another word.

I sat down that evening and drafted a long handwritten letter, setting out my qualifications as an art historian. They appeared a bit slender to me when I looked at them on paper.

The next morning I rewrote the letter on the hotel's finest stationery before addressing the envelope to "Job Enquiries" – as I had no name as a contact other than Trumper's – Number 1 Chelsea Terrace, London SW3.

The following afternoon I hand-delivered the missive to a girl on the front desk of the auction house, never really expecting to receive a reply. In any case, I wasn't actually sure what I would do if they did offer me a job, as I planned on returning to Melbourne in a few weeks and I still couldn't imagine how working at Trumper's would ever lead to my meeting Sir Charles.

Ten days later I received a letter from the personnel officer, saying they would like to interview me. I spent four pounds fifteen shillings of my hard-earned wages on a new dress that I could ill afford and arrived over an hour early for the interview. I ended up having to walk round the block several times. During that hour I discovered that Sir Charles really did seem to sell everything any human being could desire, as long as you had enough money to pay for it.

At last the hour was up and I marched in and presented myself at the front counter. I was taken up some stairs to an office on the top floor. The lady who interviewed me said she couldn't understand what I was doing stuck in a hotel as a chambermaid with my qualifications, until I explained to her that hotel work was the only job available to those who couldn't afford to pay their passage over to England.

She smiled before warning me that if I wanted to work at Number 1 everyone started on the front desk. If they proved to be any good they were promoted fairly quickly.

"I started on the front desk at Sotheby's," my interviewer went on to explain. I wanted to ask her how long she'd lasted.

"I'd love to come and work at Trumper's," I told her, "but I'm afraid I still have two months of my contract to complete before I can leave the Melrose Hotel."

"Then we'll have to wait for you," she replied without hesitation. "You can start at the front desk on 1st September, Miss Ross. I will confirm all the arrangements in writing by the end of the week."

I was so excited by her offer that I quite forgot why I'd applied for the job in the first place: until my interviewer sent her promised letter and I was able to decipher her signature scribbled across the foot of the page.

CHAPTER 40

athy had worked on the front desk of Trumper's Auction House for just eleven days when Simon Matthews asked her to help him prepare the catalogue for the Italian sale. He was the first to spot how, as the auction house's premier line of defence, she handled the myriad enquiries that were thrown at her without constantly having to seek a second opinion. She worked just as hard for Trumper's as she had done at the Melrose Hotel, but with a difference: she now enjoyed what she was doing.

For the first time in her life Cathy felt she was part of a family, because Rebecca Trumper was invariably relaxed and friendly with her staff, treating them all as equals. Her salary was far more generous than the bare minimum she had received from her previous employer, and the room they gave her above the butcher's shop at Number 135 was palatial in comparison with her hideaway at the back of the hotel.

Trying to find out more about her father began to seem less important to Cathy as she set about proving she was worth her place at Number 1 Chelsea Terrace. Her primary task in preparing the catalogue for the Italian sale was to check the history of every one of the fifty-nine pictures that were to come under the hammer. To this end she travelled right across London from library to library and telephoned gallery after gallery in her quest to track down every attribution. In the end only one picture completely baffled her, that of the Virgin Mary and Child, which bore no signature and had no history attached except that it had originally come from the private collection of Sir Charles Trumper and was now owned by a Mrs Kitty Bennett.

Cathy asked Simon Matthews if he could give any lead on the picture and was told by her head of department that he felt it might have come from the school of Bronzino.

Simon, who was in charge of the auction, went on to suggest that she should check through the press cuttings books.

"Almost everything you need to know about the Trumpers is in there somewhere."

"And where will I find them?"

"On the fourth floor in that funny little room at the end of the passage."

When she eventually found the cubicle that housed the files she had to brush off a layer of dust and even remove the odd cobweb as she browsed through the annual offerings. She sat on the floor, her legs tucked beneath her, as she continued to turn the pages, becoming more and more engrossed in the rise of Charles Trumper from his days when he owned his first barrow in Whitechapel to the proposed plans for Trumper's of Chelsea. Although the press references were sketchy in those early years, it was a small article in the *Evening Standard* that stopped Cathy in her tracks. The page had yellowed with age and on the top right-hand corner, barely discernible, was printed the date: 8 September 1922.

A tall man in his late twenties, unshaven and dressed in an old army greatcoat, broke into the home of Mr and Mrs Charles Trumper of 11 Gilston Road, Chelsea yesterday morning. The intruder escaped with a small oil painting thought to be of little value. Mrs Trumper, seven months pregnant with her second child, was in the house at the time and collapsed

> from the shock. She was later rushed to
> Guy's hospital by her husband.
>
> On arrival an emergency operation
> was carried out by the senior surgeon Mr
> Armitage, but their little girl was still-
> born. Mrs Trumper is expected to remain
> at Guy's hospital under observation for
> several days.
>
> The police would like to interview
> anyone who may have been in the vicinity
> at the time.

Cathy's eyes moved on to a second piece, dated some three weeks later.

> Police have come into possession of an
> abandoned army greatcoat that may have
> been worn by the man who broke into 11
> Gilston Road, Chelsea, the home of Mr
> and Mrs Charles Trumper, on the morn-
> ing of 7 September. The ownership of the
> coat has been traced to a Captain Tren-
> tham, formerly of the Royal Fusiliers, who
> until recently was serving with his
> regiment in India.

Cathy read the two pieces over and over again. Could she really be the daughter of a man who had tried to rob Sir Charles and had been responsible for the death of his second child? And where did the painting fit in? Just how had Mrs Bennett come into possession of it? More impor- tant, why had Lady Trumper taken such an interest in a seemingly unimportant oil by an unknown artist? Unable to answer any of these questions, Cathy closed the cuttings book and pushed it back to the bottom of the pile. After she had washed her hands she wanted to return downstairs and ask Lady Trumper all her questions one by one, but knew that wasn't possible.

When the catalogue had been completed and on sale for over a week Lady Trumper asked to see Cathy in her office. Cathy only hoped that some frightful mistake hadn't been unearthed, or someone hadn't come across an attribution for the Virgin Mary and Child that she should have discovered in time to be credited in the catalogue.

As Cathy stepped into her office Becky said, "My congratulations."

"Thank you," said Cathy, not quite sure what she was being praised for.

"Your catalogue has been a sell-out and we're having to rush through a reprint."

"I'm only sorry that I couldn't discover any worthwhile attribution for your husband's painting," said Cathy, feeling relieved that was not the reason Rebecca had wanted to see her. She also hoped her boss might confide in her how Sir Charles had come into possession of the little oil in the first place, and perhaps even throw some light on the connection between the Trumpers and Captain Trentham.

"I'm not that surprised," Becky replied, without offering any further explanation.

You see, I came across an article in the files that mentioned a certain Captain Guy Trentham and I wondered . . . Cathy wanted to say, but she remained silent.

"Would you like to be one of the spotters when the sale takes place next week?" Becky asked.

On the day of the Italian sale, Cathy was accused by Simon of being "full of beans" although in fact she had been unable to eat a thing that morning.

Once the sale had started, painting after painting passed its estimate and Cathy was delighted when *The Basilica of St Mark's* reached a record for a Canaletto.

When Sir Charles's little oil replaced the masterpiece she suddenly felt queasy. It must have been the way the light caught the canvas, because there was now no doubt in her mind that it too was a masterpiece. Her immediate thought was that if only she possessed two hundred pounds she would have put in a bid for it herself.

The uproar that followed once the little picture had been removed from the easel made Cathy yet more anxious. She felt the accuser might well be right in his claim that the painting was an original by Bronzino. She had never seen a better example of his classic chubby babies with their sun-lit halos. Lady Trumper and Simon placed no blame on Cathy's shoulders as they continued to assure everyone who asked that the picture was a copy and had been known to the gallery for several years.

When the sale eventually came to an end, Cathy began to check through the dockets to be sure they were in the correct order so that there could be no doubt who had purchased each item. Simon was standing a few feet away and telling a gallery owner which pictures had failed to reach their reserve price and might therefore be sold privately. She froze when she heard Lady Trumper turn to Simon, the moment the dealer had left, and say, "It's that wretched Trentham woman up to her tricks again. Did you spot the old horror at the back of the room?" Simon nodded, but had made no further comment.

It must have been about a week after the Bishop of Reims had made his pronouncement that Simon invited Cathy to dinner at his flat in Pimlico. "A little celebration," he added, explaining he had asked all those who had been directly involved with the Italian sale.

Cathy arrived that night to find several of the staff from the Old Masters department already enjoying a glass of wine, and by the time they sat down to dinner only Rebecca Trumper was not present. Once again Cathy felt aware of the family atmosphere the Trumpers created even in their absence. The guests all enjoyed a sumptuous meal of avocado soup followed by wild duck which they learned Simon had spent the whole afternoon preparing. She and a young man called Julian, who worked in the rare books department, stayed on after the others had left to help clear up.

"Don't bother with the washing-up," said Simon. "My lady who 'does' can deal with it all in the morning."

"Typical male attitude," said Cathy as she continued to wash the dishes. "However, I admit that I remained behind with an ulterior motive."

"And what might that be?" he asked as he picked up a dishcloth and made a token attempt to help Julian with the drying.

"Who is Mrs Trentham?" Cathy asked abruptly. Simon swung round to face her, so she added awkwardly, "I heard Becky mention her name to you a few minutes after the sale was over and that man in the tweed jacket who made such a fuss had disappeared."

Simon didn't answer her question for some time, as if he were weighing up what he should say. Two dry dishes later he began.

"It goes back a long way, even before my time. And don't forget I was at Sotheby's with Becky for five years before she asked me to join her at Trumper's. To be honest, I'm not sure why she and Mrs Trentham loathe each other quite so much, but what I do know is that Mrs Trentham's son Guy and Sir Charles served in the same regiment during the First World War, and that Guy Trentham was somehow involved with that painting of the Virgin Mary and Child that had to be withdrawn from the sale. The only other piece of information that I've picked up over the years is that Guy Trentham disappeared off to Australia soon after . . . hey, that was one of my finest coffee cups."

"I'm so sorry," said Cathy. "How clumsy of me." She bent down and started picking up the little pieces of china that were scattered over the kitchen floor. "Where can I find another one?"

"In the china department of Trumper's," said Simon. "They're about two shillings each." Cathy laughed. "Just take my advice," he added. "Remember that the older staff have a golden rule about Mrs Trentham."

Cathy stopped gathering the pieces.

"They don't mention her name in front of Becky unless

she raises the subject. And never refer to the name of Trentham in the presence of Sir Charles. If you did, I think he'd sack you on the spot."

"I'm not likely to be given the chance," Cathy said. "I've never even met him. In fact, the nearest I've been to the man was watching him in the seventh row at the Italian sale."

"Well, at least we can do something about that," said Simon. "How would you like to accompany me to a house-warming party the Trumpers are giving next Thursday at their new home in Eaton Square?"

"Are you serious?"

"I certainly am," replied Simon. "Anyway, I don't think Sir Charles would altogether approve of my taking Julian."

"Mightn't they consider it somewhat presumptuous for such a junior member of staff to turn up on the arm of the head of the department?"

"Not Sir Charles. He doesn't know what the word 'presumptuous' means."

Cathy spent many hours during her lunch breaks poking around the dress shops in Chelsea before she selected what she considered was the appropriate outfit for the Trumpers' house-warming party. Her final choice was a sunflower yellow dress with a large sash around the waist which the assistant who served her described as suitable for a cocktail party. Cathy became fearful at the last minute that its length, or lack of length, might be a little too daring for such a grand occasion. However, when Simon came to pick her up at 135 his immediate comment was "You'll be a sensation, I promise you." His unreserved assurance made her feel more confident – at least until they arrived on the top step of the Trumpers' home in Eaton Square.

As Simon knocked on the door of his employers' residence, Cathy only hoped that it wasn't too obvious that she had never been invited to such a beautiful house before. However, she lost all her inhibitions the moment the butler invited them inside. Her eyes immediately settled on the feast that awaited her. While others drank from the seemingly endless bottles of champagne and helped themselves from the passing trays of canapés, she turned her attention elsewhere and even began to climb the staircase, savouring each of the rare delicacies one by one.

First came a Courbet, a still life of magnificent rich reds, oranges and greens; then a Picasso of two doves surrounded by pink blossom, their beaks almost touching; after a further step her eyes fell on a Pissarro of an old woman carrying a bundle of hay, dominated by different shades of green. But she gasped when she first saw the Sisley, a stretch of the Seine with every touch of pastel shading being made to count.

"That's *my* favourite," said a voice from behind her. Cathy turned to see a tall, tousle-haired young man give her a grin that must have made many people return his smile. His dinner jacket didn't quite fit, his bow tie needed adjusting and he lounged on the banisters as if without their support he might collapse completely.

"Quite beautiful," she admitted. "When I was younger I used to try and paint a little myself, and it was Sisley who finally convinced me I shouldn't bother."

"Why?"

Cathy sighed. "Sisley completed that picture when he was seventeen and still at school."

"Good heavens," the young man said. "An expert in our presence." Cathy smiled at her new companion. "Perhaps we should sneak a look at some more works on the upper corridor?"

"Do you think Sir Charles would mind?"

"Wouldn't have thought so," the young man replied. "After all, what's the point of being a collector if other people are never given the chance to admire what you've acquired?"

Buoyed up by his confidence Cathy mounted another step. "Magnificent," she said. "An early Sickert. They hardly ever come on the market."

"You obviously work in an art gallery."

"I work at Trumper's," Cathy said proudly. "Number 1 Chelsea Terrace. And you?"

"I sort of work for Trumper's myself," he admitted. Out of the corner of her eye, Cathy saw Sir Charles appearing from a room on the upstairs landing – her first close encounter with the chairman. Like Alice, she wanted to disappear through a keyhole, but her companion remained unperturbed, seemingly quite at home.

Her host smiled at Cathy as he came down the stairs. "Hello," he said once he'd reached them. "I'm Charlie Trumper and I've already heard all about you, young lady. I saw you at the Italian sale, of course, and Becky tells me that you're doing a superb job. By the way, congratulations on the catalogue."

"Thank you, sir," said Cathy, unsure what else she should say as the chairman continued on down the stairs, delivering a rat-a-tat-tat of sentences while ignoring her companion.

"I see you've already met my son," Sir Charles added as he looked back towards her. "Don't be taken in by his donnish façade; he's every bit as much of a rogue as his father. Show her the Bonnard, Daniel." With this Sir Charles disappeared into the drawing room.

"Ah yes, the Bonnard. Father's pride and joy," said Daniel. "I can think of no better way of luring a girl into the bedroom."

"You're Daniel Trumper?"

"No. Raffles, the well-known art thief," Daniel said as he took Cathy's hand and guided her up the stairs and on into his parents' room.

"Well – what about that?" he asked.

"Stunning," was all Cathy could think of saying as she stared up at the vast Bonnard nude – of his mistress Maria drying herself – that hung above the double bed.

"Father's immensely proud of that particular lady," Daniel explained. "As he never stops reminding us, he only paid three hundred guineas for her. Almost as good as the . . ." but Daniel didn't complete the sentence.

"He has excellent taste."

"The best untrained eye in the business, Mother always says. And as he's selected every picture that hangs in this house, who's to argue with her?"

"Your mother chose none of them?"

"Certainly not. My mother's by nature a seller, while my father's a buyer, a combination unequalled since Duveen and Berenson cornered the art market."

"Those two should have ended up in gaol," said Cathy.

"Whereas," said Daniel, "I suspect my father will end up in the same place as Duveen." Cathy laughed. "And now I think we ought to go back downstairs and grab some food before it all disappears."

Once they entered the dining room Cathy watched as Daniel walked over to a table on the far side of the room and switched round two of the place cards.

"Well, I'll be blowed, Miss Ross," Daniel said, pulling back a chair for her as other guests searched for their places. "After all that unnecessary banter, I find we're sitting next to each other."

Cathy smiled as she sat down beside him and watched a rather shy-looking girl circle the table desperately hunting for her place card. Soon Daniel was answering all her questions about Cambridge while he in turn wanted to know everything about Melbourne, a city he had never visited, he told her. Inevitably the question arose, "And what do your parents do?" Cathy replied without hesitation, "I don't know. I'm an orphan."

Daniel smiled. "Then we're made for each other."

"Why's that?"

"I'm the son of a fruit and veg man and a baker's daughter from Whitechapel. An orphan from Melbourne, you say? You'll certainly be a step up the social ladder for me, that's for sure."

Cathy laughed as Daniel recalled his parents' early careers, and as the evening went on she even began to feel this might be the first man she would be willing to talk to about her somewhat unexplained and unexplainable background.

When the last course had been cleared away and they sat lingering over their coffee, Cathy noticed that the shy girl was now standing immediately behind her chair. Daniel rose to introduce her to Marjorie Carpenter, a mathematics don from Girton. It became obvious that she was Daniel's guest for the evening and had been surprised if not a little disappointed to find that she had not been seated next to him at dinner.

The three of them chatted about life at Cambridge until the Marchioness of Wiltshire banged a spoon on the table to attract everyone's attention, then made a seemingly impromptu speech. When she finally called for a toast they all stood and raised their glasses to Trumper's. The marchioness then presented Sir Charles with a silver cigar case in the form of a scale model of Trumper's and from the expression on his face it obviously brought their host considerable delight. After a witty, and Cathy suspected not impromptu, speech, Sir Charles resumed his place.

"I ought to be going," Cathy said a few minutes later. "I have an early start in the morning. It was nice to have met you, Daniel," she added, sounding suddenly formal. They shook hands like strangers.

"Talk to you soon," he said as Cathy went over to thank her hosts for what she told them had been a memorable evening. She left on her own, but not before she had checked that Simon was deep in conversation with a fair-haired young man who had recently come to work in rugs and carpets.

She walked slowly back from Eaton Square to Chelsea Terrace, savouring every moment of the evening, and was upstairs in her little flat above Number 135 a few minutes after midnight, feeling not unlike Cinderella.

As she began to undress, Cathy mused over how much she had enjoyed the party, especially Daniel's company and the joy of seeing so many of her favourite artists. She wondered if . . . Her thoughts were interrupted by the sound of a phone ringing.

As the time was now well past midnight she picked up the receiver assuming the caller must have dialled a wrong number.

"Said I'd talk to you soon," said a voice.

"Go to bed, you chump."

"I'm already in bed. Talk to you again in the morning," he added. She heard a click.

Daniel telephoned a little after eight the following morning.

"I've only just got out of the bath," she told him.

"Then you must be looking like Maria. I'd better come over and select a towel for you."

"I already have a towel safely wrapped round me, thank you."

"Pity," said Daniel. "I'm rather good at drying up. But failing that," he added before she could reply, "would you join me at Trinity on Saturday? They're holding a college feast. We only have a couple a term, so if you turn the invitation down there's no hope of seeing me again for another three months."

"In which case I'll accept. But only because I haven't had a feast since I left school."

The following Friday, having taken Saturday off from work, Cathy travelled up to Cambridge by train to find Daniel standing on the platform waiting for her. Although Trinity High Table has been known to intimidate the most confident of guests, Cathy felt quite at ease as she sat among the dons. Nevertheless she couldn't help wondering how so many survived to old age if they ate and drank like this regularly.

"Man cannot live by bread alone," was Daniel's only explanation during the seven-course meal. She imagined that the orgy must have ended when they were invited back to the master's lodge only to find she was being offered even more savouries, accompanied by a port decanter that circled endlessly and never seemed to settle or empty. She eventually escaped, but not before the clock on Trinity tower had struck midnight. Daniel escorted her to a guest room on the far side of Great Court and suggested that they might attend matins at King's the following morning.

"I'm so glad you didn't recommend I make an appearance at breakfast," said Cathy as Daniel gave her a kiss on the cheek before saying goodnight.

The little guest room that Daniel had booked Cathy into was even smaller than her digs above 135, but she fell asleep the moment she placed her head on the pillow and was woken only by a peal of bells that she assumed must be coming from King's College Chapel.

Daniel and Cathy reached the chapel door only moments before the choristers began their crocodile procession down the nave. The singing seemed even more moving than on the gramophone record that Cathy possessed, with only the choristers' pictures on the sleeve to hint what the real experience might be like.

Once the blessing had been given Daniel suggested a walk along the Backs "to get rid of any left-over cobwebs". He took her hand, not releasing it again until they had returned to Trinity an hour later for a modest lunch.

During the afternoon he showed her round the Fitzwilliam Museum, where Cathy was mesmerised by Goya's *Devil Eating the Children*. "Bit like Trinity High Table," suggested Daniel before they walked over to the Queens', where they listened to a student string quartet give a recital of a Bach fugue. By the time they left, the lights along Silver Street had started flickering.

"No supper, please," begged Cathy in mock protest as they strolled back across the Mathematical Bridge.

Daniel chuckled and, after they had collected her case from Trinity, drove her slowly back to London in his little MG.

"Thank you for a wonderful weekend," said Cathy once Daniel had parked outside 135. "In fact, 'wonderful' is quite inadequate to describe the last two days."

Daniel kissed her gently on the cheek. "Let's do it again next weekend," he suggested.

"Not a hope," said Cathy. "That is, if you meant it when you claimed you liked thin women."

"All right, let's try the whole thing without the food and perhaps even have a game of tennis this time. It may be the only way I'll ever find out the standard of the Melbourne University 2nd VI."

Cathy laughed. "And would you also thank your mother for that superb party last Thursday? It's been a truly memorable week."

"I would, but you'll probably see her before I do."

"Aren't you staying overnight with your parents?"

"No. I must get back to Cambridge – got supervisions to give at nine tomorrow."

"But I could have taken the train."

"And I would have had two hours less of your company," he said as he waved goodbye.

CHAPTER 41

he first time they slept together, in his uncomfortable single bed in his comfortable little room, Cathy knew she wanted to spend the rest of her life with Daniel. She just wished he wasn't the son of Sir Charles Trumper.

She begged him not to tell his parents that they were seeing each other so regularly. She was determined to prove herself at Trumper's, she explained, and didn't want any favours because she was going out with the boss's son.

After the silver sale, her coup over the man in the yellow tie and later her tip-off to the journalist from the *Telegraph*, she began to feel more confident about letting the Trumpers know she had fallen in love with their only child.

On the Monday following the silver sale, Becky invited Cathy to join the management board of the auction house, which up until then had consisted of only Simon, Peter Fellowes – the head of research – and Becky herself.

Becky also asked Cathy to prepare the catalogue for the autumn Impressionist sale and take on several other responsibilities, including overall supervision of the front counter. "Next stop, a place on the main board," teased Simon.

She phoned Daniel to tell him the news later that morning.

"Does that mean we can at last stop fooling my parents?"

*　　*　　*

When Daniel's father telephoned him some weeks later to say he and his mother wanted to come down to Cambridge, as they needed to discuss something "rather important" with him, Daniel invited them both to have tea in his rooms on the following Sunday, warning them he too had something "rather important" to tell them.

Daniel and Cathy spoke to each other on the telephone every day that week and she began to wonder if it might not be wise at least to warn Daniel's parents that she would also be present when they came to tea. Daniel wouldn't hear of it, claiming that it was not often he had the chance of stealing a march on his father and he had no intention of letting the moment pass without the full satisfaction of seeing their surprised faces.

"And I'll let you into another secret," said Daniel. "I've applied for a post of Professor of Mathematics at King's College, London."

"That's some sacrifice you're making, Doctor Trumper," said Cathy, "because once you come to live in London I'm never going to be able to feed you the way they do at Trinity."

"Good news. That can only mean fewer visits to my tailor."

The tea that Daniel held in the rooms could not have been a happier occasion, Cathy felt, although at first Becky seemed on edge and, if anything, became even more anxious following an unexplained telephone call from someone called Mr Baverstock.

Sir Charles's delight at the news that she and Daniel planned to be married during the Easter vacation was so obviously genuine and Becky was positively overjoyed at the whole idea of having Cathy as a daughter-in-law. Charlie surprised Cathy when he suddenly changed the subject and enquired who had painted the watercolour that hung above Daniel's desk.

"Cathy," Daniel told him. "An artist in the family at last."

"You can paint as well, young lady?" Charlie asked in disbelief.

"She certainly can," said Daniel, looking towards the watercolour. "My engagement present," he explained. "What's more, it's the only original Cathy has painted since she came to England, so it's priceless."

"Will you paint one for me?" asked Charlie, after he had studied the little watercolour more carefully.

"I'd be delighted to," Cathy replied. "But where would you hang it? In the garage?"

After tea the four of them all walked along the Backs and Cathy was disappointed that Daniel's parents seemed quite anxious to return to London and felt unable to join them for evening chapel.

When they had returned from evensong they made love in Daniel's little bed and Cathy warned him that Easter might not be a moment too soon.

"What do you mean?" he asked.

"I think my period's already a week overdue."

Daniel was so overjoyed by the news he wanted to phone his parents immediately and share his excitement with them.

"Don't be silly," said Cathy. "Nothing's confirmed yet. I only hope that your mother and father won't be too appalled when they find out."

"Appalled? They're hardly in a position to be. They didn't even get married until the week after I was born."

"How do you know that?"

"Checked the date on my birth certificate in Somerset House against the date of their marriage certificate. Fairly simple really. It seems to begin with no one was willing to admit I belonged to anyone."

That one statement convinced Cathy that she must finally clear up any possibility of her being related to Mrs Trentham before they were married. Although Daniel had taken her mind off the problem of her parentage for over a year, she couldn't face the Trumpers thinking at some later date that she had set out to deceive them or worse, was somehow related to the woman they loathed above all others. Now that Cathy had unwittingly discovered where Mrs Trentham lived she resolved to write a letter to the lady just as soon as she was back in London.

She scribbled out a rough copy on Sunday evening and rose early the following morning to pen a final draft:

---

135 Chelsea Terrace
London SW3

November 27th, 1950

Dear Mrs. Trentham,

I write to you as a complete stranger in the hope that you might be able to help me to clear up a dilemma that I have been facing for several years.

I was born in Melbourne, Australia and have never known who my parents are as I was abandoned at an early age. I was in fact brought up in an orphanage called St. Hilda's. The only memento that I have of my father's existence is a miniature Military Cross which he gave me when I was a small child. The initials "G.F.T." are inscribed down one arm.

The curator of the Royal Fusiliers Museum at Hounslow has confirmed that the medal was awarded to a Captain Guy Francis Trentham on July 22nd 1918 following his brave action at the second battle of the Marne.

Are you by any chance related to Guy, and could he be my father? I would appreciate any information you may be able to give me on this matter and I apologise for intruding on your privacy.

I look forward to hearing from you.

Yours sincerely,

Cathy Ross

Cathy dropped the envelope in the post-box on the corner of Chelsea Terrace before going into work. After years of hoping to find someone to whom she was related, Cathy found it ironic that she now wanted that same person to deny her.

The announcement of Cathy's engagement to Daniel Trumper was on the court and social page of *The Times* the following morning. Everyone at Number 1 seemed delighted by the news. Simon toasted Cathy's health in champagne during the lunch break and told everyone, "It's a Trumper plot to be certain we don't lose her to Sotheby's or Christie's." Everyone clapped except Simon who whispered in her ear, "And you're exactly the right person to put us in the same league." Funny how some people think of possibilities for you, Cathy thought, even before you consider them for yourself.

On Thursday morning Cathy picked up off the front door mat a purple envelope with her name written in spidery handwriting. She nervously opened the letter to find it contained two sheets of thick paper of the same colour. The contents perplexed her, but at the same time brought her considerable relief.

---

19 CHESTER SQUARE
LONDON
SW1

November 29th, 1950

Dear Miss Ross,

Thank you for your letter of last Monday, but I fear I can be of little assistance to you with your enquiries. I had two sons, the younger of whom is Nigel, who has recently separated. His wife now resides in Dorset, with my only grandson, Giles Raymond, aged two.

My elder son was indeed Guy Francis Trentham, who was awarded the Military Cross at the second battle

of the Marne, but he died of tuberculosis in 1922 after a
long illness. He never married and left no dependants.

The miniature version of his MC went missing soon
after Guy had paid a fleeting visit to distant relatives in
Melbourne. I am happy to learn of its reappearance after
all these years, and would be most grateful if you felt
able to return the medal to me at your earliest
convenience. I feel sure you would no longer wish
to hold on to a family heirloom now that you are fully
acquainted with its origins.

                    Yours sincerely

                    Ethel Trentham

Cathy was delighted to discover that Guy Trentham
had died the year before she was born. That meant it was
quite impossible for her to be related to the man who had
caused her future parents-in-law so much distress. The MC
must somehow have got into the hands of whoever her
father was, she concluded; on balance she felt she ought,
however reluctantly, to return the medal to Mrs Trentham
without delay.

After the revelations of Mrs Trentham's letter, Cathy
was doubtful that she would ever be able to find out who
her parents were, as she had no immediate plans to return
to Australia now that Daniel was so much part of her future.
In any case, she had begun to feel that further pursuit of
her father had become somewhat pointless.

As Cathy had already told Daniel on the day they met
that she had no idea who her parents were, she travelled
down to Cambridge that Saturday evening with a clear conscience. She was also relieved that her period had at last
begun. As the train bumped over the points on its journey
to the university city, Cathy could never remember feeling
so happy. She fingered the little cross that hung around her
neck now hanging from a gold chain Daniel had given her
on her birthday. She was sad to be wearing the memento

for the last time: she had already made the decision to send the medal back to Mrs Trentham following her weekend with Daniel.

The train drew into Cambridge station only a few minutes after its scheduled time of arrival.

Cathy picked up her small suitcase and strolled out on to the pavement, expecting to find Daniel parked and waiting for her in his MG: he had never once been late since the day they had met. She was disappointed to find no sign of him or his car, and even more surprised when twenty minutes later he still hadn't shown up. She walked back on to the station concourse and placed two pennies in the telephone box before dialling the number that went straight through to Daniel's room. The ringing tone went on and on, but she didn't need to press Button A because no one answered.

Puzzled by not being able to locate him, Cathy left the station once again and asked one of the drivers from the rank to take her to Trinity College.

When the taxi drove into New Court Cathy was even more bemused to discover Daniel's MG was parked in its usual space. She paid the fare and walked across the court to the now familiar staircase.

Cathy felt the least she could do was tease Daniel for failing to pick her up. Was this to be the sort of treatment she could expect once they were married? Was she now on the same level as any undergraduate who turned up without his weekly essay? She climbed the worn stone steps up to his room and knocked quietly on the door in case he still had a pupil with him. As there was no answer after a second knock, she pushed open the heavy wooden door, having decided that she would just have to wait around until he returned.

Her scream must have been heard by every resident on staircase C.

The first undergraduate to arrive on the scene found the prostrate body of a young woman lying face down in the middle of the floor. The student fell to his knees, dropped the books he had been carrying by her side and proceeded to be sick all over her. He took a deep breath, turned round as quickly as he could, and began to crawl back out of the study past an overturned chair. He was unable to look up again at the sight that had met him when he had first entered the room.

Doctor Trumper continued to swing gently from a beam in the centre of the room.

CHARLIE

1950-1964

CHAPTER 42

couldn't sleep for three days. On the fourth morning, along with so many of Daniel's friends, colleagues and undergraduates, I attended his funeral service at Trinity Chapel. I somehow survived that ordeal and the rest of the week, thanks not least to Daphne's organising everything so calmly and efficiently. Cathy was unable to attend the service as they were still detaining her for observation at Addenbrooke's hospital.

I stood next to Becky as the choir sang "Fast Falls the Eventide". My mind drifted as I tried to reconstruct the events of the past three days and make some sort of sense of them. After Daphne had told me that Daniel had taken his own life – whoever selected her to break the news understood the meaning of the word compassion – I immediately drove up to Cambridge, having begged her not to tell Becky anything until I knew more of what had actually happened myself. By the time I arrived at Trinity Great Court some two hours later, Daniel's body had already been removed, and they had taken Cathy off to Addenbrooke's where she was not surprisingly still in a state of shock. The police inspector in charge of the case couldn't have been more considerate. Later, I visited the morgue and identified the body, thanking God that at least Becky hadn't experienced that ice-cold room as the last place she was alone with her son.

"*Lord, with me abide . . .*"

I told the police that I could think of no reason why Daniel should want to take his own life – that in fact he had just become engaged and I had never known him happier. The inspector then showed me the suicide note: a sheet of foolscap containing a single handwritten paragraph.

"They generally write one, you know," he said.

I didn't know.

I began to read Daniel's neat academic hand:

Now that it's no longer possible for Cathy and me to marry, I have nothing left to live for. For God's sake take care of the child.

Daniel

I must have repeated those twenty-eight words to myself over a hundred times and still I couldn't make any sense out of them. A week later the doctor confirmed in his report to the coroner that Cathy was not pregnant and had certainly not suffered a miscarriage. I returned to those words again and again. Was I missing some subtle inference, or was his final message something I could never hope to comprehend fully?

"*When other helpers fail . . .*"

A forensic expert later discovered some writing paper in the grate, but it had been burnt to a cinder and the black brittle remains yielded no clue. Then they showed me an envelope that the police believed the charred letter must have been sent in and asked if I could identify the writing. I studied the stiff, thin upright hand that had written the words "Doctor Daniel Trumper" in purple ink.

"No," I lied. The letter had been hand-delivered, the detective told me, some time earlier that afternoon by a man with a brown moustache and a tweed coat. This was all the undergraduate who caught sight of him could remember, except that he seemed to know his way around.

I asked myself what that evil old lady could possibly have written to Daniel that would have caused him to take his own life; I felt sure the discovery that Guy Trentham was his father would not have been sufficient for such a drastic course of action — especially as I knew that he and Mrs Trentham had already met and come to an agreement some three years before.

The police found one other letter on Daniel's desk. It was from the Provost of King's College, London, formally offering him a Chair in Mathematics.

"And comforts flee . . ."

After I had left the mortuary I drove on to Addenbrooke's hospital, where they allowed me to spend some time at Cathy's bedside. Although her eyes were open, they betrayed no recognition of me: for nearly an hour she simply stared blankly up at the ceiling while I stood there. When I realised there was nothing I could usefully do I left quietly. The senior psychiatrist, Doctor Stephen Atkins, came bustling out of his office and asked if I could spare him a moment.

The dapper, little man in a beautifully tailored suit and large bow tie explained that Cathy was suffering from psychogenic amnesia, sometimes known as hysterical amnesia, and that it could be some time before he was able to assess what her rate of recovery might be. I thanked him and added that I would keep in constant touch. I then drove slowly back to London.

"Help of the helpless, O abide with me . . ."

Daphne was waiting for me in my office and made no comment about the lateness of the hour. I tried to thank her for such endless kindness, but explained that I had to be the one who broke the news to Becky. God knows how I carried out that responsibility without mentioning the purple envelope with its tell-tale hand-writing, but I did. Had I told Becky the full story I think she would have gone round to Chester Square that night and killed the woman there and then with her bare hands – I might even have assisted her.

They buried him amongst his own kind. The college chaplain, who must have carried out this particular duty so many times in the past, stopped to compose himself on three separation occasions.

"*In life, in death, O Lord, abide with me . . .*"

Becky and I visited Addenbrooke's together every day that week, but Doctor Atkins only confirmed that Cathy's condition remained unchanged; she had not yet spoken. Nevertheless, just the thought of her lying there alone needing our love gave us something else to worry about other than ourselves.

When we arrived back in London late on the Friday afternoon Arthur Selwyn was pacing up and down outside my office.

"Someone's broken into Cathy's flat, the lock's been forced," he said even before I had a chance to speak.

"But what could a thief possibly hope to find?"

"The police can't fathom that out either. Nothing seems to have been disturbed."

To the puzzle of what Mrs Trentham could have written to Daniel I added the mystery of what she could possibly want that belonged to Cathy. After checking over the little room myself I was none the wiser.

Becky and I continued to travel up and down to Cambridge every other day, and then midway through the third week Cathy finally spoke, haltingly to start with, then in bursts while grasping my hand. Then suddenly, without warning, she would go silent again. Sometimes she would rub her forefinger against her thumb just below her chin.

This puzzled even Doctor Atkins.

Doctor Atkins had since then, however, been able

to hold extensive conversations with Cathy on several occasions and had even started playing word games to probe her memory. It was his opinion that she had blotted out all recollection of anything connected with Daniel Trumper or with her early life in Australia. It was not uncommon in such cases, he assured us, and even gave the particular state of mind a fine Greek name.

"Should I try and get in touch with her tutor at the University of Melbourne? Or even talk to the staff of the Melrose Hotel – and see if they can throw any light on the problem?"

"No," he said, straightening his spotted bow tie. "Don't push her too hard and be prepared for that part of her mind to take some considerable time to recover."

I nodded my agreement.

"Back off" seemed to be Doctor Atkins' favourite expression. "And never forget your wife will be suffering the same trauma."

Seven weeks later they allowed us to take Cathy back to Eaton Square, where Becky had prepared a room for her. I had already transferred all Cathy's possessions from the little flat above the butcher's shop, still unsure if anything was missing following the break-in.

Becky had stored all Cathy's clothes neatly away in the wardrobe and drawers while trying to make the room look as lived in as possible. Some time before I had taken her watercolour of the Cam from above Daniel's desk and rehung it on the staircase between the Courbet and the Sisley. Yet when Cathy first walked up those stairs on the way to her new room, she passed her own painting without the slightest sign of recognition.

I enquired once again of Doctor Atkins if perhaps we should now write to the University of Melbourne and try to find out something about Cathy's past, but he still counselled against such a move, saying that she must be the one who came forward with any information, and then only when she felt able to do so, not as the result of any pressure from outside.

"But how long do you imagine it might be before her memory is fully restored?"

"Anything from fourteen days to fourteen years, from my experience."

I remember returning to Cathy's room that night, sitting on the end of her bed and holding her hand. I noticed with pleasure that a little colour had returned to her cheeks. She smiled and asked me for the first time how the "great barrow" was rumbling along.

"We've declared record profits," I told her. "But far more important, everyone wants to see you back at Number 1."

She thought about this for some time. Then quite simply she said, "I wish you were my father."

In February 1951 Nigel Trentham joined the board of Trumper's. He took his place next to Paul Merrick, to whom he gave a thin smile. I couldn't bring myself to look directly at him. He was a few years younger than me but I vainly considered no one round that table would have thought so.

The board meanwhile approved the expenditure of a further half a million pounds "to fill the gap", as Becky referred to the half-acre that had for ten years lain empty in the middle of Chelsea Terrace. "So at last Trumper's can all be housed under one roof," I declared. Trentham made no comment. My fellow-directors also agreed an allocation of one hundred thousand pounds to rebuild the Whitechapel Boys' Club which was to be renamed "The Dan Salmon Centre". I noticed Trentham whispered something in Merrick's ear.

In the event, inflation, strikes and escalating builders' costs caused the final bill for Trumper's to be nearer seven hundred and thirty thousand pounds than the estimated half-million. One outcome of this was to make it necessary for the company to offer a further rights issue in order to cover the extra expense. Another was that the building of the boys' club had to be postponed.

The rights issue was once again heavily oversubscribed, which was flattering for me personally, though I feared Mrs Trentham might be a major buyer of any new stock: I had no way of proving it. This dilution of my equity meant that I had to watch my personal holding in the company fall below forty per cent for the first time.

It was a long summer and as each day passed Cathy became a little stronger, Becky a little more communicative. Finally the doctor agreed that Cathy could return to Number 1. She came back to work the following Monday and Becky said it was almost as if she had never been away – except that no one ever mentioned the name of Daniel in her presence.

One evening, it must have been about a month later, I returned home from the office to find Cathy pacing up and down the hall. My immediate thoughts were that she must be agonising over the past. I couldn't have been more wrong.

"You've got your staffing policy all wrong," she said as I closed the door behind me.

"I beg your pardon, young lady?" I had not even been given enough time to shed my topcoat.

"It's all wrong," she repeated. "The Americans are saving thousands of dollars in their stores with time and motion studies while Trumper's are behaving as if they're still roaming around on the ark."

"Captive audience on the ark," I reminded her.

"Until it stopped raining," she replied. "Charlie, you must realise that the company could be saving at least eighty thousand a year on wages alone. I haven't been idle these last few weeks. In fact, I've put together a report to prove my point." She thrust a cardboard box into my arms and marched out of the room.

For over an hour after dinner I rummaged into the box and read through Cathy's preliminary findings. She had spotted an over-manning situation that we had all missed and characteristically explained in great detail how the situation could be dealt with without offending the unions.

Over breakfast the following morning Cathy continued to explain her findings to me as if I had never been to bed. "Are you still listening, Chairman?" she demanded. She always called me "Chairman" when she wanted to make a point. A ploy I felt sure she had picked up from Daphne.

"You're all talk," I told her, which caused even Becky to glance over the top of her paper.

"Do you want me to prove I'm right?" Cathy asked.

"Be my guest."

From that day on, whenever I carried out my morning rounds, I would invariably come across Cathy working on a different floor, questioning, watching or simply taking copious notes, often with a stop-watch in her other hand. I never asked her what she was up to and if she ever caught my eye all she would say was, "Good day, Chairman."

At weekends I could hear Cathy typing away in her room for hour after hour. Then, without warning, one morning at breakfast I discovered a thick file waiting for me in the place where I had hoped to find an egg, two rashers of bacon and the *Sunday Times*.

That afternoon I began reading through what Cathy had prepared for me. By the early evening I had come to the conclusion that the board must implement most of her recommendations without further delay.

I knew exactly what I wanted to do next but felt it needed Doctor Atkins' blessing. I phoned Addenbrooke's that evening and the ward sister kindly entrusted me with his home number. We spent over an hour on the phone. He had no fears for Cathy's future, he assured me, especially since she'd begun to remember little incidents from her past and was now even willing to talk about Daniel.

When I came down to breakfast the following morning I found Cathy sitting at the table waiting for me. She didn't say a word as I munched through my toast and marmalade pretending to be engrossed in the *Financial Times*.

"All right, I give in," she said.

"Better not," I warned her, without looking up from my paper. "Because you're item number seven on the agenda for next month's board meeting."

"But who's going to present my case?" asked Cathy, sounding anxious.

"Not me, that's for sure," I replied. "And I can't think of anyone else who'd be willing to do so."

For the next fortnight whenever I retired to bed I became aware when passing Cathy's room that the typing had stopped. I was so filled with curiosity that once I even peered through the half-open bedroom door. Cathy stood facing a mirror, by her side was a large white board resting on an easel covered in a mass of coloured pins and dotted arrows.

"Go away," she said, without even turning round. I realised there was nothing for it but to wait until the board was due to meet.

Doctor Atkins had warned me that the ordeal of having to present her case in public might turn out to be too much for the girl and I was to get her home if she began to show any signs of stress. "Be sure you don't push her too far," were his final words.

"I won't let that happen," I promised him.

That Thursday morning the board members were all seated in their places round the table by three minutes to ten. The meeting began on a quiet note, with apologies for absence, followed by the acceptance of the minutes of the last meeting. We somehow still managed to keep Cathy waiting for over an hour, because when we came to item number three on the agenda – a rubber-stamp decision to renew the company's insurance policy with the Prudential – Nigel Trentham used the opportunity simply as an excuse to irritate me – hoping, I suspected, that I would eventually lose my temper. I might have done, if he hadn't so obviously wanted me to.

"I think the time has come for a change, Mr Chairman," he said. "I suggest we transfer our business to Legal and General."

I stared down the left-hand side of the table to focus on the man whose very presence always brought back memories of Guy Trentham and what he might have looked like in late middle age. The younger brother wore a smart well-tailored double-breasted suit that successfully disguised his weight problem. However, there was nothing that could disguise the double chin or balding pate.

"I must point out to the board," I began, "that Trumper's have been with the Prudential for over thirty years. And what is more, they have never let the company down in the past. Just as important, Legal and General are highly unlikely to be able to offer more favourable terms."

"But they're in possession of two per cent of the company's stock," Trentham pointed out.

"The Pru still have five per cent," I reminded my fellow-directors, aware that once again Trentham hadn't done his homework. The argument might have been lobbed backwards and forwards for hours like a Drobny–Fraser tennis match had Daphne not intervened and called for a vote.

Although Trentham lost by seven to three, the altercation served to remind everyone round that table what his long-term purpose must be. For the past eighteen months Trentham had, with the help of his mother's money, been building up his shareholding in the company to a position I estimated to be around fourteen per cent. This would have been controllable had I not been painfully aware that the Hardcastle Trust also held a further seventeen per cent of our stock – stock which had originally been intended for Daniel but which would on the death of Mrs Trentham pass automatically to Sir Raymond's next of kin. Although Nigel Trentham lost the vote, he showed no sign of distress as he rearranged his papers, casting an aside to Paul Merrick who was seated on his left. He obviously felt confident that time was on his side.

"Item seven," I said and leaning over to Jessica asked if she would invite Miss Ross to join us. When Cathy entered the room every man around that table stood. Even Trentham half rose from his place.

Cathy placed two boards on the easel that had already been set up for her, one full of charts, the other covered in statistics. She turned to face us. I greeted her with a warm smile.

"Good morning, ladies and gentlemen," she said. She paused and checked her notes. "I should like to begin by . . ."

She may have started somewhat hesitantly, but she soon got into her stride as she explained, point by point, why the company's staffing policy was outdated and the steps we should take to rectify the situation as quickly as possible. These included early retirement for men of sixty and women of fifty-five; the leasing of shelf space, even whole floor sections, to recognised brand names, which would produce a guaranteed cash-flow without financial risk to Trumper's, as each lessee would be responsible for supplying their own staff; and a larger percentage discount on merchandise for any firms who were hoping to place orders with us for the first time. The presentation took Cathy about forty minutes, and when she concluded it was several moments before anyone round the table spoke.

If her initial presentation was good, her handling of the questions that followed was even better. She dealt with all the banking problems Tim Newman and Paul Merrick could throw at her, as well as the trade union anxieties Arthur Selwyn raised. As for Nigel Trentham, she handled him with a calm efficiency that I was only too painfully aware I could never equal. When Cathy left the boardroom an hour later all the men rose again except Trentham, who stared down at the report in front of him.

As I walked up the path that evening Cathy was on the doorstep waiting to greet me.

"Well?"

"Well?"

"Don't tease, Charlie," she scolded.

"You were appointed to be our new personnel director," I told her, grinning. For a moment even she was speechless.

"Now you've opened this can of worms, young lady," I added as I walked past her, "the board rather expects you to sort the problem out."

Cathy was so obviously thrilled by my news that I felt for the first time perhaps Daniel's tragic death might be behind us. I phoned Doctor Atkins that evening to tell him not only how Cathy had fared but that, as a result of her presentation, she had been elected to the board. However, what I didn't tell either of them was that I had been forced to agree to another of Trentham's nominations to the board in order to ensure that her appointment went through without a vote being called for.

From the day Cathy arrived at the boardroom table it was clear for all to see that she was a serious contender to succeed me as chairman and no longer simply a bright girl from Becky's fold. However, I was well aware that Cathy's advancement could only be achieved while Trentham remained unable to gain control of fifty-one per cent of Trumper's shares. I also realised that the only way he could hope to do that was by making a public bid for the company, which I accepted could well become possible once he got his hands on the money held by the Hardcastle Trust. For the first time in my life I wanted Mrs Trentham to live long enough to allow me to build the company to such a position of strength that even the Trust money would prove inadequate for Nigel Trentham to mount a successful takeover bid.

On 2 June 1953 Queen Elizabeth was crowned, four days after two men from different parts of the Commonwealth conquered Everest. Winston Churchill best summed it up when he said: "Those who have read the history of the first Elizabethan era must surely look forward with anticipation to participating in the second."

I took up the Prime Minister's challenge and Cathy threw all her energy into the personnel project the board had entrusted her with, and was able to show a saving of forty-nine thousand pounds in wages during 1953 and a further twenty-one thousand pounds in the first half of 1954. By the end of that fiscal year I felt she knew more about the running of Trumper's at staff level than anyone around that table, myself included.

During 1955 overseas sales began to fall sharply, and as Cathy no longer seemed to be extended and I was keen for her to gain experience of other departments I asked her to sort out the problems of our international department.

She took on her new position with the same enthusiasm with which she tackled everything, but during the next two years began to clash with Nigel Trentham over a number of issues, including a policy to return the difference to any customer who could prove he had paid less for a standard item when shopping at one of our rivals. Trentham argued that Trumper's customers were not interested in some imagined difference in price that could be compared with a lesser-known store, but only in quality and service, to which Cathy replied, "It isn't the customers' responsibility to be concerned with the balance-sheet, it's the board's on behalf of our shareholders."

On another occasion Trentham came near to accusing Cathy of being a communist when she suggested a "workers' share participation scheme" which she felt would create company loyalty that only the Japanese had fully understood – a country, she explained, where it was not uncommon for a company to retain ninety-eight per cent of its staff from womb to tomb. Even I was unsure about this particular idea, but Becky warned me in private that I was beginning to sound like a "fuddy duddy", which I assumed was some modern term not to be taken as a compliment.

When Legal and General failed to get our insurance business they sold their two per cent holding outright to Nigel Trentham. From that moment I became even more anxious that he might eventually get his hands on enough stock to take over the company. He also proposed another nomination to the board which, thanks to Paul Merrick seconding, was accepted.

"I should have secured that land thirty-five years ago for a mere four thousand pounds," I told Becky.

"As you have reminded us so often in the past, and what's worse," Becky reminded me, "is that Mrs Trentham is now more dangerous to us dead than alive."

Trumper's took the arrival of Elvis Presley, Teddy boys, stilettos and teenagers all in its stride. "The customers may have changed, but our standards must not be allowed to," I continually reminded the board.

In 1960 the company declared a seven hundred and fifty-seven thousand pound net profit, a fourteen per cent return on capital, and a year later went on to top this achievement by being granted a Royal Warrant from the monarch. I instructed that the House of Windsor's coat of arms should be hung above the main entrance to remind the public that the Queen shopped at the barrow on a regular basis.

I couldn't pretend that I had ever seen Her Majesty carrying one of our familiar blue bags with its silver motif of a barrow, or spotted her as she travelled up and down the escalators during peak hours, but we still received regular telephone calls from the Palace when they found themselves running short of supplies: which only proved yet again my old granpa's theory that an apple is an apple whoever bites it.

The highlight of 1961 for me was when Becky finally opened the Dan Salmon Centre in Whitechapel Road – another building that had run considerably over cost. However, I didn't regret one penny of the expenditure – despite Merrick's niggling criticism – as I watched the next generation of East End boys and girls swimming, boxing, weightlifting and playing squash, a game I just couldn't get the hang of.

Whenever I went to see West Ham play soccer on a Saturday afternoon, I would always drop in to the new club on my way home, and watch the African, West Indian and Asian children – the new East Enders – battle against each other just as determinedly as we had done against the Irish and Eastern European immigrants.

"The old order changeth, yielding place to new, And God fulfils himself in many ways, Lest one good custom should corrupt the world." Tennyson's words, chiselled in the stone on the archway above the centre, brought my mind back to Mrs Trentham, who was never far from my thoughts, especially while her three representatives sat around the boardroom table eager to carry out her bidding. Nigel, who now resided at Chester Square, seemed happy to wait for everything to fall into place before he marshalled his troops ready for the attack.

I continued to pray that Mrs Trentham would live to a grand old age as I still needed more time to prepare some blocking process to ensure that her son could never take over the company.

It was Daphne who first warned me that Mrs Trentham had taken to her bed and was receiving regular visits from the family GP. Nigel Trentham still managed to keep a smile on his face during those months of waiting.

Without warning, on 7 March 1962, Mrs Trentham, aged eighty-nine, died.

"Peacefully in her sleep," Daphne informed me.

CHAPTER 43

aphne attended Mrs Trentham's funeral, "Just to be certain that the wretched woman really was buried," she explained to Charlie later, "though it wouldn't surprise me if she found some way of rising from the dead." She went on to warn Charlie that Nigel had been overheard, even before the body had been lowered into the ground, telling everyone that we should expect thunderbolts as soon as the board met again. He only had a few days to wait.

That first Tuesday of the following month Charlie checked around the boardroom table to see that every director was present. He could sense they were all waiting to see who would strike first. Nigel Trentham and his two colleagues wore black ties like some official badge of office, reminding the board of their newly acquired status. In contrast, for the first time in Charlie's memory, Mr Baverstock wore a garish pastel-coloured tie.

Charlie had already worked out that Trentham would wait until item number six – a proposal to expand the banking facilities on the ground floor – before he made any move. The original scheme had been one of Cathy's brainchilds, and soon after returning from one of her monthly trips to the States she had presented a detailed proposal to the board. Although the new department had experienced some teething problems by the end of its second year it was just about breaking even.

The first half-hour was peaceful enough as Charlie took

the board through items one to five. But when he called for, "Item number six. The expansion of . . ."

"Let's close the bank and cut our losses," were Trentham's opening words even before Charlie had been given the chance to offer an opinion.

"For what reason?" asked Cathy defiantly.

"Because we're not bankers," said Trentham. "We're shopkeepers – or barrow pushers, as our chairman so often likes to remind us. In any case, it would give us a saving on expenditure of nearly thirty thousand pounds a year."

"But the bank is just beginning to pay its way," said Cathy. "We should be thinking of expanding the facilities, not curtailing them. And with profits in mind, who knows how much money cashed on the premises is then spent on the premises?"

"Yes, but look at the amount of extra counter space the banking hall is taking up."

"In return we give our customers a valuable service."

"And lose money hand over fist by not using the space for more profitable lines of business," fired back Trentham.

"Like what, for example?" said Cathy. "Just tell me one other department that would provide a more useful service for our customers and at the same time show a better return on our investment. Do that and I'll be the first to agree we should close down the banking hall."

"We're not a service industry. It's our duty to show a decent return on capital for our shareholders," said Trentham. "I demand a vote on this," he added, not bothering to rebut Cathy's arguments any further.

Trentham lost the vote by six to three and Charlie assumed after such an outcome they would then pass on to item number seven – a proposed staff outing to the film of *West Side Story*, playing at the Odeon, Leicester Square. However, once Jessica Allen had recorded the names for the minutes, Nigel Trentham rose quickly to his feet and said, "I have an announcement to make, Mr Chairman."

"Wouldn't it be more appropriate under 'Any other business'?" asked Charlie innocently.

"I will no longer be here when you come to discuss any other business, Mr Chairman," said Trentham coldly. He proceeded to move a piece of paper from an inside pocket, unfolded it and began reading from what was obviously a prepared script.

"I feel it is my duty to inform the board," he stated, "that within a few weeks I will be the sole owner of thirty-three per cent of Trumper's shares. When we next meet, I shall be insisting that several changes be made to the structure of the company, not least in the composition of those presently seated around this table." He stopped to stare at Cathy before he added, "I intend to leave now, in order that you can discuss more fully the implications of my statement."

He pushed back his chair as Daphne said, "I'm not quite sure I fully understand what you're suggesting, Mr Trentham."

Trentham hesitated for a moment before he replied, "Then I shall have to explain my position more fully, Lady Wiltshire."

"How kind of you."

"At the next board meeting," he continued unabashed, "I shall allow my name to be proposed and seconded as chairman of Trumper's. Should I fail to be elected, I shall immediately resign from the board and issue a press statement of my intention to make a full takeover bid for the remaining shares of the company. You must all be aware by now that I will have the necessary facility to mount such a challenge. As I only require a further eighteen per cent of the stock to become the majority shareholder, I suggest it might be wise for those of you who are currently directors to face up to the inevitable and offer your resignations in order to avoid the embarrassment of being dismissed. I look forward to seeing one or two of you again at next month's board meeting." He and his two colleagues rose and followed him out of the room.

The silence that followed was broken only by another question from Daphne.

"What's the collective noun for a group of shits?"

Everybody laughed, except Baverstock, who said under his breath, "A heap."

"So, now we've been given our battle orders," said Charlie. "Let's hope we all have the stomach for a fight." Turning to Mr Baverstock he asked, "Can you advise the board on the present position concerning those shares currently held by the Hardcastle Trust?"

The old man raised his head slowly and looked up at Charlie. "No, Mr Chairman, I cannot. Indeed, I'm sorry to have to inform the board that I, too, must tender my resignation."

"But why?" asked Becky, aghast. "You've always supported us in the past through thick and thin."

"I must apologise, Lady Trumper, but I am not at liberty to disclose my reasons."

"Couldn't you possibly reconsider your position?" Charlie asked.

"No, sir," Baverstock replied firmly.

Charlie immediately closed the meeting, despite everyone trying to talk at once, and quickly followed Baverstock out of the boardroom.

"What made you resign?" Charlie asked. "After all these years?"

"Perhaps we could meet and discuss my reasons tomorrow, Sir Charles?"

"Of course. But just tell me why you felt it necessary to leave us at exactly the time when I most need you."

Mr Baverstock stopped in his tracks. "Sir Raymond anticipated this might happen," he said quietly. "And instructed me accordingly."

"I don't understand."

"That is why we should meet tomorrow, Sir Charles."

"Do you want me to bring Becky along?"

Mr Baverstock considered this suggestion for some time before saying, "I think not. If I am to break a confidence for the first time in forty years, I'd prefer to have no other witnesses present."

When Charlie arrived at the offices of Baverstock, Dickens and Cobb the following morning, the senior partner was standing at the door waiting to greet him. Although Charlie had never once been late for an appointment with Mr Baverstock in the fourteen years they had known each other, he was touched by the old-world courtesy the solicitor always extended to him.

"Good morning, Sir Charles," said Baverstock before guiding his guest along the corridor to his office. Charlie was surprised to be offered a seat near the unlit fire rather than his usual place on the other side of the partner's desk. There wasn't a clerk or secretary in attendance on this occasion to keep a record of the meeting and Charlie also noticed that the phone on Mr Baverstock's desk had been taken off the hook. He sat back, realising that this was not going to be a short meeting.

"Many years ago when I was a young man," began Baverstock, "and I sat my pupil's exams, I swore to keep a code of confidentiality when dealing with my clients' private affairs. I think I can safely say that I have honoured that undertaking throughout my professional life. However, one of my clients, as you well know, was Sir Raymond Hardcastle and he –" There was a knock on the door and a young girl entered, carrying a tray bearing two cups of hot coffee and a sugar bowl.

"Thank you, Miss Burrows," said Baverstock as one of the cups was placed in front of him. He did not continue with his exposition until the door was closed behind her. "Where was I, old fellow?" Baverstock asked, as he dropped a sugar lump into his cup.

"Your client, Sir Raymond."

"Oh, yes," said Baverstock. "Now, Sir Raymond left a will of which you may well feel you are cognisant. What you could not know, however, is that he attached a letter to that document. It has no legal standing, as it was addressed to me in a personal capacity."

Charlie's coffee lay untouched as he listened intently to what Baverstock had to say. "It is because that letter is not a legal document but a private communication between old friends that I have decided you should be a party to its contents."

Baverstock leaned forward and opened the file that lay on the table in front of him. He removed a single sheet of paper transcribed in a bold, firm hand. "I should like to point out, Sir Charles, before I read this letter to you that it was written at a time when Sir Raymond assumed that his estate would be inherited by Daniel and not by his next of kin."

Mr Baverstock pushed his spectacles up the bridge of his nose, cleared his throat and began to read:

Dear Baverstock,

Despite everything I have done to ensure that my final wishes are carried out to the letter, it may still be possible that Ethel will find some way of seeing that my great grandson, Daniel Trumper, does not inherit the residue of my estate. If such circumstances should come about please use your common sense and allow those most affected by the decisions in my will to be privy to its finer details.

Old friend, you know exactly to whom and what I am referring.

Yours as ever

Ray.

Baverstock placed the letter back on the table and said, "I fear he knew my little weaknesses every bit as much as his daughter's." Charlie smiled for he appreciated the ethical dilemma with which the old lawyer was so obviously grappling.

"Now, before I make reference to the will itself I must let you into another confidence."

Charlie nodded.

"You are painfully aware, Sir Charles, that Mr Nigel Trentham is now the next of kin. However, it should not pass unobserved that the will is so worded that Sir Raymond couldn't even bring himself actually to name him as the recipient. I suspect that he hoped that Daniel might produce progeny of his own who would have taken precedence over his grandson.

"The current position is that Mr Nigel Trentham will, as Sir Raymond's closest living descendant, be entitled to the shares in Trumper's and the residue of the Hardcastle estate – a considerable fortune, which I can confirm would provide him with adequate funds to mount a full takeover bid for your company. However, that was not my purpose in wanting to see you this morning. No, that was because there is one clause in the will you could not have previously been aware of. After taking into account Sir Raymond's letter, I believe it to be nothing less than my duty to inform you of its import."

Baverstock burrowed into his file and retrieved a sheaf of papers, sealed in wax and bound in pink ribbon.

"The first eleven clauses of Sir Raymond's testament took me some considerable time to compose. However, their substance is not relevant to the issue at hand. They relate to minor legacies left by my client to nephews, nieces and cousins who have already received the sums bequeathed.

"Clauses twelve to twenty-one go on to name charities, clubs and academic institutions with which Sir Raymond had long been associated and they too have received the benefit of his munificence. But it is clause twenty-two that I consider crucial." Baverstock cleared his throat once again before looking down at the will and turning over several pages.

"'The residue of my estate shall pass to Mr Daniel Trumper of Trinity College, Cambridge, but should he fail to survive my daughter Ethel Trentham then that sum shall be equally divided between his offspring. Should he have no issue, then the estate shall pass to my closest living descendant.' Now to the relevant paragraph, Sir Charles. 'If these circumstances arise I instruct my executors to go to any lengths they feel necessary to find someone entitled to make a claim on my inheritance. In order that this option might be properly executed, I also deem that final payment of the residue of the estate shall not be made until a further two years after my daughter's death.'"

Charlie was about to ask a question when Mr Baverstock raised his hand.

· "It has become clear to me," continued Baverstock, "that Sir Raymond's purpose in including clause twenty-two was simply to give you enough time to marshal your forces and fight any hostile takeover bid Mr Nigel Trentham might have in mind.

"Sir Raymond also left instructions that, at a suitable time following his daughter's death, an advertisement should be placed in *The Times*, the *Telegraph*, the *Guardian* and any other newspaper I considered appropriate when seeking to discover if there were any other persons who feel they might have some claim on the estate. If this should be the case, they can then do so by making direct contact with this firm. Thirteen such relations have already received the sum of one thousand pounds each, but it is just possible there could be other cousins or distant relatives of whom Sir Raymond was unaware who may still be entitled to make such a claim. This provision simply gave the old man an excuse for the two-year clause. As I understand it, Sir Raymond was quite happy to allocate another thousand pounds to some unknown relative if at the same time it afforded you some breathing space. By the way," said Baverstock, "I have decided to add the *Yorkshire Post* and the *Huddersfield Daily Examiner* to the list of newspapers named in the will because of the family connections in that county."

"What a shrewd old buzzard he must have been," said Charlie. "I only wish I'd known him."

"I think I can say with some confidence, Sir Charles, that you would have liked him."

"It was also extremely kind of you to put me in the picture, old fellow."

"Not at all. I feel sure," said Baverstock, "that had he been placed in my position it is no more and certainly no less than Sir Raymond would have done himself."

"If only I'd told Daniel the truth about his father . . ."

"If you save your energies for the quick," said Baverstock, "it is possible Sir Raymond's foresight may still not have been wasted."

On 7 March 1962, the day on which Mrs Trentham had died, Trumper's shares stood at one pound two shillings on the FT Index; only four weeks later they had risen by a further three shillings.

Tim Newman's first piece of advice to Charlie was to cling on to every share he still possessed and under no circumstances during the next couple of years to agree to any further rights issues. If between them Charlie and Becky were able to lay their hands on any spare cash, they should purchase shares as and when they came on the market.

The problem with following this particular piece of advice was that every time a substantial block of shares did come on to the market they were immediately taken up by an unknown broker who obviously had instructions to purchase stock whatever the price. Charlie's stockbroker managed to get his hands on a few shares but only from those unwilling to trade on the open market. Charlie was loath to pay over the odds, as he had never forgotten how close he had come to bankruptcy when he last extended his credit. By the end of the year Trumper's shares stood at one pound seventeen shillings. There were even fewer sellers left in the market place after the *Financial Times* had warned their readers of a possible takeover battle for the company and gone on to predict it would take place within the next eighteen months.

"That damned paper seems to be as well briefed as any member of the board," Daphne complained to Charlie at their next meeting, adding that she no longer bothered with the minutes of past meetings as she could always read an excellent summary of what had taken place on the front page of the *Financial Times*, which appeared to have been dictated to them verbatim. As she delivered these words her eyes never left Paul Merrick.

The paper's latest story was inaccurate in only one small detail, as the battle for Trumper's was no longer taking place in the boardroom. As soon as it became known that a two-year holding clause existed in Sir Raymond's will Nigel Trentham and his nominees had stopped attending the monthly meetings.

Trentham's absence particularly annoyed Cathy, as quarter after quarter the new in-house bank began to show increased profits. She found herself addressing her opinions to three empty chairs – though she too suspected Merrick was reporting back every detail to Chester Square. As if to compound matters, in 1963 Charlie informed the shareholders at the AGM that the company would be declaring another record profit for the year.

"You may have spent a lifetime building up Trumper's only to hand it over on a plate to the Trenthams," Tim Newman reflected.

"There's certainly no need for Mrs Trentham to be turning in her grave," admitted Charlie. "Ironic, after all she managed during her life that it's only by her death that she's been given the chance to deliver the *coup de grâce*."

When, early in 1964, the shares rose yet again – this time to over two pounds – Charlie was informed by Tim Newman that Nigel Trentham was still in the market place with instructions to buy.

"But where's he getting hold of all the extra cash that would be needed to bankroll such an operation – when he's still not yet got his hands on his grandfather's money?"

"I picked up a hint from a former colleague," replied Tim Newman, "that a leading merchant bank has granted him a large overdraft facility in anticipation of his gaining control of the Hardcastle Trust. Only wish you had a grandfather who'd left you a fortune," he added.

"I did," said Charlie.

Nigel Trentham chose Charlie's sixty-fourth birthday to announce to the world that he would be making a full bid for Trumper's shares at a price of two pounds four shillings, a mere seven weeks before he was entitled to lay claim to his inheritance. Charlie still felt confident that with the help of friends and institutions like the Prudential – as well as some shareholders who were waiting for the price to rise even higher – he could still lay his hands on almost forty per cent of the stock. Tim Newman estimated that Trentham must now have at least twenty per cent, but once he was able to add the Trust's seventeen per cent he might then be in possession of as much as forty-two to forty-three. Picking up the extra eight or nine per cent required to gain control should not prove too hard for him, Newman warned Charlie.

That night Daphne threw a birthday party in Charlie's honour at her home in Eaton Square which Cathy was unable to attend, as she was in New York on a buying trip. No one mentioned the name of Trentham until the port had been passed round for a second time, when a slightly maudlin Charlie recited the relevant clause in Sir Raymond's will, which he explained had been put there with the sole purpose of trying to save him.

"I give you Sir Raymond Hardcastle," said Charlie, raising his glass. "A good man to have in your team."

"Sir Raymond," the guests echoed, all raising their glasses, with the exception of Daphne.

"What's the problem, old gel?" asked Percy. "Port not up to scratch?"

"No, as usual it's you lot who aren't. You've all totally failed to work out what Sir Raymond expected of you."

"What *are* you on about, old gel?"

"I should have thought it was obvious for anyone to

see, especially you, Charlie," she said, turning from her husband to the guest of honour.

"I'm with Percy – I haven't a clue what you're on about."

By now everyone round the table had fallen silent, while they concentrated on what Daphne had to say.

"It's quite simple really," continued Daphne. "Sir Raymond obviously didn't consider it likely that Mrs Trentham would outlive Daniel."

"So?" said Charlie.

"And I also doubt if he thought for one moment that Daniel would have any children before he died."

"Possibly not," said Charlie.

"And we are all painfully aware that Nigel Trentham was a last resort – otherwise Sir Raymond would happily have named him in his will as the next beneficiary and not have been willing to pass his fortune on to an offspring of Guy Trentham, whom he had never even met. He also wouldn't have added the words: should he have no issue then the estate shall pass to my closest living descendant."

"Where's all this leading?" asked Becky.

"Back to the clause Charlie has just recited. 'Please go to any lengths you feel necessary to find someone entitled to make a claim on my inheritance.'" Daphne read from the jottings she had scribbled in biro on her damask table-cloth. "Are those the correct words, Mr Baverstock?" she asked.

"They are, Lady Wiltshire, but I still don't see –"

"Because you're as blind as Charlie," said Daphne. "Thank God one of us is still sober. Mr Baverstock, please remind us all of Sir Raymond's instructions for placing the advertisement."

Mr Baverstock touched his lips with his napkin, folded the linen square neatly and placed it in front of him. "An advertisement should be placed in *The Times*, the *Telegraph* and the *Guardian* and any other newspaper I consider relevant and appropriate."

"I consider relevant and appropriate," said Daphne,

slowly enunciating each word. "As broad a hint as you might hope from a sober man, I would have thought." Every eye was now fixed on Daphne and no one attempted to interrupt her. "Can't you see those are the crucial words?" she asked. "Because if Guy Trentham did have any other children, you certainly wouldn't find them by advertising in the London *Times*, the *Telegraph*, the *Guardian*, *Yorkshire Post* or for that matter the *Huddersfield Daily Examiner*."

Charlie dropped his slice of birthday cake back on to his plate and looked across at Mr Baverstock. "Good heavens, she's right, you know."

"She certainly may not be wrong," admitted Baverstock, shuffling uneasily in his chair. "And I apologise for my lack of imagination, because as Lady Wiltshire rightly points out, I've been a blind fool by not following my master's instructions when he advised me to use my common sense. He so obviously worked out that Guy might well have fathered other children and that such offspring were most unlikely to be found in England."

"Well done, Mr Baverstock," said Daphne. "I do believe I should have gone to university and read for the bar."

Mr Baverstock felt unable to correct her on this occasion.

"There may still be time," said Charlie. "After all, there's another seven weeks left before the inheritance has to be handed over, so let's get straight back to work. By the way, thank you," he added, bowing towards Daphne.

Charlie rose from his chair and headed towards the nearest phone. "The first thing I'm going to need is the sharpest lawyer in Australia." Charlie checked his watch. "And preferably one who doesn't mind getting up early in the morning."

Mr Baverstock cleared his throat.

During the next two weeks, large box advertisements appeared in every newspaper on the Australian continent with a circulation of over fifty thousand. Each reply was quickly followed up with an interview by a firm of solicitors in Sydney that Mr Baverstock had been happy to recommend. Every evening Charlie was telephoned by Trevor Roberts, the senior partner, who remained on the end of the line for several hours when Charlie would learn the latest news that had been gathered from their offices in Sydney, Melbourne, Perth, Brisbane and Adelaide. However, after three weeks of sorting out the cranks from the genuine enquirers Roberts came up with only three candidates who fulfilled all the necessary criteria. However, once they had been interviewed by a partner of the firm they also failed to prove any direct relationship with any member of the Trentham family.

Roberts had discovered that there were seventeen Trenthams on the national register, most of them from Tasmania, but none of those could show any direct lineage with Guy Trentham or his mother, although one old lady from Hobart who had emigrated from Ripon after the war was able to present a legitimate claim for a thousand pounds, as it turned out she was a third cousin of Sir Raymond.

Charlie thanked Mr Roberts for his continued diligence but told him not to let up, as he didn't care how many staff were allocated to the job night or day.

At the final board meeting to be called before Nigel Trentham officially came into his inheritance, Charlie briefed his colleagues on the latest news from Australia.

"Doesn't sound too hopeful to me," said Newman. "After all, if there is another Trentham around he or she must be well over thirty and surely would have made a claim by now."

"Agreed, but Australia's an awfully big place and they might even have left the country."

"Never give up, do you?" remarked Daphne.

"Be that as it may," said Arthur Selwyn, "I feel the time is long overdue for us to try and come to some agreement with Trentham, if there is to be a responsible takeover of the company. In the interests of Trumper's and its customers, I would like to see if it is at all possible for the principals involved to come to some amicable arrangement –"

"Amicable arrangement!" said Charlie. "The only arrangement Trentham would agree to is that he sits in this chair with a built-in majority on the board while I am left twiddling my thumbs in a retirement home."

"That may well be the case," said Selwyn. "But I must point out, Mr Chairman, that we still have a duty to our shareholders."

"He's right," said Daphne. "You'll have to try, Charlie, for the long-term good of the company you founded." She added quietly, "However much it hurts."

Becky nodded her agreement and Charlie turned to ask Jessica to make an appointment with Trentham at his earliest convenience. Jessica returned a few minutes later to let the board know that Nigel Trentham had no interest in seeing any of them before the March board, when he would be happy to accept their resignations in person.

"Seventh of March: two years to the day since the death of his mother," Charlie reminded the board.

"And Mr Roberts is holding for you on the other line," Jessica reported.

Charlie rose and strode out of the room. The moment he reached the phone he grabbed at it as a drowning sailor might a lifeline. "Roberts, what have you got for me?"

"Guy Trentham!"

"But he's already buried in a grave in Ashurst."

"But not before his body was removed from a gaol in Melbourne."

"A gaol? I thought he died of tuberculosis."

"I don't think you can die of tuberculosis while you're hanging from the end of a six-foot rope, Sir Charles."

"Hanged?"

"For the murder of his wife, Anna Helen," said the solicitor.

"But did they have any children?"

"There's no way of knowing the answer to that."

"Why the hell not?"

"It's against the law for the prison service to release the names of the next of kin to anyone."

"But why, for heaven's sake?"

"For their own protection."

"But this could only be to their benefit."

"They've heard that one before. Indeed, I have had it pointed out to me that in this particular case we've already advertised for claimants from one coast to the other. What's worse, if any of Trentham's offspring had changed their name, for understandable reasons, we've little chance of tracing him or her at all. But be assured I'm still working flat out on it, Sir Charles."

"Get me an interview with the chief of police."

"It won't make any difference, Sir Charles. He won't –" began Roberts, but Charlie had already hung up.

"You're mad," said Becky, as she helped her husband pack a suitcase an hour later.

"True," agreed Charlie. "But this may well be the last chance I have of keeping control of the company, and I'm not willing to do it on the end of a phone, let alone twelve thousand miles away. I have to be there myself, so at least I know it's me who's failed and not a third party."

"But what exactly are you hoping to find when you get there?"

Charlie looked across at his wife as he fastened his suitcase. "I suspect only Mrs Trentham knows the answer to that."

CHAPTER 44

hen, thirty-four hours later on a warm, sunlit evening, Flight 012 touched down at Kingsford Smith airport in Sydney, Charlie felt what he most needed was a good night's sleep. After he had checked through customs he was met by a tall young man dressed in a light beige suit who stepped forward and introduced himself as Trevor Roberts, the lawyer who had been recommended by Baverstock. Roberts had thick, rusty-coloured hair and an even redder complexion. He was of a solid build and looked as if he might still spend his Saturday afternoons in a different type of court. He immediately took over Charlie's laden trolley and pushed it smartly towards the exit marked "Car park".

"No need to check this lot into a hotel," said Roberts as he held the door open for Charlie. "Just leave everything in the car."

"Is this good legal advice you're giving me?" asked Charlie, already out of breath trying to keep up with the young man.

"It certainly is, Sir Charles, because we've no time to waste." He brought the trolley to a halt at the kerbside and a chauffeur heaved the bags into the boot while Charlie and Mr Roberts climbed into the back. "The British Governor-General has invited you for drinks at six at his residence, but I also need you to be on the last flight to Melbourne tonight. As we only have six days left, we can't afford to waste any of them being in the wrong city."

Charlie knew he was going to like Mr Roberts from the moment the Australian passed over a thick file. Charlie began to listen attentively to the young lawyer as he went over the proposed schedule for the next three days. While the car travelled towards the outskirts of the city, Charlie continued to pay attention to everything he had to say, only occasionally asking for something to be repeated or gone over in greater detail as he tried to accustom himself to the difference in style between Mr Roberts and any solicitor he had dealt with in England. When he had asked Mr Baverstock to find him the sharpest young lawyer in Sydney, Charlie hadn't imagined that he would select someone in quite such a different mould from his old friend.

As the car sped along the highway towards the Governor-General's residence Roberts, with several files balanced on his knees, continued with his detailed briefing. "We're only attending this cocktail party with the Governor-General," he explained, "in case during the next few days we need some help in opening heavy doors. Then we're off to Melbourne because every time someone from my office comes up with anything that might be described as a lead it always seems to end up on the Chief Commissioner of Police's desk in that city. I've made an appointment for you to see the new chief in the morning, but as I warned you the commissioner's not proving to be at all co-operative with my people."

"Why's that?"

"He's recently been appointed to the job, and is now desperately trying to prove that everyone will be treated impartially – except 'Poms'."

"So what's his problem?"

"Like all second-generation Australians he hates the British, or at least he has to pretend he does." Roberts grinned. "In fact, I think there's only one group of people he dislikes more."

"Criminals?"

"No, lawyers," replied Roberts. "So now you'll realise why the odds are stacked against us."

"Have you managed to get anything out of him at all?"

"Not a lot. Most of what he has been willing to reveal was already on public record, namely that on 27 July 1926 Guy Trentham, in a fit of temper, killed his wife by stabbing her several times while she was taking a bath. He then held her under the water so as to be sure that she didn't survive – page sixteen in your file. We also know that on 23 April 1927 he was hanged for the crime, despite several appeals for clemency to the Governor-General. What we've been quite unable to discover is if he was survived by any children. The Melbourne *Age* was the one newspaper that carried a report of the trial, and they made no mention of a child. However, that's hardly surprising, as the judge would have ruled against any such reference in court unless it threw some light on the crime."

"But what about the wife's maiden name? Surely that's a better route to take."

"You're not going to like this, Sir Charles," said Roberts.

"Try me."

"Her name was Smith – Anna Helen Smith – that's why we concentrated what little time we had on Trentham."

"But you've still come up with no firm leads?"

"I'm afraid not," said Roberts. "If there was a child in Australia at the time bearing the name of Trentham we certainly haven't been able to trace them. My staff have interviewed every Trentham that's shown up on the national register, including one from Coorabulka that has a population of eleven and takes three days to reach by car and foot."

"Despite your valiant efforts, Roberts, my guess is there might still be some stones we need to look under."

"Possibly," said Roberts. "I even began to wonder if perhaps Trentham had changed his name when he first came to Australia, but the chief of police was able to confirm that the file he holds in Melbourne is under the name of Guy Francis Trentham."

"So if the name's unchanged then surely any child would be traceable?"

"Not necessarily. I dealt with a case quite recently in which I had a client whose husband was sent to gaol for manslaughter. She reverted to her maiden name, which she also gave to her only child and was able to show me a foolproof system for then having the original name expunged from the records. Also, remember that in this case we're dealing with a child who could have been born any time between 1923 and 1925 and the removal of just one piece of paper could well have been enough to eliminate any connection he or she might have with Guy Trentham. If that's the case, finding such a child in a country the size of Australia would be like searching for the proverbial needle in the haystack."

"But I've only got six days," said Charlie plaintively.

"Don't remind me," said Roberts, as the car drove through the gates of the Governor-General's residence at Government House, dropping its speed to a more sedate pace as they continued up the drive. "I've allocated one hour for this party, no more," the young lawyer warned. "All I want out of the Governor-General is a promise that he'll telephone the chief of police in Melbourne before our meeting tomorrow, to ask him to be as co-operative as possible. But when I say we must leave, Sir Charles, I mean we must leave."

"Understood," said Charlie, feeling like a private back on parade in Edinburgh.

"By the way," said Roberts, "the Governor-General is Sir Oliver Williams. Sixty-one, former Guards officer, comes from some place called Tunbridge Wells."

Two minutes later they were striding into the grand ballroom of Government House.

"So glad you could make it, Sir Charles," said a tall, elegantly dressed man who wore a double-breasted striped suit and a Guards tie.

"Thank you, Sir Oliver."

"And how was the journey over, old chap?"

"Five stops for refuelling and not one airport that knew how to brew a decent cup of tea."

"Then you'll need one of these," suggested Sir Oliver, handing Charlie a large whisky that he removed deftly from a passing tray. "And to think," continued the diplomat, "they're predicting that our grandchildren will be able to fly the entire journey from London to Sydney non-stop in less than a day. Still, yours was a lot less unpleasant an experience than the early settlers had to endure."

"A small compensation." Charlie couldn't think of a more appropriate reply as he considered what a contrast Mr Baverstock's nominee in Australia was to the Queen's representative.

"Now, do tell me what brings you to Sydney," continued the Governor-General. "Are we to anticipate that the second biggest barrow in the world is about to be pushed round to this side of the globe?"

"No, Sir Oliver. You'll be saved that. I'm here on a brief private visit, trying to sort out some family business."

"Well, if there's anything I can do to assist you," said his host, taking a gin from another passing tray, "just let me know."

"That's kind of you, Sir Oliver, because I do need your help over one small matter."

"And what might that be?" asked his host, at the same moment allowing his eyes to wander over Charlie's shoulder in the direction of some late arrivals.

"You could call the chief of police in Melbourne and ask him to be as co-operative as possible when I visit him tomorrow morning."

"Consider the call made, old fellow," said Sir Oliver as he leaned forward to shake the hand of an Arab sheikh. "And don't forget, Sir Charles, if there's anything I can do to help – and I mean anything – just let me know. Ah, *Monsieur l'Ambassadeur, comment allez-vous?*"

Charlie suddenly felt exhausted. He spent the rest of the hour just trying to remain on his feet while talking to diplomats, politicians and businessmen, all of whom seemed well acquainted with the biggest barrow in the world. Eventually a firm touch on his elbow from Roberts signalled that the proprieties had been observed and he must now leave for the airport.

On the flight to Melbourne Charlie was just about able to stay awake, even if his eyes weren't always open. In answer to a question from Roberts he confirmed that the Governor-General had agreed to telephone the chief of police the following morning. "But I'm not certain he appreciated how important it was."

"I see," said Roberts. "Then I'll be back in touch with his office first thing tomorrow. Sir Oliver's not renowned for remembering promises he makes at cocktail parties. 'If there's anything I can do to assist you, old chap, and I mean anything,'" – which even managed to elicit a sleepy grin from Charlie.

At Melbourne airport another car was waiting for them. Charlie was whisked away, and this time he did fall asleep and didn't wake again until they drew up outside the Windsor Hotel some twenty minutes later. The manager showed his guest to the Prince Edward suite and as soon as he had been left on his own Charlie quickly undressed, had a shower and climbed into bed. A few minutes later he fell into a heavy sleep. However, he still woke around four the next morning.

Propped uncomfortably up in bed supported by foam rubber pillows that wouldn't stay in one place, Charlie spent the next three hours going through Roberts's files. The man might not have looked or sounded like Baverstock but the same stamp of thoroughness was evident on every page. By the time Charlie let the last file drop to the floor he had to accept that Roberts's firm had covered every angle and followed up every lead; his only hope now rested with a cantankerous Melbourne policeman.

Charlie had a cold shower at seven and a hot breakfast just after eight. Although his only appointment that day was at ten o'clock he was pacing round his suite long before Roberts was due to pick him up at nine thirty, aware that if nothing came out of this meeting he might as well pack his bags and fly back to England that afternoon. At least that would give Becky the satisfaction of being proved right.

At nine twenty-nine Roberts knocked on his door; Charlie wondered how long the young lawyer had been standing outside in the corridor waiting. Roberts reported that he had already telephoned the Governor-General's office and that Sir Oliver had promised to call the chief of police within the hour.

"Good. Now tell me everything you know about the man."

"Mike Cooper is forty-seven, efficient, prickly and brash. Climbed up through the ranks but still finds it necessary to prove himself to everyone, especially when he's in the presence of a lawyer, perhaps because crime statistics for Melbourne have risen at an even faster rate than our Test averages against England."

"You said yesterday he was second generation. So where does he hail from?"

Roberts checked his file. "His father emigrated to Australia at the turn of the century from somewhere called Deptford."

"Deptford?" repeated Charlie with a grin. "That's almost home territory." He checked his watch. "Shall we be off? I think I'm more than ready to meet Mr Cooper."

When twenty minutes later Roberts held open the door of the police headquarters for his client, they were greeted with a large formal photograph of a man in his late forties that made Charlie feel every day of his sixty-four years.

After Roberts had supplied the officer on duty with their names they were kept waiting for only a few minutes before Charlie was ushered through to the chief's office.

The policeman's lips formed a reluctant smile when he shook hands with Charlie. "I am not sure there's a lot I can do to help you, Sir Charles," began Cooper, motioning him to take a seat. "Despite your Governor-General taking the trouble to call me." He ignored Roberts, who remained standing a few feet behind his client.

"I know that accent," said Charlie, not taking the offered chair.

"I beg your pardon?" replied Cooper, who also remained standing.

"Half a crown to a pound says your father hails from London."

"Yes, you're right."

"And the East End of that city would be my bet."

"Deptford," said the chief.

"I knew it the moment you opened your mouth," said Charlie now sinking back into a leather chair. "I come from Whitechapel myself. So where was he born?"

"Deptford Church Street," said the chief. "Just off –"

"Just a stone's throw away from my part of the world," said Charlie in a thick Cockney accent.

Roberts had not yet uttered a word, let alone given a professional opinion.

"Millwall supporter, I suppose," said Charlie.

"The Gunners," said Cooper, firmly.

"What a load of rubbish," said Charlie. "Arsenal are the only team I know who read the names of the crowd to the players."

The chief laughed. "I agree," he said. "I've almost given up hope for them this season. So who do you support?"

"I'm a West Ham man myself."

"And you were hoping I'd co-operate with you?"

Charlie laughed. "Well, we did let you beat us in the Cup."

"In 1930," said Cooper, laughing.

"We've got long memories down at Upton Park."

"Well, I never expected you to have an accent like that, Sir Charles."

"Call me Charlie, all my friends do. And another thing, Mike, do you want him out of the way?" Charlie cocked a thumb at Trevor Roberts who still hadn't been offered a seat.

"Might help," said the chief.

"Wait outside for me, Roberts," said Charlie, not even bothering to glance in the direction of his lawyer.

"Yes, Sir Charles." Roberts turned and started walking towards the door.

Once they were alone Charlie leaned across the desk and said, "Soddin' lawyers, they're all the same. Overpaid toffee-nosed Brussels sprouts, charge the earth and then expect you to do all the work."

Cooper laughed. "Especially when you're a grasshopper," he confided.

Charlie laughed. "Haven't heard a copper described that way since I left Whitechapel." The older man leaned forward. "This is between you and me, Mike. Two East End boys together. Can you tell me anything about Guy Francis Trentham that *he* doesn't know?" Charlie pointed his thumb towards the door.

"I'm afraid there isn't a lot Roberts hasn't already dug up, to be fair to him, Sir Charles."

"Charlie."

"Charlie. Look, you already know that Trentham murdered his wife and you must be aware by now that he was later hanged for the crime."

"Yes, but what I need to know, Mike, is, were there any children?" Charlie held his breath as the policeman seemed to hesitate.

Cooper looked down at a charge sheet that lay on the desk in front of him. "It says here, wife (deceased), one daughter."

Charlie tried not to leap out of his chair. "Don't suppose that piece of paper tells you her name?"

"Margaret Ethel Trentham," said the chief.

Charlie knew he didn't have to re-check the name in the files that Roberts had left with him overnight. There hadn't been a Margaret Ethel Trentham mentioned in any of them. He could recall the names of the three Trenthams born in Australia between 1923 and 1925, and all of those were boys.

"Date of birth?" he hazarded.

"No clue, Charlie," said Cooper. "It wasn't the girl who was being charged." He pushed the piece of paper over the desk, so that his visitor could read everything he had already been told. "They didn't bother too much with those sort of details in the twenties."

"Anything else in that file you think might 'elp an East End boy not on his 'ome ground?" asked Charlie, only hoping he wasn't overdoing it.

Cooper studied the papers in the Trentham file for some time before he offered an opinion. "There are two entries on our records that might just be of some use to you. The first was pencilled in by my predecessor and there's an even earlier entry from the chief before him which I suppose just might be of interest."

"I'm all ears, Mike."

"Chief Parker was paid a visit on 24 April 1927 by a Mrs Ethel Trentham, the deceased's mother."

"Good God," said Charlie, unable to hide his surprise. "But why?"

"No reason given, nor any record of what was said at that meeting either. Sorry."

"And the second entry?"

"That concerns another visitor from England enquiring after Guy Trentham. This time on 23 August 1947" – the police chief looked down at the file again to check the name – "a Mr Daniel Trentham."

Charlie went cold as he gripped the arms of his chair.

"You all right?" asked Cooper, sounding genuinely concerned.

"Fine," said Charlie. "It's only the effects of jet-lag. Any reason given for Daniel Trentham's visit?"

"According to the attached note, he claimed to be the deceased's son," said the chief. Charlie tried not to show any emotion. The policeman sat back in his chair. "So now you know every bit as much about the case as I do."

"You've been very 'elpful, Mike," said Charlie as he pushed himself up to his feet before leaning across to shake hands. "And if you should ever find yourself back in Dept-ford, look me up. I'd be only too happy to take you to see a real football team."

Cooper smiled and continued to trade stories with Charlie as the two men made their way out of his office to the lift. Once they were on the ground floor the policeman accompanied him to the steps of police headquarters, where Charlie shook hands with the chief once again before joining Trevor Roberts in the car.

"Right, Roberts, it seems we've got ourselves some work to do."

"May I be permitted to ask one question before we begin, Sir Charles?"

"Be my guest."

"What happened to your accent?"

"I only save that for special people, Mr Roberts. The Queen, Winston Churchill and when I'm serving a customer on the barrow. Today I felt it necessary to add Melbourne's chief of police to my list."

"I can't begin to think what you said about me and my profession."

"I told him you were an overpaid, toffee-nosed boy scout who expected me to do all the work."

"And did he offer an opinion?"

"Thought I might have been a little too restrained."

"That's not hard to believe," said Roberts. "But were you able to prise any fresh information out of him?"

"I certainly was," said Charlie. "It seems Guy Trentham had a daughter."

"A daughter?" repeated Roberts, unable to hide his excitement. "But did Cooper let you know her name, or anything about her?"

"Margaret Ethel, but our only other clue is that Mrs Trentham, Guy's mother, paid a visit to Melbourne in 1927. Cooper didn't know why."

"Good heavens," said Roberts. "You've achieved more in twenty minutes than I achieved in twenty days."

"Ah, but I had the advantage of birth," said Charlie

with a grin. "Now where would an English lady have rested her genteel head in this city around that time?"

"Not my home town," admitted Roberts. "But my partner Neil Mitchell should be able to tell us. His family settled in Melbourne over a hundred years ago."

"So what are we waiting for?"

Neil Mitchell frowned when his colleague put the same question to him. "I haven't a clue," he admitted, "but my mother's sure to know." He picked up his phone and started dialling. "She's Scottish, so she'll try and charge us for the information." Charlie and Trevor Roberts stood in front of Mitchell's desk and waited, one patiently, one impatiently. After a few preliminaries expected of a son, he put his question and listened carefully to her reply.

"Thank you, Mother, invaluable as always," he said. "See you at the weekend," he added before putting down the phone.

"Well?" said Charlie.

"The Victoria Country Club apparently was the only place someone from Mrs Trentham's background would have dreamed of staying in the twenties," Mitchell said. "In those days Melbourne only had two decent hotels and the other one was strictly for visiting businessmen."

"Does the place still exist?" asked Roberts.

"Yes, but it's badly run-down nowadays. What I imagine Sir Charles would describe as 'seedy'."

"Then telephone ahead and let them know you want a table for lunch in the name of Sir Charles Trumper. And stress Sir Charles."

"Certainly, Sir Charles," said Roberts. "And which accent will we be using on this occasion?"

"Can't tell you that until I've weighed up the opposition," said Charlie as they made their way back to the car.

"Ironic when you think about it," said Roberts, as the car headed out on to the freeway.

"Ironic?"

"Yes," said Roberts. "If Mrs Trentham went to all this trouble to remove her granddaughter's very existence from the records, she must have required the services of a first-class lawyer to do so."

"So?"

"So there must be a file buried somewhere in this city that would tell us everything we need to know."

"Possibly, but one thing's for certain: we don't have enough time to discover whose filing cabinet it's hidden in."

When they arrived at the Victoria Country Club they found the manager standing in the hallway waiting to greet them. He led his distinguished guest through to a quiet table in the alcove. Charlie was only disappointed to find how young he was.

Charlie chose the most expensive items from the *à la carte* section of the menu, then selected a 1957 bottle of Chambertin. Within moments he was receiving attention from every waiter in the room.

"And what are you up to this time, Sir Charles?" asked Roberts, who had satisfied himself with the set menu.

"Patience, young man," Charlie said in mock disdain as he tried to cut into an overcooked, tough piece of lamb with a blunt knife. He eventually gave in, and ordered a vanilla ice-cream, confident they couldn't do much harm to that. When finally the coffee was served, the oldest waiter in the room came slowly over to offer them both a cigar.

"A Monte Cristo, please," said Charlie, removing a pound note from his wallet and placing it on the table in front of him. A large old humidor was opened for his inspection. "Worked here for a long time, have you?" Charlie added.

"Forty years last month," said the waiter, as another pound note landed on top of the first.

"Good memory?"

"I like to think so, sir," said the waiter, staring at the two banknotes.

"Remember someone called Mrs Trentham? English,

strait-laced, might have stayed for a couple of weeks or more round 1927," said Charlie, pushing the notes towards the old man.

"Remember her?" said the waiter. "I'll never forget her. I was a trainee in those days and she did nothing except grumble the whole time about the food and the service. Wouldn't drink anything but water, said she didn't trust Australian wines and refused to spend good money on the French ones – that's why I always ended up having to serve on her table. End of the month, she ups and offs without a word and didn't even leave me a tip. You bet I remember her."

"That sounds like Mrs Trentham all right," said Charlie. "But did you ever find out why she came to Australia in the first place?" He removed a third pound note from his wallet and placed it on top of the others.

"I've no idea, sir," said the waiter sadly. "She never talked to anyone from morning to night, and I'm not sure even Mr Sinclair-Smith would know the answer to that question."

"Mr Sinclair-Smith?"

The waiter motioned over his shoulder to the far corner of the room where an elderly gentleman sat alone, a napkin tucked into his collar. He was busy attacking a large piece of Stilton. "The present owner," the waiter explained. "His father was the only person Mrs Trentham ever spoke civilly to."

"Thank you," said Charlie. "You've been most helpful." The waiter pocketed the three banknotes. "Would you be kind enough to ask the manager if I could have a word with him?"

"Certainly, sir," said the old waiter, who closed the humidor and scurried away.

"The manager is far too young to remember –"

"Just keep your eyes open, Mr Roberts, and possibly you might just learn a trick or two they failed to teach you in the business contracts class at law school," said Charlie as he clipped the end of his cigar.

The manager arrived at their table. "You asked to see me, Sir Charles?"

"I wonder if Mr Sinclair-Smith would care to join me for a liqueur?" said Charlie, passing the young man one of his cards.

"I'll have a word with him immediately, sir," said the manager who at once turned and walked towards the other table.

"It's back to the lobby for you, Roberts," said Charlie, "as I suspect that my conduct over the next half-hour might just offend your professional ethics." He glanced across the room, where the old man was now studying his card.

Roberts sighed, rose from his chair and left.

A large smile appeared on Mr Sinclair-Smith's podgy lips. He pushed himself up out of his chair and waddled over to join his English visitor.

"Sinclair-Smith," he said in a high-pitched English accent before offering a limp hand.

"Good of you to join me, old chap," said Charlie. "I know a fellow countryman when I see one. Can I interest you in a brandy?" The waiter scurried away.

"How kind of you, Sir Charles. I can only hope that my humble establishment has provided you with a reasonable cuisine."

"Excellent," said Charlie. "But then you were recommended," he said as he exhaled a plume of cigar smoke.

"Recommended?" said Sinclair-Smith, trying not to sound too surprised. "May I ask by whom?"

"My ancient aunt, Mrs Ethel Trentham."

"Mrs Trentham? Good heavens, Mrs Trentham, we haven't seen the dear lady since my late father's time."

Charlie frowned as the old waiter returned with two large brandies.

"I do hope she's keeping well, Sir Charles."

"Never better," said Charlie. "And she wished to be remembered to you."

"How kind of her," replied Sinclair-Smith, swirling the brandy round in his balloon. "And what a remarkable memory, because I was only a young man at the time and had just started working in the hotel. She must now be . . ."

"Over ninety," said Charlie. "And do you know the family still has no idea why she ever came to Melbourne in the first place," he added.

"Nor me," said Sinclair-Smith as he sipped his brandy.

"You never spoke to her?"

"No, never," said Sinclair-Smith. "Although my father and your aunt had many long conversations, he never once confided in me what passed between them."

Charlie tried not to show his frustration at this piece of information. "Well, if you don't know what she was up to," he said, "I don't suppose there's anyone alive who does."

"Oh, I wouldn't be so sure of that," said Sinclair-Smith. "Slade would know – that is, if he hasn't gone completely ga-ga."

"Slade?"

"Yes, a Yorkshireman who worked at the club under my father, in the days when we still had a resident chauffeur. In fact, the whole time Mrs Trentham stayed at the club she always insisted on using Slade. Said no one else should drive her."

"Is he still around?" asked Charlie as he blew out another large cloud of smoke.

"Good heavens no," said Sinclair-Smith. "Retired years ago. Not even sure he's still alive."

"Do you get back to the old country much nowadays?" enquired Charlie, convinced that he had extracted every piece of relevant information that could be gained from this particular source.

"No, unfortunately what with . . ."

For the next twenty minutes, Charlie settled back and enjoyed his cigar as he listened to Sinclair-Smith on everything from the demise of the Empire to the parlous state of English cricket. Eventually Charlie called for the bill, at which the owner took his leave and slipped discreetly away.

The old waiter shuffled back the moment he saw another pound note appear on the tablecloth.

"Something you needed, sir?"

"Does the name Slade mean anything to you?"

"Old Walter Slade, the club's chauffeur?"

"That's the man."

"Retired years ago."

"I know that much, but is he still alive?"

"No idea," said the waiter. "Last I heard of him he lived somewhere out in the Ballarat area."

"Thank you," said Charlie, as he stubbed out his cigar in the ash-tray, removed another pound note and left to join Roberts in the lobby.

"Telephone your office immediately," he instructed his solicitor. "Ask them to track down a Walter Slade who may be living at somewhere called Ballarat."

Roberts hurried off in the direction of the telephone sign, while Charlie paced up and down the corridor praying the old man was still alive. His solicitor returned a few minutes later. "Am I allowed to know what you're up to this time, Sir Charles?" he asked as he passed over a piece of paper with Walter Slade's address printed out in capital letters.

"No good, that's for sure," said Charlie, as he took in the information. "Don't need you for this one, young man, but I will require the car. See you back at the office – and I can't be sure when." He gave a small wave as he pushed through the swing doors leaving a bemused Roberts standing on his own in the lobby.

Charlie handed over the slip of paper to the chauffeur who studied the address. "But it's nearly a hundred miles," said the man, looking over his shoulder.

"Then we haven't a moment to waste, have we?"

The driver switched on the engine and swung out of the country club forecourt. He drove past the Melbourne Cricket Ground where Charlie could see someone was 147 for 2. It annoyed him that on his first trip to Australia he didn't even have enough time to drop in and see the Test Match. The journey on the north highway lasted for another hour and a half, which gave Charlie easily enough time to consider what approach he would use on Mr Slade, assuming he wasn't, to quote Sinclair-Smith, "completely ga-ga". After they had sped past the sign for Ballarat, the driver pulled into a petrol station. Once the attendant had filled the tank he gave the driver some directions and it took another fifteen minutes before they came to a halt outside a small terraced house on a run-down estate.

Charlie jumped out of the car, marched up a short, weed-covered path and knocked on the front door. He waited for some time before an old lady wearing a pinafore and a pastel-coloured dress that nearly reached the ground answered his call.

"Mrs Slade?" asked Charlie.

"Yes," she replied, peering up at him suspiciously.

"Would it be possible to have a word with your husband?"

"Why?" asked the old lady. "You from the social services?"

"No, I'm from England," said Charlie. "And I've brought your husband a small bequest from my aunt Mrs Ethel Trentham, who has recently died."

"Oh, how kind of you," said Mrs Slade. "Do come in." She guided Charlie through to the kitchen, where he found an old man dressed in a cardigan, clean check shirt and baggy trousers dozing in a chair in front of the fireplace.

"There's a man come all the way from England, specially to see you, Walter."

"What's that?" said the man, raising his bony fingers to rub the sleep out of his eyes.

"A man come from England," repeated his wife. "With a present from that Mrs Trentham."

"I'm too old to drive her now." His tired eyes blinked at Charlie.

"No, Walter, you don't understand. He's a relative come all the way from England with a gift. You see, she died."

"Died?"

Both of them were now staring quizzically at Charlie

as he quickly took out his wallet and removed every note he possessed before handing the money over to Mrs Slade.

She began to count the notes slowly as Walter Slade continued to stare at Charlie, making him feel distinctly uneasy as he stood on their spotless stone floor.

"Eighty-five pounds, Walter," she told him, passing the money over to her husband.

"Why so much?" he asked. "And after so long?"

"You did her a great service," said Charlie, "and she simply wished to repay you."

The old man began to look more suspiciously at Charlie.

"She paid me at the time," he said.

"I realise that," said Charlie, "but —"

"And I've kept my mouth shut," he said.

"That's just another reason why she had cause to be grateful to you," said Charlie.

"Are you saying that you came all the way from England, just to give me eighty-five pounds?" said Mr Slade. "Doesn't make any sense to me, lad." He suddenly sounded a lot more awake.

"No, no," said Charlie, feeling that he was losing the initiative. "I've had a dozen other bequests to deliver before coming out here, but you weren't that easy to find."

"I'm not surprised. I've stopped driving these twenty years."

"You're from Yorkshire, aren't you?" said Charlie with a grin. "I'd know that accent anywhere."

"Aye, lad, and you're from London. Which means you're not to be trusted. So why did you really come to see me? Because it wasn't to give us eighty-five pounds, that's for sure."

"I can't find the little girl who was with Mrs Trentham when you drove her," said Charlie, risking everything. "You see, she's been left a large inheritance."

"Fancy that, Walter," said Mrs Slade.

Walter Slade's face registered nothing.

"And it's my duty somehow to locate her and then inform the lady of her good fortune."

Slade's face remained impassive as Charlie battled on. "And I thought you'd be the one person who might be able to help."

"No, I won't," Slade replied. "What's more you can have your money back," he added, throwing the notes at Charlie's feet. "And don't bother to show your face round these parts again, with your phoney trumped-up stories about fortunes. Show the gentleman the door, Elsie."

Mrs Slade bent down and carefully picked up the scattered notes before passing them up to Charlie. When she had handed over the last one, she silently led the stranger back towards the front door.

"I do apologise, Mrs Slade," said Charlie. "I had no intention of offending your husband."

"I know, sir," said Mrs Slade. "But then Walter has always been so proud. Heaven knows, we could have done with the money." Charlie smiled as he stuffed the bundle of notes into the old lady's pinafore and quickly put a finger up to his lips. "If you don't tell him, I won't," he said. He gave a slight bow before turning to walk back down the little path towards the car.

"I never saw no little girl," she said in a voice that barely carried. Charlie froze on the spot. "But Walter once took a snooty lady up to that orphanage on Park Hill in Melbourne. I know because I was walking out with the gardener at the time, and he told me."

Charlie turned to thank her, but she had already closed the door and disappeared back into the house.

Charlie climbed into the car, penniless and with just one name to cling on to, aware that the old man could undoubtedly have solved the entire mystery for him. Otherwise he would have said "No, I can't" and not "No, I won't" when he had asked for his help.

He cursed his stupidity several times on the long journey back to the city.

"Roberts, is there an orphanage in Melbourne?" were

Charlie's opening words as he strode into the lawyer's office.

"St Hilda's," said Neil Mitchell, before his partner could consider the question. "Yes, it's up on Park Hill somewhere. Why?"

"That's the one," said Charlie, checking his watch. "It's about seven o'clock in the morning London time and I'm shattered, so I'm off to my hotel to try and grab some sleep. In the meantime I need a few questions answered. To start with, I want to know everything that can possibly be found out about St Hilda's, starting with the names of every member of staff who worked there between 1923 and 1927, from the head concho down to the scullery maid. And if anyone's still around from that period find them because I want to see them – and within the next twenty-four hours."

Two of the staff in Mitchell's office had begun scribbling furiously as they tried to take down every word Sir Charles said.

"I also want to know the name of every child registered at that orphanage between 1923 and 1927. Remember, we're looking for a girl who couldn't have been more than four years old, and may have been called Margaret Ethel. And when you've found the answers to all those questions wake me – whatever time it is."

CHAPTER 45

Trevor Roberts arrived back at Charlie's hotel a few minutes before eight the following morning to find his client tucking into a large breakfast of eggs, tomato, mushrooms and bacon. Although Roberts looked unshaven and tired, he was the bearer of news.

"We've been in touch with the principal of St Hilda's, a Mrs Culver, and she couldn't have been more co-operative." Charlie smiled. "It turns out that nineteen children were registered with the orphanage between 1923 and 1927. Eight boys and eleven girls. Of the eleven girls we now know that nine of them didn't have a mother or father alive at the time. Of those nine we have managed to contact seven, five of whom have a relative still alive who could vouch for who their father was, one whose parents were killed in a car crash and the other who is an aboriginal. The last two, however, are proving more difficult to track down, so I thought you might like to visit St Hilda's and study the files yourself."

"What about the staff at the orphanage?"

"Only a cook survives from around that period, and she says there never was a child at St Hilda's called Trentham or any name like that, and she can't even remember a Margaret or an Ethel. So our last hope may prove to be a Miss Benson."

"Miss Benson?"

"Yes, she was the principal at the time and is now a resident at an exclusive old people's home called Maple Lodge on the other side of the city."

"Not bad, Mr Roberts," said Charlie. "But how did you manage to get Mrs Culver to be so co-operative at such short notice?"

"I resorted to methods that I suspect are more familiar to the Whitechapel school of law than Harvard, Sir Charles."

Charlie looked at him quizzically.

"It seems that St Hilda's are currently organising an appeal for a minibus –"

"A minibus?"

"So badly needed by the orphanage for trips –"

"and so you hinted that I –"

"might be possible to help with a wheel or two if –"

"they in return felt able to –"

"co-operate. Precisely."

"You're a quick learner, Roberts, I'll give you that."

"And as there's no more time to be wasted, we ought to leave for St Hilda's immediately so you can go over those files."

"But our best bet must surely be Miss Benson."

"I agree with you, Sir Charles. And I've planned for us to pay her a visit this afternoon, just as soon as you've finished at St Hilda's. By the way, when Miss Benson was principal, she was known as 'The Dragon' not only by the children but also by the staff, so there's no reason to expect she'll be any more co-operative than Walter Slade."

When Charlie arrived at the orphanage he was greeted at the front door by the principal. Mrs Culver wore a smart green dress that looked as if it might have been freshly pressed. She had obviously decided to treat her potential benefactor as if he were Nelson Rockefeller because all that was lacking was a red carpet as Charlie was ushered through to her study.

Two young lawyers who had been going assiduously through files all night and learning all there was to know about dormitory times, exeats, kitchen duties, credits and misdemeanours stood as Charlie and Trevor Roberts entered the room.

"Any further progress with those two names?" asked Roberts.

"Oh, yes, down to two. Isn't this exciting?" said Mrs Culver, as she bustled round the room moving anything that seemed to be out of place. "I was wondering –"

"We have no proof as yet," said a bleary-eyed young man, "but one of them seems to fit the bill perfectly. We can come up with no information on the girl before the age of two. What's more important, she was registered with St Hilda's at precisely the same time as Captain Trentham was awaiting execution."

"And the cook also remembers from the days when she was a scullery maid," said Mrs Culver, jumping in, "that the girl came in the middle of the night, accompanied by a well-dressed, severe-looking lady who had a lah-de-dah accent who then –"

"Enter Mrs Trentham," said Charlie. "Only the girl's name is obviously not Trentham."

The young assistant checked the notes that lay spread across the table in front of him. "No, sir," he said. "This particular girl was registered under the name of Miss Cathy Ross."

Charlie felt his legs give way as Roberts and Mrs Culver rushed forward to help him into the only comfortable chair in the room. Mrs Culver loosened his tie and undid his collar.

"Are you feeling all right, Sir Charles?" she asked. "I must say you don't look too . . ."

"Right in front of my eyes all the time," said Charlie. "Blind as a bat is how Daphne would rightly describe me."

"I'm not sure I understand," said Roberts.

"I'm not sure I do myself as yet." Charlie turned back to face the anxious messenger responsible for delivering the news.

"Did she leave St Hilda's to take up a place at Melbourne University?" he asked.

This time the assistant double-checked his notes. "Yes, sir. She signed on for the class of '42, leaving in '45."

"Where she studied history of art and English."

The assistant's eyes again scanned the papers in front of him. "That's correct, sir," he said, unable to hide his surprise.

"And did she play tennis, by any chance?"

"The occasional match for the university second six."

"But could she paint?" asked Charlie.

The assistant continued to leaf through the files.

"Oh, yes," said Mrs Culver, "and very good she was too, Sir Charles. We still have an example of her work hanging in the dining room, a woodland scene influenced by Sisley, I suspect. Indeed, I would go as far as to say – "

"May I be allowed to see the picture, Mrs Culver?"

"Of course, Sir Charles." The principal removed a key from the top right-hand drawer of her desk and said, "Please follow me."

Charlie rose unsteadily to his feet and accompanied Mrs Culver as she marched out of her study and down a long corridor towards the dining room, the door of which she proceeded to unlock. Trevor Roberts, striding behind Charlie, continued to look puzzled, but refrained from asking any questions.

As they entered the dining room Charlie stopped in his tracks and said, "I could spot a Ross at twenty paces."

"I beg your pardon, Sir Charles?"

"It's not important, Mrs Culver," Charlie said as he stood in front of the picture and stared at a woodland scene of dappled browns and greens.

"Beautiful, isn't it, Sir Charles? A real understanding of the use of colour. I would go as far as to say – "

"I wonder, Mrs Culver, if you would consider that picture to be a fair exchange for a minibus?"

"A very fair exchange," said Mrs Culver without hesitation. "In fact I feel sure . . ."

"And would it be too much to ask that you write on the back of the picture, 'painted by Miss Cathy Ross', along with the dates that she resided at St Hilda's?"

"Delighted, Sir Charles." Mrs Culver stepped forward

and lifted the picture off its hook, then turned the frame round for all to see. What Sir Charles had requested, although faded with age, was already written and clearly legible to the naked eye.

"I do apologise, Mrs Culver," said Charlie. "By now I should know better of you." He removed his wallet from an inside pocket, signed a blank cheque and passed it over to Mrs Culver.

"But how much – ?" began the astonished principal.

"Whatever it costs," was all Charlie replied, having finally found a way of rendering Mrs Culver speechless.

The three of them returned to the principal's study where a pot of tea was waiting. One of the assistants set about making two copies of everything in Cathy's file while Roberts rang ahead to the nursing home where Miss Benson resided to warn the matron to expect them within the hour. Once both tasks had been completed Charlie thanked Mrs Culver for her kindness and bade her farewell. Although she had remained silent for some time she somehow managed, "Thank you, Sir Charles. Thank you."

Charlie clung tightly on to the picture as he walked out of the orphanage and back down the path. Once he was in the car again he instructed the driver to guard the package with his life.

"Certainly sir. And where to now?"

"Maple Lodge Residential Home, on the north side," instructed Roberts, who had climbed into the other side. "I do hope you're going to explain to me what happened back there at St Hilda's. Because I am, as the good book would have it, 'sore amazed'."

"I'll tell you as much as I know myself," said Charlie. He began to explain how he had first met Cathy almost fifteen years before at a house-warming party in his home at Eaton Square. He continued with his story uninterrupted until he had arrived at the part when Miss Ross had been appointed a director of Trumper's and how since Daniel's suicide she had been unable to tell them much about her background because she still hadn't fully recovered her memory of those events that had taken place before she came to England. The lawyer's opening response to this information took Charlie by surprise.

"You can be sure it wasn't a coincidence that Miss Ross visited England in the first place, or for that matter that she applied for a job at Trumper's."

"What are you getting at?" said Charlie.

"She must have left Australia with the sole purpose of trying to find out about her father, believing him still to be alive, perhaps even living in England. That must have been her original motivation to visit London, where she undoubtedly discovered some connection between his and your family. And if you can find that link between her father, her going to England and Trumper's, you will then have your proof – proof that Cathy Ross is in fact Margaret Ethel Trentham."

"But I have no idea what that link could be," said Charlie. "And now that Cathy remembers so little of her early life in Australia, I may never be able to find out."

"Well, let's hope Miss Benson can point us in the right direction," said Roberts. "Although, as I warned you earlier, no one who knew her at St Hilda's has a good word to say for the woman."

"If Walter Slade's anything to go by, it won't be easy to get the time of day out of her. It's becoming obvious that Mrs Trentham cast a spell over everyone she came into contact with."

"I agree," said the lawyer. "That's why I didn't reveal to Mrs Campbell, the matron of Maple Lodge our reason for wanting to visit the home. I couldn't see any point in warning Miss Benson of our impending arrival. It would only give her enough time to have all her answers well prepared."

Charlie grunted his approval. "But have you come up with any ideas as to what approach we should take with her?" he asked, "because I certainly made a balls-up of my meeting with Walter Slade."

"No, I haven't. We'll just have to play it by ear and hope she'll prove to be co-operative. Though heaven knows which accent you will be required to call on this time, Sir Charles."

Moments later they were driven between two massive wrought iron gates and on down a long shaded drive which led up to a large turn-of-the-century mansion set in several acres of private grounds.

"This can't come cheap," said Charlie.

"Agreed," said Roberts. "And unfortunately they don't look as if they're in need of a minibus."

The car drew up outside a heavy oak door. Trevor Roberts jumped out and waited until Charlie had joined him before pressing the bell.

They did not have long to wait before a young nurse answered their call, then promptly escorted them down a highly polished tiled corridor to the matron's office.

Mrs Campbell was dressed in the familiar starched blue uniform, white collar and cuffs associated with her profession. She welcomed Charlie and Trevor Roberts in a deep Scottish burr, and had it not been for the uninterrupted sunshine coming through the windows, Charlie might have been forgiven for thinking that the matron of Maple Lodge Residential Home was unaware that she had ever left Scotland.

After the introductions had been completed Mrs Campbell asked how she could be of help.

"I was hoping you might allow us to have a word with one of your residents."

"Yes, of course, Sir Charles. May I enquire who it is you wish to see?" she asked.

"A Miss Benson," explained Charlie. "You see –"

"Oh, Sir Charles, haven't you heard?"

"Heard?" said Charlie.

"Yes. Miss Benson's been dead this past week. In fact, we buried her on Thursday."

For a second time that day Charlie's legs gave way and Trevor Roberts had quickly to take his client by the elbow and guided him to the nearest chair.

"Oh, I am sorry," said Matron. "I had no idea you were such a close friend." Charlie didn't say anything.

"And have you come all the way from London especially to see her?"

"Yes, he did," said Trevor Roberts. "Has Miss Benson had any other visitors from England recently?"

"No," said the matron without hesitation. "She received very few callers towards the end. One or two from Adelaide but never one from Britain," she added with an edge to her voice.

"And did she ever mention to you anyone called Cathy Ross or Margaret Trentham?"

Mrs Campbell thought deeply for a moment. "No," she said eventually. "At least, not to my recollection."

"Then I think perhaps we should leave, Sir Charles, as there's no point in taking up any more of Mrs Campbell's time."

"I agree," said Charlie quietly. "And thank you, Matron." Roberts helped him to his feet and Mrs Campbell accompanied them both back along the corridor towards the front door.

"Will you be returning to Britain shortly, Sir Charles?" she asked.

"Yes, probably tomorrow."

"Would it be a terrible inconvenience if I were to ask you to post a letter for me once you are back in London?"

"It would be my pleasure," said Charlie.

"I wouldn't have bothered you with this task in normal circumstances," said the matron, "but as it directly concerns Miss Benson . . ."

Both men stopped in their tracks and stared down at the prim Scottish lady. She also came to a halt and held her hands together in front of her.

"It's not simply that I wish to save the postage, you understand, Sir Charles, which is what most folk would accuse my clan of. In fact, the exact opposite is the case, for my only desire is to make a speedy refund to Miss Benson's benefactors."

"Miss Benson's benefactors?" said Charlie and Roberts in unison.

"Aye," the matron said, standing her full height of five feet and half an inch. "We are not in the habit at Maple Lodge of charging residents who have died, Mr Roberts. After all, as I'm sure you would agree, that would be dishonest."

"Of course it would be, Matron."

"And so, although we insist on three months' payment in advance, we also refund any sums left over when a resident has passed away. After any outstanding bills have been covered, you understand."

"I understand," said Charlie as he stared down at the lady, a look of hope in his eyes.

"So if you will be kind enough to wait just a wee moment, I'll be away and retrieve the letter from my office." She turned and headed back to her room a few yards further down the corridor.

"Start praying," said Charlie.

"I already have," said Roberts.

Mrs Campbell returned a few moments later holding an envelope which she handed over for Charlie's safekeeping. In a bold copperplate hand were written the words: The Manager, Coutts and Company, The Strand, London WC2.

"I do hope you won't find my request too much of an imposition, Sir Charles."

"It's a greater pleasure than you may ever realise, Mrs Campbell," Charlie assured her, as he bade the matron farewell.

Once they were back in the car, Roberts said, "It would be quite unethical of me to advise you as to whether you should or should not open that letter, Sir Charles. However –"

But Charlie had already ripped open the envelope and was pulling out its contents.

A cheque for ninety-two pounds was attached to a detailed, itemised bill for the years 1953 to 1964: in full and final settlement for the account of Miss Rachel Benson.

"God bless the Scots and their puritan upbringing," said Charlie, when he saw to whom the cheque had been made out.

CHAPTER 46

"If you were quick, Sir Charles, you could still catch the earlier flight," said Trevor Roberts as the car pulled into the hotel forecourt.

"Then I'll be quick," said Charlie, "as I'd like to be back in London as soon as possible."

"Right, I'll check you out, then phone the airport to see if they can change your reservation."

"Good. Although I've a couple of days to spare there are still some loose ends I'd like to tidy up at the London end."

Charlie had jumped out of the car even before the driver could reach the door to open it for him. He made a dash for his room and quickly threw all his possessions into a suitcase. He was back in the lobby twelve minutes later, had settled the bill and was making a dash towards the hotel entrance within fifteen. The driver was not only standing by the car waiting for him but the boot was already open.

Once the third door had been closed, the chauffeur immediately accelerated out of the hotel forecourt and swung the car into the fast lane, as he headed towards the freeway.

"Passport and ticket?" said Roberts.

Charlie smiled and removed them both from an inside pocket like a child having his prep list checked.

"Good, now let's hope we can still reach the airport in time."

"You've done wonders," said Charlie.

"Thank you, Sir Charles," said Roberts. "But you must understand that despite your gathering a considerable amount of evidence to substantiate your case most if it remains at best circumstantial. Although you and I may be convinced that Cathy Ross is in fact Margaret Ethel Trentham, with Miss Benson in her grave and Miss Ross unable to recall all the relevant details of her past there's no way of predicting whether a court would find in your favour."

"I hear what you're saying," said Charlie. "But at least I now have something to bargain with. A week ago I had nothing."

"True. And having watched you operate over the past few days I'm bound to say that I'd give you odds of better than fifty-fifty. But whatever you do, don't let that picture out of your sight: it's as convincing as any fingerprint. And see that at all times you keep Mrs Campbell's letter in a safe place until you've been able to make a copy. Also be sure that the original plus the accompanying cheque are then posted on to Coutts. We don't want you arrested for stealing ninety-two pounds. Now, is there anything else I can do for you this end?"

"Yes, you could try to get a written statement out of Walter Slade admitting that he took Mrs Trentham and a little girl called Margaret to St Hilda's, and that she left without her charge. You might also attempt to pin Slade down to a date."

"That might not prove easy after your encounter," suggested Roberts.

"Well, at least have a go. Then see if you can find out if Miss Benson was in receipt of any other payments from Mrs Trentham before 1953 and if so the amounts and dates. I suspect she's been receiving a banker's order every quarter for over thirty-five years, which would explain why she was able to end her days in such comparative luxury."

"Agreed, but once again it's entirely circumstantial and there's certainly no way that any bank would allow me to delve into Miss Benson's private account."

"I accept that," said Charlie. "But Mrs Culver should be able to let you know what Miss Benson was earning while she was principal and if she appeared to live beyond her salary. After all, you can always find out what St Hilda's needs other than a minibus."

Roberts began to make notes as Charlie rattled out a series of further suggestions.

"If you were able to wrap up Slade and prove there were any previous payments made to Miss Benson, I would then be in a far stronger position to ask Nigel Trentham to explain why his mother was willing to keep on doling out money to someone who was principal of an orphanage situated on the other side of the globe if it wasn't for his elder brother's offspring."

"I'll do what I can," promised Roberts. "If I come up with anything I'll contact you in London on your return."

"Thank you," said Charlie. "Now, is there anything I can do for you?"

"Yes, Sir Charles. Would you be good enough to pass on my kindest regards to Uncle Ernest?"

"Uncle Ernest?"

"Yes, Ernest Baverstock."

"Kindest regards be damned. I shall report him to the Law Society."

"I must advise you that there is no case to answer, Sir Charles, as nepotism is not yet a crime. Though to be honest it's my mother who's to blame. You see, she produced three sons, all lawyers, and the other two are now representing you in Perth and Brisbane."

The car drew up to the kerb alongside the Qantas terminal. The driver jumped out and removed the suitcases from the boot as Charlie ran off in the direction of the ticket counter, with Roberts a yard behind carrying Cathy's picture.

"Yes, you can still make the early flight to London," the girl at the check-in desk assured Charlie. "But please be quick as we'll be closing the gates in a few minutes' time." Charlie breathed a sigh of relief and turned to say goodbye to Trevor Roberts as the driver arrived with his suitcase and placed it on the weighing machine.

"Damn," said Charlie. "Can you lend me ten pounds?"

Roberts removed the notes from his wallet and Charlie quickly passed them on to the driver, who touched his cap and returned to the car.

"How do I ever begin to thank you?" he said as he shook Trevor Roberts by the hand.

"Thank Uncle Ernest, not me," said Roberts. "He talked me into dropping everything to take on this case."

Twenty minutes later Charlie was climbing up the steps of Qantas Flight 102 ready for the first stage of his journey back to London.

As the plane lifted off ten minutes after schedule Charlie settled back and tried, with the knowledge he had gained in the last three days, to begin fitting the pieces together. He accepted Roberts's theory that it was no coincidence that Cathy had come to work at Trumper's. She must have discovered some connection between them and the Trenthams, even if Charlie couldn't work out exactly what that connection was or her reason for not telling either of them in the first place. Telling them . . . ? What right did he have to comment? If only he had told Daniel, the boy might still be alive today. Because one thing was certain: Cathy could not have realised that Daniel was her half-brother, although he now feared that Mrs Trentham must have found out, then let her grandson know the awful truth.

"Evil woman," said Charlie to himself.

"I beg your pardon," said the middle-aged lady who was seated on his left.

"Oh, I'm sorry," said Charlie. "I wasn't referring to you." He returned to his reverie. Mrs Trentham must have somehow stumbled on that truth. But how? Did Cathy go to see her as well? Or was it simply the announcement of their engagement in *The Times* that alerted Mrs Trentham to an illegal liaison that Cathy and Daniel could not have been aware of themselves? Whatever the reason, Charlie realised that his chances of piecing together the complete story were now fairly remote, with Daniel and Mrs Trentham in their graves and Cathy still unable to recall much of what had happened to her before she arrived in England.

It was ironic, thought Charlie, that so much of what he had discovered in Australia had all the time been lodged in a file at Number 1 Chelsea Terrace, marked Cathy Ross, job application. But not the missing link. "Find that," Roberts had said, "and you will be able to show the connection between Cathy Ross and Guy Trentham." Charlie nodded in agreement.

Lately Cathy had been able to recollect some memories from her past, but still nothing significant when it came to recalling her early days in Australia. Doctor Atkins continued to advise Charlie not to press her, as he was delighted with her progress, especially over her willingness to talk quite openly about Daniel. But if he were to save Trumper's he surely had to press her now? He decided that one of the first calls he should make the moment the plane touched down on English soil would have to be to Doctor Atkins.

"This is your captain speaking," said a voice over the intercom. "I'm sorry to have to inform you that we have encountered a slight technical problem. Those of you seated on the right-hand side of the aircraft will be able to see that I have turned off one of the starboard engines. I can assure you that there is no need for any anxiety, as we still have three engines working at their full capacity and in any case this aircraft is capable of completing any leg of the journey on just one." Charlie was pleased to learn this piece of news. "However," continued the captain, "it is company policy, with your safety in mind, that when any such fault arises we should land at the nearest airport, in order that repairs can be carried out immediately." Charlie frowned. "As we have not yet reached the halfway point on our outward leg of the journey to Singapore, I am advised by air traffic control that we must return to Melbourne at once." A chorus of groans went up throughout the aircraft.

Charlie made some hasty calculations about how much time he had to spare before he needed to be back in London, then he remembered that the aircraft he had been originally booked on was still due out of Melbourne at eight twenty that night.

He flicked open his seat-belt, retrieved Cathy's picture from the rack above him and moved across to the nearest available first-class seat to the cabin door, his mind now fully concentrated on the problems of getting himself re-booked on the BOAC carrier bound for London.

Qantas Flight 102 touched down at Melbourne airport at seven minutes past seven. Charlie was the first off the aircraft, running as fast as he could, but having to lug Cathy's picture under one arm slowed him down and made it possible for several other passengers, who obviously had the same idea, to overtake him. However, once he'd reached the booking counter Charlie still managed to be eleventh in the queue. One by one the line shortened as those ahead of him were allocated seats. But by the time Charlie reached the front they could only offer him a standby. Despite pleading desperately with a BOAC official he could make no headway: there were several other passengers who felt it was every bit as important for them to be in London.

He walked slowly back to the Qantas desk to be informed that Flight 102 had been grounded for engine repairs and would not be taking off again until the following morning. At eight forty he watched the BOAC Comet that he had been originally booked on lift off the tarmac without him.

All the passengers were found beds for the night at one of the local airport hotels before having their tickets transferred to a ten twenty flight the following morning.

Charlie was up, dressed and back at the airport two hours before the plane was due to take off, and when the flight was finally called he was the first on board. If all went to schedule, he worked out, the plane would still touch down at Heathrow early on the Friday morning, giving him a clear day and a half to spare before Sir Raymond's two-year deadline was up.

He breathed his first sigh of relief when the Comet took off, his second as the flight passed the halfway mark to

Singapore, and his third when they had landed at Paya Lebar airport a few minutes ahead of time.

Charlie left the plane, but only to stretch his legs. He was strapped back into his seat and ready for take-off an hour later. The second stage from Singapore to Bangkok landed at Don Muang airport only thirty minutes behind schedule, but the plane then sat parked in a queue on the runway for a further hour. It was later explained that they were short-staffed at air traffic control. Despite the delay, Charlie was not unduly worried; but that didn't stop him from checking his half-hunter every few minutes. They took off an hour behind schedule.

When the aircraft landed at Palam airport in New Delhi, he began another hour of strolling around the duty free while the plane was being refuelled. He became bored by seeing the same watches, perfume and jewellery being sold to innocent transit passengers at prices he knew still had a fifty per cent mark-up on them. When the hour had passed and there had been no further announcements about re-boarding, Charlie walked over to the enquiry desk to discover what was causing the hold-up.

"There seems to be some problem with the relief crew on this section of the flight," he was told by the young woman behind the general enquiries sign. "They haven't completed their twenty-four hours' rest period, as stipulated by IATA regulations."

"So how long have they had?"

"Twenty hours," replied the girl, looking embarrassed.

"So that means we're stuck here for another four hours?"

"I'm afraid so."

"Where is the nearest phone?" Charlie asked, making no attempt to hide his irritation.

"In the far corner, sir," said the girl, pointing to her right.

Charlie joined yet another queue and when he reached the front managed to get through to the operator twice, connected to London once but to speak with Becky never.

By the time he eventually climbed back on to the aircraft, having achieved nothing, he was exhausted.

"This is Captain Parkhouse. We are sorry for the delay in this flight's taking off," said the pilot in a soothing voice. "I can only hope that the hold-up has not caused you too much inconvenience. Please fasten your seat-belts and prepare for take-off. Flight attendants place cabin doors to automatic."

The four jets rumbled into action and the plane inched forward before building up momentum as it sped along the tarmac. Then, quite suddenly, Charlie was thrown forward as the brakes were locked in place and the plane came to a screeching halt a few hundred yards from the end of the runway.

"This is your captain speaking. I am sorry to have to tell you that the hydraulic pumps that lift the undercarriage up and down at take-off and landing are indicating red on the control panel and I am not willing to risk a take-off at this time. We shall therefore have to taxi back to our stand and ask the local engineers to fix the problem as quickly as possible. Thank you for being so understanding."

It was the word "local" that worried Charlie.

Once they had disembarked from the plane, Charlie ran from airline counter to airline counter trying to find out if there were any flights bound for anywhere in Europe due out of New Delhi that night. He quickly discovered the only flight due out that night was destined for Sydney. He began to pray for the speed and efficiency of Indian engineers.

Charlie sat in a smoke-filled waiting lounge, leafing through magazine after magazine, sipping soft drink after soft drink, as he waited for any information he could garner on the fate of Flight 102. The first news he picked up was that the chief engineer had been sent for.

"Sent for?" said Charlie. "What does that mean?"

"We have sent a car for him," explained a smiling airport official in a clipped staccato accent.

"Sent a car?" said Charlie. "But why isn't he at the airport where he's needed?"

"It's his day off."

"And haven't you got any other engineers?"

"Not for a job this big," admitted the harassed official.

Charlie slapped his forehead with the palm of his hand. "And where does the chief engineer live?"

"Somewhere in New Delhi," came back the reply. "But don't you worry yourself, sir, we should have him back within the hour."

The trouble with this country, thought Charlie, is they tell you exactly what they think you want to hear.

For some reason the same official was unable to explain later why it had taken two hours to locate the chief engineer, a further hour to bring him back to the airport and yet another fifty minutes before he discovered the job would require a full team of three qualified engineers, who had themselves recently signed off for the evening.

A rickety old bus delivered all the passengers from Flight 107 to the Taj Mahal Hotel in the centre of the city where Charlie sat on his bed and spent most of the night once more attempting to make contact with Becky. When he eventually succeeded in reaching her he was cut off even before he had time to explain where he was. He didn't bother to try and sleep.

When the bus dropped them back at the airport the following morning the Indian airport official was there to greet them, his large smile still in place.

"The plane will take off on time," he promised.

On time, thought Charlie; in normal circumstances he would have laughed.

The plane did take off an hour later and when Charlie enquired of the purser at what hour they expected to land at Heathrow he was told at some time Saturday mid-afternoon: it was hard to be precise.

When the aircraft made a further unscheduled landing at Leonardo da Vinci on Saturday afternoon Charlie telephoned Becky from the airport. He didn't even give her time to speak. "I'm in Rome," he said, "and I'll need Stan to pick me up from Heathrow. As I can't be sure what time

I'll arrive, tell him to go out to the airport right now and sit tight. Got that?"

"Yes," said Becky.

"And I'll also need Baverstock back in his office, so if he's already disappeared off to the country for the weekend ask him to drop everything and return to London."

"You sound a little harassed, dear."

"Sorry," said Charlie. "It's not been the easiest of journeys."

With the picture under one arm and no interest as to what was wrong with the aircraft this time or where his suitcase might end up, he took the first European flight available that afternoon for London, and once it had taken off checked his watch every ten minutes. When the pilot crossed the English Channel at eight o'clock that evening, Charlie felt confident that four hours would still be ample time for him to register Cathy's claim – so long as Becky had tracked down Baverstock.

As the plane began to circle London in a familiar holding pattern Charlie looked out of the little oval window and stared down at the snake-like Thames.

It was another twenty minutes before the lights of the runway glared up in two straight lines at Charlie, followed by a puff of smoke as the wheels touched the ground and the plane taxied to its allotted gate. The doors of the aircraft were finally opened at eight twenty-nine.

Charlie grabbed the picture and ran all the way to passport control and on through customs.

He didn't stop until he saw a telephone box, but as he hadn't any coins to make a local call he told the operator his name and asked to transfer the charge. A moment later he was put through.

"Becky, I'm at Heathrow. Where's Baverstock?"

"On his way back from Tewkesbury. Expects to be in his office around nine thirty, latest ten."

"Good, then I'll come straight home. I should be with you in about forty minutes."

Charlie slammed down the phone, checked his watch

and realised that he hadn't left himself enough time to phone Doctor Atkins. He ran out on to the pavement, suddenly aware of the chill breeze. Stan was waiting by the car for him. Over the years the former sergeant-major had become accustomed to Charlie's impatience and drove him smoothly through the outskirts of London, ignoring the speed limit until they reached Chiswick, after which only a motor-bike could have been stopped for speeding. Despite the teeming rain he had his boss back at Eaton Square by nine sixteen.

Charlie was about halfway through telling a silent Becky all he had discovered in Australia when Baverstock phoned to say he was back at his office in High Holborn. Charlie thanked him, passed on his nephew's best wishes and then apologised for ruining his weekend.

"You won't have ruined it if your news is positive," said Baverstock.

"Guy Trentham had another child," said Charlie.

"I didn't imagine that you'd dragged me back from Tewkesbury to tell me the latest Test score from Melbourne," said Baverstock. "Male or female?"

"Female."

"Legitimate or illegitimate?"

"Legitimate."

"Then she can register her claim with the estate at any time before midnight."

"She has to register her claim with you in person?"

"That is what the will stipulates," said Baverstock. "However, if she's still in Australia she can register with Trevor Roberts, as I've given him –"

"No, she's in England and I'll have her in your office by midnight."

"Good. By the way, what's her name?" asked Baverstock. "Just so that I can prepare the paperwork."

"Cathy Ross," said Charlie. "But ask your nephew to explain everything as I haven't a moment to spare," he added, replacing the receiver before Baverstock could react. He ran out into the hall searching for Becky.

"Where's Cathy?" he shouted, as Becky appeared at the top of the stairs.

"She went to a concert at the Festival Hall. Mozart, I think she said, with some new beau from the City."

"Right, let's go," said Charlie.

"Go?"

"Yes, go," said Charlie at the top of his voice. He had already reached the door and climbed into the back seat of the car before he realised there was no driver.

He jumped out and was on his way back to the house as Becky came rushing out in the opposite direction.

"Where's Stan?"

"Probably having some supper in the kitchen."

"Right," said Charlie, passing over his own keys. "You drive, I'll talk."

"But where are we off to?"

"The Festival Hall."

"Funny," Becky said, "after all these years and I had no idea you cared for Mozart." As she took her seat behind the wheel Charlie ran round to join her in the front. She pulled out and moved deftly through the evening traffic as Charlie continued to explain the full implications of his discoveries in Australia and how imperative it was that they find Cathy before midnight. Becky listened intently but did not attempt to interrupt her husband's flow.

By the time Charlie asked her if she had any questions they were crossing Westminster Bridge, but Becky still remained silent.

Charlie waited for a few moments before he demanded, "Have you nothing to say?"

"Yes," said Becky. "Don't let's make the same mistake with Cathy as we did with Daniel."

"Namely?"

"Fail to tell her the whole truth."

"I'll have to speak to Doctor Atkins before I can even consider taking that risk," said Charlie. "But our more immediate problem is to make sure she registers in time."

"Not to mention the even more immediate problem of

where you expect me to leave the car," said Becky as they swung left into Belvedere Road and on towards the entrance of the Royal Festival Hall with its double yellow lines and "No Parking" signs.

"Right outside the front door," said Charlie, which Becky obeyed without question.

As soon as the car had come to a halt Charlie jumped out, ran across the pavement and pushed through the glass doors.

"What time does the concert end?" he asked the first uniformed official he spotted.

"Ten thirty-five, sir, but you can't leave your car there."

"And where's the manager's office?"

"Fifth floor, turn right, second door on the left as you get out of the lift. But . . ."

"Thank you," shouted Charlie, already running past him towards the lift. Becky had just about caught up with her husband by the time the light above the lift indicated G.

"Your car, sir –" said the doorman, but the lift doors were already closing on the gesticulating official.

When the lift doors slid apart at the fifth floor Charlie jumped out, looked right and saw a door to his left marked "Manager". He knocked once before charging in, to find two men dressed in dinner jackets enjoying a cigarette and listening to the concert over an intercom. They turned to see who had interrupted them.

"Good evening, Sir Charles," said the taller of the two as he rose, stubbed out his cigarette, and stepped forward. "Jackson. I'm the theatre manager. Can I help you in any way?"

"I only hope so, Mr Jackson," said Charlie. "I have to get a young lady out of your concert hall as quickly as possible. It's an emergency."

"Do you know her seat number?"

"No idea." Charlie looked towards his wife who only shook her head.

"Then follow me," said the manager, who strode straight out of the door and back towards the lift. When the doors reopened the first official Charlie had come across was now standing in front of them.

"Any problems, Ron?"

"Only that this gentleman's left his car bang outside the front door, sir."

"Then keep an eye on it, will you, Ron?" The manager pressed the third-floor button and, turning to Becky, asked, "What was the young lady wearing?"

"A burgundy dress with a white cape," said Becky urgently.

"Well done, madam," said the manager. He stepped out of the lift and led them quickly through to a side entrance adjoining the Ceremonial Box. Once inside Mr Jackson removed a small picture of the Queen opening the building in 1957 and flicked back a disguised shutter so that he could observe the audience through a one-way mirror. "A security precaution in case there's ever any trouble," he explained. The manager then unhooked two pairs of opera glasses from their little stands under the balcony and handed one each to Charlie and Becky.

"If you can locate where the lady is seated, one of my staff will discreetly pull her out." He turned to listen to the strains of the final movement for a few seconds before adding, "You've got about ten minutes before the concert ends, twelve at the most. There are no encores planned for tonight."

"You take the stalls, Becky, and I'll cover the dress circle." Charlie began to focus the little opera glasses on the audience seated below them.

They both covered the one thousand nine hundred seats, first quickly then slowly up and down each row. Neither could spot Cathy in the stalls or dress circle.

"Try the boxes on the other side, Sir Charles," suggested the manager.

Two pairs of glasses swung over to the far side of the theatre. There was still no sign of Cathy, so Charlie and

Becky turned their attention back to the main auditorium, once again scanning quickly over the seats.

The conductor brought his baton down for the final time at ten thirty-two and the applause followed in waves as Charlie and Becky searched the standing throng until the lights eventually went up and the audience began to make their way out of the theatre.

"You keep on looking, Becky. I'll go out front and see if I can spot them as they're leaving." He dashed out of the Ceremonial Box and down the stairs followed by Jackson, nearly knocking over a man who was leaving the box below them. Charlie turned to apologise.

"Hello, Charlie, I didn't know you liked Mozart," a voice said.

"I never used to but suddenly he's top of the pops," said Charlie, unable to mask his delight.

"Of course," said the manager. "The one place you couldn't see was the box below ours."

"May I introduce –"

"We haven't time for that," said Charlie. "Just follow me." He grabbed Cathy by the arm. "Mr Jackson, would you be kind enough to ask Becky, my wife, to explain to this gentleman why I need Cathy. You can have her back after midnight," said Charlie, smiling at the bemused young man. "And thank you, Mr Jackson."

He checked his watch: ten forty. "We still have enough time."

"Enough time for what, Charlie?" said Cathy as she found herself being pulled across the foyer and out on to Belvedere Road. The uniformed man was now standing to attention by the car.

"Thank you, Ron," said Charlie as he tried to open the front door. "Damn, Becky's locked it," he said. He turned to watch a cab as it came off the waiting rank. He hailed it.

"I say, old fellow," said a man standing in the front of the taxi queue, "I think you'll find that's my cab."

"She's just about to give birth," said Charlie as he

opened the door and pushed the wafer-thin Cathy into the back of the taxi.

"Oh, jolly good luck," said the man, taking a pace backwards.

"Where to, guvn'r?" asked the cabbie.

"One hundred and ten High Holborn and don't hang about," said Charlie.

"I think we're more likely to find a solicitor than a gynaecologist at that particular address," suggested Cathy. "And I do hope you've a worthwhile explanation as to why I'm missing dinner with the one man who's asked me out on a date in weeks."

"Not right now," Charlie confessed. "All I need you to do for the moment is sign a document before midnight, then I promise the explanations will follow."

The taxi pulled up outside the solicitor's office a few minutes after eleven. Charlie stepped out of the cab to find Baverstock was standing by the door waiting to greet them.

"That'll be eight and six, guvn'r."

"Oh, God," said Charlie, "I haven't got any money."

"That's the way he treats all his girls," said Cathy, as she passed the cabbie a ten-shilling note.

They both followed Baverstock through to his office where a set of documents was already laid out on his desk. "Since you called I have had a long conversation with my nephew in Australia," said Baverstock, facing Charlie. "So I think I'm well acquainted with everything that took place while you were over there."

"Which is more than I am," said Cathy, sounding bewildered.

"All in good time," said Charlie. "Explanations later." He turned back to Baverstock. "So what happens now?"

"Miss Ross must sign here, here and here," the solicitor said without further explanation, indicating a space between two pencilled crosses at the bottom of three separate sheets of paper. "As you are in no way related to the beneficiary or a beneficiary yourself, Sir Charles, you may care to act as the witness to Miss Ross's signature."

Charlie nodded, placed a pair of opera glasses beside the contract and took a pen from his inside pocket.

"You've always taught me in the past, Charlie, to read documents carefully before putting my signature to them."

"Forget everything I've taught you in the past, my girl, and just sign where Mr Baverstock is pointing."

Cathy signed all three documents without another word.

"Thank you, Miss Ross," said Mr Baverstock. "And now if you could both bear with me for one moment, I must inform Mr Birkenshaw of what has taken place."

"Birkenshaw?" said Charlie.

"Mr Trentham's solicitor. I must obviously let him know immediately that his client is not the only person who has registered a claim to the Hardcastle estate."

Cathy, looking even more bewildered, turned to Charlie.

"Later," said Charlie. "I promise."

Baverstock dialled the seven digits of a Chelsea number.

No one spoke as they waited for the telephone to be answered. Eventually Mr Baverstock heard a sleepy voice say, "Kensington 7192."

"Good evening, Birkenshaw, Baverstock here. Sorry to have to bother you at this time of night. Indeed, I wouldn't have done so if I hadn't considered the circumstances fully warranted such an intrusion on your privacy. But may I first ask what time you make it?"

"Have I heard you correctly?" said Birkenshaw, his voice now sounding more alert. "You've telephoned me in the middle of the night to ask what the time is?"

"Precisely," said Baverstock. "You see, I need to confirm that it is still before the witching hour. So do be a good fellow and tell me what time you make it."

"I make it eleven seventeen, but I fail to understand –"

"I make it eleven sixteen," said Baverstock, "but on the matter of time I am happy to bow to your superior judgment. The purpose of this call, by the way," he continued, "is to let you know that a second person – who appears to be a more direct descendant of Sir Raymond than your client – has laid claim to the Hardcastle estate."

"What's her name?"

"I suspect you already know that," replied the old lawyer before he replaced the telephone. "Damn," he said, looking across at Charlie, "I should have recorded the conversation."

"Why?"

"Because Birkenshaw is never going to admit that he said 'her'."

CHAPTER 47

"Are you saying that Guy Trentham was my father?" asked Cathy. "But how . . . ?"

After waking up Doctor Atkins, a man more used to being disturbed during the night, Charlie felt able to explain to Cathy what he had discovered during his visit to Australia, and how everything had been borne out by the information she had supplied to Becky when she first applied for a job at Trumper's. Baverstock listened intently, nodding from time to time, while regularly checking the copious notes he had made following a long conversation with his nephew in Sydney.

Cathy listened to everything Charlie had to report and although she now had some recollections of her life in Australia, she was still fairly vague about her days at the university of Melbourne, and could remember almost nothing of St Hilda's, while the name Miss Benson just didn't register at all.

"I've tried so hard to recall more details of what happened before I came to England, but nothing much comes back despite the fact that I can remember almost everything that took place after I landed at Southampton. Doctor Atkins isn't that optimistic, is he?"

"There are no rules is all he keeps reminding me."

Around four the following morning Charlie phoned for a taxi to take them back to Eaton Square, having agreed with Baverstock that he should set up a face-to-face meeting with the other side as soon as it could be arranged. When they returned home Cathy was so exhausted that she went straight to bed but as Charlie's time-clock didn't allow him to sleep he closeted himself in the study and continued his mental search for the missing link, only too aware of the legal battle that lay ahead of him even if he succeeded.

The following day he and Cathy travelled up to Cambridge together and spent a fraught afternoon in Doctor Atkins' little office at Addenbrooke's. For his part the consultant seemed far more interested in the file on Cathy that had been supplied by Mrs Culver than the fact she might in some way be related to Mrs Trentham and therefore eligible to inherit the Hardcastle Trust.

He took her slowly through each item in the file – art classes, credits, misdemeanours, tennis matches, Melbourne Church of England Girls' Grammar School, University of Melbourne – but he always met with the same response: deep thought, but only vague recollections. He tried word associations – Melbourne, Miss Benson, cricket, ship, hotel – to which he received the replies, Australia, Hedges, scorer, Southampton, long hours.

"Scorer" was the only word that interested Doctor Atkins but pressed further Cathy's only memories of Australia remained a sketchy description of Melbourne Grammar School, some clear recollections of the university and a boy called Mel Nicholls, followed by a long trip on a ship to London. She could even tell them the names of Pam and Maureen who had travelled over with her, but not where they came from.

Cathy went into great detail when the subject turned to the Melrose Hotel and Charlie was able to confirm the accuracy of Cathy's recollections of her early life at Trumper's.

The description of her first meeting with Daniel, down to his changing the place cards at the Trumpers' housewarming party, brought tears to Charlie's eyes. But on the subject of her parentage and the names of Margaret Ethel Trentham and Miss Rachel Benson she still had nothing to offer.

By six o'clock Cathy was drained. Doctor Atkins took Charlie on one side and warned him that in his opinion it was most unlikely that she would remember much more of what took place in her life before she arrived in London. Perhaps minor incidents might come back to her from time to time, but nothing of any real significance.

"I'm sorry, I wasn't much help to you, was I?" said Cathy as Charlie drove her back to London.

He took her hand. "We're not beaten yet," he promised her, although he was beginning to feel that Trevor Roberts's odds of fifty-fifty of proving that Cathy was the rightful claimant to the Hardcastle Trust were looking distinctly optimistic.

Becky was there to welcome them home and the three of them had a quiet supper together. Charlie made no reference to what had taken place at Cambridge earlier in the day until after Cathy had retired to her room. When Becky heard how Cathy had responded to Doctor Atkins' examination she insisted that from now on the girl was to be left in peace.

"I lost Daniel because of that woman," she told her husband. "I'm not willing to lose Cathy as well. If you're going to continue your fight for Trumper's you must do it without involving her."

Charlie nodded his agreement though he wanted to shout out: How am I expected to save everything I've built up from being taken away from me by yet another Trentham without being allowed to push Cathy to the brink?

Just before he switched out the bedroom light the phone rang. It was Trevor Roberts calling from Sydney, but his news did not advance their cause. Walter Slade had refused to release any new information on Ethel Trentham and wouldn't even sign a document confirming he had driven her. Charlie once again cursed himself for the crass way he had handled the interview with the old Yorkshireman.

"And the bank?" he asked, not sounding too hopeful.

"The Commercial Bank of Australia say they wouldn't allow access to the details of Miss Benson's private account unless we could prove a crime had been committed. What Mrs Trentham did to Cathy might well be described as evil, but I fear it wasn't strictly criminal."

"It hasn't been a good day for either of us," admitted Charlie.

"Never forget that the other side doesn't know that."

"True, but how much *do* they know?"

"My uncle's told me about Birkenshaw's slip of the tongue with 'her', so my bet is they know almost as much as we do. When you confront them, better assume they do, while at the same time never stop looking for that missing link."

After Charlie had put down the phone, he lay awake for some time and didn't move again until he could hear Becky breathing deeply. Then he slid out of bed, donned his dressing-gown and crept down to his study. He opened a notebook and began to write out every fact he had gathered during the last few days in the hope that it might just trigger off some memory. The following morning Cathy found him slumped, head on his desk, sound asleep.

"I don't deserve you, Charlie," she whispered, kissing him on the forehead. He stirred and raised his eyes.

"We're winning," he said sleepily and even managed a smile, but he realised from the expression on her face that she didn't believe him.

Becky joined them for breakfast an hour later and talked of everything except the face-to-face meeting that had been arranged to take place in Mr Baverstock's rooms that afternoon.

As Charlie stood up to leave the table, Cathy said, quite unexpectedly, "I'd like to be present at the show-down."

"Do you think that's wise?" asked Becky, glancing anxiously towards her husband.

"Perhaps not," said Cathy. "But I'm still certain I want to be there, not just learn about the outcome later, second-hand."

"Good girl," said Charlie. "The meeting will be at three in Baverstock's office, when we will get the chance to present our case. Trentham's lawyer will be joining us at four. I'll pick you up at two thirty, but if you want to change your mind before then, it won't worry me in the slightest."

Becky turned to see how Cathy had reacted to this suggestion and was disappointed.

When Charlie marched in to his office at exactly eight thirty, Daphne and Arthur Selwyn were already waiting for him as instructed.

"Coffee for three and please, no interruptions," Charlie told Jessica, placing his night's work on the desk in front of him.

"So where do we start?" asked Daphne, and for the next hour and a half they rehearsed questions, statements and tactics that could be used when dealing with Trentham and Birkenshaw, trying to second-guess every situation that might arise.

By the time a light lunch was sent in just before twelve they all felt drained; no one spoke for some time.

"It's important for you to remember that you're dealing with a different Trentham this time," said Arthur Selwyn eventually, as he dropped a sugar lump into his coffee.

"They're all as bad as each other as far as I'm concerned," said Charlie.

"Perhaps Nigel's every bit as resolute as his brother, but I don't believe for one moment that he has his mother's cunning – or Guy's ability to think on his feet."

"Just what are you getting at, Arthur?" asked Daphne.

"When you all meet this afternoon Charlie must keep Trentham talking as much as possible, because I've noticed over the years during board meetings that he often says one sentence too many and simply ends up defeating his own case. I'll never forget the time he was against the staff having their own canteen because of the loss of revenue it was bound to incur, until Cathy pointed out that the food came out of the same kitchen as the restaurant and we actually ended up making a small profit on what would otherwise have been thrown away."

Charlie considered this statement as he took another bite out of his sandwich.

"Wonder what his advisors are telling him are my weak points."

"Your temper," said Daphne. "You've always lived on a short fuse. So don't give them the chance to light it."

At one o'clock Daphne and Arthur Selwyn left Charlie in peace. After the door had closed behind them Charlie removed his jacket, went over to the sofa, lay down and for the next hour slept soundly. At two o'clock Jessica woke him. He smiled up at her, feeling fully refreshed: another legacy from the war.

He returned to his desk and read through his notes once again before leaving his office to walk three doors down the corridor and pick up Cathy. He quite expected her to have changed her mind but she already had her coat on and was sitting waiting for him. They drove over to Baverstock's office arriving a full hour before Trentham and Birkenshaw were due to put in an appearance.

The old lawyer listened carefully to Charlie as he presented his case, occasionally nodding or making further notes, though from the expression on his face Charlie had no way of knowing what he really felt.

When Charlie had come to the end of his monologue Baverstock put his fountain pen down on the desk and leaned back in his chair. For some time he didn't speak.

"I am impressed by the logic of your argument, Sir Charles," he said eventually, as he leant forward and placed the palms of his hands on the desk in front of him. "And indeed with the evidence you have gathered. However, I'm bound to say that without the corroboration of your main witness and also with no written affidavits from either

Walter Slade or Miss Benson, Mr Birkenshaw will be quick to point out that your claim is based almost entirely on circumstantial evidence.

"None the less," he continued, "we shall have to see what the other side has to offer. I find it hard to believe following my conversation with Birkenshaw on Saturday night that your findings will come as a complete revelation to his client."

The clock on his mantelpiece struck a discreet four chimes; Baverstock checked his pocket watch. There was no sign of the other side and soon the old solicitor started drumming his fingers on the desk. Charlie began to wonder if this was simply tactics on behalf of his adversary.

Nigel Trentham and his lawyer finally appeared at twelve minutes past four; neither of them seemed to feel it was necessary to apologise for their lateness.

Charlie stood up when Mr Baverstock introduced him to Victor Birkenshaw, a tall, thin man, not yet fifty, prematurely balding with what little hair he had left combed over the top of his head in thin grey strands. The only characteristic he seemed to have in common with Baverstock was that their clothes appeared to have come from the same tailor. Birkenshaw sat down in one of the two vacant seats opposite the old lawyer without acknowledging that Cathy was even in the room. He removed a pen from his top pocket, took out a pad from his briefcase and rested it on his knee.

"My client, Mr Nigel Trentham, has come to lay claim to his inheritance as the rightful heir to the Hardcastle Trust," he began, "as clearly stated in Sir Raymond's last will and testament."

"Your client," said Baverstock, picking up Birkenshaw's rather formal approach, "may I remind you, is not named in Sir Raymond's will, and a dispute has now arisen as to who is the rightful next of kin. Please don't forget that Sir Raymond insisted that I call this meeting, should the need arise, in order to adjudicate on his behalf."

"My client," came back Birkenshaw, "is the second son of the late Gerald and Margaret Ethel Trentham and the grandson of Sir Raymond Hardcastle. Therefore, following the death of Guy Trentham, his elder brother, he must surely be the legitimate heir."

"Under the terms of the will, I am bound to accept your client's claim," agreed Baverstock. "Unless it can be shown that Guy Trentham is survived by a child or children. We already know that Guy was the father of Daniel Trumper –"

"That has never been proven to my client's satisfaction," said Birkenshaw, busily writing down Baverstock's words.

"It was proven sufficiently to Sir Raymond's satisfaction for him to name Daniel in his will in preference to your client. And following the meeting between Mrs Trentham and her grandson we have every reason to believe that she also was in no doubt as to who Daniel's father was. Otherwise why did she bother to come to an extensive agreement with him?"

"This is all conjecture," said Birkenshaw. "Only one fact is certain: the gentleman in question is no longer with us, and as far as anyone knows produced no children of his own." He still did not look in Cathy's direction while she sat listening silently as the ball was tossed backwards and forwards between the two professionals.

"We were happy to accept that without question," said Charlie, intervening for the first time. "But what we didn't know until recently was that Guy Trentham had a second child called Margaret Ethel."

"What proof do you have for such an outrageous claim?" said Birkenshaw, sitting bolt upright.

"The proof is in the bank statement that I sent round to your home on Sunday morning."

"A statement, I might say," said Birkenshaw, "that should not have been opened by anyone other than my client." He glanced towards Nigel Trentham who was busy lighting a cigarette.

"I agree," said Charlie, his voice rising. "But I thought I'd take a leaf out of Mrs Trentham's book for a change."

Baverstock winced, fearing his friend might be on the verge of losing his temper.

"Whoever the girl was," continued Charlie, "she somehow managed to get her name on to police files as Guy Trentham's only surviving child and to paint a picture that remained on the dining room wall of a Melbourne orphanage for over twenty years. A painting, I might add, that could not be reproduced by anyone other than the person who originally created it. Better than a fingerprint, wouldn't you say? Or is that also conjecture?"

"The only thing the painting proves," retorted Birkenshaw, "is that Miss Ross resided at an orphanage in Melbourne at some time between 1924 and 1945. However, I'm given to understand that she is quite unable to recall any details of her life at that orphanage, or indeed anything about its principal. Is that not the case, Miss Ross?" He turned to face Cathy directly for the first time.

She nodded her reluctant agreement, but still didn't speak.

"Some witness," said Birkenshaw, not attempting to disguise the sarcasm. "She can't even support the story you are putting forward on her behalf. Her name is Cathy Ross, that much we do know, despite your so-called evidence there's nothing to link her with Sir Raymond Hardcastle."

"There are several people who can support her 'story', as you call it," said Charlie, jumping back in. Baverstock raised an eyebrow as no evidence had been placed before him to corroborate such a statement, even if he did want to believe what Sir Charles was saying.

"Knowing that she was brought up in an orphanage in Melbourne doesn't add up to corroboration," said Birkenshaw, pushing back a strand of hair that had fallen across his forehead. "I repeat, even if we were to accept all your wild claims about some imagined meeting between Mrs Trentham and Miss Benson, that still doesn't prove Miss Ross is of the same blood as Guy Trentham."

"Perhaps you'd like to check her blood group for yourself?" said Charlie. This time Mr Baverstock raised both eyebrows: the subject of blood groups had never been referred to by either party before.

"A blood group, I might add, Sir Charles, that is shared by half the world's population." Birkenshaw tugged the lapels of his jacket.

"Oh, so you've already checked it?" said Charlie with a look of triumph. "So there must be some doubt in your mind."

"There's no doubt in my mind as to who is the rightful heir to the Hardcastle estate," Birkenshaw said, before turning to face Baverstock. "How long are we expected to drag out this farce?" His question was followed by an exasperated sigh.

"As long as it takes for someone to convince me who is the rightful heir to Sir Raymond's estate," said Baverstock, his voice remaining cold and authoritative.

"What more do you want?" Birkenshaw asked. "My client has nothing to hide, whereas Miss Ross seems to have nothing to offer."

"Then perhaps you could explain, Birkenshaw, to my satisfaction," said Baverstock, "why Mrs Ethel Trentham made regular payments over several years to a Miss Benson, the principal of St Hilda's Orphanage in Melbourne, where I think we all now accept Miss Ross lived between 1927 and 1942?"

"I didn't have the privilege of representing Mrs Trentham, or indeed Miss Benson, so I'm in no position to offer an opinion. Nor, sir, for that matter, are you."

"Perhaps your client is aware of the reason for those payments and *would* care to offer an opinion," interjected Charlie. They both turned to Nigel Trentham who calmly stubbed out the remains of his cigarette but still made no attempt to speak.

"There's no reason why my client should be expected to answer any such hypothetical question," Birkenshaw suggested.

"But if your client is so unwilling to speak for himself," said Baverstock, "it makes it all the more difficult for me to accept that he has nothing to hide."

"That, sir, is unworthy of you," said Birkenshaw. "You of all people are well aware that when a client is represented by a lawyer it is understood he may not necessarily wish to speak. In fact, it was not even obligatory for Mr Trentham to attend this meeting."

"This isn't a court of law," said Baverstock sharply. "In any case, I suspect Mr Trentham's grandfather would not have approved of such tactics."

"Are you denying my client his legal rights?"

"Certainly not. However, if because of his unwillingness to offer any opinion I feel unable to come to a decision myself I may have to recommend to both parties that this matter be settled in a court of law, as stated clearly in clause twenty-seven of Sir Raymond's will."

Yet another clause that he didn't know about, Charlie reflected ruefully.

"But such a case might take years just to reach the courts," Birkenshaw pointed out. "Furthermore, it could end up in vast expenses to both sides. I cannot believe that would have been Sir Raymond's purpose."

"That may be so," said Baverstock. "But at least it would ensure that your client was given the opportunity to explain those quarterly payments to a jury – that is, if he knew anything about them."

For the first time Birkenshaw seemed to hesitate but Trentham still didn't speak. He just sat there, drawing on a second cigarette.

"A jury might also consider Miss Ross to be nothing more than an opportunist," suggested Birkenshaw, changing tack. "An opportunist who, having stumbled upon rather a good tale, managed to get herself over to England where she then made the facts fit in neatly with her own circumstances."

"Very neatly indeed," said Charlie. "Didn't she do well at the age of three to get herself registered at an orphanage in Melbourne? At exactly the same time as Guy Trentham was locked up in the local jail – "

"Coincidence," said Birkenshaw.

"– having been left there by Mrs Trentham, who then makes out a quarterly payment to the principal of that orphanage which mysteriously ceases the moment Miss Benson dies. That must have been some secret she was keeping."

"Once again circumstantial and, what's more, inadmissible," said Birkenshaw.

Nigel Trentham leaned forward and was about to make a comment when his lawyer placed his right hand firmly on his arm. "We shall not fall for those sort of bully-boy tactics, Sir Charles, that I suspect are more commonplace in the Whitechapel Road than in Lincoln's Inn."

Charlie leapt out of his chair, his fist clenched, and took a pace towards Birkenshaw.

"Calm yourself, Sir Charles," said Baverstock sharply.

Charlie reluctantly came to a halt a couple of feet in front of Birkenshaw, who did not flinch. After a moment's hesitation he recalled Daphne's advice and returned to his chair: Trentham's lawyer continued to stare defiantly at him.

"As I was saying," said Birkenshaw, "my client has nothing to hide. And he will certainly not find it necessary to resort to physical violence to prove his case."

Charlie unclenched his fist but did not lower his voice: "I do hope your client will resort to answering leading counsel when he enquires as to why his mother continued to pay large sums of money to someone from the other side of the world whom she, so you claim, never met. And why a Mr Walter Slade, a chauffeur with the Victoria Country Club, took Mrs Trentham to St Hilda's on 20 April 1927 accompanied by a little girl of Cathy's age called Margaret, but left without her. And I'll bet if we ask a judge to delve into Miss Benson's bank account, we'll find that those payments go back to within a day of when Miss Ross was registered at St Hilda's. After all, we already know that the banker's order was cancelled the week Miss Benson died."

Once again Baverstock appeared horrified by Charlie's reckless nerve, and raised a hand in the hope that he might stop any further outbursts.

Birkenshaw in contrast couldn't resist a wry smile. "Sir Charles, in default of your being represented by a lawyer, I really should remind you of one or two home truths. For a start, let me make one point abundantly clear: my client has assured me that he had never heard of Miss Benson until yesterday. In any case, no English judge has the jurisdiction to delve into an Australian bank account unless he has reason to believe a crime has been committed in both countries. What is more, Sir Charles, two of your key witnesses are sadly in their graves while the third, Mr Walter Slade, will not be making any trips to London. What is more, you won't be able to subpoena him.

"So now let us turn to your claim, Sir Charles, that a jury would be surprised if my client did not appear in the witness box to answer on behalf of his mother. I suspect they would be even more staggered to learn that the principal witness in this case, the claimant, was also unwilling to take the stand to answer on her own behalf because she has little or no recollection of what actually took place at the time in question. I do not believe that you could find a counsel in the land who would be willing to put Miss Ross through such an ordeal if the only words she is likely to utter in reply to every question put to her in the witness box were, 'Sorry, I can't remember.' Or is it possible that she simply has nothing credible to say? Let me assure you, Sir Charles, we would be only too happy to go to court, because you would be laughed out of it."

Charlie could tell from the look on Baverstock's face that he was beaten. He glanced sadly across at Cathy whose expression had not changed for the past hour.

Baverstock slowly removed his spectacles and made great play of cleaning them with a handkerchief he had taken out of his top pocket. Eventually he spoke: "I confess, Sir Charles, that I cannot see any good reason to take up the courts' time with this case. In fact, I believe it would be irresponsible of me to do so, unless of course Miss Ross is able to produce some fresh evidence of her identity that has so far not been considered or at least can corroborate all the statements you have made on her behalf." He turned to Cathy. "Miss Ross, is there anything you would like to say at this juncture?"

All four men turned their attention to Cathy who, sitting quietly, was rubbing a thumb against the inside of her forefinger, just below her chin. "I apologise, Miss Ross," said Baverstock. "I didn't realise that you had been trying to gain my attention."

"No, no, it is I who should apologise, Mr Baverstock," said Cathy. "I always do that when I'm nervous. It reminds me of the piece of jewellery that my father gave me when I was a child."

"The piece of jewellery your father gave you?" said Mr Baverstock quietly, not sure that he had heard her correctly.

"Yes," said Cathy. She undid the top button of her blouse and took out the miniature medal that hung from the end of a gold chain.

"Your father gave you that?" said Charlie.

"Oh, yes," said Cathy. "It's the only tangible memory I have of him."

"May I see the necklace, please?" asked Baverstock.

"Certainly," said Cathy, slipping the gold chain over her head and passing the medal to Charlie. He examined the miniature for some time before handing it on to Mr Baverstock.

"Although I'm no expert on medals I think it's a miniature MC," said Charlie.

"Wasn't Guy Trentham awarded the MC?" asked Baverstock.

"Yes, he was," said Birkenshaw, "and he also went to Harrow, but simply wearing their old school tie doesn't prove my client was his brother. In fact, it doesn't prove anything and certainly couldn't be produced as evidence in a court of law. After all, there must be hundreds of MCs still around. Indeed, Miss Ross could have picked up such a medal in any junk shop in London once she'd planned to make the facts surrounding Guy Trentham fit in with her background. You can't really expect us to fall for that old trick, Sir Charles."

"I can assure you, Mr Birkenshaw, that this particular medal was given to me by my father," said Cathy, looking directly at the lawyer. "He may not have been entitled to wear it, but I will never forget him placing it around my neck."

"That can't possibly be my brother's MC," said Nigel Trentham, speaking for the first time. "What's more, I can prove it."

"You can prove what?" asked Baverstock.

"Are you certain – ?" began Birkenshaw, but this time it was Trentham who placed a hand firmly on his lawyer's arm.

"I will prove to your satisfaction, Mr Baverstock," continued Trentham, "that the medal you now have in front of you could not have been the MC won by my brother."

"And just how do you propose to do that?" asked Baverstock.

"Because Guy's medal was unique. After he had been awarded his MC my mother sent the original to Spink's and at her request they printed Guy's initials down the edge of one of the arms. Those initials can only be seen under a magnifying glass. I know, because the medal he was presented with on the Marne still stands on the mantelpiece of my home in Chester Square. If a miniature had ever existed my mother would have had his initials stamped on it in exactly the same way."

No one spoke as Baverstock opened a drawer in his desk and took out an ivory-handled magnifying glass that he normally used to decipher illegible handwriting. He held up the medal to the light and studied the edges of the little silver arms one by one.

"You're quite right," admitted Baverstock, as he looked back up at Trentham. "Your case is proven." He passed both the medal and the magnifying glass over to Mr

Birkenshaw who in turn studied the MC for some time before returning the medal to Cathy with a slight bow of the head. He turned to his client and asked, "Were your brother's initials G.F.T.?"

"Yes, that's right. Guy Francis Trentham."

"Then I can only wish that you had kept your mouth shut."

BECKY

1964-1971

CHAPTER 48

When Charlie burst into the drawing room that evening it was the first time that I really believed Guy Trentham was finally dead.

I sat in silence while my husband strode around the room recalling with relish every last detail of the confrontation that had taken place in Mr Baverstock's office earlier that afternoon.

I have loved four men in my life with emotions ranging from adoration to devotion, but only Charlie encompassed the entire spectrum. Yet, even in his moment of triumph, I knew it would be left to me to take away from him the thing he most loved.

Within a fortnight of that fateful meeting, Nigel Trentham had agreed to part with his shares at the market price. Now that interest rates had risen to eight per cent it was hardly surprising that he had little stomach for a protracted and bitter wrangle over any claim he might or might not have to the Hardcastle estate.

Mr Baverstock, on behalf of the Trust, purchased all his stock at a cost of a little over seven million pounds. The old solicitor then advised Charlie that he should call a special board meeting as it was his duty to inform Companies House of what had taken place. He also warned Charlie that he must, within fourteen

711

days, circulate all other shareholders with the details of the transaction.

It had been a long time since I'd looked forward to a board meeting with such anticipation.

Although I was among the first to take my place at the boardroom table that morning, every other director was present long before the meeting was scheduled to begin.

"Apologies for absence?" requested the chairman on the dot of ten.

"Nigel Trentham, Roger Gibbs and Hugh Folland," Jessica intoned in her best matter-of-fact voice.

"Thank you. Minutes of the last meeting," said Charlie. "Is it your wish that I should sign those minutes as a true record?"

I glanced round the faces at the boardroom table. Daphne, dressed in a perky yellow outfit, was doodling away all over her minutes. Tim Newman was looking as suave as ever and simply nodded, while Simon took a sip from the glass of water in front of him and when he caught my eye raised it in a mock toast. Ned Denning whispered something inaudible in Bob Makins's ear while Cathy placed a tick by item number two. Only Paul Merrick looked as if he wasn't enjoying the occasion. I turned my attention back to Charlie.

As no one appeared to be showing any dissent, Jessica folded back the last page of the minutes to allow Charlie to scrawl his signature below the bottom line. I noticed Charlie smile when he re-read the final instruction the board had given him on the last occasion we had met: "Chairman to try and come to some amicable agreement with Mr Nigel Trentham concerning the orderly takeover of Trumper's."

"Matters arising from the minutes?" Charlie asked. Still no one else spoke, so once again Charlie's eyes returned to the agenda. "Item number four, the future of – " he began, but then every one of us tried to speak at once.

When some semblance of order had been regained, Charlie suggested that it might be wise if the chief executive were to bring us up to date on the latest position. I joined the "Hear, hears" and nods that greeted this suggestion.

"Thank you, Mr Chairman," said Arthur Selwyn, removing some papers from a briefcase by the side of his chair. The rest of the board waited patiently. "Members of the board will be aware that," he began, sounding like the senior civil servant he had once been, "following the announcement by Mr Nigel Trentham that it was no longer his intention to mount a takeover bid for Trumper's, the company's shares subsequently fell from their peak of two pounds four shillings to their present price of one pound nineteen shillings."

"We're all capable of following the vagaries of the stock market," said Daphne, butting in. "What I would like to know is: what has happened to Trentham's personal shareholding?"

I didn't join in with the chorus of approval that followed as I already knew every last detail of the agreement.

"Mr Trentham's stock," said Mr Selwyn, continuing as if he had not been interrupted, "was, following an agreement reached between his lawyers and Miss Ross's, acquired a fortnight ago by Mr Baverstock on behalf of the Hardcastle Trust at a cost of two pounds one shilling per share."

"And will the rest of the board ever be privy to what brought about this cosy little arrangement?" asked Daphne.

"It has recently come to light," answered Selwyn, "that Mr Trentham has, during the past year, been building up a considerable holding in the company on borrowed money, causing him to accumulate a large overdraft – an overdraft, I am given to understand, he can no longer sustain. With that in mind he has sold his personal holding in the company – some twenty-eight per cent – direct to the Hardcastle Trust at the going market rate."

"Has he now?" said Daphne.

"Yes," said Charlie. "And it may also interest the board to know that during the past week I have received three letters of resignation, from Mr Trentham, Mr Folland and Mr Gibbs, which I took the liberty of accepting on your behalf."

"That was indeed a liberty," said Daphne sharply.

"You feel we shouldn't have accepted their resignations?"

"I certainly do, Mr Chairman."

"May one ask your reasons, Lady Wiltshire?"

"They're purely selfish, Mr Chairman." I thought I detected a chuckle in her voice, as Daphne waited to be sure she had the full attention of the board. "You see, I'd been looking forward to proposing that all three of them should be sacked."

Few members of the board were able to keep a straight face at this suggestion.

"Not to be recorded in the minutes," said Charlie, turning towards Jessica. "Thank you, Mr Selwyn, for an admirable summary of the present situation. Now, as I cannot believe there is anything to be gained by continuing to rake over those particular coals, let us move on to item number five, the banking hall."

Charlie sat back contentedly while Cathy reported to us that the new facility was making a respectable monthly return and she could see no reason why the figures should not continue to improve for the foreseeable future. "In fact," she said, "I believe the time has come for Trumper's to offer its regular customers their own credit card as . . ."

I stared at the miniature MC that hung from a gold chain around Cathy's neck, the missing link that Mr Roberts always insisted had to exist. Cathy was still unable to recall a great deal of what had taken place in her life before she had come to work in London, but I agreed with Doctor Atkins' assessment that we should no longer waste our time with the past but let her concentrate on the future.

None of us doubted that when the time came to select a new chairman we wouldn't have far to look. The only problem I had to face now was how to convince the present chairman that perhaps the time had come for him to make way for someone younger.

"Do you have any strong feelings about upper limits, Mr Chairman?" asked Cathy.

"No, no, it all makes good sense to me," said Charlie, sounding unusually vague.

"I'm not so sure that I'm able to agree with you on this occasion, Mr Chairman," said Daphne.

"And why's that, Lady Wiltshire?" asked Charlie, smiling benignly.

"Partly because you haven't been listening to a single word that's been said for about the last ten minutes," Daphne declared, "so how can you possibly know what you're agreeing to?"

"Guilty," said Charlie. "I confess my mind was on the other side of the world. However," he continued, "I did read Cathy's report on the subject and I suggest that the upper limits will have to vary from customer to customer, according to their credit rating, and we may well need to employ some new staff in future who have been trained in the City, rather than on the high street. Even so, I shall still require a detailed timetable if we're to consider seriously the introduction of such a scheme, which should be ready for presentation at the next board meeting. Is that possible, Miss Ross?" Charlie asked firmly, no doubt hoping that yet another example of his well-known "thinking on his feet" had released him from the jaws of Daphne.

"I will have everything ready for the board to consider at least a week before our next meeting."

"Thank you," said Charlie. "Item number six. Accounts."

I listened intently as Selwyn presented the latest figures, department by department. Once again I became aware of Cathy questioning and probing whenever she felt we were not being given a full enough explanation for any loss or innovation. She sounded like a better informed, more professional version of Daphne.

"What are we now projecting will be the profit forecast for the year 1965?" she asked.

"Approximately nine hundred and twenty thousand pounds," replied Selwyn, running his finger down a column of figures.

That was the moment when I realised what had to be achieved before I could convince Charlie he should announce his retirement.

"Thank you, Mr Selwyn. Shall we move on to item number seven?" said Charlie. "The appointment of Miss Cathy Ross as deputy chairman of the board." Removing his glasses, Charlie added, "I don't feel it will be necessary for me to make a long speech on why—"

"Agreed," said Daphne. "It therefore gives me considerable pleasure to propose Miss Ross as deputy chairman of Trumper's."

"I should like to second that proposal," volunteered Arthur Selwyn. I could only smile at the sight of Charlie with his mouth wide open, but he still managed to ask, "Those in favour?" I raised my hand along with all but one director.

Cathy rose and gave a short acceptance speech in which she thanked the board for their confidence in her and assured them of her total commitment to the future of the company.

"Any other business?" asked Charlie, as he began stacking up his papers.

"Yes," replied Daphne. "Having had the pleasure

of proposing Miss Ross as deputy chairman I feel the time has come for me to hand in my resignation."

"But why?" asked Charlie, looking shocked.

"Because I shall be sixty-five next month, Mr Chairman, and I consider that to be a proper age to make way for younger blood."

"Then I can only say –" began Charlie and this time none of us tried to stop him making a long and heartfelt speech. When he had finished we all banged the table with the palm of a hand.

Once order had been regained, Daphne said simply, "Thank you. I could not have expected such dividends from a sixty-pound investment."

Within weeks of Daphne leaving the company, whenever a sensitive issue came under discussion with the board Charlie would admit to me after the meeting was over that he missed the marchioness's particular brand of maddening common sense.

"And I wonder if you'll miss me and my nagging tongue quite as much when I hand in my resignation?" I asked.

"What are you talking about, Becky?"

"Only that I'll be sixty-five in a couple of years and intend to follow Daphne's example."

"But –"

"No buts, Charlie," I told him. "Number 1 now runs itself – more than competently since I stole young Richard Cartwright from Christie's. In any case, Richard ought to be offered my place on the main board. After all, he's taking most of the responsibility without gaining any of the credit."

"Well, I'll tell you one thing," Charlie retorted defiantly, "I don't intend to resign, not even when I'm seventy."

During 1965, we opened three new departments: "Teenagers", which specialised in clothes and records with its own coffee shop attached; a travel agency, to cope with the growing demand for holidays abroad; and a gift department, "for the man who has everything". Cathy also recommended to the board that after nearly twenty years perhaps the whole barrow needed a face-lift. Charlie told me that he wasn't quite sure about such a radical upheaval, reminding me of the Fordian theory that one should never invest in anything that eats or needs to be repainted. But as Arthur Selwyn and the other directors seemed in no doubt that a refurbishment programme was long overdue he only put up token resistance.

I kept to my promise – or threat as Charlie saw it – and resigned three months after my sixty-fifth birthday, leaving Charlie as the only director who still survived from the original board.

For the first time in my recollection, Charlie admitted that he was beginning to feel his age. Whenever he called for the minutes of the last meeting, he admitted, he would look around the boardroom table and realise how little he had in common with most of his fellow directors. The "bright new sparks", as Daphne referred to them, financiers, takeover specialists, and public relations men, all of whom seemed somehow detached from the one element that had always mattered to Charlie – the customer.

They talked of deficit financing, loan option schemes and the necessity to have their own computer, often without bothering to seek Charlie's opinion.

"What can I do about it?" Charlie asked me after a board meeting at which he admitted he had hardly opened his mouth.

He scowled when he had heard my recommendation.

The following month Arthur Selwyn announced at the company's AGM that the pre-tax profits for 1966 would be £1,078,600. Charlie stared down at me as I nodded firmly from the front row. He waited for "Any other business" before he rose to tell the assembled company that he felt the time had come for him to resign. Someone else must push the barrow into the seventies, he suggested.

Everyone in the room looked shocked. They spoke of the end of an era, "no possible replacement", and said that it would never be the same again; but not one of them suggested Charlie should reconsider his position.

Twenty minutes later he declared the meeting closed.

CHAPTER 49

It was Jessica Allen who told the new chairman that a Mr Corcran had phoned from the Lefevre Gallery to say that he accepted her offer of one hundred and ten thousand pounds.

Cathy smiled. "Now all we have to do is agree on a date and send out the invitations. Can you get Becky on the line for me, Jessica."

The first action Cathy had proposed to the board after being elected unanimously as the third chairman of Trumper's was to appoint Charlie as Life President and hold a dinner in his honour at the Grosvenor House Hotel. The occasion was attended by all Trumper's staff, their husbands, wives and many of the friends Charlie and Becky had made over nearly seven decades. Charlie took his place at the top table that night, one of the one thousand, seven hundred and seventy people who filled the great ballroom.

There followed a five-course meal that even Percy was unable to fault. After Charlie had been supplied with a brandy and had lit up a large Trumper's cigar, he leaned over and whispered to Becky, "I wish your father could have seen this spread." He added, "Of course, he wouldn't have come – unless he'd supplied everything from the meringues glacés to the bread rolls."

"I wish Daniel could have shared the evening with us as well," Becky replied quietly. A few moments later Cathy stood and delivered a speech that could have left no one in any doubt that they had elected the right person to follow Charlie. She ended by inviting the assembled company to toast the health of the founder and first Life President. After the applause had died away, she bent down and removed something from beneath her chair. "Charlie," she said, "this is a small memento from us all to thank you for the sacrifice you once made in order to keep Trumper's afloat." Cathy turned and handed over an oil painting to Charlie, who beamed in anticipation until he saw what the subject was. His mouth opened and his cigar fell on the table as he stared in disbelief. It was some time before he could let go of *The Potato Eaters* and rise to respond to the calls of "Speech, speech!"

Charlie began by reminding his audience once again how everything had begun with his grandfather's barrow in Whitechapel, a barrow that now stood proudly in the food hall of Trumper's. He paid tribute to the colonel, long since dead, to the pioneers of the company, Mr Crowther and Mr Hadlow, as well as to two of the original staff, Bob Makins and Ned Denning, both of whom had retired only weeks before he himself had. He ended with Daphne, Marchioness of Wiltshire, who had loaned them their first sixty pounds to make it all possible.

"I wish I was fourteen years old again," he said wistfully. "Me, my barrow and my regulars in the Whitechapel Road. Those were the 'appiest days of my life. Because at 'eart, you see, I'm a simple fruit and vegetable man." Everybody laughed, except Becky, who gazed up at her husband and recalled an eight-year-old boy in short trousers, cap in hand, standing outside her father's shop, hoping to get a free bun.

"I'm proud to 'ave built the biggest barrow in the world and tonight to be among those who 'ave 'elped me push it from the East End all the way into Chelsea Terrace. I'll miss you all – and I can only 'ope you'll allow me back into Trumper's from time to time."

As Charlie sat down, his staff rose to cheer him. He leaned over, took Becky by the hand and said, "Forgive me, but I forgot to tell 'em it was you what founded it in the first place."

Becky, who had never been to a football match in her life, had to spend hours listening to her husband on the subject of the World Cup, and how no fewer than three West Ham players had been selected for the England squad.

For the first four weeks after Charlie had retired as chairman he seemed quite content to allow Stan to drive him from Sheffield to Manchester, and from Liverpool to Leeds, so they could watch the early rounds together.

When England won a place in the semi-final, Charlie used every contact he could think of to obtain two stand tickets, and his efforts were rewarded when the home side won a place in the final.

However, despite those contacts, a willingness to pay over the odds, and even writing to Alf Ramsey, the England team manager, Charlie still failed to get even a standing ticket for the final. He told Becky that he had come to the reluctant conclusion that he and Stan would have to watch the match on television.

On the morning of the game, Charlie came down to breakfast to find two stand tickets wedged in the toast rack. He was unable to eat his eggs and bacon for sheer excitement. "You're a genius, Mrs Trumper," he said several times, interspersed with: "However did you manage it?"

"Contacts," was all Becky would say, resolved not to let Charlie know that the new computer had revealed that Mrs Ramsey held an account at Trumper's, and Cathy had suggested she should join that select group of customers who received a ten per cent discount.

The four–two victory over West Germany, with three goals scored by Geoff Hurst of West Ham, not only brought Charlie to the edge of delirium but even made Becky briefly wonder if her husband had now put Trumper's behind him and would allow Cathy a free hand as chairman.

Yet within a week of returning home from Wembley Stadium Charlie seemed perfectly content just to potter around the house, but it was during the second week that Becky realised something had to be done if she wasn't to be driven mad – as well as lose most of her domestic staff at

Eaton Square. On the Monday of the third week, she dropped into Trumper's to see the manager of the travel department and during the fourth week tickets were delivered from the offices of Cunard to Lady Trumper – for a trip to New York on the *Queen Mary* – followed by an extensive tour of the United States.

"I do hope she can run the barrow without me," said Charlie, as they were driven down to Southampton.

"I expect she'll just about scrape by," said Becky, who had planned that they should be away for at least three months, to be sure that Cathy had a free hand to get on with the refurbishment programme, which they both suspected Charlie would have done everything in his power to hold up.

Becky became even more convinced this would have been the case the moment Charlie had walked into Bloomingdale's and started grumbling about the lack of proper space allocated to view the goods. She moved him on to Macy's where he complained of the non-existent service, and when they arrived in Chicago he told Henry Field that he no longer cared for the window displays that had at one time been the hallmark of the great store. "Far too garish, even for America," he assured the owner. Becky would have mentioned the words "tact and subtlety" had Henry Field not agreed with his old friend's every pronouncement while placing the blame firmly on a new manager who believed in "flower power" whatever that was.

Dallas, San Francisco and Los Angeles were no better, and when three months later Becky and Charlie climbed back on board the great liner in New York, the name of Trumper's was once again on Charlie's lips. Becky began to dread what might happen when they set foot back on English soil.

She only hoped that five days of calm seas and a warm Atlantic breeze might help them relax and allow Charlie to forget Trumper's for a few moments. But he spent most of the voyage back explaining his new ideas for revolutionising the company, ideas he felt should be put into operation the moment they reached London. It was then that Becky decided she had to make a stand on Cathy's behalf.

"But you're not even a member of the board any longer," Becky reminded him, as she lay on the deck sunbathing.

"I'm the Life President," he insisted, after he had finished telling her his latest idea for tagging garments to combat shoplifting.

"But that's a purely honorary position."

"Poppycock. I intend to make my views felt whenever –"

"Charlie, that's not fair on Cathy. She's no longer the junior director of a family venture but chairman of a vast public company. The time has surely come for you to stay away from Trumper's and allow Cathy to push the barrow along on her own."

"So what am I expected to do?"

"I don't know, Charlie, and I don't care. But whatever you do it's no longer going to take place anywhere near Chelsea Terrace. Do I make myself clear?"

Charlie would have replied if a deck officer hadn't come to a halt beside them.

"Sorry to interrupt you, sir."

"You're not interrupting anything," said Charlie. "So what do you want me to do? Arrange a mutiny or organise the deck tennis draw?"

"Both those are the purser's responsibility, Sir Charles," said the young man. "But the captain wonders if you would be kind enough to join him on the bridge. He's received a cablegram from London which he feels you would want to know about immediately."

"I hope it's not bad news," said Becky, as she sat up quickly and placed the novel she had been trying to read on the deck beside her. "I told them not to contact us unless it was an emergency."

"Rubbish," said Charlie. "You're such an old pessimist. With you a bottle is always half empty." He stood up and stretched himself before accompanying the young officer along the after-deck towards the bridge, explaining how he would organise a mutiny. Becky followed a yard behind, offering no further comment.

As the officer escorted them on to the bridge the captain turned to greet them.

"A cablegram has just come over the wires from London, Sir Charles, which I thought you would want to see immediately." He handed the message over.

"Damn, I've left my glasses back on the deck," Charlie mumbled. "Becky, you'd better read it to me." He passed the slip of paper to his wife.

Becky opened the cablegram, her fingers trembling slightly and read the message to herself first as Charlie studied his wife's face for a clue as to its contents.

"Come on then, what is it? Half full or half empty?"

"It's a request from Buckingham Palace," she replied.

"What did I tell you," said Charlie, "you can't leave them to do anything for themselves. First day of the month, bath soap, she prefers lavender; toothpaste, he likes Euthymol, and loo paper . . . I did warn Cathy – "

"No, I don't think it's the loo paper Her Majesty is fussing about on this occasion," said Becky.

"So what's the problem?" asked Charlie.

"They want to know what title you'll take."

"Title?" said Charlie.

"Yes," said Becky, turning to face her husband. "Lord Trumper of where?"

Becky was surprised and Cathy somewhat relieved to discover how quickly Lord Trumper of Whitechapel appeared to become absorbed in the daily workings of the upper house. Becky's fears of his continually interfering with the day-to-day business of the company evaporated the moment Charlie had donned the red ermine. For his wife, the routine brought back memories of those days during the Second World War when Charlie had worked under Lord Woolton in the Ministry of Food and she could never be sure what time of night he'd arrive home.

Six months after being told by Becky he was not to go anywhere near Trumper's, Charlie announced that he had been invited to become a member of the Agricultural Committee, where he felt he could once again use his expertise to the benefit of his fellow-members. He even returned to his old routine of rising at four thirty each morning so that he could catch up with those parliamentary papers that always needed to be read before important meetings.

Whenever Charlie returned home for dinner in the evening he was always full of news about some clause he had proposed in committee that day, or how an old duffer had taken up the House's time during the afternoon with countless amendments to the hare coursing bill.

When in 1970 Britain applied to join the Common Market Charlie told his wife that he had been approached by the Chief Whip to chair a sub-committee on food distribution in Europe and felt it was his duty to accept. From that day on, whenever Becky came down for breakfast she would discover countless order papers or copies of the Lords' daily *Hansard* strewn untidily all the way from Charlie's study to the kitchen, where the inevitable note had been left to explain that he had to attend yet another early sub-committee meeting or briefing from some continental supporter of Britain's entry into Europe who happened to be in London. Until then Becky had no idea how hard members of the upper house were expected to work.

Becky continued to keep in touch with Trumper's by regular Monday morning visits. She would always go in at a time when business was fairly quiet, and to her surprise had become Charlie's main source of information as to what was happening at the store.

She always enjoyed spending a couple of hours strolling through the different departments. She couldn't help noticing how quickly fashions changed, and how Cathy always managed to keep a step ahead of her rivals, while never giving regular customers cause to grumble about unnecessary change.

Becky's final call was inevitably at the auction house to

see whose paintings were due to come under the hammer. It had been some time since she had handed over her responsibility to Richard Cartwright, the former chief auctioneer, but he always made himself available to show her round the latest preview of pictures to be auctioned. "Minor Impressionists on this occasion," he assured her.

"Now at major prices," Becky replied as she studied works by Pissarro, Bonnard and Vuillard. "But we'll still have to make sure Charlie doesn't find out about this lot."

"He already has," Richard warned her. "Dropped in last Thursday on his way to the Lords, put a reserve on three lots and even found time to complain about our estimates. Claimed he had bought a large Renoir oil from you called *L'homme à la Pêche* only a few years ago for the price I was now expecting him to pay for a small pastel by Pissarro that was nothing more than a study for a major work."

"I suspect he might be right about that," said Becky as she flicked through the catalogue to check the different estimates. "And heaven help your balance sheet if he finds out that you failed to reach the reserve price on any picture he's interested in. When I ran this department he was always known as 'our loss leader'."

As they were chatting an assistant walked over to join them, nodded politely to Lady Trumper and handed Richard a note. He studied the message before turning to Becky. "The chairman wonders if you would be kind enough to drop in and see her before you leave. Something she needs to discuss with you fairly urgently."

Richard accompanied her to the lift on the ground floor, where Becky thanked him once again for indulging an old lady.

As the lift travelled grudgingly upwards – something else that Cathy wanted to change as part of the refurbishment plan – Becky pondered on why the chairman could possibly want to see her and only hoped that she wasn't going to have to cancel dinner with them that night, as their guests were to be David and Barbara Field.

Although Cathy had moved out of Eaton Square some

eighteen months before into a spacious flat in Chelsea Cloisters they still managed dinner together at least once a month, and Cathy was always invited back to the house whenever the Fields or the Bloomingdales were in town. Becky knew that David Field, who still sat on the board of the great Chicago store, would be disappointed if Cathy was unable to keep her appointment that night, especially as the American couple were due to return home the following day.

Jessica ushered Becky straight through to the chairman's office, where she found Cathy on the phone, her brow unusually furrowed. While she waited for the chairman to finish her call, Becky stared out of the bay window at the empty wooden bench on the far side of the road and thought of Charlie, who had happily swapped it for the red leather benches of the House of Lords.

Once Cathy had replaced the receiver, she immediately asked, "How's Charlie?"

"You tell me," said Becky. "I see him for the occasional dinner during the week and he has even been known to attend breakfast on a Sunday. But that's about it. Has he been seen in Trumper's lately?"

"Not that often. To be honest, I still feel guilty about banning him from the store."

"No need to feel any guilt," Becky told her. "I've never seen the man happier."

"I'm relieved to hear it," said Cathy. "But right now I need Charlie's advice on a more urgent matter."

"And what's that?"

"Cigars," said Cathy. "I had David Field on the phone earlier to say that his father would like a dozen boxes of his usual brand and not to bother to send them round to the Connaught because he'll be only too happy to pick them up when he comes to dinner tonight."

"So what's the problem?"

"Neither David Field nor the tobacco department have the slightest idea what his father's usual brand is. It seems Charlie always dealt with the order personally."

"You could check the old invoices."

"First thing I did," said Cathy. "But there's no record of any transaction ever taking place. Which surprised me, because if I remember correctly old Mr Field regularly had a dozen boxes sent over to the Connaught whenever he came to London." Cathy's brow furrowed again. "That was something I always considered curious. After all, when you think about it, he must have had a large tobacco department in his own store."

"I'm sure he did," said Becky, "but it wouldn't have stocked any brands from Havana."

"Havana? I'm not with you."

"Some time in the fifties US Customs banned the import of all Cuban cigars into America and David's father, who had been smoking a particular brand of Havanas long before anyone had heard of Fidel Castro, saw no reason why he shouldn't be allowed to continue to indulge himself with what he considered was no more than his 'Goddamn right'."

"So how did Charlie get round the problem?"

"Charlie used to go down to the tobacco department, pick up a dozen boxes of the old man's favourite brand, return to his office, remove the bands around each cigar, then replace them with an innocuous Dutch label before putting them back in an unidentifiable Trumper's box. He always made sure that there was a ready supply on hand for Mr Field in case he ever ran out. Charlie felt it was the least we could do to repay all the hospitality the Fields had lavished on us over the years."

Cathy nodded her understanding. "But I still need to know which brand of Cuban cigar is nothing more than Mr Field's 'Goddamn right'."

"I've no idea," admitted Becky. "As you say, Charlie never allowed anyone else to handle the order."

"Then someone's going to have to ask Charlie, either to come in and complete the order himself or at least tell us which brand Mr Field is addicted to. So where can I expect to find the Life President at eleven thirty on a Monday morning?"

"Hidden away in some committee room at the House of Lords would be my bet."

"No, he's not," said Cathy. "I've already phoned the Lords and they assured me he hadn't been seen this morning – and what's more they weren't expecting him again this week."

"But that's not possible," said Becky. "He virtually lives in the place."

"That's what I thought," said Cathy. "Which is why I called down to Number 1 to ask for your help."

"I'll sort this out in a trice," said Becky. "If Jessica can put me through to the Lords, I know exactly the right person to speak to."

Jessica returned to her office, looked up the number and, as soon as she had been connected, put the call through to the chairman's desk, where Becky picked up the receiver.

"House of Lords?" said Becky. "Message board please . . . Is Mr Anson there? No, well, I'd still like to leave an urgent message for Lord Trumper . . . of Whitechapel . . . Yes, I think he's in an agricultural sub-committee this morning . . . Are you sure? . . . That can't be possible . . . You do know my husband? . . . Well, that's a relief . . . Does he . . . ? How interesting . . . No, thank you . . . No, I won't leave a message and please don't trouble Mr Anson. Goodbye."

Becky replaced the phone and looked up to find Cathy and Jessica staring at her like two children at bedtime waiting to hear the end of a story.

"Charlie hasn't been seen in the Lords this morning. There isn't an agricultural sub-committee. He's not even a member of the full committee, and what's more they haven't set eyes on him for the past three months."

"But I don't understand," said Cathy. "How have you been getting through to him in the past?"

"With a special number supplied by Charlie that I keep by the hall phone in Eaton Square. It connects me to a

Lords messenger called Mr Anson, who always seems to know exactly where Charlie can be found at any time of the day or night."

"And does this Mr Anson exist?" asked Cathy.

"Oh, yes," said Becky. "But it seems he works on another floor of the Lords and on this occasion I was put through to general enquiries."

"So what happens whenever you do get through to Mr Anson?"

"Charlie usually rings back within the hour."

"So there's nothing to stop you phoning Mr Anson now?"

"I'd rather not for the moment," said Becky. "I think I'd prefer to find out what Charlie's been up to for the past two years. Because one thing's for certain, Mr Anson isn't going to tell me."

"But Mr Anson can't be the only person who knows," said Cathy. "After all, Charlie doesn't live in a vacuum." They both swung round to face Jessica.

"Don't look at me," said Jessica. "He hasn't had any contact with this office since the day you banned him from Chelsea Terrace. If Stan didn't come in to the canteen for lunch from time to time I wouldn't even know Charlie was still alive."

"Of course," said Becky, snapping her fingers. "Stan's the one person who must know what's going on. He still picks up Charlie first thing in the morning and brings him home last thing at night. Charlie couldn't get away with anything unless his driver was fully in his confidence."

"Right, Jessica," said Cathy as she checked her diary. "Start by cancelling my lunch with the managing director of Moss Bros, then tell my secretary I'll take no calls and no interruptions until we find out exactly what our Life President has been up to. When you've done that, go down and see if Stan's in the canteen and if he is phone me back immediately."

Jessica almost ran out of the room as Cathy turned her attention back to Becky.

"Do you think he might have a mistress?" said Becky quietly.

"Night and day for nearly two years at the age of seventy? If he has, we ought to enter him as the Bull of the Year at the Royal Agricultural Show."

"Then what can he be up to?"

"My bet is that he's taking his master's degree at London University," said Cathy. "It's always riled Charlie whenever you tease him about never properly completing his education."

"But I'd have come across the relevant books and papers all over the house."

"You already have, but they were only the books and papers he intended you to see. Don't let's forget how cunning he was when he took his BA. He fooled you for eight years."

"Perhaps he's taken a job with one of our rivals."

"Not his style," said Cathy. "He's far too loyal for that. In any case, we'd know which store it was within days, the staff and management alike would be only too happy to keep reminding us. No, it has to be simpler than that." The private phone rang on Cathy's desk. She grabbed the receiver and listened carefully before saying, "Thank you, Jessica. We're on our way."

"Let's go," she said, replacing the phone and jumping up from behind her desk. "Stan's just finishing his lunch." She headed towards the door. Becky quickly followed and without another word they took the lift to the ground floor where Joe, the senior doorman, was surprised to see the chairman and Lady Trumper hail a taxi when both their drivers were patiently waiting for them on meters.

A few minutes later Stan appeared through the same door and climbed behind the wheel of Charlie's Rolls before proceeding at a gentle pace towards Hyde Park Corner, oblivious of the taxi that was following him. The Rolls continued down Piccadilly and on through Trafalgar Square before taking a left in the direction of the Strand.

"He's going to King's College," said Cathy. "I knew I was right – it has to be his master's degree."

"But Stan's not stopping," said Becky, as the Rolls passed the college entrance and weaved its way into Fleet Street.

"I can't believe he's bought a newspaper," said Cathy.

"Or taken a job in the City," Becky added as the Rolls drove on down towards the Mansion House.

"I've got it," said Becky triumphantly, as the Rolls left the City behind them and nosed its way into the East End. "He's been working on some project at his boys' club in Whitechapel."

Stan continued east until he finally brought the car to a halt outside the Dan Salmon Centre.

"But it doesn't make any sense," said Cathy. "If that's all he wanted to do with his spare time why didn't he tell you the truth in the first place? Why go through such an elaborate charade?"

"I can't work that one out either," said Becky. "In fact, I confess I'm even more baffled."

"Well, let's at least go in and find out what he's up to."

"No," said Becky, placing a hand on Cathy's arm. "I need to sit and think for a few moments before I decide what to do next. If Charlie is planning something he doesn't want us to know about, I'd hate to be the one who spoils his bit of fun, especially when it was me who banned him from going into Trumper's in the first place."

"All right," said Cathy. "So why don't we just go back to my office and say nothing of our little discovery? After all, we can always phone Mr Anson at the Lords, who as we know will make sure Charlie returns your call within the hour. That will give me easily enough time to sort out David Field and the problem of his cigars."

Becky nodded her agreement and instructed the bemused cabbie to return to Chelsea Terrace. As the taxi swung round in a circle to begin its journey back towards the West End, Becky glanced out of the rear window at the

Centre named after her father. "Stop," she said without warning. The cabbie threw on the brakes and brought the taxi to a sudden halt.

"What's the matter?" asked Cathy.

Becky pointed out of the back window, her eyes now fixed on a figure who was walking down the steps of the Dan Salmon Centre dressed in a grubby old suit and flat cap.

"I don't believe it," said Cathy.

Becky quickly paid off the cab driver while Cathy jumped out and began to follow Stan as he headed off down the Whitechapel Road.

"Where can he be going?" asked Cathy, as they kept Stan well within their sights. The shabbily dressed chauffeur continued to march along the pavement, leaving any old soldier who saw him in no doubt of his former profession while causing the two ladies who were pursuing him to have occasionally to break into a run.

"It ought to be Cohen's the tailors," said Becky. "Because heaven knows the man looks as if he could do with a new suit."

But Stan came to a halt some yards before the tailor's shop. Then, for the first time, they both saw another man, also dressed in an old suit and flat cap, standing beside a brand-new barrow on which were printed the words: "Charlie Salmon, the honest trader. Founded 1969".

"I don't offer you these at two pounds, ladies," declared a voice as loud as that of any of the youngsters on the pitches nearby, "not one pound, not even fifty pence. No, I'm going to give 'em away for twenty pence."

Cathy and Becky watched in amazement as Stan Russell touched his cap to Charlie, then began to fill a woman's basket, so that his master could deal with the next customer.

"So what'll it be today, Mrs Bates? I've got some lovely bananas just flown in from the West Indies. Ought to be selling 'em at ninety pence the bunch, but to you, my old duck, fifty pence, but be sure you don't tell the neighbours."

"What about those 'tatoes, Charlie?" said a heavily made-up, middle-aged woman who pointed suspiciously at a box on the front of the barrow.

"As I stand 'ere, Mrs Bates, new in from Jersey today and I'll tell you what I'll do. I'll sell 'em at the same price as my so-called rivals are still peddling their old ones for. Could I be fairer, I ask?"

"I'll take four pounds, Mr Salmon."

"Thank you, Mrs Bates. Serve the lady, Stan, while I deal with the next customer." Charlie stepped across to the other side of the barrow.

"And 'ow nice to see you this fine afternoon, Mrs Singh. Two pounds of figs, nuts and raisins, if my memory serves me right. And how is Doctor Singh keeping?"

"Very busy, Mr Salmon, very busy."

"Then we must see that 'e's well fed, mustn't we?" said Charlie. "Because if this weather takes a turn for the worse, I may need to come and seek 'is advice about my sinus trouble. And 'ow's little Suzika?"

"She's just passed three A-levels, Mr Salmon, and will be going to London University in September to read engineering."

"Can't see the point of it myself," said Charlie as he selected some figs. "Engineerin', you say. What will they think of next? Knew a girl once from these parts who took 'erself off to university and a fat lot of good it did 'er. Spent the rest of 'er life living off 'er 'usband, didn't she? My old granpa always used to say –"

Becky burst out laughing. "So what do we do now?" she asked.

"Go back to Eaton Square, then you can look up Mr Anson's number at the Lords and give him a call. That way at least we can be sure that Charlie will contact you within the hour."

Cathy nodded her agreement but both of them remained transfixed as they watched the oldest dealer in the market ply his trade.

"I don't offer you these at two pounds," he declared,

holding up a cabbage in both hands. "I don't offer 'em for one pound, not even fifty pence."

"No, I'll give 'em away for twenty pence," whispered Becky under her breath.

"No, I'll give 'em away for twenty pence," shouted Charlie at the top of his voice.

"You do realise," said Becky as they crept back out of the market, "that Charlie's grandfather carried on to the ripe old age of eighty-three and died only a few feet from where His Lordship is standing now."

"He's come a long way since then," said Cathy, as she raised her hand to hail a taxi.

"Oh, I don't know," Becky replied. "Only about a couple of miles – as the crow flies."

THE
PRODIGAL
DAUGHTER

To Peter, Joy, Alison
Clare and Simon

Prologue

'PRESIDENT OF THE UNITED STATES,' she replied.

'I can think of more rewarding ways of bankrupting myself,' said her father, as he removed the half-moon spectacles from the end of his nose and peered at his daughter over the top of his newspaper.

'Don't be frivolous, Papa. President Roosevelt proved to us that there can be no greater calling than public service.'

'The only thing Roosevelt proved . . .' began her father. Then he stopped and returned to his paper, realising that his daughter would consider the remark flippant.

The girl continued as if she were only too aware of what was going through her father's mind. 'I realise it would be pointless for me to pursue such an ambition without your support. My sex will be enough of a liability without adding the disadvantage of a Polish background.'

The newspaper barrier between father and daughter was abruptly removed. 'Don't ever speak disloyally of the Poles,' he said. 'History has proved us to be an honourable race who never go back on our word. My father was a baron . . .'

'Yes, I know, so was my grandfather, but he's not around now to help me become President.'

'More's the pity,' he said, sighing, 'as he would undoubtedly have made a great leader of our people.'

'Then why shouldn't his granddaughter?'

'No reason at all,' he said, as he stared into the steel grey eyes of his only child.

'Well then, Papa, will you help me? I can't hope to succeed without your financial backing.'

Her father hesitated before replying, placing the glasses back on the end of his nose and slowly folding his copy of the Chicago *Tribune*.

'I'll make a deal with you, my dear; after all that's what politics is about. If the result of the New Hampshire Primary turns out to be satisfactory, I'll back you to the hilt. If not, you must drop the whole idea.'

'What's your definition of satisfactory?' came back the immediate reply.

Again the man hesitated, weighing his words. 'If you win the Primary or capture over thirty per cent of the vote, I'll go all the way to the convention floor with you, even if it means I end up destitute.'

The girl relaxed for the first time during the conversation. 'Thank you, Papa. I couldn't have asked for more.'

'No, you certainly couldn't,' he replied. 'Now can I get back to finding out just how the Cubs could possibly have lost the seventh game of the series to the Tigers?'

'They were undoubtedly the weaker team, as the 9–3 score indicates.'

'Young lady, you may imagine you know a thing or two about politics but I can assure you that you know absolutely nothing about baseball,' the man said, as his wife entered the room. He turned his heavy frame towards her. 'Our daughter wants to run for President of the United States. What do you think about that?'

The girl looked up at her eagerly, waiting for a reply.

'I'll tell you what I think,' said the mother. 'I think it's well past her bedtime and I blame you for keeping her up so late.'

'Yes, I suppose you're right,' the husband said. 'Off you go to bed, little one.'

She came to her father's side, kissed him on the cheek and whispered, 'Thank you, Papa.'

The man's eyes followed his eleven-year-old daughter as she left the room and he noticed that the fingers on her right hand were clenched, making a small tight fist, something she always did when she was angry or determined. He suspected she was both on this occasion, but he realised that it would be pointless to try and explain to his wife that their only child was no ordinary mortal. He had long ago abandoned any attempt to involve his wife in his own ambitions, and was at least thankful that she was incapable of dampening their daughter's.

He returned to the Chicago Cubs and had to admit that his daughter's judgment might even be right on that subject.

Florentyna Rosnovski never referred to the conversation again for twenty-two years, but when she did she assumed her father would keep his end of the bargain. After all, the Polish are an honourable race who never go back on their word.

The Past

1934–1968

1

IT HAD NOT BEEN an easy birth, but then for Abel and Zaphia Rosnovski nothing had ever been easy, and in their own ways they had both become philosophical about that. Abel had wanted a son, an heir who would one day be chairman of the Baron Group. By the time the boy was ready to take over, Abel was confident that his own name would stand alongside those of Ritz and Statler and by then the Baron would be the largest hotel group in the world. Abel had paced up and down the colourless corridor of St. Luke's Hospital waiting for the first cry, his slight limp becoming more pronounced as each hour passed. Occasionally he twisted the silver band that encircled his wrist and stared at the name so neatly engraved on it. He turned and retraced his steps once again, to see Doctor Dodek heading towards him.

'Congratulations, Mr. Rosnovski,' he called.

'Thank you,' said Abel eagerly.

'You have a beautiful girl,' the doctor said as he reached him.

'Thank you,' repeated Abel, quietly, trying not to show his disappointment. He then followed the obstetrician into a little room at the other end of the corridor. Through an observation window Abel was confronted with a row of wrinkled faces. The doctor pointed to the father's first-born. Unlike the others her little fingers were curled into a tight fist. Abel had read somewhere that a child was not expected to do that for at least three weeks. He smiled, proudly.

Mother and daughter remained at St. Luke's for another six days and Abel visited them every morning, leaving his hotel only when the last breakfast had been served, and every afternoon after the last lunch guest had left the dining room. Telegrams, flowers and the recent fashion of greeting cards surrounded Zaphia's iron-framed bed, reassuring evidence that other people too rejoiced in the birth. On the seventh day mother and unnamed child – Abel had considered six boys' names – returned home.

On the anniversary of the second week of their daughter's birth they named her Florentyna, after Abel's sister. Once the infant had been installed in the newly decorated nursery at the top of the house, Abel would spend hours simply staring down at his daughter, watching her sleep and wake, knowing that he must work even harder than he had in the past to ensure the child's future. He was determined that Florentyna would be given a better start in life than he had been. Not for her the dirt and deprivation of his childhood or the humiliation of arriving on the eastern seaboard of America as an immigrant with little more than a few valueless Russian rubles sewn into the jacket of an only suit.

He would ensure that Florentyna was given the formal education he had lacked, not that he had a lot to complain about. Franklin D. Roosevelt lived in the White House and Abel's little group of hotels looked as if they were going to survive the Depression. America had been good to this immigrant.

Whenever he sat alone with his daughter in the upstairs nursery he would reflect on his past, and dream of her future.

When he had first arrived in the United States he had found a job in a little butcher's shop on the lower East Side of New York, where he worked for two long years before filling a vacancy at the Plaza Hotel as a junior waiter. From Abel's first day, Sammy, the old maître d', had treated him as though he was the lowest form of life. After four years, a slave trader would have been impressed by the work and unheard-of overtime that the lowest form of life did in order to reach

the exalted position as Sammy's assistant head waiter in the
Oak Room. During those early years Abel spent five afternoons a week poring over books at Columbia University, and
after dinner had been cleared away read on late into the
night.

His rivals wondered when he slept.

Abel was not sure how his newly-acquired degree could
advance him while he still only waited on tables in the Oak
Room of the Plaza Hotel. The question was answered for him
by a well-fed Texan called Mr. Davis Leroy, who had
watched Abel serving guests solicitously for a week. Mr.
Leroy, the owner of eleven hotels, then offered Abel the
position of assistant manager at his flagship, the Richmond
Continental in Chicago, with the sole responsibility of running the restaurants.

Abel was brought back to the present when Florentyna
turned over and started to thump the side of her crib. He
extended a finger which his daughter grabbed like a lifeline
thrown from a sinking ship. She started to bite the finger with
what she imagined were teeth . . .

When Abel first arrived in Chicago he found the Richmond Continental badly run down. It didn't take him long to
discover why. The manager, Desmond Pacey, was cooking
the books and as far as Abel could tell probably had been for
the past thirty years. The new assistant manager spent his
first six months gathering together the proof he needed to nail
Pacey and then presented to his employer a dossier containing all the facts. When Davis Leroy realised what had been
going on behind his back he immediately sacked Pacey,
replacing him with his new protégé. This spurred Abel on to
work even harder and he became so convinced that he could
turn the fortunes of the Richmond Group around that when
Leroy's ageing sister put up for sale her twenty-five per cent
of the company's stock Abel cashed everything he owned to
purchase them. Davis Leroy was touched by his young
manager's personal commitment to the company and proved
it by appointing him managing director of the group.

From that moment they became partners, a professional

bond that developed into a close friendship. Abel would have been the first to appreciate how hard it was for a Texan to acknowledge a Pole as an equal. For the first time since he had settled in America, he felt secure – until he found out that the Texans were every bit as proud a clan as the Poles.

Abel still couldn't accept what had happened. If only Davis had confided in him, told him the truth about the extent of the group's financial trouble – who wasn't having problems during the Depression? – between them they could have sorted something out. At the age of sixty-two Davis Leroy had been informed by his bank that his overdraft was no longer covered by the value of the hotels and that they required further security before they would agree to pay next month's wages. In response to the bank's ultimatum, Davis Leroy had had a quiet dinner with his daughter and retired to the Presidential Suite on the twelfth floor with two bottles of bourbon. Then he had opened the window and jumped. Abel would never forget standing on the corner of Michigan Avenue at four in the morning having to identify a body he could recognise only by the jacket his mentor had worn the previous night. The lieutenant investigating the death had remarked that it had been the seventh suicide in Chicago that day. It didn't help. How could the policeman possibly know how much Davis Leroy had done for him, or how much more he had intended to return that friendship in the future? In a hastily composed will Davis had bequeathed the remaining seventy-five per cent of the Richmond Group stock to his managing director, writing to Abel that although the stock was worthless one hundred per cent ownership of the group might give him a better chance to negotiate new terms with the bank.

Florentyna's eyes opened, and she started to howl. Abel picked her up lovingly, immediately regretting the decision as he felt the damp clammy bottom. He changed her nappy quickly, drying the child carefully, before making a triangle of the cloth, not allowing the big pins anywhere near her body: any midwife would have nodded her approval at his deftness. Florentyna closed her eyes and nodded back to sleep on her father's shoulder. 'Ungrateful brat,' he murmured fondly as he kissed her on the cheek.

After Davis Leroy's funeral Abel had visited Kane and Cabot, the Richmond Group's bankers in Boston, and pleaded with one of the directors not to put the eleven hotels up for sale on the open market. He tried to convince the bank that if only they would back him, he could – given time – turn the balance sheet from red into black. The smooth, cold man behind the expensive partner's desk had proved intractable. 'I must act in the bank's best interests,' he had used as an excuse. Abel would never forget the humiliation of having to call a man of his own age 'sir' and still leave empty-handed. The man must have had the soul of a cash register not to realise how many people were affected by his decision. Abel promised himself, for the hundredth time, that one day he would get even with Mr. William 'Ivy League' Kane.

Abel had travelled back to Chicago that night thinking that nothing else could go wrong in his life, only to find the Richmond Continental burned to the ground and the police accusing him of arson. Arson it proved to be, but at the hands of Desmond Pacey, bent on revenge. When arrested, he admitted readily to the crime as his only interest was the downfall of Abel. Pacey would have succeeded if the insurance company had not come to Abel's rescue. Until that moment, he had wondered if he would not have been better off in the Russian prisoner-of-war camp he had escaped from before fleeing to America. But then his luck turned when an anonymous backer who, Abel concluded, must have been Mr. David Maxton of the Stevens Hotel, purchased the Richmond Group and offered Abel his old position as managing director and a chance to prove he could run the company at a profit.

Abel recalled how he had been reunited with Zaphia, the self-assured girl he had first met on board the ship that had brought them to America. How immature she had made him feel then, but not when they re-met and he discovered she was a waitress at the Stevens.

Two years had passed since then and, although the newly named Baron Group had failed to make a profit in 1933, they lost only twenty-three thousand dollars, greatly helped by Chicago's celebration of its centenary when over a million tourists had visited the city to enjoy the World's Fair.

Once Pacey had been convicted of arson, Abel had only to wait for the insurance money to be paid before he could set about rebuilding the hotel in Chicago. He had used the interim period to visit the other ten hotels in the group, sacking staff who showed the same pecuniary tendencies as Desmond Pacey and replacing them from the long lines of unemployed that stretched across America.

Zaphia began to resent Abel's journeys from Charleston to Mobile, from Houston to Memphis, continually checking over his hotels in the south. But Abel realised that if he was to keep his side of the bargain with the anonymous backer there would be little time to sit around at home, however much he adored his daughter. He had been given ten years to repay the bank loan; if he succeeded, a clause in the contract stipulated he would be allowed to purchase the remaining sixty per cent of the company's stock for a further three million dollars. Zaphia thanked God each night for what they already had and pleaded with him to slow down, but nothing was going to stop Abel from trying to fulfil that aim.

'Your dinner's ready,' shouted Zaphia at the top of her voice.

Abel pretended he hadn't heard and continued to stare down at his sleeping daughter.

'Didn't you hear me? Dinner is ready.'

'What? No, dear. Sorry. Just coming.' Abel reluctantly rose to join his wife for dinner. Florentyna's rejected red eiderdown lay on the floor beside her cot. Abel picked up the fluffy quilt and placed it carefully on top of the blanket that covered his daughter. He never wanted her to feel the cold. She smiled in her sleep. Was she having her first dream? Abel wondered, as he switched out the light.

2

FLORENTYNA'S CHRISTENING WAS something every-one present was to remember – except Florentyna, who slept through the entire proceedings. After the ceremony at the Holy Name Cathedral on North Wabash, the guests made their way to the Stevens Hotel. Abel took a private room in the hotel and invited over a hundred guests to celebrate the occasion. His closest friend, George Novak, a fellow Pole who had occupied the bunk above him on the boat coming over from Europe, was to be one Kum while one of Zaphia's cousins, Janina, was to be the other.

The guests devoured a traditional ten-course dinner including pierogi and bigos while Abel sat at the head of the table accepting gifts on behalf of his daughter which included a silver rattle, U.S. savings bonds, a copy of *Huckleberry Finn* and, finest of all, a beautiful antique emerald ring from Abel's unnamed benefactor. He only hoped that the man gained as much pleasure in the giving as his daughter later showed in the receiving. To mark the occasion, Abel presented his daughter with a large brown teddy bear with red eyes.

'It looks like Franklin D. Roosevelt,' said George, holding the bear up for all to see. 'This calls for a second christening – F.D.R.'

Abel raised his glass. 'Mr. President,' he toasted – a name the bear never relinquished.

The party finally came to an end around three o'clock in the morning, when Abel had to requisition a laundry trolley from the hotel to transport all the gifts home. George waved to Abel as he headed up North Michigan Avenue pushing the trolley before him.

The happy father began whistling to himself as he recalled every moment of the wonderful evening. Only when Mr. President fell off the trolley for a third time did he realise how crooked his path down Lake Shore Drive must have been. He picked up the bear and wedged it in the centre of the gifts and was about to attempt a straighter path when a hand touched his shoulder. Abel jumped round, ready to defend with his life anyone who wanted to steal Florentyna's first possessions. He stared up into the face of a young policeman.

'Maybe you can explain why you are pushing a Stevens Hotel laundry trolley down Michigan Avenue at three in the morning?'

'Yes, officer,' replied Abel.

'Well, let's start with what's in the packages.'

'Other than Franklin D. Roosevelt, I can't be certain.'

The policeman immediately arrested Abel on suspicion of theft. While the recipient of the gifts slept soundly under her red eiderdown in the little nursery at the top of their house on Rigg Street, her father spent a sleepless night on an old horsehair mattress in a cell at the local jail. George appeared at the court house first thing in the morning to verify Abel's story.

The next day Abel purchased a four-door maroon Buick from Peter Sosnkowski, who ran a secondhand car lot in the Polish neighbourhood.

Abel began to resent having to leave Chicago and his beloved Florentyna even for a few days, fearing he might miss her first step, her first word or her first anything. From her birth, he had supervised her daily routine, never allowing Polish to be spoken in the house: he was determined there would be no trace of a Polish accent that would make her feel ill at ease in society.

Abel had intently waited for her first word, hoping it would be 'Papa', while Zaphia feared it might be some Polish word that would reveal that she had not been speaking English to her first-born when they were alone.

'My daughter is an American,' Abel had explained to Zaphia, 'and she must therefore speak English. Too many Poles continue to converse in their own language, thus ensuring that their children spend their entire lives in the north-west corner of Chicago being described as "Stupid Polacks" and ridiculed by everyone else they come across.'

'Except our countrymen who still feel some loyalty to the Polish empire,' said Zaphia defensively.

'The Polish empire? What century are you living in, Zaphia?'

'The twentieth century,' she said, her voice rising.

'Along with Dick Tracy and Famous Funnies, no doubt?'

'Hardly the attitude of someone whose ultimate ambition is to return to Warsaw as the first Polish ambassador.'

'I've told you never to mention that, Zaphia. Never.'

Zaphia, whose English remained irredeemably shaky, didn't reply but later grumbled to her cousins on the subject and continued to speak Polish only when Abel was out of the house. She was not impressed by the fact, so often trotted out by Abel, that General Motors's turnover was greater than Poland's budget.

By 1935, Abel was convinced that America had turned the corner and that the Depression was a thing of the past, so he decided the time had come to build the new Chicago Baron on the site of the old Richmond Continental. He appointed an architect and began spending more time in the Windy City and less on the road, as he was determined the hotel would turn out to be the finest in the Mid-West.

The Chicago Baron was completed in May 1936 and opened by the Democratic mayor, Edward J. Kelly. Both Illinois Senators were dancing attendance, only too aware of Abel's burgeoning power.

'Looks like a million dollars,' said J. Hamilton Lewis, the senior Senator.

'You wouldn't be far wrong,' said Abel, as he admired the thickly carpeted public rooms, the high stucco ceilings and the decorations in pastel shades of green. The final touch had been the dark green embossed B that adorned everything from the towels in the bathrooms to the flag that fluttered on the top of the forty-two storey building.

'This hotel already bears the hallmark of success,' said J. Hamilton Lewis, addressing the two thousand assembled guests, 'because, my friends, it is the man and not the building who will always be known as the Chicago Baron.' Abel was delighted by the roar that went up and smiled to himself. His public relations adviser had supplied that line to the Senator's speech writer earlier in the week.

Abel was beginning to feel at ease among big businessmen and senior politicians. Zaphia, however, had not adapted to her husband's change in fortunes and hovered uncertainly in the background, drinking a little too much champagne, and finally crept away before the dinner was served with a lame excuse about wanting to see that Florentyna was safely asleep. Abel accompanied his flushed wife towards the revolving door in silent irritation. Zaphia neither cared for nor understood success on Abel's scale and preferred to ignore his new world. She was only too aware how much this annoyed Abel and couldn't resist saying, 'Don't hurry home', as he bundled her into a cab.

'I won't,' he told the revolving door as he returned, pushing it so hard that it went around three more times after he had left it.

He returned to the hotel foyer to find Alderman Henry Osborne waiting for him.

'This must be the high point in your life,' the alderman remarked.

'High point? I've just turned thirty,' said Abel.

A camera flashed as he placed an arm around the tall, darkly handsome politician. Abel smiled towards the cameraman, enjoying the treatment he was receiving as a celebrity, and said, just loud enough for eavesdroppers to hear, 'I'm going to put Baron hotels right across the globe. I intend to be to America what César Ritz was to Europe. Stick with me, Henry, and you'll enjoy the ride.' The city alderman and Abel walked together into the dining room and once they were out of earshot Abel added: 'Join me for lunch tomorrow, Henry, if you can spare the time. There's something I need to discuss with you.'

'Delighted, Abel. A mere city alderman is always available for the Chicago Baron.'

They both laughed heartily, though neither thought the remark particularly funny.

It turned out to be another late night for Abel. When he returned home he went straight to the spare room, to be sure he didn't wake Zaphia – or that's what he told her the next morning.

When Abel came into the kitchen to join Zaphia for breakfast Florentyna was sitting in her high chair smearing a bowlful of cereal enthusiastically round her mouth and biting at most things that remained within arms' reach – even if they weren't food. He kissed her on the forehead, the only place that seemed to have missed the cereal, and sat down to a plate of waffles and maple syrup. When he had finished, Abel rose from his chair and told Zaphia that he would be having lunch with Henry Osborne.

'I don't like that man,' said Zaphia, with feeling.

'I'm not crazy about him myself,' replied Abel. 'But never forget he's well placed in City Hall to be able to do us a lot of favours.'

'And a lot of harm.'

'Don't lose any sleep over that. You can leave the handling of Alderman Osborne to me,' said Abel as he brushed his wife's cheek and turned to leave.

'Presidunk,' said a voice, and both parents turned to stare at Florentyna, who was gesticulating at the floor where the eight-month-old Franklin D. Roosevelt lay on his furry face.

Abel laughed, picked up the much-loved teddy bear and placed him in the space Florentyna had left for him on the high chair.

'Pres-i-dent,' said Abel slowly and firmly.

'Presidunk,' insisted Florentyna.

Abel laughed again and patted Franklin D. Roosevelt on the head. So F.D.R. was responsible not only for the New Deal but also for Florentyna's first political utterance.

Abel left the house to find his chauffeur waiting for him beside the new Cadillac. Abel's driving had become worse as the car he could afford improved. When he bought a Cadillac, George had advised a driver to go with it. That morning he asked the chauffeur to drive slowly as they approached the Gold Coast. Abel stared up at the gleaming glass of the Chicago Baron and marvelled that there was no other place on earth where a man could achieve so much so quickly. What the Chinese would have been happy to strive for in ten generations, he had achieved in less than fifteen years.

He leaped out of the car before his chauffeur could run around to open the door, walked briskly into the hotel and took the private express elevator to the forty-second floor where he spent the morning checking over every problem with which the new hotel was faced: one of the passenger elevators wasn't functioning properly; two waiters had been involved in a knife fight in the kitchen and had been sacked by George even before Abel had arrived; and the list of damages after the opening looked suspiciously high – Abel would have to check into possible theft by waiters being recorded in the books as breakage. He left nothing to chance in any of his hotels from who was staying in the Presidential Suite to the price of the eight thousand fresh bread rolls the catering department needed every week. He spent the morning dealing with queries, problems and decisions, stopping only when Alderman Osborne was ushered into Abel's office by his secretary.

'Good morning, Baron,' said Henry, patronisingly referring to the Rosnovski family title.

In Abel's younger days as a junior waiter at the Plaza in New York the title had been scornfully mimicked to his face. At the Richmond Continental when he was assistant manager it had figured in whispered jokes behind his back. Lately everyone mouthed the prefix with respect.

'Good morning, Alderman,' said Abel, glancing at the clock on his desk. It was five past one. 'Shall we have lunch?'

Abel guided Henry into the adjoining private dining room. To a casual observer Henry Osborne would hardly have seemed a natural soul-mate for Abel. Educated at Choate and then Harvard, as he continually reminded Abel, he had later served as a young lieutenant with the Marines in the World War. At six feet, with a full head of black hair lightly sprinkled with grey, he looked younger than his history insisted he had to be.

The two men had first met as a result of the fire at the old Richmond Continental. Henry was then working for the Great Western Casualty Insurance Company, which had, for as long as anyone could remember, insured the Richmond Group. Abel had been taken aback when Henry had suggested that a small cash payment would ensure a swifter flow of the claim papers through the head office. Abel did not possess a 'small cash payment' in those days; although the claim eventually found its way through, as Henry also believed in Abel's future.

Abel had learned for the first time about men who could be bought.

By the time Henry Osborne was elected to the Chicago City Council as an alderman, Abel *could* afford a small cash payment, and the building permit for the new Baron proceeded through City Hall as though on roller skates. When Henry later announced that he would be running for the United States House of Representatives for the Ninth District of Illinois, Abel was among the first to send a sizeable cheque for his campaign fund. While Abel remained wary of his new ally personally, he recognised that a tame politician could be of great help to the Baron Group. Abel took care to ensure that none of the small cash payments – he did not think of them as bribes, even to himself – was on the record, and felt confident that he could terminate the arrangement as and when it suited him.

The dining room was decorated in the same delicate shades of green as the rest of the hotel, but there was no sign of the embossed B anywhere in the room. The furniture was nineteenth century, and entirely in oak. Around the walls hung oil portraits from the same period, almost all imported. With the door closed, it was possible to imagine that one was in another world far away from the hectic pace of a modern hotel.

Abel took his place at the head of an ornate table that could have comfortably seated eight guests but that day was laid for only two.

'It's like being in a bit of old England,' said Henry, taking in the room.

'Not to mention Poland,' replied Abel, as a uniformed waiter served smoked salmon, while another poured them both a glass of Bouchard Chablis.

Henry stared down at the full plate in front of him. 'Now I can see why you're putting on so much weight, Baron.'

Abel frowned, and quickly changed the subject. 'Are you going to the Cubs' game tomorrow?'

'What's the point? They have a worse home record than the Republicans. Not that my absence will discourage the *Tribune* from describing the match as a close-fought battle bearing no relation to the score and but for a different set of circumstances, the Cubs would have pulled off a famous victory.'

Abel laughed.

'One thing's for sure,' continued Henry, 'you'll never see a night game at Wrigley Field. That ghastly innovation of playing under floodlights won't catch on in Chicago.'

'That's what you said about beer cans last year.'

It was Henry's turn to frown. 'You didn't ask me to lunch to hear my views on baseball or beer cans, Abel, so what little plan can I assist you with this time?'

'Simple. I want to ask your advice on what I should do about William Kane.'

Henry seemed to choke. I must speak to the chef: there shouldn't be any bones in smoked salmon, thought Abel before he continued.

'You once told me, Henry, in graphic detail what had

happened when your path crossed Mr. Kane's and how he ended up defrauding you of money. Well, Kane did far worse than that to me. During the Depression he put the squeeze on Davis Leroy, my partner and closest friend, and was the direct cause of Leroy's suicide. To make matters worse Kane refused to support me when I wanted to take over the management of the hotels and try to put the group on a sound financial footing.'

'Who did back you in the end?' asked Henry.

'A private investor with the Continental Trust. The manager has never told me in so many words, but I've always suspected it was David Maxton.'

'The owner of the Stevens Hotel?'

'The same.'

'What makes you think it was him?'

'When I had the reception for my wedding and again for Florentyna's christening at the Stevens, the bill was covered by my backer.'

'That's hardly conclusive.'

'Agreed, but I'm certain it's Maxton, because he once offered me the chance to run the Stevens. I told him I was more interested in finding a backer for the Richmond Group, and within a week his bank in Chicago came up with the money from someone who could not reveal their identity because it would clash with their day to day business interests.'

'That's a little more convincing. But tell me what you have in mind for William Kane,' said Henry as he toyed with his wine glass and waited for Abel to continue.

'Something that shouldn't take up a lot of your time, Henry, but might well prove to be rewarding for you both financially and, as you hold Kane in the same high regard as I do, personally.'

'I'm listening,' said Henry, still not looking up from his glass.

'I want to lay my hands on a substantial shareholding in Kane's Boston bank.'

'You won't find that easy,' said Henry. 'Most of the stock is held in a family trust that cannot be sold without his personal concurrence.'

'You seem very well informed,' said Abel.

'Common knowledge,' said Henry.

Abel didn't believe him. 'So let's start by finding out the name of every shareholder in Kane and Cabot and see if any of them are interested in parting with their stock at a price considerably above par.'

Abel watched Henry's eyes light up as he began to work out how much might be in this transaction for him if he could make a deal with both sides.

'If he ever found out he'd play very rough,' said Henry.

'He's not going to find out,' said Abel. 'And even if he did we'd be at least two moves ahead of him. Do you think you are capable of doing the job?'

'I can try. What did you have in mind?'

Abel realised Henry was trying to find out what payment he might expect, but he hadn't finished yet. 'I want a written report the first day of every month showing Kane's share-holdings in any company, his business commitments and all details you can obtain of his private life. I want everything you come up with, however trivial it may seem.'

'I repeat, that won't be easy,' said Henry.

'Will a thousand dollars a month make the task easier?'

'Fifteen hundred certainly would,' replied Henry.

'A thousand dollars a month for the first six months. If you prove yourself, I'll raise the figure to fifteen hundred.'

'It's a deal,' said Henry.

'Good,' said Abel as he took his wallet from his inside pocket and extracted a cheque already made out to cash for one thousand dollars.

Henry studied the cheque. 'You were pretty confident I would fall into line, weren't you?'

'No, not altogether,' said Abel, as he removed a second cheque from his wallet and showed it to Henry. It was made out for fifteen hundred dollars. 'If you come up with some winners in the first six months, you'll only have lost three thousand dollars.'

Both men laughed.

'Now to a more pleasant subject,' said Abel. 'Are we going to win?'

'The Cubs?'

'No, the election.'

'Sure, Landon is in for a whipping. The Kansas Sunflower can't hope to beat F.D.R.' said Henry. 'As the President reminded us, that particular flower is yellow, has a black heart, is useful as parrot food and always dies before November.'

Abel laughed again. 'And how about you personally?'

'No worries. The seat has always been safe for the Democrats. The difficult thing was winning the nomination, not the election.'

'I look forward to your being a Congressman, Henry.'

'I'm sure you do, Abel, and I shall look forward to serving you as well as my other constituents.'

Abel looked at him quizzically. 'Considerably better, I should hope,' he commented as a sirloin steak that almost covered the plate was placed in front of him while another glass was filled with a Côte de Beaune 1929. The rest of the lunch was spent discussing Gabby Hartnett's injury problems, Jesse Owens's four gold medals at the Berlin Olympics, and the possibility that Hitler would invade Poland.

'Never,' said Henry, and started to reminisce about the courage of the Poles at Mons in the Great War.

Abel didn't comment on the fact that no Polish regiment had seen action at Mons.

At two thirty-seven Abel was back at his desk, considering the problems of the Presidential Suite and the eight thousand fresh bread rolls.

He did not arrive home from the Baron that night until nine o'clock, only to find Florentyna already asleep. But she woke immediately as her father entered the nursery and smiled up at him.

'Presidunk, Presidunk, Presidunk.'

Abel smiled. 'Not me. You perhaps, but not me.' He

picked his daughter up and kissed her on the cheek and sat with her while she repeated her one-word vocabulary over and over again.

3

IN NOVEMBER 1936, HENRY OSBORNE was elected to the United States House of Representatives for the Ninth District of Illinois. His majority was slightly smaller than his predecessor's, a fact which could be attributed only to his indolence as Roosevelt had carried every state except Vermont and Maine, and in Congress the Republicans were down to seventeen Senators and one hundred and three Representatives. But all that Abel cared about was that his man had a seat in the House, and he immediately offered him the chairmanship of the Planning Committee of the Baron Group. Henry gratefully accepted.

Abel channelled all his energy into building more and more hotels – with the help of Congressman Osborne, who seemed able to fix building permits wherever the Baron next desired. Abel always paid Henry for these favours with used notes. He had no idea what Henry did with the money, but it was evident that some of it had to be falling into the right hands, and he had no wish to know the details.

Despite his deteriorating relationship with Zaphia, Abel still wanted a son and began to despair when his wife failed to conceive. He initially blamed Zaphia, who longed for a second child, but eventually she nagged him into seeing a doctor. Abel was humiliated to learn that he had a low sperm count: the doctor attributed this to early malnutrition and told him that it was most unlikely he would ever be a father again. From that moment the subject was closed, and Abel lavished all his affections and hopes on Florentyna, who grew like a weed. The only thing in Abel's life that grew faster was the Baron Group. He built a new hotel in the north, and another in the south, while modernising and streamlining the older hotels already in the group.

At the age of four, Florentyna attended her first nursery school. She insisted that Abel and Franklin D. Roosevelt accompany her on the opening day. Most of the other girls were chaperoned by women whom Abel was surprised to discover were not always their mothers but often nannies and, in one case, as he was gently corrected, a governess. That night he told Zaphia that he wanted someone similarly qualified to take charge of Florentyna.

'What for?' asked Zaphia sharply.

'So that no one in that school starts life with an advantage over our daughter.'

'I think it's a stupid waste of money. What would such a person be able to do for her that I can't?'

Abel didn't reply, but the next morning, he placed advertisements in the Chicago *Tribune*, the *New York Times* and the London *Times*, seeking applicants for the post of governess, stating clearly the terms offered. Hundreds of replies came in from all over the country from highly qualified women who wanted to work for the chairman of the Baron Group. Letters arrived from Radcliffe, Vassar and Smith; there was even one from the Federal Reformatory for Women in Alderson, West Virginia. But it was the reply from a lady who had obviously never heard of the Chicago Baron that intrigued him most.

The Old Rectory
Much Hadham
Hertfordshire

12 September 1938

Dear Sir,

In reply to your advertisement in the personal column on the front page of today's issue of *The Times*, I should like to be considered for the post of governess to your daughter.

I am thirty-two years of age, and I am the sixth daughter of The Rev. L. H. Tredgold, and a spinster of the parish of Much Hadham in Hertfordshire. I am at present teaching in the local grammar school and assisting my father in his work as Rural Dean.

I was educated at Cheltenham Ladies' College where I studied Latin, Greek, French and English for my higher matriculation, before taking up a closed scholarship to Newnham College, Cambridge. At the university, I sat my finals gaining first-class awards in all three parts of the Modern Language tripos. I do not hold a Bachelor of Arts degree from the university, as their statutes preclude such awards to women.

I am available for interview at any time and I would welcome the opportunity to work in the New World.

I have the honour to remain, Sir,
Your obedient servant,
W. Tredgold

Abel found it hard to accept that there was such an institution as Cheltenham Ladies' College or indeed such a place as Much Hadham, and he was certainly suspicious of claims of first-class awards without degrees.

He asked his secretary to place a call to Washington. When he was finally put through to the person he wished to speak to he read the letter aloud.

The voice from Washington confirmed that every claim in the letter could be accurate; there was no reason to doubt its credibility.

'Are you sure there really is an establishment called Cheltenham Ladies' College?' Abel insisted.

'Most certainly I am, Mr. Rosnovski. I was educated there myself,' replied the British ambassador's secretary.

That night Abel read the letter over again, this time to Zaphia.

'What do you think?' he asked, although he had already made up his mind.

'I don't like the sound of her,' said Zaphia, not looking up from the magazine she was reading. 'If we must have someone, why can't she be an American?'

'Think of the advantages Florentyna would have if she

were tutored by an English governess.' Abel paused. 'She'd even be company for you.'

This time Zaphia did look up from her magazine. 'Why? Are you hoping she'll educate me as well?'

Abel made no reply.

The following morning he sent a cable to Much Hadham, offering Miss Tredgold the position of governess.

Three weeks later when Abel went to pick up the lady from the Twentieth Century Limited at the La Salle Street Station, he knew immediately he had made the right decision. As she stood alone on the platform, three suitcases of differing sizes and vintages by her side, she could not have been anyone but Miss Tredgold. She was tall, thin and slightly imperious, and the bun that crowned her head gave her fully two inches in height over her employer.

Zaphia, however, treated Miss Tredgold as an intruder who had come to undermine her maternal position, and when she accompanied her to her daughter's room, Florentyna was nowhere to be seen. Two eyes peered suspiciously from under the bed. Miss Tredgold spotted the girl first and fell on her knees.

'I am afraid I won't be able to help you very much if you remain there, child. I'm far too big to live under a bed.'

Florentyna burst out laughing and crawled out.

'What a funny voice you have,' she said. 'Where do you come from?'

'England,' said Miss Tredgold, taking a seat beside her on the bed.

'Where's that?'

'About a week away.'

'Yes, but how far?'

'That would depend on how you travelled during the week. How many ways could I have travelled such a long distance? Can you think of three?'

Florentyna concentrated. 'From my house I'd take a bicycle and when I'd reached the end of America I'd take a . . .'

Neither of them noticed that Zaphia had left the room.

It was only a few days before Florentyna turned Miss Tredgold into the brother and sister she could never have.

Florentyna would spend hours just listening to her new companion, and Abel watched with pride as the middle-aged spinster – he could never think of her as thirty-two, his own age – taught his four-year-old daughter a range of subjects he would have liked to know more about himself.

Abel asked George one morning if he could name Henry VIII's six wives; if he couldn't it might be wise for them to acquire two more governesses from Cheltenham Ladies' College before Florentyna ended up knowing more than they did. Zaphia did not want to know about Henry VIII or his wives, as she still felt Florentyna should be brought up according to simple Polish traditions, but she had long since given up trying to convince Abel on that subject. Zaphia carried out a routine that made it possible for her to avoid the new governess most of the day.

Miss Tredgold's daily routine on the other hand owed as much to the discipline of a Grenadier Guards' officer as to the teachings of Maria Montessori. Florentyna rose at seven o'clock and with a straight spine that never touched the back of the chair received instruction in table manners and posture until she had left the breakfast room. Between seven thirty and seven forty-five Miss Tredgold would pick out two or three items from the Chicago *Tribune*, read and discuss them with her and then question her on them an hour later. Florentyna took an immediate interest in what the President was doing, perhaps because he seemed to be named after her bear. Miss Tredgold found she had to use a considerable amount of her spare time diligently learning the strange American system of government to be certain no question that her ward might ask would go unanswered.

From nine to twelve, Florentyna and F.D.R. attended nursery school where they indulged in the more normal pursuits of her contemporaries. When Miss Tredgold came to pick her up each afternoon it was easy to discern whether Florentyna had selected the clay, the scissors and paste or the finger painting that day. At the end of every play-school session she was taken straight home for a bath and change of clothes with a 'Tut, tut,' and the occasional 'I just don't know'.

In the afternoon, Miss Tredgold and Florentyna would set off on some expedition which Miss Tredgold had carefully planned that morning without Florentyna's knowledge – although this didn't stop Florentyna always trying to find out in advance what her governess had arranged.

'What are we going to do today?' or 'Where are we going?' Florentyna would demand.

'Be patient, child.'

'Can we still do it if it rains?'

'Only time will tell. But if we can't, be assured I shall have a contingency plan.'

'What's a 'tingency plan?' asked Florentyna, puzzled.

'Something you need when everything else you have planned is no longer possible,' Miss Tredgold explained.

Among such afternoon expeditions were walks around the park, visits to the zoo, even the occasional ride on the top of a trolley car, which Florentyna considered a great treat. Miss Tredgold also used the time to give her charge the first introduction to a few words of French, and she was pleasantly surprised to find that her ward showed a natural aptitude for languages. Once they had returned home, there would be half an hour with Mama before tea, followed by another bath before Florentyna was tucked up in bed by seven o'clock. Miss Tredgold would then read a few lines from the Bible or Mark Twain – not that the Americans seemed to know the difference, Miss Tredgold said in a moment of what she imagined was frivolity – and having turned the nursery light out she sat with her charge and F.D.R. until they had both fallen asleep.

This routine was slavishly adhered to and broken only on such rare occasions as birthdays or national holidays when Miss Tredgold allowed Florentyna to accompany her to the United Artists theatre on West Randolph Street to see films such as *Snow White and the Seven Dwarfs* but not before Miss Tredgold had been to the show the previous week in order to ascertain that it was suitable for her ward. Walt Disney met with Miss Tredgold's approval, as did Laurence Olivier playing Heathcliff pursued by Merle Oberon, a film she went to watch three Thursdays running on her afternoon off at a cost of twenty cents a showing. She was able to convince herself it was worth sixty cents; after all, *Wuthering Heights* was a classic.

Miss Tredgold never stopped Florentyna asking questions about the Nazis, the New Deal and even a 'home run', although sometimes she obviously didn't understand the answers. The young girl soon discovered that her mother was not always able to satisfy her curiosity, and on several occasions Miss Tredgold, in order not to render an inaccurate answer, had to disappear into her room and consult the *Encyclopaedia Britannica*.

At the age of five Florentyna attended kindergarten at the Girls Latin School of Chicago where within a week she was moved up a grade because she was so far ahead of her contemporaries. In her world everything looked wonderful. She had Mama and Papa, Miss Tredgold and Franklin D. Roosevelt, and as far as her horizon could reach nothing seemed to be unobtainable.

Only the 'best families', as Abel described them, sent their children to the Latin School, and it came as something of a shock to Miss Tredgold that when she asked some of Florentyna's friends back for tea the invitations were politely declined. Florentyna's best friends, Mary Gill and Susie Jacobson, came regularly; but some of the parents of the other girls would make lame excuses for not accepting and Miss Tredgold soon came to realise that although the Chicago Baron might well have broken the chains of poverty he was still unable to break into some of the better drawing rooms in Chicago. Zaphia did not help, making little effort to get to know the other parents, let alone join any of their charity committees, hospital boards or the clubs to which so many of them seemed to belong.

Miss Tredgold did the best she could to help, but as she was only a servant in the eyes of most of the parents it was not easy for her. She prayed that Florentyna would never learn of these prejudices – but it was not to be.

Florentyna sailed through the first grade, more than holding her own academically with the group, and only her size reminded everyone that she was a year younger.

Abel was too busy building up his own empire to give much thought to his social standing or any problems Miss Tredgold might be facing. The group was showing steady progress with Abel looking well set by 1938 to be on target to repay the loan to his backer. In fact Abel was predicting profits of two hundred and fifty thousand dollars for the year, despite his heavy building programme.

His real worries were not in the nursery or the hotels, but almost five thousand miles away in his beloved homeland. His worst fears were realised when on September 1st, 1939, Hitler marched into Poland, and Britain declared war on Germany two days later. With the outbreak of another war Abel seriously considered leaving control of the Baron Group to George – who was turning out to be a trusty lieutenant – while he sailed off to London to join the Polish army in exile. George and Zaphia managed to talk him out of the idea, so he concentrated instead on raising cash and sending the money to the British Red Cross, while lobbying Democratic politicians to join the war alongside the British.

'F.D.R. needs all the friends he can get,' Florentyna heard her father declare one morning.

By the last quarter of 1939, Abel, with the help of a small loan from the First City Bank of Chicago, became the one hundred per cent owner of the Baron Group. He predicted in the annual report that profits for 1940 would be over half a million dollars.

Franklin D. Roosevelt – the one with the red eyes and the fluffy brown fur – rarely left Florentyna's side even when she progressed to second grade. Miss Tredgold considered that perhaps the time had come to leave F.D.R. at home. In normal circumstances she would have insisted, there might have been a few tears and the matter would have been resolved; but against her better judgment she let the child have her own way. It was a decision that turned out to be one of Miss Tredgold's rare mistakes.

Every Monday, the boys of the Latin School joined the girls to be tutored in French by the modern languages teacher, Mademoiselle Mettinet. For everyone except Florentyna, this was a first, painful introduction to the language. As the class chanted *boucher*, *boulanger*, and *épicier* after Mademoiselle, Florentyna, more out of boredom than bravado, began holding a conversation with F.D.R. in French. Her neighbour, a tall, rather lazy boy named Edward Winchester, who seemed unable to grasp the difference between *le* and *la*, leaned over and told Florentyna to stop showing off. Florentyna reddened. 'I was only trying to explain to F.D.R. the difference between the masculine and the feminine.'

'Were you?' said Edward. 'Well, I'll show you *le différence*, Mademoiselle Know-All,' and in a fit of fury he grabbed F.D.R. and with all the strength he could muster tore one of the bear's arms from its body. Florentyna remained rooted to her seat in shock as Edward then took the inkwell out of his desk and poured the contents over the bear's head.

Mademoiselle Mettinet, who had never approved of having boys in the same class as girls, rushed to the back of the room, but it was too late. F.D.R. was already royal blue from head to toe and sat on the floor in the middle of a circle of stuffing from his severed arm. Florentyna grabbed her favourite friend, tears diluting the puddled ink. Mademoiselle Mettinet marched Edward to the headmaster's office and instructed the other children to sit in silence until she returned.

Florentyna crawled around the floor, trying hopelessly to put the stuffing back into F.D.R., when a fair-haired girl Florentyna had never liked leaned over and hissed, 'Serves you right, stupid Polack.' The class giggled at the girl's remark and some of them started to chant, 'Stupid Polack, stupid Polack, stupid Polack.' Florentyna clung on to F.D.R. and prayed for Mademoiselle Mettinet's return.

It seemed like hours although it was only a few minutes before the French mistress reappeared, with Edward looking suitably crestfallen following in her wake. The chanting stopped the moment Mademoiselle Mettinet entered the room, but Florentyna couldn't even make herself look up. In the unnatural silence, Edward walked up to Florentyna and apologised in a voice that was as loud as it was unconvincing. He returned to his seat and grinned at his classmates.

When Miss Tredgold picked her charge up from school that afternoon she could hardly miss noticing that the child's face was red from crying and that she walked with a bowed head clinging on to a blue-faced F.D.R. by his remaining arm. Miss Tredgold coaxed the whole story out of Florentyna before they reached home. She then gave the child her favourite supper of hamburger and ice cream, two dishes of which she normally disapproved, and put her to bed early, hoping she would quickly fall asleep. After a futile hour with nail brush and soap spent trying to clean up the indelibly stained bear, Miss Tredgold was forced to concede defeat. As she laid the damp animal by Florentyna's side, a small voice from under the bedcovers said, 'Thank you, Miss Tredgold. F.D.R. needs all the friends he can get.'

When Abel returned a little after ten o'clock – he had taken to arriving home late almost every night – Miss Tredgold sought a private meeting with him. Abel was surprised by the request and led her at once through to his study. During the eighteen months she had been in his employ Miss Tredgold had always reported the week's progress to Mr. Rosnovski on Sunday mornings between ten and ten thirty while Florentyna was attending Mass with her mother at the Holy Name Cathedral. Miss Tredgold's reports were always clear and accurate; if anything she had a tendency to underestimate the child's achievements.

'What's the problem, Miss Tredgold?' asked Abel, trying to sound unworried. With such a break in routine he dreaded the thought that she might want to give in her notice. Miss

Tredgold repeated the story of what had happened at school that day.

Abel became redder and redder in the face as the story progressed and was scarlet before Miss Tredgold came to the end.

'Intolerable,' was his first word. 'Florentyna must be removed immediately. I shall personally see Miss Allen tomorrow and tell her exactly what I think of her and her school. I am sure that you will approve of my decision, Miss Tredgold.'

'No, sir, I do not,' came back an unusually sharp reply.

'I beg your pardon?' said Abel in disbelief.

'I believe you are as much to blame as the parents of Edward Winchester.'

'I?' said Abel. 'Why?'

'You should have told your daughter a long time ago the significance of being Polish and how to deal with any problems that might arise because of it. You should have explained the Americans' deep-seated prejudice against the Poles, a prejudice that is in my own opinion every bit as reprehensible as the English attitude towards the Irish, and only a few steps away from the Nazis' barbaric behaviour towards the Jews.'

Abel remained silent. It was a long time since anyone had told him he was wrong about anything.

'Do you have anything else to say?' he asked when he had recovered.

'Yes, Mr. Rosnovski. If you remove Florentyna from Girls Latin, I shall give in my notice immediately. If on the first occasion the child encounters some problem you choose to run away from it, how can I hope to teach her to cope with life? Watching my own country at war because we wanted to go on believing Hitler was a reasonable man, if slightly misguided, I can hardly be expected to pass on the same misconstruction of events to Florentyna. It will be heartbreaking for me to have to leave her, because I could not love Florentyna more if she were my own child, but I cannot approve of disguising the real world because you have

enough money to keep the truth conveniently hidden for a
few more years. I must apologise for my frankness, Mr.
Rosnovski, as I feel I have gone too far, but I cannot
condemn other people's prejudices while at the same time
condoning yours.'

Abel sank back into his seat before replying. 'Miss Tredgold, you should have been an ambassador, not a governess.
Of course you're right. What would you advise me to do?'

Miss Tredgold, who was still standing – she would never
have dreamed of sitting in her employer's presence unless she
was with Florentyna – hesitated.

'The child should rise thirty minutes earlier each day for
the next month and be taught Polish history. She must learn
why Poland is a great nation, and why the Poles were willing
to challenge the might of Germany when alone they could
never have hoped for victory. Then she will be able to face
those who goad her about her ancestry with knowledge not
ignorance.'

Abel looked her squarely in the eyes. 'I see now what
George Bernard Shaw meant when he said that you have to
meet the English governess to discover why Britain is great.'

They both laughed.

'I'm surprised you don't want to make more of your life,
Miss Tredgold,' said Abel, suddenly aware that what he had
said might have sounded offensive. If it had, Miss Tredgold
gave no sign of being offended.

'My father had six daughters. He had hoped for a boy, but
it was not to be.'

'And what of the other five?'

'They are all married,' she replied without bitterness.

'And you?'

'He once said to me that I was born to be a teacher and that
the Lord's plan took us all in its compass so perhaps I might
teach someone who does have a destiny.'

'Let us hope so, Miss Tredgold.' Abel would have called
her by her first name but he did not know what it was. All he
knew was she signed herself 'W. Tredgold' in a way that did
not invite further enquiry. He smiled up at her.

'Will you join me in a drink, Miss Tredgold?'

'Thank you, Mr. Rosnovski. A little sherry would be most pleasant.'

Abel poured her a dry sherry and himself a large whisky.

'How bad is F.D.R.?'

'Maimed for life, I fear, which will only make the child love him the more. In the future I have decided that F.D.R. must reside at home and will only travel when accompanied by me.'

'You're beginning to sound like Eleanor Roosevelt talking about the President.'

Miss Tredgold laughed once more and sipped her sherry. 'May I offer one more suggestion concerning Florentyna?'

'Certainly,' said Abel, who proceeded to listen intently to Miss Tredgold's recommendation. By the time they had finished their second drink, Abel had nodded his approval.

'Good,' said Miss Tredgold, 'then, with your permission, I will deal with that at the first possible opportunity.'

'Certainly,' repeated Abel. 'Of course, when it comes to these morning sessions, it may not be practical for me to do a whole month without a break.' Miss Tredgold was about to speak when Abel added, 'There may be appointments that I cannot re-schedule at such short notice, as I am sure you will understand.'

'You must, Mr. Rosnovski, do what you think best, and if you find there is something more important than your daughter's future I am sure it is she who will understand.'

Abel knew when he was beaten. He cancelled all appointments outside Chicago for a full month and rose each morning thirty minutes early. Even Zaphia approved of Miss Tredgold's idea.

The first day Abel started by telling Florentyna how he had been born in a forest in Poland and adopted by a trapper's family, and how later he had been befriended by a great Baron who took him into his castle in Slonim, on the Polish–Russian border. 'He treated me like his own son,' Abel told her.

As the days went by, Abel revealed to his daughter how his

sister Florentyna, after whom she had been named, joined him in the castle and the way he discovered the Baron was his real father.

'I know, I know how you found out,' cried Florentyna.

'How can you know, little one?'

'He only had one nipple,' said Florentyna. 'It must be, it must be. I've seen you in the bath. You only have one nipple, so you had to be his son. All the boys at school have two . . .' Abel and Miss Tredgold stared at the child in disbelief as she continued, '. . . but if I'm your daughter, why have I got two?'

'Because it's only passed from father to son and is almost unknown in daughters.'

'It's not fair. I want only one.'

Abel began laughing. 'Well, perhaps if you have a son, he'll have only one.'

'Time for you to braid your hair and get ready for school,' said Miss Tredgold.

'But it's just getting exciting.'

'Do as you are told, child.'

Florentyna reluctantly left her father and went to the bathroom.

'What do you think is going to happen tomorrow, Miss Tredgold?' she asked, on the way to school.

'I have no idea, child, but as Mr. Asquith once advised, wait and see.'

'Was Mr. Asquith in the castle with Papa?'

In the days that followed Abel explained what life was like in a Russian prison camp and what had caused him to limp. He went on to teach his daughter the stories the Baron had told him in the dungeons over twenty years before. Florentyna followed the stories of the legendary Polish hero Tadeusz Kosciuszko and all the other great figures through to the present day, while Miss Tredgold pointed to a map of Europe she had pinned on the bedroom wall.

He finally explained to his daughter how he had come into possession of the silver band that he wore on his wrist.

'What does it say?' demanded Florentyna, staring at the tiny engraved letters.

'Try to read the words, little one,' said Abel.

'Bar-on Ab-el Ros-nov-ski,' she stuttered out. 'But that's your name,' she insisted.

'And it was my father's.'

After a few more days Florentyna could answer all her father's questions, even if Abel couldn't always answer all of hers.

At school, Florentyna daily expected Edward Winchester to pick on her again, but he seemed to have forgotten the incident, and on one occasion even offered to share an apple with her.

Not everyone in the class, however, had forgotten, and one girl in particular, a fat, rather dull classmate, took special pleasure in whispering the words 'Stupid Polack' within her hearing.

Florentyna did not retaliate immediately, but waited until some weeks later when the girl, having come at the bottom of the class in a history test while Florentyna came top, announced, 'At least I'm not a Polack.' Edward Winchester frowned, but some of the class giggled.

Florentyna waited for total silence before she spoke. 'True. You're not a Polack, you're a third generation American, with a history that goes back about a hundred years. Mine can be traced for a thousand, which is why you are bottom in history and I am top.'

No one in the class ever referred to the subject again. When Miss Tredgold heard the story on the way home she smiled.

'Shall we tell Papa this evening?' asked Florentyna.

'No, my dear. Pride has never been a virtue. There are some occasions on which it is wise to remain silent.'

The six-year-old girl nodded thoughtfully before asking: 'Do you ever think a Pole could be President of the United States?'

'Certainly, if the American people can overcome their own prejudice.'

'And how about a Catholic?'

'That will become irrelevant, even in my lifetime.'
'And a woman?' added Florentyna.
'That might take a little longer, child.'

That night Miss Tredgold reported to Mr. Rosnovski that his lessons had proved worthwhile.

'And when will you carry out the second part of your plan, Miss Tredgold?' Abel asked.

'Tomorrow,' she replied, smiling.

At three thirty the following afternoon Miss Tredgold was standing on the corner of the street, waiting for her ward to finish school. Florentyna came chattering out through the gates and they had walked for several blocks before she noticed that they were not taking their usual route home.

'Where are we going, Miss Tredgold?'

'Patience, child, and all will be revealed.'

Miss Tredgold smiled while Florentyna seemed more concerned with telling her how well she had done in an English test that morning, a monologue which she kept up all the way to Menomonee Street, where Miss Tredgold began to take more interest in the numbers on the doors than in Florentyna's real and imagined achievements.

At last they came to a halt outside a newly painted red door which displayed the number two hundred and eighteen. Miss Tredgold rapped on the door twice with her gloved knuckle. Florentyna stood by her side, silent for the first time since leaving school. A few moments passed before the door opened to reveal a man dressed in a grey sweater and blue jeans.

'I've come in response to your advertisement in the *Sun-Times*,' Miss Tredgold said before the man had a chance to speak.

'Ah, yes,' he replied. 'Will you come in?'

Miss Tredgold entered the house followed by a puzzled Florentyna. They were conducted through a narrow hall covered in photographs and multi-coloured rosettes before reaching the back door which led out to a yard.

Florentyna saw them immediately. They were in a basket

on the far side of the yard and she ran towards them. Six yellow labrador puppies snuggled up close to their mother. One of them left the warmth of the clan and limped out of the basket towards Florentyna.

'This one's lame,' said Florentyna, immediately picking up the puppy and studying the animal's leg.

'Yes, I'm afraid so,' admitted the breeder. 'But there are still five others in perfect condition for you to choose from.'

'What will happen if nobody takes her?'

'I suppose . . .' – the breeder hesitated – 'she will have to be put to sleep.'

Florentyna stared desperately at Miss Tredgold as she clung to the dog, who was busily licking her face.

'I want this one,' said Florentyna without hesitation, fearful of Miss Tredgold's reaction.

'How much will that be?' asked Miss Tredgold, as she opened her purse.

'No charge, ma'am. I'm happy to see that one go to a good home.'

'Thank you,' said Florentyna. 'Thank you.'

The puppy's tail never stopped wagging all the way to its new home while to Miss Tredgold's surprise Florentyna's tongue never wagged once. In fact, she didn't let go of her new pet until she was safely back inside the kitchen. Zaphia and Miss Tredgold watched as the young labrador limped across the kitchen floor towards a bowl of warm milk.

'She reminds me of Papa,' said Florentyna.

'Don't be impertinent, child,' said Miss Tredgold.

Zaphia stifled a smile. 'Well, Florentyna, what are you going to call her?'

'Eleanor.'

4

THE FIRST TIME FLORENTYNA ran for President was in 1940 at the age of six. Miss Evans, her teacher in second grade, decided to hold a mock election. The boys from the Latin School were invited to join the contest, and Edward Winchester, whom Florentyna had never quite forgiven for pouring blue ink over her bear, was chosen to run as the surrogate Wendell Willkie. Florentyna naturally ran as F.D.R.

It was agreed that each candidate would give a five-minute talk to the remaining twenty-seven members of the two classes. Miss Tredgold, without wishing to influence Florentyna, listened to her deliver her oration thirty-one times – or was it thirty-two? – as she remarked to Mr. Rosnovski the Sunday morning before the great election.

Florentyna read the political columns of the Chicago *Tribune* out loud each day to Miss Tredgold searching for any scrap of information she could add to her speech. Kate Smith seemed to be singing 'God Bless America' everywhere and the Dow Jones Index had passed 150 for the first time: whatever that was, it seemed to favour the sitting candidate. Florentyna also read about the progress of the war in Europe, and the launching of a 36,600-ton battleship U.S.S. *Washington*, the first fighting vessel America had built in nineteen years.

'Why are we building a battleship if the President has promised that the American people will never have to go to war?'

'I presume it's in the best interest of our own defence,' suggested Miss Tredgold, who was furiously knitting socks for the boys back home. 'Just in case the Germans decided to attack us.'

'They wouldn't dare,' said Florentyna.

The day that Trotsky was slain with an ice pick in Mexico, Miss Tredgold kept the paper away from her charge, while on another morning she was quite unable to explain what nylons were and why the first 72,000 pairs were sold out in eight hours, the shops limiting the sale to two per customer.

Miss Tredgold, whose legs were habitually clad in beige lisle stockings of a shade optimistically entitled 'Allure', studied the item frowningly. 'I'm sure I shall never wear nylons,' she declared, and indeed she never did.

When election day came, Florentyna's head was crammed with facts and figures, some of which she did not understand but they gave her the confidence to feel she would win. The only problem that still concerned her was that Edward was bigger than her. Florentyna imagined that this was a definite advantage as she had read that twenty-seven of the thirty-two Presidents of the United States had been taller than their rivals.

The two contestants tossed a newly-minted Jefferson nickel to decide the order of speaking. Florentyna won and chose to speak first, a mistake she never made again in her life. She walked to the front of the class, a frail figure, and mindful of Miss Tredgold's final words of advice – 'Stand up straight, child. Remember you're not a question mark' – she stood bolt upright in the centre of the raised wooden platform in front of Miss Evans's desk and waited to be told she could begin. Her first few sentences came choking out. She explained her policies for ensuring the nation's finances remained stable while at the same time promising to keep the United States out of the war. 'There is no need for one American to die because the nations of Europe cannot stay at peace,' she declared – a sentence from one of Mr. Roosevelt's speeches that she had learned by heart. Mary Gill started to applaud, but Florentyna took no notice and went on talking while, at the same time, pushing her dress down nervously with damp hands. Her last few sentences came out in a great rush, and she sat down to a lot of clapping and smiles.

Edward Winchester rose to follow her and a few of the boys from his class cheered him as he walked up to the blackboard. It was the first time Florentyna realised that some of the votes had been decided even before the speeches began. She only hoped that was true for her side as well. Edward told his classmates that winning at kickball was the same as winning for your country, and in any case Willkie stood for all the things that their parents believed in. Did they want to vote against the wishes of their fathers and mothers, because if they did support F.D.R. they would lose everything? This line was greeted with a splutter of applause, so he repeated it. At the end of his speech, Edward was also rewarded with claps and smiles, but Florentyna convinced herself they were no louder or more widespread than hers had been.

After Edward had sat down, Miss Evans congratulated both candidates and asked the twenty-seven voters to take a blank page from their notebooks and write down the name of Edward or Florentyna, according to whom they felt should be President. Pens dipped furiously into inkwells, scratched across paper. Voting slips were blotted, folded, and then passed forward to Miss Evans. When the teacher had received the last one, she began to unfold the little squares and place them in front of her in separate piles, a process that seemed to take hours. The whole classroom remained silent throughout the count which in itself was an unusual event. Once Miss Evans had completed the unfolding she counted the twenty-seven slips of paper slowly and carefully, and then double-checked them.

'The result of the mock election' – Florentyna held her breath – 'for President of the United States is thirteen votes for Edward Winchester' – Florentyna nearly cheered, she had won – '. . . and twelve votes for Florentyna Rosnovski. Two people left their papers blank, which is called abstaining.' Florentyna couldn't believe it. 'I therefore declare Edward Winchester, representing Wendell Willkie, to be the new President.'

It was the only election F.D.R. lost that year, but Florentyna was unable to disguise her disappointment and ran to hide in the girls' locker room to be sure no one could see her crying. When she came out she found Mary Gill and Susie Jacobson waiting for her.

'It doesn't matter,' said Florentyna, trying to put a brave face on the result. 'At least I know both of you supported me.'

'We couldn't.'

'Why couldn't you?' asked Florentyna in disbelief.

'We didn't want Miss Evans to know that we weren't sure how to spell your name,' said Mary.

On the way home, after Miss Tredgold had heard the story seven times, she made so bold as to ask if the child had learned anything from the exercise.

'Oh, yes,' replied Florentyna emphatically. 'I'm going to marry a man with a very simple name.'

Abel laughed when he heard the story that night and repeated it to Henry Osborne over dinner. 'Better keep your eye on her, Henry, because it won't be long before she's after your seat.'

'I've got at least fifteen years before she can vote and by then I'll be ready to hand the constituency over to her.'

'What are you doing about convincing the International Relations Committee that we ought to be in this war?'

'F.D.R. will do nothing until the result of the election is known. Everybody is aware of that, including Hitler.'

'If that's so, I only pray that Britain won't lose before we join in, because America will have to wait until November to confirm F.D.R. as President.'

During the year Abel appointed architects for two more hotels in Washington and San Francisco and had begun his first project in Canada, the Montreal Baron. Although his thoughts were rarely far from the success of the group, something else still remained on his mind.

He wanted to be in Europe, and it wasn't to build hotels.

At the end of the autumn term, Florentyna got her first spanking. In later life she always associated this with snow.

Her classmates decided to build a massive snowman and each member of the class had to bring something with which to decorate him. The snowman ended up with raisin eyes, a carrot nose, potato ears, an old pair of garden gloves, a cigar and a hat supplied by Florentyna. On the last day of the term all the parents were invited to view the snowman and many of them remarked on its hat. Florentyna beamed with pride until her father and mother arrived. Zaphia burst out laughing but Abel was not amused at the sight of his fine silk topper on the head of a grinning snowman. When they arrived home Florentyna was taken to her father's study and given a long lecture on the irresponsibility of taking things that did not belong to her. Abel bent her over his knee and gave her three hard slaps with a hairbrush.

That Saturday night was one she would never forget.

That Sunday morning was one America would always remember.

The Rising Sun appeared over Pearl Harbor on the wings of hostile aircraft and crippled the U.S. battle fleet, virtually wiping out the base and killing 2,403 Americans. The United States declared war on Japan the following day and Germany three days later.

Abel immediately summoned George to inform him that he was going to join the American forces before they sailed for Europe. George protested, Zaphia pleaded and Florentyna cried. Miss Tredgold did not venture an opinion.

Abel knew he only had to settle one final thing before leaving America. He called for Henry.

'Did you spot the announcement in the *Wall Street Journal*, Henry? I nearly missed the item myself because of all the news about Pearl Harbor.'

'You mean the merger of Lester's with Kane and Cabot, which I predicted in last month's report? Yes, I already have the full details.' Henry passed over a file to Abel. 'I guessed that's what you wanted to see me about.'

Abel flipped through the file until he found the relevant article, underlined in red by Henry. He read the paragraph twice and then started to tap his fingers on the table. 'The first mistake Kane has made.'

'I think you might be right,' said Henry.

'You're earning your fifteen hundred dollars a month, Henry.'

'Perhaps it's time to make it two thousand.'

'Why?'

'Because of Article Seven of the new bank's rules.'

'What made him allow the new clause to be inserted in the first place?' said Abel.

'To protect himself. It has obviously never occurred to Mr. Kane that someone might be trying to destroy him, but by exchanging all his shares in Kane and Cabot for the equivalent Lester shares he's lost control of one bank and not gained control of the new one because of Lester's being so much larger. While he only holds eight per cent of the shares in the new venture he has insisted on that clause to be sure that he can stop any transaction for three months, including the appointment of a new chairman.'

'So all we have to do is get hold of eight per cent of Lester's stock and use his own specially inserted clause against him as and when it suits us.' Abel paused. 'I don't imagine that will be easy.'

'That's why I've asked you for a raise.'

Abel found the task of being accepted for service in the armed forces considerably more difficult than he had at first imagined. The army was none too polite about his sight, his weight, his heart or his general physical condition. Only after some string-pulling did he manage to secure a job as a quartermaster with the Fifth Army under General Mark Clark who was waiting to sail to Africa. Abel jumped at the one chance to be involved in the war and disappeared to officers' training school. Miss Tredgold did not realise until he had left Rigg Street how much Florentyna was going to miss her father. She tried to convince the child that the war would not last long but she did not believe her own words. Miss Tredgold had read too much history.

Abel returned from training school as a major, slimmer and younger looking, but Florentyna hated seeing her father in uniform, because everyone else she knew in uniform was going away to somewhere beyond Chicago and they never seemed to come back. In February, Abel waved goodbye and left New York on the S.S. *Borinquen*. Florentyna, who was still only seven, was convinced goodbye meant for ever. Mother assured daughter that Papa would return home very quickly.

Like Miss Tredgold, Zaphia did not believe that – and this time neither did Florentyna.

Florentyna progressed to fourth grade, where she was appointed secretary of her class – which meant she kept weekly minutes of class meetings. When she read her report aloud to the rest of the class each week, no one in the fourth grade showed much interest, but in the heat and dust of Algiers, Abel, torn between laughter and tears, read each line of his daughter's earnest work as if it were the latest best-seller. Florentyna's most recent fad, much approved of by Miss Tredgold, was the Brownies, which allowed her to wear a uniform like her father. Not only did she enjoy dressing up in the smart brown outfit but she soon discovered that she could cover the sleeves with different coloured badges for such enterprises as varied as helping in the kitchen to collecting used stamps. Florentyna was awarded so many badges so quickly that Miss Tredgold was kept busy sewing them on and trying to find a new space for each one. Knots, cooking, gymnastics, animal care, handicrafts, stamps, hiking, followed quickly one after the other. 'It would have been easier if you had been an octopus,' said Miss Tredgold. But final victory was to be hers when her charge won a badge for needlework and had to sew the little yellow triangle on for herself.

When Florentyna progressed to the fifth grade, where the two schools joined together for most classes, Edward Winchester was appointed President of his class, mainly because of his feats on the sports field, while Florentyna held the post of secretary despite having better grades than anyone else including Edward. Her only disasters were in geometry, where she came second, and in the art room. Miss Tredgold always enjoyed rereading Florentyna's reports and positively relished the remarks of the art teacher. 'Perhaps if Florentyna splashed more paint on the paper than on everything that surrounded it, she might hope to become an artist rather than a plasterer and decorator.'

But the line Miss Tredgold quoted whenever she was asked about Florentyna's academic achievements came from her home-room teacher. 'This pupil mustn't cry when she is second.'

As the months passed Florentyna became aware that many of the children in her class had fathers involved in the war. She soon discovered that hers was not the only home that had to face separation. Miss Tredgold enrolled Florentyna in ballet and piano lessons to keep every moment of her spare time occupied. She even allowed her to take Eleanor to the K-9 Corps as a useful pet, but the labrador was sent home because she limped. Florentyna wished they would do the same to her father. When the summer holidays came Miss Tredgold, with the approval of Zaphia, extended their horizons to New York and Washington, despite the travel restrictions imposed by the war. Zaphia took advantage of her daughter's absence to attend charity meetings in aid of Polish soldiers returning from the front.

Florentyna was thrilled by her first trip to New York even though she had to leave Eleanor behind. There were sky-scrapers, big department stores, Central Park and more people than she had ever seen before; but despite all the excitement, it was Washington she most wanted to visit. The journey was Florentyna's first in an airplane, and Miss Tredgold's as well, and as the plane followed the line of the Potomac River into Washington's National Airport, Florentyna stared down in awe at the White House, the Washington Monument, the Lincoln Memorial, and the as yet unfinished Jefferson Building. She wondered if it would

be a memorial or a monument and asked Miss Tredgold to
explain the difference. Miss Tredgold hesitated and said they
would have to look the two words up in Webster's Dictionary
when they returned to Chicago, as she couldn't be certain
there was a difference. It was the first time that Florentyna
realised Miss Tredgold didn't know everything.

'It's just like in the pictures,' she said as she stared down
out of the tiny airplane window at the Capitol.

'What did you expect?' said Miss Tredgold.

Henry Osborne had organised a special visit to the White
House and a chance to watch the Senate and House in
session. Once she entered the gallery of the Senate Chamber
Florentyna was mesmerised, as each speaker rose at his desk
to speak. Miss Tredgold had to drag her away as one might a
boy from a football game, but it didn't stop her continually
asking Henry Osborne more and more questions. He was
surprised by the knowledge the nine-year-old girl already
possessed even if she was the daughter of the Chicago Baron.

Florentyna and Miss Tredgold spent the night at the
Willard Hotel. Her father had not yet built a Baron in
Washington although Congressman Osborne assured them
that one was in the pipeline; in fact, he added, the site had
already been fixed.

'What does "fixed" mean, Mr. Osborne?'

Florentyna received no satisfactory reply either from
Henry Osborne or from Miss Tredgold, and decided to look
that up in Webster's Dictionary as well.

That night Miss Tredgold tucked the child up in a large
hotel bed and left the room, assuming that after such a long
day her charge would quickly fall asleep. Florentyna waited
for a few minutes before switching the light back on. She then
retrieved her guide to the White House from under the
pillow. F.D.R. in a black cloak stared up at her. 'There can be
no greater calling than public service' was printed boldly on
the line underneath his name. She read the booklet twice
through, but it was the final page that fascinated her most.
She started to memorise it and fell asleep a few minutes after
one, the light still on.

During the return flight home Florentyna studied the back page again carefully while Miss Tredgold read of the progress of the war in the Washington *Times-Herald*. Italy had virtually surrendered, although it was clear that the Germans still believed they could win. Florentyna didn't interrupt Miss Tredgold's reading once between Washington and Chicago, and she wondered as the child was so quiet if she was exhausted from the travel. On returning home she allowed Florentyna to go to bed early, but not before she had written a thank-you letter to Congressman Osborne. When Miss Tredgold came to put the light out, Florentyna was still studying the guide to the White House.

It was exactly ten thirty when Miss Tredgold went down to the kitchen to make her nightly cup of cocoa before retiring to bed. On returning she heard what sounded like a chant. She tiptoed slowly to Florentyna's bedroom door, and stood alert, listening to the firmly whispered words. 'One, Washington; two, Adams; three, Jefferson; four, Madison.' She went through every President without a mistake. 'Thirty-one, Hoover; thirty-two, F.D.R.; thirty-three, Unknown; thirty-four, Unknown; thirty-five, thirty-six, thirty-seven, thirty-eight, thirty-nine, forty, forty-one, Unknown; forty-two . . .' There was a moment's silence then: 'One Washington; two, Adams; three, Jefferson . . .' Miss Tredgold tiptoed back to her room and lay awake for some time staring at the ceiling, her untouched cocoa going cold beside her as she recalled her father's words: 'You were born to be a teacher and the Lord's plan takes us all in its compass: perhaps you will teach someone of destiny.' The President of the United States, Florentyna Rosnovski? No, thought Miss Tredgold, Florentyna was right. She would have to marry someone with a simple name.

Florentyna rose the next morning, bade Miss Tredgold *bonjour* and disappeared into the bathroom. After feeding Eleanor, who now seemed to eat more than she did, Florentyna read in the Chicago *Tribune* that F.D.R. and Churchill had conferred on the unconditional surrender of Italy and told her mother joyfully that meant Papa would be home soon.

Zaphia said she hoped she was right and commented to Miss Tredgold how well she thought Florentyna was looking. 'And how did you enjoy Washington, my dear?'

'Very much, Mama. I think I'll live there one day.'

'Why, Florentyna, what would you do in Washington?'

Florentyna looked up and met Miss Tredgold's eye. She hesitated for a few seconds and then turned back to her mother. 'I don't know. I just thought Washington was a nice city. Would you please pass the marmalade, Miss Tredgold?'

5

FLORENTYNA COULDN'T BE SURE how many of her weekly letters were reaching her father because they had to be mailed to a depot in New York for checking before they were sent on to wherever Major Rosnovski was stationed at the time.

The replies came back spasmodically, and sometimes Florentyna would receive as many as three letters in one week and then no word for three months. If a whole month passed without a letter, she began to believe her father had been killed in action. Miss Tredgold explained that that was not possible since the army always sent a telegram to inform a family if a relative was killed or missing. Each morning, Florentyna would be the first to go downstairs to search through the mail for her father's handwriting or the dreaded telegram. When she did receive a letter from her father she often found some of the words were blocked out with black ink. She tried holding them up to the light over the breakfast table but still she couldn't decipher them. Miss Tredgold told her that this was for her father's own safety, as he might have inadvertently written something that could be useful to the enemy if the letter had fallen into the wrong hands.

'Why would the Germans be interested in the fact that I am second in geometry?' asked Florentyna.

Miss Tredgold ignored the question and asked if she had enough to eat.

'I'd like another bit of toast.'

'A piece, child, a piece. A bit is something you put in a horse's mouth.'

Every six months Miss Tredgold would take her charge, accompanied by Eleanor, to Monroe Street to sit on a high stool with the dog on a box by her side, to smile at a flash bulb so that Major Rosnovski could watch his daughter and the labrador grow up by photograph.

'We can't have him not recognising his only child when he returns home, can we?' she declared.

Florentyna would print her age and Eleanor's age in dog years firmly on the back of each photo and in a letter add the details of her progress at school, how she enjoyed tennis and swimming in the summer and football and basketball in the winter, also how her bookshelves were stacked with his old cigar boxes full of butterflies caught in a wonderful net that Mama had given her for Christmas. She added that Miss Tredgold had carefully chloroformed the butterflies before she pinned them and identified each one with its Latin name; how her mother had joined some charity committee and started taking an interest in the Polish League for Women; how she was growing vegetables in her victory garden, how she and Eleanor didn't like the meat shortage but that she liked bread and butter pudding while Eleanor preferred crunchy biscuits. She always ended each letter in the same way: 'Please come home tomorrow'.

The war stretched into 1944, and Florentyna followed the progress of the Allies in the Chicago *Tribune* and by listening to Edward R. Murrow's reports from London on the radio. Eisenhower became her idol and she nursed a secret admiration for General George Patton because he seemed to be a little bit like her father. On June 6th, the invasion of Western Europe was launched. Florentyna imagined that her father was on the beachhead and she was unable to understand how he could possibly hope to survive. She followed the Allies in their drive towards Paris on the map of Europe that Miss Tredgold had pinned to her playroom wall during the days of her lessons in Polish history. She began to believe that the war was at last coming to an end and that her father would soon return home.

She took to sitting hour after hour on the doorstep of their house on Rigg Street with Eleanor by her side watching the corner of the block. But the hours turned into days, the days into weeks, and Florentyna only became distracted from her vigil by the fact that both Presidential conventions were to be held in Chicago during the summer vacation, which gave her the opportunity to see her political hero in person.

The Republicans chose Thomas E. Dewey as their candidate in June, and later in July the Democrats again selected Roosevelt. Congressman Osborne took Florentyna along to the Amphitheatre to hear the President make his acceptance speech to the Convention. She was puzzled by the fact that whenever she saw Congressman Osborne, he was accompanied by a different woman. She must ask Miss Tredgold about that; she would be sure to have an explanation. After the candidate's speech, Florentyna stood in a long line waiting to shake hands with the President, but she was so nervous that she didn't look up as he was wheeled by.

It was the most exciting day of her life, and on the walk home she confided her interest in politics to Congressman Osborne. He did not point out to her that despite the war there wasn't a woman sitting in the Senate, and there were only two women in Congress.

In November Florentyna wrote to her father to tell him something she imagined he hadn't heard. F.D.R. had won a fourth term. She waited months for his reply.

And then the telegram came.

Miss Tredgold could not extract the missive from the mail before the child spotted the small buff envelope. Her governess immediately carried the telegram to Mrs. Rosnovski in the drawing room with a trembling Florentyna following in her wake, holding on to her skirt, with Eleanor a pace behind them. Zaphia tore the envelope open with nervous fingers, read the contents and burst into hysterical tears. 'No, no,' Florentyna cried. 'It can't be true, Mama. Tell me he's only missing,' and snatched the telegram from her speechless mother to read the contents. It read: MY WAR IS OVER, AM RETURNING HOME SOONEST, LOVE ABEL. Florentyna let out a whoop of joy and jumped on the back of Miss Tredgold, who fell into a chair that normally she would never have sat in. Eleanor, as if aware the usual codes could be broken, also jumped on the chair and started licking both of them while Zaphia burst out laughing.

Miss Tredgold could not convince Florentyna that 'soonest' might turn out to take some time since the army conducted a rigid system in deciding who should come home first, awarding points to those who had served the longest or had been wounded in battle. Florentyna remained optimistic but the weeks passed slowly.

One evening when she was returning home clutching yet another Brownie badge, this time for life-saving, she spotted a light shining through a small window that had not been lit for over three years. She forgot her life-saving achievement immediately, ran all the way down the street and had nearly beaten the door down before Miss Tredgold came to answer it. She dashed upstairs to her father's study, where she found him deep in conversation with her mother. She threw her arms around him and would not let go until finally he pushed her back to take a careful look at his eleven-year-old daughter.

'You're so much more beautiful than your photographs.'

'And you're in one piece, Papa.'

'Yes, and I won't be going away again.'

'Not without me, you won't,' said Florentyna, and clung on to him once more.

For the next few days, she pestered her father to tell her stories of the war. Had he met General Eisenhower? No. General Patton? Yes, for about ten minutes. General Bradley? Yes. Had he seen any Germans? No, but on one occasion he had helped to rescue a platoon that had been ambushed by the enemy at Remagen.

'And what happened –?'

'Enough, enough, young lady. You're worse than a staff sergeant on drill parade.'

Florentyna was so excited by her father's homecoming that she was an hour late for bed that night and still didn't sleep. Miss Tredgold reminded her how lucky she was that her Papa had returned without injury or disfigurement, unlike so many fathers of the children in her class.

When Florentyna heard that Edward Winchester's father had lost an arm at somewhere called Bastogne, she tried to tell him how sorry she was.

Abel quickly returned to the routine of his work. No one had recognised him when he first strode into the Baron: he had lost so much weight and looked so thin that the duty manager asked him who he was. The first decision Abel had to make was to order five new suits from Brooks Brothers because none of his pre-war clothes fitted him.

George Novak, as far as Abel could deduce from the annual reports he had been through, had kept the group on an even keel in his absence, even if he had taken no great strides forward. It was also from George that he learned that Henry Osborne had been re-elected to Congress for a fifth term. He asked his secretary to call Washington.

'Congratulations, Henry. Consider yourself elected to the board.'

'Thank you, Abel. You'll be glad to learn,' said Henry, 'that I have acquired six per cent of Lester's stock while you've been away rustling up gourmet dinners on Primus stoves for our top military brass.'

'Well done, Henry. What hope is there of getting our hands on the magic eight per cent?'

'A very good chance,' replied Henry. 'Peter Parfitt, who expected to be chairman of Lester's before Kane arrived on the scene, has been removed from the board and has about as much affection for Kane as a mongoose has for a cobra.

Parfitt has made it very clear that he is willing to part with his two per cent.'

'Then what's stopping us?'

'He's demanding a million dollars for his holding, because I'm sure he's worked out that his shares are all you need to topple Kane, and there are not many stockholders left for me to buy from. But a million is way above the ten per cent over current stock value that you authorised me to proceed at.'

Abel studied the figures that Henry had left on his desk for him. 'Offer him seven hundred and fifty thousand,' he said.

George was thinking about far smaller sums when he next spoke to Abel. 'I allowed Henry a loan in your absence and he still hasn't paid the money back,' he admitted.

'A loan?'

'Henry's description, not mine,' said George.

'Who's kidding who? How much?' said Abel.

'Five thousand dollars. I'm sorry, Abel.'

'Forget it. If that's the only mistake you've made in the last three years, I'm a lucky man. What do you imagine Henry spends the money on?'

'Wine, women and song. There's nothing particularly original about our Congressman. There's also a rumour around the Chicago bars that he's started gambling quite heavily.'

'That's all I need from the latest member of the board. Keep an eye on him and let me know if the situation gets any worse.'

George nodded.

'And now I want to talk about expansion. With Washington pumping three hundred million dollars a day into the economy we must be prepared for a boom the like of which America has never experienced before. We must also start building Barons in Europe while land is cheap and most people are only thinking about survival. Let's begin with London.'

'For God's sake, Abel, the place is as flat as a pancake.'

'All the better to build on, my dear.'

*

'Miss Tredgold,' said Zaphia, 'I'm going to a fashion show this afternoon in aid of the Chicago Symphony Orchestra and I might not be back before Florentyna's bedtime.'

'Very good, Mrs. Rosnovski,' said Miss Tredgold.

'I'd like to go,' said Florentyna.

Both women stared at the child in surprise.

'But it's only two days before your exams,' said Zaphia, anticipating that Miss Tredgold would thoroughly disapprove of Florentyna attending something as frivolous as a fashion show. 'What are you meant to be doing this afternoon?'

'Medieval history,' replied Miss Tredgold without hesitation. 'Charlemagne through to the Council of Trent.'

Zaphia was sad that her daughter was not being allowed to take an interest in feminine pursuits but rather was expected to act as a surrogate son, filling the gap for her husband's disappointment at not having a boy.

'Then perhaps we'd better leave it for another time,' she said. Zaphia would have liked to put her foot down but realised that if Abel found out both she and Florentyna would suffer for it later.

However, for once Miss Tredgold surprised her.

'I am not sure I agree with you, Mrs. Rosnovski,' she said. 'The occasion might well be the ideal one to introduce the child to the world of fashion and indeed of society.' Turning to Florentyna, she added, 'And a break from your studies a few days before exams can do you no harm.'

Zaphia looked at Miss Tredgold with new respect. 'Perhaps you would like to come yourself?' she added. It was the first time Zaphia had seen Miss Tredgold blush.

'No, thank you, no, I couldn't possibly.' She hesitated. 'I have letters, yes, letters to attend to, and I've set aside this afternoon to pen them.'

That afternoon, Zaphia was waiting by the main school gate dressed in a pink suit in place of Miss Tredgold in her usual sensible navy. Florentyna thought her mother looked extremely smart.

She wanted to run all the way to the fashion show and

when she actually arrived she found it hard to remain still even though her seat was in the front row. She could have touched the haughty models as they picked their way gracefully down the brilliantly lit catwalk. As the pleated skirts swirled and dipped, tight-waisted jackets were taken off to reveal elegantly bare shoulders, and sophisticated ladies in floating yards of pale organza topped with silk hats drifted silently to unknown assignations behind a red velvet curtain. Florentyna sat entranced. When the last model had turned a full circle, signalling the show had ended, a press photographer asked Zaphia if he could take her picture. 'Mama,' said Florentyna urgently as he was setting up his tripod, 'you must wear your hat further forward if you want to be thought chic.'

Mother obeyed child for the first time.

When Miss Tredgold tucked Florentyna into bed that night she asked if she had enjoyed the experience.

'Oh, yes,' said Florentyna. 'I had no idea clothes could make you look so good.'

Miss Tredgold smiled, a little wistfully.

'And did you realise that they raised over eight thousand dollars for the Chicago Symphony Orchestra? Even Papa would have been impressed by that.'

'Indeed he would,' said Miss Tredgold, 'and one day you will have to decide how to use your wealth for the benefit of other people. It is not always easy being born with money.'

The next day, Miss Tredgold pointed out to Florentyna a picture of her mother in *Women's Wear Daily* under the caption, 'Baroness Rosnovski, who enters the fashion scene in Chicago'.

'When can I go to a fashion show again?' asked Florentyna.

'Not until you have been through Charlemagne and the Council of Trent,' said Miss Tredgold.

'I wonder what Charlemagne wore when he was crowned Holy Roman Emperor,' said Florentyna.

That night, locked into her room, with only the light of a

torch to go by, she let down the hem of her school skirt and took two inches in at the waist.

Florentyna was now in her last term of middle school and Abel hoped she might win the coveted Upper School Scholarship. Florentyna was aware that her father could afford to send her to Upper School if she failed to win a scholarship, but she had plans for the money her father would save each year if she was awarded free tuition. She had studied hard that year, but she had no way of knowing how well she had done when the final examination came to an end, as one hundred and twenty-two Illinois children had entered for the examination but only four scholarships were to be awarded. Florentyna had been warned by Miss Tredgold that she would not learn the result for at least a month. 'Patience is a virtue,' Miss Tredgold reminded her, and added with mock horror that she would return to England on the next boat if Florentyna did not come in the first three places.

'Don't be silly, Miss Tredgold, I shall be first,' Florentyna replied confidently, but as the days of the month went by she began to regret her bragging and confided to Eleanor during a long walk that she might have written cosine when she had meant sine in one of the geometry questions, and created an impossible triangle. 'Perhaps I shall come in second,' she ventured over breakfast one morning.

'Then I shall move to the employ of the parents of the child who comes first,' said Miss Tredgold imperturbably.

Abel smiled as he looked up from his copy of the morning paper. 'If you win a scholarship,' he said, 'you will have saved me one thousand dollars a year. If you come top, two thousand dollars.'

'Yes, Papa, and I have plans for that.'

'Oh do you, young lady? And may I enquire what you have in mind?'

'If I win a scholarship, I want you to invest the money in Baron Group shares until I'm twenty-one, and if I'm first I want you to do the same for Miss Tredgold.'

'Good gracious, no,' said Miss Tredgold, stretching to her

full height, 'that would be most improper. I do apologise, Mr. Rosnovski, for Florentyna's impudence.'

'It's not impudence, Papa. If I finish top, half the credit must go to Miss Tredgold.'

'If not more,' said Abel, 'and I'll agree to your demands. But on one condition.' He folded his paper carefully.

'What's that?' said Florentyna.

'How much do you have in your savings account, young lady?'

'Three hundred and twelve dollars,' came back the immediate reply.

'Very well, if you fail to finish in the first four you must sacrifice the three hundred and twelve dollars to help me pay the tuition you haven't saved.'

Florentyna hesitated. Abel waited and Miss Tredgold did not comment.

'I agree,' said Florentyna at last.

'I have never bet in my life,' said Miss Tredgold, 'and I can only hope my dear father does not live to learn of this.'

'It should not concern you, Miss Tredgold.'

'It certainly does, Mr. Rosnovski. If the child is willing to gamble her only three hundred and twelve dollars on the strength of what I have managed to do for her then I must repay in kind and also offer three hundred and twelve dollars towards her education if she fails to win a scholarship.'

'Bravo,' said Florentyna, and threw her arms around her governess.

'A fool and his money are soon parted,' declared Miss Tredgold.

'Agreed,' said Abel, 'for I have lost.'

'What do you mean, Papa?' asked Florentyna. Abel turned over the newspaper to reveal a small headline that read 'The Chicago Baron's Daughter Wins Top Scholarship'.

'Mr. Rosnovski, you knew all the time.'

'True, Miss Tredgold, but it is you who have turned out to be the better poker player.'

Florentyna was overjoyed and spent the last few days of

her life at Middle School as the class heroine. Even Edward
Winchester congratulated her.

'Let's go and have a drink to celebrate,' he suggested.

'What?' said Florentyna. 'I've never had a drink before.'

'No time like the present,' said Edward, and led her to a
small classroom in the boys' end of the school. Once they
were inside, he locked the door. 'Don't want to be caught,' he
explained. Florentyna stood in admiring disbelief as Edward
lifted the lid of his desk and took out a bottle of beer, which he
prised open with a nickel. He poured the flat brown liquid
into two dirty glasses, also extracted from the desk, and
passed one over to Florentyna.

'Bottoms up,' said Edward.

'What does that mean?' asked Florentyna.

'Just drink the stuff,' he said, but Florentyna watched him
take a gulp before she plucked up the courage to try a sip.
Edward rummaged around in his jacket pocket and took out
a crumpled packet of Lucky Strikes. Florentyna couldn't
believe her eyes. The nearest she had been to a cigarette was
the advertisement she had heard on the radio which said:
'Lucky Strike means fine tobacco. Yes, Lucky Strike means
fine tobacco,' a theme that had driven Miss Tredgold mad.
Without speaking, Edward removed one of the cigarettes
from the packet, placed it between his lips, lit it and started
puffing away. He blew some smoke recklessly into the middle
of the room. Florentyna was mesmerised as he extracted a
second cigarette and placed it between her lips. She did not
dare to move as he struck another match and held the flame
to the end of the cigarette. She stood quite still for fear it
would catch her hair on fire.

'Inhale, you silly girl,' he said, so she puffed three or four
times very quickly and then started coughing.

'You can take the thing out of your mouth, you know,' he
said.

'Of course I know,' she said quickly, removing the cigarette the way she remembered Jean Harlow did in *Saratoga*.

'Good,' said Edward, and drank a large draught of his
beer.

'Good,' said Florentyna, and did the same. For the next few minutes, she kept in time with Edward as he puffed his cigarette and gulped the beer.

'Great, isn't it?' said Edward.

'Great,' replied Florentyna.

'Like another?'

'No, thank you.' Florentyna coughed. 'But it was great.'

'I've been smoking and drinking for several weeks,' announced Edward.

'Yes, I can tell,' said Florentyna.

A bell sounded in the hall, and Edward quickly returned the beer, cigarettes and two butts to his desk before unlocking the door. Florentyna walked slowly back to her classroom. She felt dizzy and sick when she reached her desk and worse when she returned home an hour later, unaware that the smell of Lucky Strikes was still on her breath. Miss Tredgold did not comment and put her to bed immediately.

The next morning Florentyna woke in terrible discomfort, scabious eruptions on her chest and face. She looked at herself in the mirror and burst into tears.

'Chicken pox,' declared Miss Tredgold to Zaphia.

Chicken pox, the doctor confirmed later, and Miss Tredgold brought Abel to visit Florentyna in her room after the doctor had completed his examination.

'What's wrong with me?' asked Florentyna anxiously.

'I can't imagine,' said her father mendaciously. 'Looks like one of the plagues of Egypt to me. What do you think, Miss Tredgold?'

'I have only seen the like of it once before, and that was with a man in my father's parish who smoked, but of course that doesn't apply in this case.'

Abel kissed his daughter on the cheek, and he and Miss Tredgold both left the room.

'Did we pull it off?' asked Abel when they had reached his study.

'I cannot be certain, Mr. Rosnovski, but I would be willing to wager one dollar that Florentyna never smokes again.'

Abel took out his wallet from an inside pocket, removed a

dollar bill and then replaced it.

'No, I think not, Miss Tredgold. I am too aware what happens when I bet with you.'

Florentyna once heard her headmistress remark that some incidents in history are so powerful in their impact that everyone can tell you exactly where they were when they first heard the news.

On April 12th, 1945, at four forty-seven Abel was talking to a man representing a product called Pepsi-Cola who was pressing him to try out the drink in all the Baron hotels. Zaphia was shopping in Marshall Field's and Miss Tredgold had just come out of the United Artists Theatre where she had seen Humphrey Bogart in *Casablanca* for the third time. Florentyna was in her room looking up the word 'teen-ager' in Webster's Dictionary. The word was not yet acknowledged by Webster's when Franklin D. Roosevelt died in Warm Springs, Georgia.

Of all the tributes to the late President Florentyna read during the next few days, the one she kept for the rest of her life was from the New York *Post*. It read simply:

Washington, April 19th – Following are the latest casualties in the military services including next of kin.

ARMY – NAVY DEAD

ROOSEVELT, Franklin D., Commander-in-Chief, wife Mrs. Anna Eleanor Roosevelt, The White House.

6

ENTERING UPPER SCHOOL AT Girls Latin prompted Florentyna's second trip to New York, as the only establishments that stocked the official school uniform were Marshall Field's in Chicago and, for shoes, Abercrombie & Fitch in New York. Abel snorted and declared it was inverted snobbery of the worst kind. Nevertheless as he had to travel to New York to check on the newly opened Baron, he agreed as a special treat to accompany Miss Tredgold and his eleven-year-old daughter on their journey to Madison Avenue.

Abel had long considered New York to be the only major city in the world not to boast a first-class hotel. He admired the Plaza, the Pierre and the Carlyle but did not think that any of the three held a candle to Claridge's in London, the George V in Paris or the Danieli in Venice, and only those achieved the standards he was trying to reproduce for the New York Baron.

Florentyna was aware that Papa was spending more and more time in New York, and it saddened her that the affection between her father and mother now seemed to be a thing of the past. The rows were becoming so frequent that she wondered if she was in any way to blame.

Once Miss Tredgold had purchased everything on the list that was available at Marshall Field's – three blue sweaters (navy), three blue skirts (navy), four shirts (white), six blue bloomers (dark), six pairs of grey socks (light), one navy-blue silk dress with white collar and cuffs – she planned the trip to New York.

Florentyna and Miss Tredgold took the train to Grand Central Station and on arrival in New York went straight to Abercrombie & Fitch where they selected two pairs of brown Oxfords.

'Such sensible shoes,' proclaimed Miss Tredgold. 'Nobody who wears Abercrombies needs fear going through life with flat feet.' They then proceeded on to Fifth Avenue. Miss Tredgold had walked several yards before she realised she was on her own. Turning around, she observed Florentyna's nose pressed against the pane of Elizabeth Arden's. She walked quickly back to join her. 'Ten shades of lipstick for the sophisticated woman,' read the sign in the window.

'Rose red is my favourite,' said Florentyna hopefully.

'The school rules are very clear,' said Miss Tredgold authoritatively. 'No lipstick, no nail polish, and no jewelry except a ring and a watch.'

Florentyna reluctantly left the rose-red lipstick and joined her governess on her march up Fifth Avenue towards the Plaza Hotel where her father was expecting them at the Palm Court for tea. Abel could not resist returning to the hotel where he had served his apprenticeship as a junior waiter, and although he recognised no one except Old Sammy, the head waiter in the Oak Room, everyone knew exactly who he was.

After macaroons and ice cream for Florentyna, a cup of coffee for Abel, and lemon tea and a watercress sandwich for Miss Tredgold, Abel returned to work. Miss Tredgold checked her New York itinerary and took Florentyna to the top of the Empire State Building. As the elevator reached the one hundred and second floor Florentyna felt quite giddy and they both burst out laughing when they discovered fog had come in from the East River and they couldn't even see as far as the Chrysler Building. Miss Tredgold checked her list again and decided that their time would be better spent visiting the Metropolitan Museum. Mr. Francis Henry Taylor, the director, had just acquired a large canvas by Pablo Picasso. The oil painting turned out to be a woman with two heads and one breast coming out of her shoulder.

'What do you think of that?' asked Florentyna.

'Not a lot,' said Miss Tredgold. 'I rather suspect that when he was at school he received the same sort of art reports as you do now.'

Florentyna always enjoyed staying in one of her father's hotels when she was on a trip. She would happily spend hours walking around trying to pick up mistakes the hotel was making. After all, she pointed out to Miss Tredgold, they had their investment to consider. Over dinner that night in the Grill Room of the New York Baron, Florentyna told her father that she didn't think much of the hotel shops.

'What's wrong with them?' asked Abel, mouthing questions without paying much attention to the answers.

'Nothing you can point to easily,' said Florentyna, 'except that they are all dreadfully dull compared with real shops like the ones on Fifth Avenue.'

Abel scribbled a note on the back of his menu, 'shops dreadfully dull', and doodled around it carefully before he said: 'I shall not be returning to Chicago with you tomorrow, Florentyna.'

For once Florentyna was silent.

'Some problems have arisen with the hotel at this end and I must stay behind to see they don't get out of hand,' he said, sounding a little too well rehearsed.

Florentyna gripped her father's hand. 'Try and come back tomorrow. Eleanor and I always miss you.'

Once Florentyna had returned to Chicago Miss Tredgold set about preparing her for Upper School. Each day they would spend two hours studying a different subject but Florentyna was allowed to choose whether they should work in the mornings or the afternoons. The only exception to this rule was on Thursdays, when their sessions took place in the morning as it was Miss Tredgold's afternoon off.

At two o'clock promptly every Thursday she would leave the house and not return until seven that night. She never explained where she was going, and Florentyna never summoned up the courage to ask. But as the holiday progressed

Florentyna became more and more curious about where Miss Tredgold spent her time, until finally she resolved to discover for herself.

After a Thursday morning of Latin and a light lunch together in the kitchen, Miss Tredgold said goodbye to Florentyna and retired to her room. As two o'clock struck she opened the front door of the house and headed off down the street carrying a large canvas bag. Florentyna watched her carefully through her bedroom window. Once Miss Tredgold had turned the corner of Rigg Street, Florentyna dashed out and ran all the way to the end of the block. She peered around to see her mentor waiting at a bus stop just ten yards away. She could feel her heart beating at the thought of not being able to follow Miss Tredgold any farther. Within minutes she watched a bus draw up and come to a halt. She was about to turn back for home when she noticed Miss Tredgold disappear up the circular staircase of the double-decker. Without hesitation, Florentyna ran and jumped on to the moving platform, then quickly made her way to the front of the bus.

When the ticket collector asked her where she was going Florentyna suddenly realised she had no idea of her destination.

'How far do you go?' she asked.

The collector looked at her suspiciously. 'The Loop,' he replied.

'One single for the Loop then,' said Florentyna confidently.

'That'll be fifteen cents,' said the conductor.

Florentyna fumbled in her jacket pocket to discover she had only ten cents.

'How far can I go for ten cents?'

'Rylands School,' came back the reply.

Florentyna passed over the money, praying that Miss Tredgold would reach her destination before she would have to get off, while not giving any thought to how she would make the return journey.

She sat low in her seat and watched carefully each time the

bus came to a halt, but even after she had counted twelve stops Miss Tredgold still did not appear as the bus travelled along Lake Front, passing the University of Chicago.

'Your stop is next,' the conductor said firmly.

When the bus next came to a halt at Seventy-first Street, Florentyna knew she was beaten. She stepped down reluctantly on to the pavement thinking about the long walk home and determined that the following week she would have enough money to cover the journey both ways.

She stood unhappily watching the bus as it travelled a few hundred yards farther down the street before coming to a stop once more. A figure stepped out into the road which could only have been Miss Tredgold. She disappeared down a side street, looking as if she knew exactly where she was going.

Florentyna ran as hard as she could, but when she reached the corner, breathless, there was no sign of Miss Tredgold. Florentyna walked slowly down the street wondering where her governess could have gone. Perhaps into one of the houses, or might she have taken another side street? Florentyna decided she would walk to the end of the road and if she failed to spot her quarry then she would have to make her way home.

Just at the point when she was considering turning back she came into an opening that faced a large wrought-iron archway which had embossed on it in gold: South Shore Country Club.

Florentyna didn't consider for a moment that Miss Tredgold could be inside, but out of curiosity she peered through the gates.

'What do you want?' said a uniformed guard standing on the other side.

'I was looking for my governess,' said Florentyna lamely.

'What's her name?'

'Miss Tredgold,' Florentyna said unflinchingly.

'She's already gone into the club house,' said the guard, pointing towards a Victorian building surrounded by trees about a quarter of a mile up a steep rise.

Florentyna marched boldly through, without another word, staying on the path because 'Keep off the grass' signs were displayed every few yards. She kept her eye on the club house and had ample time to leap behind a tree when she saw Miss Tredgold emerge. She hardly recognised the lady dressed in red and yellow check tweed trousers, a heavy Fair Isle sweater and heavy brown brogues. A bag of golf clubs was slung comfortably over one shoulder.

Florentyna stared at her governess, mesmerised.

Miss Tredgold walked towards the first tee where she put down her bag and took out a ball. She placed it on a tee at her feet and selected a club from her bag. After a few practice swings she steadied herself, addressed the ball and hit it firmly down the middle of the fairway. Florentyna couldn't believe her eyes. She wanted to applaud but instead ran forward to hide behind another tree as Miss Tredgold marched off down the fairway.

Miss Tredgold's second shot landed only twenty yards from the edge of the green. Florentyna ran forward to a clump of trees at the side of the fairway and watched Miss Tredgold chip her ball up on to the green and hole it with two putts. Florentyna was left in no doubt that Miss Tredgold had been playing the game for some considerable time.

Miss Tredgold then removed a small white card from her jacket pocket and wrote on it, before heading towards the second tee. As she did so she gazed towards the second green, which was to the left of where Florentyna was hidden. Once again Miss Tredgold steadied herself, addressed the ball and swung, but this time she sliced her shot and the ball ended up only fifteen yards away from Florentyna's hiding place.

Florentyna looked up at the trees but they had not been made for climbing other than by a cat. She held her breath and crouched behind the widest but could not resist watching Miss Tredgold as she studied the lay of her ball. Miss Tredgold muttered something inaudible and then selected a club. Florentyna let out her breath as Miss Tredgold swung. The ball climbed high and straight before landing in the middle of the fairway again.

Florentyna watched Miss Tredgold replace her club in the bag.

'I should have kept a straighter arm on the first shot and then we would never have met.'

Florentyna assumed Miss Tredgold was admonishing herself yet again, and remained behind the tree.

'Come here, child.' Florentyna obediently ran out but said nothing.

Miss Tredgold took another ball from the side pocket of her bag and placed it on the ground in front of her. She selected a club and handed it to her charge.

'Try to hit the ball in that direction,' she said, pointing towards a flag about a hundred yards away.

Florentyna held the club awkwardly before taking several swings at the ball, on each occasion removing what Miss Tredgold called 'divots'. At last she managed to push it twenty yards towards the fairway. She beamed with pleasure.

'I see we are in for a long afternoon,' declared Miss Tredgold resignedly.

'I am sorry,' said Florentyna. 'Can you ever forgive me?'

'For following me, yes. But for the state of your golf, no. We shall have to start with the basics, as it seems in the future I am no longer to have Thursday afternoons to myself, now you have discovered my father's only sin.'

Miss Tredgold taught Florentyna how to play golf with the same energy and application as if it were Latin or Greek. By the end of the summer Florentyna's favourite afternoon was Thursday.

Upper School was very different from Middle School. There was a new teacher for every subject rather than one teacher for everything except gym. The pupils had to move from room to room for their classes, and for many of the activities the girls joined forces with the boys' school. Florentyna's favourite subjects were current affairs, Latin, French and English, although she couldn't wait for her twice-weekly biology classes because they gave her the chance to admire the school's collection of bugs under the microscope.

'Insects, dear child. You must refer to the little creatures as insects,' Miss Tredgold insisted.

'Actually, Miss Tredgold, they're nematodes.'

Florentyna also continued to take an interest in clothes and noticed that the mode for short dresses caused by the enforced economies of war was fast becoming outdated and that once again skirts were nearly reaching the ground. She was unable to do much about experimenting with fashion, as the school uniform was the same year in and year out; the children's department of Marshall Field's, it seemed, was not a great contributor to *Vogue*. However, she studied all the relevant magazines in the library and pestered her mother to take her to more shows. For Miss Tredgold, on the other hand, who had never allowed any man to see her knees, even in the self-denying days of Lend-Lease, the new fashion only proved she had been right all along.

At the end of Florentyna's first year in Upper School the modern languages mistress decided to put on a performance of *Saint Joan* in French. As Florentyna was the only pupil who could think in the language, she was chosen to play the Maid of Orleans and rehearsed for hours in the old nursery with Miss Tredgold playing every other part as well as being prompter and cue reader. Even when Florentyna was word-perfect, Miss Tredgold sat loyally through the daily one-woman shows.

'Only the Pope and I give audiences for one,' she told Florentyna as the phone rang.

'It's for you,' said Miss Tredgold.

Florentyna always enjoyed receiving phone calls, although it was not a practice that Miss Tredgold encouraged.

'Hello, it's Edward. I need your help.'

'Why? Don't tell me you've learnt to read?'

'No hope of that, silly. But I've been given the part of the Dauphin and I can't pronounce all the words.'

Florentyna tried not to laugh. 'Come around at five thirty and you can join the daily rehearsals. Although I must warn you, Miss Tredgold has been making a very good Dauphin up to now.'

Edward came around every night at five thirty and although Miss Tredgold occasionally frowned when 'the boy' lapsed back into an American accent he was 'just about ready' by the day of the dress rehearsal.

When the night of the performance itself came, Miss Tredgold instructed Florentyna and Edward that under no circumstances must they look out into the audience hoping to spot their parents, otherwise those watching the performance would not believe in the characters they were portraying. Most unprofessional, Miss Tredgold considered, and reminded Florentyna that Mr. Noël Coward once left a performance of *Romeo and Juliet* because Mr. John Gielgud looked straight at him during a soliloquy. Florentyna was convinced, though in truth she had no idea who Mr. John Gielgud or Mr. Noël Coward were.

When the curtain went up, Florentyna did not once look beyond the footlights. Miss Tredgold considered her efforts 'most commendable', and during the intermission particularly commented to Florentyna's mother on the scene in which the Maid is alone in the centre of the stage and talks to her voices. 'Moving', was Miss Tredgold's description. 'Unquestionably moving'. When the curtain finally fell, Florentyna received a rapturous ovation, even from those who had not been able to follow every word in French. Edward stood a pace behind her, relieved to have come through the ordeal without too many mistakes. Glowing with excitement, Florentyna removed her make-up, her first experience of lipstick and powder, changed back into her school uniform and joined her mother and Miss Tredgold with the other parents who were having coffee in the dining hall. Several people came over to congratulate her on her performance including the headmaster of the Boys Latin School.

'A remarkable achievement for a girl of her age,' he told Mrs. Rosnovski. 'Though when you think about it she is only a couple of years younger than Saint Joan was when she challenged the entire might of the French establishment.'

'Saint Joan didn't have to learn someone else's lines in a foreign language,' said Zaphia, feeling pleased with herself.

Florentyna did not take in her mother's words as her eyes were searching the crowded hall for her father.

'Where's Papa?' she asked.

'He couldn't make it tonight.'

'But he promised,' said Florentyna. 'He *promised*.' Tears welled up in her eyes as she suddenly realised why Miss Tredgold had told her not to look beyond the footlights.

'You must remember, child, that your father is a very busy man. He has a small empire to run.'

'So did Saint Joan,' said Florentyna.

When Florentyna went to bed that night, Miss Tredgold came to turn out her light.

'Papa doesn't love Mama any more, does he?'

The bluntness of the question took Miss Tredgold by surprise and it was a few moments before she recovered.

'Of only one thing I am certain, child, and that is that they both love you.'

'Then why has Papa stopped coming home?'

'That I cannot explain but whatever his reasons we must be very understanding and grown-up,' said Miss Tredgold, brushing back a lock of hair that had fallen over Florentyna's forehead.

Florentyna felt very ungrown-up and wondered if Saint Joan had been so unhappy when she lost her beloved France. When Miss Tredgold closed the door quietly Florentyna put her hand under the bed to feel the reassuring wet nose of Eleanor. 'At least I'll always have you,' she whispered. Eleanor clambered up from her hiding place on to the bed and settled down next to Florentyna, facing the door: a quick retreat to her basket in the kitchen might prove necessary if Miss Tredgold reappeared.

Florentyna did not see her father during that summer vacation and had long stopped believing the stories that the growing hotel empire was keeping him away from Chicago. Whenever she mentioned him to her mother, Zaphia's replies were often bitter. Florentyna also found out from overheard telephone conversations that she was consulting lawyers.

Each day Florentyna would take Eleanor for a walk down Michigan Avenue in the hope that she might see her father's car drive by. One Wednesday, she decided to make a break in her routine and walk on the west side of the Avenue to study the stores that set the fashions for the Windy City. Eleanor was delighted to be reunited with the magnificent lampposts that had recently been placed for her at twenty-yard intervals. Florentyna had already purchased a wedding dress and a ball gown with her five dollars a week pocket money and was coveting an elegant five-hundred-dollar evening dress in the window of Martha Weathereds' on the corner of Oak Street when she saw her father's reflection in the glass. She turned, overjoyed, to see him coming out of Spaulding's on the opposite side of the street. Without a thought she dashed out into the road not looking either way as she called her father's name. A yellow cab jammed on its brakes and swerved violently, the driver aware of a flash of blue skirt then the heavy thud as the cab made contact. The rest of the traffic came to a screeching halt as the cab driver saw a stout, well-dressed man, followed by a policeman, run out into the middle of the road. A moment later Abel and the taxi driver stood in a state of shock staring down at the lifeless body. 'She's dead,' said the policeman, shaking his head, as he took out his notebook from his top pocket.

Abel fell on his knees, trembling. He looked up at the policeman. 'And the worst thing about it is I am to blame.'

'No, Papa, it was my fault,' wept Florentyna. 'I should never have rushed out into the road. I killed Eleanor by not thinking.'

The driver of the taxi that had hit the labrador explained that he had had no choice, he had to hit the dog to avoid colliding with the girl.

Abel nodded, picked up his daughter and carried her to the side of the road, not letting her look back at Eleanor's mangled body. He placed Florentyna in the back of his car and returned to the policeman.

'My name is Abel Rosno –'

'I know who you are, sir.'

'Can I leave everything to you, officer?'

'Yes, sir,' said the policeman, not looking up from his notebook.

Abel returned to his chauffeur and told him to drive them to the Baron. Abel held his daughter's hand as they walked through the crowded hotel corridor to the private elevator that whisked them to the forty-second floor. George met them when the gates sprang open. He was about to greet his goddaughter with a Polish quip when he saw the look on her face.

'Ask Miss Tredgold to come over immediately, George.'

'Of course,' said George, and disappeared into his own office.

Abel sat and listened to several stories about Eleanor without interrupting before tea and sandwiches arrived but Florentyna managed only a sip of milk. Then without any warning she changed the subject.

'Why don't you ever come home, Papa?' she asked.

Abel poured himself another cup of tea, a little spilling into the saucer. 'I've wanted to come home many times, and I hated missing *Saint Joan*, but your mother and I are going to be divorced.'

'Oh no, it can't be true. Papa . . .'

'It's my fault, little one. I have not been a good husband and . . .'

Florentyna threw her arms around her father. 'Does that mean I will never see you again?'

'No. I have made an agreement with your mother that you shall remain in Chicago while you are at school, but you will spend the rest of the time with me in New York. Of course you can always talk to me on the telephone whenever you want to.'

Florentyna remained silent as Abel gently stroked her hair.

Some time passed before there was a knock on the door and Miss Tredgold entered, her long dress swishing across the carpet as she came quickly to Florentyna's side.

'Can you take her home please, Miss Tredgold?'

'Of course, Mr. Rosnovski.' Florentyna was still tearful. 'Come with me, child,' she said. Bending down, she whispered, 'Try not to show your feelings.'

The twelve-year-old girl kissed her father on the forehead, took Miss Tredgold's hand and left.

When the door closed, Abel, not having been brought up by Miss Tredgold, sat alone and wept.

7

IT WAS AT THE beginning of her second year in Upper School that Florentyna first became aware of Pete Welling. He was sitting in a corner of the music room, playing the latest Broadway hit, 'Almost Like Being in Love' on the piano. He was slightly out of tune but Florentyna assumed it must be the piano. Pete didn't seem to notice her as she passed him, so she turned around and walked back again, but to no avail. He put a hand nonchalantly through his fair wavy hair and continued playing the piano, so she marched off pretending she hadn't seen him. By lunchtime the next day she knew that he was two grades above her, where he lived, that he was vice-captain of the football team, president of his class, and nearly seventeen. Her friend Susie Jacobson warned her that others had trod the same path without a great deal of success.

'But I assure you,' replied Florentyna, 'I have something to offer that will prove irresistible.'

That afternoon she sat down and composed what she imagined to be her first love letter. After much deliberation she chose purple ink and wrote in a bold slanting hand:

My dear Pete,
      I knew you were something special the first time I saw

you. I think you play the piano beautifully. Would you like
to come and listen to some records at my place?
                              Very sincerely,
                              Florentyna (Rosnovski)

Florentyna waited for the break before she crept down the
corridor, imagining every eye to be on her as she searched for
Pete Welling's hall locker. When she found it, she checked his
name against the number on the top of the locker. Forty-
two – she felt that was a good omen – and opened his locker
door, left her letter on top of a maths book, where he couldn't
miss it and returned to her classroom, palms sweating. She
checked her own locker, on the hour every hour, expecting
his reply, but none was forthcoming. After a week had
passed, she began to despair until she saw Pete sitting on the
steps of the chapel combing his hair. How daring to break
two school rules at once, she thought. Florentyna decided
this was her chance to find out if he had ever received her
invitation.

She walked boldly towards him, but with only a yard to go
she wished he would disappear in a cloud of dust because she
couldn't think of anything to say. She stood still like a lamb in
the gaze of a python but he saved her by saying, 'Hi.'

'Hi,' she managed. 'Did you ever find my letter?'

'Your letter?'

'Yes, I wrote to you last Monday about coming over to
play some records at my place. I've got "Silent Night", and
most of Bing Crosby's latest hits. Have you heard him
singing "White Christmas"?' she asked, playing her trump
card.

'Oh, it was you who wrote that letter,' he said.

'Yes, I saw you play against Francis Parker last week. You
were fantastic. Who are you playing next?'

'It's in the school calendar,' he said, putting his comb into
an inside pocket and looking over her shoulder.

'I'll be in the stands.'

'I'm sure you will,' he said as a tall blonde from the senior class wearing little white socks that Florentyna felt sure were not official school uniform ran over to Pete and asked if he had been waiting long.

'No, only a couple of minutes,' said Pete, and put his arm around her waist before turning back to Florentyna. 'I'm afraid you'll just have to get in line. But perhaps your time will come,' he said, laughing. 'In any case, I think Crosby's a square. Bix Beiderbecke is my man.'

As they walked away, Florentyna could hear him telling the blonde, 'That was the girl who sent me the note.' The blonde looked back over her shoulder and started laughing. 'She's probably still a virgin,' Pete added.

Florentyna went to the girls' locker room and hid until everyone else had gone home, dreading that they would all laugh at her once the story had gone the rounds. She didn't sleep that night, and the next morning she studied the other girls' faces but couldn't see any signs of sniggers or stares and decided to confide in Susie Jacobson to discover if the news was out. When Florentyna had finished her story, Susie burst out laughing.

'Not you as well,' Susie said.

Florentyna felt a lot better after Susie told her how far down the line she actually was. It gave her the courage to ask Susie if she knew what a virgin was.

'I'm not certain,' said Susie. 'Why do you ask?'

'Because Pete said I was probably one.'

'Then I think I must be one as well. I once overheard Mary Alice Beckman saying it was when a boy made love to you and nine months later you had a baby. Like Miss Horton told us about elephants, but they take two years.'

'I wonder what it feels like?'

'According to all the magazines Mary Alice keeps in her locker, it's dreamy.'

'Do you know anyone who's tried?'

'Margie McCormick claims she has.'

'She would claim anything, and if she has, why hasn't she had a baby?'

'She said she took "precautions", whatever they are.'

'If it's anything like having a period, I can't believe it's worth all the trouble,' said Florentyna.

'Agreed,' said Susie. 'I got mine again yesterday. Do you think men have the same problem?'

'Not a chance,' said Florentyna. 'They always end up with the best of every deal. Obviously we get the periods and the babies and they get shaving and the draft, but I shall have to ask Miss Tredgold about that.'

'I'm not sure she'll know,' said Susie.

'Miss Tredgold,' said Florentyna sounding confident, 'knows everything.'

That evening when Miss Tredgold was approached by a puzzled Florentyna, she did not hesitate to sit the child down and explain the birth process to her in the fullest details, warning her of the consequences of a rash desire to experiment. Florentyna sat and listened to Miss Tredgold in silence. When she had finished Florentyna asked, 'Then why is so much fuss made about the whole thing?'

'Modern society and loose morals make a lot of demands on girls, but always remember that each of us makes our own decision as to what others think of us and, more importantly, what we think of ourselves.'

'She *did* know all about becoming pregnant and having babies,' Florentyna said to Susie the next day with great authority.

'Does that mean you're going to remain a virgin?' asked Susie.

'Oh, yes,' said Florentyna. 'Miss Tredgold is still one.'

'But what about "precautions"?' demanded Susie.

'You don't need them if you remain a virgin,' Florentyna said, passing on her newly acquired knowledge.

The only other event of importance that year for Florentyna was her confirmation. Although Father O'Reilly, a young priest from the Holy Name Cathedral, officially instructed her, Miss Tredgold, resolutely suppressing the Church of England tenets of her youth, studied the Roman Catholic 'Orders in Confirmation' and took Florentyna painstakingly through her preparation, leaving her in no doubt of the obligations that her promises to our dear Lord brought upon her. The Roman Catholic Archbishop of Chicago, assisted by Father O'Reilly, administered the confirmation, and both Abel and Zaphia attended the service. Their divorce having been completed, they sat in separate pews.

Florentyna wore a simple white dress with a high neck, the hem falling a few inches below the knee. She had made the dress herself, with – when she was asleep – a little help from Miss Tredgold. The original design had come from a photograph in *Paris Match* of a dress worn by Princess Elizabeth. Miss Tredgold had brushed Florentyna's long dark hair for over an hour until it shone. She even allowed it to fall to her shoulders. Although she was only thirteen, the young confirmand looked stunning.

'My goddaughter is beautiful,' said George as he stood next to Abel in the front pew of the church.

'I know,' said Abel.

'No, I'm serious,' said George. 'Very soon there is going to be a line of men banging on the Baron's castle door demanding the hand of his only daughter.'

'As long as she's happy, I don't mind who she marries.'

After the service was over the family had a celebration dinner in Abel's private rooms at the Baron. Florentyna received gifts from her family and friends, including a beautiful leather-bound version of the Douai Bible from Miss Tredgold, but the present she treasured most was the one her father had kept safely until he felt she was old enough to appreciate it, the antique ring that had been given to Florentyna on her christening by the man who had put his faith in Papa and backed the Baron Group.

'I must write and thank him,' said Florentyna.

'You can't, my dear, as I am not certain who he is. I honoured my part of the bargain long ago, so now I will probably never discover his true identity.'

She slipped the antique ring on to the third finger of her left hand and throughout the rest of the day her eyes returned again and again to the sparkling little emeralds.

8

'How WILL YOU BE voting in the Presidential election, madam?' asked the smartly dressed young man.

'I shall not be voting,' said Miss Tredgold, continuing down the street.

'Shall I put you down as "Don't know"?' said the man, running to keep up with her.

'Most certainly not,' said Miss Tredgold. 'I made no such suggestion.'

'Am I to understand you don't wish to state your preference?'

'I am quite happy to state my preference, young man, but as I come from Much Hadham in England it is unlikely to influence either Mr. Truman or Mr. Dewey.'

The man conducting the Gallup Poll retreated, but Florentyna watched him carefully because she had read somewhere that the results of such polls were now being taken seriously by all leading politicians.

It was 1948, and America was in the middle of another election campaign. Unlike the Olympics, the race for the White House was re-run every four years, war or peace. Florentyna remained loyal to the Democrats but did not see how President Truman could possibly hold on to the White House after two such unpopular years as President. The Republican candidate, Thomas E. Dewey, had a lead of over eight per cent in the latest Gallup Poll and looked certain of victory.

Florentyna followed both campaigns closely and was delighted when Margaret Chase Smith beat three men to be chosen as the Republican Senatorial candidate for Maine. For the first time, the American people were able to follow the election on television. Abel had installed an R.C.A. set at Rigg Street only months before he departed, but during term time Miss Tredgold would not allow Florentyna to watch 'that new-fangled machine' for more than one hour a day. 'It can never be a substitute for the written word,' she declared. 'I agree with Professor Chester L. Dawes of Harvard,' she added. 'Too many instant decisions will be made in front of the cameras that will later be regretted.'

Although she did not fully agree with Miss Tredgold's sentiments at the time, Florentyna selected her hour carefully, always choosing the C.B.S. evening news, during which Douglas Edwards would give the campaign round-up, over Ed Sullivan's more popular 'Toast of the Town'. However, she still found time to listen to Ed Murrow on the radio. After all his broadcasts from London during the war, she, like so many other millions of Americans, remained loyal to his every word. She felt it was the least she could do.

During the summer vacation Florentyna parked herself in Congressman Osborne's campaign headquarters and, along with scores of other volunteers of assorted ages and ability, filled envelopes with 'A Message from your Congressman' and a bumper sticker that said in bold print 'Re-elect Osborne'. She and a pale, angular youth who never proffered any opinions would then lick the flap of each envelope and place it on a pile according to district, for hand delivery by another helper. By the end of each day her mouth and lips were covered in gum and she would return home feeling thirsty and sick.

One Thursday the receptionist in charge of the telephone enquiries asked if Florentyna could take her place while she took a break for lunch.

'Of course,' said Florentyna with tremendous excitement, and jumped into the vacated seat before the pale youth could volunteer.

'There shouldn't be any problems,' the receptionist said. 'Just say Congressman Osborne's office, and if you're not sure of anything, look it up in the campaign handbook. Everything you need to know is in there,' she added, pointing to the thick booklet by the side of the phone.

'I'll be just fine,' said Florentyna.

She sat in the exalted chair, staring at the phone, willing it to ring. She didn't have to wait long. The first caller was a man who wanted to know where he voted. That's a strange question, thought Florentyna.

'At the polls,' she said, a little pertly.

'Sure, I know that, you stupid bitch,' came back the reply. 'But where is my polling place?'

Florentyna was speechless for a moment, and then asked, very politely, where he lived.

'In the Seventh Precinct.'

Florentyna flicked through her guide. 'You should vote at Saint Chrysostom's Church on Dearborn Street.'

'Where's that?'

Florentyna studied the map. 'The church is located five blocks from the lake shore and fifteen blocks north of the Loop.' The phone clicked and immediately rang again.

'Is that Osborne's headquarters?'

'Yes, sir,' said Florentyna.

'Well, you can tell that lazy bastard I wouldn't vote for him if he was the only candidate alive.' The phone clicked again and Florentyna felt queasier than she had been when she was licking envelopes. She let the bell ring three times before she could summon up the courage to lift the receiver to answer.

'Hello,' she said nervously. 'This is Congressman Osborne's headquarters. Miss Rosnovski speaking.'

'Hello, my dear, my name is Daisy Bishop, and I will need a car to take my husband to the polls on election day because he lost both his legs in the last war.'

'Oh, I'm so sorry,' said Florentyna.

'Don't worry yourself, young lady. We wouldn't let wonderful Mr. Roosevelt down.'

'But Mr. Roosevelt is . . . Yes, of course you wouldn't. Can I please take down your telephone number and address?'

'Mr. and Mrs. Bishop, 653 West Buena Street, MA4–4816.'

'We will phone you on election morning to let you know what time the car will pick you up. Thank you for supporting the Democratic ticket, Mrs. Bishop,' said Florentyna.

'We always do, my dear. Goodbye and good luck.'

'Goodbye,' said Florentyna, who took a deep breath and felt a little better. She wrote down a '2' in brackets – after the Bishops' name and placed the note in the file marked 'Transportation for Election Day'. Then she waited for the next call.

It was some minutes before the phone sounded again and by then Florentyna had fully regained her confidence.

'Good morning, is this the Osborne office?'

'Yes, sir,' said Florentyna.

'My name is Melvin Crudick and I want to know Congressman Osborne's views on the Marshall Plan.'

'The what plan?' said Florentyna.

'The Marshall Plan,' enunciated the voice authoritatively.

Florentyna frantically flipped the pages of the campaign handbook that she had been promised would reveal everything.

'Are you still there?' barked the voice.

'Yes, sir,' said Florentyna. 'I just wanted to be sure you were given a full and detailed answer on the Congressman's views. If you would be kind enough to wait one moment.'

At last Florentyna found the Marshall Plan and read through Henry Osborne's words on the subject.

'Hello, sir.'

'Yes,' said the voice, and Florentyna started to read it out loud.

' "Congressman Osborne approves of the Marshall Plan." ' There was a long silence.

'Yes, I know he does,' said the voice from the other end.

Florentyna felt weak. 'Yes, he does support the plan,' she repeated.

'*Why* does he?' said the voice.

'Because it will benefit everyone in his district,' said Florentyna firmly, feeling rather pleased with herself.

'Pray tell me, how can giving six billion American dollars to Europe help the Ninth District of Illinois?' Florentyna could feel the perspiration on her forehead. 'Miss, you may inform your Congressman that because of your personal incompetence I shall be voting Republican on this occasion.'

Florentyna put the phone down and was considering running out of the door when the receptionist returned from her lunch. Florentyna did not know what to tell her.

'Anything interesting?' the girl asked as she resumed her place. 'Or was it the usual mixture of weirdos, perverts and cranks who have got nothing better to do with their lunch break?'

'Nothing special,' said Florentyna, nervously, 'except I think I've lost the vote of a Mr. Crudick.'

'Not Mad Mel again? What was it this time, the House Un-American Activities Committee, the Marshall Plan or the slums of Chicago?'

Florentyna returned happily to licking envelopes.

On election day, Florentyna arrived at campaign headquarters at eight o'clock in the morning and spent the day telephoning registered Democrats to be sure they had voted. 'Never forget,' said Henry Osborne in his final pep talk to his voluntary helpers, 'no man has ever lived in the White House who hasn't carried Illinois.'

Florentyna felt very proud to think she was helping to elect a President and didn't take a break all day. At eight o'clock that evening, Miss Tredgold came to collect her. She had worked twelve hours without a rest, but never once did she stop talking all the way home.

'Do you think Mr. Truman will win?' she asked finally.

'Only if he gets more than fifty per cent of the votes cast,' said Miss Tredgold.

'Wrong,' said Florentyna. 'It is possible to win a Presidential election in the United States by winning more electoral college votes than your opponent while failing to secure a majority of the plebiscite.' She then proceeded to give Miss Tredgold a brief lesson on how the American political system worked.

'Such a thing would never have happened if only dear George III had known where America was,' said Miss Tredgold. 'And I daily become aware that it will not be long before you have no further need of me, child.'

It was the first time Florentyna had ever considered that Miss Tredgold would not spend the rest of her life with her.

When they reached home, Florentyna sat down in her father's old chair to watch the early returns, but she was so tired that she dozed off in front of the fire. She, like most of America, went to sleep believing that Thomas Dewey had won the election. When Florentyna woke the next morning, she dashed downstairs to fetch the *Tribune*. Her fears were confirmed: 'Dewey Defeats Truman' ran the headline, and it took half an hour of radio bulletins and confirmation by her mother before Florentyna believed that Truman had been returned to the White House. An eleven o'clock decision had been made by the night editor of the *Tribune* to run a headline that he would not live down for the rest of his life. At least he had been right about Henry Osborne being returned to Congress for a sixth term.

When Florentyna went back to Girls Latin the next day, her home-room teacher called for her and made it quite clear that the election was now over and that the time had come to settle down and do some serious studying. Miss Tredgold agreed, and Florentyna worked with the same enthusiasm for her school exams as she had for President Truman.

During the year, she made the junior varsity hockey team, in which she played right wing without distinction and even managed to squeeze into the school's third tennis VI on one occasion. When the summer term was drawing to a close all the pupils received a note reminding them that if they wished to run for the Student Council their names must be sent to the headmaster of Boys Latin by the first Monday of the new school year. There were six representatives on the Council elected from both schools, and no one could remember a year when they had not all come from the twelfth grade. Nevertheless many of Florentyna's classmates suggested that she should allow her name to be put forward. Edward Winchester, who had years before given up trying to beat Florentyna at anything except arm wrestling, volunteered to help her.

'But anyone who helps me would have to be talented, good looking, popular and charismatic,' she teased.

'For once I agree with you,' said Edward. 'Any fool taking on such a cause will need every advantage possible to overcome the problem of their candidate being stupid, ugly, unapproachable and dull.'

'In which case it might be wise for me to wait another year.'

'Never,' said Edward. 'I can see no hope of improvement in such a short time. In any case, I want you on the council this year.'

'Why?'

'Because if you're the only eleventh grade student elected you'll be a near cert for President next year.'

'Really thought the whole thing through, haven't you?'

'And I would be willing to bet everything in my piggy bank that you have too.'

'Perhaps . . .' said Florentyna quietly.

'Perhaps?'

'Perhaps I'll consider running for the Student Council a year earlier.'

During the summer vacation, which Florentyna spent with her father at the New York Baron, she noticed that many of the big department stores now had millinery departments and wondered why there were not more shops specialising only in clothes. She spent hours in Best's, Saks and in Bonwit Teller's where she bought herself her first strapless evening dress – observing the different customers and comparing their individual preferences with those of shoppers who frequented Bloomingdale's, Altman's and Macy's. In the evening over dinner she would regale her father with all the knowledge she had acquired that day. Abel was so impressed by the speed with which Florentyna assimilated new facts that he began to explain to her in some detail how the Baron Group worked. By the end of her holiday, he was delighted with how much she had picked up about stock control, cash flow, advance reservations, the Employment Act of 1940, and even the cost of eight thousand fresh bread rolls. He warned George that his job as managing director of the group might be in jeopardy in the not-too-distant future.

'I don't think it's my job she's after, Abel.'

'No?' said Abel.

'No,' said George. 'It's yours.'

Abel took Florentyna to the airport on the final day of her holiday and presented her with a black-and-white Polaroid camera.

'Papa, what a fantastic present. Won't I be the neatest thing at school?'

'It's a bribe,' said Abel.

'A bribe?'

'Yes. George tells me you want to be Chairman of the Baron Group.'

'I think I'll start with the Student Council,' said Florentyna.

Abel laughed. 'Make sure you win a *place* on the Council first,' he said, then kissed his daughter on the cheek and waved goodbye as she disappeared up the steps of the waiting plane.

'I've decided to run.'

'Good,' said Edward. 'I have already compiled a list of every student in both schools. You must put a tick by all those who you feel are certain to support you and a cross by those who won't, so that I can work on the don't knows and firm up the backing of your supporters.'

'Very professional. How many people are running?'

'So far fifteen candidates for six places. There are four candidates you can't hope to beat, but it will be a close contest after that. I thought you'd be interested to know that Pete Welling is running.'

'That creep,' said Florentyna.

'Oh, I was led to believe that you were hopelessly in love with him.'

'Don't be so ridiculous, Edward, he's a sap. Let's go through the school lists.'

The election was due to take place at the end of the second week of the new school year, so the candidates had only ten days to gather votes. Many of Florentyna's friends dropped in at Rigg Street to assure her of their support. She was surprised to find some support where she least expected it, while other classmates whom she imagined were friends told Edward they would never back her. Florentyna discussed this problem with Miss Tredgold who warned her that if you ever run for any office which might bring you privilege or profit, it will always be your contemporaries who do not want to see you succeed in your ambitions. You need have no fear of those who are older or younger than yourself; they know you will never be their rival.

All the candidates had to write a mini-election address setting out the reason they wanted to be on the Student Council. Florentyna's was checked over by Abel, who refused to add or subtract anything, and by Miss Tredgold, who only commented on the grammar.

Voting was all day Friday at the end of the second week and the result was always announced by the headmaster after assembly the following Monday morning. It was a terrible weekend for Florentyna, and Miss Tredgold spent the entire time saying, 'Settle down, child.' Even Edward, who played tennis with her on Sunday afternoon, hardly raised a sweat, winning 6–0, 6–0.

'It wouldn't take Jack Kramer to tell you that you're not concentrating – "child".'

'Oh, do be quiet, Edward. I don't care whether I'm elected to the Student Council or not.'

Florentyna woke up at five o'clock on Monday morning and was dressed and ready for breakfast by six. She read the paper through three times from cover to cover and Miss Tredgold did not utter a word to her until it was time to leave for school.

'Remember, my dear, that Lincoln lost more elections than he won but still became President.'

'Yes, but I'd like to start out with a win,' said Florentyna.

The assembly hall was packed by nine o'clock. Morning prayers and the headmaster's announcements seemed to take for ever; Florentyna's eyes stared at the floor.

'And now I shall read the results of the Student Council election,' said the headmaster. 'There were fifteen candidates and six have been elected to the Council:

1st	Jason Morton (President)	109
2nd	Cathy Long	87
3rd	Roger Dingle	85
4th	Eddie Bell	81
5th	Jonathan Lloyd	79

The headmaster coughed and the room remained silent. 'Sixth Florentyna Rosnovski with seventy-six votes. The runner-up was Pete Welling with seventy-five votes. The first Council meeting will be in my office at ten thirty this morning. Assembly dismissed.'

Florentyna was overwhelmed and threw her arms around Edward.

'Don't forget – President next year.'

At the first Council meeting that morning, Florentyna, as junior member, was appointed Secretary.

'That will teach you to come in last,' laughed the new President, Jason Morton.

Back to writing notes that nobody else reads, thought Florentyna. But at least this time I can type them and perhaps next year I will be President. She looked up at the boy whose thin, sensitive face and seemingly shy manner had won him so many votes.

'Now privileges,' said Jason briskly, unaware of her gaze. 'The President is allowed to drive a car, while on one day a week the girls can wear pastel-coloured shirts and the boys can wear loafers instead of Oxfords. Council members are allowed to sign out of study hall when involved in school responsibilities and they can award demerits to any pupil who breaks a school rule.'

So that's what I fought so hard for, thought Florentyna, the chance to wear a pastel-coloured shirt and award demerits.

When she returned home that night Florentyna told Miss Tredgold every detail of what had happened, and she glowed with pride as she repeated the full result along with her new responsibilities.

'Who is poor Peter Welling,' enquired Miss Tredgold, 'who failed to be elected by only one vote?'

'Serves him right,' said Florentyna. 'Do you know what I said to that creep when I passed him in the corridor?'

'No, I'm sure I don't,' said Miss Tredgold apprehensively.

' "Now *you'll* have to get in line, but perhaps your time will come," ' she said, and burst out laughing.

'That was unworthy of you, Florentyna, and indeed of me. Be sure you never in your life express such an opinion again. The hour of triumph is not a time to belittle your rivals, rather it is a time to be magnanimous.'

Miss Tredgold rose from her seat and retired to her room.

When Florentyna went to lunch the next day, Jason Morton took the seat next to her. 'We're going to see a lot of each other now that you've been elected to the Student Council,' he said and smiled. Florentyna didn't smile back because Jason had the same reputation among the pupils of Girls Latin as Pete Welling, and she was determined not to make a fool of herself a second time.

Over lunch, they discussed the problem of the school orchestra's trip to Boston and what to do about the number of boys who had been caught smoking. Student councillors were limited in the punishments they were allowed to impose, and study hall detention on Saturday morning was about the most extreme terror they could evoke. Jason told

Florentyna that if they went so far as to report the smokers to the headmaster, it would undoubtedly mean expulsion for the students involved. A dilemma had arisen among the councillors because no one feared Saturday's detention and equally no one believed they ever would be reported to the headmaster.

'If we allow the smoking to go on,' said Jason, 'very soon we will have no authority at all, unless we're determined to make a positive stand in full Council right from the beginning.'

Florentyna agreed with him and was surprised by his next question.

'Would you be up to a game of tennis on Saturday afternoon?'

Florentyna remained silent for a moment. 'Yes,' she said, trying to sound casual as she remembered that he was captain of the tennis team and her backhand was awful.

'Good, I'll pick you up at three o'clock. Will that be okay?'

'Fine,' said Florentyna, hoping she still sounded uninterested.

'That tennis dress is far too short,' said Miss Tredgold.

'I know,' said Florentyna, 'but it's last year's, and I've grown since then.'

'With whom are you playing?'

'Jason Morton.'

'You really cannot play tennis in a dress like that with a young man.'

'It's either this or the nude,' said Florentyna.

'Don't be cheeky with me, child. I shall allow you to wear the garment on this occasion, but be assured I shall have acquired a new dress for you by Monday afternoon.'

The front doorbell rang. 'He seems to have arrived,' said Miss Tredgold.

Florentyna picked up her racket and ran to the door.

'Don't run, child. Let the young man wait a little. We can't have him knowing how you feel about him, can we?'

Florentyna blushed, tied back her long dark hair with a ribbon and walked slowly to the front door.

'Hi, Jason,' she said, her voice casual again. 'Won't you come in?'

Jason, who was dressed in a smart tennis outfit that looked as if it had been purchased that morning, couldn't take his eyes off Florentyna. 'What a dress,' he ventured, and was about to say more when he saw Miss Tredgold leaving the room. He hadn't realised until that moment what a good figure Florentyna had. The moment he set eyes on Miss Tredgold he knew why he had never been allowed to find out.

'It's last year's, I'm afraid,' continued Florentyna, looking down at her slim legs. 'It's awful, isn't it?'

'No, I think it's swell. Come on, I've reserved a court for three thirty and someone else will grab it if we're a minute late.'

'Good heavens,' said Florentyna as she closed the front door. 'Is that yours?'

'Yes. Don't you think it's fantastic?'

'I would say, if asked to venture an opinion, that it had seen better days.'

'Oh, really,' said Jason. 'I thought it was rather snazzy.'

'If I knew what the word meant I might be able to agree with you. Pray, sir,' she said mockingly, 'am I expected to ride in that machine or help push it?'

'That is a genuine pre-war Packard.'

'Then it deserves an early burial,' said Florentyna as she took her seat in the front, suddenly realising how much of her legs were showing.

'Has anyone taught you how to propel this lump of metal in a forward direction?' she enquired sweetly.

'No, not exactly,' said Jason.

'What?' said Florentyna in disbelief.

'I'm told driving is mostly common sense.'

Florentyna pushed down the handle of her door, opening it slightly, as if to get out. Jason put his hand on her thigh.

'Don't be silly, Tyna. I was taught by my father and I've been driving for nearly a year.'

Florentyna blushed, closed the door again and had to admit to herself that he drove rather well all the way to the tennis club even if the car did rattle and bump a little as it went over the holes in the road.

The tennis match was a desperate affair for Florentyna trying hard to win a point while Jason tried hard to lose one. Somehow Jason managed to win by only 6–2, 6–1.

'What I need is a Coke,' he said at the end of the match.

'What I need is a coach,' said Florentyna.

He laughed and took her hand as they left the court, and even though she felt sweaty and hot, he did not let her hand go until they reached the bar at the back of the club house. He bought one Coke and they sat drinking it from two straws in the corner of the room. When they had finished, Jason drove her home. On reaching Rigg Street, he leaned over and kissed her on the lips. Florentyna did not respond, more out of shock than for any other reason.

'Why don't you come to the movies with me tonight?' he said. '*On the Town* is showing at the United Artists Theatre.'

'Well, I normally . . . Yes, I'd like that,' said Florentyna.

'Good, then I'll pick you up at seven.'

Florentyna watched the car as it chugged away, and tried to think of some reason that would persuade her mother she had to be out that evening. She found Miss Tredgold preparing tea in the kitchen.

'A good game, child?' asked Miss Tredgold.

'Not for him, I'm afraid. By the way he wants to take me to' – she hesitated – 'to Orchestra Hall for a concert this evening so I won't need any dinner.'

'How nice,' said Miss Tredgold. 'Be sure you're back before eleven or your mother will worry.'

Florentyna ran upstairs, sat on the end of the bed and started to think about what she could possibly wear that evening, how awful her hair looked and whether she could steal some of her mother's make-up. She stood in front of the mirror wondering how she could make her breasts look bigger without holding her breath all night.

At seven o'clock Jason returned dressed in a red sloppy Joe sweater and khakis and was met at the door by Miss Tredgold.

'How do you do, young man.'

'How do you do, ma'am,' said Jason.

'Would you like to come into the drawing room?'

'Thank you,' said Jason.

'And what is the concert you're taking Florentyna to?'

'The concert?'

'Yes, I wondered who was playing,' said Miss Tredgold. 'I read a good review of Beethoven's Third in the morning paper.'

'Oh, yeah, Beethoven's Third,' said Jason, as Florentyna appeared on the stairs. Both Miss Tredgold and Jason were stunned. One approved while the other didn't. Florentyna was wearing a green dress that fell just below the knee and revealed the sheerest nylon stockings with dark seams down the back. She walked slowly down the stairs, her long legs unsteady in high-heeled shoes, her small breasts looking larger than usual, her dark shining hair hanging down on her shoulders, reminiscent of Jennifer Jones and making Florentyna appear a lot older than her fifteen years. The only item she wore to which Miss Tredgold could take no exception was the watch she herself had given to Florentyna on her thirteenth birthday.

'Come on, Jason, or we'll be late,' said Florentyna, wanting to avoid any conversation with Miss Tredgold.

'Sure thing,' said Jason. Florentyna did not look back once for fear of being turned into a pillar of salt.

'Be sure she's home before eleven, young man,' commanded Miss Tredgold.

'Sure thing,' repeated Jason as he closed the front door. 'Where did you find her?'

'Miss Tredgold?'

'Yes, she's straight out of a Victorian novel. "Be sure she's home before eleven, young man," ' he mimicked as he opened the car door for her.

'Don't be rude,' said Florentyna, and smiled at him coquettishly.

There was a long line outside the theatre and Florentyna spent most of the time standing beside Jason facing the wall, fearing someone might recognise her. Once inside Jason quickly guided her to the back row with an air of having been there before.

She took her seat and when the lights went down she began to relax for the first time – but not for long. Jason leaned over, put his hand around her shoulder and started kissing her. She began to enjoy the sensation as he forced her lips open and their tongues touched for the first time. Then he broke away and they watched the titles go up on the screen. Florentyna liked Gene Kelly. Jason leaned over again and pressed his mouth against hers. Her lips parted. Almost immediately she felt a hand on her breast. She tried to remove his fingers but once again his backhand was too strong for her. After a few seconds she came up for air and took a quick look at the Statue of Liberty before Jason returned with his other hand and fondled her other breast. This time she managed to push him away but for only a few moments. Annoyed, he took out a packet of Camels and lit one. Florentyna couldn't believe what was happening. After a few puffs he stubbed the cigarette out and placed a hand between her legs. In near panic she stopped any further advance by squeezing her thighs closely together.

'Oh, come on,' said Jason. 'Don't be such a prude or you'll end up like Miss Tredgold,' and he bent over to kiss her once again.

'For heaven's sake, Jason, let's watch the movie.'

'Don't be silly. No one goes to a movie house to watch a film.' He put his hand back on her leg. 'Don't tell me you haven't done it before. Hell, you're nearly sixteen. What are you hoping to be? The oldest virgin in Chicago?'

Florentyna jumped up and pushed her way out, stumbling over several pairs of feet before she reached the aisle. Without straightening her dress she ran out of the theatre as fast as she could. Once outside, she attempted to run, but couldn't manage much more than walking pace in her mother's high heels, so she took the shoes off and ran in her stockinged feet. When she reached the front door of her house she tried to compose herself, hoping she could get up to her room without bumping into Miss Tredgold, but she failed. Miss Tredgold's bedroom door was ajar and as Florentyna tiptoed past, she said, 'Concert over early, my dear?'

'Yes ... no ... I mean I didn't feel very well,' said Florentyna, and she ran into her own room before Miss Tredgold could ask any more questions. She went to bed that night still trembling.

She woke early the next morning and although still angry with Jason she found herself laughing at what had taken place and even determined to go and see the film again, on her own this time. She liked Gene Kelly, but it was the first time she had seen her *real* idol on the screen, and she couldn't get over how skinny and vulnerable he looked.

At Student Council the next day, Florentyna could not make herself look at Jason while he was stating in a quiet firm voice that some senior boys who were not members of Council were becoming casual about their dress. He also added that the next person caught smoking would have to be reported to the headmaster or his own reputation as President would be undermined. Everyone except Florentyna nodded their agreement.

'Good, then I'll put a notice on the bulletin board to that effect.'

As soon as the meeting was over, Florentyna slipped off to class before anyone could speak to her. She finished her homework late that evening and did not set off for Rigg Street until a few minutes after six o'clock. As she reached the main school door, it started to rain and she remained under the archway hoping the storm would blow over quickly. As she stood there, Jason walked straight past her with a girl from twelfth grade. She watched them climb into his car and she bit her lip. The rain came down harder, so she decided to return to her classroom and type up the minutes of the Student Council meeting. On her way back into school she passed a small crowd studying a notice on the board confirming the Council's attitude to sloppy dress and smoking.

Florentyna took about an hour to complete the minutes of the Council meeting, partly because her mind wandered continually back to Jason's double standards. The rain had stopped by the time she had finished her typing and she closed her typewriter case and placed the minutes in the top drawer. As she walked back down the corridor, she thought she heard a noise coming from the boys' locker room. No one except members of Student Council was allowed to remain in school after seven o'clock without special permission so she turned back to see who it was. When she was a few yards away from the locker room the light under the door went off. She walked over and opened the door and switched the light back on. It was some time before Florentyna focused on the figure standing in the corner, trying to hide a cigarette behind his back, but he knew she had seen it.

'Pete,' she said in surprise.

'Well, Miss Student Councillor, you've caught me once and for all. Two major offences in one day. In school after hours, and smoking. Bang goes my chance of making Harvard,' Pete Welling said as he ground out the cigarette on the stone floor. The vision returned of the Student Council President stubbing out his cigarette the night before in the back of an unlit cinema.

'Jason Morton is hoping to go to Harvard, isn't he?'

'Yes. What's that got to do with it?' said Pete. 'Nothing will stop him making the Ivy League.'

'I just remembered. No girl is allowed in the boys' locker room at any time.'

'Yes, but you're a member of . . .'

'Good night, Pete.'

Florentyna began to enjoy her new authority and took her duties and responsibilities on the Student Council very seriously, so much so that as the year passed Miss Tredgold feared Florentyna's studies were suffering because of it. She did not comment on the matter to Mrs. Rosnovski, rather she considered it her duty to find a solution. She hoped that Florentyna's attitude might be nothing more than an adolescent phase of misplaced enthusiasm. Even Miss Tredgold, despite past experience of these problems, was surprised by how quickly Florentyna had changed since being entrusted with a little power.

By the middle of the second term Miss Tredgold realised the problem was past that stage and fast becoming out of control. Florentyna was beginning to take herself, and not her work, far too seriously. Her end-of-term report was far from good by her normal high standards, and Florentyna's home-room teacher more than hinted that she was becoming high-handed with some of the other students and giving out demerits a little too freely.

Miss Tredgold could not help noticing that Florentyna had not been receiving as many invitations to parties as she had in the past and her old friends did not seem to visit Rigg Street quite so frequently, except for the loyal Edward Winchester . . . Miss Tredgold liked that boy.

Matters did not improve during the summer term and Florentyna began to be evasive when Miss Tredgold broached the subject of uncompleted homework. Zaphia, who had compensated for the loss of a husband by gaining ten pounds, was uncooperative. 'I haven't noticed anything unusual,' was her only comment when Miss Tredgold tried to discuss the problem.

Miss Tredgold pursed her lips and began to despair when one morning at breakfast Florentyna was downright rude when asked what she had planned to do for the weekend.

'I'll let you know if it concerns you,' she said without looking up from *Vogue*. Mrs. Rosnovski showed no sign of noticing, so Miss Tredgold maintained a stony silence, judging that sooner or later the child was bound to come a cropper.

It came sooner.

9

'THERE'S NO REASON FOR you to be that confident,' said Edward.

'Why? Who's going to beat me? I've been on the Council

for nearly a year and everyone else on it is graduating,' said Florentyna, lounging back in one of the horsehair chairs reserved for members of the Student Council.

Edward remained standing. 'Yes, I realise that, but not everyone likes you.'

'What do you mean?'

'A lot of people think that since you've been on the Council you've become a bit too big for your boots.'

'I hope you're not among them, Edward.'

'No, I'm not. But I am worried that if you don't bother to mix a little more with the students in the lower grades you might be beaten.'

'Don't be silly. Why should I bother to get to know them when they already know me?' she asked, fiddling with some papers on the arm of her chair.

'What's come over you, Florentyna? You didn't act like this a year ago,' said Edward, looking down.

'If you don't like the way I carry out my duties, go and support someone else.'

'It has nothing to do with the way you carry out your duties – everyone acknowledges you've been the best Secretary anyone can remember – but different qualities are needed for President.'

'Thank you for the advice, Edward, but you will discover that I can survive without it.'

'Then you won't want me to help you this year?'

'Edward, you still haven't got the message. It's not a case of not wanting you but simply not needing you.'

'I wish you luck, Florentyna, and I only hope I'm proved wrong.'

'I don't need your luck either. Some things in this life depend on ability.'

Florentyna did not repeat this conversation to Miss Tredgold.

At the end of the academic year, Florentyna was surprised to find that she had finished first in only Latin and French, and overall had fallen to third in the class. Miss Tredgold read her school report carefully and it confirmed her worst fears, but she concluded there was no point in making any adverse comment to the child as she had stopped taking anyone's advice unless it confirmed her own opinions. Once again, Florentyna spent the summer vacation in New York with her father, who allowed her to work as an assistant in one of the hotel shops.

Florentyna rose early each morning and dressed in the pastel green uniform of a junior member of the hotel staff. She threw all her energy into learning how the little fashion shop was run and was soon putting forward new ideas to Miss Parker, the manageress, who was impressed – and not just because she was the Baron's daughter. As the days passed, Florentyna gained more confidence and, conscious of the power of her privileged position, she stopped wearing the shop uniform and even started to order some of the junior sales staff around. She was, however, sufficiently cautious never to do this in front of Miss Parker.

One Friday, when Miss Parker was in her office checking the morning's petty cash, Jessie Kovats, a junior sales assistant, arrived ten minutes late. Florentyna was standing at the door waiting for her.

'You're late again,' said Florentyna, but Jessie didn't bother to reply.

'Did you hear me, Miss Kovats?' demanded Florentyna.

'Sure did,' said Jessie, hanging up her raincoat.

'Then what is your excuse this time?'

'For you, I don't have to have an excuse.'

'We'll see about that,' said Florentyna, starting off towards Miss Parker's office.

'Don't bother yourself, bossy boots, I've had enough of you in any case,' said Jessie, who walked into Miss Parker's office and closed the door behind her. Florentyna pretended to tidy the counter while she waited for Jessie to return. A few minutes later the young assistant came out of the office, put her coat back on and left the shop without another word. Florentyna felt pleased with the result of her admonition. A few minutes later Miss Parker came out of her office.

'Jessie tells me she's leaving the shop because of you.'

'Miss Kovats is hardly a great loss,' volunteered Florentyna. 'She didn't exactly pull her weight.'

'That is not the point, Florentyna. I have to continue to run this shop after you return to school.'

'Perhaps by then we shall have weeded out the Jessie Kovats of this world who shouldn't, after all, be wasting my father's time and money.'

'Miss Rosnovski, this is a team. Not everyone can be clever and bright, or even hard-working, but within their limited abilities they do the best they can, and there have been no complaints in the past.'

'Could that possibly be because my father is too busy to keep a watchful eye on you, Miss Parker?'

Miss Parker visibly flushed and steadied herself on the counter. 'I think the time has come for you to work in another of your father's shops. I have served him for nearly twenty years and he has never once spoken to me in such a discourteous way.'

'Perhaps the time has come for *you* to work in another shop,' said Florentyna, 'and preferably not my father's.' Walking out of the front door, she made straight for the hotel's private elevator and pressed the button marked forty-two. On arrival, Florentyna informed her father's secretary that she needed to speak to him immediately.

'He's chairing a board meeting at the moment, Miss Rosnovski.'

'Then interrupt him and tell him that I wish to see him.'

The secretary hesitated, then buzzed through to Mr. Rosnovski.

'I thought I told you not to disturb me, Miss Deneroff.'

'I apologise, sir, but your daughter is here and insists on seeing you.'

There was a pause. 'All right, send her in.'

'I am sorry, Papa, but this is something that can't wait,' Florentyna said as she entered the room, feeling suddenly less sure of herself as the eight men around the board-room table rose. Abel guided her through to his own office.

'Well, what is it that can't wait, my darling?'

'It's Miss Parker. She's stuffy, incompetent and stupid,' said Florentyna, and she poured out to her father her version of what had happened that morning with Jessie Kovats.

Abel's fingers never stopped tapping on the desk top as he listened to her tale. When she came to the end he flicked a switch on his intercom. 'Please ask Miss Parker in the fashion shop to come up immediately.'

'Thank you, Papa.'

'Florentyna, would you be kind enough to wait next door while I deal with Miss Parker.'

'Of course, Papa.'

A few minutes later, Miss Parker appeared, still looking flushed. Abel asked her what had happened. She gave an accurate account of the altercation, confining her view of Florentyna to the fact that she was a competent assistant but had been the sole reason that Miss Kovats, a long-serving member of her staff, had left. Others, Miss Parker pointed out, might leave too if Florentyna persisted with her attitude. Abel listened, barely controlling his anger. He gave Miss Parker his opinion and told her she would receive a letter by hand confirming his decision.

'If that is what you wish, sir,' said Miss Parker, and left.

Abel buzzed his secretary. 'Would you please ask my daughter to come back in, Miss Deneroff.'

Florentyna strode in. 'Did you tell Miss Parker what you thought, Papa?'

'Yes, I did.'

'She'll find it hard to get another job.'

'She won't need to.'

'Won't need to?'

'No, I gave her a raise and extended her contract,' he said, leaning forward and placing both hands firmly on his desk. 'If you ever treat a member of my staff that way again, I'll put you over my knee and thrash you, and it won't be a gentle tap with a hairbrush. Jessie Kovats has already left because of your insufferable behaviour and it is obvious no one in that shop likes you.'

Florentyna stared at her father in disbelief, then burst into tears.

'And you can save your tears for someone else,' continued Abel remorselessly. 'They don't impress me. I shouldn't have to remind you that I have a company to run. Another week of you and I would have had a crisis on my hands. You will now go down to Miss Parker and apologise for your disgraceful behaviour. You will also stay away from my shops until I decide you are ready to work in them again. And that is the last time you interrupt one of my board meetings. Do you understand?'

'But, Papa –'

'No buts. You will apologise to Miss Parker immediately.'

Florentyna ran out of her father's office and returned to her room in tears, packed her bags, left her green pastel dress on the bedroom floor and took a cab to the airport. Thirty-minutes later she was back in Chicago.

On learning of her departure, Abel phoned Miss Tredgold, who listened to what had taken place with dismay but not with surprise.

When Florentyna arrived home, her mother was still away at a health spa trying to shed a few unwanted pounds. Only Miss Tredgold was there to greet her.

'You're back a week early, I observe.'

'Yes, I got bored with New York.'

'Don't lie, child.'

'Must you pick on me as well?' said Florentyna, and ran upstairs to her room. That weekend she locked herself in and only crept down to the kitchen at odd times for meals. Miss Tredgold made no attempt to see her.

On the first day of school Florentyna put on one of the smart pastel shirts with the new style button-down collar she had bought at Bergdorf Goodman. She knew it would make every other girl at Girls Latin jealous. She was going to show them all how a future President of the Student Council should behave. As no member of Council could be elected for two weeks, she wore a different coloured shirt every day and took upon herself the responsibilities of President. She even started to think about what type of car she would talk her father into buying for her when she had won the election. At all times she avoided Edward Winchester, who had also put his own name forward for the Council, and she laughed openly at any comments made about his popularity. On the Monday of the third week, Florentyna went to morning assembly to hear herself confirmed as the new student President.

When Miss Allen, the headmistress, had read out the full list Florentyna could not believe her ears. She had not even finished in the first six. In fact, she was only barely the runner-up, and of all people Edward Winchester had been elected President. As she left the hall, no one commiserated with her and she spent the day in a silent daze at the back of the classroom. When she returned home that night, she crept up to Miss Tredgold's room and knocked gently on the door.

'Come.'

Florentyna opened the door slowly and looked towards Miss Tredgold who was reading at her desk.

'They didn't make me President,' she said quietly. 'In fact, they didn't even elect me to the Council.'

'I know,' Miss Tredgold replied, closing her Bible.

'How can you have known?' asked Florentyna.

'Because I wouldn't have voted for you myself.' The governess paused. 'But that's an end of the matter, child.'

Florentyna ran across the room and threw her arms around Miss Tredgold, who held her tightly.

'Good, now we shall have to start rebuilding bridges. Dry your tears, my dear, and we shall begin immediately. There is no time to be lost. Pad and pencil are needed.'

Florentyna wrote down the list dictated by Miss Tredgold and did not argue with any of her instructions. That night she wrote long letters to her father, Miss Parker (enclosing another letter for Jessie Kovats), Edward Winchester, and finally, although the name was not on her list, to Miss Tredgold. The next day she went to confession with Father O'Reilly. On returning to school Florentyna helped the newly-appointed Secretary with her first minutes, showing her the system she had found worked most satisfactorily. She wished the new President luck and promised that she would help him and his Council if she was ever needed. She spent the next week answering any queries that came up from the student councillors, but never volunteered advice. When Edward met her in the corridor a few days later he told her that the Council had voted to allow her to keep all her privileges. Miss Tredgold advised her to accept the offer with courtesy but at no time to take advantage of it. Florentyna put all her New York shirts in the bottom drawer and locked them away.

A few days later the headmistress called for her. Florentyna feared it would take longer to regain her respect, however determined she was to do so. When Florentyna arrived at her study the tiny, immaculately dressed woman gave her a friendly smile and motioned to a comfortable seat by her side.

'You must have been very disappointed by the election results.'

'Yes, Miss Allen,' said Florentyna, assuming she was to receive further chastisement.

'But by all accounts you have learned greatly from the experience, and I suspect you will be wanting to make amends.'

'It's too late, Miss Allen, I leave at the end of the year and can now never be President.'

'True, true. So we must look for other mountains to climb. I retire at the end of this year having been headmistress for twenty-five years, and I confess there is little left that I wish to achieve. The boys and girls of Latin have excellent admission records to Harvard, Yale, Radcliffe and Smith and we have always been better than every school in Illinois and as good as any on the east coast. However, there is one achievement that has eluded me.'

'What's that, Miss Allen?'

'The boys have won every major scholarship to the Ivy League universities at least once, Princeton three times, but one scholarship has eluded the girls for a quarter of a century.

That is the James Adams Woolson Prize Scholarship in Classics at Radcliffe. I wish to enter your name for that scholarship. Should you win the prize my cup will be full.'

'I would like to try,' said Florentyna, 'but my record lately . . .'

'Indeed,' said the headmistress, 'but as Mrs. Churchill pointed out to Winston when he was surprisingly beaten in an election, "that may yet turn out to be a blessing in disguise".'

' "Some disguise." ' They both smiled.

That night Florentyna studied the entry form for the James Adams Woolson Prize. The scholarship was open to every girl in America between the ages of sixteen and eighteen on July 1st of that year. There were three papers, one for Latin, one for Greek and a general paper on current affairs.

During the ensuing weeks, Florentyna spoke only Latin and Greek to Miss Tredgold before breakfast, and every weekend Miss Allen assigned her three general questions to be completed by the following Monday morning. As the examination day drew nearer, Florentyna became aware that the hopes of the whole school were with her. She sat awake at night with Cicero, Virgil, Plato and Aristotle, and every morning after breakfast she would write five hundred words on such varied subjects as the Twenty-Second Amendment or the significance of President Truman's power over Congress during the Korean War – even on the impact that television would have by going nationwide.

At the end of each day, Miss Tredgold checked through Florentyna's work, adding footnotes and comments before they would both collapse into bed, only to be up at six thirty the next morning to work their way through further old scholarship examination papers. Far from gaining confidence, Florentyna confided to Miss Tredgold that she became more frightened as each day passed.

The prize exam was set for early March at Radcliffe, and on the eve of the fateful day Florentyna unlocked her bottom drawer and took out her favourite shirt. Miss Tredgold accompanied her to the station and the few words they spoke on the way were in Greek. Her final words were: 'Don't spend the longest time on the easiest question.'

When they reached the platform, Florentyna felt an arm encircle her waist and a rose appeared in front of her.

'Edward, you nut.'

'That is not the way to address the President of the Student Council. Don't bother to come back if you fail to win the Woolson prize,' he said, and kissed her on the cheek.

Neither of them noticed the smile on Miss Tredgold's face.

Florentyna found an empty carriage and remembered very little of the journey, as she rarely looked up from her copy of the *Oresteia*.

When she arrived in Boston, she was met by a Ford 'Woody' station wagon which took her and four other girls who must have been on the same train to the Radcliffe Yard. During the journey spasmodic exchanges of polite conversation punctuated long, tense silences. Florentyna was relieved to find that she had been put in a residential house at 55 Garden Street in a room of her own: she hoped she would be able to conceal how nervous she was.

At six o'clock, the girls all met in Longfellow Hall where the Dean of Instruction, Mrs. Wilma Kirby-Miller, went over the details of the examination.

'Tomorrow, ladies, between nine and twelve, you will write the Latin paper and in the afternoon between three and six the Greek paper. The following morning you will complete the examination with a general paper. It would be foolish to wish everyone success as you cannot all expect to win the Woolson Prize, so I will only express the hope that when you have completed the three papers, each and every one of you will feel that you could not have done better.'

Florentyna returned to her room in Garden Street conscious of how little she knew and feeling very lonely. She went down to the ground floor and called her mother and Miss Tredgold on the pay phone. The next morning she woke at three and read a few pages of Aristotle's *Politics* but nothing would stick. When she came down at seven, she walked around the Radcliffe Yard several times before going to

Agassiz House for breakfast. She found two telegrams awaiting her, one from her father, wishing her luck and inviting her
to join him for a trip to Europe during the summer holiday,
and the second from Miss Tredgold which read: 'The only
thing we have to fear is fear itself.'

After breakfast, she walked once again around the yard,
this time with several other silent girls, before taking her
place in Longfellow Hall. Two hundred and forty-three girls
waited for the clock to chime nine, when the proctors allowed
them to open the little brown envelopes placed on the desk in
front of them. Florentyna read through the Latin paper once
quickly and then again carefully, before selecting those
questions that she felt best capable of answering. At twelve,
the clock struck again and her blue books were taken away
from her. She returned to her room and read Greek for two
hours, eating a solitary Hershey bar for lunch. In the afternoon she attempted three more questions in Greek. At six she
was still writing amendments when the paper had to be
handed in. She walked back to her little room in Garden
Street exhausted, fell on to the narrow bed and didn't stir
until it was time to eat. Over a late dinner, she listened to the
same conversations with different accents from Philadelphia
to Houston, and from Detroit to Atlanta: it was comforting to
discover that everyone was as nervous about the outcome of
the examination as she was. Florentyna knew that almost
everyone who took the scholarship examination would be
offered a place at Radcliffe, and twenty-two could be
awarded scholarships; but only one could win the James
Adams Woolson Prize.

On the second day she opened the brown envelope containing the general paper, fearing the worst but relaxed a
little when she read the first question: 'What changes do you
imagine would have taken place in America if the Twenty-
Second Amendment had been passed before Roosevelt became President?' She began to write furiously.

On Florentyna's return to Chicago, Miss Tredgold was
standing on the platform waiting for her.

'I shall not ask if you consider you have won the prize, my dear, only if you did as well as you had hoped.'

'Yes,' said Florentyna, after some thought. 'If I don't win a scholarship, it will be because I am not good enough.'

'You can ask for no more, child, and neither can I, so the time has come to tell you that I shall be returning to England in July.'

'Why?' said Florentyna, stunned.

'What do you imagine there is left for me to do for you, now that you're off to university? I have been offered the post of head of the classics department at a girls' school in the West Country, starting in September, and I have accepted.'

' "You could not leave me if you knew how much I loved you." '

Miss Tredgold smiled at the quotation and produced the next line. ' "It is because of how much I love you that I must now leave you, Perdano." '

Florentyna took her hand and Miss Tredgold smiled at the beautiful young woman who could already make men's heads turn as they passed by.

The last three weeks at school were not easy for Florentyna as she waited for the exam results. She tried to assure Edward that at least he was certain to gain a place at Harvard.

'They have more sports fields than lecture halls,' she teased, 'so you can't fail.'

He could fail and she knew it, and as each day passed, the hopes of both turned to fears. Florentyna had been told that the results of the examination would be known on April 14th. On that morning the headmistress called Florentyna to her study and sat her in a corner of the room while she called the registrar at Radcliffe. The registrar already had several people holding to speak to her. At last she took Miss Allen's call.

'Would you be kind enough to let me know if a Miss Florentyna Rosnovski has won a scholarship to Radcliffe?' asked the headmistress.

There was a long pause. 'How do you spell that name?'

'R-O-S-N-O-V-S-K-I.'

Another pause. Florentyna clenched her fist. Then the registrar's voice, audible to them both, came over the line: 'No, I am sorry to tell you that Miss Rosnovski's name is not among the list of scholars but over seventy per cent of those who took the scholarship examination will be offered a place at Radcliffe and will be hearing from us in the next few days.'

Neither Miss Allen nor Florentyna could mask their disappointment. As Florentyna came out of the study she found Edward waiting for her. He threw his arms around her and almost shouted, 'I'm going to Harvard. And how about you? Did you win the Woolson?' But he could see the answer in her face. 'I'm sorry,' he said. 'How thoughtless of me,' and held her in his arms as the tears came. Some younger girls who passed them giggled. Edward took her home and she, Miss Tredgold and her mother ate dinner together in silence.

Two weeks later, on Parents' Day, Miss Allen presented Florentyna with the school Classics Prize, but it was no consolation. Her mother and Miss Tredgold applauded politely but Florentyna had told her father not to come to Chicago as there was nothing particular to celebrate.

After the presentation, Miss Allen tapped the lectern in front of her before she started to speak. 'In all my years at Girls Latin,' said the headmistress in clear, resonant tones, 'it was no secret that I wanted a pupil to win the James Adams Woolson Prize Scholarship to Radcliffe.' Florentyna stared down at the wooden floorboard between her feet. 'And this year,' continued Miss Allen, 'I was convinced that we had produced our finest scholar in twenty-five years and that my dream would be realised. Some weeks ago, I phoned Radcliffe to discover our entrant had not won a scholarship. But today I received a telegram which is nevertheless worth reading to you.'

Florentyna sat back, hoping her father was not responsible for some embarrassing message of congratulation.

Miss Allen put on her reading spectacles. ' "Name of Florentyna Rosnovski not announced among general scholars because happy to inform you she is winner of James Adams Woolson Prize. Please telegraph acceptance." ' The room erupted as pupils and parents cheered. Miss Allen raised a hand, and the hall fell silent. 'After twenty-five years I should have remembered that the Woolson is always announced separately at a later date. You must put it down to old age.' There was a polite ripple of laughter before Miss Allen continued: 'There are those of us here who believe that Florentyna will go on to serve her college and country in a manner that can only reflect well upon this school. I now have only one wish left: that I live long enough to witness it.'

Florentyna stood and looked towards her mother. Large tears were coursing down her cheeks.

No one present would have realised that the lady seated bolt upright next to Zaphia, staring straight in front of her, was revelling in the applause.

So much happiness and sadness now surrounded Florentyna, but nothing was to compare with her farewell to Miss Tredgold. On the train journey from Chicago to New York, during which Florentyna tried to express her love and gratitude, she handed the older woman an envelope.

'What's this, child?' asked Miss Tredgold.

'The four thousand shares of the Baron Group which we have earned over the past four years.'

'But that includes your shares as well as mine, my dear.'

'No,' said Florentyna, 'it doesn't take into account my saving on the Woolson Prize Scholarship.'

Miss Tredgold made no reply.

An hour later, Miss Tredgold stood on the dock in New York harbour waiting to board her ship, finally to release her charge to adult life.

'I shall think of you from time to time, my dear,' she said, 'and hope that my father was right about destiny.' Florentyna kissed Miss Tredgold on both cheeks and watched her mount the gangplank. When she reached the deck, Miss Tredgold turned, waved a gloved hand once and then hailed a porter, who picked up her bags and followed the stern-looking lady towards the private cabins. She did not look back at Florentyna, who stood like a statue on the quayside

holding back the tears because she knew Miss Tredgold
would not approve.

When Miss Tredgold reached her berth, she tipped the
boy fifty cents and locked the door.

Winifred Tredgold sat on the end of the bunk and wept
unashamedly.

10

FLORENTYNA HAD NOT BEEN SO unsure about any-
thing since her first day at the Girls Latin School. When she
returned from her summer holiday in Europe with her father,
a thick manila envelope from Radcliffe was awaiting her. It
contained all the details of when and where she should
report, what to wear, a course catalogue and the 'red book'
outlining Radcliffe rules. Florentyna sat in bed studiously
taking in page after page of information until she came to
Rule 11a: 'If you entertain a man in your room for tea, at all
times the door must be kept ajar, and all four feet must
always be touching the floor.' Florentyna burst out laughing
at the thought that the first time she made love it might be
standing up, behind an open door, holding a cup of tea.

As the time drew nearer for her to leave Chicago, she
began to realise just how much she had depended on Miss
Tredgold. She packed three large suitcases which included
all the new clothes she had bought on her European trip. Her
mother, looking elegant in the latest Chanel suit, drove
Florentyna to the station. When she boarded the train she
was suddenly aware it was the first time she had travelled
anywhere for any period of time without knowing somebody
at the other end.

She arrived in Boston to find New England a beautiful
contrast of September greens and browns. An old yellow
school bus was waiting to transport students to the campus.
As the ancient vehicle crossed the Charles, Florentyna
looked through the back window to see the sun glinting off

the dome of the State House. A few sails dotted the water and eight enthusiastic students were pulling their oars through the wash while an older man on a bicycle shouted orders through a megaphone as he rode along the towpath. When the bus came to a halt at Radcliffe, a middle-aged woman in academic dress herded the freshmen into Longfellow Hall, where Florentyna had taken the Woolson exam. There they were briefed on which hall they would live in during their first year, and their rooms were allocated to them. Florentyna drew room seven in Whitman Hall. A sophomore helped her carry her bags across to Whitman and then left her to unpack.

The room smelled as if the painters had moved out only the day before. It was clear that she was to share with two other girls: there were three beds, three chests of drawers, three desks, three desk chairs, three desk lamps, three pillows, three bedspreads and three sets of blankets, according to the check list that was left on the inside of the door. As there was no sign of her roommates she chose the bed nearest the window and started to unpack. She was just about to unlock the last suitcase when the door was flung open and a large trunk landed in the middle of the room.

'Hi,' said a voice that sounded to Florentyna more like a foghorn than a freshman from Radcliffe. 'My name is Bella Hellaman. I'm from San Francisco.'

Bella shook hands with Florentyna, who immediately regretted the act as she smiled up at the six-foot giant who must have weighed well over two hundred pounds. Bella looked like a double bass and sounded like a tuba. She began to size up the room.

'I knew they wouldn't have a bed large enough for me,' was her next pronouncement. 'My headmistress did warn me that I should have applied to a man's college.'

Florentyna burst out laughing.

'You won't laugh so loud when I keep you awake all night. I toss and turn so much you'll think you're on board a ship,' Bella warned as she pushed open the window above Florentyna's bed to let in the cold Boston air. 'What time do they serve dinner at this place? I haven't had a decent meal since I left California.'

'I've no idea, but it's all in the red book,' said Florentyna, picking her copy up from the side of her bed. She started flicking through the pages until she reached 'Meals, times of'. 'Dinner, six thirty to seven thirty.'

'Then at the stroke of six thirty,' Bella said, 'I shall be under starter's orders at the dining-room door. Have you found out where the gymnasium is?'

'To be honest, I haven't,' said Florentyna, grinning. 'It wasn't high on my list of priorities for the first day.'

There was a knock on the door, and Bella shouted, 'Come in.' Florentyna later learned that it had not been a shout, just her normal speaking voice. Into the room stepped a Dresden china blonde, dressed in a neat dark blue suit and with not a hair out of place. She smiled, revealing a set of small, even teeth. Bella smiled back at her as though her dinner had arrived early.

'My name is Wendy Brinklow. I think I'm sharing a room with you.' Florentyna wanted to warn her about Bella's handshake but it was too late. She stood and watched Wendy cringe.

'You'll have to sleep over there,' Bella said, pointing to the remaining bed. 'You don't by any chance know where the gymnasium is, do you?'

'Why should Radcliffe need a gymnasium?' said Wendy as Bella helped her in with her suitcases. Bella and Wendy started to unpack and Florentyna fiddled with her books, trying not to make it too obvious that she was fascinated by what came out of Bella's suitcases. First there were goalie pads, a breast pad, and two pairs of cleats, then a face mask which Florentyna tried on, two hockey sticks and finally a pair of hockey gloves. Wendy had all her clothes in neat little piles packed away in her drawer before Bella had even worked out where to put her hockey sticks. Eventually she just threw them under the bed.

When they had finished unpacking, the three girls set off for the dining hall. Bella was the first to reach the cafeteria line and loaded her plate so full with meat and vegetables that she had to balance it on the palm of her hand. Florentyna helped herself to what she considered a normal amount and Wendy managed a couple of spoonfuls of salad. Florentyna was beginning to feel they resembled Goldilocks's three bears.

Two of them had the sleepless night Bella had promised Florentyna, and it was several weeks before either she or Wendy managed eight hours of uninterrupted sleep. Years later Florentyna discovered that she could sleep anywhere, even in a crowded airport lounge, thanks to spending her freshman year with Bella.

Bella was the first freshman to play goalie for the Radcliffe varsity and she spent the year happily terrifying anyone who dared to try to score against her. She always shook hands with the few who did. Wendy spent a lot of the time being chased by men who visited the campus and some of the time being caught. She also passed more hours reading the Kinsey Report than her class notes.

'Darlings,' she said, eyes saucer wide, 'it's a serious piece of academic work written by a distinguished professor.'

'The first academic work to sell over a million copies,' commented Bella, as she picked up her hockey sticks and left the room.

Wendy, seated in front of the one mirror in the room, started checking her lipstick.

'Who's it this time?' asked Florentyna.

'No one in particular,' she replied. 'But Dartmouth has sent their tennis team over to play Harvard and I couldn't think of a more pleasant way to spend the afternoon. Do you want to come along?'

'No thanks, but I would like to know the secret of how you find them,' said Florentyna, looking at herself appraisingly in the mirror. 'I can't remember when anyone other than Edward last asked me out.'

'It doesn't take a lot of research,' said Wendy. 'Perhaps you put them off.'

'How?' asked Florentyna, turning towards her.

Wendy put down her lipstick and picked up a comb. 'You're too obviously bright and intelligent, and not many men can handle that. You frighten them and that's not good for their egos.'

Florentyna laughed.

'I'm serious. How many men would have dared to approach your beloved Miss Tredgold, let alone make a pass at her?'

'So what do you suggest I do about it?' asked Florentyna.

'You're good-looking enough, and I don't know anyone with a better dress sense, so just act dumb and massage their ego; then they feel they have to take care of you. It always works for me.'

'But how do you stop them thinking they have the right to jump into bed with you after one hamburger?'

'Oh, I usually get three or four steaks before I let them try anything. And just occasionally I say yes.'

'That's all very well, but how did you handle it the first time?'

'God knows,' said Wendy. 'I can't remember that far back.'

Florentyna laughed again.

'If you come to the tennis with me you might get lucky. After all, there'll be five other men from Dartmouth, not to mention the six on the Harvard team.'

'No, I can't,' Florentyna said regretfully. 'I still have an essay on Oedipus to complete by six o'clock.'

'And we all know what happened to him,' said Wendy, grinning.

Despite their different interests, the three girls became inseparable, and Florentyna and Wendy would always spend Saturday afternoons watching Bella play hockey. Wendy even learned to scream 'Kill 'em,' from the sidelines, although it didn't sound very convincing. It was a hectic first year and Florentyna enjoyed regaling her father with stories of Radcliffe, Bella and Wendy.

She had to study hard as her adviser, Miss Rose, was quick

to point out that the Woolson Scholarship came up for renewal every year and that it would do neither of their reputations any good if the prize were withdrawn. At the end of the year her grades were more than satisfactory, and she had also found time to join the Debating Society and was made freshman representative for the Radcliffe Democratic Club. But she felt her greatest achievement was trouncing Bella on the Fresh Pond golf course by seven shots.

In the summer vacation of 1952, Florentyna only spent two weeks in New York with her father because she had applied to be a page at the Chicago convention.

Once Florentyna had returned to her mother in Chicago she threw herself back into politics. The Republican Party convention had been held in the city two weeks earlier and the G.O.P. had chosen Dwight D. Eisenhower and Richard Nixon as their candidates. Florentyna couldn't see how the Democrats would come up with anyone to challenge Eisenhower, the biggest national hero since Teddy Roosevelt. 'I like Ike' buttons were everywhere.

When on July 21st the Democratic convention opened, Florentyna was given the job of showing VIPs to their seats on the speakers' platform. During those four days she learned two things of value. The first was the importance of contacts and the second the vanity of politicians. Twice during the four days she placed Senators in the wrong seats, and they could not have made more fuss if she had ushered them into the electric chair. The brightest moment of her week came when a good-looking young Congressman from Massachusetts asked her where she was at college.

'When I was at Harvard,' he said, 'I spent far too much of my time at Radcliffe. They tell me now it's the other way around.'

Florentyna wanted to say something witty and bright that he would remember but nothing came out, and it was many years before she saw John Kennedy again.

The climax of the convention came when she watched the delegates select Adlai Stevenson as their standard-bearer.

She had greatly admired him when he was Governor of
Illinois, but Florentyna did not believe that such an
academic man could hope to defeat Eisenhower on election
day. Despite the shouting, cheering and singing of 'Happy
Days Are Here Again', few other people in that hall seemed
to believe it either.

Once the convention was over, Florentyna went back to
Henry Osborne's headquarters to try to help him retain his
seat in Congress. This time she was put in charge of the
switchboard enquiries but the responsibility gave her little
pleasure as she had known for some time that the Congressman was not respected by his party workers let alone by his
constituents. His reputation as a drinker and his second
divorce were not helping him with the middle-class voters in
his district.

Florentyna found him all too casual and glib about the
trust the voters had placed in him, and she began to see why
people had so little faith in their elected representatives.
That faith took another blow when Eisenhower's Vice-
Presidential candidate, Richard Nixon, addressed the nation
on September 23rd to explain away an eighteen thousand
dollar slush fund which he claimed had been set up for him
by a group of millionaire backers as 'necessary political
expenses' and for 'exposing Communists'.

On the day of the election, Florentyna and her fellow
workers were half-hearted about both of their candidates and
those feelings were reflected at the polls. Eisenhower won the
election by the largest popular vote in American history,
33,936,234 to 27,314,992. Among the casualties removed in
the landslide was Representative Osborne.

Disenchanted with politics, Florentyna returned to Radcliffe
for her sophomore year, and put all her energy into her
studies. Bella had been elected captain of hockey, the first
sophomore to be so honoured. Wendy claimed to have fallen
in love with a Dartmouth tennis player named Roger and,
taking fashion advice from Florentyna, started studying
bridal gowns in *Vogue*. Although they now all had single

rooms in Whitman, the three girls still saw each other regularly. Florentyna never missed a hockey game, come rain or snow, both of which Cambridge frequently endured, while Wendy introduced her to several men who never quite seemed worthy of a third or fourth steak.

It was halfway through the spring semester that Florentyna returned to her room to find Wendy sitting on the floor in tears.

'What's the matter?' asked Florentyna. 'Your mid-terms? You haven't flunked them?'

'No, it's much worse than that.'

'What could be worse than that?'

'I'm pregnant.'

'What?' said Florentyna, kneeling down and putting an arm around her. 'How can you be so sure?'

'This is the second month I've missed my period.'

'Well, that's not conclusive, and if the worse comes to the worst, we know Roger wants to marry you.'

'He may not be the father.'

'Oh, my God,' said Florentyna. 'Who is?'

'I think it must have been Bob, the football player from Princeton. You met him, remember?'

Florentyna didn't. There had been quite a few during the year and she wasn't sure what to do next when Wendy couldn't even be certain of the father's name. All three girls sat up late into the night with Bella displaying a gentleness and understanding Florentyna would never have thought possible. It was decided that if Wendy missed her next period she would have to make an appointment to see the university gynaecologist, Doctor MacLeod.

Wendy did miss her next period, and asked Bella and Florentyna to accompany her when she went to Doctor MacLeod's office on Brattle Street. The doctor informed Wendy's class Dean of her pregnancy that night and no one was surprised by her decision. Wendy's father arrived the next day and thanked them both for all they had done before taking his daughter back to Nashville. It all happened so suddenly that neither of them could believe they wouldn't see

Wendy again. Florentyna felt helpless and wondered if she could have done more.

At the end of her sophomore year, Florentyna began to believe she could win a coveted Phi Beta Kappa key. She was fast losing her interest in university politics; a combination of McCarthy and Nixon was not inspiring, and she became even more disillusioned by an incident that occurred at the end of the summer holidays.

Florentyna had returned to work for her father in New York. She had learned a lot since the 'Jessie Kovats' incident. In fact Abel was now happy to leave her in charge of various Baron shops when their managers were on vacation.

During one lunch break she tried to avoid a smartly dressed middle-aged man who was passing through the hotel lobby at the same time, but he spotted her, and shouted:

'Hi, Florentyna.'

'Hello, Henry,' she said with little enthusiasm.

He leaned forward and gripped her on both arms before kissing her on the cheek.

'It's your lucky day, my dear,' he said.

'Why?' asked Florentyna, genuinely puzzled.

'I have been stood up by my date tonight and I'm going to give you the chance to take her place.'

Get lost, is what she would have said if Henry Osborne had not been a director of the Baron Group, and she was about to make some suitable excuse when he added, 'I've got tickets for *Can-Can*.'

Since her arrival in New York Florentyna had been trying to get seats for Broadway's latest smash hit and had been told they were sold out for eight weeks, by which time she would have returned to Radcliffe. She hesitated for a moment and then said, 'Thank you, Henry.'

They agreed to meet at Sardi's, where they had a drink before walking over to the Shubert Theatre. The show lived up to Florentyna's expectation and she realised it would have been churlish of her not to accept Henry's invitation to supper afterwards. He took her to the Rainbow Room and it was there that the trouble started. He had three double scotches before the first course arrived and although he was not the first person to put a hand on her knee he was the first of her father's friends to do so. By the time they came to the end of the meal Henry had drunk so much he was barely coherent.

In the cab on the way back to the Baron, he stubbed out his cigarette and tried to kiss her. She squeezed herself into the corner of the cab, but it didn't deter him. She had no idea how to handle a drunk and didn't know until then how persistent they could be. When they reached the Baron, he insisted on accompanying Florentyna to her room, and she felt unable to refuse his overtures for fear any public row would reflect badly on her father. Once they were in the private elevator he tried to kiss her again and when they reached her small apartment on the forty-first floor Henry forced his way into her room as she opened the door. He immediately went over to the small bar and poured himself another large scotch. Florentyna regretted that her father was in France and that George would have left the hotel to go home long ago. She wasn't quite sure what to do next.

'Don't you think you should leave now, Henry?'

'What?' slurred Henry. 'Before the fun has begun?' He lurched towards her. 'A girl ought to show how grateful she is when a fellow has taken her to the best show in town and given her a first-class meal.'

'I am grateful, Henry, but I am also tired, and I would like to go to bed.'

'Exactly what I had in mind.'

Florentyna felt quite sick as he almost fell on her and ran his hands down her back, stopping only when he reached her buttocks.

'Henry, you had better leave before you do something you'll regret,' Florentyna said, feeling she sounded a little absurd.

'I'm not gonna regret anything,' he said as he tried to force down the zip on the back of her dress. 'And neither will you.'

Florentyna tried to push him away, but he was far too

strong for her, so she began hitting him on the side of the arms.

'Don't put up too much of a fight, my dear,' he panted. 'I know you really want it, and I'll show you a thing or two those college boys won't know about.'

Florentyna's knees gave way and she collapsed on to the carpet with Henry on top of her, knocking the phone from a table on to the floor.

'That's better,' he said, 'I like a bit of spirit.'

He grabbed at her again, pinioning her arms above her head with one hand. He started moving his other hand up her thigh. With all the force she could muster she freed an arm and slapped Henry across the face but it only made him grab her hair tightly and push her dress up above her waist. There was a rip and Henry laughed drunkenly.

'It would have been easier . . . if you had taken the damned thing off . . . in the first place,' he said in breathless grunts as he extended the tear.

Florentyna stared helplessly backwards and saw a heavy crystal vase holding some roses next to where the phone had stood. With her free arm she pulled Henry towards her and started kissing him passionately on the face and neck.

'That's more like it,' he said, releasing her other arm.

Slowly she reached backwards for the vase. When she had it firmly in her hand, she broke away and brought the vase crashing down on the back of his skull. His head slumped forward and it took all her strength to push him off her. Florentyna's first reaction when she saw the blood pouring from his scalp was to fear that she had killed him. There was a loud knock on the door.

Startled, Florentyna tried to stand up, but she felt too weak in the knees. The knock came again, even louder, but this time accompanied by a voice that could belong to only one person. Florentyna staggered to the door and opened it to find Bella taking up the whole space between the jambs.

'You look awful.'

'I feel awful.' Florentyna stared down at her tattered Balenciaga evening dress.

'Who did that to you?'

Florentyna took a pace backwards and pointed to the motionless body of Henry Osborne.

'Now I see why your phone was off the hook,' said Bella as she strode over to the prostrate body. 'Got less than he deserved, I see.'

'Is he still alive?' asked Florentyna weakly.

Bella, knelt over him and checked his pulse, replying, 'Unfortunately, yes. It's only a flesh wound. He wouldn't have lived if I'd hit him. Now all he'll have to show for his trouble is a large bump on his head in the morning, which is not enough for a jerk like that. I think I'll throw him out of the window,' she added, picking Henry up and chucking him over her shoulder as if he were a sack of potatoes.

'No, Bella. We're on the forty-first floor.'

'He won't notice the first forty,' said Bella, and started walking towards the window.

'No, no,' said Florentyna.

Bella grinned before turning back. 'I'll be generous this time and put him in the freight elevator. The management can deal with him as they see fit.' Florentyna did not argue as Bella strode past her with Henry still over her shoulder. She returned a few moments later looking as if she had saved a penalty against Vassar.

'I've sent him to the basement,' she said with glee.

Florentyna was sitting on the floor sipping a Rémy Martin.

'Bella, am I ever going to be wooed romantically?'

'I'm the wrong person to ask. No one has ever tried to rape me, let alone be romantic.'

Florentyna fell into her arms laughing. 'Thank God you came when you did. Why are you here, not that I'm complaining?'

'Little Miss Efficiency has forgotten that I'm being put up in the hotel tonight because I'm playing hockey in New York tomorrow. The Devils against the Angels.'

'But they're both men's teams.'

'That's what they think, and don't interrupt. When I arrived at the desk they had no reservation in my name and the receptionist told me the hotel was packed, so I thought I would come up and complain to the management. Give me a pillow and I'll be happy to sleep in the bath.'

Florentyna held her head in her hands.

'Why are you crying?'

'I'm not, I'm laughing. Bella, you deserve a king-size bed and you shall have one.' Florentyna put the phone back on the hook and then picked up the receiver.

'Yes, Miss Rosnovski?'

'Is the Presidential Suite free tonight?'

'Yes, miss.'

'Please register it in the name of Miss Bella Hellaman and charge it to me. She'll be down to confirm in a minute.'

'Certainly, miss. How will I recognise Miss Hellaman?'

The next morning Henry Osborne called and begged Florentyna not to tell her father what had taken place the night before, pleading with her that it wouldn't have happened if he had not drunk so much and adding plaintively that he could not afford to lose his place on the board. Florentyna stared down at the red bloodstain on the carpet and reluctantly agreed.

11

WHEN ABEL RETURNED FROM Paris he was appalled to learn that one of his directors had been found drunk in a freight elevator, and had needed seventeen stitches in his scalp.

'No doubt Henry is claiming he tripped over a dumb-waiter,' said Abel, before he unlocked his private drawer, took out an unmarked file and added another note to it.

'More likely a dumb blonde,' laughed George.

Abel nodded.

'Are you going to do anything about Henry?' George asked.

'Not at the moment. He's still useful as long as he has contacts in Washington. In any case, I'm up to my eyes with buildings in London and Paris and now I see the board wants me to look at possibilities in Amsterdam, Geneva, Cannes and Edinburgh. Not to mention the fact that Zaphia is threatening to take me to court if I don't increase her alimony.'

'Perhaps the easy way out would be to pension Henry off?' suggested George.

'Not quite yet,' replied Abel. 'There is still a reason why I need him.'

George couldn't think of even one.

'We'll kill 'em,' said Bella. Bella's decision to challenge Harvard's ice hockey team to a field hockey match came as no surprise to anyone except the Harvard team who politely declined the invitation without comment. Bella immediately took out a half-page advertisement in the Harvard *Crimson* which read:

'Harvard Jocks Flunk Radcliffe Challenge.'

The enterprising editor of the *Crimson*, who had seen the advertisement before it went to press, decided to interview Bella so she ended up on the front page as well. A photograph of Bella wearing her mask and pads, and brandishing a hockey stick, ran with the caption: 'She's more frightening when she takes the mask off.' Bella was delighted with the picture and with the caption.

Within a week Harvard had offered to send its third XI team to Radcliffe. Bella refused, demanding varsity players only. A compromise was reached, with Harvard making up a team of four varsity players, four junior varsity players and three third XI players. A date was chosen and the necessary preparations were made. The undergraduates at Radcliffe began to get quite chauvinistic about the challenge, and Bella became a cult figure on campus.

'More figure than cult,' she told Florentyna.

Bella's tactics for trying to win the match were later described by the Harvard *Crimson* as nothing short of diabolical. When the Harvard team arrived in their bus they were met by eleven amazons with hockey sticks slung over their shoulders. The fit young men were immediately whisked off for lunch. Members of the Harvard squad never normally drink a drop before a match but as the girls, without exception, ordered beers, they felt honour-bound to join them. Most of the men managed three cans before lunch and also enjoyed the excellent wine served throughout the meal. None of the Harvard men thought to comment on Radcliffe's generosity or to ask if they were breaking any college rules. All twenty-two ended the lunch with a glass of champagne to toast the fortunes of both colleges.

The eleven Harvard men were then escorted to their locker room, where they found another magnum of champagne awaiting them. The eleven happy ladies left them to change. When the Harvard captain led his team out on to the hockey field he was met by a crowd of over five hundred spectators and eleven strapping girls whom he had never seen before in his life. Eleven other ladies, not unknown to the captain, were finding it hard to remain awake in the stand. Harvard was 3–0 down by half-time and was lucky to lose only 7–0. The Harvard *Crimson* might well have described Bella as a cheat, but the Boston *Globe* declared her to be a woman of great enterprise.

The captain of the Harvard team immediately challenged Bella to a replay against the full varsity squad. 'Exactly what I wanted in the first place,' she told Florentyna. Bella accepted by sending a telegram from one side of Cambridge Common to the other. It read: 'Your place or mine?' Radcliffe had to arrange for several cars to transport their supporters, their ranks swelled by Harvard's decision to put on a dance that evening after the game. Florentyna drove Bella and three other members of the team to the field across the river in her newly acquired 1952 Oldsmobile, with hockey sticks, shin pads and goalie pads piled high in the trunk.

When they arrived, they did not meet up with any of the Harvard team before they reached the playing field. This time they were greeted by a crowd of three thousand, which included President Conant of Harvard and President Jordan of Radcliffe.

Bella's tactics again bordered on the dubious: each of her girls had clearly been instructed to play the man and not to concentrate too much on the ball. Ruthless hacking at vulnerable shins enabled them to hold Harvard to a scoreless first half.

The Radcliffe team nearly scored in the first minute of the second half which inspired them to rise above their normal game and it began to look as if the match might end in a draw when the Harvard centre forward, a man only slightly smaller than Bella, broke through and looked poised to score. He had reached the edge of the circle when Bella came charging out of her cage and hit him flat out with a shoulder charge. That was the last he remembered of the match and he departed a few seconds later on a stretcher. Both referees blew their whistles at once and a penalty was awarded to Harvard with only a minute to go. Their left wing was selected to take the shot. The five-foot-nine, slimly built man waited for the two teams to line up. He cracked the ball sharply to the right inner who lofted a shot straight into Bella's chest-pad. It dropped at her feet, and she kicked it to the right, where it landed back in front of the diminutive left wing. Bella charged at the slight figure, and gentle people in the crowd covered their eyes, but this time she had met her match. The left wing sidestepped deftly leaving the Radcliffe captain spread-eagled on the ground and himself ample time to flick the ball into the back of the net. The whistle blew and Radcliffe had lost 1–0.

It was the only occasion on which Florentyna had seen Bella cry, despite the crowd giving her a standing ovation as she led her team off the field. Although defeated Bella ended up with two compensations: the U.S. Women's Hockey Team selected her to play for her country, and she had met her future husband.

Florentyna was introduced to Claude Lamont at the reception after the match. He looked even smaller in his neat blue blazer and grey flannel trousers than he had on the field.

'Little sweetheart, isn't he?' said Bella, patting him on the head. 'Amazing goal.' Florentyna was surprised that Claude did not seem to object. All he said was, 'Didn't she play a first-class game?'

Bella and Florentyna returned to their rooms in Radcliffe and changed for the dance. Claude accompanied both girls to the hall, which Bella compared with a cattle show as the men swarmed around her old roommate. They all wanted to dance the jitterbug with her, so Claude was dispatched to fetch enough food and drink to feed an army, which Bella disposed of while she watched her friend in a whirl of Trigère silk on the dance floor.

Florentyna first saw him sitting talking to a girl in the corner of the room while she was dancing. He must have been about six feet in height with wavy fair hair and a tan that only proved he did not spend his winter vacations in Cambridge. As she looked he turned towards the dance floor and their eyes met. Florentyna turned quickly away and tried to concentrate on what her partner was saying – something about America moving into the computer age and how he was going to climb on the bandwagon. When the dance ended, the talkative partner took her back to Bella. Florentyna turned to find him by her side.

'Have you had something to eat?' he asked.

'No,' she lied.

'Would you like to join my table?'

'Thank you,' she said, and left Bella and Claude discussing the relative merits of the value of wing to wing passing, comparing field hockey with ice hockey.

For the first few minutes neither of them spoke. He brought some food over from the buffet and then they both tried to speak at once. His name was Scott Forbes and he was majoring in history at Harvard. Florentyna had read about him in Boston's society columns, as the heir to the Forbes family business and one of the most sought-after young men in America. She wished it was otherwise. What's in a name, she said to herself, and she told him hers. It didn't seem to register.

'A pretty name for a beautiful woman,' he said. 'I'm sorry we haven't met before.' Florentyna smiled. He added, 'Actually I was at Radcliffe a few weeks ago, playing in the infamous hockey game when we lost 7–0.'

'You played in that match? I didn't notice you.'

'I'm not surprised. I spent most of the time on the ground feeling sick. I had never drunk so much in my life. Bella Hellaman may look big to you when you're sober, but she looks like a Sherman tank when you're drunk.'

Florentyna laughed and sat happily listening to Scott tell stories of Harvard, his family and his life in Boston. For the rest of the evening she danced only with one man and when the night came to an end he accompanied her back to Radcliffe.

'Can I see you tomorrow?' Scott asked.

'Yes, of course.'

'Why don't we drive out to the country and have lunch together?'

'I'd like that.'

Florentyna and Bella spent most of that night telling each other about their respective partners.

'Do you think it matters that he's straight out of the Social Register?'

'Not if he's a man worth taking seriously,' replied Bella, aware of just how real Florentyna's fears were. 'I have no idea if Claude is on any social register,' she added.

The next morning, Scott Forbes drove Florentyna out into the countryside in his old M.G. She had never been happier in her life. They went to lunch in a little restaurant in Dedham that was full of people whom Scott seemed to know. Florentyna was introduced to a Lowell, a Winthrop, a Cabot and another Forbes. She was relieved to see Edward Winchester coming towards her from a corner table, leading an attractive dark-haired girl by the hand – at least, Florentyna thought, I know someone. She was astonished at how handsome and happy Edward looked and soon found out why, when he introduced his fiancée, Danielle.

'You two ought to get on famously,' said Edward.

'Why?' asked Florentyna, smiling at the girl.

'Danielle is French, and I've been telling her for a long time that I might have been the Dauphin but even when I declared you were a witch, you had to teach me how to pronounce *sorcière*.'

As Florentyna watched them depart hand in hand, Scott said quietly, '*Je n'aurais jamais pensé que je tomberais amoureux d'une sorcière.*'

Florentyna chose a simple meal of sole and agreed with his selection of Muscadet, grateful for her knowledge of food and wine, and was surprised to find at four o'clock that they were the only two left in the restaurant, with a head waiter hinting that the time might have come to prepare for the evening meal. When they returned to Radcliffe Scott kissed her gently on the cheek and said he would call her tomorrow.

He phoned during lunch the next day to ask if she could bear to watch him play ice hockey for the junior varsity against Penn on Saturday and suggested dinner together afterwards.

Florentyna accepted, masking her delight, for she couldn't wait to see him again. It seemed the longest week in her life.

On Saturday morning she made one important decision about her weekend with Scott. She packed a small suitcase and put it in the boot of the car before driving to the rink long before the face-off. She sat in the bleachers, waiting for Scott to arrive. For a moment she feared he might not feel the same way about her when they met for a third time but he dispelled that fear in a moment when he waved and skated across the ice towards her.

'Bella said I can't come home if you lose.'

'Perhaps I don't want you to,' he said, as he glided slantingly away.

She watched the game, becoming colder and colder. Scott hardly seemed to touch the puck all afternoon, but he still managed to get slammed repeatedly into the boards. She decided that it was a stupid sport but that she would not tell him so. After the match was over, she sat in her car waiting for him to change; then another reception and at last they were on their own. He took her to Locke-Ober's where again he seemed to know everyone, but this time she did not recognise anybody other than those she had seen in the fashionable magazines. He didn't notice, as he could not have been more attentive, which helped Florentyna relax. Once more, they were the last to leave, and he drove her back to her car. He kissed her gently on the lips.

'Would you like to come to lunch at Radcliffe tomorrow?'

'I can't,' he said. 'I have a paper to finish in the morning, and I'm not sure I can complete it before two o'clock. You couldn't bear joining me for tea?'

'Of course I will, silly.'

'What a pity. If I had known I would have booked you a room in the guest quarters.'

'What a pity,' echoed Florentyna, thinking of the un-opened suitcase lying in the trunk of her car.

The next day, Scott picked her up shortly after three and took her back to his rooms for tea. She smiled as he closed the door, remembering that it was still not allowed at Radcliffe. His room was considerably larger than hers and on his desk was a picture of an aristocratic, slightly severe-looking lady who could only have been his mother. As Florentyna took in the room she realised that none of the furniture belonged to Harvard.

After he had given her tea they listened to America's new singing idol, Elvis Presley, before Scott put on the no longer skinny Sinatra singing 'South of the Border' and they danced, each wondering what was in the other's mind. When they sat down on the sofa, he kissed her at first gently, then with passion. He seemed reluctant to go any further and Florentyna was both too shy and too ignorant to help him. Suddenly he placed a hand over her breast as if waiting for Florentyna's reaction. At last his hand moved to the top of

her dress and fumbled with the first button. Florentyna made
no attempt to stop him as he continued with the second. Soon
he was kissing her, first on the shoulder, then on her breast.
Florentyna wanted him so badly that she almost made the
next move herself, but quite suddenly he stood up and took
off his shirt. In response she quickly slipped out of her dress
and let her shoes fall to the floor. They made their way to the
bed, clumsily trying to remove what was left of each other's
clothing. For a moment they stared at each other before
climbing on to the bed. To her surprise the pleasure of
making love seemed to be over in seconds.

'I'm sorry, I was awful,' said Florentyna.

'No, no, it was me.' He paused. 'I might as well admit it,
that was my first time.'

'Not you as well?' she said, and they both burst out
laughing.

They lay in each other's arms for the rest of the evening,
and made love twice more, each time with greater pleasure
and confidence. When Florentyna woke in the morning,
cramped and rather tired but exultantly happy, she felt
instinctively they would spend the rest of their lives together.
For the remainder of that term they saw one another every
weekend, and sometimes during the week as well.

In the spring vacation, they met secretly in New York and
Florentyna spent the happiest three days she could remember. *On the Waterfront, Limelight* and, on Broadway, *South
Pacific* preceded the '21' club, Sardi's and even the Oak Room
at the Plaza. In the morning they shopped, visited the Frick
and walked through the park. When she returned home at
night her arms were laden with presents that ended up by the
side of her bed.

The spring term was idyllic and they were rarely out of
each other's company. As it drew to a close, Scott invited
Florentyna to spend a week in Marblehead during the spring
vacation to meet his parents.

'I know they'll love you,' he said, as he put her on the train
to Chicago.

'I hope so,' she replied.

Florentyna spent hours telling her mother how wonderful Scott was and how much she was bound to love him. Zaphia was delighted to see her daughter so happy, and genuinely looked forward to meeting Scott's parents. She prayed Florentyna had found someone with whom she could spend the rest of her life and not make an impulsive decision that she would later regret. Florentyna selected yards of different coloured silks from Marshall Field's and passed the evenings designing a dress she felt certain would capture the heart of Scott's mother.

The letter came on a Monday, and Florentyna immediately recognised Scott's handwriting. She tore the envelope open in happy anticipation but it contained only a short note saying that because of a change in his family plans he would have to postpone her trip to Marblehead. Florentyna read the letter again and again, looking for some hidden message. Remembering only how happily they had parted she decided to call his home.

'The Forbes residence,' said a voice that sounded like the butler's.

'May I speak to Mr. Scott Forbes?' Florentyna could hear her voice quiver as she said his name.

'Who is calling him, ma'am?'

'Florentyna Rosnovski.'

'I'll see if he's in, ma'am.'

Florentyna clutched the phone and waited impatiently for Scott's reassuring voice.

'He's not at home at the moment, ma'am, but I will leave a message saying that you called.'

Florentyna didn't believe him and an hour later called again.

The voice said, 'He is still not back ma'am,' so she waited until eight that evening, when the same voice announced that he was at dinner.

'Then please tell him I'm calling.'

'Yes, ma'am.'

The voice returned a few moments later and said perceptibly less politely, 'He cannot be disturbed.'

'I don't believe it. I don't believe you've told him who it is.'

'Madam, I can assure you –'

Another voice came on the line, a lady's, with the ring of habitual authority.

'Who is this calling?'

'My name is Florentyna Rosnovski. I was hoping to speak to Scott as . . .'

'Miss Rosenovski, Scott is having dinner with his fiancée at the moment and cannot be disturbed.'

'His fiancée?' whispered Florentyna, her nails drawing blood from the palm of her hand.

'Yes, Miss Rosenovski.' The phone went dead. It took several seconds for the news to sink in, then Florentyna said out loud, 'Oh, my God, I think I'll die,' and fainted.

She woke to find her mother by the side of her bed.

'Why?' was Florentyna's first word.

'Because he wasn't good enough for you. The right man won't allow his mother to select the person he spends the rest of his life with.'

Once Florentyna returned to Cambridge matters did not improve. She was unable to concentrate on any serious work and often spent hours on her bed in tears. Nothing Bella could do or say seemed to help and she could devise no better tactic than belittlement, 'Not the sort of man I would want on my team.' Other men asked Florentyna for dates but she didn't accept any of them. Her father and mother became so worried for her that they even spoke to each other about the problem.

Finally when Florentyna was near to failing a course, Miss Rose warned her that she had a lot of work to do if she still hoped to win her Phi Beta Kappa key. Florentyna remained indifferent. During the summer vacation she stayed at home in Chicago, accepting no invitations to parties or dinners. She helped her mother choose some new clothes but bought none for herself. She read all the details of the 'society wedding of the year' as the Boston *Globe* referred to the marriage of Scott Forbes to Cynthia Knowles, but it only made her cry again. The arrival of a wedding invitation from Edward Winchester did not help. Later she tried to remove Scott from her thoughts by going to New York and working unheard-of hours for her father at the New York Baron. As the holiday drew to a close she dreaded returning to Radcliffe for her final year. No amount of advice from her father or sympathy from her mother seemed to improve matters. They both began to despair when she showed no interest in the preparations for her twenty-first birthday.

It was a few days before Florentyna was due to return to Radcliffe that she saw Edward across Lake Shore Drive. He looked as unhappy as she felt. Florentyna waved and smiled. He waved back but didn't smile. They stood and stared at each other until Edward crossed the road.

'How's Danielle?' she asked.

He stared at her. 'Haven't you heard?'

'Heard what?' said Florentyna.

He continued to stare at her as if he couldn't get out the words. 'She's dead.'

Florentyna gazed back at him in disbelief.

'She was driving too fast, showing off in my new Austin-Healey, and she turned the car over. I lived, she died.'

'Oh, my God,' Florentyna said, putting her arms around him. 'How selfish I've been.'

'No, I knew you had your own troubles.'

'Nothing compared with yours. Are you going back to Harvard?'

'I have to. Danielle's father insisted, said he would never forgive me if I didn't. So now I have something to work for. Don't cry, Florentyna, because once I start I can't stop.'

Florentyna shuddered. 'Oh, my God, how selfish I've been,' she repeated.

'Come over to Harvard some time. We'll play tennis and you can help me with my French verbs. It will be like old times.'

'Will it?' she said, wistfully. 'I wonder.'

12

WHEN FLORENTYNA RETURNED TO Radcliffe, she was greeted by a two-hundred-page course catalogue that took her three evenings to digest. From the catalogue she could choose one elective course outside her major area of study. Miss Rose suggested she ought to take up something new, something she might never have another chance to study in depth.

Florentyna had heard, as every other member of the university had, that Professor Luigi Ferpozzi would be spending a year as guest lecturer at Harvard, and conducting a seminar once a week. Since winning his Nobel Peace Prize he had roamed the world receiving accolades, and when he was awarded an honorary degree from Oxford the citation described him as the only man with whom the Pope and the President were in total agreement, other than God. The world's leading authority on Italian architecture had chosen Baroque Rome for his overall subject. 'City of the Eye and the Mind' was to be the title of his first lecture. The synopsis in the course catalogue was tempting: Gianlorenzo Bernini, the artist aristocrat, and Francesco Borromini, the stone cutter's son, transformed the Eternal City of the Caesars and the Popes into the most recognisable capital in the world. Prerequisites: knowledge of Latin and Italian, with German and French highly recommended. Limited to thirty students.

Miss Rose was not optimistic about Florentyna's chances of being among the chosen few. 'They tell me there is already a line from the Widener Library to Boston Common just to see him, not to mention the fact that he is a well known misogynist.'

'So was Julius Caesar.'

'When I was in the common room last night he didn't treat me like Cleopatra,' said Miss Rose. 'But I do admire the fact that he flew with Bomber Command during the Second World War. He was personally responsible for saving half the churches in Italy by seeing that the planes did not fly over important buildings.'

'Well, I want to be one of his chosen disciples,' said Florentyna.

'Do you?' said Miss Rose, drily. 'Well, if you fail,' she added laughing – as she scribbled a note for Professor Ferpozzi – 'you can always sign up for one of those science survey courses. They seem to have no limit on numbers.'

'Rocks for Jocks,' said Florentyna disparagingly. 'Not me. I'm off to ensnare Professor Ferpozzi.'

The next morning at eight thirty, a full hour before the professor was officially available to see anyone that day, Florentyna climbed the marble steps of the Widener Library. Once in the building, she took the elevator – large enough to hold herself and one book – to the top floor where the senior professors had offices under the eaves. An earlier generation had obviously decided that being far removed from zealous students more than made up for the long climb or the inconvenience of an always occupied elevator.

Once Florentyna had reached the top of the building she found herself standing in front of a frosted door. The name 'Professor Ferpozzi' was newly stencilled in black paint on the glass. She recalled that in 1945 it was this man who had sat with President Conant in Munich and between them they had decided the fate of German architecture: what should be preserved and what should be razed. She was only too aware that she shouldn't bother him for at least another hour. She half turned, intent on retreat, but the elevator was already disappearing to a lower floor. Turning again, she knocked boldly on the door. Then she heard the crash.

'Madonna! Whoever that is, go away. You have caused me

to break my favourite teapot,' said an angry voice whose mother tongue could only have been Italian.

Florentyna stifled the impulse to run and instead slowly turned the door knob. She put her head round the door and looked into a room that must have had walls, but there was no way of knowing because books and periodicals were stacked from floor to ceiling as if they had taken the place of bricks and mortar.

In the middle of the clutter stood a professorial figure who could have been anywhere between forty and seventy. A tall man, he wore an old Harris tweed jacket and grey flannel trousers that looked as though they had been acquired from a secondhand shop or inherited from his grandfather. He was holding a brown china handle that moments before had been attached to a teapot. At his feet lay a teabag surrounded by fragments of brown china.

'I have been in possession of that teapot for over thirty years. I loved it second only to the *Pietà*, young woman. How do you intend to replace it?'

'As Michelangelo is not available to sculpt you another, I will have to go to Woolworth's and buy one.'

The professor smiled despite himself. 'What do you want?' he asked, picking up the teabag but leaving the remains of his teapot on the floor.

'To enroll in your course,' Florentyna replied.

'I do not care for women at the best of times,' he said, not facing her. 'And certainly not for one who causes me to break my teapot before breakfast. Do you possess a name?'

'Rosnovski.'

He stared at her for a moment before sitting at his desk and dropping the teabag into an ashtray. He scribbled briefly. 'Rosnovski, you have the thirtieth place.'

'But you don't know my grades or qualifications.'

'I am quite aware of your qualifications,' he said ominously. 'For next week's group discussion you will prepare a paper on' – he hesitated for a moment – 'on one of Borromini's earlier works, San Carlo alle Quattro Fontane. Good day,' he added, as Florentyna scribbled furiously on her notepad. He returned to the remains of his teapot, without giving her another thought.

Florentyna left, closing the door quietly behind her. She walked slowly down the marble steps trying to compose her thoughts. Why had he accepted her so quickly? How could he have known anything about her?

During the following week she spent long days in the crypts of the Fogg Museum poring over learned journals, making slides of the reproductions of Borromini's plans for San Carlo, even checking his lengthy expense list to see how much the remarkable building had cost. She also found time to visit the china department of Shreve, Crump & Lowe.

When Florentyna had completed the paper, she rehearsed it the night before and felt confident about the outcome; a confidence that evaporated the moment she arrived at Professor Ferpozzi's seminar. The room was already packed with expectant students and when she checked the list pinned to the wall she was horrified to discover that she was the only non-graduate present, the only non-Fine Arts student and the only woman on the course. A projector was placed on his desk facing a large white screen.

'Ah, the home wrecker returns,' the professor said, as Florentyna took the one remaining seat at the front. 'For those of you who have not come across Miss Rosnovski before, do not invite her home for tea.' He smiled at his own remark and tapped his pipe on the corner of the desk, a sign that he wished the class to commence.

'Miss Rosnovski,' he said with confidence, 'is going to give us a talk on Borromini's Oratorio di San Filippo Neri.' Florentyna's heart sank. 'No, no.' He smiled a second time. 'I am mistaken, it was, if I remember correctly, the Church of San Carlo.'

For twenty minutes Florentyna delivered her paper, showing slides and answering questions. Ferpozzi hardly stirred from behind his pipe, other than to correct her occasional mispronunciation of seventeenth-century Roman coins.

When Florentyna finally sat down, he nodded thoughtful-

ly and declared, 'A fine presentation of the work of a genius.'
She relaxed for the first time that day as Ferpozzi rose briskly
to his feet. 'Now it is my painful duty to show you the
contrast, and I want everyone to make notes in preparation
for a full discussion next week.' Ferpozzi shuffled over to the
projector and flicked his first slide into place. A building
shone up on the screen behind the professor's desk.

Florentyna stared in dismay at a ten-year-old picture of
the Chicago Baron towering above a cluster of elegant
small-scale apartment buildings on Michigan Avenue.
There was an eerie silence in the room, and one or two
students were staring at her to see how she reacted.

'Barbaric, isn't it?' Ferpozzi's smile returned. 'I am not
referring only to the building, which is a worthless piece of
plutocratic self-congratulation, but to the overall effect that
this edifice has on the city around it. Note the way the tower
breaks the eye's sense of symmetry and balance in order to
make certain that it's the only building we shall look at.' He
flicked a second slide up on to the screen. This time it
revealed the San Francisco Baron. 'A slight improvement,'
he declared, staring into the darkness at his attentive audience, 'but only because since the earthquake of 1906 the city
ordinances in San Francisco do not allow buildings to be
more than twenty storeys in height. Now let's travel abroad,'
he continued, turning to face the screen again. Up on the
screen came the Cairo Baron, its gleaming windows reflecting the chaos and poverty of the slums huddled on top of each
other in the distance.

'Who can blame the natives for backing the occasional
revolution when such a monument to Mammon is placed in
their midst while they try to survive in mud hovels that don't
even stretch to electricity?' Inexorably, the professor produced slides of the Barons in London, Johannesburg and
Paris, before saying, 'I want your critical opinion on all of
these monstrosities by next week. Do they have any
architectural value, can they be justified on financial grounds
and will they ever be seen by your grandchildren? If so, why?
Good day.'

Everyone filed out of the professor's room except Florentyna who unwrapped the brown paper parcel by her side.

'I have brought you a farewell present,' she said, and stood up, holding out an earthenware teapot. Just at the moment Ferpozzi opened his hands, she let go and the teapot fell to the ground at his feet and shattered into several pieces.

He stared at the fragments on the floor. 'I deserved no less,' he said, and smiled at her.

'That,' she rejoined, determined to say her piece, 'was unworthy of a man of your reputation.'

'Absolutely right,' he said, 'but I had to discover if you had backbone. So many women don't, you know.'

'Do you imagine your position allows you . . .'

He waved a dismissive hand. 'Next week I shall read your defence of your father's empire with interest, young woman, and I shall be only too happy to be found wanting.'

'Did you imagine I would be returning?' she said.

'Oh yes, Miss Rosnovski. If you are half the woman my colleagues claim you are, I shall have a battle on my hands next week.'

Florentyna left, just stopping herself from slamming the door behind her.

For seven days she talked with architecture professors, Boston's city planners and international urban conservationists. She telephoned her father, mother and George Novak before coming to the reluctant conclusion that, although they all had different excuses, Professor Ferpozzi had not exaggerated. She returned to the top of the library a week later and sat at the back of the room, dreading what her fellow students would have come up with.

Professor Ferpozzi stared at her as she sank into her seat. He then tapped his pipe into an ashtray and addressed the class. 'You will leave your essays on the corner of my desk at the end of this session, but today I want to discuss the influence of Borromini's work on European churches during the century after his death.' Ferpozzi then delivered a lecture of such colour and authority that his thirty students hung on every word. When he had finished he selected a sandy-haired young man in the front row to prepare next week's paper on Borromini's first meeting with Bernini.

Once again, Florentyna remained seated while all the other students filed out, leaving their essays on the corner of Ferpozzi's desk. When they were alone, she handed him a brown paper parcel. He unwrapped it to find a Royal Worcester 'Viceroy' teapot in bone china, dated 1912. 'Magnificent,' he said. 'And it will remain so as long as no one drops it.' They both laughed. 'Thank you, young lady.'

'Thank you,' Florentyna replied, 'for not putting me through any further humiliation.'

'Your admirable restraint, unusual in a woman, made it clear that it was unnecessary. I hope you will forgive me, but it would have been equally reprehensible not to try and influence someone who will one day control the largest hotel empire in the world.' Such a thought had never crossed Florentyna's mind until that moment. 'Please assure your father that I always stay in a Baron whenever I have to travel. The rooms, the food and the service are quite the most acceptable of any of the major groups, and there is never anything to complain about once you are *inside* the hotel looking out. Be sure you learn as much about the stonecutter's son as I know about the empire-builder from Slonim. Being an immigrant is something your father and I will always be proud to have in common. Good day, young lady.'

Florentyna left the office below the eaves of Widener sadly aware of how little she knew of the workings of her father's empire.

During that year she concentrated hard on her modern language studies, but she could always be found on Tuesday afternoons sitting on a pile of books listening intently to Professor Ferpozzi's lectures. It was President Conant who remarked at dinner one night that it was sad that his learned colleague was having the kind of friendship with Florentyna that he really should have had thirty years before.

Graduation day at Radcliffe was a colourful affair. Proud, smartly dressed parents mingled with professors swathed in the scarlet, purple and multi-coloured hoods appropriate to their degrees. The academics glided about, resembling a convocation of bishops, informing the visitors how well their offspring had done, sometimes with a little considerate licence. In the case of Florentyna there was no need for exaggeration, for she had graduated summa cum laude and had been elected to Phi Beta Kappa earlier in the year.

It was a day of celebration and sadness for Florentyna and Bella, who were to live on opposite sides of America, one in New York and the other in San Francisco. Bella had proposed to Claude on February 28th of their junior year – 'Couldn't wait for Leap Year,' she explained – and they had been married in the Houghton chapel at Harvard during the spring vacation. Claude had insisted on, and Bella had agreed to, 'Love, honour and obey'. Florentyna had realised then how lucky they both were when Claude said to her at the reception, 'Isn't Bella beautiful?'

Florentyna smiled and turned to Bella who was saying that it was sad Wendy was not with them. 'Not that she ever did a day's work,' added Bella, grinning.

'Florentyna could not have worked harder in her final year, and frankly no one will be surprised by her achievements,' said Miss Rose.

'I am sure she owes a great deal to you, Miss Rose,' Abel replied.

'No, no, but I was hoping to convince Florentyna to return to Cambridge and carry out some research work for a Ph.D. and then join the faculty, but she seems to have other ideas.'

'We certainly do,' said Abel. 'Florentyna will be joining the Baron Group as a director, with special responsibilities for the leasing of the shops in the hotels. They have grown out of control in the last few years and I fear I have been neglecting them.'

'You didn't tell me that was what you had in mind, Florentyna,' boomed Bella. 'I thought you said . . .'

'Shhhhh, Bella,' said Florentyna, putting a finger to her lips.

'Now what's this, young lady? Have you been keeping a secret from me?'

'Now's not the time or place, Papa.'

'Oh, come on, don't keep us in suspense,' said Edward. 'Is it the United Nations or General Motors who feel they cannot survive without you?'

'I must confess,' said Miss Rose, 'now that you have gained the highest qualifications this university can award I should be fascinated to know how you intend to use them.'

'Hoping to be a Rockette, perhaps,' said Claude.

'That's the nearest anyone has been yet,' said Florentyna.

Everyone laughed except Florentyna's mother.

'Well, if you can't find a job in New York, you can always come and work in San Francisco,' said Bella.

'I'll bear the offer in mind,' said Florentyna lightly.

To her relief, further discussion of her future was impossible because the graduation ceremony was about to begin. George Kennan, the former U.S. ambassador to Russia, delivered the address. His speech was received enthusiastically. Florentyna particularly enjoyed the quotation from Bismarck which ended his peroration: 'Let us leave just a few tasks for our children to perform.'

'You'll deliver that address one day,' said Edward, as they passed Tricentennial Hall.

'And pray, sir, what will be my chosen subject?'

'The problems of being the first woman President.'

Florentyna laughed. 'You still believe it, don't you?'

'And so do you, even if it will always fall upon me to remind you.'

Edward had been seen regularly with Florentyna during the year, and friends hoped they might soon announce their engagement, but Edward knew that would never be. This was one woman who would always be unattainable, he thought. They were destined to be close friends, never lovers.

After Florentyna had packed her last few belongings and said goodbye to her mother, she checked that she had left nothing in her room and sat on the end of her bed reflecting on her time at Radcliffe. All she had to show for it was that she had arrived with three suitcases and was leaving with six and a Bachelor of Arts degree. A crimson ice hockey pennant once given to her by Scott was all that remained on the wall. Florentyna unpinned the pennant, held it for a moment, then dropped it into a waste-paper basket.

She sat in the back of the car with her father as the chauffeur drove out of the campus for the last time.

'Could you drive a little slower?' she asked.

'Certainly, ma'am.'

Florentyna turned and stared out of the rear window until the spires of Cambridge were no longer visible above the trees, and there was nothing left of her past to see.

13

THE CHAUFFEUR BROUGHT THE Rolls-Royce to a halt at the traffic lights on Arlington Street on the west side of the Public Garden. He waited for the lights to turn green while Florentyna chatted with her father about their forthcoming trip to Europe.

Just as the lights changed, another Rolls passed in front of them, turning off Commonwealth Avenue. Another graduate and parent were deep in conversation in the back.

'I sometimes think it would have been better for you to have gone to Yale, Richard,' she said.

Richard's mother looked at him approvingly. He already had the fine aristocratic looks that had attracted her to his father over twenty years before, and now he had made it five generations of the family who had graduated from Harvard.

'Why Yale?' he asked gently, pulling his mother back from her reminiscences.

'Well, it might have been more healthy for you to get away from the introverted air of Boston.'

'Don't let father hear you say that. He would consider such a suggestion nothing less than treason.'

'But do you have to return to Harvard Business School, Richard? Surely there must be other business schools?'

'Like father, I want to be a banker. If I'm going to follow in his footsteps, Yale isn't equipped to tie Harvard's laces,' he said mockingly.

A few minutes later the Rolls came to a halt outside a large house on Beacon Hill. The front door opened and a butler stood in the doorway.

'We have about an hour before the guests arrive,' said Richard, checking his watch. 'I'll go and change immediately. Mother, perhaps we could meet up a little before seven thirty in the West Room?' He even sounded like his father, she thought.

Richard bounded up the stairs two at a time; in most houses he could have managed three. His mother followed behind at a more leisurely pace, her hand never once touching the banister rail.

The butler watched them disappear before returning to the pantry. Mrs. Kane's cousin, Henry Cabot Lodge, would be joining them for dinner, so he needed to double-check that everything below stairs was perfect.

Richard stood in the shower smiling at the thought of his mother's concern. He had always wanted to graduate from Harvard and improve on his father's achievements. He couldn't wait to enroll at the business school next fall, although he had to admit he was looking forward to taking Mary Bigelow to Barbados that summer. He had met Mary in the rehearsal rooms of the music society and later they were both invited to play in the university string quartet. The pert little lady from Vassar played the violin far better than he performed on the cello. When he eventually serenaded the reluctant Mary into bed he found she was again the better tuned, despite her pretence at inexperience. Since those days he had also discovered she was highly-strung.

Richard turned the dial to 'cold' for a brief moment before leaping out, drying and changing into evening dress. He checked himself in the mirror: double-breasted. Richard suspected he would be the only person that night wearing the latest fashion – not that it mattered when you were a little over six feet, slim and dark. Mary had once said that he looked good in everything from jock strap to morning coat.

He went downstairs and waited in the West Room for his mother to join him. When she appeared the butler served them both with a drink.

'Good heavens, are double-breasted suits back in fashion?' she enquired.

'You had better believe it. The very latest thing, Mother.'

'I can't believe it,' she said. 'I remember . . .'

The butler coughed. They both looked around. 'The Honourable Henry Cabot Lodge,' he announced.

'Henry,' said Richard's mother.

'Kate, my dear,' he replied, before kissing her on the cheek. Kate smiled; her cousin was wearing a double-breasted jacket.

Richard smiled, because it looked twenty years old.

Richard and Mary Bigelow returned from Barbados almost as brown as the natives. They stopped off in New York to have dinner with Richard's parents, who thoroughly approved of his choice. After all, she was the great-niece of Alan Lloyd, who had succeeded Richard's grandfather as chairman of the family bank.

As soon as Richard had returned to the Red House, their Boston residence on Beacon Hill, he quickly settled down and prepared himself for the business school. Everyone had warned him it was the most demanding course at the university with the largest drop-out rate, but once the term had started even he was surprised by how little free time he had to enjoy other pursuits. Mary began to despair when he had to relinquish his place in the string quartet and could manage to see her only at weekends.

At the end of his first year she suggested they take another vacation in Barbados and was disappointed to find he intended to stay put in Boston and continue studying.

When Richard returned for his final year he was determined to finish at or near the top of his class, and his father warned him not to relax until after the last exam paper had been completed. His father had added that if he did not make the top ten per cent he needn't apply for a position at the bank. He would not be accused of nepotism.

At Christmas, Richard rejoined his parents in New York, but remained for only three days before returning to Boston. His mother became quite anxious about the pressure he was putting himself under, but Richard's father pointed out that it was only for another six months. Then he could relax for the rest of his life. Kate reserved her opinion; she hadn't seen her husband relax in twenty-five years.

At Easter, Richard called his mother to say he ought to remain in Boston during the brief spring vacation, but she managed to convince him he should come down for his father's birthday. He agreed but added that he would have to return to Harvard the next morning.

Richard arrived at the family home on East Sixty-eighth Street just after four o'clock on the afternoon of his father's birthday. His mother was there to greet him as were his sisters, Virginia and Lucy. His mother thought he looked drawn and tired, and she longed for his exams to be over. Richard knew that his father would not break his routine at the bank for anyone's birthday. He would arrive home a few minutes after seven.

'What have you bought for Daddy's birthday?' enquired Virginia.

'I was waiting to seek your advice,' said Richard flatteringly, having quite forgotten about a present.

'That's what I call leaving it until the last moment,' said Lucy. 'I bought my present for him three weeks ago.'

'I know the very thing he needs,' said his mother. 'A pair of gloves. His old ones are nearly worn out.'

'Dark blue, leather, with no pattern,' said Richard laughing. 'I'll go to Bloomingdale's and choose a pair right now.'

He strode down Lexington Avenue, falling in with the pace

of the city. He was already looking forward to joining his father in the fall, and felt confident that if there were no distractions in the last few months he would come out in that top ten per cent. He would emulate his father and one day be chairman of the bank. He smiled at the thought. He pushed open the doors of Bloomingdale's, strode up the steps and asked an assistant where he could buy some gloves. As he began making his way through the crowded store, he glanced at his watch. There would be plenty of time to change for dinner before his father returned. He looked up at the two girls behind the glove counter. He smiled; the wrong one smiled back.

The smiling girl came quickly forward. She was a honey blonde with a little too much lipstick and one more button undone than Bloomingdale's could possibly have approved of. Richard couldn't help but admire such confidence. A small name tag pinned over her left breast read 'Maisie Bates'.

'Can I help you, sir?' she asked.

'Yes,' said Richard. He glanced towards the dark-haired girl. 'I need a pair of gloves, dark blue, leather and no pattern,' he said without letting his eyes return to the blonde.

Maisie selected a pair and put them on Richard's hands, pushing the leather slowly down each finger and then holding them up for him to admire.

'If they don't suit you, you could try another pair.'

'No, that's just fine,' he said. 'Do I pay you or the other girl?'

'I can take care of you.'

'Damn,' said Richard under his breath. He left reluctantly, determined he would return the next day. Until that afternoon he had considered love at first sight the most ridiculous cliché, fit only for readers of women's magazines.

His father was delighted with the 'sensible' present, as he referred to the gloves over dinner that night, and even more delighted with Richard's progress at business school.

'If you are in the top ten per cent I shall be happy to

consider offering you a position of trainee at the bank,' he said for the thousandth time.

Virginia and Lucy grinned. 'What if Richard comes out number one, Daddy? Will you make him chairman?' asked Lucy.

'Don't be frivolous, my girl. If Richard ever becomes chairman it will be because he will have earned the position after years of dedicated, hard work.' He turned to his son. 'Now, when are you returning to Harvard?'

Richard was about to say tomorrow, when he said, 'I think tomorrow.'

'Quite right,' was all his father commented.

The next day Richard returned not to Harvard, but to Bloomingdale's where he headed straight for the glove counter. Before he had any chance of letting the other girl serve him, Maisie pounced; he could do nothing about it, except purchase another pair of gloves and return home.

The following morning, Richard returned to Bloomingdale's for a third time and studied ties on the next counter until Maisie was busy serving a customer and the other girl was free. He then marched confidently up to the counter and waited for her to serve him. To Richard's horror, Maisie disengaged herself in mid-sentence from her customer and rushed over while the other girl took her place.

'Another pair of gloves?' giggled the blonde.

'Yes . . . Yes,' he said lamely.

Richard left Bloomingdale's with yet another pair of gloves – dark blue, leather with no pattern.

The following day, he told his father he was still in New York because he had to gather some data from Wall Street to complete a paper. As soon as his father had left for the bank, he headed off to Bloomingdale's. This time he had a plan for ensuring he spoke to the other girl. He marched up to the glove counter fully expecting Maisie to rush up, when the other assistant came forward to serve him.

'Good morning, sir,' she said.

'Oh, good morning,' said Richard, suddenly at a loss for words.

'Can I help you?'

'No – I mean yes. I would like a pair of gloves,' he added unconvincingly.

'Yes, sir. Have you considered dark blue? In leather? I'm sure we have your size – unless we're sold out.'

Richard looked at the name on her lapel badge: Jessie Kovats. She passed him the gloves. He tried them on. They didn't fit. He tried another pair and looked towards Maisie. She grinned at him encouragingly. He grinned nervously back. Miss Kovats handed him another pair of gloves. This time they fitted perfectly.

'I think that's what you're looking for,' said Jessie.

'No, not really,' said Richard.

Jessie lowered her voice and said, 'I'll go and rescue Maisie. Why don't you ask her out? I'm sure she'll say yes.'

'Oh, no,' said Richard. 'You don't understand. It's not her I want to take out – it's you.'

Jessie looked totally surprised.

'Will you have dinner with me tonight?'

'Yes,' she said shyly.

'Shall I pick you up at your home?'

'No. Let's meet at the restaurant.'

'Where would you like to go?'

Jessie didn't reply.

'Allen's at Seventy-third and Third?' Richard suggested.

'Yes, fine,' was all Jessie said.

'Around eight suit you?'

'Around eight,' said Jessie.

Richard left Bloomingdale's with what he wanted – and it wasn't a pair of gloves.

Richard couldn't remember a time when he had spent all day thinking about a girl, but from the moment Jessie had said 'Yes', he had thought of nothing else.

Richard's mother was delighted that he had decided to spend another day in New York and wondered if Mary

Bigelow was in town. Yes, she decided, when she passed the bathroom and heard Richard singing 'Once I had a secret love'.

Richard gave an unusual amount of thought to what he should wear that evening. He decided against a suit, finally selecting a dark blue blazer and a pair of grey flannel slacks. He also spent a little longer looking at himself in the mirror. Too Ivy League, he feared, but there wasn't much he could do about that at short notice.

He left the house on Sixty-eighth Street just before seven to avoid having to explain to his father why he was still in town. It was a crisp, clear evening and he arrived at Allen's a few minutes after seven thirty and ordered himself a Budweiser. Every few moments he checked his watch as the minute hand climbed up towards eight, and then every few seconds once it had passed the agreed hour, wondering if he would be disappointed when he saw her again.

He wasn't.

She stood in the doorway looking radiant in a simple blue dress that he assumed had come from Bloomingdale's, though any woman would have known it was a Ben Zuckerman. Her eyes searched the room. At last she saw Richard walking towards her.

'I am sorry to be late . . .' she began.

'It's not important. What's important is that you came.'

'You thought I wouldn't?'

'I wasn't sure,' Richard said, smiling. They stood staring at each other. 'I'm sorry, I don't know your name,' he said, not wanting to admit he had seen it every day at Bloomingdale's.

She hesitated. 'Jessie Kovats. And yours?'

'Richard Kane,' he said, offering her his hand. She took it, and he found himself not wanting to let go.

'And what do you do when you're not buying gloves at Bloomingdale's?' asked Jessie.

'I'm at Harvard Business School.'

'I'm surprised they didn't teach you that most people only have two hands.'

He laughed, already delighted that it wasn't going to be her looks alone that would make the evening memorable.

'Shall we sit down?' suggested Richard, taking her arm and leading her to his table.

Jessie began to study the menu on the blackboard.

'Salisbury steak?' she enquired.

'A hamburger by any other name,' said Richard.

She laughed and he was surprised that she had picked up his out of context quotation so quickly, and then felt guilty, because as the evening progressed it became obvious that she had seen more plays, read more novels and even attended more concerts than he had. It was the first time in his life he regretted his single-minded dedication to studying.

'Do you live in New York?' he asked.

'Yes,' she said, as she sipped the third coffee Richard had allowed the waiter to pour. 'With my parents.'

'Which part of town?' he asked.

'East Fifty-seventh Street,' Jessie replied.

'Then let's walk,' he said, taking her hand.

Jessie smiled her agreement and they zigzagged back across the city together. To make the journey take longer Richard stopped to gaze at shop windows which he would normally have passed on the trot. Jessie's knowledge of fashion and shop management was daunting. Richard felt sorry that she had left school at sixteen to work in the Baron Hotel before going to Bloomingdale's.

It took them nearly an hour to cover the sixteen blocks. When they reached Fifty-seventh Street, Jessie stopped outside a small old apartment house.

'This is where my parents live,' she said. He held on to her hand.

'I hope you will see me again,' said Richard.

'I'd like that,' said Jessie, not sounding very enthusiastic.

'Tomorrow?' asked Richard diffidently.

'Tomorrow?' queried Jessie.

'Yes. Why don't we go to the Blue Angel and see Bobby Short?' He took her hand again. 'It's a little more romantic than Allen's.'

Jessie seemed uncertain, as if the request was causing her a problem.

'Not if you don't want to,' he added.

'I'd love to,' she said in a whisper.

'I'm having dinner with my father, so why don't I pick you up around ten o'clock?'

'No, no,' said Jessie. 'I'll meet you there. It's only two blocks away.'

'Ten o'clock then.' He leaned forward and kissed her on the cheek. It was the first time he was aware of a delicate perfume. 'Goodnight, Jessie,' he said, and walked away.

Richard began to whistle Dvorak's *Cello Concerto* and by the time he arrived home, had reached the end of the first movement. He couldn't recall an evening he had enjoyed more. He fell asleep thinking about Jessie instead of Galbraith or Freedman. The next morning he accompanied his father down to Wall Street and spent a day in the *Journal*'s library, taking only a short break for lunch. In the evening, over dinner, he told his father about the research he had been doing on reverse take-over bids and feared he might have sounded a little too enthusiastic.

After dinner, he went off to his room. He made sure that no one noticed him slip out of the front door a few minutes before ten. Once he had reached the Blue Angel he checked his table and returned to the foyer to wait for Jessie.

He could feel his heart beating and wondered why that had never happened with Mary Bigelow. When Jessie arrived, he kissed her on the cheek and led her into the lounge. Bobby Short's voice came floating through the air: 'Are you telling me the truth or am I just another lie?'

As Richard and Jessie walked in, Short raised his arm. Richard found himself acknowledging the wave although he had seen the artist only once before and had never been introduced to him.

They were guided to a table in the centre of the room where to Richard's surprise Jessie chose the seat with her back to the piano.

Richard ordered a bottle of Chablis and asked Jessie about her day.

'Richard, there is something I must —'

'Hi, Richard.' He looked away.

Standing by the table was another man dressed in dark blue blazer and grey flannel slacks.

'Hi, Steve. May I introduce Jessie Kovats – Steve Mellon. Steve and I were at Harvard together.'

'Seen the Yankees lately?' asked Steve.

'No,' said Richard. 'I only follow winners.'

'Like Eisenhower. With his handicap you would have thought he had been to Yale.' They chatted on for a few minutes. Jessie made no effort to interrupt them. 'Ah, she's arrived at last,' said Steve, looking towards the door. 'See you, Richard. Nice to have met you, Jessie.'

During the evening Richard told Jessie about his plans to come to New York and work at Lester's, his father's bank. She was such an intent listener he only hoped he hadn't been boring her. He enjoyed himself even more than the previous night and when they left he waved to Bobby Short as if they had grown up together. When they reached Jessie's home he kissed her on the lips for the first time. For a moment she responded, but then she said, 'Good night' and disappeared into the old apartment building.

The next morning he returned to Boston. As soon as he arrived back at the Red House he phoned Jessie: was she free to go to a concert on Friday? She said she was and for the first time in his life he crossed days off a calendar. Mary phoned him later in the week and he tried to explain to her as gently as possible why he was no longer available.

When the weekend came it was memorable. The New York Philharmonic, *Dial M for Murder* – Jessie even seemed to enjoy the New York Knicks. Richard reluctantly returned to Harvard on Sunday night. The next four months were going to be long weeks and short weekends. He phoned Jessie every day and they were rarely apart at weekends.

He began to dread Mondays.

*

During one Monday morning lecture, on the '29 crash, Richard found he couldn't concentrate. How was he going to explain to his father that he had fallen in love with a girl who worked behind the gloves, scarves and woollen hats counter at Bloomingdale's? Even to himself, Richard couldn't understand why such a bright, attractive girl could be so unambitious. If only Jessie had been given the opportunities he had had . . . He scribbled her name on the top of his class notes. His father was going to have to learn to live with it. He stared at what he had written: Jessie Kane.

When Richard arrived back in New York that weekend, he made an excuse to his mother about running out of razor blades. His mother suggested that he use his father's.

'No, no, it's all right,' said Richard. 'I need some of my own. In any case, we don't use the same brand.'

Kate Kane thought this was strange because she knew they did.

Richard had to run the eight blocks to Bloomingdale's to be sure he would make the store before it closed. When he reached the glove counter, Jessie was nowhere to be seen. Maisie was standing in a corner filing her fingernails.

'Is Jessie around?' he asked her breathlessly.

'No, she's already gone home – she left a few minutes ago. She can't have gone far. Aren't you . . .?'

Richard ran out on to Lexington Avenue. He searched for Jessie's face among the figures hurrying home. He would have given up if he hadn't recognised the flash of red, a scarf he had given her. She was on the other side of the street, walking towards Fifth Avenue. Her apartment was in the opposite direction; somewhat guiltily he decided to follow her. When she reached Scribner's on Forty-eighth Street, he stopped and watched her go into the bookshop. If she wanted something to read, surely she could have picked it up at Bloomingdale's? He was puzzled. He peered through the window as Jessie talked to a sales clerk, who left her for a few moments and then returned with two books. He could just make out their titles: *The Affluent Society* by John Kenneth Galbraith and *Inside Russia Today* by John Gunther. Jessie signed for them – which surprised Richard – and left as he ducked around the corner.

'Who *is* she?' said Richard out loud as he watched her double back and enter Bendel's. The doorman saluted respectfully, leaving a distinct impression of recognition. Once again Richard peered through the window to see sales ladies fluttering around Jessie with more than casual respect. An older lady appeared with a package, which Jessie had obviously been expecting. She opened it to reveal a full-length evening dress in red. Jessie smiled and nodded as the sales lady placed the dress in a brown and white box. Then, mouthing the words 'Thank you', Jessie turned towards the door without even signing for her purchase. Richard barely managed to avoid colliding with her as she hastened out of the store to jump into a cab.

He grabbed a taxi that an old lady had originally thought was hers, and told the driver to follow Jessie's cab. 'Like the movies, isn't it?' said the cab driver. Richard didn't reply. When the cab passed the small apartment house outside of which they normally parted, he began to feel queasy. The taxi in front continued for another hundred yards and came to a halt outside a dazzling new apartment house complete with a uniformed doorman, who was quick to open the door for Jessie. With astonishment and anger, Richard jumped out of his cab and started to make his way up to the door through which she had disappeared.

'That'll be ninety-five cents, fella,' said a voice behind him.

'Oh, sorry,' said Richard. He thrust his hand into his pocket and took out a note, hurriedly pushing it at the cab driver, not thinking about the change.

'Thanks, buddy,' said the driver, clutching on to the five-dollar bill. 'Someone sure is happy today.'

Richard hurried through the door of the building and managed to catch Jessie as she stepped into the elevator. She stared at him but didn't speak.

'Who are you?' demanded Richard as the elevator door closed. The other two occupants stared in front of them with a look of studied indifference as the elevator glided up to the second floor.

'Richard,' she stammered. 'I was going to tell you everything this evening. I never seemed to find the right opportunity.'

'Like hell you were going to tell me,' he said, following her out of the elevator and into an apartment. 'Stringing me along with a pack of lies for nearly three months. Well, now the time has come for the truth.'

He pushed his way past her brusquely as she opened the door. He looked beyond her into the apartment while she stood helplessly in the passageway. At the end of the entrance hall there was a large living room with a fine oriental rug and a magnificent Georgian bureau. A handsome grandfather clock stood opposite a side table on which there was a bowl of fresh anemones. The room was impressive even by the standards of Richard's own home.

'Nice place you've got yourself for a salesgirl,' he said sharply. 'I wonder which of your lovers pays for this?'

Jessie took a pace towards him and slapped him so hard that her own palm stung. 'How dare you?' she said. 'Get out of my home.'

As she said the words, she started to cry. Richard took her in his arms.

'Oh, God, I'm sorry,' he said. 'That was a terrible thing to suggest. Please forgive me. It's just that I love you so much and imagined I knew you so well, and now I find I don't know a thing about you.'

'Richard, I love you too and I'm sorry I hit you. I didn't want to deceive you, but there's no one else – I promise you that.' She touched his cheek.

'It was the least I deserved,' he said as he kissed her.

Clasped tightly in one another's arms, they sank on to the sofa and for some moments remained almost motionless. Gently he stroked her hair until her tears subsided. Jessie slipped her fingers through the gap between his top two shirt buttons.

'Do you want to sleep with me?' she asked quietly.

'No,' he replied. 'I want to stay awake with you all night.'

Without speaking further, they undressed and made love, gently and shyly at first, afraid to hurt each other, desperately trying to please. Finally, with her head on his shoulder, they talked.

'I love you,' said Richard. 'I have since the first moment I saw you. Will you marry me? Because I don't give a damn who you are, Jessie, or what you do, but I know I must spend the rest of my life with you.'

'I want to marry you too, Richard, but first I have to tell you the truth.'

She pulled Richard's jacket over her naked body as he lay silent waiting for her to speak.

'My name is Florentyna Rosnovski,' she began, and then told Richard everything about herself. Florentyna explained why she had taken the name of Jessie Kovats – so that she would be treated like any other sales girl while she learned the trade, and not like the daughter of the Chicago Baron. Richard never spoke once during her revelation and remained silent when she came to the end.

'Have you stopped loving me already?' she asked. 'Now that you know who I really am?'

'Darling,' said Richard very quietly. 'My father hates your father.'

'What do you mean?'

'Just that the only time I ever heard your father's name mentioned in his presence, he flew completely off the handle, saying your father's sole purpose in life seemed to be a desire to ruin the Kane family.'

'What? Why?' said Florentyna, shocked. 'I've never heard of your father. How do they even know each other? You must be mistaken.'

'I wish I were,' said Richard, and repeated the little his mother had once told him about the quarrel with her father.

'Oh, my God. That must have been the "Judas" my father referred to when he changed banks after twenty-five years,' she said. 'What shall we do?'

'Tell them the truth,' said Richard. 'That we met innocently, fell in love and now we're going to be married. And that nothing they can do will stop us.'

'Let's wait for a few weeks,' said Florentyna.

'Why?' asked Richard. 'Do you think your father can talk you out of marrying me?'

'No, Richard,' she said, touching him gently as she placed her head back on his shoulder. 'Never, my darling. But let's find out if we can do anything to break the news gently before we present them both with a *fait accompli*. Anyway, maybe they won't feel as strongly as you imagine. After all, you said the problem with the Richmond Group was over twenty years ago.'

'They still feel every bit as strongly, I promise you that. My father would be outraged if he saw us together, let alone thought we were considering marriage.'

'All the more reason to leave it for a little before we break the news to them. That will give us time to consider the best way to go about it.'

He kissed her again. 'I love you, Jessie.'

'Florentyna.'

'That's something else I'm going to have to get used to,' he said.

To begin, Richard allocated one afternoon a week to researching the feud between the two fathers, but after a time it became an obsession, biting heavily into his attendance at lectures. The Chicago Baron's attempt to get Richard's father removed from his own board would have made a good case study for the Harvard Business School. The more he discovered the more Richard realised that his father and Florentyna's were formidable rivals. Richard's mother spoke of the feud as if she had needed to discuss it with someone for years.

'Why are you taking such an interest in Mr. Rosnovski?' she asked.

'I came across his name when I was going through some back copies of the *Wall Street Journal*.' The truth, he thought, but a lie.

Florentyna took a day off from Bloomingdale's and flew to Chicago to tell her mother what had happened. When Florentyna pressed her as to what she knew of the row she spoke for almost an hour without interruption. Florentyna hoped her mother was exaggerating but a few carefully worded questions over dinner with George Novak made it painfully obvious that she hadn't been.

Every weekend the two lovers exchanged their knowledge, which only added to the catalogue of hate.

'It all seems so petty,' said Florentyna. 'Why don't they just meet and talk it over? I think they would get on rather well together.'

'I agree,' said Richard. 'But which one of us is going to try telling them that?'

'Both of us are going to have to, sooner or later.'

As the weeks passed Richard could not have been more attentive and kind. Although he tried to take Florentyna's mind off 'sooner or later' with regular visits to the theatre, the New York Philharmonic and long walks through the park, their conversation always drifted back to their parents.

Even during a cello recital which Richard gave her in her flat, Florentyna's mind was occupied by her father – how could be so obdurate? As the Brahms sonata came to an end Richard put down his bow and stared into her grey eyes.

'We have got to tell them soon,' he said, taking her in his arms.

'I know we must. I just don't want to hurt my father.'

'I know.'

She looked down at the floor. 'Next Friday, Papa will be back from Washington.'

'Then it's next Friday,' said Richard quietly, not letting her go.

As Florentyna watched Richard drive away that night she wondered if she would be strong enough to keep her resolve.

On the Friday, Richard ducked his morning lecture and travelled down to New York in time to spend the rest of the day with Florentyna.

They spent that afternoon going over what they would say when they respectively faced their parents. At seven o'clock the two left Florentyna's apartment on Fifty-seventh Street. They walked without talking. When they reached Park Avenue they stopped at the light.

'Will you marry me?'

It was the last question on Florentyna's mind as she braced herself to meet her father. A tear trickled down her cheek, a tear that she felt had no right to be there on the happiest moment of her life. Richard took a ring out of a little red box – a sapphire set in diamonds. He placed it on the third finger of her left hand. He tried to stop the tears by kissing her. They broke and stared at each other for a moment, then he turned and strode away.

They had agreed to meet again at the apartment as soon as their ordeal was over. She stared at the ring on her finger, next to the antique one, her favourite of the past.

As Richard walked up Park Avenue he went over the sentences he had so carefully composed in his mind and found himself on Sixty-eighth Street long before he felt he had completed the rehearsal.

He found his father in the drawing room drinking the usual Teacher's and soda before changing for dinner. His mother was complaining that his sister didn't eat enough. 'I think Virginia plans to be the thinnest thing in New York.' Richard wanted to laugh.

'Hello, Richard, I was expecting you earlier.'

'Yes,' said Richard. 'I had to see someone before I came home.'

'Who?' said his mother, not sounding particularly interested.

'The woman I am going to marry.'

They both looked at him astonished; it certainly wasn't the opening sentence Richard had planned so carefully.

His father was the first to recover. 'Don't you think you're a bit young? I feel sure you and Mary can afford to wait a little longer.'

'It's not Mary I intend to marry.'

'Not Mary?' said his mother.

'No,' said Richard. 'Her name is Florentyna Rosnovski.'

Kate Kane turned white.

'The daughter of Abel Rosnovski?' William Kane said without expression.

'Yes, Father,' said Richard firmly.

'Is this some sort of joke, Richard?'

'No, Father. We met in unusual circumstances and fell in love without either of us realising there was a misunderstanding between our parents.'

'Misunderstanding? Misunderstanding?' he repeated. 'Don't you realise that jumped-up Polish immigrant spends most of his life trying to get me thrown off my own board – and once nearly succeeded? And you describe that as a "misunderstanding"? Richard, you will never see the daughter of that crook again if you hope to sit on the board of Lester's Bank. Have you thought about that?'

'Yes, Father, I have, and it will make no difference to my decision. I have met the woman with whom I intend to spend the rest of my life and I am proud that she would even consider being my wife.'

'She has tricked and ensnared you so that she and her father can finally take the bank away from me. Can't you see through their plan?'

'Even you can't believe something as preposterous as that, Father.'

'Preposterous? He once accused me of being responsible for killing his partner, Davis Leroy, when I . . .'

'Father, Florentyna knew nothing of the circumstances surrounding your quarrel until she met me. How can you be so irrational?'

'She has told you she's pregnant, so you will have to marry her.'

'Father, that was unworthy of you. Florentyna has never put the slightest pressure on me from the moment we met. On the contrary.' Richard turned to his mother. 'Won't you both meet her and then you'll understand how it came about?'

Kate was going to reply when Richard's father shouted, 'No. Never,' and turning to his wife, he asked her to leave them alone. As she left, Richard could see that his mother was weeping.

'Now listen to me, Richard. If you marry the Rosnovski girl I will cut you off without a penny.'

'You suffer like generations of our family, Father, from imagining money can buy everything. Your son is not for sale.'

'But you could marry Mary Bigelow – such a respectable girl, and from our own background.'

Richard laughed. 'Someone as wonderful as Florentyna couldn't be replaced by a suitable Brahmin family friend.'

'Don't you mention our heritage in the same breath as that stupid Polack.'

'Father, I never thought I would have to listen to such pathetic prejudice from a normally sober person.'

William Kane took a pace towards his son. Richard never flinched. His father stopped in his tracks. 'Get out,' he said. 'You're no longer a member of my family. Never . . .'

Richard left the room. As he walked across the hall he became aware that his mother was leaning hunched against the banister. He went to her and took her in his arms. She whispered, 'I'll always love you,' and released him when she heard her husband come into the corridor.

Richard closed the front door gently behind him. He was back on Sixty-eighth Street. His only thought was how Florentyna had managed to face her own encounter. He hailed a cab and without looking back directed it to Florentyna's apartment.

He had never felt so free in his life.

When he reached Fifty-seventh Street he asked the doorman if Florentyna had returned. She hadn't, so he waited under the canopy, beginning to fear she might not have been able to get away. He was deep in thought and didn't notice when another cab came to a halt at the kerb and the frail figure of Florentyna stepped out. She was holding a tissue to a bleeding lip. She rushed towards him and they quickly went upstairs to the privacy of the apartment.

'I love you, Richard,' were her first words.

'I love you, too,' said Richard, and took her in his arms, holding her tightly as if it would solve their problems.

Florentyna didn't let go of Richard as he spoke.

'He threatened to cut me off without a penny if I married you,' he told her. 'When will they understand we don't care a damn about their money? I tried appealing to my mother for support, but even she couldn't control my father's temper. He insisted that she leave the room. I've never seen him treat my mother that way before. She was weeping, which only made my resolve stronger. I left him in mid-sentence. God knows, I hope he doesn't take it out on Virginia and Lucy. What happened when you told your father?'

'He hit me,' said Florentyna very quietly. 'For the first time in my life. I think he'll kill you if he finds us together. Richard darling, we must get out of here before he discovers where we are, and he's bound to try the apartment first. I'm so frightened.'

'No need for you to be frightened. We'll leave tonight and go as far away as possible and to hell with them both.'

'How quickly can you pack?' asked Florentyna.

'I can't,' said Richard. 'I can never return home now. You pack your things and then we'll go. I've got about a hundred dollars with me and my cello which is still in the bedroom. How do you feel about marrying a hundred-dollar man?'

'As much as a sales girl can hope for, I suppose – and to think I dreamed of being a kept woman. Next you'll be wanting a dowry.' Florentyna rummaged in her bag. 'Well, I've got two hundred and twelve dollars and an American Express card. You owe me fifty-six dollars, Richard Kane, but I'll consider repayment at a dollar a year.'

'I think I like the idea of a dowry better,' said Richard.

In thirty minutes Florentyna was packed. Then she sat down at her desk, scrawled a note to her father explaining she would never be willing to see him again unless he would accept Richard. She left the envelope on the table by the side of her bed.

Richard hailed a cab. 'Idlewild,' he said after placing Florentyna's three suitcases and his cello in the boot.

Once they had reached the airport Florentyna made a phone call. She was relieved when it was answered. When she told Richard the news he booked a flight.

At seven thirty the American Airlines Super Constellation 1049 taxied out on to the runway to start its seven-hour flight.

Richard helped Florentyna with her seatbelt. She smiled at him.

'Do you know how much I love you, Mr. Kane?'

'Yes, I think so – Mrs. Kane,' he replied.

'You'll live to regret your actions tonight.'

He didn't reply immediately, but just sat motionless, staring in front of him. Then all he said was, 'You will never contact him again.'

She left the room without replying.

He sat alone in the crimson leather chair; time was suspended. He didn't hear the phone ring several times. The butler knocked quietly on the door and entered the room.

'A Mr. Abel Rosnovski on the line, sir. Are you in?'

William Kane felt a sharp pain in the pit of his stomach. He knew he had to take the call. He rose from his chair and only by a supreme effort stopped himself from collapsing back into it. He walked over to the phone and picked it up.

'William Kane speaking.'

'This is Abel Rosnovski.'

'Indeed, and when exactly did you think of setting up your daughter with my son? At the time, no doubt, when you failed so conspicuously to cause the downfall of my bank.'

'Don't be such a damn . . .' Abel checked himself before continuing. 'I want this marriage stopped every bit as much as you do. I never tried to take away your son. I only learned of his existence today. I love my daughter even more than I hate you and I don't want to lose her. Can't we get together and work something out between us?'

'No,' said William Kane.

'What's the good of raking over the past now, Kane? If you

know where they are, perhaps we can stop them. That's what you want too. Or are you so goddam proud that you'll stand by and watch your son marry my girl rather than help?'

William Kane hung up the phone and walked back to the leather chair.

The butler returned. 'Dinner is served, sir.'

'No dinner, and I'm not at home.'

'Yes, sir,' said the butler and left the room.

William Kane sat alone. No one disturbed him until eight o'clock the next morning.

14

WHEN FLIGHT 1049 LANDED at San Francisco's International Airport, Florentyna hoped it hadn't been too short notice. Richard had hardly placed a foot on the tarmac when he saw a massive woman charge towards them and throw her arms around Florentyna. Florentyna still couldn't get her arms around Bella.

'You don't give a girl much time, do you? Calling just as you're boarding the plane.'

'I'm sorry, Bella, I didn't know until . . .'

'Don't be silly. Claude and I had been grumbling that we didn't have anything to do this evening.'

Florentyna laughed and introduced the two of them to Richard.

'Is that all the luggage you have?' queried Bella, staring down at the three suitcases and the cello.

'We had to leave in rather a hurry,' explained Florentyna.

'Well, there's always been a home for you here,' said Bella, immediately picking up two of the suitcases.

'Thank God for you, Bella. You haven't changed a bit,' said Florentyna.

'I have in one respect. I'm six months pregnant. It's just

that I'm like a giant panda – nobody's noticed.'

The two girls dodged in and out of the airport traffic to the parking lot with Richard carrying the cello and Claude following in their wake. During the journey into San Francisco, Bella revealed that Claude had become an associate in the law firm of Pillsbury, Madison and Sutro.

'Hasn't he done well?' she said.

'And Bella's the senior physical education teacher at the local high school, and they haven't lost a hockey game since she joined them,' said Claude with equal pride.

'And what do you do?' said Bella, prodding a finger into Richard's chest. 'From your luggage I can only assume that you're an out-of-work musician.'

'Not exactly,' said Richard, laughing. 'I'm a would-be banker, and I shall be looking for a job tomorrow.'

'When are you getting married?'

'Not for three weeks at least,' said Florentyna. 'I want to be married in a church, and they'll have to read the banns first.'

'So you'll be living in sin,' declared Claude as he drove past the 'San Francisco Welcomes Careful Drivers' sign. 'Quite the modern couple. I always wanted to, but Bella wouldn't hear of it.'

'And why did you leave New York so suddenly?' asked Bella, ignoring Claude's comment.

Florentyna explained how she had met Richard and the historic feud that existed between their fathers. Bella and Claude listened incredulously to the story, both remaining unusually silent, until the car came to a halt.

'This is our home,' said Claude, putting on the brakes firmly and leaving the car in first gear.

Florentyna got out on the side of a steep hill not quite overlooking the bay.

'We go higher up the hill when Claude becomes a partner,' said Bella. 'But this will have to do for now.'

'It's fantastic,' said Florentyna as they entered the little house. She smiled when she saw hockey sticks in the umbrella stand.

'I'll take you straight to your room so you can unpack.'

Bella led the two guests up a small winding staircase to the spare room on the top floor. 'It may not be the Presidential Suite at the Baron, but it's better than joining the communes on the streets.'

It was some weeks before Florentyna discovered that Bella and Claude had spent the afternoon lugging their double bed up the stairs to the spare room and carrying the two singles back down so that Richard and Florentyna could spend their first night together.

It was four a.m. in New York when they finally climbed into bed.

'Well, now that Grace Kelly is no longer available, I suppose I'm stuck with you. Although I think Claude may be right. Perhaps we should live in sin.'

'If you and Claude lived together in sin, no one in San Francisco would even notice.'

'Any regrets so far?'

'Yes. I always hoped I'd end up with a man who slept on the left-hand side of the bed.'

In the morning, after a Bella-type breakfast, Florentyna and Richard scoured the papers for jobs.

'We must try and find something quickly. I don't think our money will last for more than a month,' said Florentyna.

'It may be easier for you. I can't believe that many banks will offer me a job without a degree or at least a reference from my father.'

'Don't worry,' said Florentyna, ruffling his hair. 'We can beat both our fathers.'

Richard turned out to be right. It took Florentyna only three days and her prospective employers one phone call to the personnel director at Bloomingdale's before she was offered a position at a young fashion shop called 'Wayout Columbus' which had advertised for a 'bright sales assistant' in the *Chronicle*. It was only another week before the manager realised what a bargain they had picked up.

Richard, on the other hand, plodded around San Francisco from bank to bank. The personnel director always asked him to call back and when he did there suddenly 'wasn't a position available at the present time' for someone with his qualifications. As the day of the wedding drew nearer Richard became increasingly anxious.

'You can't blame them,' he told Florentyna. 'They all do a lot of business with my father and they don't want to upset him.'

'Bunch of cowards. Can you think of anyone who has had a row with Lester's Bank and therefore refuses to deal with them?'

Richard buried his head in his hands and considered the question for a few moments. 'Only the Bank of America. My father had a quarrel with them once over a stop-loss guarantee which they took rather a long time to honour and it resulted in a considerable loss in interest. He swore he would never do business with them again. It's worth a try – I'll give them a call tomorrow.'

When the manager interviewed him the next day he asked if the reason Richard had applied to work at the Bank of America was the well known disagreement with his father.

'Yes, sir,' replied Richard.

'Good, then we both have something in common. You will start on Monday as a junior teller, and if you are indeed the son of William Kane I don't imagine you will stay in that position for long.'

On the Saturday of their third week in San Francisco, Richard and Florentyna were married in a simple ceremony at St. Edward's Church on California Street. Father O'Reilly – accompanied by Florentyna's mother – flew in from Chicago to conduct the service. Claude gave the bride away and then ran round to Richard's side to be best man while Bella was the matron of honour, gargantuan in a pink maternity smock. The six celebrated that night with a dinner at DiMaggio's on Fisherman's Wharf. Richard and Florentyna's combined weekly salaries didn't cover the final bill, so Zaphia came to the rescue.

'If you four want to eat out again,' added Zaphia, 'just give me a call and I'll be out on the next plane.'

Bride and groom crept into bed at one o'clock in the morning.

'I never thought I would end up married to a bank teller.'

'I never thought I would end up married to a shop assistant, but sociologically it ought to make an ideal partnership.'

'Let's hope it doesn't end with sociology,' said Florentyna, turning off the light.

Abel tried every means at his disposal to discover where Florentyna had disappeared. After days of phone calls, telegrams, and even efforts to involve the police, he realised there was only one lead left open. He dialled a number in Chicago.

'Hello,' said a voice every bit as cold as William Kane's.

'You must know why I'm ringing.'

'I can guess.'

'How long have you known about Florentyna and Richard Kane?'

'About three months. Florentyna flew up to Chicago and told me all about him. Later I met Richard at the wedding. She didn't exaggerate. He's a rare man.'

'Do you know where they are right now?' demanded Abel.

'Yes.'

'Where?'

'Find out for yourself.' The line went dead. Someone else who didn't want to help.

On the desk in front of him lay an unopened file containing details of his forthcoming trip to Europe. He flicked over the pages. Two airplane tickets, two reservations in London, Edinburgh and Cannes. Two opera tickets, two theatre tickets, but now only one person was going. Florentyna would not be opening the Edinburgh Baron or the Cannes Baron.

He sank into a fitful sleep from which he didn't want to be woken. George found him slumped at his desk at eight o'clock the next morning.

He promised Abel by the time he had returned from Europe he would have located Florentyna, but Abel now realised after reading Florentyna's letter again and again that even if he did she wouldn't agree to see him.

15

'I WOULD LIKE TO borrow thirty-four thousand dollars,' said Florentyna.

'What do you need the money for?' said Richard coldly.

'I want to take over the lease for a building on Nob Hill to open a fashion shop.'

'What are the terms of the lease?'

'Ten years, with an option to renew.'

'What security can you offer against the loan?'

'I own three thousand shares in the Baron Group.'

'But that's a private company,' said Richard, 'and the shares are in effect worthless as they can't be traded over the counter.'

'But the Baron Group is worth fifty million of anybody's money and my shares represent one per cent of the company.'

'How did you come into possession of these shares?'

'My father is the chairman of the company and he gave them to me on my twenty-first birthday.'

'Then why don't you borrow the money direct from him?'

'Oh, hell,' said Florentyna. 'Will they be that demanding?'

'I'm afraid so, Jessie.'

'Are all bank managers going to be as tough as you? They never treated me like this in Chicago.'

'That's because they had the security of your father's account. Anyone who doesn't know you is not going to be as accommodating. A loan manager has to consider that every new transaction will *not* be repaid, so unless his risk is covered twice over it's his job that will be on the line. When you borrow money you must always look across the table and consider the other person's point of view. Everyone who wants to borrow money is sure they are on to a winner, but the manager knows that over fifty per cent of deals put up to him will eventually fail, or at best break even. So the manager has to pick and choose carefully to be certain he can always see a way of retrieving his money. My father used to say that most financial deals saw a return of one per cent for the bank, which didn't allow you the opportunity to make a one hundred per cent loss more than once every five years.'

'That all makes sense, so how do I answer, "Why don't you go to your father"?'

'Tell the truth. Remember, banking is based on trust, and if they know you're always being straight with them, they'll stand by you when you are going through hard times.'

'You still haven't answered the question.'

'You simply say: my father and I quarrelled over a family matter and now I wish to succeed in my own right.'

'Do you think that will work?'

'I don't know, but if it does, at least you'll have started with all your cards on the table. Right, let's go back over it again.'

'Must we?'

'Yes. No one owes you money, Jessie.'

'I would like to borrow thirty-four thousand dollars.'

'What do you need the money for?'

'I would like to take over –'

'Supper's ready,' roared Bella.

'Rescued,' said Florentyna.

'Only until after we've eaten. How many banks are you seeing on Monday?'

'Three. Bank of California, Wells Fargo and Crocker. Why don't I pop along to the Bank of America and you can simply pass the thirty-four thousand over the counter?'

'Because there are no mixed prisons in America.'

Claude put his head around the door. 'Hurry up, you two, or there won't be any left.'

*

George spent as much of his time following up leads on Florentyna as he did being managing director of the Baron Group. He was determined to come up with some concrete results before Abel returned from Europe.

George had a little more success in one quarter than Abel. Zaphia was pleased to inform him that she was making regular trips to the coast to see the happily married couple. It took George only one phone call to a travel agent in Chicago to discover that these trips had been to San Francisco. Within twenty-four hours he had Florentyna's address and phone number. On one occasion, George even managed a brief conversation with his goddaughter, but she was fairly reticent with him.

Henry Osborne made a pretext at wanting to help, but it soon became obvious that he only wished to know what was going on in Abel's life. He even tried to press George into lending him some more money.

'You'll have to wait until Abel returns,' George told him sharply.

'I am not sure I can last that long.'

'I'm sorry, Henry, but I don't have the authority to sanction personal loans.'

'Not even to a board member? You may live to regret that decision, George. After all, I know a lot more about how the group got started than you do, and I am sure there are others who would be willing to pay me for such information.'

George always arrived at Idlewild Airport thirty minutes early whenever Abel was returning from Europe. He knew the Baron, like a newly appointed director, would be impatient to learn of any developments within the group. But this time he felt certain Abel's opening question would be on a different subject.

As always Abel was one of the first through Customs and once he and George were seated in the back of the company Cadillac, he wasted no time on small talk.

'What news?' demanded Abel, only too aware that George would know to what he was referring.

'Some good, some bad,' said George as he pressed a button by the side window. Abel watched a sheet of glass glide up between the driver and the passenger section of the car. He tapped his finger on the side pane impatiently as he waited. 'Florentyna continues to be in touch with her mother. She's living in a small apartment in San Francisco with some old friends from Radcliffe days.'

'Married?'

'Yes.'

Abel didn't speak for some moments as if taking in the finality of the statement.

'And the Kane boy?' he asked.

'He's found a job in a bank. It seems a lot of people turned him down because word got around that he didn't complete Harvard Business School and his father wouldn't supply a reference. Not many people were willing to employ him if as a consequence they antagonised William Kane. He was finally hired as a junior teller with the Bank of America, at a salary way below what he might have expected with his qualifications.'

'And Florentyna?'

'She's working as the assistant manager in a fashion shop called "Wayout Columbus" near Golden Gate Park. She's also been trying to borrow money from several banks.'

'Why?' said Abel, sounding worried. 'Is she in any sort of trouble?'

'No, she's looking for capital to open her own shop.'

'How much is she hoping to raise?'

'She needs thirty-four thousand dollars for the lease on a small building that's become vacant on Nob Hill.'

Abel considered the information for a moment. 'See that she gets the money. Make it look as if the transaction is an ordinary bank loan and be sure that it's not traceable back to me.' He started tapping on the window again. 'This must always remain between the two of us, George.'

'Anything you say, Abel.'

'And keep me informed of every move she makes, however trivial.'

'What about Richard Kane?'

'I'm not interested in him,' said Abel. 'Now, what's the bad news?'

'Trouble with Henry Osborne again. It seems he owes money everywhere, and I'm fairly certain his only source of income is you. He's still making threats – about revealing that you condoned bribes in the early days when you had taken over the group. Says he's kept all the papers from the first day he met you, when he claims he fixed an extra payment after the fire at the old Richmond in Chicago. He's telling everyong that he now has a file on you three inches thick.'

'I'll deal with Henry in the morning,' said Abel.

Abel was fully up to date on the group's activities when Henry arrived for his private meeting. Abel looked up at him: the heavy drinking and the debts were beginning to take their toll. For the first time, Abel thought Henry looked older than his years.

'I need a little money to get me through a tricky period,' said Henry even before they had shaken hands. 'I've been a bit unlucky.'

'Again, Henry? You should know better at your age. How much do you need this time?'

'Ten thousand would see me through,' said Henry.

'Ten thousand,' said Abel, spitting out the words. 'What do you think I am, a gold mine? It was only five thousand last time.'

'Inflation,' said Henry, trying to laugh.

'This is the last time, do you understand me?' said Abel as he took out his cheque book. 'Come begging once more and I'll remove you from the board and turn you out without a penny.'

'You're a real friend, Abel. I swear I'll never come back again – I promise you that. Never again.' Abel watched Henry take a cigar from the humidor on the table in front of him and light it. George hadn't done that in twenty years. 'Thanks, Abel. You'll never regret your decision.'

Henry sauntered out of the office drawing on the cigar. Abel waited for the door to be closed, then buzzed for George. He appeared moments later.

'What happened?'

'I gave in for the last time,' said Abel. 'I don't know why – it cost me ten thousand.'

'Ten thousand?' said George, sighing. 'You can be sure he'll be back again. I'd be willing to put money on that.'

'He'd better not,' said Abel, 'because I'm through with him. Whatever he's done for me in the past it's now quits. Anything new about my girl?'

'I've set up a facility for Florentyna with the Crocker National Bank of San Francisco,' said George. 'She has an appointment next Monday with the loan officer. The agreement will appear to her as one of the bank's ordinary loan transactions, with no special favours. In fact, they're charging her half a per cent more than usual so there can be no reason for her to be suspicious. What she doesn't know is that the money is covered by your guarantee.'

'Thanks, George, that's perfect. I'll bet you ten dollars she pays off the loan within two years and never needs to go back for another. Keep me briefed on everything she's up to. Everything.'

Florentyna visited three banks the following Monday. The Bank of California showed some interest, Wells Fargo none and Crocker asked her to call back. Richard was surprised and delighted.

'What terms did they discuss?'

'The Bank of California say they would want eight per cent and require to hold the deeds of the lease. Crocker wants eight and a half per cent, the deeds *and* my shares in the Baron Group.'

'Fair terms considering you have no banking history with them, but it will mean you must make a twenty-five per cent profit before taxes, just to break even.'

'I've worked it all out on paper, Richard, and I think I'll make thirty-two per cent in the first year.'

'I studied those figures last night, Jessie, and you're being overly optimistic. You have no hope of achieving that. In fact, I think the company will lose between seven and ten thousand dollars in the first year – so you'll just have to hope they believe in your long-term future.'

'That's exactly what the loan officer said.'

'When are they going to let you know their decision?'

'By the end of the week. It's worse than waiting for exam results.'

'You've done well, Kane,' said the manager. 'And I am advising head office to promote you. What I have in mind . . .'

The phone buzzed on the manager's desk. He picked it up and listened.

'It's for you,' he said, surprised, before passing it to Richard.

'The Bank of California said their loans committee had turned me down, but Crocker said yes. Oh, Richard, isn't that wonderful?'

'Yes, ma'am, it's good news indeed,' said Richard avoiding the manager's eye.

'Well, that's very kind of you to say so, Mr. Kane. Now I also have this sociological problem and I was wondering if you could help in some way.'

'Perhaps if you were to come around to the bank, ma'am, we could discuss it in greater detail.'

'What a great idea. I've always had this fantasy of making love in a bank vault surrounded by money. Lots and lots of Benjamin Franklins staring at me.'

'I agree with your proposition, ma'am, and I'll call you and confirm at the first possible opportunity.'

'Don't leave it too long or I may decide to move my account.'

'We always try to be of service at the Bank of America, ma'am.'

'If you look at my account, there's not much sign of it.'

The phone clicked.

*

'Where are we having the celebration?' asked Richard.

'I told you over the phone – in the bank vaults.'

'Darling, when you called I was in private conference with the manager, and he was offering me the number three post in the overseas department.'

'That's fantastic. Then it's a double celebration. Let's go to Chinatown and have five takeaways and five giant Cokes.'

'Why five, Jessie?'

'Because Bella will be joining us. Incidentally, Mr. Kane, I prefer it when you call me "ma'am".'

'No, I think I'll stick with Jessie. It reminds me how far you've come since we met.'

Claude arrived that evening carrying a bottle of champagne under each arm. 'Let's open one immediately and celebrate,' said Bella.

'Agreed,' said Florentyna. 'But what about the other one?'

'It's to be saved for some special occasion that none of us could have anticipated,' Claude said firmly.

Richard opened the first bottle and poured out four glasses while Florentyna put the second in the corner of the fridge.

She signed the lease on the tiny building on Nob Hill the next day and the Kanes moved into the small apartment above the shop. Florentyna, Bella and Richard spent their weekends painting and cleaning while Claude, the most artistic of the four, printed the name 'Florentyna's' in royal blue above the shop window. A month later they were ready to open.

During her first week as owner, manageress and clerk, Florentyna contacted all the main wholesalers who had dealt with her father in New York. In no time she had a shop full of goods and ninety days' credit.

Florentyna opened the little shop on August 1st, 1958. She always remembered the date because just after midnight Bella produced a twelve-pound baby.

Florentyna had sent out a large mailing announcing the opening of the store, choosing the day before the government raised postage stamps from three cents to four. She had also stolen an assistant named Nancy Ching – who had Maisie's charm but fortunately not Maisie's I.Q. – from her old employers, 'Wayout Columbus'. On the morning of the opening, the two girls stood by the door in hopeful anticipation but only one person came into the shop the whole day and all he wanted to know was the way to the Mark Hopkins. The next morning, a young woman came in and spent an hour looking at all the shirts they had in from New York. She tried on several but left without purchasing anything. In the afternoon a middle-aged lady fussed about for a long time and finally bought a pair of gloves.

'How much will that be?' she asked.

'Nothing,' said Florentyna.

'Nothing?' queried the lady.

'That's correct. You are the first customer to make a purchase at Florentyna's and there will be no charge.'

'How kind of you,' said the lady. 'I shall tell all my friends.'

'You never gave me any gloves when I shopped at Bloomingdale's, Miss Kovats,' said Richard that evening. 'You'll be bankrupt by the end of the month if you go on like that.'

But this time his judgment proved wrong. The lady turned out to be President of the Junior League in San Francisco and one word from her was worth more than a full-page advertisement in the San Francisco *Chronicle*.

For the first few weeks Florentyna seemed to be working an eighteen-hour day, for as soon as the doors closed she would check the inventory while Richard went over the books. As the months passed she began to wonder how the little shop could ever hope to make a profit.

At the end of her first year they invited Bella and Claude to join in celebrating the loss of seven thousand three hundred and eighty dollars.

'We've got to achieve better results next year,' said Florentyna firmly.

'Why?' said Richard.

'Because our grocery bills are going to be larger.'

'Is Bella coming to live with us?'

'No. I'm pregnant.'

Richard was overjoyed and his only anxiety was that he couldn't stop Florentyna from working right up until the day she went into hospital. They celebrated the end of their second year with a small profit of two thousand dollars and a large son of nine pounds three ounces. He only had one nipple.

The decision on what they would call their first born, if it was a boy, had been decided weeks before.

George Novak was both shocked and delighted to be chosen as a godfather for Florentyna's son. Although he didn't admit as much, Abel was also pleased, for he welcomed any opportunity to find out what was happening in his daughter's life.

The day before the christening, George flew out to Los Angeles to check on the progress of the new Baron. Abel was determined to have the building complete by the middle of September in order that John Kennedy could open it while he was on the campaign trail. George then flew on to San Francisco confident that Abel's deadline would be met.

By nature, George took a long time to like people and even longer to trust them. It was not so with Richard Kane. George took to him immediately, and once he was able to see for himself what Florentyna had achieved in such a short time it became obvious that she could not have done it without her husband's common sense and cautious approach. George intended to leave Abel in no doubt how he felt about the boy when he returned to New York.

After a quiet dinner the two men played backgammon at a dollar a point, and discussed the christening. 'Not at all like Florentyna's,' George confided to Richard, who laughed at the thought of his reluctant father-in-law spending a night in jail.

'You seem to throw doubles all the time,' said George, sipping the Rémy Martin Richard had poured for him.

'My father . . .' said Richard, and then hesitated for a moment, 'always accused me of being a bad loser if I made any mention of doubles.'

George laughed. 'And how is your father?'

'I've no idea. There's been no contact with him since Jessie and I were married.' George still couldn't get used to hearing his goddaughter being referred to as Jessie. When he was told the reason why, he knew it would amuse Abel.

'I'm sorry your father seems to be reacting the same way as Abel,' said George.

'I remain in touch with my mother,' continued Richard sipping his brandy, 'but I can see no end to my father's attitude, especially while Abel continues to try and increase his holding in Lester's.'

'Are you sure of that?' asked George, sounding surprised.

'Two years ago every banker on Wall Street knew what he was up to.'

'Abel is now so set in his ways,' said George, 'I can't make him listen to reason. But I don't believe he will cause any more trouble at the moment,' he added, before returning to his brandy. Richard didn't enquire why: he realised that if George wanted to explain he would.

'You see, if Kennedy wins the election,' George continued, once he had put the glass down, 'Abel has an outside chance of a minor appointment in the new administration. I put it no higher than that.'

'Our ambassador to Poland, no doubt,' said Florentyna as she came into the room carrying a tray laden with coffee cups. 'He would be the first Polish immigrant to be so honoured. I've known about that ambition ever since our trip to Europe.'

George didn't reply.

'Is Henry Osborne behind this?' asked Florentyna.

'No, he doesn't even know about it,' said George, relaxing back in his chair. 'Your father no longer places any trust in him. Since Henry lost his seat in Congress he has proved unreliable, to say the least, and your father is even considering removing him from the board.'

'At last Papa has woken up to what a nasty piece of work Henry really is.'

'I think he has always known, but there's no denying Henry was useful to your father when he was in Washington. Personally I think he is still dangerous despite being removed from Congress.'

'Why?' asked Florentyna from her seat in the corner of the room.

'Because I suspect he knows too much about the enmity between Abel and Richard's father, and if he gets into any more debt I fear he may trade that information with Mr. Kane direct.'

'Never,' said Richard.

'How can you be so sure?' asked George.

'You mean after all these years you don't know?' Richard asked.

George stared from one to the other. 'Know what?'

'Obviously not,' said Florentyna.

'You'll need a double,' said Richard, and poured George another large brandy before continuing.

'Henry Osborne hates my father even more than Abel does.'

'What? Why?' said George, leaning forward.

'Henry was married to my grandmother, after my grandfather died.' Richard poured himself another coffee before continuing. 'Many years ago when he was a young man, he tried to part my grandmother from a small family fortune. Osborne didn't succeed because *my* father, aged only seventeen, discovered that his Harvard military background was nothing more than a front and proceeded to throw him out of his own home.'

'Omój Jezu!' said George. 'I wonder if Abel knows any of this.' He hadn't noticed it was his turn to throw the dice.

'Of course he does,' said Florentyna. 'It must have been the deciding factor for employing Henry in the first place. He needed someone on his side who he could be certain would never open his mouth to Kane.'

'How did you find out?'

'Pieced it together when Richard discovered I wasn't Jessie Kovats. Most of the stuff on Henry is in a file locked in the bottom of Papa's desk.'

'I thought I was too old to learn so much in one day,' said George.

'Your day's learning hasn't begun,' said Richard. 'Henry Osborne never went to Harvard, never served in the war, and his real name is Vittorio Togna.'

George didn't speak, just opened his mouth.

'We also know that Papa has six per cent of Lester's Bank. Just imagine the problems he would cause if he could lay his hands on another two per cent,' said Florentyna.

'We think he's trying to buy that two per cent from Peter Parfitt, the deposed chairman of Lester's, with the final aim of removing my father from his own board,' Richard added.

'That may have been right in the past.'

'Why not now?' queried Florentyna.

'Abel won't become involved with anything as silly as removing your father from the bank while Kennedy has him in mind for Warsaw. So you need have no fear in that direction. And perhaps that might make you consider coming as my guest to see the candidate open the new Baron in Los Angeles?'

'Is there any hope of Richard being invited as well?'

'You know the answer to that, Florentyna.'

'Another game, George?' said Richard, changing the subject.

'No, thank you. I know a winner when I see one.' He removed his wallet from an inside pocket and handed over eleven dollars. 'Mind you, I still blame the doubles.'

16

NANCY CHING HAD RUN the shop well while Florentyna was away in the hospital, but with Kane junior safely parked in a crib in the back room Florentyna was only too happy to return to work. She explained to Miss Tredgold when she sent the first photos of them together that she was hoping to be a responsible mother until it became impossible not to employ someone. 'Not that I'll find anyone like you outside of Much Hadham,' she added.

During the first two years of their marriage, both she and Richard had concentrated on building their careers. When Florentyna acquired her second shop, Richard also advanced another rung on the bank ladder.

Florentyna would have liked to spend more time concentrating on fashion trends rather than the day-to-day finances but she felt unable to ask Richard to spend every night on her books after he had returned from the bank. She discussed her bold ideas for the future with Nancy, who was a little sceptical about placing so many orders for small sizes.

'It may suit me' – the petite Chinese girl grinned – 'but not most American women.'

'I don't agree. Small is going to be beautiful and we must be the first to anticipate it. If American women think it's the trend, we are going to witness a skinny revolution the like of which will even make you look fat.'

Nancy laughed. 'Looking at your future orders for 4s and 6s, you'd better be right.'

Neither Richard nor Florentyna brought up the vexed subject of their families after George's visit since they both despaired of any reconciliation. They both spoke to their mothers on the phone from time to time, and although Richard received letters from his two sisters, he was particularly sad that he was not invited to attend Virginia's wedding. This unhappy state of affairs might have drifted on indefinitely had it not been for two events. The first was hard to avoid, while the second was caused by the wrong person picking up the phone.

The first occurred because it was Los Angeles's turn to open a Baron. Florentyna followed its progress with great interest while she was preparing to open her third shop. The new hotel was completed in September 1960 and Florentyna took the afternoon off to watch Senator John Kennedy perform the opening ceremony. She stood at the back of a large crowd that had come to see the candidate while she kept an eye on her father. He seemed to her a lot older and had certainly put on weight. From those who were surrounding him it was obvious that he was now well connected in Democratic circles. She wondered if Kennedy were elected would her father be offered 'the chance to serve under him'. Florentyna was impressed by the competent speech of welcome Abel made, but she was mesmerised by the young Presidential candidate who seemed to her to embody the new America. After she had heard him she passionately wanted John Kennedy to be the next President. As soon as the speech in San Francisco was over, she left the newly opened Baron resolved to give time and send money to the Ninth District of Illinois for the Kennedy campaign, although she suspected her father had already contributed a sum that would make her own efforts appear minuscule. Richard remained unshakeably Republican and a supporter of Nixon.

'No doubt you remember what Eisenhower said when he was asked about your standard-bearer?' Florentyna teased.

'Something unflattering, I'm sure.'

'A journalist asked him "What major decisions has the Vice-President participated in?"'

'And what was Ike's reply?'
'If you give me a week, I might think of one.'

During the remaining weeks of the campaign, Florentyna spent what free time she had addressing envelopes and answering phone calls at the Party's headquarters in San Francisco. Unlike the past two elections, she was convinced the Democrats had found a man in whom she could place unreserved support. The final television debate between the candidates re-awakened in her the political ambitions so nearly buried by Henry Osborne. Kennedy's charisma and political insight were dazzling, while Florentyna was left to wonder how anyone who had followed the campaign could possibly vote Republican. Richard pointed out to her that charisma and good looks were not to be traded for a future policy and a proven record, even if it had to include a five o'clock shadow.

All through the election night Richard and Florentyna sat up watching the results. The twists, the turns and the upsets lasted all the way to California, where by the smallest margin in American electoral history Kennedy became President. Florentyna was ecstatic about the final outcome, while Richard maintained that Kennedy would never have made it without Mayor Daley and the Cook County ballot boxes – or lack of them.

'Would you vote the Democratic ticket if I were running for office?'

'It would depend on your policies. I'm a banker, not a sentimentalist.'

'Well, unsentimental banker, I want to open a fourth shop.'

'What?' said Richard.

'There's a bargain going in San Diego, a building with a lease of only two years to run but it could be renewable.'

'How much?'

'Thirty thousand dollars.'

'You're mad, Jessie. That's your projected profits for this year gone in expansion.'

'And while you're on the subject of expansion, I'm pregnant again.'

When the thirty-fifth President delivered his Inaugural Address Florentyna and Richard watched the ceremony on television in the apartment above the main shop.

'*Let the word go forth, from this time and place, to friend and foe alike, that the torch has been passed to a new generation of Americans, born in this century, tempered by war, disciplined by a hard and bitter peace*' – Florentyna's eyes never once left the man in whom so many people had placed their trust. When President Kennedy concluded his speech with the words, '*Ask not what your country can do for you. Ask what you can do for your country,*' Florentyna watched the crowd rise and found herself joining in the applause. She wondered how many people were clapping in other homes throughout America. She turned to Richard.

'Not bad for a Democrat,' he said, aware he was also clapping.

Florentyna smiled. 'Do you think my father is there?'

'Undoubtedly.'

'So now we sit and wait for the appointment.'

George wrote the next day to confirm that Abel had been in Washington for the celebrations. He ended on the words: 'Your father seems confident about going to Warsaw, and I am equally sure that if he is offered the position, it will be easier to get him to meet Richard.'

'What a friend George has turned out to be,' said Florentyna.

'To Abel as well as to us,' said Richard thoughtfully.

Each day Florentyna checked the new appointments as they were released by Press Secretary Pierre Salinger. But no announcement concerning the Polish ambassador was forthcoming.

17

WHEN FLORENTYNA DID SEE her father's name in the paper, she could hardly miss it: the banner headline was all across the front page:

THE CHICAGO BARON ARRESTED

Florentyna read the story in disbelief.

NEW YORK—Abel Rosnovski, the international hotelier, known as the Chicago Baron, was arrested at eight thirty this morning at an apartment on East Fifty-seventh Street by agents of the FBI. The arrest took place after his return the previous night from a business trip to Turkey where he had opened the Istanbul Baron, the latest in his chain of hotels. Rosnovski was charged by the FBI with bribery and corruption of government officials in fourteen different states. The FBI also wants to question ex-Congressman Henry Osborne who has not been seen in Chicago for the past fortnight.

Rosnovski's defence attorney, H. Trafford Jilks, made a statement denying the charges and added that his client had a full explanation which would exonerate him completely. Rosnovski was granted bail in his own recognisance of ten thousand dollars.

The news story went on to report that rumours had been

circulating in Washington for some time that the White House had been considering Mr. Rosnovski as America's next ambassador to Poland.

That night Florentyna lay awake wondering how it could have all happened, and what her father must be going through. She assumed Henry was involved in some way, and decided to follow every scrap of information that was reported in the papers. Richard tried to comfort her by saying there were very few businessmen alive who had not at some stage in their careers been involved in a little bribery.

Three days before the trial was due to begin the Justice Department found Henry Osborne in New Orleans. He was arrested, charged and immediately turned State's evidence. The FBI asked Judge Prescott for a postponement to discuss with ex-Congressman Osborne the contents of a dossier on Rosnovski that had recently come into their possession. Judge Prescott granted the FBI a further four weeks to prepare their case.

The press soon discovered that Osborne, in order to clear his considerable debts, had sold the file that he had compiled over ten years while serving as a director of the Baron Group, to a firm of private investigators in Chicago. How the file had then come into the hands of the FBI remained a mystery.

Florentyna was fearful that with Henry Osborne as star witness for the prosecution her father might have to serve a long jail sentence. After another sleepless night, Richard suggested she ought to contact her father. She agreed, and wrote him a long letter assuring him of her support and her belief in his innocence. She was about to lick the envelope when she walked over to her desk, took out her favourite picture of her son and sent it to his grandfather.

Four hours before the trial was due to begin Henry Osborne was found hanging in his cell by a guard bringing in his breakfast. He had used a Harvard tie.

'Why did Henry commit suicide?' Florentyna asked her mother on the phone later that morning.

'Oh, that's easy to explain,' replied Zaphia. 'Henry

thought the private investigator who cleared his debts wanted the file for the sole purpose of blackmailing your father.'

'And what was the real reason?' asked Florentyna.

'The file had been purchased anonymously in Chicago on behalf of William Kane, who then passed it on to the FBI.'

Florentyna could only feel hatred whenever she thought about William Kane; she couldn't stop herself from taking it out on Richard. But it was obvious that Richard was every bit as angry about his father's behaviour, which Florentyna discovered when she overheard a phone conversation between him and his mother.

'That was pretty tough,' said Florentyna when he finally put the phone down.

'Yes it was. My poor mother's getting it from both sides.'

'We haven't reached the last act of this tragedy,' said Florentyna. 'Papa has wanted to return to Warsaw for as long as I can remember. Now he will never forgive your father.'

Once the trial began, Florentyna followed the proceedings each day by phoning her mother in the evening after Zaphia had returned from the courtroom. When she listened to her mother's view on the day's happenings she wasn't always convinced they both wanted the same outcome.

'The trial is beginning to go in your father's favour,' she said in the middle of the week.

'How can you be so sure?' asked Florentyna.

'Since the FBI has lost its star witness their case hasn't stood up to much cross-examination. H. Trafford Jilks is making Henry Osborne sound like Pinocchio with a nose that is just about touching the ground.'

'Does that mean Papa will be proved innocent?'

'I wouldn't have thought so, but the courtroom officials are predicting that the FBI will end up having to make a deal.'

'What sort of deal?'

'Well, if your father pleads guilty to some minor offences, they will drop the main charges.'

'Will he get away with a fine?' asked Florentyna anxiously.

'If he's lucky. But Judge Prescott is tough, so he may still end up in jail.'

'Let's hope it's just a fine.'

Zaphia made no comment.

'Six months' suspended sentence for the Chicago Baron,' Florentyna heard the newscaster say on her car radio as she was driving to pick up Richard from the bank. She nearly collided with the Buick in front of her and pulled over into a 'no parking' zone so that she could concentrate on what the newscaster had to say.

'The FBI has dropped all the main indictments of bribery against Abel Rosnovski – known as the Chicago Baron – and the defendant pleaded guilty to misdemeanours on two minor counts of attempting to improperly influence a public official. The jury was dismissed. In his summing up Judge Prescott said: "The right to do business does not include the right to suborn public officials. Bribery is a crime and a worse crime when condoned by an intelligent and competent man, who should not need to stoop to such levels.

' "In other countries," the Judge added, "bribery might be an accepted way of life, but that is not the case in the United States." Judge Prescott gave Rosnovski a six months' suspended sentence and a twenty-five thousand dollar fine.

'In other news, President Kennedy has agreed to accompany the Vice-President to Dallas this fall . . .' Florentyna turned off the radio to find someone tapping on the side window. She wound it down.

'Do you know that you're in a restricted area, ma'am?'

'Yes,' replied Florentyna.

'I'm afraid it's going to cost you ten dollars.'

*

'Twenty-five thousand dollars and a six months' suspended sentence. It could have been worse,' said George in the car on the way back to the Baron.

'Don't forget that I lost Poland,' said Abel, 'but that's all history now. Purchase the two per cent of the Lester's shares we need from Parfitt, even if it costs a million. That will make up the eight per cent of Lester's that I need to invoke Article Seven of their by-laws and then I can slaughter William Kane in his own board room.'

George nodded sadly.

A few days later the State Department announced that the next American ambassador to Warsaw would be John Moors Cabot.

18

THE MORNING AFTER JUDGE PRESCOTT'S verdict the second event occurred. The extension of the apartment phone rang in the shop and because Nancy was removing the light summer clothes from the window, replacing them with the new autumn collection, Florentyna answered it.

'Oh, I wondered if Mr. Kane was in,' said a lady's voice. She sounded a long way off.

'No, I'm sorry, he has already left for the bank. Would you like to leave a message? It's Florentyna Kane speaking.'

There was no immediate reply and then a voice said: 'It's Katherine Kane – please don't hang up.'

'Why should I do that, Mrs. Kane?' said Florentyna, her knees feeling so weak that she sank into a chair beside the phone.

'Because you must hate me, my dear, and I can't blame you,' Richard's mother said quickly.

'No, of course I don't hate you. Would you like Richard to call you back when he comes home?'

'Oh, no. My husband doesn't realise that I'm in touch with him. He would be very angry if he ever found out. No, what I was really hoping for will finally depend on you.'

'On me?'

'Yes. I desperately want to visit you and Richard and see my grandson – if you'll allow me.'

'I'd like that very much, Mrs. Kane,' said Florentyna, not sure how she could sound more welcoming.

'Oh, how understanding of you. My husband is going to a conference in Mexico in three weeks' time and I could fly out on the Friday. Only I would have to be back first thing on Monday morning.'

When Richard heard the news he went straight to the refrigerator. Florentyna followed, bewildered. She smiled as he stripped the gold foil from Claude's bottle of Krug and began pouring.

Three weeks later Florentyna accompanied Richard to the airport to welcome his mother.

'But you're beautiful,' were Florentyna's first words as she greeted the elegant, slim lady who showed not the slightest sign of having spent the last six hours on a plane. 'And you make me feel terribly pregnant.'

'What were you expecting, my dear? An ogre with red horns and a long black tail?'

Florentyna laughed as Katherine Kane put an arm through hers and they walked off together, temporarily forgetting her son.

Richard was relieved to see how quickly the two of them became friends. When they arrived back at the flat Katherine reacted in the time-honoured way when she set eyes on her first grandchild.

'I do wish your father could see his grandson,' she said. 'But I fear it's now reached a stage where he won't even allow the subject to be discussed.'

'Do you know any more than we do about what is happening between the two men?' asked Richard.

'I wouldn't have thought so. Your father refused to let the bank support Davis Leroy when his hotel group collapsed, and Florentyna's father therefore blames my husband for the subsequent suicide of Mr. Leroy. The whole unfortunate episode might have ended there if Henry Osborne hadn't come on to the scene.' She sighed. 'I pray to God the problem will be sorted out in my lifetime.'

'I fear one of them will have to die before the other comes to his senses,' said Richard. 'They are both so confoundedly obstinate.'

The four of them had a wonderful weekend together even if Kate's grandson did spend most of his time throwing his toys on to the floor. When they drove Katherine back to the airport on Sunday night she agreed to come and see them the next time her husband was away on business. Katherine's last words to Florentyna were, 'If only you and my husband could meet, he would be in no doubt why Richard fell in love with you.'

As she turned to wave goodbye, her grandson repeated his one-word vocabulary: 'Dada'. Katherine Kane laughed, 'What chauvinists men are. That was also Richard's first word. Has anyone ever told you what yours was, Florentyna?'

Annabel came screaming into this world a few weeks later, and Richard and Florentyna had a double celebration at the end of the year when Florentyna delivered a nineteen thousand one hundred and seventy-four dollar profit. Richard decided to mark the occasion by spending a small part of those profits on a golf membership of the Olympic Club.

Richard was given more responsibility in the overseas department of the bank, and started coming home an hour later. Florentyna decided the time had come to employ a full-time nanny so that she could concentrate on her work in the shops. She realised that she would never find a Miss Tredgold but Bella recommended a black girl called Carol who had graduated from high school the year before and was finding it hard to secure employment. Their son threw his arms around Carol the moment he met her. It brought home to Florentyna that prejudice was something children learn from their elders.

19

'I CAN'T BELIEVE IT,' said Florentyna. 'I never thought it would happen. What wonderful news. But what made him change his mind?'

'He's not getting any younger,' said Katherine Kane, her voice crackling down the phone, 'and he's frightened that if he and Richard don't patch up their differences soon he will retire from Lester's without a son on the board. He also believes that the man most likely to succeed him in the chair is Jake Thomas, and as Mr. Thomas is only two years older than Richard, he certainly won't want a younger Kane in the board room.'

'I wish Richard was at home so I could tell him the news, but since he's been promoted to head of the overseas department he rarely gets back before seven. He'll be so pleased. I'll try not to show how nervous I am about meeting your husband,' said Florentyna.

'Not half as nervous as he is about meeting you. But have no fears, my dear, he's preparing the fatted calf for his prodigal son. Have you heard anything from your father since I last spoke to you?'

'No, nothing. I fear there's never going to be a fatted calf for the prodigal daughter.'

'Don't give up. Something may yet arise that makes him see the light. We'll all put our heads together when you come to New York.'

'I would love to believe it was still possible for Papa to be reconciled, but I've almost given up hope.'

'Well, let's be thankful that one father has at least come to his senses,' said Katherine. 'I'll fly out to see you and fix up all the details.'

'How soon can you come?'

'I could get away this weekend.'

When Richard came home that evening he was overjoyed by the news, and once he had finished reading the next chapter of *Winnie the Pooh* to his son, he settled down to listen to the details of his mother's news.

'We could go to New York around November,' said Richard.

'I'm not sure I can wait that long.'

'You've waited for over three years.'

'Yes, but that's different.'

'You always want everything to have happened yesterday, Jessie. That reminds me, I read your proposal for the new shop in San Diego.'

'And?'

'Basically the idea makes a lot of sense and I approve.'

'Good heavens. What next? I never thought I would hear such words from you, Mr. Kane.'

'Now hold on, Jessie, it doesn't get my whole-hearted support because the one part of your expansion programme I don't understand is the necessity to employ your own designer.'

'That's easy enough to explain,' said Florentyna. 'Although we now have five shops my expenditure on buying clothes remains as high as forty per cent of turnover. If my own garments were designed for me, I would have two obvious advantages. First, I could cut down my immediate expenditure, and second we would be continually advertising our own product.'

'It also has a major disadvantage,' suggested Richard.

'What's that?'

'There can be no rebate on clothes returned within ninety days if we already own them.'

'Agreed,' said Florentyna. 'But the more we expand the more that problem will diminish. And if I choose the right designer we'll end up with our trade-mark clothes also being sold by our rivals.'

'Has that proved worthwhile for other designers?'

'In the case of Pierre Cardin, the designer became more famous than the shops.'

'Finding such a man won't be easy.'

'Didn't I find you, Mr. Kane?'

'No, Jessie, I found you.'

Florentyna smiled. 'Two children, a sixth shop, and you're going to be invited to join the board of Lester's. Most important of all I have a chance to meet your father. What more could we want?'

'It hasn't happened yet.'

'Typical banker. Whatever the forecast, you expect it to rain by mid-afternoon.'

Annabel started to cry.

'See what I mean?' said Richard. 'Your daughter's at it again.'

'Why is it always my daughter who is bad and your son who is good?'

Despite Florentyna's desire to travel to New York immediately after Kate had returned to the east coast, she was more than fully occupied with opening the new shop in San Diego, keeping an eye on the other five shops, and somehow looking for the right designer, while still trying to be a mother. As the day for their journey to New York grew nearer she became more and more nervous. She selected her own wardrobe carefully and bought several new outfits for the children. She even purchased a new shirt with a thin red stripe running through it for Richard, but she doubted that he would wear it except at weekends. Florentyna lay awake each night anxious that Richard's father might not approve of her, but Richard kept reminding her of Katherine's words: 'Not half as nervous as he is.'

To celebrate the opening of the sixth shop and the imminent reconciliation with his father, Richard took Florentyna to a performance of *The Nutcracker* by the Italian State Ballet

Company at the War Memorial Opera House. Richard didn't care much for the ballet himself but he was surprised to find Florentyna equally as restless during the performance. As soon as the house lights went up for the intermission he asked if anything was wrong.

'Yes. I've been waiting over an hour to find out who designed those fabulous costumes.' Florentyna started to thumb through her programme.

'I would have described them as outrageous,' said Richard.

'That's because you're colour-blind,' said Florentyna. Having found what she was looking for she started reading the programme notes to Richard. 'His name is Gianni di Ferranti. His biography says he was born in Milan in 1931 and that this is his first tour with the Italian State Ballet Company since leaving the Institute of Modern Art in Florence. I wonder if he would consider resigning from the company and working for me?'

'I wouldn't, with the inside information I have on the company,' said Richard, helpfully.

'Perhaps he's more adventurous than you, darling.'

'Or just mad. After all, he is Italian.'

'Well, there's only one way to find out,' said Florentyna, standing up.

'And how do you propose doing that?'

'By going backstage.'

'But you'll miss the second half of the performance.'

'The second half might not change my whole life,' said Florentyna, stepping into the aisle.

Richard followed her out of the building and they made their way around the outside to the stage door. A young security guard pushed open his window.

'Can I help you?' he asked, sounding as if it were the last thing he wanted to do.

'Yes,' Florentyna said confidently. 'I have an appointment with Gianni di Ferranti.'

Richard looked at his wife disapprovingly.

'Your name, please,' said the guard, picking up a phone.

'Florentyna Kane.'

The guard repeated the name into the mouthpiece, listened for a moment, then replaced the receiver.

'He says he's never heard of you.'

Florentyna was taken aback for a moment but Richard took out his wallet and placed a twenty-dollar bill on the ledge in front of the guard.

'Perhaps he has heard of me,' said Richard.

'You better go and find out,' said the guard, casually removing the note. 'Through the door, take the corridor to your right, second door on the left,' he added before slamming down the window.

Richard led Florentyna through the entrance.

'Most businessmen are involved in a little bribery at some stage in their careers,' she teased.

'Now don't get annoyed just because your lie failed,' said Richard, grinning.

When they reached the room, Florentyna knocked firmly and peered around the door.

A tall, dark-haired Italian was seated in one corner of the room eating spaghetti with a fork. Florentyna's first reaction was one of admiration. He was wearing a pair of tailored jeans and blue blazer over a casual open-necked shirt. But the thing that struck her most was the young man's long, artistic fingers. The moment he saw Florentyna he rose gracefully to his feet.

'Gianni,' she began expansively. 'What a privilege –'

'No,' said the man in a soft Italian accent. 'He's in the washroom.'

Richard smirked and received a sharp kick on the ankle. Florentyna was about to speak again when the door opened and in walked a man no more than five feet five, nearly bald, and from the programme notes she knew he was not yet thirty. His clothes were beautifully cut, but the pasta had had a greater effect on his waistline than it had had on his friend.

'Who are these people, Valerio?'

'Mrs. Florentyna Kane,' said Florentyna before the young man could speak. 'And this is my husband, Richard.'

'What do you want?' he asked, not looking at her while taking the seat opposite his companion.

'To offer you a job as my designer.'

'Not another one,' he said, throwing his hands in the air.

Florentyna took a deep breath. 'Who else has spoken to you?'

'In New York, Yves Saint Laurent. In Los Angeles, Pierre Cardin. In Chicago, Balmain. Need I go on?'

'But did they offer you a percentage of the profits?'

'What profits?' Richard wanted to ask, but remembered the kick on the ankle.

'I already have six shops and we have plans for another six in the pipeline,' Florentyna continued impulsively. She hoped that Gianni di Ferranti hadn't noticed her husband's eyebrows rise dramatically at her words.

'The turnover could be millions within a few years,' she continued.

'Saint Laurent's turnover already is,' said di Ferranti, still not turning to face her.

'Yes, but what did they offer you?'

'Twenty-five thousand dollars a year, and one per cent of the profits.'

'I'll offer you twenty thousand and five per cent.'

The Italian waved a dismissive hand.

'Twenty-five thousand dollars and ten per cent?' she said.

The Italian laughed, rose from his chair and opened the door for Florentyna and Richard to leave. She stood firm.

'You are the sort of person who would expect Zeffirelli to be available to design your next shop while still hoping to retain Luigi Ferpozzi as honorary adviser. Not that I could expect you to understand what I'm talking about,' he added.

'Luigi,' said Florentyna, haughtily, 'is a dear friend of mine.'

The Italian placed his hands on his hips and roared with laughter. 'You Americans are all the same. Next you'll be saying you designed the Pope's vestments.'

Richard had some sympathy with him.

'Your bluff is called, signora. Ferpozzi came to see the show in Los Angeles only last week and spoke to me at length about my work. Now at least I have found a way to be rid of you.' Di Ferranti left the door open and picked up the phone on his dressing table and without another word dialled a 213 number.

No one spoke while they waited for the call to be answered. Eventually Florentyna heard a voice which she thought she recognised.

'Luigi?' said di Ferranti. 'It's Gianni. I have an American lady with me called Mrs. Kane who claims she is a friend of yours.'

He listened for a few moments, his smile becoming broader.

He turned to Florentyna. 'He says he doesn't know anyone called Mrs. Kane, and perhaps you would feel more at home on Alcatraz?'

'No, I wouldn't care for Alcatraz,' said Florentyna. 'But tell him he thinks my father built it.'

Gianni di Ferranti repeated Florentyna's sentiments over the phone. As he listened to the reply his face became puzzled. He finally looked back at her. 'Luigi says to offer you a cup of tea. But only if you've brought your own pot.'

It took Florentyna two lunches, one dinner with Richard, one with her bankers, and an advance big enough to move Gianni and his friend Valerio from Milan to a new home in San Francisco to persuade the little Italian to join her as the company's new in-house designer. Florentyna was confident that this was the breakthrough she had been looking for. In the excitement of convincing Gianni she quite forgot they were only six days away from going to New York to meet Richard's father.

Florentyna and Richard were having breakfast that Monday morning when his face turned so white that she thought he was going to faint.

'What's the matter, darling?'

He pointed to the front page of the *Wall Street Journal* as if unable to speak. Florentyna read the bald announcement and silently handed the paper back to her husband. He read the statement slowly for a second time to be certain he understood the full implications. The brevity and force of the words were stunning. 'William Lowell Kane, the President and Chairman of Lester's Bank, resigned after Friday's board meeting.'

Richard knew that the city would put the worst interpretation possible on such a sudden departure, made without explanation or any suggestion of illness, especially as his only son, a banker, had not been invited to take his place on the board. He put his arms around Florentyna and held her close to his chest.

'Does it mean our trip to New York will be cancelled?'

'Not unless your father was the cause.'

'It can't happen – I won't *let* it happen. Not after waiting so long.'

The phone rang and Richard leaned over to answer it, not letting go of Florentyna.

'Hello?'

'Richard, it's mother. I've been trying to get away from the house. Have you heard the news?'

'Yes, I've just read it in the *Wall Street Journal*. What in heaven's name made father resign?'

'I'm not certain of all the details myself, but as far as I can gather, Mr. Rosnovski has held six per cent of the bank's shares for the past ten years, and for some reason he only needed eight per cent to be able to remove your father from the chair.'

'To invoke Article Seven,' said Richard.

'Yes, that's right. But I'm still not sure what that means.'

'Well, father had the clause put into the bank's by-laws to protect himself from ever being taken over. He considered the clause was foolproof because only someone in possession of eight per cent or more could challenge his authority. He never imagined anyone other than the family could ever get their hands on such a large stake in the company. Father would never have given up his fifty-one per cent of Kane and

Cabot to become chairman of Lester's if he had felt an outsider could remove him.'

'But that still doesn't explain why he had to resign.'

'I suppose Florentyna's father somehow got hold of another two per cent. That would have given him the same powers as father and made life at the bank impossible for him as chairman.'

'But how could he make life impossible?' It was now obvious to Richard that his father had not even confided in Kate about what was happening at the bank.

'Among the safeguards that Article Seven stipulates, if I remember correctly,' Richard continued, 'is that anyone in possession of eight per cent of the shares can hold up any transaction the bank is involved in for three months. I know from the bank's audit that Mr. Rosnovski held six per cent. I suppose he obtained the other two per cent from Peter Parfitt.'

'No, he didn't get the shares from Parfitt,' said Kate. 'I know your father managed to secure those shares by getting an old friend to purchase them for considerably more than they were worth, which is why he has felt so relaxed and confident about the future lately.'

'Then the real mystery is how Mr. Rosnovski got hold of the other two per cent. I know no one on the board who would have parted with their own shares unless . . .'

'Your three minutes are up, ma'am.'

'Where are you, Mother?'

'I'm in a pay phone. Your father has forbidden any of us to contact you ever again, and he never wants to set eyes on Florentyna.'

'But this has nothing to do with her, she's . . .'

'I'm sorry, ma'am, but your three minutes are up.'

'I'll pay for the call, operator.'

'I'm sorry, sir, but the call has been disconnected.'

Richard replaced the phone reluctantly.

Florentyna looked up. 'Can you forgive me, darling, for having a father who was involved in such a terrible thing? I know I will never forgive him.'

'Never prejudge anyone, Jessie,' said Richard, as he stroked her hair. 'I suspect that if we ever discover the whole truth we shall find that the blame is fairly evenly distributed on both sides. Now, young lady, you have two children and six stores to worry about and I, no doubt, have irate customers waiting for me at the bank. Put this whole incident behind you because I am convinced that the worst is now over.'

Florentyna continued to cling to her husband, thankful for the strength of his words, even if she did not believe them.

Abel read the announcement of William Kane's resignation in the *Wall Street Journal* the same day. He picked up the phone, dialled Lester's Bank and asked to speak to the new chairman. A few seconds later Jake Thomas came on the line.
'Good morning, Mr. Rosnovski.'

'Good morning, Mr. Thomas. I'm just phoning to confirm that I shall release this morning my eight per cent holding in Lester's to you personally for two million dollars.'

'Thank you, Mr. Rosnovski, that's most generous of you.'

'No need to thank me, Mr. Chairman. It's no more than we agreed on when you sold me your two per cent.'

Florentyna realised that it would take a considerable time to recover from the blow inflicted by her father. She wondered how it was still possible to love him and to hate him at the same time. She tried to concentrate on her fast-growing empire and to put the thought of never seeing her father again out of her mind.

Another blow, not as personal, but every bit as tragic for Florentyna was delivered on November 22nd, 1963. Richard called her from the bank, something he had never done before, to tell her that President Kennedy had been shot in Dallas, and early reports feared he might die.

20

FLORENTYNA'S NEWLY ACQUIRED ITALIAN designer Gianni di Ferranti, had come up with the idea of putting a small entwined double F on the collar or hem of all his garments. It looked most impressive and only added to the company's reputation. Although Gianni was the first to admit that it was nothing more than a copy of an idea that Yves Saint Laurent had used, nevertheless it worked.

Florentyna found time to fly to Los Angeles to check on a property that was up for sale on Rodeo Drive in Beverly Hills. Once she had seen it, she told Richard she had plans for a seventh Florentyna's. He said he would need to study the figures carefully before he could advise her if she should take up the offer, but he was under such pressure at the bank that it might have to wait a few days.

Not for the first time Florentyna felt the need of a partner or at least a financial director, now that Richard was so overworked. She would have liked to ask him to join her but she felt diffident about suggesting it.

'You'll have to put an advertisement in the *Chronicle* and see how many replies you get,' said Richard. 'I'll help you screen them and we can interview the short list together.'

Florentyna followed Richard's instructions, and within days the letters had flooded in from bankers, lawyers and accountants, all of whom showed considerable interest in the appointment. Richard helped Florentyna sift through the replies. Halfway through the evening he paused over a particular letter and said: 'I'm crazy.'

'I know, my darling, that's why I married you.'

'We've wasted four hundred dollars.'

'Why? You felt sure the advertisement would turn out to be a worthwhile investment.'

Richard handed her the letter he had been reading.

'Seems well qualified,' said Florentyna, after she had read it through. 'Since he's at the Bank of America, you must have your own opinion as to whether he's a suitable man to be my financial director.'

'He's eminently suitable. But who do you imagine will fill his position if he leaves the bank to join you?'

'I've no idea.'

'Well, since he's my boss, it might be me,' said Richard.

Florentyna burst out laughing. 'And to think I didn't have the courage to ask you. Still, I consider it four hundred dollars well spent – partner.'

Richard Kane left the Bank of America four weeks later and joined his wife as a fifty per cent partner and the Financial Director of Florentyna Inc. of San Francisco, Los Angeles and San Diego.

Another election went by. Florentyna didn't become involved because she was so overworked with her expanding empire. She admitted to Richard that she couldn't trust Johnson while she despised Goldwater. Richard put a bumper sticker on their car which Florentyna immediately tore off:

$$Au \ + \ H^2O \ = \ 1964$$

They agreed not to discuss the subject again, although Florentyna did gloat over the Democratic landslide that followed in November.

During the next year, their two children grew more quickly than the company, and on their son's fifth birthday they opened two more Florentyna's: in Chicago and Boston. Richard remained cautious about the speed at which the

shops were springing up but Florentyna's pace never faltered. With so many new customers wanting to wear Gianni
di Ferranti's clothes, she spent most of her spare time
combing cities for prime sites.

By 1966 there was only one important city that did not
boast a Florentyna's. She realised it might be years before a
site fell vacant on the only avenue fit for the Florentyna's of
New York.

21

'YOU'RE A STUBBORN OLD fool, Abel.'

'I know, but I can't turn the clock back now.'

'Well, I can tell you, nothing's going to stop me accepting
the invitation.'

Abel looked up from his bed. He had hardly left the
penthouse since that severe bout of 'flu six months before.
After he had returned from an extensive trip to Poland,
George was almost his only contact with the outside world.
He knew his oldest friend was right, and he had to admit that
it was tempting. He wondered if Kane would be going. He
found himself hoping so, but he doubted it. The man was
every bit as stubborn as he was . . .

George voiced Abel's thoughts. 'I bet William Kane will
be there.'

Abel made no comment. 'Have you the final run-down on
Warsaw?'

'Yes,' said George sharply, angry that Abel had changed
the subject. 'All the agreements are signed and John Gronowski couldn't have been more cooperative.'

John Gronowski, the first Polish ambassador to Warsaw, reflected
Abel. *He would never recover from . . .*

'Your trip to Poland last year has achieved everything you
could have hoped for. You will live to open the Warsaw
Baron.'

'I always wanted Florentyna to open it,' said Abel quietly.

'Then invite her, but don't expect any sympathy from me. All you have to do is acknowledge Richard's existence. And even you must have woken up to the fact that their marriage is a success, otherwise *that* wouldn't be on the mantelpiece.' George stared across the room. There, propped up in front of a vase, stood an unanswered invitation.

Everyone in New York seemed to be there when Florentyna Kane opened her new boutique on Fifth Avenue. Florentyna, wearing a green dress that had been specially designed for her with the now famous double F on the high collar, stood near the entrance of the shop, greeting each of her guests and offering them a glass of champagne. Katherine Kane, accompanied by her daughter Lucy, was among the first to arrive and very quickly the floor was crowded with people whom Florentyna either knew very well or had never seen before. George Novak arrived a little later and delighted Florentyna by his first request – to be introduced to the Kanes.

'Will Mr. Rosnovski be coming later?' Lucy asked innocently.

'I'm afraid not,' said George. 'I told him that he was a stubborn old fool to miss such a good party. Is Mr. Kane here?'

'No, he's not been well lately and rarely leaves the house nowadays,' said Kate, and she then confided to George a piece of news that delighted him.

'How is my father?' Florentyna whispered into George's ear.

'Not well. I left him in bed in the penthouse. Perhaps when he hears that tonight you're going to . . .'

'Perhaps,' said Florentyna. She took Kate by the arm and introduced her to Zaphia. For a moment, neither of the old ladies spoke. Then Zaphia said, 'It's wonderful to meet you at last. Is your husband with you?'

The room became so crowded that it was almost impossible to move, and the ringing laughter and chatter left Florentyna in no doubt how well the opening was going, but now she had only one thing on her mind: dinner that evening.

*

Outside, a large crowd had gathered on the corner of Fifty-sixth Street to stare at what was going on and the traffic on Fifth Avenue had nearly come to a standstill as men and women, young and old, peered through the large plate glass windows.

A man stood in a doorway on the far side of the road. He wore a black coat, a scarf around his neck and a hat pulled well down on his head. It was a cold evening and the wind was whistling down Fifth Avenue. Not a day for old men, he thought, and wondered if after all it had been wise to leave the warmth of his bed. But he was determined that nothing would prevent his witnessing the opening of this shop. He fiddled with the silver band around his wrist and remembered the new will he had made, not leaving the heirloom to his daughter as he had originally promised.

He smiled as he watched young people surge in and out of the splendid shop. Through the window he could just make out his ex-wife talking to George, and then he saw Florentyna and a tear trickled down his lined cheek. She was even more beautiful than he remembered her. He wanted to cross the road that divided them and say, 'George was right, I've been a stubborn old fool for far too long. Can you possibly forgive me?' but instead he just stood and stared, his feet remaining fixed to the ground. He saw a young man by his daughter's side, tall, self-assured and aristocratic; he could only be the son of William Kane. A fine man, George had told him. How had he described him? Florentyna's strength. Abel wondered if Richard hated him and feared that he must. The old man turned up his collar, took one last look at his beloved daughter and turned to retrace his steps back to the Baron.

As he walked away from the shop he saw another man heading slowly along the pavement. He was taller than Abel, but his walk was just as unsteady. Their eyes met, but only for a moment, and as they passed each other the taller of the old men raised his hat. Abel returned the compliment and they continued on their separate ways without a word.

*

'Thank heavens, the last one has gone,' said Florentyna. 'And only just enough time for a bath before changing for dinner.'

Katherine Kane kissed her and said, 'See you in an hour.'

Florentyna locked the front door of the shop and, holding her children's hands tightly, she walked with them towards the Pierre. It would be the first time since her childhood she had stayed in a hotel in New York other than the Baron.

'Another day of triumph for you, my darling,' said Richard.

'To be followed by a night?'

'Oh, stop fussing, Jessie. Father will adore you.'

'It's been such a long time, Richard.'

Richard followed her through the front door of the Pierre, then caught up with his wife and put his arm around her. 'Ten wasted years, but now we have the chance to make up for the past.' Richard guided his family towards the elevator. 'I'll make sure that the children are washed and dressed while you have your bath.'

Florentyna lay in the bath, wondering how the evening would turn out. From the moment Kate Kane had told her of Richard's father's desire to see them all, she had feared he would change his mind once again; but now the meeting was only an hour away. She wondered if Richard was having the same misgivings. She stepped out of the bath, dried herself before putting on a hint of Joy, her favourite perfume, and a long blue dress especially chosen for the occasion: Kate had told her that her husband's favourite colour was blue. She hunted through her jewelry for something simple and slipped on the antique ring given to her so long ago by her father's backer. When she was fully dressed she stared at herself critically in the mirror: thirty-three, no longer young enough to wear mini skirts, nor old enough to be elegant.

Richard came in from the adjoining room. 'You look stunning,' he said. 'The old man will fall in love with you on sight.' Florentyna smiled and brushed the children's hair while Richard changed. Their son, now seven, was wearing his first suit and looked quite grown-up; Annabel had on a red dress with a white ribbon around the hem: she had no problem with the latest mini fashion.

'I think we're all ready,' said Florentyna when Richard reappeared. She couldn't believe her eyes: he was wearing a shirt with a thin red stripe running through it.

The chauffeur opened the door of their hired Lincoln and Florentyna followed her children into the back. Richard sat in front. As the car drove slowly through the crowded New York streets Florentyna sat in silence. Richard leaned over and touched her hand. The chauffeur brought the car to a stop outside a small elegant brownstone apartment on Sixty-eighth Street.

'Now, children, remember you must be on your best behaviour,' said Florentyna.

'Yes, Mummy,' they said in unison, unawed by the thought of at last meeting one of their grandfathers.

Before they had even stepped out of the car the front door of the house was opened by an elderly man in a morning coat who bowed slightly.

'Good evening, ma'am,' he said. 'And how nice to see you again, Mr. Richard.'

Kate was waiting in the hall to greet them. Florentyna's eyes were immediately drawn to an oil painting of a beautiful woman who sat in a crimson leather chair, hands resting in her lap.

'Richard's grandmother,' said Kate. 'I never knew her, but it's easy to see why she was considered one of the beauties of her day.'

Florentyna continued to stare.

'Is something wrong, my dear?' Kate asked.

'The ring,' she said, barely in a whisper.

'Yes, it's beautiful, isn't it?' said Kate, holding up her hand to display a diamond and sapphire ring. 'William gave it to me when he asked me to be his wife.'

'No, the other one in the portrait,' said Florentyna.

'The antique one, yes, quite magnificent. It had been in the family for generations but I fear it's been lost for some years. When I remarked on its disappearance to William he said he knew nothing of it.'

Florentyna raised her right hand and Kate stared down at the antique ring in disbelief. They all looked at the oil painting – there was absolutely no doubt.

'It was a christening present,' said Florentyna. 'Only I never knew who gave it to me.'

'Oh, my God,' said Richard. 'It never crossed my mind . . .'

'And my father still doesn't know,' said Florentyna.

A maid bustled into the hall. 'Excuse me, ma'am, I've told Mr. Kane that everybody has arrived. He asked if Richard and his wife would be kind enough to go up on their own.'

'You go on up,' said Kate. 'I'll join you in a few minutes with the children.'

Florentyna took her husband's arm and climbed the stairs, nervously fingering the antique ring. They entered the room to find William Lowell Kane sitting in the crimson leather chair by the fire. Such a fine-looking man, thought Florentyna, realising for the first time what her husband would look like when he was old.

'Father,' said Richard, 'I would like you to meet my wife.'

Florentyna stepped forward, to be greeted by a warm and gentle smile on William Kane's face.

Richard waited for his father's response but Florentyna knew that the old man would never speak to her now.

22

ABEL PICKED UP THE phone by the side of his bed. 'Find George for me. I need to get dressed.' Abel read the letter again. He couldn't believe William Kane had been his backer.

When George arrived, Abel didn't speak. He just handed

over the letter. George read it slowly. 'Oh, my God,' he said.

'I must attend the funeral.'

George and Abel arrived at Trinity Church in Boston a few minutes after the service had begun. They stood behind the last row of respectful mourners. Richard and Florentyna stood on each side of Kate. Three senators, five congressmen, two bishops, most of the chairmen of the leading banks and the publisher of the *Wall Street Journal* were all there. The chairman and every director of the Lester's board were also present.

'Do you think they can forgive me?' asked Abel.

George did not reply.

'Will you go and see them?'

'Yes, of course.'

'Thank you, George. I hope William Kane had a friend as good as you.'

Abel sat up in bed looking towards the door every few moments. When it eventually opened he hardly recognised the beautiful lady who had once been his 'little one'. He smiled defiantly as he stared over the top of his half-moon spectacles. George remained by the door as Florentyna ran to the side of the bed and threw her arms around her father – a long hug that couldn't make up for ten wasted years, he told her.

'So much to talk about,' he continued. 'Chicago, Poland, politics, the shops . . . But first, Richard. Can he ever believe I didn't know until yesterday that his father was my backer?'

'Yes, Papa, because he only discovered it himself a day before you, and we are still not sure how you found out.'

'A letter from the lawyers of the First National Bank of Chicago who had been instructed not to inform me until after his death. What a fool I've been,' Abel added. 'Will Richard see me?' he asked, his voice sounding very frail.

'He wants to meet you so much, he and the children are waiting downstairs.'

'Send for them, send for them,' Abel said, his voice rising. George smiled and disappeared.

'And do you still want to be President?' Abel asked.

'Of the Baron Group?'

'No, of the United States. Because if you do, I well remember my end of the bargain. All the way to the convention floor even if it means I end up destitute.'

Florentyna smiled, but made no comment.

A few moments later there was a knock at the door. Abel tried to push himself up as Richard came into the room, followed by the children. The head of the Kane family walked forward and shook hands warmly with his father-in-law.

'Good morning, sir,' he said. 'It's an honour to meet you.'

Abel couldn't get any words out so Florentyna introduced him to Annabel and his grandson.

'And what is your name?' demanded the old man.

'William Abel Kane.'

Abel gripped the boy's hand. 'I am proud to have my name linked with that of your other grandfather.

'You will never begin to know how sad I am about your father,' he said turning to Richard. 'I never realised. So many mistakes over so many years. It didn't cross my mind, even for a moment, that your father could have been my benefactor. God knows, I wish I could be given one chance to thank him personally.'

'He would have understood,' said Richard. 'But there was a clause in the deeds of the family trust which didn't allow him to reveal his identity because of the potential conflict between his professional and private interests. He would never have considered making an exception to any rule. That's why his customers trusted him with their life savings.'

'Even if it resulted in his own death?' asked Florentyna.

'I've been just as obdurate,' said Abel.

'That's hindsight,' said Richard. 'None of us could have known that Henry Osborne would cross our paths.'

'Your father and I met, you know, the day he died,' said Abel.

Florentyna and Richard stared at him in disbelief.

'Oh, yes,' said Abel. 'We passed each other on Fifth Avenue – he had come to watch the opening of your new shop. He raised his hat to me. It was enough, quite enough.'

Soon they were talking of happier days; both laughed a little and cried a lot.

'You must forgive us, Richard,' said Abel. 'The Polish are a sentimental race.'

'I know,' he replied. 'My children are half Polish.'

'Can you join me for dinner tonight?'

'Of course,' said Richard.

'Have you ever experienced a real Polish feast, my boy?'

'Every Christmas for the past ten years,' Richard replied.

Abel laughed, then talked of the future and how he saw the progress of his group. 'We ought to have one of your shops in every hotel,' he told Florentyna.

She agreed.

Abel had only one other request of Florentyna: that she and Richard would accompany him on his journey to Warsaw in nine months' time for the opening of the latest Baron. Richard assured him both of them would be there.

During the following months Abel was reunited with his daughter and quickly grew to respect his son-in-law. George had been right about the boy all along – why *had* he been so stubborn?

He confided in Richard that he wanted their return to Poland to be one Florentyna would never forget. Abel had asked his daughter to open the Baron Warsaw but she had insisted that only the President of the group could perform such a task, although she was anxious about her father's health.

Every week Florentyna and her father would follow the progress of the new hotel. As the time drew nearer for the opening the old man even practised his speech in front of her.

The whole family travelled to Warsaw together. They inspected the first Western hotel to be built behind the Iron

Curtain, to be reassured that it was everything Abel had promised.

The opening ceremony took place in the massive gardens in front of the hotel. The Polish Minister of Tourism made the opening speech welcoming the guests. He then called upon the President of the Baron Group to say a few words before performing the opening ceremony.

Abel's speech was delivered exactly as he had written it and at its conclusion the thousand guests on the lawn rose and cheered.

The Minister of Tourism then handed a large pair of scissors to the President of the Baron Group. Florentyna cut the ribbon that ran across the entrance of the hotel and said, 'I declare the Baron Warsaw open.'

Florentyna had travelled to Slonim to scatter the ashes of her father in his birthplace. As she stood on the land where her father had been born she vowed never to forget her family's origins.

Richard tried to comfort her, but in the short time he had come to know his father-in-law he had recognised the many qualities he had passed on to his daughter.

Florentyna realised that she could never come to terms with their short reconciliation. She still had so much to tell her father and even more to learn from him. She continually thanked George for the time they had been allowed to share as a family, knowing the loss was every bit as deep for him. The last Baron Rosnovski was left on his native soil while his only child and oldest friend returned to America.

The Present

1968–1982

23

FLORENTYNA KANE'S APPOINTMENT AS chairman of the Baron Group was confirmed at the board meeting the day she returned from Warsaw. Richard's first piece of advice was that they should transfer the head office of Florentyna's from San Francisco to New York. A few days later the two of them flew back to stay in their little home on Nob Hill for the last time. They spent the next four weeks in California, making the necessary arrangements for their move, which included leaving the west coast operation in the competent hands of their senior manager and putting Nancy Ching in overall charge of the two shops in San Francisco. When it came to saying goodbye to Bella and Claude, Florentyna assured her closest friends that she would be flying back to the coast on a regular basis.

'Going as suddenly as you came,' said Bella.

It was only the second time she had seen Bella cry.

Once they had settled down in New York, Richard recommended that Florentyna should make the shops a subsidiary of the Baron Group so that the companies could be consolidated for tax purposes. Florentyna agreed and made George Novak President for life on his sixty-fifth birthday, giving him a salary that even Abel would have considered generous. Florentyna became chairman of the group and Richard its chief executive.

Richard found them a magnificent new home on East Sixty-fourth Street. They continued to live on the forty-second floor of the New York Baron while their new home was being decorated. William was enrolled at the fashionable Buckley school like his father before him, while Annabel went to Spence. Carol thought perhaps the time had come to look for another job, but at the mere mention of the subject, Annabel would burst into tears.

Florentyna spent every waking hour learning from George how the Baron Group was run. At the end of her first year as chairman, George Novak's private qualms as to whether his goddaughter would have the toughness necessary to run such a huge empire were entirely allayed, especially after her stand in the south on equal pay for Baron Group employees whatever their colour.

'She has inherited her father's genius,' George told Richard. 'All she lacks now is experience.'

'Time will take care of that,' Richard predicted.

Richard made a full report to the board on the state of the company after Florentyna's first year as chairman. The group declared a profit of over twenty-seven million dollars despite a heavy worldwide building schedule and the drop in the value of the dollar caused by the escalating war in Vietnam. Richard then presented his ideas to the board for a comprehensive investment programme for the seventies. He ended his report by recommending that this sort of exercise should be taken over by a bank.

'Agreed,' said Florentyna, 'but I still look upon you as a banker.'

'Don't remind me,' said Richard. 'Only with the turnover we now generate in more than fifty currencies and the fees we pay to the many financial institutions we employ, perhaps the time has come for us to control our own bank.'

'Isn't it nearly impossible nowadays to buy a bank outright?' asked Florentyna. 'And almost as hard to fulfil the government requirements for a licence to run one?'

'Yes it is, but we already own eight per cent of Lester's and we know what problems that created for my father. This time let's turn it to our advantage. What I should like to recommend to the board is . . .'

The following day Richard wrote to Jake Thomas, the chairman of Lester's, seeking a private interview. The letter he received in reply was guarded to the point of hostility. Their secretaries agreed on a time and place for the meeting.

When Richard entered the chairman's office Jake Thomas rose from behind his desk and ushered him into a seat before returning to the leather chair that had been occupied by Richard's father for more than twenty years. The bookcases were not as full or the flowers as fresh as Richard remembered. The chairman's greeting was formal and short but Richard was not cowed by Thomas's approach as he knew that he was bargaining from strength. There was no small talk.

'Mr. Thomas, I feel that as I hold eight per cent of Lester's stock and have now moved to New York, the time has come for me to take my rightful place on the board of the bank.'

It was obvious from Jake Thomas's first words that he had anticipated what was on Richard's mind. 'I think in normal circumstances that might have been a good idea, Mr. Kane, but as the board has quite recently filled its last place perhaps the alternative would be for you to sell your stock in the bank.'

It was exactly the answer Richard had expected. 'Under no circumstances would I part with my family shares, Mr. Thomas. My father built this bank up to be one of the most respected financial institutions in America, and I intend to be closely involved in its future.'

'That's a pity, Mr. Kane, because I am sure you are aware that your father did not leave the bank in the happiest of circumstances and I feel certain we could have offered you a reasonable price for your shares.'

'Better than the price my father-in-law offered you for yours?' said Richard.

Jake Thomas's cheeks flushed brick-red. 'I see you have only come here to be destructive,' he said.

'I have often found in the past that construction must be preceded by a little destruction, Mr. Thomas.'

'I don't think you hold enough cards to make this house tumble,' the chairman retorted.

'No one knows better than you that two per cent may suffice,' said Richard.

'I can see no point in prolonging this conversation, Mr. Kane.'

'For the time being, I agree with you, but you can be sure that it will be continued in the not too distant future,' said Richard.

He rose to leave. Jake Thomas did not accept his out-stretched hand.

'If that's his attitude, we must declare war,' said Florentyna.

'Brave words,' said Richard, 'but before we make our next move I want to consult my father's old lawyer, Thaddeus Cohen. There's nothing he doesn't know about Lester's bank. Perhaps if we combine our knowledge we can come up with something.'

Florentyna agreed. 'George once told me something my father thought of doing if he failed to remove your father even when he had eight per cent.'

Richard listened intently as Florentyna outlined the plan.

'Do you think that might work in this case?' she asked her husband.

'We just might pull it off, but it would be one hell of a risk.'

'The only thing we have to fear is fear itself,' said Florentyna.

'Jessie, when will you learn that F.D.R. was a politician, not a banker?'

Richard spent most of the next four days locked in consultation with Thaddeus Cohen at the city office of Cohen, Cohen, Yablons and Cohen.

'The only person who now holds eight per cent of Lester's stock is you,' he assured Richard from behind his desk. 'Even Jake Thomas has only two per cent. If your father had known that Thomas could only afford to hold on to Abel Rosnovski's stock for a few days, he might well have called his bluff and held on to the chair.'

The old family lawyer leaned back, placing both hands on top of his bald head.

'That piece of information will make victory even sweeter,' said Richard. 'Do you have the names of all the shareholders?'

'I'm still in possession of the names of the registered stockholders at the time that your father was the bank's chief executive. But by now it may be so out-of-date as to be rendered virtually useless. I don't have to remind someone with your training that you are entitled under state law to demand a formal inspection of the shareholders' list.'

'And I can imagine how long Thomas would take to release that.'

'Around Christmas would be my guess,' said Thaddeus Cohen, allowing himself a thin smile.

'What do you imagine would happen if I called an extraordinary meeting and gave a full account of how Jake Thomas sold his own stock in order to remove my father from the board?'

'You wouldn't gain a great deal from such an exercise, apart from embarrassing a few people. Jake Thomas would see that the meeting was held on an inconvenient day and badly attended. He would also undoubtedly obtain a fifty-one per cent proxy vote against any resolution you put forward. Into the bargain I suspect Mr. Thomas would use such a move by you to re-wash dirty linen in public which would only add a further stain to your father's reputation. No, I think Mrs. Kane has come up with the best idea so far and, if I may be permitted to say so, it is typical of her father's boldness in such matters.'

'But if we should fail?'

'I am not a betting man, but I'd back a Kane and Rosnovski against Jake Thomas any day.'

'If I agree, when should we launch the bid?' asked Richard.

'April 1st,' Thaddeus Cohen said unhesitatingly.

'Why that date in particular?'

'Because it's the right length of time before everyone has to file their tax returns to be fairly certain that quite a number of people will be in need of some spare cash.'

Richard went over the detailed plan with Thaddeus Cohen again, and that night he explained it in full to Florentyna.

'How much do we stand to lose if we fail?' was her first question.

'Roughly?'

'Roughly.'

'Thirty-seven million dollars.'

'That's pretty rough,' said Florentyna.

'We don't exactly lose the money, but all our capital will be locked up in Lester's stock and that would put a severe restriction on the cash flow for the rest of the group, if we didn't control the bank.'

'What does Mr. Cohen think of our chances of pulling that off?'

'Better than fifty-fifty. My father would never have considered going ahead with such odds,' added Richard.

'But my father would have,' said Florentyna. 'He always considered a glass to be half full, never half empty.'

'Thaddeus Cohen was right.'

'About what?'

'About you. He warned me that if you were anything like your father, prepare for battle.'

During the next three months Richard spent most of his time with accountants, lawyers and tax consultants, who had all the paperwork completed for him by March 15th. That afternoon, he booked space on every major financial page in America for April 1st and informed the advertising departments that the copy would arrive by hand twenty-four hours prior to publication. He couldn't help reflecting on the date, and wondered if it would be he or Jake Thomas who would end up the fool. During the final two weeks Richard and Thaddeus Cohen checked over the plan again and again to be certain they hadn't overlooked anything and could be confident that the details of 'Operation Bust a Gut' remained known to only three people.

On the morning of April 1st, Richard sat in his office and studied the full-page advertisement in the *Wall Street Journal*:

The Baron Group announces that it will offer fourteen dollars for every Lester's Bank share. The current market value of Lester's shares is eleven dollars and a quarter. Any persons wishing to take advantage of this offer should contact their broker or write direct for details to Mr. Robin Oakley, Chase Manhattan Bank, One Chase Manhattan Plaza, New York, N.Y. 10005. This offer remains open until July 15th.

In his article on the facing page, Vermont Royster pointed out that this bold bid to take over Lester's must have had the support of Chase Manhattan, which would be holding the stock of the Baron Group as security. The columnist went on to predict that if the bid succeeded Richard Kane would undoubtedly be appointed the new chairman, a position his father had held for more than twenty years. If, on the other hand, the move failed, the Baron Group might find themselves with severe cash restrictions placed on their reserves for several years as the group would be encumbered with a large minority shareholding without actually controlling the bank. Richard could not have summed up the situation more accurately himself.

Florentyna called Richard's office to congratulate her husband on the way he had carried out 'Operation Bust a Gut'. 'Like Napoleon, you have remembered that the first rule of war is surprise.'

'Well, let's hope JakeThomas is not my Waterloo.'

'You're such a pessimist, Mr. Kane. Just remember, Mr. Thomas is probably sitting in the nearest men's room at this moment, and he doesn't have a secret weapon and you do.'

'I do?' said Richard.

'Yes. Me.' The phone clicked and rang again immediately.

'Mr. Thomas of Lester's Bank on the line for you, Mr. Kane.'

I wonder if he has a phone in the men's room, thought Richard. 'Put him through,' he said, understanding for the first time a little of what the confrontation between his father and Abel Rosnovski must have been like.

'Mr. Kane, I thought we ought to see if we can sort out our differences. Perhaps I was a little over-cautious in not offering you a place on the board immediately.'

'I'm no longer interested in a place on the board, Mr. Thomas.'

'No? But I thought that –'

'No. I am now interested only in the chair.'

'You do realise that if you fail to secure fifty-one per cent of Lester's stock by July 15th, we could institute immediate changes in the allocation of bearers' stock and voting shares that will diminish the value of the stock you already hold? And I feel I should add that the members of the board already control between them forty per cent of Lester's stock, and I intend to contact all the other shareholders by telegram today with a recommendation not to take up your offer. Once I am in possession of another eleven per cent, you will have lost a small fortune.'

'That's a risk I'm willing to take,' said Richard.

'Well, if that's your attitude, Kane, I shall call a full shareholders' meeting for July 23rd. If you haven't obtained your fifty-one per cent by then I shall personally see to it that you are kept out of any dealing with this bank for as long as I am chairman.' Without warning Thomas's tone changed from bullying to ingratiating. 'Now perhaps you might like to reconsider your position.'

'When I left your office, Mr. Thomas, I made it clear what I had in mind. Nothing has changed.' Richard put the phone down, opened his diary to July 23rd and put a line through the page, writing across it: *Stockholders meeting, Lester's Bank*, with a large question mark. He received Jake Thomas's telegram to all stockholders that afternoon.

Every morning Richard followed the response to his advertisement with calls to Thaddeus Cohen and Chase Manhattan. By the end of the first week they had picked up thirty-one per cent of the shares, which with Richard's own eight per cent meant that they held thirty-nine per cent in all. If Thomas had in fact started with forty per cent, it was going to be a tight finish.

Two days later Richard received a detailed letter sent by Jake Thomas to all shareholders in which he advised strongly against consideration of the offer from the Baron Group. 'Your interests would be transferred into the hands of a company which until recently was controlled by a man convicted of bribery and corruption,' stated the final paragraph. Richard was disgusted by Jake Thomas's personal attack on Abel and he had never seen anything make Florentyna so angry.

'We are going to beat him, aren't we?' she asked, her fingers clenched into a tight fist.

'It will be close. I know they have over forty per cent among the directors and their friends. As of four o'clock this afternoon we have forty-one per cent, so it's a battle for the last nineteen per cent that will decide who wins on July 23rd.'

By the end of the month Richard heard nothing from Jake Thomas, which made him wonder if he had already captured fifty-one per cent, but with only eight weeks left until the stockholders' meeting it was Richard's turn to read over breakfast a full-page advertisement that made his heartbeat hit one hundred and twenty. On page thirty-seven of the *Wall Street Journal* Jake Thomas had made an announcement on behalf of Lester's. They were offering two million shares of authorised but previously unoffered stock to be sold for a newly set-up pension fund on behalf of the bank's employees.

In an interview with the *Journal*'s chief reporter, Thomas explained that this was a major step in profit sharing and that the funding of retirement income would be a model to the nation both inside and outside the banking community.

Richard swore uncharacteristically as he left the table and walked towards the phone, leaving his coffee to go cold.

'What did you say?' asked Florentyna.

'Balls,' he repeated, and passed over the paper. She read the news while Richard was dialling.

'What does it mean?'

'It means that, even if we do acquire fifty-one per cent of the present stock, with Thomas's authorised issue of a further two million new shares – which you can be sure would be sold only to the institutions – it'll be impossible to defeat the bastard on July 23rd.'

'Is it legal?' enquired Florentyna.

'That's what I'm about to find out,' said Richard.

Thaddeus Cohen gave him an immediate reply. 'It's legal, unless you succeed in getting a judge to stop them. I'm having the necessary papers drawn up now, but I warn you, if we are not granted a preliminary injunction you will never be chairman of Lester's.'

During the next twenty-four hours Richard found himself rushing in and out of lawyers' offices and courtrooms. He signed three affidavits and a judge in chambers heard the case for an injunction. This was followed by a special expedited appeal in front of a three-judge panel which, after a day of deliberation, decided by two to one in favour of holding up the share offering until the day after the extraordinary general meeting. Richard had won the battle but not the war; when he returned to his office the next morning he found he still had only forty-six per cent of the stock needed to defeat Jake Thomas.

'He must have the rest,' said Florentyna forlornly.

'I don't think so,' replied Richard.

'Why not?' she asked.

'Because he would not have bothered with that smoke screen exercise of the pension fund shares if he already had fifty-one per cent.'

'Good thinking, Mr. Kane.'

'The truth is,' said Richard, 'that he believes *we* have fifty-one per cent. So where is the missing five per cent?'

During the last few days of June, Richard had to be stopped from phoning Chase Manhattan every hour to discover if they had received any more shares. When July

15th came he had forty-nine per cent, and was acutely aware that in exactly eight days Thomas would be able to issue new voting shares that would make it virtually impossible for him ever to gain control of Lester's. Because of the cash flow requirements of the Baron Group, he would have to dump some of his Lester's shares immediately – no doubt, as Jake Thomas had predicted, at a considerable loss. He found himself mumbling 'two per cent, only two per cent', several times during the day.

With only a week to go Richard found it hard to concentrate on the new hotel fire regulations pending before Congress when Mary Preston rang.

'I don't know a Mary Preston,' Richard told his secretary.

'She says you would remember her as Mary Bigelow.'

Richard smiled, wondering what she could possibly want. He hadn't seen her since leaving Harvard. He picked up his phone. 'Mary, what a surprise. Or are you only phoning to complain about bad service at one of the Baron hotels?'

'No, no complaints, although we once spent a night at a Baron if you can remember that far back.'

'How could I forget?' he said, not remembering.

'No, I was only calling to seek your advice. Some years ago my great-uncle, Alan Lloyd, left me three per cent of Lester's. I received a letter from a Mr. Jake Thomas last week asking me to pledge those shares to the board and not to deal with you.'

Richard held his breath and could hear his heart beat.

'Are you still there, Richard?'

'Yes, Mary. I was just thinking. Well, the truth is . . .'

'Now don't start a long speech, Richard. Why don't you and your wife come and spend a night in Florida with my husband and me and then you can advise us.'

'Florentyna doesn't return from San Francisco until Sunday . . .'

'Then come on your own. I know Max would love to meet you.'

'Let me see if I can re-arrange a couple of things and then I will call you back within the hour.'

Richard phoned Florentyna who told him to drop every-thing and go on his own. 'On Monday morning we will be able to wave goodbye to Jake Thomas once and for all.'

Richard then informed Thaddeus Cohen of the news, who was delighted. 'On my list the stock is still under the name of Alan Lloyd.'

'Well, it's now in the name of Mrs. Max Preston.'

'I don't give a damn what her name is, just go and get it.'

Richard flew down on Saturday afternoon and was met at the West Palm beach airport by Mary's chauffeur who drove him out to the Prestons. When Richard first saw the house Mary was living in he wondered how they could fill it without about twenty children. The vast mansion stood on the far side of a golf course on the Inter-coastal Waterway. It took six minutes to drive from the Lion Lodge gates to the imposing forty steps in front of the house. Mary was standing on the top step waiting to greet him. She was dressed in a well-cut riding outfit. Her fair hair still touched her shoul-ders. As Richard looked up at her he recalled what had first attracted him nearly fifteen years before.

The butler whisked away Richard's overnight bag and ushered him into a bedroom large enough to hold a small convention. On the end of the bed was a riding outfit.

Mary and Richard rode around the grounds before dinner, and although there was no sign of Max she said he was expected about seven. Richard was thankful that Mary never went beyond a canter. It had been a long time since he had ridden with her and he knew he was going to be stiff in the morning. When they returned to the house Richard had a bath and changed into a dark suit before going down to the drawing room a little after seven. The butler poured him a sherry. When Mary floated into the room in a delicate off-the-shoulder evening dress the butler handed her a large whisky without waiting to be asked.

'I am sorry, Richard, but Max has just phoned to say he has been held up in Dallas and won't be back until late tomorrow afternoon. He will be very disappointed not to meet you.' Before Richard could comment, she added: 'Now let's go and have dinner and you can explain to me why the Baron Group needs my three per cent.'

Richard took her slowly through the story of what had happened since his father had taken over from her great-uncle. He hardly noticed the first two courses of dinner, he became so intent.

'So with my three per cent,' said Mary, 'the bank can return safely into the hands of the Kanes?'

'Yes,' said Richard. 'Five per cent is still missing, but as we already have forty-nine per cent, you can put us over the top.'

'That's simple enough,' said Mary, as the soufflé dish was whisked away. 'I shall speak to my broker on Monday and arrange everything. Let's go and have a celebration brandy in the library.'

'You don't know what a relief that will be,' said Richard, rising from his chair and following his hostess down a long corridor.

The library turned out to be the size of a basketball court with almost as many seats. Mary poured Richard a coffee while the butler offered him a Hine. She told the butler that that was all she needed for the rest of the evening and sat down next to Richard on the sofa.

'Quite like old times,' said Mary, edging towards him.

Richard agreed as he came back from his daydreams of being chairman of Lester's. He was enjoying the brandy and hardly noticed Mary rest her head on his shoulder. After she had poured him a second brandy he couldn't miss that her hand had shifted on to his leg. He took another sip of cognac. Suddenly and without warning she threw her arms around Richard and kissed him on the lips. When she eventually released him, he laughed and said, 'Just like old times.' He stood up and poured himself a large black coffee. 'What's keeping Max in Dallas?'

'Gas piping,' said Mary, without much enthusiasm. Richard remained standing by the mantelpiece.

During the next hour he learned all about gas piping and a little about Max. When the clock struck twelve he suggested it might be time to turn in. She made no comment, just rose from her seat and accompanied him up the vast staircase to his room. She walked away before he could kiss her good night.

Richard found it hard to sleep as his mind was a mixture of elation at having secured Mary's three per cent of Lester's coupled with his plans for how the take-over of the bank would be carried out with a minimum of disruption. He realised that, even as ex-chairman, Jake Thomas could still be a nuisance and was considering ways of controlling Thomas's anger at losing the take-over battle when he heard a slight click from the bedroom door. He glanced towards it to see the handle turning, and then the door itself pushed slowly open. Mary stood silhouetted, wearing a see-through pink negligee.

'Are you still awake?'

Richard lay motionless, wondering if he could get away with pretending to be asleep. But he was aware she might have seen him move, so he said, sleepily, 'Yes.' He was amused by the thought that this was not a time for thinking on his feet.

Mary padded over to the edge of the bed and sat down. 'Would you like anything?'

'A good night's sleep,' said Richard.

'I can think of two ways of helping you achieve that,' said Mary, leaning forward and stroking the back of his head. 'You could take a sleeping pill, or we could make love.'

'That's a nice idea, but I've already taken the sleeping pill,' said Richard, drowsily.

'It doesn't seem to have had the desired effect, so perhaps we should try the second remedy,' said Mary. She lifted the negligee over her head, allowing it to fall to the floor. Then without another word she slipped under the covers, drawing herself close to Richard. Richard could feel that her firm figure was that of a woman who did a lot of exercise and had had no children.

'Hell, I wish I hadn't taken that pill,' said Richard, 'or at least I could stay another night.'

Mary started kissing Richard's neck while running a hand down his back until she reached between his legs.

Christ, thought Richard, I'm only human. And then a door slammed. Mary threw back the covers, grabbed her negligee, ran across the room, and disappeared faster than a thief when a hall light is turned on. Richard pulled the sheets back over his body and listened to a murmur of conversation which he couldn't make out. He spent the rest of the night in a fitful sleep.

When he came down to breakfast the next morning, he found Mary chatting to an elderly man who must once have been very handsome.

The man rose and shook Richard by the hand. 'Allow me to introduce myself. I'm Max Preston,' he said. 'Although I hadn't planned to be with you this weekend, my business finished early and I managed to catch the last flight out of Dallas. I certainly wouldn't have wanted you to leave my home without having experienced true southern hospitality.' Max and Richard chatted over breakfast about the problems they were both facing on Wall Street. They were deep into the effects of Nixon's new tax regulations when the butler announced that the chauffeur was waiting to take Mr. Kane to the airport.

The Prestons accompanied Richard down the forty steps to the waiting car, where Richard turned and kissed Mary on the cheek, thanked her for all she had done and shook Max warmly by the hand.

'I hope we shall meet again,' said Max.

'That's a nice idea. Why don't you give me a call when you're next in New York?' Mary smiled at him gently.

Mary and Max Preston waved as the Rolls-Royce glided down the long drive. Once his plane had taken off, Richard felt a tremendous sense of relief. The stewardess served him a cocktail and he began to think about his plans for Monday. To his delight Florentyna was waiting for him on his return to Sixty-fourth Street.

'The shares are ours,' he told her triumphantly and went over the full details during dinner. They fell asleep on the sofa by the fire a little before midnight, Florentyna's hand resting on his leg.

The next morning Richard placed a call through to Jake Thomas to inform him he was now in possession of fifty-one per cent.

Richard could hear an intake of breath.

'As soon as the certificates are in my lawyer's hands, I shall come over to the bank and let you know how I expect the transition to be carried out.'

'Of course,' said Thomas resignedly. 'May I ask from whom you obtained the last two per cent?'

'Yes, from an old friend of mine, Mary Preston.'

There was a pause at the other end. 'Not Mrs. Max Preston of Florida?' asked Jake Thomas.

'Yes,' said Richard triumphantly.

'Then you needn't bother to come over, Mr. Kane, because Mrs. Preston lodged her three per cent of Lester's with us four weeks ago and we have been in possession of the stock certificates for some time.' The phone clicked. It was Richard's turn to gasp.

When Richard told Florentyna about the new development all she could say was: 'You should have slept with the damned woman. I bet Jake Thomas would have.'

'Would you have slept with Scott Forbes in the same circumstances?'

'Good God, no, Mr. Kane.'

'Precisely, Jessie.'

Richard spent another sleepless night thinking of how that final two per cent might still be acquired. It was obvious that both sides now had forty-nine per cent of the stock. Thaddeus Cohen had already warned him that he must face reality and start thinking of ways to recoup the maximum amount of cash for the shares he already had. Perhaps he should take a leaf out of Abel's book and sell heavily the day before the meeting. Richard continued to toss and turn as useless ideas rushed through his mind. He turned over once again and tried to catch some sleep precisely when Florentyna woke with a start.

'Are you awake?' she asked quietly.

'Yes, chasing two per cent.'

'So am I. Do you remember your mother telling us that someone had purchased two per cent from a Mr. Peter Parfitt on behalf of your father to stop my father getting his hands on it?'

'Yes, I do,' said Richard.

'Well, perhaps they haven't heard about our offer.'

'My darling, it's been in every paper in the United States.'

'So have the Beatles, but not everyone has heard of them.'

'I suppose it's worth a try,' said Richard, picking up the phone by the side of his bed.

'Who are you calling? The Beatles?'

'No, my mother.'

'At four o'clock in the morning? You can't ring your mother in the middle of the night.'

'I can and I must.'

'I wouldn't have told you if I'd known you might do that.'

'Darling, there are only two and a half days to go before I lose you thirty-seven million dollars, and the owner of the shares we need so badly might live in Australia.'

'Good point, Mr Kane.'

Richard dialled the number and waited. A sleepy voice answered the phone.

'Mother?'

'Yes, Richard. What time is it?'

'Four o'clock in the morning. I'm sorry to bother you, but there is no one else I can turn to. Now please listen carefully. You once said that a friend of father's bought two per cent of Lester's shares from Peter Parfitt to keep the stock from falling into the hands of Florentyna's father. Can you remember who it was?'

There was a pause. 'Yes, I think so. It will come back to me if you hold on a minute. Yes, it was an old friend from England, a banker who had been at Harvard with your father. The name will come in a moment.' Richard held his breath. Florentyna sat up in bed.

'Dudley, Colin Dudley, the chairman of . . . oh dear, I can't remember.'

'Don't worry, Mother, that's enough to be getting on with. You go back to sleep.'

'What a thoughtful and considerate son you are,' said Kate Kane as she put the phone down.

'Now what, Richard?'

'Just make breakfast.'

Florentyna kissed him on the forehead and disappeared.

Richard picked up the phone. 'International operator, please. What time is it in London?'

'Seven minutes past nine.'

Richard flicked through his personal phone book and said, 'Please connect me to 01-735-7227.'

He waited impatiently. A voice came on the line.

'Bank of America.'

'Put me through to Jonathan Coleman, please.'

Another wait.

'Jonathan Coleman.'

'Good morning, Jonathan, it's Richard Kane.'

'Nice to hear from you, Richard. What are you up to?'

'I need some information urgently. Which bank is Colin Dudley chairman of?'

'Hold on a minute, Richard, and I'll look him up in the *Bankers' Year Book*.' Richard could hear the pages turning. 'Robert Fraser and Company,' came back the reply. 'Only now he's Sir Colin Dudley.'

'What's his number?'

'493-3211.'

'Thank you, Jonathan. I'll give you a call when I'm next in London.'

Richard wrote the number on the corner of an envelope and dialled the international operator again as Florentyna came into the bedroom.

'Getting anywhere?'

'I'm about to find out. Operator, can you please get me a number in London, 493-3211.' Florentyna sat on the end of the bed while Richard waited.

'Robert Fraser and Company.'

'May I speak to Sir Colin Dudley, please.'

'Who shall I say is calling, sir?'

'Richard Kane of the Baron Group, New York.'

'Hold on please, sir.'

Richard waited again.

'Good morning. Dudley here.'

'Good morning, Sir Colin. My name is Richard Kane. I think you knew my father?'

'Of course. We were at Harvard together. Good chap, your old man. I was very sad to read about his death. Wrote to your mother at the time. Where are you calling from?'

'New York.'

'Get up early, you Americans, don't you? So what can I do for you?'

'Do you still own two per cent of Lester's Bank shares?' Richard held his breath again.

'Yes, I do. Paid a bloody king's ransom for them. Still, can't complain. Your father did me a few favours in his time.'

'Would you consider selling them, Sir Colin?'

'If you're willing to offer me a sensible price.'

'How much would you consider sensible?'

There was a long pause. 'Eight hundred thousand dollars.'

'I accept,' said Richard, without hesitation, 'but I must be able to pick them up tomorrow, and I'm not risking a courier service. If I bank-transfer the money, can you have all the paperwork done by the time I arrive?'

'Simple, dear boy,' Dudley said without demur. 'I'll also have a car meet you at the airport and put at your disposal while you're in London.'

'Thank you, Sir Colin.'

'Go easy with the "Sir", young fellow. I've reached that age when I prefer to be called by my Christian name. Just let me know when you expect to arrive and everything will be ready for you.'

'Thank you . . . Colin.'

Richard put the phone down.

'You're not getting dressed, are you?'

'I certainly am. I won't get any more sleep tonight. Now where's my breakfast?'

By six o'clock, Richard was booked on the nine fifteen flight from Kennedy Airport. He had also booked himself on a return flight the following morning at eleven arriving back in New York by one thirty-five the following afternoon, giving him twenty-four hours to spare before the stockholders' meeting at two o'clock on Wednesday.

'Running things a bit close, aren't we?' said Florentyna, 'but, fear not, I believe in you. By the way, William is expecting you to bring him back a model of a red London bus.'

'You're always making these major commitments on my behalf. It's a heavy load I carry as the chief executive of your group.'

'I know, dear, and to think it's only because you sleep with the chairman.'

By seven Richard was seated at his office desk writing explicit instructions for the transfer of the eight hundred thousand dollars by telex to Robert Fraser and Company, Albemarle Street, London W.1. Richard knew the money would be in Sir Colin Dudley's bank long before he was. At seven thirty he was driven to the airport and he checked in. The 747 took off on time and he arrived at London's Heathrow at ten o'clock that night. Sir Colin Dudley had been as good as his word. A driver was waiting to pick him up and whisk him off to the Baron. The manager had put him in the Davis Leroy Suite. The Presidential Suite, he explained, was already occupied by Mr. Jagger. The rest of his group had taken over the ninth floor.

'I don't think I know the group,' said Richard. 'What area do they specialise in?'

'Singing,' said the manager.

When Richard checked at the reception desk, there was a message waiting for him from Sir Colin suggesting they meet at the bank at nine the following morning.

Richard dined quietly in his rooms and called Florentyna to bring her up to date before going to bed.

'Hang in there, Mr. Kane. We're all depending on you.'

Richard woke at seven and packed before going down to breakfast. His father had always gone on about the kippers in London, so he ordered them with some anticipation. When he had finished the last morsel, he realised that they were so good that he would undoubtedly bore his own son with the same story for many years to come. After breakfast, he walked round Hyde Park to kill the hour before the bank opened. The park was green and the flowerbeds a mass of untouched roses. He couldn't help but compare its beauty to Central Park, and recalled that London still had five royal parks of a similar size.

As nine o'clock struck, Richard walked in the front door of Robert Fraser and Company in Albemarle Street only a few hundred yards from the Baron. A secretary ushered him through to Sir Colin Dudley's office.

'Had a feeling you'd be on time, old fellow, so I have everything prepared for you. I once remember finding your father sitting on the doorstep with the milk bottles. Everybody drank black coffee that day.'

Richard laughed.

'Your eight hundred thousand dollars arrived before close of business yesterday so all I have to do is sign the share certificates over to you in the presence of a witness.' Sir Colin flicked a switch. 'Can you come in, Margaret?' Sir Colin's private secretary watched the chairman of one bank sign the transfer certificates so that the recipient could become the chairman of another bank.

Richard checked over the documents, carefully signed his part of the agreement and was handed a receipt for eight hundred thousand dollars.

'Well, I hope that all the trouble you've taken in coming yourself will ensure that you become the chairman of Lester's, old chap.'

Richard stared at the elderly man with the white walrus

moustache, bald head and military bearing. 'I had no idea you realised . . .'

'Wouldn't want you Americans to think we're altogether asleep over here. Now you bustle off and catch the eleven o'clock from Heathrow and you'll make your meeting easily: not many of my customers pay as promptly as you do. By the way, congratulations on that moon chappie.'

'What?' said Richard.

'You've put a man on the moon.'

'Good heavens,' said Richard.

'No, not quite,' said Sir Colin, 'but I'm sure that's what NASA has planned next.'

Richard laughed and thanked Sir Colin again. He walked quickly back to the Baron, literally humming. He knew exactly what it felt like to be the man on the moon. He had left his overnight bag with the porter so he was able to check out quickly, and Sir Colin's chauffeur drove him back to Heathrow. Richard entered Terminal Three well in time to check in for the eleven o'clock flight. He was going to be back in New York with twenty-four hours to spare: if his father had had to make the same transaction before he became chairman the process would have taken at least two weeks.

Richard sat in the Clipper Club lounge toying with a Martini while reading in *The Times* about Rod Laver's fourth Wimbledon triumph, unable to see the fog descending outside. It wasn't until thirty minutes later that an announcement warned passengers that there would be a short delay on all flights. An hour later, they called Richard's flight, but as he walked across the tarmac he could see the fog growing denser by the minute. He sat in his seat, belt fastened, reading a copy of the previous week's *Time* magazine, willing himself not to look outside, waiting to feel the plane move. Nixon, he read, had named the first women generals, Colonel Elizabeth Hoisington and Colonel Anne Mae Hays; no doubt the first Nixon initiative that Florentyna would approve of, he thought.

'We are sorry to announce that this flight has been delayed until further notice because of fog.' A groan went up inside the first-class cabin. 'Passengers should return to the terminal where they will be issued with luncheon vouchers and advised when to reboard the aircraft. Pan American apologises for the delay and hopes it will not cause any great inconvenience.' Richard had to smile, despite himself. Back inside the terminal, he went around to every ticket counter to discover who had the first plane out. It turned out to be an Air Canada flight to Montreal. He reserved a seat, after being told that his Pan Am flight to New York was now the twenty-seventh in line for departure. He then checked the flights out of Montreal to New York. There was one every two hours and the flying time was just over an hour. He pestered Pan American and Air Canada every thirty minutes but the polite bland reply remained unvaried: 'I'm sorry, sir, we can do nothing until the fog lifts.'

At two in the afternoon, he called Florentyna to warn her about the delay.

'Not impressive, Mr. Kane. While you're on the phone, did you manage to pick up a red London bus for William?'

'Damn. I completely forgot.'

'Not doing very well today, Mr. Kane. Better try the duty-free gift shop, hadn't we?'

Richard found an airport shop that sold several sizes of London buses. He selected a large plastic one and paid for it with the last of his English money. With the bus safely under his arm he decided to use his luncheon voucher. He sat down to the worst airport lunch he had ever had: one thin piece of beef about an inch square that had been misleadingly described as a minute steak on the menu, along with three tired lettuce leaves posing as a side salad. He checked his watch. It was already three o'clock. For two hours, he tried to read a copy of *The French Lieutenant's Woman* but he was so anxious listening to every radio announcement that he never got past page four.

At seven o'clock, after Richard had walked around Terminal Three several times, he began to think it would soon be too late for planes to take off whatever the weather. The loudspeaker forbodingly warned of an important announcement to follow shortly. He stood like a statue as the words came out. 'We are sorry to announce that all flights out of Heathrow have been cancelled until tomorrow morning with the exception of Iran Air Flight 006 to Jeddah and Air Canada flight 009 to Montreal.' Richard had been saved by his foresight: he knew the Air Canada flight would be completely sold out within minutes. Once again he sat in a first-class lounge. Although the flight was further delayed it was eventually called a few minutes after eight. Richard almost cheered when the 747 took off a little after nine o'clock. Thereafter he found himself checking his watch every few minutes. The flight was uneventful except for more appalling food and the plane eventually landed at Montreal airport shortly before eleven.

Richard sprinted to the American Airlines counter to discover that he had missed the last flight to New York by a few minutes. He swore out loud.

'Don't worry, sir, there is a flight at ten twenty-five tomorrow morning.'

'What time does it arrive in New York?'

'Eleven thirty.'

'Two hours and thirty minutes to spare,' he said out loud. 'It's a bit tight. Can I hire a private plane?' The clerk looked at his watch, 'Not at this time of night, sir.'

Richard thumped the desk and reserved a seat and took a room in the Airport Baron and phoned Florentyna.

'Where are you now?' she asked.

'The Airport Baron, Montreal.'

'Curiouser and curiouser.'

Richard explained what had happened.

'Poor darling. Did you remember the red London bus?'

'Yes, I'm clinging on to it, but my overnight bag is still on the Pam Am flight to New York.'

'And the stock certificates?'

'They are in my briefcase and have never left my side.'

'Well done, Mr. Kane. I'll have a car waiting for you at the airport and Mr. Cohen and I will be at the stockholders' meeting at Lester's clutching on to our forty-nine per cent. So if you're in possession of your two per cent, Jake Thomas will be on the dole by this time tomorrow.'

'How can you be so cool about it?'

'You've never let me down yet. Sleep well.'

Richard did not sleep well, and was back at the American Airlines terminal hours before the plane was due for boarding. There was a slight delay but the captain was still anticipating that he could land at Kennedy by eleven thirty. Richard had no baggage and felt confident he could now make the meeting with at least half an hour to spare. For the first time in over twenty-four hours he began to relax, and even made some notes for his first speech as Lester's chairman.

When the 707 arrived at Kennedy it began to circle the airport. Richard looked out of his little window and could clearly see the building in Wall Street that he had to be at within two hours. He thumped his knee in anger. At last the plane descended a few hundred feet, only to start circling again.

'This is Captain James McEwen speaking. I am sorry for this delay, but we have been put into a holding pattern because of traffic congestion. It seems there are some delayed flights from London now arriving into New York.' Richard wondered if the Pan American flight from Heathrow would land before he did.

Five minutes, ten minutes, fifteen minutes. Richard checked the agenda. Item number one – a motion to reject the take-over bid by the Baron Group. Item number two – the issue of new voting shares. If they couldn't prove they had fifty-one per cent, Jake Thomas would close the proceedings within minutes of the meeting starting. The plane began to descend and the wheels touched the ground at twelve twenty-seven. Richard sprinted through the terminal. He passed his chauffeur on the run, who quickly followed him to the car park, where Richard once again checked his watch. An hour and twenty minutes to spare. He was going to make the meeting comfortably.

'Step on it,' said Richard.

'Yes, sir,' said the chauffeur as he moved into the left-hand lane of the Van Wyck Expressway. Richard heard the siren a few minutes later and a policeman on a motorcycle overtook the car and waved them on to the hard shoulder. The policeman parked and walked slowly towards Richard who had already leaped out of the car. Richard tried to explain it was a matter of life and death.

'It always is,' said the officer. 'Either that or "My wife is having a baby".' Richard left his chauffeur to deal with the policeman while he tried to hail a passing cab: but they were all full. Sixteen minutes later the policeman let them go. It was one twenty-nine as they crossed the Brooklyn Bridge and turned on to F.D.R. Drive. Richard could see the giant skyscrapers of Wall Street in the distance but the cars were bumper to bumper all the way. It was six minutes to two before they reached Wall Street when Richard could bear it no longer and jumped out of the car, briefcase under one arm, a red London bus under the other, and sprinted the last three blocks, dodging slow pedestrians and fast honking cab drivers. He heard the clock at Trinity Church chime two as he reached Bowling Green and prayed that it was fast as he raced up the steps of the Lester's building, suddenly realising he didn't know where the meeting was being held.

'Fifty-first floor, sir,' the doorman informed him.

The 30 to 60 elevator was full with the post-lunch hour crowd and it stopped at 31 – 33 – 34 – 42 – 44 – 47 – 50 – 51. Richard jumped out of the elevator and ran down the corridor following the red arrow that indicated where the meeting was taking place. As he arrived in the crowded room, one or two faces turned to look at him. There must have been over five hundred people seated listening to the chairman, but he was the only shareholder sweating from head to toe. He was greeted by the sight of a cool Jake Thomas, who gave him a knowing smile from the platform. Richard realised he was too late. Florentyna was sitting in the front row, her head bowed. He took a seat at the back of the room and listened to the chairman of Lester's.

'All of us believe that the decision that has been made

today is in the best interests of the bank. In the circumstances that your board of directors faced, no one will have been surprised by my request, and Lester's will now continue its traditional role as one of America's great financial institutions. Item number two,' said Jake Thomas. Richard felt sick. 'My final task as chairman of Lester's is to propose that the new chairman be Mr. Richard Kane.'

Richard could not believe his ears. A little old lady rose from her seat in the front row and said that she would like to second the motion because she felt that Mr. Kane's father had been one of the finest chairmen the bank had ever had. There was a round of applause as the old lady sat down.

'Thank you,' said Jake Thomas. 'Those in favour of the resolution?' Richard stared into the body of the hall as hands shot into the air.

'Those against.' Jake Thomas looked down from the platform. 'Good, the resolution is carried unanimously. I am now happy to invite your new chairman to address you. Ladies and gentlemen, Mr. Richard Kane.' Richard walked forward and everyone stood up and applauded. As he passed Florentyna he handed her the red bus.

'Glad you accomplished *something* on your trip to London,' she whispered.

Richard walked, dazed, on to the platform. Jake Thomas shook his hand warmly and then took a seat on the end of the row.

'I have little to say on this occasion,' began Richard, 'other than to assure you that I wish Lester's to carry on in the same tradition as it did under my father and that I will dedicate myself to that end.' Unable to think of anything else to add, he smiled and said, 'I thank you for your attendance today and look forward to seeing you all at the annual meeting.' There followed another round of applause and the shareholders began to disperse chattering.

As soon as they could escape from those who wished to talk to Richard, either to congratulate him or tell him how they felt Lester's should be run, Florentyna led him away to the chairman's office. He stood and stared at the portrait of his father that hung over the fireplace and turned to his wife.

'How did you manage it, Jessie?'

'Well, I remembered a piece of advice my governess taught me when I was younger. Contingency, Miss Tredgold used to say. Always have a contingency plan ready in case it rains. When you called from Montreal I was afraid there might be an outside chance it would pour, and you wouldn't make the meeting. So I rang Thaddeus Cohen and explained what my contingency plan was, and he spent the morning drawing up the necessary documents.'

'What documents?' said Richard.

'Patience, Mr. Kane. I do feel after my triumph that I have the right to spin out this tale a little longer.'

Richard remained impatiently silent.

'When I had the vital document in my hand, I phoned Jake Thomas and asked if he could see me twenty minutes before the stockholders' meeting was due to start. Had you arrived in time, I would have cancelled the confrontation with Mr. Thomas, but you didn't.'

'But your plan . . .'

'My father – no fool – told me once a skunk, always a skunk, and he turned out to be right. At the meeting with Thomas I informed him that we were in possession of fifty-one per cent of Lester's stock. He was disbelieving until I mentioned the name of Sir Colin Dudley and then he turned quite pale. I placed the whole bundle of certificates on the table in front of him and, before he could check them, told him that if he sold me his two per cent before two o'clock I would still pay him the full fourteen dollars per share. I added that he must also sign a document saying he would resign as chairman and make no attempt to interfere in any future dealings involving Lester's Bank. For good measure, although it was not in the contract, he must propose you for chairman.'

'My God, Jessie, you have the nerve of ten men.'

'No. One woman.'

Richard laughed. 'What was Thomas's response?'

'Asked what I would do if he refused. If you refuse, I told

him, we'll sack you publicly without compensation for loss of office. Then I pointed out to him that he would have to sell his stock for the best price he could get on the open market because as long as we had fifty-one per cent of Lester's he would play no part in the future of the bank.'

'And then?'

'He signed there and then without even consulting his fellow directors.'

'Brilliant, Jessie, both in conception and execution.'

'Thank you, Mr. Kane. I do hope that now you are chairman of a bank you won't be running all over the world getting yourself delayed, missing meetings and having nothing to show for your troubles other than a model of a red London bus. By the way, did you remember to bring a present for Annabel?'

Richard looked embarrassed. Florentyna bent down and handed him an F.A.O. Schwarz shopping bag. He lifted out a package that showed a picture of a toy typewriter on the outside with 'Made in England' printed all along the bottom of the box.

'Just not your day is it, Mr. Kane? By the way, Neil Armstrong got back quicker than you did. Perhaps we should invite him to join the board?'

Richard read Vermont Royster's article in the *Wall Street Journal* the next morning:

Mr. Richard Kane seems to have won a bloodless coup in his bid to become chairman of Lester's. There was no vote taken by shareholders at the extraordinary meeting, and his succession to the chair was proposed by the retiring incumbent, Jake Thomas, and carried unanimously.

Many stockholders present at the meeting referred to the traditions and standards set by the late William Lowell Kane, the present chairman's father. Lester's stock ended the day up two points on the New York Exchange.

'That's the last we'll hear of Jake Thomas,' said Florentyna.

24

RICHARD HAD NEVER HEARD of Major Abanjo before that morning. Neither had anyone else in America other than those who took an over-zealous interest in the affairs of Nambawe, Central Africa's smallest state. Nevertheless, it was Major Abanjo who caused Richard to run late for his most important appointment that day, the eleventh birthday party of his only son.

When Richard arrived back at the apartment on Sixty-fourth Street, Major Abanjo was driven from his mind by Annabel, who had a few minutes earlier poured a pot of tea over William's hand because she wasn't receiving enough attention. She hadn't realised that it was boiling hot. It seemed that Carol had been in the kitchen fussing over the birthday cake at the time. Annabel was getting even less attention now that William was screaming at the top of his voice and all the other children had to be sent home. A few minutes later Annabel was also screaming, after Richard had placed her across his knee and administered six hard whacks with his slipper before both children were put to bed – William with two aspirins and an ice pack to help him sleep and Annabel as a further punishment. Eleven candles – and one to grow on – had burned themselves down to the icing on the large cake that remained untouched on the dining-room table.

'I'm afraid William will have a scar on his right hand for the rest of his life,' said Florentyna after she had checked to see that her son was at last asleep.

'Still, he took it like a man.'

'I don't agree,' said Florentyna. 'He never once grumbled.'

'It probably wouldn't have happened if I had been on time,' said Richard, ignoring her comment. 'Damn Major Abanjo.'

'Who is Major Abanjo?' asked Florentyna.

'A young army officer who was behind the coup in Nambawe today.'

'Why should a little African state stop you being on time for William's birthday party?'

'That little African state has an outstanding five-year loan agreement of three hundred million dollars that Lester's led on in 1966 and the repayment date is due in three months' time.'

'We are in for three hundred million dollars?' said Florentyna, flabbergasted.

'No, no,' said Richard. 'We covered the first fifteen per cent of the loan, and the remaining eighty-five million was divided among thirty-seven other financial institutions.'

'Can we survive a loss of forty-five million dollars?'

'Yes we can, as long as the Baron Group remains our friend,' said Richard, smiling at his wife. 'It's three years' profits down the drain, not to mention a severe blow to our reputation with the other thirty-seven banks involved and the inevitable drop in our stock price tomorrow.'

Lester's stock price dropped the next day by more than Richard had anticipated, for two reasons. The newly self-appointed President of Nambawe, General Abanjo, announced that he had no intention of honouring previous government commitments made with any 'fascist regime' including America, Britain, France, Germany and Japan. Richard wondered how many Russian bankers were boarding planes to Central Africa at that moment.

The second reason became apparent when a reporter from the *Wall Street Journal* called Richard and asked him if he had any statement to make about the coup.

'I really have nothing to say,' said Richard, trying to sound as if the whole episode were about as troublesome to him as brushing a fly off his sleeve. 'I feel sure the problem will sort itself out during the next few days. After all, the loan is only one of many that Lester's is involved with at the present time.'

'Mr. Jake Thomas might not agree with that opinion,' said the journalist.

'You have spoken to Mr. Thomas?' said Richard in disbelief.

'Yes, he called the *Journal* earlier today and had an off-the-record conversation with our publisher, leaving us in no doubt that he would be surprised if Lester's could survive such a demand on cash flow.'

'No comment,' said Richard curtly, and put the phone down.

At Richard's request, Florentyna called a board meeting of the Baron Group to ensure enough financial backing to see that Lester's could survive a run on its stock. To their surprise, George was not at all convinced that the Baron Group should enmesh itself in Lester's problems. He told them that he had never approved of using the Baron shares as security for the take-over of the bank in the first place.

'I remained silent at the time but I'm not willing to do so on a second occasion,' he said, his hands resting on the board-room table. 'Abel never liked throwing good money after bad whatever his personal involvement. He used to say that anyone could *talk* about future profits and start spending money they hadn't yet earned. Have you considered that we might both end up going bankrupt?'

'The sum involved is not that large to the Baron Group,' said Richard.

'Abel always considered any loss caused ten times the problem of any profit,' George told him. 'And what outstanding loans do you have to other countries around the world which could be taken over while we are asleep in bed?'

'Only one outside the E.E.C., and that's a loan of two hundred million to the Shah of Iran. Again we are the lead bank with a commitment of thirty million, but Iran has never missed an interest payment by so much as an hour.'

'When is their final payment due?' asked George.

Richard flicked through a bulky file that lay on the table in front of him and ran his forefinger down a column of figures. Although nettled by George's attitude, he was pleased to be well-prepared for any query that might arise.

'June 19th, 1978.'

'Then I want an assurance you won't involve the bank again when the loan comes up for renewal,' said George firmly.

'What?' said Richard. 'The Shah is as safe as the Bank of England —'

'Which hasn't proved to be so solid lately.'

Richard was beginning to look angry and was about to respond when Florentyna interrupted.

'Hold on, Richard. If Lester's agrees not to renew its loan with the Shah in 1978, or involve itself in any further Third World commitments, George, will you in turn agree to the Baron Group's underwriting the forty-five million loss on the African contract?'

'No, I'd still need some more convincing.'

'Like what?' said Richard.

'Richard, you don't have to raise your voice. I am still the President of the Baron Group and have given thirty years of my life to building the company up to its present position. I don't intend at this late stage to watch that achievement demolished in thirty minutes.'

'I'm sorry,' said Richard. 'I haven't had much sleep for the last four days. What would you like to know, George?'

'Other than the agreement with the Shah, is Lester's committed to any other loans over ten million?'

'No,' said Richard. 'Most major country to country loans are serviced by the prime banks like Chase or Chemical and we end up with only a tiny percentage of the capital sum. Obviously Jake Thomas felt that Nambawe, which is rich in copper and manganite, was as sure a bet as he could hope to find.'

'We already know, to our cost, that Mr. Thomas is fallible,' said George. 'So, what other loans above five million remain outstanding to the bank?'

'Two,' replied Richard. 'One with General Electricity in Australia for seven million, which is secured by the government, and one with ICI in London. Both are five-year loans with set payment dates and so far repayments have been met on schedule.'

'So if the group wrote off the forty-five million, how long would it take Lester's to recoup the loss?'

'That would depend on the percentage any lender required and over what period of time the money was loaned.'

'Fifteen per cent over five years.'

'Fifteen per cent?' repeated Richard, shocked.

'The Baron Group is not a charity, Richard, and as long as I am President it is not in business to prop up ailing banks. We are hoteliers by trade and have shown a seventeen per cent return on our money over the past thirty years. If we loaned you forty-five million, could you pay it back in five years at fifteen per cent?'

Richard hesitated, scribbled some figures on the pad in front of him and checked his file before he spoke. 'Yes, I am confident we could repay every penny in five years, even assuming the African contract is a total write-off,' he said quietly.

'I think we must treat the contract precisely that way,' said George. 'My informants tell me that the former head of state, King Erobo, has escaped to London, taken up residence at Claridge's and is looking at a house which is for sale in Chelsea Square. It appears he has more money stashed away in Switzerland than anyone other than the Shah, so I feel he is unlikely to return to Africa in a hurry – and I can't say I blame him.' Richard tried to smile as George continued. 'Subject to all you have told us being confirmed by the Baron's auditors, I agree to covering the African loan on the terms stated, and I wish you luck, Richard. I'll also let you in on a little secret: Abel didn't like Jake Thomas any more than you do, which is what tipped the balance for me.' George closed his file. 'I hope you will both excuse me now as I have a lunch appointment with Conrad Hilton and he has never once been late in thirty years.'

When George had closed the door behind him, Richard turned to Florentyna. 'Jesus, whose side does he think he's on?'

'Ours,' replied Florentyna. 'Now I know why my father happily trusted him to run the group while he went off to fight the Germans.'

A statement in the *Wall Street Journal* the following day, confirming that the Baron Group had underwritten Lester's loans, caused the bank's stocks to rise again and Richard settled down to what he called 'my five years of drudgery'.

'What are you going to do about Jake Thomas?'

'Ignore him,' said Richard. 'Time is on my side. No bank in New York will employ him once it's known that he is willing to run to the press whenever he has a disagreement with his past employers.'

'But how will anyone ever find out?'

'Darling, if the *Wall Street Journal* knows, everybody knows.'

Richard turned out to be right; the whole story was repeated back to him over a lunch he had with a director of Bankers Trust only a week later. The director went on to remark, 'That man's broken the golden rule of banking. From now on, he'll even find it hard to open a current account.'

William recovered from his burns far more quickly than Florentyna had expected and returned to school a few days later with a scar on his hand too small even to impress his friends. For the first few days after the accident Annabel looked away every time she saw the scar and seemed genuinely contrite.

'Do you think he's forgiven me?' she asked her mother.

'Of course, my darling. William is just like his father – forgets any quarrel by the next morning.'

*

Florentyna considered that the time had come for her to make a tour of the Baron hotels in Europe. Her staff worked out a detailed itinerary which took in Rome, Paris, Madrid, Lisbon, Berlin, Amsterdam, Stockholm, London and even Warsaw. She felt a new confidence in leaving George in control, she told Richard as they were driven to the airport. He agreed and then reminded her that they had never been apart for as long as three weeks since the day they had met.

'You'll survive, darling.'

'I'll miss you, Jessie.'

'Now, don't you get all sentimental. You know that I have to work for the rest of my life to make sure that my husband can continue posing as chairman of a New York bank.'

'I love you,' said Richard.

'I love you too,' said Florentyna. 'But you still owe me fifteen million and fifty-six dollars.'

'Where does the fifty-six come from?' said Richard.

'From our days in San Francisco. You've never repaid me that fifty-six dollars I lent you before we were married.'

'*You* said it was a dowry.'

'No, you said it was a dowry. I said it was a loan. I think I shall have to take George's advice about how it should be repaid as soon as I return. Perhaps fifteen per cent over five years would seem reasonable, Mr. Kane, which means you must now owe me around four hundred dollars.' She leaned up and kissed him goodbye.

Richard was driven back to New York by the chauffeur and on arrival at his office he immediately phoned Cartier's in London. He gave clear instructions what he required and said it had to be ready in eighteen days.

The time had come for Richard to prepare his annual general report for the bank. The red African figure maddened him. Without it, Lester's would have shown a healthy profit: so much for hoping he would beat Jake Thomas's figures in his first year. All that the stockholders would remember was a thumping loss compared with 1970.

Richard followed Florentyna's detailed schedule with interest every day and made sure that he caught up with her by phone at least once in every capital. She seemed pleased by most of what she had seen, and although she had a few ideas for changes she had to admit that the hotels on the Continent were well run by the group's European directors. Any excess expenditure had been caused by her own demands for higher standards of architecture. When she phoned from Paris Richard passed on the news that William had won the class mathematics prize and that he was now confident that his son would be accepted by St. Paul's. And since the hot water incident Annabel had tried a little harder at school and had even scraped herself off the bottom of the class. She considered it the best news Richard had given her.

'Where's your next stop?' Richard asked.

'London,' she replied.

'Great. I've got a feeling I know someone you'll want to call when you're there,' he said with a chuckle, and went to bed feeling better than he had for some days.

He heard from Florentyna a lot earlier than he had expected. Around six o'clock the next morning Richard was in a deep sleep, dreaming that he and General Abanjo were having a shoot-out; Richard pulled the trigger, the bullet fired. Then the phone rang. He woke up and lifted the receiver, expecting to hear General Abanjo's last words.

'I love you.'

'What?' he said.

'I love you.'

'Jessie, do you know what time it is?'

'A few minutes after twelve.'

'It's eight minutes past six in New York.'

'I only wanted to tell you how much I love my diamond brooch.'

Richard smiled.

'I'm going to wear it to lunch with Sir Colin and Lady Dudley. They are due to arrive any minute to take me to the Mirabelle, so I must say goodbye. Talk to you tomorrow – my today.'

'You're a nut.'

'By the way, I don't know if it's of any interest to you, but there's a reporter on the midday news here in England saying something about a certain General Abanjo being killed in a counter-coup in some Central African state and the old king will be returning home tomorrow to a hero's welcome.'

'What?'

'The king is just being interviewed now so I'll repeat what he's saying. "My government intends to honour all the debts it has incurred with our friends in the western world."'

'What?' repeated Richard, once again.

'He looks such a nice fellow now that he's got the crown back on his head. Good night, Mr. Kane. Sleep well.'

As Richard was leaping up and down on his bed, there was a knock on Florentyna's door, and Sir Colin and Lady Dudley came into her suite.

'Are you ready, young lady?' asked Sir Colin.

'I certainly am,' said Florentyna.

'You look very pleased with yourself. No doubt the reinstatement of King Erobo has brought the roses back to your cheeks.'

'Well informed as you are, Sir Colin, that is not the reason,' said Florentyna as she glanced down at the card that lay on the table in front of her and read the words again.

> I hope that this will be acceptable security until I can return the fifty-six dollars, plus interest.
>
> Mr. Kane

'What a lovely brooch you're wearing,' said Lady Dudley. 'It's a donkey, isn't it? Does that signify anything in particular?'

'It certainly does, Lady Dudley. It means the giver intends to vote for Nixon again.'

'Then you have to give him elephant cuff-links in return,' said Sir Colin.

'You know, Richard was right: it doesn't pay to underestimate the British,' said Florentyna.

*

After lunch Florentyna phoned Miss Tredgold at her school. The school secretary put her through to the staff room. Miss Tredgold, it turned out, did not need to be informed about the late General Abanjo, but seemed more interested in all the news about William and Annabel. Florentyna's second call was to Sotheby's – this time in person. On arrival she asked to see one of the heads of department.

'It may be many years before such a collector's item comes under the hammer, Mrs. Kane,' the expert told her.

'I understand,' said Florentyna. 'But please let me know the moment it does.'

'Certainly, madam,' said the expert as he wrote down Florentyna's name and address.

When Florentyna returned to New York three weeks later she settled down to institute the changes she had been considering on her European tour. By the end of 1972, with her energy, George's wisdom and Gianni di Ferranti's genius, she was able to show an increased profit. Thanks to King Erobo being as good as his word, Richard also declared a handsome profit.

On the night of the annual stockholders' meeting, Richard, Florentyna and George went out for a celebration dinner. Even though George had officially retired on his sixty-fifth birthday, he still came into his office every morning at eight o'clock. It had taken only twenty-four hours for everyone at the Baron to realise his retirement party had been a misnomer. Florentyna began to appreciate how lonely George must be now that he had lost most of his contemporaries and how close he had been to her father. She never once suggested that he should slow down, because she knew it was pointless, and it gave her particular happiness whenever George took Annabel and William on outings. Both the children called him 'Grandpapa' which brought tears to his eyes and always guaranteed them a large ice cream.

Florentyna thought she knew how much George did for the group but the truth only came home to her after his retirement could no longer be postponed. George died peacefully in his sleep in October 1972. In his will, he left everything to the Polish Red Cross. A short note addressed to Richard asked him to act as his executor.

Richard carried out George's every wish to the letter and even travelled to Warsaw accompanied by Florentyna to meet the President of the Polish Red Cross to discuss how George's donation could best be put to use. When they returned to New York Florentyna sent a directive to all managers in the group that the finest suite in each hotel was no longer to be the Presidential Suite but was to be renamed the 'George Novak Suite'.

When Richard woke the morning after they had returned from Warsaw, Florentyna, who had been waiting impatiently for him to open his eyes, told her husband that although George had taught her so much in life, he had now added to her learning even in death.

'What are you talking about?'

'George left everything he possessed to charity, but never once referred to the fact that my father rarely made charitable contributions other than the occasional gift to Polish or political causes. I'm every bit as remiss myself, and if you hadn't added a footnote to the group's annual general report concerning tax relief for charitable donations, I would never have given the matter a second thought.'

'As I'm sure you're not planning for something after your death, what do you have in mind?'

'Why don't we set up a foundation in memory of both our fathers? Let's bring the two families together. What they failed to do in their lifetime, let us do in ours.'

Richard sat up and stared at his wife as she got out of bed and continued to talk as she walked towards the bathroom.

'The Baron Group should donate one million dollars a year to the foundation,' she said.

'Spending only the income, never the capital,' he interjected.

Florentyna closed the bathroom door, which gave Richard a few moments to consider her proposal. He could still be surprised by her bold, sweeping approach to any new venture, even if, as he suspected, she had not thought through who would run the day-to-day administration of such an enterprise once it had taken off. He smiled to himself when the bathroom door reopened.

'We could spend the income derived from such a trust on first-generation immigrants who are not getting the chance of a decent education.'

'And also create scholarships for exceptionally gifted children whatever their background,' said Richard, getting out of bed.

'Brilliant, Mr. Kane, and let us hope that occasionally the same person will qualify for both.'

'Your father would have,' said Richard as he disappeared into the bathroom.

Thaddeus Cohen insisted on coming out of retirement to draw up the deeds of the foundation to cover the wishes of both Kanes. It took him over a month. When the trust fund was launched, the national press welcomed the financial commitment as another example of how Richard and Florentyna Kane were able to combine bold originality with common sense.

A reporter from the Chicago *Sun-Times* phoned Thaddeus Cohen to enquire why the foundation was so named. Cohen explained that 'Remagen' had been chosen because it was the battlefield on which Colonel Rosnovski had unknowingly saved the life of Captain Kane.

'I had no idea they had met on a battlefield,' said a young voice.

'Neither did they,' replied Thaddeus Cohen. 'It was only discovered after their deaths.'

'Fascinating. Tell me, Mr. Cohen, who is going to be the first trustee of the Remagen Foundation?'

'Professor Luigi Ferpozzi.'

Both Lester's Bank and the Baron Group set new records for the following year as Richard established himself as a force on Wall Street and Florentyna visited her hotels in the

Middle East and Africa. King Erobo held a banquet in Florentyna's honour when she arrived in Nambawe, and although she promised to build a hotel in the capital city she wouldn't be drawn into an explanation why Lester's had not been among the banks involved with the king's latest international loan.

William had a good first year at St. Paul's, showing the same flair for maths which his father had before him. As they had been taught by the same master, both father and son avoided asking for any comparison. Annabel did not progress as quickly as William, although her teacher had to admit she had improved, even if she had fallen in love with Bob Dylan.

'Who's he?' asked Florentyna.

'I don't know,' said Richard, 'but I'm told he's doing for Annabel what Sinatra did for you twenty-five years ago.'

When Florentyna started her sixth year as chairman of the group she found she was beginning to repeat herself. Richard seemed to find new challenges all the time, while Gianni di Ferranti appeared to be well in control of the chain of shops without bothering to ask her anything other than where to send the cheques. The Baron Group was now so efficient, and her management team so competent, that no one showed a great deal of concern one morning when Florentyna didn't come into the office.

That evening, when Richard was sitting in the crimson leather chair by the fire reading *The Billion Dollar Killing*, she expressed her thoughts out loud.

'I'm bored.'

Richard made no comment.

'It's time I did something with my life other than build on my father's achievements,' she added.

Richard smiled but didn't look up from his book.

25

'YOU'RE ALLOWED THREE GUESSES as to who this is.'

'Am I given any clues?' asked Florentyna, annoyed that she knew the voice but couldn't quite place it.

'Good-looking, intelligent and a national idol.'

'Paul Newman.'

'Feeble. Try again.'

'Robert Redford.'

'Worse still. One more chance.'

'I need another clue.'

'Appalling at French, not much better at English and still in love with you.'

'Edward. Edward Winchester. A voice from the past – only you don't sound as if you've changed a bit.'

'Wishful thinking. I'm over forty, and by the way so will you be next year.'

'How can I be when I'm only twenty-four this year?'

'What, again?'

'No, I have been on ice for the last fifteen years.'

'Not from what I've read about you. You go from strength to strength.'

'And how about you?'

'I'm a partner in a law firm in Chicago: Winston and Strawn.'

'Married?'

'No, I've decided to wait for you.'

Florentyna laughed. 'If you've taken this long to phone and propose, I should warn you that I've been married for

over fifteen years and I have a son of fourteen and a daughter
of twelve.'

'All right then, I won't propose, but I would like to see you.
It's a private matter.'

'A private matter? Sounds intriguing.'

'If I were to fly to New York one day next week, would you
have lunch with me?'

'I'd enjoy that.' Florentyna flicked over the pages of her
calendar. 'How about next Tuesday?'

'Suits me. Shall we say the Four Seasons, one o'clock?'

'I'll be there.'

Florentyna put down the phone and sat back in her chair.
Other than Christmas cards and the odd letter, she had had
very little contact with Edward for sixteen years. She walked
across to the mirror and studied herself. A few small lines
were beginning to appear around the eyes and mouth. She
turned sideways to confirm that she had kept her slim figure.
She didn't feel old. There was no denying that she had a
daughter who could already make young men stop in the
street for a second glance, and a teenage son she now had to
look up to. It wasn't fair. Richard didn't look forty: a few
white tufts appearing at the sides of the temples and the hair
perhaps a shade thinner than it had been, but he was every
bit as slim and vigorous as the day they had met. She
admired the fact that he still found time to play squash at the
Harvard Club twice a week and practise the cello most
weekends. Edward's phone call made her think of middle
age for the first time; how morbid. She would be thinking of
death next. Thaddeus Cohen had died the previous year;
only her mother and Kate Kane remained of that generation.

Florentyna tried to touch her toes and couldn't, so she
returned to the monthly statements of the Baron Group for
reassurance. London was still not paying its way, even
though the hotel occupied one of the finest sites in Mayfair.
Somehow the English seemed to combine impossible wage
demands with high unemployment and staff shortages all
at the same time. In Riyadh they had had to clear out

almost the entire management because of theft, and in Poland the government would still not allow the group to take any exchangeable currency out of the country. But despite these minor problems, all of which could be sorted out by her management team, the company was in good shape.

Florentyna had confidently assured Richard that the Baron Group profits would be over forty-one million for 1974, whereas Lester's would be lucky to touch eighteen million. Richard, however, had predicted that Lester's profits would pass the Baron Group's by 1974. She feigned disdain but knew when it came to financial forecasts he was rarely wrong.

Her thoughts floated back to Edward when the phone rang. Gianni di Ferranti wondered if she would like to see his new collection for the Paris show, which put her old classmate out of her mind until one o'clock the following Tuesday.

Florentyna arrived at the Four Seasons a few minutes after one, wearing one of Gianni's new dresses in midi-length bottle-green silk with a sleeveless jacket over it. She wondered if she would still recognise Edward. She walked up the wide staircase to find him waiting for her on the top step. She privately hoped she had aged as well as he had.

'Edward,' she cried, 'you haven't changed a bit.' He laughed. 'No, no,' mocked Florentyna, 'I've always liked grey hair and the extra weight suits you. I wouldn't expect anything less of a distinguished lawyer from my home town.'

He kissed her on both cheeks like a French general and then she put her arm through his as they followed the maître d' through to their table. A bottle of champagne awaited them.

'Champagne. How lovely. What are we celebrating?'

'Just being with you again, my dear.' Edward noticed that Florentyna seemed to be lost in thought. 'Is something wrong?' he enquired.

'No. I was just remembering myself sitting on the floor at Girls Latin, crying, while you tore the arm off Franklin D. Roosevelt and then poured royal-blue ink over his head.'

'You deserved it, you were a dreadful little show-off. F.D.R. didn't. Poor little bear. Is he still around?'

'Oh, yes. He's taken up residence in my daughter's bedroom and as she has managed to keep his remaining arm and both legs I can only reluctantly conclude that Annabel handles young men better than I did.'

Edward laughed. 'Shall we order? I have so much to talk to you about. It's been fun following your career on the television and in the papers but I want to see if you've changed.'

Florentyna ordered salmon and a side salad while Edward chose the prime rib with asparagus.

'I'm intrigued.'

'By what?' asked Edward.

'Why a Chicago lawyer would fly all the way to New York just to see an hotelier.'

'I do not come as a Chicago lawyer and I have no interest in talking to an hotelier. I come as treasurer of the Cook County Democratic Party.'

'I gave one hundred thousand dollars to the Chicago Democrats last year,' said Florentyna. 'Mind you, Richard donated one hundred thousand to the New York Republicans.'

'I don't want your money, Florentyna, although I know you have supported the Ninth District financially at every election. It's you I want.'

'That's a new line,' she said, grinning. 'Men have stopped saying that to me lately. You know, Edward,' she continued, her tone changing, 'I've been so overworked during the last few years, I barely have had the time to vote, let alone become personally involved. What's more, since Watergate I found Nixon detestable, Agnew worse, and with Muskie a non-runner I was only left with George McGovern, who didn't exactly inspire me.'

'But surely . . .'

'I also have a husband, two young children, and a two hundred million dollar company to run.'

'And what are you going to do for the next twenty years?'

She smiled to herself. 'Turn it into a billion dollar company.'

'In other words, just repeat yourself. Now I agree with you about McGovern and Nixon – one was too good and the other too bad – and I don't see anyone on the horizon who excites me.'

'So now you want me to run for President in '76?'

'No, I want you to run for Congress as the representative of the Ninth District of Illinois.'

Florentyna dropped her fork. 'If I remember the job specification correctly, it's an eighteen-hour day, forty-two thousand five hundred dollars a year, no family life, and your constituents are allowed to be as rude to you as they like. Worst of all, you are required to live in the Ninth District of Illinois.'

'That wouldn't be so bad. The Baron is in the Ninth District, and besides, it's just a stepping-stone.'

'To what?'

'To the Senate.'

'When the whole state can be rude to you.'

'And then the Presidency.'

'When the rest of the world can join in. Edward, this is not Girls Latin and I don't have two lives, one which can run my hotels and one . . .'

'And one in which you can give back some of what you have taken from others.'

'That was a bit rough, Edward.'

'Yes, it certainly was. I apologise. But I have always believed you could play a role in national politics, as you did once yourself, and I feel the time is right, especially as I am now convinced you haven't changed.'

'But I haven't been involved in politics at a grass-roots level, let alone a national level, for years.'

'Florentyna, you know as well as I do that most people in Congress have neither your experience nor your intelligence. That goes for most Presidents, come to think of it.'

'I'm flattered, Edward, but not convinced.'

'Well, I can tell you that a group of us in Chicago are convinced you should come home and run for the Ninth District.'

'Henry Osborne's old seat?'

'Yes. The Democrat who won back Osborne's seat in '54 is retiring this session and Mayor Daley wants a strong candidate to ward off any Republican challenger.'

'A Polish woman?'

'With the woman *Time* said ran behind only Jackie Kennedy and Margaret Mead in the nation's esteem.'

'You're mad, Edward. Who needs it?'

'I suspect you do, Florentyna. Just give me one day in your life, come to Chicago and meet the people who want you. Express in your own words how you feel about the future of our country. Won't you at least do that for me?'

'All right, I'll think about it and call you in a few days. But I warn you, Richard will think I'm nuts.'

On that count Florentyna turned out to be wrong. Richard had arrived home late that night after a trip to Boston, and told her over breakfast that she had been talking in her sleep.

'What did I say?'

Richard stared at her. 'Something I have always suspected,' he replied.

'And what was that?'

'Can I afford to run?'

Florentyna made no reply.

'Why did Edward want to see you for lunch so urgently?'

'He wants me to return to Chicago and stand for Congress.'

'So that's what brought it on. Well, I think you should consider the offer seriously, Jessie. For a long time you have been critical of the fact that competent women don't go into politics. And you have always been outspoken about the abilities of those who do enter public life. Now you can stop complaining and do something about it.'

'But what about the Baron Group?'

'The Rockefeller family managed to survive when Nelson became Governor; no doubt the Kane family will survive somehow. In any case, the group now employs twenty-seven thousand people, so I imagine we can find ten men to take your place.'

'Thank you, Mr. Kane. But how do I live in Illinois while you're in New York?'

'That's easily solved. I'll fly to Chicago every weekend. Wednesday nights you can fly to New York and now that Carol has agreed to stay it shouldn't be too unsettling for the children. When you're elected, I'll take the shuttle down to Washington Wednesday nights.'

'You sound as though you've been thinking about this for some time, Mr. Kane.'

Florentyna flew out to Chicago a week later and was met at O'Hare airport by Edward. It was pouring, and the wind was blowing so hard that even Edward, tightly clutching a large umbrella with both hands, could only just protect her from the rain.

'Now I know why I wanted to come back to Chicago,' she said as she scampered into the car, cold and wet. They were driven into the city while Edward briefed her on the people she would meet.

'They're all party workers and faithful stalwarts who have only read about you or have seen you on television. They'll be surprised to find that you only have two arms, two legs, and a head like any one of them.'

'How many do you expect to be at the meeting?'

'Around sixty. Seventy would be exceptional.'

'And all you want me to do is meet them, and then say a few words about my feelings on national affairs?'

'Yes.'

'Then I can return home?'

'If that's what you want to do.'

The car came to a halt outside the Cook County Democratic headquarters on Randolph Street where Florentyna was greeted by a Mrs. Kalamich, a fat homely woman who led her through to the main hall. Florentyna was shocked to find it was packed with people, some standing at the back. As she walked in, they began to applaud.

'You told me there would only be a few people, Edward,' she whispered.

'I am as surprised as you are. I expected about seventy, not over three hundred.'

Florentyna suddenly felt nervous as she was introduced to the members of the selection committee, and then led on to the stage. She sat next to Edward, aware of how cold the room was and how the hall was full of people with hope in their eyes, people who enjoyed so few of the privileges she took for granted. How different this room was from her own board room, full of men in Brooks Brothers suits who ordered Martinis before dinner. For the first time in her life she felt embarrassed by her wealth and hoped it didn't show.

Edward rose from his chair in the centre of the platform.

'Ladies and gentlemen, it is my privilege tonight to introduce a woman who has gained the respect and admiration of the American people. She has built up one of the largest financial empires in the world, and I believe she could now build a political career of the same dimensions. I hope she will launch that career in this room tonight. Ladies and gentlemen, Mrs. Florentyna Kane.'

Florentyna rose nervously to her feet. She wished she had spent more time preparing her speech.

'Thank you, Mr. Winchester, for your kind words. It's wonderful to be back in Chicago, my home town, and I appreciate so many of you turning out for me on this cold, wet night.

'I, like you, feel let down by the political leaders of the day. I believe in a strong America, and if I were to enter the political arena I would dedicate myself to those words Franklin D. Roosevelt said in this city over thirty years ago:

"There can be no greater calling than public service."

'My father came to Chicago as an immigrant from Poland and only in America could he have achieved the success he did. Each of us must play our role in the destiny of the country we love, and I shall always remember your kindness in inviting me to be considered as your candidate. Be assured that I shall not make my final decision lightly. I have not come with a long prepared speech as I would prefer to answer the questions you consider important.'

She sat down and three hundred people applauded enthusiastically. When the noise had died down, Florentyna answered questions on subjects ranging from the U.S. bombing of Cambodia to legalised abortion, from Watergate to the energy crisis. It was the first time she had attended any meeting without all the facts and figures at her fingertips, and she was surprised to find how strongly she felt on so many issues. After she had answered the final question, over an hour later, the crowd rose and started chanting 'Kane for Congress', refusing to stop until she left the platform. It was one of those rare moments in her life when she wasn't sure what to do next. Edward came to her rescue.

'I knew they would love you,' said Edward, obviously delighted.

'But I was awful,' she shouted back, above the noise.

'Then I can't wait to find out what you're like when you're good.'

Edward led her off the platform as the crowd surged forward. A pale man in a wheelchair managed to touch her arm. She turned.

'This is Sam,' said Edward. 'Sam Hendrick. He lost both his legs in Vietnam.'

'Mrs. Kane,' he said. 'You won't remember me; we once licked envelopes together in this hall for Stevenson. If you decide to run for Congress, my wife and I will work night and day to see you are elected. Many of us in Chicago have always believed you would come home and represent us.' His wife, who stood behind the chair, nodded and smiled.

'Thank you,' said Florentyna. She turned and tried to walk to the exit, but it was blocked by outstretched hands and well-wishers. She was stopped again at the door, this time by a girl of about twenty-five who told her, 'I lived in your old room in Whitman and Radcliffe and, like you, once stood in Soldier Field and listened to President Kennedy. America needs another Kennedy. Why shouldn't it be a woman?'

Florentyna stared at the eager, intense young face. 'I've graduated and work in Chicago now,' the girl continued, 'but the day you run, a thousand students from Illinois will be on the streets to see that you are elected.'

Florentyna tried to catch her name but was pushed on by the crowd. At last Edward managed to bustle her through the throng and into a waiting car which drove them back to the airport. She didn't speak during the journey. When they arrived at O'Hare, the black chauffeur jumped out and opened the door for her. She thanked him.

'It's a pleasure, Mrs. Kane. I want to thank you for the stand you took for my people in the south. We won't forget that you led our struggle for equal pay and all the hotels in the country had to follow. I hope I'll have a chance to vote for you.'

'Thank you again,' said Florentyna, smiling.

Edward took her to the terminal and guided her to the departure gate.

'Made your flight in good time. Thank you for coming, Florentyna. Please let me know when you have made up your mind.' He paused. 'If you feel you can't go ahead with the nomination, I shall always understand.' He kissed her lightly on the cheek and left.

On the flight back, Florentyna sat alone thinking about what had happened that night and how unprepared she had been for such a demonstration. She wished her father could have been in the hall to witness it.

A stewardess asked for her drink order.

'Nothing, thank you.'

'Is there anything else I can do for you, Mrs. Kane?'

Florentyna looked up, surprised that the young girl knew her name.

'I used to work in one of your hotels.'

'Which one?' asked Florentyna.

'The Detroit Baron. Barons would always be the first choice for stewardesses for a stop-over. If only America was governed the way you run your hotels, we wouldn't be in the trouble we're in now,' she said before moving on down the aisle.

Florentyna flicked through a copy of *Newsweek*. Under the headline 'How far does Watergate reach?' she studied the faces of Ehrlichman, Haldeman and Dean before closing the magazine. On the cover was a picture of Richard Nixon and the caption: 'When was the President told?'

A little after midnight, she arrived back at East Sixty-fourth Street. Richard was sitting up in the crimson chair by the fire. He rose to greet her.

'Well, did they ask you to run for President of the United States?'

'No. But how do you feel about Congresswoman Kane?'

Florentyna phoned Edward the next day. 'I am willing to put my name forward as the Democratic candidate for Congress,' she said.

'Thank you. I ought to try and express my thoughts more fully, but for now – thank you.'

'Edward, may I know who would have been the candidate if I had said no?'

'They were pressing me to run myself. But I told them I had a better candidate in mind. As I'm certain this time round you'll take advice, even if you became President.'

'I never did become Class President.'

'I did, and I've still ended up serving you.'

'Where do I start, coach?'

'The Primary will be in March, so you'd better reserve every weekend between now and the fall.'

'I already have, starting this weekend – and can you tell

me who was the young woman from Radcliffe who stopped me at the door and talked about Kennedy?'

'Janet Brown. In spite of her age, she's already one of the most respected case workers in the city's Human Services department.'

'Do you have her phone number?'

During the week Florentyna informed the Baron board of directors of her decision. They appointed Richard co-chairman of the group and elected two new directors.

Florentyna called Janet Brown and offered her a job as her full-time political assistant and was delighted by Janet's immediate acceptance. She then added two new secretaries to her staff for political work only. Finally she called the Chicago Baron and instructed them to leave the thirty-eighth floor free, warning them she would need the entire floor left at her disposal for at least a year.

'Taking it seriously, aren't we?' said Richard later that evening.

'Indeed I am, because I'm going to have to work very hard if you're ever going to be the First Gentleman.'

26

'ARE YOU EXPECTING MUCH opposition?'

'Nothing of real consequence,' said Edward. 'There may be a protest candidate or two, but as the committee is fully behind you, the real fight should be with the Republicans.'

'Do we know who their candidate is likely to be?'

'Not yet. My spies tell me it's between two men, Ray Buck, who seems to be the choice of the retiring member, and Stewart Lyle, who's served on the City Council for the past eight years. They'll both run a good campaign, but that's not our immediate problem. With so little time left, we must concentrate on the Democratic Primary.'

'How many people do you think will vote in the Primary?' asked Florentyna.

'Can't be certain. All we do know is that there are roughly one hundred and fifty thousand registered Democrats and that the turnout is usually between forty-five and fifty per cent. So that would point to around seventy or eighty thousand.'

Edward unfolded a large map of Chicago and placed it in front of Florentyna.

'The boundaries of the constituency are marked in red and run from Chicago Avenue in the south to the Evanston border in the north, from Ravenswood and Western Highway in the west to the lake in the east.'

'The district hasn't changed since the days of Henry Osborne,' said Florentyna, 'so it should all come back to me very quickly.'

'Let's hope so, because our main task is to see that as many Democrats in that area are aware of who you are through the press, advertising, television and public appearances. Whenever they open their newspaper, turn on the radio or watch TV Florentyna Kane must be with them. The voters must feel you are everywhere and they must believe your only interest is in them. In fact, there can be no major function in Chicago between now and March 19th at which you are not present.'

'Suits me,' said Florentyna. 'I've already set up my campaign headquarters in the Chicago Baron, which my father had the foresight to build in the heart of the district. I propose to spend weekends here and any free days during the week at home with my family, so where do you want me to start?'

'I've called a press conference for next Monday, to be held at Democratic headquarters. A short speech followed by a question-and-answer session, and then we'll serve them coffee so you can meet all the key people individually. As you enjoy thinking fast on your feet, you should relish meeting the press.'

'Any particular advice?'

'No, just be yourself.'

'You may live to regret that.'

Edward's judgment turned out to be right. After Florentyna had made a short opening statement the questions came thick and fast. Under his breath, Edward whispered the names of the various journalists as each rose to his feet.

The first was Mike Royko, of the Chicago *Daily News*.

'Why do you think it appropriate that a New York millionairess should run for the Ninth District of Illinois?'

'In this context,' said Florentyna standing to take the questions, 'I am not a New York millionairess. I was born in St. Luke's Hospital and brought up on Rigg Street. My father, who came to this country with nothing but the clothes he stood in, founded the Baron Group right here in the Ninth District. I believe we must always fight to ensure that any immigrant arriving on our shores today, whether he be from Vietnam or Poland, has the opportunity to achieve the same goals as my father did.'

Edward pointed to another journalist for the next question.

'Do you consider it a disadvantage to be a woman when seeking public office?'

'Perhaps to a limited or ill-informed person I would have to answer yes, but not with any intelligent voter who puts the issues before outdated prejudices. Which of you if involved in a traffic accident on the way home today would think twice if the first doctor on the scene turned out to be a woman? I hope the issue of sex will soon be as irrelevant as that of religion. It seems a century ago that people asked John F. Kennedy if he thought the Presidency might change because he was a Roman Catholic. I notice nowadays the question never arises with Teddy Kennedy. Women are already playing leading roles in other nations. Golda Meir in Israel and Indira Gandhi in India are just two examples. I consider it sad that in a nation of two hundred and thirty million people women number not one of the hundred Senators and only sixteen out of the four hundred and thirty-four members of Congress.'

'What does your husband feel about you wearing the trousers in your family?' demanded an unsolicited questioner. Laughter broke out in certain parts of the room and Florentyna waited for complete silence.

'He's far too intelligent and successful for such a pathetic question to occur to him.'

'What is your attitude on Watergate?'

'A sad episode in American political history which I hope will be behind us before too long, but not forgotten.'

'Do you feel President Nixon should resign?'

'That's a moral decision and one for the President to make himself.'

'Would you resign if you were President?'

'I wouldn't have to break into any hotels. I already own one hundred and forty-three.' A burst of laughter followed by applause gave Florentyna a little more confidence.

'Do you think the President should be impeached?'

'That's a question Congress will have to decide based on the evidence the Judiciary Committee is considering, including the White House tapes, if and when President Nixon releases them. But the resignation of the Attorney-General, Elliot Richardson, a man whose integrity has never been in question, should ring warning bells for the general public.'

'Where do you stand on abortion?'

'I shall not fall into the trap that Senator Mason did only last week when asked the same question, to which he replied, "Gentlemen, that one's below the belt".' Florentyna waited for the laughter to die down before saying in a more serious tone. 'I am a Roman Catholic by birth and upbringing, so I feel strongly about the protection of the unborn child. However, I also believe there are situations in which it is both necessary and indeed morally correct for a qualified doctor to carry out an abortion.'

'Can you give an example?'

'Rape would be an obvious one, and also in a case where the mother's health is in danger.'

'Isn't that against the teachings of your church?'

'That is correct, but I have always believed in the separation of church and state. Any person who runs for public office must be willing to take stands on certain issues that will not please all of the people all of the time. I think Edmund Burke summed it up better than I could hope to do when he said, "Your representative owes you, not his industry only, but his judgment, and he betrays instead of serving you, if he sacrifices it to your opinion."'

Edward sensed the effect of the last statement and promptly rose from his chair. 'Well, ladies and gentlemen of the press, I think the time has come to adjourn for coffee, which will give you the opportunity to meet Florentyna Kane personally – although I am sure by now you know why we feel she is the right person to represent the Ninth District in Congress.'

For the next hour, Florentyna faced a further barrage of personal and political questions, some of which, had they been put to her in the privacy of her own home, she would have found objectionable, but she was quickly learning that one cannot be a public figure and hope to maintain a private stance on anything. When the last journalist had left, she collapsed into a chair, not even having had the time to drink one cup of coffee.

'You were great,' said Janet Brown. 'Didn't you think so, Mr. Winchester?'

Edward smiled. 'Good, not great, but I blame myself for not warning you about the difference between being chairman of a private company and running for public office.'

'What are you getting at?' asked Florentyna, surprised.

'Some of those journalists are very powerful and they talk to hundreds of thousands of people every day through their columns. They want to tell their readers that they know you personally and once or twice you were a little too aloof, and with the man from the *Tribune* you were just plain rude.'

'Was that the man who asked about who wore the trousers?'

'Yes.'

'What was I supposed to say?'

'Turn it into a joke.'

'It wasn't funny, Edward, and it was he who was rude.'

'Possibly, but he's not the one who's running for public office and you are, so he can say what he likes. And don't ever forget his column is read by more than five hundred thousand people in Chicago every day including most of your constituents.'

'So you want me to compromise myself?'

'No, I want you to get elected. When you're in the House, you can prove to everyone that they were right in voting for you. But just now you're an unknown commodity with a lot going against you. You're a woman, you're Polish and you're a millionairess. That combination is going to arouse just about every form of prejudice or jealousy in most ordinary people. The way to counter those feelings is always to appear humorous, kind and interested in people who do not share the privileges you have.'

'Edward, it's not me who should be running for public office, it's you.'

Edward shook his head. 'I know you're the right person, Florentyna, but I realise now that it will take a little time for you to adjust to your new environment. Thank God you've always been a quick learner. By the way, I don't disagree with the sentiments you voiced so vociferously, but as you seem to like quoting statesmen of the past, don't forget Jefferson's comment to Adams: "You can't lose votes with a speech you didn't make."'

Again Edward turned out to be right: the press the next day gave Florentyna a mixed reception, and the *Tribune* reporter called her the worst sort of opportunistic carpet-bagger he had ever had the misfortune to come across on the political trail – surely Chicago could find a local person? Otherwise he would have to recommend for the first time that his readers vote Republican. Florentyna was horrified and adjusted quickly to the fact that a journalist's ego was sometimes even more sensitive than a politician's. She settled down to working five days a week in Chicago, meeting people, talking to the press, appearing on television, fund raising and then going over it all again whenever she saw Richard. Even Edward was beginning to feel confident that the tide was turning her way, when the first blow came.

'Ralph Brooks? Who on earth is Ralph Brooks?' asked Florentyna.

'A local lawyer, very bright and very ambitious. I'd always thought his sights were set on the State's Attorney's office en route to the federal bench, but it seems I'm wrong. I wonder who put him up to this?'

'Is he a serious candidate?' Florentyna asked.

'He certainly is. A local boy, educated at the University of Chicago before going on to Yale Law School.'

'Age?' asked Florentyna.

'Late thirties.'

'And of course he's good-looking?'

'Very,' said Edward. 'When he rises in court every woman on the jury wants him to win. I always avoid opposing him if I can.'

'Does this Olympian have any disadvantages?'

'Naturally. Any man who has been a lawyer in this city is bound to have made a few enemies, and I know for certain Mayor Daley won't be overjoyed about his entry into the race, since Ralph Brooks is an obvious rival for his son.'

'What am I expected to do about him?'

'Nothing,' said Edward. 'When asked, you simply give the standard answer: say it's democracy at work and may the best man – or woman – win.'

'He's left himself with only five weeks before the Primary.'

'Sometimes that's a clever tactic; he'll hope you've run out of steam. The one good thing to come out of this is that Mr. Brooks will have killed any complacency among our workers. Everyone will now know they have a fight on their hands, which will be good training for when we face the Republicans.'

Florentyna was reassured that Edward still sounded confident, although he confided in Janet Brown later that it was going to be one hell of a fight. During the next five weeks Florentyna learned just how much of a fight. Everywhere she went, Ralph Brooks seemed to have been there just before her. Every time she made a press statement on a major issue, Brooks had given his opinion the night before. But as the day of the Primary drew nearer, she learned to play Brooks at his own game, and beat him at it. However, just at the point when the opinion polls showed she was holding her lead he played an ace that Florentyna hadn't foreseen. She read the details on the front page of the Chicago *Tribune*.

'Brooks Challenges Kane to Debate' ran the headline. She knew that with all his court experience and practice at cross-examination he was bound to be a formidable opponent. Within minutes of the paper hitting the streets, the phone in her headquarters was besieged with queries from the press. Would she accept the challenge? Was she avoiding him? Didn't the people of Chicago have the right to see both candidates debate the issues? Janet held them off while Florentyna held a hasty conference with Edward. It lasted for three minutes, during which Florentyna wrote out a statement for Janet to read to all enquirers.

'Florentyna Kane is delighted to accept the invitation to debate Ralph Brooks and looks forward to the encounter.'

During the week Edward appointed a representative to consult with Brooks's campaign manager in determining the time and place for the debate.

The Thursday before the Primary was the date agreed by both sides; the venue was to be the Bernard Horwich Jewish Community Centre on West Touhy. Once the local C.B.S.-TV affiliate had agreed to cover the debate, both candidates knew that the outcome of the election might well depend on the confrontation. Florentyna spent days preparing her speech and answering questions shot at her by Edward, Janet and Richard. It brought back memories of Miss Tredgold and their preparation for the Woolson Prize Scholarship.

On the night of the debate every seat in the Community Centre was taken. People were standing at the back while others sat on window sills. Richard had flown in from New York for the occasion, and he and Florentyna arrived a half hour before the debate was due to begin. She went through the usual ordeal of television make-up while Richard found himself a seat in the front row.

She was greeted by warm applause as she entered the hall and took her seat on the stage. Ralph Brooks arrived moments later to an equally tumultuous applause. He pushed back his hair rather self-consciously as he strode across the floor. No woman in the room took her eyes from him, including Florentyna. The chairman of the Ninth District Democratic Congressional Committee welcomed them both before taking them to one side to remind them that they would each make an opening speech, which would be followed by a question-and-answer session, and then they would be invited to make a closing statement. They both nodded; the chairman was only repeating what had been agreed to by their representatives days before. He then took a new half-dollar from his pocket and Florentyna stared at the head of John Kennedy. The chairman spun the coin, and she called heads. Kennedy looked up at her again.

'I'll speak second,' she said, not even hesitating.

Without another word, they walked back on to the stage. Florentyna took a seat on the right of Edward while Ralph Brooks sat on his left. At eight o'clock, the moderator banged the gavel and called the meeting to order. 'Mr. Brooks will address you first and then Mrs. Kane will speak. The speeches will be followed by a question-and-answer session.'

Ralph Brooks rose and Florentyna stared up at the tall, handsome man. She had to admit it: if a film director had been casting for the role of President, Ralph Brooks would be given the part. From the moment he started to speak, Florentyna was in no doubt that she would not have to travel beyond Chicago to face a more formidable rival. Brooks was relaxed and assured, his delivery was professional without sounding glib.

'Ladies and gentlemen, fellow Democrats,' he began. 'I stand before you tonight, a local man who has made his way in life right here in Chicago. My great-grandfather was born in this city and for four generations the Brooks family has practised law from our offices on La Salle Street, always serving this community to the best of our ability. I offer myself today as your candidate for Congress in the belief that representatives of the people should always come from the grass-roots of their community. I do not have the vast wealth that is at the disposal of my opponent, but I bring a dedication to and care for this district that I hope you will feel surpasses wealth.' There was an outburst of applause, but Florentyna could see several people who were not joining in. 'On the issues of crime prevention, housing, public transportation and health, I have for several years sought to promote public good in the courts of Chicago. I now seek the opportunity to promote your interests in the United States House of Representatives.'

Florentyna listened intently to each well delivered phrase and was not surprised when Brooks sat down to applause that was loud and sustained. Edward rose to make Florentyna's introduction. When he had finished, she stood up – and wanted to run out of the hall. Richard smiled up at her from the front row and she regained her confidence.

'My father came to America over fifty years ago,' she began, 'having escaped first from the Germans and then from the Russians. After educating himself in New York he came to Chicago where he founded the hotel group of which I have the privilege of being chairman, right here in the Ninth District. A group that now employs twenty-seven thousand people in every state of America. When my father's career was at its zenith, he left this country to fight the Germans again and he returned to America with a Bronze Star. I was born in this city and went to high school not a mile from this hall, a Chicago education that made it possible for me to go to college. Now I have returned home wishing to represent the people who made my American dream possible.'

Loud applause greeted Florentyna's words, but she noticed once again that several people did not join in. 'I hope I will not be prevented from holding office because I was born with wealth. If that were to be a disqualification, Jefferson, Roosevelt and Kennedy would never have held office. I hope I will not be prevented because my father was an immigrant. If that were the case, then one of the greatest mayors this community has ever known, Anton Cermak, would never have worked in City Hall, and if I am to be prevented because I am a woman, then half the population of America must be disqualified along with me.' This was greeted with loud applause from all parts of the hall. Florentyna drew a deep breath.

'I do not apologise for being the daughter of an immigrant. I do not apologise for being wealthy. I do not apologise for being a woman, and I will never be apologetic about wanting to represent the people of Chicago in the United States Congress.' The applause was deafening. 'If it is not my destiny to represent you, I shall support Mr. Brooks. If, on the other hand, I have the honour of being selected to be your candidate, you can be assured that I shall tackle the problems that Chicago faces with the same dedication and energy I put into making my company one of the most successful hotel groups in the world.'

Florentyna sat down to continuing applause and looked towards her husband, who was smiling. She relaxed for the first time and stared into the hall where some people even stood to applaud although she was only too aware most of them were on her staff. She checked her watch: eight twenty-eight. She had timed it perfectly. 'Laugh-In' was almost due on TV and the Chicago Black Hawks would be warming up on channel nine. There would be a lot of changing of channels in the next few minutes. Judging by the frown on Ralph Brooks's face he was equally aware of the scheduling.

After questions – which brought no surprises – and the closing statements, Florentyna and Richard left the hall surrounded by well-wishers and returned to their room at the Baron. They waited nervously for a bellboy to deliver the first edition of the papers. The overall verdict was in favour of Florentyna. Even the *Tribune* said it had been a very close-run affair.

During the last three days of the campaign before the Primary, Florentyna pounded pavement, pressed flesh and walked the entire route of the St. Patrick's Day Parade before literally collapsing into a hot bath every night. She was woken by Richard each morning with a cup of hot coffee, after which she started the whole mad process again.

'The great day has at last arrived,' said Richard.

'Not a moment too soon,' said Florentyna. 'I am not sure my legs can go through anything like this ever again.'

'Have no fear. All will be revealed tonight,' said Richard from behind a copy of *Fortune*.

Florentyna rose and dressed in a simple blue suit of a crease-resistant fabric: although she still felt crumpled at the end of each day. She put on what Miss Tredgold would have called sensible shoes, having already worn out two pairs on the campaign trail. After breakfast, she and Richard walked down to the local school. She cast her vote for Florentyna Kane. It felt strange. Richard as a registered New York Republican remained outside.

In a heavier turnout than Edward had predicted, 49,312 other people voted for Florentyna that day, while 42,972 voted for Ralph Brooks.

Florentyna Kane had won her first election.

The Grand Old Party candidate turned out to be Stewart Lyle, who was an easier opponent than Ralph Brooks. He was an old-fashioned Republican who was always charming and courteous and who did not believe in personal confrontation. Florentyna liked him from the day they met and had no doubt that, if elected, he would have represented the district with compassion, but after Nixon had resigned on August 9th and Ford had pardoned the ex-President, the Democrats looked set for a landslide win.

Florentyna was among those elected on the bandwagon. She captured the Ninth District of Illinois with a majority over the Republican candidate of more than 27,000. Richard was the first to congratulate her.

'I am so proud of you, my darling,' he smiled mischievously. 'Mind you, I'm sure Mark Twain would have been as well.'

'Why Mark Twain?' asked Florentyna, puzzled.

'Because it was he who said: "Suppose you were an idiot and suppose you were a member of Congress. But I repeat myself."'

27

WILLIAM AND Annabel joined their father and mother for Christmas at the Kane family house on Cape Cod. Florentyna enjoyed having the children around her for the festivities, and they soon recharged all her human batteries.

William, nearly fifteen, was already talking about going to Harvard and spent every afternoon poring over maths books that even Richard didn't understand. Annabel spent most of her holiday on the phone talking long distance about boys to different school friends until Richard finally had to explain to her how the Bell Telephone Company made its money. Florentyna read Michener's *Centennial* and under pressure from her daughter listened to Roberta Flack singing 'Killing Me Softly With His Song' loudly, again and again. Richard got so sick of the record he begged Annabel to turn the damn thing over. She did, and for the first time Richard listened to a popular record he knew he would enjoy for the rest of his life. Annabel was puzzled when she saw her mother smile at the lyrics her father seemed entranced by:

> Jessie come home, there's a hole in the bed
> where you slept, and now it's getting cold.
> Jessie, the blues . . .

When the Christmas vacation came to an end Florentyna flew back to New York with Richard. It took her a week of going over reports on the Baron Group and being briefed by the heads of each department before she felt she had covered everything that had happened in her absence.

During the year they had completed hotels in Brisbane and Johannesburg, and were refurbishing old Barons in Nashville and Cleveland. In Florentyna's absence, Richard had slowed the forward planning programme down a little but had still managed to increase the profits to a record forty-five million dollars for the year ending 1974. Florentyna was in no position to complain, as Lester's was on target to show a massive increase in the credit column that year.

Florentyna's only anxiety was that Richard, for the first time in his life, was beginning to look his age: lines were appearing on his forehead and around his eyes that could only have resulted from continual and considerable stress. When she taxed him with working uncivilised hours (even his cello practice seemed less frequent) he chided her that it was a hard road to toil when one wanted to be First Gentleman.

Congresswoman Kane flew into Washington in early January. She had sent Janet Brown on to the capital in December to head up her Congressional staff and work out the transition with her predecessor's office. When Florentyna joined her, everything seemed to be organised, down to the George Novak Suite at the Washington Baron. Janet had made herself indispensable during the previous six months, and Florentyna was well prepared when the first session of the 94th Congress was ready to open. Janet had allocated the $227,270 a year each House member is permitted to staff the office. She did this with stringent care, placing the emphasis on competence in her selection whatever the age of any applicant. She had appointed a personal secretary to Florentyna named Louise Drummond, a legislative assistant, a press secretary, four legislative correspondents to research issues as well as to handle mail, two further secretaries and a receptionist. In addition, Florentyna had left three case workers in her district office under a capable Polish field representative.

Florentyna had been assigned rooms on the seventh floor

of the Longworth Building, the oldest and middle of the three House buildings. Janet told her that her office had been occupied in the past by Lyndon Johnson, John Lindsay and Pete McCloskey. '"Hear no evil, see no evil, speak no evil,"' she commented. Florentyna's new office suite was only two hundred yards from the Capitol, and she could always go directly to the chamber on the little subway if the weather was inclement or if she wished to avoid the ubiquitous herded groups of Washington sightseers.

Florentyna's personal office was a modest-sized room already cluttered with massive brown congressional furniture, a wooden desk, a large brown leather sofa, several dark, uncomfortable chairs and two glass-fronted cabinets. From the way the office had been left, it was easy to believe that the previous occupant had been male.

Florentyna quickly filled the bookcases with a copy of the U.S. Code, the Rules of the House, the Hurd Annotated Illinois Revised Statutes, and Carl Sandburg's six-volume biography of Lincoln, one of her favourite works despite his party. She then hung some water colours of her own choice on the drab cream walls in an effort to cover the nail holes left by the previous tenant. On her desk she placed a family photograph taken outside their first shop in San Francisco and when she discovered that each member of Congress was entitled to plants from the botanical gardens, she instructed Janet to claim their maximum allocation as well as arranging for fresh flowers on her desk every Monday.

She also asked Janet to decorate the front office in a way that was both welcoming and dignified; under no circumstances were there to be any portraits of her on view. Florentyna disliked the way most her colleagues filled their reception areas with self-laudatory memorabilia.

She reluctantly agreed to place the flag of Illinois and the United States flag behind her desk.

On the afternoon before Congress convened she held a reception for her family and campaign workers. Richard and Kate flew down with the children, and Edward accompanied Florentyna's mother and Father O'Reilly from Chicago.

Florentyna had sent out nearly one hundred invitations to friends and supporters all across the country, and to her surprise over seventy people turned up.

During the celebrations she took Edward aside and invited him to join the board of the Baron Group; full of champagne, he accepted and then forgot about the offer until he received a letter from Richard confirming the appointment and adding that it would be valuable for Florentyna to have two board-room views to consider while she concentrated on her political career.

When Richard and Florentyna climbed into yet another Baron king-size bed that night, he told her once more how proud he was of her achievement.

'I couldn't have done it without your support, Mr. Kane.'

'There was no suggestion that I supported you, Jessie, though I reluctantly admit to considerable pleasure at your victory. Now I must catch up with the group's European forecasts before I switch off the light on my side of the bed.'

'I do wish you would slow down a bit, Richard.'

'I can't, my darling. Neither of us can. That's why we're so good for each other.'

'Am I good for you?' asked Florentyna.

'In a word, no. If I could have it all back, I would have married Maisie and saved the money on several pairs of gloves.'

'Good God, I wonder what Maisie is up to nowadays.'

'Still in Bloomingdale's. Having given up any hope of me, she's married a travelling salesman, so I suppose I am stuck with you. Now can I get down to reading this report?'

She took the report out of his hand and dropped it on the floor.

'No, darling.'

When the first session of the 94th Congress opened Speaker Carl Albert, dressed sombrely in a dark suit, took his place on the podium and banged his gavel as he gazed down into the semi-circle of members seated in their green leather chairs. Florentyna turned in her place and smiled up at Richard and her family, who had been allocated places in the gallery above. When she looked around the chamber at her colleagues, she couldn't help thinking that they were the worst-dressed group of people she had ever seen in her life. Her bright-red wool suit, in the latest midi fashion, made her conspicuous by exception.

The Speaker asked the House chaplain, the Reverend Edward Latch, to pronounce the benediction. This was followed by an opening speech by the leaders of both parties and an address by the Speaker. Mr. Albert reminded Congressmen that they should keep their speeches brief and to refrain from making too much noise in the chamber while others were at the podium. He then adjourned the session and everyone left the chamber to attend some of the dozens of receptions given on the opening day.

'Is that all you have to do, Mummy?' asked Annabel.

Florentyna laughed. 'No, darling, that's just the opening session; the real work starts tomorrow.'

Even Florentyna was surprised the next morning. Her mail contained one hundred and sixty-one items, including two out-of-date Chicago papers, six 'Dear Colleague' letters, from Congressmen she had yet to meet, fourteen invitations to trade association receptions, seven letters from special interest groups; several invitations to address meetings – some out of Chicago and Washington – three dozen letters from constituents, two requests to be placed on her mailing list, fifteen résumés from hopeful job-seekers, and a note from Carl Albert to say that she had been placed on the Appropriations and Small Businesses committees.

The mail looked manageable compared with the ceaseless telephone demands for everything from Florentyna's official photograph to press interviews. The Washington reporters from the Chicago papers called regularly, but Florentyna was also contacted by the local Washington press, who were always intrigued by new female additions to Congress, especially those who did not resemble all-in wrestlers. Florentyna

quickly learned the names she should know, including those
of Maxine Cheshire and Betty Beale, as well as David Broder
and Joe Alsop. Before the end of March, she had been the
subject of a front-page 'Style' interview in the *Post* and had
appeared in Washingtonian Magazine's 'New Stars on the
Hill'. She turned down the continual invitations to appear on
'Panorama', and began to question where the proper balance
lay between gaining visibility, which would be of use in
influencing issues, and losing all her free time to the media.

During those first few weeks, Florentyna seemed to do
nothing except run very fast trying to remain on the same
spot. She considered herself fortunate to be the Illinois
delegation's choice for a vacancy on the powerful Appropriations Committee, the first freshman in years to be so honoured, but discovered nothing had been left to chance when
she opened a scrawled note from Mayor Daley which simply
read, 'You owe me one'.

Florentyna found her new world fascinating but it felt
rather like being back at school as she searched the corridors
for committee rooms, sprinted through the underground to
the Capitol to record her vote, met with lobbyists, studied
briefing books and signed hundreds of letters. The idea
of getting a signature machine grew increasingly appealing.

An elderly Democratic colleague from Chicago advised
her on the wisdom of sending out a constituent newsletter to
her one hundred and eighty thousand households every two
months. 'Remember, my dear,' he added, 'it may appear as
though you are doing nothing more than papering the Ninth
District, but there are only three ways of assuring your
re-election: the frank, the frank and the frank.'

He also advised Florentyna to assign two of her district
staffers to clip every article from the local newspapers that
referred to a constituent. Voters began receiving congratulations on their weddings, births, community achievements –
and even basketball victories now that eighteen-year-olds
had the vote. Florentyna always added a personal word or
two in Polish where appropriate, quietly thanking her

mother for disobeying her father's orders over the teaching of Polish.

With the help of Janet, who was always in the office before her and still there when she left, Florentyna slowly got on top of the paperwork, and by the July 4th recess she was almost in control. She had not yet spoken on the floor and had said very little in any committee hearings. Sandra Read, a House colleague from New York, had advised her to spend the first six months listening, the second six months thinking and the third six months speaking occasionally.

'What about the fourth six months?' asked Florentyna.

'You'll be campaigning for re-election,' came the reply.

On weekends she would regale Richard with stories of the bureaucratic waste of the taxpayers' money and the lunacy with which America's democratic system was conducted.

'I thought you had been elected to change all that?' he said, looking down at his wife, who was sitting cross-legged on the floor in front of him, clutching her knees.

'It will take twenty years to change anything. Are you aware that committees make decisions involving millions of dollars, but half the members haven't the slightest idea what they're voting on and the other half don't even attend but vote by proxy.'

'Then you will have to become chairman of a committee, and see to it that your members do their homework and attend hearings.'

'I can't.'

'What do you mean, you can't?' asked Richard, finally folding his morning newspaper.

'You can only become the chairman of a committee by seniority, so it's irrelevant when you reach the peak of your mental prowess. If there is someone who has been on the committee longer than you, he automatically gets the job. At this moment, of twenty-two standing committees there are three committee chairmen in their seventies, and thirteen in their sixties, which leaves only six under sixty. I've worked out that I will become chairman of the Appropriations Committee on my sixty-eighth birthday, having served twenty-eight years in the House. That is if I win the thirteen elections in between, because if you lose one, you start again. It's taken me only a few weeks to work out why so many southern states elect freshmen to Congress who are under thirty. If we ran the Baron Group the way Congress is run we'd have been bankrupt long ago.'

Florentyna was slowly coming to accept the fact that it would take years to reach the top of the political tree, and the truth was that the climb consisted of a long hard grind, known as 'serving your time'. 'Go along and get along', was the way her committee chairman put it. She decided that if it was going to be any different for her, she would have to turn the disadvantage of being a freshman into the advantage of being a woman.

It happened in a way she could never have planned. She did not speak on the House floor for the first six months, although she had sat in her seat for hours watching how the debates were conducted and learning from those who used their limited speaking time with skill. When a distinguished Republican, Robert C. L. Buchanan, announced he would be proposing an anti-abortion amendment to the Defence Appropriations Bill, Florentyna felt the time had come to deliver her maiden speech.

She wrote to the chairman and asked for permission to speak against the motion. He sent back a courteous reply, reminding her she would only be allowed five minutes and wishing her luck.

Buchanan spoke with great emotion to a silent chamber and used his five minutes with the skill of a professional House man. Florentyna thought him the worst sort of back-woodsman, and as he spoke, added some notes to her carefully prepared speech. When Buchanan sat down, Sandra Read was recognised, and she made a powerful case against the amendment although she was regularly interrupted by noisy comments from the floor. A third speaker added nothing to the debate, simply reiterating the words of Robert Buchanan, to be sure his views were on the record and would be in his local newspaper. Speaker Albert then recognised 'the distinguished gentle lady from Illinois'. Florentyna rose with some trepidation and made her way to the speaking rostrum in the well of the House, trying to keep her hands from trembling too noticeably.

'Mr. Speaker, I must apologise to the House for rising for the first time to address members on a note of controversy, but I cannot support the amendment for several reasons.' Florentyna started by talking about the role of a mother who wanted to continue a professional career. She then proceeded to outline the reasons why Congress should not adopt the amendment. She was aware of being nervous and unusually inarticulate, and after a minute or so noticed that Buchanan and the other Republican who had spoken before her were now holding a heated discussion which only encouraged some of the members in the chamber to talk among themselves while others left their seats to chat to colleagues. Soon the noise reached such a pitch that Florentyna could hardly hear the sound of her own voice. Suddenly in the middle of a sentence, she stopped speaking and stood in silence.

The Speaker banged his gavel and asked if she had yielded her time to anyone.

She turned to Carl Albert and said, 'No, Mr. Speaker, I do not intend to continue.'

'But the distinguished member was in the middle of a sentence.'

'Indeed I was, Mr. Speaker, but it has become obvious to me that there are some in this august chamber who are more interested in the sound of their own voices than in anyone else's views.' Buchanan rose to object, but was gavelled down as out of order by the Speaker. Uproar broke out, and members who had never noticed her before stared at Florentyna.

She remained at the rostrum as the Speaker went on to bang his gavel continually. When the noise died down, Florentyna continued. 'I am aware, Mr. Speaker, that it takes several years in this place before one can hope to get anything done, but I had not realised that it might take as many years before anyone would have the good manners to listen to what one had to say.'

Once again pandemonium broke out while Florentyna remained silently clutching on to the rostrum. She was now trembling from head to toe. Eventually the Speaker brought the chamber to order.

'The Honourable Member's point is well taken,' he said, staring down at the two offenders, who looked more than a little embarrassed. 'I have mentioned this habit to the House on several occasions in the past. It has taken a new member to remind us how discourteous we have become. Perhaps the distinguished gentle lady from Illinois would now like to resume.' Florentyna checked the point she had reached in her notes. The House waited in expectant silence.

She was about to continue when a hand rested firmly on her shoulder. She turned to see a smiling Sandra Read by her side. 'Sit down. You've beaten them all. If you speak now it can only spoil the effect you've created. As soon as the next speaker rises, leave the chamber immediately.' Florentyna nodded, yielded the remainder of her time, before returning to her seat.

Speaker Albert recognised the next speaker and Florentyna walked towards the Speaker's gallery exit with Sandra Read. When they reached the doors Sandra left her with the words, 'Well done. Now you're on your own.'

Florentyna did not understand what Sandra had meant until she walked into the lobby and found herself surrounded by reporters.

'Can you step outside?' asked an interviewer from C.B.S. Florentyna followed him where she was met by television cameras, reporters and flash bulbs.

'Do you think that Congress is a disgrace?'

'Will your stand help the pro-choice advocates?'

'How would you change the procedure?'

'Did you plan the whole exercise?'

Question after question came flying at Florentyna, and before the evening was out Senator Mike Mansfield, the Democratic Majority Leader in the Senate, had called to

congratulate her and she had been asked by Barbara Walters
to appear on the 'Today' show.

The following morning the *Washington Post*'s version of
events in the chamber made it sound as though Florentyna
had single-handedly caused a declaration of war. Richard
called to read the caption underneath her photograph on the
front page of the *New York Times*: 'Woman of courage arrives
in Congress', and as the morning wore on it became obvious
that Congresswoman Kane had become famous overnight
because she *hadn't* made a speech. Phyllis Mills, a Representative from Pennsylvania, warned her the following day
that she had better choose her next subject carefully because
the Republicans would be lying in wait for her with sharpened knives.

'Perhaps I should quit while I'm ahead,' said Florentyna.

When the initial furore had subsided and her mail had
dropped from one thousand letters per week back to the usual
three hundred, Florentyna began to settle down to building a
serious reputation. In Chicago that reputation was already
growing as she found from her twice-monthly visits. Her
constituents were coming to believe that she could actually
influence the course of events. This worried Florentyna
because she was quickly discovering how little room a politician has for manoeuvre outside the established guidelines. At
a local level, however, she felt that she could help people who
were often simply overwhelmed by the bureaucratic system.
She decided to add another staff member to the Chicago
office to handle the extra case work.

Richard was delighted to see how rewarding Florentyna
found her new career, and tried to take as much pressure off
her as possible when it came to the day-to-day business of the
Baron Group. Edward Winchester helped considerably by
taking on some of the responsibilities, both in New York and
Chicago. In Chicago, Edward had gained considerable sway
in the smoke-filled rooms as Mayor Daley recognised the
need for a new breed of political operative in the wake of the
1972 Presidential election. It seemed Daley's old supporters
were coming to terms with Florentyna's future. Richard was

full of praise for Edward's contribution as a member of the board and was already considering inviting him to join Lester's as well.

No sooner had Florentyna completed her first year in Congress than she complained to Richard that she would soon have to start campaigning again.

'What a crazy system that sends you to the House for only two years; no sooner have you settled into the place than you have to recycle the campaign bumper stickers.'

'How would you change it?' asked Richard

'Well, senators are in a far better position, coming up for election only every six years, so I think I would make Congressional terms at least four years in length.'

When she repeated her grouse to Edward in Chicago he was sympathetic but pointed out that in her case she didn't look as if she would have any real opposition from the Democrats or the Republicans.

'What about Ralph Brooks?'

'He seems to have his eye firmly set on the State's Attorney's office since his recent marriage. Perhaps with his wife's social background she doesn't want to see him in Washington politics.'

'Don't believe it,' said Florentyna. 'He'll be back.'

In September, Florentyna flew to New York and, together with Richard, drove William up to Concord, New Hampshire, to start his fifth-form year at St. Paul's. The car was packed with more stereo equipment, Rolling Stones records and athletic gear than books. Annabel was now in her first year at the Madeira so she could be near her mother, but she still showed no signs of wanting to follow Florentyna to Radcliffe.

Florentyna was disappointed that Annabel's sole interests always seemed to centre on boys and parties. Not once during the holidays did she discuss her progress at school or even open a book. She avoided her brother's company and would even change the subject whenever William's name came up in conversation. It became more obvious every day that she was jealous of her brother's achievements.

Carol did the best she could to keep her occupied but on two occasions Annabel disobeyed her father and once returned home from a date hours after she had agreed.

Florentyna was relieved when the time came for Annabel to return to school as she had decided not to overreact to her daughter's holiday escapades. She hoped it was nothing more than an adolescent stage she was passing through.

Struggling to survive in a man's world was nothing new for Florentyna and she began her second year in Congress with considerably more confidence. Life at the Baron had been a little sheltered in comparison with politics. After all, she had been the chairman of the group and Richard had always been there by her side. Edward was quick to point out that perhaps having to fight a little harder than any man was no bad preparation for the time when she would have to face new rivals. When Richard asked her how many of her colleagues she considered capable of holding down a place on the board of the Baron Group, she had to admit that there were very few.

Florentyna enjoyed her second year far more than her first, and there were many highlights: in February she successfully sponsored an amendment to a Bill which exempted from any taxation scientific publications selling under ten thousand copies per issue. In April she fought several provisions in Reagan's budget proposal. In May, she and Richard received an invitation to a reception at the White House for Queen Elizabeth II. But the most pleasing aspect of the whole year was the feeling that for the first time she was actually influencing issues that affected her constituents' lives.

The invitation that gave her the most pleasure that year came from Transportation Secretary William Coleman to view the tall ships enter New York Harbour in honour of the Bicentennial. It reminded her that America also had a history she could be proud of.

In all, it was a memorable year for Florentyna, and the only sad event that occurred was the death of her mother who had been afflicted with respiratory trouble for many months. For over a year Zaphia had dropped out of Chicago life at the very moment when she had been dominating the society columns. She had told Florentyna as far back as 1968, when she had brought the revolutionary Saint Laurent show to the Windy City, 'These new fashions simply don't compliment a woman of my age.' After that she was rarely seen at any of the major charity events and her name soon began to disappear from the embossed notepaper used for such occasions. She was happy to spend hours listening to stories about her grandchildren, and she often offered a word of motherly advice that her daughter had grown to respect.

Florentyna had wanted a quiet funeral. As she stood by the grave – with her son and daughter on each side of her – listening to the words of Father O'Reilly, she realised that she could no longer hope for privacy, even in death. As the coffin was lowered into the grave the flash bulbs continued to pop until the earth had completely covered the wooden casket and the last of the Rosnovskis was buried.

During the final few weeks before the Presidential election, Florentyna spent more of her time in Chicago, leaving Janet in Washington to run the office. After Representative Wayne Hayes admitted paying a member of his staff fourteen thousand dollars a year salary even though she could not type a word or answer the phone, Janet and Louise put in for a rise.

'Yes, but Miss Ray is supplying a service for Mr. Hayes that I have not yet found necessary in my office,' said Florentyna.

'But the problem in this office is the other way around,' said Louise.

'What do you mean?' asked Florentyna.

'We spend our life being propositioned by members who think we're a Capitol Hill perk.'

'How many members have propositioned you, Louise?' said Florentyna, laughing.

'Over a couple of dozen,' said Louise.

'And how many have you accepted?'

'Three,' said Louise, grinning.

'And how many have propositioned you?' said Florentyna, turning to Janet.

'Three,' said Janet.

'And how many did you accept?'

'Three,' said Janet.

When they had stopped laughing, Florentyna said, 'Well, perhaps Joan Mondale was right. What the Democrats do to their secretaries, the Republicans do to the country. You both get a rise.'

Edward turned out to be accurate about her selection. She was unopposed as the Democratic candidate, and the Primary for the Ninth District was virtually a walkover. Stewart Lyle, who ran again as the Republican candidate, admitted privately to her that he now had little chance. 'Re-elect Kane' stickers seemed to be everywhere.

Florentyna looked forward to a new session of Congress with a Democratic President in the White House. The Republicans had selected Jerry Ford after a tough battle with Governor Reagan, while the Democrats had chosen Jimmy Carter, a man she had barely heard of until the New Hampshire Primary.

Ford's Primary battle against Ronald Reagan did not enhance the President's cause and the American people had still not forgiven him for pardoning Nixon. On the personal front, Ford seemed incapable of avoiding naïve mistakes such as bumping his head on helicopter doors and falling down airplane steps. And during a television debate with Carter, Florentyna sat horrified when he suggested that there was no Soviet domination of Eastern Europe. 'Tell the Polish people that,' she said indignantly to the small screen.

The Democratic candidate committed his share of mistakes as well, but in the end it seemed to Richard that

Carter's image as an anti-Washington, evangelical Christian, when viewed against the problems Ford had inherited from his links with Nixon, would be enough to give Carter the election by a small margin.

'Then why was I returned with an increased majority?' Florentyna demanded.

'Because many Republicans voted for you but not for Carter.'

'Were you among them?'

'I plead the Fifth Amendment.'

28

RICHARD WORE A SMART dark suit on the day of the Inauguration but was sorry the President had insisted that no one wear morning dress. The Kane family watched the new President deliver a speech that lacked the charisma of Kennedy or the wisdom of Roosevelt but its simple message of Christian honesty above all else captured the mood of the moment. America wanted a decent, homespun man in the White House and everyone was willing him to succeed. President Ford sat on his immediate left; President Nixon was conspicuously absent. Florentyna felt the tone for Carter's Administration was set with the words:

'I have no dream to set forth today, but rather urge a fresh faith in the old dream. We have learned that "more" is not necessarily "better"; that even our great nation has recognised limits, and that we can neither answer all questions nor solve all problems.'

The Washington crowds were delighted when the new President, the First Lady and their daughter Amy walked down Pennsylvania Avenue hand in hand to the White House, and it was obvious that the Secret Service were quite unprepared for such a break with tradition.

'Dancer is on the move,' said one of them over his two-way radio. 'God help us if we are going to have four years of spontaneous gestures.'

That evening the Kanes attended one of the seven 'People's Parties', as Carter had named them, to commemorate the Inauguration. Florentyna was dressed in a new Gianni di Ferranti gown of white with a faint trace of gold thread which kept the camera bulbs flashing all night. During the evening they were both introduced to the President, who seemed to Florentyna to be as shy in person as he was in public.

When Florentyna took her seat on the floor of the chamber for the start of the 95th Congress it felt like returning to school, with all the back-slapping, hand shaking, hugging and noisy discussion about what members had been up to during the recess.

'Glad to see you won again.'

'Was it a hard campaign?'

'Don't imagine you'll be able to select your own committee now that Mayor Daley is dead.'

'What did you think of Jimmy's address?'

The new Speaker, Tip O'Neill, took his place in the centre of the podium, banged his gavel, called everyone to order and the whole process began again.

Florentyna had moved up two places on the Appropriations Committee, following one retirement and one defeat since the last election. She now understood how the committee system worked but still feared it would be many years and several elections before she made any real headway for the causes she espoused. Richard had suggested she concentrate on a field in which she could gain more public recognition and she had wavered between abortion and tax reform. Richard counselled against too close an association with abortion and reminded her of how her colleagues referred to Elizabeth Holtzman as 'Congressperson Holzperson'. Florentyna agreed in principle but was no nearer deciding what her special subject should be when the subject chose itself.

A debate of the Defence Appropriations Bill was taking

place on the floor of the House, and Florentyna sat listening as members casually discussed the allocation of billions of dollars on defence spending. She did not sit on the Defence Sub-Committee on which Robert C. L. Buchanan was the ranking Republican, but she was deeply interested in his opinions. Buchanan was reminding the House that Defence Secretary Brown had recently asserted that the Russians now had the capability to destroy American satellites in space. Buchanan went on to demand that the new President spend more money on defence and less in other areas. Florentyna still considered Buchanan the worst sort of conservative fool and in a moment of anger rose to challenge him. Everyone in the chamber remembered their last confrontation and knew that Buchanan would have to allow her to state her case.

'Would the Congressman yield for a question?'

'I yield to the gentle lady from Illinois.'

'I am grateful to the distinguished gentleman and would like to enquire where the extra money for these grandiose military schemes will come from?'

Buchanan rose slowly to his feet. He wore a three-piece tweed suit and his silver hair was parted neatly to the right. He rocked from leg to leg like a cavalry officer on a cold parade ground. 'These "grandiose schemes" are no more and no less than those requested by the committee on which I serve and, if I remember correctly, that committee still has a majority from the party which the distinguished member from Illinois represents.' Loud laughter greeted Buchanan's remarks. Florentyna stood up a second time; Buchanan immediately gave way again.

'I am still bound to enquire of the distinguished gentleman from Tennessee where he intends to get this money. From education, hospitals, welfare perhaps?' The chamber was silent.

'I would not take it from anyone, ma'am, but I would warn the gentle lady from Illinois that if there is not enough money for defence we may not need any money for education, hospitals or welfare.'

Buchanan picked up a document from his table and

informed the House of the exact figures spent in the previous
year's budget in all the departments Florentyna had mentioned. They showed that in real terms defence spending had
dropped more than all the others. 'It's members like the
gentle lady who come to the chamber without facts, equipped
with nothing more than a vague feeling that defence spending is too high, that make the Kremlin leaders rub their
hands with glee while the reputation of the House is at the
same time diminished. It is the type of ill-informed attitude
that tied the hands of President Roosevelt and left us so little
time to come to terms with the menace of Hitler.'

Florentyna wished she had never entered the chamber that
afternoon as members from both sides echoed their agreement. As soon as Buchanan had finished his remarks she left
the floor and returned quickly to her office.

'Janet, I want all the committee reports from the Appropriations Sub-Committee on Defence for the last ten years,
and ask my legislative researchers to join us immediately,'
she said even before she reached her desk.

'Yes, ma'am,' said Janet, somewhat surprised, as
Florentyna had never mentioned defence in the three years
she had known her. The staffers filed in and sank on to
Florentyna's old sofa.

'For the next few months I plan to concentrate on defence
matters. I need you to go over the reports of the sub-
committee during the last ten years and mark up any relevant passages. I am trying to get a realistic appraisal of
America's military strength, if we were called upon to defend
ourselves against an attack from the Soviets.' The four
assistants were writing furiously. 'I want all the major works
on the subject including the CIA Team A and Team B
evaluations, and I want to be briefed when lectures or
seminars on defence or related matters take place in
Washington. I want all press comments from the *Washington
Post*, the *New York Times*, *Newsweek* and *Time* put in a file for
me every Friday night. No one must be able to quote
something I haven't had a chance to consider.'

The assistants were as surprised as Janet because they had

been concentrating their efforts on small business and tax reform for over two years. They were not going to have many free weekends during the coming months. Once they had departed Florentyna picked up the phone and dialled five digits. When a secretary answered, she requested an appointment with the Majority Leader.

'Of course, Mrs. Kane. I will ask Mr. Chadwick to call you later today.'

Florentyna was ushered into the Majority Leader's office at ten o'clock the next morning.

'Mark, I want to be put on the Appropriations Sub-Committee on Defence.'

'I wish it were that easy, Florentyna.'

'I know, Mark. But this is the first favour I've asked for in three years.'

'There is only one slot open on that sub-committee and so many members are twisting my arm it's amazing that I'm not permanently in splints. Nevertheless, I'll give your request my serious consideration.' He made a note on the pad in front of him. 'By the way, Florentyna, the League of Women Voters is holding its annual meeting in my district, and they've invited me to make the key speech on the opening day. Now I know how popular you are with the League and I was hoping you might find it possible to fly up and do the speech of introduction.'

'I'll give your request my serious consideration,' said Florentyna, smiling.

She received a note from the Speaker's office two days later informing her of her appointment as the junior member of the Appropriations Sub-Committee on Defence. Three weeks later she flew to Texas and told the League of Women Voters that as long as there were men like Mark Chadwick in Congress they need have no fears for America's well-being. The women applauded loudly while Florentyna turned to find Mark grinning – with one arm behind his back.

During the summer vacation the whole family went to California. They spent the first ten days in San Francisco with Bella and her family in their new home, high up on the hill, now overlooking the bay.

Claude had become a partner in the law firm, and Bella had been appointed an assistant headmistress. If anything, Richard decided, Claude was a little thinner and Bella a little larger than when they had last seen them.

The holiday would have been enjoyed by everyone if Annabel hadn't frequently disappeared off on her own. Bella gripping a hockey stick firmly in her hand left Florentyna in no doubt how she would have dealt with the girl.

Florentyna tried to keep harmony between the two families, but a confrontation was unavoidable when Bella found Annabel in the attic smoking pot and asked what she thought she was doing.

'Mind your own business,' she said, as she inhaled once more.

When Florentyna lost her temper with Annabel she informed her mother that if she took more interest in *her* welfare and less in that of her constituents perhaps she could have expected a little more from her.

When Richard heard the story he immediately ordered Annabel to pack and accompanied her back to the east coast while Florentyna and William travelled on to Los Angeles for the rest of their holiday.

Florentyna spent an unhappy time phoning Richard twice a day to find out how Annabel was. She and William returned home a week early.

In September, William entered his freshman year at Harvard, taking up residence in the Yard, on the top floor of Gray's Hall, making the fifth generation of Kanes that had been educated at Cambridge. Annabel returned to the Madeira School, where she seemed to make little progress despite the fact that she started spending most weekends under her parents' watchful eyes in Washington.

During the next session of Congress Florentyna allocated all her spare time to reading the defence papers and books her staffers put in front of her. She became engrossed in the problems the nation faced if it wished to remain strategically safe. She read papers by experts, spoke to Assistant Secretaries at the Defence Department, and studied the major U.S. treaties with her NATO allies. She visited the Air Force SAC headquarters, toured U.S. bases in Europe and the Far East, observed army manoeuvres in North Carolina and California, even spent a weekend submerged in a nuclear submarine. She sought meetings with admirals and generals, as well as having discussions with privates and non-commissioned officers, but she never once raised her voice in the House chamber and only asked questions in committee hearings, where she was often struck by the fact that the most expensive weapons were not always the most effective. She began to realise that the military had a long way to go in improving its readiness, which had not been fully tested since the Cuba confrontation. After a year of listening and studying she came to the conclusion that Buchanan had been right and it was she who had been the fool. America had no choice but to increase defence spending while Russia remained so openly aggressive. She was surprised to find how much she enjoyed her new discipline and realised much how her views had been changed when a colleague openly referred to her as a hawk.

She studied all the papers on the M-X missile system, when it came under the jurisdiction of the House Armed Services Committee. As soon as the so-called Simon Amendment to hold up the authorisation of the system appeared on the calendar she asked Chairman Galloway to be recognised during the debate.

Florentyna listened intently as other members gave their views for and against the amendment. Robert Buchanan gave a considered speech against it. When he took his seat Florentyna was surprised the Speaker called on her next. She rose to a packed house. Representative Buchanan said in a voice loud enough to carry, 'We are now about to hear the views of an expert.' One or two Republicans seated near him laughed as Florentyna walked to the front of the podium. She placed her notes on the lectern in front of her.

'Mr. Speaker, I address the House as a convinced supporter of the M-X missile. America cannot afford to delay any
further the defence of this country because a group of Congressmen claim they want more time to read the relevant
documents. Those papers have been available to every member of the House for over a year. It hardly needs a course in
speed reading for members to have done their homework
before today. The truth is that this amendment is nothing
more than a delaying tactic for members who are opposed to
the M-X missile system. I condemn those members as men
with their heads in the sand, heads that will remain in the
sand until the Russians have made their first pre-emptive
strike. Don't they realise America must also have a first-
strike capability?

'I approve of the Polaris submarine system but we cannot
hope to push all our nuclear problems out to sea, especially
now that navy intelligence informs us that the Russians have
a submarine that can travel at a speed of forty knots and
remain below the ocean for four years – four years, Mr.
Speaker – without returning to base. The argument that the
citizens of Nevada and Utah are in more danger from the
M-X system than anyone else is spurious. The land where
the missiles would be deployed is already owned by the
government and is at present occupied by one thousand nine
hundred and eighty sheep and three hundred and seventy
cows. I do not believe the American people need to be
mollycoddled on the subject of the nation's safety. They have
elected us to carry out long-term decisions, not to go on
talking while we become weaker by the minute. Some members of Congress would make Nero appear to the American
people as a man who was giving a violin concert in aid of the
Rome fire brigade.'

When the laughter had diminished, Florentyna became
very grave. 'Have members so quickly forgotten that in 1935
more people worked for the Ford Motor Company than
served in the United States armed forces? Have we also
forgotten that in the same year we had a smaller army than

Czechoslovakia, a country since trampled on by Germany and Russia in turn? We had a navy half the size of that of France, a country humiliated by the Germans while we sat and watched, and an air force that even Hollywood didn't bother to hire for war movies. When the threat of Hitler first arose we could not have rattled a sabre at him. We must be certain such a situation can never arise again.

'The American people have never seen the enemy on the beaches of California or on the docksides of New York, but that does not mean that the enemy does not exist. As late as 1950, Russia had as many combat planes as the United States, four times as many troops and thirty tank divisions to America's one. We must never allow ourselves to be at such a disadvantage again. Equally I pray that our great nation will never be involved in another débâcle such as Vietnam, and that none of us will live to see another American die in combat. But our enemies must always be aware that we will meet aggression head on. Like the eagle that bestrides our standard, we will hover always alert to the defence of our friends and the protection of our citizens.'

Some members on the floor of the House started to applaud.

'To each American who says our defence expenditure is too costly, I reply let them look to the countries behind the Iron Curtain and see that no price is too high to pay for the democratic freedom we take for granted in this country. The Iron Curtain is drawn across East Germany, Czechoslovakia, Hungary and Poland, with Afghanistan and Yugoslavia guarding their borders in daily expectation of that curtain being drawn still further, perhaps even reaching the Middle East. After that the Soviets will not be satisfied until it encircles the entire globe.' The House was so silent that Florentyna dropped her voice before she continued. 'Many nations have through history played their role in the protection of the free world. That responsibility has now been passed to the leaders of this commonwealth. Let our grandchildren never say we shirked that responsibility in a cheap exchange for popularity. Let us assure America's freedom by being willing to make a sacrifice now. Let us be able to say to every American that we did not shirk our duty in the face of danger. Let there be in this House no Nero, no fiddler, no fire and no victory for our enemies.'

Members in the chamber cheered while Florentyna remained standing. The Speaker repeated his attempts to gavel the meeting to order. When the last cheer had died she spoke almost in a whisper.

'Let that sacrifice never again be the lives of America's youth, or replaced by the dangerous illusion that we can keep peace in the world without providing for its defence against aggression. Adequately protected, America can exert her influence without fear, govern without terror and still remain the bastion of the free world. Mr. Speaker, I oppose the Simon Amendment as irrelevant, and worse, irresponsible.'

Florentyna took her seat and she was quickly surrounded by colleagues from both sides who praised her speech. The press heaped further praise on her the next day and all the networks included passages from her speech in their evening bulletins. Florentyna was shocked at how glibly they described her as an expert on defence. Two papers even talked of her as a future Vice-President.

Once again Florentyna's mail rose to over a thousand letters a week, but there were three letters that particularly moved her. The first was a dinner invitation from an ailing Hubert Humphrey. She accepted but, like the other guests, did not attend. The second came from Robert Buchanan, simply written in a bold hand:

'I salute you, madam.'

The third was an anonymous scrawled note from Ohio:

'You are a commie traitor bent on destroying America with impossible defence commitments. The gas chamber is too good a place for people like you. You should be strung up with that dummy Ford and that pimp Carter. Why don't you get back to the kitchen where you belong, bitch?'

'How would one reply?' asked Janet, stunned by the letter.

'You can't, Janet. Repudiating that sort of mindless prejudice is beyond even your skilful hand. Let's be thankful
that ninety-nine per cent of the letters are from fair-minded
people who wish to express their views honestly. Though I
confess if I knew his address I'd be tempted to reply for the
first time in my life, "Up Yours".'

After a hectic week during which she seemed to be perpet-
ually pursued by phone messages, Florentyna spent a quiet
weekend with Richard. William was home from Harvard
and was quick to show his mother a cartoon from the *Boston
Globe* depicting her as a heroine with the head of an eagle,
punching a bear on the nose. Annabel phoned from school to
tell her mother that she wouldn't be home that weekend.

Florentyna played tennis with her son that Saturday and it
took her only a few minutes to realise how fit he was and what
a dreadful state she was in. She couldn't pretend walking
around golf courses kept her in any real shape. With each
shot it became more obvious that William wasn't trying very
hard. She was relieved to be told that he couldn't play
another set because he had a date that evening. She scribbled
a note to Janet to order an exercycle from Hammacher
Schlemmer.

Over dinner that night Richard told Florentyna that he
wanted to build a Baron in Madrid and that he was thinking
of sending Edward to check the building sites.

'Why Edward?'

'He's asked to go. He's working almost full-time for the
group now and has even rented an apartment in New York.'

'What can have happened to his law practice?'

'He's become counsel to the firm and says that if you can
change your whole career at forty, why shouldn't he? Since
Daley's death he hasn't found it a full-time job proving
you're worth a place in Congress. I must say he's like a
schoolboy who's found himself locked up in a candy store.
It's taken a great load off my shoulders. He's the only man I
know who works as hard as you.'

'What a good friend he has turned out to be.'

'Yes, I agree. You do realise he's in love with you, don't you?'

'What?' said Florentyna.

'Oh, I don't mean he wants to leap into bed with you, not that I could blame him if he did. No, he simply adores you, but he would never admit it to anyone, although it wouldn't take a blind man to see that.'

'But I never –'

'No, of course you haven't, my darling. Do you think I would have been considering putting him on the board of Lester's if I thought I might lose my wife to him?'

'I wish he would find himself a wife.'

'He'll never marry anyone as long as you are around, Jessie. Just be thankful that you have two men who adore you.'

When Florentyna returned to Washington after the weekend she was greeted with another pile of the invitations that had been coming in with increasing frequency. She sought Edward's advice as to what she should do about them.

'Select about half a dozen of the major invitations to places where your views can be expected to reach the maximum number of people, and explain to the others that your work load does not permit you to accept at the moment. But remember to end each letter of refusal with a personal handwritten line. One day when you are seeking a bigger audience than the Ninth District of Illinois there will be people whose only contact with you will be that letter, and on that alone they will decide whether they are for or against you.'

'You're a wise old thing, Edward.'

'Ah, but you mustn't forget I'm a year older than you, my dear.'

Florentyna took Edward's advice and spent two hours every night dealing with the letters prompted by her speech on defence. At the end of five weeks she had answered every one, by which time her mail had almost returned to normal proportions. She accepted invitations to speak at Princeton and the University of California at Berkeley. She also addressed the cadets of West Point and the midshipmen at Annapolis and was to be the guest of Max Cleveland at a Washington lunch to honour Vietnam veterans. Everywhere she went Florentyna was introduced as one of America's leading authorities on defence. She became so involved and fascinated by the subject that it terrified her how little she really knew and only made her study the subject even more intensively. Somehow she kept up with her work in Chicago, but the more she became a public figure the more she had to assign tasks to her staff. She appointed two more assistants to her Washington office and another in Chicago at her own expense. She was now spending over one hundred thousand dollars a year out of her own pocket. Richard described it as reinvesting in America.

29

'ANYTHING THAT CAN'T WAIT?' asked Florentyna, glancing down at a desk full of correspondence that had arrived that morning. The 95th Congress was winding down and most members were once again more concerned about being re-elected than about sitting in Washington working on legislation. At this stage of the session assistants were spending almost all their time dealing with constituency problems rather than concentrating on national affairs. Florentyna disliked a system that made hypocrites of normally honest people as soon as another election loomed.

'There are three matters that I ought to draw to your attention,' said Janet in her habitually efficient manner. 'The first is that your voting record can hardly be described as exemplary. It has fallen from eighty-nine per cent during the last session to seventy-one per cent this session and your opponents are bound to jump on that fact, claiming that you are losing interest in your job and should be replaced.'

'But the reason I've been missing votes is that I've been visiting defence bases and accepting so many out-of-state engagements. I can't help it if half my colleagues want me to speak in their districts.'

'*I* am aware of that,' said Janet, 'but you can't expect the voters of Chicago to be pleased that you're in California and Princeton when they expect you to be in Washington. It might be wise for you to accept no more invitations from other members or well-wishers until the next session and if you make most of the votes during the last few weeks we may push you back above eighty per cent.'

'Keep reminding me, Janet. What's second?'

'Ralph Brooks has been elected State's Attorney of Chicago, so he should be out of your hair for a while.'

'I wonder,' said Florentyna, scribbling a note on her pad to remind herself to write and congratulate him. Janet placed a copy of the Chicago *Tribune* in front of her. Mr. and Mrs. Brooks stared up at her. The caption read: 'The new State's Attorney attends charity concert in aid of the Chicago Symphony Orchestra.'

'Doesn't miss a trick, does he?' commented Florentyna. 'I bet his voting record would always be over eighty per cent. And the third thing?'

'You have a meeting with Don Short at ten a.m.'

'Don Short?'

'He's a director of Aerospace Plan, Research and Development Inc. (A.P.R.D.),' said Janet. 'You agreed to see him because his company has a contract with the government to build radar stations for tracking enemy missiles. They are now bidding for the new navy contract to put their equipment into American warships.'

'Now I remember,' said Florentyna. 'Somebody produced an excellent paper on the subject. Dig it out for me, will you?'

Janet passed over a brown manila file. 'I think you'll find everything is in there.'

Florentyna smiled and flicked quickly through the papers. 'Ah, yes, it all comes back. I shall have one or two pointed questions for Mr. Short.'

For the next hour she dictated letters before reading through the briefing file. She found time to jot down several questions before Mr. Short arrived.

'Congresswoman, this is a great honour,' said Don Short, thrusting out his hand as Janet accompanied him into Florentyna's room as ten o'clock struck. 'We at Aerospace Plan look upon you as one of the last bastions of hope for the free world.'

It was very rare for Florentyna to dislike someone on sight, but it was clear that Don Short was going to fall firmly into that category. Around five foot seven and twenty pounds overweight, he was a man in his early fifties and nearly bald except for a few strands of black hair which had been carefully combed over the dome of his head. He wore a check suit and carried a brown leather Gucci briefcase. Before Florentyna had acquired her present hawkish reputation she had never been visited by the Don Shorts of this world, as no one thought it worthwhile to lobby her. However, since she had been on the Defence Sub-Committee Florentyna had received endless invitations to dinners, travel-free junkets, and had even been sent gifts ranging from bronze model F-15s to manganese nodules encased in lucite.

Florentyna only accepted those invitations that were relevant to the issues she was working on at the time, and with the exception of a model of Concorde she returned every gift she had been sent with a polite note. She kept the statue of Concorde on her desk to remind everyone that she believed in excellence whichever country was responsible. She had been told that Margaret Thatcher had a replica of Apollo 11 on her desk in the House of Commons and she assumed it was there for the same reason.

Janet left the two of them alone and Florentyna ushered Don Short into a comfortable chair. He crossed his legs, giving Florentyna a glimpse of hairless skin where his trousers failed to meet his sock.

'A nice office you have here. Are those your children?' he asked, jabbing a pudgy finger at the photos on Florentyna's desk.

'Yes,' said Florentyna.

'Such good-looking kids – take after their mother.' He laughed nervously.

'I think you wanted to talk to me about the XR-108, Mr. Short?'

'That's right; but do call me Don. We believe it's the one piece of equipment the U.S. Navy cannot afford to be without. The XR-108 can track and pinpoint an enemy missile at a distance of over ten thousand miles. Once the XR-108 is installed in every American carrier, the Russians will never dare attack America, because America will always be sailing the high seas, guarding her people while they sleep.' Mr. Short stopped almost as if he were expecting applause. 'What is more, my company's equipment can photograph every missile site in Russia,' he continued, 'and beam the picture straight on to a television screen in the White House Situation Room. The Russians can't even go to the john without us taking a photo of them.' Mr. Short laughed again.

'I have studied the capabilities of the XR-108 in depth, Mr. Short, and I wonder why Boeing claims it can produce essentially the same piece of equipment at only seventy-two per cent of your price.'

'Our equipment is far more sophisticated, Mrs. Kane, and we have a proven record in the field, having already supplied the U.S. Army.'

'Your company did not complete the tracking stations for the Army by the date specified in your contract, and handed the government a cost over-run of seventeen per cent on the original estimate – or, to be more precise – twenty-three million dollars.' Florentyna had not once looked at her notes.

Don Short started to lick his lips. 'Well, I'm afraid inflation has taken its toll on everyone, not least the aerospace industry. Perhaps if you could spare a little time to meet our board members, the problem would become clearer to you. We might even arrange a dinner.'

'I rarely attend dinners, Mr. Short. I have long believed that the only person who makes any profit over dinner is the maître d'.'

Don Short laughed again. 'No, no, I meant a testimonial dinner in your honour. We would invite, say, five hundred people at fifty dollars a head which you could add to your campaign fund, or to whatever you need the cash for,' he added, almost in a whisper.

Florentyna was about to throw the man out when her secretary arrived with some coffee. By the time Louise left, Florentyna had controlled her temper and made a decision.

'How does that work, Mr. Short?'

'Well, my company likes to give a helping hand to its friends. We understand some of your bills for re-election can be pretty steep, so we hold a dinner to raise a little cash and if all the guests don't turn up but still send their fifty dollars – well, who's to know?'

'As you say, Mr. Short, who's to know?'

'Shall I set that up then?'

'Why don't you, Mr. Short?'

'I knew we could work together.'

Florentyna just managed a tight-lipped smile as Don Short offered a moist hand before Janet showed him out.

'I'll be in touch, Florentyna,' he said, turning back.

'Thank you.'

As soon as the door closed the voting bells started to ring. Florentyna glanced up at the clock on which tiny white bulbs were flashing to show that she still had five minutes to reach the chamber. 'Well, there's one I can pick up,' she said, and left to run to the elevator reserved for members of Congress. When she reached the basement she jumped on the subway that went between Longworth and the Capitol and took a seat next to Bob Buchanan.

'How are you going to vote?' he asked.

'Good heavens,' said Florentyna, 'I don't even know what we are voting for or against yet.'

Her thoughts were still focused on Don Short and what she was going to do about his dinner.

'You're okay this time. It's lifting the retirement age cap from sixty-five to seventy, and on that one I am sure we can both vote the same way.'

'It's only a plot to keep old men like you in Congress, and see that I never get to chair any committees.'

'Wait until you're sixty-five, Florentyna. Then you might feel differently.'

The subway reached the basement of the Capitol and the two representatives took the elevator up to the chamber together. It pleased Florentyna that this diehard Republican now looked upon her as a fully fledged member of the club. When they reached the chamber they rested on the brass rail at the back, waiting for their names to be called.

'I never enjoy standing on your side of the chamber,' he said. 'After all these years, it still feels strange.'

'Some of us are quite human, you know, and I'll let you in on a secret: my husband voted for Jerry Ford.'

'Wise man, your husband,' chuckled Buchanan.

'Perhaps your wife voted for Jimmy Carter?'

The old man suddenly looked sad. 'She died last year,' he said.

'I *am* sorry,' said Florentyna. 'I had no idea.'

'No, no, my dear. I realised that, but rejoice in your family because they are not always with you, and the one thing I have discovered is that this place can only be a poor substitute for a real family, whatever you imagine you achieve. They've started calling the Bs so I will leave you to your thoughts . . . I shall find standing on this side of the aisle more pleasant in the future.'

Florentyna smiled and reflected how their mutual respect had been conceived in mutual mistrust. She was thankful that the party differences so crudely displayed on election platforms disappeared in the privacy of everyday work. A few moments later, they called the Ks and once she had punched her card into the voting pocket she went back to her office and phoned Bill Pearson, the Majority whip, to ask for an immediate interview.

'Must it be this minute?'

'This minute, Bill.'

'I suppose you want me to put you on the Foreign Affairs Committee.'

'No, it's far more serious than that.'

'Then you had better come around right away.'

Bill Pearson puffed away at his pipe as he listened to Florentyna recount what had happened in her office that morning. 'We know a lot of this sort of thing goes on, but we're rarely able to prove it. Your Mr. Short seems to have provided an ideal chance to catch someone with their radar scanner in the pie. You go through with the whole charade, Florentyna, and keep me briefed. The moment they hand over any money we'll jump on Aerospace Plan like a ton of bricks, and if in the end we can't prove anything, at least the exercise might make other members of Congress think twice before getting themselves involved in these sorts of shenanigans.'

Over the weekend Florentyna told Richard about Don Short, but he showed no surprise. 'The problem's a simple one. Some Congressmen have only their salaries to live on, so the temptation to pick up cash must sometimes be overwhelming, especially if they are fighting for a seat they could lose and have no assured job to fall back on.'

'If that's the case, why did Mr. Short bother with me?'

'That's also easy to explain. I receive half a dozen personal approaches a year at the bank. The sort of people who offer bribes imagine no one can resist the chance to make a quick buck without Uncle Sam finding out, because that's the way they would react themselves. You would be surprised how many millionaires would sell their mothers for ten thousand dollars in cash.'

Don Short phoned during the week and confirmed that a testimonial dinner had been arranged in Florentyna's honour at the Mayflower Hotel. He expected about five hundred people to be present. Florentyna thanked him, then buzzed

Louise on the intercom and asked her to write the date in the appointment book.

Because of the pressure Florentyna was under with Congressional business and out-of-state trips over the next few weeks, she nearly missed Don Short's testimonial dinner altogether. She was on the floor of the House supporting a colleague's amendment to a Small Businesses Bill, when Janet hurried into the chamber.

'Have you forgotten the Aerospace Plan dinner?'

'No, but it's not for another week,' said Florentyna.

'If you check your card, you'll find it's tonight and you're due there in twenty minutes,' said Janet. 'And don't forget there are five hundred people waiting for you.'

Florentyna apologised to her colleague and quickly left the chamber and ran to the Longworth garage. She drove out into the Washington night well above the speed limit. She turned off Connecticut Avenue at De Sales Street and left her car in a lot before walking through the side entrance of the Mayflower. She was a few minutes late, her thoughts far from collected, and arrived to find Don Short, dressed in a tight-fitting dinner jacket, standing in the lobby waiting to greet her. Florentyna suddenly realised that she had not had time to change and hoped that the dress she was wearing did not look too casual.

'We've taken a private room,' he said as he led her towards the lift.

'I didn't realise the Mayflower had a banquet room that could seat five hundred,' she said as the elevator doors closed.

Don Short laughed. 'That's a good one,' he said and led his guest into a room that – had it been packed – would have held twenty people. He introduced her to everyone present, which took a few moments; there were only fourteen guests.

Over dinner, Florentyna listened to Don Short's blue stories and tales of Aerospace Plan's triumphs. She wasn't sure that she could get through the whole evening without exploding. At the end of the dinner Don rose from his seat, tapped a spoon on his empty glass and made a fulsome speech about his close friend Florentyna Kane. The applause when he sat down was as loud as one could hope for from fourteen people. Florentyna made a short reply of thanks and managed to escape a few minutes after eleven, at least grateful that the Mayflower had provided an excellent meal.

Don Short escorted her back to the parking lot and as she climbed into her car, he handed her an envelope. 'I'm sorry so few people turned up, but at least all the absentees sent in their fifty dollars.' He grinned as he closed the car door.

After Florentyna had driven back to the Baron, she tore open the envelope and studied the contents: a cheque for twenty-four thousand three hundred dollars made out to cash.

She told Bill Pearson the whole story the following morning and handed over the envelope. 'This,' he said, waving the cheque, 'is going to open a whole can of worms.' He smiled and locked the twenty-four thousand three hundred dollars away in his desk.

Florentyna left for the weekend, feeling she had carried out her part of the exercise rather well. Even Richard congratulated her. 'Although we could have done with the cash ourselves,' he said.

'What do you mean?' asked Florentyna.

'I think the Baron's profits are going to take a big drop this year.'

'Good heavens, why?'

'A series of financial decisions implemented by President Carter which are harming the hotels while ironically helping the bank – we have inflation running at fifteen per cent while prime rate is sixteen. I fear the expense account business trip is the first cutback for most companies who have discovered the telephone is cheaper. So we are not filling all our rooms and we end up having to raise the prices – which only gives the business community even more reason to cut back on business travel. Into the bargain, food prices have rocketed while wages are trying to keep up with inflation.'

'Every other hotel group must be faced with the same problem.'

'Yes, but the decision to move the corporate offices out of the New York Baron last year turned out to be far more expensive than I budgeted for. 450 Park Avenue may be a good address but we could have built two hotels in the south in exchange for having that on our letterhead.'

'But that decision released three floors in the New York hotel which allowed us to operate the new banquet rooms.'

'And still the hotel only made a profit of two million while sitting on real estate worth forty million.'

'But there has to be a Baron in the centre of New York. You couldn't think of selling our most prestigious hotel.'

'Until it loses money.'

'But our reputation . . .'

'Your father was never sentimental about reputation when measured against profits.'

'So what are we doing about it?'

'I'm going to commission McKinsey and Company to carry out a detailed assessment of the whole group. They will give us an interim report in three months, and complete the study in twelve months. I've already spoken to a Mr. Michael Hogan at McKinsey – he's drawing up a proposal.'

'Surely moving in the top consultants in New York will cost us even more money?'

'Yes, it'll be expensive, but I wouldn't be surprised to discover that it will save us a considerable amount in the long run. We must remember that modern hotels all around the world are serving different customers from those your father built Barons for. I want to be sure we're not missing something that's staring us in the face.'

'But can't our senior executives give us that sort of advice?'

'When McKinsey moved into Bloomingdale's,' said Richard, 'they recommended that the store should change the location of seventeen of its counters from their traditional positions. Simple, you might say, but the profits were up twenty-one per cent in the following year when none of the executive staff had considered any changes were necessary. Perhaps we face the same problem without realising it.'

'Hell, I feel so out of touch.'

'Don't worry, Jessie darling, nothing is going to be acted on that doesn't meet with your full approval.'

'And how is the bank surviving?'

'Ironically, Lester's is making more money on loans and overdrafts than at any time since the Depression. My decision to move into gold when Carter won the election has paid off handsomely. If Carter is re-elected, I shall buy more gold. If Reagan captures the White House I shall sell the same day. But don't you worry. As long as you keep earning your fifty-seven thousand five hundred a year as a Congresswoman, I'll sleep easy knowing we have something to fall back on in bad times. By the way, have you told Edward about Don Short and the twenty-four thousand dollars?'

'Twenty-four thousand three hundred. No, I haven't spoken to him in days, and when I do all he wants to talk about is how to run a hotel group.'

'I'm inviting him to join the Lester's board at the annual meetings. It will be the bank next.'

'He'll be running the whole show soon,' said Florentyna.

'That's exactly what I'm planning for when I become the First Gentleman.'

When Florentyna arrived back in Washington, she was surprised to find there was no message awaiting her from Bill Pearson. His secretary told her that he was in California campaigning, which reminded her how close the election was. Janet was quick to point out that the legislature was sleeping on its feet again, waiting for the new session, and that perhaps it might be wise for Florentyna to spend more time in Chicago.

On Thursday, Bill Pearson phoned from California to tell Florentyna that he had spoken with the ranking Republican and the chairman of the Defence Sub-Committee, and they both felt it would cause more trouble than it was worth to raise the issue before the election. He asked her not to declare the donation, because his investigation would be hampered.

Florentyna strongly disagreed with his advice and even considered raising the whole issue with the ranking committee members herself, but when she phoned Edward he counselled against such a move on the grounds that the whip's office undoubtedly possessed more information about bribery than she did, and it might look as if she were working behind their backs. Florentyna reluctantly agreed to wait until after the election.

Somehow Florentyna – with continual reminders from Janet – managed to push her voting record up to over eighty per cent by the end of the session, but only at the cost of turning down every invitation outside Washington that appeared in front of her, and she suspected there had been a whole lot more that Janet had prevented from landing on her desk. When Congress adjourned, Florentyna returned to Chicago to prepare for another election.

She was surprised to find, during the campaign, that she spent a considerable part of her time sitting in the Cook County Democratic headquarters on Randolph Street. Although Carter's first year had not lived up to the expectations of the American voters, it was well known that the local Republicans were finding it hard to convince anyone to run against Florentyna. To keep her occupied, her staff sent her off to speak on behalf of other Democratic candidates in the state as often as possible.

In the end, Stewart Lyle agreed to run again but only after he had made it clear to his committee that he was not going to stomp around the district night and day or waste any more of his money. The G.O.P. was not pleased with Lyle when he said in a private conversation – forgetting that nothing was private during an election campaign – 'There is only one difference between Kane and the late Mayor Daley – Kane is honest.'

The Ninth District of Illinois agreed with Stewart Lyle and sent Florentyna back to Congress with a slightly increased majority, but she noted the loss of fifteen of her colleagues from the House and three from the Senate. Among the casualties was Bill Pearson.

Florentyna called Bill at his home in California several times to commiserate, but he was always out. Each time she left a message on the answering machine, but he did not return her calls. She discussed the problem with Richard and Edward, who both advised her to see the Majority Leader immediately.

When Mark Chadwick heard the story he was horrified and said he would be in touch with Bill Pearson at once and speak to her later that day. Mark was as good as his word and phoned back to report something that chilled Florentyna: Bill Pearson had denied any knowledge of the twenty-four thousand three hundred dollars and was claiming that he had never discussed a bribe case with Florentyna. Pearson had reminded Chadwick that if Florentyna had received twenty-four thousand three hundred dollars from any source she was bound by law to report it either as a campaign contribution or as income. No mention of the money had been made on her campaign forms and, under House rules, she was not entitled to receive an honorarium of over seven hundred and fifty dollars from anyone. Florentyna explained to the Majority Leader that Bill Pearson had asked her not to declare the money. Mark assured Florentyna that he believed her but was not quite clear how she was going to prove that Pearson was lying. It was common knowledge, he added, that Pearson had been in financial trouble since his second divorce. 'Two alimonies when you're out of work would flatten most good men,' he pointed out.

Florentyna agreed to let Mark make a full investigation while she remained silent on the matter. Don Short rang during the week to congratulate her on her victory and to remind her that the contract with the Navy for the missile programme was up for discussion in the sub-committee that Thursday. Florentyna bit her lip after Don Short's next statement: 'I'm glad you cashed the cheque because I'm sure the money came in useful at election time.'

Florentyna immediately asked the Majority Leader to

postpone the vote on the missile programme until he had completed his enquiry on Bill Pearson. Mark Chadwick explained that he couldn't comply with her request because the allocated funds would go elsewhere if the decision were held up. Although Defence Secretary Brown didn't care which company was awarded the contract, he had warned them that all hell would break loose if a decision were postponed any longer. Finally, Chadwick reminded Florentyna of her own speech about members who held up defence contracts. She didn't waste any time arguing.

'Are you getting anywhere with your enquiries, Mark?'

'Yes. We know the cheque was cashed at the Riggs National Bank on Pennsylvania Avenue.'

'My bank, and my branch,' said Florentyna in disbelief.

'By a lady of about forty-five who wore dark glasses.'

'Is there any good news?' she asked.

'Yes,' replied Mark. 'The manager considered the sum large enough to make a note of the bill numbers in case some query arose later. How about that for irony?' She tried to smile. 'Florentyna, in my opinion, you have two choices. You can blast the entire thing open at Thursday's meeting or you can keep quiet until I have the whole messy business sorted out. One thing you can't do is talk publicly about Bill Pearson's involvement until I get to the bottom of it.'

'What do you want me to do?'

'The party would probably prefer you to keep quiet, but I know what I would do if the decision was left to me.'

'Thank you, Mark.'

'No one's going to love you for it. But that's never stopped you in the past.'

When Defence Sub-Committee chairman Thomas Lee gavelled the hearing to order, Florentyna had already been in her seat for several minutes making notes. The radar satellite contract was the sixth item on the agenda and she did not speak on the first five items. When she looked towards the press table and the seats occupied by the public she could not avoid the smiling Don Short.

'Item number six,' said the chairman, stifling a slight yawn at the length each subject on the agenda was taking. 'We must discuss today the three companies that have bid on the Navy's missile project. The Defence Department Office of Procurement will make the final decision, but they are still waiting our considered opinion. Who would like to open the discussion?'

Florentyna raised her hand.

'Congresswoman Kane.'

'I have no particular preference, Mr. Chairman, between Boeing and Grumman but under no circumstances could I support the Aerospace Plan bid.' Don Short's face turned ashen with disbelief.

'Can you tell the committee why you feel so strongly against Aerospace Plan, Mrs. Kane?'

'Certainly, Mr. Chairman. My reasons arise from a personal experience. Some weeks ago an employee of Aerospace Plan came to visit me in my offices in order to go over the reasons why his company should be awarded this contract. Later he attempted to bribe me with a cheque for twenty-four thousand three hundred dollars in exchange for my vote today. That man is now in this room and will no doubt have to answer to the courts for his actions later.'

When the chairman of the committee had finally brought the meeting back to order, Florentyna explained how the testimonial dinner had worked and she named Don Short as the man who had given her the money. She turned to look at him, but he had vanished. Florentyna continued her statement but avoided making any reference to Bill Pearson. She still considered that to be a party matter, but when she finished her story she couldn't help noticing that two other members of the committee were as white as Don Short had been.

'In view of this serious allegation made by my colleague, I intend to delay any decision on this item until a full enquiry has been carried out,' Chairman Lee announced.

Florentyna thanked him and left for her office immediately. She walked down the corridor, surrounded by reporters, but made no reply to any of their insistent questions.

She talked to Richard on the phone that night, and he warned her that the next few days were not going to be pleasant.

'Why, Richard? I've only told the truth.'

'I know. But now there are a group of people fighting for their lives on that committee and they only see you as the enemy, so you can forget the Marquis of Queensberry rules.'

When she read the papers the next morning, she found out exactly what Richard had meant.

'Congresswoman Kane Accuses Aerospace Plan of Bribery', ran one headline while another read, 'Company Lobbyist Claims Member of Congress Took Money as Campaign Contribution'. Once Florentyna had seen that most of the papers were running roughly the same story she jumped out of bed, dressed quickly, went without breakfast and drove straight to the Capitol. When she reached her office she studied all the papers in detail, and without exception they all wanted to know where the twenty-four thousand three hundred dollars had disappeared. 'And so do I,' said Florentyna out loud. The headline in the Chicago *Sun-Times* was the most unfortunate: 'Representative Kane Accuses Space Company of Bribery After Cheque Cashed'. True, but misleading.

Richard called to say that Edward was already on his way down from New York and not to talk to the press until she had spoken with him. She would not have been able to in any case because the FBI sent two senior agents to interview her at ten o'clock that morning.

In the presence of Edward and the Majority Leader, Florentyna made a complete statement. The FBI men asked her not to inform the press of Bill Pearson's involvement until they had completed their own investigation. Once again, she reluctantly agreed.

During the day some members of the House went out of their way to congratulate her. Others conspicuously avoided her.

In a lead story in the Chicago *Tribune* that afternoon the

paper wanted to know where the twenty-four thousand three hundred dollars had disappeared. They said it was their unfortunate duty to remind the public that Congresswoman Kane's father had been tried and found guilty of bribery of a public official in the Chicago courts in 1962. Florentyna could almost hear Ralph Brooks calling from the State Attorney's office to let them have all the salient details.

Edward helped Florentyna to keep her temper and Richard flew down from New York every night to be with her. Three days and three nights passed, while the papers kept the story running and Ralph Brooks made a statement from the State Attorney's office saying: 'Much as I admire Mrs. Kane and believe in her innocence I feel it might be wise in the circumstances for her to step down from Congress until the FBI investigation is completed.' It made Florentyna even more determined to stay put, especially when Mark Chadwick phoned to tell her not to give up. It could only be a matter of time before the guilty man was brought to justice.

On the fourth day, with no more news from the FBI, Florentyna was at her lowest point when a reporter from the *Washington Post* phoned.

'Mrs. Kane, may I ask how you feel about Congressman Buchanan's statement on Aerogate?'

'Has he turned against me as well?' she asked quietly.

'Hardly,' said the voice from the other end of the line. 'I'll read what he said. I quote: "I have known Representative Kane for nearly five years as a bitter adversary and she is many things that drive me to despair but, as we say in Tennessee, you'll have to swim to the end of the river to find anyone more honest. If Mrs. Kane is not to be trusted, then I do not know one honest person in either chamber of Congress."'

Florentyna phoned Bob Buchanan a few minutes later.

'Now don't you go thinking I'm getting soft in my old age,' he barked. 'You put a foot wrong in that chamber and I'll cut it off.' Florentyna laughed for the first time in days.

It was a cold December wind that whistled across the east front of the Capitol as Florentyna walked back alone to the

Longworth Building after the last vote that day. The newsboy on the corner was shouting out the evening headlines.
She couldn't catch what he was saying – something, someone, arrested. She ran towards the boy, fumbling in her
pocket for a coin, but all she could find was a twenty-dollar
bill.

'I can't change that,' the boy said.

'Don't bother,' said Florentyna as she grabbed the paper
and read the lead story first quickly and then slowly. 'Former
Congressman Bill Pearson,' she read aloud as if she wanted
to be sure the newsboy could hear, 'has been arrested by the
FBI in Fresno, California, in connection with the Aerogate
scandal. Over seventeen thousand dollars in cash was found
hidden in the rear bumper of his new Ford. He was taken to
the nearest police station, questioned and later charged with
grand larceny and three other misdemeanours. The young
woman who was with him at the time was also charged, as an
accomplice.'

Florentyna leaped up and down in the snow as the newsboy quickly pocketed the twenty dollars and ran to sell his
papers on another corner. He had always been warned about
those Hill types.

'My congratulations on the news, Mrs. Kane.' The maître
d'hôtel of the Jockey Club was the first of several to comment
that evening. Richard had flown down from New York to
take Florentyna to a celebration dinner. On her way into the
oak-panelled room, other politicians and members of
Washington society came over to say how pleased they were
that the truth was at last out. Florentyna smiled at each one
of them, a Washington smile that she had learned to develop
after nearly five years in politics.

The next day the Chicago *Tribune* and the *Sun-Times* came
out with glowing tributes to their representative's ability to
stay calm in a crisis. Florentyna gave a wry smile, determined to back her own judgment in the future. Any comment
from Ralph Brooks's office was conspicuously absent. Edward sent a large bunch of freesias, while William sent a

telegram from Harvard: SEE YOU TONIGHT IF YOU'RE NOT THE WOMAN IN FRESNO STILL BEING HELD FOR FURTHER QUESTION- ING. Annabel arrived home seemingly unaware of her mother's recent problems to announce she had been accepted at Radcliffe. Her headmistress at the Madeira School later confided to Florentyna that her daughter's acceptance had turned out to be a very close thing, although it couldn't have hurt that Mr. Kane had been at Harvard and that she herself had attended Radcliffe. Florentyna was surprised that her reputation was such that she could in- fluence her daughter's future without lifting a finger and confessed to Richard later what a relief it was that Annabel's life was more settled.

Richard asked his daughter in what subject she planned to major.

'Psychology and social relations,' Annabel replied without hesitation.

'Psychology and social relations are not real subjects but merely an excuse to talk about yourself for three years,' Richard declared.

William, now a sophomore at Harvard, nodded in sage agreement with his father, and later asked the old man if he could up his allowance to five hundred dollars a term.

When an amendment to the Health Bill, prohibiting abor- tions after ten weeks, came up on the calendar, Florentyna spoke for the first time since the Aerogate scandal. As she rose from her place, she was greeted with friendly smiles and a ripple of applause from both sides of the aisle. Florentyna made a powerful plea for the life of the mother over that of the unborn child, reminding Congress that there were only eighteen other members who could even experience preg- nancy. Bob Buchanan rose from his place and referred to the distinguished lady from Chicago as the worst sort of simple- ton who would be claiming next that you could not discuss a future space programme unless one had circled the moon and he pointed out that there was only one member in either house who had managed that.

*

Within a few days Don Short and his twenty-four thousand three hundred dollars seemed to be a thing of the past as Florentyna returned to her normal hectic Congressional schedule. She had moved up two more notches on the Appropriations Committee, and when she looked around the table she began to feel like an old-timer.

30

WHEN FLORENTYNA RETURNED TO Chicago she found Democrats were voicing aloud their fears that having Jimmy Carter in the White House might not necessarily help their chances. Gone were the days when an incumbent could take it for granted that he would be returned to the Oval Office and take with him those of his party who were fighting marginal seats. Richard reminded Florentyna that Eisenhower was the last President to complete two terms.

The Republicans were also beginning to flex their muscles and after the announcement that Jerry Ford would not seek the Presidency, George Bush and Ronald Reagan appeared to be the front runners. In the corridors of Congress it was being openly suggested that Edward Kennedy should run against Carter.

Florentyna continued her daily work in the House and avoided being associated with either camp, although she received overtures from both campaign managers and more than her usual allocation of White House invitations. She remained non-committal, as she wasn't convinced that either candidate was right to lead the party in 1980.

While others spent their time campaigning, Florentyna put pressure on the President to take a stronger line when dealing with heads of state from the Warsaw Pact and pressed for a firmer commitment to NATO; but she appeared to make little headway. When Jimmy Carter told an astonished audience that he was surprised the Russians could go back on their word, Florentyna said despairingly to Janet that any Pole in Chicago could have told him that.

But her final split with the President came when the so-called students took over the American Embassy in Tehran on November 4, 1979, and held fifty-three Americans hostage. The President appeared to do little except make 'Born Again' speeches and say his hands were tied. Florentyna proceeded to bombard the White House by every means at her disposal, demanding that the President should stand up for America. When eventually he did attempt a rescue mission, it aborted, resulting in a sad loss of reputation for the United States in the eyes of the rest of the world.

During a defence debate on the floor of the House soon after this humiliating exercise, Florentyna departed from her notes to deliver an off-the-cuff remark. 'How can a nation that possesses the energy, genius and originality to put a man on the moon fail to land three helicopters safely in a desert?' She had momentarily forgotten that the proceedings of the House were now televised and all three networks showed that part of her speech on their evening news bulletins.

She didn't need to remind Richard of George Novak's wisdom in insisting on not renewing Lester's loan to the Shah and when the Russians marched over the Afghanistan border, Richard cancelled their holiday to watch the Olympics in Moscow.

The Republicans went to Detroit in July and chose Ronald Reagan with George Bush as his running mate. A few weeks later the Democrats came to New York and the Party confirmed Jimmy Carter with even less enthusiasm than they had showed for Adlai Stevenson. When the victorious Carter entered Madison Square Garden, even the balloons refused to come down from the ceiling.

Florentyna tried to continue her work in a Congress that was uncertain which would be the majority party in a few months' time. She pushed through amendments on the Defence Appropriations Bill and the Paperwork Reduction Act. As the election drew nearer, she began to fear that the fight for her own seat might be close when the Republicans replaced Stewart Lyle with an enthusiastic young advertising executive, Ted Simmons.

With Janet prodding her, she once again pushed her voting record up to around eighty per cent by only accepting invitations to speak in Washington or Illinois during the last six months prior to the election.

Carter and Reagan seemed to be living in Chicago, flying in and out of Illinois like two cuckoos in one clock. The polls were declaring it was too close to call, but Florentyna was not convinced after she had seen the candidates debate in Cleveland in front of a television audience estimated at one hundred million Americans. The next day Bob Buchanan told her that Reagan might not have won the debate, but he sure as hell hadn't lost it, and for someone trying to remove the White House incumbent that was all important.

As election day drew nearer, the issue of the hostages became more and more a focal point in the minds of the American people, who began to doubt that Carter could ever resolve the problem. On the streets of Chicago, supporters told Florentyna that they would return her to Congress, but they could not back Carter for a second term. Richard said he knew exactly how they felt and predicted that Reagan would win easily. Florentyna took his view seriously and spent the last few weeks of the campaign working as if she were an unknown candidate fighting her first election. Her efforts were not helped by a torrential rainstorm in Chicago that pounded the streets right up until election day.

When the last vote had been counted even she was surprised by the size of the Reagan victory, which took the Senate with him on his coat tails and only just failed to capture the House for the Republicans.

Florentyna was returned to Congress with her majority cut to twenty-five thousand. She flew into Washington, battered but not beaten a few hours before the hostages returned.

The new President lifted the spirit of the nation with his Inaugural Address. Richard, sitting in a morning coat,

smiled all the way through the speech and applauded loudly
at the section he quoted to Florentyna for several years after.

> We hear much of special interest groups, but our concern
> must be for a special interest group that has been too long
> neglected. It knows no sectional boundaries, crosses
> ethnic and racial divisions and political party lines. It is
> made up of men and women who raise our food, patrol our
> streets, man our mines and factories, teach our children,
> keep our homes and heal us when we're sick. Profession-
> als, industrialists, shopkeepers, clerks, cabbies and truck
> drivers. They are, in short, we the people, this breed called
> Americans.

After the speech had been enthusiastically received the
President gave a final wave to the crowd in front of the main
stand and turned to leave the podium.

Two Secret Service men guided him through a human
aisle created by the guard of honour.

Once the Presidential party had reached the bottom of the
steps, Mr. Reagan and the First Lady climbed into the back
of a large limousine obviously unwilling to follow the example of the Carters and walk down Constitution Avenue to
their new home. As the car moved slowly off, one of the Secret
Service men flicked a switch on his two-way radio. 'Rawhide
returns to Crown' was all he said, and then, staring through a
pair of binoculars, followed the limousine all the way to the
White House gates.

When Florentyna returned to Congress in January 1981, it
was a different Washington. Republicans no longer needed to
beg support for every measure they espoused, because elected
representatives knew the country was demanding change.
Florentyna enjoyed the new challenge of studying the programme Reagan sent up to the Hill and was only too happy to
support great sections of it.

She had become so preoccupied with amendments to the

Reagan budget and defence programme that Janet had to
point out to her an item in the Chicago *Tribune* which might
eventually remove her from the House.

Senator Nichols of Illinois announced this morning that
he would not be seeking re-election to the Senate in 1982.

Florentyna was sitting at her desk, taking in the significance of this statement when the editor of the Chicago
Sun-Times called to ask her if she would be entering the race
for the Senate in 1982. Florentyna realised that it was only
natural for the press to speculate on her candidacy after three
and a half terms as a representative.

'It doesn't seem that long ago,' she teased, 'that your
distinguished journal was suggesting I should resign.'

'There was an English Prime Minister who once said that
a week was a long time in politics! So where do you stand,
Florentyna?'

'It's never crossed my mind,' she said, laughing.

'That's one statement no one is going to believe, and I am
certainly not going to print. Try again.'

'Why are you pushing me so hard when I still have over a
year to decide?'

'You haven't heard?'

'Heard what?' she asked.

'At a press conference held this morning at City Hall the
State's Attorney announced that he's a candidate.'

'Ralph Brooks To Run For Senate,' ran the banner headline
across the afternoon editions of the state's papers. Many
reporters mentioned in their columns that Florentyna had
not yet made a decision on whether she would challenge the
State's Attorney. Once again pictures of Mr. and Mrs.
Brooks stared up at Florentyna. The damn man seems to get
better looking all the time, she grumbled. Edward called
from New York to say he thought she should run but advised
her to hold back until the Brooks publicity machine ran out of
steam. 'You might even be able to orchestrate your

announcement so that it looks as if you are bowing to public pressure.'

'Who are the party faithful backing?'

'My estimate is 60–40 in your favour, but since I'm no longer even a committeeman it's hard to predict. Don't forget it's over a year to the Primary so there's no need to rush in, especially now that Brooks has made his move. You can sit and wait until the time suits you.'

'Why do you think he announced so early?'

'To try and frighten you off, I suppose. Maybe he figures you might hold back until 1984.'

'Perhaps that's a good idea.'

'No, I don't agree. Never forget what happened to John Culver in Iowa. He decided to wait because he felt it would be easier later when weaker opposition was around so his personal assistant ran instead of him and won the seat.'

'I'll think about it and let you know.'

The truth was that Florentyna thought of little else during the next few weeks, because she knew that if she could beat Brooks this time, he would be finished once and for all. She was in no doubt that Ralph Brooks still had ambitions that stretched about sixteen blocks beyond the Senate. On Janet's advice, she now accepted every major invitation to speak in the state and turned down almost all other outside commitments. 'That will give you a chance to find out how the land lies,' said Janet.

'Keep nagging me, Janet.'

'Don't worry, I will. That's what you pay me for.'

Florentyna found herself flying to Chicago twice a week for nearly six months and her voting record in Congress was barely above sixty per cent. Ralph Brooks had the advantage of not living in Washington four days a week or having his record in court expressed in percentage terms. Added to that, Chicago's Mayor Jane Byrne was only halfway through her first term. There were those who said one woman in Illinois politics was quite enough. Nevertheless Florentyna felt confident after she had covered most of the state that Edward had been right, she did have a 60–40 chance of defeating

Ralph Brooks. In truth she believed that defeating Brooks might be harder than getting elected to the Senate, as the mid-term election traditionally ran against the White House incumbent.

One day Florentyna did leave clear in her diary was for the annual meeting of the Vietnam Veterans of America. They had chosen Chicago for the celebrations and invited Senator John Tower of Texas and Florentyna to be the key speakers. The Illinois press was quick to point out the respect with which outsiders treated their favourite daughter. The paper went on to say that the very fact that the vets could couple her with the chairman of the Senate's Armed Services Committee was high praise indeed.

Florentyna was carrying a full load in the House. She successfully sponsored the 'good Samaritan' amendment to the Superfund Act, making its implementation more flexible for companies that made genuine efforts to dispose of toxic wastes. Even Bob Buchanan supported her Good Samaritan amendment.

While she was leaning on the rail at the back of the chamber waiting for the vote on the final passage of her amendment, he told her that he hoped she would run for the Senate seat.

'You're only saying that because you want to see me out of this place.'

He chuckled. 'That would have been one compensation, I must admit, but I don't think you can stay here much longer if you're destined to live in the White House.'

Florentyna looked at him in astonishment. He didn't even glance towards her but continued to gaze into the packed chamber.

'I have no doubt you'll get there. I just thank God I won't be alive to witness your inauguration,' he continued before going off to vote for Florentyna's amendment.

Whenever Florentyna went to Chicago she avoided the question of her candidacy for the Senate, although it was obviously on everyone else's mind. Edward pointed out to her that if she did not run this time it might be her last chance for twenty years as Ralph Brooks was still only forty-four and it would be virtually impossible to defeat him once he was the incumbent.

'Especially when he has "the Brooks charisma",' mocked Florentyna in reply. 'In any case,' she continued, 'who would be willing to wait twenty years?'

'Harold Stassen,' Edward replied.

Florentyna laughed. 'And everyone knows how well he did. I'll have to make up my mind one way or the other before I speak to the Vietnam Vets.'

Florentyna and Richard spent the weekend at Cape Cod and were joined by Edward on the Saturday evening.

Late into the night they discussed every alternative facing Florentyna as well as the effect it would have on Edward's work at the Baron if he were to be in charge of the campaign. When they retired to bed in the early hours of Sunday morning they had come to one conclusion.

The International Room of the Conrad Hilton Hotel was packed with two thousand men and the only other women in sight were waitresses. Richard had accompanied Florentyna to Chicago and was seated next to Senator Tower. When Florentyna rose to address the gathering she was trembling. She began by assuring the vets of her commitment to a strong America and then went on to tell them of her pride in her father when he had been awarded the Bronze Star by President Truman, and of her greater pride in them for having served their country in America's first unpopular war. The veterans whistled and banged their tables in delight. She reminded them of her commitment to the M-X missile system and her determination that Americans would live in fear of no one, especially the Soviets.

'I want Moscow to know,' she said, 'that there may be some men in Congress who would be happy to compromise America's position but not this woman.' The vets cheered again. 'The present isolationist policy President Reagan seems determined to pursue will not help Poland in its present crisis or whichever nation the Russians decide to attack next. At some point we must stand firm, and we cannot afford to wait until the Soviets have camped along the Canadian border.' Even Senator Tower showed his approval of that sentiment.

Florentyna waited for complete silence before saying, 'I have chosen tonight, while I am assembled with a group of people whom everyone in America admires, to say that as long as there are men and women who are willing to serve their country as you have done, I hope to continue to serve in the public life of this great nation, and to that end I intend to submit my name as a candidate for the United States Senate.'

Few people in the room heard the word 'Senate' because pandemonium broke out. Everyone in the gathering who could stand, stood and those who couldn't banged their tables. Florentyna ended her address with the words, 'I pledge myself to an America that does not fear war from any aggressor. At the same time, I pray that you are the last group of veterans this country ever needs.'

When she sat down, the cheering lasted for several minutes and Senator Tower went on to praise Florentyna for one of the finest speeches he had ever heard.

Edward flew in from New York to mastermind the campaign while Janet kept in daily touch from Washington. Money flowed in from every quarter; the work that Florentyna had put in for her constituents was now beginning to pay off. With twelve weeks to go to the Primary, the polls consistently showed a 58–42 lead for candidate Kane across the state.

All through the campaign, Florentyna's assistants were willing to work late into the night, but even they could not arrange for her to be in two places at once. Ralph Brooks criticised her voting record along with the lack of real results she had achieved as a representative in Congress. Some of his attacks began to hit home while Brooks continued to show the energy of a ten year old. Despite this, he didn't seem to make much headway as the polls settled around 55–45 in her favour. Word reached Florentyna that Ralph Brooks's camp was feeling despondent and his campaign contributions were drying up.

Richard flew into Chicago every weekend and the two of them lived out of suitcases, often sleeping in the homes of downstate volunteers. One of Florentyna's younger campaign workers drove them tirelessly around the state in a small blue Chevette. Florentyna was shaking hands outside factory gates on the outskirts of cities before breakfast, attending grange meetings in the rural towns of Illinois before lunch, but somehow she still found time to fit in occasional banking associations and editorial boards in Chicago during the afternoon before the inevitable evening speech and a welcome night at the Baron. During the same period somehow she never missed the monthly meetings of the Remagen Trust.

When she did eat, it was endless Dutch-treat breakfasts and pot-luck dinners. At night before falling into bed she would jot down some more facts and figures – picked up in that day's travels – into a dog-eared black briefing book that was never far from her side. She fell asleep trying to remember names, countless names of people who would be insulted if she ever forgot the role they had played in her campaign. Richard would return to New York on Sunday night every bit as tired as Florentyna. Never once did he complain or bother his wife with any problems facing the bank or the Baron Group. She smiled up at him as they said goodbye at yet another cold February airport: she noticed he was wearing a pair of the blue leather gloves he had bought for his father in Bloomingdale's over twenty years before.

'I still have one more pair to go through Jessie, before I can start looking for another woman,' he said, and left her smiling.

Each morning Florentyna rose more determined. If she was sad about anything, it was how little she saw of William and Annabel. William, now sporting a Fidel Castro moustache, looked set for a summa cum laude while Annabel brought a different young man home each vacation.

From past experience, Florentyna had learned to expect a thunderbolt to land some time during an election campaign, but she had not imagined that a meteorite would accompany it. During the past year, Chicago had been shaken by a series of brutal local murders committed by a man the press had dubbed 'the Chicago Cut-throat'. After the killer had slashed the throat of each of his victims, he carved a heart on their foreheads to leave the police in no doubt who had struck again. More and more in public gatherings Florentyna and Ralph Brooks found that they were being tackled on the question of law and order. At night the streets of Chicago were almost deserted because of the reputation of the killer whom the police were unable to apprehend. To Florentyna's relief, the murderer was caught one night on the Northwestern University campus after he had been taken by surprise while in the act of attacking a college girl.

Florentyna made a statement the next morning in praise of the Chicago police force and wrote a personal note to the officer who made the arrest. She supposed that was the end of the matter until she read the morning paper. Ralph Brooks had announced that he was personally going to prosecute the case against the Chicago Cut-throat even if it resulted in his sacrificing the Senate seat. It was a brilliant stroke that even Florentyna had to admire. Papers all across the nation ran pictures of the handsome State's Attorney next to that of the vicious killer.

The trial began five weeks before the Primary and proceedings had obviously been speeded up because of the State's Attorney's influence. It meant Ralph Brooks was on the front page every day, demanding the death penalty so that the people of Chicago could once again walk the streets safely at night. Florentyna made press statement after press statement on the energy crisis, airport noise regulations, grain price supports, even Russia's troops movements on the Polish border after martial law was instituted and the Solidarity leaders were locked up, but she couldn't knock the

State's Attorney off the front page. At a meeting with the editorial board of the *Tribune*, Florentyna complained good-naturedly to the editor, who was apologetic but pointed out that Ralph Brooks was selling newspapers. Florentyna sat in her Washington office, impotently aware that she had no effective way of countering her opponent.

In the hope that the clash might give her a chance to shine for a change, she challenged Ralph Brooks to a public debate. But the State's Attorney informed the press that he could not consider any such confrontation while so grave a public responsibility rested on his shoulders. 'If I lose my chance to represent the good people of Illinois because of this decision, so be it,' he repeated again and again. Florentyna watched another percentage point slip away.

On the day that the Chicago Cut-throat was convicted, the polls showed that Florentyna's lead had fallen to 52–48. There were two weeks to go.

Florentyna was planning to spend those last fourteen days stumping through the state when the meteorite landed.

Richard phoned the Tuesday after the trial had ended to tell her that Annabel's roommate had called to say Annabel had not returned to Radcliffe on Sunday night, and she hadn't heard from her since. Florentyna flew to New York immediately. Richard informed the police and hired a private detective to find his daughter, and then sent Florentyna back to Chicago after the police had assured her that they would do whatever they could.

When Florentyna arrived back in Chicago she walked around in a daze, phoning Richard every hour, but he had no news for her. With a week to go, the polls showed Florentyna leading only 51–49 and Edward tried to make her concentrate on the campaign but the words of Bob Buchanan kept coming back to her. '*This place can only be a poor substitute for a real family.*' She began to wonder if only . . . After a bad weekend during which Florentyna felt she had lost more votes than she had gained, Richard called in excitement to say that Annabel had been found and that she had been in New York the whole time.

'Thank God,' said Florentyna, tears of relief welling up in her eyes. 'Is she all right?'

'She's okay, and resting in Mount Sinai hospital.'

'What happened?' asked Florentyna anxiously.

'She's had an abortion.'

Florentyna flew back to New York that morning to be with her daughter. On the return flight she thought she recognised a Party worker sitting a few rows back. There was something about his smile. Once she had arrived at the hospital she discovered that Annabel had not even realised she had been reported missing. Edward begged Florentyna to return to Chicago as the media were continually asking where she was. Although they had managed to keep Annabel's private life out of the newspapers, they were becoming highly suspicious of why Florentyna was in New York rather than Illinois. For the first time, she ignored Edward's advice.

Ralph Brooks was quick to leap in and suggest that she had returned to New York because there was a crisis at the Baron Group and that that had always been her first priority. With Edward pulling and Annabel pushing, Florentyna returned to Chicago on Monday night to find every paper in Illinois saying the election was too close to call.

On the Tuesday morning Florentyna read the headline that she most dreaded: 'Candidate's Daughter Has Abortion'. The article that followed revealed every detail, even down to the bed Annabel was in. 'Keep your head down and pray,' was all Edward said as he dragged her through a nerve-racking day.

Florentyna rose at six o'clock on election day and Edward drove her to as many polling places as she could reach in fourteen hours. At every stop, campaign workers waved blue and white 'Kane for Senate' placards and handed out leaflets on Florentyna's positions on the major issues. At one stop a voter asked Florentyna for her views on abortion. Florentyna looked at the woman indignantly and said, 'I can assure you that my views haven't changed,' before realising that the question was totally innocent.

Her workers were tireless in their efforts to get out every Kane supporter, and Florentyna didn't stop working until the polls closed. She prayed that she had held on in the way Carter had against Ford in 1976. Richard flew in that night with news that Annabel had returned to Radcliffe and was feeling fine.

When Florentyna returned to the Baron, husband and wife sat alone in their suite. Three televisions were tuned into the networks as the returns came in from all over the state deciding which one of them would be chosen to oppose the Republican candidate in November. At eleven o'clock, Florentyna had a two per cent lead. At twelve o'clock Brooks was one per cent ahead. At two o'clock, Florentyna had edged back into the lead by less than one per cent. At three o'clock she fell asleep in Richard's arms. He did not wake her when he knew the outcome because he wanted her to sleep.

A little later he nodded off himself and woke with a start to find her looking out of the window, her fist clenched. The television kept flashing up the result: Ralph Brooks selected as Democratic candidate for the Senate by seven thousand one hundred and eighteen votes, a margin of less than half a per cent. On the screen was a picture of Brooks waving and smiling to his supporters.

Florentyna turned around and stared at the screen once more. Her eyes did not rest on the triumphant State's Attorney but on a man standing directly behind him. Now she knew where she had seen that smile before.

Florentyna's political career had come to a halt. She was now out of Congress and would have to wait another two years before she could even hope to re-enter public life. After Annabel's problems, she wondered if the time had come to return to the Baron Group and a more private existence. Richard didn't agree.

'I would be sorry if you gave up politics after all the time you have put into it.'

'Perhaps that's the point. If I hadn't become so involved with my own life and taken a little more interest in Annabel, she might not be facing an identity crisis.'

'An identity crisis. That's the sort of garbage I'd expect to hear from one of her sociology professors, not from you. I haven't noticed William collapsing under the strain of an "identity crisis". Darling, Annabel has had an affair and was careless; it's as simple as that. If everyone who took a lover was considered abnormal, there would only be a few of us strange ones left. What she most needs at this moment is to be treated as a friend by you.'

Florentyna dropped everything and took Annabel to Barbados that summer. During long walks along the beach, she learned of the affair her daughter had had with someone at Vassar; Florentyna still couldn't get used to the idea of men going to women's colleges. Annabel wouldn't name the man and tried to explain that although she still liked him, she didn't want to spend the rest of her life with him. 'Did you marry the first man you went to bed with?' she asked. Florentyna didn't reply immediately, and then told her about Scott Forbes.

'What a creep,' said Annabel after she had heard the story. 'How lucky you were to find Dad in Bloomingdale's.'

'No, Annabel, as your father continually reminds me, he did the finding.'

Mother and daughter grew closer together in those few days than they had been for years. Richard and William joined them in the second week of the holiday, and they spent fourteen days together getting plump and brown.

Richard was delighted to find Annabel and Florentyna so relaxed in each other's company and touched when his daughter started referring to William as 'my big brother'. Richard and Annabel regularly beat William and Florentyna at golf in the afternoons before spending long evenings chatting over dinner.

When the holiday came to an end they were all sad to be returning home. Florentyna confessed that she did not feel like throwing herself back into the political fray, until Annabel insisted that the last thing she wanted was a mother who sat home and cooked.

It felt strange to Florentyna that she would not be fighting a campaign herself that year. During her battle with Brooks for the Senate, the Democrats had selected Noel Silverman, a capable young Chicago attorney, to run for her seat in Congress. Some members of the committee admitted that they would have held up the decision if they thought Brooks had had the slightest chance of winning the party's nomination for the Senate.

Many voters asked Florentyna to run as an independent candidate but she knew the party would not approve, especially as they would be looking for another Senatorial representative in two years' time: the other United States Senator, David Rodgers, had repeatedly made it clear that he would not be running for re-election in 1984.

Florentyna flew into Chicago to speak on behalf of Noel Silverman on several occasions and was delighted when he won the seat, even if only by three thousand two hundred and twenty-three votes.

Florentyna faced the fact that she would now have to spend two years in the political wilderness and it didn't ease the pain when she read the Chicago *Tribune*'s headline the day after the election:

BROOKS ROMPS HOME IN SENATE RACE

The Future

1982–1995

31

WILLIAM FIRST BROUGHT JOANNA CABOT home at Christmas. Florentyna knew instinctively that they would be married, and not just because her father turned out to be a distant relation of Richard's. Joanna was dark-haired, slim and graceful – and shyly expressive of her obvious feelings for William. For his part William was attentive and conspicuously proud of the young woman who stood quietly by his side. 'I suppose I might have expected you to produce a son who has been educated in New York, lived in Washington and Chicago but ends up returning to Boston to choose his wife,' Florentyna teased.

'William is your son as well,' Richard reminded her. 'And what makes you think he'll marry Joanna, anyway?'

Florentyna just laughed. 'I predict Boston in the spring.' She turned out to be wrong: they had to wait until the summer.

William was in his final year as an undergraduate, and had taken his business boards and was waiting anxiously to be accepted at the Harvard Business School.

'In my day,' said Richard, 'you waited until you had finished school and had made a little money before you thought about marriage.'

'That just isn't true, Richard. You left Harvard early to marry me and for several weeks afterwards I kept you.'

'You never told me that, Dad,' said William.

'Your father has what in politics is called a selective memory.'

William left laughing.

'I still think . . .'

'They're in love, Richard. Have you grown so old you can't see what's staring you in the face?'

'No, but . . .'

'You're not yet fifty and you're already acting like an old fuddy-duddy. William is almost the same age as you when you married me. Well, haven't you anything to say?'

'No. You're just like all politicians: you keep interrupting.'

The Kanes went to stay with the Cabots early in the new year, and Richard immediately liked John Cabot, Joanna's father, and was surprised that, with so many friends in common, they had not met before. Joanna had two younger sisters, who spent the weekend running around Richard.

'I've changed my mind,' Richard said that Saturday night in bed. 'I think Joanna is just what William needs.'

Florentyna put on an extreme mid-European accent and asked: 'What if Joanna had been a little Polish immigrant who sold gloves in Bloomingdale's?'

Richard took Florentyna in his arms and said, 'I would have told him not to buy three pairs of gloves because it would work out cheaper just to marry the girl.'

Preparations for the forthcoming wedding seemed complicated and demanding to Florentyna, who remembered vividly how simply she and Richard had been married and how Bella and Claude had lugged the double bed up the stairs in San Francisco. Luckily Mrs. Cabot wanted to handle all the arrangements herself, and whenever something was expected of the Kanes, Annabel was only too happy to leap forward as the family representative.

In early January, Florentyna returned to Washington to clear out her office. Colleagues in Washington stopped and chatted with her as if she hadn't left the House. Janet was waiting for her with a pile of letters, most of them from people saying how sorry they were that Florentyna would not be returning to Congress but hoping that she would run for the Senate again in two years' time.

Florentyna answered every one of them but couldn't help wondering if something might go wrong in 1984 as well. If it did that would finish her political career completely.

Florentyna left the Capitol for New York only to find herself getting in everyone's way. The Baron Group and Lester's were being competently run by Richard and Edward. The group had changed considerably since Richard had implemented the many improvements suggested by McKinsey and Company. She was continually surprised by the new Baron of Beef restaurants that could now be found on every ground floor and thought she would never get used to the computer banks alongside the hairdresser's in the hotel lobby. When Florentyna went to see Gianni to check on the progress of the shops, he assumed she had only come in for a new dress.

During those first few months away from Washington, Florentyna became more restless than she could remember. She travelled to Poland twice and could only feel despair for her countrymen as she looked around at the devastation. She wondered where the Russians would strike next. Florentyna took advantage of these journeys to meet European leaders who continually referred to their fear that America was becoming more and more isolationist with each succeeding President.

When she returned to America once again the question of whether she should run for the Senate loomed in front of her. Janet, who had remained on Florentyna's staff, began to discuss tactics with Edward Winchester which included regular trips to Chicago for Florentyna who accepted any speaking engagements in Illinois that came her way. Florentyna felt relieved when Senator Rodgers called her over the Easter recess to say that he hoped she would run for his seat the following year and added that she could rely on his backing.

As Florentyna checked over the Chicago newspapers each week she could not help noticing that Ralph Brooks was already making a name for himself in the Senate. He had somehow managed to get on the prestigious Foreign Relations Committee as well as the Agriculture Committee – so important to Illinois farmers. He was also the only freshman Senator to be appointed to the Democratic Task Force on Regulatory Reform.

It made her more determined, not less.

William and Joanna's wedding turned out to be one of the happiest days of Florentyna's life. Her twenty-two-year-old son standing in tails next to his bride brought back to her memories of his father in San Francisco. The silver band hung loosely on his left wrist, and Florentyna smiled as she noticed the little scar on his right hand. Joanna, although she looked shy and demure, had already rid her future husband of some of his more eccentric habits, among them several gaudy ties and the Fidel Castro moustache William had been so proud of before he had met her. Grandmother Kane, as everyone now referred to Kate, was looking more and more like a pale-blue battleship in full steam as she ploughed through the guests, kissing some while allowing others – those few older than herself – to kiss her. At seventy-five she was still elegant without a suggestion of a failing faculty. She was also the one member of the family who could remonstrate with Annabel and get away with it.

After a memorable reception laid on by Joanna's parents at their Beacon Hill home – it included four hours of dancing to the ageless music of the Lester Lanin orchestra, William and his bride flew off to Europe for their honeymoon while Richard and Florentyna returned to New York. Florentyna knew that the time was fast approaching when she would have to make an announcement about the Senate seat, and she decided to phone the retiring Senator and seek his advice on how he would like her to word any statement.

She called David Rodgers at his office in the Dirksen Building. As she dialled the number, it struck her how odd it was that they now saw so little of each other when only a few months previously, they had spent half of their lives within a two hundred yard radius. The Senator wasn't in, so she left a

message to say that she had called. He did not return her call
for several days and finally his secretary rang to explain that
his schedule had been impossibly tight. Florentyna reflected
on the fact that this wasn't David Rodgers's style. She hoped
that she was just imagining the rebuff until she discussed
what was going on with Edward.

'There's a rumour going around that he wants his wife to
take over the seat,' he told her.

'Betty Rodgers? But she's always claimed she couldn't
abide public life. I can't believe she'd choose to continue his
now that David's retiring.'

'Well, don't forget that since her children left home three
years ago she's been on the Chicago City Council. Perhaps
that's given her the taste for higher things.'

'How serious do you think she is?'

'I don't know, but a couple of phone calls and I can find
out.'

Florentyna found out even before Edward because she had
a call from one of her ex-assistants in Chicago, who said the
Cook County party machine was talking about Mrs. Rodgers
as if she were already the candidate.

Edward called back later the same day to say that he had
discovered that the state committee was holding a caucus to
consider putting Betty Rodgers's name up as the candidate,
although the polls indicated that over eighty per cent of
registered Democrats supported Florentyna as David
Rodgers's successor. 'It doesn't help,' added Edward, 'that
Senator Brooks is openly backing Betty Rodgers.'

'Surprise, surprise,' said Florentyna. 'What do you think
my next move ought to be?'

'I don't think you can do anything at the moment. I know
you have strong support on the committee and it's very much
in the balance, so perhaps it might be wise not to become too
closely involved. Just go on working in Chicago and appear
to remain above it all.'

'But what if she is chosen?'

'Then you will have to run as an independent candidate
and beat her.'

'It's almost impossible to overcome the party machine, as you reminded me a few months back, Edward.'

'Truman did.'

Florentyna heard a few minutes after the meeting was over that the committee had voted by a majority of 6–5 to place Betty Rodgers's name forward as the official Democratic candidate for the Senate at a full caucus meeting later in the month. David Rodgers and Ralph Brooks had both voted against Florentyna.

She couldn't believe that only six people could make such an important decision and during the following week she had two unpleasant phone conversations, one with Rodgers, the other with Brooks, who both pleaded with her to put party unity before personal ambition. 'The sort of hypocrisy you'd expect from a Democrat,' commented Richard.

Many of Florentyna's supporters begged her to fight but she was not convinced, especially when the state chairman called and asked her to announce formally, for the unity of the party, that she would not be a candidate on this occasion. After all, he pointed out, Betty will probably only do one six-year term.

Which will be long enough for Ralph Brooks, Florentyna thought.

She listened to much advice over the next few days, but on a trip to Washington it was Bob Buchanan who told her to read *Julius Caesar* more carefully.

'The whole play?' asked Florentyna.

'No, I should concentrate on Mark Antony if I were you, my dear.'

Florentyna called the Democratic Party chairman and told him she was willing to come to the caucus and state that she was not a candidate, but she was unwilling to endorse Betty Rodgers.

The chairman readily accepted the compromise.

The meeting was held ten days later at the Democratic State Central Commitee in the Bismarck Hotel on West Randolph Street, and when Florentyna arrived the hall was already packed. She could sense from the loud applause she received as she entered the room that the meeting might not go as smoothly as the committee had planned.

Florentyna took her assigned seat on the platform at the end of the second row. The chairman sat in the middle of the front row behind a long table with two Senators, Rodgers and Brooks, on his right and left. Betty Rodgers sat next to her husband and didn't once look at Florentyna. The secretary and treasurer completed the front row. The chairman gave Florentyna a polite nod when she appeared. The other committee members sat in the second row with Florentyna. One of them whispered, 'You were crazy not to put up a fight.'

At eight o'clock the chairman invited David Rodgers to address the meeting. The Senator had always been respected as a diligent worker for his constituents, but even his closest aides would not have described him as an orator. He started by thanking everyone for their support in the past and expressed the hope that they would now pass that loyalty on to his wife. He gave a rambling talk on his work during the last twenty-four years as a Senator and sat down to what might at best, have been described as polite applause.

The chairman spoke next, outlining his reasons for proposing Betty Rodgers as the next candidate. 'At least it will be easy for the voters to remember her name.' He laughed as did one or two people on the platform but surprisingly few in the body of the hall. He then went on to spend the next ten minutes expounding the virtues of Betty Rodgers and the work she had done as a city councillor. He spoke to a silent hall. And sat down to a smattering of applause. He waited a moment, then, in a perfunctory fashion, introduced Florentyna.

She had made no notes because she wanted what she had to say to sound off the cuff, even though she had been rehearsing every word for the past ten days. Richard had wanted to accompany her but she told him not to bother as everything had been virtually decided before the first word was spoken. The truth was that she did not want him there because his support might cast doubt on her apparent innocence.

When the chairman sat down, Florentyna came foward to the centre of the stage and stood right in front of Ralph Brooks.

'Mr. Chairman, I have come to Chicago today to announce that I am not a candidate for the United States Senate.'

She paused and there were cries of 'Why not?' and 'Who stopped you?'

She went on as though she had heard nothing. 'I have had the privilege of serving my district in Chicago for six years in the United States House of Representatives and I look forward to working for the best interests of the people in the future. I have always believed in party unity –'

'But not party fixing,' someone shouted.

Once again, Florentyna ignored the interruption. 'So I shall be happy to back the candidate you select to be on the Democratic ticket,' she said, trying to sound convincing.

An uproar started, amid which cries of 'Senator Kane, Senator Kane' were clearly audible.

David Rodgers looked pointedly at Florentyna as she continued. 'To my supporters, I say that there may come another time and another place, but it will not be tonight, so let us remember in this key state that it is the Republicans we have to defeat, not ourselves. If Betty Rodgers becomes the next Senator, I feel certain that she will serve the party with the same ability we have grown to expect from her husband. Should the Republicans capture the seat, you can be assured that I shall devote myself to seeing we win it back in six years' time. Whatever the outcome, the committee can depend on my support in this crucial state during election year.'

Florentyna quickly resumed her seat in the second row as her supporters cheered and cheered.

When the chairman had brought everybody to order, which he tried to do as quickly as possible, he called upon the next United States Senator from Illinois, Mrs. Betty Rodgers, to address the meeting. Until then, Florentyna had kept her head bowed but she could not resist glancing up at her adversary. Betty Rodgers clearly had not been prepared for any opposition and looked in an agitated state as she fidgeted with her notes. She read a prepared speech, sometimes almost in a whisper, and although it was well researched the delivery made her husband sound like Cicero. Florentyna felt sad and embarrassed for her and almost started to feel guilty about her own tactics but she still despised the committee for putting Betty Rodgers through such an ordeal. She began to wonder to what extremes Ralph Brooks would go to keep her out of the Senate. When Betty Rodgers sat down she was shaking like jelly, and Florentyna quietly left the platform and stepped out of a side door so that she would no longer embarrass them. She hailed a cab and asked the driver to take her to O'Hare airport.

'Sure thing, Mrs. Kane,' came back the reply. 'I do hope you're going to run for the Senate again. You'll win the seat easy this time.'

'No, I shall not be running,' Florentyna said flatly. 'The Democratic candidate will be Betty Rodgers.'

'Who's she?' asked the taxi driver.

'Senator Rodgers's wife.'

'What's she know about the job? Her husband wasn't that hot,' he said testily, and drove the rest of the way in silence. It gave Florentyna the opportunity to reflect that she would *have* to run as an independent candidate if she were ever going to have any chance of winning a seat in the Senate. Her biggest anxiety was splitting the vote with Betty Rodgers and letting a Republican take the seat. The party would never forgive her if that was the eventual outcome. It would spell the end of her political career. Brooks now looked as if he were going to win either way. She cursed herself for not beating him when she had the chance.

The cab came to a halt outside the terminal building. As she paid the driver he said, 'It still doesn't make sense to me. I'll tell you, lady, my wife thinks you're going to be President. I can't see it myself because I could never vote for a woman.'

Florentyna laughed.

'No offence meant, lady.'

'No offence taken,' she said, and doubled his tip.

She checked her watch and made her way to the boarding gate: another thirty minutes before take-off. She bought copies of *Time* and *Newsweek* from the news-stand. Bush on both covers: the first shots of the Presidential campaign were being fired. She looked up at the telemonitor to check the New York gate number: '12C'. It amused her to think of the extremes the officials at O'Hare would go to in order to avoid 'Gate 13'. She sat down in a red plastic swivel chair and began to read the profile on George Bush. She became so engrossed in the article that she did not hear the loudspeaker. The message was repeated. 'Mrs. Florentyna Kane, please go to the nearest white courtesy telephone.'

Florentyna continued reading about the Zapata Oil company executive who had gone through the House, the Republican National Committee, the CIA and the U.S. Mission in China to become Vice-President. A TWA passenger representative came over and touched her lightly on the shoulder. She looked up.

'Mrs. Kane, isn't that for you?' the young man said, pointing at a loudspeaker.

Florentyna listened. 'Yes, it is, thank you.' She walked across the lounge to the nearest phone. At times like this, she always imagined one of the children had been involved in an accident and even now she had to remind herself that Annabel was over twenty-one and William was married. She picked up the phone.

Senator Rodgers's voice came over loud and clear. 'Florentyna, is that you?'

'Yes it is,' she replied.

'Thank God I caught you. Betty has decided she doesn't want to run after all. She feels the campaign would be too great a strain on her. Can you come back before this place is torn apart?'

'What for?' asked Florentyna, her mind in a whirl.

'Can't you hear what's going on here?' said Rodgers.

Florentyna listened to cries of 'Kane, Kane, Kane', as clear as Rodgers's own voice.

'They want to endorse you as the official candidate and no one is going to leave until you return.'

Florentyna's fingers clenched into a fist. 'I am not interested, David.'

'But Florentyna, I thought . . .'

'Not unless I have the backing of the committee and you personally propose my name in nomination.'

'Florentyna, anything you say. Betty always thought you were the right person for the job. It was just that Ralph Brooks pushed her into it.'

'Ralph Brooks?'

'Yes, but Betty now realises that was nothing more than a self-serving exercise. So for God's sake come back.'

'I'm on my way.' Florentyna almost ran down the corridor to the taxi stand. A cab shot up to her side.

'Where to this time, Mrs. Kane?'

She smiled. 'Back to where we started.'

'I suppose you know where you're going, but I can't understand how an ordinary guy like me is meant to put any faith in politicians I just don't know.'

Florentyna prayed that the driver would be silent on the return journey so that she could compose her thoughts, but this time he treated her to a diatribe: on his wife, whom he ought to leave; his mother-in-law, who wouldn't leave him; his son, who was on drugs and didn't work, and his daughter, who was living in a California commune run by a religious cult. 'What a bloody country – beg your pardon, Mrs. Kane,' he said as they drew up beside the hall. God, how she'd wanted to tell him to shut up. She paid him for the second time that evening.

'Maybe I will vote for you after all when you run for President,' he said. She smiled. 'And I could work on the people who ride this cab – there must be at least three hundred each week.'

Florentyna shuddered – another lesson learned.

She tried to collect her thoughts as she entered the building. The audience had risen from their seats and were cheering wildly. Some clapped their hands above their heads while others stood on chairs. The first person to greet her on the platform was Senator Rodgers, and then his wife, who gave Florentyna a smile of relief. The chairman shook her hand heartily. Senator Brooks was nowhere to be seen: sometimes she really hated politics. She turned to face her supporters in the hall and they cheered even louder: sometimes she really loved politics.

Florentyna stood in the centre of the stage, but it was five minutes before the chairman could bring the meeting to order. When there was complete silence, she simply said: 'Thomas Jefferson once remarked: "I have returned sooner than I expected." I am happy to accept your nomination for the United States Senate.'

She was not allowed to deliver a further word that night as they thronged around her. A little after twelve thirty she crept into her room at the Chicago Baron. Immediately she picked up the phone and started dialling 212, forgetting that it was one thirty in New York.

'Who is it?' said a drowsy voice.

'Mark Antony.'

'Who?'

'I come to bury Betty, not to praise her.'

'Jessie, have you gone mad?'

'No, but I have been endorsed as the Democratic candidate for the United States Senate.' Florentyna explained how it had come about.

'George Orwell said a lot of terrible things were going to happen round about now, but he made no mention of you waking me up in the middle of the night just to announce you are going to be a Senator.'

'I just thought you would like to be the first to know.'

'Perhaps you'd better call Edward.'

'Do you think I ought to? You've already reminded me that it's one thirty in New York.'

'I know it is, but why should I be the only person you wake up in the middle of the night to misquote *Julius Caesar* to?'

*

Senator Rodgers kept his word and backed Florentyna throughout her whole campaign. For the first time in years she was free of pressures from Washington and could devote all her energies to an election. This time there were no thunderbolts or meteors that could not be contained, although Ralph Brooks's lukewarm support on one occasion and implied praise of her Republican opponent on another did not help her cause.

The main interest in the country that year was the Presidential campaign. The major surprise was the choice of the Democratic Presidential candidate, a man who had come from nowhere to beat Walter Mondale and Edward Kennedy in the Primaries with his programme dubbed the 'Fresh Approach'. The candidate visited Illinois on no less than six occasions during the campaign, appearing with Florentyna every time.

On the day of the election, the Chicago papers said once again that the Senate race was too close to call. The pollsters were wrong and the loquacious cab driver was right because at eight thirty Central time, the Republican candidate conceded an overwhelming victory for Florentyna. Later the pollsters tried to explain away their statistical errors by speculating that many men would not admit they were going to vote for a woman. Either way it didn't matter, because the new President-elect's telegram said it all:

WELCOME BACK TO WASHINGTON, SENATOR KANE.

32

NINETEEN EIGHTY-FIVE WAS to be a year for funerals, which made Florentyna feel every day of her fifty-one years.

She returned to Washington to find she had been allocated a suite in the Russell Building, a mere six hundred yards from her old Congressional office in the Longworth Building. For several days while she was settling in, she found herself still driving into the Longworth garage rather than the Russell courtyard. She also couldn't get used to being addressed as Senator, especially by Richard, who could mouth the title in such a way as to make it sound like a term of abuse. 'You may imagine your status has increased but they still haven't given you a raise in salary. I can't wait for you to be President,' he added. 'Then at least you will earn as much as one of the bank's Vice-Presidents.'

Florentyna's salary might not have risen, but her expenses had, as once again she surrounded herself with a team many Senators would envy. She would have been the first to acknowledge the advantage of a strong financial base outside the world of politics. Most of her old team returned and were supplemented by new assistants who were in no doubt about Florentyna's future. Her office in the Russell Building was in suite four hundred and forty. The other four rooms were now occupied by the fourteen assistants, led by the intrepid Janet Brown, whom Florentyna had decided long ago was married to her job. In addition, Florentyna now had four offices throughout Illinois with three assistants working in each of them.

Her new office overlooked the courtyard, with its fountain and cobble-stoned parking area. The green lawn would be a popular lunch place for Senate assistants during the warm weather, and for an army of squirrels in the winter.

Florentyna told Richard that she estimated she would be paying out of her own pocket over two hundred thousand dollars a year more than her Senatorial allowance, an amount which varies from Senator to Senator depending on the size of their state and its population, she explained to her husband. Richard smiled and made a mental note to donate exactly the same sum to the Republican Party.

No sooner had the Illinois State Seal been affixed to her office door than Florentyna received the telegram. It was simple and stark: WINIFRED TREDGOLD PASSED AWAY ON THURSDAY AT ELEVEN O'CLOCK.

It was the first time Florentyna was aware of Miss Tredgold's Christian name. She checked her watch, made two overseas calls and then buzzed for Janet to explain where she would be for the next forty-eight hours. By one o'clock that afternoon she was on board Concorde, and she arrived in London three hours and twenty-five minutes later at nine twenty-five. The chauffeur-driven car she had ordered was waiting for her as she emerged from Customs and drove her down the M4 motorway to Wiltshire. She checked into the Lansdowne Arms Hotel and read Saul Bellow's *The Dean's December* until three o'clock in the morning to counter the jet-lag. Before turning the light out she called Richard.

'Where are you?' were his first words.

'I'm booked into a small hotel at Calne in Wiltshire, England.'

'Why, pray? Is the Senate doing a fact-finding mission on English pubs?'

'No, my darling. Miss Tredgold has died, and I'm attending the funeral tomorrow.'

'I'm sorry,' said Richard. 'If you had let me know I would have come with you. We both have a lot to thank that lady for.' Florentyna smiled. 'When will you be coming home?'

'Tomorrow evening's Concorde.'

'Sleep well, Jessie. I'll be thinking of you – and Miss Tredgold.'

At nine thirty the next morning a maid brought in a breakfast tray of kippers, toast with Cooper's Oxford marmalade, coffee and a copy of the London *Times*. She sat in bed savouring every moment, an indulgence she would never have allowed herself in Washington. By ten thirty she had absorbed *The Times* and was not surprised to discover the British were having the same problems with inflation and unemployment as those that prevailed in America. Florentyna got up and dressed in a simple black knitted suit. The only jewelry she wore was the little watch that Miss Tredgold had given her on her thirteenth birthday.

The hotel porter told her that the church was about a mile away and as the morning was so clear and crisp she decided to walk. What the local had failed to point out to her was that the journey was uphill the whole way and his 'about' was a 'guesstimate'. As she strode along, she reflected on how little exercise she had taken lately, despite the pristine exercycle now lodged at Cape Cod. She had also allowed the jogging mania to pass her by.

The tiny Norman church, surrounded by oaks and elms, was perched on the side of the hill. On the noticeboard was an appeal for twenty-five thousand pounds to save the church roof; according to a little blob of red on a thermometer over one thousand pounds had already been collected. To Florentyna's surprise, she was met in the vestry by a waiting verger and led to a place in the front pew next to an imperious lady who could only have been the headmistress.

The church was far fuller than Florentyna had expected, and the school had supplied the choir. The service was simple and the address given by the parish priest left Florentyna in no doubt that Miss Tredgold had continued to teach others with the same dedication and common sense that had influenced the whole of Florentyna's life. She tried not to cry during the address as she knew Miss Tredgold would not have approved, but she nearly succumbed when they sang her governess's favourite hymn, 'Rock of Ages'.

When the service was over, Florentyna filed back with the rest of the congregation through the Norman porch and stood in the little churchyard to watch the mortal remains of Winifred Tredgold disappear into the ground. The headmistress, a carbon copy of Miss Tredgold – Florentyna found it hard to believe that such women still existed –said she would like to show Florentyna something of the school before she left. On their way back through the grounds, she learned that Miss Tredgold had never talked about Florentyna except to her two or three closest friends, but when the headmistress opened the door of a small bedroom in a cottage on the school estate, Florentyna could no longer hold back the tears. By the bed was a photograph of a vicar whom Florentyna recognised as Miss Tredgold's father and by its side, in a small silver Victorian frame, stood a picture of Florentyna graduating from Girls Latin next to an old Bible. In the bedside drawer, they discovered every one of Florentyna's letters written over the past thirty years; the last one remained unopened by her bed.

'Did she know I had been elected to the Senate?' Florentyna asked diffidently.

'Oh, yes, the whole school prayed for you that day. It was the last occasion on which Miss Tredgold read the lesson in chapel, and before she died she asked me to write to tell you that she felt her father had been right, and she had indeed taught a woman of destiny. My dear, you must not cry, her belief in God was so unshakeable that she died in total peace with this world. Miss Tredgold also asked me to give you her Bible and this envelope, which you must not open until you have returned home. It's something she bequeathed you in her will.'

As Florentyna left, she thanked the headmistress for all her kindness and added that she had been touched and surprised at being met by the verger when no one knew she was coming.

'Oh, you should not have been surprised, child,' said the

headmistress. 'I never doubted for a moment that you would come.'

Florentyna travelled back to London clutching the envelope. She longed to open it, like a child who has seen a package in the hall but knows it is for his birthday the following day. She caught Concorde at six thirty that evening, arriving back at Dulles by five thirty p.m. She was seated at her desk in the Russell Building by six thirty the same evening. She stared at the envelope marked 'Florentyna Kane' and then slowly tore it open. She pulled out the contents, four thousand Baron Group stock. Miss Tredgold had died presumably unaware that she was worth over a half a million dollars. Florentyna took out her pen and wrote out a cheque for twenty-five thousand pounds for a new church roof in memory of Miss Winifred Tredgold and sent the shares to Professor Ferpozzi to be placed at the disposal of the Remagen Trust. When Richard heard the story he told Florentyna that his father had once acted in the same way, but the sum required had been only five hundred pounds. 'It seems even God is affected by inflation,' he added.

Washington was preparing for another inauguration. On this occasion Senator Kane was placed in the VIP stand from which the new incumbent was to make his speech. She listened intently to the blueprint for American policy over the next four years, now referred to by everyone as the 'Fresh Approach'.

'You're getting nearer the podium every time,' Richard had told her at breakfast.

Florentyna glanced around among her colleagues and friends in a Washington where she now felt at ease. Senator Ralph Brooks, a row in front of her, was even nearer the President. His eyes never left the podium.

Florentyna found herself on the Defence Sub-Committee of the Appropriations Committee and on the Environment and Public Works Committee. She was also asked to chair the Committee on Small Business. Her days once again resembled a never-ending chase for more hours. Janet and her assistants would brief her in lifts, cars, planes, en route to vote on the floor, and even on the run between committee rooms. Florentyna was tireless in her efforts to complete her daily schedule and all fourteen staffers wondered how much they could pile on her before she cracked under the strain. In the Senate, Florentyna quickly enhanced the reputation she had made for herself in the House of Representatives by speaking only on matters on which she was well briefed, and then with compassion and common sense. She still remained silent on issues on which she did not consider herself well informed. She voted against her party on several defence matters and twice over the new energy policy provoked by the latest war in the Middle East.

As the only Democratic woman Senator, she received invitations to speak all over the nation and other Senators soon learned that Florentyna Kane was not the token Democratic woman in the Senate but someone whom they could never afford to underestimate.

Florentyna was pleased to find how often she was invited to the inner sanctum of the Majority Leader's office to discuss matters of policy as well as party problems.

During her first session as a Senator, Florentyna sponsored an amendment on the Small Business Bill, giving generous tax concessions to companies who exported over thirty-five per cent of their products. For a long time she had believed that companies who did not seek to sell their goods in an overseas market were suffering from the same delusions of grandeur as the English in the mid-century, and that if they were not careful, Americans would enter the twenty-first century with the same problems that the British had failed to come to terms with in the 1980s.

In her first three months she had answered five thousand four hundred and sixteen letters, voted seventy-nine times, spoken on eight occasions in the chamber, fourteen times outside and missed lunch on forty-three of the last ninety days.

'I don't need to diet,' she told Janet, 'I weigh less than

when I was twenty-four and opened my first shop in San Francisco.'

The second death was every bit as much of a shock because the whole family had spent the previous weekend together in Cape Cod.

The maid reported to the butler that Mrs. Kate Kane had not come down to breakfast as the grandfather clock chimed eight. 'Then she must be dead,' said the butler.

Kate Kane was seventy-nine when she failed to come down for breakfast and the family gathered for a Brahmin funeral. The service was held at Trinity Church, Copley Square and could not have been in greater contrast to the service for Miss Tredgold, for this time the bishop addressed a congregation who between them could have walked from Boston to San Francisco on their own land. All the Kanes and Cabots were present along with two other Senators and a Congressman. Almost everyone who had ever known Grandmother Kane, and a good many of those who had not, filled the pews behind Richard and Florentyna.

Florentyna glanced across at William and Joanna. Joanna looked as though she would be giving birth in about a month, and it made Florentyna feel sad that Kate had not lived long enough to become Great-Grandmother Kane.

After the funeral, they spent a sombre family weekend in the Red House on Beacon Hill. Florentyna would never forget Kate's tireless efforts to bring her husband and son together. Richard was now the sole head of the Kane family, which Florentyna realised would add further responsibility to his already impossible work load. She also knew that he would not complain and it made her feel guilty that she was unable to do much about making his life any easier.

Like a typical Kane, Kate's will was sensible and prudent; the bulk of the estate was left to Richard and his sisters, Lucy and Virginia, and large settlements were made on William and Annabel. William was to receive two million dollars on his thirtieth birthday. Annabel, on the other hand, was to live off the interest of a further two million until she was forty-five or had two legitimate children. Grandmother Kane hadn't missed much.

In Washington, the battle for the mid-term election had already begun and Florentyna was glad to have a six-year term before she faced the voters again, giving her a chance for the first time to do some real work without the biennial break for party squabbles. Nevertheless, so many of her colleagues invited her to speak in their states that she seemed to be working just as hard, and the only request she politely refused was in Tennessee: she explained she could not speak against Bob Buchanan, who was seeking re-election for the last time.

The little white card which Louise gave her each night was always filled with appointments from dawn to dusk indicating the routine for the following day:

'7.45: breakfast with a visiting foreign minister of defence. 9.00: staff meeting. 9.30: Defence Sub-Committee hearing. 11.30: interview with Chicago *Tribune*. 12.30: lunch with six Senate colleagues to discuss defence budget. 2.00: weekly radio broadcast. 2.30: photo on Capitol steps with Illinois 4-H'ers. 3.15: staff briefing on Small Business Bill. 5.30: drop by reception of Associated General Contractors. 7.00: cocktail party at French Embassy. 8.00: dinner with Donald Graham of the *Washington Post*. 11.00: phone Richard at the Denver Baron.'

As a Senator, Florentyna was able to reduce her trips to Illinois to every other weekend. On every other Friday, she would catch the U.S. Air flight to Providence, where she would be met by Richard on his way up from New York. They would then drive out on Route Six to the Cape, which gave them a chance to catch up with each other's week.

Richard and Florentyna spent their free weekends in Cape Cod, which had become their family home since Kate's death, Richard having given the Red House to William and Joanna.

On Saturday mornings, they would lounge around reading newspapers and magazines. Richard might play the cello while Florentyna would look over the paperwork she had brought with her from Washington. When weather permitted, they played golf in the afternoon and whatever the weather, backgammon in the evening. Florentyna always ended up owing Richard a couple of hundred dollars which he said he would donate to the Republican Party if she ever honoured her gambling debts. Florentyna always queried the value of giving to the Massachusetts Republican Party, but Richard pointed out that he also supported a Republican Governor and Senator in New York.

Patriotically, Joanna gave birth to a son on Washington's birthday, and they christened him Richard. Suddenly Florentyna was a grandmother.

People magazine stopped describing her as the most elegant lady in Washington and started calling her the best-looking grandmother in America. This caused a flurry of letters of protest including hundreds of photographs of other glamorous grannies for the editor to consider, which only made Florentyna even more popular.

The rumours that she would be a strong contender for the Vice-Presidency in 1988 started in July when the Small Business Association made her Illinoisan of the Year and a *Newsweek* poll voted her Woman of the Year. Whenever she was questioned on the subject, she reminded her enquirers that she had been in the Senate for less than a year and that her first priority was to represent her state in Congress, although she couldn't help noticing that she was being invited to the White House more and more often for sessions with the President. It was the first time that being the one woman in the majority party was turning out to be an advantage.

Florentyna learned of Bob Buchanan's death when she asked why the flag on the Russell Building was at half-mast. The funeral was on the Wednesday when she was due to offer an amendment to the Public Health Service Act in the Senate and address a seminar on defence at the Woodrow Wilson

International Centre for Scholars. She cancelled one, postponed the other and flew to Nashville, Tennessee.

Both of the state's Senators and its seven remaining Congressmen were present. Florentyna stood next to her House colleagues in silent tribute. As they waited to go into the Lutheran chapel, one of them told her that Bob had five sons and one daughter. Gerald, the youngest, had been killed in Vietnam. She thanked God that Richard had been too old and William too young to be sent to that pointless war.

Steven, the eldest boy, led the Buchanan family into the chapel. Tall and thin, with a warm open face, he could only have been the son of Bob and when Florentyna spoke to him after the service he revealed the same southern charm and straight approach that had endeared his father to her. Florentyna was delighted when she learned that Steven was going to run for his father's seat in the coming special election.

'It will give me someone new to quarrel with,' she said, smiling.

'He greatly admired you,' said Steven.

Florentyna was not prepared to see her photograph all over the major newspapers the next morning being described as a gallant lady. Janet placed a *New York Times* editorial on top of her press clippings for her to read:

> Representative Buchanan had not been well known to the citizens of New York, but it was a comment on his service in Congress that Senator Kane flew to Tennessee to attend his funeral. It is the sort of gesture that is rarely seen in politics today and is just another reason why Senator Kane is one of the most respected legislators in either House.

Florentyna was rapidly becoming the most sought-after politician in Washington. Even the President admitted that the demands on her time weren't running far short of his. But among the invitations that came that year there was one she accepted with considerable pride. Harvard invited her to run for election to the Board of Overseers in the spring and to address the Graduation Day ceremony that June. Even Richard put a note in his diary to keep the day free.

Florentyna looked up the list of those who had preceded her in this honour – from George Marshall outlining the plan to reconstruct post-war Europe to Alexander Solzhenitsyn describing the West as decadent and lacking in spiritual values.

Florentyna spent many hours preparing her Harvard address, aware that the media traditionally gave the speech considerable coverage. She practised paragraphs daily in front of a mirror, in the bath, even on the golf course with Richard. She wrote the complete text herself – in longhand, but accepted numerous amendments from Janet, Richard and Edward on its content.

The day before she was due to deliver the speech, Florentyna received a telephone call from Sotheby's. She listened to the head of the department and agreed to his suggestion. When they had settled on a maximum price, he said he would let her know the outcome immediately after the auction. Florentyna felt the timing could not have been better. She flew up to Boston that night, to be met at Logan airport by an enthusiastic young undergraduate who drove her into Cambridge and dropped her off at the Faculty Club. President Bok greeted her in the foyer and congratulated her on her election to the board, and then took her through to be introduced to the other overseers, who numbered among the thirty, two Nobel Prize winners, one for literature and one for science; two ex-cabinet secretaries, an Army general, a judge, an oil tycoon and two other university Presidents. Florentyna sat through the meeting amused by how courteous the overseers all were to one another and she could not help but contrast their approach with that of a House committee.

The guest room they put at her disposal brought back memories of Florentyna's student days and she even had to phone Richard from the corridor. He was in Albany dealing with some tax problems caused by Jack Kemp, the new Republican Governor of New York State.

'I'll be with you for the lunch,' he promised. 'By the way, I see tomorrow's speech was worthy of a mention by Dan Rather on C.B.S. 'News' tonight. It had better be good if you hope to keep me from watching the Yankees on channel eleven.'

'Just see you are in your place on time, Mr. Kane.'

'Just you make sure it's as good as your speech to the Vietnam Veterans of America, because I'm travelling a long way to hear you, Senator.'

'How could I have fallen in love with you, Mr. Kane?'

'It was, if I remember rightly, "Adopt an Immigrant Year", and we Bostonians were exhibiting our usual social conscience.'

'Why did it continue after the end of the year?'

'I decided it was my duty to spend the rest of my life with you.'

'Good decision, Mr. Kane.'

'I wish I were with you now, Jessie.'

'You wouldn't if you could see the room they've given me. I've only a single bed, so you would be spending the night on the floor. Be on time tomorrow, because I want you to hear this speech.'

'I will. But I must say it's taking you a long time to convert me to a Democrat.'

'I'll try again tomorrow. Good night, Mr. Kane.'

Richard was woken the next morning by the telephone at the Albany Baron. He assumed it would be Florentyna on the line with some Senatorial comment, but it turned out to be New York Air to say there would be no flights out of Albany that day because of a one-day action by maintenance workers that was affecting every airline.

'Christ,' said Richard, uncharacteristically, then jumped into a cold shower where he added some other new words to his vocabulary. Once he was dry, he tried to get dressed while dialling the front desk. He dropped the phone and had to start again.

'I want a rental car at the front entrance immediately,' he said, dropped the phone again and finished dressing. He then called Harvard, but they had no idea where Senator Kane was at that particular moment. He left a message explaining what had happened, ran downstairs, skipped breakfast and picked up the keys to a Ford Executive. Richard was held up in the rush-hour traffic and it took him another thirty minutes to find Route 90 East. He checked his watch: he would only have to do a steady sixty to be in Cambridge in time for the speech at two o'clock. He knew how much this one meant to Florentyna, and he was determined not to be late.

The last few days had been a nightmare, so much so he hadn't bothered Florentyna with the theft in Cleveland, the kitchen walk-out in San Francisco, the seizing of the hotel in Cape Town, tax problems over his mother's estate – all happening while the price of gold was collapsing because of the civil war in South Africa. Richard tried to put all these problems out of his mind. Florentyna could always tell when he was tired or over-anxious, and he did not want her to be worrying about situations he knew he could sort out eventually. Richard wound the car window down to let in some fresh air.

The rest of the weekend he was going to do nothing but sleep and play the cello; it would be the first break they had both had for over a month. No children, as William would be in Boston with his own family and Annabel in Mexico – leaving nothing more strenuous to consider than a round of golf for two whole days. He wished he didn't feel so tired. 'Damn,' he said out loud. He'd forgotten the roses – had planned to send them to Florentyna from the airport as usual.

Florentyna was given two messages just before lunch. The man from Sotheby's phoned to say that she had been successful in her bid, and a college porter delivered Richard's news. She was delighted by the first and disappointed by the second, although she smiled at the thought that Richard would be worrying about the roses. Thanks to Sotheby's, she now had something for him he had wanted all his life.

Florentyna had spent the morning in the formal graduation proceedings at the Tercentenary Theatre. The sight of all three networks setting up their cameras on the lawn for the afternoon ceremony made her feel even more nervous, and she hoped no one noticed that she had eaten almost nothing at lunch.

At one forty-five, the overseers left for the yard where alumni reunion classes had already gathered. She thought back to her own class . . . Bella . . . Wendy . . . Scott . . . Edward . . . and now she had returned, as Edward had predicted, as Senator Kane. She took her seat on the platform outside the Tercentenary Theatre next to President Horner of Radcliffe and looked down at the card on the other chair beside her. It read, 'Mr. Richard Kane – husband of Senator Kane'. She smiled at how much that would have annoyed him, and scribbled underneath, 'What took you so long?' She must remember to leave the card on the mantelpiece. Florentyna knew that if Richard arrived after the ceremony had begun he would have to find a seat on the lawn. The announcement of elections, conferring of honorary degrees, and reports of gifts received by the university, was followed by an address from President Bok. Florentyna sat and listened as he introduced her. She scanned the rows in front of her, as far as her eye could see, but was still unable to spot Richard.

'President Horner, distinguished visitors, ladies and gentlemen. It is a great honour for me today to present one of Radcliffe's most distinguished alumnae, a woman who has captured the imagination of the American people. Indeed, I know many of us believe that Radcliffe will one day have *two* Presidents.' Seventeen thousand guests burst into spontaneous applause. 'Ladies and gentlemen, Senator Florentyna Kane.'

Florentyna was shaking when she rose from her seat. She checked her notes as the great television lights were switched on, momentarily blinding her so that she could see nothing but a blur of faces. She prayed Richard's was among them.

'President Bok, President Horner. I stand before you more nervous now than I was when I first came to Radcliffe thirty-three years ago and I couldn't find the dining room for two days because I was too frightened to ask anyone.' The laughter eased Florentyna's tension. 'Now I see seated in front of me men and women, and if I recall correctly from my Radcliffe rule book, men may only enter the bedrooms "between the hours of three and five p.m." and "must at all times keep both feet on the ground". If the rule still exists today, I am bound to ask how the poor things ever get any sleep.'

The laughter continued for several seconds before Florentyna was able to start again. 'Over thirty years ago I was educated at this great university and it has set the standard for everything I have tried to achieve in my life. The pursuit of excellence has always been to Harvard of paramount importance and it is a relief to find in this changing world that the standards attained today by your graduates are even higher than they were in my generation. There is a tendency among the old to say that the youth of today do not compare with their forefathers. I am reminded of a carving on the side of one of the tombs of the Pharaohs which translated reads: "The young are lazy and preoccupied with themselves and will surely cause the downfall of the world as we know it."'

The graduates cheered while the parents laughed. 'Winston Churchill once said: "When I was sixteen, I thought my parents knew nothing. When I was twenty-one, I was shocked to discover how much they had picked up in the last five years."' The parents applauded and the students smiled. 'America is often looked upon as a great monolithic land mass, with a vast centralised economy. It is neither of these things. It is two hundred and twenty-five million people who make up something more diverse, more complicated, more exciting, than any other nation on earth and I envy all of you who wish to play a role in the future of our country and feel sorry for those who do not. Harvard University is famous for its tradition of service in medicine, teaching, the law, religion and the arts. It must be thought a modern tragedy that more young people do not consider politics an honourable and worthwhile profession. We must change the atmosphere in the corridors of power so that the very brightest of our youth does not dismiss, virtually without consideration, a career in public life.

'None of us has ever doubted for a moment the integrity of Washington, Adams, Jefferson or Lincoln. Why shouldn't we today produce another generation of statesmen who will bring back to our vocabulary the words duty, pride and honour without such a suggestion being greeted with sarcasm or scorn?

'This great university produced John Kennedy, who once said when receiving an honorary degree from Yale, "And now I have the best of both worlds, a Harvard education and a Yale degree."'

When the laughter had died down, Florentyna continued: 'I, Mr. President, have the best of every world, a Radcliffe education and a Radcliffe degree.'

Seventeen thousand people rose to their feet and it was a considerable time before Florentyna could continue. She smiled as she thought how proud Richard would be, because he had suggested that line to her when she was rehearsing in the bath, and she had not been sure that it would work.

'As young Americans, take pride in your country's past achievements, but strive to make them nothing more than history. Defy old myths, break new barriers, challenge the future, so that at the end of this century, people will say of us that our achievements rank alongside those of the Greeks, the Romans and the British in advancing freedom and a just society for all people on this planet. Let no barriers be unassailable and no aims too high and when the crazy whirligig of time is over, let it be possible for you to say as Franklin D. Roosevelt did, "There is a mysterious cycle in human events. To some generations much is given, of other generations much is expected, but this generation of Americans has a rendezvous with destiny."'

Once again, everyone on the lawn broke into spontaneous

applause. When it subsided, Florentyna lowered her voice almost to a whisper. 'My fellow alumni, I say to you, I am bored by cynics, I despise belittlers, I loathe those who think there is something sophisticated and erudite in running our nation down, because I am convinced that this generation of our youth, who will take the United States into the twenty-first century, has another rendezvous with destiny. I pray that many of them are present today.'

When Florentyna sat down she was the only person who remained seated. Journalists were to remark the next day that even the cameramen whistled. Florentyna looked down aware that she had made a favourable impression on the crowd, but she still needed Richard for final confirmation. Mark Twain's words came back to her: 'Sorrow can take care of itself, but to get the true benefit of joy, you must share it.' As Florentyna was led off the stage, the students cheered and waved, but her eyes searched only for Richard. Making her way out of the Tercentenary Yard, she was stopped by dozens of people, but her thoughts remained elsewhere.

Florentyna heard the words, 'Who will tell her?' while she was trying to listen to a student who was going to Zimbabwe to teach English. She swung around to stare at the troubled face of Matina Horner, the Radcliffe President.

'It's Richard, isn't it?' said Florentyna quickly.

'Yes, I'm afraid so. He has been involved in a car accident.'

'Where is he?'

'In Newton-Wellesley Hospital, about ten miles away. You must leave immediately.'

'How bad is it?'

'Not good, I'm afraid.'

A police escort rushed Florentyna down the Massachusetts Turnpike to the Route 16 exit as she prayed, Let him live. Let him live.

As soon as the police car arrived outside the main entrance of the hospital she ran up the steps. A doctor was waiting for her.

'Senator Kane, I'm Nicholas Eyre, chief of surgery. We need your permission to operate.'

'Why? Why do you need to operate?'

'Your husband has severe head injuries. And it's our only chance to save him.'

'Can I see him?'

'Yes, of course.' He led her quickly to the emergency room where Richard lay unconscious beneath a plastic sheet, a tube coming out of his mouth, his skull encased in stained white gauze. Florentyna collapsed on to the bedside chair and stared down at the floor, unable to bear the sight of her mutilated husband. Would the brain damage be permanent or could he recover?

'What happened?' she asked the surgeon.

'The police can't be certain, but a witness said your husband veered across the divider on the turnpike for no apparent reason and collided with a tractor-trailer. There seems to have been no mechanical fault with the car he was driving, so they can only conclude he fell asleep at the wheel.'

Florentyna steeled herself to raise her eyes and look again at the man she loved.

'Can we operate, Mrs. Kane?'

'Yes,' said a faint voice that only an hour before had brought thousands of people to their feet. She was led into a corridor and sat alone. A nurse came up. They needed a signature; she scribbled her name. How many times had she done that today?

She sat alone in the corridor, a strange hunched up figure in an elegant dress, on the little wooden chair. She remembered how she had met Richard in Bloomingdale's when she thought he had fallen for Maisie; how they made love only moments after their first row and how they had run away and with the help of Bella and Claude she had become Mrs. Kane; the births of William and Annabel; that twenty-dollar bill that fixed the meeting in San Francisco with Gianni; returning to New York as partners to run the Baron Group and Lester's; how he had then made Washington possible; how she had smiled when he played the cello for her; how he had laughed when she beat him at golf. She had always wanted to achieve so much for him, and he had always been selfless in his love for her. He must live so that she could devote herself to making him well again.

In times of helplessness one suddenly believes in God. Florentyna fell on her knees and begged for her husband's life.

Hours passed before Dr. Eyre returned to her side. Florentyna looked up hopefully.

'Your husband died a few minutes ago,' was all the surgeon said.

'Did he say anything to you before he died?' Florentyna asked.

The chief of surgery looked embarrassed.

'Whatever it was my husband said, I should like to know, Dr. Eyre.'

The surgeon hesitated. 'All he said, Mrs. Kane, was, "Tell Jessie I love her".'

Florentyna bowed her head.

The widow knelt alone and prayed.

It was the second funeral of a Kane in Trinity Church in as many months. William stood between two Mrs. Kanes dressed in black, as the bishop reminded them that in death there is life.

Florentyna sat alone in her room that night and cared no longer for this life. In the hall lay a package marked: 'Fragile, Sotheby Parke Bernet, contents one cello, Stradivarius.'

William accompanied his mother back to Washington on Monday; the news-stand at Logan airport was ablaze with headlines from her speech. Florentyna didn't even notice.

William remained at the Baron with his mother for three days until she sent him back to his wife. For hours Florentyna would sit alone in a room full of Richard's past. His cello, his photographs, even the last unfinished game of back-gammon.

Florentyna began to arrive at the Senate by mid-morning.

Janet couldn't get her to answer her mail except for the hundreds of letters and telegrams expressing sorrow at Richard's death. She failed to show up at committee meetings and forgot appointments with people who had travelled great distances to see her. On one occasion, she even missed presiding over the Senate, a chore Senators took in turn when the Vice-President was absent – for a defence debate. Even her most ardent admirers doubted if she would ever fully regain her impetuous enthusiasm for politics.

As the weeks turned into months, Florentyna began to lose her best assistants who feared she no longer had the ambition for herself that they had once had for her. Complaints from her constituents, low key for the first six months after Richard's death, now turned to an angry rumble, but still Florentyna went aimlessly about her daily routine. Senator Brooks quite openly suggested an early retirement for the good of the party, and continued to voice this opinion in the smoke-filled rooms of Illinois's political headquarters. Florentyna's name began to disappear from the White House guest lists and she was no longer seen at the cocktail parties held by Mrs. John Sherman Cooper, Mrs. Lloyd Dreegar or Mrs. George Renchard.

Both William and Edward travelled regularly to Washington in an effort to try to stop her from thinking about Richard, and to bring her back to taking an interest in her work. Neither of them succeeded.

Florentyna spent a quiet Christmas at the Red House in Boston. William and Joanna found it difficult to adapt to the change that had taken place in so short a time. The once elegant and incisive lady had become listless and dull. It was an unhappy Christmas for everyone except the ten-month-old Richard who was learning to hoist himself up by pulling on anything he could get hold of. When Florentyna returned to Washington in the New Year, matters did not improve, and even Edward began to despair.

Janet Brown waited nearly a year before she told Florentyna that she had been offered the job of administrative assistant in Senator Hart's office.

'You must accept the offer, my dear. There is nothing left for you here. I shall serve out my term and then retire.'

Janet too pleaded with Florentyna but it had no effect.

Florentyna glanced through her mail, barely noticing a letter from Bella chiding her about not turning up for their daughter's wedding, and signed some more letters that she hadn't written or even bothered to read. When she checked her watch, it was six o'clock. An invitation from Senator Pryor to a small reception lay on the desk in front of her. Florentyna dropped the smartly embossed card into the waste-paper basket, picked up a copy of the *Washington Post* and decided to walk home alone. She had never once felt alone when Richard had been alive.

She came out of the Russell Building, crossed Delaware Avenue and cut over the grass of Union Station Plaza. Soon Washington would be a blaze of colours. The fountain splashed as she came to the paved walkway. She reached the steps leading down to New Jersey Avenue and decided to rest for a moment on the park bench. There was nothing to rush home for. She began to recall the look on Richard's face as Jake Thomas welcomed him as chairman of Lester's. He did look a fool standing there with a large red London bus under his arm. Reminiscing about such incidents in their life together brought her as near to happiness now as she ever expected to achieve.

'You're on my bench.'

Florentyna blinked and looked to her side. A man wearing dirty jeans and an open brown shirt with holes in the sleeves sat on the other end of the bench, staring at her suspiciously. He had not shaved for several days, which made it hard for Florentyna to determine his age.

'I'm sorry, I didn't realise it was your bench.'

'Been my bench, Danny's bench, these last thirteen years,' said the grimy face. 'Before that it was Ted's and when I go Matt gets it.'

'Matt?' repeated Florentyna uncomprehendingly.

'Yeah, Matt the Grain. He's asleep behind parking lot sixteen waiting for me to die.' The tramp chuckled. 'But I tell you the way he goes through that grain alcohol, Matt will never take over this bench. You not thinking of staying long, are you lady?'

'No, I hadn't planned to,' said Florentyna.

'Good,' said Danny.

'What do you do during the day?'

'Oh, this and that. Always know where we can get soup from church kitchens, and some of that stuff they throw out from the swanky restaurants can keep me going for days. I had the best part of a steak at the Monocle yesterday. I think I'll try the Baron tonight.'

Florentyna tried not to show her feelings. 'You don't work?'

'Who'd give Danny work? I haven't had a job in fifteen years – since I left the Army back in '70. Nobody wanted this old vet, should have died for my country in Nam – would have made things easier for everyone.'

'How many vets are there like you?'

'In Washington?'

'Yes, in Washington.'

'Hundreds.'

'Hundreds?' repeated Florentyna.

'Not as bad as some cities. New York they throw you in jail as quick as look at you. When are you thinking of going, lady?' he said eyeing her suspiciously.

'Soon. May I ask . . .?'

'You ask too many questions, so it's my turn. Okay if I have the paper when you leave?'

'The *Washington Post*?'

'Good quality, that,' said Danny.

'You read it?'

'No.' He laughed. 'I wrap myself up in it, keeps me warm as a hamburger if I stay very still.'

She passed him the paper. She stood up and smiled at Danny, noticing for the first time that he had only one leg.

'Wouldn't have a quarter to spare an old soldier?'

Florentyna rummaged through her bag. She had only a

ten-dollar bill and thirty-seven cents in change. She handed the money to Danny.

He stared at her offering in disbelief. 'There's enough here for both Matt and me to have some real food,' he exclaimed. The tramp paused and looked at her more closely. 'I know you, lady,' Danny said suspiciously. 'You're that Senator lady. Matt always says he's going to get an appointment with you and explain a thing or two about how you spend government money. But I told him what those little receptionists do when they see the likes of us walk in – they call the capital cops and grab the disinfectant. Don't even ask us to sign the guest book. I told Matt not to waste his valuable time.'

Florentyna watched Danny as he began to make himself comfortable on his bench by covering himself very professionally with the *Washington Post*. 'Any case, I told him you would be much too busy to bother with him, and so would the other ninety-nine.' He turned his back on the distinguished Senator from Illinois and lay very still. Florentyna said good night before walking down the steps to the street where she was met by a policeman outside the entrance to the underground parking lot.

'The man on that bench?'

'Yes, Senator,' said the officer. 'Danny, Danny One-Leg; he didn't cause you any trouble, I hope?'

'No, not at all,' said Florentyna. 'Does he sleep there every night?'

'Has for the past ten years, which is how long I've been on the force. Cold nights, he moves to a grate behind the Capitol. He's harmless enough, not like some of those at the back of lot sixteen.'

Florentyna lay awake the rest of the night only nodding off occasionally as she thought about Danny One-Leg and the hundreds suffering from the same plight as his. At seven thirty the next morning she was back in her office on Capitol Hill. The first person to arrive was Janet at eight thirty, and she was shocked to find Florentyna's head buried in *The Modern Welfare Society* by Arthur Quern. Florentyna looked up.

'Janet, I want all the current unemployment figures, broken down into states, and then into ethnic groups. I also need to know, with the same breakdowns, how many people are on social security and what percentage have not worked for over two years. Then I want you to find out how many of them have served in the armed forces. Compile a list of every leading authority. . . You're crying, Janet.'

'Yes, I am,' she said.

Florentyna came from behind her desk and put her arms round her. 'It's over, my dear, let's forget the past and get this show back on the road.'

33

IT TOOK EVERYONE IN Congress only a month to discover that Senator Kane was back with a vengeance. And when the President phoned her personally, she knew that her attacks on his Fresh Approach were coming home to the one house where things could be changed.

'Florentyna, I'm eighteen months away from election day and you are taking my Fresh Approach campaign apart. Do you want the Republicans to win the next election?'

'No, of course not, but with your Fresh Approach we only spent in one year on welfare what we spent on defence in six weeks. Do you realise how many people in this country don't even eat one square meal a day?'

'Yes, Florentyna, I do . . .'

'Do you also know what the figures are for people who sleep on the streets each night in America? Not India, not Africa, not Asia; I'm talking about America. And how many of those people haven't had a job in ten years; not ten weeks or ten months but ten years, Mr. President?'

'Florentyna, whenever you call me Mr. President I know I'm in trouble. What do you of all people expect me to do?

You have always been among those Democrats who advocate a strong defence programme.'

'And I still do, but there are millions of people across America who wouldn't give a damn if the Russians came marching down Pennsylvania Avenue right now, because they don't believe they could be any worse off.'

'I hear what you're saying, but you've become a hawk in dove's clothing, and those sort of statements may make wonderful headlines for you, but what do you expect me to do about it?'

'Set up a Presidential commission to look into how our welfare money is spent. I already have three of my staff working on the problem at the moment and I intend to present some of the facts they are unearthing about misuse of funds at the earliest date. I can promise you, Mr. President, the figures will make your hair curl.'

'Have you forgotten I'm nearly bald, Florentyna?' She laughed. 'I like the idea of a commission.' The President paused. 'I could even float the concept at my next press conference.'

'Why don't you do that, Mr. President? And tell them about the man who has been sleeping on a bench for thirteen years little more than a stone's throw away from the White House while you slumbered in the Lincoln bedroom. A man who lost a leg in Vietnam and doesn't even know he is entitled to sixty-three dollars a week compensation from the Veterans Administration. And if he did, he wouldn't know how to collect it, because his local V.A. office is in Texas, and if in an inspired moment they decided to send a cheque to him where would they address it? A park bench, near the Capitol?'

'Danny One-Leg,' said the President.

'So you know about Danny?'

'Who doesn't? He's had more good publicity in two weeks than I've had in two years. I'm even considering an amputation. I fought for my country in Korea, you know.'

'And you've managed to take care of yourself ever since.'

'Florentyna, if I set up a Presidential commission on welfare, will you give it your support?'

'I certainly will, Mr. President.'

'And will you stop attacking Texas?'

'That was unfortunate. A junior researcher of mine discovered Danny had come from Texas. But do you realise that in spite of the illegal immigrant problem, over twenty per cent of the people of Texas have an annual income of less than . . .?'

'I know, I know, Florentyna, but *you* seem to forget that my Vice-President comes from Houston and he hasn't had a day's rest since Danny One-Leg hit the front pages.'

'Poor old Pete,' said Florentyna. 'He will be the first Vice-President who has had something to worry about, other than where his next meal is coming from.'

'And you mustn't be hard on Pete, he plays his role.'

'You mean balances the ticket so that you can stay in the White House.'

'Florentyna, you're a wicked lady, and I warn you that I intend to open my press conference next Thursday by saying I have come up with a brilliant idea.'

'*You*'ve come up with the idea?'

'Yes,' said the President. 'There must be some compensation for taking the heat all the time. I repeat that I have come up with this brilliant idea of a Presidential commission on "Waste in Welfare" and . . .' the President hesitated for a minute '. . . that Senator Kane has agreed to be the chairman. Now will that keep you quiet for a few days?'

'Yes,' said Florentyna, 'and I'll try to report within one year so that you have time before the election to describe to the voters your bold new plans to sweep away the cobwebs of the past and usher in the Fresh Approach.'

'Florentyna.'

'I'm sorry, Mr. President. I couldn't resist that.'

Janet didn't know where Florentyna was going to find the time to chair such an important commission. Her appointment books already needed the assistant with the smallest handwriting to complete each page.

'I need three hours clear every day for the next six months,' said Florentyna.

'Sure thing,' said Janet. 'How do you feel about two o'clock to five o'clock every morning?'

'Suits me,' said Florentyna, 'but I'm not sure we could get anyone else to sit on a commission under those conditions.' Florentyna smiled. 'And we're going to need more assistants.'

Janet had already filled all the vacancies that had been created from resignations during the past few months. She had appointed a new press secretary, a new speech writer, and four more legislative researchers from some of the outstanding young college graduates who were now banging on Florentyna's door. 'Let's be thankful that the Baron Group can afford the extra cost,' Janet added.

Once the President had made his announcement, Florentyna set to work. Her commission consisted of twenty members, plus a professional support staff of eleven. She divided the commission itself, so that half were professional people who had never needed welfare in their lives nor given the subject much thought until asked to do so by Florentyna, while the other half were currently on welfare, or unemployed. A clean-shaven Danny, wearing his first suit, joined Florentyna's staff as a full-time adviser. The originality of the idea took Washington by surprise. Article after article was written on Senator Kane's 'Park Bench Commissioners'. Danny One-Leg told stories that made the other half of the committee realise how deep-seated the problem was and how many abuses still needed to be corrected, so that those in genuine need received fair recompense.

Among those who were questioned by the committee were Matt the Grain, who now slept on the bench Danny had vacated, and 'Charlie Wendon', an ingenious convict from Leavenworth who, for a parole deal arranged by Florentyna, told the committee how he had been able to milk a thousand dollars a week out of welfare before the police caught up with him. The man had so many aliases he was no longer sure of his own name; at one point he had supported seventeen wives, forty-one dependent children and nineteen dependent parents, all of whom were non-existent except on the national welfare computer. Florentyna thought he might be exaggerating until he showed the commission how to get the President of the United States on to the computer as unemployed, with two dependent children, living with his ageing mother at 1600 Pennsylvania Avenue, Washington, D.C. Wendon also went on to confirm something she had already feared, that he was small fry compared with the professional crime syndicates who thought nothing of raking in fifty thousand dollars a week through phony welfare recipients.

She later discovered that Danny One-Leg's real name was on the computer and that someone else had been collecting his money for the past thirteen years. It didn't take a lot longer to discover that Matt the Grain and several of his friends from parking lot sixteen were also on the computer although they had never received a penny themselves.

Florentyna went on to prove that there were over a million people entitled to aid who were not receiving it, while, at the same time, the money was disappearing elsewhere. She became convinced that there was no need to ask Congress for more money, just for safeguards designed to ensure that the annual pay-out of over ten billion dollars was reaching the right people. Many of those who needed help simply couldn't read or write, and so never returned to the government office once they had been presented with long forms to complete. Their names became an easy source of income for even a small-time crook. When Florentyna presented her report to the President ten months later, he sent a series of new safeguards to Congress for their immediate consideration. He also announced that he would be drawing up a new Welfare Reform Programme before the election. The press was fascinated by the way Florentyna had got the President's name and address on the unemployment computer; from MacNelly to Peters, the cartoonists had a field day, while the

FBI made a series of welfare fraud arrests right across the country.

The press praised the President for his initiative, and the *Washington Post* declared that Senator Kane had done more in one year for those in genuine need than the New Deal and the Great Society put together. This was indeed a 'fresh approach'; Florentyna had to smile. Rumours began to circulate that she would replace Pete Parkin as Vice-President when the election came round. On Monday she was on the cover of *Newsweek* for the first time and across the bottom ran the words: 'America's First Woman Vice-President?' Florentyna was far too shrewd a politician to be fooled by press speculation. She knew that when the time came, the President would stick with Parkin, balance the ticket and be sure of the south. Much as he admired Florentyna, the President wanted another four years in the White House.

Once again, Florentyna's biggest problem in life was in determining priorities among the many issues and people that competed for her attention. Among the requests from Senators to help them with their campaigns was one from Ralph Brooks. Brooks, who never lost the opportunity to describe himself as the state's senior Senator, had recently been appointed chairman of the Senate Energy Committee, which kept him in the public eye. He had received considerable praise for his handling of the oil tycoons and leaders of big business. Florentyna was aware that he never spoke well of her in private, but when proof of this came back to her she dismissed it as unimportant. She was surprised, however, when he asked her to share a TV commercial spot with him, saying how well they worked together and the importance of both Illinois Senators being Democratic. After she'd been urged to cooperate by the party chairman in Chicago, Florentyna agreed, although she had not spoken to her Senate colleague more than a couple of times a month during her entire term in Congress. She hoped her endorsement might patch up their differences. It didn't. Two years later when she came up for re-election, his support for her was rarely above a whisper.

As the Presidential election drew nearer, more and more Senators seeking re-election asked Florentyna to speak on their behalf. During the last six months of 1988 she rarely spent a weekend at home; even the President invited her to join him in several campaign appearances. He had been delighted by the public reaction to the Kane Commission report on welfare, and he agreed to the one request Florentyna made of him, although he knew Pete Parkin and Ralph Brooks would be furious when they heard.

Florentyna had had little or no social life since Richard's death, although she had managed to spend an occasional weekend with William, Joanna and her two-year-old grandson Richard at the Red House on Beacon Hill. Whenever she found a weekend free to be back at the Cape, Annabel would join her.

Edward, who was now chairman of the Baron Group and vice-chairman of Lester's Bank, reported to her at least once a week, producing results even Richard would have been proud of. On Cape Cod he would join her for golf, but unlike the results of her battles with Richard, Florentyna always won. Each time she did she would donate her winnings to the local Republican club in Richard's memory. The local G.O.P. man obligingly recorded the gifts as coming from an anonymous donor as Florentyna's constituents would have been hard put to understand her reasons for supporting both sides.

Edward left Florentyna in no doubt of his feelings for her and once hesitantly went so far as to propose. Florentyna kissed her closest friend gently on the cheek. 'I will never marry again,' she said, 'but if you ever beat me at a round of golf, I'll reconsider your offer.' Edward immediately started taking golf lessons, but Florentyna was always too good for him.

When the press got hold of the news that Senator Kane had been chosen to deliver the key speech at the Democratic convention in Detroit, they again started writing about her as a possible Presidential candidate in 1992. Edward became excited about these suggestions, but she reminded him that they had also considered forty-three other candidates in the last six months. As the President had predicted, Pete Parkin was livid when the suggestion was voiced that the Vice-Presidency would be handed to Florentyna but eventually calmed down when he realised that the President had no intention of dropping him from the ticket. It only convinced Florentyna that the Vice-President was going to be her biggest rival if she did decide to run in four years' time.

The President and Pete Parkin were re-nominated at a dull party convention, with only a handful of dissenters and favourite sons to keep the delegates awake. Florentyna wistfully recalled livelier conventions, such as the G.O.P.'s 1976 mêlée, during which Nelson Rockefeller had pulled a phone socket out of the floor in the Kansas City convention hall.

Florentyna's key speech was received by the delegates in decibels second only to those accorded to the President's speech of acceptance, and it caused posters and campaign buttons to appear on the final day with the words: 'Kane for '92'. Only in America could ten thousand campaign buttons appear overnight, thought Florentyna, and she took one home for young Richard. Her Presidential campaign was beginning without her even lifting a finger.

During the final weeks before the election, Florentyna travelled to almost as many marginal states as the President himself and the press suggested that her unstinting loyalty might well have been a factor in the Democrats' slim victory. Ralph Brooks was returned to the Senate with a slightly increased majority. It reminded Florentyna that her own re-election to the Senate was now only two years away.

When the first session of the 101st Congress opened, Florentyna found that many of her colleagues in both houses were openly letting her know of their support should she decide to put her name forward for the Presidency. She realised that some of them would be saying exactly the same thing to Pete Parkin, but she made a note of each one and always sent a handwritten letter of thanks the same day.

Her hardest task before facing re-election for the Senate was to steer the new Welfare Bill through both houses, and the job took up most of her time. She personally sponsored seven amendments to the bill which included the federal government being responsible for all costs, setting a nation-wide minimum income, and a major overhaul of social security. She spent hours badgering, cajoling, coaxing and almost bribing her colleagues until the bill became law. She stood behind the President when he signed the new Act in the Rose Garden. Cameras rolled and shutters clicked from the ring of press photographers standing behind a cordoned-off area. It was the greatest single achievement of Florentyna's political career. The President delivered a self-serving state-ment and then rose to shake Florentyna's hand. 'This is the lady whom we can thank for "The Kane Act",' he said and whispered in her ear, 'Good thing the V.P.'s in South America or I would never hear the end of it.'

Press and public alike praised the skill and determination with which Senator Kane had guided the bill through Con-gress and the *New York Times* said that if she achieved nothing more in her political career, she would have placed on the books a piece of legislation that would stand the test of time. Under the new law, no one in genuine need would forfeit his rights, while at the other end of the scale, those who played the 'Welfare Charade' would now end up behind bars.

As soon as the fuss had blown over, Florentyna tried to return to the normal daily life of a Senator. Janet warned her that she must spend more time in the state now that the election was less than nine months away. Nearly all the senior members of the party offered their services to Florentyna when she came up for re-election, but it was the President who broke into a heavy schedule to support her and drew the biggest crowd when he spoke at the convention hall in Chicago. As they walked up the steps together to the strains of 'Happy Days Are Here Again' he whispered, 'Now, I am going to get my revenge for all the flak you've given me over the past five years.'

The President described Florentyna as the woman who had given him more problems than his wife and now he heard she wanted to sleep in his bed at the White House. When the laughter died down, he added, 'And if she does aspire to that great office, America could not be better served.'

The next day the press suggested that the statement was a direct snub to Pete Parkin and that Florentyna would have the backing of the President if she decided to run. The President denied this interpretation of what he had said, but from that moment on Florentyna was placed in the unfortunate position of being the front-runner for 1992. When the results of her Senate race came in even Florentyna was surprised by the size of her victory, as most Democratic Senators had lost ground in the usual mid-term election swing against the White House. Florentyna's overwhelming victory confirmed the party's view that it had found not only a standard-bearer but something far more important: a winner.

The week of the first session of the 102nd Congress opened with Florentyna's picture on the cover of *Time*. Full profiles of her life, giving the details of her playing St. Joan at Girls Latin and winning the Woolson Scholarship to Radcliffe, were meticulously chronicled. They even explained why her late husband had called her Jessie. She had become the best known woman in America. 'This charming fifty-six-year-old woman,' said *Time* in its summation, 'is both intelligent and witty. Only beware when you see her hand clench into a tight fist because it's then she becomes a heavyweight.'

During the new session, Florentyna tried to carry out the normal duties of a Senator but she was daily being asked by colleagues, friends and the press when she would be making a statement about her intentions to run or not for the White House. She tried to sidetrack them by taking more interest in

the major issues of the day. At the time Quebec elected a
left-wing government, she flew to Canada to participate in
exploratory talks with British Columbia, Alberta, Saskatch-
ewan and Manitoba about federation with America. The
press followed her and after she returned to Washington, the
media stopped describing her as a politician but America's
first stateswoman.

Pete Parkin was already informing anyone and everyone
who wanted to listen that he intended to run, and an official
announcement was considered imminent. The Vice-
President was five years older than Florentyna and she knew
this would be his last opportunity to hear 'Hail to the Chief'
played for him. Florentyna felt it might be her only chance.
She remembered Margaret Thatcher telling her when she
stood for Prime Minister, 'The only difference between the
leader of a party being a man or a woman is, if a woman loses,
the men won't give you a second chance.'

Florentyna had no doubt what Bob Buchanan would have
advised had he still been alive. Read *Julius Caesar*, my dear,
but this time Brutus and not Mark Antony.

She and Edward spent a quiet weekend together at Cape
Cod, and while he lost yet another golf match they discussed
the tide in the affairs of one woman, the flood and the possible
fortune.

By the time that Edward returned to New York and
Florentyna to Washington, the decision had finally been
made.

34

'. . . AND TO THAT END I declare my candidacy for
the office of President of the United States.'

Florentyna gazed into the Senate Caucus Room at the
three hundred and fifty applauding members of the audience

who occupied a space that the sergeant-at-arms insisted should only hold three hundred. Television camera crews and press photographers lobbed and dodged to prevent their frames from being filled with the backs of anonymous heads. Florentyna remained standing during the prolonged applause that followed her announcement. When the noise had finally ebbed Edward stepped up to face the battery of microphones at the podium.

'Ladies and gentlemen,' he said. 'I know the candidate will be delighted to answer your questions.'

Half the people in the room started to speak at once and Edward nodded to a man in the third row to indicate that he could ask the first question.

'Albert Hunt of the *Wall Street Journal*,' he said. 'Senator Kane, who do you think will be your toughest opponent?'

'The Republican candidate,' she said without hesitation. There was a ripple of laughter and some applause. Edward smiled and called for the next question.

'Senator Kane, is this really a bid to be Pete Parkin's running mate?'

'No, I am not interested in the office of Vice-President,' replied Florentyna. 'At best it's a period of stagnation while you wait around in the hope of doing the real job. At worst I am reminded of Nelson Rockefeller's words: "Don't take the number two spot unless you're up for a four-year advanced seminar in political science and a lot of state funerals." I'm not in the mood for either.'

'Do you feel America is ready for a woman President?'

'Yes, I do, otherwise I would not be willing to run for the office, but I will be in a better position to answer that question on November 3rd.'

'Do you think the Republicans might select a woman?'

'No, they don't have the courage for such a bold move. They will watch the Democrats make a success of the idea and copy it when the next election comes around.'

'Do you feel you have enough experience to hold this office?'

'I have been a wife, a mother, the chairman of a multimillion dollar corporation, a member of the House for eight years and a Senator for seven. In the public career I've chosen, the Presidency is the number one spot. So, yes, I believe I am now qualified for that job.'

'Do you expect the success of your Welfare Act to help you with the votes of the poor and black communities?'

'I hope the Act will bring me support from every sector. My main intent with that piece of legislation was to ensure that both those who contribute to welfare through taxation and those who benefit from the legislation will feel that the provisions made are both just and humane in a modern society.'

'After the Russian invasion of Yugoslavia, would your administration take a harder line with the Kremlin?'

'After Hungary, Czechoslovakia, Afghanistan, Poland and now Yugoslavia, the latest Soviet offensive on the Pakistan border reinforces my long-standing conviction that we must remain vigilant in the defence of our people. We must always remember that the fact that the two biggest oceans on earth have protected us in the past is no guarantee of our safety in the future.'

'The President has described you as a hawk in dove's clothing.'

'I'm not sure if that's a comment on my dress or my looks, but I suspect that the combination of those two birds looks not unlike the American eagle.'

'Do you feel we can keep a special relationship with Europe after the election results in France and Britain?'

'The decision of the French to return to a Gaullist government while the British voted for a new Labour Administration does not greatly concern me. Jacques Chirac and Roy Hattersley have both proved to be good friends of America in the past, and I see no reason why that should change in the future.'

'Do you expect Ralph Brooks's support for your campaign?'

It was the first question that had taken Florentyna by surprise. 'Perhaps you should ask him, but naturally I hope that Senator Brooks will feel pleased by my decision.' She could think of nothing else to add.

'Senator Kane, do you approve of the current Primary system?'

'No. Although I am not a supporter of a national Primary, the present system is by any standards archaic. America seems to have developed a process for the selection of a President that is more responsive to the demands of the network news programmes than it is to the needs of modern government. It also encourages dilettante candidates. To-day, you have a better chance of becoming President if you are temporarily out of work, having been left several million by your grandmother. You then have four years off to devote to running around the country collecting delegates, while the people best qualified for the job are probably doing a full day's work elsewhere. If I became President, I would seek to send a bill to the Congress which would not handicap anyone from running for the Presidency through lack of time or money. We must reinstate the age-old precept that anyone born in this country, with both the desire to serve and the ability to do the job, will not find themselves disqualified before the first voter goes to the polls.'

The questions continued to come at Florentyna from all parts of the room and she took the last one over an hour later.

'Senator Kane, if you become President, will you be like Washington and never tell a lie or like Nixon and have your own definition of the truth?'

'I cannot promise I will never lie. We all lie, sometimes to protect a friend or a member of our family, and if I was President perhaps to protect one's country. Sometimes we lie just because we don't want to be found out. The one thing I can assure you of is that I am the only woman in America who has never been able to lie about her age.' When the laughter died down Florentyna remained standing. 'I would like to end this press conference by saying that whatever the outcome of my decision today, I wish to express my thanks as an American for the fact that the daughter of an immigrant has found it possible to run for the highest office in the land. I do not believe such an ambition would be attainable in any other country in the world.'

Florentyna's life began to change the moment she left the room; four Secret Service agents formed a circle around the candidate, the lead one skilfully creating a passage for her through the mass of people.

Florentyna smiled when Brad Staimes introduced himself and explained that for the duration of her candidacy, there would always be four agents with her night and day, working in eight-hour shifts. Florentyna couldn't help noticing that two of the agents were women whose build and physical appearance closely resembled her own. She thanked Mr. Staimes but never quite became used to seeing one of the agents whenever she turned her head. The agents' tiny earphones distinguished them from well-wishers and Florentyna recalled the story about an elderly lady who attended a Nixon rally in 1972. She approached a Nixon aide at the end of the candidate's speech and said she would definitely vote for his re-election because he obviously sympathised with those who, like herself, were hard of hearing.

Following the press conference, Edward chaired a strategy meeting in Florentyna's office to work out a rough schedule for the coming campaign. The Vice-President had announced some time before that he was a candidate and several other contestants had thrown their hats into the ring, but the press had already decided that the real battle was going to be between Kane and Parkin.

Edward had lined up a formidable team of pollsters, finance chairmen and policy advisers who were well supplemented by Florentyna's seasoned staff in Washington led by Janet Brown.

First Edward outlined his day-by-day plan leading up to the first Primary in New Hampshire, and from there to California, all the way to the convention floor in Detroit. Florentyna had tried to arrange for the convention to be held in Chicago, but the Vice-President vetoed the idea; he wasn't challenging Florentyna on her home ground. He reminded the Democratic committee that the choice of Chicago and the riots that followed might have been the single reason that Humphrey lost to Nixon in 1968.

Florentyna had already faced the fact that it would be almost impossible for her to beat the Vice-President in the southern states so it was vital that she should get off to a strong start in New England and the Mid-West. She agreed that during the next three months she would devote seventy-five per cent of her energies to the campaign, and for several hours her team threw around ideas for the best use of that time. It was also agreed that she would make regular trips to the major cities that voted in the first three Primaries and, if she made a strong showing in New Hampshire, a traditionally conservative area, they would plan their forward strategy accordingly.

Florentyna dealt with as much of her Senate work as possible between making frequent trips to New Hampshire, Vermont and Massachusetts. Edward had chartered a six-seater Lear jet for her with two pilots available around the clock so that she could leave Washington at a moment's notice. All three Primary states had set up strong campaign headquarters, and everywhere Florentyna went she spotted as many 'Kane for President' posters and bumper stickers as she did for Pete Parkin.

With only seven weeks left until the first Primary Florentyna began to spend more and more of her time chasing the one hundred and forty-seven thousand registered Democrats in the state. Edward did not expect her to capture more than thirty per cent of the votes, but he felt that might well be enough to win the Primary and persuade doubters that she was an electoral asset. Florentyna needed every delegate she could secure before they arrived in the south, even if possible to pass the magic one thousand six hundred and sixty-six by the time she reached the convention hall in Detroit.

The early signs were good. Florentyna's private pollster, Kevin Palumbo, assured her that the race with the Vice-President was running neck and neck, and Gallup and Harris seemed to confirm that view. Only seven per cent of the voters said they would not under any circumstances vote for a woman, but Florentyna knew just how important seven per cent could be if the final outcome was close.

Florentyna's schedule included brief stops at over one hundred and fifty of New Hampshire's two hundred and fifty small towns. Despite the hectic nature of each day, she grew to love the classical New England milltowns, the crustiness of the Granite State's farmers and the stark beauty of its winter landscape.

She served as a starter for a dogsled race in Franconia and visited the most northerly settlement near the Canadian border. She learned to respect the penetrating insights of local newspaper editors, many of whom had retired from high-level jobs with national magazines and news services. She avoided discussions of one particular issue after discovering that New Hampshire residents stoutly defended their right to oppose a state income tax, thus attracting a host of high-income professionals from across the Massachusetts border.

More than once she had occasion to be thankful for the death of William Loeb, the newspaper publisher, whose outrageous misuse of the Manchester *Union Leader* had single-handedly destroyed the candidacies of Edmund Muskie and George Bush before her. It was no secret that Loeb had had no time for women in politics.

Edward was able to report that money was flowing into their headquarters in Chicago and 'Kane for President' offices were springing up in every state. Some of them had more volunteers than they could physically accommodate; the overspill turned dozens of living rooms and garages throughout America into makeshift campaign headquarters.

In the final seven days before the first Primary, Florentyna was interviewed by Barbara Walters, Dan Rather and Frank Reynolds, as well as appearing on all three morning news programmes. As Andy Miller, her press secretary, pointed out, fifty-two million people watched her interview with Barbara Walters and it would have taken over five hundred years to shake the hands of that number of voters in White

River Junction. Nevertheless her local managers still saw to it that she visited nearly every old people's home in the state.

Despite this, Florentyna had to pound the streets of New Hampshire towns, shaking hands with papermill workers in Berlin, as well as with the somewhat inebriated denizens of the VFW and American Legion posts, which seemed to exist in every town. She learned to work the ski-lift lines in the smaller hills rather than the famous resorts which were often peopled by a majority of non-voting visitors from New York or Massachusetts.

If she failed with this tiny electorate of the northern tip of America, Florentyna knew it would raise major doubts about her credibility as a candidate.

Whenever she arrived in a city, Edward was always there to meet her and he never let her stop until the moment she stepped back on to her plane.

Edward told her that they could thank heaven for the curiosity value of a woman candidate. His advance team never had to worry about filling any hall where Florentyna was to speak with potted plants rather than with Granite State voters.

Pete Parkin, who had a good luck streak with funeral duty, proved that the Vice-President had little else to do; he spent even more time in the state than Florentyna could. When the day of the Primary came, Edward was able to show that someone in the Kane team had contacted by phone, letter or personal visit one hundred and twenty-five thousand of the one hundred and forty-seven thousand registered Democrats but, he added, obviously so had Pete Parkin because many of them had remained non-committal and some even hostile.

On the final evening, Florentyna held a rally in Manchester which over three thousand people attended. When Janet told her that tomorrow she would be about one-fiftieth of the way through the campaign, Florentyna replied, 'Or already finished.' She went to her motel room a little after midnight followed by the camera crews of C.B.S., N.B.C., A.B.C., Cable News and four agents from the Secret Service, all of whom were convinced she was going to win.

The voters of New Hampshire woke up to drifting snow and icy winds. Florentyna spent the day driving from polling place to polling place thanking the party faithful until the last poll closed. At eleven minutes past nine, C.B.S. was the first to tell the national audience that the turnout was estimated at forty-seven per cent, which Dan Rather considered high in view of the weather conditions. The early voting pattern showed that the pollsters had proved right: Florentyna and Pete Parkin were running neck and neck, each taking over the lead during the night but never by more than a couple of percentage points. Florentyna sat in her motel room with Edward, Janet, her closest assistants and two Secret Service agents, watching the final results come in.

'The outcome couldn't have been closer if they had planned it,' said Jessica Savitch, who announced the result first for N.B.C. 'Senator Kane thirty-one per cent, Vice-President Parkin thirty, Senator Bill Bradley sixteen per cent and the rest of the voters scattered among five others who in my opinion,' added Savitch, 'needn't bother to book a hotel room for the next Primary.'

Florentyna recalled her father's words: *If the result of the New Hampshire Primary turns out to be satisfactory . . .*

She left for Massachusetts with six delegates committed to her; Pete Parkin had five. The national press declared no winner but five losers. Only three candidates were seen in Massachusetts, and Florentyna seemed to have buried the bogey that as a woman she couldn't be a serious contender.

In Massachusetts she had fourteen days to capture as many of the one hundred and eleven delegates as possible, and here her work pattern hardly varied. Each day she would carry out the schedule that Edward had organised for her, a programme that ensured that the candidate met as many voters as possible and found some way to get on the morning or evening news.

Florentyna posed with babies, union leaders and Italian restaurateurs; she ate scallops, linguine, Portuguese sweetbread and cranberries; she rode the MTA, the Nantucket ferry and the Alameda bus line the length of the Massachusetts Turnpike; she jogged on beaches, hiked in the Berkshires and shopped in Boston's Quincy Market, all in an effort to prove she had the stamina of any man. Nursing her aching body in a hot bath, she came to the conclusion that had her father remained in Russia, her route to the Presidency of the U.S.S.R. couldn't have been any harder.

In Massachusetts, Florentyna held off Pete Parkin for a second time, taking forty-seven delegates to the Vice-President's thirty-nine. The same day in Vermont, she captured eight of the state's twelve delegates. Because of the upsets already achieved by Florentyna, the political pollsters were saying that more people were answering 'Yes' when asked 'Could a woman win the Presidential election?' But even she was amused when she read that six per cent of the voters had not realised that Senator Kane was a woman. The press was quick to point out that her next big test would be in the south, where the Florida, Georgia and Alabama Primaries all fell on the same day. If she could hold on there she had a real chance, because the Democratic race had become a private battle between herself and the Vice-President. Bill Bradley, having secured only eleven per cent of the votes in Massachusetts, had dropped out because of lack of funds although his name remained on the ballot in several states and no one doubted he would be a serious candidate sometime in the future. Bradley had been Florentyna's first choice as running mate, and she already had the New Jersey Senator on her short list for consideration for Vice-President.

When the Florida ballots were counted, it came as no surprise that the Vice-President had taken sixty-two of the one hundred delegates and he repeated the trend in Georgia by winning 40–23, followed by Alabama where he captured twenty-eight of the forty-five voters, But Pete Parkin was not, as he had promised the press, 'trouncing the little lady when she puts her elegant toes in the south'. Parkin was increasingly trying to outdo Florentyna as a champion of the military, but his choice of legislation setting up the so-called 'Fort

Gringo Line' along the Mexican–American border was beginning to rebound on him in the south-west, where he had imagined he was unbeatable.

Edward and his team were now working several Primaries ahead as they criss-crossed back and forth across the country; Florentyna thanked heaven for her ample campaign funds as the Lear jet touched down in state after state. Her energy remained boundless and if anything it was the Vice-President who began to stammer and sound tired and hoarse at the end of each day. Both candidates had to fit in trips to San Juan, and when Puerto Rico held its Primary in mid-March, twenty-five of the forty-one delegates favoured Florentyna. Two days later, she arrived back in her home state for the Illinois Primary, trailing Parkin 164–194.

The Windy City came to a standstill as its inhabitants welcomed their favourite daughter, giving her every one of the one hundred and seventy-nine Illinois delegates so that she went back into the lead with three hundred and forty-three delegates. However, when they moved on to New York, Connecticut, Wisconsin and Pennsylvania, the Vice-President eroded the lead until he arrived in Texas trailing only five hundred and ninety-one to Florentyna's six hundred and fifty-five.

No one was surprised when Pete Parkin took one hundred per cent of the delegates in his home state; they hadn't had a President since Lyndon Baines Johnson and the male half of Texas believed that while J. R. Ewing might have had his faults, he had been right about a woman's place being in the home. The Vice-President left his ranch outside Houston with a lead of seven hundred and forty-three to Florentyna's six hundred and fifty-five.

Travelling round the country under such tremendous daily pressure, both candidates found an off-the-cuff remark or an unwary comment could easily turn out to be tomorrow's headline. Pete Parkin was the first to make a gaffe when he got Peru mixed up with Paraguay and the photographers went wild when he rode in a chauffeured Mercedes through Flint on one of his motorcades. Nor was Florentyna without her mishaps. In Alabama, when asked if she would consider a black running mate as Vice-President, she replied, 'Of course, I've already considered the idea.' It took repeated statements to persuade the press that she had not already invited one of America's black leaders to join her ticket.

Her biggest mistake, however, was in Virginia. She addressed the University of Virginia Law School on the parole system and the changes she would like to make if she became President. The speech had been written and researched for her by one of the assistants in Washington who had been with Florentyna since her days as a Congresswoman. She read the text through carefully the night before, making only a few minor changes, admiring the way the piece had been put together, and delivered the speech to a crowded hall of law students who received it enthusiastically. When she left for an evening meeting of the Charlottesville Rotary Club to talk on the problems facing cattle farmers, she dismissed all thought of the earlier speech until she read the local paper the next morning during breakfast at the Boar's Head Inn.

The Richmond *News-Leader* came out with a story that all the national papers picked up immediately. A local journalist covering the biggest scoop of his life suggested that Florentyna's speech was outstanding because it had been written by one of Senator Kane's most trusted staff members, Allen Clarence, who was an ex-convict himself, having been given a six-month jail sentence with a year's probation before going to work for Florentyna. Few of the papers pointed out that the offence had been drunken driving without a licence, and that Clarence had been released on appeal after three months. When questioned by the press on what she intended to do about Mr. Clarence, she said, 'Nothing'.

Edward told her that she must fire him immediately, however unfair it might seem, because those sections of the press who were against her – not to mention Pete Parkin – were having a field day repeating that one of her most trusted members of staff was an ex-con. 'Can you imagine who will be running the jails in this country if that woman is elected?' became Parkin's hourly off-the-cuff remark. Eventually Allen Clarence voluntarily resigned, but by then the damage had been done. By the time they reached California, Pete Parkin had increased his lead, with nine hundred and ninety-one delegates to Florentyna's eight hundred and eighty-three.

When Florentyna arrived in San Francisco, Bella was there to meet her at the airport. She might have put on thirty years, but she still hadn't lost any pounds. By her side stood Claude, one enormous son and one skinny daughter. Bella ran towards Florentyna the moment she saw her, only to be blocked by burly Secret Service agents. She was rescued by a hug from the candidate. 'I've never seen anything like her,' muttered one of the Secret Service men. 'She could kick start a Jumbo.' Hundreds of people stood at the perimeter of the tarmac chanting 'President Kane', and Florentyna, accompanied by Bella, walked straight over to them. Hands flew in Florentyna's direction, a reaction that never failed to lift her spirits. The placards read 'California for Kane' and for the first time the majority of the crowd was made up of men. When she turned to leave them and go into the terminal she saw scrawled all over the side of a wall in red, 'Do you want a Polack bitch for President?' and underneath in white, 'Yes'.

Bella, now the headmistress of one of the largest schools in California, had also, after Florentyna had won a seat in the Senate, become the city's Democratic committee chairwoman.

'I always knew you would run for President, so I thought I had better make certain of San Francisco.'

Bella did make certain, with her one thousand so-called volunteers banging on every door. California's split personality – conservative in the south, liberal in the north – made it hard to be the kind of centrist candidate Florentyna wanted to be. But her efficiency, compassion and intelligence converted even some of the most hardened Marin County left-wingers and Orange County Birchers. San Francisco's turnout was second only to Chicago's. Florentyna wished she had fifty-one Bellas because the vote in San Francisco was enough to give her sixty-nine per cent of the state. It had been Bella who had made it possible for Florentyna to arrive in Detroit for the convention with one hundred and twenty-eight more delegates than Parkin.

Over a celebration dinner, Bella warned Florentyna that the biggest problem she was facing was not 'I'll never vote for a woman' but that 'She has too much money'.

'Not that old chestnut. I can't do any more about that,' said Florentyna. 'I've already put my own Baron stock into the foundation.'

'That's the point – no one knows what the foundation does. I realise it helps children in some way, but how many children, and how much money is involved?'

'The trust last year spent over three million dollars on 3,112 immigrants from under-privileged backgrounds. Added to that, four hundred and two gifted children won Remagen Scholarships to American universities and one went on to be our first Rhodes Scholar to Oxford.'

'I wasn't aware of that,' said Bella, 'but I'm continually reminded that Pete Parkin built a feeble little library for the University of Texas at Austin. He's made sure that the building is as well known as the Widener Library at Harvard.'

'So what do you feel Florentyna should be doing?' asked Edward.

'Why don't you let Professor Ferpozzi hold his own press conference? He's a man the public will take notice of. After that everyone will know that Florentyna Kane cares about other people and spends her own money on them to prove it.'

The next day, Edward worked on placing articles in selected magazines and organised a press conference. They ended up with a small piece in most journals and newspapers, but *People* magazine did a cover picture of Florentyna with Albert Schmidt, the Remagen Rhodes Scholar. When it was discovered that Albert was a German immigrant whose grandparents had fled from Europe after escaping from a prisoner-of-war camp, David Hartman interviewed the young man the next day on 'Good Morning, America'. After that he seemed to be getting more publicity than Florentyna.

On her way back to Washington that weekend, Florentyna heard that the Governor of Colorado, whom she had never particularly considered a friend or political ally, had endorsed her without advance warning at a solar energy symposium in Boulder. Her approach to industry and conservation, he told the convention, offered the resource-rich western states their best hope for the future.

That day ended on an even higher note when Reuters tapped out the news right across America that the Welfare Department had delivered their first major report since the implementation of the Kane Act. For the first time since Florentyna's overhaul of the social service system, the number of welfare recipients leaving the register in a given year had surpassed the number of new applicants coming on.

Florentyna's financial backing was always a problem as even the most ardent supporters assumed she could foot her own campaign bills. Parkin, with the backing of the oil tycoons led by Marvin Snyder of Blade Oil, had never had to face the same problem. But during the next few days campaign contributions flowed in to Florentyna's office, along with telegrams of support and good wishes.

Influential journalists in London, Paris, Bonn and Tokyo began to tell their readers that if America wanted a President of international status and credibility there was no contest between Florentyna Kane and the cattle farmer from Texas.

Florentyna was delighted whenever she read these articles, but Edward reminded her that neither the readers nor the writers could pull any levers on any voting machines in America, although he felt for the first time they had Parkin on the run. He was also quick to point out that there were still more than four hundred of the three thousand three hundred and thirty-one delegates who after the Primaries and caucuses remained undecided. The political pundits estimated that two hundred of them were leaning towards the Vice-President while about a hundred would come out in favour of Florentyna. It looked as if it was going to be the closest convention roll call since Reagan ran against Ford.

*

After California, Florentyna returned to Washington with another suitcase full of dirty clothes. She knew she would have to cajole, coax and twist the arms of those four hundred delegates who still remained undecided. During the next four weeks, she spoke personally to three hundred and eighty-eight of them, some of them three or four times. It was always the women she found the least helpful, although it was obvious they were all enjoying the attention that was being showered on them, especially as in a month's time no one would ever phone them again.

Edward ordered a computer terminal for Florentyna's suite at the convention which had on-line access to the records at campaign headquarters. Information on all four hundred and twelve delegates who remained uncommitted, along with a short life history of each, right down to their hotel rooms in Detroit, was available. When he reached the convention city, he intended to be ready to put his final plan into operation.

For five days during the next week, Florentyna made certain she was never far from a television set. The Republicans were at the Cow Palace, San Francisco, haggling over whom they wanted to lead them, no one having excited the voters during the Primaries.

The choice of Russell Warner came as no surprise to Florentyna. He had been campaigning for the Presidency ever since he had become Governor of Ohio. The press's description of Warner as a good Governor in a bad year reminded Florentyna that her main task would be to defeat Parkin. Once again, Florentyna felt it was going to be easier to defeat the Republican standard-bearer than the opposition within her own party.

The weekend before the convention, Florentyna and Edward joined the family on Cape Cod. Exhausted, Florentyna still managed to beat Edward in a round of golf, and she thought he looked even more tired than she felt. She was thankful that the Baron was run so well by its new, young directors, who now included William.

Florentyna and Edward were both due to fly into Detroit on Monday morning where they had taken over yet another Baron. The hotel would be filled with Florentyna's staff, supporters, the press and one hundred and twenty-four of those uncommitted delegates.

As she said good night to Edward and then to the Secret Service men and women – whom she was beginning to treat as her adopted family – on Sunday night, Florentyna knew the next four days were going to be the most important in her political career.

35

WHEN JACK GERMOND OF the *Baltimore Sun* asked Florentyna on the plane when she had started working on her acceptance speech, she replied, 'Since my eleventh birthday.'

On the flight from New York to Detroit Metro Airport, Florentyna had read through her acceptance speech, already drafted in case she was nominated on the first ballot. Edward had predicted that she would not secure victory on the first roll call, but Florentyna felt she had to be prepared for any eventuality.

Her advisers considered the result was much more likely to be known after the second or even the third ballot by which time Senator Bradley would have released his one hundred and eighty-nine delegates.

During the previous week, she had drawn up a short list of four people whom she thought worthy of consideration to join her on the ticket as Vice-President. Bill Bradley still led the field and Florentyna felt he was her natural successor to the White House, but she was also considering Sam Nunn, Gary Hart and David Pryor.

Florentyna's thoughts were interrupted when the plane landed and she looked out of the windows to see a large, excited crowd awaiting her. She couldn't help wondering how many of them would also be there tomorrow when Pete Parkin arrived. She checked her hair in her compact mirror; a few white strands were showing in the dark hair but she made no attempt to disguise them, and she smiled at the thought that Pete Parkin's hair had remained the same implausible colour for the past thirty years. Florentyna wore a simple linen suit and her only piece of jewelry was a diamond-studded donkey.

Florentyna unbuckled her seat belt, rose and ducked her head under the overhead compartment. She stepped into the aisle and as she turned to leave, everyone in the plane began applauding. She suddenly realised that if she lost the nomination, this would be the last time that she would see them all together. Florentyna shook hands with all the members of the press corps, some of whom had been on the trail with her for five months. A crew member opened the cabin door and Florentyna stepped out on to the staircase, squinting into the July sun. The crowd let up a yell of 'There she is', and Florentyna walked down the steps and straight towards the waving banners because she always found that direct contact with the voters recharged her. As she touched the tarmac, she was once again surrounded by the Secret Service who dreaded crowds they could never control. She might sometimes think of being assassinated when she was alone, but never when she was in a crowd. Florentyna clasped outstretched hands and greeted as many people as possible before Edward guided her away to the waiting motorcade.

A line of ten small new Fords reminded her that Detroit had finally come to terms with the energy crisis. If Pete Parkin were to make the mistake of being driven in a Mercedes in this city, she would be the Democratic choice before Alabama cast its first vote. Secret Service men filled the first two cars while Florentyna was in the third, with Edward in front by the driver. Florentyna's personal doctor

rode in the fourth and her staff filled the remaining six
'mighty midgets', as the new small Ford had been dubbed. A
press corps bus followed at the rear with police outriders
dotted up and down the motorcade.

The front car moved off at a snail's pace so that Florentyna
could wave to the crowds, but as soon as they reached
Interstate 94, the cars travelled into Detroit at a steady fifty
miles an hour.

For twenty minutes Florentyna relaxed in the back seat
during the drive into the mid-town New Centre area, where
the motorcade exited at Woodward Avenue, turned south
towards the river, and slowed down to about five miles an
hour as the crowds filled the street to catch a glimpse of
Senator Kane. Florentyna's organising committee in Detroit
had distributed one hundred thousand handbills showing
the exact route she would take when she arrived in the city,
and her supporters cheered her all the way to the Baron
Hotel east of the Renaissance Centre on the Detroit River.
The Secret Service begged her to change the route but she
wouldn't hear of it.

Dozens of photographers and television crews were poised
awaiting her arrival as Florentyna stepped out of her car and
climbed the steps of the Detroit Baron; the whole area was lit
up by flashbulbs and arc lights. Once she was inside the hotel
lobby, the Secret Service men whisked her away to the
twenty-fourth floor, which had been reserved for her personal use. She quickly checked over the George Novak Suite to
see that everything she required was there because she knew
that this was going to be her prison for the next four days.
The only reason she would leave that room would be either to
accept the nomination as the Democratic Party candidate or
to declare her support for Pete Parkin.

A bank of telephones had been installed so that Florentyna
could keep in touch with the four hundred and twelve
wavering delegates. She spoke to thirty-eight of them before
dinner that night and then sat up until two o'clock the next
morning, going over the names and backgrounds of those
whom her team genuinely felt had not made up their minds.

Next morning, the Detroit *Free Press* was filled with pictures of her arrival in Detroit, though in truth she knew Pete Parkin would receive the same enthusiastic coverage tomorrow. At least she was relieved that the President had decided to remain on the sidelines when it came to supporting either candidate. The press had already treated that as a moral victory for Florentyna.

She put the newspaper down and began to watch the closed circuit television to see what was going on in the convention hall during the first morning. She also kept an eye on all three channels at lunchtime in case any one network came up with some exclusive piece of news that the other two had missed and on which the press would demand her instant reaction.

During the day, thirty-one of the wavering delegates were brought to meet her on the twenty-fourth floor. As the hour progressed, they were served coffee, iced tea, hot tea and cocktails. Florentyna stuck to iced tea or she would have been drunk by eleven o'clock.

She watched in silence as Pete Parkin arrived in *Air Force II* at the Detroit airport. One assistant told her that his crowd was smaller than the one that had turned out for her yesterday, while another said it was larger. She made a mental note of the assistant who said that Parkin's crowd was larger today and decided to listen to his opinions more carefully in the future.

Pete Parkin made a short speech at a specially set-up podium on the tarmac, his Vice-Presidential seal of office glistening in the sun. He said how delighted he was to be in the city that could rightly describe itself as the car capital of the world. 'I should know,' he added, 'I've owned Fords all my life.' Florentyna smiled.

By the end of two days under 'house arrest', Florentyna had complained so much about being cooped up all day that on Tuesday morning the Secret Service took her down in a freight lift so that she could stroll along the river front and enjoy the fresh air and the low skyline of Windsor, Canada, on the opposite bank. She had gone only a few paces before she was surrounded by well-wishers who wanted to shake her hand.

When she returned, Edward had some good news: five uncommitted delegates had decided to vote for her on the first ballot. He estimated that they only needed another seventy-three to be over the magic one thousand six hundred and sixty-six. On the monitor she followed the programme on the floor of the convention hall. A black school superintendent from Delaware expounded Florentyna's virtues and when she mentioned her name the blue placards filled the hall with 'Kane for President'. During the speech that followed red placards demanding 'Parkin for President' were in equal abundance. She paced around the suite until one thirty by which time she had seen forty-three more delegates and spoken on the phone to another fifty-eight.

The second day of the convention was devoted to the major platform speeches on policy, finance, welfare, defence and the key speech by Senator Pryor. Time and time again, delegates would declare that whichever of the two great candidates was selected, they would go on to beat the Republicans in November; but most of the delegates on the floor kept up a steady hum of conversation, all but oblivious to the men and women on the platform who might well make up a Democratic cabinet.

Florentyna broke away from the welfare debate to have a drink with two delegates from Nevada who were still undecided. She realised their next stop would probably be Parkin, who would also promise them their new highway, hospital, university or whatever excuse they came up with to visit both candidates. At least tomorrow night they would have to come down finally in someone's favour. She told Edward she wanted a fence put up in the middle of the room.

'Why?' asked Edward.

'So that wavering delegates have somewhere to sit when they come to meet me.'

Reports flowed in during the day about what Pete Parkin was up to, which seemed to be much the same as Florentyna except that he was booked into the Westin Hotel at the

Renaissance Centre. As neither of them could go into the convention arena, their daily routines continued: delegates, phone calls, press statements, meetings with party officials, and finally bed without much sleep.

On Wednesday, Florentyna was dressed by six o'clock in the morning and was driven quickly to the convention hall. Once they had arrived at the Joe Louis Arena, she was shown the passage she would walk down to deliver her acceptance speech if she were the chosen candidate. She walked out on to the platform and stood in front of the banked microphones, staring out at the twenty-one thousand empty seats. The tall, thin placards that rose from the floor high into the air proudly proclaimed the name of every state from Alabama to Wyoming. She made a special note of where the Illinois delegation would be seated so that she could wave to them the moment she entered the hall.

An enterprising photographer who had slept under a seat in the convention hall all night began taking photographs of her before he was smartly ushered out of the hall by the Secret Service. Florentyna smiled as she looked toward the ceiling where two hundred thousand red, white and blue balloons waited to cascade down on the victor. She had read somewhere that it would have taken fifty college students, using bicycle pumps, one week to fill them with air.

'Okay for testing, Senator Kane?' said an impersonal voice from she could not tell where.

'My fellow Americans, this is the greatest moment in my life, and I intend to . . .'

'That's fine, Senator. Loud and clear,' said the chief electrician as he walked up through the empty seats. Pete Parkin was scheduled to go through the same routine at seven o'clock.

Florentyna was driven back to her hotel where she had breakfast with her closest staff, who were all nervous and laughed at each other's jokes, however feeble, but fell silent whenever she spoke. They watched Pete Parkin doing his usual morning jog for the television crews; it made them all hysterical when someone in an N.B.C. windcheater holding a mini-camera accelerated past a breathless Vice-President three times to get a better picture.

The roll call vote was due to start at nine that evening. Edward had set up fifty phone lines direct to every state chairman on the convention floor so that he could be in constant touch if something unexpected happened. Florentyna was seated behind a desk with only two phones, but at the single touch of a button she had access to any of the fifty lines. While the hall was beginning to fill they tested each line and Edward pronounced that they were ready for anything, and now all they could do was use every minute left to contact more delegates. By five-thirty that evening, Florentyna had spoken to three hundred and ninety-two of them in three days.

By seven o'clock the Joe Louis Arena was almost packed, although there was still a full hour to go until the names were placed in nomination. No one who had travelled to Detroit wanted to miss one minute of the unfolding drama.

At seven-thirty, Florentyna watched the party officials begin to take their seats on the stage and she remembered her days as a page at the Chicago Convention when she had first met John Kennedy. She knew then that they had all been told to arrive at certain times; the later you were asked the more senior you were. Forty years on, and she was hoping to be asked last.

The biggest cheer of the evening was reserved for Senator Bill Bradley, who had already announced he would address the convention if there was a deadlock after the first ballot. At seven forty-five, the Speaker of the House of Representatives, Marty Lynch, rose and tried to bring the convention to order but he could scarcely make himself heard above the klaxons, whistles, drums, bugles and cries of 'Kane' and 'Parkin' from supporters trying to outscream each other. Florentyna sat watching the scene but showed no sign of emotion. When finally there was a semblance of order, the chairman introduced Mrs. Bess Gardner, who had been chosen to record the votes, although everyone in the hall knew that the results would flash up on to the vast video screen above her head before she even had a chance to confirm them.

At eight o'clock the chairman brought his gavel down; some saw the little wooden hammer hit the base but no one heard it. For another twenty minutes the noise continued as the chairman still made no impression on the delegates. Eventually at eight twenty-three Marty Lynch could be heard asking Rich Daley, the mayor of Chicago, to place the name of Senator Kane in nomination; ten more minutes of noise before the mayor was able to deliver his nominating speech. Florentyna and her staff sat in silence through a speech that described her public record in the most glowing terms. She also listened attentively when Senator Ralph Brooks nominated Pete Parkin. The reception of both proposals by the delegates would have made a full symphony orchestra sound like a tin whistle. Nominations for Bill Bradley and the usual handful of predictable favourite sons followed in quick succession.

At nine o'clock, the chairman looked down into the body of the hall and called upon Alabama to cast its vote. Florentyna sat staring at the screen like a prisoner about to face trial by jury – wanting to know the verdit even before she had heard the evidence. The perspiring chairman of the Alabama delegation picked up his microphone and shouted, 'The great state of Alabama, the heart of the south, casts twenty-eight votes for Vice-President Parkin and seventeen votes for Senator Kane.' Although everyone had known how Alabama was going to vote since March 11th, over four months before, this didn't stop Parkin posters from being waved frantically, and it was another twelve minutes before the chairman was able to call on Alaska.

'Alaska, the forty-ninth state to join the Union, casts seven of its votes for Senator Kane, the forty-second President of the United States, three for Pete Parkin and one for Senator Bradley.' It was the turn of Florentyna's followers to unleash a prolonged uproar in support of their candidate, but Parkin led the field for the first half hour until California declared two hundred and fourteen for Senator Kane, ninety-two for Parkin.

'God bless Bella,' said Florentyna, but had to watch the Vice-President go back into the lead with the help of Florida, Georgia and Idaho. When they reached the state of Illinois the convention nearly came to a halt. Mrs. Kalamich, who had welcomed Florentyna the first night in Chicago nearly twenty years before, had been chosen as vice-chairman of the Illinois Democratic Party in convention year to deliver the verdict of her delegates.

'Mr. Chairman, this is the greatest moment of my life' – Florentyna smiled as Mrs. Kalamich continued – 'to say to you that the great state of Illinois is proud to cast every one of its one hundred and seventy-nine votes for its favourite daughter and the first woman President of the United States, Senator Florentyna Kane.' The Kane supporters went berserk as she took the lead for the second time, but Florentyna knew her rival would create the same effect when the moment came for Texas to declare their allegiance, and in fact Parkin went ahead for a second time with one thousand four hundred and forty delegates to Florentyna's one thousand three hundred and seventy-one after his home state had given their verdict. Bill Bradley had picked up ninety-seven delegates along the way and now looked certain to end up with enough votes to prevent there being an outright winner on the first round.

As the chairman pressed forward with each state – Utah, Vermont, Virginia – the network computers were already flashing up on the screen that there would be no winner on the first ballot, but it was ten forty-seven before Tom Brokaw announced the first round verdict: one thousand five hundred and twenty-two for Senator Kane, one thousand four hundred and eighty for Vice-President Parkin, one hundred and eighty-nine for Senator Bradley and one hundred and forty for favourite sons.

The chairman told the delegates that Senator Bradley would now address them. Another eleven minutes passed before he could speak. Florentyna had talked to him on the phone every day of the convention and steadfastly avoided asking him to join her ticket as Vice-President, because she felt such an offer would smack of bribery rather than of choosing him because she felt he was the right man to succeed her. Although Ralph Brooks was the favourite for the post in the Parkin camp, Florentyna couldn't help wondering if Pete Parkin had already offered Bradley the chance to join him.

At last the senior Senator from New Jersey was able to address the convention. 'My fellow members of the Democratic Party,' he began. 'I thank you for the support you have given me during this election year, but the time has come for me to withdraw from this Presidential race and release my delegates to vote the way their conscience guides them.' The hall fell almost silent. Bradley spoke for several minutes about the sort of person he wanted to see in the White House but did not openly support either candidate. He closed with the words: 'I pray you will select the right person to lead our country,' and was cheered for several minutes after he had returned to his seat.

By this time, most people in suite 2400 of the Baron had no nails left; only Florentyna remained outwardly calm, although Edward noticed that her fist was clenched. He quickly returned to work on the green section of his master printout, which showed only the Bradley delegates, but there wasn't much he could do while they were all on the floor except phone the chairman of each state committee and keep them working. The phones came ringing back; it seemed that the Bradley delegates were also split down the middle. Some of them would even continue to vote for Bradley in the second round in case the convention became deadlocked and had to turn to him in the end.

The second roll call vote started at eleven twenty-one with Alabama, Alaska and Arizona showing no changes. The balloting dragged on from state to state until they recorded the Wyoming decision at twelve twenty-three. At the end of the second round, the convention was still undecided, with the only important change being that Pete Parkin had taken a slight lead – 1,629–1,604 – while ninety-eight delegates had remained uncommitted or faithful to Senator Bradley.

At twelve thirty-seven the chairman said, 'Enough is enough, we'll start the roll call again tomorrow evening at seven o'clock.'

'Why not first thing tomorrow morning?' asked one of Florentyna's sleepless, young aides as he was leaving the arena.

'As the boss pointed out,' said Janet, 'elections are run for the benefit of the networks, and ten o'clock tomorrow morning just isn't prime time.'

'Are the networks going to be responsible for which candidate we choose?' he asked.

They both laughed. The sleepless aide repeated the same comment twenty-four hours later – when neither of them laughed.

The exhausted delegates slumped off to their rooms, aware that on a third ballot most states freed their delegates from their original pledges, which meant that they could now vote any way they pleased. Edward and his team didn't know where to start, but they picked up the printout and went through each delegate from Alabama to Wyoming for a third time that night, hoping they would have a plan for every state by eight o'clock the next morning.

Florentyna hardly slept that night and at ten past six she walked back into the living room of her suite in a dressing gown to find Edward still poring over the lists.

'I'll need you at eight,' he said, not looking up at her.

'Good morning,' she said, and kissed him on the forehead.

'Good morning.'

Florentyna stretched and yawned. 'What happens at eight?'

'We speak to thirty Bradley and undeclared delegates an hour all through the day. I want you to have spoken to at least two hundred and fifty by five this afternoon. We'll have all six phones manned every minute of that time so that there will never be less than two people waiting to speak to you.'

'Won't eight be a little early?' asked Florentyna.

'No,' said Edward. 'But I won't bother the west coast delegates until after lunch.'

Florentyna returned to her room realising yet again how much thought Edward had put into her whole campaign, and she remembered Richard saying how lucky she was to have two men who adored her.

At eight o'clock, she started work with a large glass of orange juice by her side. As the morning proceeded, the team became more convinced that the first roll call that evening would give the majority to their candidate. The feeling in that room was turning to one of victory.

At ten forty Bill Bradley rang to say that if his delegates caused another deadlock he was going to recommend they vote for Florentyna. Florentyna thanked him.

At eleven thirty-seven Edward passed Florentyna the phone. This time it wasn't a well-wisher.

'It's Pete Parkin here. I think we ought to get together. Can I come and see you immediately?'

Florentyna wanted to say 'I'm far too busy' but only said 'Yes'.

'I'll be right over.'

'Whatever can he want?' said Edward as Florentyna handed him back the phone.

'I have no idea, but we don't have long to wait before we find out.'

Pete Parkin arrived via the freight lift with two Secret Service agents and his campaign manager.

After unnatural pleasantries had been exchanged – the two candidates hadn't spoken to each other for the past six months – and coffee poured, the contenders were left alone. They sat in comfortable chairs facing each other. They might as well have been discussing the weather, not which one of them should rule the Western world. The Texan got straight down to business.

'I am prepared to make a deal with you, Florentyna.'

'I'm listening.'

'If you withdraw I'll offer you the Vice-Presidency.'

'You must be –'

'Hear me out, Florentyna,' said Parkin, putting up his massive hand like a traffic cop. 'If you accept my offer, I will only serve one term if elected, and then I'll support you for the job in 1996 with full White House backing. You're five years younger than I am and there is no reason why you shouldn't complete two full terms.'

Over the previous thirty minutes Florentyna had thought of many reasons why her rival might want to see her, but she had not been prepared for this.

'If you don't accept my offer and I win tonight, I'll be giving the number two spot to Ralph Brooks, who has already confirmed that he is willing to run.'

'I'll call you by two this afternoon,' was all that Florentyna said.

Once Pete Parkin had left with his aides, Florentyna discussed the offer with Edward and Janet, who both felt that they had come too far to give in now. 'Who knows what the situation might be in four years' time?' Edward pointed out. 'You might be like Humphrey trying to recover from Johnson. In any case, we only need a deadlock this time and Bradley's delegates will push us comfortably over the top on the fourth ballot.'

'And I bet Parkin knows that,' added Janet.

Florentyna sat motionless listening to her different advisers and then asked to be left alone.

Florentyna phoned Pete Parkin at one forty-three and politely declined his offer, explaining she was confident that she was going to win on the first ballot that night. He made no reply.

By two o'clock the press had got hold of the news of the secret meeting and the phones in suite 2400 never stopped as they tried to find out what had happened. Edward kept Florentyna concentrating on the delegates and with each call she was becoming more and more assured that Pete Parkin's move had been made more out of desperation than confidence. 'He's played his final card,' said Janet, smirking.

At six o'clock everyone in suite 2400 was back in front of the television: there were no longer any delegates left to speak to; they were all on the convention floor. Edward still had his phone bank linked up to all the state chairmen and the early reports back from them indicated that the feeling they had picked up votes all through the day was accurate.

Exactly at the point when Florentyna relaxed and felt confident for the first time, the bombshell fell. Edward had just handed her yet another iced tea when C.B.S. flashed up on the screen 'Newsbreak' and a camera went over to Dan Rather, who told a stunned audience only fifteen minutes before the roll call was due to start that he was about to interview Vice-President Parkin on the reason for his secret meeting with Senator Kane. The C.B.S. camera panned down on the florid face of the big Texan and to Florentyna's horror, the whole thing was going out live on the vast screen in the convention hall. She remembered that the Rules Committee had decided to allow anything to go up on the screen that might affect the delegates; this was meant to stop rumours spreading around the convention hall about what was really going on outside, to be sure that what had happened between Ford and Reagan in the 1980 convention over the picking of a running mate could never happen again. It was the first time that the delegates in the hall had been unanimously silent for four days.

The camera switched back to the C.B.S. interviewer.

'Mr. Vice-President, we know you had a meeting with Senator Kane today. Can you tell me the reason you asked to see her?'

'Certainly, Dan. It was first and foremost because I am interested in the unity of my party and above all, Dan, in beating the Republicans.'

Florentyna and her staff were mesmerised. She could see the delegates on the floor hanging on every word and she was helpless to do anything but listen.

'Can I ask what took place at that meeting?'

'I asked Senator Kane if she would be willing to serve as

my Vice-President and make up a Democratic team that would be unbeatable.'

'How did she reply to your suggestion?'

'She said she wanted to think the offer over. You see, Dan, I believe together we can lick the Republicans.'

'Ask him what my final answer was,' said Florentyna, but it was no use; the cameras were already switching to a half-crazed convention hall ready for the first vote. Edward phoned C.B.S. and demanded equal time for Florentyna. Dan Rather agreed to interview Senator Kane immediately, but Florentyna knew that they were already too late. Once the voting had started the committee had agreed that nothing would go on that screen except the ballot tally. No doubt they would have to revise the rule by the next convention, but all Florentyna could think of was Miss Tredgold's views on television: '*Too many instant decisions will be made that will later be regretted.*'

The chairman banged his gavel and called upon Alabama to begin the roll call and the Camellia State showed a two-vote switch to Parkin. When Florentyna lost one delegate from Alaska and two from Arizona she knew her only hope was another deadlock so that she could put her version of the meeting with Parkin on television before the next vote. She sat and watched herself lose one vote here and a couple there but when Illinois held firm she hoped the tide might turn. Edward and the team had been working the phones non stop.

Then the next blow came.

Edward received a call from one of his campaign managers on the floor to say that Parkin assistants had started a rumour in the hall that Florentyna had accepted his offer. A rumour he knew Florentyna would never be able to trace back directly to Parkin or have time to rebut. Although as each state's turn came to vote, Edward fought to stem the tide. When they reached West Virginia, Parkin only needed twenty-five more delegates to go over the top. They gave him twenty-one, so he needed four from the penultimate state, Wisconsin. Florentyna was confident that all three delegates from Wyoming, the final state to vote, would remain loyal to her.

'The great state of Wisconsin, mindful of its responsibility tonight' – once again the hall was totally silent – 'and believing in the unity of the party above all personal considerations gives all its eleven votes to the next President of the United States, Pete Parkin.'

The delegates went berserk. In suite 2400 the result was met with stunned silence.

Florentyna had been beaten by a cheap but brilliant trick. And its true genius was that if she denied everything and gave her version of Parkin's behaviour, the Democrats might well lose the White House to the Republicans and she would be made the scapegoat.

Thirty minutes later, Pete Parkin arrived at the Joe Louis Arena amid cheers and the strains of 'Happy Days Are Here Again'. He spent another twelve minutes waving to the delegates and when at last he managed to bring the hall to silence he said: 'I hope to stand on this platform tomorrow night with the greatest lady in America and place before the nation a team that will whip the Republicans so that those elephants will never forget it.'

Once again the delegates roared their approval. During the next hour Florentyna's staff crept back to their rooms until Edward was left alone with her.

'Do I accept?'

'You have no choice. If you don't, and the Democrats lose, the blame will be placed at your door.'

'And if I tell the truth?'

'It will be misunderstood; they will say you're a bad loser after your opponent had held out the olive branch of reconciliation. And don't forget President Ford predicted ten years ago that the first woman President would have to have been Vice-President before the American people would find the idea acceptable.'

'That might be true, but if Richard Nixon were alive today,' said Florentyna bitterly, 'he would be on the phone to Pete Parkin congratulating him on a trick far superior to any he pulled off against Muskie or Humphrey.' Florentyna yawned. 'I'm going to bed, Edward, I will have made a decision by the morning.'

At eight thirty Pete Parkin sent an emissary to ask if Florentyna had made up her mind. She replied that she wanted to see him again in private.

This time, Parkin arrived with three television companies in tow and as many reporters who could get hold of red press passes. When they were alone, Florentyna found it hard to control her temper even though she had decided not to remonstrate with Parkin but simply asked if he would confirm that he intended to serve one term.

'Yes,' he said, looking Florentyna straight in the eye.

'And at the next election you'll give me your full backing?'

'You have my word on that,' he said.

'On those terms I'm willing to serve as Vice-President.'

When he had left the room, Edward listened to what had taken place and said, 'We know exactly what his word is worth.'

As she entered the convention hall later that night, Florentyna was greeted by a cascade of noise. Pete Parkin held her hand up high, and the delegates once more roared their approval. Only Ralph Brooks looked sour.

Florentyna felt her acceptance speech as Vice-Presidential candidate was below her best, but they cheered her just the same. However, the biggest cheer of the evening was raised for Pete Parkin when he addressed the delegates; after all, he had been introduced as their new hero, the man who had brought honest unity to the party.

Florentyna flew to Boston and retreated to Cape Cod the next morning after a nauseating press conference with the Democratic candidate, who kept referring to her as 'that great little lady from Illinois'.

When they parted, in full view of the press, he kissed her on the cheek. She felt like a prostitute who had accepted his money and found it was too late to change her mind about going to bed.

36

TAKING ADVANTAGE OF THE fact that the campaign did not start until after Labour Day, Florentyna returned to Washington to catch up on her neglected Senatorial duties. She even found time to visit Chicago.

She spoke to Pete Parkin on the phone every day and certainly he could not have been more friendly and cooperative about fitting in with her arrangements. They agreed to meet at his White House office to discuss the final plan for the campaign. Florentyna tried to fulfil all her other commitments before the meeting so she could devote herself entirely to electioneering during the last nine weeks.

On September 2nd, accompanied by Edward and Janet, Florentyna arrived at the west wing of the White House to be greeted by Ralph Brooks, who clearly remained a trusted lieutenant of the candidate. She was determined not to be the cause of any friction between herself and Brooks so near the election, especially as she knew that Brooks had expected to be the Vice-Presidential candidate himself. Senator Brooks took them from the reception area through to Pete Parkin's office. It was the first time Florentyna had seen the room she might occupy in a few weeks, and she was surprised by the warmth, with its yellow walls and ivory moulding. Fresh flowers sat on Parkin's mahogany desk, and the walls were hung with Remington oil paintings. Parkin's love of the west, Florentyna thought. The late summer sun flooded in through the south-facing windows.

Pete Parkin jumped up from behind his desk and came

over to greet her, just a little too effusively. Then they all sat around a table in the centre of the room.

'I think you all know Ralph,' said Pete Parkin with a slightly uncomfortable laugh. 'He's worked out a campaign strategy which I am sure you'll find most impressive.'

Ralph Brooks unfolded a large map of the United States on the table in front of them. 'I feel the main consideration to keep uppermost in our minds is that to capture the White House we must have two hundred and seventy electoral college votes. Although it is obviously important and satisfying to win the popular vote, as we all know it's still the electoral college which selects the next President. For this reason, I have coloured the states black that I feel we have least chance of winning, and white those that are traditionally safe in the Democrat column. That leaves the key marginal states which I've marked in red, which between them make up one hundred and seventy-one electoral college votes.

'I believe both Pete and Florentyna should visit all the red states at least once, but Pete should concentrate his energies in the south while Florentyna spends most of her time in the north. Only California, with its massive forty-five electoral votes, will have to be visited by both of you regularly. During the sixty-two days left before the election, we must use every spare minute on states where we have a genuine chance and make only token visits to those fringe areas we captured in the 1964 landslide. As for our own white states, we must be prepared to visit them all once so that we cannot be accused of taking them for granted. I consider Ohio a no-hoper as it's Russell Warner's home state, but we mustn't let the Republicans assume Florida is theirs just because Warner's running mate was once the state's senior Senator. Now I've also worked out a daily routine for you both, starting next Monday,' he continued, handing the candidate and Florentyna separate sheaves of paper, 'and I think you should be in contact with each other at least twice a day, at eight o'clock in the morning and eleven o'clock at night, always Central Time.'

Florentyna found herself impressed by the work Ralph Brooks had put in before the briefing and could appreciate why Parkin had become so reliant on him. For the next hour Brooks answered queries that arose from his plan, and agreement was reached on their basic strategy for the campaign. At twelve thirty, the Vice-President and Florentyna walked on to the north portico of the White House to speak to the press. Ralph Brooks seemed to have statistics for everything: The press, he warned them, were divided like everyone else. One hundred and fifty papers with twenty-two million readers were already supporting the Democrats, while one hundred and forty-two with twenty-one point seven million readers were backing the Republicans. If they needed to know, he added, he could supply the relevant facts for any paper in the country.

Florentyna looked out across the lawn at Lafayette Square, dotted with lunchtime strollers and picnickers. If elected, she would rarely again be able to visit Washington's parks and memorials. Not unaccompanied, anyway. Parkin escorted her back to the Vice-President's office when the press had asked all the usual questions and received the usual answers. When they returned to the office they found that Parkin's Filipino stewards had set up lunch on the conference table. Florentyna came away from the meeting feeling a lot better about how matters were working out, especially since the Vice-President had twice in Brooks's hearing referred to their earlier agreement concerning 1996. Still Florentyna considered that it would be a long time before she could totally trust Parkin.

On September 7th she flew into Chicago to start her part of the election campaign but found that even though the press was still hard put to keep up with the daily routine she put herself through, she lacked the drive that had been a trademark of her earlier campaigning.

The Brooks plan ran smoothly for the first few days as Florentyna travelled through Illinois, Massachusetts and New Hampshire. She met with no surprises until she arrived in New York where the press was waiting in large numbers at the Albany airport. They wanted to know her views about Pete Parkin's treatment of Mexican Chicanos. Florentyna confessed that she didn't know what they were talking about, so they told her that the candidate had said that he had never had any trouble with Chicanos on his ranch; they were like his own children. Civil rights leaders were up in arms all over the country and all Florentyna could think of to say was, 'I am sure he has been misunderstood or else his words have been taken out of context.'

Russell Warner, the Republican candidate, said there could be no misunderstanding. Pete Parkin was simply a racist. Florentyna kept repudiating these statements although she suspected they were rooted in truth. Both Florentyna and Pete Parkin had to break off from their scheduled plans to fly to Alabama and attend the funeral of Ralph Abernathy. Ralph Brooks described the death of an aide as timely. When Florentyna heard what he had said she nearly swore at him in front of the press.

Florentyna continued her travels through Pennsylvania, West Virginia and Virginia, before going on to California, where she was joined by Edward. Bella and Claude took them out to a restaurant in Chinatown. The manager gave them a corner alcove where no one could see them, or more important, hear them, but the relaxed break only lasted for a few hours before Florentyna had to fly on to Los Angeles.

The press was becoming bored with the petty squabbles between Parkin and Warner over everything except real issues, and when the two candidates appeared together on a television debate in Pittsburgh, the universal opinion was that they had both lost, and that the only person of Presidential stature in the whole campaign was turning out to be Senator Kane. Many journalists expressed the view that it was a tragedy that Senator Kane had ever let it be known she was willing to be Pete Parkin's running mate.

'I'll write what really happened in my memoirs,' she told Edward. 'Only by then who will care?'

'In truth, no one,' replied Edward. 'How many Americans could tell you the name of Harry Truman's Vice-President?'

The next day, Pete Parkin flew into Los Angeles to join Florentyna for one of their few joint appearances. She met him at the airport. He walked off *Air Force II* holding up Missouri's *Unterrified Democrat*, the only paper which had run as its headline 'Parkin Wins Debate'. Florentyna had to admire the way he could make a rhinoceros look thin-skinned. California was to be the last stop before returning to their own states, and they held a final rally in the Rose Bowl. Parkin and Florentyna were surrounded by stars, half of whom were on stage for the free publicity they were guaranteed whichever candidate was in town. Along with Dustin Hoffman, Al Pacino and Jane Fonda, Florentyna spent most of her time signing autographs. She didn't know what to say to the girl who, puzzled by her signature, asked: 'Which was your last movie?'

The following morning, Florentyna flew back to Chicago while Pete Parkin left for Texas. As soon as Florentyna's 707 touched down in the Windy City, she was greeted by a crowd of over thirty thousand people, the biggest any candidate had had on the campaign trail.

On the morning of the election she voted at the elementary school in the Ninth District, in the presence of the usual group of reporters from the networks and the press. She smiled for them, knowing she would be forgotten news within a week if the Democrats lost. She spent the day going from committee room to polling places to television studio, and ended up back at her suite in the Chicago Baron a few minutes after the polls had closed.

Florentyna indulged herself with her first really long hot bath in over five months and a change of clothes that was not affected by whom she was spending the evening with. Then she was joined by William, Joanna, Annabel and Richard who, at the age of six, was being allowed to watch his first election. Edward arrived just after ten thirty and for the first time in his life saw Florentyna with her shoes off and her feet propped up on a table.

'Miss Tredgold wouldn't have approved.'

'Miss Tredgold never had to do seven months of campaigning without a break,' she replied.

In a room full of food, drink, family and friends, Florentyna watched the results come in from the east coast. It was obvious from the moment that New Hampshire went to the Democrats and Massachusetts to the Republicans that they were all in for a long night. Florentyna was delighted that the weather had been dry right across the nation that day. She had never forgotten Theodore H. White telling her that America always voted Republican until five on election day. From that time on, working men and women on their way home decide whether to stop at the polls; if they do and *only* if they do, the country will go Democratic. It looked as though a lot of them had stopped by, but she wondered if it would turn out to be enough. By midnight, the Democrats had taken Illinois and Texas but lost Ohio and Pennsylvania and when the voting machines closed down in California, three hours after New York, America still hadn't elected a President. The private polls conducted outside the voting stations proved only that the nation's largest state wasn't wild about either candidate.

At the George Novak Suite in the Chicago Baron, some ate, some drank, some slept. But Florentyna remained wide awake throughout the whole proceedings and at two thirty-three, C.B.S. announced the result she had been waiting for: California had been won by the Democrats, the returns showing 50.2 to 49.8, a margin of a mere three hundred and thirty-two thousand votes, giving the election to Parkin. Florentyna picked up the phone by her side.

'Are you calling the President-elect to congratulate him?' asked Edward.

'No,' said Florentyna. 'I'm calling Bella to thank her for putting him there.'

37

FLORENTYNA SPENT THE NEXT few days in Cape Cod having a total rest, only to find she kept waking at six each morning with nothing to do except wait for the morning papers. She was delighted when Edward joined her on Wednesday, but couldn't get used to him affectionately addressing her as 'V.P.'

Pete Parkin had already called a press conference at his Texas ranch to say he would not be naming his cabinet until the New Year. Florentyna returned to Washington on November 14th, for the lame-duck session of Congress, and prepared for her move from the Russell Building to the White House. Although her time was fully occupied in the Senate and Illinois, it came as a surprise to her that she spoke to the President-elect only two or three times a week and then on the phone. Congress adjourned two weeks after Thanksgiving, and Florentyna returned to Cape Cod for a family Christmas with a grandson who kept calling her Grannie President.

'Not yet,' she replied.

On January 9th the President arrived in Washington and held a press conference to announce his cabinet. Although Florentyna had not been consulted on his new appointments no one was expecting any real surprises: Charles Selover was made Secretary of Defence and would have been everyone's choice. Paul Rowe retained his position as Director of the CIA, Pierre Levale became Attorney-General and Michael

Brewer, National Security Adviser. Florentyna didn't raise an eyebrow until he came to his choice for Secretary of State. She sat in disbelief when the President declared: 'Chicago can rightly be proud of having produced the Vice-President as well as the Secretary of State.'

By Inauguration Day, Florentyna's personal belongings in the Baron had been packed up and were all ready for delivery to the Vice-President's official residence on Observatory Circle. The huge Victorian house seemed grotesquely large for a family of one. For this Inauguration, Florentyna's whole family sat in seats one row behind Pete Parkin's wife and daughters, while Florentyna sat on one side of the President, Ralph Brooks sat immediately behind him. When she stepped forward to take the oath of office, her only thought was to wish that Richard were there by her side to remind her she was getting closer and closer. Glancing sideways at Pete Parkin, she concluded that Richard would still have voted Republican.

The Chief Justice, William Rehnquist, gave her a warm smile as she repeated after him the oath of office for the Vice-President.

'"I do solemnly swear that I will support and defend the Constitution of the United States against all enemies, foreign and domestic. . . ."'

'"I do solemnly swear that I will support and defend the Constitution of the United States against all enemies, foreign and domestic. . . ."'

Florentyna's words sounded clear and confident, perhaps because she had learned the oath by heart. Annabel winked at her as she returned to her seat amid deafening applause.

After the Chief Justice administered the Presidential oath to Parkin, Florentyna listened intently as America's new chief executive delivered his Inaugural Address about which she had not been consulted and hadn't even seen in final draft until the night before. Once again he referred to her as the greatest little lady in the land.

After the Inauguration ceremony was over, Parkin, Brooks and Florentyna joined Congressional leaders for lunch in the Capitol. Her Senate colleagues gave Florentyna a warm welcome when she took her place on the dais. After lunch they climbed into limousines for the drive down Pennsylvania Avenue that would lead the Inaugural parade. Sitting in the enclosed viewing stand in front of the White House, Florentyna watched the floats, marching bands and assorted governors roll by representing every one of the fifty states. She stood and applauded when the farmers of Illinois saluted her, and then after making a token visit to every one of the Inaugural balls she spent her first night in the Vice-President's house and realised the closer she got to the top, the more alone she became.

The next morning, the President held his first cabinet meeting. This time Ralph Brooks sat on his right-hand side. The group, visibly tired from the seven Inaugural balls the night before, assembled in the Cabinet Room. Florentyna sat at the far end of the long oval table, surrounded by men with whose views she had rarely been in accord in the past, aware that she was going to have to spend four years battling against them before she could hope to form her own cabinet. She wondered how many of them knew about her deal with Parkin.

As soon as Florentyna had settled into her wing of the White House, she appointed Janet as head of her personal office. Many of the positions left vacant by Parkin's staff she also filled with her old team from the campaign and Senate days.

Of the remaining staff she inherited, she quickly learned how valuable their skills and special qualifications would have been had they not disappeared one by one as the President offered them executive branch jobs. Within three months, Parkin had denuded her office of all the most competent staff, even reaching into her inner circle of advisers.

Florentyna tried not to show her anger when the President

offered Janet the position of Under Secretary of the Department of Health and Human Service.

Janet didn't hesitate over the new opportunity: and in a handwritten letter to the President she accepted the great compliment he had paid her but explained in detail why she felt unable to consider any government position other than to serve the Vice-President.

'If you can wait four years, so can I,' she explained.

Florentyna had often read that the life of the Vice-President was, to quote John Nance Garner, 'not worth a bucketful of warm spit', but even she was surprised to find how little real work she had to do compared with her days in Congress. She had received more letters when she had been a Senator. Everyone seemed to write to the President or their Congressman. Even the people had worked out that the Vice-President had no power. Florentyna enjoyed presiding over the Senate for important debates, because it kept her in contact with colleagues who would be helping her again in four years' time. They made sure she was aware of what was being said covertly in the halls of Congress, as well as on the House and Senate floor. Many Senators used her to get messages through to the President, but as time went by she began to wonder whom she should use for the same purpose, as the days turned into weeks in which Pete Parkin did not bother to consult her on any major issue.

During her first year as Vice-President, Florentyna made goodwill tours to Brazil and Japan, attended the funerals of Willy Brandt in Berlin and Edward Heath in London, carried out on-site inspections of three natural disasters and chaired so many special task forces that she felt qualified to publish her own guide to how the government works.

The first year went slowly, the second even slower. The only highlight was being sent to represent the government at the crowning of King Charles III in Westminster Abbey after Queen Elizabeth II's abdication in 1994. Florentyna stayed with Ambassador John Sawyer at Winfield House, conscious of how similar their respective roles were in the matter of form over substance. She seemed to spend hours chatting about how the world was run and what the President was doing on subjects such as the building up of Russian troops on the Pakistan border. She gained most of her information from the *Washington Post* and envied Ralph Brooks's real involvement as Secretary of State. Although she kept herself well informed as to what was going on in the world at large, for only the second time in her life she was bored. She longed for 1996, fearing her years as Vice-President would yield very few positive results.

Once *Air Force II* had landed back at Andrews, Florentyna returned to her work and spent the rest of the week checking through the State and CIA traffic that had piled up in her absence abroad. She rested over the weekend despite C.B.S. informing the public that the dollar had suffered as a result of the international crisis. The Russians were massing more forces on the Pakistan border, a fact which the President had dismissed in his weekly press conference as 'not of great importance'. The Russians, he assured the assembled journalists, were not interested in crossing any borders into countries that had treaties with the United States.

During the following week the panic seemed to subside and the dollar recovered. 'It's a cosmetic recovery' – Florentyna pointed out to Janet – 'caused by the Russians. The international brokers are reporting that the Bank of Moscow is selling gold which is exactly what they did before invading Afghanistan. I do wish bankers would not treat history on a week-to-week basis.'

Although several politicians and journalists contacted Florentyna to stress their fears, she could only placate them as she watched proceedings from the wings. She even considered making an appointment to see the President but by Friday evening most Americans were on their way home for a peaceful weekend convinced the immediate danger had passed. Florentyna remained in her office in the West Wing that Friday evening and read through the cables from ambassadors and agents on the Indian sub-continent. The more she read the more she felt unable to share the President's relaxed stance. As there was very little she could do about it, she neatly stacked up the papers, put them into a special red folder and prepared to go home. She checked her watch. Six thirty-two. Edward had flown down from New York, and she was due to join him for dinner at seven thirty. She was laughing about the thought of filing her own papers when Janet rushed into the office.

'There's an intelligence report that the Russians are mobilising,' she said.

'Where's the President?' was Florentyna's immediate reaction.

'I've no idea. I saw him leaving the White House by helicopter about three hours ago.'

Florentyna reopened her file and stared back down at the cables while Janet remained standing in front of her desk.

'Well, who *will* know where he is?'

'You can be sure Ralph Brooks does,' said Janet.

'Get me the Secretary of State on the line.'

Janet left for her own office while Florentyna checked through the reports again. She quickly went over the salient points raised by the American ambassador in Islamabad before rereading the assessments of General Pierce Dixon, the chairman of the joint chiefs of staff.

The Russians, it was reliably documented, now had ten divisions of troops on the Afghanistan-Pakistan border and their forces had been multiplying over the past few days. It was known that half their Pacific fleet was sailing towards Karachi, while two battlegroups were carrying out 'exercises' in the Indian Ocean. General Dixon directed an increased intelligence watch when it was confirmed that fifty MIG 25s and SU 7s had landed at Kabul military airport at six that evening. Florentyna checked her watch: nine minutes past seven.

'Where is the bloody man?' she said out loud. Her phone buzzed.

'The Secretary of State on the line for you,' said Janet. Florentyna waited for several seconds.

'What can I do for you?' asked Ralph Brooks, sounding as if Florentyna had interrupted him.

'Where is the President?' she asked for a third time.

'At this moment he's on *Air Force I*,' said Brooks quickly.

'Stop lying, Ralph. It's transparent, even on the phone. Now tell me where the President is.'

'Halfway to California.'

'If we have the Soviets on the move and an increased intelligence watch, why hasn't he been advised to return?'

'We have advised him, but he has to land to refuel.'

'As you well know, *Air Force I* doesn't need to refuel for that length of journey.'

'He isn't on *Air Force I*.'

'Why the hell not?'

No reply came.

'I suggest you level with me, Ralph, even if it's only to save your own skin.'

There was a further pause.

'He was on his way to see a friend in California when the crisis broke.'

'I don't believe it,' said Florentyna. 'Who does he think he is? The President of France?'

'I have everything under control,' said Brooks, ignoring her comment. 'His plane will touch down at Colorado airport in a few minutes' time. The President will immediately transfer to an Air Force F15 and be back in Washington within two hours.

'What type of aircraft is he on at the moment?' asked Florentyna.

'A private 737 owned by Marvin Snyder of Blade Oil.'

'Can the President enter the secure National Command System network from the plane?' asked Florentyna. No reply was forthcoming. 'Did you hear what I said?' she rapped out.

'Yes,' said Ralph. 'The truth is that the plane doesn't have complete security.'

'Are you telling me that over the next two hours any ham radio enthusiast could tune into a conversation between the President and the chairman of the joint chiefs of staff?'

'Yes,' admitted Ralph.

'I'll see you in the Situation Room,' said Florentyna, and slammed down the phone.

She came out of her office almost on the run. Two surprised Secret Service officers quickly followed her as she headed down the narrow staircase past small portraits of former Presidents. Washington faced her on the bottom of the stairs before she turned into the wide corridor that led to the Situation Room. The security guard already had the door open that led into the secretarial section. She passed through a room of buzzing telexes and noisy typewriters while yet another security man opened the oak-panelled door of the Situation Room for her. Her Secret Service men remained outside as she marched in.

Ralph Brooks was seated in the President's chair giving orders to a bevy of military personnel. Four of the remaining nine seats were already occupied – around a table that almost took up the whole room. Immediately to the right of Brooks sat the Secretary of Defence, Charles Selover, and on his right the Director of the CIA, Paul Rowe. Opposite them sat the chairman of the joint chiefs of staff, General Dixon, and the National Security Adviser, Michael Brewer. The door at the end of the room that led into the Communications area was wide open.

Brooks swung around to face her. Florentyna had never seen him with his coat off and a shirt button undone.

'No panic,' he said. 'I'm on top of everything. I'm confident the Russians won't make any move before the President returns.'

'I don't expect that's what the Russians have in mind,' said Florentyna. 'While the President is unexplainably absent, we must be prepared for them to make any move that suits them.'

'Well, it's not your problem, Florentyna. The President has left me in control.'

'On the contrary, it *is* my problem,' said Florentyna firmly refusing to take a seat. 'In the absence of the President the responsibility for all military matters passes to me.'

'Now listen, Florentyna, I'm running the shop, and I don't want you interfering.' The gentle buzz of conversation between personnel around the room came to an abrupt halt as Brooks stared angrily at Florentyna. She picked up the nearest phone. 'Put the Attorney-General on the screen.'

'Yes, ma'am,' said the operator.

A few seconds later Pierre Levale's face appeared on one of the six televisions encased in the oak panelling along the side of the wall.

'Good evening, Pierre, it's Florentyna Kane. We have an increased intelligence watch on our hands and for reasons I am not willing to discuss the President is indisposed. Will you make it clear to the Secretary of State who holds executive responsibility in such a situation?'

Everyone in the room stood still and stared up at the worried face on the screen. The lines on Pierre Levale's face had never been more pronounced. They all knew he had been a Parkin appointment, but he had shown on past occasions that he thought more highly of the rule of law than of the President.

'The Constitution is not always clear on these matters,' he began, 'especially after the Bush-Haig showdown, following the attempt on Ronald Reagan's life. But, in my judgment, in the President's absence all power is vested in the Vice-President, and that is how I would advise the Senate.'

'Thank you, Pierre,' said Florentyna still looking at the screen. 'Please put that in writing and see that a copy is on the President's desk immediately on completion.' The Attorney-General disappeared from the screen.

'Now that that's settled, Ralph, brief me quickly.'

Brooks reluctantly vacated the President's chair, while a staff officer opened a small panel below the light switch by the door. He pressed a button and the beige curtain that stretched along the wall behind the President's chair opened. A large screen came down from the ceiling with a map of the world on it.

Charles Selover, the Secretary of Defence, rose from his chair as different coloured lights shone all over the map. 'The lights indicate the position of all known hostile forces,' he said as Florentyna swung around to face the map. 'The red ones are submarines, the green ones aircraft, and the blue ones full army divisions.'

'A West Point plebe looking at that map could tell you exactly what the Russians have in mind,' said Florentyna, as she stared at the mass of red lights in the Indian Ocean, green lights at Kabul airport and blue lights stretched along Afghanistan's border with Pakistan.

Paul Rowe then confirmed that the Russians had been massing armies on the Pakistan border for several days and within the last hour a coded message from a CIA agent behind the lines suggested that the Soviets intended to cross the border of Pakistan at ten o'clock Eastern Standard Time. He handed her a set of decoded cables and answered each of her questions as they arose

'The President told me,' said Brooks pointedly when Florentyna had read the final message, 'that he feels Pakistan is not another Poland and that the Russians wouldn't dare to go beyond the Afghanistan border.'

'I think we are about to find out if his judgment is sound,' she said.

'The President,' he added, 'has been in touch with Moscow during the week, as well as the Prime Minister of England, the President of France and the West German Chancellor. They all seem to agree with his assessment.'

'Since then the situation has changed radically,' said Florentyna sharply. 'It's obvious that I shall have to speak to the Soviet President myself.'

Once again Brooks hesitated. 'Immediately,' Florentyna added. Brooks picked up the phone. Everyone in the room waited while the circuit was linked. Florentyna had never spoken to President Romanov before and she could feel her heart beating. She knew her phone would be monitored to pick up the slightest reaction she unwittingly displayed, as it would be for the Soviet leader. It was always said that it was this device that had enabled the Russians to run roughshod over Jimmy Carter.

A few minutes later Gorbachev came on the line. 'Good evening, Mrs. Kane,' he said, not acknowledging her title, his voice as clear as if he were in the next room. After four years at the Court of St. James the Russian President's accent was minimal and his command of the language impressive. 'May I ask where President Parkin is?'

Florentyna could feel her mouth go dry. The Soviet President continued before she could reply.

'In California with his mistress, no doubt.' It didn't surprise Florentyna that the Russian President knew more about Parkin's movements than she did. It was now obvious why the Russians had chosen ten o'clock to cross the Pakistan border.

'You're right,' said Florentyna. 'And as he will be indisposed for at least another two hours you will have to deal with me. I therefore wish you to be left in no doubt that I am taking full Presidential responsibility in his absence.' She could feel small beads of sweat but didn't dare to touch her forehead.

'I see,' said the former head of the KGB. 'Then may I ask what is the purpose of this call?'

'Don't be naïve, Mr. President. I want you to understand that if you put one member of your armed forces over the border with Pakistan, America will retaliate immediately.'

'That would be very brave of you, Mrs. Kane,' he said.

'You obviously don't understand the American political system, Mr. President. It requires no 'bravery' at all. As Vice-President I am the one person in America who has nothing to lose and everything to gain.' This time the silence was not of her making. Florentyna felt her confidence growing. He had given her the chance to continue before he could reply. 'If you do not turn your battle fleet south, withdraw all ten army divisions from the border with Pakistan and fly your MIG 25s and SU 7s back to Moscow, I shall not hesitate to attack you on land, sea and air. Do you understand?'

The phone went dead.

Florentyna swivelled around.

By now the room was a buzz again with professionals who

had previously only played 'games' in this situation and now waited like Florentyna to see if all their training, experience and knowledge was about to be tested.

Ralph Brooks held a hand over the mouthpiece of his phone and reported that the President had landed in Colorado and wanted to speak to Florentyna. She picked up the red security phone by her side.

'Florentyna? Is that you?' came down the phone in a broad Texas accent.

'Yes, Mr. President.'

'Now hear me, lady. Ralph has briefed me and I am on my way back immediately. I'll be with you in under two hours. So don't do anything rash – and be sure the press don't get to hear of my absence.'

'Yes, Mr. President.' The phone went dead.

'General Dixon?' she said, not bothering to look at Brooks.

'Yes, ma'am,' said the four-star general who had not spoken until then.

'How quickly can we mobilise a retaliatory force into the battle area?' she asked the chief of staff.

'Within the hour, I could have ten squadrons of F 111's in the air from our bases in Europe, directed towards targets in the U.S.S.R. The Mediterranean Fleet is in almost constant contact with the Russians, but perhaps we should move it closer to the Indian Ocean.'

'How long would it take to reach the Indian Ocean?'

'Two to four days, ma'am.'

'Then issue the order, General. And, if possible, make it two.'

Florentyna didn't have to wait long for the next report to come up on the screen. It was the one she feared most. The Russian fleet still ploughed on relentlessly towards Karachi while more and more Soviet divisions were massing at Salabad and Asadabadon on the Afghanistan border.

'Get me the President of Pakistan,' said Florentyna.

He was on the line in moments.

'Where is President Parkin?' was his first question.

'Not you as well?' Florentyna wanted to say, but in fact replied, 'On his way back from Camp David. He will be with us shortly.' She briefed him on the actions she had taken to date and made it clear how far she was willing to go.

'Thank God for one brave man,' said Murbaze Bhutto.

'Just stay on the open line and we will keep you briefed if anything changes,' said Florentyna, ignoring the compliment.

'Shall I get the Russian President back?' asked Ralph Brooks.

'No,' said Florentyna. 'Get me the Prime Minister of Britain, the President of France and the Chancellor of West Germany.'

'She checked her watch: seven thirty-five. Within twenty minutes Florentyna had spoken to all three leaders. The British agreed to her plan, the French were sceptical but would cooperate, while the Germans were unhelpful.

The next piece of information Florentyna received was that Russian MIG 25s at Kabul Military Airport were being prepared for take-off.

Immediately she ordered General Dixon to place all forces on standby. Brooks leaned forward to protest but by then everyone present had placed their careers in the hands of one woman. Many of them watched her closely and noted she showed no emotion.

General Dixon came back into the Situation Room. 'Ma'am, the F111's are now ready for take-off, the Sixth Fleet is steaming full speed towards the Indian Ocean and a brigade of paratroopers can be dropped at Landi Kotal on to the borders of Pakistan within six hours.'

'Good,' said Florentyna quietly. The telex continued to rap out the message that the Russians were still advancing on every front.

'Don't you think we should renew contact with Gorbachev before it's too late?' asked Brooks. Florentyna noticed his hands were shaking.

'Why should we contact him? I have nothing to add. If we turn back now it will always be too late,' said Florentyna quietly.

'But we must try to negotiate a compromise, or by this time

tomorrow the President will look like a jackass,' said Brooks standing over her.

'Why?' asked Florentyna.

'Because in the end you will have to give in.'

Florentyna made no reply but swivelled back in her chair to face General Dixon who was standing by her side.

'In one hour, ma'am, we will be over Soviet airspace.'

'Understood,' said Florentyna.

Ralph Brooks picked up the ringing phone by his side. General Dixon returned to the Operations Room.

'The President is preparing to land at Andrews Air Force Base. He'll be with us in twenty minutes,' Brooks told Florentyna. 'Talk to the Russians and tell them to back off until he returns.'

'No,' said Florentyna. 'If the Russians don't turn back now you can be certain they will let the whole world know exactly where the President was at the moment they crossed the Afghanistan border. In any case I am still convinced they will turn back.'

'You've gone mad, Florentyna,' he shouted, rising from his chair.

'I don't think I have ever been saner,' she replied.

'Do you imagine the American people will thank you for involving them in a war over Pakistan?' asked Brooks.

'It's not Pakistan we're discussing,' said Florentyna. 'India will be next, followed by West Germany, France, Britain and finally Canada. And you, Ralph, would still be looking for excuses to avoid any confrontation even when the Soviets were marching down Constitution Avenue.'

'If that's your attitude I wash my hands of the whole affair,' said Brooks.

'And no doubt you will receive the same footnote in history as the last person who carried out that ignominious act.'

'Then I shall tell the President you overruled me and countermanded my orders,' said Brooks, his voice rising with every word.

Florentyna looked up at the handsome man who was now red in the face. 'Ralph, if you're going to wet your pants, can you please go and do it in the little boys' room and not the Situation Room?'

Brooks stormed out.

'Twenty-seven minutes to go, and still no sign of the Russians turning back,' whispered Dixon in her ear. A message came through on the telex that the fifty MIG 25s and SU 7s were taking off and would be over Pakistan air space within thirty-four minutes.

General Dixon was back by her side. 'Twenty-three minutes, ma'am.'

'How do you feel, General?' Florentyna tried to sound relaxed.

'Better than the day I marched into Berlin as a lieutenant, ma'am.'

Florentyna asked a staff major to check all three networks. She began to realise what Kennedy had been through over Cuba. The major pressed some buttons in front of him. C.B.S. was showing a Popeye cartoon, N.B.C. a basketball game and A.B.C. an old Ronald Reagan movie. She checked through everything on the little TV screen once again but there was no change. Now she could only pray she would be given enough time to be proved right. She sipped at a cup of coffee that had been left at her elbow. It tasted bitter. She pushed it to one side as President Parkin stormed into the room, followed by Brooks. The President was wearing an open-necked shirt, a sports jacket and check trousers.

'What the hell is going on?' were his first words. Florentyna had stepped out of the President's chair, when General Dixon came forward.

'Twenty minutes to go ma'am.'

'Now brief me quickly, Florentyna,' demanded Parkin, taking his place in the President's chair. She sat down on the President's right and told him what she had done right up to the moment he walked in.

'You fool,' he shouted when she had finished. 'Why didn't you listen to Ralph? He would never have got us into this trouble.'

'I am aware of exactly what the Secretary of State would have done presented with the same set of circumstances,' said Florentyna coldly.

'General Dixon,' said the President, turning his back on Florentyna. 'What is the exact position of your forces?' The general briefed President Parkin. Maps continually flashing up on the screen behind him showed the latest Russian position.

'In sixteen minutes' time the F 111 bombers will be over enemy territory.'

'Get me the President of Pakistan,' said Parkin, banging the table in front of him.

'He's holding on an open line,' said Florentyna quietly.

The President grabbed the phone, hunched his shoulders over the table and started speaking in a confidential tone.

'I'm sorry it's worked out this way, but I have no choice but to reverse the Vice-President's decision. She didn't understand the full implication of her actions. Now I don't want you to feel that we are deserting you. Be assured we will negotiate a peaceful withdrawal from your territory at the first possible opportunity,' said Parkin.

'For God's sake you can't desert us now,' said Bhutto.

'I must do what is best for all of us,' replied Parkin.

'Like you did in Afghanistan.'

Parkin ignored the comment and slammed down the phone.

'General?'

'Yes, sir,' said Dixon stepping forward.

'How much time have I got?'

He looked up at the small digital clock, suspended from the ceiling in front of him. 'Eleven minutes and eighteen seconds,' he said.

'Now listen and listen carefully. The Vice-President took on too much responsibility in my absence and I must now find a way out of this mess without egg landing on all our faces. I'm sure you agree, General.'

'Anything you say, Mr. President, but in the circumstances I'd stick with it.'

'There are wider considerations that go beyond the military. So I want you to –'

A yell went up from the far side of the room from a hitherto unknown colonel. For a moment he stopped even the President speaking.

'What is it?' shouted Parkin.

The colonel now stood to attention. 'The Russian fleet has turned back and is now heading south,' he said, reading a cable.

The President was speechless. The colonel continued, 'The MIG 25s and SU 7s are flying north-west to Moscow.' A cheer went up drowning the rest of the colonel's pronouncement. Telexes buzzed out confirmation all over the room.

'General,' said Parkin, turning to the chairman of the joint chiefs, 'we've won. It's a triumphant day for you and America.' He hesitated for a moment before adding, 'And I want to know that I'm proud to have led my country through this hour of peril.'

No one in the Situation Room laughed, and Brooks quickly added, 'Congratulations, Mr. President.' Everyone started cheering again, while several personnel walked over to congratulate Florentyna.

'General, bring your boys home. They've carried out a fantastic operation. Congratulations, you too did a great job.'

'Thank you, Mr. President,' said General Dixon. 'But I feel the praise should go to –'

The President turned to Ralph Brooks and said, 'This calls for a celebration, Ralph. All of you will remember this day for the rest of your lives. The day we showed the world America couldn't be pushed around.'

Florentyna was now standing in the corner as if she had had nothing to do with what had happened in that room. She left a few minutes later as the President continually ignored her. She returned to her office on the first floor and put away the red file, slamming the cabinet closed, before returning home. No wonder Richard had never voted Democrat.

*

'A gentleman's been waiting for you since seven thirty,' were the first words the butler said when she returned to her home on Observatory Circle.

'Good God,' said Florentyna out loud and rushed through to the drawing room where she found Edward, eyes closed, slumped on the sofa in front of the fire. She kissed him on the forehead and he woke immediately.

'Ah, my dear, been rescuing the world from a fate worse than death, no doubt?'

'Something like that,' said Florentyna, pacing up and down as she told Edward everything that had happened at the White House that evening. Edward had never seen her so angry.

'Well, I'll say one thing for Pete Parkin,' Edward said, when she had reached the end of her story, 'he's consistent.'

'He won't be after tomorrow.'

'What do you mean?'

'Precisely that. Because I'm going to hold a press conference in the morning to let everybody know exactly what happened. I'm sick and tired of his devious and irresponsible behaviour, and I know that most people who were in the Situation Room tonight will confirm everything I've told you.'

'That would be both rash and irresponsible,' said Edward, staring into the fire in front of him.

'Why?' asked Florentyna, surprised.

'Because America would be left with a lame-duck President. You might be the hero of the hour, but within days you would be despised.'

'But –' began Florentyna.

'No buts. On this occasion you will have to swallow your pride and be satisfied with using what happened tonight as a weapon to remind Parkin of his agreement over the one-term presidency.'

'And let him get away with it?'

'And let *America* get away with it,' said Edward, firmly.

Florentyna continued pacing and didn't speak for several

minutes. 'You're right,' she said finally. 'I was being short-sighted. Thank you.'

'So might I have been if I had experienced what you went through at first hand.'

Florentyna laughed. 'Come on,' she said and stopped pacing for the first time. 'Let's have something to eat. You must be starving.'

'No, no,' said Edward, looking at his watch. 'Although I must confess, V.P., that you're the first girl who's kept me waiting three and a half hours for a dinner date.'

Early the next morning the President phoned her.

'That was a great job you did yesterday, Florentyna, and I appreciate the way you carried out the earlier part of the operation.'

'You hardly showed it at the time, Mr. President,' she said, barely controlling her anger.

'I intend to address the nation today,' said Parkin, ignoring Florentyna's comment, 'and although this isn't the time to tell them I shall not be seeking re-election, when the time does come I shall remember your loyalty.'

'Thank you, Mr. President,' was all Florentyna could manage to say.

The President addressed the nation at eight o'clock that night on all three networks. Other than a passing mention of Florentyna he left the distinct impression that he had been in complete control of operations when the Russians turned back.

One or two national newspapers suggested that the Vice-President had been involved in the negotiations with the Russian leader, but as Florentyna was not available to confirm this Parkin's version went almost unchallenged.

Two days later Florentyna was sent to Paris for the funeral of Giscard d'Estaing. By the time she returned to Washington the public was worked up about the final game of the World Series and Parkin was a national hero.

*

With the first Primary little more than eight months away, she told Edward that the time had come to start planning for the 1996 Presidential campaign. To that end, Florentyna accepted invitations to speak all over America, and during the year she addressed voters in thirty-three states. She was delighted to find that wherever she went the public took it for granted she was going to be the next President. Her relationship with Pete Parkin remained cordial, but she had had to remind the President that the time was drawing near for him to make the announcement about his intentions to serve only one term in office, so that she could officially launch her campaign.

One Monday in July, when she had returned to Washington from a speaking engagement in Nebraska, she found a note from the President saying that he would be making those intentions clear in a statement to the nation that Thursday. Edward had already started work on a strategic outline for a '96 campaign so that, as soon as the President had announced that he would not be running again, the Kane effort would be ready to move into top gear.

'His timing is perfect, V.P.,' he said. 'We have fourteen months before the election campaign, and you needn't even declare you're the candidate before October.'

Florentyna sat alone in the Vice-President's office that Thursday evening waiting for the President to deliver his statement. The three networks were carrying his speech and all of them had talked of the rumour that, at sixty-five, Parkin was not considering a second term. Florentyna waited impatiently as a camera panned down from the façade of the White House and into the Oval Office, where President Parkin sat behind his desk.

'My fellow Americans,' he began, 'I have always believed in keeping you informed of my plans as I do not want any speculation about my personal future, as to whether I shall be running again for this onerous office in fourteen months' time' – Florentyna smiled – 'I therefore wish to take this opportunity to make my intentions clear so that I can complete this session without involving myself in party politics.' Florentyna nearly leaped out of her seat in delight as Parkin now leaned forward in what the press referred to as 'his sincere stance' before continuing. 'The President's job is here in the Oval Office serving the people and to that end I announce that although I shall be a candidate for President at the next election, I will leave the electioneering to my Republican opponents while I continue to work for your best interests in the White House. I hope you will allow me the privilege of serving you for another four years. God bless you all.'

Florentyna was speechless for some moments. Finally she picked up the phone by her side and dialled the Oval Office. A woman's voice answered.

'I'm on my way to see the President immediately.' Florentyna slammed down the phone and walked out of her room towards the Oval Office.

The President's private secretary met her at the door. 'The President is in conference right now, but I expect him to be free at any moment.'

Florentyna paced up and down the corridor for thirty-seven minutes before she was finally shown in.

Her first words were, 'Pete Parkin. You're a liar and a cheat,' spitting out the words even before the door had closed.

'Now just a minute, Florentyna, I feel for the good of the nation . . .'

'For the good of Pete Parkin, who can't keep his end of any bargain, God help this country. Well, I can tell you one thing, I am not willing to run as your Vice-President for a second term.'

'I'm sorry to hear that,' said the President, sitting down in his chair and making a note on the pad in front of him, 'but I naturally accept your decision with regret. Not that it would have made a lot of difference.'

'What do you mean?' said Florentyna.

'I wasn't intending to ask you to join me on the ticket for a second time, but you have made the whole problem a lot easier for me by refusing to be considered. The party will now understand why I had to look to someone else for the coming election.'

'You would lose the election if I ran against you.'

'No, Florentyna, we would both lose and the Republicans might even win the Senate and the House. That wouldn't make you the most popular little lady in town.'

'You won't get my backing in Chicago. No President has ever won the election without Illinois and they will never forgive you.'

'They might if I replaced one Senator from the state with another.'

Florentyna turned cold. 'You wouldn't dare,' she said.

'If I pick Ralph Brooks, I think you will find he's a popular enough choice. So will the people of Illinois when I say that I see him as my natural successor in five years' time.'

Florentyna left without another word. She must have been the only person who had ever slammed the Oval Office door.

38

WHEN FLORENTYNA WENT OVER the details of the Parkin meeting for Edward the following Saturday on the golf course at Cape Cod, he confessed that the news came as no great surprise.

'He may not be much of a President, but he knows more about Machiavellian politics than Nixon and Johnson put together.'

'I should have listened to you in Detroit when you warned me this would happen.'

'What did your father always say about Henry Osborne? Once a skunk, always a skunk.'

There was a slight breeze and Florentyna threw a few blades of grass into the air to determine its direction. Satisfied, she took a ball from her golf bag, set it up and hit a long drive. To her surprise the wind took the ball slightly to the right and into some brush.

'Didn't properly anticipate the wind, V.P., did you?' volunteered Edward. 'I can only believe this must be my day to beat you, Florentyna.' He hit his ball right down the centre of the fairway, but twenty yards shorter than Florentyna's.

'Things are bad, Edward, but not yet that bad,' she said, smiling, and proceeded to take the first hole with a chip out of the rough and a long putt.

'Early days,' said Edward, as they were about to tee off on the second hole. He asked Florentyna about her future plans.

'Parkin is right: I can't make a fuss as such an outburst would only play into the hands of the Republicans; so I have decided to be realistic about my future.'

'And what does that mean?'

'I'll see this fourteen months out as Vice-President and then I'd like to return to New York as chairman of the Baron Group. I've had an almost unique view of the company since my continual travelling around the globe, and I think I shall be able to institute some new ideas that could put us far ahead of any of our competitors.'

'Then it sounds as though we have an interesting time ahead of us,' Edward said, smiling as he joined her to walk to the second green. He tried to concentrate on his game while Florentyna went on talking.

'I would also like to join the board of Lester's. Richard always wanted me to find out how a bank worked from the inside. He never stopped telling me he paid his directors a higher salary than the President of the United States.'

'You'll have to consult William on that, not me.'

'Why?' asked Florentyna.

'Because he's taking over as chairman on January 1st next year. He knows more about banking than I ever will. He's inherited all Richard's natural instincts for high finance. I'll stay on as a director for a few more years, but I'm confident that the bank couldn't be in better hands.'

'Is he old enough for such a responsibility?'

'Same age as you were when you first became chairman of

the Baron Group,' said Edward.

'Well, at least we'll have one President in the family,' Florentyna said as she missed a two-foot putt.

'One hole each, V.P.' Edward marked his card and studied the two hundred and ten yard dog-leg that lay in front of him. 'Now I know how you intend to occupy half of your time. So do you have anything planned for the other half?'

'Yes,' said Florentyna. 'The Remagen Trust has lacked direction since the death of Professor Ferpozzi. I have decided to head it up myself. Do you know how much the trust has on deposit nowadays?'

'No, but it would only take one phone call to find out,' said Edward, trying to concentrate on his swing.

'I'll save you a quarter,' said Florentyna. 'Twenty-nine million dollars, bringing in an annual income of nearly four million dollars. Edward, the time has come to build the first Remagen University with major scholarships for the children of first-generation immigrants.'

'And remember, V.P., gifted children, whatever their background,' said Edward, teeing up.

'You're sounding more and more like Richard every day,' she laughed.

Edward swung. 'I wish my golf was as good as his,' he added as he watched his little white ball head high and far before hitting a tree.

Florentyna didn't seem to notice. And after she had hit her ball firmly down the middle of the fairway, they both walked off in different directions. They could not continue their conversation until they had reached the green where Florentyna went on talking about where the new university would be built, how many students it should admit in its first year, who should be the first President. She ended up losing the third and fourth holes. Florentyna began to concentrate on her game but still had to scramble to square the match by the ninth.

'I shall be particularly pleased to give your hundred dollars to the Republican party today,' Florentyna said.

'Nothing would give me more pleasure than seeing Parkin and Brooks bite the dust.'

Florentyna sighed as she hit a bad short iron from the tee towards the tenth green.

'I'm far from beaten yet,' said Edward.

Florentyna ignored him. 'What a waste my years in government have been,' she said.

'No, I can't agree with that,' said Edward, still practising his swings. 'Six years in Congress, a further eight in the Senate and ending up the first woman Vice-President. And I suspect history will ultimately record your role over the invasion of Pakistan far more accurately than Parkin has felt necessary. Even if you have achieved less than you'd hoped, you've made the task a lot easier for the next woman who wants to go the whole way. Ironically I believe if you were the Democratic candidate at the next election, you would win easily.'

'The public opinion polls certainly agree with you.' Florentyna tried to concentrate, but sliced her tee shot. 'Damn,' she said as her ball disappeared into the woods.

'You're not at the top of your game today, V.P.,' said Edward. He proceeded to win the tenth and eleventh holes but then threw away the twelfth and thirteenth with over-anxious putts.

'I think we should build a Baron in Moscow,' said Florentyna when they had reached the fourteenth green. 'That was always my father's ultimate ambition. Did I ever tell you that the Minister for Tourism, Mikhail Zokovlov, has long tried to interest me in the idea? I have to go on that frightful culture trip to Moscow next month which will be a wonderful opportunity to discuss the idea with him in greater detail. Thank God for the Bolshoi Ballet, borsch and caviar. At least they've never tried to get me in bed with some handsome young man.'

'Not while they know about our golf deal,' chuckled Edward.

They split the fourteenth and fifteenth and Edward won the sixteenth hole. 'We are about to discover what you are like under pressure,' said Florentyna.

Edward proceeded to lose the seventeenth by missing a putt of only three feet so that the match rested on the last hole. Florentyna drove well, but Edward, thanks to a lucky bounce off the edge of a small rise, came within a few feet of her. He put his second shot only twenty yards from the green and found it hard to suppress a smile as they walked down the centre of the fairway together.

'You have a long way to go yet, Edward,' said Florentyna, as she sent her ball flying into a sand trap.

Edward laughed.

'I would remind you how good I am with a sand wedge and putter,' said Florentyna, and proved her point by pitching the ball only four feet from the hole.

Edward chipped up from twenty yards to within six feet.

'This may be the last chance you'll ever have,' she said.

Edward held his putter firmly and jabbed at the ball and watched it teeter on the edge of the hole before disappearing into the cup. He threw his club high into the air and cheered.

'You haven't won yet,' said Florentyna, 'but no doubt it will be the nearest you'll ever get.' She steadied herself as she checked the line between ball and hole. If she sank her putt, the match was halved and she was off the hook.

'Don't let the helicopters distract you,' Edward said.

'The only thing that is distracting me, Edward, is you. Be warned, you will not succeed. Since the rest of my life depends on this shot, you can be assured that I shall not make a mistake. In fact,' she said, taking a step back, 'I shall wait until the helicopters have passed over.'

Florentyna stared up into the sky and waited for the four helicopters to fly past. Their chopping noise grew louder and louder.

'Did you have to go to quite such lengths to win, Edward?' she asked as one of the helicopters began to descend.

'What the hell is going on?' said Edward anxiously.

'I have no idea,' said Florentyna. 'But I suspect we are about to find out.'

Her skirt whipped around her legs as the first helicopter landed a few yards off the green of the eighteenth hole. Even as the blades continued to rotate an army colonel leaped out and rushed over to Florentyna. A second officer jumped out and stood by the helicopter, carrying a small black briefcase. Florentyna and Edward stared at the colonel as he stood to attention and saluted.

'Madam President,' he said. 'The President is dead.'

Florentyna clenched her hand into a tight fist as the eighteenth hole was surrounded by agents from the Secret Service. She glanced again at the black nuclear command briefcase which was now her sole responsibility, the trigger she hoped she would never have to pull. It was only the second time in her life she felt what real responsibility meant.

'How did it happen?' she asked calmly.

The colonel continued in clipped tones. 'The President returned from his morning jog and retired to his room to shower and change for breakfast. It was over twenty minutes before any of us felt that something might be wrong so I was sent to check, but it was already too late. The doctor said he must have had a massive coronary. He has had two minor heart attacks during the last year, but on both occasions we managed to keep them out of the press.'

'How many people know of his death?'

'Three members of his personal staff, his doctor, Mrs. Parkin and the Attorney-General, whom I informed immediately. On his instructions, I was detailed to find you and see that the oath of office is administered as quickly as is convenient. I am then to accompany you to the White House where the Attorney-General is waiting to announce the details of the President's death. The Attorney-General hopes that these arrangements meet with your approval.'

'Thank you, Colonel. We had better return to my home immediately.'

Florentyna, accompanied by Edward, the colonel, the officer with the black box and four Secret Service agents, climbed aboard the Army aircraft. As the chopper whirled up into the air, Florentyna gazed down at the eighteenth green where her ball, a diminishing white speck, remained four feet from the hole. A few minutes later, the helicopter landed on the grass in front of Florentyna's Cape Cod house while the other three remained hovering overhead.

Florentyna led them all into the living room, where young Richard was playing with his father and Bishop O'Reilly, who had flown in for a quiet weekend.

'Why are there helicopters flying over the house, Grandma?' Richard asked.

Florentyna explained to her grandson what had happened. William and Joanna rose from their chairs, not sure what to say.

'What do we do next, Colonel?' asked Florentyna.

'We'll need a Bible,' said the colonel, 'and the oath of office.'

Florentyna went to her study table in the corner of the room and from the top drawer took out Miss Tredgold's Bible. A copy of the Presidential oath was not as easy to find. Edward thought it might be in Theodore White's *The Making of the President: 1972*, which he remembered was in the library. He was right.

The colonel phoned the Attorney-General, and checked that the wording was correct. Pierre Levale then spoke to Bishop O'Reilly and explained how he should administer the oath.

In the living room of her Cape Cod home, Florentyna Kane stood beside her family, with Colonel Max Perkins and Edward Winchester acting as witnesses. She took the Bible in her right hand and repeated the words after Bishop O'Reilly.

'I, Florentyna Kane, do solemnly swear that I will faithfully execute the office of President of the United States and will to the best of my ability, preserve, protect and defend the Constitution of the United States, so help me God.'

Thus Florentyna Kane became the forty-third President of the United States.

William was the first to congratulate his mother and then they all tried to join in at once.

'I think we should leave for Washington, Madam President,' the colonel suggested a few minutes later.

'Of course.' Florentyna turned to the old family priest. 'Thank you, Monsignor,' she said. But the bishop did not reply; for the first time in his life, the little Irishman was lost for words. 'I shall need you to perform another ceremony for me in the near future.'

'And what might that be, my dear?'

'As soon as we have a free weekend Edward and I are going to be married.' Edward looked even more surprised and delighted than the moment he heard Florentyna had become President. 'I remembered a little too late,' she continued, 'that if you fail to complete a hole in match-play competition, it is automatically awarded to your opponent.'

Edward took her in his arms as Florentyna said, 'My darling, I will need your wisdom and your strength, but most of all your love.'

'You've had them for nearly forty years already, V.P. I mean . . .'

Everyone laughed.

'I think we should leave now, Madam President,' the colonel prompted. Florentyna nodded in agreement as the phone rang. Edward walked over to the desk and picked it up. 'It's Ralph Brooks. Says he needs to speak to you urgently.'

'Would you apologise to the Secretary of State, Edward, and explain I am not available at the moment.' Edward was about to convey the message when she added, 'And ask him if he would be kind enough to join me at the White House.'

Edward smiled as the forty-third President of the United States walked towards the door. The colonel accompanying her pressed a switch on his two-way radio and spoke softly into it: 'Baroness returning to Crown. The contract has been signed.'

The End